Charles John Huffam Dickens (7 February 1812 – 9 June 1870) was an English writer and social critic. He created some of the world's best-known fictional characters and is regarded by many as the greatest novelist of the Victorian era. His works enjoyed unprecedented popularity during his lifetime, and by the 20th century critics and scholars had recognised him as a literary genius. His novels and short stories are still widely read today.

Born in Portsmouth, Dickens left school to work in a factory when his father was incarcerated in a debtors' prison. Despite his lack of formal education, he edited a weekly journal for 20 years, wrote 15 novels, five novellas, hundreds of short stories and non-fiction articles, lectured and performed readings extensively, was an indefatigable letter writer, and campaigned vigorously for children's rights, education, and other social reforms. (Source: Wikipedia)

Literary works:
The Pickwick Papers
Oliver Twist
Nicholas Nickleby
The Old Curiosity Shop
Barnaby Rudge
A Christmas Carol
Martin Chuzzlewit
The Chimes
The Cricket on the Hearth
Dombey and Son
The Haunted Man
David Copperfield
Bleak House
Hard Times
Little Dorrit
A Tale of Two Cities
Great Expectations
Our Mutual Friend

THE OLD CURIOSITY SHOP
&
GREAT EXPECTATIONS
CHARLES DICKENS

PRINCE CLASSICS

Contents

THE OLD CURIOSITY SHOP — — — **13**

CHAPTER 1 — — — 13

CHAPTER 2 — — — 21

CHAPTER 3 — — — 25

CHAPTER 4 — — — 30

CHAPTER 5 — — — 35

CHAPTER 6 — — — 40

CHAPTER 7 — — — 45

CHAPTER 8 — — — 50

CHAPTER 9 — — — 56

CHAPTER 10 — — — 62

CHAPTER 11 — — — 66

CHAPTER 12 — — — 71

CHAPTER 13 — — — 76

CHAPTER 14 — — — 82

CHAPTER 15 — — — 86

CHAPTER 16 — — — 91

CHAPTER 17 — — — 95

CHAPTER 18 — — — 100

CHAPTER 19 — — — 104

CHAPTER 20 — — — 110

CHAPTER 21 — — — 114

CHAPTER 22 — — — 119

CHAPTER 23 — — — 123

CHAPTER 24 — — — 128

CHAPTER 25 — — — 132

CHAPTER 26 — — — 137

CHAPTER 27 — — — 141

CHAPTER 28 — — — 147

CHAPTER 29 — — — 151

CHAPTER 30 — — — 157

CHAPTER 31 — — — 161

CHAPTER 32 — — — 167

CHAPTER 33 — — — 170

CHAPTER 34 — — — 176

CHAPTER 35 — — — 180

CHAPTER 36 — 186
CHAPTER 37 — 190
CHAPTER 38 — 194
CHAPTER 39 — 200
CHAPTER 40 — 204
CHAPTER 41 — 209
CHAPTER 42 — 214
CHAPTER 43 — 219
CHAPTER 44 — 223
CHAPTER 45 — 229
CHAPTER 46 — 233
CHAPTER 47 — 238
CHAPTER 48 — 242
CHAPTER 49 — 248
CHAPTER 50 — 252
CHAPTER 51 — 258
CHAPTER 52 — 262
CHAPTER 53 — 268
CHAPTER 54 — 272
CHAPTER 55 — 278
CHAPTER 56 — 281
CHAPTER 57 — 288
CHAPTER 58 — 291
CHAPTER 59 — 297
CHAPTER 60 — 301
CHAPTER 61 — 307
CHAPTER 62 — 311
CHAPTER 63 — 317
CHAPTER 64 — 321
CHAPTER 65 — 327
CHAPTER 66 — 331
CHAPTER 67 — 340
CHAPTER 68 — 345
CHAPTER 69 — 349
CHAPTER 70 — 355
CHAPTER 71 — 359
CHAPTER 72 — 364
CHAPTER 73 — 369

GREAT EXPECTATIONS 377

Chapter I 377

Chapter II 380

Chapter III 385

Chapter IV 389

Chapter V 394

Chapter VI 401

Chapter VII 402

Chapter VIII 409

Chapter IX 417

Chapter X 421

Chapter XI 426

Chapter XII 435

Chapter XIII 438

Chapter XIV 443

Chapter XV 444

Chapter XVI 452

Chapter XVII 455

Chapter XVIII 460

Chapter XIX 469

Chapter XX 478

Chapter XXI 484

Chapter XXII 487

Chapter XXIII 495

Chapter XXIV 500

Chapter XXV 504

Chapter XXVI 509

Chapter XXVII 514

Chapter XXVIII 519

Chapter XXIX 523

Chapter XXX 531

Chapter XXXI   537

Chapter XXXII   541

Chapter XXXIII   544

Chapter XXXIV   549

Chapter XXXV   553

Chapter XXXVI   558

Chapter XXXVII   562

Chapter XXXVIII   567

Chapter XXXIX   575

Chapter XL   583

Chapter XLI   592

Chapter XLII   596

Chapter XLIII   600

Chapter XLIV   604

Chapter XLV   609

Chapter XLVI   614

Chapter XLVII   618

Chapter XLVIII   623

Chapter XLIX   627

Chapter L   633

Chapter LI   636

Chapter LII   641

Chapter LIII   645

Chapter LIV   653

Chapter LV   661

Chapter LVI   666

Chapter LVII   670

Chapter LVIII   678

Chapter LIX   683

About Author   687

THE OLD CURIOSITY SHOP
&
GREAT EXPECTATIONS

THE OLD CURIOSITY SHOP

CHAPTER 1

Although I am an old man, night is generally my time for walking. In the summer I often leave home early in the morning, and roam about fields and lanes all day, or even escape for days or weeks together; but, saving in the country, I seldom go out until after dark, though, Heaven be thanked, I love its light and feel the cheerfulness it sheds upon the earth, as much as any creature living.

I have fallen insensibly into this habit, both because it favours my infirmity and because it affords me greater opportunity of speculating on the characters and occupations of those who fill the streets. The glare and hurry of broad noon are not adapted to idle pursuits like mine; a glimpse of passing faces caught by the light of a street-lamp or a shop window is often better for my purpose than their full revelation in the daylight; and, if I must add the truth, night is kinder in this respect than day, which too often destroys an air-built castle at the moment of its completion, without the least ceremony or remorse.

That constant pacing to and fro, that never-ending restlessness, that incessant tread of feet wearing the rough stones smooth and glossy—is it not a wonder how the dwellers in narrows ways can bear to hear it! Think of a sick man in such a place as Saint Martin's Court, listening to the footsteps, and in the midst of pain and weariness obliged, despite himself (as though it were a task he must perform) to detect the child's step from the man's, the slipshod beggar from the booted exquisite, the lounging from the busy, the dull heel of the sauntering outcast from the quick tread of an expectant pleasure-seeker—think of the hum and noise always being present to his sense, and of the stream of life that will not stop, pouring on, on, on, through all his restless dreams, as if he were condemned to lie, dead but conscious, in a noisy churchyard, and had no hope of rest for centuries to come.

Then, the crowds for ever passing and repassing on the bridges (on those which are free of toll at last), where many stop on fine evenings looking listlessly down upon the water with some vague idea that by and by it runs between green banks which grow wider and wider until at last it joins the broad vast sea—where some halt to rest from heavy loads and think as they look over the parapet that to smoke and lounge away one's life, and lie sleeping in the sun upon a hot tarpaulin, in a dull, slow, sluggish barge, must be happiness unalloyed—and where some, and a very different class, pause with heavier loads than they, remembering to have heard or read in old time that drowning was not a hard death, but of all means of suicide the easiest and best.

Covent Garden Market at sunrise too, in the spring or summer, when the fragrance of sweet flowers is in the air, over-powering even the unwholesome streams of last night's debauchery, and driving the dusky thrush, whose cage has hung outside a garret window all night long, half mad with joy! Poor bird! the only neighbouring thing at all akin to the other little captives, some of whom, shrinking from the hot hands of drunken purchasers, lie drooping on the path already, while others, soddened by close contact, await the time when they shall be watered and freshened up to please more sober company, and make old clerks who pass them on their road to business, wonder what has filled their breasts with visions of the country.

But my present purpose is not to expatiate upon my walks. The story I am about to relate, and to which I shall recur at intervals, arose out of one of these rambles; and thus I have been led to speak of them by way of preface.

One night I had roamed into the City, and was walking slowly on in my usual way, musing upon a great many things, when I was arrested by an inquiry, the purport of which did not reach me, but which seemed to be addressed to myself, and was preferred in a soft sweet voice that struck me very pleasantly. I turned hastily round and found at my elbow a pretty little girl, who begged to be directed to a certain street at a considerable distance, and indeed in quite another quarter of the town.

'It is a very long way from here,' said I, 'my child.'

'I know that, sir,' she replied timidly. 'I am afraid it is a very long way, for I came from there to-night.'

'Alone?' said I, in some surprise.

'Oh, yes, I don't mind that, but I am a little frightened now, for I had lost my road.'

'And what made you ask it of me? Suppose I should tell you wrong?'

'I am sure you will not do that,' said the little creature,' you are such a very old gentleman, and walk so slow yourself.'

I cannot describe how much I was impressed by this appeal and the energy with which it was made, which brought a tear into the child's clear eye, and made her slight figure tremble as she looked up into my face.

'Come,' said I, 'I'll take you there.'

She put her hand in mine as confidingly as if she had known me from her cradle, and we trudged away together; the little creature accommodating her pace to mine, and rather seeming to lead and take care of me than I to be protecting her. I observed that every now and then she stole a curious look at my face, as if to make quite sure that I was not deceiving her, and that these glances (very sharp and keen they were too) seemed to increase her confidence at every repetition.

For my part, my curiosity and interest were at least equal to the child's, for child she certainly was, although I thought it probable from what I could make out, that her very small and delicate frame imparted a peculiar youthfulness to her appearance. Though more scantily attired than she might have been she was dressed with perfect neatness, and betrayed no marks of poverty or neglect.

'Who has sent you so far by yourself?' said I.

'Someone who is very kind to me, sir.'

'And what have you been doing?'

'That, I must not tell,' said the child firmly.

There was something in the manner of this reply which caused me to look at the little creature with an involuntary expression of surprise; for I wondered what kind of errand it might be that occasioned her to be prepared for questioning. Her quick eye seemed to read my thoughts, for as it met mine she added that there was no harm in what she had been doing, but it was a great secret—a secret which she did not even know herself.

This was said with no appearance of cunning or deceit, but with an unsuspicious frankness that bore the impress of truth. She walked on as before, growing more familiar with me as we proceeded and talking cheerfully by the way, but she said no more about her home, beyond remarking that we were going quite a new road and asking if it were a short one.

While we were thus engaged, I revolved in my mind a hundred different explanations of the riddle and rejected them every one. I really felt ashamed to take advantage of the ingenuousness or grateful feeling of the child for the purpose of gratifying my curiosity. I love these little people; and it is not a slight thing when they, who are so fresh from God, love us. As I had felt pleased at first by her confidence I determined to deserve it, and to do credit to the nature which had prompted her to repose it in me.

There was no reason, however, why I should refrain from seeing the person who had inconsiderately sent her to so great a distance by night and alone, and as it was not improbable that if she found herself near home she might take farewell of me and deprive me of the opportunity, I avoided the most frequented ways and took the most intricate, and thus it was not until we arrived in the street itself that she knew where we were. Clapping her hands with pleasure and running on before me for a short distance, my little acquaintance stopped at a door and remaining on the step till I came up knocked at it when I joined her.

A part of this door was of glass unprotected by any shutter, which I did not observe at first, for all was very dark and silent within, and I was anxious (as indeed the child was also) for an answer to our summons. When she had knocked twice or thrice there was a noise as if some person were moving inside, and at length a faint light appeared through the glass which, as it approached very slowly, the bearer having to make his way through a great many scattered articles, enabled me to see both what kind of person it was who advanced and what kind of place it was through which he came.

It was an old man with long grey hair, whose face and figure as he held the light above his head and looked before him as he approached, I could plainly see. Though much altered by age, I fancied I could recognize in his spare and slender form something of that delicate mould which I had noticed in the child. Their bright blue eyes were certainly alike, but his face was so deeply furrowed and so very full of care, that here all resemblance ceased.

The place through which he made his way at leisure was one of those receptacles for old and curious things which seem to crouch in odd corners of this town and to hide their musty treasures from the public eye in jealousy and distrust. There were suits of mail standing like ghosts in armour here and there, fantastic carvings brought from monkish cloisters, rusty weapons of various kinds, distorted figures in china and wood and iron and ivory: tapestry and strange furniture that might have been designed in dreams. The haggard aspect of the little old man was wonderfully suited to the place; he might have groped among old churches and tombs and deserted houses and gathered all the spoils with his own hands. There was nothing in the whole collection but was in keeping with himself nothing that looked older or more worn than he.

As he turned the key in the lock, he surveyed me with some astonishment which was not diminished when he looked from me to my companion. The door being opened, the child addressed him as grandfather, and told him the little story of our companionship.

'Why, bless thee, child,' said the old man, patting her on the head, 'how couldst thou miss thy way? What if I had lost thee, Nell!'

'I would have found my way back to you, grandfather,' said the child boldly; 'never fear.'

The old man kissed her, then turning to me and begging me to walk in, I did so. The door was closed and locked. Preceding me with the light, he led me through the place I had already seen from without, into a small sitting-room behind, in which was another door opening into a kind of closet, where I saw a little bed that a fairy might have slept in, it looked so very small and was so prettily arranged. The child took a candle and tripped into this little room, leaving the old man and me together.

'You must be tired, sir,' said he as he placed a chair near the fire, 'how can I thank you?'

'By taking more care of your grandchild another time, my good friend,' I replied.

'More care!' said the old man in a shrill voice, 'more care of Nelly! Why, who ever loved a child as I love Nell?'

He said this with such evident surprise that I was perplexed what answer to make, and the more so because coupled with something feeble and wandering in his manner, there were in his face marks of deep and anxious thought which convinced me that he could not be, as I had been at first inclined to suppose, in a state of dotage or imbecility.

'I don't think you consider—' I began.

'I don't consider!' cried the old man interrupting me, 'I don't consider her! Ah, how little you know of the truth! Little Nelly, little Nelly!'

It would be impossible for any man, I care not what his form of speech might be, to express more affection than the dealer in curiosities did, in these four words. I waited for him to speak again, but he rested his chin upon his hand and shaking his head twice or thrice fixed his eyes upon the fire.

While we were sitting thus in silence, the door of the closet opened, and the child returned, her light brown hair hanging loose about her neck, and her face flushed with the haste she had made to rejoin us. She busied herself immediately in preparing supper, and while she was thus engaged I remarked that the old man took an opportunity of observing me more closely than he had done yet. I was surprised to see that all this time everything was done by the child, and that there appeared to be no other persons but ourselves in the house. I took advantage of a moment when she was absent to venture a hint on this point, to which the old man replied that there were few grown persons as trustworthy or as careful as she.

'It always grieves me,' I observed, roused by what I took to be his selfishness, 'it always grieves me to contemplate the initiation of children into the ways of life, when they are scarcely more than infants. It checks their confidence and simplicity—two of the best qualities that Heaven gives them—and demands that they share our sorrows before they are capable of entering into our enjoyments.'

'It will never check hers,' said the old man looking steadily at me, 'the springs are too deep. Besides, the children of the poor know but few pleasures. Even the cheap delights of childhood must be bought and paid for.'

16

'But—forgive me for saying this—you are surely not so very poor'—said I.

'She is not my child, sir,' returned the old man. 'Her mother was, and she was poor. I save nothing—not a penny—though I live as you see, but'—he laid his hand upon my arm and leant forward to whisper—'she shall be rich one of these days, and a fine lady. Don't you think ill of me because I use her help. She gives it cheerfully as you see, and it would break her heart if she knew that I suffered anybody else to do for me what her little hands could undertake. I don't consider!'—he cried with sudden querulousness, 'why, God knows that this one child is the thought and object of my life, and yet he never prospers me—no, never!'

At this juncture, the subject of our conversation again returned, and the old man motioning to me to approach the table, broke off, and said no more.

We had scarcely begun our repast when there was a knock at the door by which I had entered, and Nell bursting into a hearty laugh, which I was rejoiced to hear, for it was childlike and full of hilarity, said it was no doubt dear old Kit coming back at last.

'Foolish Nell!' said the old man fondling with her hair. 'She always laughs at poor Kit.'

The child laughed again more heartily than before, and I could not help smiling from pure sympathy. The little old man took up a candle and went to open the door. When he came back, Kit was at his heels.

Kit was a shock-headed, shambling, awkward lad with an uncommonly wide mouth, very red cheeks, a turned-up nose, and certainly the most comical expression of face I ever saw. He stopped short at the door on seeing a stranger, twirled in his hand a perfectly round old hat without any vestige of a brim, and resting himself now on one leg and now on the other and changing them constantly, stood in the doorway, looking into the parlour with the most extraordinary leer I ever beheld. I entertained a grateful feeling towards the boy from that minute, for I felt that he was the comedy of the child's life.

'A long way, wasn't it, Kit?' said the little old man.

'Why, then, it was a goodish stretch, master,' returned Kit.

'Of course you have come back hungry?'

'Why, then, I do consider myself rather so, master,' was the answer.

The lad had a remarkable manner of standing sideways as he spoke, and thrusting his head forward over his shoulder, as if he could not get at his voice without that accompanying action. I think he would have amused one anywhere, but the child's exquisite enjoyment of his oddity, and the relief it was to find that there was something she associated with merriment in a place that appeared so unsuited to her, were quite irresistible. It was a great point too that Kit himself was flattered by the sensation he created, and after several efforts to preserve his gravity, burst into a loud roar, and so stood with his mouth wide open and his eyes nearly shut, laughing violently.

The old man had again relapsed into his former abstraction and took no notice of what passed, but I remarked that when her laugh was over, the child's bright eyes were dimmed with tears, called forth by the fullness of heart with which she welcomed her uncouth favourite after the little anxiety of the night. As for Kit himself (whose laugh had been all the time one of that sort which very little would change into a cry) he carried a large slice of bread and meat and a mug of beer into a corner, and applied himself to disposing of them with great voracity.

'Ah!' said the old man turning to me with a sigh, as if I had spoken to him but that moment, 'you don't know what you say when you tell me that I don't consider her.'

'You must not attach too great weight to a remark founded on first appearances, my friend,' said I.

'No,' returned the old man thoughtfully, 'no. Come hither, Nell.'

The little girl hastened from her seat, and put her arm about his neck.

'Do I love thee, Nell?' said he. 'Say—do I love thee, Nell, or no?'

The child only answered by her caresses, and laid her head upon his breast.

'Why dost thou sob?' said the grandfather, pressing her closer to him and glancing towards me. 'Is it because thou know'st I love thee, and dost not like that I should seem to doubt it by my question? Well, well—then let us say I love thee dearly.'

'Indeed, indeed you do,' replied the child with great earnestness, 'Kit knows you do.'

Kit, who in despatching his bread and meat had been swallowing two-thirds of his knife at every mouthful with the coolness of a juggler, stopped short in his operations on being thus appealed to, and bawled 'Nobody isn't such a fool as to say he doosn't,' after which he incapacitated himself for further conversation by taking a most prodigious sandwich at one bite.

'She is poor now'—said the old man, patting the child's cheek, 'but I say again that the time is coming when she shall be rich. It has been a long time coming, but it must come at last; a very long time, but it surely must come. It has come to other men who do nothing but waste and riot. When will it come to me!'

'I am very happy as I am, grandfather,' said the child.

'Tush, tush!' returned the old man, 'thou dost not know—how should'st thou!' then he muttered again between his teeth, 'The time must come, I am very sure it must. It will be all the better for coming late'; and then he sighed and fell into his former musing state, and still holding the child between his knees appeared to be insensible to everything around him. By this time it wanted but a few minutes of midnight and I rose to go, which recalled him to himself.

'One moment, sir,' he said, 'Now, Kit—near midnight, boy, and you still here! Get home, get home, and be true to your time in the morning, for there's work to do. Good night! There, bid him good night, Nell, and let him be gone!'

'Good night, Kit,' said the child, her eyes lighting up with merriment and kindness.

'Good night, Miss Nell,' returned the boy.

'And thank this gentleman,' interposed the old man, 'but for whose care I might have lost my little girl to-night.'

'No, no, master,' said Kit, 'that won't do, that won't.'

'What do you mean?' cried the old man.

'I'd have found her, master,' said Kit, 'I'd have found her. I'll bet that I'd find her if she was above ground, I would, as quick as anybody, master. Ha, ha, ha!'

Once more opening his mouth and shutting his eyes, and laughing like a stentor, Kit gradually backed to the door, and roared himself out.

Free of the room, the boy was not slow in taking his departure; when he had gone, and the child was occupied in clearing the table, the old man said:

'I haven't seemed to thank you, sir, for what you have done to-night, but I do thank you humbly and heartily, and so does she, and her thanks are better worth than mine. I should be sorry that you went away, and thought I was unmindful of your goodness, or careless of her—I am not indeed.'

I was sure of that, I said, from what I had seen. 'But,' I added, 'may I ask you a question?'

'Ay, sir,' replied the old man, 'What is it?'

'This delicate child,' said I, 'with so much beauty and intelligence—has she nobody to care for her but you? Has she no other companion or advisor?'

'No,' he returned, looking anxiously in my face, 'no, and she wants no other.'

'But are you not fearful,' said I, 'that you may misunderstand a charge so tender? I am sure you mean well, but are you quite certain that you know how to execute such a trust as this? I am an old man, like you, and I am actuated by an old man's concern in all that is young and promising. Do you not think that what I have seen of you and this little creature to-night must have an interest not wholly free from pain?'

'Sir,' rejoined the old man after a moment's silence. 'I have no right to feel hurt at what you say. It is true that in many respects I am the child, and she the grown person—that you have seen already. But waking or sleeping, by night or day, in sickness or health, she is the one object of my care, and if you knew of how much care, you would look on me with different eyes, you would indeed. Ah! It's a weary life for an old man—a weary, weary life—but there is a great end to gain and that I keep before me.'

Seeing that he was in a state of excitement and impatience, I turned to put on an outer coat which I had thrown off on entering the room, purposing to say no more. I was surprised to see the child standing patiently by with a cloak upon her arm, and in her hand a hat, and stick.

'Those are not mine, my dear,' said I.

'No,' returned the child, 'they are grandfather's.'

'But he is not going out to-night.'

'Oh, yes, he is,' said the child, with a smile.

'And what becomes of you, my pretty one?'

'Me! I stay here of course. I always do.'

I looked in astonishment towards the old man, but he was, or feigned to be, busied in the arrangement of his dress. From him I looked back to the slight gentle figure of the child. Alone! In that gloomy place all the long, dreary night.

She evinced no consciousness of my surprise, but cheerfully helped the old man with his cloak, and when he was ready took a candle to light us out. Finding that we did not follow as she expected, she looked back with a smile and waited for us. The old man showed by his face that he plainly understood the cause of my hesitation, but he merely signed to me with an inclination of the head to pass out of the room before him, and remained silent. I had no resource but to comply.

When we reached the door, the child setting down the candle, turned to say good night and raised her face to kiss me. Then she ran to the old man, who folded her in his arms and bade God bless her.

'Sleep soundly, Nell,' he said in a low voice, 'and angels guard thy bed! Do not forget thy prayers, my sweet.'

'No, indeed,' answered the child fervently, 'they make me feel so happy!'

'That's well; I know they do; they should,' said the old man. 'Bless thee a hundred times! Early in the morning I shall be home.'

'You'll not ring twice,' returned the child. 'The bell wakes me, even in the middle of a dream.'

With this, they separated. The child opened the door (now guarded by a shutter which I had heard the boy put up before he left the house) and with another farewell whose clear and tender note I have recalled a thousand times, held it until we had passed out. The old man paused a moment while it was gently closed and fastened on the inside, and satisfied that this was done, walked on at a slow pace. At the street-corner he stopped, and regarding me with a troubled countenance said that our ways were widely different and that he must take his leave. I would have spoken, but summoning up more alacrity than might have been expected in one of his appearance, he hurried away. I could see that twice or thrice he looked back as if to ascertain if I were still watching him, or perhaps to assure himself that I was not following at a distance. The obscurity of the night favoured his disappearance, and his figure was soon beyond my sight.

I remained standing on the spot where he had left me, unwilling to depart, and yet unknowing why I should loiter there. I looked wistfully into the street we had lately quitted, and after a time directed my steps that way. I passed and repassed the house, and stopped and listened at the door; all was dark, and silent as the grave.

Yet I lingered about, and could not tear myself away, thinking of all possible harm that might happen to the child—of fires and robberies and even murder—and feeling as if some evil must ensue if I turned my back upon the place. The closing of a door or window in the street brought me before the curiosity-dealer's once more; I crossed the road and looked up at the house to assure myself that the noise had not come from there. No, it was black, cold, and lifeless as before.

There were few passengers astir; the street was sad and dismal, and pretty well my own. A few stragglers from the theatres hurried by, and now and then I turned aside to avoid some noisy drunkard as he reeled homewards, but these interruptions were not frequent and soon ceased. The clocks struck one. Still I paced up and down, promising myself that every time should be the last, and breaking faith with myself on some new plea as often as I did so.

The more I thought of what the old man had said, and of his looks and bearing, the less I could account for what I had seen and heard. I had a strong misgiving that his nightly absence was for no good purpose. I had only come to know the fact through the innocence of the child, and though the old man was by at the time, and saw my undisguised surprise, he had preserved a strange mystery upon the subject and offered no word of explanation. These reflections naturally recalled again more strongly than before his haggard face, his wandering manner, his restless anxious looks. His affection for the child might not be inconsistent with villany of the worst kind; even that very affection was in itself an extraordinary contradiction, or how could he leave her thus? Disposed as I was to think badly of him, I never doubted that his love for her was real. I could not admit the thought, remembering what had passed between us, and the tone of voice in which he had called her by her name.

'Stay here of course,' the child had said in answer to my question, 'I always do!' What could take him from home by night, and every night! I called up all the strange tales I had ever heard of dark and secret deeds committed in great towns and escaping detection for a long series of years; wild as many of these stories were, I could not find one adapted to this mystery, which only became the more impenetrable, in proportion as I sought to solve it.

Occupied with such thoughts as these, and a crowd of others all tending to the same point, I continued to pace the street for two long hours; at length the rain began to descend heavily, and then over-powered by fatigue though no less interested than I had been at first, I engaged the nearest coach and so got home. A cheerful fire was blazing on the hearth, the lamp burnt brightly, my clock received me with its old familiar welcome; everything was quiet, warm and cheering, and in happy contrast to the gloom and darkness I had quitted.

But all that night, waking or in my sleep, the same thoughts recurred and the same images retained possession of my brain. I had ever before me the old dark murky rooms—the gaunt suits of mail with their ghostly silent air—the faces all awry, grinning from wood and stone—the dust and rust and worm that lives in wood—and alone in the midst of all this lumber and decay and ugly age, the beautiful child in her gentle slumber, smiling through her light and sunny dreams.

CHAPTER 2

After combating, for nearly a week, the feeling which impelled me to revisit the place I had quitted under the circumstances already detailed, I yielded to it at length; and determining that this time I would present myself by the light of day, bent my steps thither early in the morning.

I walked past the house, and took several turns in the street, with that kind of hesitation which is natural to a man who is conscious that the visit he is about to pay is unexpected, and may not be very acceptable. However, as the door of the shop was shut, and it did not appear likely that I should be recognized by those within, if I continued merely to pass up and down before it, I soon conquered this irresolution, and found myself in the Curiosity Dealer's warehouse.

The old man and another person were together in the back part, and there seemed to have been high words between them, for their voices which were raised to a very high pitch suddenly stopped on my entering, and the old man advancing hastily towards me, said in a tremulous tone that he was very glad I had come.

'You interrupted us at a critical moment,' said he, pointing to the man whom I had found in company with him; 'this fellow will murder me one of these days. He would have done so, long ago, if he had dared.'

'Bah! You would swear away my life if you could,' returned the other, after bestowing a stare and a frown on me; 'we all know that!'

'I almost think I could,' cried the old man, turning feebly upon him. 'If oaths, or prayers, or words, could rid me of you, they should. I would be quit of you, and would be relieved if you were dead.'

'I know it,' returned the other. 'I said so, didn't I? But neither oaths, or prayers, nor words, will kill me, and therefore I live, and mean to live.'

'And his mother died!' cried the old man, passionately clasping his hands and looking upward; 'and this is Heaven's justice!'

The other stood lounging with his foot upon a chair, and regarded him with a contemptuous sneer. He was a young man of one-and-twenty or thereabouts; well made, and certainly handsome, though the expression of his face was far from prepossessing, having in common with his manner and even his dress, a dissipated, insolent air which repelled one.

'Justice or no justice,' said the young fellow, 'here I am and here I shall stop till such time as I think fit to go, unless you send for assistance to put me out—which you won't do, I know. I tell you again that I want to see my sister.'

'Your sister!' said the old man bitterly.

'Ah! You can't change the relationship,' returned the other. 'If you could, you'd have done it long ago. I want to see my sister, that you keep cooped up here, poisoning her mind with your sly secrets and pretending an affection for her that you may work her to death, and add a few scraped shillings every week to the money you can hardly count. I want to see her; and I will.'

'Here's a moralist to talk of poisoned minds! Here's a generous spirit to scorn scraped-up shillings!' cried the old man, turning from him to me. 'A profligate, sir, who has forfeited every claim not only upon those who have the misfortune to be of his blood, but upon society which knows nothing of him but his misdeeds. A liar too,' he added, in a lower voice as he drew closer to me, 'who knows how dear she is to me, and seeks to wound me even there, because there is a stranger nearby.'

'Strangers are nothing to me, grandfather,' said the young fellow catching at the word, 'nor I to them, I hope. The best they can do, is to keep an eye to their business and leave me to mine. There's a friend of mine waiting outside, and as it seems that I may have to wait some time, I'll call him in, with your leave.'

Saying this, he stepped to the door, and looking down the street beckoned several times to some unseen person, who, to judge from the air of impatience with which these signals were accompanied, required a great quantity of persuasion to induce him to advance. At length there sauntered up, on the opposite side of the way—with a bad pretense of passing by accident—a figure conspicuous for its dirty smartness, which after a great many frowns and jerks of the head, in resistance of the invitation, ultimately crossed the road and was brought into the shop.

'There. It's Dick Swiveller,' said the young fellow, pushing him in. 'Sit down, Swiveller.'

'But is the old min agreeable?' said Mr Swiveller in an undertone.

Mr Swiveller complied, and looking about him with a propitiatory smile, observed that last week was a fine week for the ducks, and this week was a fine week for the dust; he also observed that whilst standing by the post at the street-corner, he had observed a pig with a straw in his mouth issuing out of the tobacco-shop, from which appearance he augured that another fine week for the ducks was approaching, and that rain would certainly ensue. He furthermore took occasion to apologize for any negligence that might be perceptible in his dress, on the ground that last night he had had 'the sun very strong in his eyes'; by which expression he was understood to convey to his hearers in the most delicate manner possible, the information that he had been extremely drunk.

'But what,' said Mr Swiveller with a sigh, 'what is the odds so long as the fire of soul is kindled at the taper of conwiviality, and the wing of friendship never moults a feather! What is the odds so long as the spirit is expanded by means of rosy wine, and the present moment is the least happiest of our existence!'

'You needn't act the chairman here,' said his friend, half aside.

'Fred!' cried Mr Swiveller, tapping his nose, 'a word to the wise is sufficient for them—we may be good and happy without riches, Fred. Say not another syllable. I know my cue; smart is the word. Only one little whisper, Fred—is the old min friendly?'

'Never you mind,' replied his friend.

'Right again, quite right,' said Mr Swiveller, 'caution is the word, and caution is the act.' with that, he winked as if in preservation of some deep secret, and folding his arms and leaning back in his chair, looked up at the ceiling with profound gravity.

It was perhaps not very unreasonable to suspect from what had already passed, that Mr Swiveller was not quite recovered from the effects of the powerful sunlight to which he had made allusion; but if no such suspicion had been awakened by his speech, his wiry hair, dull eyes, and sallow face would still have been strong witnesses against him. His attire was not, as he had himself hinted, remarkable for the nicest arrangement, but was in a state of disorder which strongly induced the idea that he had gone to bed in it. It consisted of a brown body-coat with a great many brass buttons up the front and only one behind, a bright check neckerchief, a plaid waistcoat, soiled white trousers, and a very limp hat, worn with the wrong side foremost, to hide a hole in the brim. The breast of his coat was ornamented with an outside pocket from which there peeped forth the cleanest end of a very large and very ill-favoured handkerchief; his dirty wristbands were pulled on as far as possible and ostentatiously folded back over his cuffs; he displayed no gloves, and carried a yellow cane having at the top a bone hand with the semblance of a ring on its little finger and a black ball in its grasp. With all these personal advantages (to which may be added a strong savour of tobacco-smoke, and a prevailing greasiness of appearance) Mr Swiveller leant back in his chair with his eyes fixed on the ceiling, and occasionally pitching his voice to the needful key, obliged the company with a few bars of an intensely dismal air, and then, in the middle of a note, relapsed into his former silence.

The old man sat himself down in a chair, and with folded hands, looked sometimes at his grandson and sometimes at his strange companion, as if he were utterly powerless and had no resource but to leave them to do as they pleased. The young man reclined against a table at no great distance from his friend, in apparent indifference to everything that had passed; and I—who felt the difficulty of any interference, notwithstanding that the old man had appealed to me, both by words and looks—made the best feint I could of being occupied in examining some of the goods that were disposed for sale, and paying very little attention to a person before me.

The silence was not of long duration, for Mr Swiveller, after favouring us with several melodious assurances that his heart was in the Highlands, and that he wanted but his Arab steed as a preliminary to the achievement of great feats of valour and loyalty, removed his eyes from the ceiling and subsided into prose again.

'Fred,' said Mr Swiveller stopping short, as if the idea had suddenly occurred to him, and speaking in the same audible whisper as before, 'is the old min friendly?'

'What does it matter?' returned his friend peevishly.

'No, but is he?' said Dick.

'Yes, of course. What do I care whether he is or not?'

Emboldened as it seemed by this reply to enter into a more general conversation, Mr Swiveller plainly laid himself out to captivate our attention.

He began by remarking that soda-water, though a good thing in the abstract, was apt to lie cold upon the stomach unless qualified with ginger, or a small infusion of brandy, which latter article he held to be preferable in all cases, saving for the one consideration of expense. Nobody venturing to dispute these positions, he proceeded to observe that the human hair was a great retainer of tobacco-smoke, and that the young gentlemen of Westminster and Eton, after eating vast quantities of apples to conceal any scent of cigars from their anxious friends, were usually detected in consequence of their heads possessing this remarkable property; when he concluded that if the Royal Society would turn their attention to the circumstance, and endeavour to find in the resources of science a means of preventing such untoward revelations, they might indeed be looked upon as benefactors to mankind. These opinions being equally incontrovertible with those he had already pronounced, he went on to inform us that Jamaica rum, though unquestionably an agreeable spirit of great richness and flavour, had the drawback of remaining constantly present to the taste next day; and nobody being venturous enough to argue this point either, he increased in confidence and became yet more companionable and communicative.

'It's a devil of a thing, gentlemen,' said Mr Swiveller, 'when relations fall out and disagree. If the wing of friendship should never moult a feather, the wing of relationship should never be clipped, but be always expanded and serene. Why should a grandson and grandfather peg away at each other with mutual wiolence when all might be bliss and concord. Why not jine hands and forgit it?'

'Hold your tongue,' said his friend.

'Sir,' replied Mr Swiveller, 'don't you interrupt the chair. Gentlemen, how does the case stand, upon the present occasion? Here is a jolly old grandfather—I say it with the utmost respect—and here is a wild, young grandson. The jolly old grandfather says to the wild young grandson, "I have brought you up and educated you, Fred; I have put you in the way of getting on in life; you have bolted a little out of course, as young fellows often do; and you shall never have another chance, nor the ghost of half a one." The wild young grandson makes answer to this and says, "You're as rich as rich can be; you have been at no uncommon expense on my account, you're saving up piles of money for my little sister that lives with you in a secret, stealthy, hugger-muggering kind of way and with no manner of enjoyment—why can't you stand a trifle for your grown-up relation?" The jolly old grandfather unto this, retorts, not only that he declines to fork out with that cheerful readiness which is always so agreeable and pleasant in a gentleman of his time of life, but that he will bow up, and call names, and make reflections whenever they meet. Then the plain question is, an't it a pity that this state of things should continue, and how much better would it be for the gentleman to hand over a reasonable amount of tin, and make it all right and comfortable?'

Having delivered this oration with a great many waves and flourishes of the hand, Mr Swiveller abruptly thrust the head of his cane into his mouth as if to prevent himself from impairing the effect of his speech by adding one other word.

'Why do you hunt and persecute me, God help me!' said the old man turning to his grandson. 'Why do you bring your proligate companions here? How often am I to tell you that my life is one of care and self-denial, and that I am poor?'

'How often am I to tell you,' returned the other, looking coldly at him, 'that I know better?'

'You have chosen your own path,' said the old man. 'Follow it. Leave Nell and me to toil and work.'

'Nell will be a woman soon,' returned the other, 'and, bred in your faith, she'll forget her brother unless he shows himself sometimes.'

'Take care,' said the old man with sparkling eyes, 'that she does not forget you when you would have her memory keenest. Take care that the day don't come when you walk barefoot in the streets, and she rides by in a gay carriage of her own.'

'You mean when she has your money?' retorted the other. 'How like a poor man he talks!'

'And yet,' said the old man dropping his voice and speaking like one who thinks aloud, 'how poor we are, and what a life it is! The cause is a young child's guiltless of all harm or wrong, but nothing goes well with it! Hope and patience, hope and patience!'

These words were uttered in too low a tone to reach the ears of the young men. Mr Swiveller appeared to think that they implied some mental struggle consequent upon the powerful effect of his address, for he poked his friend with his cane and whispered his conviction that he had administered 'a clincher,' and that he expected a commission on the profits. Discovering his mistake after a while, he appeared to grow rather sleepy and discontented, and had more than once suggested the propriety of an immediate departure, when the door opened, and the child herself appeared.

CHAPTER 3

The child was closely followed by an elderly man of remarkably hard features and forbidding aspect, and so low in stature as to be quite a dwarf, though his head and face were large enough for the body of a giant. His black eyes were restless, sly, and cunning; his mouth and chin, bristly with the stubble of a coarse hard beard; and his complexion was one of that kind which never looks clean or wholesome. But what added most to the grotesque expression of his face was a ghastly smile, which, appearing to be the mere result of habit and to have no connection with any mirthful or complacent feeling, constantly revealed the few discoloured fangs that were yet scattered in his mouth, and gave him the aspect of a panting dog. His dress consisted of a large high-crowned hat, a worn dark suit, a pair of capacious shoes, and a dirty white neckerchief sufficiently limp and crumpled to disclose the greater portion of his wiry throat. Such hair as he had was of a grizzled black, cut short and straight upon his temples, and hanging in a frowzy fringe about his ears. His hands, which were of a rough, coarse grain, were very dirty; his fingernails were crooked, long, and yellow.

There was ample time to note these particulars, for besides that they were sufficiently obvious without very close observation, some moments elapsed before any one broke silence. The child advanced timidly towards her brother and put her hand in his, the dwarf (if we may call him so) glanced keenly at all present, and the curiosity-dealer, who plainly had not expected his uncouth visitor, seemed disconcerted and embarrassed.

'Ah!' said the dwarf, who with his hand stretched out above his eyes had been surveying the young man attentively, 'that should be your grandson, neighbour!'

'Say rather that he should not be,' replied the old man. 'But he is.'

'And that?' said the dwarf, pointing to Dick Swiveller.

'Some friend of his, as welcome here as he,' said the old man.

'And that?' inquired the dwarf, wheeling round and pointing straight at me.

'A gentleman who was so good as to bring Nell home the other night when she lost her way, coming from your house.'

The little man turned to the child as if to chide her or express his wonder, but as she was talking to the young man, held his peace, and bent his head to listen.

'Well, Nelly,' said the young fellow aloud. 'Do they teach you to hate me, eh?'

'No, no. For shame. Oh, no!' cried the child.

'To love me, perhaps?' pursued her brother with a sneer.

'To do neither,' she returned. 'They never speak to me about you. Indeed they never do.'

'I dare be bound for that,' he said, darting a bitter look at the grandfather. 'I dare be bound for that Nell. Oh! I believe you there!'

'But I love you dearly, Fred,' said the child.

'No doubt!'

'I do indeed, and always will,' the child repeated with great emotion, 'but oh! If you would leave off vexing him and making him unhappy, then I could love you more.'

'I see!' said the young man, as he stooped carelessly over the child, and having kissed her, pushed her from him: 'There—get you away now you have said your lesson. You needn't whimper. We part good friends enough, if that's the matter.'

He remained silent, following her with his eyes, until she had gained her little room and closed the door; and then turning to the dwarf, said abruptly,

'Harkee, Mr—'

'Meaning me?' returned the dwarf. 'Quilp is my name. You might remember. It's not a long one—Daniel Quilp.'

'Harkee, Mr Quilp, then,' pursued the other, 'You have some influence with my grandfather there.'

'Some,' said Mr Quilp emphatically.

'And are in a few of his mysteries and secrets.'

'A few,' replied Quilp, with equal dryness.

'Then let me tell him once for all, through you, that I will come into and go out of this place as often as I like, so long as he keeps Nell here; and that if he wants to be quit of me, he must first be quit of her. What have I done to be made a bugbear of, and to be shunned and dreaded as if I brought the plague? He'll tell you that I have no natural affection; and that I care no more for Nell, for her own sake, than I do for him. Let him say so. I care for the whim, then, of coming to and fro and reminding her of my existence. I will see her when I please. That's my point. I came here to-day to maintain it, and I'll come here again fifty times with the same object and always with the same success. I said I would stop till I had gained it. I have done so, and now my visit's ended. Come Dick.'

'Stop!' cried Mr Swiveller, as his companion turned toward the door. 'Sir!'

'Sir, I am your humble servant,' said Mr Quilp, to whom the monosyllable was addressed.

'Before I leave the gay and festive scene, and halls of dazzling light, sir,' said Mr Swiveller, 'I will with your permission, attempt a slight remark. I came here, sir, this day, under the impression that the old min was friendly.'

'Proceed, sir,' said Daniel Quilp; for the orator had made a sudden stop.

'Inspired by this idea and the sentiments it awakened, sir, and feeling as a mutual friend that badgering, baiting, and bullying, was not the sort of thing calculated to expand the souls and promote the social harmony of the contending parties, I took upon myself to suggest a course which is the course to be adopted to the present occasion. Will you allow me to whisper half a syllable, sir?'

Without waiting for the permission he sought, Mr Swiveller stepped up to the dwarf, and leaning on his shoulder and stooping down to get at his ear, said in a voice which was perfectly audible to all present,

'The watch-word to the old min is—fork.'

'Is what?' demanded Quilp.

'Is fork, sir, fork,' replied Mr Swiveller slapping his pocket. 'You are awake, sir?'

The dwarf nodded. Mr Swiveller drew back and nodded likewise, then drew a little further back and nodded again, and so on. By these means he in time reached the door, where he gave a great cough to attract the dwarf's attention and gain an opportunity of expressing in dumb show, the closest confidence and most inviolable secrecy. Having performed the serious pantomime that was necessary for the due conveyance of this idea, he cast himself upon his friend's track, and vanished.

'Humph!' said the dwarf with a sour look and a shrug of his shoulders, 'so much for dear relations. Thank God I acknowledge none! Nor need you either,' he added, turning to the old man, 'if you were not as weak as a reed, and nearly as senseless.'

'What would you have me do?' he retorted in a kind of helpless desperation. 'It is easy to talk and sneer. What would you have me do?'

'What would I do if I was in your case?' said the dwarf.

'Something violent, no doubt.'

'You're right there,' returned the little man, highly gratified by the compliment, for such he evidently considered it; and grinning like a devil as he rubbed his dirty hands together. 'Ask Mrs Quilp, pretty Mrs Quilp, obedient, timid, loving Mrs Quilp. But that reminds me—I have left her all alone, and she will be anxious and know not a moment's peace till I return. I know she's always in that condition when I'm away, thought she doesn't dare to say so, unless I lead her on and tell her she may speak freely and I won't be angry with her. Oh! well-trained Mrs Quilp.'

The creature appeared quite horrible with his monstrous head and little body, as he rubbed his hands slowly round, and round, and round again—with something fantastic even in his manner of performing this slight action—and, dropping his shaggy brows and cocking his chin in the air, glanced upward with a stealthy look of exultation that an imp might have copied and appropriated to himself.

'Here,' he said, putting his hand into his breast and sidling up to the old man as he spoke; 'I brought it myself for fear of accidents, as, being in gold, it was something large and heavy for Nell to carry in her bag. She need be accustomed to such loads betimes though, neighbor, for she will carry weight when you are dead.'

'Heaven send she may! I hope so,' said the old man with something like a groan.

'Hope so!' echoed the dwarf, approaching close to his ear; 'neighbour, I would I knew in what good investment all these supplies are sunk. But you are a deep man, and keep your secret close.'

'My secret!' said the other with a haggard look. 'Yes, you're right—I—I—keep it close—very close.'

He said no more, but taking the money turned away with a slow, uncertain step, and pressed his hand upon his head like a weary and dejected man. The dwarf watched him sharply, while he passed into the little sitting-room and locked it in an iron safe above the chimney-piece; and after musing for a short space, prepared to take his leave, observing that unless he made good haste, Mrs Quilp would certainly be in fits on his return.

'And so, neighbour,' he added, 'I'll turn my face homewards, leaving my love for Nelly and hoping she may never lose her way again, though her doing so has procured me an honour I didn't expect.' With that he bowed and leered at me, and with a keen glance around which seemed to comprehend every object within his range of vision, however, small or trivial, went his way.

I had several times essayed to go myself, but the old man had always opposed it and entreated me to remain. As he renewed his entreaties on our being left alone, and adverted with many thanks to the former occasion of our being together, I willingly yielded to his persuasions, and sat down, pretending to examine some curious miniatures and a few old medals which he placed before me. It needed no great pressing to induce me to stay, for if my curiosity has been excited on the occasion of my first visit, it certainly was not diminished now.

Nell joined us before long, and bringing some needle-work to the table, sat by the old man's side. It was pleasant to observe the fresh flowers in the room, the pet bird with a green bough shading his little cage, the breath of freshness and youth which seemed to rustle through the old dull house and hover round the child. It was curious, but not so pleasant, to turn from the beauty and grace of the girl, to the stooping figure, care-worn face, and jaded aspect of the old man. As he grew weaker and more feeble, what would become of this lonely little creature; poor protector as he was, say that he died—what would be her fate, then?

The old man almost answered my thoughts, as he laid his hand on hers, and spoke aloud.

'I'll be of better cheer, Nell,' he said; 'there must be good fortune in store for thee—I do not ask it for myself, but thee. Such miseries must fall on thy innocent head without it, that I cannot believe but that, being tempted, it will come at last!'

She looked cheerfully into his face, but made no answer.

'When I think,' said he, 'of the many years—many in thy short life—that thou has lived with me; of my monotonous existence, knowing no companions of thy own age nor any childish pleasures; of the solitude in which thou has grown to be what thou art, and in which thou hast lived apart from nearly all thy kind but one old man; I sometimes fear I have dealt hardly by thee, Nell.'

'Grandfather!' cried the child in unfeigned surprise.

'Not in intention—no no,' said he. 'I have ever looked forward to the time that should enable thee to mix among the gayest and prettiest, and take thy station with the best. But I still look forward, Nell, I still look forward, and if I should be forced to leave thee, meanwhile, how have I fitted thee for struggles with the world? The poor bird yonder is as well qualified to encounter it, and be turned adrift upon its mercies—Hark! I hear Kit outside. Go to him, Nell, go to him.'

She rose, and hurrying away, stopped, turned back, and put her arms about the old man's neck, then left him and hurried away again—but faster this time, to hide her falling tears.

'A word in your ear, sir,' said the old man in a hurried whisper. 'I have been rendered uneasy by what you said the other night, and can only plead that I have done all for the best—that it is too late to retract, if I could (though I cannot)—and that I hope to triumph yet. All is for her sake. I have borne great poverty myself, and would spare her the sufferings that poverty carries with it. I would spare her the miseries that brought her mother, my own dear child, to an early grave. I would leave her—not with resources which could be easily spent or squandered away, but with what would place her beyond the reach of want for ever. You mark me sir? She shall have no pittance, but a fortune—Hush! I can say no more than that, now or at any other time, and she is here again!'

The eagerness with which all this was poured into my ear, the trembling of the hand with which he clasped my arm, the strained and starting eyes he fixed upon me, the wild vehemence and agitation of his manner, filled me with amazement. All that I had heard and seen, and a great part of what he had said himself, led me to suppose that he was a wealthy man. I could form no comprehension of his character, unless he were one of those miserable wretches who, having made gain the sole end and object of their lives and having succeeded in amassing great riches, are constantly tortured by the dread of poverty, and beset by fears of loss and ruin. Many things he had said which I had been at a loss to understand, were quite reconcilable with the idea thus presented to me, and at length I concluded that beyond all doubt he was one of this unhappy race.

The opinion was not the result of hasty consideration, for which indeed there was no opportunity at that time, as the child came directly, and soon occupied herself in preparations for giving Kit a writing lesson, of which it seemed he had a couple every week, and one regularly on that evening, to the great mirth and enjoyment both of himself and his instructress. To relate how it was a long time before his modesty could be so far prevailed upon as it admit of his sitting down in the parlour, in the presence of an unknown gentleman—how, when he did set down, he tucked up his sleeves and squared his elbows and put his face close to the copy-book and squinted horribly at the lines—how, from the very first moment of having the pen in his hand, he began to wallow in blots, and to daub himself with ink up to the very roots of his hair—how, if he did by accident form a letter properly, he immediately smeared it out again with his arm in his preparations to make another—how, at every fresh mistake, there was a fresh burst of merriment from the child and louder and not less hearty laugh from poor Kit himself—and how there was all the way through, notwithstanding, a gentle wish on her part to teach, and an anxious desire on his to learn—to relate all these particulars would no doubt occupy more space and time than they deserve. It will be sufficient to say that the lesson was given—that evening passed and night came on—that the old man again grew restless and impatient—that he quitted the house secretly at the same hour as before—and that the child was once more left alone within its gloomy walls.

And now that I have carried this history so far in my own character and introduced these personages to the reader, I shall for the convenience of the narrative detach myself from its further course, and leave those who have prominent and necessary parts in it to speak and act for themselves.

CHAPTER 4

Mr and Mrs Quilp resided on Tower Hill; and in her bower on Tower Hill Mrs Quilp was left to pine the absence of her lord, when he quitted her on the business which he had already seen to transact.

Mr Quilp could scarcely be said to be of any particular trade or calling, though his pursuits were diversified and his occupations numerous. He collected the rents of whole colonies of filthy streets and alleys by the waterside, advanced money to the seamen and petty officers of merchant vessels, had a share in the ventures of divers mates of East Indiamen, smoked his smuggled cigars under the very nose of the Custom House, and made appointments on 'Change with men in glazed hats and round jackets pretty well every day. On the Surrey side of the river was a small rat-infested dreary yard called 'Quilp's Wharf,' in which were a little wooden counting-house burrowing all awry in the dust as if it had fallen from the clouds and ploughed into the ground; a few fragments of rusty anchors; several large iron rings; some piles of rotten wood; and two or three heaps of old sheet copper, crumpled, cracked, and battered. On Quilp's Wharf, Daniel Quilp was a ship-breaker, yet to judge from these appearances he must either have been a ship-breaker on a very small scale, or have broken his ships up very small indeed. Neither did the place present any extraordinary aspect of life or activity, as its only human occupant was an amphibious boy in a canvas suit, whose sole change of occupation was from sitting on the head of a pile and throwing stones into the mud when the tide was out, to standing with his hands in his pockets gazing listlessly on the motion and on the bustle of the river at high-water.

The dwarf's lodging on Tower hill comprised, besides the needful accommodation for himself and Mrs Quilp, a small sleeping-closet for that lady's mother, who resided with the couple and waged perpetual war with Daniel; of whom, notwithstanding, she stood in no slight dread. Indeed, the ugly creature contrived by some means or other—whether by his ugliness or his ferocity or his natural cunning is no great matter—to impress with a wholesome fear of his anger, most of those with whom he was brought into daily contact and communication. Over nobody had he such complete ascendance as Mrs Quilp herself—a pretty little, mild-spoken, blue-eyed woman, who having allied herself in wedlock to the dwarf in one of those strange infatuations of which examples are by no means scarce, performed a sound practical penance for her folly, every day of her life.

It has been said that Mrs Quilp was pining in her bower. In her bower she was, but not alone, for besides the old lady her mother of whom mention has recently been made, there were present some half-dozen ladies of the neighborhood who had happened by a strange accident (and also by a little understanding among themselves) to drop in one after another, just about tea-time. This being a season favourable to conversation, and the room being a cool, shady, lazy kind of place, with some plants at the open window shutting out the dust, and interposing pleasantly enough between the tea table within and the old Tower without, it is no wonder that the ladies felt an inclination to talk and linger, especially when there are taken into account the additional inducements of fresh butter, new bread, shrimps, and watercresses.

Now, the ladies being together under these circumstances, it was extremely natural that the discourse should turn upon the propensity of mankind to tyrannize over the weaker sex, and the duty that developed upon the weaker sex to resist that tyranny and assert their rights and dignity. It was natural for four reasons: firstly, because Mrs Quilp being a young woman and notoriously under the dominion of her husband ought to be excited to rebel; secondly, because Mrs Quilp's parent was known to be laudably shrewish in her disposition and inclined to resist male authority; thirdly, because each visitor wished to show for herself how superior she was in this respect to the generality of her sex; and fourthly, because the company being accustomed to scandalise each other in pairs, were deprived of their usual subject of conversation now that they were all assembled in close friendship, and had consequently no better employment than to attack the common enemy.

Moved by these considerations, a stout lady opened the proceedings by inquiring, with an air of great concern and sympathy, how Mr Quilp was; whereunto Mr Quilp's wife's mother replied sharply, 'Oh! He was well enough—nothing much was every the matter with him— and ill weeds were sure to thrive.' All the ladies then sighed in concert, shook their heads gravely, and looked at Mrs Quilp as a martyr.

'Ah!' said the spokeswoman, 'I wish you'd give her a little of your advice, Mrs Jiniwin'— Mrs Quilp had been a Miss Jiniwin it should be observed—'nobody knows better than you, ma'am, what us women owe to ourselves.'

31

'Owe indeed, ma'am!' replied Mrs Jiniwin. 'When my poor husband, her dear father, was alive, if he had ever ventured a cross word to me, I'd have—' The good old lady did not finish the sentence, but she twisted off the head of a shrimp with a vindictiveness which seemed to imply that the action was in some degree a substitute for words. In this light it was clearly understood by the other party, who immediately replied with great approbation, 'You quite enter into my feelings, ma'am, and it's jist what I'd do myself.'

'But you have no call to do it,' said Mrs Jiniwin. 'Luckily for you, you have no more occasion to do it than I had.'

'No woman need have, if she was true to herself,' rejoined the stout lady.

'Do you hear that, Betsy?' said Mrs Jiniwin, in a warning voice. 'How often have I said the same words to you, and almost gone down my knees when I spoke 'em!'

Poor Mrs Quilp, who had looked in a state of helplessness from one face of condolence to another, coloured, smiled, and shook her head doubtfully. This was the signal for a general clamour, which beginning in a low murmur gradually swelled into a great noise in which everybody spoke at once, and all said that she being a young woman had no right to set up her opinions against the experiences of those who knew so much better; that it was very wrong of her not to take the advice of people who had nothing at heart but her good; that it was next door to being downright ungrateful to conduct herself in that manner; that if she had no respect for herself she ought to have some for other women, all of whom she compromised by her meekness; and that if she had no respect for other women, the time would come when other women would have no respect for her; and she would be very sorry for that, they could tell her. Having dealt out these admonitions, the ladies fell to a more powerful assault than they had yet made upon the mixed tea, new bread, fresh butter, shrimps, and watercresses, and said that their vexation was so great to see her going on like that, that they could hardly bring themselves to eat a single morsel.

'It's all very fine to talk,' said Mrs Quilp with much simplicity, 'but I know that if I was to die to-morrow, Quilp could marry anybody he pleased—now that he could, I know!'

There was quite a scream of indignation at this idea. Marry whom he pleased! They would like to see him dare to think of marrying any of them; they would like to see the faintest approach to such a thing. One lady (a widow) was quite certain she should stab him if he hinted at it.

'Very well,' said Mrs Quilp, nodding her head, 'as I said just now, it's very easy to talk, but I say again that I know—that I'm sure—Quilp has such a way with him when he likes, that the best looking woman here couldn't refuse him if I was dead, and she was free, and he chose to make love to her. Come!'

Everybody bridled up at this remark, as much as to say, 'I know you mean me. Let him try—that's all.' and yet for some hidden reason they were all angry with the widow, and each lady whispered in her neighbour's ear that it was very plain that said widow thought herself the person referred to, and what a puss she was!

'Mother knows,' said Mrs Quilp, 'that what I say is quite correct, for she often said so before we were married. Didn't you say so, mother?'

This inquiry involved the respected lady in rather a delicate position, for she certainly had been an active party in making her daughter Mrs Quilp, and, besides, it was not supporting the family credit to encourage the idea that she had married a man whom nobody else would have. On the other hand, to exaggerate the captivating qualities of her son-in-law would be to weaken the cause of revolt, in which all her energies were deeply engaged. Beset by these opposing considerations, Mrs Jiniwin admitted the powers of insinuation, but denied the right to govern, and with a timely compliment to the stout lady brought back the discussion to the point from which it had strayed.

'Oh! It's a sensible and proper thing indeed, what Mrs George has said!' exclaimed the old lady. 'If women are only true to themselves!—But Betsy isn't, and more's the shame and pity.'

'Before I'd let a man order me about as Quilp orders her,' said Mrs George, 'before I'd consent to stand in awe of a man as she does of him, I'd—I'd kill myself, and write a letter first to say he did it!'

This remark being loudly commended and approved of, another lady (from the Minories) put in her word:

'Mr Quilp may be a very nice man,' said this lady, 'and I supposed there's no doubt he is, because Mrs Quilp says he is, and Mrs Jiniwin says he is, and they ought to know, or nobody does. But still he is not quite a—what one calls a handsome man, nor quite a young man neither, which might be a little excuse for him if anything could be; whereas his wife is young, and is good-looking, and is a woman—which is the greatest thing after all.'

This last clause being delivered with extraordinary pathos, elicited a corresponding murmer from the hearers, stimulated by which the lady went on to remark that if such a husband was cross and unreasonable with such a wife, then—

'If he is!' interposed the mother, putting down her tea-cup and brushing the crumbs out of her lap, preparatory to making a solemn declaration. 'If he is! He is the greatest tyrant that every lived, she daren't call her soul her own, he makes her tremble with a word and even with a look, he frightens her to death, and she hasn't the spirit to give him a word back, no, not a single word.'

Notwithstanding that the fact had been notorious beforehand to all the tea-drinkers, and had been discussed and expatiated on at every tea-drinking in the neighbourhood for the last twelve months, this official communication was no sooner made than they all began to talk at once and to vie with each other in vehemence and volubility. Mrs George remarked that people would talk, that people had often said this to her before, that Mrs Simmons then and there present had told her so twenty times, that she had always said, 'No, Henrietta Simmons, unless I see it with my own eyes and hear it with my own ears, I never will believe it.' Mrs Simmons corroborated this testimony and added strong evidence of her own. The lady from the Minories recounted a successful course of treatment under which she had placed her own husband, who, from manifesting one month after marriage unequivocal symptoms of the tiger, had by this means become subdued into a perfect lamb. Another lady recounted her own personal struggle and final triumph, in the course whereof she had found it necessary to call in her mother and two aunts, and to weep incessantly night and day for six weeks. A third, who in the general confusion could secure no other listener, fastened herself upon a young woman still unmarried who happened to be amongst them, and conjured her, as she valued her own peace of mind and happiness to profit by this solemn occasion, to take example from the weakness of Mrs Quilp, and from that time forth to direct her whole thoughts to taming and subduing the rebellious spirit of man. The noise was at its height, and half the company had elevated their voices into a perfect shriek in order to drown the voices of the other half, when Mrs Jiniwin was seen to change colour and shake her forefinger stealthily, as if exhorting them to silence. Then, and not until then, Daniel Quilp himself, the cause and occasion of all this clamour, was observed to be in the room, looking on and listening with profound attention.

'Go on, ladies, go on,' said Daniel. 'Mrs Quilp, pray ask the ladies to stop to supper, and have a couple of lobsters and something light and palatable.'

'I—I—didn't ask them to tea, Quilp,' stammered his wife. 'It's quite an accident.'

'So much the better, Mrs Quilp; these accidental parties are always the pleasantest,' said the dwarf, rubbing his hands so hard that he seemed to be engaged in manufacturing, of the dirt with which they were encrusted, little charges for popguns. 'What! Not going, ladies, you are not going, surely!'

His fair enemies tossed their heads slightly as they sought their respective bonnets and shawls, but left all verbal contention to Mrs Jiniwin, who finding herself in the position of champion, made a faint struggle to sustain the character.

'And why not stop to supper, Quilp,' said the old lady, 'if my daughter had a mind?'

'To be sure,' rejoined Daniel. 'Why not?'

'There's nothing dishonest or wrong in a supper, I hope?' said Mrs Jiniwin.

'Surely not,' returned the dwarf. 'Why should there be? Nor anything unwholesome, either, unless there's lobster-salad or prawns, which I'm told are not good for digestion.'

'And you wouldn't like your wife to be attacked with that, or anything else that would make her uneasy would you?' said Mrs Jiniwin.

'Not for a score of worlds,' replied the dwarf with a grin. 'Not even to have a score of mothers-in-law at the same time—and what a blessing that would be!'

'My daughter's your wife, Mr Quilp, certainly,' said the old lady with a giggle, meant for satirical and to imply that he needed to be reminded of the fact; 'your wedded wife.'

'So she is, certainly. So she is,' observed the dwarf.

'And she has a right to do as she likes, I hope, Quilp,' said the old lady trembling, partly with anger and partly with a secret fear of her impish son-in-law.

'Hope she has!' he replied. 'Oh! Don't you know she has? Don't you know she has, Mrs Jiniwin?

'I know she ought to have, Quilp, and would have, if she was of my way of thinking.'

'Why an't you of your mother's way of thinking, my dear?' said the dwarf, turing round and addressing his wife, 'why don't you always imitate your mother, my dear? She's the ornament of her sex—your father said so every day of his life. I am sure he did.'

'Her father was a blessed creetur, Quilp, and worthy twenty thousand of some people,' said Mrs Jiniwin; 'twenty hundred million thousand.'

'I should like to have known him,' remarked the dwarf. 'I dare say he was a blessed creature then; but I'm sure he is now. It was a happy release. I believe he had suffered a long time?'

The old lady gave a gasp, but nothing came of it; Quilp resumed, with the same malice in his eye and the same sarcastic politeness on his tongue.

'You look ill, Mrs Jiniwin; I know you have been exciting yourself too much—talking perhaps, for it is your weakness. Go to bed. Do go to bed.'

'I shall go when I please, Quilp, and not before.'

'But please to do now. Do please to go now,' said the dwarf.

The old woman looked angrily at him, but retreated as he advanced, and falling back before him, suffered him to shut the door upon her and bolt her out among the guests, who were by this time crowding downstairs. Being left alone with his wife, who sat trembling in a corner with her eyes fixed upon the ground, the little man planted himself before her, and folding his arms looked steadily at her for a long time without speaking.

'Mrs Quilp,' he said at last.

'Yes, Quilp,' she replead meekly.

Instead of pursuing the theme he had in his mind, Quilp folded his arms again, and looked at her more sternly than before, while she averted her eyes and kept them on the ground.

'Mrs Quilp.'

'Yes, Quilp.'

'If ever you listen to these beldames again, I'll bite you.'

With this laconic threat, which he accompanied with a snarl that gave him the appearance of being particularly in earnest, Mr Quilp bade her clear the teaboard away, and bring the rum. The spirit being set before him in a huge case-bottle, which had originally come out of some ship's locker, he settled himself in an arm-chair with his large head and face squeezed up against the back, and his little legs planted on the table.

'Now, Mrs Quilp,' he said; 'I feel in a smoking humour, and shall probably blaze away all night. But sit where you are, if you please, in case I want you.'

His wife returned no other reply than the necessary 'Yes, Quilp,' and the small lord of the creation took his first cigar and mixed his first glass of grog. The sun went down and the stars peeped out, the Tower turned from its own proper colours to grey and from grey to black, the room became perfectly dark and the end of the cigar a deep fiery red, but still Mr Quilp went on smoking and drinking in the same position, and staring listlessly out of window with the doglike smile always on his face, save when Mrs Quilp made some involuntary movement of restlessness or fatigue; and then it expanded into a grin of delight.

CHAPTER 5

Whether Mr Quilp took any sleep by snatches of a few winks at a time, or whether he sat with his eyes wide open all night long, certain it is that he kept his cigar alight, and kindled every fresh one from the ashes of that which was nearly consumed, without requiring the assistance of a candle. Nor did the striking of the clocks, hour after hour, appear to inspire him with any sense of drowsiness or any natural desire to go to rest, but rather to increase his wakefulness, which he showed, at every such indication of the progress of the night, by a suppressed cackling in his throat, and a motion of his shoulders, like one who laughs heartily but the same time slyly and by stealth.

At length the day broke, and poor Mrs Quilp, shivering with cold of early morning and harassed by fatigue and want of sleep, was discovered sitting patiently on her chair, raising her eyes at intervals in mute appeal to the compassion and clemency of her lord, and gently reminding him by an occasion cough that she was still unpardoned and that her penance had been of long duration. But her dwarfish spouse still smoked his cigar and drank his rum without heeding her; and it was not until the sun had some time risen, and the activity and noise of city day were rife in the street, that he deigned to recognize her presence by any word or sign. He might not have done so even then, but for certain impatient tapping at the door he seemed to denote that some pretty hard knuckles were actively engaged upon the other side.

'Why dear me!' he said looking round with a malicious grin, 'it's day. Open the door, sweet Mrs Quilp!'

His obedient wife withdrew the bolt, and her lady mother entered.

Now, Mrs Jiniwin bounced into the room with great impetuosity; for, supposing her son-in-law to be still a-bed, she had come to relieve her feelings by pronouncing a strong opinion upon his general conduct and character. Seeing that he was up and dressed, and that the room appeared to have been occupied ever since she quitted it on the previous evening, she stopped short, in some embarrassment.

Nothing escaped the hawk's eye of the ugly little man, who, perfectly understanding what passed in the old lady's mind, turned uglier still in the fulness of his satisfaction, and bade her good morning, with a leer or triumph.

'Why, Betsy,' said the old woman, 'you haven't been—you don't mean to say you've been a—'

'Sitting up all night?' said Quilp, supplying the conclusion of the sentence. 'Yes she has!'

'All night?' cried Mrs Jiniwin.

'Ay, all night. Is the dear old lady deaf?' said Quilp, with a smile of which a frown was part. 'Who says man and wife are bad company? Ha ha! The time has flown.'

'You're a brute!' exclaimed Mrs Jiniwin.

'Come come,' said Quilp, wilfully misunderstanding her, of course, 'you mustn't call her names. She's married now, you know. And though she did beguile the time and keep me from my bed, you must not be so tenderly careful of me as to be out of humour with her. Bless you for a dear old lady. Here's to your health!'

'I am much obliged to you,' returned the old woman, testifying by a certain restlessness in her hands a vehement desire to shake her matronly fist at her son-in-law. 'Oh! I'm very much obliged to you!'

'Grateful soul!' cried the dwarf. 'Mrs Quilp.'

'Yes, Quilp,' said the timid sufferer.

'Help your mother to get breakfast, Mrs Quilp. I am going to the wharf this morning—

the earlier the better, so be quick.'

Mrs Jiniwin made a faint demonstration of rebellion by sitting down in a chair near the door and folding her arms as if in a resolute determination to do nothing. But a few whispered words from her daughter, and a kind inquiry from her son-in-law whether she felt faint, with a hint that there was abundance of cold water in the next apartment, routed these symptoms effectually, and she applied herself to the prescribed preparations with sullen diligence.

While they were in progress, Mr Quilp withdrew to the adjoining room, and, turning back his coat-collar, proceeded to smear his countenance with a damp towel of very unwholesome appearance, which made his complexion rather more cloudy than it was before. But, while he was thus engaged, his caution and inquisitiveness did not forsake him, for with a face as sharp and cunning as ever, he often stopped, even in this short process, and stood listening for any conversation in the next room, of which he might be the theme.

'Ah!' he said after a short effort of attention, 'it was not the towel over my ears, I thought it wasn't. I'm a little hunchy villain and a monster, am I, Mrs Jiniwin? Oh!'

The pleasure of this discovery called up the old doglike smile in full force. When he had quite done with it, he shook himself in a very doglike manner, and rejoined the ladies.

Mr Quilp now walked up to front of a looking-glass, and was standing there putting on his neckerchief, when Mrs Jiniwin happening to be behind him, could not resist the inclination she felt to shake her fist at her tyrant son-in-law. It was the gesture of an instant, but as she did so and accompanied the action with a menacing look, she met his eye in the glass, catching her in the very act. The same glance at the mirror conveyed to her the reflection of a horribly grotesque and distorted face with the tongue lolling out; and the next instant the dwarf, turning about with a perfectly bland and placid look, inquired in a tone of great affection.

'How are you now, my dear old darling?'

Slight and ridiculous as the incident was, it made him appear such a little fiend, and withal such a keen and knowing one, that the old woman felt too much afraid of him to utter a single word, and suffered herself to be led with extraordinary politeness to the breakfast-table. Here he by no means diminished the impression he had just produced, for he ate hard eggs, shell and all, devoured gigantic prawns with the heads and tails on, chewed tobacco and water-cresses at the same time and with extraordinary greediness, drank boiling tea without winking, bit his fork and spoon till they bent again, and in short performed so many horrifying and uncommon acts that the women were nearly frightened out of their wits, and began to doubt if he were really a human creature. At last, having gone through these proceedings and many others which were equally a part of his system, Mr Quilp left them, reduced to a very obedient and humbled state, and betook himself to the river-side, where he took boat for the wharf on which he had bestowed his name.

It was flood tide when Daniel Quilp sat himself down in the ferry to cross to the opposite shore. A fleet of barges were coming lazily on, some sideways, some head first, some stern first; all in a wrong-headed, dogged, obstinate way, bumping up against the larger craft, running under the bows of steamboats, getting into every kind of nook and corner where they had no business, and being crunched on all sides like so many walnut-shells; while each with its pair of long sweeps struggling and splashing in the water looked like some lumbering fish in pain. In some of the vessels at anchor all hands were busily engaged in coiling ropes, spreading out sails to dry, taking in or discharging their cargoes; in others no life was visible but two or three tarry boys, and perhaps a barking dog running to and fro upon the deck or scrambling up to look over the side and bark the louder for the view. Coming slowly on through the forests of masts was a great steamship, beating the water in short impatient strokes with her heavy paddles as though she wanted room to breathe, and advancing in her huge bulk like a sea monster among the minnows of the Thames. On either hand were long black tiers of colliers; between them vessels slowly working out of harbour with sails glistening in the sun, and creaking noise on board, re-echoed from a hundred quarters. The water and all upon it was in active motion, dancing and buoyant and bubbling up; while the old grey Tower and piles of building on the shore, with many a church-spire shooting up between, looked coldly on, and seemed to disdain their chafing, restless neighbour.

Daniel Quilp, who was not much affected by a bright morning save in so far as it spared him the trouble of carrying an umbrella, caused himself to be put ashore hard by the wharf, and proceeded thither through a narrow lane which, partaking of the amphibious character of its frequenters, had as much water as mud in its composition, and a very liberal supply of both. Arrived at his destination, the first object that presented itself to his view was a pair of very imperfectly shod feet elevated in the air with the soles upwards, which remarkable appearance was referable to the boy, who being of an eccentric spirit and having a natural taste for tumbling, was now standing on his head and contemplating the aspect of the river under these uncommon circumstances. He was speedily brought on his heels by the sound of his master's voice, and as soon as his head was in its right position, Mr Quilp, to speak expressively in the absence of a better verb, 'punched it' for him.

'Come, you let me alone,' said the boy, parrying Quilp's hand with both his elbows alternatively. 'You'll get something you won't like if you don't and so I tell you.'

'You dog,' snarled Quilp, 'I'll beat you with an iron rod, I'll scratch you with a rusty nail, I'll pinch your eyes, if you talk to me—I will.'

With these threats he clenched his hand again, and dexterously diving in between the elbows and catching the boy's head as it dodged from side to side, gave it three or four good hard knocks. Having now carried his point and insisted on it, he left off.

'You won't do it agin,' said the boy, nodding his head and drawing back, with the elbows ready in case of the worst; 'now—'

'Stand still, you dog,' said Quilp. 'I won't do it again, because I've done it as often as I want. Here. Take the key.'

'Why don't you hit one of your size?' said the boy approaching very slowly.

'Where is there one of my size, you dog?' returned Quilp. 'Take the key, or I'll brain you with it'—indeed he gave him a smart tap with the handle as he spoke. 'Now, open the counting-house.'

The boy sulkily complied, muttering at first, but desisting when he looked round and saw that Quilp was following him with a steady look. And here it may be remarked, that between this boy and the dwarf there existed a strange kind of mutual liking. How born or bred, and or nourished upon blows and threats on one side, and retorts and defiances on the other, is not to the purpose. Quilp would certainly suffer nobody to contract him but the boy, and the boy would assuredly not have submitted to be so knocked about by anybody but Quilp, when he had the power to run away at any time he chose.

'Now,' said Quilp, passing into the wooden counting-house, 'you mind the wharf. Stand upon your head agin, and I'll cut one of your feet off.'

The boy made no answer, but directly Quilp had shut himself in, stood on his head before the door, then walked on his hands to the back and stood on his head there, and then to the opposite side and repeated the performance. There were indeed four sides to the counting-house, but he avoided that one where the window was, deeming it probable that Quilp would be looking out of it. This was prudent, for in point of fact, the dwarf, knowing his disposition, was lying in wait at a little distance from the sash armed with a large piece of wood, which, being rough and jagged and studded in many parts with broken nails, might possibly have hurt him.

It was a dirty little box, this counting-house, with nothing in it but an old ricketty desk and two stools, a hat-peg, an ancient almanack, an inkstand with no ink, and the stump of one pen, and an eight-day clock which hadn't gone for eighteen years at least, and of which the minute-hand had been twisted off for a tooth-pick. Daniel Quilp pulled his hat over his brows, climbed on to the desk (which had a flat top) and stretching his short length upon it went to sleep with ease of an old practitioner; intending, no doubt, to compensate himself for the deprivation of last night's rest, by a long and sound nap.

Sound it might have been, but long it was not, for he had not been asleep a quarter of an hour when the boy opened the door and thrust in his head, which was like a bundle of badly-picked oakum. Quilp was a light sleeper and started up directly.

'Here's somebody for you,' said the boy.

'Who?'

'I don't know.'

'Ask!' said Quilp, seizing the trifle of wood before mentioned and throwing it at him with such dexterity that it was well the boy disappeared before it reached the spot on which he had stood. 'Ask, you dog.'

Not caring to venture within range of such missles again, the boy discreetly sent in his stead the first cause of the interruption, who now presented herself at the door.

'What, Nelly!' cried Quilp.

'Yes,' said the child, hesitating whether to enter or retreat, for the dwarf just roused, with his dishevelled hair hanging all about him and a yellow handkerchief over his head, was something fearful to behold; it's only me, sir.'

'Come in,' said Quilp, without getting off the desk. 'Come in. Stay. Just look out into the yard, and see whether there's a boy standing on his head.'

'No, sir,' replied Nell. 'He's on his feet.'

'You're sure he is?' said Quilp. 'Well. Now, come in and shut the door. What's your message, Nelly?'

The child handed him a letter. Mr Quilp, without changing his position further than to turn over a little more on his side and rest his chin on his hand, proceeded to make himself acquainted with its contents.

CHAPTER 6

Little Nell stood timidly by, with her eyes raised to the countenance of Mr Quilp as he read the letter, plainly showing by her looks that while she entertained some fear and distrust of the little man, she was much inclined to laugh at his uncouth appearance and grotesque attitude. And yet there was visible on the part of the child a painful anxiety for his reply, and consciousness of his power to render it disagreeable or distressing, which was strongly at variance with this impulse and restrained it more effectually than she could possibly have done by any efforts of her own.

That Mr Quilp was himself perplexed, and that in no small degree, by the contents of the letter, was sufficiently obvious. Before he had got through the first two or three lines he began to open his eyes very wide and to frown most horribly, the next two or three caused him to scratch his head in an uncommonly vicious manner, and when he came to the conclusion he gave a long dismal whistle indicative of surprise and dismay. After folding and laying it down beside him, he bit the nails of all of his ten fingers with extreme voracity; and taking it up sharply, read it again. The second perusal was to all appearance as unsatisfactory as the first, and plunged him into a profound reverie from which he awakened to another assault upon his nails and a long stare at the child, who with her eyes turned towards the ground awaited his further pleasure.

'Halloa here!' he said at length, in a voice, and with a suddenness, which made the child start as though a gun had been fired off at her ear. 'Nelly!'

'Yes, sir.'

'Do you know what's inside this letter, Nell?'

'No, sir!'

'Are you sure, quite sure, quite certain, upon your soul?'

'Quite sure, sir.'

'Do you wish you may die if you do know, hey?' said the dwarf.

'Indeed I don't know,' returned the child.

'Well!' muttered Quilp as he marked her earnest look. 'I believe you. Humph! Gone already? Gone in four-and-twenty hours! What the devil has he done with it, that's the mystery!'

This reflection set him scratching his head and biting his nails once more. While he was thus employed his features gradually relaxed into what was with him a cheerful smile, but which in any other man would have been a ghastly grin of pain, and when the child looked up again she found that he was regarding her with extraordinary favour and complacency.

'You look very pretty to-day, Nelly, charmingly pretty. Are you tired, Nelly?'

'No, sir. I'm in a hurry to get back, for he will be anxious while I am away.'

'There's no hurry, little Nell, no hurry at all,' said Quilp. 'How should you like to be my number two, Nelly?'

'To be what, sir?'

'My number two, Nelly, my second, my Mrs Quilp,' said the dwarf.

The child looked frightened, but seemed not to understand him, which Mr Quilp observing, hastened to make his meaning more distinctly.

'To be Mrs Quilp the second, when Mrs Quilp the first is dead, sweet Nell,' said Quilp, wrinkling up his eyes and luring her towards him with his bent forefinger, 'to be my wife, my little cherry-cheeked, red-lipped wife. Say that Mrs Quilp lives five year, or only four, you'll be just the proper age for me. Ha ha! Be a good girl, Nelly, a very good girl, and see if one of these days you don't come to be Mrs Quilp of Tower Hill.'

So far from being sustained and stimulated by this delightful prospect, the child shrank from him in great agitation, and trembled violently. Mr Quilp, either because frightening anybody afforded him a constitutional delight, or because it was pleasant to contemplate the death of Mrs Quilp number one, and the elevation of Mrs Quilp number two to her post and title, or because he was determined from purposes of his own to be agreeable and good-humoured at that particular time, only laughed and feigned to take no heed of her alarm.

'You shall come with me to Tower Hill and see Mrs Quilp that is, directly,' said the dwarf. 'She's very fond of you, Nell, though not so fond as I am. You shall come home with me.'

'I must go back indeed,' said the child. 'He told me to return directly I had the answer.'

'But you haven't it, Nelly,' retorted the dwarf, 'and won't have it, and can't have it, until I have been home, so you see that to do your errand, you must go with me. Reach me yonder hat, my dear, and we'll go directly.' With that, Mr Quilp suffered himself to roll gradually off the desk until his short legs touched the ground, when he got upon them and led the way from the counting-house to the wharf outside, when the first objects that presented themselves were the boy who had stood on his head and another young gentleman of about his own stature, rolling in the mud together, locked in a tight embrace, and cuffing each other with mutual heartiness.

'It's Kit!' cried Nelly, clasping her hand, 'poor Kit who came with me! Oh, pray stop them, Mr Quilp!'

'I'll stop 'em,' cried Quilp, diving into the little counting-house and returning with a thick stick, 'I'll stop 'em. Now, my boys, fight away. I'll fight you both. I'll take both of you, both together, both together!'

With which defiances the dwarf flourished his cudgel, and dancing round the combatants and treading upon them and skipping over them, in a kind of frenzy, laid about him, now on one and now on the other, in a most desperate manner, always aiming at their heads and dealing such blows as none but the veriest little savage would have inflicted. This being warmer work than they had calculated upon, speedily cooled the courage of the belligerents, who scrambled to their feet and called for quarter.

'I'll beat you to a pulp, you dogs,' said Quilp, vainly endeavoring to get near either of them for a parting blow. 'I'll bruise you until you're copper-coloured, I'll break your faces till you haven't a profile between you, I will.'

'Come, you drop that stick or it'll be worse for you,' said his boy, dodging round him and watching an opportunity to rush in; 'you drop that stick.'

'Come a little nearer, and I'll drop it on your skull, you dog,' said Quilp, with gleaming eyes; 'a little nearer—nearer yet.'

But the boy declined the invitation until his master was apparently a little off his guard, when he darted in and seizing the weapon tried to wrest it from his grasp. Quilp, who was as strong as a lion, easily kept his hold until the boy was tugging at it with his utmost power, when he suddenly let it go and sent him reeling backwards, so that he fell violently upon his head. The success of this manoeuvre tickled Mr Quilp beyond description, and he laughed and stamped upon the ground as at a most irresistible jest.

'Never mind,' said the boy, nodding his head and rubbing it at the same time; 'you see if ever I offer to strike anybody again because they say you're an uglier dwarf than can be seen anywheres for a penny, that's all.'

'Do you mean to say, I'm not, you dog?' returned Quilp.

'No!' retorted the boy.

'Then what do you fight on my wharf for, you villain?' said Quilp.

'Because he said so,' replied the boy, pointing to Kit, 'not because you an't.'

'Then why did he say,' bawled Kit, 'that Miss Nelly was ugly, and that she and my master was obliged to do whatever his master liked? Why did he say that?'

'He said what he did because he's a fool, and you said what you did because you're very wise and clever—almost too clever to live, unless you're very careful of yourself, Kit.' said Quilp, with great suavity in his manner, but still more of quiet malice about his eyes and mouth. 'Here's sixpence for you, Kit. Always speak the truth. At all times, Kit, speak the truth. Lock the counting-house, you dog, and bring me the key.'

The other boy, to whom this order was addressed, did as he was told, and was rewarded for his partizanship in behalf of his master, by a dexterous rap on the nose with the key, which brought the water into his eyes. Then Mr Quilp departed with the child and Kit in a boat, and the boy revenged himself by dancing on his head at intervals on the extreme verge of the wharf, during the whole time they crossed the river.

There was only Mrs Quilp at home, and she, little expecting the return of her lord, was just composing herself for a refreshing slumber when the sound of his footsteps roused her. She had barely time to seem to be occupied in some needle-work, when he entered, accompanied by the child; having left Kit downstairs.

'Here's Nelly Trent, dear Mrs Quilp,' said her husband. 'A glass of wine, my dear, and a biscuit, for she has had a long walk. She'll sit with you, my soul, while I write a letter.'

Mrs Quilp looked tremblingly in her spouse's face to know what this unusual courtesy might portend, and obedient to the summons she saw in his gesture, followed him into the next room.

'Mind what I say to you,' whispered Quilp. 'See if you can get out of her anything about her grandfather, or what they do, or how they live, or what he tells her. I've my reasons for knowing, if I can. You women talk more freely to one another than you do to us, and you have a soft, mild way with you that'll win upon her. Do you hear?'

'Yes, Quilp.'

'Go then. What's the matter now?'

'Dear Quilp,' faltered his wife. 'I love the child—if you could do without making me deceive her—'

The dwarf muttering a terrible oath looked round as if for some weapon with which to inflict condign punishment upon his disobedient wife. The submissive little woman hurriedly entreated him not to be angry, and promised to do as he bade her.

'Do you hear me,' whispered Quilp, nipping and pinching her arm; 'worm yourself into her secrets; I know you can. I'm listening, recollect. If you're not sharp enough, I'll creak the door, and woe betide you if I have to creak it much. Go!'

Mrs Quilp departed according to order, and her amiable husband, ensconcing himself behind the partly opened door, and applying his ear close to it, began to listen with a face of great craftiness and attention.

Poor Mrs Quilp was thinking, however, in what manner to begin or what kind of inquiries she could make; and it was not until the door, creaking in a very urgent manner, warned her to proceed without further consideration, that the sound of her voice was heard.

'How very often you have come backwards and forwards lately to Mr Quilp, my dear.'

'I have said so to grandfather, a hundred times,' returned Nell innocently.

'And what has he said to that?'

'Only sighed, and dropped his head, and seemed so sad and wretched that if you could have seen him I am sure you must have cried; you could not have helped it more than I, I know. How that door creaks!'

'It often does.' returned Mrs Quilp, with an uneasy glance towards it. 'But your grandfather—he used not to be so wretched?'

'Oh, no!' said the child eagerly, 'so different! We were once so happy and he so cheerful and contented! You cannot think what a sad change has fallen on us since.'

'I am very, very sorry, to hear you speak like this, my dear!' said Mrs Quilp. And she spoke the truth.

'Thank you,' returned the child, kissing her cheek, 'you are always kind to me, and it is a pleasure to talk to you. I can speak to no one else about him, but poor Kit. I am very happy still, I ought to feel happier perhaps than I do, but you cannot think how it grieves me sometimes to see him alter so.'

'He'll alter again, Nelly,' said Mrs Quilp, 'and be what he was before.'

'Oh, if God would only let that come about!' said the child with streaming eyes; 'but it is a long time now, since he first began to—I thought I saw that door moving!'

'It's the wind,' said Mrs Quilp, faintly. 'Began to—'

'To be so thoughtful and dejected, and to forget our old way of spending the time in the long evenings,' said the child. 'I used to read to him by the fireside, and he sat listening, and when I stopped and we began to talk, he told me about my mother, and how she once looked and spoke just like me when she was a little child. Then he used to take me on his knee, and try to make me understand that she was not lying in her grave, but had flown to a beautiful country beyond the sky where nothing died or ever grew old—we were very happy once!'

'Nelly, Nelly!' said the poor woman, 'I can't bear to see one as young as you so sorrowful. Pray don't cry.'

'I do so very seldom,' said Nell, 'but I have kept this to myself a long time, and I am not quite well, I think, for the tears come into my eyes and I cannot keep them back. I don't mind telling you my grief, for I know you will not tell it to any one again.'

Mrs Quilp turned away her head and made no answer.

'Then,' said the child, 'we often walked in the fields and among the green trees, and when we came home at night, we liked it better for being tired, and said what a happy place it was. And if it was dark and rather dull, we used to say, what did it matter to us, for it only made us remember our last walk with greater pleasure, and look forward to our next one. But now we never have these walks, and though it is the same house it is darker and much more gloomy than it used to be, indeed!'

She paused here, but though the door creaked more than once, Mrs Quilp said nothing.

'Mind you don't suppose,' said the child earnestly, 'that grandfather is less kind to me than he was. I think he loves me better every day, and is kinder and more affectionate than he was the day before. You do not know how fond he is of me!'

'I am sure he loves you dearly,' said Mrs Quilp.

'Indeed, indeed he does!' cried Nell, 'as dearly as I love him. But I have not told you the greatest change of all, and this you must never breathe again to any one. He has no sleep or rest, but that which he takes by day in his easy chair; for every night and nearly all night long he is away from home.'

'Nelly!'

'Hush!' said the child, laying her finger on her lip and looking round. 'When he comes home in the morning, which is generally just before day, I let him in. Last night he was very late, and it was quite light. I saw that his face was deadly pale, that his eyes were bloodshot, and that his legs trembled as he walked. When I had gone to bed again, I heard him groan. I got up and ran back to him, and heard him say, before he knew that I was there, that he could not bear his life much longer, and if it was not for the child, would wish to die. What shall I do! Oh! What shall I do!'

The fountains of her heart were opened; the child, overpowered by the weight of her sorrows and anxieties, by the first confidence she had ever shown, and the sympathy with which her little tale had been received, hid her face in the arms of her helpless friend, and burst into a passion of tears.

In a few minutes Mr Quilp returned, and expressed the utmost surprise to find her in this condition, which he did very naturally and with admirable effect, for that kind of acting had been rendered familiar to him by long practice, and he was quite at home in it.

'She's tired you see, Mrs Quilp,' said the dwarf, squinting in a hideous manner to imply that his wife was to follow his lead. 'It's a long way from her home to the wharf, and then she was alarmed to see a couple of young scoundrels fighting, and was timorous on the water besides. All this together has been too much for her. Poor Nell!'

Mr Quilp unintentionally adopted the very best means he could have devised for the recovery of his young visitor, by patting her on the head. Such an application from any other hand might not have produced a remarkable effect, but the child shrank so quickly from his touch and felt such an instinctive desire to get out of his reach, that she rose directly and declared herself ready to return.

'But you'd better wait, and dine with Mrs Quilp and me.' said the dwarf.

'I have been away too long, sir, already,' returned Nell, drying her eyes.

'Well,' said Mr Quilp, 'if you will go, you will, Nelly. Here's the note. It's only to say that I shall see him to-morrow or maybe next day, and that I couldn't do that little business for him this morning. Good-bye, Nelly. Here, you sir; take care of her, d'ye hear?'

Kit, who appeared at the summons, deigned to make no reply to so needless an injunction, and after staring at Quilp in a threatening manner, as if he doubted whether he might not have been the cause of Nelly shedding tears, and felt more than half disposed to revenge the fact upon him on the mere suspicion, turned about and followed his young mistress, who had by this time taken her leave of Mrs Quilp and departed.

'You're a keen questioner, an't you, Mrs Quilp?' said the dwarf, turning upon her as soon as they were left alone.

'What more could I do?' returned his wife mildly.

'What more could you do!' sneered Quilp, 'couldn't you have done something less? Couldn't you have done what you had to do, without appearing in your favourite part of the crocodile, you minx?'

'I am very sorry for the child, Quilp,' said his wife. 'Surely I've done enough. I've led her on to tell her secret she supposed we were alone; and you were by, God forgive me.'

'You led her on! You did a great deal truly!' said Quilp. 'What did I tell you about making me creak the door? It's lucky for you that from what she let fall, I've got the clue I want, for if I hadn't, I'd have visited the failure upon you, I can tell you.'

Mrs Quilp being fully persuaded of this, made no reply. Her husband added with some exultation,

'But you may thank your fortunate stars—the same stars that made you Mrs Quilp—you may thank them that I'm upon the old gentleman's track, and have got a new light. So let me hear no more about this matter now or at any other time, and don't get anything too nice for dinner, for I shan't be home to it.'

So saying, Mr Quilp put his hat on and took himself off, and Mrs Quilp, who was afflicted beyond measure by the recollection of the part she had just acted, shut herself up in her chamber, and smothering her head in the bed-clothes bemoaned her fault more bitterly than many less tender-hearted persons would have mourned a much greater offence; for, in the majority of cases, conscience is an elastic and very flexible article, which will bear a deal of stretching and adapt itself to a great variety of circumstances. Some people by prudent management and leaving it off piece by piece like a flannel waistcoat in warm weather, even contrive, in time, to dispense with it altogether; but there be others who can assume the garment and throw it off at pleasure; and this, being the greatest and most convenient improvement, is the one most in vogue.

CHAPTER 7

Fred,' said Mr Swiveller, 'remember the once popular melody of Begone dull care; fan the sinking flame of hilarity with the wing of friendship; and pass the rosy wine.'

Mr Richard Swiveller's apartments were in the neighbourhood of Drury Lane, and in addition to this convenience of situation had the advantage of being over a tobacconist's shop, so that he was enabled to procure a refreshing sneeze at any time by merely stepping out upon the staircase, and was saved the trouble and expense of maintaining a snuff-box. It was in these apartments that Mr Swiveller made use of the expressions above recorded for the consolation and encouragement of his desponding friend; and it may not be uninteresting or improper to remark that even these brief observations partook in a double sense of the figurative and poetical character of Mr Swiveller's mind, as the rosy wine was in fact represented by one glass of cold gin-and-water, which was replenished as occasion required from a bottle and jug upon the table, and was passed from one to another, in a scarcity of tumblers which, as Mr Swiveller's was a bachelor's establishment, may be acknowledged without a blush. By a like pleasant fiction his single chamber was always mentioned in a plural number. In its disengaged times, the tobacconist had announced it in his window as 'apartments' for a single gentleman, and Mr Swiveller, following up the hint, never failed to speak of it as his rooms, his lodgings, or his chambers, conveying to his hearers a notion of indefinite space, and leaving their imaginations to wander through long suites of lofty halls, at pleasure.

In this flight of fancy, Mr Swiveller was assisted by a deceptive piece of furniture, in reality a bedstead, but in semblance a bookcase, which occupied a prominent situation in his chamber and seemed to defy suspicion and challenge inquiry. There is no doubt that by day Mr Swiveller firmly believed this secret convenience to be a bookcase and nothing more; that he closed his eyes to the bed, resolutely denied the existence of the blankets, and spurned the bolster from his thoughts. No word of its real use, no hint of its nightly service, no allusion to its peculiar properties, had ever passed between him and his most intimate friends. Implicit faith in the deception was the first article of his creed. To be the friend of Swiveller you must reject all circumstantial evidence, all reason, observation, and experience, and repose a blind belief in the bookcase. It was his pet weakness, and he cherished it.

'Fred!' said Mr Swiveller, finding that his former adjuration had been productive of no effect. 'Pass the rosy.'

Young Trent with an impatient gesture pushed the glass towards him, and fell again in the moody attitude from which he had been unwillingly roused.

'I'll give you, Fred,' said his friend, stirring the mixture, 'a little sentiment appropriate to the occasion. Here's May the—'

'Pshaw!' interposed the other. 'You worry me to death with your chattering. You can be merry under any circumstances.'

'Why, Mr Trent,' returned Dick, 'there is a proverb which talks about being merry and wise. There are some people who can be merry and can't be wise, and some who can be wise (or think they can) and can't be merry. I'm one of the first sort. If the proverb's a good 'un, I suppose it's better to keep to half of it than none; at all events, I'd rather be merry and not wise, than like you, neither one nor t'other.'

'Bah!' muttered his friend, peevishly.

'With all my heart,' said Mr Swiveller. 'In the polite circles I believe this sort of thing isn't usually said to a gentleman in his own apartments, but never mind that. Make yourself at home,' adding to this retort an observation to the effect that his friend appeared to be rather 'cranky' in point of temper, Richard Swiveller finished the rosy and applied himself to the composition of another glassful, in which, after tasting it with great relish, he proposed a toast to an imaginary company.

'Gentlemen, I'll give you, if you please, Success to the ancient family of the Swivellers, and good luck to Mr Richard in particular—Mr Richard, gentlemen,' said Dick with great emphasis, 'who spends all his money on his friends and is Bah!'d for his pains. Hear, hear!'

'Dick!' said the other, returning to his seat after having paced the room twice or thrice, 'will you talk seriously for two minutes, if I show you a way to make your fortune with very little trouble?'

'You've shown me so many,' returned Dick; 'and nothing has come of any one of 'em but empty pockets—'

'You'll tell a different story of this one, before a very long time is over,' said his companion, drawing his chair to the table. 'You saw my sister Nell?'

'What about her?' returned Dick.

'She has a pretty face, has she not?'

'Why, certainly,' replied Dick. 'I must say for her that there's not any very strong family likeness between her and you.'

'Has she a pretty face,' repeated his friend impatiently.

'Yes,' said Dick, 'she has a pretty face, a very pretty face. What of that?'

'I'll tell you,' returned his friend. 'It's very plain that the old man and I will remain at daggers drawn to the end of our lives, and that I have nothing to expect from him. You see that, I suppose?'

'A bat might see that, with the sun shining,' said Dick.

'It's equally plain that the money which the old flint—rot him—first taught me to expect that I should share with her at his death, will all be hers, is it not?'

'I should said it was,' replied Dick; 'unless the way in which I put the case to him, made an impression. It may have done so. It was powerful, Fred. 'Here is a jolly old grandfather'— that was strong, I thought—very friendly and natural. Did it strike you in that way?'

'It didn't strike him,' returned the other, 'so we needn't discuss it. Now look here. Nell is nearly fourteen.'

'Fine girl of her age, but small,' observed Richard Swiveller parenthetically.

'If I am to go on, be quiet for one minute,' returned Trent, fretting at the slight interest the other appeared to take in the conversation. 'Now I'm coming to the point.'

'That's right,' said Dick.

'The girl has strong affections, and brought up as she has been, may, at her age, be easily influenced and persuaded. If I take her in hand, I will be bound by a very little coaxing and threatening to bend her to my will. Not to beat about the bush (for the advantages of the scheme would take a week to tell) what's to prevent your marrying her?'

Richard Swiveller, who had been looking over the rim of the tumbler while his companion addressed the foregoing remarks to him with great energy and earnestness of manner, no sooner heard these words than he evinced the utmost consternation, and with difficulty ejaculated the monosyllable:

'What!'

'I say, what's to prevent,' repeated the other with a steadiness of manner, of the effect of which upon his companion he was well assured by long experience, 'what's to prevent your marrying her?'

'And she "nearly fourteen"!' cried Dick.

'I don't mean marrying her now'—returned the brother angrily; 'say in two year's time, in three, in four. Does the old man look like a long-liver?'

'He don't look like it,' said Dick shaking his head, 'but these old people—there's no trusting them, Fred. There's an aunt of mine down in Dorsetshire that was going to die when I was eight years old, and hasn't kept her word yet. They're so aggravating, so unprincipled, so spiteful—unless there's apoplexy in the family, Fred, you can't calculate upon 'em, and even then they deceive you just as often as not.'

'Look at the worst side of the question then,' said Trent as steadily as before, and keeping his eyes upon his friend. 'Suppose he lives.'

'To be sure,' said Dick. 'There's the rub.'

'I say,' resumed his friend, 'suppose he lives, and I persuaded, or if the word sounds more feasible, forced Nell to a secret marriage with you. What do you think would come of that?'

'A family and an annual income of nothing, to keep 'em on,' said Richard Swiveller after some reflection.

'I tell you,' returned the other with an increased earnestness, which, whether it were real or assumed, had the same effect on his companion, 'that he lives for her, that his whole energies and thoughts are bound up in her, that he would no more disinherit her for an act of disobedience than he would take me into his favour again for any act of obedience or virtue that I could possibly be guilty of. He could not do it. You or any other man with eyes in his head may see that, if he chooses.'

'It seems improbable certainly,' said Dick, musing.

'It seems improbable because it is improbable,' his friend returned. 'If you would furnish him with an additional inducement to forgive you, let there be an irreconcilable breach, a most deadly quarrel, between you and me—let there be a pretense of such a thing, I mean, of course—and he'll do fast enough. As to Nell, constant dropping will wear away a stone; you know you may trust to me as far as she is concerned. So, whether he lives or dies, what does it come to? That you become the sole inheritor of the wealth of this rich old hunks, that you and I spend it together, and that you get into the bargain a beautiful young wife.'

'I suppose there's no doubt about his being rich'—said Dick.

'Doubt! Did you hear what he let fall the other day when we were there? Doubt! What will you doubt next, Dick?'

It would be tedious to pursue the conversation through all its artful windings, or to develope the gradual approaches by which the heart of Richard Swiveller was gained. It is sufficient to know that vanity, interest, poverty, and every spendthrift consideration urged him to look upon the proposal with favour, and that where all other inducements were wanting, the habitual carelessness of his disposition stepped in and still weighed down the scale on the same side. To these impulses must be added the complete ascendancy which his friend had long been accustomed to exercise over him—an ascendancy exerted in the beginning sorely at the expense of his friend's vices, and was in nine cases out of ten looked upon as his designing tempter when he was indeed nothing but his thoughtless, light-headed tool.

The motives on the other side were something deeper than any which Richard Swiveller entertained or understood, but these being left to their own development, require no present elucidation. The negotiation was concluded very pleasantly, and Mr Swiveller was in the act of stating in flowery terms that he had no insurmountable objection to marrying anybody plentifully endowed with money or moveables, who could be induced to take him, when he was interrupted in his observations by a knock at the door, and the consequent necessity of crying 'Come in.'

The door was opened, but nothing came in except a soapy arm and a strong gush of tobacco. The gush of tobacco came from the shop downstairs, and the soapy arm proceeded from the body of a servant-girl, who being then and there engaged in cleaning the stairs had just drawn it out of a warm pail to take in a letter, which letter she now held in her hand, proclaiming aloud with that quick perception of surnames peculiar to her class that it was for Mister Snivelling.

Dick looked rather pale and foolish when he glanced at the direction, and still more so when he came to look at the inside, observing that it was one of the inconveniences of being a lady's man, and that it was very easy to talk as they had been talking, but he had quite forgotten her.

'Her. Who?' demanded Trent.

'Sophy Wackles,' said Dick.

'Who's she?'

'She's all my fancy painted her, sir, that's what she is,' said Mr Swiveller, taking a long pull at 'the rosy' and looking gravely at his friend. 'She's lovely, she's divine. You know her.'

'I remember,' said his companion carelessly. 'What of her?'

'Why, sir,' returned Dick, 'between Miss Sophia Wackles and the humble individual who has now the honor to address you, warm and tender sentiments have been engendered, sentiments of the most honourable and inspiring kind. The Goddess Diana, sir, that calls aloud for the chase, is not more particular in her behavior than Sophia Wackles; I can tell you that.'

'Am I to believe there's anything real in what you say?' demanded his friend; 'you don't mean to say that any love-making has been going on?'

'Love-making, yes. Promising, no,' said Dick. 'There can be no action for breach, that's one comfort. I've never committed myself in writing, Fred.'

'And what's in the letter, pray?'

'A reminder, Fred, for to-night—a small party of twenty, making two hundred light fantastic toes in all, supposing every lady and gentleman to have the proper complement. I must go, if it's only to begin breaking off the affair—I'll do it, don't you be afraid. I should like to know whether she left this herself. If she did, unconscious of any bar to her happiness, it's affecting, Fred.'

To solve this question, Mr Swiveller summoned the handmaid and ascertained that Miss Sophy Wackles had indeed left the letter with her own hands; and that she had come accompanied, for decorum's sake no doubt, by a younger Miss Wackles; and that on learning that Mr Swiveller was at home and being requested to walk upstairs, she was extremely shocked and professed that she would rather die. Mr Swiveller heard this account with a degree of admiration not altogether consistent with the project in which he had just concurred, but his friend attached very little importance to his behavior in this respect, probably because he knew that he had influence sufficient to control Richard Swiveller's proceedings in this or any other matter, whenever he deemed it necessary, for the advancement of his own purposes, to exert it.

CHAPTER 8

Business disposed of, Mr Swiveller was inwardly reminded of its being nigh dinner-time, and to the intent that his health might not be endangered by longer abstinence, dispatched a message to the nearest eating-house requiring an immediate supply of boiled beef and greens for two. With this demand, however, the eating-house (having experience of its customer) declined to comply, churlishly sending back for answer that if Mr Swiveller stood in need of beef perhaps he would be so obliging as to come there and eat it, bringing with him, as grace before meat, the amount of a certain small account which had long been outstanding. Not at all intimidated by this rebuff, but rather sharpened in wits and appetite, Mr Swiveller forwarded the same message to another and more distant eating-house, adding to it by way of rider that the gentleman was induced to send so far, not only by the great fame and popularity its beef had acquired, but in consequence of the extreme toughness of the beef retailed at the obdurant cook's shop, which rendered it quite unfit not merely for gentlemanly food, but for any human consumption. The good effect of this politic course was demonstrated by the speedy arrival of a small pewter pyramid, curiously constructed of platters and covers, whereof the boiled-beef-plates formed the base, and a foaming quart-pot the apex; the structure being resolved into its component parts afforded all things requisite and necessary for a hearty meal, to which Mr Swiveller and his friend applied themselves with great keenness and enjoyment.

'May the present moment,' said Dick, sticking his fork into a large carbuncular potato, 'be the worst of our lives! I like the plan of sending 'em with the peel on; there's a charm in drawing a potato from its native element (if I may so express it) to which the rich and powerful are strangers. Ah! "Man wants but little here below, nor wants that little long!" How true that is!—after dinner.'

'I hope the eating-house keeper will want but little and that he may not want that little long,' returned his companion; but I suspect you've no means of paying for this!'

'I shall be passing present, and I'll call,' said Dick, winking his eye significantly. 'The waiter's quite helpless. The goods are gone, Fred, and there's an end of it.'

In point of fact, it would seem that the waiter felt this wholesome truth, for when he returned for the empty plates and dishes and was informed by Mr Swiveller with dignified carelessness that he would call and settle when he should be passing presently, he displayed some perturbation of spirit and muttered a few remarks about 'payment on delivery' and 'no trust,' and other unpleasant subjects, but was fain to content himself with inquiring at what hour it was likely that the gentleman would call, in order that being presently responsible for the beef, greens, and sundries, he might take to be in the way at the time. Mr Swiveller, after mentally calculating his engagements to a nicety, replied that he should look in at from two minutes before six and seven minutes past; and the man disappearing with this feeble consolation, Richard Swiveller took a greasy memorandum-book from his pocket and made an entry therein.

'Is that a reminder, in case you should forget to call?' said Trent with a sneer.

'Not exactly, Fred,' replied the imperturbable Richard, continuing to write with a businesslike air. 'I enter in this little book the names of the streets that I can't go down while the shops are open. This dinner today closes Long Acre. I bought a pair of boots in Great Queen Street last week, and made that no throughfare too. There's only one avenue to the Strand left often now, and I shall have to stop up that to-night with a pair of gloves. The roads are closing so fast in every direction, that in a month's time, unless my aunt sends me a remittance, I shall have to go three or four miles out of town to get over the way.'

'There's no fear of failing, in the end?' said Trent.

'Why, I hope not,' returned Mr Swiveller, 'but the average number of letters it take to soften her is six, and this time we have got as far as eight without any effect at all. I'll write another to-morrow morning. I mean to blot it a good deal and shake some water over it out of the pepper-castor to make it look penitent. "I'm in such a state of mind that I hardly know what I write"—blot—"if you could see me at this minute shedding tears for my past misconduct"—pepper-castor—"my hand trembles when I think"—blot again—if that don't produce the effect, it's all over.'

By this time, Mr Swiveller had finished his entry, and he now replaced his pencil in its little sheath and closed the book, in a perfectly grave and serious frame of mind. His friend discovered that it was time for him to fulfil some other engagement, and Richard Swiveller was accordingly left alone, in company with the rosy wine and his own meditations touching Miss Sophy Wackles.

'It's rather sudden,' said Dick shaking his head with a look of infinite wisdom, and running on (as he was accustomed to do) with scraps of verse as if they were only prose in a hurry; 'when the heart of a man is depressed with fears, the mist is dispelled when Miss Wackles appears; she's a very nice girl. She's like the red red rose that's newly sprung in June—there's no denying that—she's also like a melody that's sweetly played in tune. It's really very sudden. Not that there's any need, on account of Fred's little sister, to turn cool directly, but its better not to go too far. If I begin to cool at all I must begin at once, I see that. There's the chance of an action for breach, that's another. There's the chance of—no, there's no chance of that, but it's as well to be on the safe side.'

This undeveloped was the possibility, which Richard Swiveller sought to conceal even from himself, of his not being proof against the charms of Miss Wackles, and in some unguarded moment, by linking his fortunes to hers forever, of putting it out of his own power to further their notable scheme to which he had so readily become a party. For all these reasons, he decided to pick a quarrel with Miss Wackles without delay, and casting about for a pretext determined in favour of groundless jealousy. Having made up his mind on this important point, he circulated the glass (from his right hand to left, and back again) pretty freely, to enable him to act his part with the greater discretion, and then, after making some slight improvements in his toilet, bent his steps towards the spot hallowed by the fair object of his meditations.

The spot was at Chelsea, for there Miss Sophia Wackles resided with her widowed mother and two sisters, in conjunction with whom she maintained a very small day-school for young ladies of proportionate dimensions; a circumstance which was made known to the neighbourhood by an oval board over the front first-floor windows, whereupon appeared in circumambient flourishes the words 'Ladies' Seminary'; and which was further published and proclaimed at intervals between the hours of half-past nine and ten in the morning, by a straggling and solitary young lady of tender years standing on the scraper on the tips of her toes and making futile attempts to reach the knocker with a spelling-book. The several duties of instruction in this establishment were thus discharged. English grammar, composition, geography, and the use of the dumb-bells, by Miss Melissa Wackles; writing, arithmetic, dancing, music, and general fascination, by Miss Sophia Wackles; the art of needle-work, marking, and samplery, by Miss Jane Wackles; corporal punishment, fasting, and other tortures and terrors, by Mrs Wackles. Miss Melissa Wackles was the eldest daughter, Miss Sophy the next, and Miss Jane the youngest. Miss Melissa might have seen five-and-thirty summers or thereabouts, and verged on the autumnal; Miss Sophy was a fresh, good humoured, buxom girl of twenty; and Miss Jane numbered scarcely sixteen years. Mrs Wackles was an excellent but rather venomous old lady of three-score.

To this Ladies' Seminary, then, Richard Swiveller hied, with designs obnoxious to the peace of the fair Sophia, who, arrayed in virgin white, embellished by no ornament but one blushing rose, received him on his arrival, in the midst of very elegant not to say brilliant preparations; such as the embellishment of the room with the little flower-pots which always stood on the window-sill outside, save in windy weather when they blew into the area; the choice attire of the day-scholars who were allowed to grace the festival; the unwonted curls of Miss Jane Wackles who had kept her head during the whole of the preceding day screwed up tight in a yellow play-bill; and the solemn gentility and stately bearing of the old lady and her eldest daughter, which struck Mr Swiveller as being uncommon but made no further impression upon him.

The truth is—and, as there is no accounting for tastes, even a taste so strange as this may be recorded without being looked upon as a wilful and malicious invention—the truth is that neither Mrs Wackles nor her eldest daughter had at any time greatly favoured the pretensions of Mr Swiveller, being accustomed to make slight mention of him as 'a gay young man' and to sigh and shake their heads ominously whenever his name was mentioned. Mr Swiveller's conduct in respect to Miss Sophy having been of that vague and dilatory kind which is usually looked upon as betokening no fixed matrimonial intentions, the young lady herself began in course of time to deem it highly desirable, that it should be brought to an issue one way or other. Hence she had at last consented to play off against Richard Swiveller a stricken market-gardner known to be ready with his offer on the smallest encouragement, and hence—as this occasion had been specially assigned for the purpose—that great anxiety on her part for Richard Swiveller's presence which had occasioned her to leave the note he has been seen to receive. 'If he has any expectations at all or any means of keeping a wife well,' said Mrs

Wackles to her eldest daughter, 'he'll state 'em to us now or never.'—'If he really cares about me,' thought Miss Sophy, 'he must tell me so, to-night.'

But all these sayings and doings and thinkings being unknown to Mr Swiveller, affected him not in the least; he was debating in his mind how he could best turn jealous, and wishing that Sophy were for that occasion only far less pretty than she was, or that she were her own sister, which would have served his turn as well, when the company came, and among them the market-gardener, whose name was Cheggs. But Mr Cheggs came not alone or unsupported, for he prudently brought along with him his sister, Miss Cheggs, who making straight to Miss Sophy and taking her by both hands, and kissing her on both cheeks, hoped in an audible whisper that they had not come too early.

'Too early, no!' replied Miss Sophy.

'Oh, my dear,' rejoined Miss Cheggs in the same whisper as before, 'I've been so tormented, so worried, that it's a mercy we were not here at four o'clock in the afternoon. Alick has been in such a state of impatience to come! You'd hardly believe that he was dressed before dinner-time and has been looking at the clock and teasing me ever since. It's all your fault, you naughty thing.'

Hereupon Miss Sophy blushed, and Mr Cheggs (who was bashful before ladies) blushed too, and Miss Sophy's mother and sisters, to prevent Mr Cheggs from blushing more, lavished civilities and attentions upon him, and left Richard Swiveller to take care of himself. Here was the very thing he wanted, here was good cause reason and foundation for pretending to be angry; but having this cause reason and foundation which he had come expressly to seek, not expecting to find, Richard Swiveller was angry in sound earnest, and wondered what the devil Cheggs meant by his impudence.

However, Mr Swiveller had Miss Sophy's hand for the first quadrille (country-dances being low, were utterly proscribed) and so gained an advantage over his rival, who sat despondingly in a corner and contemplated the glorious figure of the young lady as she moved through the mazy dance. Nor was this the only start Mr Swiveller had of the market-gardener, for determining to show the family what quality of man they trifled with, and influenced perhaps by his late libations, he performed such feats of agility and such spins and twirls as filled the company with astonishment, and in particular caused a very long gentleman who was dancing with a very short scholar, to stand quite transfixed by wonder and admiration. Even Mrs Wackles forgot for the moment to snub three small young ladies who were inclined to be happy, and could not repress a rising thought that to have such a dancer as that in the family would be a pride indeed.

At this momentous crisis, Miss Cheggs proved herself a vigourous and useful ally, for not confining herself to expressing by scornful smiles a contempt for Mr Swiveller's accomplishments, she took every opportunity of whispering into Miss Sophy's ear expressions of condolence and sympathy on her being worried by such a ridiculous creature, declaring that she was frightened to death lest Alick should fall upon, and beat him, in the fulness of his wrath, and entreating Miss Sophy to observe how the eyes of the said Alick gleamed with love and fury; passions, it may be observed, which being too much for his eyes rushed into his nose also, and suffused it with a crimson glow.

'You must dance with Miss Cheggs,' said Miss Sophy to Dick Swiviller, after she had herself danced twice with Mr Cheggs and made great show of encouraging his advances. 'She's a nice girl—and her brother's quite delightful.'

'Quite delightful, is he?' muttered Dick. 'Quite delighted too, I should say, from the manner in which he's looking this way.'

Here Miss Jane (previously instructed for the purpose) interposed her many curls and whispered her sister to observe how jealous Mr Cheggs was.

'Jealous! Like his impudence!' said Richard Swiviller.

'His impudence, Mr Swiviller!' said Miss Jane, tossing her head. 'Take care he don't hear you, sir, or you may be sorry for it.'

'Oh, pray, Jane—' said Miss Sophy.

'Nonsense!' replied her sister. 'Why shouldn't Mr Cheggs be jealous if he likes? I like that, certainly. Mr Cheggs has a good a right to be jealous as anyone else has, and perhaps he may have a better right soon if he hasn't already. You know best about that, Sophy!'

Though this was a concerted plot between Miss Sophy and her sister, originating in humane intentions and having for its object the inducing Mr Swiviller to declare himself in time, it failed in its effect; for Miss Jane being one of those young ladies who are prematurely shrill and shrewish, gave such undue importance to her part that Mr Swiviller retired in dudgeon, resigning his mistress to Mr Cheggs and conveying a defiance into his looks which that gentleman indignantly returned.

'Did you speak to me, sir?' said Mr Cheggs, following him into a corner. 'Have the kindness to smile, sir, in order that we may not be suspected. Did you speak to me, sir'?

Mr Swiviller looked with a supercilious smile at Mr Chegg's toes, then raised his eyes from them to his ankles, from that to his shin, from that to his knee, and so on very gradually, keeping up his right leg, until he reached his waistcoat, when he raised his eyes from button to button until he reached his chin, and travelling straight up the middle of his nose came at last to his eyes, when he said abruptly,

'No, sir, I didn't.'

''Hem!' said Mr Cheggs, glancing over his shoulder, 'have the goodness to smile again, sir. Perhaps you wished to speak to me, sir.'

'No, sir, I didn't do that, either.'

'Perhaps you may have nothing to say to me now, sir,' said Mr Cheggs fiercely.

At these words Richard Swiviller withdrew his eyes from Mr Chegg's face, and travelling down the middle of his nose and down his waistcoat and down his right leg, reached his toes again, and carefully surveyed him; this done, he crossed over, and coming up the other leg, and thence approaching by the waistcoat as before, said when had got to his eyes, 'No sir, I haven't.'

'Oh, indeed, sir!' said Mr Cheggs. 'I'm glad to hear it. You know where I'm to be found, I suppose, sir, in case you should have anything to say to me?'

'I can easily inquire, sir, when I want to know.'

'There's nothing more we need say, I believe, sir?'

'Nothing more, sir'—With that they closed the tremendous dialog by frowning mutually.

Mr Cheggs hastened to tender his hand to Miss Sophy, and Mr Swiviller sat himself down in a corner in a very moody state.

Hard by this corner, Mrs Wackles and Miss Wackles were seated, looking on at the dance; and unto Mrs and Miss Wackles, Miss Cheggs occasionally darted when her partner was occupied with his share of the figure, and made some remark or other which was gall and wormwood to Richard Swiviller's soul. Looking into the eyes of Mrs and Miss Wackles for encouragement, and sitting very upright and uncomfortable on a couple of hard stools, were two of the day-scholars; and when Miss Wackles smiled, and Mrs Wackles smiled, the two little girls on the stools sought to curry favour by smiling likewise, in gracious acknowledgement of which attention the old lady frowned them down instantly, and said that if they dared to be guilty of such an impertinence again, they should be sent under convoy to their respective homes. This threat caused one of the young ladies, she being of a weak and trembling temperament, to shed tears, and for this offense they were both filed off immediately, with a dreadful promptitude that struck terror into the souls of all the pupils.

'I've got such news for you,' said Miss Cheggs approaching once more, 'Alick has been saying such things to Sophy. Upon my word, you know, it's quite serious and in earnest, that's clear.'

'What's he been saying, my dear?' demanded Mrs Wackles.

'All manner of things,' replied Miss Cheggs, 'you can't think how out he has been speaking!'

Richard Swiviller considered it advisable to hear no more, but taking advantage of a pause in the dancing, and the approach of Mr Cheggs to pay his court to the old lady, swaggered with an extremely careful assumption of extreme carelessness toward the door, passing on the way Miss Jane Wackles, who in all the glory of her curls was holding a flirtation, (as good practice when no better was to be had) with a feeble old gentleman who lodged in the parlour. Near the door sat Miss Sophy, still fluttered and confused by the attentions of Mr Cheggs, and by her side Richard Swiveller lingered for a moment to exchange a few parting words.

'My boat is on the shore and my bark is on the sea, but before I pass this door I will say farewell to thee,' murmured Dick, looking gloomily upon her.

'Are you going?' said Miss Sophy, whose heart sank within her at the result of her stratagem, but who affected a light indifference notwithstanding.

'Am I going!' echoed Dick bitterly. 'Yes, I am. What then?'

'Nothing, except that it's very early,' said Miss Sophy; 'but you are your own master, of course.'

'I would that I had been my own mistress too,' said Dick, 'before I had ever entertained a thought of you. Miss Wackles, I believed you true, and I was blest in so believing, but now I mourn that e'er I knew, a girl so fair yet so deceiving.'

Miss Sophy bit her lip and affected to look with great interest after Mr Cheggs, who was quaffing lemonade in the distance.

'I came here,' said Dick, rather oblivious of the purpose with which he had really come, 'with my bosom expanded, my heart dilated, and my sentiments of a corresponding description. I go away with feelings that may be conceived but cannot be described, feeling within myself that desolating truth that my best affections have experienced this night a stifler!'

'I am sure I don't know what you mean, Mr Swiviller,' said Miss Sophy with downcast eyes. 'I'm very sorry if—'

'Sorry, Ma'am!' said Dick, 'sorry in the possession of a Cheggs! But I wish you a very good night, concluding with this slight remark, that there is a young lady growing up at this present moment for me, who has not only great personal attractions but great wealth, and who has requested her next of kin to propose for my hand, which, having a regard for some members of her family, I have consented to promise. It's a gratifying circumstance which you'll be glad to hear, that a young and lovely girl is growing into a woman expressly on my account, and is now saving up for me. I thought I'd mention it. I have now merely to apologize for trespassing so long upon your attention. Good night.'

'There's one good thing springs out of all this,' said Richard Swiviller to himself when he had reached home and was hanging over the candle with the extinguisher in his hand, 'which is, that I now go heart and soul, neck and heels, with Fred in all his scheme about little Nelly, and right glad he'll be to find me so strong upon it. He shall know all about that to-morrow, and in the meantime, as it's rather late, I'll try and get a wink of the balmy.'

'The balmy' came almost as soon as it was courted. In a very few minutes Mr Swiviller was fast asleep, dreaming that he had married Nelly Trent and come into the property, and that his first act of power was to lay waste the market-garden of Mr Cheggs and turn it into a brick-field.

CHAPTER 9

The child, in her confidence with Mrs Quilp, had but feebly described the sadness and sorrow of her thoughts, or the heaviness of the cloud which overhung her home, and cast dark shadows on its hearth. Besides that it was very difficult to impart to any person not intimately acquainted with the life she led, an adequate sense of its gloom and loneliness, a constant fear of in some way committing or injuring the old man to whom she was so tenderly attached, had restrained her, even in the midst of her heart's overflowing, and made her timid of allusion to the main cause of her anxiety and distress.

For, it was not the monotonous days unchequered by variety and uncheered by pleasant companionship, it was not the dark dreary evenings or the long solitary nights, it was not the absence of every slight and easy pleasure for which young hearts beat high, or the knowing nothing of childhood but its weakness and its easily wounded spirit, that had wrung such tears from Nell. To see the old man struck down beneath the pressure of some hidden grief, to mark his wavering and unsettled state, to be agitated at times with a dreadful fear that his mind was wandering, and to trace in his words and looks the dawning of despondent madness; to watch and wait and listen for confirmation of these things day after day, and to feel and know that, come what might, they were alone in the world with no one to help or advise or care about them—these were causes of depression and anxiety that might have sat heavily on an older breast with many influences at work to cheer and gladden it, but how heavily on the mind of a young child to whom they were ever present, and who was constantly surrounded by all that could keep such thoughts in restless action!

And yet, to the old man's vision, Nell was still the same. When he could, for a moment, disengage his mind from the phantom that haunted and brooded on it always, there was his young companion with the same smile for him, the same earnest words, the same merry laugh, the same love and care that, sinking deep into his soul, seemed to have been present to him through his whole life. And so he went on, content to read the book of her heart from the page first presented to him, little dreaming of the story that lay hidden in its other leaves, and murmuring within himself that at least the child was happy.

She had been once. She had gone singing through the dim rooms, and moving with gay and lightsome step among their dusty treasures, making them older by her young life, and sterner and more grim by her gay and cheerful presence. But, now, the chambers were cold and gloomy, and when she left her own little room to while away the tedious hours, and sat in one of them, she was still and motionless as their inanimate occupants, and had no heart to startle the echoes—hoarse from their long silence—with her voice.

In one of these rooms, was a window looking into the street, where the child sat, many and many a long evening, and often far into the night, alone and thoughtful. None are so anxious as those who watch and wait; at these times, mournful fancies came flocking on her mind, in crowds.

She would take her station here, at dusk, and watch the people as they passed up and down the street, or appeared at the windows of the opposite houses; wondering whether those rooms were as lonesome as that in which she sat, and whether those people felt it company to see her sitting there, as she did only to see them look out and draw in their heads again. There was a crooked stack of chimneys on one of the roofs, in which, by often looking at them, she had fancied ugly faces that were frowning over at her and trying to peer into the room; and she felt glad when it grew too dark to make them out, though she was sorry too, when the man came to light the lamps in the street—for it made it late, and very dull inside. Then, she would draw in her head to look round the room and see that everything was in its place and hadn't moved; and looking out into the street again, would perhaps see a man passing with a coffin on his back, and two or three others silently following him to a house where somebody lay dead; which made her shudder and think of such things until they suggested afresh the old man's altered face and manner, and a new train of fears and speculations. If he were to die—if sudden illness had happened to him, and he were never to come home again, alive—if, one night, he should come home, and kiss and bless her as usual, and after she had gone to bed and had fallen asleep and was perhaps dreaming pleasantly, and smiling in her sleep, he should kill himself and his blood come creeping, creeping, on the ground to her own bed-room door! These thoughts were too terrible to dwell upon, and again she would have recourse to the street, now trodden by fewer feet, and darker and more silent than before. The shops were closing fast, and lights began to shine from the upper windows, as the neighbours went to bed. By degrees, these dwindled away and disappeared or were replaced, here and there, by a feeble rush-candle which was to burn all night. Still, there was one late shop at no great distance which sent forth a ruddy glare upon the pavement even yet, and looked bright and companionable. But, in a little time, this closed, the light was extinguished, and all was gloomy and quiet, except when some stray footsteps sounded on the pavement, or a neighbour, out later than his wont, knocked lustily at his house-door to rouse the sleeping inmates.

When the night had worn away thus far (and seldom now until it had) the child would close the window, and steal softly down stairs, thinking as she went that if one of those hideous faces below, which often mingled with her dreams, were to meet her by the way, rendering itself visible by some strange light of its own, how terrified she would be. But these fears vanished before a well-trimmed lamp and the familiar aspect of her own room. After praying fervently, and with many bursting tears, for the old man, and the restoration of his peace of mind and the happiness they had once enjoyed, she would lay her head upon the pillow and sob herself to sleep: often starting up again, before the day-light came, to listen for the bell and respond to the imaginary summons which had roused her from her slumber.

One night, the third after Nelly's interview with Mrs Quilp, the old man, who had been weak and ill all day, said he should not leave home. The child's eyes sparkled at the intelligence, but her joy subsided when they reverted to his worn and sickly face.

'Two days,' he said, 'two whole, clear, days have passed, and there is no reply. What did he tell thee, Nell?'

'Exactly what I told you, dear grandfather, indeed.'

'True,' said the old man, faintly. 'Yes. But tell me again, Nell. My head fails me. What was it that he told thee? Nothing more than that he would see me to-morrow or next day? That was in the note.'

'Nothing more,' said the child. 'Shall I go to him again to-morrow, dear grandfather? Very early? I will be there and back, before breakfast.'

The old man shook his head, and sighing mournfully, drew her towards him.

''Twould be of no use, my dear, no earthly use. But if he deserts me, Nell, at this moment—if he deserts me now, when I should, with his assistance, be recompensed for all the time and money I have lost, and all the agony of mind I have undergone, which makes me what you see, I am ruined, and—worse, far worse than that—have ruined thee, for whom I ventured all. If we are beggars—!'

'What if we are?' said the child boldly. 'Let us be beggars, and be happy.'

'Beggars—and happy!' said the old man. 'Poor child!'

'Dear grandfather,' cried the girl with an energy which shone in her flushed face, trembling voice, and impassioned gesture, 'I am not a child in that I think, but even if I am, oh hear me pray that we may beg, or work in open roads or fields, to earn a scanty living, rather than live as we do now.'

'Nelly!' said the old man.

'Yes, yes, rather than live as we do now,' the child repeated, more earnestly than before. 'If you are sorrowful, let me know why and be sorrowful too; if you waste away and are paler and weaker every day, let me be your nurse and try to comfort you. If you are poor, let us be poor together; but let me be with you, do let me be with you; do not let me see such change and not know why, or I shall break my heart and die. Dear grandfather, let us leave this sad place to-morrow, and beg our way from door to door.'

The old man covered his face with his hands, and hid it in the pillow of the couch on which he lay.

'Let us be beggars,' said the child passing an arm round his neck, 'I have no fear but we shall have enough, I am sure we shall. Let us walk through country places, and sleep in fields and under trees, and never think of money again, or anything that can make you sad, but rest at nights, and have the sun and wind upon our faces in the day, and thank God together! Let us never set foot in dark rooms or melancholy houses, any more, but wander up and down wherever we like to go; and when you are tired, you shall stop to rest in the pleasantest place that we can find, and I will go and beg for both.'

The child's voice was lost in sobs as she dropped upon the old man's neck; nor did she weep alone.

These were not words for other ears, nor was it a scene for other eyes. And yet other ears and eyes were there and greedily taking in all that passed, and moreover they were the ears and eyes of no less a person than Mr Daniel Quilp, who, having entered unseen when the child first placed herself at the old man's side, refrained—actuated, no doubt, by motives of the purest delicacy—from interrupting the conversation, and stood looking on with his accustomed grin. Standing, however, being a tiresome attitude to a gentleman already fatigued with walking, and the dwarf being one of that kind of persons who usually make themselves at home, he soon cast his eyes upon a chair, into which he skipped with uncommon agility, and perching himself on the back with his feet upon the seat, was thus enabled to look on and listen with greater comfort to himself, besides gratifying at the same time that taste for doing something fantastic and monkey-like, which on all occasions had strong possession of him. Here, then, he sat, one leg cocked carelessly over the other, his chin resting on the palm of his hand, his head turned a little on one side, and his ugly features twisted into a complacent grimace. And in this position the old man, happening in course of time to look that way, at length chanced to see him: to his unbounded astonishment.

The child uttered a suppressed shriek on beholding this agreeable figure; in their first surprise both she and the old man, not knowing what to say, and half doubting its reality, looked shrinkingly at it. Not at all disconcerted by this reception, Daniel Quilp preserved the same attitude, merely nodding twice or thrice with great condescension. At length, the old man pronounced his name, and inquired how he came there.

'Through the door,' said Quilp pointing over his shoulder with his thumb. 'I'm not quite small enough to get through key-holes. I wish I was. I want to have some talk with you, particularly, and in private. With nobody present, neighbour. Good-bye, little Nelly.'

Nell looked at the old man, who nodded to her to retire, and kissed her cheek.

'Ah!' said the dwarf, smacking his lips, 'what a nice kiss that was—just upon the rosy part. What a capital kiss!'

Nell was none the slower in going away, for this remark. Quilp looked after her with an admiring leer, and when she had closed the door, fell to complimenting the old man upon her charms.

'Such a fresh, blooming, modest little bud, neighbour,' said Quilp, nursing his short leg, and making his eyes twinkle very much; 'such a chubby, rosy, cosy, little Nell!'

The old man answered by a forced smile, and was plainly struggling with a feeling of the keenest and most exquisite impatience. It was not lost upon Quilp, who delighted in torturing him, or indeed anybody else, when he could.

'She's so,' said Quilp, speaking very slowly, and feigning to be quite absorbed in the subject, 'so small, so compact, so beautifully modelled, so fair, with such blue veins and such a transparent skin, and such little feet, and such winning ways—but bless me, you're nervous! Why neighbour, what's the matter? I swear to you,' continued the dwarf dismounting from the chair and sitting down in it, with a careful slowness of gesture very different from the rapidity with which he had sprung up unheard, 'I swear to you that I had no idea old blood ran so fast or kept so warm. I thought it was sluggish in its course, and cool, quite cool. I am pretty sure it ought to be. Yours must be out of order, neighbour.'

'I believe it is,' groaned the old man, clasping his head with both hands. 'There's burning fever here, and something now and then to which I fear to give a name.'

The dwarf said never a word, but watched his companion as he paced restlessly up and down the room, and presently returned to his seat. Here he remained, with his head bowed upon his breast for some time, and then suddenly raising it, said,

'Once, and once for all, have you brought me any money?'

'No!' returned Quilp.

'Then,' said the old man, clenching his hands desperately, and looking upwards, 'the child and I are lost!'

'Neighbour,' said Quilp glancing sternly at him, and beating his hand twice or thrice upon the table to attract his wandering attention, 'let me be plain with you, and play a fairer game than when you held all the cards, and I saw but the backs and nothing more. You have no secret from me now.'

The old man looked up, trembling.

'You are surprised,' said Quilp. 'Well, perhaps that's natural. You have no secret from me now, I say; no, not one. For now, I know, that all those sums of money, that all those loans, advances, and supplies that you have had from me, have found their way to—shall I say the word?'

'Aye!' replied the old man, 'say it, if you will.'

'To the gaming-table,' rejoined Quilp, 'your nightly haunt. This was the precious scheme to make your fortune, was it; this was the secret certain source of wealth in which I was to have sunk my money (if I had been the fool you took me for); this was your inexhaustible mine of gold, your El Dorado, eh?'

'Yes,' cried the old man, turning upon him with gleaming eyes, 'it was. It is. It will be, till I die.'

'That I should have been blinded,' said Quilp looking contemptuously at him, 'by a mere shallow gambler!'

'I am no gambler,' cried the old man fiercely. 'I call Heaven to witness that I never played for gain of mine, or love of play; that at every piece I staked, I whispered to myself that orphan's name and called on Heaven to bless the venture;—which it never did. Whom did it prosper? Who were those with whom I played? Men who lived by plunder, profligacy, and riot; squandering their gold in doing ill, and propagating vice and evil. My winnings would have been from them, my winnings would have been bestowed to the last farthing on a young sinless child whose life they would have sweetened and made happy. What would they have contracted? The means of corruption, wretchedness, and misery. Who would not have hoped in such a cause? Tell me that! Who would not have hoped as I did?'

'When did you first begin this mad career?' asked Quilp, his taunting inclination subdued, for a moment, by the old man's grief and wildness.

'When did I first begin?' he rejoined, passing his hand across his brow. 'When was it, that I first began? When should it be, but when I began to think how little I had saved, how long a time it took to save at all, how short a time I might have at my age to live, and how she would be left to the rough mercies of the world, with barely enough to keep her from the sorrows that wait on poverty; then it was that I began to think about it.'

'After you first came to me to get your precious grandson packed off to sea?' said Quilp.

'Shortly after that,' replied the old man. 'I thought of it a long time, and had it in my sleep for months. Then I began. I found no pleasure in it, I expected none. What has it ever brought me but anxious days and sleepless nights; but loss of health and peace of mind, and gain of feebleness and sorrow!'

'You lost what money you had laid by, first, and then came to me. While I thought you were making your fortune (as you said you were) you were making yourself a beggar, eh? Dear me! And so it comes to pass that I hold every security you could scrape together, and a bill of sale upon the—upon the stock and property,' said Quilp standing up and looking about him, as if to assure himself that none of it had been taken away. 'But did you never win?'

'Never!' groaned the old man. 'Never won back my loss!'

'I thought,' sneered the dwarf, 'that if a man played long enough he was sure to win at last, or, at the worst, not to come off a loser.'

'And so he is,' cried the old man, suddenly rousing himself from his state of despondency, and lashed into the most violent excitement, 'so he is; I have felt that from the first, I have always known it, I've seen it, I never felt it half so strongly as I feel it now. Quilp, I have dreamed, three nights, of winning the same large sum, I never could dream that dream before, though I have often tried. Do not desert me, now I have this chance. I have no resource but you, give me some help, let me try this one last hope.'

The dwarf shrugged his shoulders and shook his head.

'See, Quilp, good tender-hearted Quilp,' said the old man, drawing some scraps of paper from his pocket with a trembling hand, and clasping the dwarf's arm, 'only see here. Look at these figures, the result of long calculation, and painful and hard experience. I must win. I only want a little help once more, a few pounds, but two score pounds, dear Quilp.'

'The last advance was seventy,' said the dwarf; 'and it went in one night.'

'I know it did,' answered the old man, 'but that was the very worst fortune of all, and the time had not come then. Quilp, consider, consider,' the old man cried, trembling so much the while, that the papers in his hand fluttered as if they were shaken by the wind, 'that orphan child! If I were alone, I could die with gladness—perhaps even anticipate that doom which is dealt out so unequally: coming, as it does, on the proud and happy in their strength, and shunning the needy and afflicted, and all who court it in their despair—but what I have done, has been for her. Help me for her sake I implore you; not for mine; for hers!'

'I'm sorry I've got an appointment in the city,' said Quilp, looking at his watch with perfect self-possession, 'or I should have been very glad to have spent half an hour with you while you composed yourself, very glad.'

'Nay, Quilp, good Quilp,' gasped the old man, catching at his skirts, 'you and I have talked together, more than once, of her poor mother's story. The fear of her coming to poverty has perhaps been bred in me by that. Do not be hard upon me, but take that into account. You are a great gainer by me. Oh spare me the money for this one last hope!'

'I couldn't do it really,' said Quilp with unusual politeness, 'though I tell you what—and this is a circumstance worth bearing in mind as showing how the sharpest among us may be taken in sometimes—I was so deceived by the penurious way in which you lived, alone with Nelly—'

'All done to save money for tempting fortune, and to make her triumph greater,' cried the old man.

'Yes, yes, I understand that now,' said Quilp; 'but I was going to say, I was so deceived by that, your miserly way, the reputation you had among those who knew you of being rich, and your repeated assurances that you would make of my advances treble and quadruple the interest you paid me, that I'd have advanced you, even now, what you want, on your simple note of hand, if I hadn't unexpectedly become acquainted with your secret way of life.'

'Who is it,' retorted the old man desperately, 'that, notwithstanding all my caution, told you? Come. Let me know the name—the person.'

The crafty dwarf, bethinking himself that his giving up the child would lead to the disclosure of the artifice he had employed, which, as nothing was to be gained by it, it was well to conceal, stopped short in his answer and said, 'Now, who do you think?'

'It was Kit, it must have been the boy; he played the spy, and you tampered with him?' said the old man.

'How came you to think of him?' said the dwarf in a tone of great commiseration. 'Yes, it was Kit. Poor Kit!'

So saying, he nodded in a friendly manner, and took his leave: stopping when he had passed the outer door a little distance, and grinning with extraordinary delight.

'Poor Kit!' muttered Quilp. 'I think it was Kit who said I was an uglier dwarf than could be seen anywhere for a penny, wasn't it. Ha ha ha! Poor Kit!'

And with that he went his way, still chuckling as he went.

CHAPTER 10

Daniel Quilp neither entered nor left the old man's house, unobserved. In the shadow of an archway nearly opposite, leading to one of the many passages which diverged from the main street, there lingered one, who, having taken up his position when the twilight first came on, still maintained it with undiminished patience, and leaning against the wall with the manner of a person who had a long time to wait, and being well used to it was quite resigned, scarcely changed his attitude for the hour together.

This patient lounger attracted little attention from any of those who passed, and bestowed as little upon them. His eyes were constantly directed towards one object; the window at which the child was accustomed to sit. If he withdrew them for a moment, it was only to glance at a clock in some neighbouring shop, and then to strain his sight once more in the old quarter with increased earnestness and attention.

It had been remarked that this personage evinced no weariness in his place of concealment; nor did he, long as his waiting was. But as the time went on, he manifested some anxiety and surprise, glancing at the clock more frequently and at the window less hopefully than before. At length, the clock was hidden from his sight by some envious shutters, then the church steeples proclaimed eleven at night, then the quarter past, and then the conviction seemed to obtrude itself on his mind that it was no use tarrying there any longer.

That the conviction was an unwelcome one, and that he was by no means willing to yield to it, was apparent from his reluctance to quit the spot; from the tardy steps with which he often left it, still looking over his shoulder at the same window; and from the precipitation with which he as often returned, when a fancied noise or the changing and imperfect light induced him to suppose it had been softly raised. At length, he gave the matter up, as hopeless for that night, and suddenly breaking into a run as though to force himself away, scampered off at his utmost speed, nor once ventured to look behind him lest he should be tempted back again.

Without relaxing his pace, or stopping to take breath, this mysterious individual dashed on through a great many alleys and narrow ways until he at length arrived in a square paved court, when he subsided into a walk, and making for a small house from the window of which a light was shining, lifted the latch of the door and passed in.

'Bless us!' cried a woman turning sharply round, 'who's that? Oh! It's you, Kit!'

'Yes, mother, it's me.'

'Why, how tired you look, my dear!'

'Old master an't gone out to-night,' said Kit; 'and so she hasn't been at the window at all.' With which words, he sat down by the fire and looked very mournful and discontented.

The room in which Kit sat himself down, in this condition, was an extremely poor and homely place, but with that air of comfort about it, nevertheless, which—or the spot must be a wretched one indeed—cleanliness and order can always impart in some degree. Late as the Dutch clock showed it to be, the poor woman was still hard at work at an ironing-table; a young child lay sleeping in a cradle near the fire; and another, a sturdy boy of two or three years old, very wide awake, with a very tight night-cap on his head, and a night-gown very much too small for him on his body, was sitting bolt upright in a clothes-basket, staring over the rim with his great round eyes, and looking as if he had thoroughly made up his mind never to go to sleep any more; which, as he had already declined to take his natural rest and had been brought out of bed in consequence, opened a cheerful prospect for his relations and friends. It was rather a queer-looking family: Kit, his mother, and the children, being all strongly alike.

Kit was disposed to be out of temper, as the best of us are too often—but he looked at the youngest child who was sleeping soundly, and from him to his other brother in the clothes-basket, and from him to their mother, who had been at work without complaint since morning, and thought it would be a better and kinder thing to be good-humoured. So he rocked the cradle with his foot; made a face at the rebel in the clothes-basket, which put him in high good-humour directly; and stoutly determined to be talkative and make himself agreeable.

'Ah, mother!' said Kit, taking out his clasp-knife, and falling upon a great piece of bread and meat which she had had ready for him, hours before, 'what a one you are! There an't many such as you, I know.'

'I hope there are many a great deal better, Kit,' said Mrs Nubbles; 'and that there are, or ought to be, accordin' to what the parson at chapel says.'

'Much he knows about it,' returned Kit contemptuously. 'Wait till he's a widder and works like you do, and gets as little, and does as much, and keeps his spirit up the same, and then I'll ask him what's o'clock and trust him for being right to half a second.'

'Well,' said Mrs Nubbles, evading the point, 'your beer's down there by the fender, Kit.'

'I see,' replied her son, taking up the porter pot, 'my love to you, mother. And the parson's health too if you like. I don't bear him any malice, not I!'

'Did you tell me, just now, that your master hadn't gone out to-night?' inquired Mrs Nubbles.

'Yes,' said Kit, 'worse luck!'

'You should say better luck, I think,' returned his mother, 'because Miss Nelly won't have been left alone.'

'Ah!' said Kit, 'I forgot that. I said worse luck, because I've been watching ever since eight o'clock, and seen nothing of her.'

'I wonder what she'd say,' cried his mother, stopping in her work and looking round, 'if she knew that every night, when she—poor thing—is sitting alone at that window, you are watching in the open street for fear any harm should come to her, and that you never leave the place or come home to your bed though you're ever so tired, till such time as you think she's safe in hers.'

'Never mind what she'd say,' replied Kit, with something like a blush on his uncouth face; 'she'll never know nothing, and consequently, she'll never say nothing.'

Mrs Nubbles ironed away in silence for a minute or two, and coming to the fireplace for another iron, glanced stealthily at Kit while she rubbed it on a board and dusted it with a duster, but said nothing until she had returned to her table again: when, holding the iron at an alarmingly short distance from her cheek, to test its temperature, and looking round with a smile, she observed:

'I know what some people would say, Kit—'

'Nonsense,' interposed Kit with a perfect apprehension of what was to follow.

'No, but they would indeed. Some people would say that you'd fallen in love with her, I know they would.'

To this, Kit only replied by bashfully bidding his mother 'get out,' and forming sundry strange figures with his legs and arms, accompanied by sympathetic contortions of his face. Not deriving from these means the relief which he sought, he bit off an immense mouthful from the bread and meat, and took a quick drink of the porter; by which artificial aids he choked himself and effected a diversion of the subject.

'Speaking seriously though, Kit,' said his mother, taking up the theme afresh, after a time, 'for of course I was only in joke just now, it's very good and thoughtful, and like you, to do this, and never let anybody know it, though some day I hope she may come to know it, for I'm sure she would be very grateful to you and feel it very much. It's a cruel thing to keep the dear child shut up there. I don't wonder that the old gentleman wants to keep it from you.'

'He don't think it's cruel, bless you,' said Kit, 'and don't mean it to be so, or he wouldn't do it—I do consider, mother, that he wouldn't do it for all the gold and silver in the world. No, no, that he wouldn't. I know him better than that.'

'Then what does he do it for, and why does he keep it so close from you?' said Mrs Nubbles.

'That I don't know,' returned her son. 'If he hadn't tried to keep it so close though, I should never have found it out, for it was his getting me away at night and sending me off so much earlier than he used to, that first made me curious to know what was going on. Hark! what's that?'

'It's only somebody outside.'

'It's somebody crossing over here,' said Kit, standing up to listen, 'and coming very fast too. He can't have gone out after I left, and the house caught fire, mother!'

The boy stood, for a moment, really bereft, by the apprehension he had conjured up, of the power to move. The footsteps drew nearer, the door was opened with a hasty hand, and the child herself, pale and breathless, and hastily wrapped in a few disordered garments, hurried into the room.

'Miss Nelly! What is the matter!' cried mother and son together.

'I must not stay a moment,' she returned, 'grandfather has been taken very ill. I found him in a fit upon the floor—'

'I'll run for a doctor'—said Kit, seizing his brimless hat. 'I'll be there directly, I'll—'

'No, no,' cried Nell, 'there is one there, you're not wanted, you—you—must never come near us any more!'

'What!' roared Kit.

'Never again,' said the child. 'Don't ask me why, for I don't know. Pray don't ask me why, pray don't be sorry, pray don't be vexed with me! I have nothing to do with it indeed!'

Kit looked at her with his eyes stretched wide; and opened and shut his mouth a great many times; but couldn't get out one word.

'He complains and raves of you,' said the child, 'I don't know what you have done, but I hope it's nothing very bad.'

'I done!' roared Kit.

'He cried that you're the cause of all his misery,' returned the child with tearful eyes; 'he screamed and called for you; they say you must not come near him or he will die. You must not return to us any more. I came to tell you. I thought it would be better that I should come than somebody quite strange. Oh, Kit, what have you done? You, in whom I trusted so much, and who were almost the only friend I had!'

The unfortunate Kit looked at his young mistress harder and harder, and with eyes growing wider and wider, but was perfectly motionless and silent.

'I have brought his money for the week,' said the child, looking to the woman and laying it on the table—'and—and—a little more, for he was always good and kind to me. I hope he will be sorry and do well somewhere else and not take this to heart too much. It grieves me very much to part with him like this, but there is no help. It must be done. Good night!'

With the tears streaming down her face, and her slight figure trembling with the agitation of the scene she had left, the shock she had received, the errand she had just discharged, and a thousand painful and affectionate feelings, the child hastened to the door, and disappeared as rapidly as she had come.

The poor woman, who had no cause to doubt her son, but every reason for relying on his honesty and truth, was staggered, notwithstanding, by his not having advanced one word in his defence. Visions of gallantry, knavery, robbery; and of the nightly absences from home for which he had accounted so strangely, having been occasioned by some unlawful pursuit; flocked into her brain and rendered her afraid to question him. She rocked herself upon a chair, wringing her hands and weeping bitterly, but Kit made no attempt to comfort her and remained quite bewildered. The baby in the cradle woke up and cried; the boy in the clothes-basket fell over on his back with the basket upon him, and was seen no more; the mother wept louder yet and rocked faster; but Kit, insensible to all the din and tumult, remained in a state of utter stupefaction.

CHAPTER 11

Quiet and solitude were destined to hold uninterrupted rule no longer, beneath the roof that sheltered the child. Next morning, the old man was in a raging fever accompanied with delirium; and sinking under the influence of this disorder he lay for many weeks in imminent peril of his life. There was watching enough, now, but it was the watching of strangers who made a greedy trade of it, and who, in the intervals in their attendance upon the sick man huddled together with a ghastly good-fellowship, and ate and drank and made merry; for disease and death were their ordinary household gods.

Yet, in all the hurry and crowding of such a time, the child was more alone than she had ever been before; alone in spirit, alone in her devotion to him who was wasting away upon his burning bed; alone in her unfeigned sorrow, and her unpurchased sympathy. Day after day, and night after night, found her still by the pillow of the unconscious sufferer, still anticipating his every want, still listening to those repetitions of her name and those anxieties and cares for her, which were ever uppermost among his feverish wanderings.

The house was no longer theirs. Even the sick chamber seemed to be retained, on the uncertain tenure of Mr Quilp's favour. The old man's illness had not lasted many days when he took formal possession of the premises and all upon them, in virtue of certain legal powers to that effect, which few understood and none presumed to call in question. This important step secured, with the assistance of a man of law whom he brought with him for the purpose, the dwarf proceeded to establish himself and his coadjutor in the house, as an assertion of his claim against all comers; and then set about making his quarters comfortable, after his own fashion.

To this end, Mr Quilp encamped in the back parlour, having first put an effectual stop to any further business by shutting up the shop. Having looked out, from among the old furniture, the handsomest and most commodious chair he could possibly find (which he reserved for his own use) and an especially hideous and uncomfortable one (which he considerately appropriated to the accommodation of his friend) he caused them to be carried into this room, and took up his position in great state. The apartment was very far removed from the old man's chamber, but Mr Quilp deemed it prudent, as a precaution against infection from fever, and a means of wholesome fumigation, not only to smoke, himself, without cessation, but to insist upon it that his legal friend did the like. Moreover, he sent an express to the wharf for the tumbling boy, who arriving with all despatch was enjoined to sit himself down in another chair just inside the door, continually to smoke a great pipe which the dwarf had provided for the purpose, and to take it from his lips under any pretence whatever, were it only for one minute at a time, if he dared. These arrangements completed, Mr Quilp looked round him with chuckling satisfaction, and remarked that he called that comfort.

The legal gentleman, whose melodious name was Brass, might have called it comfort also but for two drawbacks: one was, that he could by no exertion sit easy in his chair, the seat of which was very hard, angular, slippery, and sloping; the other, that tobacco-smoke always caused him great internal discomposure and annoyance. But as he was quite a creature of Mr Quilp's and had a thousand reasons for conciliating his good opinion, he tried to smile, and nodded his acquiescence with the best grace he could assume.

This Brass was an attorney of no very good repute, from Bevis Marks in the city of London; he was a tall, meagre man, with a nose like a wen, a protruding forehead, retreating eyes, and hair of a deep red. He wore a long black surtout reaching nearly to his ankles, short black trousers, high shoes, and cotton stockings of a bluish grey. He had a cringing manner, but a very harsh voice; and his blandest smiles were so extremely forbidding, that to have had his company under the least repulsive circumstances, one would have wished him to be out of temper that he might only scowl.

Quilp looked at his legal adviser, and seeing that he was winking very much in the anguish of his pipe, that he sometimes shuddered when he happened to inhale its full flavour, and that he constantly fanned the smoke from him, was quite overjoyed and rubbed his hands with glee.

'Smoke away, you dog,' said Quilp, turning to the boy; 'fill your pipe again and smoke it fast, down to the last whiff, or I'll put the sealing-waxed end of it in the fire and rub it red hot upon your tongue.'

Luckily the boy was case-hardened, and would have smoked a small lime-kiln if anybody had treated him with it. Wherefore, he only muttered a brief defiance of his master, and did as he was ordered.

'Is it good, Brass, is it nice, is it fragrant, do you feel like the Grand Turk?' said Quilp.

Mr Brass thought that if he did, the Grand Turk's feelings were by no means to be envied, but he said it was famous, and he had no doubt he felt very like that Potentate.

'This is the way to keep off fever,' said Quilp, 'this is the way to keep off every calamity of life! We'll never leave off, all the time we stop here—smoke away, you dog, or you shall swallow the pipe!'

'Shall we stop here long, Mr Quilp?' inquired his legal friend, when the dwarf had given his boy this gentle admonition.

'We must stop, I suppose, till the old gentleman up stairs is dead,' returned Quilp.

'He he he!' laughed Mr Brass, 'oh! very good!'

'Smoke away!' cried Quilp. 'Never stop! You can talk as you smoke. Don't lose time.'

'He he he!' cried Brass faintly, as he again applied himself to the odious pipe. 'But if he should get better, Mr Quilp?'

'Then we shall stop till he does, and no longer,' returned the dwarf.

'How kind it is of you, Sir, to wait till then!' said Brass. 'Some people, Sir, would have sold or removed the goods—oh dear, the very instant the law allowed 'em. Some people, Sir, would have been all flintiness and granite. Some people, sir, would have—'

'Some people would have spared themselves the jabbering of such a parrot as you,' interposed the dwarf.

'He he he!' cried Brass. 'You have such spirits!'

The smoking sentinel at the door interposed in this place, and without taking his pipe from his lips, growled,

'Here's the gal a comin' down.'

'The what, you dog?' said Quilp.

'The gal,' returned the boy. 'Are you deaf?'

'Oh!' said Quilp, drawing in his breath with great relish as if he were taking soup, 'you and I will have such a settling presently; there's such a scratching and bruising in store for you, my dear young friend! Aha! Nelly! How is he now, my duck of diamonds?'

'He's very bad,' replied the weeping child.

'What a pretty little Nell!' cried Quilp.

'Oh beautiful, sir, beautiful indeed,' said Brass. 'Quite charming.'

'Has she come to sit upon Quilp's knee,' said the dwarf, in what he meant to be a soothing tone, 'or is she going to bed in her own little room inside here? Which is poor Nelly going to do?'

'What a remarkable pleasant way he has with children!' muttered Brass, as if in confidence between himself and the ceiling; 'upon my word it's quite a treat to hear him.'

'I'm not going to stay at all,' faltered Nell. 'I want a few things out of that room, and then I—I—won't come down here any more.'

'And a very nice little room it is!' said the dwarf looking into it as the child entered. 'Quite a bower! You're sure you're not going to use it; you're sure you're not coming back, Nelly?'

'No,' replied the child, hurrying away, with the few articles of dress she had come to remove; 'never again! Never again.'

'She's very sensitive,' said Quilp, looking after her. 'Very sensitive; that's a pity. The bedstead is much about my size. I think I shall make it my little room.'

Mr Brass encouraging this idea, as he would have encouraged any other emanating from the same source, the dwarf walked in to try the effect. This he did, by throwing himself on his back upon the bed with his pipe in his mouth, and then kicking up his legs and smoking violently. Mr Brass applauding this picture very much, and the bed being soft and comfortable, Mr Quilp determined to use it, both as a sleeping place by night and as a kind of Divan by day; and in order that it might be converted to the latter purpose at once, remained where he was, and smoked his pipe out. The legal gentleman being by this time rather giddy and perplexed in his ideas (for this was one of the operations of the tobacco on his nervous system), took the opportunity of slinking away into the open air, where, in course of time, he recovered sufficiently to return with a countenance of tolerable composure. He was soon led on by the malicious dwarf to smoke himself into a relapse, and in that state stumbled upon a settee where he slept till morning.

Such were Mr Quilp's first proceedings on entering upon his new property. He was, for some days, restrained by business from performing any particular pranks, as his time was pretty well occupied between taking, with the assistance of Mr Brass, a minute inventory of all the goods in the place, and going abroad upon his other concerns which happily engaged him for several hours at a time. His avarice and caution being, now, thoroughly awakened, however, he was never absent from the house one night; and his eagerness for some termination, good or bad, to the old man's disorder, increasing rapidly, as the time passed by, soon began to vent itself in open murmurs and exclamations of impatience.

Nell shrank timidly from all the dwarf's advances towards conversation, and fled from the very sound of his voice; nor were the lawyer's smiles less terrible to her than Quilp's grimaces. She lived in such continual dread and apprehension of meeting one or other of them on the stairs or in the passages if she stirred from her grandfather's chamber, that she seldom left it, for a moment, until late at night, when the silence encouraged her to venture forth and breathe the purer air of some empty room.

One night, she had stolen to her usual window, and was sitting there very sorrowfully— for the old man had been worse that day—when she thought she heard her name pronounced by a voice in the street. Looking down, she recognised Kit, whose endeavours to attract her attention had roused her from her sad reflections.

'Miss Nell!' said the boy in a low voice.

'Yes,' replied the child, doubtful whether she ought to hold any communication with the supposed culprit, but inclining to her old favourite still; 'what do you want?'

'I have wanted to say a word to you, for a long time,' the boy replied, 'but the people below have driven me away and wouldn't let me see you. You don't believe—I hope you don't really believe—that I deserve to be cast off as I have been; do you, miss?'

'I must believe it,' returned the child. 'Or why would grandfather have been so angry with you?'

'I don't know,' replied Kit. 'I'm sure I never deserved it from him, no, nor from you. I can say that, with a true and honest heart, any way. And then to be driven from the door, when I only came to ask how old master was—!'

'They never told me that,' said the child. 'I didn't know it indeed. I wouldn't have had them do it for the world.'

'Thank'ee, miss,' returned Kit, 'it's comfortable to hear you say that. I said I never would believe that it was your doing.'

'That was right!' said the child eagerly.

'Miss Nell,' cried the boy coming under the window, and speaking in a lower tone, 'there are new masters down stairs. It's a change for you.'

'It is indeed,' replied the child.

'And so it will be for him when he gets better,' said the boy, pointing towards the sick room.

'—If he ever does,' added the child, unable to restrain her tears.

'Oh, he'll do that, he'll do that,' said Kit. 'I'm sure he will. You mustn't be cast down, Miss Nell. Now don't be, pray!'

These words of encouragement and consolation were few and roughly said, but they affected the child and made her, for the moment, weep the more.

'He'll be sure to get better now,' said the boy anxiously, 'if you don't give way to low spirits and turn ill yourself, which would make him worse and throw him back, just as he was recovering. When he does, say a good word—say a kind word for me, Miss Nell!'

'They tell me I must not even mention your name to him for a long, long time,' rejoined the child, 'I dare not; and even if I might, what good would a kind word do you, Kit? We shall be very poor. We shall scarcely have bread to eat.'

'It's not that I may be taken back,' said the boy, 'that I ask the favour of you. It isn't for the sake of food and wages that I've been waiting about so long in hopes to see you. Don't think that I'd come in a time of trouble to talk of such things as them.'

The child looked gratefully and kindly at him, but waited that he might speak again.

'No, it's not that,' said Kit hesitating, 'it's something very different from that. I haven't got much sense, I know, but if he could be brought to believe that I'd been a faithful servant to him, doing the best I could, and never meaning harm, perhaps he mightn't—'

Here Kit faltered so long that the child entreated him to speak out, and quickly, for it was very late, and time to shut the window.

'Perhaps he mightn't think it over venturesome of me to say—well then, to say this,' cried Kit with sudden boldness. 'This home is gone from you and him. Mother and I have got a poor one, but that's better than this with all these people here; and why not come there, till he's had time to look about, and find a better!'

The child did not speak. Kit, in the relief of having made his proposition, found his tongue loosened, and spoke out in its favour with his utmost eloquence.

'You think,' said the boy, 'that it's very small and inconvenient. So it is, but it's very clean. Perhaps you think it would be noisy, but there's not a quieter court than ours in all the town.

Don't be afraid of the children; the baby hardly ever cries, and the other one is very good—besides, I'd mind 'em. They wouldn't vex you much, I'm sure. Do try, Miss Nell, do try. The little front room up stairs is very pleasant. You can see a piece of the church-clock, through the chimneys, and almost tell the time; mother says it would be just the thing for you, and so it would, and you'd have her to wait upon you both, and me to run of errands. We don't mean money, bless you; you're not to think of that! Will you try him, Miss Nell? Only say you'll try him. Do try to make old master come, and ask him first what I have done. Will you only promise that, Miss Nell?'

Before the child could reply to this earnest solicitation, the street-door opened, and Mr Brass thrusting out his night-capped head called in a surly voice, 'Who's there!' Kit immediately glided away, and Nell, closing the window softly, drew back into the room.

Before Mr Brass had repeated his inquiry many times, Mr Quilp, also embellished with a night-cap, emerged from the same door and looked carefully up and down the street, and up at all the windows of the house, from the opposite side. Finding that there was nobody in sight, he presently returned into the house with his legal friend, protesting (as the child heard from the staircase), that there was a league and plot against him; that he was in danger of being robbed and plundered by a band of conspirators who prowled about the house at all seasons; and that he would delay no longer but take immediate steps for disposing of the property and returning to his own peaceful roof. Having growled forth these, and a great many other threats of the same nature, he coiled himself once more in the child's little bed, and Nell crept softly up the stairs.

It was natural enough that her short and unfinished dialogue with Kit should leave a strong impression on her mind, and influence her dreams that night and her recollections for a long, long time. Surrounded by unfeeling creditors, and mercenary attendants upon the sick, and meeting in the height of her anxiety and sorrow with little regard or sympathy even from the women about her, it is not surprising that the affectionate heart of the child should have been touched to the quick by one kind and generous spirit, however uncouth the temple in which it dwelt. Thank Heaven that the temples of such spirits are not made with hands, and that they may be even more worthily hung with poor patch-work than with purple and fine linen!

CHAPTER 12

At length, the crisis of the old man's disorder was past, and he began to mend. By very slow and feeble degrees his consciousness came back; but the mind was weakened and its functions were impaired. He was patient, and quiet; often sat brooding, but not despondently, for a long space; was easily amused, even by a sun-beam on the wall or ceiling; made no complaint that the days were long, or the nights tedious; and appeared indeed to have lost all count of time, and every sense of care or weariness. He would sit, for hours together, with Nell's small hand in his, playing with the fingers and stopping sometimes to smooth her hair or kiss her brow; and, when he saw that tears were glistening in her eyes, would look, amazed, about him for the cause, and forget his wonder even while he looked.

The child and he rode out; the old man propped up with pillows, and the child beside him. They were hand in hand as usual. The noise and motion in the streets fatigued his brain at first, but he was not surprised, or curious, or pleased, or irritated. He was asked if he remembered this, or that. 'O yes,' he said, 'quite well—why not?' Sometimes he turned his head, and looked, with earnest gaze and outstretched neck, after some stranger in the crowd, until he disappeared from sight; but, to the question why he did this, he answered not a word.

He was sitting in his easy chair one day, and Nell upon a stool beside him, when a man outside the door inquired if he might enter. 'Yes,' he said without emotion, 'it was Quilp, he knew. Quilp was master there. Of course he might come in.' And so he did.

'I'm glad to see you well again at last, neighbour,' said the dwarf, sitting down opposite him. 'You're quite strong now?'

'Yes,' said the old man feebly, 'yes.'

'I don't want to hurry you, you know, neighbour,' said the dwarf, raising his voice, for the old man's senses were duller than they had been; 'but, as soon as you can arrange your future proceedings, the better.'

'Surely,' said the old man. 'The better for all parties.'

'You see,' pursued Quilp after a short pause, 'the goods being once removed, this house would be uncomfortable; uninhabitable in fact.'

'You say true,' returned the old man. 'Poor Nell too, what would she do?'

'Exactly,' bawled the dwarf nodding his head; 'that's very well observed. Then will you consider about it, neighbour?'

'I will, certainly,' replied the old man. 'We shall not stop here.'

'So I supposed,' said the dwarf. 'I have sold the things. They have not yielded quite as much as they might have done, but pretty well—pretty well. To-day's Tuesday. When shall they be moved? There's no hurry—shall we say this afternoon?'

'Say Friday morning,' returned the old man.

'Very good,' said the dwarf. 'So be it—with the understanding that I can't go beyond that day, neighbour, on any account.'

'Good,' returned the old man. 'I shall remember it.'

Mr Quilp seemed rather puzzled by the strange, even spiritless way in which all this was said; but as the old man nodded his head and repeated 'on Friday morning. I shall remember it,' he had no excuse for dwelling on the subject any further, and so took a friendly leave with many expressions of good-will and many compliments to his friend on his looking so remarkably well; and went below stairs to report progress to Mr Brass.

All that day, and all the next, the old man remained in this state. He wandered up and down the house and into and out of the various rooms, as if with some vague intent of bidding them adieu, but he referred neither by direct allusions nor in any other manner to the interview of the morning or the necessity of finding some other shelter. An indistinct idea he had, that the child was desolate and in want of help; for he often drew her to his bosom and bade her be of good cheer, saying that they would not desert each other; but he seemed unable to contemplate their real position more distinctly, and was still the listless, passionless creature that suffering of mind and body had left him.

We call this a state of childishness, but it is the same poor hollow mockery of it, that death is of sleep. Where, in the dull eyes of doating men, are the laughing light and life of childhood, the gaiety that has known no check, the frankness that has felt no chill, the hope that has never withered, the joys that fade in blossoming? Where, in the sharp lineaments of rigid and unsightly death, is the calm beauty of slumber, telling of rest for the waking hours that are past, and gentle hopes and loves for those which are to come? Lay death and sleep down, side by side, and say who shall find the two akin. Send forth the child and childish man together, and blush for the pride that libels our own old happy state, and gives its title to an ugly and distorted image.

Thursday arrived, and there was no alteration in the old man. But a change came upon him that evening as he and the child sat silently together.

In a small dull yard below his window, there was a tree—green and flourishing enough, for such a place—and as the air stirred among its leaves, it threw a rippling shadow on the white wall. The old man sat watching the shadows as they trembled in this patch of light, until the sun went down; and when it was night, and the moon was slowly rising, he still sat in the same spot.

To one who had been tossing on a restless bed so long, even these few green leaves and this tranquil light, although it languished among chimneys and house-tops, were pleasant things. They suggested quiet places afar off, and rest, and peace. The child thought, more than once that he was moved: and had forborne to speak. But now he shed tears—tears that it lightened her aching heart to see—and making as though he would fall upon his knees, besought her to forgive him.

'Forgive you—what?' said Nell, interposing to prevent his purpose. 'Oh grandfather, what should I forgive?'

'All that is past, all that has come upon thee, Nell, all that was done in that uneasy dream,' returned the old man.

'Do not talk so,' said the child. 'Pray do not. Let us speak of something else.'

'Yes, yes, we will,' he rejoined. 'And it shall be of what we talked of long ago—many months—months is it, or weeks, or days? which is it Nell?'

'I do not understand you,' said the child.

'It has come back upon me to-day, it has all come back since we have been sitting here. I bless thee for it, Nell!'

'For what, dear grandfather?'

'For what you said when we were first made beggars, Nell. Let us speak softly. Hush! for if they knew our purpose down stairs, they would cry that I was mad and take thee from me. We will not stop here another day. We will go far away from here.'

'Yes, let us go,' said the child earnestly. 'Let us begone from this place, and never turn back or think of it again. Let us wander barefoot through the world, rather than linger here.'

'We will,' answered the old man, 'we will travel afoot through the fields and woods, and by the side of rivers, and trust ourselves to God in the places where He dwells. It is far better to lie down at night beneath an open sky like that yonder—see how bright it is—than to rest in close rooms which are always full of care and weary dreams. Thou and I together, Nell, may be cheerful and happy yet, and learn to forget this time, as if it had never been.'

'We will be happy,' cried the child. 'We never can be here.'

'No, we never can again—never again—that's truly said,' rejoined the old man. 'Let us steal away to-morrow morning—early and softly, that we may not be seen or heard—and leave no trace or track for them to follow by. Poor Nell! Thy cheek is pale, and thy eyes are heavy with watching and weeping for me—I know—for me; but thou wilt be well again, and merry too, when we are far away. To-morrow morning, dear, we'll turn our faces from this scene of sorrow, and be as free and happy as the birds.'

And then the old man clasped his hands above her head, and said, in a few broken words, that from that time forth they would wander up and down together, and never part more until Death took one or other of the twain.

The child's heart beat high with hope and confidence. She had no thought of hunger, or cold, or thirst, or suffering. She saw in this, but a return of the simple pleasures they had once enjoyed, a relief from the gloomy solitude in which she had lived, an escape from the heartless people by whom she had been surrounded in her late time of trial, the restoration of the old man's health and peace, and a life of tranquil happiness. Sun, and stream, and meadow, and summer days, shone brightly in her view, and there was no dark tint in all the sparkling picture.

The old man had slept, for some hours, soundly in his bed, and she was yet busily engaged in preparing for their flight. There were a few articles of clothing for herself to carry, and a few for him; old garments, such as became their fallen fortunes, laid out to wear; and a staff to support his feeble steps, put ready for his use. But this was not all her task; for now she must visit the old rooms for the last time.

And how different the parting with them was, from any she had expected, and most of all from that which she had oftenest pictured to herself. How could she ever have thought of bidding them farewell in triumph, when the recollection of the many hours she had passed among them rose to her swelling heart, and made her feel the wish a cruelty: lonely and sad though many of those hours had been! She sat down at the window where she had spent so many evenings—darker far than this—and every thought of hope or cheerfulness that had occurred to her in that place came vividly upon her mind, and blotted out all its dull and mournful associations in an instant.

Her own little room too, where she had so often knelt down and prayed at night—prayed for the time which she hoped was dawning now—the little room where she had slept so peacefully, and dreamed such pleasant dreams! It was hard not to be able to glance round it once more, and to be forced to leave it without one kind look or grateful tear. There were some trifles there—poor useless things—that she would have liked to take away; but that was impossible.

This brought to mind her bird, her poor bird, who hung there yet. She wept bitterly for the loss of this little creature—until the idea occurred to her—she did not know how, or why, it came into her head—that it might, by some means, fall into the hands of Kit who would keep it for her sake, and think, perhaps, that she had left it behind in the hope that he might have it, and as an assurance that she was grateful to him. She was calmed and comforted by the thought, and went to rest with a lighter heart.

From many dreams of rambling through light and sunny places, but with some vague object unattained which ran indistinctly through them all, she awoke to find that it was yet night, and that the stars were shining brightly in the sky. At length, the day began to glimmer, and the stars to grow pale and dim. As soon as she was sure of this, she arose, and dressed herself for the journey.

The old man was yet asleep, and as she was unwilling to disturb him, she left him to slumber on, until the sun rose. He was anxious that they should leave the house without a minute's loss of time, and was soon ready.

The child then took him by the hand, and they trod lightly and cautiously down the stairs, trembling whenever a board creaked, and often stopping to listen. The old man had forgotten a kind of wallet which contained the light burden he had to carry; and the going back a few steps to fetch it seemed an interminable delay.

At last they reached the passage on the ground floor, where the snoring of Mr Quilp and his legal friend sounded more terrible in their ears than the roars of lions. The bolts of the door were rusty, and difficult to unfasten without noise. When they were all drawn back, it was found to be locked, and worst of all, the key was gone. Then the child remembered, for the first time, one of the nurses having told her that Quilp always locked both the house-doors at night, and kept the keys on the table in his bedroom.

It was not without great fear and trepidation that little Nell slipped off her shoes and gliding through the store-room of old curiosities, where Mr Brass—the ugliest piece of goods in all the stock—lay sleeping on a mattress, passed into her own little chamber.

Here she stood, for a few moments, quite transfixed with terror at the sight of Mr Quilp, who was hanging so far out of bed that he almost seemed to be standing on his head, and who, either from the uneasiness of this posture, or in one of his agreeable habits, was gasping and growling with his mouth wide open, and the whites (or rather the dirty yellows) of his eyes distinctly visible. It was no time, however, to ask whether anything ailed him; so, possessing herself of the key after one hasty glance about the room, and repassing the prostrate Mr Brass, she rejoined the old man in safety. They got the door open without noise, and passing into the street, stood still.

'Which way?' said the child.

The old man looked, irresolutely and helplessly, first at her, then to the right and left, then at her again, and shook his head. It was plain that she was thenceforth his guide and leader. The child felt it, but had no doubts or misgiving, and putting her hand in his, led him gently away.

It was the beginning of a day in June; the deep blue sky unsullied by a cloud, and teeming with brilliant light. The streets were, as yet, nearly free from passengers, the houses and shops were closed, and the healthy air of morning fell like breath from angels, on the sleeping town.

The old man and the child passed on through the glad silence, elate with hope and pleasure. They were alone together, once again; every object was bright and fresh; nothing reminded them, otherwise than by contrast, of the monotony and constraint they had left behind; church towers and steeples, frowning and dark at other times, now shone in the sun; each humble nook and corner rejoiced in light; and the sky, dimmed only by excessive distance, shed its placid smile on everything beneath.

Forth from the city, while it yet slumbered, went the two poor adventurers, wandering they knew not whither.

CHAPTER 13

Daniel Quilp of Tower Hill, and Sampson Brass of Bevis Marks in the city of London, Gentleman, one of her Majesty's attornies of the Courts of the King's Bench and Common Pleas at Westminster and a solicitor of the High Court of Chancery, slumbered on, unconscious and unsuspicious of any mischance, until a knocking on the street door, often repeated and gradually mounting up from a modest single rap to a perfect battery of knocks, fired in long discharges with a very short interval between, caused the said Daniel Quilp to struggle into a horizontal position, and to stare at the ceiling with a drowsy indifference, betokening that he heard the noise and rather wondered at the same, and couldn't be at the trouble of bestowing any further thought upon the subject.

As the knocking, however, instead of accommodating itself to his lazy state, increased in vigour and became more importunate, as if in earnest remonstrance against his falling asleep again, now that he had once opened his eyes, Daniel Quilp began by degrees to comprehend the possibility of there being somebody at the door; and thus he gradually came to recollect that it was Friday morning, and he had ordered Mrs Quilp to be in waiting upon him at an early hour.

Mr Brass, after writhing about, in a great many strange attitudes, and often twisting his face and eyes into an expression like that which is usually produced by eating gooseberries very early in the season, was by this time awake also. Seeing that Mr Quilp invested himself in his every-day garments, he hastened to do the like, putting on his shoes before his stockings, and thrusting his legs into his coat sleeves, and making such other small mistakes in his toilet as are not uncommon to those who dress in a hurry, and labour under the agitation of having been suddenly roused.

While the attorney was thus engaged, the dwarf was groping under the table, muttering desperate imprecations on himself, and mankind in general, and all inanimate objects to boot, which suggested to Mr Brass the question, 'what's the matter?'

'The key,' said the dwarf, looking viciously about him, 'the door-key—that's the matter. D'ye know anything of it?'

'How should I know anything of it, sir?' returned Mr Brass.

'How should you?' repeated Quilp with a sneer. 'You're a nice lawyer, an't you? Ugh, you idiot!'

Not caring to represent to the dwarf in his present humour, that the loss of a key by another person could scarcely be said to affect his (Brass's) legal knowledge in any material degree, Mr Brass humbly suggested that it must have been forgotten over night, and was, doubtless, at that moment in its native key-hole. Notwithstanding that Mr Quilp had a strong conviction to the contrary, founded on his recollection of having carefully taken it out, he was fain to admit that this was possible, and therefore went grumbling to the door where, sure enough, he found it.

Now, just as Mr Quilp laid his hand upon the lock, and saw with great astonishment that the fastenings were undone, the knocking came again with the most irritating violence, and the daylight which had been shining through the key-hole was intercepted on the outside by a human eye. The dwarf was very much exasperated, and wanting somebody to wreak his ill-humour upon, determined to dart out suddenly, and favour Mrs Quilp with a gentle acknowledgment of her attention in making that hideous uproar.

With this view, he drew back the lock very silently and softly, and opening the door all at once, pounced out upon the person on the other side, who had at that moment raised the knocker for another application, and at whom the dwarf ran head first: throwing out his hands and feet together, and biting the air in the fulness of his malice.

So far, however, from rushing upon somebody who offered no resistance and implored his mercy, Mr Quilp was no sooner in the arms of the individual whom he had taken for his wife than he found himself complimented with two staggering blows on the head, and two more, of the same quality, in the chest; and closing with his assailant, such a shower of buffets rained down upon his person as sufficed to convince him that he was in skilful and experienced hands. Nothing daunted by this reception, he clung tight to his opponent, and bit and hammered away with such good-will and heartiness, that it was at least a couple of minutes before he was dislodged. Then, and not until then, Daniel Quilp found himself, all flushed and dishevelled, in the middle of the street, with Mr Richard Swiveller performing a kind of dance round him and requiring to know 'whether he wanted any more?'

'There's plenty more of it at the same shop,' said Mr Swiveller, by turns advancing and retreating in a threatening attitude, 'a large and extensive assortment always on hand—country orders executed with promptitude and despatch—will you have a little more, Sir—don't say no, if you'd rather not.'

'I thought it was somebody else,' said Quilp, rubbing his shoulders, 'why didn't you say who you were?'

'Why didn't you say who you were?' returned Dick, 'instead of flying out of the house like a Bedlamite?'

'It was you that—that knocked,' said the dwarf, getting up with a short groan, 'was it?'

'Yes, I am the man,' replied Dick. 'That lady had begun when I came, but she knocked too soft, so I relieved her.' As he said this, he pointed towards Mrs Quilp, who stood trembling at a little distance.

'Humph!' muttered the dwarf, darting an angry look at his wife, 'I thought it was your fault! And you, sir—don't you know there has been somebody ill here, that you knock as if you'd beat the door down?'

'Damme!' answered Dick, 'that's why I did it. I thought there was somebody dead here.'

'You came for some purpose, I suppose,' said Quilp. 'What is it you want?'

'I want to know how the old gentleman is,' rejoined Mr Swiveller, 'and to hear from Nell herself, with whom I should like to have a little talk. I'm a friend of the family, sir—at least I'm the friend of one of the family, and that's the same thing.'

'You'd better walk in then,' said the dwarf. 'Go on, sir, go on. Now, Mrs Quilp—after you, ma'am.'

Mrs Quilp hesitated, but Mr Quilp insisted. And it was not a contest of politeness, or by any means a matter of form, for she knew very well that her husband wished to enter the house in this order, that he might have a favourable opportunity of inflicting a few pinches on her arms, which were seldom free from impressions of his fingers in black and blue colours. Mr Swiveller, who was not in the secret, was a little surprised to hear a suppressed scream, and, looking round, to see Mrs Quilp following him with a sudden jerk; but he did not remark on these appearances, and soon forgot them.

'Now, Mrs Quilp,' said the dwarf when they had entered the shop, 'go you up stairs, if you please, to Nelly's room, and tell her that she's wanted.'

'You seem to make yourself at home here,' said Dick, who was unacquainted with Mr Quilp's authority.

'I am at home, young gentleman,' returned the dwarf.

Dick was pondering what these words might mean, and still more what the presence of Mr Brass might mean, when Mrs Quilp came hurrying down stairs, declaring that the rooms above were empty.

'Empty, you fool!' said the dwarf.

'I give you my word, Quilp,' answered his trembling wife, 'that I have been into every room and there's not a soul in any of them.'

'And that,' said Mr Brass, clapping his hands once, with an emphasis, 'explains the mystery of the key!'

Quilp looked frowningly at him, and frowningly at his wife, and frowningly at Richard Swiveller; but, receiving no enlightenment from any of them, hurried up stairs, whence he soon hurried down again, confirming the report which had already been made.

'It's a strange way of going,' he said, glancing at Swiveller, 'very strange not to communicate with me who am such a close and intimate friend of his! Ah! he'll write to me no doubt, or he'll bid Nelly write—yes, yes, that's what he'll do. Nelly's very fond of me. Pretty Nell!'

Mr Swiveller looked, as he was, all open-mouthed astonishment. Still glancing furtively at him, Quilp turned to Mr Brass and observed, with assumed carelessness, that this need not interfere with the removal of the goods.

'For indeed,' he added, 'we knew that they'd go away to-day, but not that they'd go so early, or so quietly. But they have their reasons, they have their reasons.'

'Where in the devil's name are they gone?' said the wondering Dick.

Quilp shook his head, and pursed up his lips, in a manner which implied that he knew very well, but was not at liberty to say.

'And what,' said Dick, looking at the confusion about him, 'what do you mean by moving the goods?'

'That I have bought 'em, Sir,' rejoined Quilp. 'Eh? What then?'

'Has the sly old fox made his fortune then, and gone to live in a tranquil cot in a pleasant spot with a distant view of the changing sea?' said Dick, in great bewilderment.

'Keeping his place of retirement very close, that he may not be visited too often by affectionate grandsons and their devoted friends, eh?' added the dwarf, rubbing his hands hard; 'I say nothing, but is that your meaning?'

Richard Swiveller was utterly aghast at this unexpected alteration of circumstances, which threatened the complete overthrow of the project in which he bore so conspicuous a part, and seemed to nip his prospects in the bud. Having only received from Frederick Trent, late on the previous night, information of the old man's illness, he had come upon a visit of condolence and inquiry to Nell, prepared with the first instalment of that long train of fascinations which was to fire her heart at last. And here, when he had been thinking of all kinds of graceful and insinuating approaches, and meditating on the fearful retaliation which was slowly working against Sophy Wackles—here were Nell, the old man, and all the money gone, melted away, decamped he knew not whither, as if with a fore-knowledge of the scheme and a resolution to defeat it in the very outset, before a step was taken.

In his secret heart, Daniel Quilp was both surprised and troubled by the flight which had been made. It had not escaped his keen eye that some indispensable articles of clothing were gone with the fugitives, and knowing the old man's weak state of mind, he marvelled what that course of proceeding might be in which he had so readily procured the concurrence of the child. It must not be supposed (or it would be a gross injustice to Mr Quilp) that he was tortured by any disinterested anxiety on behalf of either. His uneasiness arose from a misgiving that the old man had some secret store of money which he had not suspected; and the idea of its escaping his clutches, overwhelmed him with mortification and self-reproach.

In this frame of mind, it was some consolation to him to find that Richard Swiveller was, for different reasons, evidently irritated and disappointed by the same cause. It was plain, thought the dwarf, that he had come there, on behalf of his friend, to cajole or frighten the old man out of some small fraction of that wealth of which they supposed him to have an abundance. Therefore, it was a relief to vex his heart with a picture of the riches the old man hoarded, and to expatiate on his cunning in removing himself even beyond the reach of importunity.

'Well,' said Dick, with a blank look, 'I suppose it's of no use my staying here.'

'Not the least in the world,' rejoined the dwarf.

'You'll mention that I called, perhaps?' said Dick.

Mr Quilp nodded, and said he certainly would, the very first time he saw them.

'And say,' added Mr Swiveller, 'say, sir, that I was wafted here upon the pinions of concord; that I came to remove, with the rake of friendship, the seeds of mutual violence and heart-burning, and to sow in their place, the germs of social harmony. Will you have the goodness to charge yourself with that commission, Sir?'

'Certainly!' rejoined Quilp.

'Will you be kind enough to add to it, Sir,' said Dick, producing a very small limp card, 'that that is my address, and that I am to be found at home every morning. Two distinct knocks, sir, will produce the slavey at any time. My particular friends, Sir, are accustomed to sneeze when the door is opened, to give her to understand that they are my friends and have no interested motives in asking if I'm at home. I beg your pardon; will you allow me to look at that card again?'

'Oh! by all means,' rejoined Quilp.

'By a slight and not unnatural mistake, sir,' said Dick, substituting another in its stead, 'I had handed you the pass-ticket of a select convivial circle called the Glorious Apollers of which

I have the honour to be Perpetual Grand. That is the proper document, Sir. Good morning.'

Quilp bade him good day; the perpetual Grand Master of the Glorious Apollers, elevating his hat in honour of Mrs Quilp, dropped it carelessly on the side of his head again, and disappeared with a flourish.

By this time, certain vans had arrived for the conveyance of the goods, and divers strong men in caps were balancing chests of drawers and other trifles of that nature upon their heads, and performing muscular feats which heightened their complexions considerably. Not to be behind-hand in the bustle, Mr Quilp went to work with surprising vigour; hustling and driving the people about, like an evil spirit; setting Mrs Quilp upon all kinds of arduous and impracticable tasks; carrying great weights up and down, with no apparent effort; kicking the boy from the wharf, whenever he could get near him; and inflicting, with his loads, a great many sly bumps and blows on the shoulders of Mr Brass, as he stood upon the door-steps to answer all the inquiries of curious neighbours, which was his department. His presence and example diffused such alacrity among the persons employed, that, in a few hours, the house was emptied of everything, but pieces of matting, empty porter-pots, and scattered fragments of straw.

Seated, like an African chief, on one of these pieces of matting, the dwarf was regaling himself in the parlour, with bread and cheese and beer, when he observed without appearing to do so, that a boy was prying in at the outer door. Assured that it was Kit, though he saw little more than his nose, Mr Quilp hailed him by his name; whereupon Kit came in and demanded what he wanted.

'Come here, you sir,' said the dwarf. 'Well, so your old master and young mistress have gone?'

'Where?' rejoined Kit, looking round.

'Do you mean to say you don't know where?' answered Quilp sharply. 'Where have they gone, eh?'

'I don't know,' said Kit.

'Come,' retorted Quilp, 'let's have no more of this! Do you mean to say that you don't know they went away by stealth, as soon as it was light this morning?'

'No,' said the boy, in evident surprise.

'You don't know that?' cried Quilp. 'Don't I know that you were hanging about the house the other night, like a thief, eh? Weren't you told then?'

'No,' replied the boy.

'You were not?' said Quilp. 'What were you told then; what were you talking about?'

Kit, who knew no particular reason why he should keep the matter secret now, related the purpose for which he had come on that occasion, and the proposal he had made.

'Oh!' said the dwarf after a little consideration. 'Then, I think they'll come to you yet.'

'Do you think they will?' cried Kit eagerly.

'Aye, I think they will,' returned the dwarf. 'Now, when they do, let me know; d'ye hear? Let me know, and I'll give you something. I want to do 'em a kindness, and I can't do 'em a kindness unless I know where they are. You hear what I say?'

Kit might have returned some answer which would not have been agreeable to his irascible questioner, if the boy from the wharf, who had been skulking about the room in search of anything that might have been left about by accident, had not happened to cry, 'Here's a bird! What's to be done with this?'

'Wring its neck,' rejoined Quilp.

'Oh no, don't do that,' said Kit, stepping forward. 'Give it to me.'

'Oh yes, I dare say,' cried the other boy. 'Come! You let the cage alone, and let me wring its neck will you? He said I was to do it. You let the cage alone will you.'

'Give it here, give it to me, you dogs,' roared Quilp. 'Fight for it, you dogs, or I'll wring its neck myself!'

Without further persuasion, the two boys fell upon each other, tooth and nail, while Quilp, holding up the cage in one hand, and chopping the ground with his knife in an ecstasy, urged them on by his taunts and cries to fight more fiercely. They were a pretty equal match, and rolled about together, exchanging blows which were by no means child's play, until at length Kit, planting a well-directed hit in his adversary's chest, disengaged himself, sprung nimbly up, and snatching the cage from Quilp's hands made off with his prize.

He did not stop once until he reached home, where his bleeding face occasioned great consternation, and caused the elder child to howl dreadfully.

'Goodness gracious, Kit, what is the matter, what have you been doing?' cried Mrs Nubbles.

'Never you mind, mother,' answered her son, wiping his face on the jack-towel behind the door. 'I'm not hurt, don't you be afraid for me. I've been a fightin' for a bird and won him, that's all. Hold your noise, little Jacob. I never see such a naughty boy in all my days!'

'You have been fighting for a bird!' exclaimed his mother.

'Ah! Fightin' for a bird!' replied Kit, 'and here he is—Miss Nelly's bird, mother, that they was agoin' to wring the neck of! I stopped that though—ha ha ha! They wouldn't wring his neck and me by, no, no. It wouldn't do, mother, it wouldn't do at all. Ha ha ha!'

Kit laughing so heartily, with his swoln and bruised face looking out of the towel, made little Jacob laugh, and then his mother laughed, and then the baby crowed and kicked with great glee, and then they all laughed in concert: partly because of Kit's triumph, and partly because they were very fond of each other. When this fit was over, Kit exhibited the bird to both children, as a great and precious rarity—it was only a poor linnet—and looking about the wall for an old nail, made a scaffolding of a chair and table and twisted it out with great exultation.

'Let me see,' said the boy, 'I think I'll hang him in the winder, because it's more light and cheerful, and he can see the sky there, if he looks up very much. He's such a one to sing, I can tell you!'

So, the scaffolding was made again, and Kit, climbing up with the poker for a hammer, knocked in the nail and hung up the cage, to the immeasurable delight of the whole family. When it had been adjusted and straightened a great many times, and he had walked backwards into the fire-place in his admiration of it, the arrangement was pronounced to be perfect.

'And now, mother,' said the boy, 'before I rest any more, I'll go out and see if I can find a horse to hold, and then I can buy some birdseed, and a bit of something nice for you, into the bargain.'

CHAPTER 14

As it was very easy for Kit to persuade himself that the old house was in his way, his way being anywhere, he tried to look upon his passing it once more as a matter of imperative and disagreeable necessity, quite apart from any desire of his own, to which he could not choose but yield. It is not uncommon for people who are much better fed and taught than Christopher Nubbles had ever been, to make duties of their inclinations in matters of more doubtful propriety, and to take great credit for the self-denial with which they gratify themselves.

There was no need of any caution this time, and no fear of being detained by having to play out a return match with Daniel Quilp's boy. The place was entirely deserted, and looked as dusty and dingy as if it had been so for months. A rusty padlock was fastened on the door, ends of discoloured blinds and curtains flapped drearily against the half-opened upper windows, and the crooked holes cut in the closed shutters below, were black with the darkness of the inside. Some of the glass in the window he had so often watched, had been broken in the rough hurry of the morning, and that room looked more deserted and dull than any. A group of idle urchins had taken possession of the door-steps; some were plying the knocker and listening with delighted dread to the hollow sounds it spread through the dismantled house; others were clustered about the keyhole, watching half in jest and half in earnest for 'the ghost,' which an hour's gloom, added to the mystery that hung about the late inhabitants, had already raised. Standing all alone in the midst of the business and bustle of the street, the house looked a picture of cold desolation; and Kit, who remembered the cheerful fire that used to burn there on a winter's night and the no less cheerful laugh that made the small room ring, turned quite mournfully away.

It must be especially observed in justice to poor Kit that he was by no means of a sentimental turn, and perhaps had never heard that adjective in all his life. He was only a soft-hearted grateful fellow, and had nothing genteel or polite about him; consequently, instead of going home again, in his grief, to kick the children and abuse his mother (for, when your finely strung people are out of sorts, they must have everybody else unhappy likewise), he turned his thoughts to the vulgar expedient of making them more comfortable if he could.

Bless us, what a number of gentlemen on horseback there were riding up and down, and how few of them wanted their horses held! A good city speculator or a parliamentary commissioner could have told to a fraction, from the crowds that were cantering about, what sum of money was realised in London, in the course of a year, by holding horses alone. And undoubtedly it would have been a very large one, if only a twentieth part of the gentlemen without grooms had had occasion to alight; but they had not; and it is often an ill-natured circumstance like this, which spoils the most ingenious estimate in the world.

Kit walked about, now with quick steps and now with slow; now lingering as some rider slackened his horse's pace and looked about him; and now darting at full speed up a bye-street as he caught a glimpse of some distant horseman going lazily up the shady side of the road, and promising to stop, at every door. But on they all went, one after another, and there was not a penny stirring. 'I wonder,' thought the boy, 'if one of these gentlemen knew there was nothing in the cupboard at home, whether he'd stop on purpose, and make believe that he wanted to call somewhere, that I might earn a trifle?'

He was quite tired out with pacing the streets, to say nothing of repeated disappointments, and was sitting down upon a step to rest, when there approached towards him a little clattering jingling four-wheeled chaise, drawn by a little obstinate-looking rough-coated pony, and driven by a little fat placid-faced old gentleman. Beside the little old gentleman sat a little old lady, plump and placid like himself, and the pony was coming along at his own pace and doing exactly as he pleased with the whole concern. If the old gentleman remonstrated by shaking the reins, the pony replied by shaking his head. It was plain that the utmost the pony would consent to do, was to go in his own way up any street that the old gentleman particularly wished to traverse, but that it was an understanding between them that he must do this after his own fashion or not at all.

As they passed where he sat, Kit looked so wistfully at the little turn-out, that the old gentleman looked at him. Kit rising and putting his hand to his hat, the old gentleman intimated to the pony that he wished to stop, to which proposal the pony (who seldom objected to that part of his duty) graciously acceded.

'I beg your pardon, sir,' said Kit. 'I'm sorry you stopped, sir. I only meant did you want your horse minded.'

'I'm going to get down in the next street,' returned the old gentleman. 'If you like to come on after us, you may have the job.'

Kit thanked him, and joyfully obeyed. The pony ran off at a sharp angle to inspect a lamp-post on the opposite side of the way, and then went off at a tangent to another lamp-post on the other side. Having satisfied himself that they were of the same pattern and materials, he came to a stop apparently absorbed in meditation.

'Will you go on, sir,' said the old gentleman, gravely, 'or are we to wait here for you till it's too late for our appointment?'

The pony remained immoveable.

'Oh you naughty Whisker,' said the old lady. 'Fie upon you! I'm ashamed of such conduct.'

The pony appeared to be touched by this appeal to his feelings, for he trotted on directly, though in a sulky manner, and stopped no more until he came to a door whereon was a brass plate with the words 'Witherden—Notary.' Here the old gentleman got out and helped out the old lady, and then took from under the seat a nosegay resembling in shape and dimensions a full-sized warming-pan with the handle cut short off. This, the old lady carried into the house with a staid and stately air, and the old gentleman (who had a club-foot) followed close upon her.

They went, as it was easy to tell from the sound of their voices, into the front parlour, which seemed to be a kind of office. The day being very warm and the street a quiet one, the windows were wide open; and it was easy to hear through the Venetian blinds all that passed inside.

At first there was a great shaking of hands and shuffling of feet, succeeded by the presentation of the nosegay; for a voice, supposed by the listener to be that of Mr Witherden the Notary, was heard to exclaim a great many times, 'oh, delicious!' 'oh, fragrant, indeed!' and a nose, also supposed to be the property of that gentleman, was heard to inhale the scent with a snuffle of exceeding pleasure.

'I brought it in honour of the occasion, Sir,' said the old lady.

'Ah! an occasion indeed, ma'am, an occasion which does honour to me, ma'am, honour to me,' rejoined Mr Witherden, the notary. 'I have had many a gentleman articled to me, ma'am, many a one. Some of them are now rolling in riches, unmindful of their old companion and friend, ma'am, others are in the habit of calling upon me to this day and saying, "Mr Witherden, some of the pleasantest hours I ever spent in my life were spent in this office—were spent, Sir, upon this very stool"; but there was never one among the number, ma'am, attached as I have been to many of them, of whom I augured such bright things as I do of your only son.'

'Oh dear!' said the old lady. 'How happy you do make us when you tell us that, to be sure!'

'I tell you, ma'am,' said Mr Witherden, 'what I think as an honest man, which, as the poet observes, is the noblest work of God. I agree with the poet in every particular, ma'am. The mountainous Alps on the one hand, or a humming-bird on the other, is nothing, in point of workmanship, to an honest man—or woman—or woman.'

'Anything that Mr Witherden can say of me,' observed a small quiet voice, 'I can say, with interest, of him, I am sure.'

'It's a happy circumstance, a truly happy circumstance,' said the Notary, 'to happen too upon his eight-and-twentieth birthday, and I hope I know how to appreciate it. I trust, Mr Garland, my dear Sir, that we may mutually congratulate each other upon this auspicious occasion.'

To this the old gentleman replied that he felt assured they might. There appeared to be another shaking of hands in consequence, and when it was over, the old gentleman said that, though he said it who should not, he believed no son had ever been a greater comfort to his parents than Abel Garland had been to his.

'Marrying as his mother and I did, late in life, sir, after waiting for a great many years, until we were well enough off—coming together when we were no longer young, and then being blessed with one child who has always been dutiful and affectionate—why, it's a source of great happiness to us both, sir.'

'Of course it is, I have no doubt of it,' returned the Notary in a sympathising voice. 'It's the contemplation of this sort of thing, that makes me deplore my fate in being a bachelor. There was a young lady once, sir, the daughter of an outfitting warehouse of the first respectability— but that's a weakness. Chuckster, bring in Mr Abel's articles.'

'You see, Mr Witherden,' said the old lady, 'that Abel has not been brought up like the run of young men. He has always had a pleasure in our society, and always been with us. Abel has never been absent from us, for a day; has he, my dear?'

'Never, my dear,' returned the old gentleman, 'except when he went to Margate one

Saturday with Mr Tomkinley that had been a teacher at that school he went to, and came back upon the Monday; but he was very ill after that, you remember, my dear; it was quite a dissipation.'

'He was not used to it, you know,' said the old lady, 'and he couldn't bear it, that's the truth. Besides he had no comfort in being there without us, and had nobody to talk to or enjoy himself with.'

'That was it, you know,' interposed the same small quiet voice that had spoken once before. 'I was quite abroad, mother, quite desolate, and to think that the sea was between us—oh, I never shall forget what I felt when I first thought that the sea was between us!'

'Very natural under the circumstances,' observed the Notary. 'Mr Abel's feelings did credit to his nature, and credit to your nature, ma'am, and his father's nature, and human nature. I trace the same current now, flowing through all his quiet and unobtrusive proceedings.—I am about to sign my name, you observe, at the foot of the articles which Mr Chuckster will witness; and placing my finger upon this blue wafer with the vandyked corners, I am constrained to remark in a distinct tone of voice—don't be alarmed, ma'am, it is merely a form of law—that I deliver this, as my act and deed. Mr Abel will place his name against the other wafer, repeating the same cabalistic words, and the business is over. Ha ha ha! You see how easily these things are done!'

There was a short silence, apparently, while Mr Abel went through the prescribed form, and then the shaking of hands and shuffling of feet were renewed, and shortly afterwards there was a clinking of wine-glasses and a great talkativeness on the part of everybody. In about a quarter of an hour Mr Chuckster (with a pen behind his ear and his face inflamed with wine) appeared at the door, and condescending to address Kit by the jocose appellation of 'Young Snob,' informed him that the visitors were coming out.

Out they came forthwith; Mr Witherden, who was short, chubby, fresh-coloured, brisk, and pompous, leading the old lady with extreme politeness, and the father and son following them, arm in arm. Mr Abel, who had a quaint old-fashioned air about him, looked nearly of the same age as his father, and bore a wonderful resemblance to him in face and figure, though wanting something of his full, round, cheerfulness, and substituting in its place a timid reserve. In all other respects, in the neatness of the dress, and even in the club-foot, he and the old gentleman were precisely alike.

Having seen the old lady safely in her seat, and assisted in the arrangement of her cloak and a small basket which formed an indispensable portion of her equipage, Mr Abel got into a little box behind which had evidently been made for his express accommodation, and smiled at everybody present by turns, beginning with his mother and ending with the pony. There was then a great to-do to make the pony hold up his head that the bearing-rein might be fastened; at last even this was effected; and the old gentleman, taking his seat and the reins, put his hand in his pocket to find a sixpence for Kit.

He had no sixpence, neither had the old lady, nor Mr Abel, nor the Notary, nor Mr Chuckster. The old gentleman thought a shilling too much, but there was no shop in the street to get change at, so he gave it to the boy.

'There,' he said jokingly, 'I'm coming here again next Monday at the same time, and mind you're here, my lad, to work it out.'

'Thank you, Sir,' said Kit. 'I'll be sure to be here.'

He was quite serious, but they all laughed heartily at his saying so, especially Mr Chuckster, who roared outright and appeared to relish the joke amazingly. As the pony, with a presentiment that he was going home, or a determination that he would not go anywhere else (which was the same thing) trotted away pretty nimbly, Kit had no time to justify himself, and went his way also. Having expended his treasure in such purchases as he knew would be most acceptable at home, not forgetting some seed for the wonderful bird, he hastened back as fast as he could, so elated with his success and great good fortune, that he more than half expected Nell and the old man would have arrived before him.

CHAPTER 15

Often, while they were yet pacing the silent streets of the town on the morning of their departure, the child trembled with a mingled sensation of hope and fear as in some far-off figure imperfectly seen in the clear distance, her fancy traced a likeness to honest Kit. But although she would gladly have given him her hand and thanked him for what he had said at their last meeting, it was always a relief to find, when they came nearer to each other, that the person who approached was not he, but a stranger; for even if she had not dreaded the effect which the sight of him might have wrought upon her fellow-traveller, she felt that to bid farewell to anybody now, and most of all to him who had been so faithful and so true, was more than she could bear. It was enough to leave dumb things behind, and objects that were insensible both to her love and sorrow. To have parted from her only other friend upon the threshold of that wild journey, would have wrung her heart indeed.

Why is it that we can better bear to part in spirit than in body, and while we have the fortitude to act farewell have not the nerve to say it? On the eve of long voyages or an absence of many years, friends who are tenderly attached will separate with the usual look, the usual pressure of the hand, planning one final interview for the morrow, while each well knows that it is but a poor feint to save the pain of uttering that one word, and that the meeting will never be. Should possibilities be worse to bear than certainties? We do not shun our dying friends; the not having distinctly taken leave of one among them, whom we left in all kindness and affection, will often embitter the whole remainder of a life.

The town was glad with morning light; places that had shown ugly and distrustful all night long, now wore a smile; and sparkling sunbeams dancing on chamber windows, and twinkling through blind and curtain before sleepers' eyes, shed light even into dreams, and chased away the shadows of the night. Birds in hot rooms, covered up close and dark, felt it was morning, and chafed and grew restless in their little cells; bright-eyed mice crept back to their tiny homes and nestled timidly together; the sleek house-cat, forgetful of her prey, sat winking at the rays of sun starting through keyhole and cranny in the door, and longed for her stealthy run and warm sleek bask outside. The nobler beasts confined in dens, stood motionless behind their bars and gazed on fluttering boughs, and sunshine peeping through some little window, with eyes in which old forests gleamed—then trod impatiently the track their prisoned feet had worn—and stopped and gazed again. Men in their dungeons stretched their cramp cold limbs and cursed the stone that no bright sky could warm. The flowers that sleep by night, opened their gentle eyes and turned them to the day. The light, creation's mind, was everywhere, and all things owned its power.

The two pilgrims, often pressing each other's hands, or exchanging a smile or cheerful look, pursued their way in silence. Bright and happy as it was, there was something solemn in the long, deserted streets, from which, like bodies without souls, all habitual character and expression had departed, leaving but one dead uniform repose, that made them all alike. All was so still at that early hour, that the few pale people whom they met seemed as much unsuited to the scene, as the sickly lamp which had been here and there left burning, was powerless and faint in the full glory of the sun.

Before they had penetrated very far into the labyrinth of men's abodes which yet lay between them and the outskirts, this aspect began to melt away, and noise and bustle to usurp its place. Some straggling carts and coaches rumbling by, first broke the charm, then others came, then others yet more active, then a crowd. The wonder was, at first, to see a tradesman's window open, but it was a rare thing soon to see one closed; then, smoke rose slowly from the chimneys, and sashes were thrown up to let in air, and doors were opened, and servant girls, looking lazily in all directions but their brooms, scattered brown clouds of dust into the eyes of shrinking passengers, or listened disconsolately to milkmen who spoke of country fairs, and told of waggons in the mews, with awnings and all things complete, and gallant swains to boot, which another hour would see upon their journey.

This quarter passed, they came upon the haunts of commerce and great traffic, where many people were resorting, and business was already rife. The old man looked about him with a startled and bewildered gaze, for these were places that he hoped to shun. He pressed his finger on his lip, and drew the child along by narrow courts and winding ways, nor did he seem at ease until they had left it far behind, often casting a backward look towards it, murmuring that ruin and self-murder were crouching in every street, and would follow if they scented them; and that they could not fly too fast.

Again this quarter passed, they came upon a straggling neighbourhood, where the mean houses parcelled off in rooms, and windows patched with rags and paper, told of the populous poverty that sheltered there. The shops sold goods that only poverty could buy, and sellers and buyers were pinched and griped alike. Here were poor streets where faded gentility essayed with scanty space and shipwrecked means to make its last feeble stand, but tax-gatherer and creditor came there as elsewhere, and the poverty that yet faintly struggled was hardly less squalid and manifest than that which had long ago submitted and given up the game.

This was a wide, wide track—for the humble followers of the camp of wealth pitch their tents round about it for many a mile—but its character was still the same. Damp rotten houses, many to let, many yet building, many half-built and mouldering away—lodgings, where it would be hard to tell which needed pity most, those who let or those who came to take—children, scantily fed and clothed, spread over every street, and sprawling in the dust—scolding mothers, stamping their slipshod feet with noisy threats upon the pavement—shabby fathers, hurrying with dispirited looks to the occupation which brought them 'daily bread' and little more—mangling-women, washer-women, cobblers, tailors, chandlers, driving their trades in parlours and kitchens and back room and garrets, and sometimes all of them under the same roof—brick-fields skirting gardens paled with staves of old casks, or timber pillaged from houses burnt down, and blackened and blistered by the flames—mounds of dock-weed, nettles, coarse grass and oyster-shells, heaped in rank confusion—small dissenting chapels to teach, with no lack of illustration, the miseries of Earth, and plenty of new churches, erected with a little superfluous wealth, to show the way to Heaven.

At length these streets becoming more straggling yet, dwindled and dwindled away, until there were only small garden patches bordering the road, with many a summer house innocent of paint and built of old timber or some fragments of a boat, green as the tough cabbage-stalks that grew about it, and grottoed at the seams with toad-stools and tight-sticking snails. To these succeeded pert cottages, two and two with plots of ground in front, laid out in angular beds with stiff box borders and narrow paths between, where footstep never strayed to make the gravel rough. Then came the public-house, freshly painted in green and white, with tea-gardens and a bowling green, spurning its old neighbour with the horse-trough where the waggons stopped; then, fields; and then, some houses, one by one, of goodly size with lawns, some even with a lodge where dwelt a porter and his wife. Then came a turnpike; then fields again with trees and hay-stacks; then, a hill, and on the top of that, the traveller might stop, and—looking back at old Saint Paul's looming through the smoke, its cross peeping above the cloud (if the day were clear), and glittering in the sun; and casting his eyes upon the Babel out of which it grew until he traced it down to the furthest outposts of the invading army of bricks and mortar whose station lay for the present nearly at his feet—might feel at last that he was clear of London.

Near such a spot as this, and in a pleasant field, the old man and his little guide (if guide she were, who knew not whither they were bound) sat down to rest. She had had the precaution to furnish her basket with some slices of bread and meat, and here they made their frugal breakfast.

The freshness of the day, the singing of the birds, the beauty of the waving grass, the deep green leaves, the wild flowers, and the thousand exquisite scents and sounds that floated in the air—deep joys to most of us, but most of all to those whose life is in a crowd or who live solitarily in great cities as in the bucket of a human well—sunk into their breasts and made them very glad. The child had repeated her artless prayers once that morning, more earnestly perhaps than she had ever done in all her life, but as she felt all this, they rose to her lips again. The old man took off his hat—he had no memory for the words—but he said amen, and that they were very good.

There had been an old copy of the Pilgrim's Progress, with strange plates, upon a shelf at home, over which she had often pored whole evenings, wondering whether it was true in every word, and where those distant countries with the curious names might be. As she looked back upon the place they had left, one part of it came strongly on her mind.

'Dear grandfather,' she said, 'only that this place is prettier and a great deal better than the real one, if that in the book is like it, I feel as if we were both Christian, and laid down on this grass all the cares and troubles we brought with us; never to take them up again.'

'No—never to return—never to return'—replied the old man, waving his hand towards the city. 'Thou and I are free of it now, Nell. They shall never lure us back.'

'Are you tired?' said the child, 'are you sure you don't feel ill from this long walk?'

'I shall never feel ill again, now that we are once away,' was his reply. 'Let us be stirring, Nell. We must be further away—a long, long way further. We are too near to stop, and be at rest. Come!'

There was a pool of clear water in the field, in which the child laved her hands and face, and cooled her feet before setting forth to walk again. She would have the old man refresh himself in this way too, and making him sit down upon the grass, cast the water on him with her hands, and dried it with her simple dress.

'I can do nothing for myself, my darling,' said the grandfather; 'I don't know how it is, I could once, but the time's gone. Don't leave me, Nell; say that thou'lt not leave me. I loved thee all the while, indeed I did. If I lose thee too, my dear, I must die!'

He laid his head upon her shoulder and moaned piteously. The time had been, and a very few days before, when the child could not have restrained her tears and must have wept with him. But now she soothed him with gentle and tender words, smiled at his thinking they could ever part, and rallied him cheerfully upon the jest. He was soon calmed and fell asleep, singing to himself in a low voice, like a little child.

He awoke refreshed, and they continued their journey. The road was pleasant, lying between beautiful pastures and fields of corn, about which, poised high in the clear blue sky, the lark trilled out her happy song. The air came laden with the fragrance it caught upon its way, and the bees, upborne upon its scented breath, hummed forth their drowsy satisfaction as they floated by.

They were now in the open country; the houses were very few and scattered at long intervals, often miles apart. Occasionally they came upon a cluster of poor cottages, some with a chair or low board put across the open door to keep the scrambling children from the road, others shut up close while all the family were working in the fields. These were often the commencement of a little village: and after an interval came a wheelwright's shed or perhaps a blacksmith's forge; then a thriving farm with sleepy cows lying about the yard, and horses peering over the low wall and scampering away when harnessed horses passed upon the road, as though in triumph at their freedom. There were dull pigs too, turning up the ground in search of dainty food, and grunting their monotonous grumblings as they prowled about, or crossed each other in their quest; plump pigeons skimming round the roof or strutting on the eaves; and ducks and geese, far more graceful in their own conceit, waddling awkwardly about the edges of the pond or sailing glibly on its surface. The farm-yard passed, then came the little inn; the humbler beer-shop; and the village tradesman's; then the lawyer's and the parson's, at whose dread names the beer-shop trembled; the church then peeped out modestly from a clump of trees; then there were a few more cottages; then the cage, and pound, and not unfrequently, on a bank by the way-side, a deep old dusty well. Then came the trim-hedged fields on either hand, and the open road again.

They walked all day, and slept that night at a small cottage where beds were let to travellers. Next morning they were afoot again, and though jaded at first, and very tired, recovered before long and proceeded briskly forward.

They often stopped to rest, but only for a short space at a time, and still kept on, having had but slight refreshment since the morning. It was nearly five o'clock in the afternoon, when drawing near another cluster of labourers' huts, the child looked wistfully in each, doubtful at which to ask for permission to rest awhile, and buy a draught of milk.

It was not easy to determine, for she was timid and fearful of being repulsed. Here was a crying child, and there a noisy wife. In this, the people seemed too poor; in that, too many. At length she stopped at one where the family were seated round the table—chiefly because there was an old man sitting in a cushioned chair beside the hearth, and she thought he was a grandfather and would feel for hers.

There were besides, the cottager and his wife, and three young sturdy children, brown as berries. The request was no sooner preferred, than granted. The eldest boy ran out to fetch some milk, the second dragged two stools towards the door, and the youngest crept to his mother's gown, and looked at the strangers from beneath his sunburnt hand.

'God save you, master,' said the old cottager in a thin piping voice; 'are you travelling far?'

'Yes, Sir, a long way'—replied the child; for her grandfather appealed to her.

'From London?' inquired the old man.

The child said yes.

Ah! He had been in London many a time—used to go there often once, with waggons. It was nigh two-and-thirty year since he had been there last, and he did hear say there were great changes. Like enough! He had changed, himself, since then. Two-and-thirty year was a long time and eighty-four a great age, though there was some he had known that had lived to very hard upon a hundred—and not so hearty as he, neither—no, nothing like it.

'Sit thee down, master, in the elbow chair,' said the old man, knocking his stick upon the brick floor, and trying to do so sharply. 'Take a pinch out o' that box; I don't take much myself, for it comes dear, but I find it wakes me up sometimes, and ye're but a boy to me. I should have a son pretty nigh as old as you if he'd lived, but they listed him for a so'ger—he come back home though, for all he had but one poor leg. He always said he'd be buried near the sun-dial he used to climb upon when he was a baby, did my poor boy, and his words come true—you can see the place with your own eyes; we've kept the turf up, ever since.'

He shook his head, and looking at his daughter with watery eyes, said she needn't be afraid that he was going to talk about that, any more. He didn't wish to trouble nobody, and if he had troubled anybody by what he said, he asked pardon, that was all.

The milk arrived, and the child producing her little basket, and selecting its best fragments for her grandfather, they made a hearty meal. The furniture of the room was very homely of course—a few rough chairs and a table, a corner cupboard with their little stock of crockery and delf, a gaudy tea-tray, representing a lady in bright red, walking out with a very blue parasol, a few common, coloured scripture subjects in frames upon the wall and chimney, an old dwarf clothes-press and an eight-day clock, with a few bright saucepans and a kettle, comprised the whole. But everything was clean and neat, and as the child glanced round, she felt a tranquil air of comfort and content to which she had long been unaccustomed.

'How far is it to any town or village?' she asked of the husband.

'A matter of good five mile, my dear,' was the reply, 'but you're not going on to-night?'

'Yes, yes, Nell,' said the old man hastily, urging her too by signs. 'Further on, further on, darling, further away if we walk till midnight.'

'There's a good barn hard by, master,' said the man, 'or there's travellers' lodging, I know, at the Plow an' Harrer. Excuse me, but you do seem a little tired, and unless you're very anxious to get on—'

'Yes, yes, we are,' returned the old man fretfully. 'Further away, dear Nell, pray further away.'

'We must go on, indeed,' said the child, yielding to his restless wish. 'We thank you very much, but we cannot stop so soon. I'm quite ready, grandfather.'

But the woman had observed, from the young wanderer's gait, that one of her little feet was blistered and sore, and being a woman and a mother too, she would not suffer her to go until she had washed the place and applied some simple remedy, which she did so carefully and with such a gentle hand—rough-grained and hard though it was, with work—that the child's heart was too full to admit of her saying more than a fervent 'God bless you!' nor could she look back nor trust herself to speak, until they had left the cottage some distance behind. When she turned her head, she saw that the whole family, even the old grandfather, were standing in the road watching them as they went, and so, with many waves of the hand, and cheering nods, and on one side at least not without tears, they parted company.

They trudged forward, more slowly and painfully than they had done yet, for another mile or thereabouts, when they heard the sound of wheels behind them, and looking round observed an empty cart approaching pretty briskly. The driver on coming up to them stopped his horse and looked earnestly at Nell.

'Didn't you stop to rest at a cottage yonder?' he said.

'Yes, sir,' replied the child.

'Ah! They asked me to look out for you,' said the man. 'I'm going your way. Give me your hand—jump up, master.'

This was a great relief, for they were very much fatigued and could scarcely crawl along. To them the jolting cart was a luxurious carriage, and the ride the most delicious in the world. Nell had scarcely settled herself on a little heap of straw in one corner, when she fell asleep, for the first time that day.

She was awakened by the stopping of the cart, which was about to turn up a bye-lane. The driver kindly got down to help her out, and pointing to some trees at a very short distance before them, said that the town lay there, and that they had better take the path which they would see leading through the churchyard. Accordingly, towards this spot, they directed their weary steps.

CHAPTER 16

The sun was setting when they reached the wicket-gate at which the path began, and, as the rain falls upon the just and unjust alike, it shed its warm tint even upon the resting-places of the dead, and bade them be of good hope for its rising on the morrow. The church was old and grey, with ivy clinging to the walls, and round the porch. Shunning the tombs, it crept about the mounds, beneath which slept poor humble men: twining for them the first wreaths they had ever won, but wreaths less liable to wither and far more lasting in their kind, than some which were graven deep in stone and marble, and told in pompous terms of virtues meekly hidden for many a year, and only revealed at last to executors and mourning legatees.

The clergyman's horse, stumbling with a dull blunt sound among the graves, was cropping the grass; at once deriving orthodox consolation from the dead parishioners, and enforcing last

Sunday's text that this was what all flesh came to; a lean ass who had sought to expound it also, without being qualified and ordained, was pricking his ears in an empty pound hard by, and looking with hungry eyes upon his priestly neighbour.

The old man and the child quitted the gravel path, and strayed among the tombs; for there the ground was soft, and easy to their tired feet. As they passed behind the church, they heard voices near at hand, and presently came on those who had spoken.

They were two men who were seated in easy attitudes upon the grass, and so busily engaged as to be at first unconscious of intruders. It was not difficult to divine that they were of a class of itinerant showmen—exhibitors of the freaks of Punch—for, perched cross-legged upon a tombstone behind them, was a figure of that hero himself, his nose and chin as hooked and his face as beaming as usual. Perhaps his imperturbable character was never more strikingly developed, for he preserved his usual equable smile notwithstanding that his body was dangling in a most uncomfortable position, all loose and limp and shapeless, while his long peaked cap, unequally balanced against his exceedingly slight legs, threatened every instant to bring him toppling down.

In part scattered upon the ground at the feet of the two men, and in part jumbled together in a long flat box, were the other persons of the Drama. The hero's wife and one child, the hobby-horse, the doctor, the foreign gentleman who not being familiar with the language is unable in the representation to express his ideas otherwise than by the utterance of the word 'Shallabalah' three distinct times, the radical neighbour who will by no means admit that a tin bell is an organ, the executioner, and the devil, were all here. Their owners had evidently come to that spot to make some needful repairs in the stage arrangements, for one of them was engaged in binding together a small gallows with thread, while the other was intent upon fixing a new black wig, with the aid of a small hammer and some tacks, upon the head of the radical neighbour, who had been beaten bald.

They raised their eyes when the old man and his young companion were close upon them, and pausing in their work, returned their looks of curiosity. One of them, the actual exhibitor no doubt, was a little merry-faced man with a twinkling eye and a red nose, who seemed to have unconsciously imbibed something of his hero's character. The other—that was he who took the money—had rather a careful and cautious look, which was perhaps inseparable from his occupation also.

The merry man was the first to greet the strangers with a nod; and following the old man's eyes, he observed that perhaps that was the first time he had ever seen a Punch off the stage. (Punch, it may be remarked, seemed to be pointing with the tip of his cap to a most flourishing epitaph, and to be chuckling over it with all his heart.)

'Why do you come here to do this?' said the old man, sitting down beside them, and looking at the figures with extreme delight.

'Why you see,' rejoined the little man, 'we're putting up for to-night at the public-house yonder, and it wouldn't do to let 'em see the present company undergoing repair.'

'No!' cried the old man, making signs to Nell to listen, 'why not, eh? why not?'

'Because it would destroy all the delusion, and take away all the interest, wouldn't it?' replied the little man. 'Would you care a ha'penny for the Lord Chancellor if you know'd him in private and without his wig?—certainly not.'

'Good!' said the old man, venturing to touch one of the puppets, and drawing away his hand with a shrill laugh. 'Are you going to show 'em to-night? are you?'

'That is the intention, governor,' replied the other, 'and unless I'm much mistaken, Tommy Codlin is a calculating at this minute what we've lost through your coming upon us. Cheer up, Tommy, it can't be much.'

The little man accompanied these latter words with a wink, expressive of the estimate he had formed of the travellers' finances.

To this Mr Codlin, who had a surly, grumbling manner, replied, as he twitched Punch off the tombstone and flung him into the box, 'I don't care if we haven't lost a farden, but you're too free. If you stood in front of the curtain and see the public's faces as I do, you'd know human natur' better.'

'Ah! it's been the spoiling of you, Tommy, your taking to that branch,' rejoined his companion. 'When you played the ghost in the reg'lar drama in the fairs, you believed in everything—except ghosts. But now you're a universal mistruster. I never see a man so changed.'

'Never mind,' said Mr Codlin, with the air of a discontented philosopher. 'I know better now, and p'raps I'm sorry for it.'

Turning over the figures in the box like one who knew and despised them, Mr Codlin drew one forth and held it up for the inspection of his friend:

'Look here; here's all this judy's clothes falling to pieces again. You haven't got a needle and thread I suppose?'

The little man shook his head, and scratched it ruefully as he contemplated this severe indisposition of a principal performer. Seeing that they were at a loss, the child said timidly:

'I have a needle, Sir, in my basket, and thread too. Will you let me try to mend it for you? I think I could do it neater than you could.'

Even Mr Codlin had nothing to urge against a proposal so seasonable. Nelly, kneeling down beside the box, was soon busily engaged in her task, and accomplishing it to a miracle.

While she was thus engaged, the merry little man looked at her with an interest which did not appear to be diminished when he glanced at her helpless companion. When she had finished her work he thanked her, and inquired whither they were travelling.

'N—no further to-night, I think,' said the child, looking towards her grandfather.

'If you're wanting a place to stop at,' the man remarked, 'I should advise you to take up at the same house with us. That's it. The long, low, white house there. It's very cheap.'

The old man, notwithstanding his fatigue, would have remained in the churchyard all night if his new acquaintances had remained there too. As he yielded to this suggestion a ready and rapturous assent, they all rose and walked away together; he keeping close to the box of puppets in which he was quite absorbed, the merry little man carrying it slung over his arm by a strap attached to it for the purpose, Nelly having hold of her grandfather's hand, and Mr Codlin sauntering slowly behind, casting up at the church tower and neighbouring trees such looks as he was accustomed in town-practice to direct to drawing-room and nursery windows, when seeking for a profitable spot on which to plant the show.

The public-house was kept by a fat old landlord and landlady who made no objection to receiving their new guests, but praised Nelly's beauty and were at once prepossessed in her behalf. There was no other company in the kitchen but the two showmen, and the child felt very thankful that they had fallen upon such good quarters. The landlady was very much astonished to learn that they had come all the way from London, and appeared to have no little curiosity touching their farther destination. The child parried her inquiries as well as she could, and with no great trouble, for finding that they appeared to give her pain, the old lady desisted.

'These two gentlemen have ordered supper in an hour's time,' she said, taking her into the bar; 'and your best plan will be to sup with them. Meanwhile you shall have a little taste of something that'll do you good, for I'm sure you must want it after all you've gone through to-day. Now, don't look after the old gentleman, because when you've drank that, he shall have some too.'

As nothing could induce the child to leave him alone, however, or to touch anything in which he was not the first and greatest sharer, the old lady was obliged to help him first. When they had been thus refreshed, the whole house hurried away into an empty stable where the show stood, and where, by the light of a few flaring candles stuck round a hoop which hung by a line from the ceiling, it was to be forthwith exhibited.

And now Mr Thomas Codlin, the misanthrope, after blowing away at the Pan's pipes until he was intensely wretched, took his station on one side of the checked drapery which concealed the mover of the figures, and putting his hands in his pockets prepared to reply to all questions and remarks of Punch, and to make a dismal feint of being his most intimate private friend, of believing in him to the fullest and most unlimited extent, of knowing that he enjoyed day and night a merry and glorious existence in that temple, and that he was at all times and under every circumstance the same intelligent and joyful person that the spectators then beheld him. All this Mr Codlin did with the air of a man who had made up his mind for the worst and was quite resigned; his eye slowly wandering about during the briskest repartee to observe the effect upon the audience, and particularly the impression made upon the landlord and landlady, which might be productive of very important results in connexion with the supper.

Upon this head, however, he had no cause for any anxiety, for the whole performance was applauded to the echo, and voluntary contributions were showered in with a liberality which testified yet more strongly to the general delight. Among the laughter none was more loud and frequent than the old man's. Nell's was unheard, for she, poor child, with her head drooping on his shoulder, had fallen asleep, and slept too soundly to be roused by any of his efforts to awaken her to a participation in his glee.

The supper was very good, but she was too tired to eat, and yet would not leave the old man until she had kissed him in his bed. He, happily insensible to every care and anxiety, sat listening with a vacant smile and admiring face to all that his new friend said; and it was not until they retired yawning to their room, that he followed the child up stairs.

It was but a loft partitioned into two compartments, where they were to rest, but they were well pleased with their lodging and had hoped for none so good. The old man was uneasy when he had lain down, and begged that Nell would come and sit at his bedside as she had done for so many nights. She hastened to him, and sat there till he slept.

There was a little window, hardly more than a chink in the wall, in her room, and when she left him, she opened it, quite wondering at the silence. The sight of the old church, and the graves about it in the moonlight, and the dark trees whispering among themselves, made her more thoughtful than before. She closed the window again, and sitting down upon the bed, thought of the life that was before them.

She had a little money, but it was very little, and when that was gone, they must begin to beg. There was one piece of gold among it, and an emergency might come when its worth to them would be increased a hundred fold. It would be best to hide this coin, and never produce it unless their case was absolutely desperate, and no other resource was left them.

Her resolution taken, she sewed the piece of gold into her dress, and going to bed with a lighter heart sunk into a deep slumber.

CHAPTER 17

Another bright day shining in through the small casement, and claiming fellowship with the kindred eyes of the child, awoke her. At sight of the strange room and its unaccustomed objects she started up in alarm, wondering how she had been moved from the familiar chamber in which she seemed to have fallen asleep last night, and whither she had been conveyed. But, another glance around called to her mind all that had lately passed, and she sprung from her bed, hoping and trustful.

It was yet early, and the old man being still asleep, she walked out into the churchyard, brushing the dew from the long grass with her feet, and often turning aside into places where it grew longer than in others, that she might not tread upon the graves. She felt a curious kind of pleasure in lingering among these houses of the dead, and read the inscriptions on the tombs of the good people (a great number of good people were buried there), passing on from one to another with increasing interest.

It was a very quiet place, as such a place should be, save for the cawing of the rooks who had built their nests among the branches of some tall old trees, and were calling to one another, high up in the air. First, one sleek bird, hovering near his ragged house as it swung and dangled in the wind, uttered his hoarse cry, quite by chance as it would seem, and in a sober tone as though he were but talking to himself. Another answered, and he called again, but louder than before; then another spoke and then another; and each time the first, aggravated by contradiction, insisted on his case more strongly. Other voices, silent till now, struck in from boughs lower down and higher up and midway, and to the right and left, and from the tree-tops; and others, arriving hastily from the grey church turrets and old belfry window, joined the clamour which rose and fell, and swelled and dropped again, and still went on; and all this noisy contention amidst a skimming to and fro, and lighting on fresh branches, and frequent change of place, which satirised the old restlessness of those who lay so still beneath the moss and turf below, and the strife in which they had worn away their lives.

Frequently raising her eyes to the trees whence these sounds came down, and feeling as though they made the place more quiet than perfect silence would have done, the child loitered from grave to grave, now stopping to replace with careful hands the bramble which had started from some green mound it helped to keep in shape, and now peeping through one of the low latticed windows into the church, with its worm-eaten books upon the desks, and baize of whitened-green mouldering from the pew sides and leaving the naked wood to view.

There were the seats where the poor old people sat, worn spare, and yellow like themselves; the rugged font where children had their names, the homely altar where they knelt in after life, the plain black tressels that bore their weight on their last visit to the cool old shady church. Everything told of long use and quiet slow decay; the very bell-rope in the porch was frayed into a fringe, and hoary with old age.

She was looking at a humble stone which told of a young man who had died at twenty-three years old, fifty-five years ago, when she heard a faltering step approaching, and looking round saw a feeble woman bent with the weight of years, who tottered to the foot of that same grave and asked her to read the writing on the stone. The old woman thanked her when she had done, saying that she had had the words by heart for many a long, long year, but could not see them now.

'Were you his mother?' said the child.

'I was his wife, my dear.'

She the wife of a young man of three-and-twenty! Ah, true! It was fifty-five years ago.

'You wonder to hear me say that,' remarked the old woman, shaking her head. 'You're not the first. Older folk than you have wondered at the same thing before now. Yes, I was his wife. Death doesn't change us more than life, my dear.'

'Do you come here often?' asked the child.

'I sit here very often in the summer time,' she answered, 'I used to come here once to cry and mourn, but that was a weary while ago, bless God!'

'I pluck the daisies as they grow, and take them home,' said the old woman after a short silence. 'I like no flowers so well as these, and haven't for five-and-fifty years. It's a long time, and I'm getting very old.'

Then growing garrulous upon a theme which was new to one listener though it were but a child, she told her how she had wept and moaned and prayed to die herself, when this happened; and how when she first came to that place, a young creature strong in love and grief, she had hoped that her heart was breaking as it seemed to be. But that time passed by, and although she continued to be sad when she came there, still she could bear to come, and so went on until it was pain no longer, but a solemn pleasure, and a duty she had learned to like. And now that five-and-fifty years were gone, she spoke of the dead man as if he had been her son or grandson, with a kind of pity for his youth, growing out of her own old age, and an exalting of his strength and manly beauty as compared with her own weakness and decay; and yet she spoke about him as her husband too, and thinking of herself in connexion with him, as she used to be and not as she was now, talked of their meeting in another world, as if he were dead but yesterday, and she, separated from her former self, were thinking of the happiness of that comely girl who seemed to have died with him.

The child left her gathering the flowers that grew upon the grave, and thoughtfully retraced her steps.

The old man was by this time up and dressed. Mr Codlin, still doomed to contemplate the harsh realities of existence, was packing among his linen the candle-ends which had been saved from the previous night's performance; while his companion received the compliments of all the loungers in the stable-yard, who, unable to separate him from the master-mind of

Punch, set him down as next in importance to that merry outlaw, and loved him scarcely less. When he had sufficiently acknowledged his popularity he came in to breakfast, at which meal they all sat down together.

'And where are you going to-day?' said the little man, addressing himself to Nell.

'Indeed I hardly know—we have not determined yet,' replied the child.

'We're going on to the races,' said the little man. 'If that's your way and you like to have us for company, let us travel together. If you prefer going alone, only say the word and you'll find that we shan't trouble you.'

'We'll go with you,' said the old man. 'Nell—with them, with them.'

The child considered for a moment, and reflecting that she must shortly beg, and could scarcely hope to do so at a better place than where crowds of rich ladies and gentlemen were assembled together for purposes of enjoyment and festivity, determined to accompany these men so far. She therefore thanked the little man for his offer, and said, glancing timidly towards his friend, that if there was no objection to their accompanying them as far as the race town—

'Objection!' said the little man. 'Now be gracious for once, Tommy, and say that you'd rather they went with us. I know you would. Be gracious, Tommy.'

'Trotters,' said Mr Codlin, who talked very slowly and ate very greedily, as is not uncommon with philosophers and misanthropes; 'you're too free.'

'Why what harm can it do?' urged the other.

'No harm at all in this particular case, perhaps,' replied Mr Codlin; 'but the principle's a dangerous one, and you're too free I tell you.'

'Well, are they to go with us or not?'

'Yes, they are,' said Mr Codlin; 'but you might have made a favour of it, mightn't you?'

The real name of the little man was Harris, but it had gradually merged into the less euphonious one of Trotters, which, with the prefatory adjective, Short, had been conferred upon him by reason of the small size of his legs. Short Trotters however, being a compound name, inconvenient of use in friendly dialogue, the gentleman on whom it had been bestowed was known among his intimates either as 'Short,' or 'Trotters,' and was seldom accosted at full length as Short Trotters, except in formal conversations and on occasions of ceremony.

Short, then, or Trotters, as the reader pleases, returned unto the remonstrance of his friend Mr Thomas Codlin a jocose answer calculated to turn aside his discontent; and applying himself with great relish to the cold boiled beef, the tea, and bread and butter, strongly impressed upon his companions that they should do the like. Mr Codlin indeed required no such persuasion, as he had already eaten as much as he could possibly carry and was now moistening his clay with strong ale, whereof he took deep draughts with a silent relish and invited nobody to partake—thus again strongly indicating his misanthropical turn of mind.

Breakfast being at length over, Mr Codlin called the bill, and charging the ale to the company generally (a practice also savouring of misanthropy) divided the sum-total into two fair and equal parts, assigning one moiety to himself and friend, and the other to Nelly and her grandfather. These being duly discharged and all things ready for their departure, they took farewell of the landlord and landlady and resumed their journey.

And here Mr Codlin's false position in society and the effect it wrought upon his wounded spirit, were strongly illustrated; for whereas he had been last night accosted by Mr Punch as 'master,' and had by inference left the audience to understand that he maintained that individual for his own luxurious entertainment and delight, here he was, now, painfully walking beneath the burden of that same Punch's temple, and bearing it bodily upon his shoulders on a sultry day and along a dusty road. In place of enlivening his patron with a constant fire of wit or the cheerful rattle of his quarter-staff on the heads of his relations and acquaintance, here was that beaming Punch utterly devoid of spine, all slack and drooping in a dark box, with his legs doubled up round his neck, and not one of his social qualities remaining.

Mr Codlin trudged heavily on, exchanging a word or two at intervals with Short, and stopping to rest and growl occasionally. Short led the way; with the flat box, the private luggage (which was not extensive) tied up in a bundle, and a brazen trumpet slung from his shoulder-blade. Nell and her grandfather walked next him on either hand, and Thomas Codlin brought up the rear.

When they came to any town or village, or even to a detached house of good appearance, Short blew a blast upon the brazen trumpet and carolled a fragment of a song in that hilarious tone common to Punches and their consorts. If people hurried to the windows, Mr Codlin pitched the temple, and hastily unfurling the drapery and concealing Short therewith, flourished hysterically on the pipes and performed an air. Then the entertainment began as soon as might be; Mr Codlin having the responsibility of deciding on its length and of protracting or expediting the time for the hero's final triumph over the enemy of mankind, according as he judged that the after-crop of half-pence would be plentiful or scant. When it had been gathered in to the last farthing, he resumed his load and on they went again.

Sometimes they played out the toll across a bridge or ferry, and once exhibited by particular desire at a turnpike, where the collector, being drunk in his solitude, paid down a shilling to have it to himself. There was one small place of rich promise in which their hopes were blighted, for a favourite character in the play having gold-lace upon his coat and being a meddling wooden-headed fellow was held to be a libel on the beadle, for which reason the authorities enforced a quick retreat; but they were generally well received, and seldom left a town without a troop of ragged children shouting at their heels.

They made a long day's journey, despite these interruptions, and were yet upon the road when the moon was shining in the sky. Short beguiled the time with songs and jests, and made the best of everything that happened. Mr Codlin on the other hand, cursed his fate, and all the hollow things of earth (but Punch especially), and limped along with the theatre on his back, a prey to the bitterest chagrin.

They had stopped to rest beneath a finger-post where four roads met, and Mr Codlin in his deep misanthropy had let down the drapery and seated himself in the bottom of the show, invisible to mortal eyes and disdainful of the company of his fellow creatures, when two monstrous shadows were seen stalking towards them from a turning in the road by which they had come. The child was at first quite terrified by the sight of these gaunt giants—for such they looked as they advanced with lofty strides beneath the shadow of the trees—but Short, telling her there was nothing to fear, blew a blast upon the trumpet, which was answered by a cheerful shout.

'It's Grinder's lot, an't it?' cried Mr Short in a loud key.

'Yes,' replied a couple of shrill voices.

'Come on then,' said Short. 'Let's have a look at you. I thought it was you.'

Thus invited, 'Grinder's lot' approached with redoubled speed and soon came up with the little party.

Mr Grinder's company, familiarly termed a lot, consisted of a young gentleman and a young lady on stilts, and Mr Grinder himself, who used his natural legs for pedestrian purposes and carried at his back a drum. The public costume of the young people was of the Highland kind, but the night being damp and cold, the young gentleman wore over his kilt a man's pea jacket reaching to his ankles, and a glazed hat; the young lady too was muffled in an old cloth pelisse and had a handkerchief tied about her head. Their Scotch bonnets, ornamented with plumes of jet black feathers, Mr Grinder carried on his instrument.

'Bound for the races, I see,' said Mr Grinder coming up out of breath. 'So are we. How are you, Short?' With that they shook hands in a very friendly manner. The young people being too high up for the ordinary salutations, saluted Short after their own fashion. The young gentleman twisted up his right stilt and patted him on the shoulder, and the young lady rattled her tambourine.

'Practice?' said Short, pointing to the stilts.

'No,' returned Grinder. 'It comes either to walkin' in 'em or carryin' of 'em, and they like walkin' in 'em best. It's wery pleasant for the prospects. Which road are you takin'? We go the nighest.'

'Why, the fact is,' said Short, 'that we are going the longest way, because then we could stop for the night, a mile and a half on. But three or four mile gained to-night is so many saved to-morrow, and if you keep on, I think our best way is to do the same.'

'Where's your partner?' inquired Grinder.

'Here he is,' cried Mr Thomas Codlin, presenting his head and face in the proscenium of the stage, and exhibiting an expression of countenance not often seen there; 'and he'll see his partner boiled alive before he'll go on to-night. That's what he says.'

'Well, don't say such things as them, in a spear which is dewoted to something pleasanter,' urged Short. 'Respect associations, Tommy, even if you do cut up rough.'

'Rough or smooth,' said Mr Codlin, beating his hand on the little footboard where Punch, when suddenly struck with the symmetry of his legs and their capacity for silk stockings, is accustomed to exhibit them to popular admiration, 'rough or smooth, I won't go further than the mile and a half to-night. I put up at the Jolly Sandboys and nowhere else. If you like to come there, come there. If you like to go on by yourself, go on by yourself, and do without me if you can.'

So saying, Mr Codlin disappeared from the scene and immediately presented himself outside the theatre, took it on his shoulders at a jerk, and made off with most remarkable agility.

Any further controversy being now out of the question, Short was fain to part with Mr Grinder and his pupils and to follow his morose companion. After lingering at the finger-post for a few minutes to see the stilts frisking away in the moonlight and the bearer of the drum toiling slowly after them, he blew a few notes upon the trumpet as a parting salute, and hastened with all speed to follow Mr Codlin. With this view he gave his unoccupied hand to Nell, and bidding her be of good cheer as they would soon be at the end of their journey for that night, and stimulating the old man with a similar assurance, led them at a pretty swift pace towards their destination, which he was the less unwilling to make for, as the moon was now overcast and the clouds were threatening rain.

CHAPTER 18

The Jolly Sandboys was a small road-side inn of pretty ancient date, with a sign, representing three Sandboys increasing their jollity with as many jugs of ale and bags of gold, creaking and swinging on its post on the opposite side of the road. As the travellers had observed that day many indications of their drawing nearer and nearer to the race town, such as gipsy camps, carts laden with gambling booths and their appurtenances, itinerant showmen of various kinds, and beggars and trampers of every degree, all wending their way in the same direction, Mr Codlin was fearful of finding the accommodations forestalled; this fear increasing as he diminished the distance between himself and the hostelry, he quickened his pace, and notwithstanding the burden he had to carry, maintained a round trot until he reached the threshold. Here he had the gratification of finding that his fears were without foundation, for the landlord was leaning against the door-post looking lazily at the rain, which had by this time begun to descend heavily, and no tinkling of cracked bell, nor boisterous shout, nor noisy chorus, gave note of company within.

'All alone?' said Mr Codlin, putting down his burden and wiping his forehead.

'All alone as yet,' rejoined the landlord, glancing at the sky, 'but we shall have more company to-night I expect. Here one of you boys, carry that show into the barn. Make haste in out of the wet, Tom; when it came on to rain I told 'em to make the fire up, and there's a glorious blaze in the kitchen, I can tell you.'

Mr Codlin followed with a willing mind, and soon found that the landlord had not commended his preparations without good reason. A mighty fire was blazing on the hearth and roaring up the wide chimney with a cheerful sound, which a large iron cauldron, bubbling and simmering in the heat, lent its pleasant aid to swell. There was a deep red ruddy blush upon the room, and when the landlord stirred the fire, sending the flames skipping and leaping up—when he took off the lid of the iron pot and there rushed out a savoury smell, while the bubbling sound grew deeper and more rich, and an unctuous steam came floating out, hanging in a delicious mist above their heads—when he did this, Mr Codlin's heart was touched. He sat down in the chimney-corner and smiled.

Mr Codlin sat smiling in the chimney-corner, eyeing the landlord as with a roguish look he held the cover in his hand, and, feigning that his doing so was needful to the welfare of the cookery, suffered the delightful steam to tickle the nostrils of his guest. The glow of the fire was upon the landlord's bald head, and upon his twinkling eye, and upon his watering mouth, and upon his pimpled face, and upon his round fat figure. Mr Codlin drew his sleeve across his lips, and said in a murmuring voice, 'What is it?'

'It's a stew of tripe,' said the landlord smacking his lips, 'and cow-heel,' smacking them again, 'and bacon,' smacking them once more, 'and steak,' smacking them for the fourth time, 'and peas, cauliflowers, new potatoes, and sparrow-grass, all working up together in one delicious gravy.' Having come to the climax, he smacked his lips a great many times, and taking a long hearty sniff of the fragrance that was hovering about, put on the cover again with the air of one whose toils on earth were over.

'At what time will it be ready?' asked Mr Codlin faintly.

'It'll be done to a turn,' said the landlord looking up to the clock—and the very clock had a colour in its fat white face, and looked a clock for jolly Sandboys to consult—'it'll be done to a turn at twenty-two minutes before eleven.'

'Then,' said Mr Codlin, 'fetch me a pint of warm ale, and don't let nobody bring into the room even so much as a biscuit till the time arrives.'

Nodding his approval of this decisive and manly course of procedure, the landlord retired to draw the beer, and presently returning with it, applied himself to warm the same in a small tin vessel shaped funnel-wise, for the convenience of sticking it far down in the fire and getting at the bright places. This was soon done, and he handed it over to Mr Codlin with that creamy froth upon the surface which is one of the happy circumstances attendant on mulled malt.

Greatly softened by this soothing beverage, Mr Codlin now bethought him of his companions, and acquainted mine host of the Sandboys that their arrival might be shortly looked for. The rain was rattling against the windows and pouring down in torrents, and such was Mr Codlin's extreme amiability of mind, that he more than once expressed his earnest hope that they would not be so foolish as to get wet.

At length they arrived, drenched with the rain and presenting a most miserable appearance, notwithstanding that Short had sheltered the child as well as he could under the skirts of his own coat, and they were nearly breathless from the haste they had made. But their steps were no sooner heard upon the road than the landlord, who had been at the outer door anxiously watching for their coming, rushed into the kitchen and took the cover off. The effect was electrical. They all came in with smiling faces though the wet was dripping from their clothes upon the floor, and Short's first remark was, 'What a delicious smell!'

It is not very difficult to forget rain and mud by the side of a cheerful fire, and in a bright room. They were furnished with slippers and such dry garments as the house or their own bundles afforded, and ensconcing themselves, as Mr Codlin had already done, in the warm chimney-corner, soon forgot their late troubles or only remembered them as enhancing the delights of the present time. Overpowered by the warmth and comfort and the fatigue they had undergone, Nelly and the old man had not long taken their seats here, when they fell asleep.

'Who are they?' whispered the landlord.

Short shook his head, and wished he knew himself.

'Don't you know?' asked the host, turning to Mr Codlin.

'Not I,' he replied. 'They're no good, I suppose.'

'They're no harm,' said Short. 'Depend upon that. I tell you what—it's plain that the old man an't in his right mind—'

'If you haven't got anything newer than that to say,' growled Mr Codlin, glancing at the clock, 'you'd better let us fix our minds upon the supper, and not disturb us.'

'Hear me out, won't you?' retorted his friend. 'It's very plain to me, besides, that they're not used to this way of life. Don't tell me that that handsome child has been in the habit of prowling about as she's done these last two or three days. I know better.'

'Well, who does tell you she has?' growled Mr Codlin, again glancing at the clock and from it to the cauldron, 'can't you think of anything more suitable to present circumstances than saying things and then contradicting 'em?'

'I wish somebody would give you your supper,' returned Short, 'for there'll be no peace till you've got it. Have you seen how anxious the old man is to get on—always wanting to be furder away—furder away. Have you seen that?'

'Ah! what then?' muttered Thomas Codlin.

'This, then,' said Short. 'He has given his friends the slip. Mind what I say—he has given his friends the slip, and persuaded this delicate young creetur all along of her fondness for him to be his guide and travelling companion—where to, he knows no more than the man in the moon. Now I'm not a going to stand that.'

'You're not a going to stand that!' cried Mr Codlin, glancing at the clock again and pulling his hair with both hands in a kind of frenzy, but whether occasioned by his companion's observation or the tardy pace of Time, it was difficult to determine. 'Here's a world to live in!'

'I,' repeated Short emphatically and slowly, 'am not a-going to stand it. I am not a-going to see this fair young child a falling into bad hands, and getting among people that she's no more fit for, than they are to get among angels as their ordinary chums. Therefore when they dewelope an intention of parting company from us, I shall take measures for detaining of 'em, and restoring 'em to their friends, who I dare say have had their disconsolation pasted up on every wall in London by this time.'

'Short,' said Mr Codlin, who with his head upon his hands, and his elbows on his knees, had been shaking himself impatiently from side to side up to this point and occasionally stamping on the ground, but who now looked up with eager eyes; 'it's possible that there may be uncommon good sense in what you've said. If there is, and there should be a reward, Short, remember that we're partners in everything!'

His companion had only time to nod a brief assent to this position, for the child awoke at the instant. They had drawn close together during the previous whispering, and now hastily separated and were rather awkwardly endeavouring to exchange some casual remarks in their usual tone, when strange footsteps were heard without, and fresh company entered.

These were no other than four very dismal dogs, who came pattering in one after the other, headed by an old bandy dog of particularly mournful aspect, who, stopping when the last of his followers had got as far as the door, erected himself upon his hind legs and looked round at his companions, who immediately stood upon their hind legs, in a grave and melancholy row. Nor was this the only remarkable circumstance about these dogs, for each of them wore a kind of little coat of some gaudy colour trimmed with tarnished spangles, and one of them had a cap upon his head, tied very carefully under his chin, which had fallen down upon his nose and completely obscured one eye; add to this, that the gaudy coats were all wet through and discoloured with rain, and that the wearers were splashed and dirty, and some idea may be formed of the unusual appearance of these new visitors to the Jolly Sandboys.

Neither Short nor the landlord nor Thomas Codlin, however, was in the least surprised, merely remarking that these were Jerry's dogs and that Jerry could not be far behind. So there the dogs stood, patiently winking and gaping and looking extremely hard at the boiling pot, until Jerry himself appeared, when they all dropped down at once and walked about the room in their natural manner. This posture it must be confessed did not much improve their appearance, as their own personal tails and their coat tails—both capital things in their way—did not agree together.

Jerry, the manager of these dancing dogs, was a tall black-whiskered man in a velveteen coat, who seemed well known to the landlord and his guests and accosted them with great cordiality. Disencumbering himself of a barrel organ which he placed upon a chair, and retaining in his hand a small whip wherewith to awe his company of comedians, he came up to the fire to dry himself, and entered into conversation.

'Your people don't usually travel in character, do they?' said Short, pointing to the dresses of the dogs. 'It must come expensive if they do?'

'No,' replied Jerry, 'no, it's not the custom with us. But we've been playing a little on the road to-day, and we come out with a new wardrobe at the races, so I didn't think it worth while to stop to undress. Down, Pedro!'

This was addressed to the dog with the cap on, who being a new member of the company, and not quite certain of his duty, kept his unobscured eye anxiously on his master, and was perpetually starting upon his hind legs when there was no occasion, and falling down again.

'I've got a animal here,' said Jerry, putting his hand into the capacious pocket of his coat, and diving into one corner as if he were feeling for a small orange or an apple or some such article, 'a animal here, wot I think you know something of, Short.'

'Ah!' cried Short, 'let's have a look at him.'

'Here he is,' said Jerry, producing a little terrier from his pocket. 'He was once a Toby of yours, warn't he!'

In some versions of the great drama of Punch there is a small dog—a modern innovation—supposed to be the private property of that gentleman, whose name is always Toby. This Toby has been stolen in youth from another gentleman, and fraudulently sold to the confiding hero, who having no guile himself has no suspicion that it lurks in others; but Toby, entertaining a grateful recollection of his old master, and scorning to attach himself to any new patrons, not only refuses to smoke a pipe at the bidding of Punch, but to mark his old fidelity more strongly, seizes him by the nose and wrings the same with violence, at which instance of canine attachment the spectators are deeply affected. This was the character which the little terrier in question had once sustained; if there had been any doubt upon the subject he would speedily have resolved it by his conduct; for not only did he, on seeing Short, give the strongest tokens of recognition, but catching sight of the flat box he barked so furiously at the pasteboard nose which he knew was inside, that his master was obliged to gather him up and put him into his pocket again, to the great relief of the whole company.

The landlord now busied himself in laying the cloth, in which process Mr Codlin obligingly assisted by setting forth his own knife and fork in the most convenient place and establishing himself behind them. When everything was ready, the landlord took off the cover for the last time, and then indeed there burst forth such a goodly promise of supper, that if he had offered to put it on again or had hinted at postponement, he would certainly have been sacrificed on his own hearth.

However, he did nothing of the kind, but instead thereof assisted a stout servant girl in turning the contents of the cauldron into a large tureen; a proceeding which the dogs, proof against various hot splashes which fell upon their noses, watched with terrible eagerness. At length the dish was lifted on the table, and mugs of ale having been previously set round, little Nell ventured to say grace, and supper began.

At this juncture the poor dogs were standing on their hind legs quite surprisingly; the child, having pity on them, was about to cast some morsels of food to them before she tasted it herself, hungry though she was, when their master interposed.

'No, my dear, no, not an atom from anybody's hand but mine if you please. That dog,' said Jerry, pointing out the old leader of the troop, and speaking in a terrible voice, 'lost a halfpenny to-day. He goes without his supper.'

The unfortunate creature dropped upon his fore-legs directly, wagged his tail, and looked imploringly at his master.

'You must be more careful, Sir,' said Jerry, walking coolly to the chair where he had placed the organ, and setting the stop. 'Come here. Now, Sir, you play away at that, while we have supper, and leave off if you dare.'

The dog immediately began to grind most mournful music. His master having shown him the whip resumed his seat and called up the others, who, at his directions, formed in a row, standing upright as a file of soldiers.

'Now, gentlemen,' said Jerry, looking at them attentively. 'The dog whose name's called, eats. The dogs whose names an't called, keep quiet. Carlo!'

The lucky individual whose name was called, snapped up the morsel thrown towards him, but none of the others moved a muscle. In this manner they were fed at the discretion of their master. Meanwhile the dog in disgrace ground hard at the organ, sometimes in quick time, sometimes in slow, but never leaving off for an instant. When the knives and forks rattled very much, or any of his fellows got an unusually large piece of fat, he accompanied the music with a short howl, but he immediately checked it on his master looking round, and applied himself with increased diligence to the Old Hundredth.

CHAPTER 19

Supper was not yet over, when there arrived at the Jolly Sandboys two more travellers bound for the same haven as the rest, who had been walking in the rain for some hours, and came in shining and heavy with water. One of these was the proprietor of a giant, and a little lady without legs or arms, who had jogged forward in a van; the other, a silent gentleman who earned his living by showing tricks upon the cards, and who had rather deranged the natural expression of his countenance by putting small leaden lozenges into his eyes and bringing them out at his mouth, which was one of his professional accomplishments. The name of the first of these newcomers was Vuffin; the other, probably as a pleasant satire upon his ugliness, was called Sweet William. To render them as comfortable as he could, the landlord bestirred himself nimbly, and in a very short time both gentlemen were perfectly at their ease.

'How's the Giant?' said Short, when they all sat smoking round the fire.

'Rather weak upon his legs,' returned Mr Vuffin. 'I begin to be afraid he's going at the knees.'

'That's a bad look-out,' said Short.

'Aye! Bad indeed,' replied Mr Vuffin, contemplating the fire with a sigh. 'Once get a giant shaky on his legs, and the public care no more about him than they do for a dead cabbage stalk.'

'What becomes of old giants?' said Short, turning to him again after a little reflection.

'They're usually kept in carawans to wait upon the dwarfs,' said Mr Vuffin.

'The maintaining of 'em must come expensive, when they can't be shown, eh?' remarked Short, eyeing him doubtfully.

'It's better that, than letting 'em go upon the parish or about the streets,' said Mr Vuffin. 'Once make a giant common and giants will never draw again. Look at wooden legs. If there was only one man with a wooden leg what a property he'd be!'

'So he would!' observed the landlord and Short both together. 'That's very true.'

'Instead of which,' pursued Mr Vuffin, 'if you was to advertise Shakspeare played entirely by wooden legs, it's my belief you wouldn't draw a sixpence.'

'I don't suppose you would,' said Short. And the landlord said so too.

'This shows, you see,' said Mr Vuffin, waving his pipe with an argumentative air, 'this shows the policy of keeping the used-up giants still in the carawans, where they get food and lodging for nothing, all their lives, and in general very glad they are to stop there. There was one giant—a black 'un—as left his carawan some year ago and took to carrying coach-bills about London, making himself as cheap as crossing-sweepers. He died. I make no insinuation against anybody in particular,' said Mr Vuffin, looking solemnly round, 'but he was ruining the trade;—and he died.'

The landlord drew his breath hard, and looked at the owner of the dogs, who nodded and said gruffly that he remembered.

'I know you do, Jerry,' said Mr Vuffin with profound meaning. 'I know you remember it, Jerry, and the universal opinion was, that it served him right. Why, I remember the time when old Maunders as had three-and-twenty wans—I remember the time when old Maunders had in his cottage in Spa Fields in the winter time, when the season was over, eight male and female dwarfs setting down to dinner every day, who was waited on by eight old giants in green coats, red smalls, blue cotton stockings, and high-lows: and there was one dwarf as had grown elderly and wicious who whenever his giant wasn't quick enough to please him, used to stick pins in his legs, not being able to reach up any higher. I know that's a fact, for Maunders told it me himself.'

'What about the dwarfs when they get old?' inquired the landlord.

'The older a dwarf is, the better worth he is,' returned Mr Vuffin; 'a grey-headed dwarf, well wrinkled, is beyond all suspicion. But a giant weak in the legs and not standing upright!— keep him in the caravan, but never show him, never show him, for any persuasion that can be offered.'

While Mr Vuffin and his two friends smoked their pipes and beguiled the time with such conversation as this, the silent gentleman sat in a warm corner, swallowing, or seeming to swallow, sixpennyworth of halfpence for practice, balancing a feather upon his nose, and rehearsing other feats of dexterity of that kind, without paying any regard whatever to the company, who in their turn left him utterly unnoticed. At length the weary child prevailed upon her grandfather to retire, and they withdrew, leaving the company yet seated round the fire, and the dogs fast asleep at a humble distance.

After bidding the old man good night, Nell retired to her poor garret, but had scarcely closed the door, when it was gently tapped at. She opened it directly, and was a little startled by the sight of Mr Thomas Codlin, whom she had left, to all appearance, fast asleep down stairs.

'What is the matter?' said the child.

'Nothing's the matter, my dear,' returned her visitor. 'I'm your friend. Perhaps you haven't thought so, but it's me that's your friend—not him.'

'Not who?' the child inquired.

'Short, my dear. I tell you what,' said Codlin, 'for all his having a kind of way with him that you'd be very apt to like, I'm the real, open-hearted man. I mayn't look it, but I am indeed.'

The child began to be alarmed, considering that the ale had taken effect upon Mr Codlin, and that this commendation of himself was the consequence.

'Short's very well, and seems kind,' resumed the misanthrope, 'but he overdoes it. Now I don't.'

Certainly if there were any fault in Mr Codlin's usual deportment, it was that he rather underdid his kindness to those about him, than overdid it. But the child was puzzled, and could not tell what to say.

'Take my advice,' said Codlin: 'don't ask me why, but take it. As long as you travel with us, keep as near me as you can. Don't offer to leave us—not on any account—but always stick to me and say that I'm your friend. Will you bear that in mind, my dear, and always say that it was me that was your friend?'

'Say so where—and when?' inquired the child innocently.

'O, nowhere in particular,' replied Codlin, a little put out as it seemed by the question; 'I'm only anxious that you should think me so, and do me justice. You can't think what an interest I have in you. Why didn't you tell me your little history—that about you and the poor old gentleman? I'm the best adviser that ever was, and so interested in you—so much more interested than Short. I think they're breaking up down stairs; you needn't tell Short, you know, that we've had this little talk together. God bless you. Recollect the friend. Codlin's the friend, not Short. Short's very well as far as he goes, but the real friend is Codlin—not Short.'

Eking out these professions with a number of benevolent and protecting looks and great fervour of manner, Thomas Codlin stole away on tiptoe, leaving the child in a state of extreme surprise. She was still ruminating upon his curious behaviour, when the floor of the crazy stairs and landing cracked beneath the tread of the other travellers who were passing to their beds. When they had all passed, and the sound of their footsteps had died away, one of them returned, and after a little hesitation and rustling in the passage, as if he were doubtful what door to knock at, knocked at hers.

'Yes,' said the child from within.

'It's me—Short'—a voice called through the keyhole. 'I only wanted to say that we must be off early to-morrow morning, my dear, because unless we get the start of the dogs and the conjuror, the villages won't be worth a penny. You'll be sure to be stirring early and go with us? I'll call you.'

The child answered in the affirmative, and returning his 'good night' heard him creep away. She felt some uneasiness at the anxiety of these men, increased by the recollection of their whispering together down stairs and their slight confusion when she awoke, nor was she quite free from a misgiving that they were not the fittest companions she could have stumbled on. Her uneasiness, however, was nothing, weighed against her fatigue; and she soon forgot it in sleep.

Very early next morning, Short fulfilled his promise, and knocking softly at her door, entreated that she would get up directly, as the proprietor of the dogs was still snoring, and if they lost no time they might get a good deal in advance both of him and the conjuror, who was talking in his sleep, and from what he could be heard to say, appeared to be balancing a donkey in his dreams. She started from her bed without delay, and roused the old man with so much expedition that they were both ready as soon as Short himself, to that gentleman's unspeakable gratification and relief.

After a very unceremonious and scrambling breakfast, of which the staple commodities were bacon and bread, and beer, they took leave of the landlord and issued from the door of the jolly Sandboys. The morning was fine and warm, the ground cool to the feet after the late rain, the hedges gayer and more green, the air clear, and everything fresh and healthful. Surrounded by these influences, they walked on pleasantly enough.

They had not gone very far, when the child was again struck by the altered behaviour of Mr Thomas Codlin, who instead of plodding on sulkily by himself as he had heretofore done, kept close to her, and when he had an opportunity of looking at her unseen by his companion, warned her by certain wry faces and jerks of the head not to put any trust in Short, but to reserve all confidences for Codlin. Neither did he confine himself to looks and gestures, for when she and her grandfather were walking on beside the aforesaid Short, and that little man was talking with his accustomed cheerfulness on a variety of indifferent subjects, Thomas Codlin testified his jealousy and distrust by following close at her heels, and occasionally admonishing her ankles with the legs of the theatre in a very abrupt and painful manner.

All these proceedings naturally made the child more watchful and suspicious, and she soon observed that whenever they halted to perform outside a village alehouse or other place, Mr Codlin while he went through his share of the entertainments kept his eye steadily upon her and the old man, or with a show of great friendship and consideration invited the latter to lean upon his arm, and so held him tight until the representation was over and they again went forward. Even Short seemed to change in this respect, and to mingle with his good-nature something of a desire to keep them in safe custody. This increased the child's misgivings, and made her yet more anxious and uneasy.

Meanwhile, they were drawing near the town where the races were to begin next day; for, from passing numerous groups of gipsies and trampers on the road, wending their way towards it, and straggling out from every by-way and cross-country lane, they gradually fell into a stream of people, some walking by the side of covered carts, others with horses, others with donkeys, others toiling on with heavy loads upon their backs, but all tending to the same point. The public-houses by the wayside, from being empty and noiseless as those in the remoter parts had been, now sent out boisterous shouts and clouds of smoke; and, from the misty windows, clusters of broad red faces looked down upon the road. On every piece of waste or common ground, some small gambler drove his noisy trade, and bellowed to the idle passersby to stop and try their chance; the crowd grew thicker and more noisy; gilt gingerbread in blanket-stalls exposed its glories to the dust; and often a four-horse carriage, dashing by, obscured all objects in the gritty cloud it raised, and left them, stunned and blinded, far behind.

It was dark before they reached the town itself, and long indeed the few last miles had been. Here all was tumult and confusion; the streets were filled with throngs of people—many strangers were there, it seemed, by the looks they cast about—the church-bells rang out their noisy peals, and flags streamed from windows and house-tops. In the large inn-yards waiters flitted to and fro and ran against each other, horses clattered on the uneven stones, carriage steps fell rattling down, and sickening smells from many dinners came in a heavy lukewarm breath upon the sense. In the smaller public-houses, fiddles with all their might and main were squeaking out the tune to staggering feet; drunken men, oblivious of the burden of their song, joined in a senseless howl, which drowned the tinkling of the feeble bell and made them savage for their drink; vagabond groups assembled round the doors to see the stroller woman dance, and add their uproar to the shrill flageolet and deafening drum.

Through this delirious scene, the child, frightened and repelled by all she saw, led on her bewildered charge, clinging close to her conductor, and trembling lest in the press she should be separated from him and left to find her way alone. Quickening their steps to get clear of all the roar and riot, they at length passed through the town and made for the race-course, which was upon an open heath, situated on an eminence, a full mile distant from its furthest bounds.

Although there were many people here, none of the best favoured or best clad, busily erecting tents and driving stakes in the ground, and hurrying to and fro with dusty feet and many a grumbled oath—although there were tired children cradled on heaps of straw between the wheels of carts, crying themselves to sleep—and poor lean horses and donkeys just turned loose, grazing among the men and women, and pots and kettles, and half-lighted fires, and ends of candles flaring and wasting in the air—for all this, the child felt it an escape from the town and drew her breath more freely. After a scanty supper, the purchase of which reduced her little stock so low, that she had only a few halfpence with which to buy a breakfast on the morrow, she and the old man lay down to rest in a corner of a tent, and slept, despite the busy preparations that were going on around them all night long.

And now they had come to the time when they must beg their bread. Soon after sunrise in the morning she stole out from the tent, and rambling into some fields at a short distance, plucked a few wild roses and such humble flowers, purposing to make them into little nosegays and offer them to the ladies in the carriages when the company arrived. Her thoughts were not idle while she was thus employed; when she returned and was seated beside the old man in one corner of the tent, tying her flowers together, while the two men lay dozing in another corner, she plucked him by the sleeve, and slightly glancing towards them, said, in a low voice—

'Grandfather, don't look at those I talk of, and don't seem as if I spoke of anything but what I am about. What was that you told me before we left the old house? That if they knew what we were going to do, they would say that you were mad, and part us?'

The old man turned to her with an aspect of wild terror; but she checked him by a look, and bidding him hold some flowers while she tied them up, and so bringing her lips closer to his ear, said—

'I know that was what you told me. You needn't speak, dear. I recollect it very well. It was not likely that I should forget it. Grandfather, these men suspect that we have secretly left our friends, and mean to carry us before some gentleman and have us taken care of and sent back. If you let your hand tremble so, we can never get away from them, but if you're only quiet now, we shall do so, easily.'

'How?' muttered the old man. 'Dear Nelly, how? They will shut me up in a stone room, dark and cold, and chain me up to the wall, Nell—flog me with whips, and never let me see thee more!'

'You're trembling again,' said the child. 'Keep close to me all day. Never mind them, don't look at them, but me. I shall find a time when we can steal away. When I do, mind you come with me, and do not stop or speak a word. Hush! That's all.'

'Halloa! what are you up to, my dear?' said Mr Codlin, raising his head, and yawning. Then observing that his companion was fast asleep, he added in an earnest whisper, 'Codlin's the friend, remember—not Short.'

'Making some nosegays,' the child replied; 'I am going to try and sell some, these three days of the races. Will you have one—as a present I mean?'

Mr Codlin would have risen to receive it, but the child hurried towards him and placed it in his hand. He stuck it in his buttonhole with an air of ineffable complacency for a misanthrope, and leering exultingly at the unconscious Short, muttered, as he laid himself down again, 'Tom Codlin's the friend, by G—!'

As the morning wore on, the tents assumed a gayer and more brilliant appearance, and long lines of carriages came rolling softly on the turf. Men who had lounged about all night in smock-frocks and leather leggings, came out in silken vests and hats and plumes, as jugglers or mountebanks; or in gorgeous liveries as soft-spoken servants at gambling booths; or in sturdy yeoman dress as decoys at unlawful games. Black-eyed gipsy girls, hooded in showy handkerchiefs, sallied forth to tell fortunes, and pale slender women with consumptive faces lingered upon the footsteps of ventriloquists and conjurors, and counted the sixpences with anxious eyes long before they were gained. As many of the children as could be kept within bounds, were stowed away, with all the other signs of dirt and poverty, among the donkeys, carts, and horses; and as many as could not be thus disposed of ran in and out in all intricate spots, crept between people's legs and carriage wheels, and came forth unharmed from under horses' hoofs. The dancing-dogs, the stilts, the little lady and the tall man, and all the other attractions, with organs out of number and bands innumerable, emerged from the holes and corners in which they had passed the night, and flourished boldly in the sun.

Along the uncleared course, Short led his party, sounding the brazen trumpet and revelling in the voice of Punch; and at his heels went Thomas Codlin, bearing the show as usual, and keeping his eye on Nelly and her grandfather, as they rather lingered in the rear. The child bore upon her arm the little basket with her flowers, and sometimes stopped, with timid and modest looks, to offer them at some gay carriage; but alas! there were many bolder beggars there, gipsies who promised husbands, and other adepts in their trade, and although some ladies smiled gently as they shook their heads, and others cried to the gentlemen beside them 'See, what a pretty face!' they let the pretty face pass on, and never thought that it looked tired or hungry.

There was but one lady who seemed to understand the child, and she was one who sat alone in a handsome carriage, while two young men in dashing clothes, who had just dismounted from it, talked and laughed loudly at a little distance, appearing to forget her, quite. There were many ladies all around, but they turned their backs, or looked another way, or at the two young men (not unfavourably at them), and left her to herself. She motioned away a gipsy-woman urgent to tell her fortune, saying that it was told already and had been for some years, but called the child towards her, and taking her flowers put money into her trembling hand, and bade her go home and keep at home for God's sake.

Many a time they went up and down those long, long lines, seeing everything but the horses and the race; when the bell rang to clear the course, going back to rest among the carts and donkeys, and not coming out again until the heat was over. Many a time, too, was Punch displayed in the full zenith of his humour, but all this while the eye of Thomas Codlin was upon them, and to escape without notice was impracticable.

At length, late in the day, Mr Codlin pitched the show in a convenient spot, and the spectators were soon in the very triumph of the scene. The child, sitting down with the old man close behind it, had been thinking how strange it was that horses who were such fine honest creatures should seem to make vagabonds of all the men they drew about them, when a loud laugh at some extemporaneous witticism of Mr Short's, having allusion to the circumstances of the day, roused her from her meditation and caused her to look around.

If they were ever to get away unseen, that was the very moment. Short was plying the quarter-staves vigorously and knocking the characters in the fury of the combat against the sides of the show, the people were looking on with laughing faces, and Mr Codlin had relaxed into a grim smile as his roving eye detected hands going into waistcoat pockets and groping secretly for sixpences. If they were ever to get away unseen, that was the very moment. They seized it, and fled.

They made a path through booths and carriages and throngs of people, and never once stopped to look behind. The bell was ringing and the course was cleared by the time they reached the ropes, but they dashed across it insensible to the shouts and screeching that assailed them for breaking in upon its sanctity, and creeping under the brow of the hill at a quick pace, made for the open fields.

CHAPTER 20

Day after day as he bent his steps homeward, returning from some new effort to procure employment, Kit raised his eyes to the window of the little room he had so much commended to the child, and hoped to see some indication of her presence. His own earnest wish, coupled with the assurance he had received from Quilp, filled him with the belief that she would yet arrive to claim the humble shelter he had offered, and from the death of each day's hope another hope sprung up to live to-morrow.

'I think they must certainly come to-morrow, eh mother?' said Kit, laying aside his hat with a weary air and sighing as he spoke. 'They have been gone a week. They surely couldn't stop away more than a week, could they now?'

The mother shook her head, and reminded him how often he had been disappointed already.

'For the matter of that,' said Kit, 'you speak true and sensible enough, as you always do, mother. Still, I do consider that a week is quite long enough for 'em to be rambling about; don't you say so?'

'Quite long enough, Kit, longer than enough, but they may not come back for all that.'

Kit was for a moment disposed to be vexed by this contradiction, and not the less so from having anticipated it in his own mind and knowing how just it was. But the impulse was only momentary, and the vexed look became a kind one before it had crossed the room.

'Then what do you think, mother, has become of 'em? You don't think they've gone to sea, anyhow?'

'Not gone for sailors, certainly,' returned the mother with a smile. 'But I can't help thinking that they have gone to some foreign country.'

'I say,' cried Kit with a rueful face, 'don't talk like that, mother.'

'I am afraid they have, and that's the truth,' she said. 'It's the talk of all the neighbours, and there are some even that know of their having been seen on board ship, and can tell you the name of the place they've gone to, which is more than I can, my dear, for it's a very hard one.'

'I don't believe it,' said Kit. 'Not a word of it. A set of idle chatterboxes, how should they know!'

'They may be wrong of course,' returned the mother, 'I can't tell about that, though I don't think it's at all unlikely that they're in the right, for the talk is that the old gentleman had put by a little money that nobody knew of, not even that ugly little man you talk to me about—what's his name—Quilp; and that he and Miss Nell have gone to live abroad where it can't be taken from them, and they will never be disturbed. That don't seem very far out of the way now, do it?'

Kit scratched his head mournfully, in reluctant admission that it did not, and clambering up to the old nail took down the cage and set himself to clean it and to feed the bird. His thoughts reverting from this occupation to the little old gentleman who had given him the shilling, he suddenly recollected that that was the very day—nay, nearly the very hour—at which the little old gentleman had said he should be at the Notary's house again. He no sooner remembered this, than he hung up the cage with great precipitation, and hastily explaining the nature of his errand, went off at full speed to the appointed place.

It was some two minutes after the time when he reached the spot, which was a considerable distance from his home, but by great good luck the little old gentleman had not yet arrived; at least there was no pony-chaise to be seen, and it was not likely that he had come and gone again in so short a space. Greatly relieved to find that he was not too late, Kit leant against a lamp-post to take breath, and waited the advent of the pony and his charge.

Sure enough, before long the pony came trotting round the corner of the street, looking as obstinate as pony might, and picking his steps as if he were spying about for the cleanest places, and would by no means dirty his feet or hurry himself inconveniently. Behind the pony sat the little old gentleman, and by the old gentleman's side sat the little old lady, carrying just such a nosegay as she had brought before.

The old gentleman, the old lady, the pony, and the chaise, came up the street in perfect unanimity, until they arrived within some half a dozen doors of the Notary's house, when the pony, deceived by a brass-plate beneath a tailor's knocker, came to a halt, and maintained by a sturdy silence, that that was the house they wanted.

'Now, Sir, will you ha' the goodness to go on; this is not the place,' said the old gentleman.

The pony looked with great attention into a fire-plug which was near him, and appeared to be quite absorbed in contemplating it.

'Oh dear, such a naughty Whisker!' cried the old lady. 'After being so good too, and coming along so well! I am quite ashamed of him. I don't know what we are to do with him, I really don't.'

The pony having thoroughly satisfied himself as to the nature and properties of the fire-plug, looked into the air after his old enemies the flies, and as there happened to be one of them tickling his ear at that moment he shook his head and whisked his tail, after which he appeared full of thought but quite comfortable and collected. The old gentleman having exhausted his powers of persuasion, alighted to lead him; whereupon the pony, perhaps because he held this to be a sufficient concession, perhaps because he happened to catch sight of the other brass-plate, or perhaps because he was in a spiteful humour, darted off with the old lady and stopped at the right house, leaving the old gentleman to come panting on behind.

It was then that Kit presented himself at the pony's head, and touched his hat with a smile.

'Why, bless me,' cried the old gentleman, 'the lad is here! My dear, do you see?'

'I said I'd be here, Sir,' said Kit, patting Whisker's neck. 'I hope you've had a pleasant ride, sir. He's a very nice little pony.'

'My dear,' said the old gentleman. 'This is an uncommon lad; a good lad, I'm sure.'

'I'm sure he is,' rejoined the old lady. 'A very good lad, and I am sure he is a good son.'

Kit acknowledged these expressions of confidence by touching his hat again and blushing very much. The old gentleman then handed the old lady out, and after looking at him with an approving smile, they went into the house—talking about him as they went, Kit could not help feeling. Presently Mr Witherden, smelling very hard at the nosegay, came to the window and looked at him, and after that Mr Abel came and looked at him, and after that the old gentleman and lady came and looked at him again, and after that they all came and looked at him together, which Kit, feeling very much embarrassed by, made a pretence of not observing. Therefore he patted the pony more and more; and this liberty the pony most handsomely permitted.

The faces had not disappeared from the window many moments, when Mr Chuckster in his official coat, and with his hat hanging on his head just as it happened to fall from its peg, appeared upon the pavement, and telling him he was wanted inside, bade him go in and he would mind the chaise the while. In giving him this direction Mr Chuckster remarked that he wished that he might be blessed if he could make out whether he (Kit) was 'precious raw' or 'precious deep,' but intimated by a distrustful shake of the head, that he inclined to the latter opinion.

Kit entered the office in a great tremor, for he was not used to going among strange ladies and gentlemen, and the tin boxes and bundles of dusty papers had in his eyes an awful and venerable air. Mr Witherden too was a bustling gentleman who talked loud and fast, and all eyes were upon him, and he was very shabby.

'Well, boy,' said Mr Witherden, 'you came to work out that shilling;—not to get another, hey?'

'No indeed, sir,' replied Kit, taking courage to look up. 'I never thought of such a thing.'

'Father alive?' said the Notary.

'Dead, sir.'

'Mother?'

'Yes, sir.'

'Married again—eh?'

Kit made answer, not without some indignation, that she was a widow with three children, and that as to her marrying again, if the gentleman knew her he wouldn't think of such a thing. At this reply Mr Witherden buried his nose in the flowers again, and whispered behind the nosegay to the old gentleman that he believed the lad was as honest a lad as need be.

'Now,' said Mr Garland when they had made some further inquiries of him, 'I am not going to give you anything—'

'Thank you, sir,' Kit replied; and quite seriously too, for this announcement seemed to free him from the suspicion which the Notary had hinted.

'—But,' resumed the old gentleman, 'perhaps I may want to know something more about you, so tell me where you live, and I'll put it down in my pocket-book.'

Kit told him, and the old gentleman wrote down the address with his pencil. He had scarcely done so, when there was a great uproar in the street, and the old lady hurrying to the window cried that Whisker had run away, upon which Kit darted out to the rescue, and the others followed.

It seemed that Mr Chuckster had been standing with his hands in his pockets looking carelessly at the pony, and occasionally insulting him with such admonitions as 'Stand still,'—'Be quiet,'—'Woa-a-a,' and the like, which by a pony of spirit cannot be borne. Consequently, the pony being deterred by no considerations of duty or obedience, and not having before him the slightest fear of the human eye, had at length started off, and was at that moment rattling down the street—Mr Chuckster, with his hat off and a pen behind his ear, hanging on in the rear of the chaise and making futile attempts to draw it the other way, to the unspeakable admiration of all beholders. Even in running away, however, Whisker was perverse, for he had not gone very far when he suddenly stopped, and before assistance could be rendered, commenced backing at nearly as quick a pace as he had gone forward. By these means Mr Chuckster was pushed and hustled to the office again, in a most inglorious manner, and arrived in a state of great exhaustion and discomfiture.

The old lady then stepped into her seat, and Mr Abel (whom they had come to fetch) into his. The old gentleman, after reasoning with the pony on the extreme impropriety of his conduct, and making the best amends in his power to Mr Chuckster, took his place also, and they drove away, waving a farewell to the Notary and his clerk, and more than once turning to nod kindly to Kit as he watched them from the road.

CHAPTER 21

Kit turned away and very soon forgot the pony, and the chaise, and the little old lady, and the little old gentleman, and the little young gentleman to boot, in thinking what could have become of his late master and his lovely grandchild, who were the fountain-head of all his meditations. Still casting about for some plausible means of accounting for their non-appearance, and of persuading himself that they must soon return, he bent his steps towards home, intending to finish the task which the sudden recollection of his contract had interrupted, and then to sally forth once more to seek his fortune for the day.

When he came to the corner of the court in which he lived, lo and behold there was the pony again! Yes, there he was, looking more obstinate than ever; and alone in the chaise, keeping a steady watch upon his every wink, sat Mr Abel, who, lifting up his eyes by chance and seeing Kit pass by, nodded to him as though he would have nodded his head off.

Kit wondered to see the pony again, so near his own home too, but it never occurred to him for what purpose the pony might have come there, or where the old lady and the old gentleman had gone, until he lifted the latch of the door, and walking in, found them seated in the room in conversation with his mother, at which unexpected sight he pulled off his hat and made his best bow in some confusion.

'We are here before you, you see, Christopher,' said Mr Garland smiling.

'Yes, sir,' said Kit; and as he said it, he looked towards his mother for an explanation of the visit.

'The gentleman's been kind enough, my dear,' said she, in reply to this mute interrogation, 'to ask me whether you were in a good place, or in any place at all, and when I told him no, you were not in any, he was so good as to say that—'

'—That we wanted a good lad in our house,' said the old gentleman and the old lady both together, 'and that perhaps we might think of it, if we found everything as we would wish it to be.'

As this thinking of it, plainly meant the thinking of engaging Kit, he immediately partook of his mother's anxiety and fell into a great flutter; for the little old couple were very methodical and cautious, and asked so many questions that he began to be afraid there was no chance of his success.

'You see, my good woman,' said Mrs Garland to Kit's mother, 'that it's necessary to be very careful and particular in such a matter as this, for we're only three in family, and are very quiet regular folks, and it would be a sad thing if we made any kind of mistake, and found things different from what we hoped and expected.'

To this, Kit's mother replied, that certainly it was quite true, and quite right, and quite proper, and Heaven forbid that she should shrink, or have cause to shrink, from any inquiry into her character or that of her son, who was a very good son though she was his mother, in which respect, she was bold to say, he took after his father, who was not only a good son to his mother, but the best of husbands and the best of fathers besides, which Kit could and would corroborate she knew, and so would little Jacob and the baby likewise if they were old enough, which unfortunately they were not, though as they didn't know what a loss they had had, perhaps it was a great deal better that they should be as young as they were; and so Kit's mother wound up a long story by wiping her eyes with her apron, and patting little Jacob's head, who was rocking the cradle and staring with all his might at the strange lady and gentleman.

When Kit's mother had done speaking, the old lady struck in again, and said that she was quite sure she was a very honest and very respectable person or she never would have expressed herself in that manner, and that certainly the appearance of the children and the cleanliness of the house deserved great praise and did her the utmost credit, whereat Kit's mother dropped a curtsey and became consoled. Then the good woman entered in a long and minute account of Kit's life and history from the earliest period down to that time, not omitting to make mention of his miraculous fall out of a back-parlour window when an infant of tender years, or his uncommon sufferings in a state of measles, which were illustrated by correct imitations of the plaintive manner in which he called for toast and water, day and night, and said, 'don't cry, mother, I shall soon be better;' for proof of which statements reference was made to Mrs Green, lodger, at the cheesemonger's round the corner, and divers other ladies and gentlemen in various parts of England and Wales (and one Mr Brown who was supposed to be then a corporal in the East Indies, and who could of course be found with very little trouble), within whose personal knowledge the circumstances had occurred. This narration ended, Mr Garland put some questions to Kit respecting his qualifications and general acquirements, while Mrs Garland noticed the children, and hearing from Kit's mother certain remarkable circumstances which had attended the birth of each, related certain other remarkable circumstances which had attended the birth of her own son, Mr Abel, from which it appeared that both Kit's mother and herself had been, above and beyond all other women of what condition or age soever, peculiarly hemmed in with perils and dangers. Lastly, inquiry was made into the nature and extent of Kit's wardrobe, and a small advance being made to improve the same, he was formally hired at an annual income of Six Pounds, over and above his board and lodging, by Mr and Mrs Garland, of Abel Cottage, Finchley.

It would be difficult to say which party appeared most pleased with this arrangement, the conclusion of which was hailed with nothing but pleasant looks and cheerful smiles on both sides. It was settled that Kit should repair to his new abode on the next day but one, in the morning; and finally, the little old couple, after bestowing a bright half-crown on little Jacob and another on the baby, took their leaves; being escorted as far as the street by their new attendant, who held the obdurate pony by the bridle while they took their seats, and saw them drive away with a lightened heart.

'Well, mother,' said Kit, hurrying back into the house, 'I think my fortune's about made now.'

'I should think it was indeed, Kit,' rejoined his mother. 'Six pound a year! Only think!'

'Ah!' said Kit, trying to maintain the gravity which the consideration of such a sum demanded, but grinning with delight in spite of himself. 'There's a property!'

Kit drew a long breath when he had said this, and putting his hands deep into his pockets as if there were one year's wages at least in each, looked at his mother, as though he saw through her, and down an immense perspective of sovereigns beyond.

'Please God we'll make such a lady of you for Sundays, mother! such a scholar of Jacob, such a child of the baby, such a room of the one up stairs! Six pound a year!'

'Hem!' croaked a strange voice. 'What's that about six pound a year? What about six pound a year?' And as the voice made this inquiry, Daniel Quilp walked in with Richard Swiveller at his heels.

'Who said he was to have six pound a year?' said Quilp, looking sharply round. 'Did the old man say it, or did little Nell say it? And what's he to have it for, and where are they, eh!'

The good woman was so much alarmed by the sudden apparition of this unknown piece of ugliness, that she hastily caught the baby from its cradle and retreated into the furthest corner of the room; while little Jacob, sitting upon his stool with his hands on his knees, looked full at him in a species of fascination, roaring lustily all the time. Richard Swiveller took an easy observation of the family over Mr Quilp's head, and Quilp himself, with his hands in his pockets, smiled in an exquisite enjoyment of the commotion he occasioned.

'Don't be frightened, mistress,' said Quilp, after a pause. 'Your son knows me; I don't eat babies; I don't like 'em. It will be as well to stop that young screamer though, in case I should be tempted to do him a mischief. Holloa, sir! Will you be quiet?'

Little Jacob stemmed the course of two tears which he was squeezing out of his eyes, and instantly subsided into a silent horror.

'Mind you don't break out again, you villain,' said Quilp, looking sternly at him, 'or I'll make faces at you and throw you into fits, I will. Now you sir, why haven't you been to me as you promised?'

'What should I come for?' retorted Kit. 'I hadn't any business with you, no more than you had with me.'

'Here, mistress,' said Quilp, turning quickly away, and appealing from Kit to his mother. 'When did his old master come or send here last? Is he here now? If not, where's he gone?'

'He has not been here at all,' she replied. 'I wish we knew where they have gone, for it would make my son a good deal easier in his mind, and me too. If you're the gentleman named Mr Quilp, I should have thought you'd have known, and so I told him only this very day.'

'Humph!' muttered Quilp, evidently disappointed to believe that this was true. 'That's what you tell this gentleman too, is it?'

'If the gentleman comes to ask the same question, I can't tell him anything else, sir; and I only wish I could, for our own sakes,' was the reply.

Quilp glanced at Richard Swiveller, and observed that having met him on the threshold, he assumed that he had come in search of some intelligence of the fugitives. He supposed he was right?

'Yes,' said Dick, 'that was the object of the present expedition. I fancied it possible—but let us go ring fancy's knell. I'll begin it.'

'You seem disappointed,' observed Quilp.

'A baffler, Sir, a baffler, that's all,' returned Dick. 'I have entered upon a speculation which has proved a baffler; and a Being of brightness and beauty will be offered up a sacrifice at Cheggs's altar. That's all, sir.'

The dwarf eyed Richard with a sarcastic smile, but Richard, who had been taking a rather strong lunch with a friend, observed him not, and continued to deplore his fate with mournful and despondent looks. Quilp plainly discerned that there was some secret reason for this visit and his uncommon disappointment, and, in the hope that there might be means of mischief lurking beneath it, resolved to worm it out. He had no sooner adopted this resolution, than he conveyed as much honesty into his face as it was capable of expressing, and sympathised with Mr Swiveller exceedingly.

'I am disappointed myself,' said Quilp, 'out of mere friendly feeling for them; but you have real reasons, private reasons I have no doubt, for your disappointment, and therefore it comes heavier than mine.'

'Why, of course it does,' Dick observed, testily.

'Upon my word, I'm very sorry, very sorry. I'm rather cast down myself. As we are companions in adversity, shall we be companions in the surest way of forgetting it? If you had no particular business, now, to lead you in another direction,' urged Quilp, plucking him by the sleeve and looking slyly up into his face out of the corners of his eyes, 'there is a house by the water-side where they have some of the noblest Schiedam—reputed to be smuggled, but that's between ourselves—that can be got in all the world. The landlord knows me. There's a little summer-house overlooking the river, where we might take a glass of this delicious liquor with a whiff of the best tobacco—it's in this case, and of the rarest quality, to my certain knowledge—and be perfectly snug and happy, could we possibly contrive it; or is there any very particular engagement that peremptorily takes you another way, Mr Swiveller, eh?'

As the dwarf spoke, Dick's face relaxed into a compliant smile, and his brows slowly unbent. By the time he had finished, Dick was looking down at Quilp in the same sly manner as Quilp was looking up at him, and there remained nothing more to be done but to set out for the house in question. This they did, straightway. The moment their backs were turned, little Jacob thawed, and resumed his crying from the point where Quilp had frozen him.

The summer-house of which Mr Quilp had spoken was a rugged wooden box, rotten and bare to see, which overhung the river's mud, and threatened to slide down into it. The tavern to which it belonged was a crazy building, sapped and undermined by the rats, and only upheld by great bars of wood which were reared against its walls, and had propped it up so long that even they were decaying and yielding with their load, and of a windy night might be heard to creak and crack as if the whole fabric were about to come toppling down. The house stood—if anything so old and feeble could be said to stand—on a piece of waste ground, blighted with the unwholesome smoke of factory chimneys, and echoing the clank of iron wheels and rush of troubled water. Its internal accommodations amply fulfilled the promise of the outside. The rooms were low and damp, the clammy walls were pierced with chinks and holes, the rotten floors had sunk from their level, the very beams started from their places and warned the timid stranger from their neighbourhood.

To this inviting spot, entreating him to observe its beauties as they passed along, Mr Quilp led Richard Swiveller, and on the table of the summer-house, scored deep with many a gallows and initial letter, there soon appeared a wooden keg, full of the vaunted liquor. Drawing it off into the glasses with the skill of a practised hand, and mixing it with about a third part of water, Mr Quilp assigned to Richard Swiveller his portion, and lighting his pipe from an end of a candle in a very old and battered lantern, drew himself together upon a seat and puffed away.

'Is it good?' said Quilp, as Richard Swiveller smacked his lips, 'is it strong and fiery? Does it make you wink, and choke, and your eyes water, and your breath come short—does it?'

'Does it?' cried Dick, throwing away part of the contents of his glass, and filling it up with water, 'why, man, you don't mean to tell me that you drink such fire as this?'

'No!' rejoined Quilp, 'Not drink it! Look here. And here. And here again. Not drink it!'

As he spoke, Daniel Quilp drew off and drank three small glassfuls of the raw spirit, and then with a horrible grimace took a great many pulls at his pipe, and swallowing the smoke, discharged it in a heavy cloud from his nose. This feat accomplished he drew himself together in his former position, and laughed excessively.

'Give us a toast!' cried Quilp, rattling on the table in a dexterous manner with his fist and elbow alternately, in a kind of tune, 'a woman, a beauty. Let's have a beauty for our toast and empty our glasses to the last drop. Her name, come!'

'If you want a name,' said Dick, 'here's Sophy Wackles.'

'Sophy Wackles,' screamed the dwarf, 'Miss Sophy Wackles that is—Mrs Richard Swiveller that shall be—that shall be—ha ha ha!'

'Ah!' said Dick, 'you might have said that a few weeks ago, but it won't do now, my buck. Immolating herself upon the shrine of Cheggs—'

'Poison Cheggs, cut Cheggs's ears off,' rejoined Quilp. 'I won't hear of Cheggs. Her name is Swiveller or nothing. I'll drink her health again, and her father's, and her mother's; and to all her sisters and brothers—the glorious family of the Wackleses—all the Wackleses in one glass—down with it to the dregs!'

'Well,' said Richard Swiveller, stopping short in the act of raising the glass to his lips and looking at the dwarf in a species of stupor as he flourished his arms and legs about: 'you're a jolly fellow, but of all the jolly fellows I ever saw or heard of, you have the queerest and most extraordinary way with you, upon my life you have.'

This candid declaration tended rather to increase than restrain Mr Quilp's eccentricities, and Richard Swiveller, astonished to see him in such a roystering vein, and drinking not a little himself, for company—began imperceptibly to become more companionable and confiding, so that, being judiciously led on by Mr Quilp, he grew at last very confiding indeed. Having once got him into this mood, and knowing now the key-note to strike whenever he was at a loss, Daniel Quilp's task was comparatively an easy one, and he was soon in possession of the whole details of the scheme contrived between the easy Dick and his more designing friend.

'Stop!' said Quilp. 'That's the thing, that's the thing. It can be brought about, it shall be brought about. There's my hand upon it; I am your friend from this minute.'

'What! do you think there's still a chance?' inquired Dick, in surprise at this encouragement.

'A chance!' echoed the dwarf, 'a certainty! Sophy Wackles may become a Cheggs or anything else she likes, but not a Swiveller. Oh you lucky dog! He's richer than any Jew alive; you're a made man. I see in you now nothing but Nelly's husband, rolling in gold and silver. I'll help you. It shall be done. Mind my words, it shall be done.'

'But how?' said Dick.

'There's plenty of time,' rejoined the dwarf, 'and it shall be done. We'll sit down and talk it over again all the way through. Fill your glass while I'm gone. I shall be back directly—directly.'

With these hasty words, Daniel Quilp withdrew into a dismantled skittle-ground behind the public-house, and, throwing himself upon the ground actually screamed and rolled about in uncontrollable delight.

'Here's sport!' he cried, 'sport ready to my hand, all invented and arranged, and only to be enjoyed. It was this shallow-pated fellow who made my bones ache t'other day, was it? It was his friend and fellow-plotter, Mr Trent, that once made eyes at Mrs Quilp, and leered and looked, was it? After labouring for two or three years in their precious scheme, to find that they've got a beggar at last, and one of them tied for life. Ha ha ha! He shall marry Nell. He shall have her, and I'll be the first man, when the knot's tied hard and fast, to tell 'em what they've gained and what I've helped 'em to. Here will be a clearing of old scores, here will be a time to remind 'em what a capital friend I was, and how I helped them to the heiress. Ha ha ha!'

In the height of his ecstasy, Mr Quilp had like to have met with a disagreeable check, for rolling very near a broken dog-kennel, there leapt forth a large fierce dog, who, but that his chain was of the shortest, would have given him a disagreeable salute. As it was, the dwarf remained upon his back in perfect safety, taunting the dog with hideous faces, and triumphing over him in his inability to advance another inch, though there were not a couple of feet between them.

'Why don't you come and bite me, why don't you come and tear me to pieces, you coward?' said Quilp, hissing and worrying the animal till he was nearly mad. 'You're afraid, you bully, you're afraid, you know you are.'

The dog tore and strained at his chain with starting eyes and furious bark, but there the dwarf lay, snapping his fingers with gestures of defiance and contempt. When he had sufficiently recovered from his delight, he rose, and with his arms a-kimbo, achieved a kind of demon-dance round the kennel, just without the limits of the chain, driving the dog quite wild. Having by this means composed his spirits and put himself in a pleasant train, he returned to his unsuspicious companion, whom he found looking at the tide with exceeding gravity, and thinking of that same gold and silver which Mr Quilp had mentioned.

CHAPTER 22

The remainder of that day and the whole of the next were a busy time for the Nubbles family, to whom everything connected with Kit's outfit and departure was matter of as great moment as if he had been about to penetrate into the interior of Africa, or to take a cruise round the world. It would be difficult to suppose that there ever was a box which was opened and shut so many times within four-and-twenty hours, as that which contained his wardrobe and necessaries; and certainly there never was one which to two small eyes presented such a mine of clothing, as this mighty chest with its three shirts and proportionate allowance of stockings and pocket-handkerchiefs, disclosed to the astonished vision of little Jacob. At last it was conveyed to the carrier's, at whose house at Finchley Kit was to find it next day; and the box being gone, there remained but two questions for consideration: firstly, whether the carrier would lose, or dishonestly feign to lose, the box upon the road; secondly, whether Kit's mother perfectly understood how to take care of herself in the absence of her son.

'I don't think there's hardly a chance of his really losing it, but carriers are under great temptation to pretend they lose things, no doubt,' said Mrs Nubbles apprehensively, in reference to the first point.

'No doubt about it,' returned Kit, with a serious look; 'upon my word, mother, I don't think it was right to trust it to itself. Somebody ought to have gone with it, I'm afraid.'

'We can't help it now,' said his mother; 'but it was foolish and wrong. People oughtn't to be tempted.'

Kit inwardly resolved that he would never tempt a carrier any more, save with an empty box; and having formed this Christian determination, he turned his thoughts to the second question.

'You know you must keep up your spirits, mother, and not be lonesome because I'm not at home. I shall very often be able to look in when I come into town I dare say, and I shall send you a letter sometimes, and when the quarter comes round, I can get a holiday of course; and then see if we don't take little Jacob to the play, and let him know what oysters means.'

'I hope plays mayn't be sinful, Kit, but I'm a'most afraid,' said Mrs Nubbles.

'I know who has been putting that in your head,' rejoined her son disconsolately; 'that's Little Bethel again. Now I say, mother, pray don't take to going there regularly, for if I was to see your good-humoured face that has always made home cheerful, turned into a grievous one, and the baby trained to look grievous too, and to call itself a young sinner (bless its heart) and a child of the devil (which is calling its dead father names); if I was to see this, and see little Jacob looking grievous likewise, I should so take it to heart that I'm sure I should go and list for a soldier, and run my head on purpose against the first cannon-ball I saw coming my way.'

'Oh, Kit, don't talk like that.'

'I would, indeed, mother, and unless you want to make me feel very wretched and uncomfortable, you'll keep that bow on your bonnet, which you'd more than half a mind to pull off last week. Can you suppose there's any harm in looking as cheerful and being as cheerful as our poor circumstances will permit? Do I see anything in the way I'm made, which calls upon me to be a snivelling, solemn, whispering chap, sneaking about as if I couldn't help it, and expressing myself in a most unpleasant snuffle? on the contrary, don't I see every reason why I shouldn't? just hear this! Ha ha ha! An't that as nat'ral as walking, and as good for the health? Ha ha ha! An't that as nat'ral as a sheep's bleating, or a pig's grunting, or a horse's neighing, or a bird's singing? Ha ha ha! Isn't it, mother?'

There was something contagious in Kit's laugh, for his mother, who had looked grave before, first subsided into a smile, and then fell to joining in it heartily, which occasioned Kit to say that he knew it was natural, and to laugh the more. Kit and his mother, laughing together in a pretty loud key, woke the baby, who, finding that there was something very jovial and agreeable in progress, was no sooner in its mother's arms than it began to kick and laugh, most vigorously. This new illustration of his argument so tickled Kit, that he fell backward in his chair in a state of exhaustion, pointing at the baby and shaking his sides till he rocked again. After recovering twice or thrice, and as often relapsing, he wiped his eyes and said grace; and a very cheerful meal their scanty supper was.

With more kisses, and hugs, and tears, than many young gentlemen who start upon their travels, and leave well-stocked homes behind them, would deem within the bounds of probability (if matter so low could be herein set down), Kit left the house at an early hour next morning, and set out to walk to Finchley; feeling a sufficient pride in his appearance to have warranted his excommunication from Little Bethel from that time forth, if he had ever been one of that mournful congregation.

Lest anybody should feel a curiosity to know how Kit was clad, it may be briefly remarked that he wore no livery, but was dressed in a coat of pepper-and-salt with waistcoat of canary colour, and nether garments of iron-grey; besides these glories, he shone in the lustre of a new pair of boots and an extremely stiff and shiny hat, which on being struck anywhere with the knuckles, sounded like a drum. And in this attire, rather wondering that he attracted so little attention, and attributing the circumstance to the insensibility of those who got up early, he made his way towards Abel Cottage.

Without encountering any more remarkable adventure on the road, than meeting a lad in a brimless hat, the exact counterpart of his old one, on whom he bestowed half the sixpence he possessed, Kit arrived in course of time at the carrier's house, where, to the lasting honour of human nature, he found the box in safety. Receiving from the wife of this immaculate man, a direction to Mr Garland's, he took the box upon his shoulder and repaired thither directly.

To be sure, it was a beautiful little cottage with a thatched roof and little spires at the gable-ends, and pieces of stained glass in some of the windows, almost as large as pocket-books. On one side of the house was a little stable, just the size for the pony, with a little room over it, just the size for Kit. White curtains were fluttering, and birds in cages that looked as bright as if they were made of gold, were singing at the windows; plants were arranged on either side of the path, and clustered about the door; and the garden was bright with flowers in full bloom, which shed a sweet odour all round, and had a charming and elegant appearance. Everything within the house and without, seemed to be the perfection of neatness and order. In the garden there was not a weed to be seen, and to judge from some dapper gardening-tools, a basket, and a pair of gloves which were lying in one of the walks, old Mr Garland had been at work in it that very morning.

Kit looked about him, and admired, and looked again, and this a great many times before he could make up his mind to turn his head another way and ring the bell. There was abundance of time to look about him again though, when he had rung it, for nobody came, so after ringing it twice or thrice he sat down upon his box, and waited.

He rang the bell a great many times, and yet nobody came. But at last, as he was sitting upon the box thinking about giants' castles, and princesses tied up to pegs by the hair of their heads, and dragons bursting out from behind gates, and other incidents of the like nature, common in story-books to youths of low degree on their first visit to strange houses, the door was gently opened, and a little servant-girl, very tidy, modest, and demure, but very pretty too, appeared. 'I suppose you're Christopher, sir,' said the servant-girl.

Kit got off the box, and said yes, he was.

'I'm afraid you've rung a good many times perhaps,' she rejoined, 'but we couldn't hear you, because we've been catching the pony.'

Kit rather wondered what this meant, but as he couldn't stop there, asking questions, he shouldered the box again and followed the girl into the hall, where through a back-door he descried Mr Garland leading Whisker in triumph up the garden, after that self-willed pony had (as he afterwards learned) dodged the family round a small paddock in the rear, for one hour and three quarters.

The old gentleman received him very kindly and so did the old lady, whose previous good opinion of him was greatly enhanced by his wiping his boots on the mat until the soles of his feet burnt again. He was then taken into the parlour to be inspected in his new clothes; and when he had been surveyed several times, and had afforded by his appearance unlimited satisfaction, he was taken into the stable (where the pony received him with uncommon complaisance); and thence into the little chamber he had already observed, which was very clean and comfortable: and thence into the garden, in which the old gentleman told him he would be taught to employ himself, and where he told him, besides, what great things he meant to do to make him comfortable, and happy, if he found he deserved it. All these kindnesses, Kit acknowledged with various expressions of gratitude, and so many touches of the new hat, that the brim suffered considerably. When the old gentleman had said all he had to say in the way of promise and advice, and Kit had said all he had to say in the way of assurance and thankfulness, he was handed over again to the old lady, who, summoning the little servant-girl (whose name was Barbara) instructed her to take him down stairs and give him something to eat and drink, after his walk.

Down stairs, therefore, Kit went; and at the bottom of the stairs there was such a kitchen as was never before seen or heard of out of a toy-shop window, with everything in it as bright and glowing, and as precisely ordered too, as Barbara herself. And in this kitchen, Kit sat himself down at a table as white as a tablecloth, to eat cold meat, and drink small ale, and use his knife and fork the more awkwardly, because there was an unknown Barbara looking on and observing him.

It did not appear, however, that there was anything remarkably tremendous about this strange Barbara, who having lived a very quiet life, blushed very much and was quite as embarrassed and uncertain what she ought to say or do, as Kit could possibly be. When he had sat for some little time, attentive to the ticking of the sober clock, he ventured to glance curiously at the dresser, and there, among the plates and dishes, were Barbara's little work-box with a sliding lid to shut in the balls of cotton, and Barbara's prayer-book, and Barbara's hymn-book, and Barbara's Bible. Barbara's little looking-glass hung in a good light near the window, and Barbara's bonnet was on a nail behind the door. From all these mute signs and tokens of her presence, he naturally glanced at Barbara herself, who sat as mute as they, shelling peas into a dish; and just when Kit was looking at her eyelashes and wondering—quite in the simplicity of his heart—what colour her eyes might be, it perversely happened that Barbara raised her

122

head a little to look at him, when both pair of eyes were hastily withdrawn, and Kit leant over his plate, and Barbara over her pea-shells, each in extreme confusion at having been detected by the other.

CHAPTER 23

Mr Richard Swiveller wending homeward from the Wilderness (for such was the appropriate name of Quilp's choice retreat), after a sinuous and corkscrew fashion, with many checks and stumbles; after stopping suddenly and staring about him, then as suddenly running forward for a few paces, and as suddenly halting again and shaking his head; doing everything with a jerk and nothing by premeditation;—Mr Richard Swiveller wending his way homeward after this fashion, which is considered by evil-minded men to be symbolical of intoxication, and is not held by such persons to denote that state of deep wisdom and reflection in which the actor knows himself to be, began to think that possibly he had misplaced his confidence and that the dwarf might not be precisely the sort of person to whom to entrust a secret of such delicacy and importance. And being led and tempted on by this remorseful thought into a condition which the evil-minded class before referred to would term the maudlin state or stage of drunkenness, it occurred to Mr Swiveller to cast his hat upon the ground, and moan, crying aloud that he was an unhappy orphan, and that if he had not been an unhappy orphan things had never come to this.

'Left an infant by my parents, at an early age,' said Mr Swiveller, bewailing his hard lot, 'cast upon the world in my tenderest period, and thrown upon the mercies of a deluding dwarf, who can wonder at my weakness! Here's a miserable orphan for you. Here,' said Mr Swiveller raising his voice to a high pitch, and looking sleepily round, 'is a miserable orphan!'

'Then,' said somebody hard by, 'let me be a father to you.'

Mr Swiveller swayed himself to and fro to preserve his balance, and, looking into a kind of haze which seemed to surround him, at last perceived two eyes dimly twinkling through the mist, which he observed after a short time were in the neighbourhood of a nose and mouth. Casting his eyes down towards that quarter in which, with reference to a man's face, his legs are usually to be found, he observed that the face had a body attached; and when he looked more intently he was satisfied that the person was Mr Quilp, who indeed had been in his company all the time, but whom he had some vague idea of having left a mile or two behind.

'You have deceived an orphan, Sir,' said Mr Swiveller solemnly.'

'I! I'm a second father to you,' replied Quilp.

'You my father, Sir!' retorted Dick. 'Being all right myself, Sir, I request to be left alone—instantly, Sir.'

'What a funny fellow you are!' cried Quilp.

'Go, Sir,' returned Dick, leaning against a post and waving his hand. 'Go, deceiver, go, some day, Sir, p'r'aps you'll waken, from pleasure's dream to know, the grief of orphans forsaken. Will you go, Sir?'

The dwarf taking no heed of this adjuration, Mr Swiveller advanced with the view of inflicting upon him condign chastisement. But forgetting his purpose or changing his mind before he came close to him, he seized his hand and vowed eternal friendship, declaring with an agreeable frankness that from that time forth they were brothers in everything but personal appearance. Then he told his secret over again, with the addition of being pathetic on the subject of Miss Wackles, who, he gave Mr Quilp to understand, was the occasion of any slight incoherency he might observe in his speech at that moment, which was attributable solely to the strength of his affection and not to rosy wine or other fermented liquor. And then they went on arm-in-arm, very lovingly together.

'I'm as sharp,' said Quilp to him, at parting, 'as sharp as a ferret, and as cunning as a weazel. You bring Trent to me; assure him that I'm his friend though I fear he a little distrusts me (I don't know why, I have not deserved it); and you've both of you made your fortunes—in perspective.'

'That's the worst of it,' returned Dick. 'These fortunes in perspective look such a long way off.'

'But they look smaller than they really are, on that account,' said Quilp, pressing his arm. 'You'll have no conception of the value of your prize until you draw close to it. Mark that.'

'D'ye think not?' said Dick.

'Aye, I do; and I am certain of what I say, that's better,' returned the dwarf. 'You bring Trent to me. Tell him I am his friend and yours—why shouldn't I be?'

'There's no reason why you shouldn't, certainly,' replied Dick, 'and perhaps there are a great many why you should—at least there would be nothing strange in your wanting to be my friend, if you were a choice spirit, but then you know you're not a choice spirit.'

'I not a choice spirit?' cried Quilp.

'Devil a bit, sir,' returned Dick. 'A man of your appearance couldn't be. If you're any spirit at all, sir, you're an evil spirit. Choice spirits,' added Dick, smiting himself on the breast, 'are quite a different looking sort of people, you may take your oath of that, sir.'

Quilp glanced at his free-spoken friend with a mingled expression of cunning and dislike, and wringing his hand almost at the same moment, declared that he was an uncommon character and had his warmest esteem. With that they parted; Mr Swiveller to make the best of his way home and sleep himself sober; and Quilp to cogitate upon the discovery he had made, and exult in the prospect of the rich field of enjoyment and reprisal it opened to him.

It was not without great reluctance and misgiving that Mr Swiveller, next morning, his head racked by the fumes of the renowned Schiedam, repaired to the lodging of his friend Trent (which was in the roof of an old house in an old ghostly inn), and recounted by very slow degrees what had yesterday taken place between him and Quilp. Nor was it without great surprise and much speculation on Quilp's probable motives, nor without many bitter comments on Dick Swiveller's folly, that his friend received the tale.

'I don't defend myself, Fred,' said the penitent Richard; 'but the fellow has such a queer way with him and is such an artful dog, that first of all he set me upon thinking whether there was any harm in telling him, and while I was thinking, screwed it out of me. If you had seen him drink and smoke, as I did, you couldn't have kept anything from him. He's a Salamander you know, that's what he is.'

Without inquiring whether Salamanders were of necessity good confidential agents, or whether a fire-proof man was as a matter of course trustworthy, Frederick Trent threw himself into a chair, and, burying his head in his hands, endeavoured to fathom the motives which had led Quilp to insinuate himself into Richard Swiveller's confidence;—for that the disclosure was of his seeking, and had not been spontaneously revealed by Dick, was sufficiently plain from Quilp's seeking his company and enticing him away.

The dwarf had twice encountered him when he was endeavouring to obtain intelligence of the fugitives. This, perhaps, as he had not shown any previous anxiety about them, was enough to awaken suspicion in the breast of a creature so jealous and distrustful by nature, setting aside any additional impulse to curiosity that he might have derived from Dick's incautious manner. But knowing the scheme they had planned, why should he offer to assist it? This was a question more difficult of solution; but as knaves generally overreach themselves by imputing their own designs to others, the idea immediately presented itself that some circumstances of irritation between Quilp and the old man, arising out of their secret transactions and not unconnected perhaps with his sudden disappearance, now rendered the former desirous of revenging himself upon him by seeking to entrap the sole object of his love and anxiety into a connexion of which he knew he had a dread and hatred. As Frederick Trent himself, utterly regardless of his sister, had this object at heart, only second to the hope of gain, it seemed to him the more likely to be Quilp's main principle of action. Once investing the dwarf with a design of his own in abetting them, which the attainment of their purpose would serve, it was easy to believe him sincere and hearty in the cause; and as there could be no doubt of his proving a powerful and useful auxiliary, Trent determined to accept his invitation and go to his house that night, and if what he said and did confirmed him in the impression he had formed, to let him share the labour of their plan, but not the profit.

Having revolved these things in his mind and arrived at this conclusion, he communicated to Mr Swiveller as much of his meditations as he thought proper (Dick would have been perfectly satisfied with less), and giving him the day to recover himself from his late salamandering, accompanied him at evening to Mr Quilp's house.

Mighty glad Mr Quilp was to see them, or mightily glad he seemed to be; and fearfully polite Mr Quilp was to Mrs Quilp and Mrs Jiniwin; and very sharp was the look he cast on his wife to observe how she was affected by the recognition of young Trent. Mrs Quilp was as innocent as her own mother of any emotion, painful or pleasant, which the sight of him awakened, but as her husband's glance made her timid and confused, and uncertain what to do or what was required of her, Mr Quilp did not fail to assign her embarrassment to the cause he had in his mind, and while he chuckled at his penetration was secretly exasperated by his jealousy.

Nothing of this appeared, however. On the contrary, Mr Quilp was all blandness and suavity, and presided over the case-bottle of rum with extraordinary open-heartedness.

'Why, let me see,' said Quilp. 'It must be a matter of nearly two years since we were first acquainted.'

'Nearer three, I think,' said Trent.

'Nearer three!' cried Quilp. 'How fast time flies. Does it seem as long as that to you, Mrs Quilp?'

'Yes, I think it seems full three years, Quilp,' was the unfortunate reply.

'Oh indeed, ma'am,' thought Quilp, 'you have been pining, have you? Very good, ma'am.'

'It seems to me but yesterday that you went out to Demerara in the Mary Anne,' said Quilp; 'but yesterday, I declare. Well, I like a little wildness. I was wild myself once.'

Mr Quilp accompanied this admission with such an awful wink, indicative of old rovings and backslidings, that Mrs Jiniwin was indignant, and could not forbear from remarking under her breath that he might at least put off his confessions until his wife was absent; for which act of boldness and insubordination Mr Quilp first stared her out of countenance and then drank her health ceremoniously.

'I thought you'd come back directly, Fred. I always thought that,' said Quilp setting down his glass. 'And when the Mary Anne returned with you on board, instead of a letter to say what a contrite heart you had, and how happy you were in the situation that had been provided for you, I was amused—exceedingly amused. Ha ha ha!'

The young man smiled, but not as though the theme was the most agreeable one that could have been selected for his entertainment; and for that reason Quilp pursued it.

'I always will say,' he resumed, 'that when a rich relation having two young people—sisters or brothers, or brother and sister—dependent on him, attaches himself exclusively to one, and casts off the other, he does wrong.'

The young man made a movement of impatience, but Quilp went on as calmly as if he were discussing some abstract question in which nobody present had the slightest personal interest.

'It's very true,' said Quilp, 'that your grandfather urged repeated forgiveness, ingratitude, riot, and extravagance, and all that; but as I told him "these are common faults." "But he's a scoundrel," said he. "Granting that," said I (for the sake of argument of course), "a great many young noblemen and gentlemen are scoundrels too!" But he wouldn't be convinced.'

'I wonder at that, Mr Quilp,' said the young man sarcastically.

'Well, so did I at the time,' returned Quilp, 'but he was always obstinate. He was in a manner a friend of mine, but he was always obstinate and wrong-headed. Little Nell is a nice girl, a charming girl, but you're her brother, Frederick. You're her brother after all; as you told him the last time you met, he can't alter that.'

'He would if he could, confound him for that and all other kindnesses,' said the young man impatiently. 'But nothing can come of this subject now, and let us have done with it in the Devil's name.'

'Agreed,' returned Quilp, 'agreed on my part readily. Why have I alluded to it? Just to show you, Frederick, that I have always stood your friend. You little knew who was your friend, and who your foe; now did you? You thought I was against you, and so there has been a coolness between us; but it was all on your side, entirely on your side. Let's shake hands again, Fred.'

With his head sunk down between his shoulders, and a hideous grin over-spreading his face, the dwarf stood up and stretched his short arm across the table. After a moment's hesitation, the young man stretched out his to meet it; Quilp clutched his fingers in a grip that for the moment stopped the current of the blood within them, and pressing his other hand upon his lip and frowning towards the unsuspicious Richard, released them and sat down.

This action was not lost upon Trent, who, knowing that Richard Swiveller was a mere tool in his hands and knew no more of his designs than he thought proper to communicate, saw that the dwarf perfectly understood their relative position, and fully entered into the character of his friend. It is something to be appreciated, even in knavery. This silent homage to his superior abilities, no less than a sense of the power with which the dwarf's quick perception had already invested him, inclined the young man towards that ugly worthy, and determined him to profit by his aid.

It being now Mr Quilp's cue to change the subject with all convenient expedition, lest Richard Swiveller in his heedlessness should reveal anything which it was inexpedient for the women to know, he proposed a game at four-handed cribbage, and partners being cut for, Mrs Quilp fell to Frederick Trent, and Dick himself to Quilp. Mrs Jiniwin being very fond of cards was carefully excluded by her son-in-law from any participation in the game, and had assigned to her the duty of occasionally replenishing the glasses from the case-bottle; Mr Quilp from that moment keeping one eye constantly upon her, lest she should by any means procure a taste of the same, and thereby tantalising the wretched old lady (who was as much attached to the case-bottle as the cards) in a double degree and most ingenious manner.

But it was not to Mrs Jiniwin alone that Mr Quilp's attention was restricted, as several other matters required his constant vigilance. Among his various eccentric habits he had a humorous one of always cheating at cards, which rendered necessary on his part, not only a close observance of the game, and a sleight-of-hand in counting and scoring, but also involved the constant correction, by looks, and frowns, and kicks under the table, of Richard Swiveller, who being bewildered by the rapidity with which his cards were told, and the rate at which the pegs travelled down the board, could not be prevented from sometimes expressing his surprise and incredulity. Mrs Quilp too was the partner of young Trent, and for every look that passed between them, and every word they spoke, and every card they played, the dwarf had eyes and ears; not occupied alone with what was passing above the table, but with signals that might be exchanging beneath it, which he laid all kinds of traps to detect; besides often treading on his wife's toes to see whether she cried out or remained silent under the infliction, in which latter case it would have been quite clear that Trent had been treading on her toes before. Yet, in the most of all these distractions, the one eye was upon the old lady always, and if she so much as stealthily advanced a tea-spoon towards a neighbouring glass (which she often did), for the purpose of abstracting but one sup of its sweet contents, Quilp's hand would overset it in the very moment of her triumph, and Quilp's mocking voice implore her to regard her precious health. And in any one of these his many cares, from first to last, Quilp never flagged nor faltered.

At length, when they had played a great many rubbers and drawn pretty freely upon the case-bottle, Mr Quilp warned his lady to retire to rest, and that submissive wife complying, and being followed by her indignant mother, Mr Swiveller fell asleep. The dwarf beckoning his remaining companion to the other end of the room, held a short conference with him in whispers.

'It's as well not to say more than one can help before our worthy friend,' said Quilp, making a grimace towards the slumbering Dick. 'Is it a bargain between us, Fred? Shall he marry little rosy Nell by-and-by?'

'You have some end of your own to answer, of course,' returned the other.

'Of course I have, dear Fred,' said Quilp, grinning to think how little he suspected what the real end was. 'It's retaliation perhaps; perhaps whim. I have influence, Fred, to help or oppose. Which way shall I use it? There are a pair of scales, and it goes into one.'

'Throw it into mine then,' said Trent.

'It's done, Fred,' rejoined Quilp, stretching out his clenched hand and opening it as if he had let some weight fall out. 'It's in the scale from this time, and turns it, Fred. Mind that.'

'Where have they gone?' asked Trent.

Quilp shook his head, and said that point remained to be discovered, which it might be, easily. When it was, they would begin their preliminary advances. He would visit the old man, or even Richard Swiveller might visit him, and by affecting a deep concern in his behalf, and imploring him to settle in some worthy home, lead to the child's remembering him with gratitude and favour. Once impressed to this extent, it would be easy, he said, to win her in a year or two, for she supposed the old man to be poor, as it was a part of his jealous policy (in common with many other misers) to feign to be so, to those about him.

'He has feigned it often enough to me, of late,' said Trent.

'Oh! and to me too!' replied the dwarf. 'Which is more extraordinary, as I know how rich he really is.'

'I suppose you should,' said Trent.

'I think I should indeed,' rejoined the dwarf; and in that, at least, he spoke the truth.

After a few more whispered words, they returned to the table, and the young man rousing Richard Swiveller informed him that he was waiting to depart. This was welcome news to Dick, who started up directly. After a few words of confidence in the result of their project had been exchanged, they bade the grinning Quilp good night.

Quilp crept to the window as they passed in the street below, and listened. Trent was pronouncing an encomium upon his wife, and they were both wondering by what enchantment she had been brought to marry such a misshapen wretch as he. The dwarf after watching their retreating shadows with a wider grin than his face had yet displayed, stole softly in the dark to bed.

In this hatching of their scheme, neither Trent nor Quilp had had one thought about the happiness or misery of poor innocent Nell. It would have been strange if the careless profligate, who was the butt of both, had been harassed by any such consideration; for his high opinion of his own merits and deserts rendered the project rather a laudable one than otherwise; and if he had been visited by so unwonted a guest as reflection, he would—being a brute only in the gratification of his appetites—have soothed his conscience with the plea that he did not mean to beat or kill his wife, and would therefore, after all said and done, be a very tolerable, average husband.

CHAPTER 24

It was not until they were quite exhausted and could no longer maintain the pace at which they had fled from the race-ground, that the old man and the child ventured to stop, and sit down to rest upon the borders of a little wood. Here, though the course was hidden from their view, they could yet faintly distinguish the noise of distant shouts, the hum of voices, and the beating of drums. Climbing the eminence which lay between them and the spot they had left, the child could even discern the fluttering flags and white tops of booths; but no person was approaching towards them, and their resting-place was solitary and still.

Some time elapsed before she could reassure her trembling companion, or restore him to a state of moderate tranquillity. His disordered imagination represented to him a crowd of persons stealing towards them beneath the cover of the bushes, lurking in every ditch, and peeping from the boughs of every rustling tree. He was haunted by apprehensions of being led captive to some gloomy place where he would be chained and scourged, and worse than all, where Nell could never come to see him, save through iron bars and gratings in the wall. His terrors affected the child. Separation from her grandfather was the greatest evil she could dread; and feeling for the time as though, go where they would, they were to be hunted down, and could never be safe but in hiding, her heart failed her, and her courage drooped.

In one so young, and so unused to the scenes in which she had lately moved, this sinking of the spirit was not surprising. But, Nature often enshrines gallant and noble hearts in weak bosoms—oftenest, God bless her, in female breasts—and when the child, casting her tearful eyes upon the old man, remembered how weak he was, and how destitute and helpless he would be if she failed him, her heart swelled within her, and animated her with new strength and fortitude.

'We are quite safe now, and have nothing to fear indeed, dear grandfather,' she said.

'Nothing to fear!' returned the old man. 'Nothing to fear if they took me from thee! Nothing to fear if they parted us! Nobody is true to me. No, not one. Not even Nell!'

'Oh! do not say that,' replied the child, 'for if ever anybody was true at heart, and earnest, I am. I am sure you know I am.'

'Then how,' said the old man, looking fearfully round, 'how can you bear to think that we are safe, when they are searching for me everywhere, and may come here, and steal upon us, even while we're talking?'

'Because I'm sure we have not been followed,' said the child. 'Judge for yourself, dear grandfather: look round, and see how quiet and still it is. We are alone together, and may ramble where we like. Not safe! Could I feel easy—did I feel at ease—when any danger threatened you?'

'True, too,' he answered, pressing her hand, but still looking anxiously about. 'What noise was that?'

'A bird,' said the child, 'flying into the wood, and leading the way for us to follow.' You remember that we said we would walk in woods and fields, and by the side of rivers, and how happy we would be—you remember that? But here, while the sun shines above our heads, and everything is bright and happy, we are sitting sadly down, and losing time. See what a pleasant path; and there's the bird—the same bird—now he flies to another tree, and stays to sing. Come!'

When they rose up from the ground, and took the shady track which led them through the wood, she bounded on before, printing her tiny footsteps in the moss, which rose elastic from so light a pressure and gave it back as mirrors throw off breath; and thus she lured the old man on, with many a backward look and merry beck, now pointing stealthily to some lone bird as it perched and twittered on a branch that strayed across their path, now stopping to listen to the songs that broke the happy silence, or watch the sun as it trembled through the leaves, and stealing in among the ivied trunks of stout old trees, opened long paths of light. As they passed onward, parting the boughs that clustered in their way, the serenity which the child had first assumed, stole into her breast in earnest; the old man cast no longer fearful looks behind, but felt at ease and cheerful, for the further they passed into the deep green shade, the more they felt that the tranquil mind of God was there, and shed its peace on them.

At length the path becoming clearer and less intricate, brought them to the end of the wood, and into a public road. Taking their way along it for a short distance, they came to a lane, so shaded by the trees on either hand that they met together over-head, and arched the narrow way. A broken finger-post announced that this led to a village three miles off; and thither they resolved to bend their steps.

The miles appeared so long that they sometimes thought they must have missed their road. But at last, to their great joy, it led downwards in a steep descent, with overhanging banks over which the footpaths led; and the clustered houses of the village peeped from the woody hollow below.

It was a very small place. The men and boys were playing at cricket on the green; and as the other folks were looking on, they wandered up and down, uncertain where to seek a humble lodging. There was but one old man in the little garden before his cottage, and him they were timid of approaching, for he was the schoolmaster, and had 'School' written up over his window in black letters on a white board. He was a pale, simple-looking man, of a spare and meagre habit, and sat among his flowers and beehives, smoking his pipe, in the little porch before his door.

'Speak to him, dear,' the old man whispered.

'I am almost afraid to disturb him,' said the child timidly. 'He does not seem to see us. Perhaps if we wait a little, he may look this way.'

They waited, but the schoolmaster cast no look towards them, and still sat, thoughtful and silent, in the little porch. He had a kind face. In his plain old suit of black, he looked pale and meagre. They fancied, too, a lonely air about him and his house, but perhaps that was because the other people formed a merry company upon the green, and he seemed the only solitary man in all the place.

They were very tired, and the child would have been bold enough to address even a schoolmaster, but for something in his manner which seemed to denote that he was uneasy or distressed. As they stood hesitating at a little distance, they saw that he sat for a few minutes at a time like one in a brown study, then laid aside his pipe and took a few turns in his garden, then approached the gate and looked towards the green, then took up his pipe again with a sigh, and sat down thoughtfully as before.

As nobody else appeared and it would soon be dark, Nell at length took courage, and when he had resumed his pipe and seat, ventured to draw near, leading her grandfather by the hand. The slight noise they made in raising the latch of the wicket-gate, caught his attention. He looked at them kindly but seemed disappointed too, and slightly shook his head.

Nell dropped a curtsey, and told him they were poor travellers who sought a shelter for the night which they would gladly pay for, so far as their means allowed. The schoolmaster looked earnestly at her as she spoke, laid aside his pipe, and rose up directly.

'If you could direct us anywhere, sir,' said the child, 'we should take it very kindly.'

'You have been walking a long way,' said the schoolmaster.

'A long way, Sir,' the child replied.

'You're a young traveller, my child,' he said, laying his hand gently on her head. 'Your grandchild, friend?'

'Aye, Sir,' cried the old man, 'and the stay and comfort of my life.'

'Come in,' said the schoolmaster.

Without further preface he conducted them into his little school-room, which was parlour and kitchen likewise, and told them that they were welcome to remain under his roof till morning. Before they had done thanking him, he spread a coarse white cloth upon the table, with knives and platters; and bringing out some bread and cold meat and a jug of beer, besought them to eat and drink.

The child looked round the room as she took her seat. There were a couple of forms, notched and cut and inked all over; a small deal desk perched on four legs, at which no doubt the master sat; a few dog's-eared books upon a high shelf; and beside them a motley collection of peg-tops, balls, kites, fishing-lines, marbles, half-eaten apples, and other confiscated property of idle urchins. Displayed on hooks upon the wall in all their terrors, were the cane and ruler; and near them, on a small shelf of its own, the dunce's cap, made of old newspapers and decorated with glaring wafers of the largest size. But, the great ornaments of the walls were certain moral sentences fairly copied in good round text, and well-worked sums in simple addition and multiplication, evidently achieved by the same hand, which were plentifully pasted all round the room: for the double purpose, as it seemed, of bearing testimony to the excellence of the school, and kindling a worthy emulation in the bosoms of the scholars.

'Yes,' said the old schoolmaster, observing that her attention was caught by these latter specimens. 'That's beautiful writing, my dear.'

'Very, Sir,' replied the child modestly, 'is it yours?'

'Mine!' he returned, taking out his spectacles and putting them on, to have a better view of the triumphs so dear to his heart. 'I couldn't write like that, now-a-days. No. They're all done by one hand; a little hand it is, not so old as yours, but a very clever one.'

As the schoolmaster said this, he saw that a small blot of ink had been thrown on one of the copies, so he took a penknife from his pocket, and going up to the wall, carefully scraped it out. When he had finished, he walked slowly backward from the writing, admiring it as one might contemplate a beautiful picture, but with something of sadness in his voice and manner which quite touched the child, though she was unacquainted with its cause.

'A little hand indeed,' said the poor schoolmaster. 'Far beyond all his companions, in his learning and his sports too, how did he ever come to be so fond of me! That I should love him is no wonder, but that he should love me—' and there the schoolmaster stopped, and took off his spectacles to wipe them, as though they had grown dim.

'I hope there is nothing the matter, sir,' said Nell anxiously.

'Not much, my dear,' returned the schoolmaster. 'I hoped to have seen him on the green to-night. He was always foremost among them. But he'll be there to-morrow.'

'Has he been ill?' asked the child, with a child's quick sympathy.

'Not very. They said he was wandering in his head yesterday, dear boy, and so they said the day before. But that's a part of that kind of disorder; it's not a bad sign—not at all a bad sign.'

The child was silent. He walked to the door, and looked wistfully out. The shadows of night were gathering, and all was still.

'If he could lean upon anybody's arm, he would come to me, I know,' he said, returning into the room. 'He always came into the garden to say good night. But perhaps his illness has only just taken a favourable turn, and it's too late for him to come out, for it's very damp and there's a heavy dew. It's much better he shouldn't come to-night.'

The schoolmaster lighted a candle, fastened the window-shutter, and closed the door. But after he had done this, and sat silent a little time, he took down his hat, and said he would go and satisfy himself, if Nell would sit up till he returned. The child readily complied, and he went out.

She sat there half-an-hour or more, feeling the place very strange and lonely, for she had prevailed upon the old man to go to bed, and there was nothing to be heard but the ticking of an old clock, and the whistling of the wind among the trees. When he returned, he took his seat in the chimney corner, but remained silent for a long time. At length he turned to her, and speaking very gently, hoped she would say a prayer that night for a sick child.

'My favourite scholar!' said the poor schoolmaster, smoking a pipe he had forgotten to light, and looking mournfully round upon the walls. 'It is a little hand to have done all that, and waste away with sickness. It is a very, very little hand!'

CHAPTER 25

After a sound night's rest in a chamber in the thatched roof, in which it seemed the sexton had for some years been a lodger, but which he had lately deserted for a wife and a cottage of his own, the child rose early in the morning and descended to the room where she had supped last night. As the schoolmaster had already left his bed and gone out, she bestirred herself to make it neat and comfortable, and had just finished its arrangement when the kind host returned.

He thanked her many times, and said that the old dame who usually did such offices for him had gone to nurse the little scholar whom he had told her of. The child asked how he was, and hoped he was better.

'No,' rejoined the schoolmaster shaking his head sorrowfully, 'no better. They even say he is worse.'

'I am very sorry for that, Sir,' said the child.

The poor schoolmaster appeared to be gratified by her earnest manner, but yet rendered more uneasy by it, for he added hastily that anxious people often magnified an evil and thought it greater than it was; 'for my part,' he said, in his quiet, patient way, 'I hope it's not so. I don't think he can be worse.'

The child asked his leave to prepare breakfast, and her grandfather coming down stairs, they all three partook of it together. While the meal was in progress, their host remarked that the old man seemed much fatigued, and evidently stood in need of rest.

'If the journey you have before you is a long one,' he said, 'and don't press you for one day, you're very welcome to pass another night here. I should really be glad if you would, friend.'

He saw that the old man looked at Nell, uncertain whether to accept or decline his offer; and added,

'I shall be glad to have your young companion with me for one day. If you can do a charity to a lone man, and rest yourself at the same time, do so. If you must proceed upon your journey, I wish you well through it, and will walk a little way with you before school begins.'

'What are we to do, Nell?' said the old man irresolutely, 'say what we're to do, dear.'

It required no great persuasion to induce the child to answer that they had better accept the invitation and remain. She was happy to show her gratitude to the kind schoolmaster by busying herself in the performance of such household duties as his little cottage stood in need of. When these were done, she took some needle-work from her basket, and sat herself down upon a stool beside the lattice, where the honeysuckle and woodbine entwined their tender stems, and stealing into the room filled it with their delicious breath. Her grandfather was basking in the sun outside, breathing the perfume of the flowers, and idly watching the clouds as they floated on before the light summer wind.

As the schoolmaster, after arranging the two forms in due order, took his seat behind his desk and made other preparations for school, the child was apprehensive that she might be in the way, and offered to withdraw to her little bedroom. But this he would not allow, and as he seemed pleased to have her there, she remained, busying herself with her work.

'Have you many scholars, sir?' she asked.

The poor schoolmaster shook his head, and said that they barely filled the two forms.

'Are the others clever, sir?' asked the child, glancing at the trophies on the wall.

'Good boys,' returned the schoolmaster, 'good boys enough, my dear, but they'll never do like that.'

A small white-headed boy with a sunburnt face appeared at the door while he was speaking, and stopping there to make a rustic bow, came in and took his seat upon one of the forms. The white-headed boy then put an open book, astonishingly dog's-eared upon his knees, and thrusting his hands into his pockets began counting the marbles with which they were filled; displaying in the expression of his face a remarkable capacity of totally abstracting his mind from the spelling on which his eyes were fixed. Soon afterwards another white-headed little boy came straggling in, and after him a red-headed lad, and after him two more with white heads, and then one with a flaxen poll, and so on until the forms were occupied by a dozen boys or thereabouts, with heads of every colour but grey, and ranging in their ages from four years old to fourteen years or more; for the legs of the youngest were a long way from the floor when he sat upon the form, and the eldest was a heavy good-tempered foolish fellow, about half a head taller than the schoolmaster.

At the top of the first form—the post of honour in the school—was the vacant place of the little sick scholar, and at the head of the row of pegs on which those who came in hats or caps were wont to hang them up, one was left empty. No boy attempted to violate the sanctity of seat or peg, but many a one looked from the empty spaces to the schoolmaster, and whispered his idle neighbour behind his hand.

Then began the hum of conning over lessons and getting them by heart, the whispered jest and stealthy game, and all the noise and drawl of school; and in the midst of the din sat the poor schoolmaster, the very image of meekness and simplicity, vainly attempting to fix his mind upon the duties of the day, and to forget his little friend. But the tedium of his office reminded him more strongly of the willing scholar, and his thoughts were rambling from his pupils—it was plain.

None knew this better than the idlest boys, who, growing bolder with impunity, waxed louder and more daring; playing odd-or-even under the master's eye, eating apples openly and without rebuke, pinching each other in sport or malice without the least reserve, and cutting their autographs in the very legs of his desk. The puzzled dunce, who stood beside it to say his lesson out of book, looked no longer at the ceiling for forgotten words, but drew closer to the master's elbow and boldly cast his eye upon the page; the wag of the little troop squinted and made grimaces (at the smallest boy of course), holding no book before his face, and his approving audience knew no constraint in their delight. If the master did chance to rouse himself and seem alive to what was going on, the noise subsided for a moment and no eyes met his but wore a studious and a deeply humble look; but the instant he relapsed again, it broke out afresh, and ten times louder than before.

Oh! how some of those idle fellows longed to be outside, and how they looked at the open door and window, as if they half meditated rushing violently out, plunging into the woods, and being wild boys and savages from that time forth. What rebellious thoughts of the cool river, and some shady bathing-place beneath willow trees with branches dipping in the water, kept tempting and urging that sturdy boy, who, with his shirt-collar unbuttoned and flung back as far as it could go, sat fanning his flushed face with a spelling-book, wishing himself a whale, or a tittlebat, or a fly, or anything but a boy at school on that hot, broiling day! Heat! ask that other boy, whose seat being nearest to the door gave him opportunities of gliding out into the garden and driving his companions to madness by dipping his face into the bucket of the well and then rolling on the grass—ask him if there were ever such a day as that, when even the bees were diving deep down into the cups of flowers and stopping there, as if they had made up their minds to retire from business and be manufacturers of honey no more. The day was made for laziness, and lying on one's back in green places, and staring at the sky till its brightness forced one to shut one's eyes and go to sleep; and was this a time to be poring over musty books in a dark room, slighted by the very sun itself? Monstrous!

Nell sat by the window occupied with her work, but attentive still to all that passed, though sometimes rather timid of the boisterous boys. The lessons over, writing time began; and there being but one desk and that the master's, each boy sat at it in turn and laboured at his crooked copy, while the master walked about. This was a quieter time; for he would come and look over the writer's shoulder, and tell him mildly to observe how such a letter was turned in such a copy on the wall, praise such an up-stroke here and such a down-stroke there, and bid him take it for his model. Then he would stop and tell them what the sick child had said last night, and how he had longed to be among them once again; and such was the poor schoolmaster's gentle and affectionate manner, that the boys seemed quite remorseful that they had worried him so much, and were absolutely quiet; eating no apples, cutting no names, inflicting no pinches, and making no grimaces, for full two minutes afterwards.

'I think, boys,' said the schoolmaster when the clock struck twelve, 'that I shall give an extra half-holiday this afternoon.'

At this intelligence, the boys, led on and headed by the tall boy, raised a great shout, in the midst of which the master was seen to speak, but could not be heard. As he held up his hand, however, in token of his wish that they should be silent, they were considerate enough to leave off, as soon as the longest-winded among them were quite out of breath.

'You must promise me first,' said the schoolmaster, 'that you'll not be noisy, or at least, if you are, that you'll go away and be so—away out of the village I mean. I'm sure you wouldn't disturb your old playmate and companion.'

There was a general murmur (and perhaps a very sincere one, for they were but boys) in the negative; and the tall boy, perhaps as sincerely as any of them, called those about him to witness that he had only shouted in a whisper.

'Then pray don't forget, there's my dear scholars,' said the schoolmaster, 'what I have asked you, and do it as a favour to me. Be as happy as you can, and don't be unmindful that you are blessed with health. Good-bye all!'

'Thank'ee, Sir,' and 'good-bye, Sir,' were said a good many times in a variety of voices, and the boys went out very slowly and softly. But there was the sun shining and there were the birds singing, as the sun only shines and the birds only sing on holidays and half-holidays; there were the trees waving to all free boys to climb and nestle among their leafy branches; the hay, entreating them to come and scatter it to the pure air; the green corn, gently beckoning towards wood and stream; the smooth ground, rendered smoother still by blending lights and shadows, inviting to runs and leaps, and long walks God knows whither. It was more than boy could bear, and with a joyous whoop the whole cluster took to their heels and spread themselves about, shouting and laughing as they went.

'It's natural, thank Heaven!' said the poor schoolmaster, looking after them. 'I'm very glad they didn't mind me!'

It is difficult, however, to please everybody, as most of us would have discovered, even without the fable which bears that moral, and in the course of the afternoon several mothers and aunts of pupils looked in to express their entire disapproval of the schoolmaster's proceeding. A few confined themselves to hints, such as politely inquiring what red-letter day or saint's day the almanack said it was; a few (these were the profound village politicians) argued that it was a slight to the throne and an affront to church and state, and savoured of revolutionary principles, to grant a half-holiday upon any lighter occasion than the birthday of the Monarch; but the majority expressed their displeasure on private grounds and in plain terms, arguing that to put the pupils on this short allowance of learning was nothing but an act of downright robbery and fraud: and one old lady, finding that she could not inflame or irritate the peaceable schoolmaster by talking to him, bounced out of his house and talked at him for half-an-hour outside his own window, to another old lady, saying that of course he would deduct this half-holiday from his weekly charge, or of course he would naturally expect to have an opposition started against him; there was no want of idle chaps in that neighbourhood (here the old lady raised her voice), and some chaps who were too idle even to be schoolmasters, might soon find that there were other chaps put over their heads, and so she would have them take care, and look pretty sharp about them. But all these taunts and vexations failed to elicit one word from the meek schoolmaster, who sat with the child by his side—a little more dejected perhaps, but quite silent and uncomplaining.

Towards night an old woman came tottering up the garden as speedily as she could, and meeting the schoolmaster at the door, said he was to go to Dame West's directly, and had best run on before her. He and the child were on the point of going out together for a walk, and without relinquishing her hand, the schoolmaster hurried away, leaving the messenger to follow as she might.

They stopped at a cottage-door, and the schoolmaster knocked softly at it with his hand. It was opened without loss of time. They entered a room where a little group of women were gathered about one, older than the rest, who was crying very bitterly, and sat wringing her hands and rocking herself to and fro.

'Oh, dame!' said the schoolmaster, drawing near her chair, 'is it so bad as this?'

'He's going fast,' cried the old woman; 'my grandson's dying. It's all along of you. You shouldn't see him now, but for his being so earnest on it. This is what his learning has brought him to. Oh dear, dear, dear, what can I do!'

'Do not say that I am in any fault,' urged the gentle school-master. 'I am not hurt, dame. No, no. You are in great distress of mind, and don't mean what you say. I am sure you don't.'

'I do,' returned the old woman. 'I mean it all. If he hadn't been poring over his books out of fear of you, he would have been well and merry now, I know he would.'

The schoolmaster looked round upon the other women as if to entreat some one among them to say a kind word for him, but they shook their heads, and murmured to each other that they never thought there was much good in learning, and that this convinced them. Without saying a word in reply, or giving them a look of reproach, he followed the old woman who had summoned him (and who had now rejoined them) into another room, where his infant friend, half-dressed, lay stretched upon a bed.

He was a very young boy; quite a little child. His hair still hung in curls about his face, and his eyes were very bright; but their light was of Heaven, not earth. The schoolmaster took a seat beside him, and stooping over the pillow, whispered his name. The boy sprung up, stroked his face with his hand, and threw his wasted arms round his neck, crying out that he was his dear kind friend.

'I hope I always was. I meant to be, God knows,' said the poor schoolmaster.

'Who is that?' said the boy, seeing Nell. 'I am afraid to kiss her, lest I should make her ill. Ask her to shake hands with me.'

The sobbing child came closer up, and took the little languid hand in hers. Releasing his again after a time, the sick boy laid him gently down.

'You remember the garden, Harry,' whispered the schoolmaster, anxious to rouse him, for a dulness seemed gathering upon the child, 'and how pleasant it used to be in the evening time? You must make haste to visit it again, for I think the very flowers have missed you, and are less gay than they used to be. You will come soon, my dear, very soon now—won't you?'

136

The boy smiled faintly—so very, very faintly—and put his hand upon his friend's grey head. He moved his lips too, but no voice came from them; no, not a sound.

In the silence that ensued, the hum of distant voices borne upon the evening air came floating through the open window. 'What's that?' said the sick child, opening his eyes.

'The boys at play upon the green.'

He took a handkerchief from his pillow, and tried to wave it above his head. But the feeble arm dropped powerless down.

'Shall I do it?' said the schoolmaster.

'Please wave it at the window,' was the faint reply. 'Tie it to the lattice. Some of them may see it there. Perhaps they'll think of me, and look this way.'

He raised his head, and glanced from the fluttering signal to his idle bat, that lay with slate and book and other boyish property upon a table in the room. And then he laid him softly down once more, and asked if the little girl were there, for he could not see her.

She stepped forward, and pressed the passive hand that lay upon the coverlet. The two old friends and companions—for such they were, though they were man and child—held each other in a long embrace, and then the little scholar turned his face towards the wall, and fell asleep.

The poor schoolmaster sat in the same place, holding the small cold hand in his, and chafing it. It was but the hand of a dead child. He felt that; and yet he chafed it still, and could not lay it down.

CHAPTER 26

Almost broken-hearted, Nell withdrew with the schoolmaster from the bedside and returned to his cottage. In the midst of her grief and tears she was yet careful to conceal their real cause from the old man, for the dead boy had been a grandchild, and left but one aged relative to mourn his premature decay.

She stole away to bed as quickly as she could, and when she was alone, gave free vent to the sorrow with which her breast was overcharged. But the sad scene she had witnessed, was not without its lesson of content and gratitude; of content with the lot which left her health and freedom; and gratitude that she was spared to the one relative and friend she loved, and to live and move in a beautiful world, when so many young creatures—as young and full of hope as she—were stricken down and gathered to their graves. How many of the mounds in that old churchyard where she had lately strayed, grew green above the graves of children! And though she thought as a child herself, and did not perhaps sufficiently consider to what a bright and happy existence those who die young are borne, and how in death they lose the pain of seeing others die around them, bearing to the tomb some strong affection of their hearts (which makes the old die many times in one long life), still she thought wisely enough, to draw a plain and easy moral from what she had seen that night, and to store it, deep in her mind.

Her dreams were of the little scholar: not coffined and covered up, but mingling with angels, and smiling happily. The sun darting his cheerful rays into the room, awoke her; and now there remained but to take leave of the poor schoolmaster and wander forth once more.

By the time they were ready to depart, school had begun. In the darkened room, the din of yesterday was going on again: a little sobered and softened down, perhaps, but only a very little, if at all. The schoolmaster rose from his desk and walked with them to the gate.

It was with a trembling and reluctant hand, that the child held out to him the money which the lady had given her at the races for her flowers: faltering in her thanks as she thought how small the sum was, and blushing as she offered it. But he bade her put it up, and stooping to kiss her cheek, turned back into his house.

They had not gone half-a-dozen paces when he was at the door again; the old man retraced his steps to shake hands, and the child did the same.

'Good fortune and happiness go with you!' said the poor schoolmaster. 'I am quite a solitary man now. If you ever pass this way again, you'll not forget the little village-school.'

'We shall never forget it, sir,' rejoined Nell; 'nor ever forget to be grateful to you for your kindness to us.'

'I have heard such words from the lips of children very often,' said the schoolmaster, shaking his head, and smiling thoughtfully, 'but they were soon forgotten. I had attached one young friend to me, the better friend for being young—but that's over—God bless you!'

They bade him farewell very many times, and turned away, walking slowly and often looking back, until they could see him no more. At length they had left the village far behind, and even lost sight of the smoke among the trees. They trudged onward now, at a quicker pace, resolving to keep the main road, and go wherever it might lead them.

But main roads stretch a long, long way. With the exception of two or three inconsiderable clusters of cottages which they passed, without stopping, and one lonely road-side public-house where they had some bread and cheese, this highway had led them to nothing—late in the afternoon—and still lengthened out, far in the distance, the same dull, tedious, winding course, that they had been pursuing all day. As they had no resource, however, but to go forward, they still kept on, though at a much slower pace, being very weary and fatigued.

The afternoon had worn away into a beautiful evening, when they arrived at a point where the road made a sharp turn and struck across a common. On the border of this common, and close to the hedge which divided it from the cultivated fields, a caravan was drawn up to rest; upon which, by reason of its situation, they came so suddenly that they could not have avoided it if they would.

It was not a shabby, dingy, dusty cart, but a smart little house upon wheels, with white dimity curtains festooning the windows, and window-shutters of green picked out with panels of a staring red, in which happily-contrasted colours the whole concern shone brilliant. Neither was it a poor caravan drawn by a single donkey or emaciated horse, for a pair of horses in pretty good condition were released from the shafts and grazing on the frouzy grass. Neither was it a gipsy caravan, for at the open door (graced with a bright brass knocker) sat a Christian lady, stout and comfortable to look upon, who wore a large bonnet trembling with bows. And that it was not an unprovided or destitute caravan was clear from this lady's occupation, which was the very pleasant and refreshing one of taking tea. The tea-things, including a bottle of rather suspicious character and a cold knuckle of ham, were set forth upon a drum, covered with a white napkin; and there, as if at the most convenient round-table in all the world, sat this roving lady, taking her tea and enjoying the prospect.

138

It happened that at that moment the lady of the caravan had her cup (which, that everything about her might be of a stout and comfortable kind, was a breakfast cup) to her lips, and that having her eyes lifted to the sky in her enjoyment of the full flavour of the tea, not unmingled possibly with just the slightest dash or gleam of something out of the suspicious bottle—but this is mere speculation and not distinct matter of history—it happened that being thus agreeably engaged, she did not see the travellers when they first came up. It was not until she was in the act of getting down the cup, and drawing a long breath after the exertion of causing its contents to disappear, that the lady of the caravan beheld an old man and a young child walking slowly by, and glancing at her proceedings with eyes of modest but hungry admiration.

'Hey!' cried the lady of the caravan, scooping the crumbs out of her lap and swallowing the same before wiping her lips. 'Yes, to be sure—Who won the Helter-Skelter Plate, child?'

'Won what, ma'am?' asked Nell.

'The Helter-Skelter Plate at the races, child—the plate that was run for on the second day.'

'On the second day, ma'am?'

'Second day! Yes, second day,' repeated the lady with an air of impatience. 'Can't you say who won the Helter-Skelter Plate when you're asked the question civilly?'

'I don't know, ma'am.'

'Don't know!' repeated the lady of the caravan; 'why, you were there. I saw you with my own eyes.'

Nell was not a little alarmed to hear this, supposing that the lady might be intimately acquainted with the firm of Short and Codlin; but what followed tended to reassure her.

'And very sorry I was,' said the lady of the caravan, 'to see you in company with a Punch; a low, practical, wulgar wretch, that people should scorn to look at.'

'I was not there by choice,' returned the child; 'we didn't know our way, and the two men were very kind to us, and let us travel with them. Do you—do you know them, ma'am?'

'Know 'em, child!' cried the lady of the caravan in a sort of shriek. 'Know them! But you're young and inexperienced, and that's your excuse for asking sich a question. Do I look as if I know'd 'em, does the caravan look as if it know'd 'em?'

'No, ma'am, no,' said the child, fearing she had committed some grievous fault. 'I beg your pardon.'

It was granted immediately, though the lady still appeared much ruffled and discomposed by the degrading supposition. The child then explained that they had left the races on the first day, and were travelling to the next town on that road, where they purposed to spend the night. As the countenance of the stout lady began to clear up, she ventured to inquire how far it was. The reply—which the stout lady did not come to, until she had thoroughly explained that she went to the races on the first day in a gig, and as an expedition of pleasure, and that her presence there had no connexion with any matters of business or profit—was, that the town was eight miles off.

This discouraging information a little dashed the child, who could scarcely repress a tear

139

as she glanced along the darkening road. Her grandfather made no complaint, but he sighed heavily as he leaned upon his staff, and vainly tried to pierce the dusty distance.

The lady of the caravan was in the act of gathering her tea equipage together preparatory to clearing the table, but noting the child's anxious manner she hesitated and stopped. The child curtseyed, thanked her for her information, and giving her hand to the old man had already got some fifty yards or so away, when the lady of the caravan called to her to return.

'Come nearer, nearer still,' said she, beckoning to her to ascend the steps. 'Are you hungry, child?'

'Not very, but we are tired, and it's—it is a long way.'

'Well, hungry or not, you had better have some tea,' rejoined her new acquaintance. 'I suppose you are agreeable to that, old gentleman?'

The grandfather humbly pulled off his hat and thanked her. The lady of the caravan then bade him come up the steps likewise, but the drum proving an inconvenient table for two, they descended again, and sat upon the grass, where she handed down to them the tea-tray, the bread and butter, the knuckle of ham, and in short everything of which she had partaken herself, except the bottle which she had already embraced an opportunity of slipping into her pocket.

'Set 'em out near the hind wheels, child, that's the best place,' said their friend, superintending the arrangements from above. 'Now hand up the teapot for a little more hot water, and a pinch of fresh tea, and then both of you eat and drink as much as you can, and don't spare anything; that's all I ask of you.'

They might perhaps have carried out the lady's wish, if it had been less freely expressed, or even if it had not been expressed at all. But as this direction relieved them from any shadow of delicacy or uneasiness, they made a hearty meal and enjoyed it to the utmost.

While they were thus engaged, the lady of the caravan alighted on the earth, and with her hands clasped behind her, and her large bonnet trembling excessively, walked up and down in a measured tread and very stately manner, surveying the caravan from time to time with an air of calm delight, and deriving particular gratification from the red panels and the brass knocker. When she had taken this gentle exercise for some time, she sat down upon the steps and called 'George'; whereupon a man in a carter's frock, who had been so shrouded in a hedge up to this time as to see everything that passed without being seen himself, parted the twigs that concealed him, and appeared in a sitting attitude, supporting on his legs a baking-dish and a half-gallon stone bottle, and bearing in his right hand a knife, and in his left a fork.

'Yes, Missus,' said George.

'How did you find the cold pie, George?'

'It warn't amiss, mum.'

'And the beer,' said the lady of the caravan, with an appearance of being more interested in this question than the last; 'is it passable, George?'

'It's more flatterer than it might be,' George returned, 'but it an't so bad for all that.'

To set the mind of his mistress at rest, he took a sip (amounting in quantity to a pint or thereabouts) from the stone bottle, and then smacked his lips, winked his eye, and nodded his head. No doubt with the same amiable desire, he immediately resumed his knife and fork, as a practical assurance that the beer had wrought no bad effect upon his appetite.

The lady of the caravan looked on approvingly for some time, and then said,

'Have you nearly finished?'

'Wery nigh, mum.' And indeed, after scraping the dish all round with his knife and carrying the choice brown morsels to his mouth, and after taking such a scientific pull at the stone bottle that, by degrees almost imperceptible to the sight, his head went further and further back until he lay nearly at his full length upon the ground, this gentleman declared himself quite disengaged, and came forth from his retreat.

'I hope I haven't hurried you, George,' said his mistress, who appeared to have a great sympathy with his late pursuit.

'If you have,' returned the follower, wisely reserving himself for any favourable contingency that might occur, 'we must make up for it next time, that's all.'

'We are not a heavy load, George?'

'That's always what the ladies say,' replied the man, looking a long way round, as if he were appealing to Nature in general against such monstrous propositions. 'If you see a woman a driving, you'll always perceive that she never will keep her whip still; the horse can't go fast enough for her. If cattle have got their proper load, you never can persuade a woman that they'll not bear something more. What is the cause of this here?'

'Would these two travellers make much difference to the horses, if we took them with us?' asked his mistress, offering no reply to the philosophical inquiry, and pointing to Nell and the old man, who were painfully preparing to resume their journey on foot.

'They'd make a difference in course,' said George doggedly.

'Would they make much difference?' repeated his mistress. 'They can't be very heavy.'

'The weight o' the pair, mum,' said George, eyeing them with the look of a man who was calculating within half an ounce or so, 'would be a trifle under that of Oliver Cromwell.'

Nell was very much surprised that the man should be so accurately acquainted with the weight of one whom she had read of in books as having lived considerably before their time, but speedily forgot the subject in the joy of hearing that they were to go forward in the caravan, for which she thanked its lady with unaffected earnestness. She helped with great readiness and alacrity to put away the tea-things and other matters that were lying about, and, the horses being by that time harnessed, mounted into the vehicle, followed by her delighted grandfather. Their patroness then shut the door and sat herself down by her drum at an open window; and, the steps being struck by George and stowed under the carriage, away they went, with a great noise of flapping and creaking and straining, and the bright brass knocker, which nobody ever knocked at, knocking one perpetual double knock of its own accord as they jolted heavily along.

CHAPTER 27

When they had travelled slowly forward for some short distance, Nell ventured to steal a look round the caravan and observe it more closely. One half of it—that moiety in which the comfortable proprietress was then seated—was carpeted, and so partitioned off at the further end as to accommodate a sleeping-place, constructed after the fashion of a berth on board ship, which was shaded, like the little windows, with fair white curtains, and looked comfortable enough, though by what kind of gymnastic exercise the lady of the caravan ever contrived to get into it, was an unfathomable mystery. The other half served for a kitchen, and was fitted up with a stove whose small chimney passed through the roof. It held also a closet or larder, several chests, a great pitcher of water, and a few cooking-utensils and articles of crockery. These latter necessaries hung upon the walls, which, in that portion of the establishment devoted to the lady of the caravan, were ornamented with such gayer and lighter decorations as a triangle and a couple of well-thumbed tambourines.

The lady of the caravan sat at one window in all the pride and poetry of the musical instruments, and little Nell and her grandfather sat at the other in all the humility of the kettle and saucepans, while the machine jogged on and shifted the darkening prospect very slowly. At first the two travellers spoke little, and only in whispers, but as they grew more familiar with the place they ventured to converse with greater freedom, and talked about the country through which they were passing, and the different objects that presented themselves, until the old man fell asleep; which the lady of the caravan observing, invited Nell to come and sit beside her.

'Well, child,' she said, 'how do you like this way of travelling?'

Nell replied that she thought it was very pleasant indeed, to which the lady assented in the case of people who had their spirits. For herself, she said, she was troubled with a lowness in that respect which required a constant stimulant; though whether the aforesaid stimulant was derived from the suspicious bottle of which mention has been already made or from other sources, she did not say.

'That's the happiness of you young people,' she continued. 'You don't know what it is to be low in your feelings. You always have your appetites too, and what a comfort that is.'

Nell thought that she could sometimes dispense with her own appetite very conveniently; and thought, moreover, that there was nothing either in the lady's personal appearance or in her manner of taking tea, to lead to the conclusion that her natural relish for meat and drink had at all failed her. She silently assented, however, as in duty bound, to what the lady had said, and waited until she should speak again.

Instead of speaking, however, she sat looking at the child for a long time in silence, and then getting up, brought out from a corner a large roll of canvas about a yard in width, which she laid upon the floor and spread open with her foot until it nearly reached from one end of the caravan to the other.

'There, child,' she said, 'read that.'

Nell walked down it, and read aloud, in enormous black letters, the inscription, 'JARLEY'S WAX-WORK.'

'Read it again,' said the lady, complacently.

'Jarley's Wax-Work,' repeated Nell.

'That's me,' said the lady. 'I am Mrs Jarley.'

Giving the child an encouraging look, intended to reassure her and let her know, that,

142

although she stood in the presence of the original Jarley, she must not allow herself to be utterly overwhelmed and borne down, the lady of the caravan unfolded another scroll, whereon was the inscription, 'One hundred figures the full size of life,' and then another scroll, on which was written, 'The only stupendous collection of real wax-work in the world,' and then several smaller scrolls with such inscriptions as 'Now exhibiting within'—'The genuine and only Jarley'—'Jarley's unrivalled collection'—'Jarley is the delight of the Nobility and Gentry'—'The Royal Family are the patrons of Jarley.' When she had exhibited these leviathans of public announcement to the astonished child, she brought forth specimens of the lesser fry in the shape of hand-bills, some of which were couched in the form of parodies on popular melodies, as 'Believe me if all Jarley's wax-work so rare'—'I saw thy show in youthful prime'—'Over the water to Jarley;' while, to consult all tastes, others were composed with a view to the lighter and more facetious spirits, as a parody on the favourite air of 'If I had a donkey,' beginning,

If I know'd a donkey wot wouldn't go

To see Mrs JARLEY'S wax-work show,

Do you think I'd acknowledge him? Oh no no!

Then run to Jarley's—

—besides several compositions in prose, purporting to be dialogues between the Emperor of China and an oyster, or the Archbishop of Canterbury and a dissenter on the subject of church-rates, but all having the same moral, namely, that the reader must make haste to Jarley's, and that children and servants were admitted at half-price. When she had brought all these testimonials of her important position in society to bear upon her young companion, Mrs Jarley rolled them up, and having put them carefully away, sat down again, and looked at the child in triumph.

'Never go into the company of a filthy Punch any more,' said Mrs Jarley, 'after this.'

'I never saw any wax-work, ma'am,' said Nell. 'Is it funnier than Punch?'

'Funnier!' said Mrs Jarley in a shrill voice. 'It is not funny at all.'

'Oh!' said Nell, with all possible humility.

'It isn't funny at all,' repeated Mrs Jarley. 'It's calm and—what's that word again—critical?—no—classical, that's it—it's calm and classical. No low beatings and knockings about, no jokings and squeakings like your precious Punches, but always the same, with a constantly unchanging air of coldness and gentility; and so like life, that if wax-work only spoke and walked about, you'd hardly know the difference. I won't go so far as to say, that, as it is, I've seen wax-work quite like life, but I've certainly seen some life that was exactly like wax-work.'

'Is it here, ma'am?' asked Nell, whose curiosity was awakened by this description.

'Is what here, child?'

'The wax-work, ma'am.'

'Why, bless you, child, what are you thinking of? How could such a collection be here, where you see everything except the inside of one little cupboard and a few boxes? It's gone on in the other wans to the assembly-rooms, and there it'll be exhibited the day after to-morrow. You are going to the same town, and you'll see it I dare say. It's natural to expect that you'll see it, and I've no doubt you will. I suppose you couldn't stop away if you was to try ever so much.'

'I shall not be in the town, I think, ma'am,' said the child.

'Not there!' cried Mrs Jarley. 'Then where will you be?'

'I—I—don't quite know. I am not certain.'

'You don't mean to say that you're travelling about the country without knowing where you're going to?' said the lady of the caravan. 'What curious people you are! What line are you in? You looked to me at the races, child, as if you were quite out of your element, and had got there by accident.'

'We were there quite by accident,' returned Nell, confused by this abrupt questioning. 'We are poor people, ma'am, and are only wandering about. We have nothing to do;—I wish we had.'

'You amaze me more and more,' said Mrs Jarley, after remaining for some time as mute as one of her own figures. 'Why, what do you call yourselves? Not beggars?'

'Indeed, ma'am, I don't know what else we are,' returned the child.

'Lord bless me,' said the lady of the caravan. 'I never heard of such a thing. Who'd have thought it!'

She remained so long silent after this exclamation, that Nell feared she felt her having been induced to bestow her protection and conversation upon one so poor, to be an outrage upon her dignity that nothing could repair. This persuasion was rather confirmed than otherwise by the tone in which she at length broke silence and said,

'And yet you can read. And write too, I shouldn't wonder?'

'Yes, ma'am,' said the child, fearful of giving new offence by the confession.

'Well, and what a thing that is,' returned Mrs Jarley. 'I can't!'

Nell said 'indeed' in a tone which might imply, either that she was reasonably surprised to find the genuine and only Jarley, who was the delight of the Nobility and Gentry and the peculiar pet of the Royal Family, destitute of these familiar arts; or that she presumed so great a lady could scarcely stand in need of such ordinary accomplishments. In whatever way Mrs Jarley received the response, it did not provoke her to further questioning, or tempt her into any more remarks at the time, for she relapsed into a thoughtful silence, and remained in that state so long that Nell withdrew to the other window and rejoined her grandfather, who was now awake.

At length the lady of the caravan shook off her fit of meditation, and, summoning the driver to come under the window at which she was seated, held a long conversation with him in a low tone of voice, as if she were asking his advice on an important point, and discussing the pros and cons of some very weighty matter. This conference at length concluded, she drew in her head again, and beckoned Nell to approach.

'And the old gentleman too,' said Mrs Jarley; 'for I want to have a word with him. Do you want a good situation for your grand-daughter, master? If you do, I can put her in the way of getting one. What do you say?'

'I can't leave her,' answered the old man. 'We can't separate. What would become of me without her?'

'I should have thought you were old enough to take care of yourself, if you ever will be,' retorted Mrs Jarley sharply.

'But he never will be,' said the child in an earnest whisper. 'I fear he never will be again. Pray do not speak harshly to him. We are very thankful to you,' she added aloud; 'but neither of us could part from the other if all the wealth of the world were halved between us.'

Mrs Jarley was a little disconcerted by this reception of her proposal, and looked at the old man, who tenderly took Nell's hand and detained it in his own, as if she could have very well dispensed with his company or even his earthly existence. After an awkward pause, she thrust her head out of the window again, and had another conference with the driver upon some point on which they did not seem to agree quite so readily as on their former topic of discussion; but they concluded at last, and she addressed the grandfather again.

'If you're really disposed to employ yourself,' said Mrs Jarley, 'there would be plenty for you to do in the way of helping to dust the figures, and take the checks, and so forth. What I want your grand-daughter for, is to point 'em out to the company; they would be soon learnt, and she has a way with her that people wouldn't think unpleasant, though she does come after me; for I've been always accustomed to go round with visitors myself, which I should keep on doing now, only that my spirits make a little ease absolutely necessary. It's not a common offer, bear in mind,' said the lady, rising into the tone and manner in which she was accustomed to address her audiences; 'it's Jarley's wax-work, remember. The duty's very light and genteel, the company particularly select, the exhibition takes place in assembly-rooms, town-halls, large rooms at inns, or auction galleries. There is none of your open-air wagrancy at Jarley's, recollect; there is no tarpaulin and sawdust at Jarley's, remember. Every expectation held out in the handbills is realised to the utmost, and the whole forms an effect of imposing brilliancy hitherto unrivalled in this kingdom. Remember that the price of admission is only sixpence, and that this is an opportunity which may never occur again!'

Descending from the sublime when she had reached this point, to the details of common life, Mrs Jarley remarked that with reference to salary she could pledge herself to no specific sum until she had sufficiently tested Nell's abilities, and narrowly watched her in the performance of her duties. But board and lodging, both for her and her grandfather, she bound herself to provide, and she furthermore passed her word that the board should always be good in quality, and in quantity plentiful.

Nell and her grandfather consulted together, and while they were so engaged, Mrs Jarley with her hands behind her walked up and down the caravan, as she had walked after tea on the dull earth, with uncommon dignity and self-esteem. Nor will this appear so slight a circumstance as to be unworthy of mention, when it is remembered that the caravan was in uneasy motion all the time, and that none but a person of great natural stateliness and acquired grace could have forborne to stagger.

'Now, child?' cried Mrs Jarley, coming to a halt as Nell turned towards her.

'We are very much obliged to you, ma'am,' said Nell, 'and thankfully accept your offer.'

'And you'll never be sorry for it,' returned Mrs Jarley. 'I'm pretty sure of that. So as that's all settled, let us have a bit of supper.'

In the meanwhile, the caravan blundered on as if it too had been drinking strong beer and was drowsy, and came at last upon the paved streets of a town which were clear of passengers, and quiet, for it was by this time near midnight, and the townspeople were all abed. As it was too late an hour to repair to the exhibition room, they turned aside into a piece of waste ground that lay just within the old town-gate, and drew up there for the night, near to another caravan, which, notwithstanding that it bore on the lawful panel the great name of Jarley, and was employed besides in conveying from place to place the wax-work which was its country's pride, was designated by a grovelling stamp-office as a 'Common Stage Waggon,' and numbered too—seven thousand odd hundred—as though its precious freight were mere flour or coals!

This ill-used machine being empty (for it had deposited its burden at the place of exhibition, and lingered here until its services were again required) was assigned to the old man as his sleeping-place for the night; and within its wooden walls, Nell made him up the best bed she could, from the materials at hand. For herself, she was to sleep in Mrs Jarley's own travelling-carriage, as a signal mark of that lady's favour and confidence.

She had taken leave of her grandfather and was returning to the other waggon, when she was tempted by the coolness of the night to linger for a little while in the air. The moon was shining down upon the old gateway of the town, leaving the low archway very black and dark; and with a mingled sensation of curiosity and fear, she slowly approached the gate, and stood still to look up at it, wondering to see how dark, and grim, and old, and cold, it looked.

There was an empty niche from which some old statue had fallen or been carried away hundreds of years ago, and she was thinking what strange people it must have looked down upon when it stood there, and how many hard struggles might have taken place, and how many murders might have been done, upon that silent spot, when there suddenly emerged from the black shade of the arch, a man. The instant he appeared, she recognised him—Who could have failed to recognise, in that instant, the ugly misshapen Quilp!

The street beyond was so narrow, and the shadow of the houses on one side of the way so deep, that he seemed to have risen out of the earth. But there he was. The child withdrew into a dark corner, and saw him pass close to her. He had a stick in his hand, and, when he had got clear of the shadow of the gateway, he leant upon it, looked back—directly, as it seemed, towards where she stood—and beckoned.

To her? oh no, thank God, not to her; for as she stood, in an extremity of fear, hesitating whether to scream for help, or come from her hiding-place and fly, before he should draw nearer, there issued slowly forth from the arch another figure—that of a boy—who carried on his back a trunk.

'Faster, sirrah!' cried Quilp, looking up at the old gateway, and showing in the moonlight like some monstrous image that had come down from its niche and was casting a backward glance at its old house, 'faster!'

'It's a dreadful heavy load, Sir,' the boy pleaded. 'I've come on very fast, considering.'

'You have come fast, considering!' retorted Quilp; 'you creep, you dog, you crawl, you measure distance like a worm. There are the chimes now, half-past twelve.'

He stopped to listen, and then turning upon the boy with a suddenness and ferocity that made him start, asked at what hour that London coach passed the corner of the road. The boy replied, at one.

'Come on then,' said Quilp, 'or I shall be too late. Faster—do you hear me? Faster.'

The boy made all the speed he could, and Quilp led onward, constantly turning back to threaten him, and urge him to greater haste. Nell did not dare to move until they were out of sight and hearing, and then hurried to where she had left her grandfather, feeling as if the very passing of the dwarf so near him must have filled him with alarm and terror. But he was sleeping soundly, and she softly withdrew.

As she was making her way to her own bed, she determined to say nothing of this adventure, as upon whatever errand the dwarf had come (and she feared it must have been in search of them) it was clear by his inquiry about the London coach that he was on his way homeward, and as he had passed through that place, it was but reasonable to suppose that they were safer from his inquiries there, than they could be elsewhere. These reflections did not remove her own alarm, for she had been too much terrified to be easily composed, and felt as if she were hemmed in by a legion of Quilps, and the very air itself were filled with them.

The delight of the Nobility and Gentry and the patronised of Royalty had, by some process of self-abridgment known only to herself, got into her travelling bed, where she was snoring peacefully, while the large bonnet, carefully disposed upon the drum, was revealing its glories by the light of a dim lamp that swung from the roof. The child's bed was already made upon the floor, and it was a great comfort to her to hear the steps removed as soon as she had entered, and to know that all easy communication between persons outside and the brass knocker was by this means effectually prevented. Certain guttural sounds, too, which from time to time ascended through the floor of the caravan, and a rustling of straw in the same direction, apprised her that the driver was couched upon the ground beneath, and gave her an additional feeling of security.

Notwithstanding these protections, she could get none but broken sleep by fits and starts all night, for fear of Quilp, who throughout her uneasy dreams was somehow connected with the wax-work, or was wax-work himself, or was Mrs Jarley and wax-work too, or was himself, Mrs Jarley, wax-work, and a barrel organ all in one, and yet not exactly any of them either. At length, towards break of day, that deep sleep came upon her which succeeds to weariness and over-watching, and which has no consciousness but one of overpowering and irresistible enjoyment.

CHAPTER 28

Sleep hung upon the eyelids of the child so long, that, when she awoke, Mrs Jarley was already decorated with her large bonnet, and actively engaged in preparing breakfast. She received Nell's apology for being so late with perfect good humour, and said that she should not have roused her if she had slept on until noon.

'Because it does you good,' said the lady of the caravan, 'when you're tired, to sleep as long as ever you can, and get the fatigue quite off; and that's another blessing of your time of life—you can sleep so very sound.'

'Have you had a bad night, ma'am?' asked Nell.

'I seldom have anything else, child,' replied Mrs Jarley, with the air of a martyr. 'I sometimes wonder how I bear it.'

Remembering the snores which had proceeded from that cleft in the caravan in which the proprietress of the wax-work passed the night, Nell rather thought she must have been dreaming of lying awake. However, she expressed herself very sorry to hear such a dismal account of her state of health, and shortly afterwards sat down with her grandfather and Mrs Jarley to breakfast. The meal finished, Nell assisted to wash the cups and saucers, and put them in their proper places, and these household duties performed, Mrs Jarley arrayed herself in an exceedingly bright shawl for the purpose of making a progress through the streets of the town.

'The wan will come on to bring the boxes,' said Mrs Jarley, and you had better come in it, child. I am obliged to walk, very much against my will; but the people expect it of me, and public characters can't be their own masters and mistresses in such matters as these. How do I look, child?'

Nell returned a satisfactory reply, and Mrs Jarley, after sticking a great many pins into various parts of her figure, and making several abortive attempts to obtain a full view of her own back, was at last satisfied with her appearance, and went forth majestically.

The caravan followed at no great distance. As it went jolting through the streets, Nell peeped from the window, curious to see in what kind of place they were, and yet fearful of encountering at every turn the dreaded face of Quilp. It was a pretty large town, with an open square which they were crawling slowly across, and in the middle of which was the Town-Hall, with a clock-tower and a weather-cock. There were houses of stone, houses of red brick, houses of yellow brick, houses of lath and plaster; and houses of wood, many of them very old, with withered faces carved upon the beams, and staring down into the street. These had very little winking windows, and low-arched doors, and, in some of the narrower ways, quite overhung the pavement. The streets were very clean, very sunny, very empty, and very dull. A few idle men lounged about the two inns, and the empty market-place, and the tradesmen's doors, and some old people were dozing in chairs outside an alms-house wall; but scarcely any passengers who seemed bent on going anywhere, or to have any object in view, went by; and if perchance some straggler did, his footsteps echoed on the hot bright pavement for minutes afterwards. Nothing seemed to be going on but the clocks, and they had such drowsy faces, such heavy lazy hands, and such cracked voices that they surely must have been too slow. The very dogs were all asleep, and the flies, drunk with moist sugar in the grocer's shop, forgot their wings and briskness, and baked to death in dusty corners of the window.

Rumbling along with most unwonted noise, the caravan stopped at last at the place of exhibition, where Nell dismounted amidst an admiring group of children, who evidently supposed her to be an important item of the curiosities, and were fully impressed with the belief that her grandfather was a cunning device in wax. The chests were taken out with all convenient despatch, and taken in to be unlocked by Mrs Jarley, who, attended by George and another man in velveteen shorts and a drab hat ornamented with turnpike tickets, were waiting to dispose their contents (consisting of red festoons and other ornamental devices in upholstery work) to the best advantage in the decoration of the room.

They all got to work without loss of time, and very busy they were. As the stupendous collection were yet concealed by cloths, lest the envious dust should injure their complexions, Nell bestirred herself to assist in the embellishment of the room, in which her grandfather also was of great service. The two men being well used to it, did a great deal in a short time; and Mrs Jarley served out the tin tacks from a linen pocket like a toll-collector's which she wore for the purpose, and encouraged her assistants to renewed exertion.

While they were thus employed, a tallish gentleman with a hook nose and black hair, dressed in a military surtout very short and tight in the sleeves, and which had once been frogged and braided all over, but was now sadly shorn of its garniture and quite threadbare— dressed too in ancient grey pantaloons fitting tight to the leg, and a pair of pumps in the winter of their existence—looked in at the door and smiled affably. Mrs Jarley's back being then towards him, the military gentleman shook his forefinger as a sign that her myrmidons were not to apprise her of his presence, and stealing up close behind her, tapped her on the neck, and cried playfully 'Boh!'

'What, Mr Slum!' cried the lady of the wax-work. 'Lot! who'd have thought of seeing you here!'

'Pon my soul and honour,' said Mr Slum, 'that's a good remark. 'Pon my soul and honour that's a wise remark. Who would have thought it! George, my faithful feller, how are you?'

George received this advance with a surly indifference, observing that he was well enough for the matter of that, and hammering lustily all the time.

'I came here,' said the military gentleman turning to Mrs Jarley—''pon my soul and honour I hardly know what I came here for. It would puzzle me to tell you, it would by Gad. I wanted a little inspiration, a little freshening up, a little change of ideas, and—'Pon my soul and honour,' said the military gentleman, checking himself and looking round the room, 'what a devilish classical thing this is! by Gad, it's quite Minervian.'

'It'll look well enough when it comes to be finished,' observed Mrs Jarley.

'Well enough!' said Mr Slum. 'Will you believe me when I say it's the delight of my life to have dabbled in poetry, when I think I've exercised my pen upon this charming theme? By the way—any orders? Is there any little thing I can do for you?'

'It comes so very expensive, sir,' replied Mrs Jarley, 'and I really don't think it does much good.'

'Hush! No, no!' returned Mr Slum, elevating his hand. 'No fibs. I'll not hear it. Don't say it don't do good. Don't say it. I know better!'

'I don't think it does,' said Mrs Jarley.

'Ha, ha!' cried Mr Slum, 'you're giving way, you're coming down. Ask the perfumers, ask the blacking-makers, ask the hatters, ask the old lottery-office-keepers—ask any man among 'em what my poetry has done for him, and mark my words, he blesses the name of Slum. If he's an honest man, he raises his eyes to heaven, and blesses the name of Slum—mark that! You are acquainted with Westminster Abbey, Mrs Jarley?'

'Yes, surely.'

'Then upon my soul and honour, ma'am, you'll find in a certain angle of that dreary pile, called Poets' Corner, a few smaller names than Slum,' retorted that gentleman, tapping himself expressively on the forehead to imply that there was some slight quantity of brain behind it. 'I've got a little trifle here, now,' said Mr Slum, taking off his hat which was full of scraps of paper, 'a little trifle here, thrown off in the heat of the moment, which I should say was exactly the thing you wanted to set this place on fire with. It's an acrostic—the name at this moment is Warren, and the idea's a convertible one, and a positive inspiration for Jarley. Have the acrostic.'

'I suppose it's very dear,' said Mrs Jarley.

'Five shillings,' returned Mr Slum, using his pencil as a toothpick. 'Cheaper than any prose.'

'I couldn't give more than three,' said Mrs Jarley.

'—And six,' retorted Slum. 'Come. Three-and-six.'

Mrs Jarley was not proof against the poet's insinuating manner, and Mr Slum entered the order in a small note-book as a three-and-sixpenny one. Mr Slum then withdrew to alter the acrostic, after taking a most affectionate leave of his patroness, and promising to return, as soon as he possibly could, with a fair copy for the printer.

As his presence had not interfered with or interrupted the preparations, they were now far advanced, and were completed shortly after his departure. When the festoons were all put up as tastily as they might be, the stupendous collection was uncovered, and there were displayed, on a raised platform some two feet from the floor, running round the room and parted from the rude public by a crimson rope breast high, divers sprightly effigies of celebrated characters, singly and in groups, clad in glittering dresses of various climes and times, and standing more or less unsteadily upon their legs, with their eyes very wide open, and their nostrils very much inflated, and the muscles of their legs and arms very strongly developed, and all their countenances expressing great surprise. All the gentlemen were very pigeon-breasted and very blue about the beards; and all the ladies were miraculous figures; and all the ladies and all the gentlemen were looking intensely nowhere, and staring with extraordinary earnestness at nothing.

When Nell had exhausted her first raptures at this glorious sight, Mrs Jarley ordered the room to be cleared of all but herself and the child, and, sitting herself down in an arm-chair in the centre, formally invested Nell with a willow wand, long used by herself for pointing out the characters, and was at great pains to instruct her in her duty.

'That,' said Mrs Jarley in her exhibition tone, as Nell touched a figure at the beginning of the platform, 'is an unfortunate Maid of Honour in the Time of Queen Elizabeth, who died from pricking her finger in consequence of working upon a Sunday. Observe the blood which is trickling from her finger; also the gold-eyed needle of the period, with which she is at work.'

All this, Nell repeated twice or thrice: pointing to the finger and the needle at the right times: and then passed on to the next.

'That, ladies and gentlemen,' said Mrs Jarley, 'is Jasper Packlemerton of atrocious memory, who courted and married fourteen wives, and destroyed them all, by tickling the soles of their feet when they were sleeping in the consciousness of innocence and virtue. On being brought to the scaffold and asked if he was sorry for what he had done, he replied yes, he was sorry for having let 'em off so easy, and hoped all Christian husbands would pardon him the offence. Let this be a warning to all young ladies to be particular in the character of the gentlemen of their choice. Observe that his fingers are curled as if in the act of tickling, and that his face is represented with a wink, as he appeared when committing his barbarous murders.'

When Nell knew all about Mr Packlemerton, and could say it without faltering, Mrs Jarley passed on to the fat man, and then to the thin man, the tall man, the short man, the old lady who died of dancing at a hundred and thirty-two, the wild boy of the woods, the woman who poisoned fourteen families with pickled walnuts, and other historical characters and interesting but misguided individuals. And so well did Nell profit by her instructions, and so apt was she to remember them, that by the time they had been shut up together for a couple of hours, she was in full possession of the history of the whole establishment, and perfectly competent to the enlightenment of visitors.

Mrs Jarley was not slow to express her admiration at this happy result, and carried her young friend and pupil to inspect the remaining arrangements within doors, by virtue of which the passage had been already converted into a grove of green-baize hung with the inscription she had already seen (Mr Slum's productions), and a highly ornamented table placed at the upper end for Mrs Jarley herself, at which she was to preside and take the money, in company with his Majesty King George the Third, Mr Grimaldi as clown, Mary Queen of Scots, an anonymous gentleman of the Quaker persuasion, and Mr Pitt holding in his hand a correct model of the bill for the imposition of the window duty. The preparations without doors had not been neglected either; a nun of great personal attractions was telling her beads on the little portico over the door; and a brigand with the blackest possible head of hair, and the clearest possible complexion, was at that moment going round the town in a cart, consulting the miniature of a lady.

It now only remained that Mr Slum's compositions should be judiciously distributed; that the pathetic effusions should find their way to all private houses and tradespeople; and that the parody commencing 'If I know'd a donkey,' should be confined to the taverns, and circulated only among the lawyers' clerks and choice spirits of the place. When this had been done, and Mrs Jarley had waited upon the boarding-schools in person, with a handbill composed expressly for them, in which it was distinctly proved that wax-work refined the mind, cultivated the taste, and enlarged the sphere of the human understanding, that indefatigable lady sat down to dinner, and drank out of the suspicious bottle to a flourishing campaign.

CHAPTER 29

Unquestionably Mrs Jarley had an inventive genius. In the midst of the various devices for attracting visitors to the exhibition, little Nell was not forgotten. The light cart in which the Brigand usually made his perambulations being gaily dressed with flags and streamers, and the Brigand placed therein, contemplating the miniature of his beloved as usual, Nell was accommodated with a seat beside him, decorated with artificial flowers, and in this state and ceremony rode slowly through the town every morning, dispersing handbills from a basket, to the sound of drum and trumpet. The beauty of the child, coupled with her gentle and timid bearing, produced quite a sensation in the little country place. The Brigand, heretofore a source of exclusive interest in the streets, became a mere secondary consideration, and to be important only as a part of the show of which she was the chief attraction. Grown-up folks began to be interested in the bright-eyed girl, and some score of little boys fell desperately in love, and constantly left enclosures of nuts and apples, directed in small-text, at the wax-work door.

This desirable impression was not lost on Mrs Jarley, who, lest Nell should become too cheap, soon sent the Brigand out alone again, and kept her in the exhibition room, where she described the figures every half-hour to the great satisfaction of admiring audiences. And these audiences were of a very superior description, including a great many young ladies' boarding-schools, whose favour Mrs Jarley had been at great pains to conciliate, by altering the face and costume of Mr Grimaldi as clown to represent Mr Lindley Murray as he appeared when engaged in the composition of his English Grammar, and turning a murderess of great renown into Mrs Hannah More—both of which likenesses were admitted by Miss Monflathers, who was at the head of the head Boarding and Day Establishment in the town, and who condescended to take a Private View with eight chosen young ladies, to be quite startling from their extreme correctness. Mr Pitt in a nightcap and bedgown, and without his boots, represented the poet Cowper with perfect exactness; and Mary Queen of Scots in a dark wig, white shirt-collar, and male attire, was such a complete image of Lord Byron that the young ladies quite screamed when they saw it. Miss Monflathers, however, rebuked this enthusiasm, and took occasion to reprove Mrs Jarley for not keeping her collection more select: observing that His Lordship had held certain opinions quite incompatible with wax-work honours, and adding something about a Dean and Chapter, which Mrs Jarley did not understand.

Although her duties were sufficiently laborious, Nell found in the lady of the caravan a very kind and considerate person, who had not only a peculiar relish for being comfortable herself, but for making everybody about her comfortable also; which latter taste, it may be remarked, is, even in persons who live in much finer places than caravans, a far more rare and uncommon one than the first, and is not by any means its necessary consequence. As her popularity procured her various little fees from the visitors on which her patroness never demanded any toll, and as her grandfather too was well-treated and useful, she had no cause of anxiety in connexion with the wax-work, beyond that which sprung from her recollection of Quilp, and her fears that he might return and one day suddenly encounter them.

Quilp indeed was a perpetual night-mare to the child, who was constantly haunted by a vision of his ugly face and stunted figure. She slept, for their better security, in the room where the wax-work figures were, and she never retired to this place at night but she tortured herself—she could not help it—with imagining a resemblance, in some one or other of their death-like faces, to the dwarf, and this fancy would sometimes so gain upon her that she would almost believe he had removed the figure and stood within the clothes. Then there were so many of them with their great glassy eyes—and, as they stood one behind the other all about her bed, they looked so like living creatures, and yet so unlike in their grim stillness and silence, that she had a kind of terror of them for their own sakes, and would often lie watching their dusky figures until she was obliged to rise and light a candle, or go and sit at the open window and feel a companionship in the bright stars. At these times, she would recall the old house and the window at which she used to sit alone; and then she would think of poor Kit and all his kindness, until the tears came into her eyes, and she would weep and smile together.

Often and anxiously at this silent hour, her thoughts reverted to her grandfather, and she would wonder how much he remembered of their former life, and whether he was ever really mindful of the change in their condition and of their late helplessness and destitution. When they were wandering about, she seldom thought of this, but now she could not help considering what would become of them if he fell sick, or her own strength were to fail her.

He was very patient and willing, happy to execute any little task, and glad to be of use; but he was in the same listless state, with no prospect of improvement—a mere child—a poor, thoughtless, vacant creature—a harmless fond old man, susceptible of tender love and regard for her, and of pleasant and painful impressions, but alive to nothing more. It made her very sad to know that this was so—so sad to see it that sometimes when he sat idly by, smiling and nodding to her when she looked round, or when he caressed some little child and carried it to and fro, as he was fond of doing by the hour together, perplexed by its simple questions, yet patient under his own infirmity, and seeming almost conscious of it too, and humbled even before the mind of an infant—so sad it made her to see him thus, that she would burst into tears, and, withdrawing into some secret place, fall down upon her knees and pray that he might be restored.

But, the bitterness of her grief was not in beholding him in this condition, when he was at least content and tranquil, nor in her solitary meditations on his altered state, though these were trials for a young heart. Cause for deeper and heavier sorrow was yet to come.

One evening, a holiday night with them, Nell and her grandfather went out to walk. They had been rather closely confined for some days, and the weather being warm, they strolled a long distance. Clear of the town, they took a footpath which struck through some pleasant fields, judging that it would terminate in the road they quitted and enable them to return that way. It made, however, a much wider circuit than they had supposed, and thus they were tempted onward until sunset, when they reached the track of which they were in search, and stopped to rest.

It had been gradually getting overcast, and now the sky was dark and lowering, save where the glory of the departing sun piled up masses of gold and burning fire, decaying embers of which gleamed here and there through the black veil, and shone redly down upon the earth. The wind began to moan in hollow murmurs, as the sun went down carrying glad day elsewhere; and a train of dull clouds coming up against it, menaced thunder and lightning. Large drops of rain soon began to fall, and, as the storm clouds came sailing onward, others supplied the void they left behind and spread over all the sky. Then was heard the low rumbling of distant thunder, then the lightning quivered, and then the darkness of an hour seemed to have gathered in an instant.

Fearful of taking shelter beneath a tree or hedge, the old man and the child hurried along the high road, hoping to find some house in which they could seek a refuge from the storm, which had now burst forth in earnest, and every moment increased in violence. Drenched with the pelting rain, confused by the deafening thunder, and bewildered by the glare of the forked lightning, they would have passed a solitary house without being aware of its vicinity, had not a man, who was standing at the door, called lustily to them to enter.

'Your ears ought to be better than other folks' at any rate, if you make so little of the chance of being struck blind,' he said, retreating from the door and shading his eyes with his hands as the jagged lightning came again. 'What were you going past for, eh?' he added, as he closed the door and led the way along a passage to a room behind.

'We didn't see the house, sir, till we heard you calling,' Nell replied.

'No wonder,' said the man, 'with this lightning in one's eyes, by-the-by. You had better stand by the fire here, and dry yourselves a bit. You can call for what you like if you want anything. If you don't want anything, you are not obliged to give an order. Don't be afraid of that. This is a public-house, that's all. The Valiant Soldier is pretty well known hereabouts.'

'Is this house called the Valiant Soldier, Sir?' asked Nell.

'I thought everybody knew that,' replied the landlord. 'Where have you come from, if you don't know the Valiant Soldier as well as the church catechism? This is the Valiant Soldier, by James Groves—Jem Groves—honest Jem Groves, as is a man of unblemished moral character, and has a good dry skittle-ground. If any man has got anything to say again Jem Groves, let him say it to Jem Groves, and Jem Groves can accommodate him with a customer on any terms from four pound a side to forty.'

With these words, the speaker tapped himself on the waistcoat to intimate that he was the Jem Groves so highly eulogized; sparred scientifically at a counterfeit Jem Groves, who was sparring at society in general from a black frame over the chimney-piece; and, applying a half-emptied glass of spirits and water to his lips, drank Jem Groves's health.

The night being warm, there was a large screen drawn across the room, for a barrier against the heat of the fire. It seemed as if somebody on the other side of this screen had been insinuating doubts of Mr Groves's prowess, and had thereby given rise to these egotistical expressions, for Mr Groves wound up his defiance by giving a loud knock upon it with his knuckles and pausing for a reply from the other side.

'There an't many men,' said Mr Groves, no answer being returned, 'who would ventur' to cross Jem Groves under his own roof. There's only one man, I know, that has nerve enough for that, and that man's not a hundred mile from here neither. But he's worth a dozen men, and I let him say of me whatever he likes in consequence—he knows that.'

In return for this complimentary address, a very gruff hoarse voice bade Mr Groves 'hold his noise and light a candle.' And the same voice remarked that the same gentleman 'needn't waste his breath in brag, for most people knew pretty well what sort of stuff he was made of.'

'Nell, they're—they're playing cards,' whispered the old man, suddenly interested. 'Don't you hear them?'

'Look sharp with that candle,' said the voice; 'it's as much as I can do to see the pips on the cards as it is; and get this shutter closed as quick as you can, will you? Your beer will be the worse for to-night's thunder I expect.—Game! Seven-and-sixpence to me, old Isaac. Hand over.'

'Do you hear, Nell, do you hear them?' whispered the old man again, with increased earnestness, as the money chinked upon the table.

'I haven't seen such a storm as this,' said a sharp cracked voice of most disagreeable quality, when a tremendous peal of thunder had died away, 'since the night when old Luke Withers won thirteen times running on the red. We all said he had the Devil's luck and his own, and as it was the kind of night for the Devil to be out and busy, I suppose he was looking over his shoulder, if anybody could have seen him.'

'Ah!' returned the gruff voice; 'for all old Luke's winning through thick and thin of late years, I remember the time when he was the unluckiest and unfortunatest of men. He never took a dice-box in his hand, or held a card, but he was plucked, pigeoned, and cleaned out completely.'

'Do you hear what he says?' whispered the old man. 'Do you hear that, Nell?'

The child saw with astonishment and alarm that his whole appearance had undergone a complete change. His face was flushed and eager, his eyes were strained, his teeth set, his breath came short and thick, and the hand he laid upon her arm trembled so violently that she shook beneath its grasp.

'Bear witness,' he muttered, looking upward, 'that I always said it; that I knew it, dreamed of it, felt it was the truth, and that it must be so! What money have we, Nell? Come! I saw you with money yesterday. What money have we? Give it to me.'

'No, no, let me keep it, grandfather,' said the frightened child. 'Let us go away from here. Do not mind the rain. Pray let us go.'

'Give it to me, I say,' returned the old man fiercely. 'Hush, hush, don't cry, Nell. If I spoke sharply, dear, I didn't mean it. It's for thy good. I have wronged thee, Nell, but I will right thee yet, I will indeed. Where is the money?'

'Do not take it,' said the child. 'Pray do not take it, dear. For both our sakes let me keep it, or let me throw it away—better let me throw it away, than you take it now. Let us go; do let us go.'

'Give me the money,' returned the old man, 'I must have it. There—there—that's my dear Nell. I'll right thee one day, child, I'll right thee, never fear!'

She took from her pocket a little purse. He seized it with the same rapid impatience which had characterised his speech, and hastily made his way to the other side of the screen. It was impossible to restrain him, and the trembling child followed close behind.

The landlord had placed a light upon the table, and was engaged in drawing the curtain of the window. The speakers whom they had heard were two men, who had a pack of cards and some silver money between them, while upon the screen itself the games they had played were scored in chalk. The man with the rough voice was a burly fellow of middle age, with large black whiskers, broad cheeks, a coarse wide mouth, and bull neck, which was pretty freely displayed as his shirt collar was only confined by a loose red neckerchief. He wore his hat, which was of a brownish-white, and had beside him a thick knotted stick. The other man, whom his companion had called Isaac, was of a more slender figure—stooping, and high in the shoulders—with a very ill-favoured face, and a most sinister and villainous squint.

'Now old gentleman,' said Isaac, looking round. 'Do you know either of us? This side of the screen is private, sir.'

'No offence, I hope,' returned the old man.

'But by G—, sir, there is offence,' said the other, interrupting him, 'when you intrude yourself upon a couple of gentlemen who are particularly engaged.'

'I had no intention to offend,' said the old man, looking anxiously at the cards. 'I thought that—'

'But you had no right to think, sir,' retorted the other. 'What the devil has a man at your time of life to do with thinking?'

'Now bully boy,' said the stout man, raising his eyes from his cards for the first time, 'can't you let him speak?'

The landlord, who had apparently resolved to remain neutral until he knew which side of the question the stout man would espouse, chimed in at this place with 'Ah, to be sure, can't you let him speak, Isaac List?'

'Can't I let him speak,' sneered Isaac in reply, mimicking as nearly as he could, in his shrill voice, the tones of the landlord. 'Yes, I can let him speak, Jemmy Groves.'

'Well then, do it, will you?' said the landlord.

Mr List's squint assumed a portentous character, which seemed to threaten a prolongation of this controversy, when his companion, who had been looking sharply at the old man, put a timely stop to it.

'Who knows,' said he, with a cunning look, 'but the gentleman may have civilly meant to ask if he might have the honour to take a hand with us!'

'I did mean it,' cried the old man. 'That is what I mean. That is what I want now!'

'I thought so,' returned the same man. 'Then who knows but the gentleman, anticipating our objection to play for love, civilly desired to play for money?'

The old man replied by shaking the little purse in his eager hand, and then throwing it down upon the table, and gathering up the cards as a miser would clutch at gold.

'Oh! That indeed,' said Isaac; 'if that's what the gentleman meant, I beg the gentleman's pardon. Is this the gentleman's little purse? A very pretty little purse. Rather a light purse,' added Isaac, throwing it into the air and catching it dexterously, 'but enough to amuse a gentleman for half an hour or so.'

'We'll make a four-handed game of it, and take in Groves,' said the stout man. 'Come, Jemmy.'

The landlord, who conducted himself like one who was well used to such little parties, approached the table and took his seat. The child, in a perfect agony, drew her grandfather aside, and implored him, even then, to come away.

'Come; and we may be so happy,' said the child.

'We will be happy,' replied the old man hastily. 'Let me go, Nell. The means of happiness are on the cards and the dice. We must rise from little winnings to great. There's little to be won here; but great will come in time. I shall but win back my own, and it's all for thee, my darling.'

'God help us!' cried the child. 'Oh! what hard fortune brought us here?'

'Hush!' rejoined the old man laying his hand upon her mouth, 'Fortune will not bear chiding. We must not reproach her, or she shuns us; I have found that out.'

'Now, mister,' said the stout man. 'If you're not coming yourself, give us the cards, will you?'

'I am coming,' cried the old man. 'Sit thee down, Nell, sit thee down and look on. Be of good heart, it's all for thee—all—every penny. I don't tell them, no, no, or else they wouldn't play, dreading the chance that such a cause must give me. Look at them. See what they are and what thou art. Who doubts that we must win!'

'The gentleman has thought better of it, and isn't coming,' said Isaac, making as though he would rise from the table. 'I'm sorry the gentleman's daunted—nothing venture, nothing have—but the gentleman knows best.'

'Why I am ready. You have all been slow but me,' said the old man. 'I wonder who is more anxious to begin than I.'

As he spoke he drew a chair to the table; and the other three closing round it at the same time, the game commenced.

The child sat by, and watched its progress with a troubled mind. Regardless of the run of luck, and mindful only of the desperate passion which had its hold upon her grandfather, losses and gains were to her alike. Exulting in some brief triumph, or cast down by a defeat, there he sat so wild and restless, so feverishly and intensely anxious, so terribly eager, so ravenous for the paltry stakes, that she could have almost better borne to see him dead. And yet she was the innocent cause of all this torture, and he, gambling with such a savage thirst for gain as the most insatiable gambler never felt, had not one selfish thought!

On the contrary, the other three—knaves and gamesters by their trade—while intent upon their game, were yet as cool and quiet as if every virtue had been centered in their breasts. Sometimes one would look up to smile to another, or to snuff the feeble candle, or to glance at the lightning as it shot through the open window and fluttering curtain, or to listen to some louder peal of thunder than the rest, with a kind of momentary impatience, as if it put him out; but there they sat, with a calm indifference to everything but their cards, perfect philosophers in appearance, and with no greater show of passion or excitement than if they had been made of stone.

The storm had raged for full three hours; the lightning had grown fainter and less frequent; the thunder, from seeming to roll and break above their heads, had gradually died away into a deep hoarse distance; and still the game went on, and still the anxious child was quite forgotten.

CHAPTER 30

At length the play came to an end, and Mr Isaac List rose the only winner. Mat and the landlord bore their losses with professional fortitude. Isaac pocketed his gains with the air of a man who had quite made up his mind to win, all along, and was neither surprised nor pleased.

Nell's little purse was exhausted; but although it lay empty by his side, and the other players had now risen from the table, the old man sat poring over the cards, dealing them as they had been dealt before, and turning up the different hands to see what each man would have held if they had still been playing. He was quite absorbed in this occupation, when the child drew near and laid her hand upon his shoulder, telling him it was near midnight.

'See the curse of poverty, Nell,' he said, pointing to the packs he had spread out upon the table. 'If I could have gone on a little longer, only a little longer, the luck would have turned on my side. Yes, it's as plain as the marks upon the cards. See here—and there—and here again.'

'Put them away,' urged the child. 'Try to forget them.'

'Try to forget them!' he rejoined, raising his haggard face to hers, and regarding her with an incredulous stare. 'To forget them! How are we ever to grow rich if I forget them?'

The child could only shake her head.

'No, no, Nell,' said the old man, patting her cheek; 'they must not be forgotten. We must make amends for this as soon as we can. Patience—patience, and we'll right thee yet, I promise thee. Lose to-day, win to-morrow. And nothing can be won without anxiety and care—nothing. Come, I am ready.'

'Do you know what the time is?' said Mr Groves, who was smoking with his friends. 'Past twelve o'clock—'

'—And a rainy night,' added the stout man.

'The Valiant Soldier, by James Groves. Good beds. Cheap entertainment for man and beast,' said Mr Groves, quoting his sign-board. 'Half-past twelve o'clock.'

'It's very late,' said the uneasy child. 'I wish we had gone before. What will they think of us! It will be two o'clock by the time we get back. What would it cost, sir, if we stopped here?'

'Two good beds, one-and-sixpence; supper and beer one shilling; total two shillings and sixpence,' replied the Valiant Soldier.

Now, Nell had still the piece of gold sewn in her dress; and when she came to consider the lateness of the hour, and the somnolent habits of Mrs Jarley, and to imagine the state of consternation in which they would certainly throw that good lady by knocking her up in the middle of the night—and when she reflected, on the other hand, that if they remained where they were, and rose early in the morning, they might get back before she awoke, and could plead the violence of the storm by which they had been overtaken, as a good apology for their absence—she decided, after a great deal of hesitation, to remain. She therefore took her grandfather aside, and telling him that she had still enough left to defray the cost of their lodging, proposed that they should stay there for the night.

'If I had had but that money before—If I had only known of it a few minutes ago!' muttered the old man.

'We will decide to stop here if you please,' said Nell, turning hastily to the landlord.

'I think that's prudent,' returned Mr Groves. 'You shall have your suppers directly.'

Accordingly, when Mr Groves had smoked his pipe out, knocked out the ashes, and placed it carefully in a corner of the fire-place, with the bowl downwards, he brought in the bread and cheese, and beer, with many high encomiums upon their excellence, and bade his guests fall to, and make themselves at home. Nell and her grandfather ate sparingly, for both were occupied with their own reflections; the other gentlemen, for whose constitutions beer was too weak and tame a liquid, consoled themselves with spirits and tobacco.

As they would leave the house very early in the morning, the child was anxious to pay for their entertainment before they retired to bed. But as she felt the necessity of concealing her little hoard from her grandfather, and had to change the piece of gold, she took it secretly from its place of concealment, and embraced an opportunity of following the landlord when he went out of the room, and tendered it to him in the little bar.

'Will you give me the change here, if you please?' said the child.

Mr James Groves was evidently surprised, and looked at the money, and rang it, and looked at the child, and at the money again, as though he had a mind to inquire how she came by it. The coin being genuine, however, and changed at his house, he probably felt, like a wise landlord, that it was no business of his. At any rate, he counted out the change, and gave it her. The child was returning to the room where they had passed the evening, when she fancied she saw a figure just gliding in at the door. There was nothing but a long dark passage between this door and the place where she had changed the money, and, being very certain that no person had passed in or out while she stood there, the thought struck her that she had been watched.

But by whom? When she re-entered the room, she found its inmates exactly as she had left them. The stout fellow lay upon two chairs, resting his head on his hand, and the squinting man reposed in a similar attitude on the opposite side of the table. Between them sat her grandfather, looking intently at the winner with a kind of hungry admiration, and hanging upon his words as if he were some superior being. She was puzzled for a moment, and looked round to see if any else were there. No. Then she asked her grandfather in a whisper whether anybody had left the room while she was absent. 'No,' he said, 'nobody.'

It must have been her fancy then; and yet it was strange, that, without anything in her previous thoughts to lead to it, she should have imagined this figure so very distinctly. She was still wondering and thinking of it, when a girl came to light her to bed.

The old man took leave of the company at the same time, and they went up stairs together. It was a great, rambling house, with dull corridors and wide staircases which the flaring candles seemed to make more gloomy. She left her grandfather in his chamber, and followed her guide to another, which was at the end of a passage, and approached by some half-dozen crazy steps. This was prepared for her. The girl lingered a little while to talk, and tell her grievances. She had not a good place, she said; the wages were low, and the work was hard. She was going to leave it in a fortnight; the child couldn't recommend her to another, she supposed? Instead she was afraid another would be difficult to get after living there, for the house had a very indifferent character; there was far too much card-playing, and such like. She was very much mistaken if some of the people who came there oftenest were quite as honest as they might be, but she wouldn't have it known that she had said so, for the world. Then there were some rambling allusions to a rejected sweetheart, who had threatened to go a soldiering—a final promise of knocking at the door early in the morning—and 'Good night.'

The child did not feel comfortable when she was left alone. She could not help thinking of the figure stealing through the passage down stairs; and what the girl had said did not tend to reassure her. The men were very ill-looking. They might get their living by robbing and murdering travellers. Who could tell?

Reasoning herself out of these fears, or losing sight of them for a little while, there came the anxiety to which the adventures of the night gave rise. Here was the old passion awakened again in her grandfather's breast, and to what further distraction it might tempt him Heaven only knew. What fears their absence might have occasioned already! Persons might be seeking for them even then. Would they be forgiven in the morning, or turned adrift again! Oh! why had they stopped in that strange place? It would have been better, under any circumstances, to have gone on!

At last, sleep gradually stole upon her—a broken, fitful sleep, troubled by dreams of falling from high towers, and waking with a start and in great terror. A deeper slumber followed this—and then—What! That figure in the room.

A figure was there. Yes, she had drawn up the blind to admit the light when it should be dawn, and there, between the foot of the bed and the dark casement, it crouched and slunk along, groping its way with noiseless hands, and stealing round the bed. She had no voice to cry for help, no power to move, but lay still, watching it.

On it came—on, silently and stealthily, to the bed's head. The breath so near her pillow, that she shrunk back into it, lest those wandering hands should light upon her face. Back again it stole to the window—then turned its head towards her.

The dark form was a mere blot upon the lighter darkness of the room, but she saw the turning of the head, and felt and knew how the eyes looked and the ears listened. There it remained, motionless as she. At length, still keeping the face towards her, it busied its hands in something, and she heard the chink of money.

Then, on it came again, silent and stealthy as before, and replacing the garments it had taken from the bedside, dropped upon its hands and knees, and crawled away. How slowly it seemed to move, now that she could hear but not see it, creeping along the floor! It reached the door at last, and stood upon its feet. The steps creaked beneath its noiseless tread, and it was gone.

The first impulse of the child was to fly from the terror of being by herself in that room—to have somebody by—not to be alone—and then her power of speech would be restored. With no consciousness of having moved, she gained the door.

There was the dreadful shadow, pausing at the bottom of the steps.

She could not pass it; she might have done so, perhaps, in the darkness without being seized, but her blood curdled at the thought. The figure stood quite still, and so did she; not boldly, but of necessity; for going back into the room was hardly less terrible than going on.

The rain beat fast and furiously without, and ran down in plashing streams from the thatched roof. Some summer insect, with no escape into the air, flew blindly to and fro, beating its body against the walls and ceiling, and filling the silent place with murmurs. The figure moved again. The child involuntarily did the same. Once in her grandfather's room, she would be safe.

It crept along the passage until it came to the very door she longed so ardently to reach. The child, in the agony of being so near, had almost darted forward with the design of bursting into the room and closing it behind her, when the figure stopped again.

The idea flashed suddenly upon her—what if it entered there, and had a design upon the old man's life! She turned faint and sick. It did. It went in. There was a light inside. The figure was now within the chamber, and she, still dumb—quite dumb, and almost senseless—stood looking on.

The door was partly open. Not knowing what she meant to do, but meaning to preserve him or be killed herself, she staggered forward and looked in. What sight was that which met her view!

The bed had not been lain on, but was smooth and empty. And at a table sat the old man himself; the only living creature there; his white face pinched and sharpened by the greediness which made his eyes unnaturally bright—counting the money of which his hands had robbed her.

160

CHAPTER 31

With steps more faltering and unsteady than those with which she had approached the room, the child withdrew from the door, and groped her way back to her own chamber. The terror she had lately felt was nothing compared with that which now oppressed her. No strange robber, no treacherous host conniving at the plunder of his guests, or stealing to their beds to kill them in their sleep, no nightly prowler, however terrible and cruel, could have awakened in her bosom half the dread which the recognition of her silent visitor inspired. The grey-headed old man gliding like a ghost into her room and acting the thief while he supposed her fast asleep, then bearing off his prize and hanging over it with the ghastly exultation she had witnessed, was worse—immeasurably worse, and far more dreadful, for the moment, to reflect upon—than anything her wildest fancy could have suggested. If he should return—there was no lock or bolt upon the door, and if, distrustful of having left some money yet behind, he should come back to seek for more—a vague awe and horror surrounded the idea of his slinking in again with stealthy tread, and turning his face toward the empty bed, while she shrank down close at his feet to avoid his touch, which was almost insupportable. She sat and listened. Hark! A footstep on the stairs, and now the door was slowly opening. It was but imagination, yet imagination had all the terrors of reality; nay, it was worse, for the reality would have come and gone, and there an end, but in imagination it was always coming, and never went away.

The feeling which beset the child was one of dim uncertain horror. She had no fear of the dear old grandfather, in whose love for her this disease of the brain had been engendered; but the man she had seen that night, wrapt in the game of chance, lurking in her room, and counting the money by the glimmering light, seemed like another creature in his shape, a monstrous distortion of his image, a something to recoil from, and be the more afraid of, because it bore a likeness to him, and kept close about her, as he did. She could scarcely connect her own affectionate companion, save by his loss, with this old man, so like yet so unlike him. She had wept to see him dull and quiet. How much greater cause she had for weeping now!

The child sat watching and thinking of these things, until the phantom in her mind so increased in gloom and terror, that she felt it would be a relief to hear the old man's voice, or, if he were asleep, even to see him, and banish some of the fears that clustered round his image. She stole down the stairs and passage again. The door was still ajar as she had left it, and the candle burning as before.

She had her own candle in her hand, prepared to say, if he were waking, that she was uneasy and could not rest, and had come to see if his were still alight. Looking into the room, she saw him lying calmly on his bed, and so took courage to enter.

Fast asleep. No passion in the face, no avarice, no anxiety, no wild desire; all gentle, tranquil, and at peace. This was not the gambler, or the shadow in her room; this was not even the worn and jaded man whose face had so often met her own in the grey morning light; this was her dear old friend, her harmless fellow-traveller, her good, kind grandfather.

She had no fear as she looked upon his slumbering features, but she had a deep and weighty sorrow, and it found its relief in tears.

'God bless him!' said the child, stooping softly to kiss his placid cheek. 'I see too well now, that they would indeed part us if they found us out, and shut him up from the light of the sun and sky. He has only me to help him. God bless us both!'

Lighting her candle, she retreated as silently as she had come, and, gaining her own room once more, sat up during the remainder of that long, long, miserable night.

At last the day turned her waning candle pale, and she fell asleep. She was quickly roused by the girl who had shown her up to bed; and, as soon as she was dressed, prepared to go down to her grandfather. But first she searched her pocket and found that her money was all gone—not a sixpence remained.

The old man was ready, and in a few seconds they were on their road. The child thought he rather avoided her eye, and appeared to expect that she would tell him of her loss. She felt she must do that, or he might suspect the truth.

'Grandfather,' she said in a tremulous voice, after they had walked about a mile in silence, 'do you think they are honest people at the house yonder?'

'Why?' returned the old man trembling. 'Do I think them honest—yes, they played honestly.'

'I'll tell you why I ask,' rejoined Nell. 'I lost some money last night—out of my bedroom, I am sure. Unless it was taken by somebody in jest—only in jest, dear grandfather, which would make me laugh heartily if I could but know it—'

'Who would take money in jest?' returned the old man in a hurried manner. 'Those who take money, take it to keep. Don't talk of jest.'

'Then it was stolen out of my room, dear,' said the child, whose last hope was destroyed by the manner of this reply.

'But is there no more, Nell?' said the old man; 'no more anywhere? Was it all taken—every farthing of it—was there nothing left?'

'Nothing,' replied the child.

'We must get more,' said the old man, 'we must earn it, Nell, hoard it up, scrape it together, come by it somehow. Never mind this loss. Tell nobody of it, and perhaps we may regain it. Don't ask how;—we may regain it, and a great deal more;—but tell nobody, or trouble may come of it. And so they took it out of thy room, when thou wert asleep!' he added in a compassionate tone, very different from the secret, cunning way in which he had spoken until now. 'Poor Nell, poor little Nell!'

The child hung down her head and wept. The sympathising tone in which he spoke, was quite sincere; she was sure of that. It was not the lightest part of her sorrow to know that this was done for her.

'Not a word about it to any one but me,' said the old man, 'no, not even to me,' he added hastily, 'for it can do no good. All the losses that ever were, are not worth tears from thy eyes, darling. Why should they be, when we will win them back?'

'Let them go,' said the child looking up. 'Let them go, once and for ever, and I would never shed another tear if every penny had been a thousand pounds.'

'Well, well,' returned the old man, checking himself as some impetuous answer rose to his lips, 'she knows no better. I ought to be thankful of it.'

'But listen to me,' said the child earnestly, 'will you listen to me?'

'Aye, aye, I'll listen,' returned the old man, still without looking at her; 'a pretty voice. It has always a sweet sound to me. It always had when it was her mother's, poor child.'

'Let me persuade you, then—oh, do let me persuade you,' said the child, 'to think no more of gains or losses, and to try no fortune but the fortune we pursue together.'

'We pursue this aim together,' retorted her grandfather, still looking away and seeming to confer with himself. 'Whose image sanctifies the game?'

'Have we been worse off,' resumed the child, 'since you forgot these cares, and we have been travelling on together? Have we not been much better and happier without a home to shelter us, than ever we were in that unhappy house, when they were on your mind?'

'She speaks the truth,' murmured the old man in the same tone as before. 'It must not turn me, but it is the truth; no doubt it is.'

'Only remember what we have been since that bright morning when we turned our backs upon it for the last time,' said Nell, 'only remember what we have been since we have been free of all those miseries—what peaceful days and quiet nights we have had—what pleasant times we have known—what happiness we have enjoyed. If we have been tired or hungry, we have been soon refreshed, and slept the sounder for it. Think what beautiful things we have seen, and how contented we have felt. And why was this blessed change?'

He stopped her with a motion of his hand, and bade her talk to him no more just then, for he was busy. After a time he kissed her cheek, still motioning her to silence, and walked on, looking far before him, and sometimes stopping and gazing with a puckered brow upon the ground, as if he were painfully trying to collect his disordered thoughts. Once she saw tears in his eyes. When he had gone on thus for some time, he took her hand in his as he was accustomed to do, with nothing of the violence or animation of his late manner; and so, by degrees so fine that the child could not trace them, he settled down into his usual quiet way, and suffered her to lead him where she would.

When they presented themselves in the midst of the stupendous collection, they found, as Nell had anticipated, that Mrs Jarley was not yet out of bed, and that, although she had suffered some uneasiness on their account overnight, and had indeed sat up for them until past eleven o'clock, she had retired in the persuasion, that, being overtaken by storm at some distance from home, they had sought the nearest shelter, and would not return before morning. Nell immediately applied herself with great assiduity to the decoration and preparation of the room, and had the satisfaction of completing her task, and dressing herself neatly, before the beloved of the Royal Family came down to breakfast.

'We haven't had,' said Mrs Jarley when the meal was over, 'more than eight of Miss Monflathers's young ladies all the time we've been here, and there's twenty-six of 'em, as I was told by the cook when I asked her a question or two and put her on the free-list. We must try 'em with a parcel of new bills, and you shall take it, my dear, and see what effect that has upon 'em.'

The proposed expedition being one of paramount importance, Mrs Jarley adjusted Nell's bonnet with her own hands, and declaring that she certainly did look very pretty, and reflected credit on the establishment, dismissed her with many commendations, and certain needful directions as to the turnings on the right which she was to take, and the turnings on the left which she was to avoid. Thus instructed, Nell had no difficulty in finding out Miss Monflathers's Boarding and Day Establishment, which was a large house, with a high wall, and a large garden-gate with a large brass plate, and a small grating through which Miss Monflathers's parlour-maid inspected all visitors before admitting them; for nothing in the shape of a man—no, not even a milkman—was suffered, without special license, to pass that gate. Even the tax-gatherer, who was stout, and wore spectacles and a broad-brimmed hat, had the taxes handed through the grating. More obdurate than gate of adamant or brass, this gate of Miss Monflathers's frowned on all mankind. The very butcher respected it as a gate of mystery, and left off whistling when he rang the bell.

As Nell approached the awful door, it turned slowly upon its hinges with a creaking noise, and, forth from the solemn grove beyond, came a long file of young ladies, two and two, all with open books in their hands, and some with parasols likewise. And last of the goodly procession came Miss Monflathers, bearing herself a parasol of lilac silk, and supported by two smiling teachers, each mortally envious of the other, and devoted unto Miss Monflathers.

Confused by the looks and whispers of the girls, Nell stood with downcast eyes and suffered the procession to pass on, until Miss Monflathers, bringing up the rear, approached her, when she curtseyed and presented her little packet; on receipt whereof Miss Monflathers commanded that the line should halt.

'You're the wax-work child, are you not?' said Miss Monflathers.

'Yes, ma'am,' replied Nell, colouring deeply, for the young ladies had collected about her, and she was the centre on which all eyes were fixed.

'And don't you think you must be a very wicked little child,' said Miss Monflathers, who was of rather uncertain temper, and lost no opportunity of impressing moral truths upon the tender minds of the young ladies, 'to be a wax-work child at all?'

Poor Nell had never viewed her position in this light, and not knowing what to say, remained silent, blushing more deeply than before.

'Don't you know,' said Miss Monflathers, 'that it's very naughty and unfeminine, and a perversion of the properties wisely and benignantly transmitted to us, with expansive powers to be roused from their dormant state through the medium of cultivation?'

The two teachers murmured their respectful approval of this home-thrust, and looked at Nell as though they would have said that there indeed Miss Monflathers had hit her very hard. Then they smiled and glanced at Miss Monflathers, and then, their eyes meeting, they exchanged looks which plainly said that each considered herself smiler in ordinary to Miss Monflathers, and regarded the other as having no right to smile, and that her so doing was an act of presumption and impertinence.

'Don't you feel how naughty it is of you,' resumed Miss Monflathers, 'to be a wax-work child, when you might have the proud consciousness of assisting, to the extent of your infant powers, the manufactures of your country; of improving your mind by the constant contemplation of the steam-engine; and of earning a comfortable and independent subsistence of from two-and-ninepence to three shillings per week? Don't you know that the harder you are at work, the happier you are?'

'"How doth the little—"' murmured one of the teachers, in quotation from Doctor Watts.

'Eh?' said Miss Monflathers, turning smartly round. 'Who said that?'

Of course the teacher who had not said it, indicated the rival who had, whom Miss Monflathers frowningly requested to hold her peace; by that means throwing the informing teacher into raptures of joy.

'The little busy bee,' said Miss Monflathers, drawing herself up, 'is applicable only to genteel children.

"In books, or work, or healthful play"

is quite right as far as they are concerned; and the work means painting on velvet, fancy needle-work, or embroidery. In such cases as these,' pointing to Nell, with her parasol, 'and in the case of all poor people's children, we should read it thus:

"In work, work, work. In work alway

Let my first years be past,

That I may give for ev'ry day

Some good account at last."'

A deep hum of applause rose not only from the two teachers, but from all the pupils, who were equally astonished to hear Miss Monflathers improvising after this brilliant style; for although she had been long known as a politician, she had never appeared before as an original poet. Just then somebody happened to discover that Nell was crying, and all eyes were again turned towards her.

There were indeed tears in her eyes, and drawing out her handkerchief to brush them away, she happened to let it fall. Before she could stoop to pick it up, one young lady of about fifteen or sixteen, who had been standing a little apart from the others, as though she had no recognised place among them, sprang forward and put it in her hand. She was gliding timidly away again, when she was arrested by the governess.

'It was Miss Edwards who did that, I know,' said Miss Monflathers predictively. 'Now I am sure that was Miss Edwards.'

It was Miss Edwards, and everybody said it was Miss Edwards, and Miss Edwards herself admitted that it was.

'Is it not,' said Miss Monflathers, putting down her parasol to take a severer view of the offender, 'a most remarkable thing, Miss Edwards, that you have an attachment to the lower classes which always draws you to their sides; or, rather, is it not a most extraordinary thing that all I say and do will not wean you from propensities which your original station in life have unhappily rendered habitual to you, you extremely vulgar-minded girl?'

'I really intended no harm, ma'am,' said a sweet voice. 'It was a momentary impulse, indeed.'

'An impulse!' repeated Miss Monflathers scornfully. 'I wonder that you presume to speak of impulses to me'—both the teachers assented—'I am astonished'—both the teachers were astonished—'I suppose it is an impulse which induces you to take the part of every grovelling and debased person that comes in your way'—both the teachers supposed so too.

'But I would have you know, Miss Edwards,' resumed the governess in a tone of increased severity, 'that you cannot be permitted—if it be only for the sake of preserving a proper example and decorum in this establishment—that you cannot be permitted, and that you shall not be permitted, to fly in the face of your superiors in this exceedingly gross manner. If you have no reason to feel a becoming pride before wax-work children, there are young ladies here who have, and you must either defer to those young ladies or leave the establishment, Miss Edwards.'

This young lady, being motherless and poor, was apprenticed at the school—taught for nothing—teaching others what she learnt, for nothing—boarded for nothing—lodged for nothing—and set down and rated as something immeasurably less than nothing, by all the dwellers in the house. The servant-maids felt her inferiority, for they were better treated; free to come and go, and regarded in their stations with much more respect. The teachers were infinitely superior, for they had paid to go to school in their time, and were paid now. The pupils cared little for a companion who had no grand stories to tell about home; no friends to come with post-horses, and be received in all humility, with cake and wine, by the governess; no deferential servant to attend and bear her home for the holidays; nothing genteel to talk about, and nothing to display. But why was Miss Monflathers always vexed and irritated with the poor apprentice—how did that come to pass?

Why, the gayest feather in Miss Monflathers's cap, and the brightest glory of Miss Monflathers's school, was a baronet's daughter—the real live daughter of a real live baronet— who, by some extraordinary reversal of the Laws of Nature, was not only plain in features but dull in intellect, while the poor apprentice had both a ready wit, and a handsome face and figure. It seems incredible. Here was Miss Edwards, who only paid a small premium which had been spent long ago, every day outshining and excelling the baronet's daughter, who learned all the extras (or was taught them all) and whose half-yearly bill came to double that of any other young lady's in the school, making no account of the honour and reputation of her pupilage. Therefore, and because she was a dependent, Miss Monflathers had a great dislike to Miss Edwards, and was spiteful to her, and aggravated by her, and, when she had compassion on little Nell, verbally fell upon and maltreated her as we have already seen.

'You will not take the air to-day, Miss Edwards,' said Miss Monflathers. 'Have the goodness to retire to your own room, and not to leave it without permission.'

The poor girl was moving hastily away, when she was suddenly, in nautical phrase, 'brought to' by a subdued shriek from Miss Monflathers.

'She has passed me without any salute!' cried the governess, raising her eyes to the sky. 'She has actually passed me without the slightest acknowledgment of my presence!'

The young lady turned and curtsied. Nell could see that she raised her dark eyes to the face of her superior, and that their expression, and that of her whole attitude for the instant, was one of mute but most touching appeal against this ungenerous usage. Miss Monflathers only tossed her head in reply, and the great gate closed upon a bursting heart.

'As for you, you wicked child,' said Miss Monflathers, turning to Nell, 'tell your mistress that if she presumes to take the liberty of sending to me any more, I will write to the legislative authorities and have her put in the stocks, or compelled to do penance in a white sheet; and you may depend upon it that you shall certainly experience the treadmill if you dare to come here again. Now ladies, on.'

The procession filed off, two and two, with the books and parasols, and Miss Monflathers, calling the Baronet's daughter to walk with her and smooth her ruffled feelings, discarded the two teachers—who by this time had exchanged their smiles for looks of sympathy—and left them to bring up the rear, and hate each other a little more for being obliged to walk together.

CHAPTER 32

Mrs Jarley's wrath on first learning that she had been threatened with the indignity of Stocks and Penance, passed all description. The genuine and only Jarley exposed to public scorn, jeered by children, and flouted by beadles! The delight of the Nobility and Gentry shorn of a bonnet which a Lady Mayoress might have sighed to wear, and arrayed in a white sheet as a spectacle of mortification and humility! And Miss Monflathers, the audacious creature who presumed, even in the dimmest and remotest distance of her imagination, to conjure up the degrading picture, 'I am a'most inclined,' said Mrs Jarley, bursting with the fulness of her anger and the weakness of her means of revenge, 'to turn atheist when I think of it!'

But instead of adopting this course of retaliation, Mrs Jarley, on second thoughts, brought out the suspicious bottle, and ordering glasses to be set forth upon her favourite drum, and sinking into a chair behind it, called her satellites about her, and to them several times recounted, word for word, the affronts she had received. This done, she begged them in a kind of deep despair to drink; then laughed, then cried, then took a little sip herself, then laughed and cried again, and took a little more; and so, by degrees, the worthy lady went on, increasing in smiles and decreasing in tears, until at last she could not laugh enough at Miss Monflathers, who, from being an object of dire vexation, became one of sheer ridicule and absurdity.

'For which of us is best off, I wonder,' quoth Mrs Jarley, 'she or me! It's only talking, when all is said and done, and if she talks of me in the stocks, why I can talk of her in the stocks, which is a good deal funnier if we come to that. Lord, what does it matter, after all!'

Having arrived at this comfortable frame of mind (to which she had been greatly assisted by certain short interjectional remarks of the philosophical George), Mrs Jarley consoled Nell with many kind words, and requested as a personal favour that whenever she thought of Miss Monflathers, she would do nothing else but laugh at her, all the days of her life.

So ended Mrs Jarley's wrath, which subsided long before the going down of the sun. Nell's anxieties, however, were of a deeper kind, and the checks they imposed upon her cheerfulness were not so easily removed.

That evening, as she had dreaded, her grandfather stole away, and did not come back until the night was far spent. Worn out as she was, and fatigued in mind and body, she sat up alone, counting the minutes, until he returned—penniless, broken-spirited, and wretched, but still hotly bent upon his infatuation.

'Get me money,' he said wildly, as they parted for the night. 'I must have money, Nell. It shall be paid thee back with gallant interest one day, but all the money that comes into thy hands, must be mine—not for myself, but to use for thee. Remember, Nell, to use for thee!'

What could the child do with the knowledge she had, but give him every penny that came into her hands, lest he should be tempted on to rob their benefactress? If she told the truth (so thought the child) he would be treated as a madman; if she did not supply him with money, he would supply himself; supplying him, she fed the fire that burnt him up, and put him perhaps beyond recovery. Distracted by these thoughts, borne down by the weight of the sorrow which she dared not tell, tortured by a crowd of apprehensions whenever the old man was absent, and dreading alike his stay and his return, the colour forsook her cheek, her eye grew dim, and her heart was oppressed and heavy. All her old sorrows had come back upon her, augmented by new fears and doubts; by day they were ever present to her mind; by night they hovered round her pillow, and haunted her in dreams.

It was natural that, in the midst of her affliction, she should often revert to that sweet young lady of whom she had only caught a hasty glance, but whose sympathy, expressed in one slight brief action, dwelt in her memory like the kindnesses of years. She would often think, if she had such a friend as that to whom to tell her griefs, how much lighter her heart would be—that if she were but free to hear that voice, she would be happier. Then she would wish that she were something better, that she were not quite so poor and humble, that she dared address her without fearing a repulse; and then feel that there was an immeasurable distance between them, and have no hope that the young lady thought of her any more.

It was now holiday-time at the schools, and the young ladies had gone home, and Miss Monflathers was reported to be flourishing in London, and damaging the hearts of middle-aged gentlemen, but nobody said anything about Miss Edwards, whether she had gone home, or whether she had any home to go to, whether she was still at the school, or anything about her. But one evening, as Nell was returning from a lonely walk, she happened to pass the inn where the stage-coaches stopped, just as one drove up, and there was the beautiful girl she so well remembered, pressing forward to embrace a young child whom they were helping down from the roof.

Well, this was her sister, her little sister, much younger than Nell, whom she had not seen (so the story went afterwards) for five years, and to bring whom to that place on a short visit, she had been saving her poor means all that time. Nell felt as if her heart would break when she saw them meet. They went a little apart from the knot of people who had congregated about the coach, and fell upon each other's neck, and sobbed, and wept with joy. Their plain and simple dress, the distance which the child had come alone, their agitation and delight, and the tears they shed, would have told their history by themselves.

They became a little more composed in a short time, and went away, not so much hand in hand as clinging to each other. 'Are you sure you're happy, sister?' said the child as they passed where Nell was standing. 'Quite happy now,' she answered. 'But always?' said the child. 'Ah, sister, why do you turn away your face?'

Nell could not help following at a little distance. They went to the house of an old nurse, where the elder sister had engaged a bed-room for the child. 'I shall come to you early every morning,' she said, 'and we can be together all the day.'

'Why not at night-time too? Dear sister, would they be angry with you for that?'

Why were the eyes of little Nell wet, that night, with tears like those of the two sisters? Why did she bear a grateful heart because they had met, and feel it pain to think that they would shortly part? Let us not believe that any selfish reference—unconscious though it might have been—to her own trials awoke this sympathy, but thank God that the innocent joys of others can strongly move us, and that we, even in our fallen nature, have one source of pure emotion which must be prized in Heaven!

By morning's cheerful glow, but oftener still by evening's gentle light, the child, with a respect for the short and happy intercourse of these two sisters which forbade her to approach and say a thankful word, although she yearned to do so, followed them at a distance in their walks and rambles, stopping when they stopped, sitting on the grass when they sat down, rising when they went on, and feeling it a companionship and delight to be so near them. Their evening walk was by a river's side. Here, every night, the child was too, unseen by them, unthought of, unregarded; but feeling as if they were her friends, as if they had confidences and trusts together, as if her load were lightened and less hard to bear; as if they mingled their sorrows, and found mutual consolation. It was a weak fancy perhaps, the childish fancy of a young and lonely creature; but night after night, and still the sisters loitered in the same place, and still the child followed with a mild and softened heart.

She was much startled, on returning home one night, to find that Mrs Jarley had commanded an announcement to be prepared, to the effect that the stupendous collection would only remain in its present quarters one day longer; in fulfilment of which threat (for all announcements connected with public amusements are well known to be irrevocable and most exact), the stupendous collection shut up next day.

'Are we going from this place directly, ma'am?' said Nell.

'Look here, child,' returned Mrs Jarley. 'That'll inform you.' And so saying Mrs Jarley produced another announcement, wherein it was stated, that, in consequence of numerous inquiries at the wax-work door, and in consequence of crowds having been disappointed in obtaining admission, the Exhibition would be continued for one week longer, and would re-open next day.

'For now that the schools are gone, and the regular sight-seers exhausted,' said Mrs Jarley, 'we come to the General Public, and they want stimulating.'

Upon the following day at noon, Mrs Jarley established herself behind the highly-ornamented table, attended by the distinguished effigies before mentioned, and ordered the doors to be thrown open for the readmission of a discerning and enlightened public. But the first day's operations were by no means of a successful character, inasmuch as the general public, though they manifested a lively interest in Mrs Jarley personally, and such of her waxen satellites as were to be seen for nothing, were not affected by any impulses moving them to the payment of sixpence a head. Thus, notwithstanding that a great many people continued to stare at the entry and the figures therein displayed; and remained there with great perseverance, by the hour at a time, to hear the barrel-organ played and to read the bills; and notwithstanding that they were kind enough to recommend their friends to patronise the exhibition in the like manner, until the door-way was regularly blockaded by half the population of the town, who, when they went off duty, were relieved by the other half; it was not found that the treasury was any the richer, or that the prospects of the establishment were at all encouraging.

In this depressed state of the classical market, Mrs Jarley made extraordinary efforts to stimulate the popular taste, and whet the popular curiosity. Certain machinery in the body of the nun on the leads over the door was cleaned up and put in motion, so that the figure shook its head paralytically all day long, to the great admiration of a drunken, but very Protestant, barber over the way, who looked upon the said paralytic motion as typical of the degrading effect wrought upon the human mind by the ceremonies of the Romish Church and discoursed upon that theme with great eloquence and morality. The two carters constantly passed in and out of the exhibition-room, under various disguises, protesting aloud that the sight was better worth the money than anything they had beheld in all their lives, and urging the bystanders, with tears in their eyes, not to neglect such a brilliant gratification. Mrs Jarley sat in the pay-place, chinking silver moneys from noon till night, and solemnly calling upon the crowd to take notice that the price of admission was only sixpence, and that the departure of the whole collection, on a short tour among the Crowned Heads of Europe, was positively fixed for that day week.

'So be in time, be in time, be in time,' said Mrs Jarley at the close of every such address. 'Remember that this is Jarley's stupendous collection of upwards of One Hundred Figures, and that it is the only collection in the world; all others being imposters and deceptions. Be in time, be in time, be in time!'

CHAPTER 33

As the course of this tale requires that we should become acquainted, somewhere hereabouts, with a few particulars connected with the domestic economy of Mr Sampson Brass, and as a more convenient place than the present is not likely to occur for that purpose, the historian takes the friendly reader by the hand, and springing with him into the air, and cleaving the same at a greater rate than ever Don Cleophas Leandro Perez Zambullo and his familiar travelled through that pleasant region in company, alights with him upon the pavement of Bevis Marks.

The intrepid aeronauts alight before a small dark house, once the residence of Mr Sampson Brass.

In the parlour window of this little habitation, which is so close upon the footway that the passenger who takes the wall brushes the dim glass with his coat sleeve—much to its improvement, for it is very dirty—in this parlour window in the days of its occupation by Sampson Brass, there hung, all awry and slack, and discoloured by the sun, a curtain of faded green, so threadbare from long service as by no means to intercept the view of the little dark room, but rather to afford a favourable medium through which to observe it accurately. There was not much to look at. A rickety table, with spare bundles of papers, yellow and ragged from long carriage in the pocket, ostentatiously displayed upon its top; a couple of stools set face to face on opposite sides of this crazy piece of furniture; a treacherous old chair by the fire-place, whose withered arms had hugged full many a client and helped to squeeze him dry; a second-hand wig box, used as a depository for blank writs and declarations and other small forms of law, once the sole contents of the head which belonged to the wig which belonged to the box, as they were now of the box itself; two or three common books of practice; a jar of ink, a pounce box, a stunted hearth-broom, a carpet trodden to shreds but still clinging with the tightness of desperation to its tacks—these, with the yellow wainscot of the walls, the smoke-discoloured ceiling, the dust and cobwebs, were among the most prominent decorations of the office of Mr Sampson Brass.

But this was mere still-life, of no greater importance than the plate, 'Brass, Solicitor,' upon the door, and the bill, 'First floor to let to a single gentleman,' which was tied to the knocker. The office commonly held two examples of animated nature, more to the purpose of this history, and in whom it has a stronger interest and more particular concern.

Of these, one was Mr Brass himself, who has already appeared in these pages. The other was his clerk, assistant, housekeeper, secretary, confidential plotter, adviser, intriguer, and bill of cost increaser, Miss Brass—a kind of amazon at common law, of whom it may be desirable to offer a brief description.

Miss Sally Brass, then, was a lady of thirty-five or thereabouts, of a gaunt and bony figure, and a resolute bearing, which if it repressed the softer emotions of love, and kept admirers at a distance, certainly inspired a feeling akin to awe in the breasts of those male strangers who had the happiness to approach her. In face she bore a striking resemblance to her brother, Sampson—so exact, indeed, was the likeness between them, that had it consorted with Miss Brass's maiden modesty and gentle womanhood to have assumed her brother's clothes in a frolic and sat down beside him, it would have been difficult for the oldest friend of the family to determine which was Sampson and which Sally, especially as the lady carried upon her upper lip certain reddish demonstrations, which, if the imagination had been assisted by her attire, might have been mistaken for a beard. These were, however, in all probability, nothing more than eyelashes in a wrong place, as the eyes of Miss Brass were quite free from any such natural impertinencies. In complexion Miss Brass was sallow—rather a dirty sallow, so to speak—but this hue was agreeably relieved by the healthy glow which mantled in the extreme tip of her laughing nose. Her voice was exceedingly impressive—deep and rich in quality, and, once heard, not easily forgotten. Her usual dress was a green gown, in colour not unlike the curtain of the office window, made tight to the figure, and terminating at the throat, where it was fastened behind by a peculiarly large and massive button. Feeling, no doubt, that simplicity and plainness are the soul of elegance, Miss Brass wore no collar or kerchief except upon her head, which was invariably ornamented with a brown gauze scarf, like the wing of the fabled vampire, and which, twisted into any form that happened to suggest itself, formed an easy and graceful head-dress.

Such was Miss Brass in person. In mind, she was of a strong and vigorous turn, having from her earliest youth devoted herself with uncommon ardour to the study of law; not wasting her speculations upon its eagle flights, which are rare, but tracing it attentively through all the slippery and eel-like crawlings in which it commonly pursues its way. Nor had she, like many persons of great intellect, confined herself to theory, or stopped short where practical usefulness begins; inasmuch as she could ingross, fair-copy, fill up printed forms with perfect accuracy, and, in short, transact any ordinary duty of the office down to pouncing a skin of parchment or mending a pen. It is difficult to understand how, possessed of these combined attractions, she should remain Miss Brass; but whether she had steeled her heart against mankind, or whether those who might have wooed and won her, were deterred by fears that, being learned in the law, she might have too near her fingers' ends those particular statutes which regulate what are familiarly termed actions for breach, certain it is that she was still in a state of celibacy, and still in daily occupation of her old stool opposite to that of her brother Sampson. And equally certain it is, by the way, that between these two stools a great many people had come to the ground.

One morning Mr Sampson Brass sat upon his stool copying some legal process, and viciously digging his pen deep into the paper, as if he were writing upon the very heart of the party against whom it was directed; and Miss Sally Brass sat upon her stool making a new pen preparatory to drawing out a little bill, which was her favourite occupation; and so they sat in silence for a long time, until Miss Brass broke silence.

'Have you nearly done, Sammy?' said Miss Brass; for in her mild and feminine lips, Sampson became Sammy, and all things were softened down.

'No,' returned her brother. 'It would have been all done though, if you had helped at the right time.'

'Oh yes, indeed,' cried Miss Sally; 'you want my help, don't you?—you, too, that are going to keep a clerk!'

'Am I going to keep a clerk for my own pleasure, or because of my own wish, you provoking rascal!' said Mr Brass, putting his pen in his mouth, and grinning spitefully at his sister. 'What do you taunt me about going to keep a clerk for?'

It may be observed in this place, lest the fact of Mr Brass calling a lady a rascal, should occasion any wonderment or surprise, that he was so habituated to having her near him in a man's capacity, that he had gradually accustomed himself to talk to her as though she were really a man. And this feeling was so perfectly reciprocal, that not only did Mr Brass often call Miss Brass a rascal, or even put an adjective before the rascal, but Miss Brass looked upon it as quite a matter of course, and was as little moved as any other lady would be by being called an angel.

'What do you taunt me, after three hours' talk last night, with going to keep a clerk for?' repeated Mr Brass, grinning again with the pen in his mouth, like some nobleman's or gentleman's crest. 'Is it my fault?'

'All I know is,' said Miss Sally, smiling drily, for she delighted in nothing so much as irritating her brother, 'that if every one of your clients is to force us to keep a clerk, whether we want to or not, you had better leave off business, strike yourself off the roll, and get taken in execution, as soon as you can.'

'Have we got any other client like him?' said Brass. 'Have we got another client like him now—will you answer me that?'

'Do you mean in the face?' said his sister.

'Do I mean in the face!' sneered Sampson Brass, reaching over to take up the bill-book, and fluttering its leaves rapidly. 'Look here—Daniel Quilp, Esquire—Daniel Quilp, Esquire—Daniel Quilp, Esquire—all through. Whether should I take a clerk that he recommends, and says, "this is the man for you," or lose all this, eh?'

Miss Sally deigned to make no reply, but smiled again, and went on with her work.

'But I know what it is,' resumed Brass after a short silence. 'You're afraid you won't have as long a finger in the business as you've been used to have. Do you think I don't see through that?'

'The business wouldn't go on very long, I expect, without me,' returned his sister composedly. 'Don't you be a fool and provoke me, Sammy, but mind what you're doing, and do it.'

Sampson Brass, who was at heart in great fear of his sister, sulkily bent over his writing again, and listened as she said:

'If I determined that the clerk ought not to come, of course he wouldn't be allowed to come. You know that well enough, so don't talk nonsense.'

Mr Brass received this observation with increased meekness, merely remarking, under his breath, that he didn't like that kind of joking, and that Miss Sally would be 'a much better fellow' if she forbore to aggravate him. To this compliment Miss Sally replied, that she had a relish for the amusement, and had no intention to forego its gratification. Mr Brass not caring, as it seemed, to pursue the subject any further, they both plied their pens at a great pace, and there the discussion ended.

While they were thus employed, the window was suddenly darkened, as by some person standing close against it. As Mr Brass and Miss Sally looked up to ascertain the cause, the top sash was nimbly lowered from without, and Quilp thrust in his head.

'Hallo!' he said, standing on tip-toe on the window-sill, and looking down into the room. 'Is there anybody at home? Is there any of the Devil's ware here? Is Brass at a premium, eh?'

'Ha, ha, ha!' laughed the lawyer in an affected ecstasy. 'Oh, very good, Sir! Oh, very good indeed! Quite eccentric! Dear me, what humour he has!'

'Is that my Sally?' croaked the dwarf, ogling the fair Miss Brass. 'Is it Justice with the bandage off her eyes, and without the sword and scales? Is it the Strong Arm of the Law? Is it the Virgin of Bevis?'

'What an amazing flow of spirits!' cried Brass. 'Upon my word, it's quite extraordinary!'

'Open the door,' said Quilp, 'I've got him here. Such a clerk for you, Brass, such a prize, such an ace of trumps. Be quick and open the door, or if there's another lawyer near and he should happen to look out of window, he'll snap him up before your eyes, he will.'

It is probable that the loss of the phoenix of clerks, even to a rival practitioner, would not have broken Mr Brass's heart; but, pretending great alacrity, he rose from his seat, and going to the door, returned, introducing his client, who led by the hand no less a person than Mr Richard Swiveller.

'There she is,' said Quilp, stopping short at the door, and wrinkling up his eyebrows as he looked towards Miss Sally; 'there is the woman I ought to have married—there is the beautiful Sarah—there is the female who has all the charms of her sex and none of their weaknesses. Oh Sally, Sally!'

To this amorous address Miss Brass briefly responded 'Bother!'

'Hard-hearted as the metal from which she takes her name,' said Quilp. 'Why don't she change it—melt down the brass, and take another name?'

'Hold your nonsense, Mr Quilp, do,' returned Miss Sally, with a grim smile. 'I wonder you're not ashamed of yourself before a strange young man.'

'The strange young man,' said Quilp, handing Dick Swiveller forward, 'is too susceptible himself not to understand me well. This is Mr Swiveller, my intimate friend—a gentleman of good family and great expectations, but who, having rather involved himself by youthful indiscretion, is content for a time to fill the humble station of a clerk—humble, but here most enviable. What a delicious atmosphere!'

If Mr Quilp spoke figuratively, and meant to imply that the air breathed by Miss Sally Brass was sweetened and rarefied by that dainty creature, he had doubtless good reason for what he said. But if he spoke of the delights of the atmosphere of Mr Brass's office in a literal sense, he had certainly a peculiar taste, as it was of a close and earthy kind, and, besides being frequently impregnated with strong whiffs of the second-hand wearing apparel exposed for sale in Duke's Place and Houndsditch, had a decided flavour of rats and mice, and a taint of mouldiness. Perhaps some doubts of its pure delight presented themselves to Mr Swiveller, as he gave vent to one or two short abrupt sniffs, and looked incredulously at the grinning dwarf.

'Mr Swiveller,' said Quilp, 'being pretty well accustomed to the agricultural pursuits of sowing wild oats, Miss Sally, prudently considers that half a loaf is better than no bread. To be out of harm's way he prudently thinks is something too, and therefore he accepts your brother's offer. Brass, Mr Swiveller is yours.'

'I am very glad, Sir,' said Mr Brass, 'very glad indeed. Mr Swiveller, Sir, is fortunate enough to have your friendship. You may be very proud, Sir, to have the friendship of Mr Quilp.'

Dick murmured something about never wanting a friend or a bottle to give him, and also gasped forth his favourite allusion to the wing of friendship and its never moulting a feather; but his faculties appeared to be absorbed in the contemplation of Miss Sally Brass, at whom he stared with blank and rueful looks, which delighted the watchful dwarf beyond measure. As to the divine Miss Sally herself, she rubbed her hands as men of business do, and took a few turns up and down the office with her pen behind her ear.

'I suppose,' said the dwarf, turning briskly to his legal friend, 'that Mr Swiveller enters upon his duties at once? It's Monday morning.'

'At once, if you please, Sir, by all means,' returned Brass.

'Miss Sally will teach him law, the delightful study of the law,' said Quilp; 'she'll be his guide, his friend, his companion, his Blackstone, his Coke upon Littleton, his Young Lawyer's Best Companion.'

'He is exceedingly eloquent,' said Brass, like a man abstracted, and looking at the roofs of the opposite houses, with his hands in his pockets; 'he has an extraordinary flow of language. Beautiful, really.'

'With Miss Sally,' Quilp went on, 'and the beautiful fictions of the law, his days will pass like minutes. Those charming creations of the poet, John Doe and Richard Roe, when they first dawn upon him, will open a new world for the enlargement of his mind and the improvement of his heart.'

'Oh, beautiful, beautiful! Beau-ti-ful indeed!' cried Brass. 'It's a treat to hear him!'

'Where will Mr Swiveller sit?' said Quilp, looking round.

'Why, we'll buy another stool, sir,' returned Brass. 'We hadn't any thoughts of having a gentleman with us, sir, until you were kind enough to suggest it, and our accommodation's not extensive. We'll look about for a second-hand stool, sir. In the meantime, if Mr Swiveller will take my seat, and try his hand at a fair copy of this ejectment, as I shall be out pretty well all the morning—'

'Walk with me,' said Quilp. 'I have a word or two to say to you on points of business. Can you spare the time?'

'Can I spare the time to walk with you, sir? You're joking, sir, you're joking with me,' replied the lawyer, putting on his hat. 'I'm ready, sir, quite ready. My time must be fully occupied indeed, sir, not to leave me time to walk with you. It's not everybody, sir, who has an opportunity of improving himself by the conversation of Mr Quilp.'

The dwarf glanced sarcastically at his brazen friend, and, with a short dry cough, turned upon his heel to bid adieu to Miss Sally. After a very gallant parting on his side, and a very cool and gentlemanly sort of one on hers, he nodded to Dick Swiveller, and withdrew with the attorney.

Dick stood at the desk in a state of utter stupefaction, staring with all his might at the beauteous Sally, as if she had been some curious animal whose like had never lived. When the dwarf got into the street, he mounted again upon the window-sill, and looked into the office for a moment with a grinning face, as a man might peep into a cage. Dick glanced upward at him, but without any token of recognition; and long after he had disappeared, still stood gazing upon Miss Sally Brass, seeing or thinking of nothing else, and rooted to the spot.

Miss Brass being by this time deep in the bill of costs, took no notice whatever of Dick, but went scratching on, with a noisy pen, scoring down the figures with evident delight, and working like a steam-engine. There stood Dick, gazing now at the green gown, now at the brown head-dress, now at the face, and now at the rapid pen, in a state of stupid perplexity, wondering how he got into the company of that strange monster, and whether it was a dream and he would ever wake. At last he heaved a deep sigh, and began slowly pulling off his coat.

Mr Swiveller pulled off his coat, and folded it up with great elaboration, staring at Miss Sally all the time; then put on a blue jacket with a double row of gilt buttons, which he had originally ordered for aquatic expeditions, but had brought with him that morning for office purposes; and, still keeping his eye upon her, suffered himself to drop down silently upon Mr Brass's stool. Then he underwent a relapse, and becoming powerless again, rested his chin upon his hand, and opened his eyes so wide, that it appeared quite out of the question that he could ever close them any more.

When he had looked so long that he could see nothing, Dick took his eyes off the fair object of his amazement, turned over the leaves of the draft he was to copy, dipped his pen into the inkstand, and at last, and by slow approaches, began to write. But he had not written half-a-dozen words when, reaching over to the inkstand to take a fresh dip, he happened to raise his eyes. There was the intolerable brown head-dress—there was the green gown—there, in short, was Miss Sally Brass, arrayed in all her charms, and more tremendous than ever.

This happened so often, that Mr Swiveller by degrees began to feel strange influences creeping over him—horrible desires to annihilate this Sally Brass—mysterious promptings to knock her head-dress off and try how she looked without it. There was a very large ruler on the table; a large, black, shining ruler. Mr Swiveller took it up and began to rub his nose with it.

From rubbing his nose with the ruler, to poising it in his hand and giving it an occasional flourish after the tomahawk manner, the transition was easy and natural. In some of these flourishes it went close to Miss Sally's head; the ragged edges of the head-dress fluttered with the wind it raised; advance it but an inch, and that great brown knot was on the ground: yet still the unconscious maiden worked away, and never raised her eyes.

Well, this was a great relief. It was a good thing to write doggedly and obstinately until he was desperate, and then snatch up the ruler and whirl it about the brown head-dress with the consciousness that he could have it off if he liked. It was a good thing to draw it back, and rub his nose very hard with it, if he thought Miss Sally was going to look up, and to recompense himself with more hardy flourishes when he found she was still absorbed. By these means Mr Swiveller calmed the agitation of his feelings, until his applications to the ruler became less fierce and frequent, and he could even write as many as half-a-dozen consecutive lines without having recourse to it—which was a great victory.

CHAPTER 34

In course of time, that is to say, after a couple of hours or so, of diligent application, Miss Brass arrived at the conclusion of her task, and recorded the fact by wiping her pen upon the green gown, and taking a pinch of snuff from a little round tin box which she carried in her pocket. Having disposed of this temperate refreshment, she arose from her stool, tied her papers into a formal packet with red tape, and taking them under her arm, marched out of the office.

Mr Swiveller had scarcely sprung off his seat and commenced the performance of a maniac hornpipe, when he was interrupted, in the fulness of his joy at being again alone, by the opening of the door, and the reappearance of Miss Sally's head.

'I am going out,' said Miss Brass.

'Very good, ma'am,' returned Dick. 'And don't hurry yourself on my account to come back, ma'am,' he added inwardly.

'If anybody comes on office business, take their messages, and say that the gentleman who attends to that matter isn't in at present, will you?' said Miss Brass.

'I will, ma'am,' replied Dick.

'I shan't be very long,' said Miss Brass, retiring.

'I'm sorry to hear it, ma'am,' rejoined Dick when she had shut the door. 'I hope you may be unexpectedly detained, ma'am. If you could manage to be run over, ma'am, but not seriously, so much the better.'

Uttering these expressions of good-will with extreme gravity, Mr Swiveller sat down in the client's chair and pondered; then took a few turns up and down the room and fell into the chair again.

'So I'm Brass's clerk, am I?' said Dick. 'Brass's clerk, eh? And the clerk of Brass's sister—clerk to a female Dragon. Very good, very good! What shall I be next? Shall I be a convict in a felt hat and a grey suit, trotting about a dockyard with my number neatly embroidered on my uniform, and the order of the garter on my leg, restrained from chafing my ankle by a twisted belcher handkerchief? Shall I be that? Will that do, or is it too genteel? Whatever you please, have it your own way, of course.'

As he was entirely alone, it may be presumed that, in these remarks, Mr Swiveller addressed himself to his fate or destiny, whom, as we learn by the precedents, it is the custom of heroes to taunt in a very bitter and ironical manner when they find themselves in situations of an unpleasant nature. This is the more probable from the circumstance of Mr Swiveller directing his observations to the ceiling, which these bodily personages are usually supposed to inhabit—except in theatrical cases, when they live in the heart of the great chandelier.

'Quilp offers me this place, which he says he can insure me,' resumed Dick after a thoughtful silence, and telling off the circumstances of his position, one by one, upon his fingers; 'Fred, who, I could have taken my affidavit, would not have heard of such a thing, backs Quilp to my astonishment, and urges me to take it also—staggerer, number one! My aunt in the country stops the supplies, and writes an affectionate note to say that she has made a new will, and left me out of it—staggerer, number two. No money; no credit; no support from Fred, who seems to turn steady all at once; notice to quit the old lodgings—staggerers, three, four, five, and six! Under an accumulation of staggerers, no man can be considered a free agent. No man knocks himself down; if his destiny knocks him down, his destiny must pick him up again. Then I'm very glad that mine has brought all this upon itself, and I shall be as careless as I can, and make myself quite at home to spite it. So go on my buck,' said Mr Swiveller, taking his leave of the ceiling with a significant nod, 'and let us see which of us will be tired first!'

Dismissing the subject of his downfall with these reflections, which were no doubt very profound, and are indeed not altogether unknown in certain systems of moral philosophy, Mr Swiveller shook off his despondency and assumed the cheerful ease of an irresponsible clerk.

As a means towards his composure and self-possession, he entered into a more minute examination of the office than he had yet had time to make; looked into the wig-box, the books, and ink-bottle; untied and inspected all the papers; carved a few devices on the table with a sharp blade of Mr Brass's penknife; and wrote his name on the inside of the wooden coal-scuttle. Having, as it were, taken formal possession of his clerkship in virtue of these proceedings, he opened the window and leaned negligently out of it until a beer-boy happened to pass, whom he commanded to set down his tray and to serve him with a pint of mild porter, which he drank upon the spot and promptly paid for, with the view of breaking ground for a system of future credit and opening a correspondence tending thereto, without loss of time. Then, three or four little boys dropped in, on legal errands from three or four attorneys of the Brass grade: whom Mr Swiveller received and dismissed with about as professional a manner, and as correct and comprehensive an understanding of their business, as would have been shown by a clown in a pantomime under similar circumstances. These things done and over, he got upon his stool again and tried his hand at drawing caricatures of Miss Brass with a pen and ink, whistling very cheerfully all the time.

He was occupied in this diversion when a coach stopped near the door, and presently afterwards there was a loud double-knock. As this was no business of Mr Swiveller's, the person not ringing the office bell, he pursued his diversion with perfect composure, notwithstanding that he rather thought there was nobody else in the house.

In this, however, he was mistaken; for, after the knock had been repeated with increased impatience, the door was opened, and somebody with a very heavy tread went up the stairs and into the room above. Mr Swiveller was wondering whether this might be another Miss Brass, twin sister to the Dragon, when there came a rapping of knuckles at the office door.

'Come in!' said Dick. 'Don't stand upon ceremony. The business will get rather complicated if I've many more customers. Come in!'

'Oh, please,' said a little voice very low down in the doorway, 'will you come and show the lodgings?'

Dick leant over the table, and descried a small slipshod girl in a dirty coarse apron and bib, which left nothing of her visible but her face and feet. She might as well have been dressed in a violin-case.

'Why, who are you?' said Dick.

To which the only reply was, 'Oh, please will you come and show the lodgings?'

There never was such an old-fashioned child in her looks and manner. She must have been at work from her cradle. She seemed as much afraid of Dick, as Dick was amazed at her.

'I hav'n't got anything to do with the lodgings,' said Dick. 'Tell 'em to call again.'

'Oh, but please will you come and show the lodgings,' returned the girl; 'It's eighteen shillings a week and us finding plate and linen. Boots and clothes is extra, and fires in winter-time is eightpence a day.'

'Why don't you show 'em yourself? You seem to know all about 'em,' said Dick.

'Miss Sally said I wasn't to, because people wouldn't believe the attendance was good if they saw how small I was first.'

'Well, but they'll see how small you are afterwards, won't they?' said Dick.

'Ah! But then they'll have taken 'em for a fortnight certain,' replied the child with a shrewd look; 'and people don't like moving when they're once settled.'

'This is a queer sort of thing,' muttered Dick, rising. 'What do you mean to say you are—the cook?'

'Yes, I do plain cooking;' replied the child. 'I'm housemaid too; I do all the work of the house.'

'I suppose Brass and the Dragon and I do the dirtiest part of it,' thought Dick. And he might have thought much more, being in a doubtful and hesitating mood, but that the girl again urged her request, and certain mysterious bumping sounds on the passage and staircase seemed to give note of the applicant's impatience. Richard Swiveller, therefore, sticking a pen behind each ear, and carrying another in his mouth as a token of his great importance and devotion to business, hurried out to meet and treat with the single gentleman.

He was a little surprised to perceive that the bumping sounds were occasioned by the progress up-stairs of the single gentleman's trunk, which, being nearly twice as wide as the staircase, and exceedingly heavy withal, it was no easy matter for the united exertions of the single gentleman and the coachman to convey up the steep ascent. But there they were, crushing each other, and pushing and pulling with all their might, and getting the trunk tight and fast in all kinds of impossible angles, and to pass them was out of the question; for which sufficient reason, Mr Swiveller followed slowly behind, entering a new protest on every stair against the house of Mr Sampson Brass being thus taken by storm.

To these remonstrances, the single gentleman answered not a word, but when the trunk was at last got into the bed-room, sat down upon it and wiped his bald head and face with his handkerchief. He was very warm, and well he might be; for, not to mention the exertion of getting the trunk up stairs, he was closely muffled in winter garments, though the thermometer had stood all day at eighty-one in the shade.

'I believe, sir,' said Richard Swiveller, taking his pen out of his mouth, 'that you desire to look at these apartments. They are very charming apartments, sir. They command an uninterrupted view of—of over the way, and they are within one minute's walk of—of the corner of the street. There is exceedingly mild porter, sir, in the immediate vicinity, and the contingent advantages are extraordinary.'

'What's the rent?' said the single gentleman.

'One pound per week,' replied Dick, improving on the terms.

'I'll take 'em.'

'The boots and clothes are extras,' said Dick; 'and the fires in winter time are—'

'Are all agreed to,' answered the single gentleman.

'Two weeks certain,' said Dick, 'are the—'

'Two weeks!' cried the single gentleman gruffly, eyeing him from top to toe. 'Two years. I shall live here for two years. Here. Ten pounds down. The bargain's made.'

'Why you see,' said Dick, 'my name is not Brass, and—'

'Who said it was? My name's not Brass. What then?'

'The name of the master of the house is,' said Dick.

'I'm glad of it,' returned the single gentleman; 'it's a good name for a lawyer. Coachman, you may go. So may you, Sir.'

Mr Swiveller was so much confounded by the single gentleman riding roughshod over him at this rate, that he stood looking at him almost as hard as he had looked at Miss Sally. The single gentleman, however, was not in the slightest degree affected by this circumstance, but proceeded with perfect composure to unwind the shawl which was tied round his neck, and then to pull off his boots. Freed of these encumbrances, he went on to divest himself of his other clothing, which he folded up, piece by piece, and ranged in order on the trunk. Then, he pulled down the window-blinds, drew the curtains, wound up his watch, and, quite leisurely and methodically, got into bed.

'Take down the bill,' were his parting words, as he looked out from between the curtains; 'and let nobody call me till I ring the bell.'

With that the curtains closed, and he seemed to snore immediately.

'This is a most remarkable and supernatural sort of house!' said Mr Swiveller, as he walked into the office with the bill in his hand. 'She-dragons in the business, conducting themselves like professional gentlemen; plain cooks of three feet high appearing mysteriously from under ground; strangers walking in and going to bed without leave or licence in the middle of the day! If he should be one of the miraculous fellows that turn up now and then, and has gone to sleep for two years, I shall be in a pleasant situation. It's my destiny, however, and I hope Brass may like it. I shall be sorry if he don't. But it's no business of mine—I have nothing whatever to do with it!'

CHAPTER 35

Mr Brass on returning home received the report of his clerk with much complacency and satisfaction, and was particular in inquiring after the ten-pound note, which, proving on examination to be a good and lawful note of the Governor and Company of the Bank of England, increased his good-humour considerably. Indeed he so overflowed with liberality and condescension, that, in the fulness of his heart, he invited Mr Swiveller to partake of a bowl of punch with him at that remote and indefinite period which is currently denominated 'one of these days,' and paid him many handsome compliments on the uncommon aptitude for business which his conduct on the first day of his devotion to it had so plainly evinced.

It was a maxim with Mr Brass that the habit of paying compliments kept a man's tongue oiled without any expense; and, as that useful member ought never to grow rusty or creak in turning on its hinges in the case of a practitioner of the law, in whom it should be always glib and easy, he lost few opportunities of improving himself by the utterance of handsome speeches and eulogistic expressions. And this had passed into such a habit with him, that, if he could not be correctly said to have his tongue at his fingers' ends, he might certainly be said to have it anywhere but in his face: which being, as we have already seen, of a harsh and repulsive character, was not oiled so easily, but frowned above all the smooth speeches—one of nature's beacons, warning off those who navigated the shoals and breakers of the World, or of that dangerous strait the Law, and admonishing them to seek less treacherous harbours and try their fortune elsewhere.

While Mr Brass by turns overwhelmed his clerk with compliments and inspected the ten-pound note, Miss Sally showed little emotion and that of no pleasurable kind, for as the tendency of her legal practice had been to fix her thoughts on small gains and gripings, and to whet and sharpen her natural wisdom, she was not a little disappointed that the single gentleman had obtained the lodgings at such an easy rate, arguing that when he was seen to have set his mind upon them, he should have been at the least charged double or treble the usual terms, and that, in exact proportion as he pressed forward, Mr Swiveller should have hung back. But neither the good opinion of Mr Brass, nor the dissatisfaction of Miss Sally, wrought any impression upon that young gentleman, who, throwing the responsibility of this and all other acts and deeds thereafter to be done by him, upon his unlucky destiny, was quite resigned and comfortable: fully prepared for the worst, and philosophically indifferent to the best.

'Good morning, Mr Richard,' said Brass, on the second day of Mr Swiveller's clerkship. 'Sally found you a second-hand stool, Sir, yesterday evening, in Whitechapel. She's a rare fellow at a bargain, I can tell you, Mr Richard. You'll find that a first-rate stool, Sir, take my word for it.'

'It's rather a crazy one to look at,' said Dick.

'You'll find it a most amazing stool to sit down upon, you may depend,' returned Mr Brass. 'It was bought in the open street just opposite the hospital, and as it has been standing there a month of two, it has got rather dusty and a little brown from being in the sun, that's all.'

'I hope it hasn't got any fevers or anything of that sort in it,' said Dick, sitting himself down discontentedly, between Mr Sampson and the chaste Sally. 'One of the legs is longer than the others.'

'Then we get a bit of timber in, Sir,' retorted Brass. 'Ha, ha, ha! We get a bit of timber in, Sir, and that's another advantage of my sister's going to market for us. Miss Brass, Mr Richard is the—'

'Will you keep quiet?' interrupted the fair subject of these remarks, looking up from her papers. 'How am I to work if you keep on chattering?'

'What an uncertain chap you are!' returned the lawyer. 'Sometimes you're all for a chat. At another time you're all for work. A man never knows what humour he'll find you in.'

'I'm in a working humour now,' said Sally, 'so don't disturb me, if you please. And don't take him,' Miss Sally pointed with the feather of her pen to Richard, 'off his business. He won't do more than he can help, I dare say.'

Mr Brass had evidently a strong inclination to make an angry reply, but was deterred by prudent or timid considerations, as he only muttered something about aggravation and a vagabond; not associating the terms with any individual, but mentioning them as connected with some abstract ideas which happened to occur to him. They went on writing for a long time in silence after this—in such a dull silence that Mr Swiveller (who required excitement) had several times fallen asleep, and written divers strange words in an unknown character with his eyes shut, when Miss Sally at length broke in upon the monotony of the office by pulling out the little tin box, taking a noisy pinch of snuff, and then expressing her opinion that Mr Richard Swiveller had 'done it.'

'Done what, ma'am?' said Richard.

'Do you know,' returned Miss Brass, 'that the lodger isn't up yet— that nothing has been seen or heard of him since he went to bed yesterday afternoon?'

'Well, ma'am,' said Dick, 'I suppose he may sleep his ten pound out, in peace and quietness, if he likes.'

'Ah! I begin to think he'll never wake,' observed Miss Sally.

'It's a very remarkable circumstance,' said Brass, laying down his pen; 'really, very remarkable. Mr Richard, you'll remember, if this gentleman should be found to have hung himself to the bed-post, or any unpleasant accident of that kind should happen—you'll remember, Mr Richard, that this ten pound note was given to you in part payment of two years' rent? You'll bear that in mind, Mr Richard; you had better make a note of it, sir, in case you should ever be called upon to give evidence.'

Mr Swiveller took a large sheet of foolscap, and with a countenance of profound gravity, began to make a very small note in one corner.

'We can never be too cautious,' said Mr Brass. 'There is a deal of wickedness going about the world, a deal of wickedness. Did the gentleman happen to say, Sir—but never mind that at present, sir; finish that little memorandum first.'

Dick did so, and handed it to Mr Brass, who had dismounted from his stool, and was walking up and down the office.

'Oh, this is the memorandum, is it?' said Brass, running his eye over the document. 'Very good. Now, Mr Richard, did the gentleman say anything else?'

'No.'

'Are you sure, Mr Richard,' said Brass, solemnly, 'that the gentleman said nothing else?'

'Devil a word, Sir,' replied Dick.

'Think again, Sir,' said Brass; 'it's my duty, Sir, in the position in which I stand, and as an honourable member of the legal profession—the first profession in this country, Sir, or in any other country, or in any of the planets that shine above us at night and are supposed to be inhabited—it's my duty, Sir, as an honourable member of that profession, not to put to you a leading question in a matter of this delicacy and importance. Did the gentleman, Sir, who took the first floor of you yesterday afternoon, and who brought with him a box of property—a box of property—say anything more than is set down in this memorandum?'

'Come, don't be a fool,' said Miss Sally.

Dick looked at her, and then at Brass, and then at Miss Sally again, and still said 'No.'

'Pooh, pooh! Deuce take it, Mr Richard, how dull you are!' cried Brass, relaxing into a smile. 'Did he say anything about his property?—there!'

'That's the way to put it,' said Miss Sally, nodding to her brother.

'Did he say, for instance,' added Brass, in a kind of comfortable, cozy tone—'I don't assert that he did say so, mind; I only ask you, to refresh your memory—did he say, for instance, that he was a stranger in London—that it was not his humour or within his ability to give any references—that he felt we had a right to require them—and that, in case anything should happen to him, at any time, he particularly desired that whatever property he had upon the premises should be considered mine, as some slight recompense for the trouble and annoyance I should sustain—and were you, in short,' added Brass, still more comfortably and cozily than before, 'were you induced to accept him on my behalf, as a tenant, upon those conditions?'

'Certainly not,' replied Dick.

'Why then, Mr Richard,' said Brass, darting at him a supercilious and reproachful look, 'it's my opinion that you've mistaken your calling, and will never make a lawyer.'

'Not if you live a thousand years,' added Miss Sally. Whereupon the brother and sister took each a noisy pinch of snuff from the little tin box, and fell into a gloomy thoughtfulness.

Nothing further passed up to Mr Swiveller's dinner-time, which was at three o'clock, and seemed about three weeks in coming. At the first stroke of the hour, the new clerk disappeared. At the last stroke of five, he reappeared, and the office, as if by magic, became fragrant with the smell of gin and water and lemon-peel.

'Mr Richard,' said Brass, 'this man's not up yet. Nothing will wake him, sir. What's to be done?'

'I should let him have his sleep out,' returned Dick.

'Sleep out!' cried Brass; 'why he has been asleep now, six-and-twenty hours. We have been moving chests of drawers over his head, we have knocked double knocks at the street-door, we have made the servant-girl fall down stairs several times (she's a light weight, and it don't hurt her much,) but nothing wakes him.'

'Perhaps a ladder,' suggested Dick, 'and getting in at the first-floor window—'

'But then there's a door between; besides, the neighbours would be up in arms,' said Brass.

'What do you say to getting on the roof of the house through the trap-door, and dropping down the chimney?' suggested Dick.

'That would be an excellent plan,' said Brass, 'if anybody would be—' and here he looked very hard at Mr Swiveller—'would be kind, and friendly, and generous enough, to undertake it. I dare say it would not be anything like as disagreeable as one supposes.'

Dick had made the suggestion, thinking that the duty might possibly fall within Miss Sally's department. As he said nothing further, and declined taking the hint, Mr Brass was fain to propose that they should go up stairs together, and make a last effort to awaken the sleeper by some less violent means, which, if they failed on this last trial, must positively be succeeded by stronger measures. Mr Swiveller, assenting, armed himself with his stool and the large ruler, and repaired with his employer to the scene of action, where Miss Brass was already ringing a hand-bell with all her might, and yet without producing the smallest effect upon their mysterious lodger.

'There are his boots, Mr Richard!' said Brass.

'Very obstinate-looking articles they are too,' quoth Richard Swiveller. And truly, they were as sturdy and bluff a pair of boots as one would wish to see; as firmly planted on the ground as if their owner's legs and feet had been in them; and seeming, with their broad soles and blunt toes, to hold possession of their place by main force.

'I can't see anything but the curtain of the bed,' said Brass, applying his eye to the keyhole of the door. 'Is he a strong man, Mr Richard?'

'Very,' answered Dick.

'It would be an extremely unpleasant circumstance if he was to bounce out suddenly,' said Brass. 'Keep the stairs clear. I should be more than a match for him, of course, but I'm the master of the house, and the laws of hospitality must be respected.—Hallo there! Hallo, hallo!'

While Mr Brass, with his eye curiously twisted into the keyhole, uttered these sounds as a means of attracting the lodger's attention, and while Miss Brass plied the hand-bell, Mr Swiveller put his stool close against the wall by the side of the door, and mounting on the top and standing bolt upright, so that if the lodger did make a rush, he would most probably pass him in its onward fury, began a violent battery with the ruler upon the upper panels of the door. Captivated with his own ingenuity, and confident in the strength of his position, which he had taken up after the method of those hardy individuals who open the pit and gallery doors of theatres on crowded nights, Mr Swiveller rained down such a shower of blows, that the noise of the bell was drowned; and the small servant, who lingered on the stairs below, ready to fly at a moment's notice, was obliged to hold her ears lest she should be rendered deaf for life.

Suddenly the door was unlocked on the inside, and flung violently open. The small servant flew to the coal-cellar; Miss Sally dived into her own bed-room; Mr Brass, who was not remarkable for personal courage, ran into the next street, and finding that nobody followed him, armed with a poker or other offensive weapon, put his hands in his pockets, walked very slowly all at once, and whistled.

Meanwhile, Mr Swiveller, on the top of the stool, drew himself into as flat a shape as possible against the wall, and looked, not unconcernedly, down upon the single gentleman, who appeared at the door growling and cursing in a very awful manner, and, with the boots in his hand, seemed to have an intention of hurling them down stairs on speculation. This idea, however, he abandoned. He was turning into his room again, still growling vengefully, when his eyes met those of the watchful Richard.

'Have you been making that horrible noise?' said the single gentleman.

'I have been helping, sir,' returned Dick, keeping his eye upon him, and waving the ruler gently in his right hand, as an indication of what the single gentleman had to expect if he attempted any violence.

'How dare you then,' said the lodger, 'Eh?'

To this, Dick made no other reply than by inquiring whether the lodger held it to be consistent with the conduct and character of a gentleman to go to sleep for six-and-twenty hours at a stretch, and whether the peace of an amiable and virtuous family was to weigh as nothing in the balance.

'Is my peace nothing?' said the single gentleman.

'Is their peace nothing, sir?' returned Dick. 'I don't wish to hold out any threats, sir—indeed the law does not allow of threats, for to threaten is an indictable offence—but if ever you do that again, take care you're not sat upon by the coroner and buried in a cross road before you wake. We have been distracted with fears that you were dead, Sir,' said Dick, gently sliding to the ground, 'and the short and the long of it is, that we cannot allow single gentlemen to come into this establishment and sleep like double gentlemen without paying extra for it.'

'Indeed!' cried the lodger.

'Yes, Sir, indeed,' returned Dick, yielding to his destiny and saying whatever came uppermost; 'an equal quantity of slumber was never got out of one bed and bedstead, and if you're going to sleep in that way, you must pay for a double-bedded room.'

Instead of being thrown into a greater passion by these remarks, the lodger lapsed into a broad grin and looked at Mr Swiveller with twinkling eyes. He was a brown-faced sun-burnt man, and appeared browner and more sun-burnt from having a white nightcap on. As it was clear that he was a choleric fellow in some respects, Mr Swiveller was relieved to find him in such good humour, and, to encourage him in it, smiled himself.

The lodger, in the testiness of being so rudely roused, had pushed his nightcap very much on one side of his bald head. This gave him a rakish eccentric air which, now that he had leisure to observe it, charmed Mr Swiveller exceedingly; therefore, by way of propitiation, he expressed his hope that the gentleman was going to get up, and further that he would never do so any more.

'Come here, you impudent rascal!' was the lodger's answer as he re-entered his room.

Mr Swiveller followed him in, leaving the stool outside, but reserving the ruler in case of a surprise. He rather congratulated himself on his prudence when the single gentleman, without notice or explanation of any kind, double-locked the door.

'Can you drink anything?' was his next inquiry.

Mr Swiveller replied that he had very recently been assuaging the pangs of thirst, but that he was still open to 'a modest quencher,' if the materials were at hand. Without another word spoken on either side, the lodger took from his great trunk, a kind of temple, shining as of polished silver, and placed it carefully on the table.

Greatly interested in his proceedings, Mr Swiveller observed him closely. Into one little chamber of this temple, he dropped an egg; into another some coffee; into a third a compact piece of raw steak from a neat tin case; into a fourth, he poured some water. Then, with the aid of a phosphorus-box and some matches, he procured a light and applied it to a spirit-lamp which had a place of its own below the temple; then, he shut down the lids of all the little chambers; then he opened them; and then, by some wonderful and unseen agency, the steak was done, the egg was boiled, the coffee was accurately prepared, and his breakfast was ready.

'Hot water—' said the lodger, handing it to Mr Swiveller with as much coolness as if he had a kitchen fire before him—'extraordinary rum—sugar—and a travelling glass. Mix for yourself. And make haste.'

Dick complied, his eyes wandering all the time from the temple on the table, which seemed to do everything, to the great trunk which seemed to hold everything. The lodger took his breakfast like a man who was used to work these miracles, and thought nothing of them.

'The man of the house is a lawyer, is he not?' said the lodger.

Dick nodded. The rum was amazing.

'The woman of the house—what's she?'

'A dragon,' said Dick.

The single gentleman, perhaps because he had met with such things in his travels, or perhaps because he was a single gentleman, evinced no surprise, but merely inquired 'Wife or sister?'—'Sister,' said Dick.—'So much the better,' said the single gentleman, 'he can get rid of her when he likes.'

'I want to do as I like, young man,' he added after a short silence; 'to go to bed when I like, get up when I like, come in when I like, go out when I like—to be asked no questions and be surrounded by no spies. In this last respect, servants are the devil. There's only one here.'

'And a very little one,' said Dick.

'And a very little one,' repeated the lodger. 'Well, the place will suit me, will it?'

'Yes,' said Dick.

'Sharks, I suppose?' said the lodger.

Dick nodded assent, and drained his glass.

'Let them know my humour,' said the single gentleman, rising. 'If they disturb me, they lose a good tenant. If they know me to be that, they know enough. If they try to know more, it's a notice to quit. It's better to understand these things at once. Good day.'

'I beg your pardon,' said Dick, halting in his passage to the door, which the lodger prepared to open. 'When he who adores thee has left but the name—'

'What do you mean?'

'—But the name,' said Dick—'has left but the name—in case of letters or parcels—'

'I never have any,' returned the lodger.

'Or in the case anybody should call.'

'Nobody ever calls on me.'

'If any mistake should arise from not having the name, don't say it was my fault, Sir,' added Dick, still lingering.—'Oh blame not the bard—'

'I'll blame nobody,' said the lodger, with such irascibility that in a moment Dick found himself on the staircase, and the locked door between them.

Mr Brass and Miss Sally were lurking hard by, having been, indeed, only routed from the keyhole by Mr Swiveller's abrupt exit. As their utmost exertions had not enabled them to overhear a word of the interview, however, in consequence of a quarrel for precedence, which, though limited of necessity to pushes and pinches and such quiet pantomime, had lasted the whole time, they hurried him down to the office to hear his account of the conversation.

This Mr Swiveller gave them—faithfully as regarded the wishes and character of the single gentleman, and poetically as concerned the great trunk, of which he gave a description more remarkable for brilliancy of imagination than a strict adherence to truth; declaring, with many strong asseverations, that it contained a specimen of every kind of rich food and wine, known in these times, and in particular that it was of a self-acting kind and served up whatever was required, as he supposed by clock-work. He also gave them to understand that the cooking apparatus roasted a fine piece of sirloin of beef, weighing about six pounds avoir-dupoise, in two minutes and a quarter, as he had himself witnessed, and proved by his sense of taste; and further, that, however the effect was produced, he had distinctly seen water boil and bubble up when the single gentleman winked; from which facts he (Mr Swiveller) was led to infer that the lodger was some great conjuror or chemist, or both, whose residence under that roof could not fail at some future days to shed a great credit and distinction on the name of Brass, and add a new interest to the history of Bevis Marks.

There was one point which Mr Swiveller deemed it unnecessary to enlarge upon, and that was the fact of the modest quencher, which, by reason of its intrinsic strength and its coming close upon the heels of the temperate beverage he had discussed at dinner, awakened a slight degree of fever, and rendered necessary two or three other modest quenchers at the public-house in the course of the evening.

CHAPTER 36

As the single gentleman after some weeks' occupation of his lodgings, still declined to correspond, by word or gesture, either with Mr Brass or his sister Sally, but invariably chose Richard Swiveller as his channel of communication; and as he proved himself in all respects a highly desirable inmate, paying for everything beforehand, giving very little trouble, making no noise, and keeping early hours; Mr Richard imperceptibly rose to an important position in the family, as one who had influence over this mysterious lodger, and could negotiate with him, for good or evil, when nobody else durst approach his person.

If the truth must be told, even Mr Swiveller's approaches to the single gentleman were of a very distant kind, and met with small encouragement; but, as he never returned from a monosyllabic conference with the unknown, without quoting such expressions as 'Swiveller, I know I can rely upon you,'—'I have no hesitation in saying, Swiveller, that I entertain a regard for you,'—'Swiveller, you are my friend, and will stand by me I am sure,' with many other short speeches of the same familiar and confiding kind, purporting to have been addressed by the single gentleman to himself, and to form the staple of their ordinary discourse, neither Mr Brass nor Miss Sally for a moment questioned the extent of his influence, but accorded to him their fullest and most unqualified belief.

But quite apart from, and independent of, this source of popularity, Mr Swiveller had another, which promised to be equally enduring, and to lighten his position considerably.

He found favour in the eyes of Miss Sally Brass. Let not the light scorners of female fascination erect their ears to listen to a new tale of love which shall serve them for a jest; for Miss Brass, however accurately formed to be beloved, was not of the loving kind. That amiable virgin, having clung to the skirts of the Law from her earliest youth; having sustained herself by their aid, as it were, in her first running alone, and maintained a firm grasp upon them ever since; had passed her life in a kind of legal childhood. She had been remarkable, when a tender prattler for an uncommon talent in counterfeiting the walk and manner of a bailiff: in which character she had learned to tap her little playfellows on the shoulder, and to carry them off to imaginary sponging-houses, with a correctness of imitation which was the surprise and delight of all who witnessed her performances, and which was only to be exceeded by her exquisite manner of putting an execution into her doll's house, and taking an exact inventory of the chairs and tables. These artless sports had naturally soothed and cheered the decline of her widowed father: a most exemplary gentleman (called 'old Foxey' by his friends from his extreme sagacity,) who encouraged them to the utmost, and whose chief regret, on finding that he drew near to Houndsditch churchyard, was, that his daughter could not take out an attorney's certificate and hold a place upon the roll. Filled with this affectionate and touching sorrow, he had solemnly confided her to his son Sampson as an invaluable auxiliary; and from the old gentleman's decease to the period of which we treat, Miss Sally Brass had been the prop and pillar of his business.

It is obvious that, having devoted herself from infancy to this one pursuit and study, Miss Brass could know but little of the world, otherwise than in connection with the law; and that from a lady gifted with such high tastes, proficiency in those gentler and softer arts in which women usually excel, was scarcely to be looked for. Miss Sally's accomplishments were all of a masculine and strictly legal kind. They began with the practice of an attorney and they ended with it. She was in a state of lawful innocence, so to speak. The law had been her nurse. And, as bandy-legs or such physical deformities in children are held to be the consequence of bad nursing, so, if in a mind so beautiful any moral twist or handiness could be found, Miss Sally Brass's nurse was alone to blame.

It was upon this lady, then, that Mr Swiveller burst in full freshness as something new and hitherto undreamed of, lighting up the office with scraps of song and merriment, conjuring with inkstands and boxes of wafers, catching three oranges in one hand, balancing stools upon his chin and penknives on his nose, and constantly performing a hundred other feats with equal ingenuity; for with such unbendings did Richard, in Mr Brass's absence, relieve the tedium of his confinement. These social qualities, which Miss Sally first discovered by accident, gradually made such an impression upon her, that she would entreat Mr Swiveller to relax as though she were not by, which Mr Swiveller, nothing loth, would readily consent to do. By these means a friendship sprung up between them. Mr Swiveller gradually came to look upon her as her brother Sampson did, and as he would have looked upon any other clerk. He imparted to her the mystery of going the odd man or plain Newmarket for fruit, ginger-beer, baked potatoes, or even a modest quencher, of which Miss Brass did not scruple to partake. He would often persuade her to undertake his share of writing in addition to her own; nay, he would sometimes reward her with a hearty slap on the back, and protest that she was a devilish good fellow, a jolly dog, and so forth; all of which compliments Miss Sally would receive in entire good part and with perfect satisfaction.

One circumstance troubled Mr Swiveller's mind very much, and that was that the small servant always remained somewhere in the bowels of the earth under Bevis Marks, and never came to the surface unless the single gentleman rang his bell, when she would answer it and immediately disappear again. She never went out, or came into the office, or had a clean face, or took off the coarse apron, or looked out of any one of the windows, or stood at the street-door for a breath of air, or had any rest or enjoyment whatever. Nobody ever came to see her, nobody spoke of her, nobody cared about her. Mr Brass had said once, that he believed she was a 'love-child' (which means anything but a child of love), and that was all the information Richard Swiveller could obtain.

'It's of no use asking the dragon,' thought Dick one day, as he sat contemplating the features of Miss Sally Brass. 'I suspect if I asked any questions on that head, our alliance would be at an end. I wonder whether she is a dragon by-the-bye, or something in the mermaid way. She has rather a scaly appearance. But mermaids are fond of looking at themselves in the glass, which she can't be. And they have a habit of combing their hair, which she hasn't. No, she's a dragon.'

'Where are you going, old fellow?' said Dick aloud, as Miss Sally wiped her pen as usual on the green dress, and uprose from her seat.

'To dinner,' answered the dragon.

'To dinner!' thought Dick, 'that's another circumstance. I don't believe that small servant ever has anything to eat.'

'Sammy won't be home,' said Miss Brass. 'Stop till I come back. I sha'n't be long.'

Dick nodded, and followed Miss Brass—with his eyes to the door, and with his ears to a little back parlour, where she and her brother took their meals.

'Now,' said Dick, walking up and down with his hands in his pockets, 'I'd give something—if I had it—to know how they use that child, and where they keep her. My mother must have been a very inquisitive woman; I have no doubt I'm marked with a note of interrogation somewhere. My feelings I smother, but thou hast been the cause of this anguish, my—upon my word,' said Mr Swiveller, checking himself and falling thoughtfully into the client's chair, 'I should like to know how they use her!'

After running on, in this way, for some time, Mr Swiveller softly opened the office door, with the intention of darting across the street for a glass of the mild porter. At that moment he caught a parting glimpse of the brown head-dress of Miss Brass flitting down the kitchen stairs. 'And by Jove!' thought Dick, 'she's going to feed the small servant. Now or never!'

First peeping over the handrail and allowing the head-dress to disappear in the darkness below, he groped his way down, and arrived at the door of a back kitchen immediately after

Miss Brass had entered the same, bearing in her hand a cold leg of mutton. It was a very dark miserable place, very low and very damp: the walls disfigured by a thousand rents and blotches. The water was trickling out of a leaky butt, and a most wretched cat was lapping up the drops with the sickly eagerness of starvation. The grate, which was a wide one, was wound and screwed up tight, so as to hold no more than a little thin sandwich of fire. Everything was locked up; the coal-cellar, the candle-box, the salt-box, the meat-safe, were all padlocked. There was nothing that a beetle could have lunched upon. The pinched and meagre aspect of the place would have killed a chameleon. He would have known, at the first mouthful, that the air was not eatable, and must have given up the ghost in despair. The small servant stood with humility in presence of Miss Sally, and hung her head.

'Are you there?' said Miss Sally.

'Yes, ma'am,' was the answer in a weak voice.

'Go further away from the leg of mutton, or you'll be picking it, I know,' said Miss Sally.

The girl withdrew into a corner, while Miss Brass took a key from her pocket, and opening the safe, brought from it a dreary waste of cold potatoes, looking as eatable as Stonehenge. This she placed before the small servant, ordering her to sit down before it, and then, taking up a great carving-knife, made a mighty show of sharpening it upon the carving-fork.

'Do you see this?' said Miss Brass, slicing off about two square inches of cold mutton, after all this preparation, and holding it out on the point of the fork.

The small servant looked hard enough at it with her hungry eyes to see every shred of it, small as it was, and answered, 'yes.'

'Then don't you ever go and say,' retorted Miss Sally, 'that you hadn't meat here. There, eat it up.'

This was soon done. 'Now, do you want any more?' said Miss Sally.

The hungry creature answered with a faint 'No.' They were evidently going through an established form.

'You've been helped once to meat,' said Miss Brass, summing up the facts; 'you have had as much as you can eat, you're asked if you want any more, and you answer, 'no!' Then don't you ever go and say you were allowanced, mind that.'

With those words, Miss Sally put the meat away and locked the safe, and then drawing near to the small servant, overlooked her while she finished the potatoes.

It was plain that some extraordinary grudge was working in Miss Brass's gentle breast, and that it was that which impelled her, without the smallest present cause, to rap the child with the blade of the knife, now on her hand, now on her head, and now on her back, as if she found it quite impossible to stand so close to her without administering a few slight knocks. But Mr Swiveller was not a little surprised to see his fellow-clerk, after walking slowly backwards towards the door, as if she were trying to withdraw herself from the room but could not accomplish it, dart suddenly forward, and falling on the small servant give her some hard blows with her clenched hand. The victim cried, but in a subdued manner as if she feared to raise her voice, and Miss Sally, comforting herself with a pinch of snuff, ascended the stairs, just as Richard had safely reached the office.

CHAPTER 37

The single gentleman among his other peculiarities—and he had a very plentiful stock, of which he every day furnished some new specimen—took a most extraordinary and remarkable interest in the exhibition of Punch. If the sound of a Punch's voice, at ever so remote a distance, reached Bevis Marks, the single gentleman, though in bed and asleep, would start up, and, hurrying on his clothes, make for the spot with all speed, and presently return at the head of a long procession of idlers, having in the midst the theatre and its proprietors. Straightway, the stage would be set up in front of Mr Brass's house; the single gentleman would establish himself at the first floor window; and the entertainment would proceed, with all its exciting accompaniments of fife and drum and shout, to the excessive consternation of all sober votaries of business in that silent thoroughfare. It might have been expected that when the play was done, both players and audience would have dispersed; but the epilogue was as bad as the play, for no sooner was the Devil dead, than the manager of the puppets and his partner were summoned by the single gentleman to his chamber, where they were regaled with strong waters from his private store, and where they held with him long conversations, the purport of which no human being could fathom. But the secret of these discussions was of little importance. It was sufficient to know that while they were proceeding, the concourse without still lingered round the house; that boys beat upon the drum with their fists, and imitated Punch with their tender voices; that the office-window was rendered opaque by flattened noses, and the key-hole of the street-door luminous with eyes; that every time the single gentleman or either of his guests was seen at the upper window, or so much as the end of one of their noses was visible, there was a great shout of execration from the excluded mob, who remained howling and yelling, and refusing consolation, until the exhibitors were delivered up to them to be attended elsewhere. It was sufficient, in short, to know that Bevis Marks was revolutionised by these popular movements, and that peace and quietness fled from its precincts.

Nobody was rendered more indignant by these proceedings than Mr Sampson Brass, who, as he could by no means afford to lose so profitable an inmate, deemed it prudent to pocket his lodger's affront along with his cash, and to annoy the audiences who clustered round his door by such imperfect means of retaliation as were open to him, and which were confined to the trickling down of foul water on their heads from unseen watering pots, pelting them with fragments of tile and mortar from the roof of the house, and bribing the drivers of hackney cabriolets to come suddenly round the corner and dash in among them precipitately. It may, at first sight, be matter of surprise to the thoughtless few that Mr Brass, being a professional gentleman, should not have legally indicted some party or parties, active in the promotion of the nuisance, but they will be good enough to remember, that as Doctors seldom take their own prescriptions, and Divines do not always practise what they preach, so lawyers are shy of meddling with the Law on their own account: knowing it to be an edged tool of uncertain application, very expensive in the working, and rather remarkable for its properties of close shaving, than for its always shaving the right person.

'Come,' said Mr Brass one afternoon, 'this is two days without a Punch. I'm in hopes he has run through 'em all, at last.'

'Why are you in hopes?' returned Miss Sally. 'What harm do they do?'

'Here's a pretty sort of a fellow!' cried Brass, laying down his pen in despair. 'Now here's an aggravating animal!'

'Well, what harm do they do?' retorted Sally.

'What harm!' cried Brass. 'Is it no harm to have a constant hallooing and hooting under one's very nose, distracting one from business, and making one grind one's teeth with vexation? Is it no harm to be blinded and choked up, and have the king's highway stopped with a set of screamers and roarers whose throats must be made of—of—'

'Brass,' suggested Mr Swiveller.

'Ah! of brass,' said the lawyer, glancing at his clerk, to assure himself that he had suggested the word in good faith and without any sinister intention. 'Is that no harm?'

The lawyer stopped short in his invective, and listening for a moment, and recognising the well-known voice, rested his head upon his hand, raised his eyes to the ceiling, and muttered faintly, 'There's another!'

Up went the single gentleman's window directly.

'There's another,' repeated Brass; 'and if I could get a break and four blood horses to cut into the Marks when the crowd is at its thickest, I'd give eighteen-pence and never grudge it!'

The distant squeak was heard again. The single gentleman's door burst open. He ran violently down the stairs, out into the street, and so past the window, without any hat, towards the quarter whence the sound proceeded—bent, no doubt, upon securing the strangers' services directly.

'I wish I only knew who his friends were,' muttered Sampson, filling his pocket with papers; 'if they'd just get up a pretty little Commission de lunatico at the Gray's Inn Coffee House and give me the job, I'd be content to have the lodgings empty for one while, at all events.'

With which words, and knocking his hat over his eyes as if for the purpose of shutting out even a glimpse of the dreadful visitation, Mr Brass rushed from the house and hurried away.

As Mr Swiveller was decidedly favourable to these performances, upon the ground that looking at a Punch, or indeed looking at anything out of window, was better than working; and as he had been, for this reason, at some pains to awaken in his fellow clerk a sense of their beauties and manifold deserts; both he and Miss Sally rose as with one accord and took up their positions at the window: upon the sill whereof, as in a post of honour, sundry young ladies and gentlemen who were employed in the dry nurture of babies, and who made a point of being present, with their young charges, on such occasions, had already established themselves as comfortably as the circumstances would allow.

The glass being dim, Mr Swiveller, agreeably to a friendly custom which he had established between them, hitched off the brown head-dress from Miss Sally's head, and dusted it carefully therewith. By the time he had handed it back, and its beautiful wearer had put it on again (which she did with perfect composure and indifference), the lodger returned with the show and showmen at his heels, and a strong addition to the body of spectators. The exhibitor disappeared with all speed behind the drapery; and his partner, stationing himself by the side of the Theatre, surveyed the audience with a remarkable expression of melancholy, which became more remarkable still when he breathed a hornpipe tune into that sweet musical instrument which is popularly termed a mouth-organ, without at all changing the mournful expression of the upper part of his face, though his mouth and chin were, of necessity, in lively spasms.

The drama proceeded to its close, and held the spectators enchained in the customary manner. The sensation which kindles in large assemblies, when they are relieved from a state of breathless suspense and are again free to speak and move, was yet rife, when the lodger, as usual, summoned the men up stairs.

'Both of you,' he called from the window; for only the actual exhibitor—a little fat man—prepared to obey the summons. 'I want to talk to you. Come both of you!'

'Come, Tommy,' said the little man.

'I an't a talker,' replied the other. 'Tell him so. What should I go and talk for?'

'Don't you see the gentleman's got a bottle and glass up there?' returned the little man.

'And couldn't you have said so at first?' retorted the other with sudden alacrity. 'Now, what are you waiting for? Are you going to keep the gentleman expecting us all day? haven't you no manners?'

With this remonstrance, the melancholy man, who was no other than Mr Thomas Codlin, pushed past his friend and brother in the craft, Mr Harris, otherwise Short or Trotters, and hurried before him to the single gentleman's apartment.

'Now, my men,' said the single gentleman; 'you have done very well. What will you take? Tell that little man behind, to shut the door.'

'Shut the door, can't you?' said Mr Codlin, turning gruffly to his friend. 'You might have knowed that the gentleman wanted the door shut, without being told, I think.'

Mr Short obeyed, observing under his breath that his friend seemed unusually 'cranky,' and expressing a hope that there was no dairy in the neighbourhood, or his temper would certainly spoil its contents.

The gentleman pointed to a couple of chairs, and intimated by an emphatic nod of his head that he expected them to be seated. Messrs Codlin and Short, after looking at each other with considerable doubt and indecision, at length sat down—each on the extreme edge of the chair pointed out to him—and held their hats very tight, while the single gentleman filled a couple of glasses from a bottle on the table beside him, and presented them in due form.

'You're pretty well browned by the sun, both of you,' said their entertainer. 'Have you been travelling?'

Mr Short replied in the affirmative with a nod and a smile. Mr Codlin added a corroborative nod and a short groan, as if he still felt the weight of the Temple on his shoulders.

'To fairs, markets, races, and so forth, I suppose?' pursued the single gentleman.

'Yes, sir,' returned Short, 'pretty nigh all over the West of England.'

'I have talked to men of your craft from North, East, and South,' returned their host, in rather a hasty manner; 'but I never lighted on any from the West before.'

'It's our reg'lar summer circuit is the West, master,' said Short; 'that's where it is. We takes the East of London in the spring and winter, and the West of England in the summer time. Many's the hard day's walking in rain and mud, and with never a penny earned, we've had down in the West.'

'Let me fill your glass again.'

'Much obleeged to you sir, I think I will,' said Mr Codlin, suddenly thrusting in his own and turning Short's aside. 'I'm the sufferer, sir, in all the travelling, and in all the staying at home. In town or country, wet or dry, hot or cold, Tom Codlin suffers. But Tom Codlin isn't to complain for all that. Oh, no! Short may complain, but if Codlin grumbles by so much as a word—oh dear, down with him, down with him directly. It isn't his place to grumble. That's quite out of the question.'

'Codlin an't without his usefulness,' observed Short with an arch look, 'but he don't always keep his eyes open. He falls asleep sometimes, you know. Remember them last races, Tommy.'

'Will you never leave off aggravating a man?' said Codlin. 'It's very like I was asleep when five-and-tenpence was collected, in one round, isn't it? I was attending to my business, and couldn't have my eyes in twenty places at once, like a peacock, no more than you could. If I an't a match for an old man and a young child, you an't neither, so don't throw that out against me, for the cap fits your head quite as correct as it fits mine.'

'You may as well drop the subject, Tom,' said Short. 'It isn't particular agreeable to the gentleman, I dare say.'

'Then you shouldn't have brought it up,' returned Mr Codlin; 'and I ask the gentleman's pardon on your account, as a giddy chap that likes to hear himself talk, and don't much care what he talks about, so that he does talk.'

Their entertainer had sat perfectly quiet in the beginning of this dispute, looking first at one man and then at the other, as if he were lying in wait for an opportunity of putting some further question, or reverting to that from which the discourse had strayed. But, from the point where Mr Codlin was charged with sleepiness, he had shown an increasing interest in the discussion: which now attained a very high pitch.

'You are the two men I want,' he said, 'the two men I have been looking for, and searching after! Where are that old man and that child you speak of?'

'Sir?' said Short, hesitating, and looking towards his friend.

'The old man and his grandchild who travelled with you—where are they? It will be worth your while to speak out, I assure you; much better worth your while than you believe. They left you, you say—at those races, as I understand. They have been traced to that place, and there lost sight of. Have you no clue, can you suggest no clue, to their recovery?'

'Did I always say, Thomas,' cried Short, turning with a look of amazement to his friend, 'that there was sure to be an inquiry after them two travellers?'

'You said!' returned Mr Codlin. 'Did I always say that that 'ere blessed child was the most interesting I ever see? Did I always say I loved her, and doated on her? Pretty creetur, I think I hear her now. "Codlin's my friend," she says, with a tear of gratitude a trickling down her little eye; "Codlin's my friend," she says—"not Short. Short's very well," she says; "I've no quarrel with Short; he means kind, I dare say; but Codlin," she says, "has the feelings for my money, though he mayn't look it."'

Repeating these words with great emotion, Mr Codlin rubbed the bridge of his nose with his coat-sleeve, and shaking his head mournfully from side to side, left the single gentleman to infer that, from the moment when he lost sight of his dear young charge, his peace of mind and happiness had fled.

'Good Heaven!' said the single gentleman, pacing up and down the room, 'have I found these men at last, only to discover that they can give me no information or assistance! It would have been better to have lived on, in hope, from day to day, and never to have lighted on them, than to have my expectations scattered thus.'

'Stay a minute,' said Short. 'A man of the name of Jerry—you know Jerry, Thomas?'

'Oh, don't talk to me of Jerrys,' replied Mr Codlin. 'How can I care a pinch of snuff for Jerrys, when I think of that 'ere darling child? "Codlin's my friend," she says, "dear, good, kind Codlin, as is always a devising pleasures for me! I don't object to Short," she says, "but I cotton to Codlin." Once,' said that gentleman reflectively, 'she called me Father Codlin. I thought I should have bust!'

'A man of the name of Jerry, sir,' said Short, turning from his selfish colleague to their new acquaintance, 'wot keeps a company of dancing dogs, told me, in a accidental sort of way, that he had seen the old gentleman in connexion with a travelling wax-work, unbeknown to him. As they'd given us the slip, and nothing had come of it, and this was down in the country that he'd been seen, I took no measures about it, and asked no questions—But I can, if you like.'

'Is this man in town?' said the impatient single gentleman. 'Speak faster.'

'No he isn't, but he will be to-morrow, for he lodges in our house,' replied Mr Short rapidly.

'Then bring him here,' said the single gentleman. 'Here's a sovereign a-piece. If I can find these people through your means, it is but a prelude to twenty more. Return to me to-morrow, and keep your own counsel on this subject—though I need hardly tell you that; for you'll do so for your own sakes. Now, give me your address, and leave me.'

The address was given, the two men departed, the crowd went with them, and the single gentleman for two mortal hours walked in uncommon agitation up and down his room, over the wondering heads of Mr Swiveller and Miss Sally Brass.

CHAPTER 38

Kit—for it happens at this juncture, not only that we have breathing time to follow his fortunes, but that the necessities of these adventures so adapt themselves to our ease and inclination as to call upon us imperatively to pursue the track we most desire to take—Kit, while the matters treated of in the last fifteen chapters were yet in progress, was, as the reader may suppose, gradually familiarising himself more and more with Mr and Mrs Garland, Mr Abel, the pony, and Barbara, and gradually coming to consider them one and all as his particular private friends, and Abel Cottage, Finchley, as his own proper home.

Stay—the words are written, and may go, but if they convey any notion that Kit, in the plentiful board and comfortable lodging of his new abode, began to think slightingly of the poor fare and furniture of his old dwelling, they do their office badly and commit injustice. Who so mindful of those he left at home—albeit they were but a mother and two young babies—as Kit? What boastful father in the fulness of his heart ever related such wonders of his infant prodigy, as Kit never wearied of telling Barbara in the evening time, concerning little Jacob? Was there ever such a mother as Kit's mother, on her son's showing; or was there ever such comfort in poverty as in the poverty of Kit's family, if any correct judgment might be arrived at, from his own glowing account!

And let me linger in this place, for an instant, to remark that if ever household affections and loves are graceful things, they are graceful in the poor. The ties that bind the wealthy and the proud to home may be forged on earth, but those which link the poor man to his humble hearth are of the truer metal and bear the stamp of Heaven. The man of high descent may love the halls and lands of his inheritance as part of himself: as trophies of his birth and power; his associations with them are associations of pride and wealth and triumph; the poor man's attachment to the tenements he holds, which strangers have held before, and may to-morrow occupy again, has a worthier root, struck deep into a purer soil. His household gods are of flesh and blood, with no alloy of silver, gold, or precious stone; he has no property but in the affections of his own heart; and when they endear bare floors and walls, despite of rags and toil and scanty fare, that man has his love of home from God, and his rude hut becomes a solemn place.

Oh! if those who rule the destinies of nations would but remember this—if they would but think how hard it is for the very poor to have engendered in their hearts, that love of home from which all domestic virtues spring, when they live in dense and squalid masses where social decency is lost, or rather never found—if they would but turn aside from the wide thoroughfares and great houses, and strive to improve the wretched dwellings in bye-ways where only Poverty may walk—many low roofs would point more truly to the sky, than the loftiest steeple that now rears proudly up from the midst of guilt, and crime, and horrible disease, to mock them by its contrast. In hollow voices from Workhouse, Hospital, and jail, this truth is preached from day to day, and has been proclaimed for years. It is no light matter—no outcry from the working vulgar—no mere question of the people's health and comforts that may be whistled down on Wednesday nights. In love of home, the love of country has its rise; and who are the truer patriots or the better in time of need—those who venerate the land, owning its wood, and stream, and earth, and all that they produce? or those who love their country, boasting not a foot of ground in all its wide domain!

Kit knew nothing about such questions, but he knew that his old home was a very poor place, and that his new one was very unlike it, and yet he was constantly looking back with grateful satisfaction and affectionate anxiety, and often indited square-folded letters to his mother, enclosing a shilling or eighteenpence or such other small remittance, which Mr Abel's liberality enabled him to make. Sometimes being in the neighbourhood, he had leisure to call upon her, and then great was the joy and pride of Kit's mother, and extremely noisy the satisfaction of little Jacob and the baby, and cordial the congratulations of the whole court, who listened with admiring ears to the accounts of Abel Cottage, and could never be told too much of its wonders and magnificence.

Although Kit was in the very highest favour with the old lady and gentleman, and

Mr Abel, and Barbara, it is certain that no member of the family evinced such a remarkable partiality for him as the self-willed pony, who, from being the most obstinate and opinionated pony on the face of the earth, was, in his hands, the meekest and most tractable of animals. It is true that in exact proportion as he became manageable by Kit he became utterly ungovernable by anybody else (as if he had determined to keep him in the family at all risks and hazards), and that, even under the guidance of his favourite, he would sometimes perform a great variety of strange freaks and capers, to the extreme discomposure of the old lady's nerves; but as Kit always represented that this was only his fun, or a way he had of showing his attachment to his employers, Mrs Garland gradually suffered herself to be persuaded into the belief, in which she at last became so strongly confirmed, that if, in one of these ebullitions, he had overturned the chaise, she would have been quite satisfied that he did it with the very best intentions.

Besides becoming in a short time a perfect marvel in all stable matters, Kit soon made himself a very tolerable gardener, a handy fellow within doors, and an indispensable attendant on Mr Abel, who every day gave him some new proof of his confidence and approbation. Mr Witherden the notary, too, regarded him with a friendly eye; and even Mr Chuckster would sometimes condescend to give him a slight nod, or to honour him with that peculiar form of recognition which is called 'taking a sight,' or to favour him with some other salute combining pleasantry with patronage.

One morning Kit drove Mr Abel to the Notary's office, as he sometimes did, and having set him down at the house, was about to drive off to a livery stable hard by, when this same Mr Chuckster emerged from the office door, and cried 'Woa-a-a-a-a!'—dwelling upon the note a long time, for the purpose of striking terror into the pony's heart, and asserting the supremacy of man over the inferior animals.

'Pull up, Snobby,' cried Mr Chuckster, addressing himself to Kit. 'You're wanted inside here.'

'Has Mr Abel forgotten anything, I wonder?' said Kit as he dismounted.

'Ask no questions, Snobby,' returned Mr Chuckster, 'but go and see. Woa-a-a then, will you? If that pony was mine, I'd break him.'

'You must be very gentle with him, if you please,' said Kit, 'or you'll find him troublesome. You'd better not keep on pulling his ears, please. I know he won't like it.'

To this remonstrance Mr Chuckster deigned no other answer, than addressing Kit with a lofty and distant air as 'young feller,' and requesting him to cut and come again with all speed. The 'young feller' complying, Mr Chuckster put his hands in his pockets, and tried to look as if he were not minding the pony, but happened to be lounging there by accident.

Kit scraped his shoes very carefully (for he had not yet lost his reverence for the bundles of papers and the tin boxes,) and tapped at the office-door, which was quickly opened by the Notary himself.

'Oh! come in, Christopher,' said Mr Witherden.

'Is that the lad?' asked an elderly gentleman, but of a stout, bluff figure—who was in the room.

'That's the lad,' said Mr Witherden. 'He fell in with my client, Mr Garland, sir, at this very door. I have reason to think he is a good lad, sir, and that you may believe what he says.

Let me introduce Mr Abel Garland, sir—his young master; my articled pupil, sir, and most particular friend:—my most particular friend, sir,' repeated the Notary, drawing out his silk handkerchief and flourishing it about his face.

'Your servant, sir,' said the stranger gentleman.

'Yours, sir, I'm sure,' replied Mr Abel mildly. 'You were wishing to speak to Christopher, sir?'

'Yes, I was. Have I your permission?'

'By all means.'

'My business is no secret; or I should rather say it need be no secret here,' said the stranger, observing that Mr Abel and the Notary were preparing to retire. 'It relates to a dealer in curiosities with whom he lived, and in whom I am earnestly and warmly interested. I have been a stranger to this country, gentlemen, for very many years, and if I am deficient in form and ceremony, I hope you will forgive me.'

'No forgiveness is necessary, sir;—none whatever,' replied the Notary. And so said Mr Abel.

'I have been making inquiries in the neighbourhood in which his old master lived,' said the stranger, 'and I learn that he was served by this lad. I have found out his mother's house, and have been directed by her to this place as the nearest in which I should be likely to find him. That's the cause of my presenting myself here this morning.'

'I am very glad of any cause, sir,' said the Notary, 'which procures me the honour of this visit.'

'Sir,' retorted the stranger, 'you speak like a mere man of the world, and I think you something better. Therefore, pray do not sink your real character in paying unmeaning compliments to me.'

'Hem!' coughed the Notary. 'You're a plain speaker, sir.'

'And a plain dealer,' returned the stranger. 'It may be my long absence and inexperience that lead me to the conclusion; but if plain speakers are scarce in this part of the world, I fancy plain dealers are still scarcer. If my speaking should offend you, sir, my dealing, I hope, will make amends.'

Mr Witherden seemed a little disconcerted by the elderly gentleman's mode of conducting the dialogue; and as for Kit, he looked at him in open-mouthed astonishment: wondering what kind of language he would address to him, if he talked in that free and easy way to a Notary. It was with no harshness, however, though with something of constitutional irritability and haste, that he turned to Kit and said:

'If you think, my lad, that I am pursuing these inquiries with any other view than that of serving and reclaiming those I am in search of, you do me a very great wrong, and deceive yourself. Don't be deceived, I beg of you, but rely upon my assurance. The fact is, gentlemen,' he added, turning again to the Notary and his pupil, 'that I am in a very painful and wholly unexpected position. I came to this city with a darling object at my heart, expecting to find no obstacle or difficulty in the way of its attainment. I find myself suddenly checked and stopped short, in the execution of my design, by a mystery which I cannot penetrate. Every effort I have made to penetrate it, has only served to render it darker and more obscure; and I am afraid to stir openly in the matter, lest those whom I anxiously pursue, should fly still farther from me. I assure you that if you could give me any assistance, you would not be sorry to do so, if you knew how greatly I stand in need of it, and what a load it would relieve me from.'

There was a simplicity in this confidence which occasioned it to find a quick response in the breast of the good-natured Notary, who replied, in the same spirit, that the stranger had not mistaken his desire, and that if he could be of service to him, he would, most readily.

Kit was then put under examination and closely questioned by the unknown gentleman, touching his old master and the child, their lonely way of life, their retired habits, and strict seclusion. The nightly absence of the old man, the solitary existence of the child at those times, his illness and recovery, Quilp's possession of the house, and their sudden disappearance, were all the subjects of much questioning and answer. Finally, Kit informed the gentleman that the premises were now to let, and that a board upon the door referred all inquirers to Mr Sampson Brass, Solicitor, of Bevis Marks, from whom he might perhaps learn some further particulars.

'Not by inquiry,' said the gentleman shaking his head. 'I live there.'

'Live at Brass's the attorney's!' cried Mr Witherden in some surprise: having professional knowledge of the gentleman in question.

'Aye,' was the reply. 'I entered on his lodgings t'other day, chiefly because I had seen this very board. It matters little to me where I live, and I had a desperate hope that some intelligence might be cast in my way there, which would not reach me elsewhere. Yes, I live at Brass's—more shame for me, I suppose?'

'That's a mere matter of opinion,' said the Notary, shrugging his shoulders. 'He is looked upon as rather a doubtful character.'

'Doubtful?' echoed the other. 'I am glad to hear there's any doubt about it. I supposed that had been thoroughly settled, long ago. But will you let me speak a word or two with you in private?'

Mr Witherden consenting, they walked into that gentleman's private closet, and remained there, in close conversation, for some quarter of an hour, when they returned into the outer office. The stranger had left his hat in Mr Witherden's room, and seemed to have established himself in this short interval on quite a friendly footing.

'I'll not detain you any longer now,' he said, putting a crown into Kit's hand, and looking towards the Notary. 'You shall hear from me again. Not a word of this, you know, except to your master and mistress.'

'Mother, sir, would be glad to know—' said Kit, faltering.

'Glad to know what?'

'Anything—so that it was no harm—about Miss Nell.'

'Would she? Well then, you may tell her if she can keep a secret. But mind, not a word of this to anybody else. Don't forget that. Be particular.'

'I'll take care, sir,' said Kit. 'Thankee, sir, and good morning.'

Now, it happened that the gentleman, in his anxiety to impress upon Kit that he was not to tell anybody what had passed between them, followed him out to the door to repeat his caution, and it further happened that at that moment the eyes of Mr Richard Swiveller were turned in that direction, and beheld his mysterious friend and Kit together.

It was quite an accident, and the way in which it came about was this. Mr Chuckster, being a gentleman of a cultivated taste and refined spirit, was one of that Lodge of Glorious Apollos whereof Mr Swiveller was Perpetual Grand. Mr Swiveller, passing through the street in the execution of some Brazen errand, and beholding one of his Glorious Brotherhood intently gazing on a pony, crossed over to give him that fraternal greeting with which Perpetual Grands are, by the very constitution of their office, bound to cheer and encourage their disciples. He had scarcely bestowed upon him his blessing, and followed it with a general remark touching the present state and prospects of the weather, when, lifting up his eyes, he beheld the single gentleman of Bevis Marks in earnest conversation with Christopher Nubbles.

'Hallo!' said Dick, 'who is that?'

'He called to see my Governor this morning,' replied Mr Chuckster; 'beyond that, I don't know him from Adam.'

'At least you know his name?' said Dick.

To which Mr Chuckster replied, with an elevation of speech becoming a Glorious Apollo, that he was 'everlastingly blessed' if he did.

'All I know, my dear feller,' said Mr Chuckster, running his fingers through his hair, 'is, that he is the cause of my having stood here twenty minutes, for which I hate him with a mortal and undying hatred, and would pursue him to the confines of eternity if I could afford the time.'

While they were thus discoursing, the subject of their conversation (who had not appeared to recognise Mr Richard Swiveller) re-entered the house, and Kit came down the steps and joined them; to whom Mr Swiveller again propounded his inquiry with no better success.

'He is a very nice gentleman, Sir,' said Kit, 'and that's all I know about him.'

Mr Chuckster waxed wroth at this answer, and without applying the remark to any particular case, mentioned, as a general truth, that it was expedient to break the heads of Snobs, and to tweak their noses. Without expressing his concurrence in this sentiment, Mr Swiveller after a few moments of abstraction inquired which way Kit was driving, and, being informed, declared it was his way, and that he would trespass on him for a lift. Kit would gladly have declined the proffered honour, but as Mr Swiveller was already established in the seat beside him, he had no means of doing so, otherwise than by a forcible ejectment, and therefore, drove briskly off—so briskly indeed, as to cut short the leave-taking between Mr Chuckster and his Grand Master, and to occasion the former gentleman some inconvenience from having his corns squeezed by the impatient pony.

As Whisker was tired of standing, and Mr Swiveller was kind enough to stimulate him by shrill whistles, and various sporting cries, they rattled off at too sharp a pace to admit of much conversation: especially as the pony, incensed by Mr Swiveller's admonitions, took a particular fancy for the lamp-posts and cart-wheels, and evinced a strong desire to run on the pavement and rasp himself against the brick walls. It was not, therefore, until they had arrived at the stable, and the chaise had been extricated from a very small doorway, into which the pony dragged it under the impression that he could take it along with him into his usual stall, that Mr Swiveller found time to talk.

'It's hard work,' said Richard. 'What do you say to some beer?'

Kit at first declined, but presently consented, and they adjourned to the neighbouring bar together.

'We'll drink our friend what's-his-name,' said Dick, holding up the bright frothy pot; '—that was talking to you this morning, you know—I know him—a good fellow, but eccentric—very—here's what's-his-name!'

Kit pledged him.

'He lives in my house,' said Dick; 'at least in the house occupied by the firm in which I'm a sort of a—of a managing partner—a difficult fellow to get anything out of, but we like him—we like him.'

'I must be going, sir, if you please,' said Kit, moving away.

'Don't be in a hurry, Christopher,' replied his patron, 'we'll drink your mother.'

'Thank you, sir.'

'An excellent woman that mother of yours, Christopher,' said Mr Swiveller. 'Who ran to catch me when I fell, and kissed the place to make it well? My mother. A charming woman. He's a liberal sort of fellow. We must get him to do something for your mother. Does he know her, Christopher?'

Kit shook his head, and glancing slyly at his questioner, thanked him, and made off before he could say another word.

'Humph!' said Mr Swiveller pondering, 'this is queer. Nothing but mysteries in connection with Brass's house. I'll keep my own counsel, however. Everybody and anybody has been in my confidence as yet, but now I think I'll set up in business for myself. Queer—very queer!'

After pondering deeply and with a face of exceeding wisdom for some time, Mr Swiveller drank some more of the beer, and summoning a small boy who had been watching his proceedings, poured forth the few remaining drops as a libation on the gravel, and bade him carry the empty vessel to the bar with his compliments, and above all things to lead a sober and temperate life, and abstain from all intoxicating and exciting liquors. Having given him this piece of moral advice for his trouble (which, as he wisely observed, was far better than half-pence) the Perpetual Grand Master of the Glorious Apollos thrust his hands into his pockets and sauntered away: still pondering as he went.

CHAPTER 39

All that day, though he waited for Mr Abel until evening, Kit kept clear of his mother's house, determined not to anticipate the pleasures of the morrow, but to let them come in their full rush of delight; for to-morrow was the great and long looked-for epoch in his life—to-morrow was the end of his first quarter—the day of receiving, for the first time, one fourth part of his annual income of Six Pounds in one vast sum of Thirty Shillings—to-morrow was to be a half-holiday devoted to a whirl of entertainments, and little Jacob was to know what oysters meant, and to see a play.

All manner of incidents combined in favour of the occasion: not only had Mr and Mrs Garland forewarned him that they intended to make no deduction for his outfit from the great amount, but to pay it him unbroken in all its gigantic grandeur; not only had the unknown gentleman increased the stock by the sum of five shillings, which was a perfect god-send and in itself a fortune; not only had these things come to pass which nobody could have calculated upon, or in their wildest dreams have hoped; but it was Barbara's quarter too—Barbara's quarter, that very day—and Barbara had a half-holiday as well as Kit, and Barbara's mother was going to make one of the party, and to take tea with Kit's mother, and cultivate her acquaintance.

To be sure Kit looked out of his window very early that morning to see which way the clouds were flying, and to be sure Barbara would have been at hers too, if she had not sat up so late over-night, starching and ironing small pieces of muslin, and crimping them into frills, and sewing them on to other pieces to form magnificent wholes for next day's wear. But they were both up very early for all that, and had small appetites for breakfast and less for dinner, and were in a state of great excitement when Barbara's mother came in, with astonishing accounts of the fineness of the weather out of doors (but with a very large umbrella notwithstanding, for people like Barbara's mother seldom make holiday without one), and when the bell rang for them to go up stairs and receive their quarter's money in gold and silver.

Well, wasn't Mr Garland kind when he said 'Christopher, here's your money, and you have earned it well;' and wasn't Mrs Garland kind when she said 'Barbara, here's yours, and I'm much pleased with you;' and didn't Kit sign his name bold to his receipt, and didn't Barbara sign her name all a trembling to hers; and wasn't it beautiful to see how Mrs Garland poured out Barbara's mother a glass of wine; and didn't Barbara's mother speak up when she said 'Here's blessing you, ma'am, as a good lady, and you, sir, as a good gentleman, and Barbara, my love to you, and here's towards you, Mr Christopher;' and wasn't she as long drinking it as if it had been a tumblerful; and didn't she look genteel, standing there with her gloves on; and wasn't there plenty of laughing and talking among them as they reviewed all these things upon the top of the coach, and didn't they pity the people who hadn't got a holiday!

But Kit's mother, again—wouldn't anybody have supposed she had come of a good stock and been a lady all her life! There she was, quite ready to receive them, with a display of tea-things that might have warmed the heart of a china-shop; and little Jacob and the baby in such a state of perfection that their clothes looked as good as new, though Heaven knows they were old enough! Didn't she say before they had sat down five minutes that Barbara's mother was exactly the sort of lady she expected, and didn't Barbara's mother say that Kit's mother was the very picture of what she had expected, and didn't Kit's mother compliment Barbara's mother on Barbara, and didn't Barbara's mother compliment Kit's mother on Kit, and wasn't Barbara herself quite fascinated with little Jacob, and did ever a child show off when he was wanted, as that child did, or make such friends as he made!

'And we are both widows too!' said Barbara's mother. 'We must have been made to know each other.'

'I haven't a doubt about it,' returned Mrs Nubbles. 'And what a pity it is we didn't know each other sooner.'

'But then, you know, it's such a pleasure,' said Barbara's mother, 'to have it brought about by one's son and daughter, that it's fully made up for. Now, an't it?'

To this, Kit's mother yielded her full assent, and tracing things back from effects to causes, they naturally reverted to their deceased husbands, respecting whose lives, deaths, and burials, they compared notes, and discovered sundry circumstances that tallied with wonderful exactness; such as Barbara's father having been exactly four years and ten months older than Kit's father, and one of them having died on a Wednesday and the other on a Thursday, and both of them having been of a very fine make and remarkably good-looking, with other extraordinary coincidences. These recollections being of a kind calculated to cast a shadow on the brightness of the holiday, Kit diverted the conversation to general topics, and they were soon in great force again, and as merry as before. Among other things, Kit told them about his old place, and the extraordinary beauty of Nell (of whom he had talked to Barbara a thousand times already); but the last-named circumstance failed to interest his hearers to anything like the extent he had supposed, and even his mother said (looking accidentally at Barbara at the same time) that there was no doubt Miss Nell was very pretty, but she was but a child after all, and there were many young women quite as pretty as she; and Barbara mildly observed that she should think so, and that she never could help believing Mr Christopher must be under a mistake—which Kit wondered at very much, not being able to conceive what reason she had for doubting him. Barbara's mother too, observed that it was very common for young folks to change at about fourteen or fifteen, and whereas they had been very pretty before, to grow up quite plain; which truth she illustrated by many forcible examples, especially one of a young man, who, being a builder with great prospects, had been particular in his attentions to Barbara, but whom Barbara would have nothing to say to; which (though everything happened for the best) she almost thought was a pity. Kit said he thought so too, and so he did honestly, and he wondered what made Barbara so silent all at once, and why his mother looked at him as if he shouldn't have said it.

However, it was high time now to be thinking of the play; for which great preparation was required, in the way of shawls and bonnets, not to mention one handkerchief full of oranges and another of apples, which took some time tying up, in consequence of the fruit having a tendency to roll out at the corners. At length, everything was ready, and they went off very fast; Kit's mother carrying the baby, who was dreadfully wide awake, and Kit holding little Jacob in one hand, and escorting Barbara with the other—a state of things which occasioned the two mothers, who walked behind, to declare that they looked quite family folks, and caused Barbara to blush and say, 'Now don't, mother!' But Kit said she had no call to mind what they said; and indeed she need not have had, if she had known how very far from Kit's thoughts any love-making was. Poor Barbara!

At last they got to the theatre, which was Astley's: and in some two minutes after they had reached the yet unopened door, little Jacob was squeezed flat, and the baby had received divers concussions, and Barbara's mother's umbrella had been carried several yards off and passed back to her over the shoulders of the people, and Kit had hit a man on the head with the handkerchief of apples for 'scrowdging' his parent with unnecessary violence, and there was a great uproar. But, when they were once past the pay-place and tearing away for very life with their checks in their hands, and, above all, when they were fairly in the theatre, and seated in such places that they couldn't have had better if they had picked them out, and taken them beforehand, all this was looked upon as quite a capital joke, and an essential part of the entertainment.

Dear, dear, what a place it looked, that Astley's; with all the paint, gilding, and looking-glass; the vague smell of horses suggestive of coming wonders; the curtain that hid such gorgeous mysteries; the clean white sawdust down in the circus; the company coming in and taking their places; the fiddlers looking carelessly up at them while they tuned their instruments, as if they didn't want the play to begin, and knew it all beforehand! What a glow was that, which burst upon them all, when that long, clear, brilliant row of lights came slowly up; and what the feverish excitement when the little bell rang and the music began in good earnest, with strong parts for the drums, and sweet effects for the triangles! Well might Barbara's mother say to Kit's mother that the gallery was the place to see from, and wonder it wasn't much dearer than the boxes; well might Barbara feel doubtful whether to laugh or cry, in her flutter of delight.

Then the play itself! the horses which little Jacob believed from the first to be alive, and the ladies and gentlemen of whose reality he could be by no means persuaded, having never seen or heard anything at all like them—the firing, which made Barbara wink—the forlorn lady, who made her cry—the tyrant, who made her tremble—the man who sang the song with the lady's-maid and danced the chorus, who made her laugh—the pony who reared up on his hind legs when he saw the murderer, and wouldn't hear of walking on all fours again until he was taken into custody—the clown who ventured on such familiarities with the military man in boots—the lady who jumped over the nine-and-twenty ribbons and came down safe upon the horse's back—everything was delightful, splendid, and surprising! Little Jacob applauded till his hands were sore; Kit cried 'an-kor' at the end of everything, the three-act piece included; and Barbara's mother beat her umbrella on the floor, in her ecstasies, until it was nearly worn down to the gingham.

In the midst of all these fascinations, Barbara's thoughts seemed to have been still running on what Kit had said at tea-time; for, when they were coming out of the play, she asked him, with an hysterical simper, if Miss Nell was as handsome as the lady who jumped over the ribbons.

'As handsome as her?' said Kit. 'Double as handsome.'

'Oh Christopher! I'm sure she was the beautifullest creature ever was,' said Barbara.

'Nonsense!' returned Kit. 'She was well enough, I don't deny that; but think how she was dressed and painted, and what a difference that made. Why you are a good deal better looking than her, Barbara.'

'Oh Christopher!' said Barbara, looking down.

'You are, any day,' said Kit, '—and so's your mother.'

Poor Barbara!

What was all this though—even all this—to the extraordinary dissipation that ensued, when Kit, walking into an oyster-shop as bold as if he lived there, and not so much as looking at the counter or the man behind it, led his party into a box—a private box, fitted up with red curtains, white table-cloth, and cruet-stand complete—and ordered a fierce gentleman with whiskers, who acted as waiter and called him, him Christopher Nubbles, 'sir,' to bring three dozen of his largest-sized oysters, and to look sharp about it! Yes, Kit told this gentleman to look sharp, and he not only said he would look sharp, but he actually did, and presently came running back with the newest loaves, and the freshest butter, and the largest oysters, ever seen. Then said Kit to this gentleman, 'a pot of beer'—just so—and the gentleman, instead of replying, 'Sir, did you address that language to me?' only said, 'Pot o' beer, sir? Yes, sir,' and went off and fetched it, and put it on the table in a small decanter-stand, like those which blind-men's dogs carry about the streets in their mouths, to catch the half-pence in; and both Kit's mother and Barbara's mother declared as he turned away that he was one of the slimmest and gracefullest young men she had ever looked upon.

Then they fell to work upon the supper in earnest; and there was Barbara, that foolish Barbara, declaring that she could not eat more than two, and wanting more pressing than you would believe before she would eat four: though her mother and Kit's mother made up for it pretty well, and ate and laughed and enjoyed themselves so thoroughly that it did Kit good to see them, and made him laugh and eat likewise from strong sympathy. But the greatest miracle of the night was little Jacob, who ate oysters as if he had been born and bred to the business—sprinkled the pepper and the vinegar with a discretion beyond his years—and afterwards built a grotto on the table with the shells. There was the baby too, who had never closed an eye all night, but had sat as good as gold, trying to force a large orange into his mouth, and gazing intently at the lights in the chandelier—there he was, sitting up in his mother's lap, staring at the gas without winking, and making indentations in his soft visage with an oyster-shell, to that degree that a heart of iron must have loved him! In short, there never was a more successful supper; and when Kit ordered in a glass of something hot to finish with, and proposed Mr and Mrs Garland before sending it round, there were not six happier people in all the world.

But all happiness has an end—hence the chief pleasure of its next beginning—and as it was now growing late, they agreed it was time to turn their faces homewards. So, after going a little out of their way to see Barbara and Barbara's mother safe to a friend's house where they were to pass the night, Kit and his mother left them at the door, with an early appointment for returning to Finchley next morning, and a great many plans for next quarter's enjoyment. Then, Kit took little Jacob on his back, and giving his arm to his mother, and a kiss to the baby, they all trudged merrily home together.

CHAPTER 40

Full of that vague kind of penitence which holidays awaken next morning, Kit turned out at sunrise, and, with his faith in last night's enjoyments a little shaken by cool daylight and the return to every-day duties and occupations, went to meet Barbara and her mother at the appointed place. And being careful not to awaken any of the little household, who were yet resting from their unusual fatigues, Kit left his money on the chimney-piece, with an inscription in chalk calling his mother's attention to the circumstance, and informing her that it came from her dutiful son; and went his way, with a heart something heavier than his pockets, but free from any very great oppression notwithstanding.

Oh these holidays! why will they leave us some regret? why cannot we push them back, only a week or two in our memories, so as to put them at once at that convenient distance whence they may be regarded either with a calm indifference or a pleasant effort of recollection! why will they hang about us, like the flavour of yesterday's wine, suggestive of headaches and lassitude, and those good intentions for the future, which, under the earth, form the everlasting pavement of a large estate, and, upon it, usually endure until dinner-time or thereabouts!

Who will wonder that Barbara had a headache, or that Barbara's mother was disposed to be cross, or that she slightly underrated Astley's, and thought the clown was older than they had taken him to be last night? Kit was not surprised to hear her say so—not he. He had already had a misgiving that the inconstant actors in that dazzling vision had been doing the same thing the night before last, and would do it again that night, and the next, and for weeks and months to come, though he would not be there. Such is the difference between yesterday and today. We are all going to the play, or coming home from it.

However, the Sun himself is weak when he first rises, and gathers strength and courage as the day gets on. By degrees, they began to recall circumstances more and more pleasant in their nature, until, what between talking, walking, and laughing, they reached Finchley in such good heart, that Barbara's mother declared she never felt less tired or in better spirits. And so said Kit. Barbara had been silent all the way, but she said so too. Poor little Barbara! She was very quiet.

They were at home in such good time that Kit had rubbed down the pony and made him as spruce as a race-horse, before Mr Garland came down to breakfast; which punctual and industrious conduct the old lady, and the old gentleman, and Mr Abel, highly extolled. At his usual hour (or rather at his usual minute and second, for he was the soul of punctuality) Mr Abel walked out, to be overtaken by the London coach, and Kit and the old gentleman went to work in the garden.

This was not the least pleasant of Kit's employments. On a fine day they were quite a family party; the old lady sitting hard by with her work-basket on a little table; the old gentleman digging, or pruning, or clipping about with a large pair of shears, or helping Kit in some way or other with great assiduity; and Whisker looking on from his paddock in placid contemplation of them all. To-day they were to trim the grape-vine, so Kit mounted half-way up a short ladder, and began to snip and hammer away, while the old gentleman, with a great interest in his proceedings, handed up the nails and shreds of cloth as he wanted them. The old lady and Whisker looked on as usual.

'Well, Christopher,' said Mr Garland, 'and so you have made a new friend, eh?'

'I beg your pardon, Sir?' returned Kit, looking down from the ladder.

'You have made a new friend, I hear from Mr Abel,' said the old gentleman, 'at the office!'

'Oh! Yes Sir, yes. He behaved very handsome, Sir.'

'I'm glad to hear it,' returned the old gentlemen with a smile. 'He is disposed to behave more handsomely still, though, Christopher.'

'Indeed, Sir! It's very kind in him, but I don't want him to, I'm sure,' said Kit, hammering stoutly at an obdurate nail.

'He is rather anxious,' pursued the old gentleman, 'to have you in his own service—take care what you're doing, or you will fall down and hurt yourself.'

'To have me in his service, Sir?' cried Kit, who had stopped short in his work and faced about on the ladder like some dexterous tumbler. 'Why, Sir, I don't think he can be in earnest when he says that.'

'Oh! But he is indeed,' said Mr Garland. 'And he has told Mr Abel so.'

'I never heard of such a thing!' muttered Kit, looking ruefully at his master and mistress.

'I wonder at him; that I do.'

'You see, Christopher,' said Mr Garland, 'this is a point of much importance to you, and you should understand and consider it in that light. This gentleman is able to give you more money than I—not, I hope, to carry through the various relations of master and servant, more kindness and confidence, but certainly, Christopher, to give you more money.'

'Well,' said Kit, 'after that, Sir—'

'Wait a moment,' interposed Mr Garland. 'That is not all. You were a very faithful servant to your old employers, as I understand, and should this gentleman recover them, as it is his purpose to attempt doing by every means in his power, I have no doubt that you, being in his service, would meet with your reward. Besides,' added the old gentleman with stronger emphasis, 'besides having the pleasure of being again brought into communication with those to whom you seem to be very strongly and disinterestedly attached. You must think of all this, Christopher, and not be rash or hasty in your choice.'

Kit did suffer one twinge, one momentary pang, in keeping the resolution he had already formed, when this last argument passed swiftly into his thoughts, and conjured up the realization of all his hopes and fancies. But it was gone in a minute, and he sturdily rejoined that the gentleman must look out for somebody else, as he did think he might have done at first.

'He has no right to think that I'd be led away to go to him, sir,' said Kit, turning round again after half a minute's hammering. 'Does he think I'm a fool?'

'He may, perhaps, Christopher, if you refuse his offer,' said Mr Garland gravely.

'Then let him, sir,' retorted Kit; 'what do I care, sir, what he thinks? why should I care for his thinking, sir, when I know that I should be a fool, and worse than a fool, sir, to leave the kindest master and mistress that ever was or can be, who took me out of the streets a very poor and hungry lad indeed—poorer and hungrier perhaps than even you think for, sir—to go to him or anybody? If Miss Nell was to come back, ma'am,' added Kit, turning suddenly to his mistress, 'why that would be another thing, and perhaps if she wanted me, I might ask you now and then to let me work for her when all was done at home. But when she comes back, I see now that she'll be rich as old master always said she would, and being a rich young lady, what could she want of me? No, no,' added Kit, shaking his head sorrowfully, 'she'll never want me any more, and bless her, I hope she never may, though I should like to see her too!'

Here Kit drove a nail into the wall, very hard—much harder than was necessary—and having done so, faced about again.

'There's the pony, sir,' said Kit—'Whisker, ma'am (and he knows so well I'm talking about him that he begins to neigh directly, Sir)—would he let anybody come near him but me, ma'am? Here's the garden, sir, and Mr Abel, ma'am. Would Mr Abel part with me, Sir, or is there anybody that could be fonder of the garden, ma'am? It would break mother's heart, Sir, and even little Jacob would have sense enough to cry his eyes out, ma'am, if he thought that Mr Abel could wish to part with me so soon, after having told me, only the other day, that he hoped we might be together for years to come—'

There is no telling how long Kit might have stood upon the ladder, addressing his master and mistress by turns, and generally turning towards the wrong person, if Barbara had not at that moment come running up to say that a messenger from the office had brought a note, which, with an expression of some surprise at Kit's oratorical appearance, she put into her master's hand.

'Oh!' said the old gentleman after reading it, 'ask the messenger to walk this way.' Barbara tripping off to do as she was bid, he turned to Kit and said that they would not pursue the subject any further, and that Kit could not be more unwilling to part with them, than they would be to part with Kit; a sentiment which the old lady very generously echoed.

'At the same time, Christopher,' added Mr Garland, glancing at the note in his hand, 'if the gentleman should want to borrow you now and then for an hour or so, or even a day or so, at a time, we must consent to lend you, and you must consent to be lent.—Oh! here is the young gentleman. How do you do, Sir?'

This salutation was addressed to Mr Chuckster, who, with his hat extremely on one side, and his hair a long way beyond it, came swaggering up the walk.

'Hope I see you well sir,' returned that gentleman. 'Hope I see you well, ma'am. Charming box this, sir. Delicious country to be sure.'

'You want to take Kit back with you, I find?' observed Mr Garland.

'I have got a chariot-cab waiting on purpose,' replied the clerk. 'A very spanking grey in that cab, sir, if you're a judge of horse-flesh.'

Declining to inspect the spanking grey, on the plea that he was but poorly acquainted with such matters, and would but imperfectly appreciate his beauties, Mr Garland invited Mr Chuckster to partake of a slight repast in the way of lunch. That gentleman readily consenting, certain cold viands, flanked with ale and wine, were speedily prepared for his refreshment.

At this repast, Mr Chuckster exerted his utmost abilities to enchant his entertainers, and impress them with a conviction of the mental superiority of those who dwelt in town; with which view he led the discourse to the small scandal of the day, in which he was justly considered by his friends to shine prodigiously. Thus, he was in a condition to relate the exact circumstances of the difference between the Marquis of Mizzler and Lord Bobby, which it appeared originated in a disputed bottle of champagne, and not in a pigeon-pie, as erroneously reported in the newspapers; neither had Lord Bobby said to the Marquis of Mizzler, 'Mizzler, one of us two tells a lie, and I'm not the man,' as incorrectly stated by the same authorities; but 'Mizzler, you know where I'm to be found, and damme, sir, find me if you want me'—which, of course, entirely changed the aspect of this interesting question, and placed it in a very different light. He also acquainted them with the precise amount of the income guaranteed by the Duke of Thigsberry to Violetta Stetta of the Italian Opera, which it appeared was payable quarterly, and not half-yearly, as the public had been given to understand, and which was exclusive, and not inclusive (as had been monstrously stated,) of jewellery, perfumery, hair-powder for five footmen, and two daily changes of kid-gloves for a page. Having entreated the old lady and gentleman to set their minds at rest on these absorbing points, for they might rely on his statement being the correct one, Mr Chuckster entertained them with theatrical chit-chat and the court circular; and so wound up a brilliant and fascinating conversation which he had maintained alone, and without any assistance whatever, for upwards of three-quarters of an hour.

'And now that the nag has got his wind again,' said Mr Chuckster rising in a graceful manner, 'I'm afraid I must cut my stick.'

Neither Mr nor Mrs Garland offered any opposition to his tearing himself away (feeling, no doubt, that such a man could ill be spared from his proper sphere of action), and therefore Mr Chuckster and Kit were shortly afterwards upon their way to town; Kit being perched upon the box of the cabriolet beside the driver, and Mr Chuckster seated in solitary state inside, with one of his boots sticking out at each of the front windows.

When they reached the Notary's house, Kit followed into the office, and was desired by Mr Abel to sit down and wait, for the gentleman who wanted him had gone out, and perhaps might not return for some time. This anticipation was strictly verified, for Kit had had his dinner, and his tea, and had read all the lighter matter in the Law-List, and the Post-Office Directory, and had fallen asleep a great many times, before the gentleman whom he had seen before, came in; which he did at last in a very great hurry.

He was closeted with Mr Witherden for some little time, and Mr Abel had been called in to assist at the conference, before Kit, wondering very much what he was wanted for, was summoned to attend them.

'Christopher,' said the gentleman, turning to him directly he entered the room, 'I have found your old master and young mistress.'

'No, Sir! Have you, though?' returned Kit, his eyes sparkling with delight. 'Where are they, Sir? How are they, Sir? Are they—are they near here?'

'A long way from here,' returned the gentleman, shaking his head. 'But I am going away to-night to bring them back, and I want you to go with me.'

'Me, Sir?' cried Kit, full of joy and surprise.

'The place,' said the strange gentleman, turning thoughtfully to the Notary, 'indicated by this man of the dogs, is—how far from here—sixty miles?'

'From sixty to seventy.'

'Humph! If we travel post all night, we shall reach there in good time to-morrow morning. Now, the only question is, as they will not know me, and the child, God bless her, would think that any stranger pursuing them had a design upon her grandfather's liberty—can I do better than take this lad, whom they both know and will readily remember, as an assurance to them of my friendly intentions?'

'Certainly not,' replied the Notary. 'Take Christopher by all means.'

'I beg your pardon, Sir,' said Kit, who had listened to this discourse with a lengthening countenance, 'but if that's the reason, I'm afraid I should do more harm than good—Miss Nell, Sir, she knows me, and would trust in me, I am sure; but old master—I don't know why, gentlemen; nobody does—would not bear me in his sight after he had been ill, and Miss Nell herself told me that I must not go near him or let him see me any more. I should spoil all that you were doing if I went, I'm afraid. I'd give the world to go, but you had better not take me, Sir.'

'Another difficulty!' cried the impetuous gentleman. 'Was ever man so beset as I? Is there nobody else that knew them, nobody else in whom they had any confidence? Solitary as their lives were, is there no one person who would serve my purpose?'

'Is there, Christopher?' said the Notary.

'Not one, Sir,' replied Kit.—'Yes, though—there's my mother.'

'Did they know her?' said the single gentleman.

'Know her, Sir! why, she was always coming backwards and forwards. They were as kind to her as they were to me. Bless you, Sir, she expected they'd come back to her house.'

'Then where the devil is the woman?' said the impatient gentleman, catching up his hat. 'Why isn't she here? Why is that woman always out of the way when she is most wanted?'

In a word, the single gentleman was bursting out of the office, bent upon laying violent hands on Kit's mother, forcing her into a post-chaise, and carrying her off, when this novel kind of abduction was with some difficulty prevented by the joint efforts of Mr Abel and the Notary, who restrained him by dint of their remonstrances, and persuaded him to sound Kit upon the probability of her being able and willing to undertake such a journey on so short a notice.

This occasioned some doubts on the part of Kit, and some violent demonstrations on that of the single gentleman, and a great many soothing speeches on that of the Notary and Mr Abel. The upshot of the business was, that Kit, after weighing the matter in his mind and considering it carefully, promised, on behalf of his mother, that she should be ready within two hours from that time to undertake the expedition, and engaged to produce her in that place, in all respects equipped and prepared for the journey, before the specified period had expired.

Having given this pledge, which was rather a bold one, and not particularly easy of redemption, Kit lost no time in sallying forth, and taking measures for its immediate fulfilment.

CHAPTER 41

Kit made his way through the crowded streets, dividing the stream of people, dashing across the busy road-ways, diving into lanes and alleys, and stopping or turning aside for nothing, until he came in front of the Old Curiosity Shop, when he came to a stand; partly from habit and partly from being out of breath.

It was a gloomy autumn evening, and he thought the old place had never looked so dismal as in its dreary twilight. The windows broken, the rusty sashes rattling in their frames, the deserted house a dull barrier dividing the glaring lights and bustle of the street into two long lines, and standing in the midst, cold, dark, and empty—presented a cheerless spectacle which mingled harshly with the bright prospects the boy had been building up for its late inmates, and came like a disappointment or misfortune. Kit would have had a good fire roaring up the empty chimneys, lights sparkling and shining through the windows, people moving briskly to and fro, voices in cheerful conversation, something in unison with the new hopes that were astir. He had not expected that the house would wear any different aspect—had known indeed that it could not—but coming upon it in the midst of eager thoughts and expectations, it checked the current in its flow, and darkened it with a mournful shadow.

Kit, however, fortunately for himself, was not learned enough or contemplative enough to be troubled with presages of evil afar off, and, having no mental spectacles to assist his vision in this respect, saw nothing but the dull house, which jarred uncomfortably upon his previous thoughts. So, almost wishing that he had not passed it, though hardly knowing why, he hurried on again, making up by his increased speed for the few moments he had lost.

'Now, if she should be out,' thought Kit, as he approached the poor dwelling of his mother, 'and I not able to find her, this impatient gentleman would be in a pretty taking. And sure enough there's no light, and the door's fast. Now, God forgive me for saying so, but if this is Little Bethel's doing, I wish Little Bethel was—was farther off,' said Kit checking himself, and knocking at the door.

A second knock brought no reply from within the house; but caused a woman over the way to look out and inquire who that was, awanting Mrs Nubbles.

'Me,' said Kit. 'She's at—at Little Bethel, I suppose?'—getting out the name of the obnoxious conventicle with some reluctance, and laying a spiteful emphasis upon the words.

The neighbour nodded assent.

'Then pray tell me where it is,' said Kit, 'for I have come on a pressing matter, and must fetch her out, even if she was in the pulpit.'

It was not very easy to procure a direction to the fold in question, as none of the neighbours were of the flock that resorted thither, and few knew anything more of it than the name. At last, a gossip of Mrs Nubbles's, who had accompanied her to chapel on one or two occasions when a comfortable cup of tea had preceded her devotions, furnished the needful information, which Kit had no sooner obtained than he started off again.

Little Bethel might have been nearer, and might have been in a straighter road, though in that case the reverend gentleman who presided over its congregation would have lost his favourite allusion to the crooked ways by which it was approached, and which enabled him to liken it to Paradise itself, in contradistinction to the parish church and the broad thoroughfare leading thereunto. Kit found it, at last, after some trouble, and pausing at the door to take breath that he might enter with becoming decency, passed into the chapel.

It was not badly named in one respect, being in truth a particularly little Bethel—a Bethel of the smallest dimensions—with a small number of small pews, and a small pulpit, in which a small gentleman (by trade a Shoemaker, and by calling a Divine) was delivering in a by no means small voice, a by no means small sermon, judging of its dimensions by the condition of his audience, which, if their gross amount were but small, comprised a still smaller number of hearers, as the majority were slumbering.

Among these was Kit's mother, who, finding it matter of extreme difficulty to keep her eyes open after the fatigues of last night, and feeling their inclination to close strongly backed and seconded by the arguments of the preacher, had yielded to the drowsiness that overpowered her, and fallen asleep; though not so soundly but that she could, from time to time, utter a slight and almost inaudible groan, as if in recognition of the orator's doctrines. The baby in her arms was as fast asleep as she; and little Jacob, whose youth prevented him from recognising in this prolonged spiritual nourishment anything half as interesting as oysters, was alternately very fast asleep and very wide awake, as his inclination to slumber, or his terror of being personally alluded to in the discourse, gained the mastery over him.

'And now I'm here,' thought Kit, gliding into the nearest empty pew which was opposite his mother's, and on the other side of the little aisle, 'how am I ever to get at her, or persuade her to come out! I might as well be twenty miles off. She'll never wake till it's all over, and there goes the clock again! If he would but leave off for a minute, or if they'd only sing!'

But there was little encouragement to believe that either event would happen for a couple of hours to come. The preacher went on telling them what he meant to convince them of before he had done, and it was clear that if he only kept to one-half of his promises and forgot the other, he was good for that time at least.

In his desperation and restlessness Kit cast his eyes about the chapel, and happening to let them fall upon a little seat in front of the clerk's desk, could scarcely believe them when they showed him—Quilp!

He rubbed them twice or thrice, but still they insisted that Quilp was there, and there indeed he was, sitting with his hands upon his knees, and his hat between them on a little wooden bracket, with the accustomed grin on his dirty face, and his eyes fixed upon the ceiling. He certainly did not glance at Kit or at his mother, and appeared utterly unconscious of their presence; still Kit could not help feeling, directly, that the attention of the sly little fiend was fastened upon them, and upon nothing else.

But, astounded as he was by the apparition of the dwarf among the Little Bethelites, and not free from a misgiving that it was the forerunner of some trouble or annoyance, he was compelled to subdue his wonder and to take active measures for the withdrawal of his parent, as the evening was now creeping on, and the matter grew serious. Therefore, the next time little Jacob woke, Kit set himself to attract his wandering attention, and this not being a very difficult task (one sneeze effected it), he signed to him to rouse his mother.

Ill-luck would have it, however, that, just then, the preacher, in a forcible exposition of one head of his discourse, leaned over upon the pulpit-desk so that very little more of him than his legs remained inside; and, while he made vehement gestures with his right hand, and held on with his left, stared, or seemed to stare, straight into little Jacob's eyes, threatening him by his strained look and attitude—so it appeared to the child—that if he so much as moved a muscle, he, the preacher, would be literally, and not figuratively, 'down upon him' that instant. In this fearful state of things, distracted by the sudden appearance of Kit, and fascinated by the eyes of the preacher, the miserable Jacob sat bolt upright, wholly incapable of motion, strongly disposed to cry but afraid to do so, and returning his pastor's gaze until his infant eyes seemed starting from their sockets.

'If I must do it openly, I must,' thought Kit. With that he walked softly out of his pew and into his mother's, and as Mr Swiveller would have observed if he had been present, 'collared' the baby without speaking a word.

'Hush, mother!' whispered Kit. 'Come along with me, I've got something to tell you.'

'Where am I?' said Mrs Nubbles.

'In this blessed Little Bethel,' returned her son, peevishly.

'Blessed indeed!' cried Mrs Nubbles, catching at the word. 'Oh, Christopher, how have I been edified this night!'

'Yes, yes, I know,' said Kit hastily; 'but come along, mother, everybody's looking at us. Don't make a noise—bring Jacob—that's right!'

'Stay, Satan, stay!' cried the preacher, as Kit was moving off.

211

'This gentleman says you're to stay, Christopher,' whispered his mother.

'Stay, Satan, stay!' roared the preacher again. 'Tempt not the woman that doth incline her ear to thee, but harken to the voice of him that calleth. He hath a lamb from the fold!' cried the preacher, raising his voice still higher and pointing to the baby. 'He beareth off a lamb, a precious lamb! He goeth about, like a wolf in the night season, and inveigleth the tender lambs!'

Kit was the best-tempered fellow in the world, but considering this strong language, and being somewhat excited by the circumstances in which he was placed, he faced round to the pulpit with the baby in his arms, and replied aloud, 'No, I don't. He's my brother.'

'He's my brother!' cried the preacher.

'He isn't,' said Kit indignantly. 'How can you say such a thing? And don't call me names if you please; what harm have I done? I shouldn't have come to take 'em away, unless I was obliged, you may depend upon that. I wanted to do it very quiet, but you wouldn't let me. Now, you have the goodness to abuse Satan and them, as much as you like, Sir, and to let me alone if you please.'

So saying, Kit marched out of the chapel, followed by his mother and little Jacob, and found himself in the open air, with an indistinct recollection of having seen the people wake up and look surprised, and of Quilp having remained, throughout the interruption, in his old attitude, without moving his eyes from the ceiling, or appearing to take the smallest notice of anything that passed.

'Oh Kit!' said his mother, with her handkerchief to her eyes, 'what have you done! I never can go there again—never!'

'I'm glad of it, mother. What was there in the little bit of pleasure you took last night that made it necessary for you to be low-spirited and sorrowful tonight? That's the way you do. If you're happy or merry ever, you come here to say, along with that chap, that you're sorry for it. More shame for you, mother, I was going to say.'

'Hush, dear!' said Mrs Nubbles; 'you don't mean what you say I know, but you're talking sinfulness.'

'Don't mean it? But I do mean it!' retorted Kit. 'I don't believe, mother, that harmless cheerfulness and good humour are thought greater sins in Heaven than shirt-collars are, and I do believe that those chaps are just about as right and sensible in putting down the one as in leaving off the other—that's my belief. But I won't say anything more about it, if you'll promise not to cry, that's all; and you take the baby that's a lighter weight, and give me little Jacob; and as we go along (which we must do pretty quick) I'll give you the news I bring, which will surprise you a little, I can tell you. There—that's right. Now you look as if you'd never seen Little Bethel in all your life, as I hope you never will again; and here's the baby; and little Jacob, you get atop of my back and catch hold of me tight round the neck, and whenever a Little Bethel parson calls you a precious lamb or says your brother's one, you tell him it's the truest things he's said for a twelvemonth, and that if he'd got a little more of the lamb himself, and less of the mint-sauce—not being quite so sharp and sour over it—I should like him all the better. That's what you've got to say to him, Jacob.'

Talking on in this way, half in jest and half in earnest, and cheering up his mother, the children, and himself, by the one simple process of determining to be in a good humour, Kit led them briskly forward; and on the road home, he related what had passed at the Notary's house, and the purpose with which he had intruded on the solemnities of Little Bethel.

His mother was not a little startled on learning what service was required of her, and presently fell into a confusion of ideas, of which the most prominent were that it was a great honour and dignity to ride in a post-chaise, and that it was a moral impossibility to leave the children behind. But this objection, and a great many others, founded on certain articles of dress being at the wash, and certain other articles having no existence in the wardrobe of Mrs Nubbles, were overcome by Kit, who opposed to each and every of them, the pleasure of recovering Nell, and the delight it would be to bring her back in triumph.

'There's only ten minutes now, mother,' said Kit when they reached home. 'There's a bandbox. Throw in what you want, and we'll be off directly.'

To tell how Kit then hustled into the box all sorts of things which could, by no remote contingency, be wanted, and how he left out everything likely to be of the smallest use; how a neighbour was persuaded to come and stop with the children, and how the children at first cried dismally, and then laughed heartily on being promised all kinds of impossible and unheard-of toys; how Kit's mother wouldn't leave off kissing them, and how Kit couldn't make up his mind to be vexed with her for doing it; would take more time and room than you and I can spare. So, passing over all such matters, it is sufficient to say that within a few minutes after the two hours had expired, Kit and his mother arrived at the Notary's door, where a post-chaise was already waiting.

'With four horses I declare!' said Kit, quite aghast at the preparations. 'Well you are going to do it, mother! Here she is, Sir. Here's my mother. She's quite ready, sir.'

'That's well,' returned the gentleman. 'Now, don't be in a flutter, ma'am; you'll be taken great care of. Where's the box with the new clothing and necessaries for them?'

'Here it is,' said the Notary. 'In with it, Christopher.'

'All right, Sir,' replied Kit. 'Quite ready now, sir.'

'Then come along,' said the single gentleman. And thereupon he gave his arm to Kit's mother, handed her into the carriage as politely as you please, and took his seat beside her.

Up went the steps, bang went the door, round whirled the wheels, and off they rattled, with Kit's mother hanging out at one window waving a damp pocket-handkerchief and screaming out a great many messages to little Jacob and the baby, of which nobody heard a word.

Kit stood in the middle of the road, and looked after them with tears in his eyes—not brought there by the departure he witnessed, but by the return to which he looked forward. 'They went away,' he thought, 'on foot with nobody to speak to them or say a kind word at parting, and they'll come back, drawn by four horses, with this rich gentleman for their friend, and all their troubles over! She'll forget that she taught me to write—'

Whatever Kit thought about after this, took some time to think of, for he stood gazing up the lines of shining lamps, long after the chaise had disappeared, and did not return into the house until the Notary and Mr Abel, who had themselves lingered outside till the sound of the wheels was no longer distinguishable, had several times wondered what could possibly detain him.

CHAPTER 42

It behoves us to leave Kit for a while, thoughtful and expectant, and to follow the fortunes of little Nell; resuming the thread of the narrative at the point where it was left, some chapters back.

In one of those wanderings in the evening time, when, following the two sisters at a humble distance, she felt, in her sympathy with them and her recognition in their trials of something akin to her own loneliness of spirit, a comfort and consolation which made such moments a time of deep delight, though the softened pleasure they yielded was of that kind which lives and dies in tears—in one of those wanderings at the quiet hour of twilight, when sky, and earth, and air, and rippling water, and sound of distant bells, claimed kindred with the emotions of the solitary child, and inspired her with soothing thoughts, but not of a child's world or its easy joys—in one of those rambles which had now become her only pleasure or relief from care, light had faded into darkness and evening deepened into night, and still the young creature lingered in the gloom; feeling a companionship in Nature so serene and still, when noise of tongues and glare of garish lights would have been solitude indeed.

The sisters had gone home, and she was alone. She raised her eyes to the bright stars, looking down so mildly from the wide worlds of air, and, gazing on them, found new stars burst upon her view, and more beyond, and more beyond again, until the whole great expanse sparkled with shining spheres, rising higher and higher in immeasurable space, eternal in their numbers as in their changeless and incorruptible existence. She bent over the calm river, and saw them shining in the same majestic order as when the dove beheld them gleaming through the swollen waters, upon the mountain tops down far below, and dead mankind, a million fathoms deep.

The child sat silently beneath a tree, hushed in her very breath by the stillness of the night, and all its attendant wonders. The time and place awoke reflection, and she thought with a quiet hope—less hope, perhaps, than resignation—on the past, and present, and what was yet before her. Between the old man and herself there had come a gradual separation, harder to bear than any former sorrow. Every evening, and often in the day-time too, he was absent, alone; and although she well knew where he went, and why—too well from the constant drain upon her scanty purse and from his haggard looks—he evaded all inquiry, maintained a strict reserve, and even shunned her presence.

She sat meditating sorrowfully upon this change, and mingling it, as it were, with everything about her, when the distant church-clock bell struck nine. Rising at the sound, she retraced her steps, and turned thoughtfully towards the town.

She had gained a little wooden bridge, which, thrown across the stream, led into a meadow in her way, when she came suddenly upon a ruddy light, and looking forward more attentively, discerned that it proceeded from what appeared to be an encampment of gipsies, who had made a fire in one corner at no great distance from the path, and were sitting or lying round it. As she was too poor to have any fear of them, she did not alter her course (which, indeed, she could not have done without going a long way round), but quickened her pace a little, and kept straight on.

A movement of timid curiosity impelled her, when she approached the spot, to glance towards the fire. There was a form between it and her, the outline strongly developed against the light, which caused her to stop abruptly. Then, as if she had reasoned with herself and were assured that it could not be, or had satisfied herself that it was not that of the person she had supposed, she went on again.

But at that instant the conversation, whatever it was, which had been carrying on near this fire was resumed, and the tones of the voice that spoke—she could not distinguish words—sounded as familiar to her as her own.

She turned, and looked back. The person had been seated before, but was now in a standing posture, and leaning forward on a stick on which he rested both hands. The attitude was no less familiar to her than the tone of voice had been. It was her grandfather.

Her first impulse was to call to him; her next to wonder who his associates could be, and for what purpose they were together. Some vague apprehension succeeded, and, yielding to the strong inclination it awakened, she drew nearer to the place; not advancing across the open field, however, but creeping towards it by the hedge.

In this way she advanced within a few feet of the fire, and standing among a few young trees, could both see and hear, without much danger of being observed.

There were no women or children, as she had seen in other gipsy camps they had passed in their wayfaring, and but one gipsy—a tall athletic man, who stood with his arms folded, leaning against a tree at a little distance off, looking now at the fire, and now, under his black eyelashes, at three other men who were there, with a watchful but half-concealed interest in their conversation. Of these, her grandfather was one; the others she recognised as the first card-players at the public-house on the eventful night of the storm—the man whom they had called Isaac List, and his gruff companion. One of the low, arched gipsy-tents, common to that people, was pitched hard by, but it either was, or appeared to be, empty.

'Well, are you going?' said the stout man, looking up from the ground where he was lying at his ease, into her grandfather's face. 'You were in a mighty hurry a minute ago. Go, if you like. You're your own master, I hope?'

'Don't vex him,' returned Isaac List, who was squatting like a frog on the other side of the fire, and had so screwed himself up that he seemed to be squinting all over; 'he didn't mean any offence.'

'You keep me poor, and plunder me, and make a sport and jest of me besides,' said the old man, turning from one to the other. 'Ye'll drive me mad among ye.'

The utter irresolution and feebleness of the grey-haired child, contrasted with the keen and cunning looks of those in whose hands he was, smote upon the little listener's heart. But she constrained herself to attend to all that passed, and to note each look and word.

'Confound you, what do you mean?' said the stout man rising a little, and supporting himself on his elbow. 'Keep you poor! You'd keep us poor if you could, wouldn't you? That's the way with you whining, puny, pitiful players. When you lose, you're martyrs; but I don't find that when you win, you look upon the other losers in that light. As to plunder!' cried the fellow, raising his voice—'Damme, what do you mean by such ungentlemanly language as plunder, eh?'

The speaker laid himself down again at full length, and gave one or two short, angry kicks, as if in further expression of his unbounded indignation. It was quite plain that he acted the bully, and his friend the peacemaker, for some particular purpose; or rather, it would have been to any one but the weak old man; for they exchanged glances quite openly, both with each other and with the gipsy, who grinned his approval of the jest until his white teeth shone again.

The old man stood helplessly among them for a little time, and then said, turning to his assailant:

'You yourself were speaking of plunder just now, you know. Don't be so violent with me. You were, were you not?'

'Not of plundering among present company! Honour among—among gentlemen, Sir,' returned the other, who seemed to have been very near giving an awkward termination to the sentence.

'Don't be hard upon him, Jowl,' said Isaac List. 'He's very sorry for giving offence. There—go on with what you were saying—go on.'

'I'm a jolly old tender-hearted lamb, I am,' cried Mr Jowl, 'to be sitting here at my time of life giving advice when I know it won't be taken, and that I shall get nothing but abuse for my pains. But that's the way I've gone through life. Experience has never put a chill upon my warm-heartedness.'

'I tell you he's very sorry, don't I?' remonstrated Isaac List, 'and that he wishes you'd go on.'

'Does he wish it?' said the other.

'Ay,' groaned the old man sitting down, and rocking himself to and fro. 'Go on, go on. It's in vain to fight with it; I can't do it; go on.'

'I go on then,' said Jowl, 'where I left off, when you got up so quick. If you're persuaded that it's time for luck to turn, as it certainly is, and find that you haven't means enough to try it (and that's where it is, for you know, yourself, that you never have the funds to keep on long enough at a sitting), help yourself to what seems put in your way on purpose. Borrow it, I say, and, when you're able, pay it back again.'

'Certainly,' Isaac List struck in, 'if this good lady as keeps the wax-works has money, and does keep it in a tin box when she goes to bed, and doesn't lock her door for fear of fire, it seems a easy thing; quite a Providence, I should call it—but then I've been religiously brought up.'

'You see, Isaac,' said his friend, growing more eager, and drawing himself closer to the old man, while he signed to the gipsy not to come between them; 'you see, Isaac, strangers are going in and out every hour of the day; nothing would be more likely than for one of these strangers to get under the good lady's bed, or lock himself in the cupboard; suspicion would be very wide, and would fall a long way from the mark, no doubt. I'd give him his revenge to the last farthing he brought, whatever the amount was.'

'But could you?' urged Isaac List. 'Is your bank strong enough?'

'Strong enough!' answered the other, with assumed disdain. 'Here, you Sir, give me that box out of the straw!'

This was addressed to the gipsy, who crawled into the low tent on all fours, and after some rummaging and rustling returned with a cash-box, which the man who had spoken opened with a key he wore about his person.

'Do you see this?' he said, gathering up the money in his hand and letting it drop back into the box, between his fingers, like water. 'Do you hear it? Do you know the sound of gold? There, put it back—and don't talk about banks again, Isaac, till you've got one of your own.'

Isaac List, with great apparent humility, protested that he had never doubted the credit of a gentleman so notorious for his honourable dealing as Mr Jowl, and that he had hinted at the production of the box, not for the satisfaction of his doubts, for he could have none, but with a view to being regaled with a sight of so much wealth, which, though it might be deemed by some but an unsubstantial and visionary pleasure, was to one in his circumstances a source of extreme delight, only to be surpassed by its safe depository in his own personal pockets. Although Mr List and Mr Jowl addressed themselves to each other, it was remarkable that they both looked narrowly at the old man, who, with his eyes fixed upon the fire, sat brooding over it, yet listening eagerly—as it seemed from a certain involuntary motion of the head, or twitching of the face from time to time—to all they said.

'My advice,' said Jowl, lying down again with a careless air, 'is plain—I have given it, in fact. I act as a friend. Why should I help a man to the means perhaps of winning all I have, unless I considered him my friend? It's foolish, I dare say, to be so thoughtful of the welfare of other people, but that's my constitution, and I can't help it; so don't blame me, Isaac List.'

'I blame you!' returned the person addressed; 'not for the world, Mr Jowl. I wish I could afford to be as liberal as you; and, as you say, he might pay it back if he won—and if he lost—'

'You're not to take that into consideration at all,' said Jowl.

'But suppose he did (and nothing's less likely, from all I know of chances), why, it's better to lose other people's money than one's own, I hope?'

'Ah!' cried Isaac List rapturously, 'the pleasures of winning! The delight of picking up the money—the bright, shining yellow-boys—and sweeping 'em into one's pocket! The deliciousness of having a triumph at last, and thinking that one didn't stop short and turn back, but went half-way to meet it! The—but you're not going, old gentleman?'

'I'll do it,' said the old man, who had risen and taken two or three hurried steps away, and now returned as hurriedly. 'I'll have it, every penny.'

'Why, that's brave,' cried Isaac, jumping up and slapping him on the shoulder; 'and I respect you for having so much young blood left. Ha, ha, ha! Joe Jowl's half sorry he advised you now. We've got the laugh against him. Ha, ha, ha!'

'He gives me my revenge, mind,' said the old man, pointing to him eagerly with his shrivelled hand: 'mind—he stakes coin against coin, down to the last one in the box, be there many or few. Remember that!'

'I'm witness,' returned Isaac. 'I'll see fair between you.'

'I have passed my word,' said Jowl with feigned reluctance, 'and I'll keep it. When does this match come off? I wish it was over.—To-night?'

'I must have the money first,' said the old man; 'and that I'll have to-morrow—'

'Why not to-night?' urged Jowl.

'It's late now, and I should be flushed and flurried,' said the old man. 'It must be softly done. No, to-morrow night.'

'Then to-morrow be it,' said Jowl. 'A drop of comfort here. Luck to the best man! Fill!'

The gipsy produced three tin cups, and filled them to the brim with brandy. The old man turned aside and muttered to himself before he drank. Her own name struck upon the listener's ear, coupled with some wish so fervent, that he seemed to breathe it in an agony of supplication.

'God be merciful to us!' cried the child within herself, 'and help us in this trying hour! What shall I do to save him!'

The remainder of their conversation was carried on in a lower tone of voice, and was sufficiently concise; relating merely to the execution of the project, and the best precautions for diverting suspicion. The old man then shook hands with his tempters, and withdrew.

They watched his bowed and stooping figure as it retreated slowly, and when he turned his head to look back, which he often did, waved their hands, or shouted some brief encouragement. It was not until they had seen him gradually diminish into a mere speck upon the distant road, that they turned to each other, and ventured to laugh aloud.

'So,' said Jowl, warming his hands at the fire, 'it's done at last. He wanted more persuading than I expected. It's three weeks ago, since we first put this in his head. What'll he bring, do you think?'

'Whatever he brings, it's halved between us,' returned Isaac List.

The other man nodded. 'We must make quick work of it,' he said, 'and then cut his acquaintance, or we may be suspected. Sharp's the word.'

List and the gipsy acquiesced. When they had all three amused themselves a little with their victim's infatuation, they dismissed the subject as one which had been sufficiently discussed, and began to talk in a jargon which the child did not understand. As their discourse appeared to relate to matters in which they were warmly interested, however, she deemed it the best time for escaping unobserved; and crept away with slow and cautious steps, keeping in the shadow of the hedges, or forcing a path through them or the dry ditches, until she could emerge upon the road at a point beyond their range of vision. Then she fled homeward as quickly as she could, torn and bleeding from the wounds of thorns and briars, but more lacerated in mind, and threw herself upon her bed, distracted.

The first idea that flashed upon her mind was flight, instant flight; dragging him from that place, and rather dying of want upon the roadside, than ever exposing him again to such terrible temptations. Then, she remembered that the crime was not to be committed until next night, and there was the intermediate time for thinking, and resolving what to do. Then, she was distracted with a horrible fear that he might be committing it at that moment; with a dread of hearing shrieks and cries piercing the silence of the night; with fearful thoughts of what he might be tempted and led on to do, if he were detected in the act, and had but a woman to struggle with. It was impossible to bear such torture. She stole to the room where the money was, opened the door, and looked in. God be praised! He was not there, and she was sleeping soundly.

She went back to her own room, and tried to prepare herself for bed. But who could sleep—sleep! who could lie passively down, distracted by such terrors? They came upon her more and more strongly yet. Half undressed, and with her hair in wild disorder, she flew to the old man's bedside, clasped him by the wrist, and roused him from his sleep.

'What's this!' he cried, starting up in bed, and fixing his eyes upon her spectral face.

'I have had a dreadful dream,' said the child, with an energy that nothing but such terrors could have inspired. 'A dreadful, horrible dream. I have had it once before. It is a dream of grey-haired men like you, in darkened rooms by night, robbing sleepers of their gold. Up, up!'

The old man shook in every joint, and folded his hands like one who prays.

'Not to me,' said the child, 'not to me—to Heaven, to save us from such deeds! This dream is too real. I cannot sleep, I cannot stay here, I cannot leave you alone under the roof where such dreams come. Up! We must fly.'

He looked at her as if she were a spirit—she might have been for all the look of earth she had—and trembled more and more.

'There is no time to lose; I will not lose one minute,' said the child. 'Up! and away with me!'

'To-night?' murmured the old man.

'Yes, to-night,' replied the child. 'To-morrow night will be too late. The dream will have come again. Nothing but flight can save us. Up!'

The old man rose from his bed: his forehead bedewed with the cold sweat of fear: and, bending before the child as if she had been an angel messenger sent to lead him where she would, made ready to follow her. She took him by the hand and led him on. As they passed the door of the room he had proposed to rob, she shuddered and looked up into his face. What a white face was that, and with what a look did he meet hers!

She took him to her own chamber, and, still holding him by the hand as if she feared to lose him for an instant, gathered together the little stock she had, and hung her basket on her arm. The old man took his wallet from her hands and strapped it on his shoulders—his staff, too, she had brought away—and then she led him forth.

Through the strait streets, and narrow crooked outskirts, their trembling feet passed quickly. Up the steep hill too, crowned by the old grey castle, they toiled with rapid steps, and had not once looked behind.

But as they drew nearer the ruined walls, the moon rose in all her gentle glory, and, from their venerable age, garlanded with ivy, moss, and waving grass, the child looked back upon the sleeping town, deep in the valley's shade: and on the far-off river with its winding track of light: and on the distant hills; and as she did so, she clasped the hand she held, less firmly, and bursting into tears, fell upon the old man's neck.

CHAPTER 43

Her momentary weakness past, the child again summoned the resolution which had until now sustained her, and, endeavouring to keep steadily in her view the one idea that they were flying from disgrace and crime, and that her grandfather's preservation must depend solely on her firmness, unaided by one word of advice or any helping hand, urged him onward and looked back no more.

While he, subdued and abashed, seemed to crouch before her, and to shrink and cower down, as if in the presence of some superior creature, the child herself was sensible of a new feeling within her, which elevated her nature, and inspired her with an energy and confidence she had never known. There was no divided responsibility now; the whole burden of their two lives had fallen upon her, and henceforth she must think and act for both. 'I have saved him,' she thought. 'In all dangers and distresses, I will remember that.'

At any other time, the recollection of having deserted the friend who had shown them so much homely kindness, without a word of justification—the thought that they were guilty, in appearance, of treachery and ingratitude—even the having parted from the two sisters—would have filled her with sorrow and regret. But now, all other considerations were lost in the new uncertainties and anxieties of their wild and wandering life; and the very desperation of their condition roused and stimulated her.

In the pale moonlight, which lent a wanness of its own to the delicate face where thoughtful care already mingled with the winning grace and loveliness of youth, the too bright eye, the spiritual head, the lips that pressed each other with such high resolve and courage of the heart, the slight figure firm in its bearing and yet so very weak, told their silent tale; but told it only to the wind that rustled by, which, taking up its burden, carried, perhaps to some mother's pillow, faint dreams of childhood fading in its bloom, and resting in the sleep that knows no waking.

The night crept on apace, the moon went down, the stars grew pale and dim, and morning, cold as they, slowly approached. Then, from behind a distant hill, the noble sun rose up, driving the mists in phantom shapes before it, and clearing the earth of their ghostly forms till darkness came again. When it had climbed higher into the sky, and there was warmth in its cheerful beams, they laid them down to sleep, upon a bank, hard by some water.

But Nell retained her grasp upon the old man's arm, and long after he was slumbering soundly, watched him with untiring eyes. Fatigue stole over her at last; her grasp relaxed, tightened, relaxed again, and they slept side by side.

A confused sound of voices, mingling with her dreams, awoke her. A man of very uncouth and rough appearance was standing over them, and two of his companions were looking on, from a long heavy boat which had come close to the bank while they were sleeping. The boat had neither oar nor sail, but was towed by a couple of horses, who, with the rope to which they were harnessed slack and dripping in the water, were resting on the path.

'Holloa!' said the man roughly. 'What's the matter here?'

'We were only asleep, Sir,' said Nell. 'We have been walking all night.'

'A pair of queer travellers to be walking all night,' observed the man who had first accosted them. 'One of you is a trifle too old for that sort of work, and the other a trifle too young. Where are you going?'

Nell faltered, and pointed at hazard towards the West, upon which the man inquired if she meant a certain town which he named. Nell, to avoid more questioning, said 'Yes, that was the place.'

'Where have you come from?' was the next question; and this being an easier one to answer, Nell mentioned the name of the village in which their friend the schoolmaster dwelt, as being less likely to be known to the men or to provoke further inquiry.

'I thought somebody had been robbing and ill-using you, might be,' said the man. 'That's all. Good day.'

Returning his salute and feeling greatly relieved by his departure, Nell looked after him as he mounted one of the horses, and the boat went on. It had not gone very far, when it stopped again, and she saw the men beckoning to her.

'Did you call to me?' said Nell, running up to them.

'You may go with us if you like,' replied one of those in the boat. 'We're going to the same place.'

The child hesitated for a moment. Thinking, as she had thought with great trepidation more than once before, that the men whom she had seen with her grandfather might, perhaps, in their eagerness for the booty, follow them, and regaining their influence over him, set hers at nought; and that if they went with these men, all traces of them must surely be lost at that spot; determined to accept the offer. The boat came close to the bank again, and before she had had any more time for consideration, she and her grandfather were on board, and gliding smoothly down the canal.

The sun shone pleasantly on the bright water, which was sometimes shaded by trees, and sometimes open to a wide extent of country, intersected by running streams, and rich with wooded hills, cultivated land, and sheltered farms. Now and then, a village with its modest spire, thatched roofs, and gable-ends, would peep out from among the trees; and, more than once, a distant town, with great church towers looming through its smoke, and high factories or workshops rising above the mass of houses, would come in view, and, by the length of time it lingered in the distance, show them how slowly they travelled. Their way lay, for the most part, through the low grounds, and open plains; and except these distant places, and occasionally some men working in the fields, or lounging on the bridges under which they passed, to see them creep along, nothing encroached on their monotonous and secluded track.

Nell was rather disheartened, when they stopped at a kind of wharf late in the afternoon, to learn from one of the men that they would not reach their place of destination until next day, and that, if she had no provision with her, she had better buy it there. She had but a few pence, having already bargained with them for some bread, but even of these it was necessary to be very careful, as they were on their way to an utterly strange place, with no resource whatever. A small loaf and a morsel of cheese, therefore, were all she could afford, and with these she took her place in the boat again, and, after half an hour's delay during which the men were drinking at the public-house, proceeded on the journey.

They brought some beer and spirits into the boat with them, and what with drinking freely before, and again now, were soon in a fair way of being quarrelsome and intoxicated. Avoiding the small cabin, therefore, which was very dark and filthy, and to which they often invited both her and her grandfather, Nell sat in the open air with the old man by her side: listening to their boisterous hosts with a palpitating heart, and almost wishing herself safe on shore again though she should have to walk all night.

They were, in truth, very rugged, noisy fellows, and quite brutal among themselves, though civil enough to their two passengers. Thus, when a quarrel arose between the man who was steering and his friend in the cabin, upon the question who had first suggested the propriety of offering Nell some beer, and when the quarrel led to a scuffle in which they beat each other fearfully, to her inexpressible terror, neither visited his displeasure upon her, but each contented himself with venting it on his adversary, on whom, in addition to blows, he bestowed a variety of compliments, which, happily for the child, were conveyed in terms, to her quite unintelligible. The difference was finally adjusted, by the man who had come out of the cabin knocking the other into it head first, and taking the helm into his own hands, without evincing the least discomposure himself, or causing any in his friend, who, being of a tolerably strong constitution and perfectly inured to such trifles, went to sleep as he was, with his heels upwards, and in a couple of minutes or so was snoring comfortably.

By this time it was night again, and though the child felt cold, being but poorly clad, her anxious thoughts were far removed from her own suffering or uneasiness, and busily engaged in endeavouring to devise some scheme for their joint subsistence. The same spirit which had supported her on the previous night, upheld and sustained her now. Her grandfather lay sleeping safely at her side, and the crime to which his madness urged him, was not committed. That was her comfort.

How every circumstance of her short, eventful life, came thronging into her mind, as they travelled on! Slight incidents, never thought of or remembered until now; faces, seen once and ever since forgotten; words scarcely heeded at the time; scenes, of a year ago and those of yesterday, mixing up and linking themselves together; familiar places shaping themselves out in the darkness from things which, when approached, were, of all others, the most remote and most unlike them; sometimes, a strange confusion in her mind relative to the occasion of her being there, and the place to which she was going, and the people she was with; and imagination suggesting remarks and questions which sounded so plainly in her ears, that she would start, and turn, and be almost tempted to reply;—all the fancies and contradictions common in watching and excitement and restless change of place, beset the child.

She happened, while she was thus engaged, to encounter the face of the man on deck, in whom the sentimental stage of drunkenness had now succeeded to the boisterous, and who, taking from his mouth a short pipe, quilted over with string for its longer preservation, requested that she would oblige him with a song.

'You've got a very pretty voice, a very soft eye, and a very strong memory,' said this gentleman; 'the voice and eye I've got evidence for, and the memory's an opinion of my own. And I'm never wrong. Let me hear a song this minute.'

'I don't think I know one, sir,' returned Nell.

'You know forty-seven songs,' said the man, with a gravity which admitted of no altercation on the subject. 'Forty-seven's your number. Let me hear one of 'em—the best. Give me a song this minute.'

Not knowing what might be the consequences of irritating her friend, and trembling with the fear of doing so, poor Nell sang him some little ditty which she had learned in happier times, and which was so agreeable to his ear, that on its conclusion he in the same peremptory manner requested to be favoured with another, to which he was so obliging as to roar a chorus to no particular tune, and with no words at all, but which amply made up in its amazing energy for its deficiency in other respects. The noise of this vocal performance awakened the other man, who, staggering upon deck and shaking his late opponent by the hand, swore that singing was his pride and joy and chief delight, and that he desired no better entertainment. With a third call, more imperative than either of the two former, Nell felt obliged to comply, and this time a chorus was maintained not only by the two men together, but also by the third man on horseback, who being by his position debarred from a nearer participation in the revels of the night, roared when his companions roared, and rent the very air. In this way, with little cessation, and singing the same songs again and again, the tired and exhausted child kept them in good humour all that night; and many a cottager, who was roused from his soundest sleep by the discordant chorus as it floated away upon the wind, hid his head beneath the bed-clothes and trembled at the sounds.

At length the morning dawned. It was no sooner light than it began to rain heavily. As the child could not endure the intolerable vapours of the cabin, they covered her, in return for her exertions, with some pieces of sail-cloth and ends of tarpaulin, which sufficed to keep her tolerably dry and to shelter her grandfather besides. As the day advanced the rain increased. At noon it poured down more hopelessly and heavily than ever without the faintest promise of abatement.

They had, for some time, been gradually approaching the place for which they were bound. The water had become thicker and dirtier; other barges, coming from it, passed them frequently; the paths of coal-ash and huts of staring brick, marked the vicinity of some great manufacturing town; while scattered streets and houses, and smoke from distant furnaces, indicated that they were already in the outskirts. Now, the clustered roofs, and piles of buildings, trembling with the working of engines, and dimly resounding with their shrieks and throbbings; the tall chimneys vomiting forth a black vapour, which hung in a dense ill-favoured cloud above the housetops and filled the air with gloom; the clank of hammers beating upon iron, the roar of busy streets and noisy crowds, gradually augmenting until all the various sounds blended into one and none was distinguishable for itself, announced the termination of their journey.

The boat floated into the wharf to which it belonged. The men were occupied directly. The child and her grandfather, after waiting in vain to thank them or ask them whither they should go, passed through a dirty lane into a crowded street, and stood, amid its din and tumult, and in the pouring rain, as strange, bewildered, and confused, as if they had lived a thousand years before, and were raised from the dead and placed there by a miracle.

CHAPTER 44

The throng of people hurried by, in two opposite streams, with no symptom of cessation or exhaustion; intent upon their own affairs; and undisturbed in their business speculations, by the roar of carts and waggons laden with clashing wares, the slipping of horses' feet upon the wet and greasy pavement, the rattling of the rain on windows and umbrella-tops, the jostling of the more impatient passengers, and all the noise and tumult of a crowded street in the high tide of its occupation: while the two poor strangers, stunned and bewildered by the hurry they beheld but had no part in, looked mournfully on; feeling, amidst the crowd, a solitude which has no parallel but in the thirst of the shipwrecked mariner, who, tost to and fro upon the billows of a mighty ocean, his red eyes blinded by looking on the water which hems him in on every side, has not one drop to cool his burning tongue.

They withdrew into a low archway for shelter from the rain, and watched the faces of those who passed, to find in one among them a ray of encouragement or hope. Some frowned, some smiled, some muttered to themselves, some made slight gestures, as if anticipating the conversation in which they would shortly be engaged, some wore the cunning look of bargaining and plotting, some were anxious and eager, some slow and dull; in some countenances, were written gain; in others, loss. It was like being in the confidence of all these people to stand quietly there, looking into their faces as they flitted past. In busy places, where each man has an object of his own, and feels assured that every other man has his, his character and purpose are written broadly in his face. In the public walks and lounges of a town, people go to see and to be seen, and there the same expression, with little variety, is repeated a hundred times. The working-day faces come nearer to the truth, and let it out more plainly.

Falling into that kind of abstraction which such a solitude awakens, the child continued to gaze upon the passing crowd with a wondering interest, amounting almost to a temporary forgetfulness of her own condition. But cold, wet, hunger, want of rest, and lack of any place in which to lay her aching head, soon brought her thoughts back to the point whence they had strayed. No one passed who seemed to notice them, or to whom she durst appeal. After some time, they left their place of refuge from the weather, and mingled with the concourse.

Evening came on. They were still wandering up and down, with fewer people about them, but with the same sense of solitude in their own breasts, and the same indifference from all around. The lights in the streets and shops made them feel yet more desolate, for with their help, night and darkness seemed to come on faster. Shivering with the cold and damp, ill in body, and sick to death at heart, the child needed her utmost firmness and resolution even to creep along.

Why had they ever come to this noisy town, when there were peaceful country places, in which, at least, they might have hungered and thirsted, with less suffering than in its squalid strife! They were but an atom, here, in a mountain heap of misery, the very sight of which increased their hopelessness and suffering.

The child had not only to endure the accumulated hardships of their destitute condition, but to bear the reproaches of her grandfather, who began to murmur at having been led away from their late abode, and demand that they should return to it. Being now penniless, and no relief or prospect of relief appearing, they retraced their steps through the deserted streets, and went back to the wharf, hoping to find the boat in which they had come, and to be allowed to sleep on board that night. But here again they were disappointed, for the gate was closed, and some fierce dogs, barking at their approach, obliged them to retreat.

'We must sleep in the open air to-night, dear,' said the child in a weak voice, as they turned away from this last repulse; 'and to-morrow we will beg our way to some quiet part of the country, and try to earn our bread in very humble work.'

'Why did you bring me here?' returned the old man fiercely. 'I cannot bear these close eternal streets. We came from a quiet part. Why did you force me to leave it?'

'Because I must have that dream I told you of, no more,' said the child, with a momentary firmness that lost itself in tears; 'and we must live among poor people, or it will come again. Dear grandfather, you are old and weak, I know; but look at me. I never will complain if you will not, but I have some suffering indeed.'

'Ah! poor, houseless, wandering, motherless child!' cried the old man, clasping his hands and gazing as if for the first time upon her anxious face, her travel-stained dress, and bruised and swollen feet; 'has all my agony of care brought her to this at last! Was I a happy man once, and have I lost happiness and all I had, for this!'

'If we were in the country now,' said the child, with assumed cheerfulness, as they walked on looking about them for a shelter, 'we should find some good old tree, stretching out his green arms as if he loved us, and nodding and rustling as if he would have us fall asleep, thinking of him while he watched. Please God, we shall be there soon—to-morrow or next day at the farthest—and in the meantime let us think, dear, that it was a good thing we came here; for we are lost in the crowd and hurry of this place, and if any cruel people should pursue us, they could surely never trace us further. There's comfort in that. And here's a deep old doorway— very dark, but quite dry, and warm too, for the wind don't blow in here—What's that!'

Uttering a half shriek, she recoiled from a black figure which came suddenly out of the dark recess in which they were about to take refuge, and stood still, looking at them.

'Speak again,' it said; 'do I know the voice?'

'No,' replied the child timidly; 'we are strangers, and having no money for a night's lodging, were going to rest here.'

There was a feeble lamp at no great distance; the only one in the place, which was a kind of square yard, but sufficient to show how poor and mean it was. To this, the figure beckoned them; at the same time drawing within its rays, as if to show that it had no desire to conceal itself or take them at an advantage. The form was that of a man, miserably clad and begrimed with smoke, which, perhaps by its contrast with the natural colour of his skin, made him look paler than he really was. That he was naturally of a very wan and pallid aspect, however, his hollow cheeks, sharp features, and sunken eyes, no less than a certain look of patient endurance, sufficiently testified. His voice was harsh by nature, but not brutal; and though his face, besides possessing the characteristics already mentioned, was overshadowed by a quantity of long dark hair, its expression was neither ferocious nor bad.

'How came you to think of resting there?' he said. 'Or how,' he added, looking more attentively at the child, 'do you come to want a place of rest at this time of night?'

'Our misfortunes,' the grandfather answered, 'are the cause.'

'Do you know,' said the man, looking still more earnestly at Nell, 'how wet she is, and that the damp streets are not a place for her?'

'I know it well, God help me,' he replied. 'What can I do!'

The man looked at Nell again, and gently touched her garments, from which the rain was running off in little streams. 'I can give you warmth,' he said, after a pause; 'nothing else. Such lodging as I have, is in that house,' pointing to the doorway from which he had emerged, 'but she is safer and better there than here. The fire is in a rough place, but you can pass the night beside it safely, if you'll trust yourselves to me. You see that red light yonder?'

They raised their eyes, and saw a lurid glare hanging in the dark sky; the dull reflection of some distant fire.

'It's not far,' said the man. 'Shall I take you there? You were going to sleep upon cold bricks; I can give you a bed of warm ashes—nothing better.'

Without waiting for any further reply than he saw in their looks, he took Nell in his arms, and bade the old man follow.

Carrying her as tenderly, and as easily too, as if she had been an infant, and showing himself both swift and sure of foot, he led the way through what appeared to be the poorest and most wretched quarter of the town; and turning aside to avoid the overflowing kennels or running waterspouts, but holding his course, regardless of such obstructions, and making his way straight through them. They had proceeded thus, in silence, for some quarter of an hour, and had lost sight of the glare to which he had pointed, in the dark and narrow ways by which they had come, when it suddenly burst upon them again, streaming up from the high chimney of a building close before them.

'This is the place,' he said, pausing at a door to put Nell down and take her hand. 'Don't be afraid. There's nobody here will harm you.'

It needed a strong confidence in this assurance to induce them to enter, and what they saw inside did not diminish their apprehension and alarm. In a large and lofty building, supported by pillars of iron, with great black apertures in the upper walls, open to the external air; echoing to the roof with the beating of hammers and roar of furnaces, mingled with the hissing of red-hot metal plunged in water, and a hundred strange unearthly noises never heard elsewhere; in this gloomy place, moving like demons among the flame and smoke, dimly and fitfully seen, flushed and tormented by the burning fires, and wielding great weapons, a faulty blow from any one of which must have crushed some workman's skull, a number of men laboured like giants. Others, reposing upon heaps of coals or ashes, with their faces turned to the black vault above, slept or rested from their toil. Others again, opening the white-hot furnace-doors, cast fuel on the flames, which came rushing and roaring forth to meet it, and licked it up like oil. Others drew forth, with clashing noise, upon the ground, great sheets of glowing steel, emitting an insupportable heat, and a dull deep light like that which reddens in the eyes of savage beasts.

Through these bewildering sights and deafening sounds, their conductor led them to where, in a dark portion of the building, one furnace burnt by night and day—so, at least, they gathered from the motion of his lips, for as yet they could only see him speak: not hear him. The man who had been watching this fire, and whose task was ended for the present, gladly withdrew, and left them with their friend, who, spreading Nell's little cloak upon a heap of ashes, and showing her where she could hang her outer-clothes to dry, signed to her and the old man to lie down and sleep. For himself, he took his station on a rugged mat before the furnace-door, and resting his chin upon his hands, watched the flame as it shone through the iron chinks, and the white ashes as they fell into their bright hot grave below.

The warmth of her bed, hard and humble as it was, combined with the great fatigue she had undergone, soon caused the tumult of the place to fall with a gentler sound upon the child's tired ears, and was not long in lulling her to sleep. The old man was stretched beside her, and with her hand upon his neck she lay and dreamed.

It was yet night when she awoke, nor did she know how long, or for how short a time, she had slept. But she found herself protected, both from any cold air that might find its way into the building, and from the scorching heat, by some of the workmen's clothes; and glancing at their friend saw that he sat in exactly the same attitude, looking with a fixed earnestness of attention towards the fire, and keeping so very still that he did not even seem to breathe. She lay in the state between sleeping and waking, looking so long at his motionless figure that at length she almost feared he had died as he sat there; and softly rising and drawing close to him, ventured to whisper in his ear.

He moved, and glancing from her to the place she had lately occupied, as if to assure himself that it was really the child so near him, looked inquiringly into her face.

'I feared you were ill,' she said. 'The other men are all in motion, and you are so very quiet.'

'They leave me to myself,' he replied. 'They know my humour. They laugh at me, but don't harm me in it. See yonder there—that's my friend.'

'The fire?' said the child.

'It has been alive as long as I have,' the man made answer. 'We talk and think together all night long.'

The child glanced quickly at him in her surprise, but he had turned his eyes in their former direction, and was musing as before.

'It's like a book to me,' he said—'the only book I ever learned to read; and many an old story it tells me. It's music, for I should know its voice among a thousand, and there are other voices in its roar. It has its pictures too. You don't know how many strange faces and different scenes I trace in the red-hot coals. It's my memory, that fire, and shows me all my life.'

The child, bending down to listen to his words, could not help remarking with what brightened eyes he continued to speak and muse.

'Yes,' he said, with a faint smile, 'it was the same when I was quite a baby, and crawled about it, till I fell asleep. My father watched it then.'

'Had you no mother?' asked the child.

'No, she was dead. Women work hard in these parts. She worked herself to death they told me, and, as they said so then, the fire has gone on saying the same thing ever since. I suppose it was true. I have always believed it.'

'Were you brought up here, then?' said the child.

'Summer and winter,' he replied. 'Secretly at first, but when they found it out, they let him keep me here. So the fire nursed me—the same fire. It has never gone out.'

'You are fond of it?' said the child.

'Of course I am. He died before it. I saw him fall down—just there, where those ashes are burning now—and wondered, I remember, why it didn't help him.'

'Have you been here ever since?' asked the child.

'Ever since I came to watch it; but there was a while between, and a very cold dreary while it was. It burned all the time though, and roared and leaped when I came back, as it used to do in our play days. You may guess, from looking at me, what kind of child I was, but for all the difference between us I was a child, and when I saw you in the street to-night, you put me in mind of myself, as I was after he died, and made me wish to bring you to the fire. I thought of those old times again, when I saw you sleeping by it. You should be sleeping now. Lie down again, poor child, lie down again!'

With that, he led her to her rude couch, and covering her with the clothes with which she had found herself enveloped when she woke, returned to his seat, whence he moved no more unless to feed the furnace, but remained motionless as a statue. The child continued to watch him for a little time, but soon yielded to the drowsiness that came upon her, and, in the dark strange place and on the heap of ashes, slept as peacefully as if the room had been a palace chamber, and the bed, a bed of down.

When she awoke again, broad day was shining through the lofty openings in the walls, and, stealing in slanting rays but midway down, seemed to make the building darker than it had been at night. The clang and tumult were still going on, and the remorseless fires were burning fiercely as before; for few changes of night and day brought rest or quiet there.

Her friend parted his breakfast—a scanty mess of coffee and some coarse bread—with the child and her grandfather, and inquired whither they were going. She told him that they sought some distant country place remote from towns or even other villages, and with a faltering tongue inquired what road they would do best to take.

'I know little of the country,' he said, shaking his head, 'for such as I, pass all our lives before our furnace doors, and seldom go forth to breathe. But there are such places yonder.'

'And far from here?' said Nell.

'Aye surely. How could they be near us, and be green and fresh? The road lies, too, through miles and miles, all lighted up by fires like ours—a strange black road, and one that would frighten you by night.'

'We are here and must go on,' said the child boldly; for she saw that the old man listened with anxious ears to this account.

'Rough people—paths never made for little feet like yours—a dismal blighted way—is there no turning back, my child?'

'There is none,' cried Nell, pressing forward. 'If you can direct us, do. If not, pray do not seek to turn us from our purpose. Indeed you do not know the danger that we shun, and how right and true we are in flying from it, or you would not try to stop us, I am sure you would not.'

'God forbid, if it is so!' said their uncouth protector, glancing from the eager child to her grandfather, who hung his head and bent his eyes upon the ground. 'I'll direct you from the door, the best I can. I wish I could do more.'

He showed them, then, by which road they must leave the town, and what course they should hold when they had gained it. He lingered so long on these instructions, that the child, with a fervent blessing, tore herself away, and stayed to hear no more.

But, before they had reached the corner of the lane, the man came running after them, and, pressing her hand, left something in it—two old, battered, smoke-encrusted penny pieces. Who knows but they shone as brightly in the eyes of angels, as golden gifts that have been chronicled on tombs?

And thus they separated; the child to lead her sacred charge farther from guilt and shame; the labourer to attach a fresh interest to the spot where his guests had slept, and read new histories in his furnace fire.

CHAPTER 45

In all their journeying, they had never longed so ardently, they had never so pined and wearied, for the freedom of pure air and open country, as now. No, not even on that memorable morning, when, deserting their old home, they abandoned themselves to the mercies of a strange world, and left all the dumb and senseless things they had known and loved, behind— not even then, had they so yearned for the fresh solitudes of wood, hillside, and field, as now, when the noise and dirt and vapour, of the great manufacturing town reeking with lean misery and hungry wretchedness, hemmed them in on every side, and seemed to shut out hope, and render escape impossible.

'Two days and nights!' thought the child. 'He said two days and nights we should have to spend among such scenes as these. Oh! if we live to reach the country once again, if we get clear of these dreadful places, though it is only to lie down and die, with what a grateful heart I shall thank God for so much mercy!'

With thoughts like this, and with some vague design of travelling to a great distance among streams and mountains, where only very poor and simple people lived, and where they might maintain themselves by very humble helping work in farms, free from such terrors as that from which they fled—the child, with no resource but the poor man's gift, and no encouragement but that which flowed from her own heart, and its sense of the truth and right of what she did, nerved herself to this last journey and boldly pursued her task.

'We shall be very slow to-day, dear,' she said, as they toiled painfully through the streets; 'my feet are sore, and I have pains in all my limbs from the wet of yesterday. I saw that he looked at us and thought of that, when he said how long we should be upon the road.'

'It was a dreary way he told us of,' returned her grandfather, piteously. 'Is there no other road? Will you not let me go some other way than this?'

'Places lie beyond these,' said the child, firmly, 'where we may live in peace, and be tempted to do no harm. We will take the road that promises to have that end, and we would not turn out of it, if it were a hundred times worse than our fears lead us to expect. We would not, dear, would we?'

'No,' replied the old man, wavering in his voice, no less than in his manner. 'No. Let us go on. I am ready. I am quite ready, Nell.'

The child walked with more difficulty than she had led her companion to expect, for the pains that racked her joints were of no common severity, and every exertion increased them. But they wrung from her no complaint, or look of suffering; and, though the two travellers proceeded very slowly, they did proceed. Clearing the town in course of time, they began to feel that they were fairly on their way.

A long suburb of red brick houses—some with patches of garden-ground, where coal-dust and factory smoke darkened the shrinking leaves, and coarse rank flowers, and where the struggling vegetation sickened and sank under the hot breath of kiln and furnace, making them by its presence seem yet more blighting and unwholesome than in the town itself—a long, flat, straggling suburb passed, they came, by slow degrees, upon a cheerless region, where not a blade of grass was seen to grow, where not a bud put forth its promise in the spring, where nothing green could live but on the surface of the stagnant pools, which here and there lay idly sweltering by the black road-side.

Advancing more and more into the shadow of this mournful place, its dark depressing influence stole upon their spirits, and filled them with a dismal gloom. On every side, and far as the eye could see into the heavy distance, tall chimneys, crowding on each other, and presenting that endless repetition of the same dull, ugly form, which is the horror of oppressive dreams, poured out their plague of smoke, obscured the light, and made foul the melancholy air. On mounds of ashes by the wayside, sheltered only by a few rough boards, or rotten pent-house roofs, strange engines spun and writhed like tortured creatures; clanking their iron chains, shrieking in their rapid whirl from time to time as though in torment unendurable, and making the ground tremble with their agonies. Dismantled houses here and there appeared, tottering to the earth, propped up by fragments of others that had fallen down, unroofed, windowless, blackened, desolate, but yet inhabited. Men, women, children, wan in their looks and ragged in attire, tended the engines, fed their tributary fire, begged upon the road, or scowled half-naked from the doorless houses. Then came more of the wrathful monsters, whose like they almost seemed to be in their wildness and their untamed air, screeching and turning round and round again; and still, before, behind, and to the right and left, was the same interminable perspective of brick towers, never ceasing in their black vomit, blasting all things living or inanimate, shutting out the face of day, and closing in on all these horrors with a dense dark cloud.

But night-time in this dreadful spot!—night, when the smoke was changed to fire; when every chimney spirited up its flame; and places, that had been dark vaults all day, now shone red-hot, with figures moving to and fro within their blazing jaws, and calling to one another with hoarse cries—night, when the noise of every strange machine was aggravated by the darkness; when the people near them looked wilder and more savage; when bands of unemployed labourers paraded the roads, or clustered by torch-light round their leaders, who told them, in stern language, of their wrongs, and urged them on to frightful cries and threats; when maddened men, armed with sword and firebrand, spurning the tears and prayers of women who would restrain them, rushed forth on errands of terror and destruction, to work no ruin half so surely as their own—night, when carts came rumbling by, filled with rude coffins (for contagious disease and death had been busy with the living crops); when orphans cried, and distracted women shrieked and followed in their wake—night, when some called for bread, and some for drink to drown their cares, and some with tears, and some with staggering feet, and some with bloodshot eyes, went brooding home—night, which, unlike the night that Heaven sends on earth, brought with it no peace, nor quiet, nor signs of blessed sleep—who shall tell the terrors of the night to the young wandering child!

And yet she lay down, with nothing between her and the sky; and, with no fear for herself, for she was past it now, put up a prayer for the poor old man. So very weak and spent, she felt, so very calm and unresisting, that she had no thought of any wants of her own, but prayed that God would raise up some friend for him. She tried to recall the way they had come, and to look in the direction where the fire by which they had slept last night was burning. She had forgotten to ask the name of the poor man, their friend, and when she had remembered him in her prayers, it seemed ungrateful not to turn one look towards the spot where he was watching.

A penny loaf was all they had had that day. It was very little, but even hunger was forgotten in the strange tranquillity that crept over her senses. She lay down, very gently, and, with a quiet smile upon her face, fell into a slumber. It was not like sleep—and yet it must have been, or why those pleasant dreams of the little scholar all night long! Morning came. Much weaker, diminished powers even of sight and hearing, and yet the child made no complaint—perhaps would have made none, even if she had not had that inducement to be silent, travelling by her side. She felt a hopelessness of their ever being extricated together from that forlorn place; a dull conviction that she was very ill, perhaps dying; but no fear or anxiety.

A loathing of food that she was not conscious of until they expended their last penny in the purchase of another loaf, prevented her partaking even of this poor repast. Her grandfather ate greedily, which she was glad to see.

Their way lay through the same scenes as yesterday, with no variety or improvement. There was the same thick air, difficult to breathe; the same blighted ground, the same hopeless prospect, the same misery and distress. Objects appeared more dim, the noise less, the path more rugged and uneven, for sometimes she stumbled, and became roused, as it were, in the effort to prevent herself from falling. Poor child! the cause was in her tottering feet.

Towards the afternoon, her grandfather complained bitterly of hunger. She approached one of the wretched hovels by the way-side, and knocked with her hand upon the door.

'What would you have here?' said a gaunt man, opening it.

'Charity. A morsel of bread.'

'Do you see that?' returned the man hoarsely, pointing to a kind of bundle on the ground. 'That's a dead child. I and five hundred other men were thrown out of work, three months ago. That is my third dead child, and last. Do you think I have charity to bestow, or a morsel of bread to spare?'

The child recoiled from the door, and it closed upon her. Impelled by strong necessity, she knocked at another: a neighbouring one, which, yielding to the slight pressure of her hand, flew open.

It seemed that a couple of poor families lived in this hovel, for two women, each among children of her own, occupied different portions of the room. In the centre, stood a grave gentleman in black who appeared to have just entered, and who held by the arm a boy.

'Here, woman,' he said, 'here's your deaf and dumb son. You may thank me for restoring him to you. He was brought before me, this morning, charged with theft; and with any other boy it would have gone hard, I assure you. But, as I had compassion on his infirmities, and thought he might have learnt no better, I have managed to bring him back to you. Take more care of him for the future.'

'And won't you give me back my son!' said the other woman, hastily rising and confronting him. 'Won't you give me back my son, Sir, who was transported for the same offence!'

'Was he deaf and dumb, woman?' asked the gentleman sternly.

'Was he not, Sir?'

'You know he was not.'

'He was,' cried the woman. 'He was deaf, dumb, and blind, to all that was good and right, from his cradle. Her boy may have learnt no better! where did mine learn better? where could he? who was there to teach him better, or where was it to be learnt?'

'Peace, woman,' said the gentleman, 'your boy was in possession of all his senses.'

'He was,' cried the mother; 'and he was the more easy to be led astray because he had them. If you save this boy because he may not know right from wrong, why did you not save mine who was never taught the difference? You gentlemen have as good a right to punish her boy, that God has kept in ignorance of sound and speech, as you have to punish mine, that you kept in ignorance yourselves. How many of the girls and boys—ah, men and women too—that are brought before you and you don't pity, are deaf and dumb in their minds, and go wrong in that state, and are punished in that state, body and soul, while you gentlemen are quarrelling among yourselves whether they ought to learn this or that?—Be a just man, Sir, and give me back my son.'

'You are desperate,' said the gentleman, taking out his snuff-box, 'and I am sorry for you.'

'I am desperate,' returned the woman, 'and you have made me so. Give me back my son, to work for these helpless children. Be a just man, Sir, and, as you have had mercy upon this boy, give me back my son!'

The child had seen and heard enough to know that this was not a place at which to ask for alms. She led the old man softly from the door, and they pursued their journey.

With less and less of hope or strength, as they went on, but with an undiminished resolution not to betray by any word or sigh her sinking state, so long as she had energy to move, the child, throughout the remainder of that hard day, compelled herself to proceed: not even stopping to rest as frequently as usual, to compensate in some measure for the tardy pace at which she was obliged to walk. Evening was drawing on, but had not closed in, when—still travelling among the same dismal objects—they came to a busy town.

Faint and spiritless as they were, its streets were insupportable. After humbly asking for relief at some few doors, and being repulsed, they agreed to make their way out of it as speedily as they could, and try if the inmates of any lone house beyond, would have more pity on their exhausted state.

They were dragging themselves along through the last street, and the child felt that the time was close at hand when her enfeebled powers would bear no more. There appeared before them, at this juncture, going in the same direction as themselves, a traveller on foot, who, with a portmanteau strapped to his back, leaned upon a stout stick as he walked, and read from a book which he held in his other hand.

It was not an easy matter to come up with him, and beseech his aid, for he walked fast, and was a little distance in advance. At length, he stopped, to look more attentively at some passage in his book. Animated with a ray of hope, the child shot on before her grandfather, and, going close to the stranger without rousing him by the sound of her footsteps, began, in a few faint words, to implore his help.

He turned his head. The child clapped her hands together, uttered a wild shriek, and fell senseless at his feet.

CHAPTER 46

It was the poor schoolmaster. No other than the poor schoolmaster. Scarcely less moved and surprised by the sight of the child than she had been on recognising him, he stood, for a moment, silent and confounded by this unexpected apparition, without even the presence of mind to raise her from the ground.

But, quickly recovering his self-possession, he threw down his stick and book, and dropping on one knee beside her, endeavoured, by such simple means as occurred to him, to restore her to herself; while her grandfather, standing idly by, wrung his hands, and implored her with many endearing expressions to speak to him, were it only a word.

'She is quite exhausted,' said the schoolmaster, glancing upward into his face. 'You have taxed her powers too far, friend.'

'She is perishing of want,' rejoined the old man. 'I never thought how weak and ill she was, till now.'

Casting a look upon him, half-reproachful and half-compassionate, the schoolmaster took the child in his arms, and, bidding the old man gather up her little basket and follow him directly, bore her away at his utmost speed.

There was a small inn within sight, to which, it would seem, he had been directing his steps when so unexpectedly overtaken. Towards this place he hurried with his unconscious burden, and rushing into the kitchen, and calling upon the company there assembled to make way for God's sake, deposited it on a chair before the fire.

The company, who rose in confusion on the schoolmaster's entrance, did as people usually do under such circumstances. Everybody called for his or her favourite remedy, which nobody brought; each cried for more air, at the same time carefully excluding what air there was, by closing round the object of sympathy; and all wondered why somebody else didn't do what it never appeared to occur to them might be done by themselves.

The landlady, however, who possessed more readiness and activity than any of them, and who had withal a quicker perception of the merits of the case, soon came running in, with a little hot brandy and water, followed by her servant-girl, carrying vinegar, hartshorn, smelling-salts, and such other restoratives; which, being duly administered, recovered the child so far as to enable her to thank them in a faint voice, and to extend her hand to the poor schoolmaster, who stood, with an anxious face, hard by. Without suffering her to speak another word, or so much as to stir a finger any more, the women straightway carried her off to bed; and, having covered her up warm, bathed her cold feet, and wrapped them in flannel, they despatched a messenger for the doctor.

The doctor, who was a red-nosed gentleman with a great bunch of seals dangling below a waistcoat of ribbed black satin, arrived with all speed, and taking his seat by the bedside of poor Nell, drew out his watch, and felt her pulse. Then he looked at her tongue, then he felt her pulse again, and while he did so, he eyed the half-emptied wine-glass as if in profound abstraction.

'I should give her,' said the doctor at length, 'a tea-spoonful, every now and then, of hot brandy and water.'

'Why, that's exactly what we've done, sir!' said the delighted landlady.

'I should also,' observed the doctor, who had passed the foot-bath on the stairs, 'I should also,' said the doctor, in the voice of an oracle, 'put her feet in hot water, and wrap them up in flannel. I should likewise,' said the doctor with increased solemnity, 'give her something light for supper—the wing of a roasted fowl now—'

'Why, goodness gracious me, sir, it's cooking at the kitchen fire this instant!' cried the landlady. And so indeed it was, for the schoolmaster had ordered it to be put down, and it was getting on so well that the doctor might have smelt it if he had tried; perhaps he did.

'You may then,' said the doctor, rising gravely, 'give her a glass of hot mulled port wine, if she likes wine—'

'And a toast, Sir?' suggested the landlady.

'Ay,' said the doctor, in the tone of a man who makes a dignified concession. 'And a toast—of bread. But be very particular to make it of bread, if you please, ma'am.'

With which parting injunction, slowly and portentously delivered, the doctor departed, leaving the whole house in admiration of that wisdom which tallied so closely with their own. Everybody said he was a very shrewd doctor indeed, and knew perfectly what people's constitutions were; which there appears some reason to suppose he did.

While her supper was preparing, the child fell into a refreshing sleep, from which they were obliged to rouse her when it was ready. As she evinced extraordinary uneasiness on learning that her grandfather was below stairs, and as she was greatly troubled at the thought of their being apart, he took his supper with her. Finding her still very restless on this head, they made him up a bed in an inner room, to which he presently retired. The key of this chamber happened by good fortune to be on that side of the door which was in Nell's room; she turned it on him when the landlady had withdrawn, and crept to bed again with a thankful heart.

The schoolmaster sat for a long time smoking his pipe by the kitchen fire, which was now deserted, thinking, with a very happy face, on the fortunate chance which had brought him so opportunely to the child's assistance, and parrying, as well as in his simple way he could, the inquisitive cross-examination of the landlady, who had a great curiosity to be made acquainted with every particular of Nell's life and history. The poor schoolmaster was so open-hearted, and so little versed in the most ordinary cunning or deceit, that she could not have failed to succeed in the first five minutes, but that he happened to be unacquainted with what she wished to know; and so he told her. The landlady, by no means satisfied with this assurance, which she considered an ingenious evasion of the question, rejoined that he had his reasons of course. Heaven forbid that she should wish to pry into the affairs of her customers, which indeed were no business of hers, who had so many of her own. She had merely asked a civil question, and to be sure she knew it would meet with a civil answer. She was quite satisfied—quite. She had rather perhaps that he would have said at once that he didn't choose to be communicative, because that would have been plain and intelligible. However, she had no right to be offended of course. He was the best judge, and had a perfect right to say what he pleased; nobody could dispute that for a moment. Oh dear, no!

'I assure you, my good lady,' said the mild schoolmaster, 'that I have told you the plain truth. As I hope to be saved, I have told you the truth.'

'Why then, I do believe you are in earnest,' rejoined the landlady, with ready good-humour, 'and I'm very sorry I have teazed you. But curiosity you know is the curse of our sex, and that's the fact.'

The landlord scratched his head, as if he thought the curse sometimes involved the other sex likewise; but he was prevented from making any remark to that effect, if he had it in contemplation to do so, by the schoolmaster's rejoinder.

'You should question me for half-a-dozen hours at a sitting, and welcome, and I would answer you patiently for the kindness of heart you have shown to-night, if I could,' he said. 'As it is, please to take care of her in the morning, and let me know early how she is; and to understand that I am paymaster for the three.'

So, parting with them on most friendly terms (not the less cordial perhaps for this last direction), the schoolmaster went to his bed, and the host and hostess to theirs.

The report in the morning was, that the child was better, but was extremely weak, and would at least require a day's rest, and careful nursing, before she could proceed upon her journey. The schoolmaster received this communication with perfect cheerfulness, observing that he had a day to spare—two days for that matter—and could very well afford to wait. As the patient was to sit up in the evening, he appointed to visit her in her room at a certain hour, and rambling out with his book, did not return until the hour arrived.

Nell could not help weeping when they were left alone; whereat, and at sight of her pale face and wasted figure, the simple schoolmaster shed a few tears himself, at the same time showing in very energetic language how foolish it was to do so, and how very easily it could be avoided, if one tried.

'It makes me unhappy even in the midst of all this kindness' said the child, 'to think that we should be a burden upon you. How can I ever thank you? If I had not met you so far from home, I must have died, and he would have been left alone.'

'We'll not talk about dying,' said the schoolmaster; 'and as to burdens, I have made my fortune since you slept at my cottage.'

'Indeed!' cried the child joyfully.

'Oh yes,' returned her friend. 'I have been appointed clerk and schoolmaster to a village a long way from here—and a long way from the old one as you may suppose—at five-and-thirty pounds a year. Five-and-thirty pounds!'

'I am very glad,' said the child, 'so very, very glad.'

'I am on my way there now,' resumed the schoolmaster. 'They allowed me the stage-coach-hire—outside stage-coach-hire all the way. Bless you, they grudge me nothing. But as the time at which I am expected there, left me ample leisure, I determined to walk instead. How glad I am, to think I did so!'

'How glad should we be!'

'Yes, yes,' said the schoolmaster, moving restlessly in his chair, 'certainly, that's very true. But you—where are you going, where are you coming from, what have you been doing since you left me, what had you been doing before? Now, tell me—do tell me. I know very little of the world, and perhaps you are better fitted to advise me in its affairs than I am qualified to give advice to you; but I am very sincere, and I have a reason (you have not forgotten it) for loving you. I have felt since that time as if my love for him who died, had been transferred to you who stood beside his bed. If this,' he added, looking upwards, 'is the beautiful creation that springs from ashes, let its peace prosper with me, as I deal tenderly and compassionately by this young child!'

The plain, frank kindness of the honest schoolmaster, the affectionate earnestness of his speech and manner, the truth which was stamped upon his every word and look, gave the child a confidence in him, which the utmost arts of treachery and dissimulation could never have awakened in her breast. She told him all—that they had no friend or relative—that she had fled with the old man, to save him from a madhouse and all the miseries he dreaded—that she was flying now, to save him from himself—and that she sought an asylum in some remote and primitive place, where the temptation before which he fell would never enter, and her late sorrows and distresses could have no place.

The schoolmaster heard her with astonishment. 'This child!'—he thought—'Has this child heroically persevered under all doubts and dangers, struggled with poverty and suffering, upheld and sustained by strong affection and the consciousness of rectitude alone! And yet the world is full of such heroism. Have I yet to learn that the hardest and best-borne trials are those which are never chronicled in any earthly record, and are suffered every day! And should I be surprised to hear the story of this child!'

What more he thought or said, matters not. It was concluded that Nell and her grandfather should accompany him to the village whither he was bound, and that he should endeavour to find them some humble occupation by which they could subsist. 'We shall be sure to succeed,' said the schoolmaster, heartily. 'The cause is too good a one to fail.'

They arranged to proceed upon their journey next evening, as a stage-waggon, which travelled for some distance on the same road as they must take, would stop at the inn to change horses, and the driver for a small gratuity would give Nell a place inside. A bargain was soon struck when the waggon came; and in due time it rolled away; with the child comfortably bestowed among the softer packages, her grandfather and the schoolmaster walking on beside the driver, and the landlady and all the good folks of the inn screaming out their good wishes and farewells.

What a soothing, luxurious, drowsy way of travelling, to lie inside that slowly-moving mountain, listening to the tinkling of the horses' bells, the occasional smacking of the carter's whip, the smooth rolling of the great broad wheels, the rattle of the harness, the cheery good-nights of passing travellers jogging past on little short-stepped horses—all made pleasantly indistinct by the thick awning, which seemed made for lazy listening under, till one fell asleep! The very going to sleep, still with an indistinct idea, as the head jogged to and fro upon the pillow, of moving onward with no trouble or fatigue, and hearing all these sounds like dreamy music, lulling to the senses—and the slow waking up, and finding one's self staring out through the breezy curtain half-opened in the front, far up into the cold bright sky with its countless stars, and downward at the driver's lantern dancing on like its namesake Jack of the swamps and marshes, and sideways at the dark grim trees, and forward at the long bare road rising up, up, up, until it stopped abruptly at a sharp high ridge as if there were no more road, and all beyond was sky—and the stopping at the inn to bait, and being helped out, and going into a room with fire and candles, and winking very much, and being agreeably reminded that

236

the night was cold, and anxious for very comfort's sake to think it colder than it was!—What a delicious journey was that journey in the waggon.

Then the going on again—so fresh at first, and shortly afterwards so sleepy. The waking from a sound nap as the mail came dashing past like a highway comet, with gleaming lamps and rattling hoofs, and visions of a guard behind, standing up to keep his feet warm, and of a gentleman in a fur cap opening his eyes and looking wild and stupefied—the stopping at the turnpike where the man was gone to bed, and knocking at the door until he answered with a smothered shout from under the bed-clothes in the little room above, where the faint light was burning, and presently came down, night-capped and shivering, to throw the gate wide open, and wish all waggons off the road except by day. The cold sharp interval between night and morning—the distant streak of light widening and spreading, and turning from grey to white, and from white to yellow, and from yellow to burning red—the presence of day, with all its cheerfulness and life—men and horses at the plough—birds in the trees and hedges, and boys in solitary fields, frightening them away with rattles. The coming to a town—people busy in the markets; light carts and chaises round the tavern yard; tradesmen standing at their doors; men running horses up and down the street for sale; pigs plunging and grunting in the dirty distance, getting off with long strings at their legs, running into clean chemists' shops and being dislodged with brooms by 'prentices; the night coach changing horses—the passengers cheerless, cold, ugly, and discontented, with three months' growth of hair in one night—the coachman fresh as from a band-box, and exquisitely beautiful by contrast:—so much bustle, so many things in motion, such a variety of incidents—when was there a journey with so many delights as that journey in the waggon!

Sometimes walking for a mile or two while her grandfather rode inside, and sometimes even prevailing upon the schoolmaster to take her place and lie down to rest, Nell travelled on very happily until they came to a large town, where the waggon stopped, and where they spent a night. They passed a large church; and in the streets were a number of old houses, built of a kind of earth or plaster, crossed and re-crossed in a great many directions with black beams, which gave them a remarkable and very ancient look. The doors, too, were arched and low, some with oaken portals and quaint benches, where the former inhabitants had sat on summer evenings. The windows were latticed in little diamond panes, that seemed to wink and blink upon the passengers as if they were dim of sight. They had long since got clear of the smoke and furnaces, except in one or two solitary instances, where a factory planted among fields withered the space about it, like a burning mountain. When they had passed through this town, they entered again upon the country, and began to draw near their place of destination.

It was not so near, however, but that they spent another night upon the road; not that their doing so was quite an act of necessity, but that the schoolmaster, when they approached within a few miles of his village, had a fidgety sense of his dignity as the new clerk, and was unwilling to make his entry in dusty shoes, and travel-disordered dress. It was a fine, clear, autumn morning, when they came upon the scene of his promotion, and stopped to contemplate its beauties.

'See—here's the church!' cried the delighted schoolmaster in a low voice; 'and that old building close beside it, is the schoolhouse, I'll be sworn. Five-and-thirty pounds a-year in this beautiful place!'

They admired everything—the old grey porch, the mullioned windows, the venerable gravestones dotting the green churchyard, the ancient tower, the very weathercock; the brown thatched roofs of cottage, barn, and homestead, peeping from among the trees; the stream that rippled by the distant water-mill; the blue Welsh mountains far away. It was for such a spot the child had wearied in the dense, dark, miserable haunts of labour. Upon her bed of ashes, and amidst the squalid horrors through which they had forced their way, visions of such scenes—beautiful indeed, but not more beautiful than this sweet reality—had been always present to her mind. They had seemed to melt into a dim and airy distance, as the prospect of ever beholding them again grew fainter; but, as they receded, she had loved and panted for them more.

'I must leave you somewhere for a few minutes,' said the schoolmaster, at length breaking the silence into which they had fallen in their gladness. 'I have a letter to present, and inquiries to make, you know. Where shall I take you? To the little inn yonder?'

'Let us wait here,' rejoined Nell. 'The gate is open. We will sit in the church porch till you come back.'

'A good place too,' said the schoolmaster, leading the way towards it, disencumbering himself of his portmanteau, and placing it on the stone seat. 'Be sure that I come back with good news, and am not long gone!'

So, the happy schoolmaster put on a bran-new pair of gloves which he had carried in a little parcel in his pocket all the way, and hurried off, full of ardour and excitement.

The child watched him from the porch until the intervening foliage hid him from her view, and then stepped softly out into the old churchyard—so solemn and quiet that every rustle of her dress upon the fallen leaves, which strewed the path and made her footsteps noiseless, seemed an invasion of its silence. It was a very aged, ghostly place; the church had been built many hundreds of years ago, and had once had a convent or monastery attached; for arches in ruins, remains of oriel windows, and fragments of blackened walls, were yet standing; while other portions of the old building, which had crumbled away and fallen down, were mingled with the churchyard earth and overgrown with grass, as if they too claimed a burying-place and sought to mix their ashes with the dust of men. Hard by these gravestones of dead years, and forming a part of the ruin which some pains had been taken to render habitable in modern times, were two small dwellings with sunken windows and oaken doors, fast hastening to decay, empty and desolate.

Upon these tenements, the attention of the child became exclusively riveted. She knew not why. The church, the ruin, the antiquated graves, had equal claims at least upon a stranger's thoughts, but from the moment when her eyes first rested on these two dwellings, she could turn to nothing else. Even when she had made the circuit of the enclosure, and, returning to the porch, sat pensively waiting for their friend, she took her station where she could still look upon them, and felt as if fascinated towards that spot.

CHAPTER 47

Kit's mother and the single gentleman—upon whose track it is expedient to follow with hurried steps, lest this history should be chargeable with inconstancy, and the offence of leaving its characters in situations of uncertainty and doubt—Kit's mother and the single gentleman, speeding onward in the post-chaise-and-four whose departure from the Notary's door we have already witnessed, soon left the town behind them, and struck fire from the flints of the broad highway.

The good woman, being not a little embarrassed by the novelty of her situation, and certain material apprehensions that perhaps by this time little Jacob, or the baby, or both, had fallen into the fire, or tumbled down stairs, or had been squeezed behind doors, or had scalded their windpipes in endeavouring to allay their thirst at the spouts of tea-kettles, preserved an uneasy silence; and meeting from the window the eyes of turnpike-men, omnibus-drivers, and others, felt in the new dignity of her position like a mourner at a funeral, who, not being greatly afflicted by the loss of the departed, recognizes his every-day acquaintance from the window of the mourning coach, but is constrained to preserve a decent solemnity, and the appearance of being indifferent to all external objects.

To have been indifferent to the companionship of the single gentleman would have been tantamount to being gifted with nerves of steel. Never did chaise inclose, or horses draw, such a restless gentleman as he. He never sat in the same position for two minutes together, but was perpetually tossing his arms and legs about, pulling up the sashes and letting them violently down, or thrusting his head out of one window to draw it in again and thrust it out of another. He carried in his pocket, too, a fire-box of mysterious and unknown construction; and as sure as ever Kit's mother closed her eyes, so surely—whisk, rattle, fizz—there was the single gentleman consulting his watch by a flame of fire, and letting the sparks fall down among the straw as if there were no such thing as a possibility of himself and Kit's mother being roasted alive before the boys could stop their horses. Whenever they halted to change, there he was— out of the carriage without letting down the steps, bursting about the inn-yard like a lighted cracker, pulling out his watch by lamp-light and forgetting to look at it before he put it up again, and in short committing so many extravagances that Kit's mother was quite afraid of him. Then, when the horses were to, in he came like a Harlequin, and before they had gone a mile, out came the watch and the fire-box together, and Kit's mother as wide awake again, with no hope of a wink of sleep for that stage.

'Are you comfortable?' the single gentleman would say after one of these exploits, turning sharply round.

'Quite, Sir, thank you.'

'Are you sure? An't you cold?'

'It is a little chilly, Sir,' Kit's mother would reply.

'I knew it!' cried the single gentleman, letting down one of the front glasses. 'She wants some brandy and water! Of course she does. How could I forget it? Hallo! Stop at the next inn, and call out for a glass of hot brandy and water.'

It was in vain for Kit's mother to protest that she stood in need of nothing of the kind. The single gentleman was inexorable; and whenever he had exhausted all other modes and fashions of restlessness, it invariably occurred to him that Kit's mother wanted brandy and water.

In this way they travelled on until near midnight, when they stopped to supper, for which meal the single gentleman ordered everything eatable that the house contained; and because Kit's mother didn't eat everything at once, and eat it all, he took it into his head that she must be ill.

'You're faint,' said the single gentleman, who did nothing himself but walk about the room. 'I see what's the matter with you, ma'am. You're faint.'

'Thank you, sir, I'm not indeed.'

'I know you are. I'm sure of it. I drag this poor woman from the bosom of her family at a minute's notice, and she goes on getting fainter and fainter before my eyes. I'm a pretty fellow! How many children have you got, ma'am?'

'Two, sir, besides Kit.'

'Boys, ma'am?'

'Yes, sir.'

'Are they christened?'

'Only half baptised as yet, sir.'

'I'm godfather to both of 'em. Remember that, if you please, ma'am. You had better have some mulled wine.'

'I couldn't touch a drop indeed, sir.'

'You must,' said the single gentleman. 'I see you want it. I ought to have thought of it before.'

Immediately flying to the bell, and calling for mulled wine as impetuously as if it had been wanted for instant use in the recovery of some person apparently drowned, the single gentleman made Kit's mother swallow a bumper of it at such a high temperature that the tears ran down her face, and then hustled her off to the chaise again, where—not impossibly from the effects of this agreeable sedative—she soon became insensible to his restlessness, and fell fast asleep. Nor were the happy effects of this prescription of a transitory nature, as, notwithstanding that the distance was greater, and the journey longer, than the single gentleman had anticipated, she did not awake until it was broad day, and they were clattering over the pavement of a town.

'This is the place!' cried her companion, letting down all the glasses. 'Drive to the wax-work!'

The boy on the wheeler touched his hat, and setting spurs to his horse, to the end that they might go in brilliantly, all four broke into a smart canter, and dashed through the streets with a noise that brought the good folks wondering to their doors and windows, and drowned the sober voices of the town-clocks as they chimed out half-past eight. They drove up to a door round which a crowd of persons were collected, and there stopped.

'What's this?' said the single gentleman thrusting out his head. 'Is anything the matter here?'

'A wedding Sir, a wedding!' cried several voices. 'Hurrah!'

The single gentleman, rather bewildered by finding himself the centre of this noisy throng, alighted with the assistance of one of the postilions, and handed out Kit's mother, at sight of whom the populace cried out, 'Here's another wedding!' and roared and leaped for joy.

'The world has gone mad, I think,' said the single gentleman, pressing through the concourse with his supposed bride. 'Stand back here, will you, and let me knock.'

Anything that makes a noise is satisfactory to a crowd. A score of dirty hands were raised directly to knock for him, and seldom has a knocker of equal powers been made to produce more deafening sounds than this particular engine on the occasion in question. Having rendered these voluntary services, the throng modestly retired a little, preferring that the single gentleman should bear their consequences alone.

'Now, sir, what do you want!' said a man with a large white bow at his button-hole, opening the door, and confronting him with a very stoical aspect.

'Who has been married here, my friend?' said the single gentleman.

'I have.'

'You! and to whom in the devil's name?'

'What right have you to ask?' returned the bridegroom, eyeing him from top to toe.

'What right!' cried the single gentleman, drawing the arm of Kit's mother more tightly through his own, for that good woman evidently had it in contemplation to run away. 'A right you little dream of. Mind, good people, if this fellow has been marrying a minor—tut, tut, that can't be. Where is the child you have here, my good fellow. You call her Nell. Where is she?'

As he propounded this question, which Kit's mother echoed, somebody in a room near at hand, uttered a great shriek, and a stout lady in a white dress came running to the door, and supported herself upon the bridegroom's arm.

'Where is she!' cried this lady. 'What news have you brought me? What has become of her?'

The single gentleman started back, and gazed upon the face of the late Mrs Jarley (that morning wedded to the philosophic George, to the eternal wrath and despair of Mr Slum the poet), with looks of conflicting apprehension, disappointment, and incredulity. At length he stammered out,

'I ask you where she is? What do you mean?'

'Oh sir!' cried the bride, 'If you have come here to do her any good, why weren't you here a week ago?'

'She is not—not dead?' said the person to whom she addressed herself, turning very pale.

'No, not so bad as that.'

'I thank God!' cried the single gentleman feebly. 'Let me come in.'

They drew back to admit him, and when he had entered, closed the door.

'You see in me, good people,' he said, turning to the newly-married couple, 'one to whom life itself is not dearer than the two persons whom I seek. They would not know me. My features are strange to them, but if they or either of them are here, take this good woman with you, and let them see her first, for her they both know. If you deny them from any mistaken regard or fear for them, judge of my intentions by their recognition of this person as their old humble friend.'

'I always said it!' cried the bride, 'I knew she was not a common child! Alas, sir! we have no power to help you, for all that we could do, has been tried in vain.'

With that, they related to him, without disguise or concealment, all that they knew of Nell and her grandfather, from their first meeting with them, down to the time of their sudden disappearance; adding (which was quite true) that they had made every possible effort to trace them, but without success; having been at first in great alarm for their safety, as well as on account of the suspicions to which they themselves might one day be exposed in consequence of their abrupt departure. They dwelt upon the old man's imbecility of mind, upon the uneasiness the child had always testified when he was absent, upon the company he had been supposed to keep, and upon the increased depression which had gradually crept over her and changed her both in health and spirits. Whether she had missed the old man in the night, and knowing or conjecturing whither he had bent his steps, had gone in pursuit, or whether they had left the house together, they had no means of determining. Certain they considered it, that there was but slender prospect left of hearing of them again, and that whether their flight originated with the old man, or with the child, there was now no hope of their return. To all this, the single gentleman listened with the air of a man quite borne down by grief and disappointment. He shed tears when they spoke of the grandfather, and appeared in deep affliction.

Not to protract this portion of our narrative, and to make short work of a long story, let it be briefly written that before the interview came to a close, the single gentleman deemed he had sufficient evidence of having been told the truth, and that he endeavoured to force upon the bride and bridegroom an acknowledgment of their kindness to the unfriended child, which, however, they steadily declined accepting. In the end, the happy couple jolted away in the caravan to spend their honeymoon in a country excursion; and the single gentleman and Kit's mother stood ruefully before their carriage-door.

'Where shall we drive you, sir?' said the post-boy.

'You may drive me,' said the single gentleman, 'to the—' He was not going to add 'inn,' but he added it for the sake of Kit's mother; and to the inn they went.

Rumours had already got abroad that the little girl who used to show the wax-work, was the child of great people who had been stolen from her parents in infancy, and had only just been traced. Opinion was divided whether she was the daughter of a prince, a duke, an earl, a viscount, or a baron, but all agreed upon the main fact, and that the single gentleman was her father; and all bent forward to catch a glimpse, though it were only of the tip of his noble nose, as he rode away, desponding, in his four-horse chaise.

What would he have given to know, and what sorrow would have been saved if he had only known, that at that moment both child and grandfather were seated in the old church porch, patiently awaiting the schoolmaster's return!

CHAPTER 48

Popular rumour concerning the single gentleman and his errand, travelling from mouth to mouth, and waxing stronger in the marvellous as it was bandied about—for your popular rumour, unlike the rolling stone of the proverb, is one which gathers a deal of moss in its wanderings up and down—occasioned his dismounting at the inn-door to be looked upon as an exciting and attractive spectacle, which could scarcely be enough admired; and drew together a large concourse of idlers, who having recently been, as it were, thrown out of employment by the closing of the wax-work and the completion of the nuptial ceremonies, considered his arrival as little else than a special providence, and hailed it with demonstrations of the liveliest joy.

Not at all participating in the general sensation, but wearing the depressed and wearied look of one who sought to meditate on his disappointment in silence and privacy, the single gentleman alighted, and handed out Kit's mother with a gloomy politeness which impressed the lookers-on extremely. That done, he gave her his arm and escorted her into the house, while several active waiters ran on before as a skirmishing party, to clear the way and to show the room which was ready for their reception.

'Any room will do,' said the single gentleman. 'Let it be near at hand, that's all.'

'Close here, sir, if you please to walk this way.'

'Would the gentleman like this room?' said a voice, as a little out-of-the-way door at the foot of the well staircase flew briskly open and a head popped out. 'He's quite welcome to it. He's as welcome as flowers in May, or coals at Christmas. Would you like this room, sir? Honour me by walking in. Do me the favour, pray.'

'Goodness gracious me!' cried Kit's mother, falling back in extreme surprise, 'only think of this!'

She had some reason to be astonished, for the person who proffered the gracious invitation was no other than Daniel Quilp. The little door out of which he had thrust his head was close to the inn larder; and there he stood, bowing with grotesque politeness; as much at his ease as if the door were that of his own house; blighting all the legs of mutton and cold roast fowls by his close companionship, and looking like the evil genius of the cellars come from underground upon some work of mischief.

'Would you do me the honour?' said Quilp.

'I prefer being alone,' replied the single gentleman.

'Oh!' said Quilp. And with that, he darted in again with one jerk and clapped the little door to, like a figure in a Dutch clock when the hour strikes.

'Why it was only last night, sir,' whispered Kit's mother, 'that I left him in Little Bethel.'

'Indeed!' said her fellow-passenger. 'When did that person come here, waiter?'

'Come down by the night-coach, this morning, sir.'

'Humph! And when is he going?'

'Can't say, sir, really. When the chambermaid asked him just now if he should want a bed, sir, he first made faces at her, and then wanted to kiss her.'

'Beg him to walk this way,' said the single gentleman. 'I should be glad to exchange a word with him, tell him. Beg him to come at once, do you hear?'

The man stared on receiving these instructions, for the single gentleman had not only displayed as much astonishment as Kit's mother at sight of the dwarf, but, standing in no fear of him, had been at less pains to conceal his dislike and repugnance. He departed on his errand, however, and immediately returned, ushering in its object.

'Your servant, sir,' said the dwarf, 'I encountered your messenger half-way. I thought you'd allow me to pay my compliments to you. I hope you're well. I hope you're very well.'

There was a short pause, while the dwarf, with half-shut eyes and puckered face, stood waiting for an answer. Receiving none, he turned towards his more familiar acquaintance.

'Christopher's mother!' he cried. 'Such a dear lady, such a worthy woman, so blest in her honest son! How is Christopher's mother? Have change of air and scene improved her? Her little family too, and Christopher? Do they thrive? Do they flourish? Are they growing into worthy citizens, eh?'

Making his voice ascend in the scale with every succeeding question, Mr Quilp finished in a shrill squeak, and subsided into the panting look which was customary with him, and which, whether it were assumed or natural, had equally the effect of banishing all expression from his face, and rendering it, as far as it afforded any index to his mood or meaning, a perfect blank.

'Mr Quilp,' said the single gentleman.

The dwarf put his hand to his great flapped ear, and counterfeited the closest attention.

'We two have met before—'

'Surely,' cried Quilp, nodding his head. 'Oh surely, sir. Such an honour and pleasure—it's both, Christopher's mother, it's both—is not to be forgotten so soon. By no means!'

'You may remember that the day I arrived in London, and found the house to which I drove, empty and deserted, I was directed by some of the neighbours to you, and waited upon you without stopping for rest or refreshment?'

'How precipitate that was, and yet what an earnest and vigorous measure!' said Quilp, conferring with himself, in imitation of his friend Mr Sampson Brass.

'I found,' said the single gentleman, 'you most unaccountably, in possession of everything that had so recently belonged to another man, and that other man, who up to the time of your entering upon his property had been looked upon as affluent, reduced to sudden beggary, and driven from house and home.'

'We had warrant for what we did, my good sir,' rejoined Quilp, 'we had our warrant. Don't say driven either. He went of his own accord—vanished in the night, sir.'

'No matter,' said the single gentleman angrily. 'He was gone.'

'Yes, he was gone,' said Quilp, with the same exasperating composure. 'No doubt he was gone. The only question was, where. And it's a question still.'

'Now, what am I to think,' said the single gentleman, sternly regarding him, 'of you, who, plainly indisposed to give me any information then—nay, obviously holding back, and sheltering yourself with all kinds of cunning, trickery, and evasion—are dogging my footsteps now?'

'I dogging!' cried Quilp.

'Why, are you not?' returned his questioner, fretted into a state of the utmost irritation. 'Were you not a few hours since, sixty miles off, and in the chapel to which this good woman goes to say her prayers?'

'She was there too, I think?' said Quilp, still perfectly unmoved. 'I might say, if I was inclined to be rude, how do I know but you are dogging my footsteps. Yes, I was at chapel.

What then? I've read in books that pilgrims were used to go to chapel before they went on journeys, to put up petitions for their safe return. Wise men! journeys are very perilous— especially outside the coach. Wheels come off, horses take fright, coachmen drive too fast, coaches overturn. I always go to chapel before I start on journeys. It's the last thing I do on such occasions, indeed.'

That Quilp lied most heartily in this speech, it needed no very great penetration to discover, although for anything that he suffered to appear in his face, voice, or manner, he might have been clinging to the truth with the quiet constancy of a martyr.

'In the name of all that's calculated to drive one crazy, man,' said the unfortunate single gentleman, 'have you not, for some reason of your own, taken upon yourself my errand? don't you know with what object I have come here, and if you do know, can you throw no light upon it?'

'You think I'm a conjuror, sir,' replied Quilp, shrugging up his shoulders. 'If I was, I should tell my own fortune—and make it.'

'Ah! we have said all we need say, I see,' returned the other, throwing himself impatiently upon a sofa. 'Pray leave us, if you please.'

'Willingly,' returned Quilp. 'Most willingly. Christopher's mother, my good soul, farewell. A pleasant journey—back, sir. Ahem!'

With these parting words, and with a grin upon his features altogether indescribable, but which seemed to be compounded of every monstrous grimace of which men or monkeys are capable, the dwarf slowly retreated and closed the door behind him.

'Oho!' he said when he had regained his own room, and sat himself down in a chair with his arms akimbo. 'Oho! Are you there, my friend? In-deed!'

Chuckling as though in very great glee, and recompensing himself for the restraint he had lately put upon his countenance by twisting it into all imaginable varieties of ugliness, Mr Quilp, rocking himself to and fro in his chair and nursing his left leg at the same time, fell into certain meditations, of which it may be necessary to relate the substance.

First, he reviewed the circumstances which had led to his repairing to that spot, which were briefly these. Dropping in at Mr Sampson Brass's office on the previous evening, in the absence of that gentleman and his learned sister, he had lighted upon Mr Swiveller, who chanced at the moment to be sprinkling a glass of warm gin and water on the dust of the law, and to be moistening his clay, as the phrase goes, rather copiously. But as clay in the abstract, when too much moistened, becomes of a weak and uncertain consistency, breaking down in unexpected places, retaining impressions but faintly, and preserving no strength or steadiness of character, so Mr Swiveller's clay, having imbibed a considerable quantity of moisture, was in a very loose and slippery state, insomuch that the various ideas impressed upon it were fast losing their distinctive character, and running into each other. It is not uncommon for human clay in this condition to value itself above all things upon its great prudence and sagacity; and Mr Swiveller, especially prizing himself upon these qualities, took occasion to remark that he had made strange discoveries in connection with the single gentleman who lodged above, which he had determined to keep within his own bosom, and which neither tortures nor cajolery should ever induce him to reveal. Of this determination Mr Quilp expressed his high approval, and setting himself in the same breath to goad Mr Swiveller on to further hints, soon made out that the single gentleman had been seen in communication with Kit, and that this was the secret which was never to be disclosed.

Possessed of this piece of information, Mr Quilp directly supposed that the single gentleman above stairs must be the same individual who had waited on him, and having assured himself by further inquiries that this surmise was correct, had no difficulty in arriving at the conclusion that the intent and object of his correspondence with Kit was the recovery of his old client and the child. Burning with curiosity to know what proceedings were afoot, he resolved to pounce upon Kit's mother as the person least able to resist his arts, and consequently the most likely to be entrapped into such revelations as he sought; so taking an abrupt leave of Mr Swiveller, he hurried to her house. The good woman being from home, he made inquiries of a neighbour, as Kit himself did soon afterwards, and being directed to the chapel be took himself there, in order to waylay her, at the conclusion of the service.

He had not sat in the chapel more than a quarter of an hour, and with his eyes piously fixed upon the ceiling was chuckling inwardly over the joke of his being there at all, when Kit himself appeared. Watchful as a lynx, one glance showed the dwarf that he had come on business. Absorbed in appearance, as we have seen, and feigning a profound abstraction, he noted every circumstance of his behaviour, and when he withdrew with his family, shot out after him. In fine, he traced them to the notary's house; learnt the destination of the carriage from one of the postilions; and knowing that a fast night-coach started for the same place, at the very hour which was on the point of striking, from a street hard by, darted round to the coach-office without more ado, and took his seat upon the roof. After passing and repassing the carriage on the road, and being passed and repassed by it sundry times in the course of the night, according as their stoppages were longer or shorter; or their rate of travelling varied, they reached the town almost together. Quilp kept the chaise in sight, mingled with the crowd, learnt the single gentleman's errand, and its failure, and having possessed himself of all that it was material to know, hurried off, reached the inn before him, had the interview just now detailed, and shut himself up in the little room in which he hastily reviewed all these occurrences.

'You are there, are you, my friend?' he repeated, greedily biting his nails. 'I am suspected and thrown aside, and Kit's the confidential agent, is he? I shall have to dispose of him, I fear. If we had come up with them this morning,' he continued, after a thoughtful pause, 'I was ready to prove a pretty good claim. I could have made my profit. But for these canting hypocrites, the lad and his mother, I could get this fiery gentleman as comfortably into my net as our old friend—our mutual friend, ha! ha!—and chubby, rosy Nell. At the worst, it's a golden opportunity, not to be lost. Let us find them first, and I'll find means of draining you of some of your superfluous cash, sir, while there are prison bars, and bolts, and locks, to keep your friend or kinsman safely. I hate your virtuous people!' said the dwarf, throwing off a bumper of brandy, and smacking his lips, 'ah! I hate 'em every one!'

This was not a mere empty vaunt, but a deliberate avowal of his real sentiments; for Mr Quilp, who loved nobody, had by little and little come to hate everybody nearly or remotely connected with his ruined client:—the old man himself, because he had been able to deceive him and elude his vigilance—the child, because she was the object of Mrs Quilp's commiseration and constant self-reproach—the single gentleman, because of his unconcealed aversion to himself—Kit and his mother, most mortally, for the reasons shown. Above and beyond that general feeling of opposition to them, which would have been inseparable from his ravenous desire to enrich himself by these altered circumstances, Daniel Quilp hated them every one.

In this amiable mood, Mr Quilp enlivened himself and his hatreds with more brandy, and then, changing his quarters, withdrew to an obscure alehouse, under cover of which seclusion he instituted all possible inquiries that might lead to the discovery of the old man and his grandchild. But all was in vain. Not the slightest trace or clue could be obtained. They had left the town by night; no one had seen them go; no one had met them on the road; the driver of no coach, cart, or waggon, had seen any travellers answering their description; nobody had fallen in with them, or heard of them. Convinced at last that for the present all such attempts were hopeless, he appointed two or three scouts, with promises of large rewards in case of their forwarding him any intelligence, and returned to London by next day's coach.

It was some gratification to Mr Quilp to find, as he took his place upon the roof, that Kit's mother was alone inside; from which circumstance he derived in the course of the journey much cheerfulness of spirit, inasmuch as her solitary condition enabled him to terrify her with many extraordinary annoyances; such as hanging over the side of the coach at the risk of his life, and staring in with his great goggle eyes, which seemed in hers the more horrible from his face being upside down; dodging her in this way from one window to another; getting nimbly down whenever they changed horses and thrusting his head in at the window with a dismal squint: which ingenious tortures had such an effect upon Mrs Nubbles, that she was quite unable for the time to resist the belief that Mr Quilp did in his own person represent and embody that Evil Power, who was so vigorously attacked at Little Bethel, and who, by reason of her backslidings in respect of Astley's and oysters, was now frolicsome and rampant.

Kit, having been apprised by letter of his mother's intended return, was waiting for her at the coach-office; and great was his surprise when he saw, leering over the coachman's shoulder like some familiar demon, invisible to all eyes but his, the well-known face of Quilp.

'How are you, Christopher?' croaked the dwarf from the coach-top. 'All right, Christopher. Mother's inside.'

'Why, how did he come here, mother?' whispered Kit.

'I don't know how he came or why, my dear,' rejoined Mrs Nubbles, dismounting with her son's assistance, 'but he has been a terrifying of me out of my seven senses all this blessed day.'

'He has?' cried Kit.

'You wouldn't believe it, that you wouldn't,' replied his mother, 'but don't say a word to him, for I really don't believe he's human. Hush! Don't turn round as if I was talking of him, but he's a squinting at me now in the full blaze of the coach-lamp, quite awful!'

In spite of his mother's injunction, Kit turned sharply round to look. Mr Quilp was serenely gazing at the stars, quite absorbed in celestial contemplation.

'Oh, he's the artfullest creetur!' cried Mrs Nubbles. 'But come away. Don't speak to him for the world.'

'Yes I will, mother. What nonsense. I say, sir—'

Mr Quilp affected to start, and looked smilingly round.

'You let my mother alone, will you?' said Kit. 'How dare you tease a poor lone woman like her, making her miserable and melancholy as if she hadn't got enough to make her so, without you. An't you ashamed of yourself, you little monster?'

'Monster!' said Quilp inwardly, with a smile. 'Ugliest dwarf that could be seen anywhere for a penny—monster—ah!'

'You show her any of your impudence again,' resumed Kit, shouldering the bandbox, 'and I tell you what, Mr Quilp, I won't bear with you any more. You have no right to do it; I'm sure we never interfered with you. This isn't the first time; and if ever you worry or frighten her again, you'll oblige me (though I should be very sorry to do it, on account of your size) to beat you.'

Quilp said not a word in reply, but walking so close to Kit as to bring his eyes within two or three inches of his face, looked fixedly at him, retreated a little distance without averting his gaze, approached again, again withdrew, and so on for half-a-dozen times, like a head in a phantasmagoria. Kit stood his ground as if in expectation of an immediate assault, but finding that nothing came of these gestures, snapped his fingers and walked away; his mother dragging him off as fast as she could, and, even in the midst of his news of little Jacob and the baby, looking anxiously over her shoulder to see if Quilp were following.

CHAPTER 49

Kit's mother might have spared herself the trouble of looking back so often, for nothing was further from Mr Quilp's thoughts than any intention of pursuing her and her son, or renewing the quarrel with which they had parted. He went his way, whistling from time to time some fragments of a tune; and with a face quite tranquil and composed, jogged pleasantly towards home; entertaining himself as he went with visions of the fears and terrors of Mrs Quilp, who, having received no intelligence of him for three whole days and two nights, and having had no previous notice of his absence, was doubtless by that time in a state of distraction, and constantly fainting away with anxiety and grief.

This facetious probability was so congenial to the dwarf's humour, and so exquisitely amusing to him, that he laughed as he went along until the tears ran down his cheeks; and more than once, when he found himself in a bye-street, vented his delight in a shrill scream, which greatly terrifying any lonely passenger, who happened to be walking on before him expecting nothing so little, increased his mirth, and made him remarkably cheerful and light-hearted.

In this happy flow of spirits, Mr Quilp reached Tower Hill, when, gazing up at the window of his own sitting-room, he thought he descried more light than is usual in a house of mourning. Drawing nearer, and listening attentively, he could hear several voices in earnest conversation, among which he could distinguish, not only those of his wife and mother-in-law, but the tongues of men.

'Ha!' cried the jealous dwarf, 'What's this! Do they entertain visitors while I'm away!'

A smothered cough from above, was the reply. He felt in his pockets for his latch-key, but had forgotten it. There was no resource but to knock at the door.

'A light in the passage,' said Quilp, peeping through the keyhole. 'A very soft knock; and, by your leave, my lady, I may yet steal upon you unawares. Soho!'

A very low and gentle rap received no answer from within. But after a second application to the knocker, no louder than the first, the door was softly opened by the boy from the wharf, whom Quilp instantly gagged with one hand, and dragged into the street with the other.

'You'll throttle me, master,' whispered the boy. 'Let go, will you.'

'Who's up stairs, you dog?' retorted Quilp in the same tone. 'Tell me. And don't speak above your breath, or I'll choke you in good earnest.'

The boy could only point to the window, and reply with a stifled giggle, expressive of such intense enjoyment, that Quilp clutched him by the throat and might have carried his threat into execution, or at least have made very good progress towards that end, but for the boy's nimbly extricating himself from his grasp, and fortifying himself behind the nearest post, at which, after some fruitless attempts to catch him by the hair of the head, his master was obliged to come to a parley.

'Will you answer me?' said Quilp. 'What's going on, above?'

'You won't let one speak,' replied the boy. 'They—ha, ha, ha!—they think you're—you're dead. Ha ha ha!'

'Dead!' cried Quilp, relaxing into a grim laugh himself. 'No. Do they? Do they really, you dog?'

'They think you're—you're drowned,' replied the boy, who in his malicious nature had a strong infusion of his master. 'You was last seen on the brink of the wharf, and they think you tumbled over. Ha ha!'

The prospect of playing the spy under such delicious circumstances, and of disappointing them all by walking in alive, gave more delight to Quilp than the greatest stroke of good fortune could possibly have inspired him with. He was no less tickled than his hopeful assistant, and they both stood for some seconds, grinning and gasping and wagging their heads at each other, on either side of the post, like an unmatchable pair of Chinese idols.

'Not a word,' said Quilp, making towards the door on tiptoe. 'Not a sound, not so much as a creaking board, or a stumble against a cobweb. Drowned, eh, Mrs Quilp! Drowned!'

So saying, he blew out the candle, kicked off his shoes, and groped his way up stairs; leaving his delighted young friend in an ecstasy of summersets on the pavement.

The bedroom-door on the staircase being unlocked, Mr Quilp slipped in, and planted himself behind the door of communication between that chamber and the sitting-room, which standing ajar to render both more airy, and having a very convenient chink (of which he had often availed himself for purposes of espial, and had indeed enlarged with his pocket-knife), enabled him not only to hear, but to see distinctly, what was passing.

Applying his eye to this convenient place, he descried Mr Brass seated at the table with pen, ink, and paper, and the case-bottle of rum—his own case-bottle, and his own particular Jamaica—convenient to his hand; with hot water, fragrant lemons, white lump sugar, and all things fitting; from which choice materials, Sampson, by no means insensible to their claims upon his attention, had compounded a mighty glass of punch reeking hot; which he was at that very moment stirring up with a teaspoon, and contemplating with looks in which a faint assumption of sentimental regret, struggled but weakly with a bland and comfortable joy. At the same table, with both her elbows upon it, was Mrs Jiniwin; no longer sipping other people's punch feloniously with teaspoons, but taking deep draughts from a jorum of her own; while her daughter—not exactly with ashes on her head, or sackcloth on her back, but preserving a very decent and becoming appearance of sorrow nevertheless—was reclining in an easy chair, and soothing her grief with a smaller allowance of the same glib liquid. There were also present, a couple of water-side men, bearing between them certain machines called drags; even these fellows were accommodated with a stiff glass a-piece; and as they drank with a great relish, and were naturally of a red-nosed, pimple-faced, convivial look, their presence rather increased than detracted from that decided appearance of comfort, which was the great characteristic of the party.

'If I could poison that dear old lady's rum and water,' murmured Quilp, 'I'd die happy.'

'Ah!' said Mr Brass, breaking the silence, and raising his eyes to the ceiling with a sigh, 'Who knows but he may be looking down upon us now! Who knows but he may be surveying of us from—from somewheres or another, and contemplating us with a watchful eye! Oh Lor!'

Here Mr Brass stopped to drink half his punch, and then resumed; looking at the other half, as he spoke, with a dejected smile.

'I can almost fancy,' said the lawyer shaking his head, 'that I see his eye glistening down at the very bottom of my liquor. When shall we look upon his like again? Never, never!' One minute we are here'—holding his tumbler before his eyes—'the next we are there'—gulping down its contents, and striking himself emphatically a little below the chest—'in the silent tomb. To think that I should be drinking his very rum! It seems like a dream.'

With the view, no doubt, of testing the reality of his position, Mr Brass pushed his tumbler as he spoke towards Mrs Jiniwin for the purpose of being replenished; and turned towards the attendant mariners.

'The search has been quite unsuccessful then?'

'Quite, master. But I should say that if he turns up anywhere, he'll come ashore somewhere about Grinidge to-morrow, at ebb tide, eh, mate?'

The other gentleman assented, observing that he was expected at the Hospital, and that several pensioners would be ready to receive him whenever he arrived.

'Then we have nothing for it but resignation,' said Mr Brass; 'nothing but resignation and expectation. It would be a comfort to have his body; it would be a dreary comfort.'

'Oh, beyond a doubt,' assented Mrs Jiniwin hastily; 'if we once had that, we should be quite sure.'

'With regard to the descriptive advertisement,' said Sampson Brass, taking up his pen. 'It is a melancholy pleasure to recall his traits. Respecting his legs now—?'

'Crooked, certainly,' said Mrs Jiniwin. 'Do you think they were crooked?' said Brass, in an insinuating tone. 'I think I see them now coming up the street very wide apart, in nankeen' pantaloons a little shrunk and without straps. Ah! what a vale of tears we live in. Do we say crooked?'

'I think they were a little so,' observed Mrs Quilp with a sob.

'Legs crooked,' said Brass, writing as he spoke. 'Large head, short body, legs crooked—'

'Very crooked,' suggested Mrs Jiniwin.

'We'll not say very crooked, ma'am,' said Brass piously. 'Let us not bear hard upon the weaknesses of the deceased. He is gone, ma'am, to where his legs will never come in question.— We will content ourselves with crooked, Mrs Jiniwin.'

'I thought you wanted the truth,' said the old lady. 'That's all.'

'Bless your eyes, how I love you,' muttered Quilp. 'There she goes again. Nothing but punch!'

'This is an occupation,' said the lawyer, laying down his pen and emptying his glass, 'which seems to bring him before my eyes like the Ghost of Hamlet's father, in the very clothes that he wore on work-a-days. His coat, his waistcoat, his shoes and stockings, his trousers, his hat, his wit and humour, his pathos and his umbrella, all come before me like visions of my youth. His linen!' said Mr Brass smiling fondly at the wall, 'his linen which was always of a particular colour, for such was his whim and fancy—how plain I see his linen now!'

'You had better go on, sir,' said Mrs Jiniwin impatiently.

'True, ma'am, true,' cried Mr Brass. 'Our faculties must not freeze with grief. I'll trouble you for a little more of that, ma'am. A question now arises, with relation to his nose.'

'Flat,' said Mrs Jiniwin.

'Aquiline!' cried Quilp, thrusting in his head, and striking the feature with his fist. 'Aquiline, you hag. Do you see it? Do you call this flat? Do you? Eh?'

'Oh capital, capital!' shouted Brass, from the mere force of habit. 'Excellent! How very good he is! He's a most remarkable man—so extremely whimsical! Such an amazing power of taking people by surprise!'

Quilp paid no regard whatever to these compliments, nor to the dubious and frightened look into which the lawyer gradually subsided, nor to the shrieks of his wife and mother-in-law, nor to the latter's running from the room, nor to the former's fainting away. Keeping his eye fixed on Sampson Brass, he walked up to the table, and beginning with his glass, drank off the contents, and went regularly round until he had emptied the other two, when he seized the case-bottle, and hugging it under his arm, surveyed him with a most extraordinary leer.

'Not yet, Sampson,' said Quilp. 'Not just yet!'

'Oh very good indeed!' cried Brass, recovering his spirits a little. 'Ha ha ha! Oh exceedingly good! There's not another man alive who could carry it off like that. A most difficult position to carry off. But he has such a flow of good-humour, such an amazing flow!'

'Good night,' said the dwarf, nodding expressively.

'Good night, sir, good night,' cried the lawyer, retreating backwards towards the door. 'This is a joyful occasion indeed, extremely joyful. Ha ha ha! oh very rich, very rich indeed, remarkably so!'

Waiting until Mr Brass's ejaculations died away in the distance (for he continued to pour them out, all the way down stairs), Quilp advanced towards the two men, who yet lingered in a kind of stupid amazement.

'Have you been dragging the river all day, gentlemen?' said the dwarf, holding the door open with great politeness.

'And yesterday too, master.'

'Dear me, you've had a deal of trouble. Pray consider everything yours that you find upon the—upon the body. Good night!'

The men looked at each other, but had evidently no inclination to argue the point just then, and shuffled out of the room. The speedy clearance effected, Quilp locked the doors; and still embracing the case-bottle with shrugged-up shoulders and folded arms, stood looking at his insensible wife like a dismounted nightmare.

CHAPTER 50

Matrimonial differences are usually discussed by the parties concerned in the form of dialogue, in which the lady bears at least her full half share. Those of Mr and Mrs Quilp, however, were an exception to the general rule; the remarks which they occasioned being limited to a long soliloquy on the part of the gentleman, with perhaps a few deprecatory observations from the lady, not extending beyond a trembling monosyllable uttered at long intervals, and in a very submissive and humble tone. On the present occasion, Mrs Quilp did not for a long time venture even on this gentle defence, but when she had recovered from her fainting-fit, sat in a tearful silence, meekly listening to the reproaches of her lord and master.

Of these Mr Quilp delivered himself with the utmost animation and rapidity, and with so many distortions of limb and feature, that even his wife, although tolerably well accustomed to his proficiency in these respects, was well-nigh beside herself with alarm. But the Jamaica rum, and the joy of having occasioned a heavy disappointment, by degrees cooled Mr Quilp's wrath; which from being at savage heat, dropped slowly to the bantering or chuckling point, at which it steadily remained.

'So you thought I was dead and gone, did you?' said Quilp. 'You thought you were a widow, eh? Ha, ha, ha, you jade.'

'Indeed, Quilp,' returned his wife. 'I'm very sorry—'

'Who doubts it!' cried the dwarf. 'You very sorry! to be sure you are. Who doubts that you're very sorry!'

'I don't mean sorry that you have come home again alive and well,' said his wife, 'but sorry that I should have been led into such a belief. I am glad to see you, Quilp; indeed I am.'

In truth Mrs Quilp did seem a great deal more glad to behold her lord than might have been expected, and did evince a degree of interest in his safety which, all things considered, was rather unaccountable. Upon Quilp, however, this circumstance made no impression, farther than as it moved him to snap his fingers close to his wife's eyes, with divers grins of triumph and derision.

'How could you go away so long, without saying a word to me or letting me hear of you or know anything about you?' asked the poor little woman, sobbing. 'How could you be so cruel, Quilp?'

'How could I be so cruel! cruel!' cried the dwarf. 'Because I was in the humour. I'm in the humour now. I shall be cruel when I like. I'm going away again.'

'Not again!'

'Yes, again. I'm going away now. I'm off directly. I mean to go and live wherever the fancy seizes me—at the wharf—at the counting-house—and be a jolly bachelor. You were a widow in anticipation. Damme,' screamed the dwarf, 'I'll be a bachelor in earnest.'

'You can't be serious, Quilp,' sobbed his wife.

'I tell you,' said the dwarf, exulting in his project, 'that I'll be a bachelor, a devil-may-care bachelor; and I'll have my bachelor's hall at the counting-house, and at such times come near it if you dare. And mind too that I don't pounce in upon you at unseasonable hours again, for I'll be a spy upon you, and come and go like a mole or a weazel. Tom Scott—where's Tom Scott?'

'Here I am, master,' cried the voice of the boy, as Quilp threw up the window.

'Wait there, you dog,' returned the dwarf, 'to carry a bachelor's portmanteau. Pack it up, Mrs Quilp. Knock up the dear old lady to help; knock her up. Halloa there! Halloa!'

With these exclamations, Mr Quilp caught up the poker, and hurrying to the door of the good lady's sleeping-closet, beat upon it therewith until she awoke in inexpressible terror, thinking that her amiable son-in-law surely intended to murder her in justification of the legs she had slandered. Impressed with this idea, she was no sooner fairly awake than she screamed violently, and would have quickly precipitated herself out of the window and through a neighbouring skylight, if her daughter had not hastened in to undeceive her, and implore her assistance. Somewhat reassured by her account of the service she was required to render, Mrs Jiniwin made her appearance in a flannel dressing-gown; and both mother and daughter, trembling with terror and cold—for the night was now far advanced—obeyed Mr Quilp's directions in submissive silence. Prolonging his preparations as much as possible, for their greater comfort, that eccentric gentleman superintended the packing of his wardrobe, and having added to it with his own hands, a plate, knife and fork, spoon, teacup and saucer, and other small household matters of that nature, strapped up the portmanteau, took it on his shoulders, and actually marched off without another word, and with the case-bottle (which he had never once put down) still tightly clasped under his arm. Consigning his heavier burden to the care of Tom Scott when he reached the street, taking a dram from the bottle for his own encouragement, and giving the boy a rap on the head with it as a small taste for himself, Quilp very deliberately led the way to the wharf, and reached it at between three and four o'clock in the morning.

'Snug!' said Quilp, when he had groped his way to the wooden counting-house, and opened the door with a key he carried about with him. 'Beautifully snug! Call me at eight, you dog.'

With no more formal leave-taking or explanation, he clutched the portmanteau, shut the door on his attendant, and climbing on the desk, and rolling himself up as round as a hedgehog, in an old boat-cloak, fell fast asleep.

Being roused in the morning at the appointed time, and roused with difficulty, after his late fatigues, Quilp instructed Tom Scott to make a fire in the yard of sundry pieces of old timber, and to prepare some coffee for breakfast; for the better furnishing of which repast he entrusted him with certain small moneys, to be expended in the purchase of hot rolls, butter, sugar, Yarmouth bloaters, and other articles of housekeeping; so that in a few minutes a savoury meal was smoking on the board. With this substantial comfort, the dwarf regaled himself to his heart's content; and being highly satisfied with this free and gipsy mode of life (which he had often meditated, as offering, whenever he chose to avail himself of it, an agreeable freedom from the restraints of matrimony, and a choice means of keeping Mrs Quilp and her mother in a state of incessant agitation and suspense), bestirred himself to improve his retreat, and render it more commodious and comfortable.

With this view, he issued forth to a place hard by, where sea-stores were sold, purchased a second-hand hammock, and had it slung in seamanlike fashion from the ceiling of the counting-house. He also caused to be erected, in the same mouldy cabin, an old ship's stove with a rusty funnel to carry the smoke through the roof; and these arrangements completed, surveyed them with ineffable delight.

'I've got a country-house like Robinson Crusoe,' said the dwarf, ogling the accommodations; 'a solitary, sequestered, desolate-island sort of spot, where I can be quite alone when I have business on hand, and be secure from all spies and listeners. Nobody near me here, but rats, and they are fine stealthy secret fellows. I shall be as merry as a grig among these gentry. I'll look out for one like Christopher, and poison him—ha, ha, ha! Business though—business—we must be mindful of business in the midst of pleasure, and the time has flown this morning, I declare.'

Enjoining Tom Scott to await his return, and not to stand upon his head, or throw a summerset, or so much as walk upon his hands meanwhile, on pain of lingering torments, the dwarf threw himself into a boat, and crossing to the other side of the river, and then speeding away on foot, reached Mr Swiveller's usual house of entertainment in Bevis Marks, just as that gentleman sat down alone to dinner in its dusky parlour.

'Dick,' said the dwarf, thrusting his head in at the door, 'my pet, my pupil, the apple of my eye, hey, hey!'

'Oh you're there, are you?' returned Mr Swiveller; 'how are you?'

'How's Dick?' retorted Quilp. 'How's the cream of clerkship, eh?'

'Why, rather sour, sir,' replied Mr Swiveller. 'Beginning to border upon cheesiness, in fact.'

'What's the matter?' said the dwarf, advancing. 'Has Sally proved unkind. "Of all the girls that are so smart, there's none like—" eh, Dick!'

'Certainly not,' replied Mr Swiveller, eating his dinner with great gravity, 'none like her. She's the sphynx of private life, is Sally B.'

'You're out of spirits,' said Quilp, drawing up a chair. 'What's the matter?'

'The law don't agree with me,' returned Dick. 'It isn't moist enough, and there's too much confinement. I have been thinking of running away.'

'Bah!' said the dwarf. 'Where would you run to, Dick?'

'I don't know' returned Mr Swiveller. 'Towards Highgate, I suppose. Perhaps the bells might strike up "Turn again Swiveller, Lord Mayor of London." Whittington's name was Dick.

I wish cats were scarcer.'

Quilp looked at his companion with his eyes screwed up into a comical expression of curiosity, and patiently awaited his further explanation; upon which, however, Mr Swiveller appeared in no hurry to enter, as he ate a very long dinner in profound silence, finally pushed away his plate, threw himself back into his chair, folded his arms, and stared ruefully at the fire, in which some ends of cigars were smoking on their own account, and sending up a fragrant odour.

'Perhaps you'd like a bit of cake'—said Dick, at last turning to the dwarf. 'You're quite welcome to it. You ought to be, for it's of your making.'

'What do you mean?' said Quilp.

Mr Swiveller replied by taking from his pocket a small and very greasy parcel, slowly unfolding it, and displaying a little slab of plum-cake extremely indigestible in appearance, and bordered with a paste of white sugar an inch and a half deep.

'What should you say this was?' demanded Mr Swiveller.

'It looks like bride-cake,' replied the dwarf, grinning.

'And whose should you say it was?' inquired Mr Swiveller, rubbing the pastry against his nose with a dreadful calmness. 'Whose?'

'Not—'

'Yes,' said Dick, 'the same. You needn't mention her name. There's no such name now. Her name is Cheggs now, Sophy Cheggs. Yet loved I as man never loved that hadn't wooden legs, and my heart, my heart is breaking for the love of Sophy Cheggs.'

With this extemporary adaptation of a popular ballad to the distressing circumstances of his own case, Mr Swiveller folded up the parcel again, beat it very flat between the palms of his hands, thrust it into his breast, buttoned his coat over it, and folded his arms upon the whole.

'Now, I hope you're satisfied, sir,' said Dick; 'and I hope Fred's satisfied. You went partners in the mischief, and I hope you like it. This is the triumph I was to have, is it? It's like the old country-dance of that name, where there are two gentlemen to one lady, and one has her, and the other hasn't, but comes limping up behind to make out the figure. But it's Destiny, and mine's a crusher.'

Disguising his secret joy in Mr Swiveller's defeat, Daniel Quilp adopted the surest means of soothing him, by ringing the bell, and ordering in a supply of rosy wine (that is to say, of its usual representative), which he put about with great alacrity, calling upon Mr Swiveller to pledge him in various toasts derisive of Cheggs, and eulogistic of the happiness of single men. Such was their impression on Mr Swiveller, coupled with the reflection that no man could oppose his destiny, that in a very short space of time his spirits rose surprisingly, and he was enabled to give the dwarf an account of the receipt of the cake, which, it appeared, had been brought to Bevis Marks by the two surviving Miss Wackleses in person, and delivered at the office door with much giggling and joyfulness.

'Ha!' said Quilp. 'It will be our turn to giggle soon. And that reminds me—you spoke of young Trent—where is he?'

Mr Swiveller explained that his respectable friend had recently accepted a responsible situation in a locomotive gaming-house, and was at that time absent on a professional tour among the adventurous spirits of Great Britain.

'That's unfortunate,' said the dwarf, 'for I came, in fact, to ask you about him. A thought has occurred to me, Dick; your friend over the way—'

'Which friend?'

'In the first floor.'

'Yes?'

'Your friend in the first floor, Dick, may know him.'

'No, he don't,' said Mr Swiveller, shaking his head.

'Don't! No, because he has never seen him,' rejoined Quilp; 'but if we were to bring them together, who knows, Dick, but Fred, properly introduced, would serve his turn almost as well as little Nell or her grandfather—who knows but it might make the young fellow's fortune, and, through him, yours, eh?'

'Why, the fact is, you see,' said Mr Swiveller, 'that they have been brought together.'

'Have been!' cried the dwarf, looking suspiciously at his companion. 'Through whose means?'

'Through mine,' said Dick, slightly confused. 'Didn't I mention it to you the last time you called over yonder?'

'You know you didn't,' returned the dwarf.

'I believe you're right,' said Dick. 'No. I didn't, I recollect. Oh yes, I brought 'em together that very day. It was Fred's suggestion.'

'And what came of it?'

'Why, instead of my friend's bursting into tears when he knew who Fred was, embracing him kindly, and telling him that he was his grandfather, or his grandmother in disguise (which we fully expected), he flew into a tremendous passion; called him all manner of names; said it was in a great measure his fault that little Nell and the old gentleman had ever been brought to poverty; didn't hint at our taking anything to drink; and—and in short rather turned us out of the room than otherwise.'

'That's strange,' said the dwarf, musing.

'So we remarked to each other at the time,' returned Dick coolly, 'but quite true.'

Quilp was plainly staggered by this intelligence, over which he brooded for some time in moody silence, often raising his eyes to Mr Swiveller's face, and sharply scanning its expression. As he could read in it, however, no additional information or anything to lead him to believe he had spoken falsely; and as Mr Swiveller, left to his own meditations, sighed deeply, and was evidently growing maudlin on the subject of Mrs Cheggs; the dwarf soon broke up the conference and took his departure, leaving the bereaved one to his melancholy ruminations.

'Have been brought together, eh?' said the dwarf as he walked the streets alone. 'My friend has stolen a march upon me. It led him to nothing, and therefore is no great matter, save in the intention. I'm glad he has lost his mistress. Ha ha! The blockhead mustn't leave the law at present. I'm sure of him where he is, whenever I want him for my own purposes, and, besides, he's a good unconscious spy on Brass, and tells, in his cups, all that he sees and hears. You're useful to me, Dick, and cost nothing but a little treating now and then. I am not sure that it may not be worth while, before long, to take credit with the stranger, Dick, by discovering your designs upon the child; but for the present we'll remain the best friends in the world, with your good leave.'

Pursuing these thoughts, and gasping as he went along, after his own peculiar fashion, Mr Quilp once more crossed the Thames, and shut himself up in his Bachelor's Hall, which, by reason of its newly-erected chimney depositing the smoke inside the room and carrying none of it off, was not quite so agreeable as more fastidious people might have desired. Such inconveniences, however, instead of disgusting the dwarf with his new abode, rather suited his humour; so, after dining luxuriously from the public-house, he lighted his pipe, and smoked against the chimney until nothing of him was visible through the mist but a pair of red and highly inflamed eyes, with sometimes a dim vision of his head and face, as, in a violent fit of coughing, he slightly stirred the smoke and scattered the heavy wreaths by which they were obscured. In the midst of this atmosphere, which must infallibly have smothered any other man, Mr Quilp passed the evening with great cheerfulness; solacing himself all the time with the pipe and the case-bottle; and occasionally entertaining himself with a melodious howl, intended for a song, but bearing not the faintest resemblance to any scrap of any piece of music, vocal or instrumental, ever invented by man. Thus he amused himself until nearly midnight, when he turned into his hammock with the utmost satisfaction.

The first sound that met his ears in the morning—as he half opened his eyes, and, finding himself so unusually near the ceiling, entertained a drowsy idea that he must have been transformed into a fly or blue-bottle in the course of the night,—was that of a stifled sobbing and weeping in the room. Peeping cautiously over the side of his hammock, he descried Mrs Quilp, to whom, after contemplating her for some time in silence, he communicated a violent start by suddenly yelling out—'Halloa!'

'Oh, Quilp!' cried his poor little wife, looking up. 'How you frightened me!'

'I meant to, you jade,' returned the dwarf. 'What do you want here? I'm dead, an't I?'

'Oh, please come home, do come home,' said Mrs Quilp, sobbing; 'we'll never do so any more, Quilp, and after all it was only a mistake that grew out of our anxiety.'

'Out of your anxiety,' grinned the dwarf. 'Yes, I know that—out of your anxiety for my death. I shall come home when I please, I tell you. I shall come home when I please, and go when I please. I'll be a Will o' the Wisp, now here, now there, dancing about you always, starting up when you least expect me, and keeping you in a constant state of restlessness and irritation. Will you begone?'

Mrs Quilp durst only make a gesture of entreaty.

'I tell you no,' cried the dwarf. 'No. If you dare to come here again unless you're sent for, I'll keep watch-dogs in the yard that'll growl and bite—I'll have man-traps, cunningly altered and improved for catching women—I'll have spring guns, that shall explode when you tread upon the wires, and blow you into little pieces. Will you begone?'

'Do forgive me. Do come back,' said his wife, earnestly.

'No-o-o-o-o!' roared Quilp. 'Not till my own good time, and then I'll return again as often as I choose, and be accountable to nobody for my goings or comings. You see the door there. Will you go?'

Mr Quilp delivered this last command in such a very energetic voice, and moreover accompanied it with such a sudden gesture, indicative of an intention to spring out of his hammock, and, night-capped as he was, bear his wife home again through the public streets, that she sped away like an arrow. Her worthy lord stretched his neck and eyes until she had crossed the yard, and then, not at all sorry to have had this opportunity of carrying his point, and asserting the sanctity of his castle, fell into an immoderate fit of laughter, and laid himself down to sleep again.

CHAPTER 51

The bland and open-hearted proprietor of Bachelor's Hall slept on amidst the congenial accompaniments of rain, mud, dirt, damp, fog, and rats, until late in the day; when, summoning his valet Tom Scott to assist him to rise, and to prepare breakfast, he quitted his couch, and made his toilet. This duty performed, and his repast ended, he again betook himself to Bevis Marks.

This visit was not intended for Mr Swiveller, but for his friend and employer Mr Sampson Brass. Both gentlemen however were from home, nor was the life and light of law, Miss Sally, at her post either. The fact of their joint desertion of the office was made known to all comers by a scrap of paper in the hand-writing of Mr Swiveller, which was attached to the bell-handle, and which, giving the reader no clue to the time of day when it was first posted, furnished him with the rather vague and unsatisfactory information that that gentleman would 'return in an hour.'

'There's a servant, I suppose,' said the dwarf, knocking at the house-door. 'She'll do.'

After a sufficiently long interval, the door was opened, and a small voice immediately accosted him with, 'Oh please will you leave a card or message?'

'Eh?' said the dwarf, looking down, (it was something quite new to him) upon the small servant.

To this, the child, conducting her conversation as upon the occasion of her first interview with Mr Swiveller, again replied, 'Oh please will you leave a card or message?'

'I'll write a note,' said the dwarf, pushing past her into the office; 'and mind your master has it directly he comes home.' So Mr Quilp climbed up to the top of a tall stool to write the note, and the small servant, carefully tutored for such emergencies, looked on with her eyes wide open, ready, if he so much as abstracted a wafer, to rush into the street and give the alarm to the police.

As Mr Quilp folded his note (which was soon written: being a very short one) he encountered the gaze of the small servant. He looked at her, long and earnestly.

'How are you?' said the dwarf, moistening a wafer with horrible grimaces.

The small servant, perhaps frightened by his looks, returned no audible reply; but it appeared from the motion of her lips that she was inwardly repeating the same form of expression concerning the note or message.

'Do they use you ill here? is your mistress a Tartar?' said Quilp with a chuckle.

In reply to the last interrogation, the small servant, with a look of infinite cunning mingled with fear, screwed up her mouth very tight and round, and nodded violently. Whether there was anything in the peculiar slyness of her action which fascinated Mr Quilp, or anything in the expression of her features at the moment which attracted his attention for some other reason; or whether it merely occurred to him as a pleasant whim to stare the small servant out of countenance; certain it is, that he planted his elbows square and firmly on the desk, and squeezing up his cheeks with his hands, looked at her fixedly.

'Where do you come from?' he said after a long pause, stroking his chin.

'I don't know.'

'What's your name?'

'Nothing.'

'Nonsense!' retorted Quilp. 'What does your mistress call you when she wants you?'

'A little devil,' said the child.

She added in the same breath, as if fearful of any further questioning, 'But please will you leave a card or message?'

These unusual answers might naturally have provoked some more inquiries. Quilp, however, without uttering another word, withdrew his eyes from the small servant, stroked his chin more thoughtfully than before, and then, bending over the note as if to direct it with scrupulous and hair-breadth nicety, looked at her, covertly but very narrowly, from under his bushy eyebrows. The result of this secret survey was, that he shaded his face with his hands, and laughed slyly and noiselessly, until every vein in it was swollen almost to bursting. Pulling his hat over his brow to conceal his mirth and its effects, he tossed the letter to the child, and hastily withdrew.

Once in the street, moved by some secret impulse, he laughed, and held his sides, and laughed again, and tried to peer through the dusty area railings as if to catch another glimpse of the child, until he was quite tired out. At last, he travelled back to the Wilderness, which was within rifle-shot of his bachelor retreat, and ordered tea in the wooden summer-house that afternoon for three persons; an invitation to Miss Sally Brass and her brother to partake of that entertainment at that place, having been the object both of his journey and his note.

It was not precisely the kind of weather in which people usually take tea in summer-houses, far less in summer-houses in an advanced state of decay, and overlooking the slimy banks of a great river at low water. Nevertheless, it was in this choice retreat that Mr Quilp ordered a cold collation to be prepared, and it was beneath its cracked and leaky roof that he, in due course of time, received Mr Sampson and his sister Sally.

'You're fond of the beauties of nature,' said Quilp with a grin. 'Is this charming, Brass? Is it unusual, unsophisticated, primitive?'

'It's delightful indeed, sir,' replied the lawyer.

'Cool?' said Quilp.

'N-not particularly so, I think, sir,' rejoined Brass, with his teeth chattering in his head.

'Perhaps a little damp and ague-ish?' said Quilp.

'Just damp enough to be cheerful, sir,' rejoined Brass. 'Nothing more, sir, nothing more.'

'And Sally?' said the delighted dwarf. 'Does she like it?'

'She'll like it better,' returned that strong-minded lady, 'when she has tea; so let us have it, and don't bother.'

'Sweet Sally!' cried Quilp, extending his arms as if about to embrace her. 'Gentle, charming, overwhelming Sally.'

'He's a very remarkable man indeed!' soliloquised Mr Brass. 'He's quite a Troubadour, you know; quite a Troubadour!'

These complimentary expressions were uttered in a somewhat absent and distracted manner; for the unfortunate lawyer, besides having a bad cold in his head, had got wet in coming, and would have willingly borne some pecuniary sacrifice if he could have shifted his present raw quarters to a warm room, and dried himself at a fire. Quilp, however—who, beyond the gratification of his demon whims, owed Sampson some acknowledgment of the part he had played in the mourning scene of which he had been a hidden witness, marked these symptoms of uneasiness with a delight past all expression, and derived from them a secret joy which the costliest banquet could never have afforded him.

It is worthy of remark, too, as illustrating a little feature in the character of Miss Sally Brass, that, although on her own account she would have borne the discomforts of the Wilderness with a very ill grace, and would probably, indeed, have walked off before the tea appeared, she no sooner beheld the latent uneasiness and misery of her brother than she developed a grim satisfaction, and began to enjoy herself after her own manner. Though the wet came stealing through the roof and trickling down upon their heads, Miss Brass uttered no complaint, but presided over the tea equipage with imperturbable composure. While Mr Quilp, in his uproarious hospitality, seated himself upon an empty beer-barrel, vaunted the place as the most beautiful and comfortable in the three kingdoms, and elevating his glass, drank to their next merry-meeting in that jovial spot; and Mr Brass, with the rain plashing down into his tea-cup, made a dismal attempt to pluck up his spirits and appear at his ease; and Tom Scott, who was in waiting at the door under an old umbrella, exulted in his agonies, and bade fair to split his sides with laughing; while all this was passing, Miss Sally Brass, unmindful of the wet which dripped down upon her own feminine person and fair apparel, sat placidly behind the tea-board, erect and grizzly, contemplating the unhappiness of her brother with a mind at ease, and content, in her amiable disregard of self, to sit there all night, witnessing the torments which his avaricious and grovelling nature compelled him to endure and forbade him to resent. And this, it must be observed, or the illustration would be incomplete, although in a business point of view she had the strongest sympathy with Mr Sampson, and would have been beyond measure indignant if he had thwarted their client in any one respect.

In the height of his boisterous merriment, Mr Quilp, having on some pretence dismissed his attendant sprite for the moment, resumed his usual manner all at once, dismounted from his cask, and laid his hand upon the lawyer's sleeve.

'A word,' said the dwarf, 'before we go farther. Sally, hark'ee for a minute.'

Miss Sally drew closer, as if accustomed to business conferences with their host which were the better for not having air.

'Business,' said the dwarf, glancing from brother to sister. 'Very private business. Lay your heads together when you're by yourselves.'

'Certainly, sir,' returned Brass, taking out his pocket-book and pencil. 'I'll take down the heads if you please, sir. Remarkable documents,' added the lawyer, raising his eyes to the ceiling, 'most remarkable documents. He states his points so clearly that it's a treat to have 'em! I don't know any act of parliament that's equal to him in clearness.'

'I shall deprive you of a treat,' said Quilp. 'Put up your book. We don't want any documents. So. There's a lad named Kit—'

Miss Sally nodded, implying that she knew of him.

'Kit!' said Mr Sampson.—'Kit! Ha! I've heard the name before, but I don't exactly call to mind—I don't exactly—'

'You're as slow as a tortoise, and more thick-headed than a rhinoceros,' returned his obliging client with an impatient gesture.

'He's extremely pleasant!' cried the obsequious Sampson. 'His acquaintance with Natural History too is surprising. Quite a Buffoon, quite!'

There is no doubt that Mr Brass intended some compliment or other; and it has been argued with show of reason that he would have said Buffon, but made use of a superfluous vowel. Be this as it may, Quilp gave him no time for correction, as he performed that office himself by more than tapping him on the head with the handle of his umbrella.

'Don't let's have any wrangling,' said Miss Sally, staying his hand. 'I've showed you that I know him, and that's enough.'

'She's always foremost!' said the dwarf, patting her on the back and looking contemptuously at Sampson. 'I don't like Kit, Sally.'

'Nor I,' rejoined Miss Brass.

'Nor I,' said Sampson.

'Why, that's right!' cried Quilp. 'Half our work is done already. This Kit is one of your honest people; one of your fair characters; a prowling prying hound; a hypocrite; a double-faced, white-livered, sneaking spy; a crouching cur to those that feed and coax him, and a barking yelping dog to all besides.'

'Fearfully eloquent!' cried Brass with a sneeze. 'Quite appalling!'

'Come to the point,' said Miss Sally, 'and don't talk so much.'

'Right again!' exclaimed Quilp, with another contemptuous look at Sampson, 'always foremost! I say, Sally, he is a yelping, insolent dog to all besides, and most of all, to me. In short, I owe him a grudge.' 'That's enough, sir,' said Sampson.

'No, it's not enough, sir,' sneered Quilp; 'will you hear me out? Besides that I owe him a grudge on that account, he thwarts me at this minute, and stands between me and an end which might otherwise prove a golden one to us all. Apart from that, I repeat that he crosses my humour, and I hate him. Now, you know the lad, and can guess the rest. Devise your own means of putting him out of my way, and execute them. Shall it be done?'

'It shall, sir,' said Sampson.

'Then give me your hand,' retorted Quilp. 'Sally, girl, yours. I rely as much, or more, on you than him. Tom Scott comes back. Lantern, pipes, more grog, and a jolly night of it!'

No other word was spoken, no other look exchanged, which had the slightest reference to this, the real occasion of their meeting. The trio were well accustomed to act together, and were linked to each other by ties of mutual interest and advantage, and nothing more was needed. Resuming his boisterous manner with the same ease with which he had thrown it off, Quilp was in an instant the same uproarious, reckless little savage he had been a few seconds before. It was ten o'clock at night before the amiable Sally supported her beloved and loving brother from the Wilderness, by which time he needed the utmost support her tender frame could render; his walk being from some unknown reason anything but steady, and his legs constantly doubling up in unexpected places.

Overpowered, notwithstanding his late prolonged slumbers, by the fatigues of the last few days, the dwarf lost no time in creeping to his dainty house, and was soon dreaming in his hammock. Leaving him to visions, in which perhaps the quiet figures we quitted in the old church porch were not without their share, be it our task to rejoin them as they sat and watched.

CHAPTER 52

After a long time, the schoolmaster appeared at the wicket-gate of the churchyard, and hurried towards them, tingling in his hand, as he came along, a bundle of rusty keys. He was quite breathless with pleasure and haste when he reached the porch, and at first could only point towards the old building which the child had been contemplating so earnestly.

'You see those two old houses,' he said at last.

'Yes, surely,' replied Nell. 'I have been looking at them nearly all the time you have been away.'

'And you would have looked at them more curiously yet, if you could have guessed what I have to tell you,' said her friend. 'One of those houses is mine.'

Without saying any more, or giving the child time to reply, the schoolmaster took her hand, and, his honest face quite radiant with exultation, led her to the place of which he spoke.

They stopped before its low arched door. After trying several of the keys in vain, the schoolmaster found one to fit the huge lock, which turned back, creaking, and admitted them into the house.

The room into which they entered was a vaulted chamber once nobly ornamented by cunning architects, and still retaining, in its beautiful groined roof and rich stone tracery, choice remnants of its ancient splendour. Foliage carved in the stone, and emulating the mastery of Nature's hand, yet remained to tell how many times the leaves outside had come and gone, while it lived on unchanged. The broken figures supporting the burden of the chimney-piece, though mutilated, were still distinguishable for what they had been—far different from the dust without—and showed sadly by the empty hearth, like creatures who had outlived their kind, and mourned their own too slow decay.

In some old time—for even change was old in that old place—a wooden partition had been constructed in one part of the chamber to form a sleeping-closet, into which the light was admitted at the same period by a rude window, or rather niche, cut in the solid wall. This screen, together with two seats in the broad chimney, had at some forgotten date been part of the church or convent; for the oak, hastily appropriated to its present purpose, had been little altered from its former shape, and presented to the eye a pile of fragments of rich carving from old monkish stalls.

An open door leading to a small room or cell, dim with the light that came through leaves of ivy, completed the interior of this portion of the ruin. It was not quite destitute of furniture. A few strange chairs, whose arms and legs looked as though they had dwindled away with age; a table, the very spectre of its race: a great old chest that had once held records in the church, with other quaintly-fashioned domestic necessaries, and store of fire-wood for the winter, were scattered around, and gave evident tokens of its occupation as a dwelling-place at no very distant time.

The child looked around her, with that solemn feeling with which we contemplate the work of ages that have become but drops of water in the great ocean of eternity. The old man had followed them, but they were all three hushed for a space, and drew their breath softly, as if they feared to break the silence even by so slight a sound.

'It is a very beautiful place!' said the child, in a low voice.

'I almost feared you thought otherwise,' returned the schoolmaster. 'You shivered when we first came in, as if you felt it cold or gloomy.'

'It was not that,' said Nell, glancing round with a slight shudder. 'Indeed I cannot tell you what it was, but when I saw the outside, from the church porch, the same feeling came over me. It is its being so old and grey perhaps.'

'A peaceful place to live in, don't you think so?' said her friend.

'Oh yes,' rejoined the child, clasping her hands earnestly. 'A quiet, happy place—a place to live and learn to die in!' She would have said more, but that the energy of her thoughts caused her voice to falter, and come in trembling whispers from her lips.

'A place to live, and learn to live, and gather health of mind and body in,' said the schoolmaster; 'for this old house is yours.'

'Ours!' cried the child.

'Ay,' returned the schoolmaster gaily, 'for many a merry year to come, I hope. I shall be a close neighbour—only next door—but this house is yours.'

Having now disburdened himself of his great surprise, the schoolmaster sat down, and drawing Nell to his side, told her how he had learnt that ancient tenement had been occupied for a very long time by an old person, nearly a hundred years of age, who kept the keys of the church, opened and closed it for the services, and showed it to strangers; how she had died not many weeks ago, and nobody had yet been found to fill the office; how, learning all this in an interview with the sexton, who was confined to his bed by rheumatism, he had been bold to make mention of his fellow-traveller, which had been so favourably received by that high authority, that he had taken courage, acting on his advice, to propound the matter to the clergyman. In a word, the result of his exertions was, that Nell and her grandfather were to be carried before the last-named gentleman next day; and, his approval of their conduct and appearance reserved as a matter of form, that they were already appointed to the vacant post.

'There's a small allowance of money,' said the schoolmaster. 'It is not much, but still enough to live upon in this retired spot. By clubbing our funds together, we shall do bravely; no fear of that.'

'Heaven bless and prosper you!' sobbed the child.

'Amen, my dear,' returned her friend cheerfully; 'and all of us, as it will, and has, in leading us through sorrow and trouble to this tranquil life. But we must look at my house now. Come!'

They repaired to the other tenement; tried the rusty keys as before; at length found the right one; and opened the worm-eaten door. It led into a chamber, vaulted and old, like that from which they had come, but not so spacious, and having only one other little room attached. It was not difficult to divine that the other house was of right the schoolmaster's, and that he had chosen for himself the least commodious, in his care and regard for them. Like the adjoining habitation, it held such old articles of furniture as were absolutely necessary, and had its stack of fire-wood.

To make these dwellings as habitable and full of comfort as they could, was now their pleasant care. In a short time, each had its cheerful fire glowing and crackling on the hearth, and reddening the pale old wall with a hale and healthy blush. Nell, busily plying her needle, repaired the tattered window-hangings, drew together the rents that time had worn in the threadbare scraps of carpet, and made them whole and decent. The schoolmaster swept and smoothed the ground before the door, trimmed the long grass, trained the ivy and creeping plants which hung their drooping heads in melancholy neglect; and gave to the outer walls a cheery air of home. The old man, sometimes by his side and sometimes with the child, lent his aid to both, went here and there on little patient services, and was happy. Neighbours, too, as they came from work, proffered their help; or sent their children with such small presents or loans as the strangers needed most. It was a busy day; and night came on, and found them wondering that there was yet so much to do, and that it should be dark so soon.

They took their supper together, in the house which may be henceforth called the child's; and, when they had finished their meal, drew round the fire, and almost in whispers—their hearts were too quiet and glad for loud expression—discussed their future plans. Before they separated, the schoolmaster read some prayers aloud; and then, full of gratitude and happiness, they parted for the night.

At that silent hour, when her grandfather was sleeping peacefully in his bed, and every sound was hushed, the child lingered before the dying embers, and thought of her past fortunes as if they had been a dream And she only now awoke. The glare of the sinking flame, reflected in the oaken panels whose carved tops were dimly seen in the dusky roof—the aged walls, where strange shadows came and went with every flickering of the fire—the solemn presence, within, of that decay which falls on senseless things the most enduring in their nature: and, without, and round about on every side, of Death—filled her with deep and thoughtful feelings, but with none of terror or alarm. A change had been gradually stealing over her, in the time of her loneliness and sorrow. With failing strength and heightening resolution, there had sprung up a purified and altered mind; there had grown in her bosom blessed thoughts and hopes, which are the portion of few but the weak and drooping. There were none to see the frail, perishable figure, as it glided from the fire and leaned pensively at the open casement; none but the stars, to look into the upturned face and read its history. The old church bell rang out the hour with a mournful sound, as if it had grown sad from so much communing with the dead and unheeded warning to the living; the fallen leaves rustled; the grass stirred upon the graves; all else was still and sleeping.

Some of those dreamless sleepers lay close within the shadow of the church—touching the wall, as if they clung to it for comfort and protection. Others had chosen to lie beneath the changing shade of trees; others by the path, that footsteps might come near them; others, among the graves of little children. Some had desired to rest beneath the very ground they had trodden in their daily walks; some, where the setting sun might shine upon their beds; some, where its light would fall upon them when it rose. Perhaps not one of the imprisoned souls had been able quite to separate itself in living thought from its old companion. If any had, it had still felt for it a love like that which captives have been known to bear towards the cell in which they have been long confined, and, even at parting, hung upon its narrow bounds affectionately.

It was long before the child closed the window, and approached her bed. Again something of the same sensation as before—an involuntary chill—a momentary feeling akin to fear—but vanishing directly, and leaving no alarm behind. Again, too, dreams of the little scholar; of the roof opening, and a column of bright faces, rising far away into the sky, as she had seen in some old scriptural picture once, and looking down on her, asleep. It was a sweet and happy dream. The quiet spot, outside, seemed to remain the same, saving that there was music in the air, and a sound of angels' wings. After a time the sisters came there, hand in hand, and stood among the graves. And then the dream grew dim, and faded.

With the brightness and joy of morning, came the renewal of yesterday's labours, the revival of its pleasant thoughts, the restoration of its energies, cheerfulness, and hope. They worked gaily in ordering and arranging their houses until noon, and then went to visit the clergyman.

He was a simple-hearted old gentleman, of a shrinking, subdued spirit, accustomed to retirement, and very little acquainted with the world, which he had left many years before to come and settle in that place. His wife had died in the house in which he still lived, and he had long since lost sight of any earthly cares or hopes beyond it.

He received them very kindly, and at once showed an interest in Nell; asking her name, and age, her birthplace, the circumstances which had led her there, and so forth. The schoolmaster had already told her story. They had no other friends or home to leave, he said, and had come to share his fortunes. He loved the child as though she were his own.

'Well, well,' said the clergyman. 'Let it be as you desire. She is very young.'

'Old in adversity and trial, sir,' replied the schoolmaster.

'God help her. Let her rest, and forget them,' said the old gentleman. 'But an old church is a dull and gloomy place for one so young as you, my child.'

'Oh no, sir,' returned Nell. 'I have no such thoughts, indeed.'

'I would rather see her dancing on the green at nights,' said the old gentleman, laying his hand upon her head, and smiling sadly, 'than have her sitting in the shadow of our mouldering arches. You must look to this, and see that her heart does not grow heavy among these solemn ruins. Your request is granted, friend.'

After more kind words, they withdrew, and repaired to the child's house; where they were yet in conversation on their happy fortune, when another friend appeared.

This was a little old gentleman, who lived in the parsonage-house, and had resided there (so they learnt soon afterwards) ever since the death of the clergyman's wife, which had happened fifteen years before. He had been his college friend and always his close companion; in the first shock of his grief he had come to console and comfort him; and from that time they had never parted company. The little old gentleman was the active spirit of the place, the adjuster of all differences, the promoter of all merry-makings, the dispenser of his friend's bounty, and of no small charity of his own besides; the universal mediator, comforter, and friend. None of the simple villagers had cared to ask his name, or, when they knew it, to store it in their memory. Perhaps from some vague rumour of his college honours which had been whispered abroad on his first arrival, perhaps because he was an unmarried, unencumbered gentleman, he had been called the bachelor. The name pleased him, or suited him as well as any other, and the Bachelor he had ever since remained. And the bachelor it was, it may be added, who with his own hands had laid in the stock of fuel which the wanderers had found in their new habitation.

The bachelor, then—to call him by his usual appellation—lifted the latch, showed his little round mild face for a moment at the door, and stepped into the room like one who was no stranger to it.

'You are Mr Marton, the new schoolmaster?' he said, greeting Nell's kind friend.

'I am, sir.'

'You come well recommended, and I am glad to see you. I should have been in the way yesterday, expecting you, but I rode across the country to carry a message from a sick mother to her daughter in service some miles off, and have but just now returned. This is our young church-keeper? You are not the less welcome, friend, for her sake, or for this old man's; nor the worse teacher for having learnt humanity.' 'She has been ill, sir, very lately,' said the schoolmaster, in answer to the look with which their visitor regarded Nell when he had kissed her cheek.

'Yes, yes. I know she has,' he rejoined. 'There have been suffering and heartache here.'

'Indeed there have, sir.'

The little old gentleman glanced at the grandfather, and back again at the child, whose hand he took tenderly in his, and held.

'You will be happier here,' he said; 'we will try, at least, to make you so. You have made great improvements here already. Are they the work of your hands?'

'Yes, sir.'

'We may make some others—not better in themselves, but with better means perhaps,' said the bachelor. 'Let us see now, let us see.'

Nell accompanied him into the other little rooms, and over both the houses, in which he found various small comforts wanting, which he engaged to supply from a certain collection of odds and ends he had at home, and which must have been a very miscellaneous and extensive one, as it comprehended the most opposite articles imaginable. They all came, however, and came without loss of time; for the little old gentleman, disappearing for some five or ten minutes, presently returned, laden with old shelves, rugs, blankets, and other household gear, and followed by a boy bearing a similar load. These being cast on the floor in a promiscuous heap, yielded a quantity of occupation in arranging, erecting, and putting away; the superintendence of which task evidently afforded the old gentleman extreme delight, and engaged him for some time with great briskness and activity. When nothing more was left to be done, he charged the boy to run off and bring his schoolmates to be marshalled before their new master, and solemnly reviewed.

'As good a set of fellows, Marton, as you'd wish to see,' he said, turning to the schoolmaster when the boy was gone; 'but I don't let 'em know I think so. That wouldn't do, at all.'

The messenger soon returned at the head of a long row of urchins, great and small, who, being confronted by the bachelor at the house door, fell into various convulsions of politeness; clutching their hats and caps, squeezing them into the smallest possible dimensions, and making all manner of bows and scrapes, which the little old gentleman contemplated with excessive satisfaction, and expressed his approval of by a great many nods and smiles. Indeed, his approbation of the boys was by no means so scrupulously disguised as he had led the schoolmaster to suppose, inasmuch as it broke out in sundry loud whispers and confidential remarks which were perfectly audible to them every one.

'This first boy, schoolmaster,' said the bachelor, 'is John Owen; a lad of good parts, sir, and frank, honest temper; but too thoughtless, too playful, too light-headed by far. That boy, my good sir, would break his neck with pleasure, and deprive his parents of their chief comfort—and between ourselves, when you come to see him at hare and hounds, taking the fence and ditch by the finger-post, and sliding down the face of the little quarry, you'll never forget it. It's beautiful!'

John Owen having been thus rebuked, and being in perfect possession of the speech aside, the bachelor singled out another boy.

'Now, look at that lad, sir,' said the bachelor. 'You see that fellow? Richard Evans his name is, sir. An amazing boy to learn, blessed with a good memory, and a ready understanding, and moreover with a good voice and ear for psalm-singing, in which he is the best among us. Yet, sir, that boy will come to a bad end; he'll never die in his bed; he's always falling asleep in sermon-time—and to tell you the truth, Mr Marton, I always did the same at his age, and feel quite certain that it was natural to my constitution and I couldn't help it.'

This hopeful pupil edified by the above terrible reproval, the bachelor turned to another.

'But if we talk of examples to be shunned,' said he, 'if we come to boys that should be a warning and a beacon to all their fellows, here's the one, and I hope you won't spare him. This is the lad, sir; this one with the blue eyes and light hair. This is a swimmer, sir, this fellow—a diver, Lord save us! This is a boy, sir, who had a fancy for plunging into eighteen feet of water, with his clothes on, and bringing up a blind man's dog, who was being drowned by the weight of his chain and collar, while his master stood wringing his hands upon the bank, bewailing the loss of his guide and friend. I sent the boy two guineas anonymously, sir,' added the bachelor, in his peculiar whisper, 'directly I heard of it; but never mention it on any account, for he hasn't the least idea that it came from me.'

Having disposed of this culprit, the bachelor turned to another, and from him to another, and so on through the whole array, laying, for their wholesome restriction within due bounds, the same cutting emphasis on such of their propensities as were dearest to his heart and were unquestionably referrable to his own precept and example. Thoroughly persuaded, in the end, that he had made them miserable by his severity, he dismissed them with a small present, and an admonition to walk quietly home, without any leapings, scufflings, or turnings out of the way; which injunction, he informed the schoolmaster in the same audible confidence, he did not think he could have obeyed when he was a boy, had his life depended on it.

Hailing these little tokens of the bachelor's disposition as so many assurances of his own welcome course from that time, the schoolmaster parted from him with a light heart and joyous spirits, and deemed himself one of the happiest men on earth. The windows of the two old houses were ruddy again, that night, with the reflection of the cheerful fires that burnt within; and the bachelor and his friend, pausing to look upon them as they returned from their evening walk, spoke softly together of the beautiful child, and looked round upon the churchyard with a sigh.

CHAPTER 53

Nell was stirring early in the morning, and having discharged her household tasks, and put everything in order for the good schoolmaster (though sorely against his will, for he would have spared her the pains), took down, from its nail by the fireside, a little bundle of keys with which the bachelor had formally invested her on the previous day, and went out alone to visit the old church.

The sky was serene and bright, the air clear, perfumed with the fresh scent of newly fallen leaves, and grateful to every sense. The neighbouring stream sparkled, and rolled onward with a tuneful sound; the dew glistened on the green mounds, like tears shed by Good Spirits over the dead. Some young children sported among the tombs, and hid from each other, with laughing faces. They had an infant with them, and had laid it down asleep upon a child's grave, in a little bed of leaves. It was a new grave—the resting-place, perhaps, of some little creature, who, meek and patient in its illness, had often sat and watched them, and now seemed, to their minds, scarcely changed.

She drew near and asked one of them whose grave it was. The child answered that that was not its name; it was a garden—his brother's. It was greener, he said, than all the other gardens, and the birds loved it better because he had been used to feed them. When he had done speaking, he looked at her with a smile, and kneeling down and nestling for a moment with his cheek against the turf, bounded merrily away.

She passed the church, gazing upward at its old tower, went through the wicket gate, and so into the village. The old sexton, leaning on a crutch, was taking the air at his cottage door, and gave her good morrow.

'You are better?' said the child, stopping to speak with him.

'Ay surely,' returned the old man. 'I'm thankful to say, much better.'

'You will be quite well soon.'

'With Heaven's leave, and a little patience. But come in, come in!' The old man limped on before, and warning her of the downward step, which he achieved himself with no small difficulty, led the way into his little cottage.

'It is but one room you see. There is another up above, but the stair has got harder to climb o' late years, and I never use it. I'm thinking of taking to it again, next summer, though.'

The child wondered how a grey-headed man like him—one of his trade too—could talk of time so easily. He saw her eyes wandering to the tools that hung upon the wall, and smiled.

'I warrant now,' he said, 'that you think all those are used in making graves.'

'Indeed, I wondered that you wanted so many.'

'And well you might. I am a gardener. I dig the ground, and plant things that are to live and grow. My works don't all moulder away, and rot in the earth. You see that spade in the centre?'

'The very old one—so notched and worn? Yes.'

'That's the sexton's spade, and it's a well-used one, as you see. We're healthy people here, but it has done a power of work. If it could speak now, that spade, it would tell you of many an unexpected job that it and I have done together; but I forget 'em, for my memory's a poor one.—That's nothing new,' he added hastily. 'It always was.'

'There are flowers and shrubs to speak to your other work,' said the child.

'Oh yes. And tall trees. But they are not so separate from the sexton's labours as you think.'

'No!'

'Not in my mind, and recollection—such as it is,' said the old man. 'Indeed they often help it. For say that I planted such a tree for such a man. There it stands, to remind me that he died. When I look at its broad shadow, and remember what it was in his time, it helps me to the age of my other work, and I can tell you pretty nearly when I made his grave.'

'But it may remind you of one who is still alive,' said the child.

'Of twenty that are dead, in connexion with that one who lives, then,' rejoined the old man; 'wife, husband, parents, brothers, sisters, children, friends—a score at least. So it happens that the sexton's spade gets worn and battered. I shall need a new one—next summer.'

The child looked quickly towards him, thinking that he jested with his age and infirmity: but the unconscious sexton was quite in earnest.

'Ah!' he said, after a brief silence. 'People never learn. They never learn. It's only we who turn up the ground, where nothing grows and everything decays, who think of such things as these—who think of them properly, I mean. You have been into the church?'

'I am going there now,' the child replied.

'There's an old well there,' said the sexton, 'right underneath the belfry; a deep, dark, echoing well. Forty year ago, you had only to let down the bucket till the first knot in the rope was free of the windlass, and you heard it splashing in the cold dull water. By little and little the water fell away, so that in ten year after that, a second knot was made, and you must unwind so much rope, or the bucket swung tight and empty at the end. In ten years' time, the water fell again, and a third knot was made. In ten years more, the well dried up; and now, if you lower the bucket till your arms are tired, and let out nearly all the cord, you'll hear it, of a sudden, clanking and rattling on the ground below; with a sound of being so deep and so far down, that your heart leaps into your mouth, and you start away as if you were falling in.'

'A dreadful place to come on in the dark!' exclaimed the child, who had followed the old man's looks and words until she seemed to stand upon its brink.

'What is it but a grave!' said the sexton. 'What else! And which of our old folks, knowing all this, thought, as the spring subsided, of their own failing strength, and lessening life? Not one!'

'Are you very old yourself?' asked the child, involuntarily.

'I shall be seventy-nine—next summer.'

'You still work when you are well?'

'Work! To be sure. You shall see my gardens hereabout. Look at the window there. I made, and have kept, that plot of ground entirely with my own hands. By this time next year I shall hardly see the sky, the boughs will have grown so thick. I have my winter work at night besides.'

He opened, as he spoke, a cupboard close to where he sat, and produced some miniature boxes, carved in a homely manner and made of old wood.

'Some gentlefolks who are fond of ancient days, and what belongs to them,' he said, 'like to buy these keepsakes from our church and ruins. Sometimes, I make them of scraps of oak, that turn up here and there; sometimes of bits of coffins which the vaults have long preserved. See here—this is a little chest of the last kind, clasped at the edges with fragments of brass plates that had writing on 'em once, though it would be hard to read it now. I haven't many by me at this time of year, but these shelves will be full—next summer.'

The child admired and praised his work, and shortly afterwards departed; thinking, as she went, how strange it was, that this old man, drawing from his pursuits, and everything around him, one stern moral, never contemplated its application to himself; and, while he dwelt upon the uncertainty of human life, seemed both in word and deed to deem himself immortal. But her musings did not stop here, for she was wise enough to think that by a good and merciful adjustment this must be human nature, and that the old sexton, with his plans for next summer, was but a type of all mankind.

Full of these meditations, she reached the church. It was easy to find the key belonging to the outer door, for each was labelled on a scrap of yellow parchment. Its very turning in the lock awoke a hollow sound, and when she entered with a faltering step, the echoes that it raised in closing, made her start.

If the peace of the simple village had moved the child more strongly, because of the dark and troubled ways that lay beyond, and through which she had journeyed with such failing feet, what was the deep impression of finding herself alone in that solemn building, where the very light, coming through sunken windows, seemed old and grey, and the air, redolent of earth and mould, seemed laden with decay, purified by time of all its grosser particles, and sighing through arch and aisle, and clustered pillars, like the breath of ages gone! Here was the broken pavement, worn, so long ago, by pious feet, that Time, stealing on the pilgrims' steps, had trodden out their track, and left but crumbling stones. Here were the rotten beam, the sinking arch, the sapped and mouldering wall, the lowly trench of earth, the stately tomb on which no epitaph remained—all—marble, stone, iron, wood, and dust—one common monument of ruin. The best work and the worst, the plainest and the richest, the stateliest and the least imposing—both of Heaven's work and Man's—all found one common level here, and told one common tale.

Some part of the edifice had been a baronial chapel, and here were effigies of warriors stretched upon their beds of stone with folded hands—cross-legged, those who had fought in the Holy Wars—girded with their swords, and cased in armour as they had lived. Some of these knights had their own weapons, helmets, coats of mail, hanging upon the walls hard by, and dangling from rusty hooks. Broken and dilapidated as they were, they yet retained their ancient form, and something of their ancient aspect. Thus violent deeds live after men upon the earth, and traces of war and bloodshed will survive in mournful shapes long after those who worked the desolation are but atoms of earth themselves.

The child sat down, in this old, silent place, among the stark figures on the tombs—they made it more quiet there, than elsewhere, to her fancy—and gazing round with a feeling of awe, tempered with a calm delight, felt that now she was happy, and at rest. She took a Bible from the shelf, and read; then, laying it down, thought of the summer days and the bright springtime that would come—of the rays of sun that would fall in aslant, upon the sleeping forms—of the leaves that would flutter at the window, and play in glistening shadows on the pavement—of the songs of birds, and growth of buds and blossoms out of doors—of the sweet air, that would steal in, and gently wave the tattered banners overhead. What if the spot awakened thoughts of death! Die who would, it would still remain the same; these sights and sounds would still go on, as happily as ever. It would be no pain to sleep amidst them.

She left the chapel—very slowly and often turning back to gaze again—and coming to a low door, which plainly led into the tower, opened it, and climbed the winding stair in darkness; save where she looked down, through narrow loopholes, on the place she had left, or caught a glimmering vision of the dusty bells. At length she gained the end of the ascent and stood upon the turret top.

Oh! the glory of the sudden burst of light; the freshness of the fields and woods, stretching away on every side, and meeting the bright blue sky; the cattle grazing in the pasturage; the smoke, that, coming from among the trees, seemed to rise upward from the green earth; the children yet at their gambols below—all, everything, so beautiful and happy! It was like passing from death to life; it was drawing nearer Heaven.

The children were gone, when she emerged into the porch, and locked the door. As she passed the school-house she could hear the busy hum of voices. Her friend had begun his labours only on that day. The noise grew louder, and, looking back, she saw the boys come trooping out and disperse themselves with merry shouts and play. 'It's a good thing,' thought the child, 'I am very glad they pass the church.' And then she stopped, to fancy how the noise would sound inside, and how gently it would seem to die away upon the ear.

Again that day, yes, twice again, she stole back to the old chapel, and in her former seat read from the same book, or indulged the same quiet train of thought. Even when it had grown dusk, and the shadows of coming night made it more solemn still, the child remained, like one rooted to the spot, and had no fear or thought of stirring.

They found her there, at last, and took her home. She looked pale but very happy, until they separated for the night; and then, as the poor schoolmaster stooped down to kiss her cheek, he thought he felt a tear upon his face.

CHAPTER 54

The bachelor, among his various occupations, found in the old church a constant source of interest and amusement. Taking that pride in it which men conceive for the wonders of their own little world, he had made its history his study; and many a summer day within its walls, and many a winter's night beside the parsonage fire, had found the bachelor still poring over, and adding to, his goodly store of tale and legend.

As he was not one of those rough spirits who would strip fair Truth of every little shadowy vestment in which time and teeming fancies love to array her—and some of which become her pleasantly enough, serving, like the waters of her well, to add new graces to the charms they half conceal and half suggest, and to awaken interest and pursuit rather than languor and indifference—as, unlike this stern and obdurate class, he loved to see the goddess crowned with those garlands of wild flowers which tradition wreathes for her gentle wearing, and which are often freshest in their homeliest shapes—he trod with a light step and bore with a light hand upon the dust of centuries, unwilling to demolish any of the airy shrines that had been raised above it, if any good feeling or affection of the human heart were hiding thereabouts. Thus, in the case of an ancient coffin of rough stone, supposed, for many generations, to contain the bones of a certain baron, who, after ravaging, with cut, and thrust, and plunder, in foreign lands, came back with a penitent and sorrowing heart to die at home, but which had been lately shown by learned antiquaries to be no such thing, as the baron in question (so they contended) had died hard in battle, gnashing his teeth and cursing with his latest breath—the bachelor stoutly maintained that the old tale was the true one; that the baron, repenting him of the evil, had done great charities and meekly given up the ghost; and that, if ever baron went to heaven, that baron was then at peace. In like manner, when the aforesaid antiquaries did argue and contend that a certain secret vault was not the tomb of a grey-haired lady who had been hanged and drawn and quartered by glorious Queen Bess for succouring a wretched priest who fainted of thirst and hunger at her door, the bachelor did solemnly maintain, against all comers, that the church was hallowed by the said poor lady's ashes; that her remains had been collected in the night from four of the city's gates, and thither in secret brought, and there deposited; and the bachelor did further (being highly excited at such times) deny the glory of Queen Bess, and assert the immeasurably greater glory of the meanest woman in her realm, who had a merciful and tender heart. As to the assertion that the flat stone near the door was not the grave of the miser who had disowned his only child and left a sum of money to the church to buy a peal of bells, the bachelor did readily admit the same, and that the place had given birth to no such man. In a word, he would have had every stone, and plate of brass, the monument only of deeds whose memory should survive. All others he was willing to forget. They might be buried in consecrated ground, but he would have had them buried deep, and never brought to light again.

It was from the lips of such a tutor, that the child learnt her easy task. Already impressed, beyond all telling, by the silent building and the peaceful beauty of the spot in which it stood— majestic age surrounded by perpetual youth—it seemed to her, when she heard these things, sacred to all goodness and virtue. It was another world, where sin and sorrow never came; a tranquil place of rest, where nothing evil entered.

When the bachelor had given her in connection with almost every tomb and flat gravestone some history of its own, he took her down into the old crypt, now a mere dull vault, and showed her how it had been lighted up in the time of the monks, and how, amid lamps depending from the roof, and swinging censers exhaling scented odours, and habits glittering with gold and silver, and pictures, and precious stuffs, and jewels all flashing and glistening through the low arches, the chaunt of aged voices had been many a time heard there, at midnight, in old days, while hooded figures knelt and prayed around, and told their rosaries of beads. Thence, he took her above ground again, and showed her, high up in the old walls, small galleries, where the nuns had been wont to glide along—dimly seen in their dark dresses so far off—or to pause like gloomy shadows, listening to the prayers. He showed her too, how the warriors, whose figures rested on the tombs, had worn those rotting scraps of armour up above—how this had been a helmet, and that a shield, and that a gauntlet—and how they had wielded the great two-handed swords, and beaten men down, with yonder iron mace. All that he told the child she treasured in her mind; and sometimes, when she awoke at night from dreams of those old times, and rising from her bed looked out at the dark church, she almost hoped to see the windows lighted up, and hear the organ's swell, and sound of voices, on the rushing wind.

The old sexton soon got better, and was about again. From him the child learnt many other things, though of a different kind. He was not able to work, but one day there was a grave to be made, and he came to overlook the man who dug it. He was in a talkative mood; and the child, at first standing by his side, and afterwards sitting on the grass at his feet, with her thoughtful face raised towards his, began to converse with him.

Now, the man who did the sexton's duty was a little older than he, though much more active. But he was deaf; and when the sexton (who peradventure, on a pinch, might have walked a mile with great difficulty in half-a-dozen hours) exchanged a remark with him about his work, the child could not help noticing that he did so with an impatient kind of pity for his infirmity, as if he were himself the strongest and heartiest man alive.

'I'm sorry to see there is this to do,' said the child when she approached. 'I heard of no one having died.'

'She lived in another hamlet, my dear,' returned the sexton. 'Three mile away.'

'Was she young?'

'Ye-yes' said the sexton; not more than sixty-four, I think. David, was she more than sixty-four?'

David, who was digging hard, heard nothing of the question. The sexton, as he could not reach to touch him with his crutch, and was too infirm to rise without assistance, called his attention by throwing a little mould upon his red nightcap.

'What's the matter now?' said David, looking up.

'How old was Becky Morgan?' asked the sexton.

'Becky Morgan?' repeated David.

'Yes,' replied the sexton; adding in a half compassionate, half irritable tone, which the old man couldn't hear, 'you're getting very deaf, Davy, very deaf to be sure!'

The old man stopped in his work, and cleansing his spade with a piece of slate he had by him for the purpose—and scraping off, in the process, the essence of Heaven knows how many Becky Morgans—set himself to consider the subject.

'Let me think' quoth he. 'I saw last night what they had put upon the coffin—was it seventy-nine?'

'No, no,' said the sexton.

'Ah yes, it was though,' returned the old man with a sigh. 'For I remember thinking she was very near our age. Yes, it was seventy-nine.'

'Are you sure you didn't mistake a figure, Davy?' asked the sexton, with signs of some emotion.

'What?' said the old man. 'Say that again.'

'He's very deaf. He's very deaf indeed,' cried the sexton petulantly; 'are you sure you're right about the figures?'

'Oh quite,' replied the old man. 'Why not?'

'He's exceedingly deaf,' muttered the sexton to himself. 'I think he's getting foolish.'

The child rather wondered what had led him to this belief, as, to say the truth, the old man seemed quite as sharp as he, and was infinitely more robust. As the sexton said nothing more just then, however, she forgot it for the time, and spoke again.

'You were telling me,' she said, 'about your gardening. Do you ever plant things here?'

'In the churchyard?' returned the sexton, 'Not I.'

'I have seen some flowers and little shrubs about,' the child rejoined; 'there are some over there, you see. I thought they were of your rearing, though indeed they grow but poorly.'

'They grow as Heaven wills,' said the old man; 'and it kindly ordains that they shall never flourish here.'

'I do not understand you.'

'Why, this it is,' said the sexton. 'They mark the graves of those who had very tender, loving friends.'

'I was sure they did!' the child exclaimed. 'I am very glad to know they do!'

'Aye,' returned the old man, 'but stay. Look at them. See how they hang their heads, and droop, and wither. Do you guess the reason?'

'No,' the child replied.

'Because the memory of those who lie below, passes away so soon. At first they tend them, morning, noon, and night; they soon begin to come less frequently; from once a day, to once a week; from once a week to once a month; then, at long and uncertain intervals; then, not at all. Such tokens seldom flourish long. I have known the briefest summer flowers outlive them.'

'I grieve to hear it,' said the child.

'Ah! so say the gentlefolks who come down here to look about them,' returned the old man, shaking his head, 'but I say otherwise. "It's a pretty custom you have in this part of the country," they say to me sometimes, "to plant the graves, but it's melancholy to see these things all withering or dead." I crave their pardon and tell them that, as I take it, 'tis a good sign for the happiness of the living. And so it is. It's nature.'

'Perhaps the mourners learn to look to the blue sky by day, and to the stars by night, and to think that the dead are there, and not in graves,' said the child in an earnest voice.

'Perhaps so,' replied the old man doubtfully. 'It may be.'

'Whether it be as I believe it is, or no,' thought the child within herself, 'I'll make this place my garden. It will be no harm at least to work here day by day, and pleasant thoughts will come of it, I am sure.'

Her glowing cheek and moistened eye passed unnoticed by the sexton, who turned towards old David, and called him by his name. It was plain that Becky Morgan's age still troubled him; though why, the child could scarcely understand.

The second or third repetition of his name attracted the old man's attention. Pausing from his work, he leant on his spade, and put his hand to his dull ear.

'Did you call?' he said.

'I have been thinking, Davy,' replied the sexton, 'that she,' he pointed to the grave, 'must have been a deal older than you or me.'

'Seventy-nine,' answered the old man with a shake of the head, 'I tell you that I saw it.'

'Saw it?' replied the sexton; 'aye, but, Davy, women don't always tell the truth about their age.'

'That's true indeed,' said the other old man, with a sudden sparkle in his eye. 'She might have been older.'

'I'm sure she must have been. Why, only think how old she looked. You and I seemed but boys to her.'

'She did look old,' rejoined David. 'You're right. She did look old.'

'Call to mind how old she looked for many a long, long year, and say if she could be but seventy-nine at last—only our age,' said the sexton.

'Five year older at the very least!' cried the other.

'Five!' retorted the sexton. 'Ten. Good eighty-nine. I call to mind the time her daughter died. She was eighty-nine if she was a day, and tries to pass upon us now, for ten year younger. Oh! human vanity!'

The other old man was not behindhand with some moral reflections on this fruitful theme, and both adduced a mass of evidence, of such weight as to render it doubtful—not whether the deceased was of the age suggested, but whether she had not almost reached the patriarchal term of a hundred. When they had settled this question to their mutual satisfaction, the sexton, with his friend's assistance, rose to go.

'It's chilly, sitting here, and I must be careful—till the summer,' he said, as he prepared to limp away.

'What?' asked old David.

'He's very deaf, poor fellow!' cried the sexton. 'Good-bye!'

'Ah!' said old David, looking after him. 'He's failing very fast. He ages every day.'

And so they parted; each persuaded that the other had less life in him than himself; and both greatly consoled and comforted by the little fiction they had agreed upon, respecting Becky Morgan, whose decease was no longer a precedent of uncomfortable application, and would be no business of theirs for half a score of years to come.

The child remained, for some minutes, watching the deaf old man as he threw out the earth with his shovel, and, often stopping to cough and fetch his breath, still muttered to himself, with a kind of sober chuckle, that the sexton was wearing fast. At length she turned away, and walking thoughtfully through the churchyard, came unexpectedly upon the schoolmaster, who was sitting on a green grave in the sun, reading.

'Nell here?' he said cheerfully, as he closed his book. 'It does me good to see you in the air and light. I feared you were again in the church, where you so often are.'

'Feared!' replied the child, sitting down beside him. 'Is it not a good place?'

'Yes, yes,' said the schoolmaster. 'But you must be gay sometimes—nay, don't shake your head and smile so sadly.'

'Not sadly, if you knew my heart. Do not look at me as if you thought me sorrowful. There is not a happier creature on earth, than I am now.'

Full of grateful tenderness, the child took his hand, and folded it between her own. 'It's God's will!' she said, when they had been silent for some time.

'What?'

'All this,' she rejoined; 'all this about us. But which of us is sad now? You see that I am smiling.'

'And so am I,' said the schoolmaster; 'smiling to think how often we shall laugh in this same place. Were you not talking yonder?'

'Yes,' the child rejoined.

'Of something that has made you sorrowful?'

There was a long pause.

'What was it?' said the schoolmaster, tenderly. 'Come. Tell me what it was.'

'I rather grieve—I do rather grieve to think,' said the child, bursting into tears, 'that those who die about us, are so soon forgotten.'

'And do you think,' said the schoolmaster, marking the glance she had thrown around, 'that an unvisited grave, a withered tree, a faded flower or two, are tokens of forgetfulness or cold neglect? Do you think there are no deeds, far away from here, in which these dead may be best remembered? Nell, Nell, there may be people busy in the world, at this instant, in whose good actions and good thoughts these very graves—neglected as they look to us—are the chief instruments.'

'Tell me no more,' said the child quickly. 'Tell me no more. I feel, I know it. How could I be unmindful of it, when I thought of you?'

'There is nothing,' cried her friend, 'no, nothing innocent or good, that dies, and is forgotten. Let us hold to that faith, or none. An infant, a prattling child, dying in its cradle, will live again in the better thoughts of those who loved it, and will play its part, through them, in the redeeming actions of the world, though its body be burnt to ashes or drowned in the deepest sea. There is not an angel added to the Host of Heaven but does its blessed work on earth in those that loved it here. Forgotten! oh, if the good deeds of human creatures could be traced to their source, how beautiful would even death appear; for how much charity, mercy, and purified affection, would be seen to have their growth in dusty graves!'

'Yes,' said the child, 'it is the truth; I know it is. Who should feel its force so much as I, in whom your little scholar lives again! Dear, dear, good friend, if you knew the comfort you have given me!'

The poor schoolmaster made her no answer, but bent over her in silence; for his heart was full.

They were yet seated in the same place, when the grandfather approached. Before they had spoken many words together, the church clock struck the hour of school, and their friend withdrew.

'A good man,' said the grandfather, looking after him; 'a kind man. Surely he will never harm us, Nell. We are safe here, at last, eh? We will never go away from here?'

The child shook her head and smiled.

'She needs rest,' said the old man, patting her cheek; 'too pale—too pale. She is not like what she was.'

'When?' asked the child.

'Ha!' said the old man, 'to be sure—when? How many weeks ago? Could I count them on my fingers? Let them rest though; they're better gone.'

'Much better, dear,' replied the child. 'We will forget them; or, if we ever call them to mind, it shall be only as some uneasy dream that has passed away.'

'Hush!' said the old man, motioning hastily to her with his hand and looking over his shoulder; 'no more talk of the dream, and all the miseries it brought. There are no dreams here. 'Tis a quiet place, and they keep away. Let us never think about them, lest they should pursue us again. Sunken eyes and hollow cheeks—wet, cold, and famine—and horrors before them all, that were even worse—we must forget such things if we would be tranquil here.'

'Thank Heaven!' inwardly exclaimed the child, 'for this most happy change!'

'I will be patient,' said the old man, 'humble, very thankful, and obedient, if you will let me stay. But do not hide from me; do not steal away alone; let me keep beside you. Indeed, I will be very true and faithful, Nell.'

'I steal away alone! why that,' replied the child, with assumed gaiety, 'would be a pleasant jest indeed. See here, dear grandfather, we'll make this place our garden—why not! It is a very good one—and to-morrow we'll begin, and work together, side by side.'

'It is a brave thought!' cried her grandfather. 'Mind, darling—we begin to-morrow!'

Who so delighted as the old man, when they next day began their labour! Who so unconscious of all associations connected with the spot, as he! They plucked the long grass and nettles from the tombs, thinned the poor shrubs and roots, made the turf smooth, and cleared it of the leaves and weeds. They were yet in the ardour of their work, when the child, raising her head from the ground over which she bent, observed that the bachelor was sitting on the stile close by, watching them in silence.

'A kind office,' said the little gentleman, nodding to Nell as she curtseyed to him. 'Have you done all that, this morning?'

'It is very little, sir,' returned the child, with downcast eyes, 'to what we mean to do.'

'Good work, good work,' said the bachelor. 'But do you only labour at the graves of children, and young people?'

'We shall come to the others in good time, sir,' replied Nell, turning her head aside, and speaking softly.

It was a slight incident, and might have been design or accident, or the child's unconscious sympathy with youth. But it seemed to strike upon her grandfather, though he had not noticed it before. He looked in a hurried manner at the graves, then anxiously at the child, then pressed her to his side, and bade her stop to rest. Something he had long forgotten, appeared to struggle faintly in his mind. It did not pass away, as weightier things had done; but came uppermost again, and yet again, and many times that day, and often afterwards. Once, while they were yet at work, the child, seeing that he often turned and looked uneasily at her, as though he were trying to resolve some painful doubts or collect some scattered thoughts, urged him to tell the reason. But he said it was nothing—nothing—and, laying her head upon his arm, patted her fair cheek with his hand, and muttered that she grew stronger every day, and would be a woman, soon.

CHAPTER 55

From that time, there sprung up in the old man's mind, a solicitude about the child which never slept or left him. There are chords in the human heart—strange, varying strings—which are only struck by accident; which will remain mute and senseless to appeals the most passionate and earnest, and respond at last to the slightest casual touch. In the most insensible or childish minds, there is some train of reflection which art can seldom lead, or skill assist, but which will reveal itself, as great truths have done, by chance, and when the discoverer has the plainest end in view. From that time, the old man never, for a moment, forgot the weakness and devotion of the child; from the time of that slight incident, he who had seen her toiling by his side through so much difficulty and suffering, and had scarcely thought of her otherwise than as the partner of miseries which he felt severely in his own person, and deplored for his own sake at least as much as hers, awoke to a sense of what he owed her, and what those miseries had made her. Never, no, never once, in one unguarded moment from that time to the end, did any care for himself, any thought of his own comfort, any selfish consideration or regard distract his thoughts from the gentle object of his love.

He would follow her up and down, waiting till she should tire and lean upon his arm— he would sit opposite to her in the chimney-corner, content to watch, and look, until she raised her head and smiled upon him as of old—he would discharge by stealth, those household duties which tasked her powers too heavily—he would rise, in the cold dark nights, to listen to her breathing in her sleep, and sometimes crouch for hours by her bedside only to touch her hand. He who knows all, can only know what hopes, and fears, and thoughts of deep affection, were in that one disordered brain, and what a change had fallen on the poor old man. Sometimes—weeks had crept on, then—the child, exhausted, though with little fatigue, would pass whole evenings on a couch beside the fire. At such times, the schoolmaster would bring in books, and read to her aloud; and seldom an evening passed, but the bachelor came in, and took his turn of reading. The old man sat and listened—with little understanding for the words, but with his eyes fixed upon the child—and if she smiled or brightened with the story, he would say it was a good one, and conceive a fondness for the very book. When, in their evening talk, the bachelor told some tale that pleased her (as his tales were sure to do), the old man would painfully try to store it in his mind; nay, when the bachelor left them, he would sometimes slip out after him, and humbly beg that he would tell him such a part again, that he might learn to win a smile from Nell.

But these were rare occasions, happily; for the child yearned to be out of doors, and walking in her solemn garden. Parties, too, would come to see the church; and those who came, speaking to others of the child, sent more; so even at that season of the year they had visitors almost daily. The old man would follow them at a little distance through the building, listening to the voice he loved so well; and when the strangers left, and parted from Nell, he would mingle with them to catch up fragments of their conversation; or he would stand for the same purpose, with his grey head uncovered, at the gate as they passed through.

They always praised the child, her sense and beauty, and he was proud to hear them! But what was that, so often added, which wrung his heart, and made him sob and weep alone, in some dull corner! Alas! even careless strangers—they who had no feeling for her, but the interest of the moment—they who would go away and forget next week that such a being lived—even they saw it—even they pitied her—even they bade him good day compassionately, and whispered as they passed.

The people of the village, too, of whom there was not one but grew to have a fondness for poor Nell; even among them, there was the same feeling; a tenderness towards her—a compassionate regard for her, increasing every day. The very schoolboys, light-hearted and thoughtless as they were, even they cared for her. The roughest among them was sorry if he missed her in the usual place upon his way to school, and would turn out of the path to ask for her at the latticed window. If she were sitting in the church, they perhaps might peep in softly at the open door; but they never spoke to her, unless she rose and went to speak to them. Some feeling was abroad which raised the child above them all.

So, when Sunday came. They were all poor country people in the church, for the castle in which the old family had lived, was an empty ruin, and there were none but humble folks for seven miles around. There, as elsewhere, they had an interest in Nell. They would gather round her in the porch, before and after service; young children would cluster at her skirts; and aged men and women forsake their gossips, to give her kindly greeting. None of them, young or old, thought of passing the child without a friendly word. Many who came from three or four miles distant, brought her little presents; the humblest and rudest had good wishes to bestow.

She had sought out the young children whom she first saw playing in the churchyard. One of these—he who had spoken of his brother—was her little favourite and friend, and often sat by her side in the church, or climbed with her to the tower-top. It was his delight to help her, or to fancy that he did so, and they soon became close companions.

It happened, that, as she was reading in the old spot by herself one day, this child came running in with his eyes full of tears, and after holding her from him, and looking at her eagerly for a moment, clasped his little arms passionately about her neck.

'What now?' said Nell, soothing him. 'What is the matter?'

'She is not one yet!' cried the boy, embracing her still more closely. 'No, no. Not yet.'

She looked at him wonderingly, and putting his hair back from his face, and kissing him, asked what he meant.

'You must not be one, dear Nell,' cried the boy. 'We can't see them. They never come to play with us, or talk to us. Be what you are. You are better so.'

'I do not understand you,' said the child. 'Tell me what you mean.'

'Why, they say,' replied the boy, looking up into her face, that you will be an Angel, before the birds sing again. But you won't be, will you? Don't leave us Nell, though the sky is bright. Do not leave us!'

The child dropped her head, and put her hands before her face.

'She cannot bear the thought!' cried the boy, exulting through his tears. 'You will not go. You know how sorry we should be. Dear Nell, tell me that you'll stay amongst us. Oh! Pray, pray, tell me that you will.'

The little creature folded his hands, and knelt down at her feet.

'Only look at me, Nell,' said the boy, 'and tell me that you'll stop, and then I shall know that they are wrong, and will cry no more. Won't you say yes, Nell?'

Still the drooping head and hidden face, and the child quite silent—save for her sobs.

'After a time,' pursued the boy, trying to draw away her hand, 'the kind angels will be glad to think that you are not among them, and that you stayed here to be with us. Willy went away, to join them; but if he had known how I should miss him in our little bed at night, he never would have left me, I am sure.'

Yet the child could make him no answer, and sobbed as though her heart were bursting. 'Why would you go, dear Nell? I know you would not be happy when you heard that we were crying for your loss. They say that Willy is in Heaven now, and that it's always summer there, and yet I'm sure he grieves when I lie down upon his garden bed, and he cannot turn to kiss me. But if you do go, Nell,' said the boy, caressing her, and pressing his face to hers, 'be fond of him for my sake. Tell him how I love him still, and how much I loved you; and when I think that you two are together, and are happy, I'll try to bear it, and never give you pain by doing wrong—indeed I never will!'

The child suffered him to move her hands, and put them round his neck. There was a tearful silence, but it was not long before she looked upon him with a smile, and promised him, in a very gentle, quiet voice, that she would stay, and be his friend, as long as Heaven would let her. He clapped his hands for joy, and thanked her many times; and being charged to tell no person what had passed between them, gave her an earnest promise that he never would.

Nor did he, so far as the child could learn; but was her quiet companion in all her walks and musings, and never again adverted to the theme, which he felt had given her pain, although he was unconscious of its cause. Something of distrust lingered about him still; for he would often come, even in the dark evenings, and call in a timid voice outside the door to know if she were safe within; and being answered yes, and bade to enter, would take his station on a low stool at her feet, and sit there patiently until they came to seek, and take him home. Sure as the morning came, it found him lingering near the house to ask if she were well; and, morning, noon, or night, go where she would, he would forsake his playmates and his sports to bear her company.

'And a good little friend he is, too,' said the old sexton to her once. 'When his elder brother died—elder seems a strange word, for he was only seven years old—I remember this one took it sorely to heart.'

The child thought of what the schoolmaster had told her, and felt how its truth was shadowed out even in this infant.

'It has given him something of a quiet way, I think,' said the old man, 'though for that he is merry enough at times. I'd wager now that you and he have been listening by the old well.'

'Indeed we have not,' the child replied. 'I have been afraid to go near it; for I am not often down in that part of the church, and do not know the ground.'

'Come down with me,' said the old man. 'I have known it from a boy. Come!'

They descended the narrow steps which led into the crypt, and paused among the gloomy arches, in a dim and murky spot.

'This is the place,' said the old man. 'Give me your hand while you throw back the cover, lest you should stumble and fall in. I am too old—I mean rheumatic—to stoop, myself.'

'A black and dreadful place!' exclaimed the child.

'Look in,' said the old man, pointing downward with his finger.

The child complied, and gazed down into the pit.

'It looks like a grave itself,' said the old man.

'It does,' replied the child.

'I have often had the fancy,' said the sexton, 'that it might have been dug at first to make the old place more gloomy, and the old monks more religious. It's to be closed up, and built over.'

The child still stood, looking thoughtfully into the vault.

'We shall see,' said the sexton, 'on what gay heads other earth will have closed, when the light is shut out from here. God knows! They'll close it up, next spring.'

'The birds sing again in spring,' thought the child, as she leaned at her casement window, and gazed at the declining sun. 'Spring! a beautiful and happy time!'

CHAPTER 56

A day or two after the Quilp tea-party at the Wilderness, Mr Swiveller walked into Sampson Brass's office at the usual hour, and being alone in that Temple of Probity, placed his hat upon the desk, and taking from his pocket a small parcel of black crape, applied himself to folding and pinning the same upon it, after the manner of a hatband. Having completed the construction of this appendage, he surveyed his work with great complacency, and put his hat on again—very much over one eye, to increase the mournfulness of the effect. These arrangements perfected to his entire satisfaction, he thrust his hands into his pockets, and walked up and down the office with measured steps.

'It has always been the same with me,' said Mr Swiveller, 'always. 'Twas ever thus—from childhood's hour I've seen my fondest hopes decay, I never loved a tree or flower but 'twas the first to fade away; I never nursed a dear Gazelle, to glad me with its soft black eye, but when it came to know me well, and love me, it was sure to marry a market-gardener.'

Overpowered by these reflections, Mr Swiveller stopped short at the clients' chair, and flung himself into its open arms.

'And this,' said Mr Swiveller, with a kind of bantering composure, 'is life, I believe. Oh, certainly. Why not! I'm quite satisfied. I shall wear,' added Richard, taking off his hat again and looking hard at it, as if he were only deterred by pecuniary considerations from spurning it with his foot, 'I shall wear this emblem of woman's perfidy, in remembrance of her with whom I shall never again thread the windings of the mazy; whom I shall never more pledge in the rosy; who, during the short remainder of my existence, will murder the balmy. Ha, ha, ha!'

It may be necessary to observe, lest there should appear any incongruity in the close of this soliloquy, that Mr Swiveller did not wind up with a cheerful hilarious laugh, which would have been undoubtedly at variance with his solemn reflections, but that, being in a theatrical mood, he merely achieved that performance which is designated in melodramas 'laughing like a fiend,'—for it seems that your fiends always laugh in syllables, and always in three syllables, never more nor less, which is a remarkable property in such gentry, and one worthy of remembrance.

The baleful sounds had hardly died away, and Mr Swiveller was still sitting in a very grim state in the clients' chair, when there came a ring—or, if we may adapt the sound to his then humour, a knell—at the office bell. Opening the door with all speed, he beheld the expressive countenance of Mr Chuckster, between whom and himself a fraternal greeting ensued.

'You're devilish early at this pestiferous old slaughter-house,' said that gentleman, poising himself on one leg, and shaking the other in an easy manner.

'Rather,' returned Dick.

'Rather!' retorted Mr Chuckster, with that air of graceful trifling which so well became him. 'I should think so. Why, my good feller, do you know what o'clock it is—half-past nine a.m. in the morning?'

'Won't you come in?' said Dick. 'All alone. Swiveller solus. "'Tis now the witching—"'

'"Hour of night!"'

'"When churchyards yawn,"'

'"And graves give up their dead."'

At the end of this quotation in dialogue, each gentleman struck an attitude, and immediately subsiding into prose walked into the office. Such morsels of enthusiasm are common among the Glorious Apollos, and were indeed the links that bound them together, and raised them above the cold dull earth.

'Well, and how are you my buck?' said Mr Chuckster, taking a stool. 'I was forced to come into the City upon some little private matters of my own, and couldn't pass the corner of the street without looking in, but upon my soul I didn't expect to find you. It is so everlastingly early.'

Mr Swiveller expressed his acknowledgments; and it appearing on further conversation that he was in good health, and that Mr Chuckster was in the like enviable condition, both gentlemen, in compliance with a solemn custom of the ancient Brotherhood to which they belonged, joined in a fragment of the popular duet of 'All's Well,' with a long shake at the end.

'And what's the news?' said Richard.

'The town's as flat, my dear feller,' replied Mr Chuckster, 'as the surface of a Dutch oven. There's no news. By-the-bye, that lodger of yours is a most extraordinary person. He quite eludes the most vigorous comprehension, you know. Never was such a feller!'

'What has he been doing now?' said Dick.

'By Jove, Sir,' returned Mr Chuckster, taking out an oblong snuff-box, the lid whereof was ornamented with a fox's head curiously carved in brass, 'that man is an unfathomable. Sir, that man has made friends with our articled clerk. There's no harm in him, but he is so amazingly slow and soft. Now, if he wanted a friend, why couldn't he have one that knew a thing or two, and could do him some good by his manners and conversation. I have my faults, sir,' said Mr Chuckster—

'No, no,' interposed Mr Swiveller.

'Oh yes I have, I have my faults, no man knows his faults better than I know mine. But,' said Mr Chuckster, 'I'm not meek. My worst enemies—every man has his enemies, Sir, and I have mine—never accused me of being meek. And I tell you what, Sir, if I hadn't more of these qualities that commonly endear man to man, than our articled clerk has, I'd steal a Cheshire cheese, tie it round my neck, and drown myself. I'd die degraded, as I had lived. I would upon my honour.'

Mr Chuckster paused, rapped the fox's head exactly on the nose with the knuckle of the fore-finger, took a pinch of snuff, and looked steadily at Mr Swiveller, as much as to say that if he thought he was going to sneeze, he would find himself mistaken.

'Not contented, Sir,' said Mr Chuckster, 'with making friends with Abel, he has cultivated the acquaintance of his father and mother. Since he came home from that wild-goose chase, he has been there— actually been there. He patronises young Snobby besides; you'll find, Sir, that he'll be constantly coming backwards and forwards to this place: yet I don't suppose that beyond the common forms of civility, he has ever exchanged half-a-dozen words with me. Now, upon my soul, you know,' said Mr Chuckster, shaking his head gravely, as men are wont to do when they consider things are going a little too far, 'this is altogether such a low-minded affair, that if I didn't feel for the governor, and know that he could never get on without me, I should be obliged to cut the connection. I should have no alternative.'

Mr Swiveller, who sat on another stool opposite to his friend, stirred the fire in an excess of sympathy, but said nothing.

'As to young Snob, sir,' pursued Mr Chuckster with a prophetic look, 'you'll find he'll turn out bad. In our profession we know something of human nature, and take my word for it, that the feller that came back to work out that shilling, will show himself one of these days in his true colours. He's a low thief, sir. He must be.'

Mr Chuckster being roused, would probably have pursued this subject further, and in more emphatic language, but for a tap at the door, which seeming to announce the arrival of somebody on business, caused him to assume a greater appearance of meekness than was perhaps quite consistent with his late declaration. Mr Swiveller, hearing the same sound, caused his stool to revolve rapidly on one leg until it brought him to his desk, into which, having forgotten in the sudden flurry of his spirits to part with the poker, he thrust it as he cried 'Come in!'

Who should present himself but that very Kit who had been the theme of Mr Chuckster's wrath! Never did man pluck up his courage so quickly, or look so fierce, as Mr Chuckster when he found it was he. Mr Swiveller stared at him for a moment, and then leaping from his stool, and drawing out the poker from its place of concealment, performed the broad-sword exercise with all the cuts and guards complete, in a species of frenzy.

'Is the gentleman at home?' said Kit, rather astonished by this uncommon reception.

Before Mr Swiveller could make any reply, Mr Chuckster took occasion to enter his indignant protest against this form of inquiry; which he held to be of a disrespectful and snobbish tendency, inasmuch as the inquirer, seeing two gentlemen then and there present, should have spoken of the other gentleman; or rather (for it was not impossible that the object of his search might be of inferior quality) should have mentioned his name, leaving it to his hearers to determine his degree as they thought proper. Mr Chuckster likewise remarked, that he had some reason to believe this form of address was personal to himself, and that he was not a man to be trifled with—as certain snobs (whom he did not more particularly mention or describe) might find to their cost.

'I mean the gentleman up-stairs,' said Kit, turning to Richard Swiveller. 'Is he at home?'

'Why?' rejoined Dick.

'Because if he is, I have a letter for him.'

'From whom?' said Dick.

'From Mr Garland.'

'Oh!' said Dick, with extreme politeness. 'Then you may hand it over, Sir. And if you're to wait for an answer, Sir, you may wait in the passage, Sir, which is an airy and well-ventilated apartment, sir.'

'Thank you,' returned Kit. 'But I am to give it to himself, if you please.'

The excessive audacity of this retort so overpowered Mr Chuckster, and so moved his tender regard for his friend's honour, that he declared, if he were not restrained by official considerations, he must certainly have annihilated Kit upon the spot; a resentment of the affront which he did consider, under the extraordinary circumstances of aggravation attending it, could but have met with the proper sanction and approval of a jury of Englishmen, who, he had no doubt, would have returned a verdict of justifiable Homicide, coupled with a high testimony to the morals and character of the Avenger. Mr Swiveller, without being quite so hot upon the matter, was rather shamed by his friend's excitement, and not a little puzzled how to act (Kit being quite cool and good-humoured), when the single gentleman was heard to call violently down the stairs.

'Didn't I see somebody for me, come in?' cried the lodger.

'Yes, Sir,' replied Dick. 'Certainly, Sir.'

'Then where is he?' roared the single gentleman.

'He's here, sir,' rejoined Mr Swiveller. 'Now young man, don't you hear you're to go up-stairs? Are you deaf?'

Kit did not appear to think it worth his while to enter into any altercation, but hurried off and left the Glorious Apollos gazing at each other in silence.

'Didn't I tell you so?' said Mr Chuckster. 'What do you think of that?'

Mr Swiveller being in the main a good-natured fellow, and not perceiving in the conduct of Kit any villany of enormous magnitude, scarcely knew what answer to return. He was relieved from his perplexity, however, by the entrance of Mr Sampson and his sister, Sally, at sight of whom Mr Chuckster precipitately retired.

Mr Brass and his lovely companion appeared to have been holding a consultation over their temperate breakfast, upon some matter of great interest and importance. On the occasion of such conferences, they generally appeared in the office some half an hour after their usual time, and in a very smiling state, as though their late plots and designs had tranquillised their minds and shed a light upon their toilsome way. In the present instance, they seemed particularly gay; Miss Sally's aspect being of a most oily kind, and Mr Brass rubbing his hands in an exceedingly jocose and light-hearted manner.

'Well, Mr Richard,' said Brass. 'How are we this morning? Are we pretty fresh and cheerful sir—eh, Mr Richard?'

'Pretty well, sir,' replied Dick.

'That's well,' said Brass. 'Ha ha! We should be as gay as larks, Mr Richard—why not? It's a pleasant world we live in sir, a very pleasant world. There are bad people in it, Mr Richard, but if there were no bad people, there would be no good lawyers. Ha ha! Any letters by the post this morning, Mr Richard?'

Mr Swiveller answered in the negative.

'Ha!' said Brass, 'no matter. If there's little business to-day, there'll be more to-morrow. A contented spirit, Mr Richard, is the sweetness of existence. Anybody been here, sir?'

'Only my friend'—replied Dick. 'May we ne'er want a—'

'Friend,' Brass chimed in quickly, 'or a bottle to give him. Ha ha! That's the way the song runs, isn't it? A very good song, Mr Richard, very good. I like the sentiment of it. Ha ha! Your friend's the young man from Witherden's office I think—yes—May we ne'er want a— Nobody else at all, been, Mr Richard?'

'Only somebody to the lodger,' replied Mr Swiveller.

'Oh indeed!' cried Brass. 'Somebody to the lodger eh? Ha ha! May we ne'er want a friend, or a——Somebody to the lodger, eh, Mr Richard?'

'Yes,' said Dick, a little disconcerted by the excessive buoyancy of spirits which his employer displayed. 'With him now.'

'With him now!' cried Brass; 'Ha ha! There let 'em be, merry and free, toor rul lol le. Eh, Mr Richard? Ha ha!'

'Oh certainly,' replied Dick.

'And who,' said Brass, shuffling among his papers, 'who is the lodger's visitor—not a lady visitor, I hope, eh, Mr Richard? The morals of the Marks you know, sir—"when lovely women stoops to folly"—and all that—eh, Mr Richard?'

'Another young man, who belongs to Witherden's too, or half belongs there,' returned Richard. 'Kit, they call him.'

'Kit, eh!' said Brass. 'Strange name—name of a dancing-master's fiddle, eh, Mr Richard? Ha ha! Kit's there, is he? Oh!'

Dick looked at Miss Sally, wondering that she didn't check this uncommon exuberance on the part of Mr Sampson; but as she made no attempt to do so, and rather appeared to exhibit a tacit acquiescence in it, he concluded that they had just been cheating somebody, and receiving the bill.

'Will you have the goodness, Mr Richard,' said Brass, taking a letter from his desk, 'just to step over to Peckham Rye with that? There's no answer, but it's rather particular and should go by hand. Charge the office with your coach-hire back, you know; don't spare the office; get as much out of it as you can—clerk's motto—Eh, Mr Richard? Ha ha!'

Mr Swiveller solemnly doffed the aquatic jacket, put on his coat, took down his hat from its peg, pocketed the letter, and departed. As soon as he was gone, up rose Miss Sally Brass, and smiling sweetly at her brother (who nodded and smote his nose in return) withdrew also.

Sampson Brass was no sooner left alone, than he set the office-door wide open, and establishing himself at his desk directly opposite, so that he could not fail to see anybody who came down-stairs and passed out at the street door, began to write with extreme cheerfulness and assiduity; humming as he did so, in a voice that was anything but musical, certain vocal snatches which appeared to have reference to the union between Church and State, inasmuch as they were compounded of the Evening Hymn and God save the King.

Thus, the attorney of Bevis Marks sat, and wrote, and hummed, for a long time, except when he stopped to listen with a very cunning face, and hearing nothing, went on humming louder, and writing slower than ever. At length, in one of these pauses, he heard his lodger's door opened and shut, and footsteps coming down the stairs. Then, Mr Brass left off writing entirely, and, with his pen in his hand, hummed his very loudest; shaking his head meanwhile from side to side, like a man whose whole soul was in the music, and smiling in a manner quite seraphic.

It was towards this moving spectacle that the staircase and the sweet sounds guided Kit; on whose arrival before his door, Mr Brass stopped his singing, but not his smiling, and nodded affably: at the same time beckoning to him with his pen.

'Kit,' said Mr Brass, in the pleasantest way imaginable, 'how do you do?'

Kit, being rather shy of his friend, made a suitable reply, and had his hand upon the lock of the street door when Mr Brass called him softly back.

'You are not to go, if you please, Kit,' said the attorney in a mysterious and yet business-like way. 'You are to step in here, if you please. Dear me, dear me! When I look at you,' said the lawyer, quitting his stool, and standing before the fire with his back towards it, 'I am reminded of the sweetest little face that ever my eyes beheld. I remember your coming there, twice or thrice, when we were in possession. Ah Kit, my dear fellow, gentleman in my profession have such painful duties to perform sometimes, that you needn't envy us—you needn't indeed!'

'I don't, sir,' said Kit, 'though it isn't for the like of me to judge.'

'Our only consolation, Kit,' pursued the lawyer, looking at him in a sort of pensive abstraction, 'is, that although we cannot turn away the wind, we can soften it; we can temper it, if I may say so, to the shorn lambs.'

'Shorn indeed!' thought Kit. 'Pretty close!' But he didn't say so.

'On that occasion, Kit,' said Mr Brass, 'on that occasion that I have just alluded to, I had a hard battle with Mr Quilp (for Mr Quilp is a very hard man) to obtain them the indulgence they had. It might have cost me a client. But suffering virtue inspired me, and I prevailed.'

'He's not so bad after all,' thought honest Kit, as the attorney pursed up his lips and looked like a man who was struggling with his better feelings.

'I respect you, Kit,' said Brass with emotion. 'I saw enough of your conduct, at that time, to respect you, though your station is humble, and your fortune lowly. It isn't the waistcoat that I look at. It is the heart. The checks in the waistcoat are but the wires of the cage. But the heart is the bird. Ah! How many sich birds are perpetually moulting, and putting their beaks through the wires to peck at all mankind!'

This poetic figure, which Kit took to be in a special allusion to his own checked waistcoat, quite overcame him; Mr Brass's voice and manner added not a little to its effect, for he discoursed with all the mild austerity of a hermit, and wanted but a cord round the waist of his rusty surtout, and a skull on the chimney-piece, to be completely set up in that line of business.

'Well, well,' said Sampson, smiling as good men smile when they compassionate their own weakness or that of their fellow-creatures, 'this is wide of the bull's-eye. You're to take that, if you please.' As he spoke, he pointed to a couple of half-crowns on the desk.

Kit looked at the coins, and then at Sampson, and hesitated.

'For yourself,' said Brass. 'From—'

'No matter about the person they came from,' replied the lawyer. 'Say me, if you like. We have eccentric friends overhead, Kit, and we mustn't ask questions or talk too much—you understand? You're to take them, that's all; and between you and me, I don't think they'll be the last you'll have to take from the same place. I hope not. Good bye, Kit. Good bye!'

With many thanks, and many more self-reproaches for having on such slight grounds suspected one who in their very first conversation turned out such a different man from what he had supposed, Kit took the money and made the best of his way home. Mr Brass remained airing himself at the fire, and resumed his vocal exercise, and his seraphic smile, simultaneously.

'May I come in?' said Miss Sally, peeping.

'Oh yes, you may come in,' returned her brother.

'Ahem!' coughed Miss Brass interrogatively.

'Why, yes,' returned Sampson, 'I should say as good as done.'

CHAPTER 57

Mr Chuckster's indignant apprehensions were not without foundation. Certainly the friendship between the single gentleman and Mr Garland was not suffered to cool, but had a rapid growth and flourished exceedingly. They were soon in habits of constant intercourse and communication; and the single gentleman labouring at this time under a slight attack of illness—the consequence most probably of his late excited feelings and subsequent disappointment—furnished a reason for their holding yet more frequent correspondence; so that some one of the inmates of Abel Cottage, Finchley, came backwards and forwards between that place and Bevis Marks, almost every day.

As the pony had now thrown off all disguise, and without any mincing of the matter or beating about the bush, sturdily refused to be driven by anybody but Kit, it generally happened that whether old Mr Garland came, or Mr Abel, Kit was of the party. Of all messages and inquiries, Kit was, in right of his position, the bearer; thus it came about that, while the single gentleman remained indisposed, Kit turned into Bevis Marks every morning with nearly as much regularity as the General Postman.

Mr Sampson Brass, who no doubt had his reasons for looking sharply about him, soon learnt to distinguish the pony's trot and the clatter of the little chaise at the corner of the street. Whenever the sound reached his ears, he would immediately lay down his pen and fall to rubbing his hands and exhibiting the greatest glee.

'Ha ha!' he would cry. 'Here's the pony again! Most remarkable pony, extremely docile, eh, Mr Richard, eh sir?'

Dick would return some matter-of-course reply, and Mr Brass standing on the bottom rail of his stool, so as to get a view of the street over the top of the window-blind, would take an observation of the visitors.

'The old gentleman again!' he would exclaim, 'a very prepossessing old gentleman, Mr Richard—charming countenance, sir—extremely calm—benevolence in every feature, sir. He quite realises my idea of King Lear, as he appeared when in possession of his kingdom, Mr Richard—the same good humour, the same white hair and partial baldness, the same liability to be imposed upon. Ah! A sweet subject for contemplation, sir, very sweet!'

Then Mr Garland having alighted and gone up-stairs, Sampson would nod and smile to Kit from the window, and presently walk out into the street to greet him, when some such conversation as the following would ensue.

'Admirably groomed, Kit'—Mr Brass is patting the pony—'does you great credit—amazingly sleek and bright to be sure. He literally looks as if he had been varnished all over.'

Kit touches his hat, smiles, pats the pony himself, and expresses his conviction, 'that Mr Brass will not find many like him.'

'A beautiful animal indeed!' cries Brass. 'Sagacious too?'

'Bless you!' replies Kit, 'he knows what you say to him as well as a Christian does.'

'Does he indeed!' cries Brass, who has heard the same thing in the same place from the same person in the same words a dozen times, but is paralysed with astonishment notwithstanding. 'Dear me!'

'I little thought the first time I saw him, Sir,' says Kit, pleased with the attorney's strong interest in his favourite, 'that I should come to be as intimate with him as I am now.'

'Ah!' rejoins Mr Brass, brim-full of moral precepts and love of virtue. 'A charming subject of reflection for you, very charming. A subject of proper pride and congratulation, Christopher. Honesty is the best policy.—I always find it so myself. I lost forty-seven pound ten by being honest this morning. But it's all gain, it's gain!'

Mr Brass slyly tickles his nose with his pen, and looks at Kit with the water standing in his eyes. Kit thinks that if ever there was a good man who belied his appearance, that man is Sampson Brass.

'A man,' says Sampson, 'who loses forty-seven pound ten in one morning by his honesty, is a man to be envied. If it had been eighty pound, the luxuriousness of feeling would have been increased. Every pound lost, would have been a hundredweight of happiness gained. The still small voice, Christopher,' cries Brass, smiling, and tapping himself on the bosom, 'is a-singing comic songs within me, and all is happiness and joy!'

Kit is so improved by the conversation, and finds it go so completely home to his feelings, that he is considering what he shall say, when Mr Garland appears. The old gentleman is helped into the chaise with great obsequiousness by Mr Sampson Brass; and the pony, after shaking his head several times, and standing for three or four minutes with all his four legs planted firmly on the ground, as if he had made up his mind never to stir from that spot, but there to live and die, suddenly darts off, without the smallest notice, at the rate of twelve English miles an hour. Then, Mr Brass and his sister (who has joined him at the door) exchange an odd kind of smile—not at all a pleasant one in its expression—and return to the society of Mr Richard Swiveller, who, during their absence, has been regaling himself with various feats of pantomime, and is discovered at his desk, in a very flushed and heated condition, violently scratching out nothing with half a penknife.

Whenever Kit came alone, and without the chaise, it always happened that Sampson Brass was reminded of some mission, calling Mr Swiveller, if not to Peckham Rye again, at all events to some pretty distant place from which he could not be expected to return for two or three hours, or in all probability a much longer period, as that gentleman was not, to say the truth, renowned for using great expedition on such occasions, but rather for protracting and spinning out the time to the very utmost limit of possibility. Mr Swiveller out of sight, Miss Sally immediately withdrew. Mr Brass would then set the office-door wide open, hum his old tune with great gaiety of heart, and smile seraphically as before. Kit coming down-stairs would be called in; entertained with some moral and agreeable conversation; perhaps entreated to mind the office for an instant while Mr Brass stepped over the way; and afterwards presented with one or two half-crowns as the case might be. This occurred so often, that Kit, nothing doubting but that they came from the single gentleman who had already rewarded his mother with great liberality, could not enough admire his generosity; and bought so many cheap presents for her, and for little Jacob, and for the baby, and for Barbara to boot, that one or other of them was having some new trifle every day of their lives.

While these acts and deeds were in progress in and out of the office of Sampson Brass, Richard Swiveller, being often left alone therein, began to find the time hang heavy on his hands. For the better preservation of his cheerfulness therefore, and to prevent his faculties from rusting, he provided himself with a cribbage-board and pack of cards, and accustomed himself to play at cribbage with a dummy, for twenty, thirty, or sometimes even fifty thousand pounds aside, besides many hazardous bets to a considerable amount.

As these games were very silently conducted, notwithstanding the magnitude of the interests involved, Mr Swiveller began to think that on those evenings when Mr and Miss Brass were out (and they often went out now) he heard a kind of snorting or hard-breathing sound in the direction of the door, which it occurred to him, after some reflection, must proceed from the small servant, who always had a cold from damp living. Looking intently that way one night, he plainly distinguished an eye gleaming and glistening at the keyhole; and having now no doubt that his suspicions were correct, he stole softly to the door, and pounced upon her before she was aware of his approach.

'Oh! I didn't mean any harm indeed, upon my word I didn't,' cried the small servant, struggling like a much larger one. 'It's so very dull, down-stairs, Please don't you tell upon me, please don't.'

'Tell upon you!' said Dick. 'Do you mean to say you were looking through the keyhole for company?'

'Yes, upon my word I was,' replied the small servant.

'How long have you been cooling your eye there?' said Dick.

'Oh ever since you first began to play them cards, and long before.'

Vague recollections of several fantastic exercises with which he had refreshed himself after the fatigues of business, and to all of which, no doubt, the small servant was a party, rather disconcerted Mr Swiveller; but he was not very sensitive on such points, and recovered himself speedily.

'Well—come in'—he said, after a little consideration. 'Here—sit down, and I'll teach you how to play.'

'Oh! I durstn't do it,' rejoined the small servant; 'Miss Sally 'ud kill me, if she know'd I come up here.'

'Have you got a fire down-stairs?' said Dick.

'A very little one,' replied the small servant.

'Miss Sally couldn't kill me if she know'd I went down there, so I'll come,' said Richard, putting the cards into his pocket. 'Why, how thin you are! What do you mean by it?'

'It ain't my fault.'

'Could you eat any bread and meat?' said Dick, taking down his hat. 'Yes? Ah! I thought so. Did you ever taste beer?'

'I had a sip of it once,' said the small servant.

'Here's a state of things!' cried Mr Swiveller, raising his eyes to the ceiling. 'She never tasted it—it can't be tasted in a sip! Why, how old are you?'

'I don't know.'

Mr Swiveller opened his eyes very wide, and appeared thoughtful for a moment; then, bidding the child mind the door until he came back, vanished straightway.

290

Presently, he returned, followed by the boy from the public-house, who bore in one hand a plate of bread and beef, and in the other a great pot, filled with some very fragrant compound, which sent forth a grateful steam, and was indeed choice purl, made after a particular recipe which Mr Swiveller had imparted to the landlord, at a period when he was deep in his books and desirous to conciliate his friendship. Relieving the boy of his burden at the door, and charging his little companion to fasten it to prevent surprise, Mr Swiveller followed her into the kitchen.

'There!' said Richard, putting the plate before her. 'First of all clear that off, and then you'll see what's next.'

The small servant needed no second bidding, and the plate was soon empty.

'Next,' said Dick, handing the purl, 'take a pull at that; but moderate your transports, you know, for you're not used to it. Well, is it good?'

'Oh! isn't it?' said the small servant.

Mr Swiveller appeared gratified beyond all expression by this reply, and took a long draught himself, steadfastly regarding his companion while he did so. These preliminaries disposed of, he applied himself to teaching her the game, which she soon learnt tolerably well, being both sharp-witted and cunning.

'Now,' said Mr Swiveller, putting two sixpences into a saucer, and trimming the wretched candle, when the cards had been cut and dealt, 'those are the stakes. If you win, you get 'em all. If I win, I get 'em. To make it seem more real and pleasant, I shall call you the Marchioness, do you hear?'

The small servant nodded.

'Then, Marchioness,' said Mr Swiveller, 'fire away!'

The Marchioness, holding her cards very tight in both hands, considered which to play, and Mr Swiveller, assuming the gay and fashionable air which such society required, took another pull at the tankard, and waited for her lead.

CHAPTER 58

Mr Swiveller and his partner played several rubbers with varying success, until the loss of three sixpences, the gradual sinking of the purl, and the striking of ten o'clock, combined to render that gentleman mindful of the flight of Time, and the expediency of withdrawing before Mr Sampson and Miss Sally Brass returned.

'With which object in view, Marchioness,' said Mr Swiveller gravely, 'I shall ask your ladyship's permission to put the board in my pocket, and to retire from the presence when I have finished this tankard; merely observing, Marchioness, that since life like a river is flowing, I care not how fast it rolls on, ma'am, on, while such purl on the bank still is growing, and such eyes light the waves as they run. Marchioness, your health. You will excuse my wearing my hat, but the palace is damp, and the marble floor is—if I may be allowed the expression—sloppy.'

As a precaution against this latter inconvenience, Mr Swiveller had been sitting for some time with his feet on the hob, in which attitude he now gave utterance to these apologetic observations, and slowly sipped the last choice drops of nectar.

'The Baron Sampsono Brasso and his fair sister are (you tell me) at the Play?' said Mr

Swiveller, leaning his left arm heavily upon the table, and raising his voice and his right leg after the manner of a theatrical bandit.

The Marchioness nodded.

'Ha!' said Mr Swiveller, with a portentous frown. ''Tis well. Marchioness!—but no matter. Some wine there. Ho!' He illustrated these melodramatic morsels by handing the tankard to himself with great humility, receiving it haughtily, drinking from it thirstily, and smacking his lips fiercely.

The small servant, who was not so well acquainted with theatrical conventionalities as Mr Swiveller (having indeed never seen a play, or heard one spoken of, except by chance through chinks of doors and in other forbidden places), was rather alarmed by demonstrations so novel in their nature, and showed her concern so plainly in her looks, that Mr Swiveller felt it necessary to discharge his brigand manner for one more suitable to private life, as he asked,

'Do they often go where glory waits 'em, and leave you here?'

'Oh, yes; I believe you they do,' returned the small servant. 'Miss Sally's such a one-er for that, she is.'

'Such a what?' said Dick.

'Such a one-er,' returned the Marchioness.

After a moment's reflection, Mr Swiveller determined to forego his responsible duty of setting her right, and to suffer her to talk on; as it was evident that her tongue was loosened by the purl, and her opportunities for conversation were not so frequent as to render a momentary check of little consequence.

'They sometimes go to see Mr Quilp,' said the small servant with a shrewd look; 'they go to a many places, bless you!'

'Is Mr Brass a wunner?' said Dick.

'Not half what Miss Sally is, he isn't,' replied the small servant, shaking her head. 'Bless you, he'd never do anything without her.'

'Oh! He wouldn't, wouldn't he?' said Dick.

'Miss Sally keeps him in such order,' said the small servant; 'he always asks her advice, he does; and he catches it sometimes. Bless you, you wouldn't believe how much he catches it.'

'I suppose,' said Dick, 'that they consult together, a good deal, and talk about a great many people—about me for instance, sometimes, eh, Marchioness?'

The Marchioness nodded amazingly.

'Complimentary?' said Mr Swiveller.

The Marchioness changed the motion of her head, which had not yet left off nodding, and suddenly began to shake it from side to side, with a vehemence which threatened to dislocate her neck.

'Humph!' Dick muttered. 'Would it be any breach of confidence, Marchioness, to relate what they say of the humble individual who has now the honour to—?'

'Miss Sally says you're a funny chap,' replied his friend.

'Well, Marchioness,' said Mr Swiveller, 'that's not uncomplimentary. Merriment, Marchioness, is not a bad or a degrading quality. Old King Cole was himself a merry old soul, if we may put any faith in the pages of history.'

'But she says,' pursued his companion, 'that you an't to be trusted.'

'Why, really Marchioness,' said Mr Swiveller, thoughtfully; 'several ladies and gentlemen— not exactly professional persons, but tradespeople, ma'am, tradespeople—have made the same remark. The obscure citizen who keeps the hotel over the way, inclined strongly to that opinion to-night when I ordered him to prepare the banquet. It's a popular prejudice, Marchioness; and yet I am sure I don't know why, for I have been trusted in my time to a considerable amount, and I can safely say that I never forsook my trust until it deserted me—never. Mr Brass is of the same opinion, I suppose?'

His friend nodded again, with a cunning look which seemed to hint that Mr Brass held stronger opinions on the subject than his sister; and seeming to recollect herself, added imploringly, 'But don't you ever tell upon me, or I shall be beat to death.'

'Marchioness,' said Mr Swiveller, rising, 'the word of a gentleman is as good as his bond—sometimes better, as in the present case, where his bond might prove but a doubtful sort of security. I am your friend, and I hope we shall play many more rubbers together in this same saloon. But, Marchioness,' added Richard, stopping in his way to the door, and wheeling slowly round upon the small servant, who was following with the candle; 'it occurs to me that you must be in the constant habit of airing your eye at keyholes, to know all this.'

'I only wanted,' replied the trembling Marchioness, 'to know where the key of the safe was hid; that was all; and I wouldn't have taken much, if I had found it—only enough to squench my hunger.'

'You didn't find it then?' said Dick. 'But of course you didn't, or you'd be plumper. Good night, Marchioness. Fare thee well, and if for ever, then for ever fare thee well—and put up the chain, Marchioness, in case of accidents.'

With this parting injunction, Mr Swiveller emerged from the house; and feeling that he had by this time taken quite as much to drink as promised to be good for his constitution (purl being a rather strong and heady compound), wisely resolved to betake himself to his lodgings, and to bed at once. Homeward he went therefore; and his apartments (for he still retained the plural fiction) being at no great distance from the office, he was soon seated in his own bed-chamber, where, having pulled off one boot and forgotten the other, he fell into deep cogitation.

'This Marchioness,' said Mr Swiveller, folding his arms, 'is a very extraordinary person— surrounded by mysteries, ignorant of the taste of beer, unacquainted with her own name (which is less remarkable), and taking a limited view of society through the keyholes of doors—can these things be her destiny, or has some unknown person started an opposition to the decrees of fate? It is a most inscrutable and unmitigated staggerer!'

When his meditations had attained this satisfactory point, he became aware of his remaining boot, of which, with unimpaired solemnity he proceeded to divest himself; shaking his head with exceeding gravity all the time, and sighing deeply.

'These rubbers,' said Mr Swiveller, putting on his nightcap in exactly the same style as he wore his hat, 'remind me of the matrimonial fireside. Cheggs's wife plays cribbage; all-fours likewise. She rings the changes on 'em now. From sport to sport they hurry her to banish her regrets, and when they win a smile from her, they think that she forgets—but she don't. By this time, I should say,' added Richard, getting his left cheek into profile, and looking complacently at the reflection of a very little scrap of whisker in the looking-glass; 'by this time, I should say, the iron has entered into her soul. It serves her right!'

Melting from this stern and obdurate, into the tender and pathetic mood, Mr Swiveller groaned a little, walked wildly up and down, and even made a show of tearing his hair, which, however, he thought better of, and wrenched the tassel from his nightcap instead. At last, undressing himself with a gloomy resolution, he got into bed.

Some men in his blighted position would have taken to drinking; but as Mr Swiveller had taken to that before, he only took, on receiving the news that Sophy Wackles was lost to him for ever, to playing the flute; thinking after mature consideration that it was a good, sound, dismal occupation, not only in unison with his own sad thoughts, but calculated to awaken a fellow-feeling in the bosoms of his neighbours. In pursuance of this resolution, he now drew a little table to his bedside, and arranging the light and a small oblong music-book to the best advantage, took his flute from its box, and began to play most mournfully.

The air was 'Away with melancholy'—a composition, which, when it is played very slowly on the flute, in bed, with the further disadvantage of being performed by a gentleman but imperfectly acquainted with the instrument, who repeats one note a great many times before he can find the next, has not a lively effect. Yet, for half the night, or more, Mr Swiveller, lying sometimes on his back with his eyes upon the ceiling, and sometimes half out of bed to correct himself by the book, played this unhappy tune over and over again; never leaving off, save for a minute or two at a time to take breath and soliloquise about the Marchioness, and then beginning again with renewed vigour. It was not until he had quite exhausted his several subjects of meditation, and had breathed into the flute the whole sentiment of the purl down to its very dregs, and had nearly maddened the people of the house, and at both the next doors, and over the way—that he shut up the music-book, extinguished the candle, and finding himself greatly lightened and relieved in his mind, turned round and fell asleep.

He awoke in the morning, much refreshed; and having taken half an hour's exercise at the flute, and graciously received a notice to quit from his landlady, who had been in waiting on the stairs for that purpose since the dawn of day, repaired to Bevis Marks; where the beautiful Sally was already at her post, bearing in her looks a radiance, mild as that which beameth from the virgin moon.

Mr Swiveller acknowledged her presence by a nod, and exchanged his coat for the aquatic jacket; which usually took some time fitting on, for in consequence of a tightness in the sleeves, it was only to be got into by a series of struggles. This difficulty overcome, he took his seat at the desk.

'I say'—quoth Miss Brass, abruptly breaking silence, 'you haven't seen a silver pencil-case this morning, have you?'

'I didn't meet many in the street,' rejoined Mr Swiveller. 'I saw one—a stout pencil-case of respectable appearance—but as he was in company with an elderly penknife, and a young toothpick with whom he was in earnest conversation, I felt a delicacy in speaking to him.'

294

'No, but have you?' returned Miss Brass. 'Seriously, you know.'

'What a dull dog you must be to ask me such a question seriously,' said Mr Swiveller. 'Haven't I this moment come?'

'Well, all I know is,' replied Miss Sally, 'that it's not to be found, and that it disappeared one day this week, when I left it on the desk.'

'Halloa!' thought Richard, 'I hope the Marchioness hasn't been at work here.'

'There was a knife too,' said Miss Sally, 'of the same pattern. They were given to me by my father, years ago, and are both gone. You haven't missed anything yourself, have you?'

Mr Swiveller involuntarily clapped his hands to the jacket to be quite sure that it was a jacket and not a skirted coat; and having satisfied himself of the safety of this, his only moveable in Bevis Marks, made answer in the negative.

'It's a very unpleasant thing, Dick,' said Miss Brass, pulling out the tin box and refreshing herself with a pinch of snuff; 'but between you and me—between friends you know, for if Sammy knew it, I should never hear the last of it—some of the office-money, too, that has been left about, has gone in the same way. In particular, I have missed three half-crowns at three different times.'

'You don't mean that?' cried Dick. 'Be careful what you say, old boy, for this is a serious matter. Are you quite sure? Is there no mistake?'

'It is so, and there can't be any mistake at all,' rejoined Miss Brass emphatically.

'Then by Jove,' thought Richard, laying down his pen, 'I am afraid the Marchioness is done for!'

The more he discussed the subject in his thoughts, the more probable it appeared to Dick that the miserable little servant was the culprit. When he considered on what a spare allowance of food she lived, how neglected and untaught she was, and how her natural cunning had been sharpened by necessity and privation, he scarcely doubted it. And yet he pitied her so much, and felt so unwilling to have a matter of such gravity disturbing the oddity of their acquaintance, that he thought, and thought truly, that rather than receive fifty pounds down, he would have the Marchioness proved innocent.

While he was plunged in very profound and serious meditation upon this theme, Miss Sally sat shaking her head with an air of great mystery and doubt; when the voice of her brother Sampson, carolling a cheerful strain, was heard in the passage, and that gentleman himself, beaming with virtuous smiles, appeared.

'Mr Richard, sir, good morning! Here we are again, sir, entering upon another day, with our bodies strengthened by slumber and breakfast, and our spirits fresh and flowing. Here we are, Mr Richard, rising with the sun to run our little course—our course of duty, sir—and, like him, to get through our day's work with credit to ourselves and advantage to our fellow-creatures. A charming reflection sir, very charming!'

While he addressed his clerk in these words, Mr Brass was, somewhat ostentatiously, engaged in minutely examining and holding up against the light a five-pound bank note, which he had brought in, in his hand.

Mr Richard not receiving his remarks with anything like enthusiasm, his employer turned his eyes to his face, and observed that it wore a troubled expression.

'You're out of spirits, sir,' said Brass. 'Mr Richard, sir, we should fall to work cheerfully, and not in a despondent state. It becomes us, Mr Richard, sir, to—'

Here the chaste Sarah heaved a loud sigh.

'Dear me!' said Mr Sampson, 'you too! Is anything the matter? Mr Richard, sir—'

Dick, glancing at Miss Sally, saw that she was making signals to him, to acquaint her brother with the subject of their recent conversation. As his own position was not a very pleasant one until the matter was set at rest one way or other, he did so; and Miss Brass, plying her snuff-box at a most wasteful rate, corroborated his account.

The countenance of Sampson fell, and anxiety overspread his features. Instead of passionately bewailing the loss of his money, as Miss Sally had expected, he walked on tiptoe to the door, opened it, looked outside, shut it softly, returned on tiptoe, and said in a whisper,

'This is a most extraordinary and painful circumstance—Mr Richard, sir, a most painful circumstance. The fact is, that I myself have missed several small sums from the desk, of late, and have refrained from mentioning it, hoping that accident would discover the offender; but it has not done so—it has not done so. Sally—Mr Richard, sir—this is a particularly distressing affair!'

As Sampson spoke, he laid the bank-note upon the desk among some papers, in an absent manner, and thrust his hands into his pockets. Richard Swiveller pointed to it, and admonished him to take it up.

'No, Mr Richard, sir,' rejoined Brass with emotion, 'I will not take it up. I will let it lie there, sir. To take it up, Mr Richard, sir, would imply a doubt of you; and in you, sir, I have unlimited confidence. We will let it lie there, Sir, if you please, and we will not take it up by any means.' With that, Mr Brass patted him twice or thrice on the shoulder, in a most friendly manner, and entreated him to believe that he had as much faith in his honesty as he had in his own.

Although at another time Mr Swiveller might have looked upon this as a doubtful compliment, he felt it, under the then-existing circumstances, a great relief to be assured that he was not wrongfully suspected. When he had made a suitable reply, Mr Brass wrung him by the hand, and fell into a brown study, as did Miss Sally likewise. Richard too remained in a thoughtful state; fearing every moment to hear the Marchioness impeached, and unable to resist the conviction that she must be guilty.

When they had severally remained in this condition for some minutes, Miss Sally all at once gave a loud rap upon the desk with her clenched fist, and cried, 'I've hit it!'—as indeed she had, and chipped a piece out of it too; but that was not her meaning.

'Well,' cried Brass anxiously. 'Go on, will you!'

'Why,' replied his sister with an air of triumph, 'hasn't there been somebody always coming in and out of this office for the last three or four weeks; hasn't that somebody been left alone in it sometimes—thanks to you; and do you mean to tell me that that somebody isn't the thief!'

'What somebody?' blustered Brass.

'Why, what do you call him—Kit.'

'Mr Garland's young man?'

'To be sure.'

'Never!' cried Brass. 'Never. I'll not hear of it. Don't tell me'—said Sampson, shaking his head, and working with both his hands as if he were clearing away ten thousand cobwebs. 'I'll never believe it of him. Never!'

'I say,' repeated Miss Brass, taking another pinch of snuff, 'that he's the thief.'

'I say,' returned Sampson violently, 'that he is not. What do you mean? How dare you? Are characters to be whispered away like this? Do you know that he's the honestest and faithfullest fellow that ever lived, and that he has an irreproachable good name? Come in, come in!'

These last words were not addressed to Miss Sally, though they partook of the tone in which the indignant remonstrances that preceded them had been uttered. They were addressed to some person who had knocked at the office-door; and they had hardly passed the lips of Mr Brass, when this very Kit himself looked in.

'Is the gentleman up-stairs, sir, if you please?'

'Yes, Kit,' said Brass, still fired with an honest indignation, and frowning with knotted brows upon his sister; 'Yes Kit, he is. I am glad to see you Kit, I am rejoiced to see you. Look in again, as you come down-stairs, Kit. That lad a robber!' cried Brass when he had withdrawn, 'with that frank and open countenance! I'd trust him with untold gold. Mr Richard, sir, have the goodness to step directly to Wrasp and Co.'s in Broad Street, and inquire if they have had instructions to appear in Carkem and Painter. That lad a robber,' sneered Sampson, flushed and heated with his wrath. 'Am I blind, deaf, silly; do I know nothing of human nature when I see it before me? Kit a robber! Bah!'

Flinging this final interjection at Miss Sally with immeasurable scorn and contempt, Sampson Brass thrust his head into his desk, as if to shut the base world from his view, and breathed defiance from under its half-closed lid.

CHAPTER 59

When Kit, having discharged his errand, came down-stairs from the single gentleman's apartment after the lapse of a quarter of an hour or so, Mr Sampson Brass was alone in the office. He was not singing as usual, nor was he seated at his desk. The open door showed him standing before the fire with his back towards it, and looking so very strange that Kit supposed he must have been suddenly taken ill.

'Is anything the matter, sir?' said Kit.

'Matter!' cried Brass. 'No. Why anything the matter?'

'You are so very pale,' said Kit, 'that I should hardly have known you.'

'Pooh pooh! mere fancy,' cried Brass, stooping to throw up the cinders. 'Never better, Kit, never better in all my life. Merry too. Ha ha! How's our friend above-stairs, eh?'

'A great deal better,' said Kit.

'I'm glad to hear it,' rejoined Brass; 'thankful, I may say. An excellent gentleman—worthy, liberal, generous, gives very little trouble—an admirable lodger. Ha ha! Mr Garland—he's well I hope, Kit—and the pony—my friend, my particular friend you know. Ha ha!'

Kit gave a satisfactory account of all the little household at Abel Cottage. Mr Brass, who seemed remarkably inattentive and impatient, mounted on his stool, and beckoning him to come nearer, took him by the button-hole.

'I have been thinking, Kit,' said the lawyer, 'that I could throw some little emoluments in your mother's way—You have a mother, I think? If I recollect right, you told me—'

'Oh yes, Sir, yes certainly.'

'A widow, I think? an industrious widow?'

'A harder-working woman or a better mother never lived, Sir.'

'Ah!' cried Brass. 'That's affecting, truly affecting. A poor widow struggling to maintain her orphans in decency and comfort, is a delicious picture of human goodness.—Put down your hat, Kit.'

'Thank you Sir, I must be going directly.'

'Put it down while you stay, at any rate,' said Brass, taking it from him and making some confusion among the papers, in finding a place for it on the desk. 'I was thinking, Kit, that we have often houses to let for people we are concerned for, and matters of that sort. Now you know we're obliged to put people into those houses to take care of 'em—very often undeserving people that we can't depend upon. What's to prevent our having a person that we can depend upon, and enjoying the delight of doing a good action at the same time? I say, what's to prevent our employing this worthy woman, your mother? What with one job and another, there's lodging—and good lodging too—pretty well all the year round, rent free, and a weekly allowance besides, Kit, that would provide her with a great many comforts she don't at present enjoy. Now what do you think of that? Do you see any objection? My only desire is to serve you, Kit; therefore if you do, say so freely.'

As Brass spoke, he moved the hat twice or thrice, and shuffled among the papers again, as if in search of something.

'How can I see any objection to such a kind offer, sir?' replied Kit with his whole heart. 'I don't know how to thank you sir, I don't indeed.'

'Why then,' said Brass, suddenly turning upon him and thrusting his face close to Kit's with such a repulsive smile that the latter, even in the very height of his gratitude, drew back, quite startled. 'Why then, it's done.'

Kit looked at him in some confusion.

'Done, I say,' added Sampson, rubbing his hands and veiling himself again in his usual oily manner. 'Ha ha! and so you shall find Kit, so you shall find. But dear me,' said Brass, 'what a time Mr Richard is gone! A sad loiterer to be sure! Will you mind the office one minute, while I run up-stairs? Only one minute. I'll not detain you an instant longer, on any account, Kit.'

Talking as he went, Mr Brass bustled out of the office, and in a very short time returned. Mr Swiveller came back, almost at the same instant; and as Kit was leaving the room hastily, to make up for lost time, Miss Brass herself encountered him in the doorway.

'Oh!' sneered Sally, looking after him as she entered. 'There goes your pet, Sammy, eh?'

'Ah! There he goes,' replied Brass. 'My pet, if you please. An honest fellow, Mr Richard, sir—a worthy fellow indeed!'

'Hem!' coughed Miss Brass.

'I tell you, you aggravating vagabond,' said the angry Sampson, 'that I'd stake my life upon his honesty. Am I never to hear the last of this? Am I always to be baited, and beset, by your mean suspicions? Have you no regard for true merit, you malignant fellow? If you come to that, I'd sooner suspect your honesty than his.'

Miss Sally pulled out the tin snuff-box, and took a long, slow pinch, regarding her brother with a steady gaze all the time.

'She drives me wild, Mr Richard, sir,' said Brass, 'she exasperates me beyond all bearing. I am heated and excited, sir, I know I am. These are not business manners, sir, nor business looks, but she carries me out of myself.'

'Why don't you leave him alone?' said Dick.

'Because she can't, sir,' retorted Brass; 'because to chafe and vex me is a part of her nature, Sir, and she will and must do it, or I don't believe she'd have her health. But never mind,' said Brass, 'never mind. I've carried my point. I've shown my confidence in the lad. He has minded the office again. Ha ha! Ugh, you viper!'

The beautiful virgin took another pinch, and put the snuff-box in her pocket; still looking at her brother with perfect composure.

'He has minded the office again,' said Brass triumphantly; 'he has had my confidence, and he shall continue to have it; he—why, where's the—'

'What have you lost?' inquired Mr Swiveller.

'Dear me!' said Brass, slapping all his pockets, one after another, and looking into his desk, and under it, and upon it, and wildly tossing the papers about, 'the note, Mr Richard, sir, the five-pound note—what can have become of it? I laid it down here—God bless me!'

'What!' cried Miss Sally, starting up, clapping her hands, and scattering the papers on the floor. 'Gone! Now who's right? Now who's got it? Never mind five pounds—what's five pounds? He's honest, you know, quite honest. It would be mean to suspect him. Don't run after him. No, no, not for the world!'

'Is it really gone though?' said Dick, looking at Brass with a face as pale as his own.

'Upon my word, Mr Richard, Sir,' replied the lawyer, feeling in all his pockets with looks of the greatest agitation, 'I fear this is a black business. It's certainly gone, Sir. What's to be done?'

'Don't run after him,' said Miss Sally, taking more snuff. 'Don't run after him on any account. Give him time to get rid of it, you know. It would be cruel to find him out!'

Mr Swiveller and Sampson Brass looked from Miss Sally to each other, in a state of bewilderment, and then, as by one impulse, caught up their hats and rushed out into the street—darting along in the middle of the road, and dashing aside all obstructions, as though they were running for their lives.

It happened that Kit had been running too, though not so fast, and having the start of them by some few minutes, was a good distance ahead. As they were pretty certain of the road he must have taken, however, and kept on at a great pace, they came up with him, at the very moment when he had taken breath, and was breaking into a run again.

'Stop!' cried Sampson, laying his hand on one shoulder, while Mr Swiveller pounced upon the other. 'Not so fast sir. You're in a hurry?'

'Yes, I am,' said Kit, looking from one to the other in great surprise.

'I—I—can hardly believe it,' panted Sampson, 'but something of value is missing from the office. I hope you don't know what.'

'Know what! good Heaven, Mr Brass!' cried Kit, trembling from head to foot; 'you don't suppose—'

'No, no,' rejoined Brass quickly, 'I don't suppose anything. Don't say I said you did. You'll come back quietly, I hope?'

'Of course I will,' returned Kit. 'Why not?'

'To be sure!' said Brass. 'Why not? I hope there may turn out to be no why not. If you knew the trouble I've been in, this morning, through taking your part, Christopher, you'd be sorry for it.'

'And I am sure you'll be sorry for having suspected me sir,' replied Kit. 'Come. Let us make haste back.'

'Certainly!' cried Brass, 'the quicker, the better. Mr Richard—have the goodness, sir, to take that arm. I'll take this one. It's not easy walking three abreast, but under these circumstances it must be done, sir; there's no help for it.'

Kit did turn from white to red, and from red to white again, when they secured him thus, and for a moment seemed disposed to resist. But, quickly recollecting himself, and remembering that if he made any struggle, he would perhaps be dragged by the collar through the public streets, he only repeated, with great earnestness and with the tears standing in his eyes, that they would be sorry for this—and suffered them to lead him off. While they were on the way back, Mr Swiveller, upon whom his present functions sat very irksomely, took an opportunity of whispering in his ear that if he would confess his guilt, even by so much as a nod, and promise not to do so any more, he would connive at his kicking Sampson Brass on the shins and escaping up a court; but Kit indignantly rejecting this proposal, Mr Richard had nothing for it, but to hold him tight until they reached Bevis Marks, and ushered him into the presence of the charming Sarah, who immediately took the precaution of locking the door.

'Now, you know,' said Brass, 'if this is a case of innocence, it is a case of that description, Christopher, where the fullest disclosure is the best satisfaction for everybody. Therefore if you'll consent to an examination,' he demonstrated what kind of examination he meant by turning back the cuffs of his coat, 'it will be a comfortable and pleasant thing for all parties.'

'Search me,' said Kit, proudly holding up his arms. 'But mind, sir—I know you'll be sorry for this, to the last day of your life.'

'It is certainly a very painful occurrence,' said Brass with a sigh, as he dived into one of Kit's pockets, and fished up a miscellaneous collection of small articles; 'very painful. Nothing here, Mr Richard, Sir, all perfectly satisfactory. Nor here, sir. Nor in the waistcoat, Mr Richard, nor in the coat tails. So far, I am rejoiced, I am sure.'

Richard Swiveller, holding Kit's hat in his hand, was watching the proceedings with great interest, and bore upon his face the slightest possible indication of a smile, as Brass, shutting one of his eyes, looked with the other up the inside of one of the poor fellow's sleeves as if it were a telescope—when Sampson turning hastily to him, bade him search the hat.

'Here's a handkerchief,' said Dick.

'No harm in that sir,' rejoined Brass, applying his eye to the other sleeve, and speaking in the voice of one who was contemplating an immense extent of prospect. 'No harm in a handkerchief Sir, whatever. The faculty don't consider it a healthy custom, I believe, Mr Richard, to carry one's handkerchief in one's hat—I have heard that it keeps the head too warm—but in every other point of view, its being there, is extremely satisfactory—extremely so.'

An exclamation, at once from Richard Swiveller, Miss Sally, and Kit himself, cut the lawyer short. He turned his head, and saw Dick standing with the bank-note in his hand.

'In the hat?' cried Brass in a sort of shriek.

'Under the handkerchief, and tucked beneath the lining,' said Dick, aghast at the discovery.

Mr Brass looked at him, at his sister, at the walls, at the ceiling, at the floor—everywhere but at Kit, who stood quite stupefied and motionless.

'And this,' cried Sampson, clasping his hands, 'is the world that turns upon its own axis, and has Lunar influences, and revolutions round Heavenly Bodies, and various games of that sort! This is human natur, is it! Oh natur, natur! This is the miscreant that I was going to benefit with all my little arts, and that, even now, I feel so much for, as to wish to let him go! But,' added Mr Brass with greater fortitude, 'I am myself a lawyer, and bound to set an example in carrying the laws of my happy country into effect. Sally my dear, forgive me, and catch hold of him on the other side. Mr Richard, sir, have the goodness to run and fetch a constable. The weakness is past and over sir, and moral strength returns. A constable, sir, if you please!'

CHAPTER 60

Kit stood as one entranced, with his eyes opened wide and fixed upon the ground, regardless alike of the tremulous hold which Mr Brass maintained on one side of his cravat, and of the firmer grasp of Miss Sally upon the other; although this latter detention was in itself no small inconvenience, as that fascinating woman, besides screwing her knuckles inconveniently into his throat from time to time, had fastened upon him in the first instance with so tight a grip that even in the disorder and distraction of his thoughts he could not divest himself of an uneasy sense of choking. Between the brother and sister he remained in this posture, quite unresisting and passive, until Mr Swiveller returned, with a police constable at his heels.

This functionary, being, of course, well used to such scenes; looking upon all kinds of robbery, from petty larceny up to housebreaking or ventures on the highway, as matters in the regular course of business; and regarding the perpetrators in the light of so many customers coming to be served at the wholesale and retail shop of criminal law where he stood behind the counter; received Mr Brass's statement of facts with about as much interest and surprise, as an undertaker might evince if required to listen to a circumstantial account of the last illness of a person whom he was called in to wait upon professionally; and took Kit into custody with a decent indifference.

'We had better,' said this subordinate minister of justice, 'get to the office while there's a magistrate sitting. I shall want you to come along with us, Mr Brass, and the—' he looked at Miss Sally as if in some doubt whether she might not be a griffin or other fabulous monster.

'The lady, eh?' said Sampson.

'Ah!' replied the constable. 'Yes—the lady. Likewise the young man that found the property.'

'Mr Richard, Sir,' said Brass in a mournful voice. 'A sad necessity. But the altar of our country sir—'

'You'll have a hackney-coach, I suppose?' interrupted the constable, holding Kit (whom his other captors had released) carelessly by the arm, a little above the elbow. 'Be so good as send for one, will you?'

'But, hear me speak a word,' cried Kit, raising his eyes and looking imploringly about him. 'Hear me speak a word. I am no more guilty than any one of you. Upon my soul I am not. I a thief! Oh, Mr Brass, you know me better. I am sure you know me better. This is not right of you, indeed.'

'I give you my word, constable—' said Brass. But here the constable interposed with the constitutional principle 'words be blowed;' observing that words were but spoon-meat for babes and sucklings, and that oaths were the food for strong men.

'Quite true, constable,' assented Brass in the same mournful tone. 'Strictly correct. I give you my oath, constable, that down to a few minutes ago, when this fatal discovery was made, I had such confidence in that lad, that I'd have trusted him with—a hackney-coach, Mr Richard, sir; you're very slow, Sir.'

'Who is there that knows me,' cried Kit, 'that would not trust me— that does not? ask anybody whether they have ever doubted me; whether I have ever wronged them of a farthing. Was I ever once dishonest when I was poor and hungry, and is it likely I would begin now! Oh consider what you do. How can I meet the kindest friends that ever human creature had, with this dreadful charge upon me!'

Mr Brass rejoined that it would have been well for the prisoner if he had thought of that before, and was about to make some other gloomy observations when the voice of the single gentleman was heard, demanding from above-stairs what was the matter, and what was the cause of all that noise and hurry. Kit made an involuntary start towards the door in his anxiety to answer for himself, but being speedily detained by the constable, had the agony of seeing Sampson Brass run out alone to tell the story in his own way.

'And he can hardly believe it, either,' said Sampson, when he returned, 'nor nobody will. I wish I could doubt the evidence of my senses, but their depositions are unimpeachable. It's of no use cross-examining my eyes,' cried Sampson, winking and rubbing them, 'they stick to their first account, and will. Now, Sarah, I hear the coach in the Marks; get on your bonnet, and we'll be off. A sad errand! a moral funeral, quite!'

'Mr Brass,' said Kit. 'Do me one favour. Take me to Mr Witherden's first.'

Sampson shook his head irresolutely.

'Do,' said Kit. 'My master's there. For Heaven's sake, take me there, first.'

'Well, I don't know,' stammered Brass, who perhaps had his reasons for wishing to show as fair as possible in the eyes of the notary. 'How do we stand in point of time, constable, eh?'

The constable, who had been chewing a straw all this while with great philosophy, replied that if they went away at once they would have time enough, but that if they stood shilly-shallying there, any longer, they must go straight to the Mansion House; and finally expressed his opinion that that was where it was, and that was all about it.

Mr Richard Swiveller having arrived inside the coach, and still remaining immoveable in the most commodious corner with his face to the horses, Mr Brass instructed the officer to remove his prisoner, and declared himself quite ready. Therefore, the constable, still holding Kit in the same manner, and pushing him on a little before him, so as to keep him at about three-quarters of an arm's length in advance (which is the professional mode), thrust him into the vehicle and followed himself. Miss Sally entered next; and there being now four inside, Sampson Brass got upon the box, and made the coachman drive on.

Still completely stunned by the sudden and terrible change which had taken place in his affairs, Kit sat gazing out of the coach window, almost hoping to see some monstrous phenomenon in the streets which might give him reason to believe he was in a dream. Alas! Everything was too real and familiar: the same succession of turnings, the same houses, the same streams of people running side by side in different directions upon the pavement, the same bustle of carts and carriages in the road, the same well-remembered objects in the shop windows: a regularity in the very noise and hurry which no dream ever mirrored. Dream-like as the story was, it was true. He stood charged with robbery; the note had been found upon him, though he was innocent in thought and deed; and they were carrying him back, a prisoner.

Absorbed in these painful ruminations, thinking with a drooping heart of his mother and little Jacob, feeling as though even the consciousness of innocence would be insufficient to support him in the presence of his friends if they believed him guilty, and sinking in hope and courage more and more as they drew nearer to the notary's, poor Kit was looking earnestly out of the window, observant of nothing,—when all at once, as though it had been conjured up by magic, he became aware of the face of Quilp.

And what a leer there was upon the face! It was from the open window of a tavern that it looked out; and the dwarf had so spread himself over it, with his elbows on the window-sill and his head resting on both his hands, that what between this attitude and his being swoln with suppressed laughter, he looked puffed and bloated into twice his usual breadth. Mr Brass, on recognising him, immediately stopped the coach. As it came to a halt directly opposite to where he stood, the dwarf pulled off his hat, and saluted the party with a hideous and grotesque politeness.

'Aha!' he cried. 'Where now, Brass? where now? Sally with you too? Sweet Sally! And Dick? Pleasant Dick! And Kit! Honest Kit!'

'He's extremely cheerful!' said Brass to the coachman. 'Very much so! Ah, sir—a sad business! Never believe in honesty any more, sir.'

'Why not?' returned the dwarf. 'Why not, you rogue of a lawyer, why not?'

'Bank-note lost in our office sir,' said Brass, shaking his head. 'Found in his hat sir—he previously left alone there—no mistake at all sir—chain of evidence complete—not a link wanting.'

'What!' cried the dwarf, leaning half his body out of window. 'Kit a thief! Kit a thief! Ha ha ha! Why, he's an uglier-looking thief than can be seen anywhere for a penny. Eh, Kit—eh? Ha ha ha! Have you taken Kit into custody before he had time and opportunity to beat me! Eh, Kit, eh?' And with that, he burst into a yell of laughter, manifestly to the great terror of the coachman, and pointed to a dyer's pole hard by, where a dangling suit of clothes bore some resemblance to a man upon a gibbet.

'Is it coming to that, Kit!' cried the dwarf, rubbing his hands violently. 'Ha ha ha ha! What a disappointment for little Jacob, and for his darling mother! Let him have the Bethel minister to comfort and console him, Brass. Eh, Kit, eh? Drive on coachey, drive on. Bye bye, Kit; all good go with you; keep up your spirits; my love to the Garlands—the dear old lady and gentleman. Say I inquired after 'em, will you? Blessings on 'em, on you, and on everybody, Kit. Blessings on all the world!'

With such good wishes and farewells, poured out in a rapid torrent until they were out of hearing, Quilp suffered them to depart; and when he could see the coach no longer, drew in his head, and rolled upon the ground in an ecstacy of enjoyment.

When they reached the notary's, which they were not long in doing, for they had encountered the dwarf in a bye street at a very little distance from the house, Mr Brass dismounted; and opening the coach door with a melancholy visage, requested his sister to accompany him into the office, with the view of preparing the good people within, for the mournful intelligence that awaited them. Miss Sally complying, he desired Mr Swiveller to accompany them. So, into the office they went; Mr Sampson and his sister arm-in-arm; and Mr Swiveller following, alone.

The notary was standing before the fire in the outer office, talking to Mr Abel and the elder Mr Garland, while Mr Chuckster sat writing at the desk, picking up such crumbs of their conversation as happened to fall in his way. This posture of affairs Mr Brass observed through the glass-door as he was turning the handle, and seeing that the notary recognised him, he began to shake his head and sigh deeply while that partition yet divided them.

'Sir,' said Sampson, taking off his hat, and kissing the two fore-fingers of his right hand beaver glove, 'my name is Brass—Brass of Bevis Marks, Sir. I have had the honour and pleasure, Sir, of being concerned against you in some little testamentary matters. How do you do, sir?'

'My clerk will attend to any business you may have come upon, Mr Brass,' said the notary, turning away.

'Thank you Sir,' said Brass, 'thank you, I am sure. Allow me, Sir, to introduce my sister— quite one of us Sir, although of the weaker sex—of great use in my business Sir, I assure you. Mr Richard, sir, have the goodness to come foward if you please—No really,' said Brass, stepping between the notary and his private office (towards which he had begun to retreat), and speaking in the tone of an injured man, 'really Sir, I must, under favour, request a word or two with you, indeed.'

'Mr Brass,' said the other, in a decided tone, 'I am engaged. You see that I am occupied with these gentlemen. If you will communicate your business to Mr Chuckster yonder, you will receive every attention.'

'Gentlemen,' said Brass, laying his right hand on his waistcoat, and looking towards the father and son with a smooth smile—'Gentlemen, I appeal to you—really, gentlemen—consider, I beg of you. I am of the law. I am styled "gentleman" by Act of Parliament. I maintain the title by the annual payment of twelve pound sterling for a certificate. I am not one of your players of music, stage actors, writers of books, or painters of pictures, who assume a station that the laws of their country don't recognise. I am none of your strollers or vagabonds. If any man brings his action against me, he must describe me as a gentleman, or his action is null and void. I appeal to you—is this quite respectful? Really gentlemen—'

'Well, will you have the goodness to state your business then, Mr Brass?' said the notary.

'Sir,' rejoined Brass, 'I will. Ah Mr Witherden! you little know the—but I will not be tempted to travel from the point, sir, I believe the name of one of these gentlemen is Garland.'

'Of both,' said the notary.

'In-deed!' rejoined Brass, cringing excessively. 'But I might have known that, from the uncommon likeness. Extremely happy, I am sure, to have the honour of an introduction to two such gentlemen, although the occasion is a most painful one. One of you gentlemen has a servant called Kit?'

'Both,' replied the notary.

'Two Kits?' said Brass smiling. 'Dear me!'

'One Kit, sir,' returned Mr Witherden angrily, 'who is employed by both gentlemen. What of him?'

'This of him, sir,' rejoined Brass, dropping his voice impressively. 'That young man, sir, that I have felt unbounded and unlimited confidence in, and always behaved to as if he was my equal—that young man has this morning committed a robbery in my office, and been taken almost in the fact.'

'This must be some falsehood!' cried the notary.

'It is not possible,' said Mr Abel.

'I'll not believe one word of it,' exclaimed the old gentleman.

Mr Brass looked mildly round upon them, and rejoined,

'Mr Witherden, sir, your words are actionable, and if I was a man of low and mean standing, who couldn't afford to be slandered, I should proceed for damages. Hows'ever, sir, being what I am, I merely scorn such expressions. The honest warmth of the other gentleman I respect, and I'm truly sorry to be the messenger of such unpleasant news. I shouldn't have put myself in this painful position, I assure you, but that the lad himself desired to be brought here in the first instance, and I yielded to his prayers. Mr Chuckster, sir, will you have the goodness to tap at the window for the constable that's waiting in the coach?'

The three gentlemen looked at each other with blank faces when these words were uttered, and Mr Chuckster, doing as he was desired, and leaping off his stool with something of the excitement of an inspired prophet whose foretellings had in the fulness of time been realised, held the door open for the entrance of the wretched captive.

Such a scene as there was, when Kit came in, and bursting into the rude eloquence with which Truth at length inspired him, called Heaven to witness that he was innocent, and that how the property came to be found upon him he knew not! Such a confusion of tongues, before the circumstances were related, and the proofs disclosed! Such a dead silence when all was told, and his three friends exchanged looks of doubt and amazement!

'Is it not possible,' said Mr Witherden, after a long pause, 'that this note may have found its way into the hat by some accident,—such as the removal of papers on the desk, for instance?'

But this was clearly shown to be quite impossible. Mr Swiveller, though an unwilling witness, could not help proving to demonstration, from the position in which it was found, that it must have been designedly secreted.

'It's very distressing,' said Brass, 'immensely distressing, I am sure. When he comes to be tried, I shall be very happy to recommend him to mercy on account of his previous good character. I did lose money before, certainly, but it doesn't quite follow that he took it. The presumption's against him—strongly against him—but we're Christians, I hope?'

'I suppose,' said the constable, looking round, 'that no gentleman here can give evidence as to whether he's been flush of money of late, Do you happen to know, Sir?'

'He has had money from time to time, certainly,' returned Mr Garland, to whom the man had put the question. 'But that, as he always told me, was given him by Mr Brass himself.'

'Yes to be sure,' said Kit eagerly. 'You can bear me out in that, Sir?'

'Eh?' cried Brass, looking from face to face with an expression of stupid amazement.

'The money you know, the half-crowns, that you gave me—from the lodger,' said Kit.

'Oh dear me!' cried Brass, shaking his head and frowning heavily. 'This is a bad case, I find; a very bad case indeed.'

'What! Did you give him no money on account of anybody, Sir?' asked Mr Garland, with great anxiety.

'I give him money, Sir!' returned Sampson. 'Oh, come you know, this is too barefaced. Constable, my good fellow, we had better be going.'

'What!' shrieked Kit. 'Does he deny that he did? ask him, somebody, pray. Ask him to tell you whether he did or not!'

'Did you, sir?' asked the notary.

'I tell you what, gentlemen,' replied Brass, in a very grave manner, 'he'll not serve his case this way, and really, if you feel any interest in him, you had better advise him to go upon some other tack. Did I, sir? Of course I never did.'

'Gentlemen,' cried Kit, on whom a light broke suddenly, 'Master, Mr Abel, Mr Witherden, every one of you—he did it! What I have done to offend him, I don't know, but this is a plot to ruin me. Mind, gentlemen, it's a plot, and whatever comes of it, I will say with my dying breath that he put that note in my hat himself! Look at him, gentlemen! see how he changes colour. Which of us looks the guilty person—he, or I?'

'You hear him, gentlemen?' said Brass, smiling, 'you hear him. Now, does this case strike you as assuming rather a black complexion, or does it not? Is it at all a treacherous case, do you think, or is it one of mere ordinary guilt? Perhaps, gentlemen, if he had not said this in your presence and I had reported it, you'd have held this to be impossible likewise, eh?'

With such pacific and bantering remarks did Mr Brass refute the foul aspersion on his character; but the virtuous Sarah, moved by stronger feelings, and having at heart, perhaps, a more jealous regard for the honour of her family, flew from her brother's side, without any previous intimation of her design, and darted at the prisoner with the utmost fury. It would undoubtedly have gone hard with Kit's face, but that the wary constable, foreseeing her design, drew him aside at the critical moment, and thus placed Mr Chuckster in circumstances of some jeopardy; for that gentleman happening to be next the object of Miss Brass's wrath; and rage being, like love and fortune, blind; was pounced upon by the fair enslaver, and had a false collar plucked up by the roots, and his hair very much dishevelled, before the exertions of the company could make her sensible of her mistake.

The constable, taking warning by this desperate attack, and thinking perhaps that it would be more satisfactory to the ends of justice if the prisoner were taken before a magistrate, whole, rather than in small pieces, led him back to the hackney-coach without more ado, and moreover insisted on Miss Brass becoming an outside passenger; to which proposal the charming creature, after a little angry discussion, yielded her consent; and so took her brother Sampson's place upon the box: Mr Brass with some reluctance agreeing to occupy her seat inside. These arrangements perfected, they drove to the justice-room with all speed, followed by the notary and his two friends in another coach. Mr Chuckster alone was left behind—greatly to his indignation; for he held the evidence he could have given, relative to Kit's returning to work out the shilling, to be so very material as bearing upon his hypocritical and designing character, that he considered its suppression little better than a compromise of felony.

At the justice-room, they found the single gentleman, who had gone straight there, and was expecting them with desperate impatience. But not fifty single gentlemen rolled into one could have helped poor Kit, who in half an hour afterwards was committed for trial, and was assured by a friendly officer on his way to prison that there was no occasion to be cast down, for the sessions would soon be on, and he would, in all likelihood, get his little affair disposed of, and be comfortably transported, in less than a fortnight.

CHAPTER 61

Let moralists and philosophers say what they may, it is very questionable whether a guilty man would have felt half as much misery that night, as Kit did, being innocent. The world, being in the constant commission of vast quantities of injustice, is a little too apt to comfort itself with the idea that if the victim of its falsehood and malice have a clear conscience, he cannot fail to be sustained under his trials, and somehow or other to come right at last; 'in which case,' say they who have hunted him down, '—though we certainly don't expect it— nobody will be better pleased than we.' Whereas, the world would do well to reflect, that injustice is in itself, to every generous and properly constituted mind, an injury, of all others the most insufferable, the most torturing, and the most hard to bear; and that many clear consciences have gone to their account elsewhere, and many sound hearts have broken, because of this very reason; the knowledge of their own deserts only aggravating their sufferings, and rendering them the less endurable.

The world, however, was not in fault in Kit's case. But Kit was innocent; and knowing this, and feeling that his best friends deemed him guilty—that Mr and Mrs Garland would look upon him as a monster of ingratitude—that Barbara would associate him with all that was bad and criminal—that the pony would consider himself forsaken—and that even his own mother might perhaps yield to the strong appearances against him, and believe him to be the wretch he seemed—knowing and feeling all this, he experienced, at first, an agony of mind which no words can describe, and walked up and down the little cell in which he was locked up for the night, almost beside himself with grief.

Even when the violence of these emotions had in some degree subsided, and he was beginning to grow more calm, there came into his mind a new thought, the anguish of which was scarcely less. The child—the bright star of the simple fellow's life—she, who always came back upon him like a beautiful dream—who had made the poorest part of his existence, the happiest and best—who had ever been so gentle, and considerate, and good—if she were ever to hear of this, what would she think! As this idea occurred to him, the walls of the prison seemed to melt away, and the old place to reveal itself in their stead, as it was wont to be on winter nights—the fireside, the little supper table, the old man's hat, and coat, and stick—the half-opened door, leading to her little room—they were all there. And Nell herself was there, and he—both laughing heartily as they had often done—and when he had got as far as this, Kit could go no farther, but flung himself upon his poor bedstead and wept.

It was a long night, which seemed as though it would have no end; but he slept too, and dreamed—always of being at liberty, and roving about, now with one person and now with another, but ever with a vague dread of being recalled to prison; not that prison, but one which was in itself a dim idea—not of a place, but of a care and sorrow: of something oppressive and always present, and yet impossible to define. At last, the morning dawned, and there was the jail itself—cold, black, and dreary, and very real indeed.

He was left to himself, however, and there was comfort in that. He had liberty to walk in a small paved yard at a certain hour, and learnt from the turnkey, who came to unlock his cell and show him where to wash, that there was a regular time for visiting, every day, and that if any of his friends came to see him, he would be fetched down to the grate. When he had given him this information, and a tin porringer containing his breakfast, the man locked him up again; and went clattering along the stone passage, opening and shutting a great many other doors, and raising numberless loud echoes which resounded through the building for a long time, as if they were in prison too, and unable to get out.

This turnkey had given him to understand that he was lodged, like some few others in the jail, apart from the mass of prisoners; because he was not supposed to be utterly depraved and irreclaimable, and had never occupied apartments in that mansion before. Kit was thankful for this indulgence, and sat reading the church catechism very attentively (though he had known it by heart from a little child), until he heard the key in the lock, and the man entered again.

'Now then,' he said, 'come on!'

'Where to, Sir?' asked Kit.

The man contented himself by briefly replying 'Wisitors;' and taking him by the arm in exactly the same manner as the constable had done the day before, led him, through several winding ways and strong gates, into a passage, where he placed him at a grating and turned upon his heel. Beyond this grating, at the distance of about four or five feet, was another exactly like it. In the space between, sat a turnkey reading a newspaper, and outside the further railing, Kit saw, with a palpitating heart, his mother with the baby in her arms; Barbara's mother with her never-failing umbrella; and poor little Jacob, staring in with all his might, as though he were looking for the bird, or the wild beast, and thought the men were mere accidents with whom the bars could have no possible concern.

But when little Jacob saw his brother, and, thrusting his arms between the rails to hug him, found that he came no nearer, but still stood afar off with his head resting on the arm by which he held to one of the bars, he began to cry most piteously; whereupon, Kit's mother and Barbara's mother, who had restrained themselves as much as possible, burst out sobbing and weeping afresh. Poor Kit could not help joining them, and not one of them could speak a word. During this melancholy pause, the turnkey read his newspaper with a waggish look (he had evidently got among the facetious paragraphs) until, happening to take his eyes off for an instant, as if to get by dint of contemplation at the very marrow of some joke of a deeper sort than the rest, it appeared to occur to him, for the first time, that somebody was crying.

'Now, ladies, ladies,' he said, looking round with surprise, 'I'd advise you not to waste time like this. It's allowanced here, you know. You mustn't let that child make that noise either. It's against all rules.'

'I'm his poor mother, sir,'—sobbed Mrs Nubbles, curtseying humbly, 'and this is his brother, sir. Oh dear me, dear me!'

'Well!' replied the turnkey, folding his paper on his knee, so as to get with greater convenience at the top of the next column. 'It can't be helped you know. He ain't the only one in the same fix. You mustn't make a noise about it!'

With that he went on reading. The man was not unnaturally cruel or hard-hearted. He had come to look upon felony as a kind of disorder, like the scarlet fever or erysipelas: some people had it—some hadn't—just as it might be.

'Oh! my darling Kit,' said his mother, whom Barbara's mother had charitably relieved of the baby, 'that I should see my poor boy here!'

'You don't believe that I did what they accuse me of, mother dear?' cried Kit, in a choking voice.

'I believe it!' exclaimed the poor woman, 'I that never knew you tell a lie, or do a bad action from your cradle—that have never had a moment's sorrow on your account, except it was the poor meals that you have taken with such good humour and content, that I forgot how little there was, when I thought how kind and thoughtful you were, though you were but a child!—I believe it of the son that's been a comfort to me from the hour of his birth until this time, and that I never laid down one night in anger with! I believe it of you Kit!—'

'Why then, thank God!' said Kit, clutching the bars with an earnestness that shook them, 'and I can bear it, mother! Come what may, I shall always have one drop of happiness in my heart when I think that you said that.'

At this the poor woman fell a-crying again, and Barbara's mother too. And little Jacob, whose disjointed thoughts had by this time resolved themselves into a pretty distinct impression that Kit couldn't go out for a walk if he wanted, and that there were no birds, lions, tigers or other natural curiosities behind those bars—nothing indeed, but a caged brother—added his tears to theirs with as little noise as possible.

Kit's mother, drying her eyes (and moistening them, poor soul, more than she dried them), now took from the ground a small basket, and submissively addressed herself to the turnkey, saying, would he please to listen to her for a minute? The turnkey, being in the very crisis and passion of a joke, motioned to her with his hand to keep silent one minute longer, for her life. Nor did he remove his hand into its former posture, but kept it in the same warning attitude until he had finished the paragraph, when he paused for a few seconds, with a smile upon his face, as who should say 'this editor is a comical blade—a funny dog,' and then asked her what she wanted.

'I have brought him a little something to eat,' said the good woman. 'If you please, Sir, might he have it?'

'Yes,—he may have it. There's no rule against that. Give it to me when you go, and I'll take care he has it.'

'No, but if you please sir—don't be angry with me sir—I am his mother, and you had a mother once—if I might only see him eat a little bit, I should go away, so much more satisfied that he was all comfortable.'

And again the tears of Kit's mother burst forth, and of Barbara's mother, and of little Jacob. As to the baby, it was crowing and laughing with its might—under the idea, apparently, that the whole scene had been invented and got up for its particular satisfaction.

The turnkey looked as if he thought the request a strange one and rather out of the common way, but nevertheless he laid down his paper, and coming round where Kit's mother stood, took the basket from her, and after inspecting its contents, handed it to Kit, and went back to his place. It may be easily conceived that the prisoner had no great appetite, but he sat down on the ground, and ate as hard as he could, while, at every morsel he put into his mouth, his mother sobbed and wept afresh, though with a softened grief that bespoke the satisfaction the sight afforded her.

While he was thus engaged, Kit made some anxious inquiries about his employers, and whether they had expressed any opinion concerning him; but all he could learn was that Mr Abel had himself broken the intelligence to his mother, with great kindness and delicacy, late on the previous night, but had himself expressed no opinion of his innocence or guilt. Kit was on the point of mustering courage to ask Barbara's mother about Barbara, when the turnkey who had conducted him, reappeared, a second turnkey appeared behind his visitors, and the third turnkey with the newspaper cried 'Time's up!'—adding in the same breath 'Now for the next party!' and then plunging deep into his newspaper again. Kit was taken off in an instant, with a blessing from his mother, and a scream from little Jacob, ringing in his ears. As he was crossing the next yard with the basket in his hand, under the guidance of his former conductor, another officer called to them to stop, and came up with a pint pot of porter in his hand.

'This is Christopher Nubbles, isn't it, that come in last night for felony?' said the man.

His comrade replied that this was the chicken in question.

'Then here's your beer,' said the other man to Christopher. 'What are you looking at? There an't a discharge in it.'

'I beg your pardon,' said Kit. 'Who sent it me?'

'Why, your friend,' replied the man. 'You're to have it every day, he says. And so you will, if he pays for it.'

'My friend!' repeated Kit.

'You're all abroad, seemingly,' returned the other man. 'There's his letter. Take hold!'

Kit took it, and when he was locked up again, read as follows.

'Drink of this cup, you'll find there's a spell in its every drop 'gainst the ills of mortality. Talk of the cordial that sparkled for Helen! Her cup was a fiction, but this is reality (Barclay and Co.'s).—If they ever send it in a flat state, complain to the Governor. Yours, R. S.'

'R. S.!' said Kit, after some consideration. 'It must be Mr Richard Swiveller. Well, its very kind of him, and I thank him heartily.'

CHAPTER 62

A faint light, twinkling from the window of the counting-house on Quilp's wharf, and looking inflamed and red through the night-fog, as though it suffered from it like an eye, forewarned Mr Sampson Brass, as he approached the wooden cabin with a cautious step, that the excellent proprietor, his esteemed client, was inside, and probably waiting with his accustomed patience and sweetness of temper the fulfilment of the appointment which now brought Mr Brass within his fair domain.

'A treacherous place to pick one's steps in, of a dark night,' muttered Sampson, as he stumbled for the twentieth time over some stray lumber, and limped in pain. 'I believe that boy strews the ground differently every day, on purpose to bruise and maim one; unless his master does it with his own hands, which is more than likely. I hate to come to this place without Sally. She's more protection than a dozen men.'

As he paid this compliment to the merit of the absent charmer, Mr Brass came to a halt; looking doubtfully towards the light, and over his shoulder.

'What's he about, I wonder?' murmured the lawyer, standing on tiptoe, and endeavouring to obtain a glimpse of what was passing inside, which at that distance was impossible— 'drinking, I suppose,—making himself more fiery and furious, and heating his malice and mischievousness till they boil. I'm always afraid to come here by myself, when his account's a pretty large one. I don't believe he'd mind throttling me, and dropping me softly into the river when the tide was at its strongest, any more than he'd mind killing a rat—indeed I don't know whether he wouldn't consider it a pleasant joke. Hark! Now he's singing!'

Mr Quilp was certainly entertaining himself with vocal exercise, but it was rather a kind of chant than a song; being a monotonous repetition of one sentence in a very rapid manner, with a long stress upon the last word, which he swelled into a dismal roar. Nor did the burden of this performance bear any reference to love, or war, or wine, or loyalty, or any other, the standard topics of song, but to a subject not often set to music or generally known in ballads; the words being these:—'The worthy magistrate, after remarking that the prisoner would find some difficulty in persuading a jury to believe his tale, committed him to take his trial at the approaching sessions; and directed the customary recognisances to be entered into for the pros-e-cu-tion.'

Every time he came to this concluding word, and had exhausted all possible stress upon it, Quilp burst into a shriek of laughter, and began again.

'He's dreadfully imprudent,' muttered Brass, after he had listened to two or three repetitions of the chant. 'Horribly imprudent. I wish he was dumb. I wish he was deaf. I wish he was blind. Hang him,' cried Brass, as the chant began again. 'I wish he was dead!'

Giving utterance to these friendly aspirations in behalf of his client, Mr Sampson composed his face into its usual state of smoothness, and waiting until the shriek came again and was dying away, went up to the wooden house, and knocked at the door.

'Come in!' cried the dwarf.

'How do you do to-night sir?' said Sampson, peeping in. 'Ha ha ha! How do you do sir? Oh dear me, how very whimsical! Amazingly whimsical to be sure!'

'Come in, you fool!' returned the dwarf, 'and don't stand there shaking your head and showing your teeth. Come in, you false witness, you perjurer, you suborner of evidence, come in!'

'He has the richest humour!' cried Brass, shutting the door behind him; 'the most amazing vein of comicality! But isn't it rather injudicious, sir—?'

'What?' demanded Quilp. 'What, Judas?'

'Judas!' cried Brass. 'He has such extraordinary spirits! His humour is so extremely playful! Judas! Oh yes—dear me, how very good! Ha ha ha!'

All this time, Sampson was rubbing his hands, and staring, with ludicrous surprise and dismay, at a great, goggle-eyed, blunt-nosed figure-head of some old ship, which was reared up against the wall in a corner near the stove, looking like a goblin or hideous idol whom the dwarf worshipped. A mass of timber on its head, carved into the dim and distant semblance of a cocked hat, together with a representation of a star on the left breast and epaulettes on the shoulders, denoted that it was intended for the effigy of some famous admiral; but, without those helps, any observer might have supposed it the authentic portrait of a distinguished merman, or great sea-monster. Being originally much too large for the apartment which it was now employed to decorate, it had been sawn short off at the waist. Even in this state it reached from floor to ceiling; and thrusting itself forward, with that excessively wide-awake aspect, and air of somewhat obtrusive politeness, by which figure-heads are usually characterised, seemed to reduce everything else to mere pigmy proportions.

'Do you know it?' said the dwarf, watching Sampson's eyes. 'Do you see the likeness?'

'Eh?' said Brass, holding his head on one side, and throwing it a little back, as connoisseurs do. 'Now I look at it again, I fancy I see a—yes, there certainly is something in the smile that reminds me of—and yet upon my word I—'

Now, the fact was, that Sampson, having never seen anything in the smallest degree resembling this substantial phantom, was much perplexed; being uncertain whether Mr Quilp considered it like himself, and had therefore bought it for a family portrait; or whether he was pleased to consider it as the likeness of some enemy. He was not very long in doubt; for, while he was surveying it with that knowing look which people assume when they are contemplating for the first time portraits which they ought to recognise but don't, the dwarf threw down the newspaper from which he had been chanting the words already quoted, and seizing a rusty iron bar, which he used in lieu of poker, dealt the figure such a stroke on the nose that it rocked again.

'Is it like Kit—is it his picture, his image, his very self?' cried the dwarf, aiming a shower of blows at the insensible countenance, and covering it with deep dimples. 'Is it the exact model and counterpart of the dog—is it—is it—is it?' And with every repetition of the question, he battered the great image, until the perspiration streamed down his face with the violence of the exercise.

Although this might have been a very comical thing to look at from a secure gallery, as a bull-fight is found to be a comfortable spectacle by those who are not in the arena, and a house on fire is better than a play to people who don't live near it, there was something in the earnestness of Mr Quilp's manner which made his legal adviser feel that the counting-house was a little too small, and a deal too lonely, for the complete enjoyment of these humours. Therefore, he stood as far off as he could, while the dwarf was thus engaged; whimpering out but feeble applause; and when Quilp left off and sat down again from pure exhaustion, approached with more obsequiousness than ever.

'Excellent indeed!' cried Brass. 'He he! Oh, very good Sir. You know,' said Sampson, looking round as if in appeal to the bruised animal, 'he's quite a remarkable man—quite!'

'Sit down,' said the dwarf. 'I bought the dog yesterday. I've been screwing gimlets into him, and sticking forks in his eyes, and cutting my name on him. I mean to burn him at last.'

'Ha ha!' cried Brass. 'Extremely entertaining, indeed!'

'Come here,' said Quilp, beckoning him to draw near. 'What's injudicious, hey?'

'Nothing Sir—nothing. Scarcely worth mentioning Sir; but I thought that song—admirably humorous in itself you know—was perhaps rather—'

'Yes,' said Quilp, 'rather what?'

'Just bordering, or as one may say remotely verging, upon the confines of injudiciousness perhaps, Sir,' returned Brass, looking timidly at the dwarf's cunning eyes, which were turned towards the fire and reflected its red light.

'Why?' inquired Quilp, without looking up.

'Why, you know, sir,' returned Brass, venturing to be more familiar: '—the fact is, sir, that any allusion to these little combinings together, of friends, for objects in themselves extremely laudable, but which the law terms conspiracies, are—you take me, sir?—best kept snug and among friends, you know.'

'Eh!' said Quilp, looking up with a perfectly vacant countenance. 'What do you mean?'

'Cautious, exceedingly cautious, very right and proper!' cried Brass, nodding his head. 'Mum, sir, even here—my meaning, sir, exactly.'

'Your meaning exactly, you brazen scarecrow,—what's your meaning?' retorted Quilp. 'Why do you talk to me of combining together? Do I combine? Do I know anything about your combinings?'

'No no, sir—certainly not; not by any means,' returned Brass.

'If you so wink and nod at me,' said the dwarf, looking about him as if for his poker, 'I'll spoil the expression of your monkey's face, I will.'

'Don't put yourself out of the way I beg, sir,' rejoined Brass, checking himself with great alacrity. 'You're quite right, sir, quite right. I shouldn't have mentioned the subject, sir. It's much better not to. You're quite right, sir. Let us change it, if you please. You were asking, sir, Sally told me, about our lodger. He has not returned, sir.'

'No?' said Quilp, heating some rum in a little saucepan, and watching it to prevent its boiling over. 'Why not?'

'Why, sir,' returned Brass, 'he—dear me, Mr Quilp, sir—'

'What's the matter?' said the dwarf, stopping his hand in the act of carrying the saucepan to his mouth.

'You have forgotten the water, sir,' said Brass. 'And—excuse me, sir—but it's burning hot.'

Deigning no other than a practical answer to this remonstrance, Mr Quilp raised the hot saucepan to his lips, and deliberately drank off all the spirit it contained, which might have been in quantity about half a pint, and had been but a moment before, when he took it off the fire, bubbling and hissing fiercely. Having swallowed this gentle stimulant, and shaken his fist at the admiral, he bade Mr Brass proceed.

'But first,' said Quilp, with his accustomed grin, 'have a drop yourself—a nice drop—a good, warm, fiery drop.'

'Why, sir,' replied Brass, 'if there was such a thing as a mouthful of water that could be got without trouble—'

'There's no such thing to be had here,' cried the dwarf. 'Water for lawyers! Melted lead and brimstone, you mean, nice hot blistering pitch and tar—that's the thing for them—eh, Brass, eh?'

'Ha ha ha!' laughed Mr Brass. 'Oh very biting! and yet it's like being tickled—there's a pleasure in it too, sir!'

'Drink that,' said the dwarf, who had by this time heated some more. 'Toss it off, don't leave any heeltap, scorch your throat and be happy!'

The wretched Sampson took a few short sips of the liquor, which immediately distilled itself into burning tears, and in that form came rolling down his cheeks into the pipkin again, turning the colour of his face and eyelids to a deep red, and giving rise to a violent fit of coughing, in the midst of which he was still heard to declare, with the constancy of a martyr, that it was 'beautiful indeed!' While he was yet in unspeakable agonies, the dwarf renewed their conversation.

'The lodger,' said Quilp, '—what about him?'

'He is still, sir,' returned Brass, with intervals of coughing, 'stopping with the Garland family. He has only been home once, Sir, since the day of the examination of that culprit. He informed Mr Richard, sir, that he couldn't bear the house after what had taken place; that he was wretched in it; and that he looked upon himself as being in a certain kind of way the cause of the occurrence.—A very excellent lodger Sir. I hope we may not lose him.'

'Yah!' cried the dwarf. 'Never thinking of anybody but yourself—why don't you retrench then—scrape up, hoard, economise, eh?'

'Why, sir,' replied Brass, 'upon my word I think Sarah's as good an economiser as any going. I do indeed, Mr Quilp.'

'Moisten your clay, wet the other eye, drink, man!' cried the dwarf. 'You took a clerk to oblige me.'

'Delighted, sir, I am sure, at any time,' replied Sampson. 'Yes, Sir, I did.'

'Then now you may discharge him,' said Quilp. 'There's a means of retrenchment for you at once.'

'Discharge Mr Richard, sir?' cried Brass.

'Have you more than one clerk, you parrot, that you ask the question? Yes.'

'Upon my word, Sir,' said Brass, 'I wasn't prepared for this--'

'How could you be?' sneered the dwarf, 'when I wasn't? How often am I to tell you that I brought him to you that I might always have my eye on him and know where he was—and that I had a plot, a scheme, a little quiet piece of enjoyment afoot, of which the very cream and essence was, that this old man and grandchild (who have sunk underground I think) should be, while he and his precious friend believed them rich, in reality as poor as frozen rats?'

'I quite understood that, sir,' rejoined Brass. 'Thoroughly.'

'Well, Sir,' retorted Quilp, 'and do you understand now, that they're not poor—that they can't be, if they have such men as your lodger searching for them, and scouring the country far and wide?'

'Of course I do, Sir,' said Sampson.

'Of course you do,' retorted the dwarf, viciously snapping at his words. 'Of course do you understand then, that it's no matter what comes of this fellow? of course do you understand that for any other purpose he's no man for me, nor for you?'

'I have frequently said to Sarah, sir,' returned Brass, 'that he was of no use at all in the business. You can't put any confidence in him, sir. If you'll believe me I've found that fellow, in the commonest little matters of the office that have been trusted to him, blurting out the truth, though expressly cautioned. The aggravation of that chap sir, has exceeded anything you can imagine, it has indeed. Nothing but the respect and obligation I owe to you, sir—'

As it was plain that Sampson was bent on a complimentary harangue, unless he received a timely interruption, Mr Quilp politely tapped him on the crown of his head with the little saucepan, and requested that he would be so obliging as to hold his peace.

'Practical, sir, practical,' said Brass, rubbing the place and smiling; 'but still extremely pleasant—immensely so!'

'Hearken to me, will you?' returned Quilp, 'or I'll be a little more pleasant, presently. There's no chance of his comrade and friend returning. The scamp has been obliged to fly, as I learn, for some knavery, and has found his way abroad. Let him rot there.'

'Certainly, sir. Quite proper.—Forcible!' cried Brass, glancing at the admiral again, as if he made a third in company. 'Extremely forcible!'

'I hate him,' said Quilp between his teeth, 'and have always hated him, for family reasons. Besides, he was an intractable ruffian; otherwise he would have been of use. This fellow is pigeon-hearted and light-headed. I don't want him any longer. Let him hang or drown—starve—go to the devil.'

'By all means, sir,' returned Brass. 'When would you wish him, sir, to—ha, ha!—to make that little excursion?'

'When this trial's over,' said Quilp. 'As soon as that's ended, send him about his business.'

'It shall be done, sir,' returned Brass; 'by all means. It will be rather a blow to Sarah, sir, but she has all her feelings under control. Ah, Mr Quilp, I often think, sir, if it had only pleased Providence to bring you and Sarah together, in earlier life, what blessed results would have flowed from such a union! You never saw our dear father, sir?—A charming gentleman. Sarah was his pride and joy, sir. He would have closed his eyes in bliss, would Foxey, Mr Quilp, if he could have found her such a partner. You esteem her, sir?'

'I love her,' croaked the dwarf.

'You're very good, Sir,' returned Brass, 'I am sure. Is there any other order, sir, that I can take a note of, besides this little matter of Mr Richard?'

'None,' replied the dwarf, seizing the saucepan. 'Let us drink the lovely Sarah.'

'If we could do it in something, sir, that wasn't quite boiling,' suggested Brass humbly, 'perhaps it would be better. I think it will be more agreeable to Sarah's feelings, when she comes to hear from me of the honour you have done her, if she learns it was in liquor rather cooler than the last, Sir.'

But to these remonstrances, Mr Quilp turned a deaf ear. Sampson Brass, who was, by this time, anything but sober, being compelled to take further draughts of the same strong bowl, found that, instead of at all contributing to his recovery, they had the novel effect of making the counting-house spin round and round with extreme velocity, and causing the floor and ceiling to heave in a very distressing manner. After a brief stupor, he awoke to a consciousness of being partly under the table and partly under the grate. This position not being the most comfortable one he could have chosen for himself, he managed to stagger to his feet, and, holding on by the admiral, looked round for his host.

Mr Brass's first impression was, that his host was gone and had left him there alone—perhaps locked him in for the night. A strong smell of tobacco, however, suggested a new train of ideas, he looked upward, and saw that the dwarf was smoking in his hammock.

'Good bye, Sir,' cried Brass faintly. 'Good bye, Sir.'

'Won't you stop all night?' said the dwarf, peeping out. 'Do stop all night!'

'I couldn't indeed, Sir,' replied Brass, who was almost dead from nausea and the closeness of the room. 'If you'd have the goodness to show me a light, so that I may see my way across the yard, sir—'

Quilp was out in an instant; not with his legs first, or his head first, or his arms first, but bodily—altogether.

'To be sure,' he said, taking up a lantern, which was now the only light in the place. 'Be careful how you go, my dear friend. Be sure to pick your way among the timber, for all the rusty nails are upwards. There's a dog in the lane. He bit a man last night, and a woman the night before, and last Tuesday he killed a child—but that was in play. Don't go too near him.'

'Which side of the road is he, sir?' asked Brass, in great dismay.

'He lives on the right hand,' said Quilp, 'but sometimes he hides on the left, ready for a spring. He's uncertain in that respect. Mind you take care of yourself. I'll never forgive you if you don't. There's the light out—never mind—you know the way—straight on!' Quilp had slily shaded the light by holding it against his breast, and now stood chuckling and shaking from head to foot in a rapture of delight, as he heard the lawyer stumbling up the yard, and now and then falling heavily down. At length, however, he got quit of the place, and was out of hearing.

The dwarf shut himself up again, and sprang once more into his hammock.

CHAPTER 63

The professional gentleman who had given Kit the consolatory piece of information relative to the settlement of his trifle of business at the Old Bailey, and the probability of its being very soon disposed of, turned out to be quite correct in his prognostications. In eight days' time, the sessions commenced. In one day afterwards, the Grand Jury found a True Bill against Christopher Nubbles for felony; and in two days from that finding, the aforesaid Christopher Nubbles was called upon to plead Guilty or Not Guilty to an Indictment for that he the said Christopher did feloniously abstract and steal from the dwelling-house and office of one Sampson Brass, gentleman, one Bank Note for Five Pounds issued by the Governor and Company of the Bank of England; in contravention of the Statutes in that case made and provided, and against the peace of our Sovereign Lord the King, his crown and dignity.

To this indictment, Christopher Nubbles, in a low and trembling voice, pleaded Not Guilty; and here, let those who are in the habit of forming hasty judgments from appearances, and who would have had Christopher, if innocent, speak out very strong and loud, observe, that confinement and anxiety will subdue the stoutest hearts; and that to one who has been close shut up, though it be only for ten or eleven days, seeing but stone walls and a very few stony faces, the sudden entrance into a great hall filled with life, is a rather disconcerting and startling circumstance. To this, it must be added, that life in a wig is to a large class of people much more terrifying and impressive than life with its own head of hair; and if, in addition to these considerations, there be taken into account Kit's natural emotion on seeing the two Mr Garlands and the little Notary looking on with pale and anxious faces, it will perhaps seem matter of no very great wonder that he should have been rather out of sorts, and unable to make himself quite at home.

Although he had never seen either of the Mr Garlands, or Mr Witherden, since the time of his arrest, he had been given to understand that they had employed counsel for him. Therefore, when one of the gentlemen in wigs got up and said 'I am for the prisoner, my Lord,' Kit made him a bow; and when another gentleman in a wig got up and said 'And I'm against him, my Lord,' Kit trembled very much, and bowed to him too. And didn't he hope in his own heart that his gentleman was a match for the other gentleman, and would make him ashamed of himself in no time!

The gentleman who was against him had to speak first, and being in dreadfully good spirits (for he had, in the last trial, very nearly procured the acquittal of a young gentleman who had had the misfortune to murder his father) he spoke up, you may be sure; telling the jury that if they acquitted this prisoner they must expect to suffer no less pangs and agonies than he had told the other jury they would certainly undergo if they convicted that prisoner. And when he had told them all about the case, and that he had never known a worse case, he stopped a little while, like a man who had something terrible to tell them, and then said that he understood an attempt would be made by his learned friend (and here he looked sideways at Kit's gentleman) to impeach the testimony of those immaculate witnesses whom he should call before them; but he did hope and trust that his learned friend would have a greater respect and veneration for the character of the prosecutor; than whom, as he well knew, there did not exist, and never had existed, a more honourable member of that most honourable profession to which he was attached. And then he said, did the jury know Bevis Marks? And if they did know Bevis Marks (as he trusted for their own character, they did) did they know the historical and elevating associations connected with that most remarkable spot? Did they believe that a man like Brass could reside in a place like Bevis Marks, and not be a virtuous and most upright character? And when he had said a great deal to them on this point, he remembered that it was an insult to their understandings to make any remarks on what they must have felt so strongly without him, and therefore called Sampson Brass into the witness-box, straightway.

Then up comes Mr Brass, very brisk and fresh; and, having bowed to the judge, like a man who has had the pleasure of seeing him before, and who hopes he has been pretty well since their last meeting, folds his arms, and looks at his gentleman as much as to say 'Here I am—full of evidence—Tap me!' And the gentleman does tap him presently, and with great discretion too; drawing off the evidence by little and little, and making it run quite clear and bright in the eyes of all present. Then, Kit's gentleman takes him in hand, but can make nothing of him; and after a great many very long questions and very short answers, Mr Sampson Brass goes down in glory.

To him succeeds Sarah, who in like manner is easy to be managed by Mr Brass's gentleman, but very obdurate to Kit's. In short, Kit's gentleman can get nothing out of her but a repetition of what she has said before (only a little stronger this time, as against his client), and therefore lets her go, in some confusion. Then, Mr Brass's gentleman calls Richard Swiveller, and Richard Swiveller appears accordingly.

Now, Mr Brass's gentleman has it whispered in his ear that this witness is disposed to be friendly to the prisoner—which, to say the truth, he is rather glad to hear, as his strength is considered to lie in what is familiarly termed badgering. Wherefore, he begins by requesting the officer to be quite sure that this witness kisses the book, then goes to work at him, tooth and nail.

'Mr Swiveller,' says this gentleman to Dick, when he had told his tale with evident reluctance and a desire to make the best of it: 'Pray sir, where did you dine yesterday?'—'Where did I dine yesterday?'—'Aye, sir, where did you dine yesterday—was it near here, sir?'—'Oh to be sure—yes—just over the way.'—'To be sure. Yes. Just over the way,' repeats Mr Brass's gentleman, with a glance at the court.—'Alone, sir?'—'I beg your pardon,' says Mr Swiveller, who has not caught the question—'Alone, sir?' repeats Mr Brass's gentleman in a voice of thunder, 'did you dine alone? Did you treat anybody, sir? Come!'—'Oh yes, to be sure—yes, I did,' says Mr Swiveller with a smile.—'Have the goodness to banish a levity, sir, which is very ill-suited to the place in which you stand (though perhaps you have reason to be thankful that it's only that place),' says Mr Brass's gentleman, with a nod of the head, insinuating that the dock is Mr Swiveller's legitimate sphere of action; 'and attend to me. You were waiting about here, yesterday, in expectation that this trial was coming on. You dined over the way. You treated somebody. Now, was that somebody brother to the prisoner at the bar?'—Mr Swiveller is proceeding to explain—'Yes or No, sir,' cries Mr Brass's gentleman—'But will you allow me—'—'Yes or No, sir'—'Yes it was, but—'—'Yes it was,' cries the gentleman, taking him up short. 'And a very pretty witness you are!'

Down sits Mr Brass's gentleman. Kit's gentleman, not knowing how the matter really stands, is afraid to pursue the subject. Richard Swiveller retires abashed. Judge, jury and spectators have visions of his lounging about, with an ill-looking, large-whiskered, dissolute young fellow of six feet high. The reality is, little Jacob, with the calves of his legs exposed to the open air, and himself tied up in a shawl. Nobody knows the truth; everybody believes a falsehood; and all because of the ingenuity of Mr Brass's gentleman.

Then come the witnesses to character, and here Mr Brass's gentleman shines again. It turns out that Mr Garland has had no character with Kit, no recommendation of him but from his own mother, and that he was suddenly dismissed by his former master for unknown reasons. 'Really Mr Garland,' says Mr Brass's gentleman, 'for a person who has arrived at your time of life, you are, to say the least of it, singularly indiscreet, I think.' The jury think so too, and find Kit guilty. He is taken off, humbly protesting his innocence. The spectators settle themselves in their places with renewed attention, for there are several female witnesses to be examined in the next case, and it has been rumoured that Mr Brass's gentleman will make great fun in cross-examining them for the prisoner.

Kit's mother, poor woman, is waiting at the grate below stairs, accompanied by Barbara's mother (who, honest soul! never does anything but cry, and hold the baby), and a sad interview ensues. The newspaper-reading turnkey has told them all. He don't think it will be transportation for life, because there's time to prove the good character yet, and that is sure to serve him. He wonders what he did it for. 'He never did it!' cries Kit's mother. 'Well,' says the turnkey, 'I won't contradict you. It's all one, now, whether he did it or not.'

Kit's mother can reach his hand through the bars, and she clasps it— God, and those to whom he has given such tenderness, only know in how much agony. Kit bids her keep a good heart, and, under pretence of having the children lifted up to kiss him, prays Barbara's mother in a whisper to take her home.

'Some friend will rise up for us, mother,' cried Kit, 'I am sure. If not now, before long. My innocence will come out, mother, and I shall be brought back again; I feel confidence in that. You must teach little Jacob and the baby how all this was, for if they thought I had ever been dishonest, when they grew old enough to understand, it would break my heart to know it, if I was thousands of miles away.—Oh! is there no good gentleman here, who will take care of her!'

The hand slips out of his, for the poor creature sinks down upon the earth, insensible. Richard Swiveller comes hastily up, elbows the bystanders out of the way, takes her (after some trouble) in one arm after the manner of theatrical ravishers, and, nodding to Kit, and commanding Barbara's mother to follow, for he has a coach waiting, bears her swiftly off.

Well; Richard took her home. And what astonishing absurdities in the way of quotation from song and poem he perpetrated on the road, no man knows. He took her home, and stayed till she was recovered; and, having no money to pay the coach, went back in state to Bevis Marks, bidding the driver (for it was Saturday night) wait at the door while he went in for 'change.'

'Mr Richard, sir,' said Brass cheerfully, 'Good evening!'

Monstrous as Kit's tale had appeared, at first, Mr Richard did, that night, half suspect his affable employer of some deep villany. Perhaps it was but the misery he had just witnessed which gave his careless nature this impulse; but, be that as it may, it was very strong upon him, and he said in as few words as possible, what he wanted.

'Money?' cried Brass, taking out his purse. 'Ha ha! To be sure, Mr Richard, to be sure, sir. All men must live. You haven't change for a five-pound note, have you sir?'

'No,' returned Dick, shortly.

'Oh!' said Brass, 'here's the very sum. That saves trouble. You're very welcome I'm sure.— Mr Richard, sir—'

Dick, who had by this time reached the door, turned round.

'You needn't,' said Brass, 'trouble yourself to come back any more, Sir.'

'Eh?'

'You see, Mr Richard,' said Brass, thrusting his hands in his pockets, and rocking himself to and fro on his stool, 'the fact is, that a man of your abilities is lost, Sir, quite lost, in our dry and mouldy line. It's terrible drudgery—shocking. I should say, now, that the stage, or the—or the army, Mr Richard—or something very superior in the licensed victualling way—was the kind of thing that would call out the genius of such a man as you. I hope you'll look in to see us now and then. Sally, Sir, will be delighted I'm sure. She's extremely sorry to lose you, Mr Richard, but a sense of her duty to society reconciles her. An amazing creature that, sir! You'll find the money quite correct, I think. There's a cracked window sir, but I've not made any deduction on that account. Whenever we part with friends, Mr Richard, let us part liberally. A delightful sentiment, sir!'

To all these rambling observations, Mr Swiveller answered not one word, but, returning for the aquatic jacket, rolled it into a tight round ball: looking steadily at Brass meanwhile as if he had some intention of bowling him down with it. He only took it under his arm, however, and marched out of the office in profound silence. When he had closed the door, he re-opened it, stared in again for a few moments with the same portentous gravity, and nodding his head once, in a slow and ghost-like manner, vanished.

He paid the coachman, and turned his back on Bevis Marks, big with great designs for the comforting of Kit's mother and the aid of Kit himself.

But the lives of gentlemen devoted to such pleasures as Richard Swiveller, are extremely precarious. The spiritual excitement of the last fortnight, working upon a system affected in no slight degree by the spirituous excitement of some years, proved a little too much for him. That very night, Mr Richard was seized with an alarming illness, and in twenty-four hours was stricken with a raging fever.

CHAPTER 64

Tossing to and fro upon his hot, uneasy bed; tormented by a fierce thirst which nothing could appease; unable to find, in any change of posture, a moment's peace or ease; and rambling, ever, through deserts of thought where there was no resting-place, no sight or sound suggestive of refreshment or repose, nothing but a dull eternal weariness, with no change but the restless shiftings of his miserable body, and the weary wandering of his mind, constant still to one ever-present anxiety—to a sense of something left undone, of some fearful obstacle to be surmounted, of some carking care that would not be driven away, and which haunted the distempered brain, now in this form, now in that, always shadowy and dim, but recognisable for the same phantom in every shape it took: darkening every vision like an evil conscience, and making slumber horrible—in these slow tortures of his dread disease, the unfortunate Richard lay wasting and consuming inch by inch, until, at last, when he seemed to fight and struggle to rise up, and to be held down by devils, he sank into a deep sleep, and dreamed no more.

He awoke. With a sensation of most blissful rest, better than sleep itself, he began gradually to remember something of these sufferings, and to think what a long night it had been, and whether he had not been delirious twice or thrice. Happening, in the midst of these cogitations, to raise his hand, he was astonished to find how heavy it seemed, and yet how thin and light it really was. Still, he felt indifferent and happy; and having no curiosity to pursue the subject, remained in the same waking slumber until his attention was attracted by a cough. This made him doubt whether he had locked his door last night, and feel a little surprised at having a companion in the room. Still, he lacked energy to follow up this train of thought; and unconsciously fell, in a luxury of repose, to staring at some green stripes on the bed-furniture, and associating them strangely with patches of fresh turf, while the yellow ground between made gravel-walks, and so helped out a long perspective of trim gardens.

He was rambling in imagination on these terraces, and had quite lost himself among them indeed, when he heard the cough once more. The walks shrunk into stripes again at the sound, and raising himself a little in the bed, and holding the curtain open with one hand, he looked out.

The same room certainly, and still by candlelight; but with what unbounded astonishment did he see all those bottles, and basins, and articles of linen airing by the fire, and such-like furniture of a sick chamber—all very clean and neat, but all quite different from anything he had left there, when he went to bed! The atmosphere, too, filled with a cool smell of herbs and vinegar; the floor newly sprinkled; the—the what? The Marchioness?

Yes; playing cribbage with herself at the table. There she sat, intent upon her game, coughing now and then in a subdued manner as if she feared to disturb him—shuffling the cards, cutting, dealing, playing, counting, pegging—going through all the mysteries of cribbage as if she had been in full practice from her cradle! Mr Swiveller contemplated these things for a short time, and suffering the curtain to fall into its former position, laid his head on the pillow again.

'I'm dreaming,' thought Richard, 'that's clear. When I went to bed, my hands were not made of egg-shells; and now I can almost see through 'em. If this is not a dream, I have woke up, by mistake, in an Arabian Night, instead of a London one. But I have no doubt I'm asleep.

Not the least.'

Here the small servant had another cough.

'Very remarkable!' thought Mr Swiveller. 'I never dreamt such a real cough as that before. I don't know, indeed, that I ever dreamt either a cough or a sneeze. Perhaps it's part of the philosophy of dreams that one never does. There's another—and another—I say!—I'm dreaming rather fast!'

For the purpose of testing his real condition, Mr Swiveller, after some reflection, pinched himself in the arm.

'Queerer still!' he thought. 'I came to bed rather plump than otherwise, and now there's nothing to lay hold of. I'll take another survey.'

The result of this additional inspection was, to convince Mr Swiveller that the objects by which he was surrounded were real, and that he saw them, beyond all question, with his waking eyes.

'It's an Arabian Night; that's what it is,' said Richard. 'I'm in Damascus or Grand Cairo. The Marchioness is a Genie, and having had a wager with another Genie about who is the handsomest young man alive, and the worthiest to be the husband of the Princess of China, has brought me away, room and all, to compare us together. Perhaps,' said Mr Swiveller, turning languidly round on his pillow, and looking on that side of his bed which was next the wall, 'the Princess may be still—No, she's gone.'

Not feeling quite satisfied with this explanation, as, even taking it to be the correct one, it still involved a little mystery and doubt, Mr Swiveller raised the curtain again, determined to take the first favourable opportunity of addressing his companion. An occasion presented itself. The Marchioness dealt, turned up a knave, and omitted to take the usual advantage; upon which Mr Swiveller called out as loud as he could—'Two for his heels!'

The Marchioness jumped up quickly and clapped her hands. 'Arabian Night, certainly,' thought Mr Swiveller; 'they always clap their hands instead of ringing the bell. Now for the two thousand black slaves, with jars of jewels on their heads!'

It appeared, however, that she had only clapped her hands for joy; for directly afterward she began to laugh, and then to cry; declaring, not in choice Arabic but in familiar English, that she was 'so glad, she didn't know what to do.'

'Marchioness,' said Mr Swiveller, thoughtfully, 'be pleased to draw nearer. First of all, will you have the goodness to inform me where I shall find my voice; and secondly, what has become of my flesh?'

The Marchioness only shook her head mournfully, and cried again; whereupon Mr Swiveller (being very weak) felt his own eyes affected likewise.

'I begin to infer, from your manner, and these appearances, Marchioness,' said Richard after a pause, and smiling with a trembling lip, 'that I have been ill.'

'You just have!' replied the small servant, wiping her eyes. 'And haven't you been a talking nonsense!'

'Oh!' said Dick. 'Very ill, Marchioness, have I been?'

'Dead, all but,' replied the small servant. 'I never thought you'd get better. Thank Heaven you have!'

Mr Swiveller was silent for a long while. By and bye, he began to talk again, inquiring how long he had been there.

'Three weeks to-morrow,' replied the servant.

'Three what?' said Dick.

'Weeks,' returned the Marchioness emphatically; 'three long, slow weeks.'

The bare thought of having been in such extremity, caused Richard to fall into another silence, and to lie flat down again, at his full length. The Marchioness, having arranged the bed-clothes more comfortably, and felt that his hands and forehead were quite cool—a discovery that filled her with delight—cried a little more, and then applied herself to getting tea ready, and making some thin dry toast.

While she was thus engaged, Mr Swiveller looked on with a grateful heart, very much astonished to see how thoroughly at home she made herself, and attributing this attention, in its origin, to Sally Brass, whom, in his own mind, he could not thank enough. When the Marchioness had finished her toasting, she spread a clean cloth on a tray, and brought him some crisp slices and a great basin of weak tea, with which (she said) the doctor had left word he might refresh himself when he awoke. She propped him up with pillows, if not as skilfully as if she had been a professional nurse all her life, at least as tenderly; and looked on with unutterable satisfaction while the patient—stopping every now and then to shake her by the hand—took his poor meal with an appetite and relish, which the greatest dainties of the earth, under any other circumstances, would have failed to provoke. Having cleared away, and disposed everything comfortably about him again, she sat down at the table to take her own tea.

'Marchioness,' said Mr Swiveller, 'how's Sally?'

The small servant screwed her face into an expression of the very uttermost entanglement of slyness, and shook her head.

'What, haven't you seen her lately?' said Dick.

'Seen her!' cried the small servant. 'Bless you, I've run away!'

Mr Swiveller immediately laid himself down again quite flat, and so remained for about five minutes. By slow degrees he resumed his sitting posture after that lapse of time, and inquired:

'And where do you live, Marchioness?'

'Live!' cried the small servant. 'Here!'

'Oh!' said Mr Swiveller.

And with that he fell down flat again, as suddenly as if he had been shot. Thus he remained, motionless and bereft of speech, until she had finished her meal, put everything in its place, and swept the hearth; when he motioned her to bring a chair to the bedside, and, being propped up again, opened a farther conversation.

'And so,' said Dick, 'you have run away?'

'Yes,' said the Marchioness, 'and they've been a tizing of me.'

'Been—I beg your pardon,' said Dick—'what have they been doing?'

'Been a tizing of me—tizing you know—in the newspapers,' rejoined the Marchioness.

'Aye, aye,' said Dick, 'advertising?'

The small servant nodded, and winked. Her eyes were so red with waking and crying, that the Tragic Muse might have winked with greater consistency. And so Dick felt.

'Tell me,' said he, 'how it was that you thought of coming here.'

'Why, you see,' returned the Marchioness, 'when you was gone, I hadn't any friend at all, because the lodger he never come back, and I didn't know where either him or you was to be found, you know. But one morning, when I was—'

'Was near a keyhole?' suggested Mr Swiveller, observing that she faltered.

'Well then,' said the small servant, nodding; 'when I was near the office keyhole—as you see me through, you know—I heard somebody saying that she lived here, and was the lady whose house you lodged at, and that you was took very bad, and wouldn't nobody come and take care of you. Mr Brass, he says, "It's no business of mine," he says; and Miss Sally, she says, "He's a funny chap, but it's no business of mine;" and the lady went away, and slammed the door to, when she went out, I can tell you. So I run away that night, and come here, and told 'em you was my brother, and they believed me, and I've been here ever since.'

'This poor little Marchioness has been wearing herself to death!' cried Dick.

'No I haven't,' she returned, 'not a bit of it. Don't you mind about me. I like sitting up, and I've often had a sleep, bless you, in one of them chairs. But if you could have seen how you tried to jump out o' winder, and if you could have heard how you used to keep on singing and making speeches, you wouldn't have believed it—I'm so glad you're better, Mr Liverer.'

'Liverer indeed!' said Dick thoughtfully. 'It's well I am a liverer. I strongly suspect I should have died, Marchioness, but for you.'

At this point, Mr Swiveller took the small servant's hand in his again, and being, as we have seen, but poorly, might in struggling to express his thanks have made his eyes as red as hers, but that she quickly changed the theme by making him lie down, and urging him to keep very quiet.

'The doctor,' she told him, 'said you was to be kept quite still, and there was to be no noise nor nothing. Now, take a rest, and then we'll talk again. I'll sit by you, you know. If you shut your eyes, perhaps you'll go to sleep. You'll be all the better for it, if you do.'

The Marchioness, in saying these words, brought a little table to the bedside, took her seat at it, and began to work away at the concoction of some cooling drink, with the address of a score of chemists. Richard Swiveller being indeed fatigued, fell into a slumber, and waking in about half an hour, inquired what time it was.

'Just gone half after six,' replied his small friend, helping him to sit up again.

'Marchioness,' said Richard, passing his hand over his forehead and turning suddenly round, as though the subject but that moment flashed upon him, 'what has become of Kit?'

He had been sentenced to transportation for a great many years, she said.

'Has he gone?' asked Dick—'his mother—how is she,—what has become of her?'

His nurse shook her head, and answered that she knew nothing about them. 'But, if I thought,' said she, very slowly, 'that you'd keep quiet, and not put yourself into another fever, I could tell you—but I won't now.'

'Yes, do,' said Dick. 'It will amuse me.'

'Oh! would it though!' rejoined the small servant, with a horrified look. 'I know better than that. Wait till you're better and then I'll tell you.'

Dick looked very earnestly at his little friend: and his eyes, being large and hollow from illness, assisted the expression so much, that she was quite frightened, and besought him not to think any more about it. What had already fallen from her, however, had not only piqued his curiosity, but seriously alarmed him, wherefore he urged her to tell him the worst at once.

'Oh there's no worst in it,' said the small servant. 'It hasn't anything to do with you.'

'Has it anything to do with—is it anything you heard through chinks or keyholes—and that you were not intended to hear?' asked Dick, in a breathless state.

'Yes,' replied the small servant.

'In—in Bevis Marks?' pursued Dick hastily. 'Conversations between Brass and Sally?'

'Yes,' cried the small servant again.

Richard Swiveller thrust his lank arm out of bed, and, gripping her by the wrist and drawing her close to him, bade her out with it, and freely too, or he would not answer for the consequences; being wholly unable to endure the state of excitement and expectation. She, seeing that he was greatly agitated, and that the effects of postponing her revelation might be much more injurious than any that were likely to ensue from its being made at once, promised compliance, on condition that the patient kept himself perfectly quiet, and abstained from starting up or tossing about.

'But if you begin to do that,' said the small servant, 'I'll leave off. And so I tell you.'

'You can't leave off, till you have gone on,' said Dick. 'And do go on, there's a darling. Speak, sister, speak. Pretty Polly say. Oh tell me when, and tell me where, pray Marchioness, I beseech you!'

Unable to resist these fervent adjurations, which Richard Swiveller poured out as passionately as if they had been of the most solemn and tremendous nature, his companion spoke thus:

'Well! Before I run away, I used to sleep in the kitchen—where we played cards, you know. Miss Sally used to keep the key of the kitchen door in her pocket, and she always come down at night to take away the candle and rake out the fire. When she had done that, she left me to go to bed in the dark, locked the door on the outside, put the key in her pocket again, and kept me locked up till she come down in the morning—very early I can tell you—and let me out. I was terrible afraid of being kept like this, because if there was a fire, I thought they might forget me and only take care of themselves you know. So, whenever I see an old rusty key anywhere, I picked it up and tried if it would fit the door, and at last I found in the dust cellar a key that did fit it.'

Here, Mr Swiveller made a violent demonstration with his legs. But the small servant immediately pausing in her talk, he subsided again, and pleading a momentary forgetfulness of their compact, entreated her to proceed.

'They kept me very short,' said the small servant. 'Oh! you can't think how short they kept me! So I used to come out at night after they'd gone to bed, and feel about in the dark for bits of biscuit, or sangwitches that you'd left in the office, or even pieces of orange peel to put into cold water and make believe it was wine. Did you ever taste orange peel and water?'

Mr Swiveller replied that he had never tasted that ardent liquor; and once more urged his friend to resume the thread of her narrative.

'If you make believe very much, it's quite nice,' said the small servant, 'but if you don't, you know, it seems as if it would bear a little more seasoning, certainly. Well, sometimes I used to come out after they'd gone to bed, and sometimes before, you know; and one or two nights before there was all that precious noise in the office—when the young man was took, I mean—I come upstairs while Mr Brass and Miss Sally was a-sittin' at the office fire; and I tell you the truth, that I come to listen again, about the key of the safe.'

Mr Swiveller gathered up his knees so as to make a great cone of the bedclothes, and conveyed into his countenance an expression of the utmost concern. But the small servant pausing, and holding up her finger, the cone gently disappeared, though the look of concern did not.

'There was him and her,' said the small servant, 'a-sittin' by the fire, and talking softly together. Mr Brass says to Miss Sally, "Upon my word," he says "it's a dangerous thing, and it might get us into a world of trouble, and I don't half like it." She says—you know her way—she says, "You're the chickenest-hearted, feeblest, faintest man I ever see, and I think," she says, "that I ought to have been the brother, and you the sister. Isn't Quilp," she says, "our principal support?" "He certainly is," says Mr Brass, "And an't we," she says, "constantly ruining somebody or other in the way of business?" "We certainly are," says Mr Brass. "Then does it signify," she says, "about ruining this Kit when Quilp desires it?" "It certainly does not signify," says Mr Brass. Then they whispered and laughed for a long time about there being no danger if it was well done, and then Mr Brass pulls out his pocket-book, and says, "Well," he says, "here it is—Quilp's own five-pound note. We'll agree that way, then," he says. "Kit's coming to-morrow morning, I know. While he's up-stairs, you'll get out of the way, and I'll clear off Mr Richard. Having Kit alone, I'll hold him in conversation, and put this property in his hat. I'll manage so, besides," he says, "that Mr Richard shall find it there, and be the evidence. And if that don't get Christopher out of Mr Quilp's way, and satisfy Mr Quilp's grudges," he says, "the Devil's in it." Miss Sally laughed, and said that was the plan, and as they seemed to be moving away, and I was afraid to stop any longer, I went down-stairs again.—There!'

The small servant had gradually worked herself into as much agitation as Mr Swiveller, and therefore made no effort to restrain him when he sat up in bed and hastily demanded whether this story had been told to anybody.

'How could it be?' replied his nurse. 'I was almost afraid to think about it, and hoped the young man would be let off. When I heard 'em say they had found him guilty of what he didn't do, you was gone, and so was the lodger—though I think I should have been frightened to tell him, even if he'd been there. Ever since I come here, you've been out of your senses, and what would have been the good of telling you then?'

'Marchioness,' said Mr Swiveller, plucking off his nightcap and flinging it to the other end of the room; 'if you'll do me the favour to retire for a few minutes and see what sort of a night it is, I'll get up.'

'You mustn't think of such a thing,' cried his nurse.

'I must indeed,' said the patient, looking round the room. 'Whereabouts are my clothes?'

'Oh, I'm so glad—you haven't got any,' replied the Marchioness.

'Ma'am!' said Mr Swiveller, in great astonishment.

'I've been obliged to sell them, every one, to get the things that was ordered for you. But don't take on about that,' urged the Marchioness, as Dick fell back upon his pillow. 'You're too weak to stand, indeed.'

'I am afraid,' said Richard dolefully, 'that you're right. What ought I to do! what is to be done!'

It naturally occurred to him on very little reflection, that the first step to take would be to communicate with one of the Mr Garlands instantly. It was very possible that Mr Abel had not yet left the office. In as little time as it takes to tell it, the small servant had the address in pencil on a piece of paper; a verbal description of father and son, which would enable her to recognise either, without difficulty; and a special caution to be shy of Mr Chuckster, in consequence of that gentleman's known antipathy to Kit. Armed with these slender powers, she hurried away, commissioned to bring either old Mr Garland or Mr Abel, bodily, to that apartment.

'I suppose,' said Dick, as she closed the door slowly, and peeped into the room again, to make sure that he was comfortable, 'I suppose there's nothing left—not so much as a waistcoat even?'

'No, nothing.'

'It's embarrassing,' said Mr Swiveller, 'in case of fire—even an umbrella would be something—but you did quite right, dear Marchioness. I should have died without you!'

CHAPTER 65

It was well for the small servant that she was of a sharp, quick nature, or the consequence of sending her out alone, from the very neighbourhood in which it was most dangerous for her to appear, would probably have been the restoration of Miss Sally Brass to the supreme authority over her person. Not unmindful of the risk she ran, however, the Marchioness no sooner left the house than she dived into the first dark by-way that presented itself, and, without any present reference to the point to which her journey tended, made it her first business to put two good miles of brick and mortar between herself and Bevis Marks.

When she had accomplished this object, she began to shape her course for the notary's office, to which—shrewdly inquiring of apple-women and oyster-sellers at street-corners, rather than in lighted shops or of well-dressed people, at the hazard of attracting notice—she easily procured a direction. As carrier-pigeons, on being first let loose in a strange place, beat the air at random for a short time before darting off towards the spot for which they are designed, so did the Marchioness flutter round and round until she believed herself in safety, and then bear swiftly down upon the port for which she was bound.

She had no bonnet—nothing on her head but a great cap which, in some old time, had been worn by Sally Brass, whose taste in head-dresses was, as we have seen, peculiar—and her speed was rather retarded than assisted by her shoes, which, being extremely large and slipshod, flew off every now and then, and were difficult to find again, among the crowd of passengers. Indeed, the poor little creature experienced so much trouble and delay from having to grope for these articles of dress in mud and kennel, and suffered in these researches so much jostling, pushing, squeezing and bandying from hand to hand, that by the time she reached the street in which the notary lived, she was fairly worn out and exhausted, and could not refrain from tears.

But to have got there at last was a great comfort, especially as there were lights still burning in the office window, and therefore some hope that she was not too late. So the Marchioness dried her eyes with the backs of her hands, and, stealing softly up the steps, peeped in through the glass door.

Mr Chuckster was standing behind the lid of his desk, making such preparations towards finishing off for the night, as pulling down his wristbands and pulling up his shirt-collar, settling his neck more gracefully in his stock, and secretly arranging his whiskers by the aid of a little triangular bit of looking glass. Before the ashes of the fire stood two gentlemen, one of whom she rightly judged to be the notary, and the other (who was buttoning his great-coat and was evidently about to depart immediately) Mr Abel Garland.

Having made these observations, the small spy took counsel with herself, and resolved to wait in the street until Mr Abel came out, as there would be then no fear of having to speak before Mr Chuckster, and less difficulty in delivering her message. With this purpose she slipped out again, and crossing the road, sat down upon a door-step just opposite.

She had hardly taken this position, when there came dancing up the street, with his legs all wrong, and his head everywhere by turns, a pony. This pony had a little phaeton behind him, and a man in it; but neither man nor phaeton seemed to embarrass him in the least, as he reared up on his hind legs, or stopped, or went on, or stood still again, or backed, or went side-ways, without the smallest reference to them—just as the fancy seized him, and as if he were the freest animal in creation. When they came to the notary's door, the man called out in a very respectful manner, 'Woa then'—intimating that if he might venture to express a wish, it would be that they stopped there. The pony made a moment's pause; but, as if it occurred to him that to stop when he was required might be to establish an inconvenient and dangerous precedent, he immediately started off again, rattled at a fast trot to the street corner, wheeled round, came back, and then stopped of his own accord.

'Oh! you're a precious creatur!' said the man—who didn't venture by the bye to come out in his true colours until he was safe on the pavement. 'I wish I had the rewarding of you—I do.'

'What has he been doing?' said Mr Abel, tying a shawl round his neck as he came down the steps.

'He's enough to fret a man's heart out,' replied the hostler. 'He is the most wicious rascal—Woa then, will you?'

'He'll never stand still, if you call him names,' said Mr Abel, getting in, and taking the reins. 'He's a very good fellow if you know how to manage him. This is the first time he has been out, this long while, for he has lost his old driver and wouldn't stir for anybody else, till this morning. The lamps are right, are they? That's well. Be here to take him to-morrow, if you please. Good night!'

And, after one or two strange plunges, quite of his own invention, the pony yielded to Mr Abel's mildness, and trotted gently off.

All this time Mr Chuckster had been standing at the door, and the small servant had been afraid to approach. She had nothing for it now, therefore, but to run after the chaise, and to call to Mr Abel to stop. Being out of breath when she came up with it, she was unable to make him hear. The case was desperate; for the pony was quickening his pace. The Marchioness hung on behind for a few moments, and, feeling that she could go no farther, and must soon yield, clambered by a vigorous effort into the hinder seat, and in so doing lost one of the shoes for ever.

Mr Abel being in a thoughtful frame of mind, and having quite enough to do to keep the pony going, went jogging on without looking round: little dreaming of the strange figure that was close behind him, until the Marchioness, having in some degree recovered her breath, and the loss of her shoe, and the novelty of her position, uttered close into his ear, the words—'I say, Sir'—

He turned his head quickly enough then, and stopping the pony, cried, with some trepidation, 'God bless me, what is this!'

'Don't be frightened, Sir,' replied the still panting messenger. 'Oh I've run such a way after you!'

'What do you want with me?' said Mr Abel. 'How did you come here?'

'I got in behind,' replied the Marchioness. 'Oh please drive on, sir—don't stop—and go towards the City, will you? And oh do please make haste, because it's of consequence. There's somebody wants to see you there. He sent me to say would you come directly, and that he knowed all about Kit, and could save him yet, and prove his innocence.'

'What do you tell me, child?'

'The truth, upon my word and honour I do. But please to drive on— quick, please! I've been such a time gone, he'll think I'm lost.'

Mr Abel involuntarily urged the pony forward. The pony, impelled by some secret sympathy or some new caprice, burst into a great pace, and neither slackened it, nor indulged in any eccentric performances, until they arrived at the door of Mr Swiveller's lodging, where, marvellous to relate, he consented to stop when Mr Abel checked him.

'See! It's the room up there,' said the Marchioness, pointing to one where there was a faint light. 'Come!'

Mr Abel, who was one of the simplest and most retiring creatures in existence, and naturally timid withal, hesitated; for he had heard of people being decoyed into strange places to be robbed and murdered, under circumstances very like the present, and, for anything he knew to the contrary, by guides very like the Marchioness. His regard for Kit, however, overcame every other consideration. So, entrusting Whisker to the charge of a man who was lingering hard by in expectation of the job, he suffered his companion to take his hand, and to lead him up the dark and narrow stairs.

He was not a little surprised to find himself conducted into a dimly-lighted sick chamber, where a man was sleeping tranquilly in bed.

'An't it nice to see him lying there so quiet?' said his guide, in an earnest whisper. 'Oh! you'd say it was, if you had only seen him two or three days ago.'

Mr Abel made no answer, and, to say the truth, kept a long way from the bed and very near the door. His guide, who appeared to understand his reluctance, trimmed the candle, and taking it in her hand, approached the bed. As she did so, the sleeper started up, and he recognised in the wasted face the features of Richard Swiveller.

'Why, how is this?' said Mr Abel kindly, as he hurried towards him. 'You have been ill?'

'Very,' replied Dick. 'Nearly dead. You might have chanced to hear of your Richard on his bier, but for the friend I sent to fetch you. Another shake of the hand, Marchioness, if you please. Sit down, Sir.'

Mr Abel seemed rather astonished to hear of the quality of his guide, and took a chair by the bedside.

'I have sent for you, Sir,' said Dick—'but she told you on what account?'

'She did. I am quite bewildered by all this. I really don't know what to say or think,' replied Mr Abel.

'You'll say that presently,' retorted Dick. 'Marchioness, take a seat on the bed, will you? Now, tell this gentleman all that you told me; and be particular. Don't you speak another word, Sir.'

The story was repeated; it was, in effect, exactly the same as before, without any deviation or omission. Richard Swiveller kept his eyes fixed on his visitor during its narration, and directly it was concluded, took the word again.

'You have heard it all, and you'll not forget it. I'm too giddy and too queer to suggest anything; but you and your friends will know what to do. After this long delay, every minute is an age. If ever you went home fast in your life, go home fast to-night. Don't stop to say one word to me, but go. She will be found here, whenever she's wanted; and as to me, you're pretty sure to find me at home, for a week or two. There are more reasons than one for that. Marchioness, a light! If you lose another minute in looking at me, sir, I'll never forgive you!'

Mr Abel needed no more remonstrance or persuasion. He was gone in an instant; and the Marchioness, returning from lighting him down-stairs, reported that the pony, without any preliminary objection whatever, had dashed away at full gallop.

'That's right!' said Dick; 'and hearty of him; and I honour him from this time. But get some supper and a mug of beer, for I am sure you must be tired. Do have a mug of beer. It will do me as much good to see you take it as if I might drink it myself.'

Nothing but this assurance could have prevailed upon the small nurse to indulge in such a luxury. Having eaten and drunk to Mr Swiveller's extreme contentment, given him his drink, and put everything in neat order, she wrapped herself in an old coverlet and lay down upon the rug before the fire.

Mr Swiveller was by that time murmuring in his sleep, 'Strew then, oh strew, a bed of rushes. Here will we stay, till morning blushes. Good night, Marchioness!'

CHAPTER 66

On awaking in the morning, Richard Swiveller became conscious, by slow degrees, of whispering voices in his room. Looking out between the curtains, he espied Mr Garland, Mr Abel, the notary, and the single gentleman, gathered round the Marchioness, and talking to her with great earnestness but in very subdued tones—fearing, no doubt, to disturb him. He lost no time in letting them know that this precaution was unnecessary, and all four gentlemen directly approached his bedside. Old Mr Garland was the first to stretch out his hand, and inquire how he felt.

Dick was about to answer that he felt much better, though still as weak as need be, when his little nurse, pushing the visitors aside and pressing up to his pillow as if in jealousy of their interference, set his breakfast before him, and insisted on his taking it before he underwent the fatigue of speaking or of being spoken to. Mr Swiveller, who was perfectly ravenous, and had had, all night, amazingly distinct and consistent dreams of mutton chops, double stout, and similar delicacies, felt even the weak tea and dry toast such irresistible temptations, that he consented to eat and drink on one condition.

'And that is,' said Dick, returning the pressure of Mr Garland's hand, 'that you answer me this question truly, before I take a bit or drop. Is it too late?'

'For completing the work you began so well last night?' returned the old gentleman. 'No. Set your mind at rest on that point. It is not, I assure you.'

Comforted by this intelligence, the patient applied himself to his food with a keen appetite, though evidently not with a greater zest in the eating than his nurse appeared to have in seeing him eat. The manner of this meal was this:—Mr Swiveller, holding the slice of toast or cup of tea in his left hand, and taking a bite or drink, as the case might be, constantly kept, in his right, one palm of the Marchioness tight locked; and to shake, or even to kiss this imprisoned hand, he would stop every now and then, in the very act of swallowing, with perfect seriousness of intention, and the utmost gravity. As often as he put anything into his mouth, whether for eating or drinking, the face of the Marchioness lighted up beyond all description; but whenever he gave her one or other of these tokens of recognition, her countenance became overshadowed, and she began to sob. Now, whether she was in her laughing joy, or in her crying one, the Marchioness could not help turning to the visitors with an appealing look, which seemed to say, 'You see this fellow—can I help this?'—and they, being thus made, as it were, parties to the scene, as regularly answered by another look, 'No. Certainly not.' This dumb-show, taking place during the whole time of the invalid's breakfast, and the invalid himself, pale and emaciated, performing no small part in the same, it may be fairly questioned whether at any meal, where no word, good or bad, was spoken from beginning to end, so much was expressed by gestures in themselves so slight and unimportant.

At length—and to say the truth before very long—Mr Swiveller had despatched as much toast and tea as in that stage of his recovery it was discreet to let him have. But the cares of the Marchioness did not stop here; for, disappearing for an instant and presently returning with a basin of fair water, she laved his face and hands, brushed his hair, and in short made him as spruce and smart as anybody under such circumstances could be made; and all this, in as brisk and business-like a manner, as if he were a very little boy, and she his grown-up nurse. To these various attentions, Mr Swiveller submitted in a kind of grateful astonishment beyond the reach of language. When they were at last brought to an end, and the Marchioness had withdrawn into a distant corner to take her own poor breakfast (cold enough by that time), he turned his face away for some few moments, and shook hands heartily with the air.

'Gentlemen,' said Dick, rousing himself from this pause, and turning round again, 'you'll excuse me. Men who have been brought so low as I have been, are easily fatigued. I am fresh again now, and fit for talking. We're short of chairs here, among other trifles, but if you'll do me the favour to sit upon the bed—'

'What can we do for you?' said Mr Garland, kindly.

'If you could make the Marchioness yonder, a Marchioness, in real, sober earnest,' returned Dick, 'I'd thank you to get it done off-hand. But as you can't, and as the question is not what you will do for me, but what you will do for somebody else who has a better claim upon you, pray sir let me know what you intend doing.'

'It's chiefly on that account that we have come just now,' said the single gentleman, 'for you will have another visitor presently. We feared you would be anxious unless you knew from ourselves what steps we intended to take, and therefore came to you before we stirred in the matter.'

'Gentlemen,' returned Dick, 'I thank you. Anybody in the helpless state that you see me in, is naturally anxious. Don't let me interrupt you, sir.'

'Then, you see, my good fellow,' said the single gentleman, 'that while we have no doubt whatever of the truth of this disclosure, which has so providentially come to light—'

'Meaning hers?' said Dick, pointing towards the Marchioness.

'—Meaning hers, of course. While we have no doubt of that, or that a proper use of it would procure the poor lad's immediate pardon and liberation, we have a great doubt whether it would, by itself, enable us to reach Quilp, the chief agent in this villany. I should tell you that this doubt has been confirmed into something very nearly approaching certainty by the best opinions we have been enabled, in this short space of time, to take upon the subject. You'll agree with us, that to give him even the most distant chance of escape, if we could help it, would be monstrous. You say with us, no doubt, if somebody must escape, let it be any one but he.'

'Yes,' returned Dick, 'certainly. That is if somebody must—but upon my word, I'm unwilling that anybody should. Since laws were made for every degree, to curb vice in others as well as in me—and so forth you know—doesn't it strike you in that light?'

The single gentleman smiled as if the light in which Mr Swiveller had put the question were not the clearest in the world, and proceeded to explain that they contemplated proceeding by stratagem in the first instance; and that their design was to endeavour to extort a confession from the gentle Sarah.

'When she finds how much we know, and how we know it,' he said, 'and that she is clearly compromised already, we are not without strong hopes that we may be enabled through her means to punish the other two effectually. If we could do that, she might go scot-free for aught I cared.'

Dick received this project in anything but a gracious manner, representing with as much warmth as he was then capable of showing, that they would find the old buck (meaning Sarah) more difficult to manage than Quilp himself—that, for any tampering, terrifying, or cajolery, she was a very unpromising and unyielding subject—that she was of a kind of brass not easily melted or moulded into shape—in short, that they were no match for her, and would be signally defeated. But it was in vain to urge them to adopt some other course. The single gentleman has been described as explaining their joint intentions, but it should have been written that they all spoke together; that if any one of them by chance held his peace for a moment, he stood gasping and panting for an opportunity to strike in again: in a word, that they had reached that pitch of impatience and anxiety where men can neither be persuaded nor reasoned with; and that it would have been as easy to turn the most impetuous wind that ever blew, as to prevail on them to reconsider their determination. So, after telling Mr Swiveller how they had not lost sight of Kit's mother and the children; how they had never once even lost sight of Kit himself, but had been unremitting in their endeavours to procure a mitigation of his sentence; how they had been perfectly distracted between the strong proofs of his guilt, and their own fading hopes of his innocence; and how he, Richard Swiveller, might keep his mind at rest, for everything should be happily adjusted between that time and night;—after telling him all this, and adding a great many kind and cordial expressions, personal to himself, which it is unnecessary to recite, Mr Garland, the notary, and the single gentleman, took their leaves at a very critical time, or Richard Swiveller must assuredly have been driven into another fever, whereof the results might have been fatal.

Mr Abel remained behind, very often looking at his watch and at the room door, until Mr Swiveller was roused from a short nap, by the setting-down on the landing-place outside, as from the shoulders of a porter, of some giant load, which seemed to shake the house, and made the little physic bottles on the mantel-shelf ring again. Directly this sound reached his ears, Mr Abel started up, and hobbled to the door, and opened it; and behold! there stood a strong man, with a mighty hamper, which, being hauled into the room and presently unpacked, disgorged such treasures as tea, and coffee, and wine, and rusks, and oranges, and grapes, and fowls ready trussed for boiling, and calves'-foot jelly, and arrow-root, and sago, and other delicate restoratives, that the small servant, who had never thought it possible that such things could be, except in shops, stood rooted to the spot in her one shoe, with her mouth and eyes watering in unison, and her power of speech quite gone. But, not so Mr Abel; or the strong man who emptied the hamper, big as it was, in a twinkling; and not so the nice old lady, who appeared so suddenly that she might have come out of the hamper too (it was quite large enough), and who, bustling about on tiptoe and without noise—now here, now there, now everywhere at once—began to fill out the jelly in tea-cups, and to make chicken broth in small saucepans, and to peel oranges for the sick man and to cut them up in little pieces, and to ply the small servant with glasses of wine and choice bits of everything until more substantial meat could be prepared for her refreshment. The whole of which appearances were so unexpected and bewildering, that Mr Swiveller, when he had taken two oranges and a little jelly, and had seen the strong man walk off with the empty basket, plainly leaving all that abundance for his use and benefit, was fain to lie down and fall asleep again, from sheer inability to entertain such wonders in his mind.

Meanwhile, the single gentleman, the Notary, and Mr Garland, repaired to a certain coffee-house, and from that place indited and sent a letter to Miss Sally Brass, requesting her, in terms mysterious and brief, to favour an unknown friend who wished to consult her, with her company there, as speedily as possible. The communication performed its errand so well, that within ten minutes of the messenger's return and report of its delivery, Miss Brass herself was announced.

'Pray ma'am,' said the single gentleman, whom she found alone in the room, 'take a chair.'

Miss Brass sat herself down, in a very stiff and frigid state, and seemed—as indeed she was—not a little astonished to find that the lodger and her mysterious correspondent were one and the same person.

'You did not expect to see me?' said the single gentleman.

'I didn't think much about it,' returned the beauty. 'I supposed it was business of some kind or other. If it's about the apartments, of course you'll give my brother regular notice, you know—or money. That's very easily settled. You're a responsible party, and in such a case lawful money and lawful notice are pretty much the same.'

'I am obliged to you for your good opinion,' retorted the single gentleman, 'and quite concur in these sentiments. But that is not the subject on which I wish to speak with you.'

'Oh!' said Sally. 'Then just state the particulars, will you? I suppose it's professional business?'

'Why, it is connected with the law, certainly.'

'Very well,' returned Miss Brass. 'My brother and I are just the same. I can take any instructions, or give you any advice.'

'As there are other parties interested besides myself,' said the single gentleman, rising and opening the door of an inner room, 'we had better confer together. Miss Brass is here, gentlemen.'

Mr Garland and the Notary walked in, looking very grave; and, drawing up two chairs, one on each side of the single gentleman, formed a kind of fence round the gentle Sarah, and penned her into a corner. Her brother Sampson under such circumstances would certainly have evinced some confusion or anxiety, but she—all composure—pulled out the tin box, and calmly took a pinch of snuff.

'Miss Brass,' said the Notary, taking the word at this crisis, 'we professional people understand each other, and, when we choose, can say what we have to say, in very few words. You advertised a runaway servant, the other day?'

'Well,' returned Miss Sally, with a sudden flush overspreading her features, 'what of that?'

'She is found, ma'am,' said the Notary, pulling out his pocket-handkerchief with a flourish. 'She is found.'

'Who found her?' demanded Sarah hastily.

'We did, ma'am—we three. Only last night, or you would have heard from us before.'

'And now I have heard from you,' said Miss Brass, folding her arms as though she were about to deny something to the death, 'what have you got to say? Something you have got into your heads about her, of course. Prove it, will you—that's all. Prove it. You have found her, you say. I can tell you (if you don't know it) that you have found the most artful, lying, pilfering, devilish little minx that was ever born.—Have you got her here?' she added, looking sharply round.

'No, she is not here at present,' returned the Notary. 'But she is quite safe.'

'Ha!' cried Sally, twitching a pinch of snuff out of her box, as spitefully as if she were in the very act of wrenching off the small servant's nose; 'she shall be safe enough from this time, I warrant you.'

'I hope so,' replied the Notary. 'Did it occur to you for the first time, when you found she had run away, that there were two keys to your kitchen door?'

Miss Sally took another pinch, and putting her head on one side, looked at her questioner, with a curious kind of spasm about her mouth, but with a cunning aspect of immense expression.

'Two keys,' repeated the Notary; 'one of which gave her the opportunities of roaming through the house at nights when you supposed her fast locked up, and of overhearing confidential consultations—among others, that particular conference, to be described to-day before a justice, which you will have an opportunity of hearing her relate; that conference which you and Mr Brass held together, on the night before that most unfortunate and innocent young man was accused of robbery, by a horrible device of which I will only say that it may be characterised by the epithets which you have applied to this wretched little witness, and by a few stronger ones besides.'

Sally took another pinch. Although her face was wonderfully composed, it was apparent that she was wholly taken by surprise, and that what she had expected to be taxed with, in connection with her small servant, was something very different from this.

'Come, come, Miss Brass,' said the Notary, 'you have great command of feature, but you feel, I see, that by a chance which never entered your imagination, this base design is revealed, and two of its plotters must be brought to justice. Now, you know the pains and penalties you are liable to, and so I need not dilate upon them, but I have a proposal to make to you. You have the honour of being sister to one of the greatest scoundrels unhung; and, if I may venture to say so to a lady, you are in every respect quite worthy of him. But connected with you two is a third party, a villain of the name of Quilp, the prime mover of the whole diabolical device, who I believe to be worse than either. For his sake, Miss Brass, do us the favour to reveal the whole history of this affair. Let me remind you that your doing so, at our instance, will place you in a safe and comfortable position—your present one is not desirable—and cannot injure your brother; for against him and you we have quite sufficient evidence (as you hear) already. I will not say to you that we suggest this course in mercy (for, to tell you the truth, we do not entertain any regard for you), but it is a necessity to which we are reduced, and I recommend it to you as a matter of the very best policy. Time,' said Mr Witherden, pulling out his watch, 'in a business like this, is exceedingly precious. Favour us with your decision as speedily as possible, ma'am.'

With a smile upon her face, and looking at each of the three by turns, Miss Brass took two or three more pinches of snuff, and having by this time very little left, travelled round and round the box with her forefinger and thumb, scraping up another. Having disposed of this likewise and put the box carefully in her pocket, she said,—

'I am to accept or reject at once, am I?'

'Yes,' said Mr Witherden.

The charming creature was opening her lips to speak in reply, when the door was hastily opened too, and the head of Sampson Brass was thrust into the room.

'Excuse me,' said the gentleman hastily. 'Wait a bit!'

So saying, and quite indifferent to the astonishment his presence occasioned, he crept in, shut the door, kissed his greasy glove as servilely as if it were the dust, and made a most abject bow.

'Sarah,' said Brass, 'hold your tongue if you please, and let me speak. Gentlemen, if I could express the pleasure it gives me to see three such men in a happy unity of feeling and concord of sentiment, I think you would hardly believe me. But though I am unfortunate— nay, gentlemen, criminal, if we are to use harsh expressions in a company like this—still, I have my feelings like other men. I have heard of a poet, who remarked that feelings were the common lot of all. If he could have been a pig, gentlemen, and have uttered that sentiment, he would still have been immortal.'

'If you're not an idiot,' said Miss Brass harshly, 'hold your peace.'

'Sarah, my dear,' returned her brother, 'thank you. But I know what I am about, my love, and will take the liberty of expressing myself accordingly. Mr Witherden, Sir, your handkerchief is hanging out of your pocket—would you allow me to—,

As Mr Brass advanced to remedy this accident, the Notary shrunk from him with an air of disgust. Brass, who over and above his usual prepossessing qualities, had a scratched face, a green shade over one eye, and a hat grievously crushed, stopped short, and looked round with a pitiful smile.

'He shuns me,' said Sampson, 'even when I would, as I may say, heap coals of fire upon his head. Well! Ah! But I am a falling house, and the rats (if I may be allowed the expression in reference to a gentleman I respect and love beyond everything) fly from me! Gentlemen— regarding your conversation just now, I happened to see my sister on her way here, and, wondering where she could be going to, and being—may I venture to say?—naturally of a suspicious turn, followed her. Since then, I have been listening.'

'If you're not mad,' interposed Miss Sally, 'stop there, and say no more.'

'Sarah, my dear,' rejoined Brass with undiminished politeness, 'I thank you kindly, but will still proceed. Mr Witherden, sir, as we have the honour to be members of the same profession—to say nothing of that other gentleman having been my lodger, and having partaken, as one may say, of the hospitality of my roof—I think you might have given me the refusal of this offer in the first instance. I do indeed. Now, my dear Sir,' cried Brass, seeing that the Notary was about to interrupt him, 'suffer me to speak, I beg.'

Mr Witherden was silent, and Brass went on.

'If you will do me the favour,' he said, holding up the green shade, and revealing an eye most horribly discoloured, 'to look at this, you will naturally inquire, in your own minds, how did I get it. If you look from that, to my face, you will wonder what could have been the cause of all these scratches. And if from them to my hat, how it came into the state in which you see it. Gentlemen,' said Brass, striking the hat fiercely with his clenched hand, 'to all these questions I answer—Quilp!'

The three gentlemen looked at each other, but said nothing.

'I say,' pursued Brass, glancing aside at his sister, as though he were talking for her information, and speaking with a snarling malignity, in violent contrast to his usual smoothness, 'that I answer to all these questions,—Quilp—Quilp, who deludes me into his infernal den, and takes a delight in looking on and chuckling while I scorch, and burn, and bruise, and maim myself—Quilp, who never once, no never once, in all our communications together, has treated me otherwise than as a dog—Quilp, whom I have always hated with my whole heart, but never so much as lately. He gives me the cold shoulder on this very matter as if he had had nothing to do with it, instead of being the first to propose it. I can't trust him. In one of his howling, raving, blazing humours, I believe he'd let it out, if it was murder, and never think of himself so long as he could terrify me. Now,' said Brass, picking up his hat again and replacing the shade over his eye, and actually crouching down, in the excess of his servility, 'what does all this lead to?—what should you say it led me to, gentlemen?—could you guess at all near the mark?'

Nobody spoke. Brass stood smirking for a little while, as if he had propounded some choice conundrum; and then said:

'To be short with you, then, it leads me to this. If the truth has come out, as it plainly has in a manner that there's no standing up against—and a very sublime and grand thing is Truth, gentlemen, in its way, though like other sublime and grand things, such as thunder-storms and that, we're not always over and above glad to see it—I had better turn upon this man than let this man turn upon me. It's clear to me that I am done for. Therefore, if anybody is to split, I had better be the person and have the advantage of it. Sarah, my dear, comparatively speaking you're safe. I relate these circumstances for my own profit.'

With that, Mr Brass, in a great hurry, revealed the whole story; bearing as heavily as possible on his amiable employer, and making himself out to be rather a saint-like and holy character, though subject—he acknowledged—to human weaknesses. He concluded thus:

'Now, gentlemen, I am not a man who does things by halves. Being in for a penny, I am ready, as the saying is, to be in for a pound. You must do with me what you please, and take me where you please. If you wish to have this in writing, we'll reduce it into manuscript immediately. You will be tender with me, I am sure. I am quite confident you will be tender with me. You are men of honour, and have feeling hearts. I yielded from necessity to Quilp, for though necessity has no law, she has her lawyers. I yield to you from necessity too; from policy besides; and because of feelings that have been a pretty long time working within me. Punish Quilp, gentlemen. Weigh heavily upon him. Grind him down. Tread him under foot. He has done as much by me, for many and many a day.'

Having now arrived at the conclusion of his discourse, Sampson checked the current of his wrath, kissed his glove again, and smiled as only parasites and cowards can.

'And this,' said Miss Brass, raising her head, with which she had hitherto sat resting on her hands, and surveying him from head to foot with a bitter sneer, 'this is my brother, is it! This is my brother, that I have worked and toiled for, and believed to have had something of the man in him!'

'Sarah, my dear,' returned Sampson, rubbing his hands feebly; 'you disturb our friends. Besides you—you're disappointed, Sarah, and, not knowing what you say, expose yourself.'

'Yes, you pitiful dastard,' retorted the lovely damsel, 'I understand you. You feared that I should be beforehand with you. But do you think that I would have been enticed to say a word! I'd have scorned it, if they had tried and tempted me for twenty years.'

'He he!' simpered Brass, who, in his deep debasement, really seemed to have changed sexes with his sister, and to have made over to her any spark of manliness he might have possessed. 'You think so, Sarah, you think so perhaps; but you would have acted quite different, my good fellow. You will not have forgotten that it was a maxim with Foxey—our revered father, gentlemen—"Always suspect everybody." That's the maxim to go through life with! If you were not actually about to purchase your own safety when I showed myself, I suspect you'd have done it by this time. And therefore I've done it myself, and spared you the trouble as well as the shame. The shame, gentlemen,' added Brass, allowing himself to be slightly overcome, 'if there is any, is mine. It's better that a female should be spared it.'

With deference to the better opinion of Mr Brass, and more particularly to the authority of his Great Ancestor, it may be doubted, with humility, whether the elevating principle laid down by the latter gentleman, and acted upon by his descendant, is always a prudent one, or attended in practice with the desired results. This is, beyond question, a bold and presumptuous doubt, inasmuch as many distinguished characters, called men of the world, long-headed customers, knowing dogs, shrewd fellows, capital hands at business, and the like, have made, and do daily make, this axiom their polar star and compass. Still, the doubt may be gently insinuated. And in illustration it may be observed, that if Mr Brass, not being over-suspicious, had, without prying and listening, left his sister to manage the conference on their joint behalf, or prying and listening, had not been in such a mighty hurry to anticipate her (which he would not have been, but for his distrust and jealousy), he would probably have found himself much better off in the end. Thus, it will always happen that these men of the world, who go through it in armour, defend themselves from quite as much good as evil; to say nothing of the inconvenience and absurdity of mounting guard with a microscope at all times, and of wearing a coat of mail on the most innocent occasions.

The three gentlemen spoke together apart, for a few moments. At the end of their consultation, which was very brief, the Notary pointed to the writing materials on the table, and informed Mr Brass that if he wished to make any statement in writing, he had the opportunity of doing so. At the same time he felt bound to tell him that they would require his attendance, presently, before a justice of the peace, and that in what he did or said, he was guided entirely by his own discretion.

'Gentlemen,' said Brass, drawing off his glove, and crawling in spirit upon the ground before them, 'I will justify the tenderness with which I know I shall be treated; and as, without tenderness, I should, now that this discovery has been made, stand in the worst position of the three, you may depend upon it I will make a clean breast. Mr Witherden, sir, a kind of faintness is upon my spirits—if you would do me the favour to ring the bell and order up a glass of something warm and spicy, I shall, notwithstanding what has passed, have a melancholy pleasure in drinking your good health. I had hoped,' said Brass, looking round with a mournful smile, 'to have seen you three gentlemen, one day or another, with your legs under the mahogany in my humble parlour in the Marks. But hopes are fleeting. Dear me!'

Mr Brass found himself so exceedingly affected, at this point, that he could say or do nothing more until some refreshment arrived. Having partaken of it, pretty freely for one in his agitated state, he sat down to write.

The lovely Sarah, now with her arms folded, and now with her hands clasped behind her, paced the room with manly strides while her brother was thus employed, and sometimes stopped to pull out her snuff-box and bite the lid. She continued to pace up and down until she was quite tired, and then fell asleep on a chair near the door.

It has been since supposed, with some reason, that this slumber was a sham or feint, as she contrived to slip away unobserved in the dusk of the afternoon. Whether this was an intentional and waking departure, or a somnambulistic leave-taking and walking in her sleep, may remain a subject of contention; but, on one point (and indeed the main one) all parties are agreed. In whatever state she walked away, she certainly did not walk back again.

Mention having been made of the dusk of the afternoon, it will be inferred that Mr Brass's task occupied some time in the completion. It was not finished until evening; but, being done at last, that worthy person and the three friends adjourned in a hackney-coach to the private office of a justice, who, giving Mr Brass a warm reception and detaining him in a secure place that he might insure to himself the pleasure of seeing him on the morrow, dismissed the others with the cheering assurance that a warrant could not fail to be granted next day for the apprehension of Mr Quilp, and that a proper application and statement of all the circumstances to the secretary of state (who was fortunately in town), would no doubt procure Kit's free pardon and liberation without delay.

And now, indeed, it seemed that Quilp's malignant career was drawing to a close, and that retribution, which often travels slowly—especially when heaviest—had tracked his footsteps with a sure and certain scent and was gaining on him fast. Unmindful of her stealthy tread, her victim holds his course in fancied triumph. Still at his heels she comes, and once afoot, is never turned aside!

Their business ended, the three gentlemen hastened back to the lodgings of Mr Swiveller, whom they found progressing so favourably in his recovery as to have been able to sit up for half an hour, and to have conversed with cheerfulness. Mrs Garland had gone home some time since, but Mr Abel was still sitting with him. After telling him all they had done, the two Mr Garlands and the single gentleman, as if by some previous understanding, took their leaves for the night, leaving the invalid alone with the Notary and the small servant.

'As you are so much better,' said Mr Witherden, sitting down at the bedside, 'I may venture to communicate to you a piece of news which has come to me professionally.'

The idea of any professional intelligence from a gentleman connected with legal matters, appeared to afford Richard any-thing but a pleasing anticipation. Perhaps he connected it in his own mind with one or two outstanding accounts, in reference to which he had already received divers threatening letters. His countenance fell as he replied,

'Certainly, sir. I hope it's not anything of a very disagreeable nature, though?'

'If I thought it so, I should choose some better time for communicating it,' replied the Notary. 'Let me tell you, first, that my friends who have been here to-day, know nothing of it, and that their kindness to you has been quite spontaneous and with no hope of return. It may do a thoughtless, careless man, good, to know that.'

Dick thanked him, and said he hoped it would.

'I have been making some inquiries about you,' said Mr Witherden, 'little thinking that I should find you under such circumstances as those which have brought us together. You are the nephew of Rebecca Swiveller, spinster, deceased, of Cheselbourne in Dorsetshire.'

'Deceased!' cried Dick.

'Deceased. If you had been another sort of nephew, you would have come into possession (so says the will, and I see no reason to doubt it) of five-and-twenty thousand pounds. As it is, you have fallen into an annuity of one hundred and fifty pounds a year; but I think I may congratulate you even upon that.'

'Sir,' said Dick, sobbing and laughing together, 'you may. For, please God, we'll make a scholar of the poor Marchioness yet! And she shall walk in silk attire, and siller have to spare, or may I never rise from this bed again!'

CHAPTER 67

Unconscious of the proceedings faithfully narrated in the last chapter, and little dreaming of the mine which had been sprung beneath him (for, to the end that he should have no warning of the business a-foot, the profoundest secrecy was observed in the whole transaction), Mr Quilp remained shut up in his hermitage, undisturbed by any suspicion, and extremely well satisfied with the result of his machinations. Being engaged in the adjustment of some accounts—an occupation to which the silence and solitude of his retreat were very favourable—he had not strayed from his den for two whole days. The third day of his devotion to this pursuit found him still hard at work, and little disposed to stir abroad.

It was the day next after Mr Brass's confession, and consequently, that which threatened the restriction of Mr Quilp's liberty, and the abrupt communication to him of some very unpleasant and unwelcome facts. Having no intuitive perception of the cloud which lowered upon his house, the dwarf was in his ordinary state of cheerfulness; and, when he found he was becoming too much engrossed by business with a due regard to his health and spirits, he varied its monotonous routine with a little screeching, or howling, or some other innocent relaxation of that nature.

He was attended, as usual, by Tom Scott, who sat crouching over the fire after the manner of a toad, and, from time to time, when his master's back was turned, imitating his grimaces with a fearful exactness. The figure-head had not yet disappeared, but remained in its old place. The face, horribly seared by the frequent application of the red-hot poker, and further ornamented by the insertion, in the tip of the nose, of a tenpenny nail, yet smiled blandly in its less lacerated parts, and seemed, like a sturdy martyr, to provoke its tormentor to the commission of new outrages and insults.

The day, in the highest and brightest quarters of the town, was damp, dark, cold and gloomy. In that low and marshy spot, the fog filled every nook and corner with a thick dense cloud. Every object was obscure at one or two yards' distance. The warning lights and fires upon the river were powerless beneath this pall, and, but for a raw and piercing chillness in the air, and now and then the cry of some bewildered boatman as he rested on his oars and tried to make out where he was, the river itself might have been miles away.

The mist, though sluggish and slow to move, was of a keenly searching kind. No muffling up in furs and broadcloth kept it out. It seemed to penetrate into the very bones of the shrinking wayfarers, and to rack them with cold and pains. Everything was wet and clammy to the touch. The warm blaze alone defied it, and leaped and sparkled merrily. It was a day to be at home, crowding about the fire, telling stories of travellers who had lost their way in such weather on heaths and moors; and to love a warm hearth more than ever.

The dwarf's humour, as we know, was to have a fireside to himself; and when he was disposed to be convivial, to enjoy himself alone. By no means insensible to the comfort of being within doors, he ordered Tom Scott to pile the little stove with coals, and, dismissing his work for that day, determined to be jovial.

To this end, he lighted up fresh candles and heaped more fuel on the fire; and having dined off a beefsteak, which he cooked himself in somewhat of a savage and cannibal-like manner, brewed a great bowl of hot punch, lighted his pipe, and sat down to spend the evening.

At this moment, a low knocking at the cabin-door arrested his attention. When it had been twice or thrice repeated, he softly opened the little window, and thrusting his head out, demanded who was there.

'Only me, Quilp,' replied a woman's voice.

'Only you!' cried the dwarf, stretching his neck to obtain a better view of his visitor. 'And what brings you here, you jade? How dare you approach the ogre's castle, eh?'

'I have come with some news,' rejoined his spouse. 'Don't be angry with me.'

'Is it good news, pleasant news, news to make a man skip and snap his fingers?' said the dwarf. 'Is the dear old lady dead?'

'I don't know what news it is, or whether it's good or bad,' rejoined his wife.

'Then she's alive,' said Quilp, 'and there's nothing the matter with her. Go home again, you bird of evil note, go home!'

'I have brought a letter,' cried the meek little woman.

'Toss it in at the window here, and go your ways,' said Quilp, interrupting her, 'or I'll come out and scratch you.'

'No, but please, Quilp—do hear me speak,' urged his submissive wife, in tears. 'Please do!'

'Speak then,' growled the dwarf with a malicious grin. 'Be quick and short about it. Speak, will you?'

'It was left at our house this afternoon,' said Mrs Quilp, trembling, 'by a boy who said he didn't know from whom it came, but that it was given to him to leave, and that he was told to say it must be brought on to you directly, for it was of the very greatest consequence.—But please,' she added, as her husband stretched out his hand for it, 'please let me in. You don't know how wet and cold I am, or how many times I have lost my way in coming here through this thick fog. Let me dry myself at the fire for five minutes. I'll go away directly you tell me to, Quilp. Upon my word I will.'

Her amiable husband hesitated for a few moments; but, bethinking himself that the letter might require some answer, of which she could be the bearer, closed the window, opened the door, and bade her enter. Mrs Quilp obeyed right willingly, and, kneeling down before the fire to warm her hands, delivered into his a little packet.

'I'm glad you're wet,' said Quilp, snatching it, and squinting at her. 'I'm glad you're cold. I'm glad you lost your way. I'm glad your eyes are red with crying. It does my heart good to see your little nose so pinched and frosty.'

'Oh Quilp!' sobbed his wife. 'How cruel it is of you!'

'Did she think I was dead?' said Quilp, wrinkling his face into a most extraordinary series of grimaces. 'Did she think she was going to have all the money, and to marry somebody she liked? Ha ha ha! Did she?'

These taunts elicited no reply from the poor little woman, who remained on her knees, warming her hands, and sobbing, to Mr Quilp's great delight. But, just as he was contemplating her, and chuckling excessively, he happened to observe that Tom Scott was delighted too; wherefore, that he might have no presumptuous partner in his glee, the dwarf instantly collared him, dragged him to the door, and after a short scuffle, kicked him into the yard. In return for this mark of attention, Tom immediately walked upon his hands to the window, and—if the expression be allowable—looked in with his shoes: besides rattling his feet upon the glass like a Banshee upside down. As a matter of course, Mr Quilp lost no time in resorting to the infallible poker, with which, after some dodging and lying in ambush, he paid his young friend one or two such unequivocal compliments that he vanished precipitately, and left him in quiet possession of the field.

'So! That little job being disposed of,' said the dwarf, coolly, 'I'll read my letter. Humph!' he muttered, looking at the direction. 'I ought to know this writing. Beautiful Sally!'

Opening it, he read, in a fair, round, legal hand, as follows:

'Sammy has been practised upon, and has broken confidence. It has all come out. You had better not be in the way, for strangers are going to call upon you. They have been very quiet as yet, because they mean to surprise you. Don't lose time. I didn't. I am not to be found anywhere. If I was you, I wouldn't either. S. B., late of B. M.'

To describe the changes that passed over Quilp's face, as he read this letter half-a-dozen times, would require some new language: such, for power of expression, as was never written, read, or spoken. For a long time he did not utter one word; but, after a considerable interval, during which Mrs Quilp was almost paralysed with the alarm his looks engendered, he contrived to gasp out,

'If I had him here. If I only had him here—'

'Oh Quilp!' said his wife, 'what's the matter? Who are you angry with?'

'—I should drown him,' said the dwarf, not heeding her. 'Too easy a death, too short, too quick—but the river runs close at hand. Oh! if I had him here! just to take him to the brink coaxingly and pleasantly,—holding him by the button-hole—joking with him,—and, with a sudden push, to send him splashing down! Drowning men come to the surface three times they say. Ah! To see him those three times, and mock him as his face came bobbing up,—oh, what a rich treat that would be!'

'Quilp!' stammered his wife, venturing at the same time to touch him on the shoulder: 'what has gone wrong?'

She was so terrified by the relish with which he pictured this pleasure to himself that she could scarcely make herself intelligible.

'Such a bloodless cur!' said Quilp, rubbing his hands very slowly, and pressing them tight together. 'I thought his cowardice and servility were the best guarantee for his keeping silence. Oh Brass, Brass—my dear, good, affectionate, faithful, complimentary, charming friend—if I only had you here!'

His wife, who had retreated lest she should seem to listen to these mutterings, ventured to approach him again, and was about to speak, when he hurried to the door, and called Tom Scott, who, remembering his late gentle admonition, deemed it prudent to appear immediately.

'There!' said the dwarf, pulling him in. 'Take her home. Don't come here to-morrow, for this place will be shut up. Come back no more till you hear from me or see me. Do you mind?'

Tom nodded sulkily, and beckoned Mrs Quilp to lead the way.

'As for you,' said the dwarf, addressing himself to her, 'ask no questions about me, make no search for me, say nothing concerning me. I shall not be dead, mistress, and that'll comfort you. He'll take care of you.'

'But, Quilp? What is the matter? Where are you going? Do say something more?'

'I'll say that,' said the dwarf, seizing her by the arm, 'and do that too, which undone and unsaid would be best for you, unless you go directly.'

'Has anything happened?' cried his wife. 'Oh! Do tell me that?'

'Yes,' snarled the dwarf. 'No. What matter which? I have told you what to do. Woe betide you if you fail to do it, or disobey me by a hair's breadth. Will you go!'

'I am going, I'll go directly; but,' faltered his wife, 'answer me one question first. Has this letter any connexion with dear little Nell? I must ask you that—I must indeed, Quilp. You cannot think what days and nights of sorrow I have had through having once deceived that child. I don't know what harm I may have brought about, but, great or little, I did it for you, Quilp. My conscience misgave me when I did it. Do answer me this question, if you please?'

The exasperated dwarf returned no answer, but turned round and caught up his usual weapon with such vehemence, that Tom Scott dragged his charge away, by main force, and as swiftly as he could. It was well he did so, for Quilp, who was nearly mad with rage, pursued them to the neighbouring lane, and might have prolonged the chase but for the dense mist which obscured them from his view and appeared to thicken every moment.

'It will be a good night for travelling anonymously,' he said, as he returned slowly, being pretty well breathed with his run. 'Stay. We may look better here. This is too hospitable and free.'

By a great exertion of strength, he closed the two old gates, which were deeply sunken in the mud, and barred them with a heavy beam. That done, he shook his matted hair from about his eyes, and tried them.—Strong and fast.

'The fence between this wharf and the next is easily climbed,' said the dwarf, when he had taken these precautions. 'There's a back lane, too, from there. That shall be my way out. A man need know his road well, to find it in this lovely place to-night. I need fear no unwelcome visitors while this lasts, I think.'

Almost reduced to the necessity of groping his way with his hands (it had grown so dark and the fog had so much increased), he returned to his lair; and, after musing for some time over the fire, busied himself in preparations for a speedy departure.

While he was collecting a few necessaries and cramming them into his pockets, he never once ceased communing with himself in a low voice, or unclenched his teeth, which he had ground together on finishing Miss Brass's note.

'Oh Sampson!' he muttered, 'good worthy creature—if I could but hug you! If I could only fold you in my arms, and squeeze your ribs, as I could squeeze them if I once had you tight—what a meeting there would be between us! If we ever do cross each other again, Sampson, we'll have a greeting not easily to be forgotten, trust me. This time, Sampson, this moment when all had gone on so well, was so nicely chosen! It was so thoughtful of you, so penitent, so good. Oh, if we were face to face in this room again, my white-livered man of law, how well contented one of us would be!'

There he stopped; and raising the bowl of punch to his lips, drank a long deep draught, as if it were fair water and cooling to his parched mouth. Setting it down abruptly, and resuming his preparations, he went on with his soliloquy.

'There's Sally,' he said, with flashing eyes; 'the woman has spirit, determination, purpose—was she asleep, or petrified? She could have stabbed him—poisoned him safely. She might have seen this coming on. Why does she give me notice when it's too late? When he sat there,—yonder there, over there,—with his white face, and red head, and sickly smile, why didn't I know what was passing in his heart? It should have stopped beating, that night, if I had been in his secret, or there are no drugs to lull a man to sleep, or no fire to burn him!'

Another draught from the bowl; and, cowering over the fire with a ferocious aspect, he muttered to himself again.

'And this, like every other trouble and anxiety I have had of late times, springs from that old dotard and his darling child—two wretched feeble wanderers! I'll be their evil genius yet. And you, sweet Kit, honest Kit, virtuous, innocent Kit, look to yourself. Where I hate, I bite. I hate you, my darling fellow, with good cause, and proud as you are to-night, I'll have my turn.——What's that?'

A knocking at the gate he had closed. A loud and violent knocking. Then, a pause; as if those who knocked had stopped to listen. Then, the noise again, more clamorous and importunate than before.

'So soon!' said the dwarf. 'And so eager! I am afraid I shall disappoint you. It's well I'm quite prepared. Sally, I thank you!'

As he spoke, he extinguished the candle. In his impetuous attempts to subdue the brightness of the fire, he overset the stove, which came tumbling forward, and fell with a crash upon the burning embers it had shot forth in its descent, leaving the room in pitchy darkness. The noise at the gate still continuing, he felt his way to the door, and stepped into the open air.

At that moment the knocking ceased. It was about eight o'clock; but the dead of the darkest night would have been as noon-day in comparison with the thick cloud which then rested upon the earth, and shrouded everything from view. He darted forward for a few paces, as if into the mouth of some dim, yawning cavern; then, thinking he had gone wrong, changed the direction of his steps; then stood still, not knowing where to turn.

'If they would knock again,' said Quilp, trying to peer into the gloom by which he was surrounded, 'the sound might guide me! Come! Batter the gate once more!'

He stood listening intently, but the noise was not renewed. Nothing was to be heard in that deserted place, but, at intervals, the distant barkings of dogs. The sound was far away—now in one quarter, now answered in another—nor was it any guide, for it often came from shipboard, as he knew.

'If I could find a wall or fence,' said the dwarf, stretching out his arms, and walking slowly on, 'I should know which way to turn. A good, black, devil's night this, to have my dear friend here! If I had but that wish, it might, for anything I cared, never be day again.'

As the word passed his lips, he staggered and fell—and next moment was fighting with the cold dark water!

For all its bubbling up and rushing in his ears, he could hear the knocking at the gate again—could hear a shout that followed it—could recognise the voice. For all his struggling and plashing, he could understand that they had lost their way, and had wandered back to the point from which they started; that they were all but looking on, while he was drowned; that they were close at hand, but could not make an effort to save him; that he himself had shut and barred them out. He answered the shout—with a yell, which seemed to make the hundred fires that danced before his eyes tremble and flicker, as if a gust of wind had stirred them. It was of no avail. The strong tide filled his throat, and bore him on, upon its rapid current.

Another mortal struggle, and he was up again, beating the water with his hands, and looking out, with wild and glaring eyes that showed him some black object he was drifting close upon. The hull of a ship! He could touch its smooth and slippery surface with his hand. One loud cry, now—but the resistless water bore him down before he could give it utterance, and, driving him under it, carried away a corpse.

It toyed and sported with its ghastly freight, now bruising it against the slimy piles, now hiding it in mud or long rank grass, now dragging it heavily over rough stones and gravel, now feigning to yield it to its own element, and in the same action luring it away, until, tired of the ugly plaything, it flung it on a swamp—a dismal place where pirates had swung in chains through many a wintry night—and left it there to bleach.

And there it lay alone. The sky was red with flame, and the water that bore it there had been tinged with the sullen light as it flowed along. The place the deserted carcass had left so recently, a living man, was now a blazing ruin. There was something of the glare upon its face. The hair, stirred by the damp breeze, played in a kind of mockery of death—such a mockery as the dead man himself would have delighted in when alive—about its head, and its dress fluttered idly in the night wind.

CHAPTER 68

Lighted rooms, bright fires, cheerful faces, the music of glad voices, words of love and welcome, warm hearts, and tears of happiness—what a change is this! But it is to such delights that Kit is hastening. They are awaiting him, he knows. He fears he will die of joy, before he gets among them.

They have prepared him for this, all day. He is not to be carried off to-morrow with the rest, they tell him first. By degrees they let him know that doubts have arisen, that inquiries are to be made, and perhaps he may be pardoned after all. At last, the evening being come, they bring him to a room where some gentlemen are assembled. Foremost among them is his good old master, who comes and takes him by the hand. He hears that his innocence is established, and that he is pardoned. He cannot see the speaker, but he turns towards the voice, and in trying to answer, falls down insensible.

They recover him again, and tell him he must be composed, and bear this like a man. Somebody says he must think of his poor mother. It is because he does think of her so much, that the happy news had overpowered him. They crowd about him, and tell him that the truth has gone abroad, and that all the town and country ring with sympathy for his misfortunes. He has no ears for this. His thoughts, as yet, have no wider range than home. Does she know it? what did she say? who told her? He can speak of nothing else.

They make him drink a little wine, and talk kindly to him for a while, until he is more collected, and can listen, and thank them. He is free to go. Mr Garland thinks, if he feels better, it is time they went away. The gentlemen cluster round him, and shake hands with him. He feels very grateful to them for the interest they have in him, and for the kind promises they make; but the power of speech is gone again, and he has much ado to keep his feet, even though leaning on his master's arm.

As they come through the dismal passages, some officers of the jail who are in waiting there, congratulate him, in their rough way, on his release. The newsmonger is of the number, but his manner is not quite hearty—there is something of surliness in his compliments. He looks upon Kit as an intruder, as one who has obtained admission to that place on false pretences, who has enjoyed a privilege without being duly qualified. He may be a very good sort of young man, he thinks, but he has no business there, and the sooner he is gone, the better.

The last door shuts behind them. They have passed the outer wall, and stand in the open air—in the street he has so often pictured to himself when hemmed in by the gloomy stones, and which has been in all his dreams. It seems wider and more busy than it used to be. The night is bad, and yet how cheerful and gay in his eyes! One of the gentlemen, in taking leave of him, pressed some money into his hand. He has not counted it; but when they have gone a few paces beyond the box for poor Prisoners, he hastily returns and drops it in.

Mr Garland has a coach waiting in a neighbouring street, and, taking Kit inside with him, bids the man drive home. At first, they can only travel at a foot pace, and then with torches going on before, because of the heavy fog. But, as they get farther from the river, and leave the closer portions of the town behind, they are able to dispense with this precaution and to proceed at a brisker rate. On the road, hard galloping would be too slow for Kit; but, when they are drawing near their journey's end, he begs they may go more slowly, and, when the house appears in sight, that they may stop—only for a minute or two, to give him time to breathe.

But there is no stopping then, for the old gentleman speaks stoutly to him, the horses mend their pace, and they are already at the garden-gate. Next minute, they are at the door.

There is a noise of tongues, and tread of feet, inside. It opens. Kit rushes in, and finds his mother clinging round his neck.

And there, too, is the ever faithful Barbara's mother, still holding the baby as if she had never put it down since that sad day when they little hoped to have such joy as this—there she is, Heaven bless her, crying her eyes out, and sobbing as never woman sobbed before; and there is little Barbara—poor little Barbara, so much thinner and so much paler, and yet so very pretty—trembling like a leaf and supporting herself against the wall; and there is Mrs Garland, neater and nicer than ever, fainting away stone dead with nobody to help her; and there is Mr Abel, violently blowing his nose, and wanting to embrace everybody; and there is the single gentleman hovering round them all, and constant to nothing for an instant; and there is that good, dear, thoughtful little Jacob, sitting all alone by himself on the bottom stair, with his hands on his knees like an old man, roaring fearfully without giving any trouble to anybody; and each and all of them are for the time clean out of their wits, and do jointly and severally commit all manner of follies.

And even when the rest have in some measure come to themselves again, and can find words and smiles, Barbara—that soft-hearted, gentle, foolish little Barbara—is suddenly missed, and found to be in a swoon by herself in the back parlour, from which swoon she falls into hysterics, and from which hysterics into a swoon again, and is, indeed, so bad, that despite a mortal quantity of vinegar and cold water she is hardly a bit better at last than she was at first. Then, Kit's mother comes in and says, will he come and speak to her; and Kit says 'Yes,' and goes; and he says in a kind voice 'Barbara!' and Barbara's mother tells her that 'it's only Kit;' and Barbara says (with her eyes closed all the time) 'Oh! but is it him indeed?' and Barbara's mother says 'To be sure it is, my dear; there's nothing the matter now.' And in further assurance that he's safe and sound, Kit speaks to her again; and then Barbara goes off into another fit of laughter, and then into another fit of crying; and then Barbara's mother and Kit's mother nod to each other and pretend to scold her—but only to bring her to herself the faster, bless you!—and being experienced matrons, and acute at perceiving the first dawning symptoms of recovery, they comfort Kit with the assurance that 'she'll do now,' and so dismiss him to the place from whence he came.

Well! In that place (which is the next room) there are decanters of wine, and all that sort of thing, set out as grand as if Kit and his friends were first-rate company; and there is little Jacob, walking, as the popular phrase is, into a home-made plum-cake, at a most surprising pace, and keeping his eye on the figs and oranges which are to follow, and making the best use of his time, you may believe. Kit no sooner comes in, than that single gentleman (never was such a busy gentleman) charges all the glasses—bumpers—and drinks his health, and tells him he shall never want a friend while he lives; and so does Mr Garland, and so does Mrs Garland, and so does Mr Abel. But even this honour and distinction is not all, for the single gentleman forthwith pulls out of his pocket a massive silver watch—going hard, and right to half a second—and upon the back of this watch is engraved Kit's name, with flourishes all over; and in short it is Kit's watch, bought expressly for him, and presented to him on the spot. You may rest assured that Mr and Mrs Garland can't help hinting about their present, in store, and that Mr Abel tells outright that he has his; and that Kit is the happiest of the happy.

There is one friend he has not seen yet, and as he cannot be conveniently introduced into the family circle, by reason of his being an iron-shod quadruped, Kit takes the first opportunity of slipping away and hurrying to the stable. The moment he lays his hand upon the latch, the pony neighs the loudest pony's greeting; before he has crossed the threshold, the pony is capering about his loose box (for he brooks not the indignity of a halter), mad to give him welcome; and when Kit goes up to caress and pat him, the pony rubs his nose against his coat, and fondles him more lovingly than ever pony fondled man. It is the crowning circumstance of his earnest, heartfelt reception; and Kit fairly puts his arm round Whisker's neck and hugs him.

But how comes Barbara to trip in there? and how smart she is again! she has been at her glass since she recovered. How comes Barbara in the stable, of all places in the world? Why, since Kit has been away, the pony would take his food from nobody but her, and Barbara, you see, not dreaming that Christopher was there, and just looking in, to see that everything was right, has come upon him unawares. Blushing little Barbara!

It may be that Kit has caressed the pony enough; it may be that there are even better things to caress than ponies. He leaves him for Barbara at any rate, and hopes she is better. Yes. Barbara is a great deal better. She is afraid—and here Barbara looks down and blushes more— that he must have thought her very foolish. 'Not at all,' says Kit. Barbara is glad of that, and coughs—Hem!—just the slightest cough possible—not more than that.

What a discreet pony when he chooses! He is as quiet now as if he were of marble. He has a very knowing look, but that he always has. 'We have hardly had time to shake hands, Barbara,' says Kit. Barbara gives him hers. Why, she is trembling now! Foolish, fluttering Barbara!

Arm's length? The length of an arm is not much. Barbara's was not a long arm, by any means, and besides, she didn't hold it out straight, but bent a little. Kit was so near her when they shook hands, that he could see a small tiny tear, yet trembling on an eyelash. It was natural that he should look at it, unknown to Barbara. It was natural that Barbara should raise her eyes unconsciously, and find him out. Was it natural that at that instant, without any previous impulse or design, Kit should kiss Barbara? He did it, whether or no. Barbara said 'for shame,' but let him do it too—twice. He might have done it thrice, but the pony kicked up his heels and shook his head, as if he were suddenly taken with convulsions of delight, and Barbara being frightened, ran away—not straight to where her mother and Kit's mother were, though, lest they should see how red her cheeks were, and should ask her why. Sly little Barbara!

When the first transports of the whole party had subsided, and Kit and his mother, and Barbara and her mother, with little Jacob and the baby to boot, had had their suppers together—which there was no hurrying over, for they were going to stop there all night—Mr Garland called Kit to him, and taking him into a room where they could be alone, told him that he had something yet to say, which would surprise him greatly. Kit looked so anxious and turned so pale on hearing this, that the old gentleman hastened to add, he would be agreeably surprised; and asked him if he would be ready next morning for a journey.

'For a journey, sir!' cried Kit.

'In company with me and my friend in the next room. Can you guess its purpose?'

Kit turned paler yet, and shook his head.

'Oh yes. I think you do already,' said his master. 'Try.'

Kit murmured something rather rambling and unintelligible, but he plainly pronounced the words 'Miss Nell,' three or four times—shaking his head while he did so, as if he would add that there was no hope of that.

But Mr Garland, instead of saying 'Try again,' as Kit had made sure he would, told him very seriously, that he had guessed right.

'The place of their retreat is indeed discovered,' he said, 'at last. And that is our journey's end.'

Kit faltered out such questions as, where was it, and how had it been found, and how long since, and was she well and happy?

'Happy she is, beyond all doubt,' said Mr Garland. 'And well, I—I trust she will be soon. She has been weak and ailing, as I learn, but she was better when I heard this morning, and they were full of hope. Sit you down, and you shall hear the rest.'

Scarcely venturing to draw his breath, Kit did as he was told. Mr Garland then related to him, how he had a brother (of whom he would remember to have heard him speak, and whose picture, taken when he was a young man, hung in the best room), and how this brother lived a long way off, in a country-place, with an old clergyman who had been his early friend. How, although they loved each other as brothers should, they had not met for many years, but had communicated by letter from time to time, always looking forward to some period when they would take each other by the hand once more, and still letting the Present time steal on, as it was the habit for men to do, and suffering the Future to melt into the Past. How this brother, whose temper was very mild and quiet and retiring—such as Mr Abel's—was greatly beloved by the simple people among whom he dwelt, who quite revered the Bachelor (for so they called him), and had every one experienced his charity and benevolence. How even those slight circumstances had come to his knowledge, very slowly and in course of years, for the Bachelor was one of those whose goodness shuns the light, and who have more pleasure in discovering and extolling the good deeds of others, than in trumpeting their own, be they never so commendable. How, for that reason, he seldom told them of his village friends; but how, for all that, his mind had become so full of two among them—a child and an old man, to whom he had been very kind—that, in a letter received a few days before, he had dwelt upon them from first to last, and had told such a tale of their wandering, and mutual love, that few could read it without being moved to tears. How he, the recipient of that letter, was directly led to the belief that these must be the very wanderers for whom so much search had been made, and whom Heaven had directed to his brother's care. How he had written for such further information as would put the fact beyond all doubt; how it had that morning arrived; had confirmed his first impression into a certainty; and was the immediate cause of that journey being planned, which they were to take to-morrow.

'In the meantime,' said the old gentleman rising, and laying his hand on Kit's shoulder, 'you have a great need of rest; for such a day as this would wear out the strongest man. Good night, and Heaven send our journey may have a prosperous ending!'

CHAPTER 69

Kit was no sluggard next morning, but, springing from his bed some time before day, began to prepare for his welcome expedition. The hurry of spirits consequent upon the events of yesterday, and the unexpected intelligence he had heard at night, had troubled his sleep through the long dark hours, and summoned such uneasy dreams about his pillow that it was best to rise.

But, had it been the beginning of some great labour with the same end in view—had it been the commencement of a long journey, to be performed on foot in that inclement season of the year, to be pursued under very privation and difficulty, and to be achieved only with great distress, fatigue, and suffering—had it been the dawn of some painful enterprise, certain to task his utmost powers of resolution and endurance, and to need his utmost fortitude, but only likely to end, if happily achieved, in good fortune and delight to Nell—Kit's cheerful zeal would have been as highly roused: Kit's ardour and impatience would have been, at least, the same.

Nor was he alone excited and eager. Before he had been up a quarter of an hour the whole house were astir and busy. Everybody hurried to do something towards facilitating the preparations. The single gentleman, it is true, could do nothing himself, but he overlooked everybody else and was more locomotive than anybody. The work of packing and making ready went briskly on, and by daybreak every preparation for the journey was completed. Then Kit began to wish they had not been quite so nimble; for the travelling-carriage which had been hired for the occasion was not to arrive until nine o'clock, and there was nothing but breakfast to fill up the intervening blank of one hour and a half. Yes there was, though. There was Barbara. Barbara was busy, to be sure, but so much the better—Kit could help her, and that would pass away the time better than any means that could be devised. Barbara had no objection to this arrangement, and Kit, tracking out the idea which had come upon him so suddenly overnight, began to think that surely Barbara was fond of him, and surely he was fond of Barbara.

Now, Barbara, if the truth must be told—as it must and ought to be—Barbara seemed, of all the little household, to take least pleasure in the bustle of the occasion; and when Kit, in the openness of his heart, told her how glad and overjoyed it made him, Barbara became more downcast still, and seemed to have even less pleasure in it than before!

'You have not been home so long, Christopher,' said Barbara—and it is impossible to tell how carelessly she said it—'You have not been home so long, that you need to be glad to go away again, I should think.'

'But for such a purpose,' returned Kit. 'To bring back Miss Nell! To see her again! Only think of that! I am so pleased too, to think that you will see her, Barbara, at last.'

Barbara did not absolutely say that she felt no gratification on this point, but she expressed the sentiment so plainly by one little toss of her head, that Kit was quite disconcerted, and wondered, in his simplicity, why she was so cool about it.

'You'll say she has the sweetest and beautifullest face you ever saw, I know,' said Kit, rubbing his hands. 'I'm sure you'll say that.'

Barbara tossed her head again.

'What's the matter, Barbara?' said Kit.

'Nothing,' cried Barbara. And Barbara pouted—not sulkily, or in an ugly manner, but just enough to make her look more cherry-lipped than ever.

There is no school in which a pupil gets on so fast, as that in which Kit became a scholar when he gave Barbara the kiss. He saw what Barbara meant now—he had his lesson by heart all at once—she was the book—there it was before him, as plain as print.

'Barbara,' said Kit, 'you're not cross with me?'

Oh dear no! Why should Barbara be cross? And what right had she to be cross? And what did it matter whether she was cross or not? Who minded her!

'Why, I do,' said Kit. 'Of course I do.'

Barbara didn't see why it was of course, at all.

Kit was sure she must. Would she think again?

Certainly, Barbara would think again. No, she didn't see why it was of course. She didn't understand what Christopher meant. And besides she was sure they wanted her up stairs by this time, and she must go, indeed—

'No, but Barbara,' said Kit, detaining her gently, 'let us part friends. I was always thinking of you, in my troubles. I should have been a great deal more miserable than I was, if it hadn't been for you.'

Goodness gracious, how pretty Barbara was when she coloured—and when she trembled, like a little shrinking bird!

'I am telling you the truth, Barbara, upon my word, but not half so strong as I could wish,' said Kit. 'When I want you to be pleased to see Miss Nell, it's only because I like you to be pleased with what pleases me—that's all. As to her, Barbara, I think I could almost die to do her service, but you would think so too, if you knew her as I do. I am sure you would.'

Barbara was touched, and sorry to have appeared indifferent.

'I have been used, you see,' said Kit, 'to talk and think of her, almost as if she was an angel. When I look forward to meeting her again, I think of her smiling as she used to do, and being glad to see me, and putting out her hand and saying, "It's my own old Kit," or some such words as those—like what she used to say. I think of seeing her happy, and with friends about her, and brought up as she deserves, and as she ought to be. When I think of myself, it's as her old servant, and one that loved her dearly, as his kind, good, gentle mistress; and who would have gone—yes, and still would go—through any harm to serve her. Once, I couldn't help being afraid that if she came back with friends about her she might forget, or be ashamed of having known, a humble lad like me, and so might speak coldly, which would have cut me, Barbara, deeper than I can tell. But when I came to think again, I felt sure that I was doing her wrong in this; and so I went on, as I did at first, hoping to see her once more, just as she used to be. Hoping this, and remembering what she was, has made me feel as if I would always try to please her, and always be what I should like to seem to her if I was still her servant. If I'm the better for that—and I don't think I'm the worse—I am grateful to her for it, and love and honour her the more. That's the plain honest truth, dear Barbara, upon my word it is!'

Little Barbara was not of a wayward or capricious nature, and, being full of remorse, melted into tears. To what more conversation this might have led, we need not stop to inquire; for the wheels of the carriage were heard at that moment, and, being followed by a smart ring at the garden gate, caused the bustle in the house, which had laid dormant for a short time, to burst again into tenfold life and vigour.

Simultaneously with the travelling equipage, arrived Mr Chuckster in a hackney cab, with certain papers and supplies of money for the single gentleman, into whose hands he delivered them. This duty discharged, he subsided into the bosom of the family; and, entertaining himself with a strolling or peripatetic breakfast, watched, with genteel indifference, the process of loading the carriage.

'Snobby's in this, I see, Sir?' he said to Mr Abel Garland. 'I thought he wasn't in the last trip because it was expected that his presence wouldn't be acceptable to the ancient buffalo.'

'To whom, Sir?' demanded Mr Abel.

'To the old gentleman,' returned Mr Chuckster, slightly abashed.

'Our client prefers to take him now,' said Mr Abel, drily. 'There is no longer any need for that precaution, as my father's relationship to a gentleman in whom the objects of his search have full confidence, will be a sufficient guarantee for the friendly nature of their errand.'

'Ah!' thought Mr Chuckster, looking out of window, 'anybody but me! Snobby before me, of course. He didn't happen to take that particular five-pound note, but I have not the smallest doubt that he's always up to something of that sort. I always said it, long before this came out. Devilish pretty girl that! 'Pon my soul, an amazing little creature!'

Barbara was the subject of Mr Chuckster's commendations; and as she was lingering near the carriage (all being now ready for its departure), that gentleman was suddenly seized with a strong interest in the proceedings, which impelled him to swagger down the garden, and take up his position at a convenient ogling distance. Having had great experience of the sex, and being perfectly acquainted with all those little artifices which find the readiest road to their hearts, Mr Chuckster, on taking his ground, planted one hand on his hip, and with the other adjusted his flowing hair. This is a favourite attitude in the polite circles, and, accompanied with a graceful whistling, has been known to do immense execution.

Such, however, is the difference between town and country, that nobody took the smallest notice of this insinuating figure; the wretches being wholly engaged in bidding the travellers farewell, in kissing hands to each other, waving handkerchiefs, and the like tame and vulgar practices. For now the single gentleman and Mr Garland were in the carriage, and the post-boy was in the saddle, and Kit, well wrapped and muffled up, was in the rumble behind; and Mrs Garland was there, and Mr Abel was there, and Kit's mother was there, and little Jacob was there, and Barbara's mother was visible in remote perspective, nursing the ever-wakeful baby; and all were nodding, beckoning, curtseying, or crying out, 'Good bye!' with all the energy they could express. In another minute, the carriage was out of sight; and Mr Chuckster remained alone on the spot where it had lately been, with a vision of Kit standing up in the rumble waving his hand to Barbara, and of Barbara in the full light and lustre of his eyes—his eyes—Chuckster's—Chuckster the successful—on whom ladies of quality had looked with favour from phaetons in the parks on Sundays—waving hers to Kit!

How Mr Chuckster, entranced by this monstrous fact, stood for some time rooted to the earth, protesting within himself that Kit was the Prince of felonious characters, and very Emperor or Great Mogul of Snobs, and how he clearly traced this revolting circumstance back to that old villany of the shilling, are matters foreign to our purpose; which is to track the rolling wheels, and bear the travellers company on their cold, bleak journey.

It was a bitter day. A keen wind was blowing, and rushed against them fiercely: bleaching the hard ground, shaking the white frost from the trees and hedges, and whirling it away like dust. But little cared Kit for weather. There was a freedom and freshness in the wind, as it came howling by, which, let it cut never so sharp, was welcome. As it swept on with its cloud of frost, bearing down the dry twigs and boughs and withered leaves, and carrying them away pell-mell, it seemed as though some general sympathy had got abroad, and everything was in a hurry, like themselves. The harder the gusts, the better progress they appeared to make. It was a good thing to go struggling and fighting forward, vanquishing them one by one; to watch them driving up, gathering strength and fury as they came along; to bend for a moment, as they whistled past; and then to look back and see them speed away, their hoarse noise dying in the distance, and the stout trees cowering down before them.

All day long, it blew without cessation. The night was clear and starlit, but the wind had not fallen, and the cold was piercing. Sometimes—towards the end of a long stage—Kit could not help wishing it were a little warmer: but when they stopped to change horses, and he had had a good run, and what with that, and the bustle of paying the old postilion, and rousing the new one, and running to and fro again until the horses were put to, he was so warm that the blood tingled and smarted in his fingers' ends—then, he felt as if to have it one degree less cold would be to lose half the delight and glory of the journey: and up he jumped again, right cheerily, singing to the merry music of the wheels as they rolled away, and, leaving the townspeople in their warm beds, pursued their course along the lonely road.

Meantime the two gentlemen inside, who were little disposed to sleep, beguiled the time with conversation. As both were anxious and expectant, it naturally turned upon the subject of their expedition, on the manner in which it had been brought about, and on the hopes and fears they entertained respecting it. Of the former they had many, of the latter few—none perhaps beyond that indefinable uneasiness which is inseparable from suddenly awakened hope, and protracted expectation.

In one of the pauses of their discourse, and when half the night had worn away, the single gentleman, who had gradually become more and more silent and thoughtful, turned to his companion and said abruptly:

'Are you a good listener?'

'Like most other men, I suppose,' returned Mr Garland, smiling. 'I can be, if I am interested; and if not interested, I should still try to appear so. Why do you ask?'

'I have a short narrative on my lips,' rejoined his friend, 'and will try you with it. It is very brief.'

Pausing for no reply, he laid his hand on the old gentleman's sleeve, and proceeded thus:

'There were once two brothers, who loved each other dearly. There was a disparity in their ages—some twelve years. I am not sure but they may insensibly have loved each other the better for that reason. Wide as the interval between them was, however, they became rivals too soon. The deepest and strongest affection of both their hearts settled upon one object.

'The youngest—there were reasons for his being sensitive and watchful—was the first to find this out. I will not tell you what misery he underwent, what agony of soul he knew, how great his mental struggle was. He had been a sickly child. His brother, patient and considerate in the midst of his own high health and strength, had many and many a day denied himself the sports he loved, to sit beside his couch, telling him old stories till his pale face lighted up with an unwonted glow; to carry him in his arms to some green spot, where he could tend the poor pensive boy as he looked upon the bright summer day, and saw all nature healthy but himself; to be, in any way, his fond and faithful nurse. I may not dwell on all he did, to make the poor, weak creature love him, or my tale would have no end. But when the time of trial came, the younger brother's heart was full of those old days. Heaven strengthened it to repay the sacrifices of inconsiderate youth by one of thoughtful manhood. He left his brother to be happy. The truth never passed his lips, and he quitted the country, hoping to die abroad.

'The elder brother married her. She was in Heaven before long, and left him with an infant daughter.

'If you have seen the picture-gallery of any one old family, you will remember how the same face and figure—often the fairest and slightest of them all—come upon you in different generations; and how you trace the same sweet girl through a long line of portraits—never growing old or changing—the Good Angel of the race—abiding by them in all reverses—redeeming all their sins—

'In this daughter the mother lived again. You may judge with what devotion he who lost that mother almost in the winning, clung to this girl, her breathing image. She grew to womanhood, and gave her heart to one who could not know its worth. Well! Her fond father could not see her pine and droop. He might be more deserving than he thought him. He surely might become so, with a wife like her. He joined their hands, and they were married.

'Through all the misery that followed this union; through all the cold neglect and undeserved reproach; through all the poverty he brought upon her; through all the struggles of their daily life, too mean and pitiful to tell, but dreadful to endure; she toiled on, in the deep devotion of her spirit, and in her better nature, as only women can. Her means and substance wasted; her father nearly beggared by her husband's hand, and the hourly witness (for they lived now under one roof) of her ill-usage and unhappiness,—she never, but for him, bewailed her fate. Patient, and upheld by strong affection to the last, she died a widow of some three weeks' date, leaving to her father's care two orphans; one a son of ten or twelve years old; the other a girl—such another infant child—the same in helplessness, in age, in form, in feature—as she had been herself when her young mother died.

'The elder brother, grandfather to these two children, was now a broken man; crushed and borne down, less by the weight of years than by the heavy hand of sorrow. With the wreck of his possessions, he began to trade—in pictures first, and then in curious ancient things. He had entertained a fondness for such matters from a boy, and the tastes he had cultivated were now to yield him an anxious and precarious subsistence.

'The boy grew like his father in mind and person; the girl so like her mother, that when the old man had her on his knee, and looked into her mild blue eyes, he felt as if awakening from a wretched dream, and his daughter were a little child again. The wayward boy soon spurned the shelter of his roof, and sought associates more congenial to his taste. The old man and the child dwelt alone together.

'It was then, when the love of two dead people who had been nearest and dearest to his heart, was all transferred to this slight creature; when her face, constantly before him, reminded him, from hour to hour, of the too early change he had seen in such another—of all the sufferings he had watched and known, and all his child had undergone; when the young man's profligate and hardened course drained him of money as his father's had, and even sometimes occasioned them temporary privation and distress; it was then that there began to beset him, and to be ever in his mind, a gloomy dread of poverty and want. He had no thought for himself in this. His fear was for the child. It was a spectre in his house, and haunted him night and day.

'The younger brother had been a traveller in many countries, and had made his pilgrimage through life alone. His voluntary banishment had been misconstrued, and he had borne (not without pain) reproach and slight for doing that which had wrung his heart, and cast a mournful shadow on his path. Apart from this, communication between him and the elder was difficult, and uncertain, and often failed; still, it was not so wholly broken off but that he learnt—with long blanks and gaps between each interval of information—all that I have told you now.

'Then, dreams of their young, happy life—happy to him though laden with pain and early care—visited his pillow yet oftener than before; and every night, a boy again, he was at his brother's side. With the utmost speed he could exert, he settled his affairs; converted into money all the goods he had; and, with honourable wealth enough for both, with open heart and hand, with limbs that trembled as they bore him on, with emotion such as men can hardly bear and live, arrived one evening at his brother's door!'

The narrator, whose voice had faltered lately, stopped.

'The rest,' said Mr Garland, pressing his hand after a pause, 'I know.'

'Yes,' rejoined his friend, 'we may spare ourselves the sequel. You know the poor result of all my search. Even when by dint of such inquiries as the utmost vigilance and sagacity could set on foot, we found they had been seen with two poor travelling showmen—and in time discovered the men themselves—and in time, the actual place of their retreat; even then, we were too late. Pray God, we are not too late again!'

'We cannot be,' said Mr Garland. 'This time we must succeed.'

'I have believed and hoped so,' returned the other. 'I try to believe and hope so still. But a heavy weight has fallen on my spirits, my good friend, and the sadness that gathers over me, will yield to neither hope nor reason.'

'That does not surprise me,' said Mr Garland; 'it is a natural consequence of the events you have recalled; of this dreary time and place; and above all, of this wild and dismal night. A dismal night, indeed! Hark! how the wind is howling!'

CHAPTER 70

Day broke, and found them still upon their way. Since leaving home, they had halted here and there for necessary refreshment, and had frequently been delayed, especially in the night time, by waiting for fresh horses. They had made no other stoppages, but the weather continued rough, and the roads were often steep and heavy. It would be night again before they reached their place of destination.

Kit, all bluff and hardened with the cold, went on manfully; and, having enough to do to keep his blood circulating, to picture to himself the happy end of this adventurous journey, and to look about him and be amazed at everything, had little spare time for thinking of discomforts. Though his impatience, and that of his fellow-travellers, rapidly increased as the day waned, the hours did not stand still. The short daylight of winter soon faded away, and it was dark again when they had yet many miles to travel.

As it grew dusk, the wind fell; its distant moanings were more low and mournful; and, as it came creeping up the road, and rattling covertly among the dry brambles on either hand, it seemed like some great phantom for whom the way was narrow, whose garments rustled as it stalked along. By degrees it lulled and died away, and then it came on to snow.

The flakes fell fast and thick, soon covering the ground some inches deep, and spreading abroad a solemn stillness. The rolling wheels were noiseless, and the sharp ring and clatter of the horses' hoofs, became a dull, muffled tramp. The life of their progress seemed to be slowly hushed, and something death-like to usurp its place.

Shading his eyes from the falling snow, which froze upon their lashes and obscured his sight, Kit often tried to catch the earliest glimpse of twinkling lights, denoting their approach to some not distant town. He could descry objects enough at such times, but none correctly. Now, a tall church spire appeared in view, which presently became a tree, a barn, a shadow on the ground, thrown on it by their own bright lamps. Now, there were horsemen, foot-passengers, carriages, going on before, or meeting them in narrow ways; which, when they were close upon them, turned to shadows too. A wall, a ruin, a sturdy gable end, would rise up in the road; and, when they were plunging headlong at it, would be the road itself. Strange turnings too, bridges, and sheets of water, appeared to start up here and there, making the way doubtful and uncertain; and yet they were on the same bare road, and these things, like the others, as they were passed, turned into dim illusions.

He descended slowly from his seat—for his limbs were numbed—when they arrived at a lone posting-house, and inquired how far they had to go to reach their journey's end. It was a late hour in such by-places, and the people were abed; but a voice answered from an upper window, Ten miles. The ten minutes that ensued appeared an hour; but at the end of that time, a shivering figure led out the horses they required, and after another brief delay they were again in motion.

It was a cross-country road, full, after the first three or four miles, of holes and cart-ruts, which, being covered by the snow, were so many pitfalls to the trembling horses, and obliged them to keep a footpace. As it was next to impossible for men so much agitated as they were by this time, to sit still and move so slowly, all three got out and plodded on behind the carriage. The distance seemed interminable, and the walk was most laborious. As each was thinking within himself that the driver must have lost his way, a church bell, close at hand, struck the hour of midnight, and the carriage stopped. It had moved softly enough, but when it ceased to crunch the snow, the silence was as startling as if some great noise had been replaced by perfect stillness.

'This is the place, gentlemen,' said the driver, dismounting from his horse, and knocking at the door of a little inn. 'Halloa! Past twelve o'clock is the dead of night here.'

The knocking was loud and long, but it failed to rouse the drowsy inmates. All continued dark and silent as before. They fell back a little, and looked up at the windows, which were mere black patches in the whitened house front. No light appeared. The house might have been deserted, or the sleepers dead, for any air of life it had about it.

They spoke together with a strange inconsistency, in whispers; unwilling to disturb again the dreary echoes they had just now raised.

'Let us go on,' said the younger brother, 'and leave this good fellow to wake them, if he can. I cannot rest until I know that we are not too late. Let us go on, in the name of Heaven!'

They did so, leaving the postilion to order such accommodation as the house afforded, and to renew his knocking. Kit accompanied them with a little bundle, which he had hung in the carriage when they left home, and had not forgotten since—the bird in his old cage—just as she had left him. She would be glad to see her bird, he knew.

The road wound gently downward. As they proceeded, they lost sight of the church whose clock they had heard, and of the small village clustering round it. The knocking, which was now renewed, and which in that stillness they could plainly hear, troubled them. They wished the man would forbear, or that they had told him not to break the silence until they returned.

The old church tower, clad in a ghostly garb of pure cold white, again rose up before them, and a few moments brought them close beside it. A venerable building—grey, even in the midst of the hoary landscape. An ancient sun-dial on the belfry wall was nearly hidden by the snow-drift, and scarcely to be known for what it was. Time itself seemed to have grown dull and old, as if no day were ever to displace the melancholy night.

A wicket gate was close at hand, but there was more than one path across the churchyard to which it led, and, uncertain which to take, they came to a stand again.

The village street—if street that could be called which was an irregular cluster of poor cottages of many heights and ages, some with their fronts, some with their backs, and some with gable ends towards the road, with here and there a signpost, or a shed encroaching on the path—was close at hand. There was a faint light in a chamber window not far off, and Kit ran towards that house to ask their way.

His first shout was answered by an old man within, who presently appeared at the casement, wrapping some garment round his throat as a protection from the cold, and demanded who was abroad at that unseasonable hour, wanting him.

''Tis hard weather this,' he grumbled, 'and not a night to call me up in. My trade is not of that kind that I need be roused from bed. The business on which folks want me, will keep cold, especially at this season. What do you want?'

'I would not have roused you, if I had known you were old and ill,' said Kit.

'Old!' repeated the other peevishly. 'How do you know I am old? Not so old as you think, friend, perhaps. As to being ill, you will find many young people in worse case than I am. More's the pity that it should be so—not that I should be strong and hearty for my years, I mean, but that they should be weak and tender. I ask your pardon though,' said the old man, 'if I spoke rather rough at first. My eyes are not good at night—that's neither age nor illness; they never were—and I didn't see you were a stranger.'

'I am sorry to call you from your bed,' said Kit, 'but those gentlemen you may see by the churchyard gate, are strangers too, who have just arrived from a long journey, and seek the parsonage-house. You can direct us?'

'I should be able to,' answered the old man, in a trembling voice, 'for, come next summer,

I have been sexton here, good fifty years. The right hand path, friend, is the road.—There is no ill news for our good gentleman, I hope?'

Kit thanked him, and made him a hasty answer in the negative; he was turning back, when his attention was caught by the voice of a child. Looking up, he saw a very little creature at a neighbouring window.

'What is that?' cried the child, earnestly. 'Has my dream come true? Pray speak to me, whoever that is, awake and up.'

'Poor boy!' said the sexton, before Kit could answer, 'how goes it, darling?'

'Has my dream come true?' exclaimed the child again, in a voice so fervent that it might have thrilled to the heart of any listener. 'But no, that can never be! How could it be—Oh! how could it!'

'I guess his meaning,' said the sexton. 'To bed again, poor boy!'

'Ay!' cried the child, in a burst of despair. 'I knew it could never be, I felt too sure of that, before I asked! But, all to-night, and last night too, it was the same. I never fall asleep, but that cruel dream comes back.'

'Try to sleep again,' said the old man, soothingly. 'It will go in time.'

'No no, I would rather that it staid—cruel as it is, I would rather that it staid,' rejoined the child. 'I am not afraid to have it in my sleep, but I am so sad—so very, very sad.'

The old man blessed him, the child in tears replied Good night, and Kit was again alone.

He hurried back, moved by what he had heard, though more by the child's manner than by anything he had said, as his meaning was hidden from him. They took the path indicated by the sexton, and soon arrived before the parsonage wall. Turning round to look about them when they had got thus far, they saw, among some ruined buildings at a distance, one single solitary light.

It shone from what appeared to be an old oriel window, and being surrounded by the deep shadows of overhanging walls, sparkled like a star. Bright and glimmering as the stars above their heads, lonely and motionless as they, it seemed to claim some kindred with the eternal lamps of Heaven, and to burn in fellowship with them.

'What light is that!' said the younger brother.

'It is surely,' said Mr Garland, 'in the ruin where they live. I see no other ruin hereabouts.'

'They cannot,' returned the brother hastily, 'be waking at this late hour—'

Kit interposed directly, and begged that, while they rang and waited at the gate, they would let him make his way to where this light was shining, and try to ascertain if any people were about. Obtaining the permission he desired, he darted off with breathless eagerness, and, still carrying the birdcage in his hand, made straight towards the spot.

It was not easy to hold that pace among the graves, and at another time he might have gone more slowly, or round by the path. Unmindful of all obstacles, however, he pressed forward without slackening his speed, and soon arrived within a few yards of the window. He approached as softly as he could, and advancing so near the wall as to brush the whitened ivy with his dress, listened. There was no sound inside. The church itself was not more quiet.

Touching the glass with his cheek, he listened again. No. And yet there was such a silence all around, that he felt sure he could have heard even the breathing of a sleeper, if there had been one there.

A strange circumstance, a light in such a place at that time of night, with no one near it.

A curtain was drawn across the lower portion of the window, and he could not see into the room. But there was no shadow thrown upon it from within. To have gained a footing on the wall and tried to look in from above, would have been attended with some danger—certainly with some noise, and the chance of terrifying the child, if that really were her habitation. Again and again he listened; again and again the same wearisome blank.

Leaving the spot with slow and cautious steps, and skirting the ruin for a few paces, he came at length to a door. He knocked. No answer. But there was a curious noise inside. It was difficult to determine what it was. It bore a resemblance to the low moaning of one in pain, but it was not that, being far too regular and constant. Now it seemed a kind of song, now a wail—seemed, that is, to his changing fancy, for the sound itself was never changed or checked. It was unlike anything he had ever heard; and in its tone there was something fearful, chilling, and unearthly.

The listener's blood ran colder now than ever it had done in frost and snow, but he knocked again. There was no answer, and the sound went on without any interruption. He laid his hand softly upon the latch, and put his knee against the door. It was secured on the inside, but yielded to the pressure, and turned upon its hinges. He saw the glimmering of a fire upon the old walls, and entered.

CHAPTER 71

The dull, red glow of a wood fire—for no lamp or candle burnt within the room—showed him a figure, seated on the hearth with its back towards him, bending over the fitful light. The attitude was that of one who sought the heat. It was, and yet was not. The stooping posture and the cowering form were there, but no hands were stretched out to meet the grateful warmth, no shrug or shiver compared its luxury with the piercing cold outside. With limbs huddled together, head bowed down, arms crossed upon the breast, and fingers tightly clenched, it rocked to and fro upon its seat without a moment's pause, accompanying the action with the mournful sound he had heard.

The heavy door had closed behind him on his entrance, with a crash that made him start. The figure neither spoke, nor turned to look, nor gave in any other way the faintest sign of having heard the noise. The form was that of an old man, his white head akin in colour to the mouldering embers upon which he gazed. He, and the failing light and dying fire, the time-worn room, the solitude, the wasted life, and gloom, were all in fellowship. Ashes, and dust, and ruin!

Kit tried to speak, and did pronounce some words, though what they were he scarcely knew. Still the same terrible low cry went on—still the same rocking in the chair—the same stricken figure was there, unchanged and heedless of his presence.

He had his hand upon the latch, when something in the form—distinctly seen as one log broke and fell, and, as it fell, blazed up—arrested it. He returned to where he had stood before—advanced a pace—another—another still. Another, and he saw the face. Yes! Changed as it was, he knew it well.

'Master!' he cried, stooping on one knee and catching at his hand. 'Dear master. Speak to me!'

The old man turned slowly towards him; and muttered in a hollow voice,

'This is another!—How many of these spirits there have been to-night!'

'No spirit, master. No one but your old servant. You know me now, I am sure? Miss Nell—where is she—where is she?'

'They all say that!' cried the old man. 'They all ask the same question. A spirit!'

'Where is she?' demanded Kit. 'Oh tell me but that,—but that, dear master!'

'She is asleep—yonder—in there.'

'Thank God!'

'Aye! Thank God!' returned the old man. 'I have prayed to Him, many, and many, and many a livelong night, when she has been asleep, He knows. Hark! Did she call?'

'I heard no voice.'

'You did. You hear her now. Do you tell me that you don't hear that?'

He started up, and listened again.

'Nor that?' he cried, with a triumphant smile, 'Can any body know that voice so well as I? Hush! Hush!'

Motioning to him to be silent, he stole away into another chamber. After a short absence (during which he could be heard to speak in a softened soothing tone) he returned, bearing in his hand a lamp.

'She is still asleep,' he whispered. 'You were right. She did not call—unless she did so in her slumber. She has called to me in her sleep before now, sir; as I have sat by, watching, I have seen her lips move, and have known, though no sound came from them, that she spoke of me. I feared the light might dazzle her eyes and wake her, so I brought it here.'

He spoke rather to himself than to the visitor, but when he had put the lamp upon the table, he took it up, as if impelled by some momentary recollection or curiosity, and held it near his face. Then, as if forgetting his motive in the very action, he turned away and put it down again.

'She is sleeping soundly,' he said; 'but no wonder. Angel hands have strewn the ground deep with snow, that the lightest footstep may be lighter yet; and the very birds are dead, that they may not wake her. She used to feed them, Sir. Though never so cold and hungry, the timid things would fly from us. They never flew from her!'

Again he stopped to listen, and scarcely drawing breath, listened for a long, long time. That fancy past, he opened an old chest, took out some clothes as fondly as if they had been living things, and began to smooth and brush them with his hand.

'Why dost thou lie so idle there, dear Nell,' he murmured, 'when there are bright red berries out of doors waiting for thee to pluck them! Why dost thou lie so idle there, when thy little friends come creeping to the door, crying "where is Nell—sweet Nell?"—and sob, and weep, because they do not see thee. She was always gentle with children. The wildest would do her bidding—she had a tender way with them, indeed she had!'

Kit had no power to speak. His eyes were filled with tears.

'Her little homely dress,—her favourite!' cried the old man, pressing it to his breast, and patting it with his shrivelled hand. 'She will miss it when she wakes. They have hid it here in sport, but she shall have it—she shall have it. I would not vex my darling, for the wide world's riches. See here—these shoes—how worn they are—she kept them to remind her of our last long journey. You see where the little feet went bare upon the ground. They told me, afterwards, that the stones had cut and bruised them. She never told me that. No, no, God bless her! and, I have remembered since, she walked behind me, sir, that I might not see how lame she was—but yet she had my hand in hers, and seemed to lead me still.'

He pressed them to his lips, and having carefully put them back again, went on communing with himself—looking wistfully from time to time towards the chamber he had lately visited.

'She was not wont to be a lie-abed; but she was well then. We must have patience. When she is well again, she will rise early, as she used to do, and ramble abroad in the healthy morning time. I often tried to track the way she had gone, but her small footstep left no print upon the dewy ground, to guide me. Who is that? Shut the door. Quick!—Have we not enough to do to drive away that marble cold, and keep her warm!'

The door was indeed opened, for the entrance of Mr Garland and his friend, accompanied by two other persons. These were the schoolmaster, and the bachelor. The former held a light in his hand. He had, it seemed, but gone to his own cottage to replenish the exhausted lamp, at the moment when Kit came up and found the old man alone.

He softened again at sight of these two friends, and, laying aside the angry manner—if to anything so feeble and so sad the term can be applied—in which he had spoken when the door opened, resumed his former seat, and subsided, by little and little into the old action, and the old, dull, wandering sound.

Of the strangers, he took no heed whatever. He had seen them, but appeared quite incapable of interest or curiosity. The younger brother stood apart. The bachelor drew a chair towards the old man, and sat down close beside him. After a long silence, he ventured to speak.

'Another night, and not in bed!' he said softly; 'I hoped you would be more mindful of your promise to me. Why do you not take some rest?'

'Sleep has left me,' returned the old man. 'It is all with her!'

'It would pain her very much to know that you were watching thus,' said the bachelor. 'You would not give her pain?'

'I am not so sure of that, if it would only rouse her. She has slept so very long. And yet I am rash to say so. It is a good and happy sleep—eh?'

'Indeed it is,' returned the bachelor. 'Indeed, indeed, it is!'

'That's well!—and the waking—' faltered the old man.

'Happy too. Happier than tongue can tell, or heart of man conceive.'

They watched him as he rose and stole on tiptoe to the other chamber where the lamp had been replaced. They listened as he spoke again within its silent walls. They looked into the faces of each other, and no man's cheek was free from tears. He came back, whispering that she was still asleep, but that he thought she had moved. It was her hand, he said—a little—a very, very little—but he was pretty sure she had moved it—perhaps in seeking his. He had known her do that, before now, though in the deepest sleep the while. And when he had said this, he dropped into his chair again, and clasping his hands above his head, uttered a cry never to be forgotten.

The poor schoolmaster motioned to the bachelor that he would come on the other side, and speak to him. They gently unlocked his fingers, which he had twisted in his grey hair, and pressed them in their own.

'He will hear me,' said the schoolmaster, 'I am sure. He will hear either me or you if we beseech him. She would, at all times.'

'I will hear any voice she liked to hear,' cried the old man. 'I love all she loved!'

'I know you do,' returned the schoolmaster. 'I am certain of it. Think of her; think of all the sorrows and afflictions you have shared together; of all the trials, and all the peaceful pleasures, you have jointly known.'

'I do. I do. I think of nothing else.'

'I would have you think of nothing else to-night—of nothing but those things which will soften your heart, dear friend, and open it to old affections and old times. It is so that she would speak to you herself, and in her name it is that I speak now.'

'You do well to speak softly,' said the old man. 'We will not wake her. I should be glad to see her eyes again, and to see her smile. There is a smile upon her young face now, but it is fixed and changeless. I would have it come and go. That shall be in Heaven's good time. We will not wake her.'

'Let us not talk of her in her sleep, but as she used to be when you were journeying together, far away—as she was at home, in the old house from which you fled together—as she was, in the old cheerful time,' said the schoolmaster.

'She was always cheerful—very cheerful,' cried the old man, looking steadfastly at him. 'There was ever something mild and quiet about her, I remember, from the first; but she was of a happy nature.'

'We have heard you say,' pursued the schoolmaster, 'that in this and in all goodness, she was like her mother. You can think of, and remember her?'

He maintained his steadfast look, but gave no answer.

'Or even one before her,' said the bachelor. 'It is many years ago, and affliction makes the time longer, but you have not forgotten her whose death contributed to make this child so dear to you, even before you knew her worth or could read her heart? Say, that you could carry back your thoughts to very distant days—to the time of your early life—when, unlike this fair flower, you did not pass your youth alone. Say, that you could remember, long ago, another child who loved you dearly, you being but a child yourself. Say, that you had a brother, long forgotten, long unseen, long separated from you, who now, at last, in your utmost need came back to comfort and console you—'

'To be to you what you were once to him,' cried the younger, falling on his knee before him; 'to repay your old affection, brother dear, by constant care, solicitude, and love; to be, at your right hand, what he has never ceased to be when oceans rolled between us; to call to witness his unchanging truth and mindfulness of bygone days, whole years of desolation. Give me but one word of recognition, brother—and never—no never, in the brightest moment of our youngest days, when, poor silly boys, we thought to pass our lives together—have we been half as dear and precious to each other as we shall be from this time hence!'

The old man looked from face to face, and his lips moved; but no sound came from them in reply.

'If we were knit together then,' pursued the younger brother, 'what will be the bond between us now! Our love and fellowship began in childhood, when life was all before us, and will be resumed when we have proved it, and are but children at the last. As many restless spirits, who have hunted fortune, fame, or pleasure through the world, retire in their decline to where they first drew breath, vainly seeking to be children once again before they die, so we, less fortunate than they in early life, but happier in its closing scenes, will set up our rest again among our boyish haunts, and going home with no hope realised, that had its growth in manhood—carrying back nothing that we brought away, but our old yearnings to each other—saving no fragment from the wreck of life, but that which first endeared it—may be, indeed, but children as at first. And even,' he added in an altered voice, 'even if what I dread to name has come to pass—even if that be so, or is to be (which Heaven forbid and spare us!)— still, dear brother, we are not apart, and have that comfort in our great affliction.'

By little and little, the old man had drawn back towards the inner chamber, while these words were spoken. He pointed there, as he replied, with trembling lips.

'You plot among you to wean my heart from her. You never will do that—never while I have life. I have no relative or friend but her—I never had—I never will have. She is all in all to me. It is too late to part us now.'

Waving them off with his hand, and calling softly to her as he went, he stole into the room. They who were left behind, drew close together, and after a few whispered words— not unbroken by emotion, or easily uttered—followed him. They moved so gently, that their footsteps made no noise; but there were sobs from among the group, and sounds of grief and mourning.

For she was dead. There, upon her little bed, she lay at rest. The solemn stillness was no marvel now.

She was dead. No sleep so beautiful and calm, so free from trace of pain, so fair to look upon. She seemed a creature fresh from the hand of God, and waiting for the breath of life; not one who had lived and suffered death.

Her couch was dressed with here and there some winter berries and green leaves, gathered in a spot she had been used to favour. 'When I die, put near me something that has loved the light, and had the sky above it always.' Those were her words.

She was dead. Dear, gentle, patient, noble Nell was dead. Her little bird—a poor slight thing the pressure of a finger would have crushed—was stirring nimbly in its cage; and the strong heart of its child mistress was mute and motionless for ever.

363

Where were the traces of her early cares, her sufferings, and fatigues? All gone. Sorrow was dead indeed in her, but peace and perfect happiness were born; imaged in her tranquil beauty and profound repose.

And still her former self lay there, unaltered in this change. Yes. The old fireside had smiled upon that same sweet face; it had passed, like a dream, through haunts of misery and care; at the door of the poor schoolmaster on the summer evening, before the furnace fire upon the cold wet night, at the still bedside of the dying boy, there had been the same mild lovely look. So shall we know the angels in their majesty, after death.

The old man held one languid arm in his, and had the small hand tight folded to his breast, for warmth. It was the hand she had stretched out to him with her last smile—the hand that had led him on, through all their wanderings. Ever and anon he pressed it to his lips; then hugged it to his breast again, murmuring that it was warmer now; and, as he said it, he looked, in agony, to those who stood around, as if imploring them to help her.

She was dead, and past all help, or need of it. The ancient rooms she had seemed to fill with life, even while her own was waning fast—the garden she had tended—the eyes she had gladdened—the noiseless haunts of many a thoughtful hour—the paths she had trodden as it were but yesterday—could know her never more.

'It is not,' said the schoolmaster, as he bent down to kiss her on the cheek, and gave his tears free vent, 'it is not on earth that Heaven's justice ends. Think what earth is, compared with the World to which her young spirit has winged its early flight; and say, if one deliberate wish expressed in solemn terms above this bed could call her back to life, which of us would utter it!'

CHAPTER 72

When morning came, and they could speak more calmly on the subject of their grief, they heard how her life had closed.

She had been dead two days. They were all about her at the time, knowing that the end was drawing on. She died soon after daybreak. They had read and talked to her in the earlier portion of the night, but as the hours crept on, she sunk to sleep. They could tell, by what she faintly uttered in her dreams, that they were of her journeyings with the old man; they were of no painful scenes, but of people who had helped and used them kindly, for she often said 'God bless you!' with great fervour. Waking, she never wandered in her mind but once, and that was of beautiful music which she said was in the air. God knows. It may have been.

Opening her eyes at last, from a very quiet sleep, she begged that they would kiss her once again. That done, she turned to the old man with a lovely smile upon her face—such, they said, as they had never seen, and never could forget—and clung with both her arms about his neck. They did not know that she was dead, at first.

She had spoken very often of the two sisters, who, she said, were like dear friends to her. She wished they could be told how much she thought about them, and how she had watched them as they walked together, by the river side at night. She would like to see poor Kit, she had often said of late. She wished there was somebody to take her love to Kit. And, even then, she never thought or spoke about him, but with something of her old, clear, merry laugh.

For the rest, she had never murmured or complained; but with a quiet mind, and manner quite unaltered—save that she every day became more earnest and more grateful to them—faded like the light upon a summer's evening.

The child who had been her little friend came there, almost as soon as it was day, with an offering of dried flowers which he begged them to lay upon her breast. It was he who had come to the window overnight and spoken to the sexton, and they saw in the snow traces of small feet, where he had been lingering near the room in which she lay, before he went to bed. He had a fancy, it seemed, that they had left her there alone; and could not bear the thought.

He told them of his dream again, and that it was of her being restored to them, just as she used to be. He begged hard to see her, saying that he would be very quiet, and that they need not fear his being alarmed, for he had sat alone by his young brother all day long when he was dead, and had felt glad to be so near him. They let him have his wish; and indeed he kept his word, and was, in his childish way, a lesson to them all.

Up to that time, the old man had not spoken once—except to her—or stirred from the bedside. But, when he saw her little favourite, he was moved as they had not seen him yet, and made as though he would have him come nearer. Then, pointing to the bed, he burst into tears for the first time, and they who stood by, knowing that the sight of this child had done him good, left them alone together.

Soothing him with his artless talk of her, the child persuaded him to take some rest, to walk abroad, to do almost as he desired him. And when the day came on, which must remove her in her earthly shape from earthly eyes for ever, he led him away, that he might not know when she was taken from him.

They were to gather fresh leaves and berries for her bed. It was Sunday—a bright, clear, wintry afternoon—and as they traversed the village street, those who were walking in their path drew back to make way for them, and gave them a softened greeting. Some shook the old man kindly by the hand, some stood uncovered while he tottered by, and many cried 'God help him!' as he passed along.

'Neighbour!' said the old man, stopping at the cottage where his young guide's mother dwelt, 'how is it that the folks are nearly all in black to-day? I have seen a mourning ribbon or a piece of crape on almost every one.'

She could not tell, the woman said.

'Why, you yourself—you wear the colour too?' he said. 'Windows are closed that never used to be by day. What does this mean?'

Again the woman said she could not tell.

'We must go back,' said the old man, hurriedly. 'We must see what this is.'

'No, no,' cried the child, detaining him. 'Remember what you promised. Our way is to the old green lane, where she and I so often were, and where you found us, more than once, making those garlands for her garden. Do not turn back!'

'Where is she now?' said the old man. 'Tell me that.'

'Do you not know?' returned the child. 'Did we not leave her, but just now?'

'True. True. It was her we left—was it?'

He pressed his hand upon his brow, looked vacantly round, and as if impelled by a sudden thought, crossed the road, and entered the sexton's house. He and his deaf assistant were sitting before the fire. Both rose up, on seeing who it was.

The child made a hasty sign to them with his hand. It was the action of an instant, but that, and the old man's look, were quite enough.

'Do you—do you bury any one to-day?' he said, eagerly.

'No, no! Who should we bury, Sir?' returned the sexton.

'Aye, who indeed! I say with you, who indeed!'

'It is a holiday with us, good Sir,' returned the sexton mildly. 'We have no work to do to-day.'

'Why then, I'll go where you will,' said the old man, turning to the child. 'You're sure of what you tell me? You would not deceive me? I am changed, even in the little time since you last saw me.'

'Go thy ways with him, Sir,' cried the sexton, 'and Heaven be with ye both!'

'I am quite ready,' said the old man, meekly. 'Come, boy, come—' and so submitted to be led away.

And now the bell—the bell she had so often heard, by night and day, and listened to with solemn pleasure almost as a living voice—rung its remorseless toll, for her, so young, so beautiful, so good. Decrepit age, and vigorous life, and blooming youth, and helpless infancy, poured forth—on crutches, in the pride of strength and health, in the full blush of promise, in the mere dawn of life—to gather round her tomb. Old men were there, whose eyes were dim and senses failing—grandmothers, who might have died ten years ago, and still been old—the deaf, the blind, the lame, the palsied, the living dead in many shapes and forms, to see the closing of that early grave. What was the death it would shut in, to that which still could crawl and creep above it!

Along the crowded path they bore her now; pure as the newly-fallen snow that covered it; whose day on earth had been as fleeting. Under the porch, where she had sat when Heaven in its mercy brought her to that peaceful spot, she passed again; and the old church received her in its quiet shade.

They carried her to one old nook, where she had many and many a time sat musing, and laid their burden softly on the pavement. The light streamed on it through the coloured window—a window, where the boughs of trees were ever rustling in the summer, and where the birds sang sweetly all day long. With every breath of air that stirred among those branches in the sunshine, some trembling, changing light, would fall upon her grave.

Earth to earth, ashes to ashes, dust to dust! Many a young hand dropped in its little wreath, many a stifled sob was heard. Some—and they were not a few—knelt down. All were sincere and truthful in their sorrow.

The service done, the mourners stood apart, and the villagers closed round to look into the grave before the pavement-stone should be replaced. One called to mind how he had seen her sitting on that very spot, and how her book had fallen on her lap, and she was gazing with a pensive face upon the sky. Another told, how he had wondered much that one so delicate as she, should be so bold; how she had never feared to enter the church alone at night, but had loved to linger there when all was quiet, and even to climb the tower stair, with no more light than that of the moon rays stealing through the loopholes in the thick old wall. A whisper went about among the oldest, that she had seen and talked with angels; and when they called to mind how she had looked, and spoken, and her early death, some thought it might be so, indeed. Thus, coming to the grave in little knots, and glancing down, and giving place to others, and falling off in whispering groups of three or four, the church was cleared in time, of all but the sexton and the mourning friends.

They saw the vault covered, and the stone fixed down. Then, when the dusk of evening had come on, and not a sound disturbed the sacred stillness of the place—when the bright moon poured in her light on tomb and monument, on pillar, wall, and arch, and most of all (it seemed to them) upon her quiet grave—in that calm time, when outward things and inward thoughts teem with assurances of immortality, and worldly hopes and fears are humbled in the dust before them—then, with tranquil and submissive hearts they turned away, and left the child with God.

Oh! it is hard to take to heart the lesson that such deaths will teach, but let no man reject it, for it is one that all must learn, and is a mighty, universal Truth. When Death strikes down the innocent and young, for every fragile form from which he lets the panting spirit free, a hundred virtues rise, in shapes of mercy, charity, and love, to walk the world, and bless it. Of every tear that sorrowing mortals shed on such green graves, some good is born, some gentler nature comes. In the Destroyer's steps there spring up bright creations that defy his power, and his dark path becomes a way of light to Heaven.

It was late when the old man came home. The boy had led him to his own dwelling, under some pretence, on their way back; and, rendered drowsy by his long ramble and late want of rest, he had sunk into a deep sleep by the fireside. He was perfectly exhausted, and they were careful not to rouse him. The slumber held him a long time, and when he at length awoke the moon was shining.

The younger brother, uneasy at his protracted absence, was watching at the door for his coming, when he appeared in the pathway with his little guide. He advanced to meet them, and tenderly obliging the old man to lean upon his arm, conducted him with slow and trembling steps towards the house.

He repaired to her chamber, straight. Not finding what he had left there, he returned with distracted looks to the room in which they were assembled. From that, he rushed into the schoolmaster's cottage, calling her name. They followed close upon him, and when he had vainly searched it, brought him home.

With such persuasive words as pity and affection could suggest, they prevailed upon him to sit among them and hear what they should tell him. Then endeavouring by every little artifice to prepare his mind for what must come, and dwelling with many fervent words upon the happy lot to which she had been removed, they told him, at last, the truth. The moment it had passed their lips, he fell down among them like a murdered man.

For many hours, they had little hope of his surviving; but grief is strong, and he recovered.

If there be any who have never known the blank that follows death—the weary void—the sense of desolation that will come upon the strongest minds, when something familiar and beloved is missed at every turn—the connection between inanimate and senseless things, and the object of recollection, when every household god becomes a monument and every room a grave—if there be any who have not known this, and proved it by their own experience, they can never faintly guess how, for many days, the old man pined and moped away the time, and wandered here and there as seeking something, and had no comfort.

Whatever power of thought or memory he retained, was all bound up in her. He never understood, or seemed to care to understand, about his brother. To every endearment and attention he continued listless. If they spoke to him on this, or any other theme—save one—he would hear them patiently for awhile, then turn away, and go on seeking as before.

On that one theme, which was in his and all their minds, it was impossible to touch. Dead! He could not hear or bear the word. The slightest hint of it would throw him into a paroxysm, like that he had had when it was first spoken. In what hope he lived, no man could tell; but that he had some hope of finding her again—some faint and shadowy hope, deferred from day to day, and making him from day to day more sick and sore at heart—was plain to all.

They bethought them of a removal from the scene of this last sorrow; of trying whether change of place would rouse or cheer him. His brother sought the advice of those who were accounted skilful in such matters, and they came and saw him. Some of the number staid upon the spot, conversed with him when he would converse, and watched him as he wandered up and down, alone and silent. Move him where they might, they said, he would ever seek to get back there. His mind would run upon that spot. If they confined him closely, and kept a strict guard upon him, they might hold him prisoner, but if he could by any means escape, he would surely wander back to that place, or die upon the road.

The boy, to whom he had submitted at first, had no longer any influence with him. At times he would suffer the child to walk by his side, or would even take such notice of his presence as giving him his hand, or would stop to kiss his cheek, or pat him on the head. At other times, he would entreat him—not unkindly—to be gone, and would not brook him near. But, whether alone, or with this pliant friend, or with those who would have given him, at any cost or sacrifice, some consolation or some peace of mind, if happily the means could have been devised; he was at all times the same—with no love or care for anything in life—a broken-hearted man.

At length, they found, one day, that he had risen early, and, with his knapsack on his back, his staff in hand, her own straw hat, and little basket full of such things as she had been used to carry, was gone. As they were making ready to pursue him far and wide, a frightened schoolboy came who had seen him, but a moment before, sitting in the church—upon her grave, he said.

They hastened there, and going softly to the door, espied him in the attitude of one who waited patiently. They did not disturb him then, but kept a watch upon him all that day. When it grew quite dark, he rose and returned home, and went to bed, murmuring to himself, 'She will come to-morrow!'

Upon the morrow he was there again from sunrise until night; and still at night he laid him down to rest, and murmured, 'She will come to-morrow!'

And thenceforth, every day, and all day long, he waited at her grave, for her. How many pictures of new journeys over pleasant country, of resting-places under the free broad sky, of rambles in the fields and woods, and paths not often trodden—how many tones of that one well-remembered voice, how many glimpses of the form, the fluttering dress, the hair that waved so gaily in the wind—how many visions of what had been, and what he hoped was yet to be—rose up before him, in the old, dull, silent church! He never told them what he thought, or where he went. He would sit with them at night, pondering with a secret satisfaction, they could see, upon the flight that he and she would take before night came again; and still they would hear him whisper in his prayers, 'Lord! Let her come to-morrow!'

The last time was on a genial day in spring. He did not return at the usual hour, and they went to seek him. He was lying dead upon the stone.

They laid him by the side of her whom he had loved so well; and, in the church where they had often prayed, and mused, and lingered hand in hand, the child and the old man slept together.

CHAPTER 73

The magic reel, which, rolling on before, has led the chronicler thus far, now slackens in its pace, and stops. It lies before the goal; the pursuit is at an end.

It remains but to dismiss the leaders of the little crowd who have borne us company upon the road, and so to close the journey.

Foremost among them, smooth Sampson Brass and Sally, arm in arm, claim our polite attention.

Mr Sampson, then, being detained, as already has been shown, by the justice upon whom he called, and being so strongly pressed to protract his stay that he could by no means refuse, remained under his protection for a considerable time, during which the great attention of his entertainer kept him so extremely close, that he was quite lost to society, and never even went abroad for exercise saving into a small paved yard. So well, indeed, was his modest and retiring temper understood by those with whom he had to deal, and so jealous were they of his absence, that they required a kind of friendly bond to be entered into by two substantial housekeepers, in the sum of fifteen hundred pounds a-piece, before they would suffer him to quit their hospitable roof—doubting, it appeared, that he would return, if once let loose, on any other terms. Mr Brass, struck with the humour of this jest, and carrying out its spirit to the utmost, sought from his wide connection a pair of friends whose joint possessions fell some halfpence short of fifteen pence, and proffered them as bail—for that was the merry word agreed upon both sides. These gentlemen being rejected after twenty-four hours' pleasantry, Mr Brass consented to remain, and did remain, until a club of choice spirits called a Grand Jury (who were in the joke) summoned him to a trial before twelve other wags for perjury and fraud, who in their turn found him guilty with a most facetious joy,—nay, the very populace entered into the whim, and when Mr Brass was moving in a hackney-coach towards the building where these wags assembled, saluted him with rotten eggs and carcases of kittens, and feigned to wish to tear him into shreds, which greatly increased the comicality of the thing, and made him relish it the more, no doubt.

To work this sportive vein still further, Mr Brass, by his counsel, moved in arrest of judgment that he had been led to criminate himself, by assurances of safety and promises of pardon, and claimed the leniency which the law extends to such confiding natures as are thus deluded. After solemn argument, this point (with others of a technical nature, whose humorous extravagance it would be difficult to exaggerate) was referred to the judges for their decision, Sampson being meantime removed to his former quarters. Finally, some of the points were given in Sampson's favour, and some against him; and the upshot was, that, instead of being desired to travel for a time in foreign parts, he was permitted to grace the mother country under certain insignificant restrictions.

These were, that he should, for a term of years, reside in a spacious mansion where several other gentlemen were lodged and boarded at the public charge, who went clad in a sober uniform of grey turned up with yellow, had their hair cut extremely short, and chiefly lived on gruel and light soup. It was also required of him that he should partake of their exercise of constantly ascending an endless flight of stairs; and, lest his legs, unused to such exertion, should be weakened by it, that he should wear upon one ankle an amulet or charm of iron. These conditions being arranged, he was removed one evening to his new abode, and enjoyed, in common with nine other gentlemen, and two ladies, the privilege of being taken to his place of retirement in one of Royalty's own carriages.

Over and above these trifling penalties, his name was erased and blotted out from the roll of attorneys; which erasure has been always held in these latter times to be a great degradation and reproach, and to imply the commission of some amazing villany—as indeed it would seem to be the case, when so many worthless names remain among its better records, unmolested.

Of Sally Brass, conflicting rumours went abroad. Some said with confidence that she had gone down to the docks in male attire, and had become a female sailor; others darkly whispered that she had enlisted as a private in the second regiment of Foot Guards, and had been seen in uniform, and on duty, to wit, leaning on her musket and looking out of a sentry-box in St James's Park, one evening. There were many such whispers as these in circulation; but the truth appears to be that, after the lapse of some five years (during which there is no direct evidence of her having been seen at all), two wretched people were more than once observed to crawl at dusk from the inmost recesses of St Giles's, and to take their way along the streets, with shuffling steps and cowering shivering forms, looking into the roads and kennels as they went in search of refuse food or disregarded offal. These forms were never beheld but in those nights of cold and gloom, when the terrible spectres, who lie at all other times in the obscene hiding-places of London, in archways, dark vaults and cellars, venture to creep into the streets; the embodied spirits of Disease, and Vice, and Famine. It was whispered by those who should have known, that these were Sampson and his sister Sally; and to this day, it is said, they sometimes pass, on bad nights, in the same loathsome guise, close at the elbow of the shrinking passenger.

The body of Quilp being found—though not until some days had elapsed—an inquest was held on it near the spot where it had been washed ashore. The general supposition was that he had committed suicide, and, this appearing to be favoured by all the circumstances of his death, the verdict was to that effect. He was left to be buried with a stake through his heart in the centre of four lonely roads.

It was rumoured afterwards that this horrible and barbarous ceremony had been dispensed with, and that the remains had been secretly given up to Tom Scott. But even here, opinion was divided; for some said Tom dug them up at midnight, and carried them to a place indicated to him by the widow. It is probable that both these stories may have had their origin in the simple fact of Tom's shedding tears upon the inquest—which he certainly did, extraordinary as it may appear. He manifested, besides, a strong desire to assault the jury; and being restrained and conducted out of court, darkened its only window by standing on his head upon the sill, until he was dexterously tilted upon his feet again by a cautious beadle.

Being cast upon the world by his master's death, he determined to go through it upon his head and hands, and accordingly began to tumble for his bread. Finding, however, his English birth an insurmountable obstacle to his advancement in this pursuit (notwithstanding that his art was in high repute and favour), he assumed the name of an Italian image lad, with whom he had become acquainted; and afterwards tumbled with extraordinary success, and to overflowing audiences.

Little Mrs Quilp never quite forgave herself the one deceit that lay so heavy on her conscience, and never spoke or thought of it but with bitter tears. Her husband had no relations, and she was rich. He had made no will, or she would probably have been poor. Having married the first time at her mother's instigation, she consulted in her second choice nobody but herself. It fell upon a smart young fellow enough; and as he made it a preliminary condition that Mrs Jiniwin should be thenceforth an out-pensioner, they lived together after marriage with no more than the average amount of quarrelling, and led a merry life upon the dead dwarf's money.

Mr and Mrs Garland, and Mr Abel, went out as usual (except that there was a change in their household, as will be seen presently), and in due time the latter went into partnership with his friend the notary, on which occasion there was a dinner, and a ball, and great extent of dissipation. Unto this ball there happened to be invited the most bashful young lady that was ever seen, with whom Mr Abel happened to fall in love. HOW it happened, or how they found it out, or which of them first communicated the discovery to the other, nobody knows. But certain it is that in course of time they were married; and equally certain it is that they were the happiest of the happy; and no less certain it is that they deserved to be so. And it is pleasant to write down that they reared a family; because any propagation of goodness and benevolence is no small addition to the aristocracy of nature, and no small subject of rejoicing for mankind at large.

The pony preserved his character for independence and principle down to the last moment of his life; which was an unusually long one, and caused him to be looked upon, indeed, as the very Old Parr of ponies. He often went to and fro with the little phaeton between Mr Garland's and his son's, and, as the old people and the young were frequently together, had a stable of his own at the new establishment, into which he would walk of himself with surprising dignity. He condescended to play with the children, as they grew old enough to cultivate his friendship, and would run up and down the little paddock with them like a dog; but though he relaxed so far, and allowed them such small freedoms as caresses, or even to look at his shoes or hang on by his tail, he never permitted any one among them to mount his back or drive him; thus showing that even their familiarity must have its limits, and that there were points between them far too serious for trifling.

He was not unsusceptible of warm attachments in his later life, for when the good bachelor came to live with Mr Garland upon the clergyman's decease, he conceived a great friendship for him, and amiably submitted to be driven by his hands without the least resistance. He did no work for two or three years before he died, but lived in clover; and his last act (like a choleric old gentleman) was to kick his doctor.

Mr Swiveller, recovering very slowly from his illness, and entering into the receipt of his annuity, bought for the Marchioness a handsome stock of clothes, and put her to school forthwith, in redemption of the vow he had made upon his fevered bed. After casting about for some time for a name which should be worthy of her, he decided in favour of Sophronia Sphynx, as being euphonious and genteel, and furthermore indicative of mystery. Under this title the Marchioness repaired, in tears, to the school of his selection, from which, as she soon distanced all competitors, she was removed before the lapse of many quarters to one of a higher grade. It is but bare justice to Mr Swiveller to say, that, although the expenses of her education kept him in straitened circumstances for half a dozen years, he never slackened in his zeal, and always held himself sufficiently repaid by the accounts he heard (with great gravity) of her advancement, on his monthly visits to the governess, who looked upon him as a literary gentleman of eccentric habits, and of a most prodigious talent in quotation.

In a word, Mr Swiveller kept the Marchioness at this establishment until she was, at a moderate guess, full nineteen years of age— good-looking, clever, and good-humoured; when he began to consider seriously what was to be done next. On one of his periodical visits, while he was revolving this question in his mind, the Marchioness came down to him, alone, looking more smiling and more fresh than ever. Then, it occurred to him, but not for the first time, that if she would marry him, how comfortable they might be! So Richard asked her; whatever she said, it wasn't No; and they were married in good earnest that day week. Which gave Mr Swiveller frequent occasion to remark at divers subsequent periods that there had been a young lady saving up for him after all.

A little cottage at Hampstead being to let, which had in its garden a smoking-box, the envy of the civilised world, they agreed to become its tenants, and, when the honey-moon was over, entered upon its occupation. To this retreat Mr Chuckster repaired regularly every Sunday to spend the day—usually beginning with breakfast—and here he was the great purveyor of general news and fashionable intelligence. For some years he continued a deadly foe to Kit, protesting that he had a better opinion of him when he was supposed to have stolen the five-pound note, than when he was shown to be perfectly free of the crime; inasmuch as his guilt would have had in it something daring and bold, whereas his innocence was but another proof of a sneaking and crafty disposition. By slow degrees, however, he was reconciled to him in the end; and even went so far as to honour him with his patronage, as one who had in some measure reformed, and was therefore to be forgiven. But he never forgot or pardoned that circumstance of the shilling; holding that if he had come back to get another he would have done well enough, but that his returning to work out the former gift was a stain upon his moral character which no penitence or contrition could ever wash away.

Mr Swiveller, having always been in some measure of a philosophic and reflective turn, grew immensely contemplative, at times, in the smoking-box, and was accustomed at such periods to debate in his own mind the mysterious question of Sophronia's parentage. Sophronia herself supposed she was an orphan; but Mr Swiveller, putting various slight circumstances together, often thought Miss Brass must know better than that; and, having heard from his wife of her strange interview with Quilp, entertained sundry misgivings whether that person, in his lifetime, might not also have been able to solve the riddle, had he chosen. These speculations, however, gave him no uneasiness; for Sophronia was ever a most cheerful, affectionate, and provident wife to him; and Dick (excepting for an occasional outbreak with Mr Chuckster, which she had the good sense rather to encourage than oppose) was to her an attached and domesticated husband. And they played many hundred thousand games of cribbage together. And let it be added, to Dick's honour, that, though we have called her Sophronia, he called her the Marchioness from first to last; and that upon every anniversary of the day on which he found her in his sick room, Mr Chuckster came to dinner, and there was great glorification.

The gamblers, Isaac List and Jowl, with their trusty confederate Mr James Groves of unimpeachable memory, pursued their course with varying success, until the failure of a spirited enterprise in the way of their profession, dispersed them in various directions, and caused their career to receive a sudden check from the long and strong arm of the law. This defeat had its origin in the untoward detection of a new associate—young Frederick Trent— who thus became the unconscious instrument of their punishment and his own.

For the young man himself, he rioted abroad for a brief term, living by his wits—which means by the abuse of every faculty that worthily employed raises man above the beasts, and so degraded, sinks him far below them. It was not long before his body was recognised by a stranger, who chanced to visit that hospital in Paris where the drowned are laid out to be owned; despite the bruises and disfigurements which were said to have been occasioned by some previous scuffle. But the stranger kept his own counsel until he returned home, and it was never claimed or cared for.

The younger brother, or the single gentleman, for that designation is more familiar, would have drawn the poor schoolmaster from his lone retreat, and made him his companion and friend. But the humble village teacher was timid of venturing into the noisy world, and had become fond of his dwelling in the old churchyard. Calmly happy in his school, and in the spot, and in the attachment of Her little mourner, he pursued his quiet course in peace; and was, through the righteous gratitude of his friend—let this brief mention suffice for that—a POOR school-master no more.

That friend—single gentleman, or younger brother, which you will—had at his heart a heavy sorrow; but it bred in him no misanthropy or monastic gloom. He went forth into the world, a lover of his kind. For a long, long time, it was his chief delight to travel in the steps of the old man and the child (so far as he could trace them from her last narrative), to halt where they had halted, sympathise where they had suffered, and rejoice where they had been made glad. Those who had been kind to them, did not escape his search. The sisters at the school—they who were her friends, because themselves so friendless—Mrs Jarley of the wax-work, Codlin, Short—he found them all; and trust me, the man who fed the furnace fire was not forgotten.

Kit's story having got abroad, raised him up a host of friends, and many offers of provision for his future life. He had no idea at first of ever quitting Mr Garland's service; but, after serious remonstrance and advice from that gentleman, began to contemplate the possibility of such a change being brought about in time. A good post was procured for him, with a rapidity which took away his breath, by some of the gentlemen who had believed him guilty of the offence laid to his charge, and who had acted upon that belief. Through the same kind agency, his mother was secured from want, and made quite happy. Thus, as Kit often said, his great misfortune turned out to be the source of all his subsequent prosperity.

Did Kit live a single man all his days, or did he marry? Of course he married, and who should be his wife but Barbara? And the best of it was, he married so soon that little Jacob was an uncle, before the calves of his legs, already mentioned in this history, had ever been encased in broadcloth pantaloons,—though that was not quite the best either, for of necessity the baby was an uncle too. The delight of Kit's mother and of Barbara's mother upon the great occasion is past all telling; finding they agreed so well on that, and on all other subjects, they took up their abode together, and were a most harmonious pair of friends from that time forth. And hadn't Astley's cause to bless itself for their all going together once a quarter—to the pit—and didn't Kit's mother always say, when they painted the outside, that Kit's last treat had helped to that, and wonder what the manager would feel if he but knew it as they passed his house!

When Kit had children six and seven years old, there was a Barbara among them, and a pretty Barbara she was. Nor was there wanting an exact facsimile and copy of little Jacob, as he appeared in those remote times when they taught him what oysters meant. Of course there was an Abel, own godson to the Mr Garland of that name; and there was a Dick, whom Mr Swiveller did especially favour. The little group would often gather round him of a night and beg him to tell again that story of good Miss Nell who died. This, Kit would do; and when they cried to hear it, wishing it longer too, he would teach them how she had gone to Heaven, as all good people did; and how, if they were good, like her, they might hope to be there too, one day, and to see and know her as he had done when he was quite a boy. Then, he would relate to them how needy he used to be, and how she had taught him what he was otherwise too poor to learn, and how the old man had been used to say 'she always laughs at Kit;' at which they would brush away their tears, and laugh themselves to think that she had done so, and be again quite merry.

He sometimes took them to the street where she had lived; but new improvements had altered it so much, it was not like the same. The old house had been long ago pulled down, and a fine broad road was in its place. At first he would draw with his stick a square upon the ground to show them where it used to stand. But he soon became uncertain of the spot, and could only say it was thereabouts, he thought, and these alterations were confusing.

Such are the changes which a few years bring about, and so do things pass away, like a tale that is told!

GREAT EXPECTATIONS

Chapter I

My father's family name being Pirrip, and my Christian name Philip, my infant tongue could make of both names nothing longer or more explicit than Pip. So, I called myself Pip, and came to be called Pip.

I give Pirrip as my father's family name, on the authority of his tombstone and my sister,—Mrs. Joe Gargery, who married the blacksmith. As I never saw my father or my mother, and never saw any likeness of either of them (for their days were long before the days of photographs), my first fancies regarding what they were like were unreasonably derived from their tombstones. The shape of the letters on my father's, gave me an odd idea that he was a square, stout, dark man, with curly black hair. From the character and turn of the inscription, "Also Georgiana Wife of the Above," I drew a childish conclusion that my mother was freckled and sickly. To five little stone lozenges, each about a foot and a half long, which were arranged in a neat row beside their grave, and were sacred to the memory of five little brothers of mine,—who gave up trying to get a living, exceedingly early in that universal struggle,—I am indebted for a belief I religiously entertained that they had all been born on their backs with their hands in their trousers-pockets, and had never taken them out in this state of existence.

Ours was the marsh country, down by the river, within, as the river wound, twenty miles of the sea. My first most vivid and broad impression of the identity of things seems to me to have been gained on a memorable raw afternoon towards evening. At such a time I found out for certain that this bleak place overgrown with nettles was the churchyard; and that Philip Pirrip, late of this parish, and also Georgiana wife of the above, were dead and buried; and that Alexander, Bartholomew, Abraham, Tobias, and Roger, infant children of the aforesaid, were also dead and buried; and that the dark flat wilderness beyond the churchyard, intersected with dikes and mounds and gates, with scattered cattle feeding on it, was the marshes; and that the low leaden line beyond was the river; and that the distant savage lair from which the wind was rushing was the sea; and that the small bundle of shivers growing afraid of it all and beginning to cry, was Pip.

"Hold your noise!" cried a terrible voice, as a man started up from among the graves at the side of the church porch. "Keep still, you little devil, or I'll cut your throat!"

A fearful man, all in coarse gray, with a great iron on his leg. A man with no hat, and with broken shoes, and with an old rag tied round his head. A man who had been soaked in water, and smothered in mud, and lamed by stones, and cut by flints, and stung by nettles, and torn by briars; who limped, and shivered, and glared, and growled; and whose teeth chattered in his head as he seized me by the chin.

"Oh! Don't cut my throat, sir," I pleaded in terror. "Pray don't do it, sir."

"Tell us your name!" said the man. "Quick!"

"Pip, sir."

"Once more," said the man, staring at me. "Give it mouth!"

"Pip. Pip, sir."

"Show us where you live," said the man. "Pint out the place!"

I pointed to where our village lay, on the flat in-shore among the alder-trees and pollards, a mile or more from the church.

The man, after looking at me for a moment, turned me upside down, and emptied my pockets. There was nothing in them but a piece of bread. When the church came to itself,—for he was so sudden and strong that he made it go head over heels before me, and I saw the steeple under my feet,—when the church came to itself, I say, I was seated on a high tombstone, trembling while he ate the bread ravenously.

"You young dog," said the man, licking his lips, "what fat cheeks you ha' got."

I believe they were fat, though I was at that time undersized for my years, and not strong.

"Darn me if I couldn't eat em," said the man, with a threatening shake of his head, "and if I han't half a mind to't!"

I earnestly expressed my hope that he wouldn't, and held tighter to the tombstone on which he had put me; partly, to keep myself upon it; partly, to keep myself from crying.

"Now lookee here!" said the man. "Where's your mother?"

"There, sir!" said I.

He started, made a short run, and stopped and looked over his shoulder.

"There, sir!" I timidly explained. "Also Georgiana. That's my mother."

"Oh!" said he, coming back. "And is that your father alonger your mother?"

"Yes, sir," said I; "him too; late of this parish."

"Ha!" he muttered then, considering. "Who d'ye live with,—supposin' you're kindly let to live, which I han't made up my mind about?"

"My sister, sir,—Mrs. Joe Gargery,—wife of Joe Gargery, the blacksmith, sir."

"Blacksmith, eh?" said he. And looked down at his leg.

After darkly looking at his leg and me several times, he came closer to my tombstone, took me by both arms, and tilted me back as far as he could hold me; so that his eyes looked most powerfully down into mine, and mine looked most helplessly up into his.

"Now lookee here," he said, "the question being whether you're to be let to live. You know what a file is?"

"Yes, sir."

"And you know what wittles is?"

"Yes, sir."

After each question he tilted me over a little more, so as to give me a greater sense of helplessness and danger.

"You get me a file." He tilted me again. "And you get me wittles." He tilted me again. "You bring 'em both to me." He tilted me again. "Or I'll have your heart and liver out." He tilted me again.

I was dreadfully frightened, and so giddy that I clung to him with both hands, and said, "If you would kindly please to let me keep upright, sir, perhaps I shouldn't be sick, and perhaps I could attend more."

He gave me a most tremendous dip and roll, so that the church jumped over its own weathercock. Then, he held me by the arms, in an upright position on the top of the stone, and went on in these fearful terms:—

"You bring me, to-morrow morning early, that file and them wittles. You bring the lot to me, at that old Battery over yonder. You do it, and you never dare to say a word or dare to make a sign concerning your having seen such a person as me, or any person sumever, and you shall be let to live. You fail, or you go from my words in any partickler, no matter how small it is, and your heart and your liver shall be tore out, roasted, and ate. Now, I ain't alone, as you may think I am. There's a young man hid with me, in comparison with which young man I am a Angel. That young man hears the words I speak. That young man has a secret way pecooliar to himself, of getting at a boy, and at his heart, and at his liver. It is in wain for a boy to attempt to hide himself from that young man. A boy may lock his door, may be warm in bed, may tuck himself up, may draw the clothes over his head, may think himself comfortable and safe, but that young man will softly creep and creep his way to him and tear him open. I am a keeping that young man from harming of you at the present moment, with great difficulty. I find it wery hard to hold that young man off of your inside. Now, what do you say?"

I said that I would get him the file, and I would get him what broken bits of food I could, and I would come to him at the Battery, early in the morning.

"Say Lord strike you dead if you don't!" said the man.

I said so, and he took me down.

"Now," he pursued, "you remember what you've undertook, and you remember that young man, and you get home!"

"Goo-good night, sir," I faltered.

"Much of that!" said he, glancing about him over the cold wet flat. "I wish I was a frog. Or a eel!"

At the same time, he hugged his shuddering body in both his arms,—clasping himself, as if to hold himself together,—and limped towards the low church wall. As I saw him go, picking his way among the nettles, and among the brambles that bound the green mounds, he looked in my young eyes as if he were eluding the hands of the dead people, stretching up cautiously out of their graves, to get a twist upon his ankle and pull him in.

When he came to the low church wall, he got over it, like a man whose legs were numbed and stiff, and then turned round to look for me. When I saw him turning, I set my face towards home, and made the best use of my legs. But presently I looked over my shoulder, and saw him going on again towards the river, still hugging himself in both arms, and picking his way with his sore feet among the great stones dropped into the marshes here and there, for stepping-places when the rains were heavy or the tide was in.

The marshes were just a long black horizontal line then, as I stopped to look after him; and the river was just another horizontal line, not nearly so broad nor yet so black; and the sky was just a row of long angry red lines and dense black lines intermixed. On the edge of the river I could faintly make out the only two black things in all the prospect that seemed to be standing upright; one of these was the beacon by which the sailors steered,—like an unhooped cask upon a pole,—an ugly thing when you were near it; the other, a gibbet, with some chains hanging to it which had once held a pirate. The man was limping on towards this latter, as if he were the pirate come to life, and come down, and going back to hook himself up again. It gave me a terrible turn when I thought so; and as I saw the cattle lifting their heads to gaze after him, I wondered whether they thought so too. I looked all round for the horrible young man, and could see no signs of him. But now I was frightened again, and ran home without stopping.

Chapter II

My sister, Mrs. Joe Gargery, was more than twenty years older than I, and had established a great reputation with herself and the neighbors because she had brought me up "by hand." Having at that time to find out for myself what the expression meant, and knowing her to have a hard and heavy hand, and to be much in the habit of laying it upon her husband as well as upon me, I supposed that Joe Gargery and I were both brought up by hand.

She was not a good-looking woman, my sister; and I had a general impression that she must have made Joe Gargery marry her by hand. Joe was a fair man, with curls of flaxen hair on each side of his smooth face, and with eyes of such a very undecided blue that they seemed to have somehow got mixed with their own whites. He was a mild, good-natured, sweet-tempered, easy-going, foolish, dear fellow,—a sort of Hercules in strength, and also in weakness.

My sister, Mrs. Joe, with black hair and eyes, had such a prevailing redness of skin that I sometimes used to wonder whether it was possible she washed herself with a nutmeg-grater instead of soap. She was tall and bony, and almost always wore a coarse apron, fastened over her figure behind with two loops, and having a square impregnable bib in front, that was stuck full of pins and needles. She made it a powerful merit in herself, and a strong reproach against Joe, that she wore this apron so much. Though I really see no reason why she should have worn it at all; or why, if she did wear it at all, she should not have taken it off, every day of her life.

Joe's forge adjoined our house, which was a wooden house, as many of the dwellings in our country were,—most of them, at that time. When I ran home from the churchyard, the forge was shut up, and Joe was sitting alone in the kitchen. Joe and I being fellow-sufferers, and having confidences as such, Joe imparted a confidence to me, the moment I raised the latch of the door and peeped in at him opposite to it, sitting in the chimney corner.

"Mrs. Joe has been out a dozen times, looking for you, Pip. And she's out now, making it a baker's dozen."

"Is she?"

"Yes, Pip," said Joe; "and what's worse, she's got Tickler with her."

At this dismal intelligence, I twisted the only button on my waistcoat round and round, and looked in great depression at the fire. Tickler was a wax-ended piece of cane, worn smooth by collision with my tickled frame.

"She sot down," said Joe, "and she got up, and she made a grab at Tickler, and she Rampaged out. That's what she did," said Joe, slowly clearing the fire between the lower bars with the poker, and looking at it; "she Ram-paged out, Pip."

"Has she been gone long, Joe?" I always treated him as a larger species of child, and as no more than my equal.

"Well," said Joe, glancing up at the Dutch clock, "she's been on the Ram-page, this last spell, about five minutes, Pip. She's a coming! Get behind the door, old chap, and have the jack-towel betwixt you."

I took the advice. My sister, Mrs. Joe, throwing the door wide open, and finding an obstruction behind it, immediately divined the cause, and applied Tickler to its further investigation. She concluded by throwing me—I often served as a connubial missile—at Joe, who, glad to get hold of me on any terms, passed me on into the chimney and quietly fenced me up there with his great leg.

"Where have you been, you young monkey?" said Mrs. Joe, stamping her foot. "Tell me directly what you've been doing to wear me away with fret and fright and worrit, or I'd have you out of that corner if you was fifty Pips, and he was five hundred Gargerys."

"I have only been to the churchyard," said I, from my stool, crying and rubbing myself.

"Churchyard!" repeated my sister. "If it warn't for me you'd have been to the churchyard long ago, and stayed there. Who brought you up by hand?"

"You did," said I.

"And why did I do it, I should like to know?" exclaimed my sister.

I whimpered, "I don't know."

"I don't!" said my sister. "I'd never do it again! I know that. I may truly say I've never had this apron of mine off since born you were. It's bad enough to be a blacksmith's wife (and him a Gargery) without being your mother."

My thoughts strayed from that question as I looked disconsolately at the fire. For the fugitive out on the marshes with the ironed leg, the mysterious young man, the file, the food, and the dreadful pledge I was under to commit a larceny on those sheltering premises, rose before me in the avenging coals.

"Hah!" said Mrs. Joe, restoring Tickler to his station. "Churchyard, indeed! You may well say churchyard, you two." One of us, by the by, had not said it at all. "You'll drive me to the churchyard betwixt you, one of these days, and O, a pr-r-recious pair you'd be without me!"

As she applied herself to set the tea-things, Joe peeped down at me over his leg, as if he were mentally casting me and himself up, and calculating what kind of pair we practically should make, under the grievous circumstances foreshadowed. After that, he sat feeling his right-side flaxen curls and whisker, and following Mrs. Joe about with his blue eyes, as his manner always was at squally times.

My sister had a trenchant way of cutting our bread and butter for us, that never varied. First, with her left hand she jammed the loaf hard and fast against her bib,—where it sometimes got a pin into it, and sometimes a needle, which we afterwards got into our mouths. Then she took some butter (not too much) on a knife and spread it on the loaf, in an apothecary kind of way, as if she were making a plaster,—using both sides of the knife with a slapping dexterity, and trimming and moulding the butter off round the crust. Then, she gave the knife a final smart wipe on the edge of the plaster, and then sawed a very thick round off the loaf: which she finally, before separating from the loaf, hewed into two halves, of which Joe got one, and I the other.

On the present occasion, though I was hungry, I dared not eat my slice. I felt that I must have something in reserve for my dreadful acquaintance, and his ally the still more dreadful young man. I knew Mrs. Joe's housekeeping to be of the strictest kind, and that my larcenous researches might find nothing available in the safe. Therefore I resolved to put my hunk of bread and butter down the leg of my trousers.

The effort of resolution necessary to the achievement of this purpose I found to be quite awful. It was as if I had to make up my mind to leap from the top of a high house, or plunge into a great depth of water. And it was made the more difficult by the unconscious Joe. In our already-mentioned freemasonry as fellow-sufferers, and in his good-natured companionship with me, it was our evening habit to compare the way we bit through our slices, by silently holding them up to each other's admiration now and then,—which stimulated us to new exertions. To-night, Joe several times invited me, by the display of his fast diminishing slice, to enter upon our usual friendly competition; but he found me, each time, with my yellow mug of tea on one knee, and my untouched bread and butter on the other. At last, I desperately considered that the thing I contemplated must be done, and that it had best be done in the least improbable manner consistent with the circumstances. I took advantage of a moment when Joe had just looked at me, and got my bread and butter down my leg.

Joe was evidently made uncomfortable by what he supposed to be my loss of appetite, and took a thoughtful bite out of his slice, which he didn't seem to enjoy. He turned it about in his mouth much longer than usual, pondering over it a good deal, and after all gulped it down like a pill. He was about to take another bite, and had just got his head on one side for a good purchase on it, when his eye fell on me, and he saw that my bread and butter was gone.

The wonder and consternation with which Joe stopped on the threshold of his bite and stared at me, were too evident to escape my sister's observation.

"What's the matter now?" said she, smartly, as she put down her cup.

"I say, you know!" muttered Joe, shaking his head at me in very serious remonstrance. "Pip, old chap! You'll do yourself a mischief. It'll stick somewhere. You can't have chawed it, Pip."

"What's the matter now?" repeated my sister, more sharply than before.

"If you can cough any trifle on it up, Pip, I'd recommend you to do it," said Joe, all aghast. "Manners is manners, but still your elth's your elth."

By this time, my sister was quite desperate, so she pounced on Joe, and, taking him by the two whiskers, knocked his head for a little while against the wall behind him, while I sat in the corner, looking guiltily on.

"Now, perhaps you'll mention what's the matter," said my sister, out of breath, "you staring great stuck pig."

Joe looked at her in a helpless way, then took a helpless bite, and looked at me again.

"You know, Pip," said Joe, solemnly, with his last bite in his cheek, and speaking in a confidential voice, as if we two were quite alone, "you and me is always friends, and I'd be the last to tell upon you, any time. But such a—" he moved his chair and looked about the floor between us, and then again at me—"such a most oncommon Bolt as that!"

"Been bolting his food, has he?" cried my sister.

"You know, old chap," said Joe, looking at me, and not at Mrs. Joe, with his bite still in his cheek, "I Bolted, myself, when I was your age—frequent—and as a boy I've been among a many Bolters; but I never see your Bolting equal yet, Pip, and it's a mercy you ain't Bolted dead."

My sister made a dive at me, and fished me up by the hair, saying nothing more than the awful words, "You come along and be dosed."

Some medical beast had revived Tar-water in those days as a fine medicine, and Mrs. Joe always kept a supply of it in the cupboard; having a belief in its virtues correspondent to its nastiness. At the best of times, so much of this elixir was administered to me as a choice restorative, that I was conscious of going about, smelling like a new fence. On this particular evening the urgency of my case demanded a pint of this mixture, which was poured down my throat, for my greater comfort, while Mrs. Joe held my head under her arm, as a boot would be held in a bootjack. Joe got off with half a pint; but was made to swallow that (much to his disturbance, as he sat slowly munching and meditating before the fire), "because he had had a turn." Judging from myself, I should say he certainly had a turn afterwards, if he had had none before.

Conscience is a dreadful thing when it accuses man or boy; but when, in the case of a boy, that secret burden co-operates with another secret burden down the leg of his trousers, it is (as I can testify) a great punishment. The guilty knowledge that I was going to rob Mrs. Joe—I never thought I was going to rob Joe, for I never thought of any of the housekeeping property as his—united to the necessity of always keeping one hand on my bread and butter as I sat, or when I was ordered about the kitchen on any small errand, almost drove me out of my mind. Then, as the marsh winds made the fire glow and flare, I thought I heard the voice outside, of the man with the iron on his leg who had sworn me to secrecy, declaring that he couldn't and wouldn't starve until to-morrow, but must be fed now. At other times, I thought, What if the young man who was with so much difficulty restrained from imbruing his hands in me should yield to a constitutional impatience, or should mistake the time, and should think himself accredited to my heart and liver to-night, instead of to-morrow! If ever anybody's hair stood on end with terror, mine must have done so then. But, perhaps, nobody's ever did?

It was Christmas Eve, and I had to stir the pudding for next day, with a copper-stick, from seven to eight by the Dutch clock. I tried it with the load upon my leg (and that made me think afresh of the man with the load on his leg), and found the tendency of exercise to bring the bread and butter out at my ankle, quite unmanageable. Happily I slipped away, and deposited that part of my conscience in my garret bedroom.

"Hark!" said I, when I had done my stirring, and was taking a final warm in the chimney corner before being sent up to bed; "was that great guns, Joe?"

"Ah!" said Joe. "There's another conwict off."

"What does that mean, Joe?" said I.

Mrs. Joe, who always took explanations upon herself, said, snappishly, "Escaped.

Escaped." Administering the definition like Tar-water.

While Mrs. Joe sat with her head bending over her needlework, I put my mouth into the forms of saying to Joe, "What's a convict?" Joe put his mouth into the forms of returning such a highly elaborate answer, that I could make out nothing of it but the single word "Pip."

"There was a convict off last night," said Joe, aloud, "after sunset-gun. And they fired warning of him. And now it appears they're firing warning of another."

"Who's firing?" said I.

"Drat that boy," interposed my sister, frowning at me over her work, "what a questioner he is. Ask no questions, and you'll be told no lies."

It was not very polite to herself, I thought, to imply that I should be told lies by her even if I did ask questions. But she never was polite unless there was company.

At this point Joe greatly augmented my curiosity by taking the utmost pains to open his mouth very wide, and to put it into the form of a word that looked to me like "sulks." Therefore, I naturally pointed to Mrs. Joe, and put my mouth into the form of saying, "her?" But Joe wouldn't hear of that, at all, and again opened his mouth very wide, and shook the form of a most emphatic word out of it. But I could make nothing of the word.

"Mrs. Joe," said I, as a last resort, "I should like to know—if you wouldn't much mind— where the firing comes from?"

"Lord bless the boy!" exclaimed my sister, as if she didn't quite mean that but rather the contrary. "From the Hulks!"

"Oh-h!" said I, looking at Joe. "Hulks!"

Joe gave a reproachful cough, as much as to say, "Well, I told you so."

"And please, what's Hulks?" said I.

"That's the way with this boy!" exclaimed my sister, pointing me out with her needle and thread, and shaking her head at me. "Answer him one question, and he'll ask you a dozen directly. Hulks are prison-ships, right 'cross th' meshes." We always used that name for marshes, in our country.

"I wonder who's put into prison-ships, and why they're put there?" said I, in a general way, and with quiet desperation.

It was too much for Mrs. Joe, who immediately rose. "I tell you what, young fellow," said she, "I didn't bring you up by hand to badger people's lives out. It would be blame to me and not praise, if I had. People are put in the Hulks because they murder, and because they rob, and forge, and do all sorts of bad; and they always begin by asking questions. Now, you get along to bed!"

I was never allowed a candle to light me to bed, and, as I went upstairs in the dark, with my head tingling,—from Mrs. Joe's thimble having played the tambourine upon it, to accompany her last words,—I felt fearfully sensible of the great convenience that the hulks were handy for me. I was clearly on my way there. I had begun by asking questions, and I was going to rob Mrs. Joe.

Since that time, which is far enough away now, I have often thought that few people know what secrecy there is in the young under terror. No matter how unreasonable the terror, so that it be terror. I was in mortal terror of the young man who wanted my heart and liver; I was in mortal terror of my interlocutor with the iron leg; I was in mortal terror of myself, from whom an awful promise had been extracted; I had no hope of deliverance through my all-powerful sister, who repulsed me at every turn; I am afraid to think of what I might have done on requirement, in the secrecy of my terror.

If I slept at all that night, it was only to imagine myself drifting down the river on a strong spring-tide, to the Hulks; a ghostly pirate calling out to me through a speaking-trumpet, as I passed the gibbet-station, that I had better come ashore and be hanged there at once, and not put it off. I was afraid to sleep, even if I had been inclined, for I knew that at the first faint dawn of morning I must rob the pantry. There was no doing it in the night, for there was no getting a light by easy friction then; to have got one I must have struck it out of flint and steel, and have made a noise like the very pirate himself rattling his chains.

As soon as the great black velvet pall outside my little window was shot with gray, I got up and went downstairs; every board upon the way, and every crack in every board calling after me, "Stop thief!" and "Get up, Mrs. Joe!" In the pantry, which was far more abundantly supplied than usual, owing to the season, I was very much alarmed by a hare hanging up by the heels, whom I rather thought I caught, when my back was half turned, winking. I had no time for verification, no time for selection, no time for anything, for I had no time to spare. I stole some bread, some rind of cheese, about half a jar of mincemeat (which I tied up in my pocket-handkerchief with my last night's slice), some brandy from a stone bottle (which I decanted into a glass bottle I had secretly used for making that intoxicating fluid, Spanish-liquorice-water, up in my room: diluting the stone bottle from a jug in the kitchen cupboard), a meat bone with very little on it, and a beautiful round compact pork pie. I was nearly going away without the pie, but I was tempted to mount upon a shelf, to look what it was that was put away so carefully in a covered earthenware dish in a corner, and I found it was the pie, and I took it in the hope that it was not intended for early use, and would not be missed for some time.

There was a door in the kitchen, communicating with the forge; I unlocked and unbolted that door, and got a file from among Joe's tools. Then I put the fastenings as I had found them, opened the door at which I had entered when I ran home last night, shut it, and ran for the misty marshes.

Chapter III

It was a rimy morning, and very damp. I had seen the damp lying on the outside of my little window, as if some goblin had been crying there all night, and using the window for a pocket-handkerchief. Now, I saw the damp lying on the bare hedges and spare grass, like a coarser sort of spiders' webs; hanging itself from twig to twig and blade to blade. On every rail and gate, wet lay clammy, and the marsh mist was so thick, that the wooden finger on the post directing people to our village—a direction which they never accepted, for they never came there—was invisible to me until I was quite close under it. Then, as I looked up at it, while it dripped, it seemed to my oppressed conscience like a phantom devoting me to the Hulks.

The mist was heavier yet when I got out upon the marshes, so that instead of my running at everything, everything seemed to run at me. This was very disagreeable to a guilty mind. The gates and dikes and banks came bursting at me through the mist, as if they cried as plainly as could be, "A boy with somebody else's pork pie! Stop him!" The cattle came upon me with like suddenness, staring out of their eyes, and steaming out of their nostrils, "Halloa, young thief!" One black ox, with a white cravat on,—who even had to my awakened conscience something of a clerical air,—fixed me so obstinately with his eyes, and moved his blunt head round in such an accusatory manner as I moved round, that I blubbered out to him, "I couldn't help it, sir! It wasn't for myself I took it!" Upon which he put down his head, blew a cloud of smoke out of his nose, and vanished with a kick-up of his hind-legs and a flourish of his tail.

All this time, I was getting on towards the river; but however fast I went, I couldn't warm my feet, to which the damp cold seemed riveted, as the iron was riveted to the leg of the man I was running to meet. I knew my way to the Battery, pretty straight, for I had been down there on a Sunday with Joe, and Joe, sitting on an old gun, had told me that when I was 'prentice to him, regularly bound, we would have such Larks there! However, in the confusion of the mist, I found myself at last too far to the right, and consequently had to try back along the river-side, on the bank of loose stones above the mud and the stakes that staked the tide out. Making my way along here with all despatch, I had just crossed a ditch which I knew to be very near the Battery, and had just scrambled up the mound beyond the ditch, when I saw the man sitting before me. His back was towards me, and he had his arms folded, and was nodding forward, heavy with sleep.

I thought he would be more glad if I came upon him with his breakfast, in that unexpected manner, so I went forward softly and touched him on the shoulder. He instantly jumped up, and it was not the same man, but another man!

And yet this man was dressed in coarse gray, too, and had a great iron on his leg, and was lame, and hoarse, and cold, and was everything that the other man was; except that he had not the same face, and had a flat broad-brimmed low-crowned felt hat on. All this I saw in a moment, for I had only a moment to see it in: he swore an oath at me, made a hit at me,—it was a round weak blow that missed me and almost knocked himself down, for it made him stumble,—and then he ran into the mist, stumbling twice as he went, and I lost him.

"It's the young man!" I thought, feeling my heart shoot as I identified him. I dare say I should have felt a pain in my liver, too, if I had known where it was.

I was soon at the Battery after that, and there was the right man,—hugging himself and limping to and fro, as if he had never all night left off hugging and limping,—waiting for me. He was awfully cold, to be sure. I half expected to see him drop down before my face and die of deadly cold. His eyes looked so awfully hungry too, that when I handed him the file and he laid it down on the grass, it occurred to me he would have tried to eat it, if he had not seen my bundle. He did not turn me upside down this time to get at what I had, but left me right side upwards while I opened the bundle and emptied my pockets.

"What's in the bottle, boy?" said he.

"Brandy," said I.

He was already handing mincemeat down his throat in the most curious manner,—more like a man who was putting it away somewhere in a violent hurry, than a man who was eating it,—but he left off to take some of the liquor. He shivered all the while so violently, that it was quite as much as he could do to keep the neck of the bottle between his teeth, without biting it off.

"I think you have got the ague," said I.

"I'm much of your opinion, boy," said he.

"It's bad about here," I told him. "You've been lying out on the meshes, and they're dreadful aguish. Rheumatic too."

"I'll eat my breakfast afore they're the death of me," said he. "I'd do that, if I was going to be strung up to that there gallows as there is over there, directly afterwards. I'll beat the shivers so far, I'll bet you."

He was gobbling mincemeat, meatbone, bread, cheese, and pork pie, all at once: staring distrustfully while he did so at the mist all round us, and often stopping—even stopping his jaws—to listen. Some real or fancied sound, some clink upon the river or breathing of beast upon the marsh, now gave him a start, and he said, suddenly,—

"You're not a deceiving imp? You brought no one with you?"

"No, sir! No!"

"Nor giv' no one the office to follow you?"

"No!"

"Well," said he, "I believe you. You'd be but a fierce young hound indeed, if at your time of life you could help to hunt a wretched warmint hunted as near death and dunghill as this poor wretched warmint is!"

Something clicked in his throat as if he had works in him like a clock, and was going to strike. And he smeared his ragged rough sleeve over his eyes.

Pitying his desolation, and watching him as he gradually settled down upon the pie, I made bold to say, "I am glad you enjoy it."

"Did you speak?"

"I said I was glad you enjoyed it."

"Thankee, my boy. I do."

I had often watched a large dog of ours eating his food; and I now noticed a decided similarity between the dog's way of eating, and the man's. The man took strong sharp sudden bites, just like the dog. He swallowed, or rather snapped up, every mouthful, too soon and too fast; and he looked sideways here and there while he ate, as if he thought there was danger in every direction of somebody's coming to take the pie away. He was altogether too unsettled in his mind over it, to appreciate it comfortably I thought, or to have anybody to dine with him, without making a chop with his jaws at the visitor. In all of which particulars he was very like the dog.

"I am afraid you won't leave any of it for him," said I, timidly; after a silence during which I had hesitated as to the politeness of making the remark. "There's no more to be got where that came from." It was the certainty of this fact that impelled me to offer the hint.

"Leave any for him? Who's him?" said my friend, stopping in his crunching of pie-crust.

"The young man. That you spoke of. That was hid with you."

"Oh ah!" he returned, with something like a gruff laugh. "Him? Yes, yes! He don't want no wittles."

"I thought he looked as if he did," said I.

The man stopped eating, and regarded me with the keenest scrutiny and the greatest surprise.

"Looked? When?"

"Just now."

"Where?"

"Yonder," said I, pointing; "over there, where I found him nodding asleep, and thought it was you."

He held me by the collar and stared at me so, that I began to think his first idea about cutting my throat had revived.

"Dressed like you, you know, only with a hat," I explained, trembling; "and—and"—I was very anxious to put this delicately—"and with—the same reason for wanting to borrow a file. Didn't you hear the cannon last night?"

"Then there was firing!" he said to himself.

"I wonder you shouldn't have been sure of that," I returned, "for we heard it up at home, and that's farther away, and we were shut in besides."

"Why, see now!" said he. "When a man's alone on these flats, with a light head and a light stomach, perishing of cold and want, he hears nothin' all night, but guns firing, and voices calling. Hears? He sees the soldiers, with their red coats lighted up by the torches carried afore, closing in round him. Hears his number called, hears himself challenged, hears the rattle of the muskets, hears the orders 'Make ready! Present! Cover him steady, men!' and is laid hands on—and there's nothin'! Why, if I see one pursuing party last night—coming up in order, Damn 'em, with their tramp, tramp—I see a hundred. And as to firing! Why, I see the mist shake with the cannon, arter it was broad day,—But this man"; he had said all the rest, as if he had forgotten my being there; "did you notice anything in him?"

"He had a badly bruised face," said I, recalling what I hardly knew I knew.

"Not here?" exclaimed the man, striking his left cheek mercilessly, with the flat of his hand.

"Yes, there!"

"Where is he?" He crammed what little food was left, into the breast of his gray jacket. "Show me the way he went. I'll pull him down, like a bloodhound. Curse this iron on my sore leg! Give us hold of the file, boy."

I indicated in what direction the mist had shrouded the other man, and he looked up at it for an instant. But he was down on the rank wet grass, filing at his iron like a madman, and not minding me or minding his own leg, which had an old chafe upon it and was bloody, but which he handled as roughly as if it had no more feeling in it than the file. I was very much afraid of him again, now that he had worked himself into this fierce hurry, and I was likewise very much afraid of keeping away from home any longer. I told him I must go, but he took no notice, so I thought the best thing I could do was to slip off. The last I saw of him, his head was bent over his knee and he was working hard at his fetter, muttering impatient imprecations at it and at his leg. The last I heard of him, I stopped in the mist to listen, and the file was still going.

Chapter IV

I fully expected to find a Constable in the kitchen, waiting to take me up. But not only was there no Constable there, but no discovery had yet been made of the robbery. Mrs. Joe was prodigiously busy in getting the house ready for the festivities of the day, and Joe had been put upon the kitchen doorstep to keep him out of the dust-pan,—an article into which his destiny always led him, sooner or later, when my sister was vigorously reaping the floors of her establishment.

"And where the deuce ha' you been?" was Mrs. Joe's Christmas salutation, when I and my conscience showed ourselves.

I said I had been down to hear the Carols. "Ah! well!" observed Mrs. Joe. "You might ha' done worse." Not a doubt of that I thought.

"Perhaps if I warn't a blacksmith's wife, and (what's the same thing) a slave with her apron never off, I should have been to hear the Carols," said Mrs. Joe. "I'm rather partial to Carols, myself, and that's the best of reasons for my never hearing any."

Joe, who had ventured into the kitchen after me as the dustpan had retired before us, drew the back of his hand across his nose with a conciliatory air, when Mrs. Joe darted a look at him, and, when her eyes were withdrawn, secretly crossed his two forefingers, and exhibited them to me, as our token that Mrs. Joe was in a cross temper. This was so much her normal state, that Joe and I would often, for weeks together, be, as to our fingers, like monumental Crusaders as to their legs.

We were to have a superb dinner, consisting of a leg of pickled pork and greens, and a pair of roast stuffed fowls. A handsome mince-pie had been made yesterday morning (which accounted for the mincemeat not being missed), and the pudding was already on the boil. These extensive arrangements occasioned us to be cut off unceremoniously in respect of breakfast; "for I ain't," said Mrs. Joe,—"I ain't a going to have no formal cramming and busting and washing up now, with what I've got before me, I promise you!"

So, we had our slices served out, as if we were two thousand troops on a forced march instead of a man and boy at home; and we took gulps of milk and water, with apologetic countenances, from a jug on the dresser. In the meantime, Mrs. Joe put clean white curtains up, and tacked a new flowered flounce across the wide chimney to replace the old one, and uncovered the little state parlor across the passage, which was never uncovered at any other time, but passed the rest of the year in a cool haze of silver paper, which even extended to the four little white crockery poodles on the mantel-shelf, each with a black nose and a basket of flowers in his mouth, and each the counterpart of the other. Mrs. Joe was a very clean housekeeper, but had an exquisite art of making her cleanliness more uncomfortable and unacceptable than dirt itself. Cleanliness is next to Godliness, and some people do the same by their religion.

My sister, having so much to do, was going to church vicariously, that is to say, Joe and I were going. In his working-clothes, Joe was a well-knit characteristic-looking blacksmith;

in his holiday clothes, he was more like a scarecrow in good circumstances, than anything else. Nothing that he wore then fitted him or seemed to belong to him; and everything that he wore then grazed him. On the present festive occasion he emerged from his room, when the blithe bells were going, the picture of misery, in a full suit of Sunday penitentials. As to me, I think my sister must have had some general idea that I was a young offender whom an Accoucheur Policeman had taken up (on my birthday) and delivered over to her, to be dealt with according to the outraged majesty of the law. I was always treated as if I had insisted on being born in opposition to the dictates of reason, religion, and morality, and against the dissuading arguments of my best friends. Even when I was taken to have a new suit of clothes, the tailor had orders to make them like a kind of Reformatory, and on no account to let me have the free use of my limbs.

Joe and I going to church, therefore, must have been a moving spectacle for compassionate minds. Yet, what I suffered outside was nothing to what I underwent within. The terrors that had assailed me whenever Mrs. Joe had gone near the pantry, or out of the room, were only to be equalled by the remorse with which my mind dwelt on what my hands had done. Under the weight of my wicked secret, I pondered whether the Church would be powerful enough to shield me from the vengeance of the terrible young man, if I divulged to that establishment. I conceived the idea that the time when the banns were read and when the clergyman said, "Ye are now to declare it!" would be the time for me to rise and propose a private conference in the vestry. I am far from being sure that I might not have astonished our small congregation by resorting to this extreme measure, but for its being Christmas Day and no Sunday.

Mr. Wopsle, the clerk at church, was to dine with us; and Mr. Hubble the wheelwright and Mrs. Hubble; and Uncle Pumblechook (Joe's uncle, but Mrs. Joe appropriated him), who was a well-to-do cornchandler in the nearest town, and drove his own chaise-cart. The dinner hour was half-past one. When Joe and I got home, we found the table laid, and Mrs. Joe dressed, and the dinner dressing, and the front door unlocked (it never was at any other time) for the company to enter by, and everything most splendid. And still, not a word of the robbery.

The time came, without bringing with it any relief to my feelings, and the company came. Mr. Wopsle, united to a Roman nose and a large shining bald forehead, had a deep voice which he was uncommonly proud of; indeed it was understood among his acquaintance that if you could only give him his head, he would read the clergyman into fits; he himself confessed that if the Church was "thrown open," meaning to competition, he would not despair of making his mark in it. The Church not being "thrown open," he was, as I have said, our clerk. But he punished the Amens tremendously; and when he gave out the psalm,—always giving the whole verse,—he looked all round the congregation first, as much as to say, "You have heard my friend overhead; oblige me with your opinion of this style!"

I opened the door to the company,—making believe that it was a habit of ours to open that door,—and I opened it first to Mr. Wopsle, next to Mr. and Mrs. Hubble, and last of all to Uncle Pumblechook. N.B. I was not allowed to call him uncle, under the severest penalties.

"Mrs. Joe," said Uncle Pumblechook, a large hard-breathing middle-aged slow man, with a mouth like a fish, dull staring eyes, and sandy hair standing upright on his head, so that he looked as if he had just been all but choked, and had that moment come to, "I have brought you as the compliments of the season—I have brought you, Mum, a bottle of sherry wine—

and I have brought you, Mum, a bottle of port wine."

Every Christmas Day he presented himself, as a profound novelty, with exactly the same words, and carrying the two bottles like dumb-bells. Every Christmas Day, Mrs. Joe replied, as she now replied, "O, Un—cle Pum-ble—chook! This is kind!" Every Christmas Day, he retorted, as he now retorted, "It's no more than your merits. And now are you all bobbish, and how's Sixpennorth of halfpence?" meaning me.

We dined on these occasions in the kitchen, and adjourned, for the nuts and oranges and apples to the parlor; which was a change very like Joe's change from his working-clothes to his Sunday dress. My sister was uncommonly lively on the present occasion, and indeed was generally more gracious in the society of Mrs. Hubble than in other company. I remember Mrs. Hubble as a little curly sharp-edged person in sky-blue, who held a conventionally juvenile position, because she had married Mr. Hubble,—I don't know at what remote period,—when she was much younger than he. I remember Mr Hubble as a tough, high-shouldered, stooping old man, of a sawdusty fragrance, with his legs extraordinarily wide apart: so that in my short days I always saw some miles of open country between them when I met him coming up the lane.

Among this good company I should have felt myself, even if I hadn't robbed the pantry, in a false position. Not because I was squeezed in at an acute angle of the tablecloth, with the table in my chest, and the Pumblechookian elbow in my eye, nor because I was not allowed to speak (I didn't want to speak), nor because I was regaled with the scaly tips of the drumsticks of the fowls, and with those obscure corners of pork of which the pig, when living, had had the least reason to be vain. No; I should not have minded that, if they would only have left me alone. But they wouldn't leave me alone. They seemed to think the opportunity lost, if they failed to point the conversation at me, every now and then, and stick the point into me. I might have been an unfortunate little bull in a Spanish arena, I got so smartingly touched up by these moral goads.

It began the moment we sat down to dinner. Mr. Wopsle said grace with theatrical declamation,—as it now appears to me, something like a religious cross of the Ghost in Hamlet with Richard the Third,—and ended with the very proper aspiration that we might be truly grateful. Upon which my sister fixed me with her eye, and said, in a low reproachful voice, "Do you hear that? Be grateful."

"Especially," said Mr. Pumblechook, "be grateful, boy, to them which brought you up by hand."

Mrs. Hubble shook her head, and contemplating me with a mournful presentiment that I should come to no good, asked, "Why is it that the young are never grateful?" This moral mystery seemed too much for the company until Mr. Hubble tersely solved it by saying, "Naterally wicious." Everybody then murmured "True!" and looked at me in a particularly unpleasant and personal manner.

Joe's station and influence were something feebler (if possible) when there was company than when there was none. But he always aided and comforted me when he could, in some way of his own, and he always did so at dinner-time by giving me gravy, if there were any. There being plenty of gravy to-day, Joe spooned into my plate, at this point, about half a pint.

A little later on in the dinner, Mr. Wopsle reviewed the sermon with some severity, and intimated—in the usual hypothetical case of the Church being "thrown open"—what kind of sermon he would have given them. After favoring them with some heads of that discourse, he remarked that he considered the subject of the day's homily, ill chosen; which was the less excusable, he added, when there were so many subjects "going about."

"True again," said Uncle Pumblechook. "You've hit it, sir! Plenty of subjects going about, for them that know how to put salt upon their tails. That's what's wanted. A man needn't go far to find a subject, if he's ready with his salt-box." Mr. Pumblechook added, after a short interval of reflection, "Look at Pork alone. There's a subject! If you want a subject, look at Pork!"

"True, sir. Many a moral for the young," returned Mr. Wopsle,—and I knew he was going to lug me in, before he said it; "might be deduced from that text."

("You listen to this," said my sister to me, in a severe parenthesis.)

Joe gave me some more gravy.

"Swine," pursued Mr. Wopsle, in his deepest voice, and pointing his fork at my blushes, as if he were mentioning my Christian name,—"swine were the companions of the prodigal. The gluttony of Swine is put before us, as an example to the young." (I thought this pretty well in him who had been praising up the pork for being so plump and juicy.) "What is detestable in a pig is more detestable in a boy."

"Or girl," suggested Mr. Hubble.

"Of course, or girl, Mr. Hubble," assented Mr. Wopsle, rather irritably, "but there is no girl present."

"Besides," said Mr. Pumblechook, turning sharp on me, "think what you've got to be grateful for. If you'd been born a Squeaker—"

"He was, if ever a child was," said my sister, most emphatically.

Joe gave me some more gravy.

"Well, but I mean a four-footed Squeaker," said Mr. Pumblechook. "If you had been born such, would you have been here now? Not you—"

"Unless in that form," said Mr. Wopsle, nodding towards the dish.

"But I don't mean in that form, sir," returned Mr. Pumblechook, who had an objection to being interrupted; "I mean, enjoying himself with his elders and betters, and improving himself with their conversation, and rolling in the lap of luxury. Would he have been doing that? No, he wouldn't. And what would have been your destination?" turning on me again. "You would have been disposed of for so many shillings according to the market price of the article, and Dunstable the butcher would have come up to you as you lay in your straw, and he would have whipped you under his left arm, and with his right he would have tucked up his frock to get a penknife from out of his waistcoat-pocket, and he would have shed your blood and had your life. No bringing up by hand then. Not a bit of it!"

Joe offered me more gravy, which I was afraid to take.

"He was a world of trouble to you, ma'am," said Mrs. Hubble, commiserating my sister.

"Trouble?" echoed my sister; "trouble?" and then entered on a fearful catalogue of all the illnesses I had been guilty of, and all the acts of sleeplessness I had committed, and all the high places I had tumbled from, and all the low places I had tumbled into, and all the injuries I had done myself, and all the times she had wished me in my grave, and I had contumaciously refused to go there.

I think the Romans must have aggravated one another very much, with their noses. Perhaps, they became the restless people they were, in consequence. Anyhow, Mr. Wopsle's Roman nose so aggravated me, during the recital of my misdemeanours, that I should have liked to pull it until he howled. But, all I had endured up to this time was nothing in comparison with the awful feelings that took possession of me when the pause was broken which ensued upon my sister's recital, and in which pause everybody had looked at me (as I felt painfully conscious) with indignation and abhorrence.

"Yet," said Mr. Pumblechook, leading the company gently back to the theme from which they had strayed, "Pork—regarded as biled—is rich, too; ain't it?"

"Have a little brandy, uncle," said my sister.

O Heavens, it had come at last! He would find it was weak, he would say it was weak, and I was lost! I held tight to the leg of the table under the cloth, with both hands, and awaited my fate.

My sister went for the stone bottle, came back with the stone bottle, and poured his brandy out: no one else taking any. The wretched man trifled with his glass,—took it up, looked at it through the light, put it down,—prolonged my misery. All this time Mrs. Joe and Joe were briskly clearing the table for the pie and pudding.

I couldn't keep my eyes off him. Always holding tight by the leg of the table with my hands and feet, I saw the miserable creature finger his glass playfully, take it up, smile, throw his head back, and drink the brandy off. Instantly afterwards, the company were seized with unspeakable consternation, owing to his springing to his feet, turning round several times in an appalling spasmodic whooping-cough dance, and rushing out at the door; he then became visible through the window, violently plunging and expectorating, making the most hideous faces, and apparently out of his mind.

I held on tight, while Mrs. Joe and Joe ran to him. I didn't know how I had done it, but I had no doubt I had murdered him somehow. In my dreadful situation, it was a relief when he was brought back, and surveying the company all round as if they had disagreed with him, sank down into his chair with the one significant gasp, "Tar!"

I had filled up the bottle from the tar-water jug. I knew he would be worse by and by. I moved the table, like a Medium of the present day, by the vigor of my unseen hold upon it.

"Tar!" cried my sister, in amazement. "Why, how ever could Tar come there?"

But, Uncle Pumblechook, who was omnipotent in that kitchen, wouldn't hear the word, wouldn't hear of the subject, imperiously waved it all away with his hand, and asked for hot gin and water. My sister, who had begun to be alarmingly meditative, had to employ herself actively in getting the gin, the hot water, the sugar, and the lemon-peel, and mixing them. For the time being at least, I was saved. I still held on to the leg of the table, but clutched it now with the fervor of gratitude.

By degrees, I became calm enough to release my grasp and partake of pudding. Mr. Pumblechook partook of pudding. All partook of pudding. The course terminated, and Mr.

Pumblechook had begun to beam under the genial influence of gin and water. I began to think I should get over the day, when my sister said to Joe, "Clean plates,—cold."

I clutched the leg of the table again immediately, and pressed it to my bosom as if it had been the companion of my youth and friend of my soul. I foresaw what was coming, and I felt that this time I really was gone.

"You must taste," said my sister, addressing the guests with her best grace—"you must taste, to finish with, such a delightful and delicious present of Uncle Pumblechook's!"

Must they! Let them not hope to taste it!

"You must know," said my sister, rising, "it's a pie; a savory pork pie."

The company murmured their compliments. Uncle Pumblechook, sensible of having deserved well of his fellow-creatures, said,—quite vivaciously, all things considered,—"Well, Mrs. Joe, we'll do our best endeavors; let us have a cut at this same pie."

My sister went out to get it. I heard her steps proceed to the pantry. I saw Mr. Pumblechook balance his knife. I saw reawakening appetite in the Roman nostrils of Mr. Wopsle. I heard Mr. Hubble remark that "a bit of savory pork pie would lay atop of anything you could mention, and do no harm," and I heard Joe say, "You shall have some, Pip." I have never been absolutely certain whether I uttered a shrill yell of terror, merely in spirit, or in the bodily hearing of the company. I felt that I could bear no more, and that I must run away. I released the leg of the table, and ran for my life.

But I ran no farther than the house door, for there I ran head-foremost into a party of soldiers with their muskets, one of whom held out a pair of handcuffs to me, saying, "Here you are, look sharp, come on!"

Chapter V

The apparition of a file of soldiers ringing down the but-ends of their loaded muskets on our door-step, caused the dinner-party to rise from table in confusion, and caused Mrs. Joe re-entering the kitchen empty-handed, to stop short and stare, in her wondering lament of "Gracious goodness gracious me, what's gone—with the—pie!"

The sergeant and I were in the kitchen when Mrs. Joe stood staring; at which crisis I partially recovered the use of my senses. It was the sergeant who had spoken to me, and he was now looking round at the company, with his handcuffs invitingly extended towards them in his right hand, and his left on my shoulder.

"Excuse me, ladies and gentleman," said the sergeant, "but as I have mentioned at the door to this smart young shaver," (which he hadn't), "I am on a chase in the name of the king, and I want the blacksmith."

"And pray what might you want with him?" retorted my sister, quick to resent his being wanted at all.

"Missis," returned the gallant sergeant, "speaking for myself, I should reply, the honor and pleasure of his fine wife's acquaintance; speaking for the king, I answer, a little job done."

This was received as rather neat in the sergeant; insomuch that Mr. Pumblechook cried audibly, "Good again!"

"You see, blacksmith," said the sergeant, who had by this time picked out Joe with his eye, "we have had an accident with these, and I find the lock of one of 'em goes wrong, and the coupling don't act pretty. As they are wanted for immediate service, will you throw your eye over them?"

Joe threw his eye over them, and pronounced that the job would necessitate the lighting of his forge fire, and would take nearer two hours than one. "Will it? Then will you set about it at once, blacksmith?" said the off-hand sergeant, "as it's on his Majesty's service. And if my men can bear a hand anywhere, they'll make themselves useful." With that, he called to his men, who came trooping into the kitchen one after another, and piled their arms in a corner. And then they stood about, as soldiers do; now, with their hands loosely clasped before them; now, resting a knee or a shoulder; now, easing a belt or a pouch; now, opening the door to spit stiffly over their high stocks, out into the yard.

All these things I saw without then knowing that I saw them, for I was in an agony of apprehension. But beginning to perceive that the handcuffs were not for me, and that the military had so far got the better of the pie as to put it in the background, I collected a little more of my scattered wits.

"Would you give me the time?" said the sergeant, addressing himself to Mr. Pumblechook, as to a man whose appreciative powers justified the inference that he was equal to the time.

"It's just gone half past two."

"That's not so bad," said the sergeant, reflecting; "even if I was forced to halt here nigh two hours, that'll do. How far might you call yourselves from the marshes, hereabouts? Not above a mile, I reckon?"

"Just a mile," said Mrs. Joe.

"That'll do. We begin to close in upon 'em about dusk. A little before dusk, my orders are. That'll do."

"Convicts, sergeant?" asked Mr. Wopsle, in a matter-of-course way.

"Ay!" returned the sergeant, "two. They're pretty well known to be out on the marshes still, and they won't try to get clear of 'em before dusk. Anybody here seen anything of any such game?"

Everybody, myself excepted, said no, with confidence. Nobody thought of me.

"Well!" said the sergeant, "they'll find themselves trapped in a circle, I expect, sooner than they count on. Now, blacksmith! If you're ready, his Majesty the King is."

Joe had got his coat and waistcoat and cravat off, and his leather apron on, and passed into the forge. One of the soldiers opened its wooden windows, another lighted the fire, another turned to at the bellows, the rest stood round the blaze, which was soon roaring. Then Joe began to hammer and clink, hammer and clink, and we all looked on.

The interest of the impending pursuit not only absorbed the general attention, but even made my sister liberal. She drew a pitcher of beer from the cask for the soldiers, and invited the sergeant to take a glass of brandy. But Mr. Pumblechook said, sharply, "Give him wine, Mum. I'll engage there's no tar in that:" so, the sergeant thanked him and said that as he preferred his drink without tar, he would take wine, if it was equally convenient. When it was given him, he drank his Majesty's health and compliments of the season, and took it all at a mouthful and smacked his lips.

"Good stuff, eh, sergeant?" said Mr. Pumblechook.

"I'll tell you something," returned the sergeant; "I suspect that stuff's of your providing."

Mr. Pumblechook, with a fat sort of laugh, said, "Ay, ay? Why?"

"Because," returned the sergeant, clapping him on the shoulder, "you're a man that knows what's what."

"D'ye think so?" said Mr. Pumblechook, with his former laugh. "Have another glass!"

"With you. Hob and nob," returned the sergeant. "The top of mine to the foot of yours,—the foot of yours to the top of mine,—Ring once, ring twice,—the best tune on the Musical Glasses! Your health. May you live a thousand years, and never be a worse judge of the right sort than you are at the present moment of your life!"

The sergeant tossed off his glass again and seemed quite ready for another glass. I noticed that Mr. Pumblechook in his hospitality appeared to forget that he had made a present of the wine, but took the bottle from Mrs. Joe and had all the credit of handing it about in a gush of joviality. Even I got some. And he was so very free of the wine that he even called for the other bottle, and handed that about with the same liberality, when the first was gone.

As I watched them while they all stood clustering about the forge, enjoying themselves so much, I thought what terrible good sauce for a dinner my fugitive friend on the marshes was. They had not enjoyed themselves a quarter so much, before the entertainment was brightened with the excitement he furnished. And now, when they were all in lively anticipation of "the two villains" being taken, and when the bellows seemed to roar for the fugitives, the fire to flare for them, the smoke to hurry away in pursuit of them, Joe to hammer and clink for them, and all the murky shadows on the wall to shake at them in menace as the blaze rose and sank, and the red-hot sparks dropped and died, the pale afternoon outside almost seemed in my pitying young fancy to have turned pale on their account, poor wretches.

At last, Joe's job was done, and the ringing and roaring stopped. As Joe got on his coat, he mustered courage to propose that some of us should go down with the soldiers and see what came of the hunt. Mr. Pumblechook and Mr. Hubble declined, on the plea of a pipe and ladies' society; but Mr. Wopsle said he would go, if Joe would. Joe said he was agreeable, and would take me, if Mrs. Joe approved. We never should have got leave to go, I am sure, but for Mrs. Joe's curiosity to know all about it and how it ended. As it was, she merely stipulated, "If you bring the boy back with his head blown to bits by a musket, don't look to me to put it together again."

The sergeant took a polite leave of the ladies, and parted from Mr. Pumblechook as from a comrade; though I doubt if he were quite as fully sensible of that gentleman's merits under arid conditions, as when something moist was going. His men resumed their muskets and fell in. Mr. Wopsle, Joe, and I, received strict charge to keep in the rear, and to speak no word after we reached the marshes. When we were all out in the raw air and were steadily moving towards our business, I treasonably whispered to Joe, "I hope, Joe, we shan't find them." and Joe whispered to me, "I'd give a shilling if they had cut and run, Pip."

We were joined by no stragglers from the village, for the weather was cold and threatening, the way dreary, the footing bad, darkness coming on, and the people had good fires in-doors and were keeping the day. A few faces hurried to glowing windows and looked after us, but none came out. We passed the finger-post, and held straight on to the churchyard. There we were stopped a few minutes by a signal from the sergeant's hand, while two or three of his men dispersed themselves among the graves, and also examined the porch. They came in again without finding anything, and then we struck out on the open marshes, through the gate at the side of the churchyard. A bitter sleet came rattling against us here on the east wind, and Joe took me on his back.

Now that we were out upon the dismal wilderness where they little thought I had been within eight or nine hours and had seen both men hiding, I considered for the first time, with great dread, if we should come upon them, would my particular convict suppose that it was I who had brought the soldiers there? He had asked me if I was a deceiving imp, and he had said I should be a fierce young hound if I joined the hunt against him. Would he believe that I was both imp and hound in treacherous earnest, and had betrayed him?

It was of no use asking myself this question now. There I was, on Joe's back, and there was Joe beneath me, charging at the ditches like a hunter, and stimulating Mr. Wopsle not to tumble on his Roman nose, and to keep up with us. The soldiers were in front of us, extending into a pretty wide line with an interval between man and man. We were taking the course I had begun with, and from which I had diverged in the mist. Either the mist was not out again yet, or the wind had dispelled it. Under the low red glare of sunset, the beacon, and the gibbet, and the mound of the Battery, and the opposite shore of the river, were plain, though all of a watery lead color.

With my heart thumping like a blacksmith at Joe's broad shoulder, I looked all about for any sign of the convicts. I could see none, I could hear none. Mr. Wopsle had greatly alarmed me more than once, by his blowing and hard breathing; but I knew the sounds by this time, and could dissociate them from the object of pursuit. I got a dreadful start, when I thought I heard the file still going; but it was only a sheep-bell. The sheep stopped in their eating and looked timidly at us; and the cattle, their heads turned from the wind and sleet, stared angrily as if they held us responsible for both annoyances; but, except these things, and the shudder of the dying day in every blade of grass, there was no break in the bleak stillness of the marshes.

The soldiers were moving on in the direction of the old Battery, and we were moving on a little way behind them, when, all of a sudden, we all stopped. For there had reached us on the wings of the wind and rain, a long shout. It was repeated. It was at a distance towards the east, but it was long and loud. Nay, there seemed to be two or more shouts raised together,—if one might judge from a confusion in the sound.

To this effect the sergeant and the nearest men were speaking under their breath, when Joe and I came up. After another moment's listening, Joe (who was a good judge) agreed, and Mr. Wopsle (who was a bad judge) agreed. The sergeant, a decisive man, ordered that the sound should not be answered, but that the course should be changed, and that his men should make towards it "at the double." So we slanted to the right (where the East was), and Joe pounded away so wonderfully, that I had to hold on tight to keep my seat.

It was a run indeed now, and what Joe called, in the only two words he spoke all the time, "a Winder." Down banks and up banks, and over gates, and splashing into dikes, and breaking among coarse rushes: no man cared where he went. As we came nearer to the shouting, it became more and more apparent that it was made by more than one voice. Sometimes, it seemed to stop altogether, and then the soldiers stopped. When it broke out again, the soldiers made for it at a greater rate than ever, and we after them. After a while, we had so run it down, that we could hear one voice calling "Murder!" and another voice, "Convicts! Runaways! Guard! This way for the runaway convicts!" Then both voices would seem to be stifled in a struggle, and then would break out again. And when it had come to this, the soldiers ran like deer, and Joe too.

The sergeant ran in first, when we had run the noise quite down, and two of his men ran in close upon him. Their pieces were cocked and levelled when we all ran in.

"Here are both men!" panted the sergeant, struggling at the bottom of a ditch. "Surrender, you two! and confound you for two wild beasts! Come asunder!"

Water was splashing, and mud was flying, and oaths were being sworn, and blows were being struck, when some more men went down into the ditch to help the sergeant, and dragged out, separately, my convict and the other one. Both were bleeding and panting and execrating and struggling; but of course I knew them both directly.

"Mind!" said my convict, wiping blood from his face with his ragged sleeves, and shaking torn hair from his fingers: "I took him! I give him up to you! Mind that!"

"It's not much to be particular about," said the sergeant; "it'll do you small good, my man, being in the same plight yourself. Handcuffs there!"

"I don't expect it to do me any good. I don't want it to do me more good than it does now," said my convict, with a greedy laugh. "I took him. He knows it. That's enough for me."

The other convict was livid to look at, and, in addition to the old bruised left side of his face, seemed to be bruised and torn all over. He could not so much as get his breath to speak, until they were both separately handcuffed, but leaned upon a soldier to keep himself from falling.

"Take notice, guard,—he tried to murder me," were his first words.

"Tried to murder him?" said my convict, disdainfully. "Try, and not do it? I took him, and giv' him up; that's what I done. I not only prevented him getting off the marshes, but I dragged him here,—dragged him this far on his way back. He's a gentleman, if you please, this villain. Now, the Hulks has got its gentleman again, through me. Murder him? Worth my while, too, to murder him, when I could do worse and drag him back!"

The other one still gasped, "He tried—he tried-to—murder me. Bear—bear witness."

"Lookee here!" said my convict to the sergeant. "Single-handed I got clear of the prison-ship; I made a dash and I done it. I could ha' got clear of these death-cold flats likewise—look at my leg: you won't find much iron on it—if I hadn't made the discovery that he was here. Let him go free? Let him profit by the means as I found out? Let him make a tool of me afresh and again? Once more? No, no, no. If I had died at the bottom there," and he made an emphatic swing at the ditch with his manacled hands, "I'd have held to him with that grip, that you should have been safe to find him in my hold."

The other fugitive, who was evidently in extreme horror of his companion, repeated, "He tried to murder me. I should have been a dead man if you had not come up."

"He lies!" said my convict, with fierce energy. "He's a liar born, and he'll die a liar. Look at his face; ain't it written there? Let him turn those eyes of his on me. I defy him to do it."

The other, with an effort at a scornful smile, which could not, however, collect the nervous working of his mouth into any set expression, looked at the soldiers, and looked about at the marshes and at the sky, but certainly did not look at the speaker.

"Do you see him?" pursued my convict. "Do you see what a villain he is? Do you see those grovelling and wandering eyes? That's how he looked when we were tried together. He never looked at me."

The other, always working and working his dry lips and turning his eyes restlessly about him far and near, did at last turn them for a moment on the speaker, with the words, "You are not much to look at," and with a half-taunting glance at the bound hands. At that point, my convict became so frantically exasperated, that he would have rushed upon him but for the interposition of the soldiers. "Didn't I tell you," said the other convict then, "that he would murder me, if he could?" And any one could see that he shook with fear, and that there broke out upon his lips curious white flakes, like thin snow.

"Enough of this parley," said the sergeant. "Light those torches."

As one of the soldiers, who carried a basket in lieu of a gun, went down on his knee to open it, my convict looked round him for the first time, and saw me. I had alighted from Joe's back on the brink of the ditch when we came up, and had not moved since. I looked at him eagerly when he looked at me, and slightly moved my hands and shook my head. I had been waiting for him to see me that I might try to assure him of my innocence. It was not at all expressed to me that he even comprehended my intention, for he gave me a look that I did not understand, and it all passed in a moment. But if he had looked at me for an hour or for a day, I could not have remembered his face ever afterwards, as having been more attentive.

The soldier with the basket soon got a light, and lighted three or four torches, and took one himself and distributed the others. It had been almost dark before, but now it seemed quite dark, and soon afterwards very dark. Before we departed from that spot, four soldiers standing in a ring, fired twice into the air. Presently we saw other torches kindled at some distance behind us, and others on the marshes on the opposite bank of the river. "All right," said the sergeant. "March."

We had not gone far when three cannon were fired ahead of us with a sound that seemed to burst something inside my ear. "You are expected on board," said the sergeant to my convict; "they know you are coming. Don't straggle, my man. Close up here."

The two were kept apart, and each walked surrounded by a separate guard. I had hold of Joe's hand now, and Joe carried one of the torches. Mr. Wopsle had been for going back, but Joe was resolved to see it out, so we went on with the party. There was a reasonably good path now, mostly on the edge of the river, with a divergence here and there where a dike came, with a miniature windmill on it and a muddy sluice-gate. When I looked round, I could see the other lights coming in after us. The torches we carried dropped great blotches of fire upon the track, and I could see those, too, lying smoking and flaring. I could see nothing else but black darkness. Our lights warmed the air about us with their pitchy blaze, and the two prisoners seemed rather to like that, as they limped along in the midst of the muskets. We could not go fast, because of their lameness; and they were so spent, that two or three times we had to halt while they rested.

After an hour or so of this travelling, we came to a rough wooden hut and a landing-place. There was a guard in the hut, and they challenged, and the sergeant answered. Then, we went into the hut, where there was a smell of tobacco and whitewash, and a bright fire, and a lamp, and a stand of muskets, and a drum, and a low wooden bedstead, like an overgrown mangle without the machinery, capable of holding about a dozen soldiers all at once. Three or four soldiers who lay upon it in their great-coats were not much interested in us, but just lifted their heads and took a sleepy stare, and then lay down again. The sergeant made some kind of report, and some entry in a book, and then the convict whom I call the other convict was drafted off with his guard, to go on board first.

My convict never looked at me, except that once. While we stood in the hut, he stood before the fire looking thoughtfully at it, or putting up his feet by turns upon the hob, and looking thoughtfully at them as if he pitied them for their recent adventures. Suddenly, he turned to the sergeant, and remarked,—

"I wish to say something respecting this escape. It may prevent some persons laying under suspicion alonger me."

"You can say what you like," returned the sergeant, standing coolly looking at him with his arms folded, "but you have no call to say it here. You'll have opportunity enough to say about it, and hear about it, before it's done with, you know."

"I know, but this is another pint, a separate matter. A man can't starve; at least I can't. I took some wittles, up at the willage over yonder,—where the church stands a'most out on the marshes."

"You mean stole," said the sergeant.

"And I'll tell you where from. From the blacksmith's."

"Halloa!" said the sergeant, staring at Joe.

"Halloa, Pip!" said Joe, staring at me.

"It was some broken wittles—that's what it was—and a dram of liquor, and a pie."

"Have you happened to miss such an article as a pie, blacksmith?" asked the sergeant, confidentially.

"My wife did, at the very moment when you came in. Don't you know, Pip?"

"So," said my convict, turning his eyes on Joe in a moody manner, and without the least glance at me,—"so you're the blacksmith, are you? Than I'm sorry to say, I've eaten your pie."

"God knows you're welcome to it,—so far as it was ever mine," returned Joe, with a saving remembrance of Mrs. Joe. "We don't know what you have done, but we wouldn't have you starved to death for it, poor miserable fellow-creatur.—Would us, Pip?"

The something that I had noticed before, clicked in the man's throat again, and he turned his back. The boat had returned, and his guard were ready, so we followed him to the landing-place made of rough stakes and stones, and saw him put into the boat, which was rowed by a crew of convicts like himself. No one seemed surprised to see him, or interested in seeing him, or glad to see him, or sorry to see him, or spoke a word, except that somebody in the boat growled as if to dogs, "Give way, you!" which was the signal for the dip of the oars. By the light of the torches, we saw the black Hulk lying out a little way from the mud of the shore, like a wicked Noah's ark. Cribbed and barred and moored by massive rusty chains, the prison-ship seemed in my young eyes to be ironed like the prisoners. We saw the boat go alongside, and we saw him taken up the side and disappear. Then, the ends of the torches were flung hissing into the water, and went out, as if it were all over with him.

Chapter VI

My state of mind regarding the pilfering from which I had been so unexpectedly exonerated did not impel me to frank disclosure; but I hope it had some dregs of good at the bottom of it.

I do not recall that I felt any tenderness of conscience in reference to Mrs. Joe, when the fear of being found out was lifted off me. But I loved Joe,—perhaps for no better reason in those early days than because the dear fellow let me love him,—and, as to him, my inner self was not so easily composed. It was much upon my mind (particularly when I first saw him looking about for his file) that I ought to tell Joe the whole truth. Yet I did not, and for the reason that I mistrusted that if I did, he would think me worse than I was. The fear of losing Joe's confidence, and of thenceforth sitting in the chimney corner at night staring drearily at my forever lost companion and friend, tied up my tongue. I morbidly represented to myself that if Joe knew it, I never afterwards could see him at the fireside feeling his fair whisker, without thinking that he was meditating on it. That, if Joe knew it, I never afterwards could see him glance, however casually, at yesterday's meat or pudding when it came on to-day's table, without thinking that he was debating whether I had been in the pantry. That, if Joe knew it, and at any subsequent period of our joint domestic life remarked that his beer was flat or thick, the conviction that he suspected tar in it, would bring a rush of blood to my face. In a word, I was too cowardly to do what I knew to be right, as I had been too cowardly to avoid doing what I knew to be wrong. I had had no intercourse with the world at that time, and I imitated none of its many inhabitants who act in this manner. Quite an untaught genius, I made the discovery of the line of action for myself.

As I was sleepy before we were far away from the prison-ship, Joe took me on his back again and carried me home. He must have had a tiresome journey of it, for Mr. Wopsle, being knocked up, was in such a very bad temper that if the Church had been thrown open, he would probably have excommunicated the whole expedition, beginning with Joe and myself. In his lay capacity, he persisted in sitting down in the damp to such an insane extent, that when his coat was taken off to be dried at the kitchen fire, the circumstantial evidence on his trousers would have hanged him, if it had been a capital offence.

By that time, I was staggering on the kitchen floor like a little drunkard, through having been newly set upon my feet, and through having been fast asleep, and through waking in the heat and lights and noise of tongues. As I came to myself (with the aid of a heavy thump between the shoulders, and the restorative exclamation "Yah! Was there ever such a boy as this!" from my sister,) I found Joe telling them about the convict's confession, and all the visitors suggesting different ways by which he had got into the pantry. Mr. Pumblechook made out, after carefully surveying the premises, that he had first got upon the roof of the forge, and had then got upon the roof of the house, and had then let himself down the kitchen chimney by a rope made of his bedding cut into strips; and as Mr. Pumblechook was very positive and drove his own chaise-cart—over everybody—it was agreed that it must be so. Mr. Wopsle, indeed, wildly cried out, "No!" with the feeble malice of a tired man; but, as he had no theory, and no coat on, he was unanimously set at naught,—not to mention his smoking hard behind, as he stood with his back to the kitchen fire to draw the damp out: which was not calculated to inspire confidence.

This was all I heard that night before my sister clutched me, as a slumberous offence to the company's eyesight, and assisted me up to bed with such a strong hand that I seemed to have fifty boots on, and to be dangling them all against the edges of the stairs. My state of mind, as I have described it, began before I was up in the morning, and lasted long after the subject had died out, and had ceased to be mentioned saving on exceptional occasions.

Chapter VII

At the time when I stood in the churchyard reading the family tombstones, I had just enough learning to be able to spell them out. My construction even of their simple meaning was not very correct, for I read "wife of the Above" as a complimentary reference to my father's exaltation to a better world; and if any one of my deceased relations had been referred to as "Below," I have no doubt I should have formed the worst opinions of that member of the family. Neither were my notions of the theological positions to which my Catechism bound me, at all accurate; for, I have a lively remembrance that I supposed my declaration that I was to "walk in the same all the days of my life," laid me under an obligation always to go through the village from our house in one particular direction, and never to vary it by turning down by the wheelwright's or up by the mill.

When I was old enough, I was to be apprenticed to Joe, and until I could assume that dignity I was not to be what Mrs. Joe called "Pompeyed," or (as I render it) pampered. Therefore, I was not only odd-boy about the forge, but if any neighbor happened to want an extra boy to frighten birds, or pick up stones, or do any such job, I was favored with the employment. In order, however, that our superior position might not be compromised thereby, a money-box was kept on the kitchen mantel-shelf, into which it was publicly made known that all my earnings were dropped. I have an impression that they were to be contributed eventually towards the liquidation of the National Debt, but I know I had no hope of any personal participation in the treasure.

Mr. Wopsle's great-aunt kept an evening school in the village; that is to say, she was a ridiculous old woman of limited means and unlimited infirmity, who used to go to sleep from six to seven every evening, in the society of youth who paid two pence per week each, for the improving opportunity of seeing her do it. She rented a small cottage, and Mr. Wopsle had the room upstairs, where we students used to overhear him reading aloud in a most dignified and terrific manner, and occasionally bumping on the ceiling. There was a fiction that Mr. Wopsle "examined" the scholars once a quarter. What he did on those occasions was to turn up his cuffs, stick up his hair, and give us Mark Antony's oration over the body of Caesar. This was always followed by Collins's Ode on the Passions, wherein I particularly venerated Mr. Wopsle as Revenge throwing his blood-stained sword in thunder down, and taking the War-denouncing trumpet with a withering look. It was not with me then, as it was in later life, when I fell into the society of the Passions, and compared them with Collins and Wopsle, rather to the disadvantage of both gentlemen.

Mr. Wopsle's great-aunt, besides keeping this Educational Institution, kept in the same room—a little general shop. She had no idea what stock she had, or what the price of anything in it was; but there was a little greasy memorandum-book kept in a drawer, which served as a Catalogue of Prices, and by this oracle Biddy arranged all the shop transactions. Biddy was Mr. Wopsle's great-aunt's granddaughter; I confess myself quite unequal to the working out of the problem, what relation she was to Mr. Wopsle. She was an orphan like myself; like me, too, had been brought up by hand. She was most noticeable, I thought, in respect of her extremities; for, her hair always wanted brushing, her hands always wanted washing, and her shoes always wanted mending and pulling up at heel. This description must be received with a week-day limitation. On Sundays, she went to church elaborated.

Much of my unassisted self, and more by the help of Biddy than of Mr. Wopsle's great-aunt, I struggled through the alphabet as if it had been a bramble-bush; getting considerably worried and scratched by every letter. After that I fell among those thieves, the nine figures, who seemed every evening to do something new to disguise themselves and baffle recognition. But, at last I began, in a purblind groping way, to read, write, and cipher, on the very smallest scale.

One night I was sitting in the chimney corner with my slate, expending great efforts on the production of a letter to Joe. I think it must have been a full year after our hunt upon the marshes, for it was a long time after, and it was winter and a hard frost. With an alphabet on the hearth at my feet for reference, I contrived in an hour or two to print and smear this epistle:—

"mI deEr JO i opE U r krWitE wEll i opE i shAl soN B haBelL 4 2 teeDge U JO aN theN wE shOrl b sO glOdd aN wEn i M preNgtD 2 u JO woT larX an blEvE ME inF xn PiP."

There was no indispensable necessity for my communicating with Joe by letter, inasmuch as he sat beside me and we were alone. But I delivered this written communication (slate and all) with my own hand, and Joe received it as a miracle of erudition.

"I say, Pip, old chap!" cried Joe, opening his blue eyes wide, "what a scholar you are! An't you?"

"I should like to be," said I, glancing at the slate as he held it; with a misgiving that the writing was rather hilly.

"Why, here's a J," said Joe, "and a O equal to anythink! Here's a J and a O, Pip, and a J-O, Joe."

I had never heard Joe read aloud to any greater extent than this monosyllable, and I had observed at church last Sunday, when I accidentally held our Prayer-Book upside down, that it seemed to suit his convenience quite as well as if it had been all right. Wishing to embrace the present occasion of finding out whether in teaching Joe, I should have to begin quite at the beginning, I said, "Ah! But read the rest, Jo."

"The rest, eh, Pip?" said Joe, looking at it with a slow, searching eye, "One, two, three. Why, here's three Js, and three Os, and three J-O, Joes in it, Pip!"

I leaned over Joe, and, with the aid of my forefinger read him the whole letter.

"Astonishing!" said Joe, when I had finished. "You ARE a scholar."

"How do you spell Gargery, Joe?" I asked him, with a modest patronage.

"I don't spell it at all," said Joe.

"But supposing you did?"

"It can't be supposed," said Joe. "Tho' I'm uncommon fond of reading, too."

"Are you, Joe?"

"On-common. Give me," said Joe, "a good book, or a good newspaper, and sit me down afore a good fire, and I ask no better. Lord!" he continued, after rubbing his knees a little, "when you do come to a J and a O, and says you, 'Here, at last, is a J-O, Joe,' how interesting reading is!"

I derived from this, that Joe's education, like Steam, was yet in its infancy. Pursuing the subject, I inquired,—

"Didn't you ever go to school, Joe, when you were as little as me?"

"No, Pip."

"Why didn't you ever go to school, Joe, when you were as little as me?"

"Well, Pip," said Joe, taking up the poker, and settling himself to his usual occupation when he was thoughtful, of slowly raking the fire between the lower bars; "I'll tell you. My father, Pip, he were given to drink, and when he were overtook with drink, he hammered away at my mother, most onmerciful. It were a'most the only hammering he did, indeed, 'xcepting at myself. And he hammered at me with a wigor only to be equalled by the wigor with which he didn't hammer at his anvil.—You're a listening and understanding, Pip?"

"Yes, Joe."

"'Consequence, my mother and me we ran away from my father several times; and then my mother she'd go out to work, and she'd say, "Joe," she'd say, "now, please God, you shall have some schooling, child," and she'd put me to school. But my father were that good in his hart that he couldn't abear to be without us. So, he'd come with a most tremenjous crowd and make such a row at the doors of the houses where we was, that they used to be obligated to have no more to do with us and to give us up to him. And then he took us home and hammered us. Which, you see, Pip," said Joe, pausing in his meditative raking of the fire, and looking at me, "were a drawback on my learning."

"Certainly, poor Joe!"

"Though mind you, Pip," said Joe, with a judicial touch or two of the poker on the top bar, "rendering unto all their doo, and maintaining equal justice betwixt man and man, my father were that good in his hart, don't you see?"

I didn't see; but I didn't say so.

"Well!" Joe pursued, "somebody must keep the pot a biling, Pip, or the pot won't bile, don't you know?"

I saw that, and said so.

"'Consequence, my father didn't make objections to my going to work; so I went to work at my present calling, which were his too, if he would have followed it, and I worked tolerable hard, I assure you, Pip. In time I were able to keep him, and I kep him till he went off in a purple leptic fit. And it were my intentions to have had put upon his tombstone that, Whatsume'er the failings on his part, Remember reader he were that good in his heart."

Joe recited this couplet with such manifest pride and careful perspicuity, that I asked him if he had made it himself.

"I made it," said Joe, "my own self. I made it in a moment. It was like striking out a horseshoe complete, in a single blow. I never was so much surprised in all my life,—couldn't credit my own ed,—to tell you the truth, hardly believed it were my own ed. As I was saying, Pip, it were my intentions to have had it cut over him; but poetry costs money, cut it how you will, small or large, and it were not done. Not to mention bearers, all the money that could be spared were wanted for my mother. She were in poor elth, and quite broke. She weren't long of following, poor soul, and her share of peace come round at last."

Joe's blue eyes turned a little watery; he rubbed first one of them, and then the other, in a most uncongenial and uncomfortable manner, with the round knob on the top of the poker.

"It were but lonesome then," said Joe, "living here alone, and I got acquainted with your sister. Now, Pip,"—Joe looked firmly at me as if he knew I was not going to agree with him;—"your sister is a fine figure of a woman."

I could not help looking at the fire, in an obvious state of doubt.

"Whatever family opinions, or whatever the world's opinions, on that subject may be, Pip, your sister is," Joe tapped the top bar with the poker after every word following, "a-fine-figure—of—a—woman!"

I could think of nothing better to say than "I am glad you think so, Joe."

"So am I," returned Joe, catching me up. "I am glad I think so, Pip. A little redness or a little matter of Bone, here or there, what does it signify to Me?"

I sagaciously observed, if it didn't signify to him, to whom did it signify?

"Certainly!" assented Joe. "That's it. You're right, old chap! When I got acquainted with your sister, it were the talk how she was bringing you up by hand. Very kind of her too, all the folks said, and I said, along with all the folks. As to you," Joe pursued with a countenance expressive of seeing something very nasty indeed, "if you could have been aware how small and flabby and mean you was, dear me, you'd have formed the most contemptible opinion of yourself!"

Not exactly relishing this, I said, "Never mind me, Joe."

"But I did mind you, Pip," he returned with tender simplicity. "When I offered to your sister to keep company, and to be asked in church at such times as she was willing and ready to come to the forge, I said to her, 'And bring the poor little child. God bless the poor little child,' I said to your sister, 'there's room for him at the forge!'"

I broke out crying and begging pardon, and hugged Joe round the neck: who dropped the poker to hug me, and to say, "Ever the best of friends; an't us, Pip? Don't cry, old chap!"

When this little interruption was over, Joe resumed:—

"Well, you see, Pip, and here we are! That's about where it lights; here we are! Now, when you take me in hand in my learning, Pip (and I tell you beforehand I am awful dull, most awful dull), Mrs. Joe mustn't see too much of what we're up to. It must be done, as I may say, on the sly. And why on the sly? I'll tell you why, Pip."

He had taken up the poker again; without which, I doubt if he could have proceeded in his demonstration.

"Your sister is given to government."

"Given to government, Joe?" I was startled, for I had some shadowy idea (and I am afraid I must add, hope) that Joe had divorced her in a favor of the Lords of the Admiralty, or Treasury.

"Given to government," said Joe. "Which I meantersay the government of you and myself."

"Oh!"

"And she an't over partial to having scholars on the premises," Joe continued, "and in partickler would not be over partial to my being a scholar, for fear as I might rise. Like a sort of rebel, don't you see?"

I was going to retort with an inquiry, and had got as far as "Why—" when Joe stopped me.

"Stay a bit. I know what you're a going to say, Pip; stay a bit! I don't deny that your sister comes the Mo-gul over us, now and again. I don't deny that she do throw us back-falls, and that she do drop down upon us heavy. At such times as when your sister is on the Ram-page, Pip," Joe sank his voice to a whisper and glanced at the door, "candor compels fur to admit that she is a Buster."

Joe pronounced this word, as if it began with at least twelve capital Bs.

"Why don't I rise? That were your observation when I broke it off, Pip?"

"Yes, Joe."

"Well," said Joe, passing the poker into his left hand, that he might feel his whisker; and I had no hope of him whenever he took to that placid occupation; "your sister's a master-mind. A master-mind."

"What's that?" I asked, in some hope of bringing him to a stand. But Joe was readier with his definition than I had expected, and completely stopped me by arguing circularly, and answering with a fixed look, "Her."

"And I ain't a master-mind," Joe resumed, when he had unfixed his look, and got back to his whisker. "And last of all, Pip,—and this I want to say very serious to you, old chap,—I see so much in my poor mother, of a woman drudging and slaving and breaking her honest hart and never getting no peace in her mortal days, that I'm dead afeerd of going wrong in the way of not doing what's right by a woman, and I'd fur rather of the two go wrong the t'other way, and be a little ill-conwenienced myself. I wish it was only me that got put out, Pip; I wish there warn't no Tickler for you, old chap; I wish I could take it all on myself; but this is the up-and-down-and-straight on it, Pip, and I hope you'll overlook shortcomings."

Young as I was, I believe that I dated a new admiration of Joe from that night. We were equals afterwards, as we had been before; but, afterwards at quiet times when I sat looking at Joe and thinking about him, I had a new sensation of feeling conscious that I was looking up to Joe in my heart.

"However," said Joe, rising to replenish the fire; "here's the Dutch-clock a working himself up to being equal to strike Eight of 'em, and she's not come home yet! I hope Uncle Pumblechook's mare mayn't have set a forefoot on a piece o' ice, and gone down."

Mrs. Joe made occasional trips with Uncle Pumblechook on market-days, to assist him in buying such household stuffs and goods as required a woman's judgment; Uncle Pumblechook being a bachelor and reposing no confidences in his domestic servant. This was market-day, and Mrs. Joe was out on one of these expeditions.

Joe made the fire and swept the hearth, and then we went to the door to listen for the chaise-cart. It was a dry cold night, and the wind blew keenly, and the frost was white and hard. A man would die to-night of lying out on the marshes, I thought. And then I looked at the stars, and considered how awful it would be for a man to turn his face up to them as he froze to death, and see no help or pity in all the glittering multitude.

"Here comes the mare," said Joe, "ringing like a peal of bells!"

The sound of her iron shoes upon the hard road was quite musical, as she came along at a much brisker trot than usual. We got a chair out, ready for Mrs. Joe's alighting, and stirred up the fire that they might see a bright window, and took a final survey of the kitchen that nothing might be out of its place. When we had completed these preparations, they drove up, wrapped to the eyes. Mrs. Joe was soon landed, and Uncle Pumblechook was soon down too, covering the mare with a cloth, and we were soon all in the kitchen, carrying so much cold air in with us that it seemed to drive all the heat out of the fire.

"Now," said Mrs. Joe, unwrapping herself with haste and excitement, and throwing her bonnet back on her shoulders where it hung by the strings, "if this boy ain't grateful this night, he never will be!"

I looked as grateful as any boy possibly could, who was wholly uninformed why he ought to assume that expression.

"It's only to be hoped," said my sister, "that he won't be Pompeyed. But I have my fears."

"She ain't in that line, Mum," said Mr. Pumblechook. "She knows better."

She? I looked at Joe, making the motion with my lips and eyebrows, "She?" Joe looked at me, making the motion with his lips and eyebrows, "She?" My sister catching him in the act, he drew the back of his hand across his nose with his usual conciliatory air on such occasions, and looked at her.

"Well?" said my sister, in her snappish way. "What are you staring at? Is the house afire?"

"—Which some individual," Joe politely hinted, "mentioned—she."

"And she is a she, I suppose?" said my sister. "Unless you call Miss Havisham a he. And

I doubt if even you'll go so far as that."

"Miss Havisham, up town?" said Joe.

"Is there any Miss Havisham down town?" returned my sister.

"She wants this boy to go and play there. And of course he's going. And he had better play there," said my sister, shaking her head at me as an encouragement to be extremely light and sportive, "or I'll work him."

I had heard of Miss Havisham up town,—everybody for miles round had heard of Miss Havisham up town,—as an immensely rich and grim lady who lived in a large and dismal house barricaded against robbers, and who led a life of seclusion.

"Well to be sure!" said Joe, astounded. "I wonder how she come to know Pip!"

"Noodle!" cried my sister. "Who said she knew him?"

"—Which some individual," Joe again politely hinted, "mentioned that she wanted him to go and play there."

"And couldn't she ask Uncle Pumblechook if he knew of a boy to go and play there? Isn't it just barely possible that Uncle Pumblechook may be a tenant of hers, and that he may sometimes—we won't say quarterly or half-yearly, for that would be requiring too much of you—but sometimes—go there to pay his rent? And couldn't she then ask Uncle Pumblechook if he knew of a boy to go and play there? And couldn't Uncle Pumblechook, being always considerate and thoughtful for us—though you may not think it, Joseph," in a tone of the deepest reproach, as if he were the most callous of nephews, "then mention this boy, standing Prancing here"—which I solemnly declare I was not doing—"that I have for ever been a willing slave to?"

"Good again!" cried Uncle Pumblechook. "Well put! Prettily pointed! Good indeed! Now Joseph, you know the case."

"No, Joseph," said my sister, still in a reproachful manner, while Joe apologetically drew the back of his hand across and across his nose, "you do not yet—though you may not think it—know the case. You may consider that you do, but you do not, Joseph. For you do not know that Uncle Pumblechook, being sensible that for anything we can tell, this boy's fortune may be made by his going to Miss Havisham's, has offered to take him into town to-night in his own chaise-cart, and to keep him to-night, and to take him with his own hands to Miss Havisham's to-morrow morning. And Lor-a-mussy me!" cried my sister, casting off her bonnet in sudden desperation, "here I stand talking to mere Mooncalfs, with Uncle Pumblechook waiting, and the mare catching cold at the door, and the boy grimed with crock and dirt from the hair of his head to the sole of his foot!"

With that, she pounced upon me, like an eagle on a lamb, and my face was squeezed into wooden bowls in sinks, and my head was put under taps of water-butts, and I was soaped, and kneaded, and towelled, and thumped, and harrowed, and rasped, until I really was quite beside myself. (I may here remark that I suppose myself to be better acquainted than any living authority, with the ridgy effect of a wedding-ring, passing unsympathetically over the human countenance.)

When my ablutions were completed, I was put into clean linen of the stiffest character, like a young penitent into sackcloth, and was trussed up in my tightest and fearfullest suit. I was then delivered over to Mr. Pumblechook, who formally received me as if he were the Sheriff, and who let off upon me the speech that I knew he had been dying to make all along: "Boy, be forever grateful to all friends, but especially unto them which brought you up by hand!"

"Good-bye, Joe!"

"God bless you, Pip, old chap!"

I had never parted from him before, and what with my feelings and what with soapsuds, I could at first see no stars from the chaise-cart. But they twinkled out one by one, without throwing any light on the questions why on earth I was going to play at Miss Havisham's, and what on earth I was expected to play at.

Chapter VIII

Mr. Pumblechook's premises in the High Street of the market town, were of a peppercorny and farinaceous character, as the premises of a cornchandler and seedsman should be. It appeared to me that he must be a very happy man indeed, to have so many little drawers in his shop; and I wondered when I peeped into one or two on the lower tiers, and saw the tied-up brown paper packets inside, whether the flower-seeds and bulbs ever wanted of a fine day to break out of those jails, and bloom.

It was in the early morning after my arrival that I entertained this speculation. On the previous night, I had been sent straight to bed in an attic with a sloping roof, which was so low in the corner where the bedstead was, that I calculated the tiles as being within a foot of my eyebrows. In the same early morning, I discovered a singular affinity between seeds and corduroys. Mr. Pumblechook wore corduroys, and so did his shopman; and somehow, there was a general air and flavor about the corduroys, so much in the nature of seeds, and a general air and flavor about the seeds, so much in the nature of corduroys, that I hardly knew which was which. The same opportunity served me for noticing that Mr. Pumblechook appeared to conduct his business by looking across the street at the saddler, who appeared to transact his business by keeping his eye on the coachmaker, who appeared to get on in life by putting his hands in his pockets and contemplating the baker, who in his turn folded his arms and stared at the grocer, who stood at his door and yawned at the chemist. The watchmaker, always poring over a little desk with a magnifying-glass at his eye, and always inspected by a group of smock-frocks poring over him through the glass of his shop-window, seemed to be about the only person in the High Street whose trade engaged his attention.

Mr. Pumblechook and I breakfasted at eight o'clock in the parlor behind the shop, while the shopman took his mug of tea and hunch of bread and butter on a sack of peas in the front premises. I considered Mr. Pumblechook wretched company. Besides being possessed by my sister's idea that a mortifying and penitential character ought to be imparted to my diet,—besides giving me as much crumb as possible in combination with as little butter, and putting such a quantity of warm water into my milk that it would have been more candid to have left the milk out altogether,—his conversation consisted of nothing but arithmetic. On my politely bidding him Good morning, he said, pompously, "Seven times nine, boy?" And how should I be able to answer, dodged in that way, in a strange place, on an empty stomach! I was hungry, but before I had swallowed a morsel, he began a running sum that lasted all through the breakfast. "Seven?" "And four?" "And eight?" "And six?" "And two?" "And ten?" And so on. And after each figure was disposed of, it was as much as I could do to get a bite or a sup, before the next came; while he sat at his ease guessing nothing, and eating bacon and hot roll, in (if I may be allowed the expression) a gorging and gormandizing manner.

For such reasons, I was very glad when ten o'clock came and we started for Miss Havisham's; though I was not at all at my ease regarding the manner in which I should acquit myself under that lady's roof. Within a quarter of an hour we came to Miss Havisham's house, which was of old brick, and dismal, and had a great many iron bars to it. Some of the windows had been walled up; of those that remained, all the lower were rustily barred. There was a courtyard in front, and that was barred; so we had to wait, after ringing the bell, until some one should come to open it. While we waited at the gate, I peeped in (even then Mr. Pumblechook said, "And fourteen?" but I pretended not to hear him), and saw that at the side of the house there was a large brewery. No brewing was going on in it, and none seemed to have gone on for a long long time.

A window was raised, and a clear voice demanded "What name?" To which my conductor replied, "Pumblechook." The voice returned, "Quite right," and the window was shut again, and a young lady came across the court-yard, with keys in her hand.

"This," said Mr. Pumblechook, "is Pip."

"This is Pip, is it?" returned the young lady, who was very pretty and seemed very proud; "come in, Pip."

Mr. Pumblechook was coming in also, when she stopped him with the gate.

"Oh!" she said. "Did you wish to see Miss Havisham?"

"If Miss Havisham wished to see me," returned Mr. Pumblechook, discomfited.

"Ah!" said the girl; "but you see she don't."

She said it so finally, and in such an undiscussible way, that Mr. Pumblechook, though in a condition of ruffled dignity, could not protest. But he eyed me severely,—as if I had done anything to him!—and departed with the words reproachfully delivered: "Boy! Let your behavior here be a credit unto them which brought you up by hand!" I was not free from apprehension that he would come back to propound through the gate, "And sixteen?" But he didn't.

My young conductress locked the gate, and we went across the courtyard. It was paved and clean, but grass was growing in every crevice. The brewery buildings had a little lane of communication with it, and the wooden gates of that lane stood open, and all the brewery beyond stood open, away to the high enclosing wall; and all was empty and disused. The cold wind seemed to blow colder there than outside the gate; and it made a shrill noise in howling in and out at the open sides of the brewery, like the noise of wind in the rigging of a ship at sea.

She saw me looking at it, and she said, "You could drink without hurt all the strong beer that's brewed there now, boy."

"I should think I could, miss," said I, in a shy way.

"Better not try to brew beer there now, or it would turn out sour, boy; don't you think so?"

"It looks like it, miss."

"Not that anybody means to try," she added, "for that's all done with, and the place will stand as idle as it is till it falls. As to strong beer, there's enough of it in the cellars already, to drown the Manor House."

"Is that the name of this house, miss?"

"One of its names, boy."

"It has more than one, then, miss?"

"One more. Its other name was Satis; which is Greek, or Latin, or Hebrew, or all three— or all one to me—for enough."

"Enough House," said I; "that's a curious name, miss."

"Yes," she replied; "but it meant more than it said. It meant, when it was given, that whoever had this house could want nothing else. They must have been easily satisfied in those days, I should think. But don't loiter, boy."

Though she called me "boy" so often, and with a carelessness that was far from complimentary, she was of about my own age. She seemed much older than I, of course, being a girl, and beautiful and self-possessed; and she was as scornful of me as if she had been one-and-twenty, and a queen.

We went into the house by a side door, the great front entrance had two chains across it outside,—and the first thing I noticed was, that the passages were all dark, and that she had left a candle burning there. She took it up, and we went through more passages and up a staircase, and still it was all dark, and only the candle lighted us.

At last we came to the door of a room, and she said, "Go in."

I answered, more in shyness than politeness, "After you, miss."

To this she returned: "Don't be ridiculous, boy; I am not going in." And scornfully walked away, and—what was worse—took the candle with her.

This was very uncomfortable, and I was half afraid. However, the only thing to be done being to knock at the door, I knocked, and was told from within to enter. I entered, therefore, and found myself in a pretty large room, well lighted with wax candles. No glimpse of daylight was to be seen in it. It was a dressing-room, as I supposed from the furniture, though much of it was of forms and uses then quite unknown to me. But prominent in it was a draped table with a gilded looking-glass, and that I made out at first sight to be a fine lady's dressing-table.

Whether I should have made out this object so soon if there had been no fine lady sitting at it, I cannot say. In an arm-chair, with an elbow resting on the table and her head leaning on that hand, sat the strangest lady I have ever seen, or shall ever see.

She was dressed in rich materials,—satins, and lace, and silks,—all of white. Her shoes were white. And she had a long white veil dependent from her hair, and she had bridal flowers in her hair, but her hair was white. Some bright jewels sparkled on her neck and on her hands, and some other jewels lay sparkling on the table. Dresses, less splendid than the dress she wore, and half-packed trunks, were scattered about. She had not quite finished dressing, for she had but one shoe on,—the other was on the table near her hand,—her veil was but half arranged, her watch and chain were not put on, and some lace for her bosom lay with those trinkets, and with her handkerchief, and gloves, and some flowers, and a Prayer-Book all confusedly heaped about the looking-glass.

It was not in the first few moments that I saw all these things, though I saw more of them in the first moments than might be supposed. But I saw that everything within my view which ought to be white, had been white long ago, and had lost its lustre and was faded and yellow. I saw that the bride within the bridal dress had withered like the dress, and like the flowers, and had no brightness left but the brightness of her sunken eyes. I saw that the dress had been put upon the rounded figure of a young woman, and that the figure upon which it now hung loose had shrunk to skin and bone. Once, I had been taken to see some ghastly waxwork at the Fair, representing I know not what impossible personage lying in state. Once, I had been taken to one of our old marsh churches to see a skeleton in the ashes of a rich dress that had been dug out of a vault under the church pavement. Now, waxwork and skeleton seemed to have dark eyes that moved and looked at me. I should have cried out, if I could.

"Who is it?" said the lady at the table.

"Pip, ma'am."

"Pip?"

"Mr. Pumblechook's boy, ma'am. Come—to play."

"Come nearer; let me look at you. Come close."

It was when I stood before her, avoiding her eyes, that I took note of the surrounding objects in detail, and saw that her watch had stopped at twenty minutes to nine, and that a clock in the room had stopped at twenty minutes to nine.

"Look at me," said Miss Havisham. "You are not afraid of a woman who has never seen the sun since you were born?"

I regret to state that I was not afraid of telling the enormous lie comprehended in the answer "No."

"Do you know what I touch here?" she said, laying her hands, one upon the other, on her left side.

"Yes, ma'am." (It made me think of the young man.)

"What do I touch?"

"Your heart."

"Broken!"

She uttered the word with an eager look, and with strong emphasis, and with a weird smile that had a kind of boast in it. Afterwards she kept her hands there for a little while, and slowly took them away as if they were heavy.

"I am tired," said Miss Havisham. "I want diversion, and I have done with men and women. Play."

I think it will be conceded by my most disputatious reader, that she could hardly have directed an unfortunate boy to do anything in the wide world more difficult to be done under the circumstances.

"I sometimes have sick fancies," she went on, "and I have a sick fancy that I want to see some play. There, there!" with an impatient movement of the fingers of her right hand; "play, play, play!"

For a moment, with the fear of my sister's working me before my eyes, I had a desperate idea of starting round the room in the assumed character of Mr. Pumblechook's chaise-cart. But I felt myself so unequal to the performance that I gave it up, and stood looking at Miss Havisham in what I suppose she took for a dogged manner, inasmuch as she said, when we had taken a good look at each other,—

"Are you sullen and obstinate?"

"No, ma'am, I am very sorry for you, and very sorry I can't play just now. If you complain of me I shall get into trouble with my sister, so I would do it if I could; but it's so new here, and so strange, and so fine,—and melancholy—." I stopped, fearing I might say too much, or had already said it, and we took another look at each other.

Before she spoke again, she turned her eyes from me, and looked at the dress she wore, and at the dressing-table, and finally at herself in the looking-glass.

"So new to him," she muttered, "so old to me; so strange to him, so familiar to me; so melancholy to both of us! Call Estella."

As she was still looking at the reflection of herself, I thought she was still talking to herself, and kept quiet.

"Call Estella," she repeated, flashing a look at me. "You can do that. Call Estella. At the door."

To stand in the dark in a mysterious passage of an unknown house, bawling Estella to a scornful young lady neither visible nor responsive, and feeling it a dreadful liberty so to roar out her name, was almost as bad as playing to order. But she answered at last, and her light came along the dark passage like a star.

Miss Havisham beckoned her to come close, and took up a jewel from the table, and tried its effect upon her fair young bosom and against her pretty brown hair. "Your own, one day, my dear, and you will use it well. Let me see you play cards with this boy."

"With this boy? Why, he is a common laboring boy!"

I thought I overheard Miss Havisham answer,—only it seemed so unlikely,—"Well? You can break his heart."

"What do you play, boy?" asked Estella of myself, with the greatest disdain.

"Nothing but beggar my neighbor, miss."

"Beggar him," said Miss Havisham to Estella. So we sat down to cards.

It was then I began to understand that everything in the room had stopped, like the watch and the clock, a long time ago. I noticed that Miss Havisham put down the jewel exactly on the spot from which she had taken it up. As Estella dealt the cards, I glanced at the dressing-table again, and saw that the shoe upon it, once white, now yellow, had never been worn. I glanced down at the foot from which the shoe was absent, and saw that the silk stocking on it, once white, now yellow, had been trodden ragged. Without this arrest of everything, this standing still of all the pale decayed objects, not even the withered bridal dress on the collapsed form could have looked so like grave-clothes, or the long veil so like a shroud.

So she sat, corpse-like, as we played at cards; the frillings and trimmings on her bridal dress, looking like earthy paper. I knew nothing then of the discoveries that are occasionally made of bodies buried in ancient times, which fall to powder in the moment of being distinctly seen; but, I have often thought since, that she must have looked as if the admission of the natural light of day would have struck her to dust.

"He calls the knaves Jacks, this boy!" said Estella with disdain, before our first game was out. "And what coarse hands he has! And what thick boots!"

I had never thought of being ashamed of my hands before; but I began to consider them a very indifferent pair. Her contempt for me was so strong, that it became infectious, and I caught it.

She won the game, and I dealt. I misdealt, as was only natural, when I knew she was lying in wait for me to do wrong; and she denounced me for a stupid, clumsy laboring-boy.

"You say nothing of her," remarked Miss Havisham to me, as she looked on. "She says many hard things of you, but you say nothing of her. What do you think of her?"

"I don't like to say," I stammered.

"Tell me in my ear," said Miss Havisham, bending down.

"I think she is very proud," I replied, in a whisper.

"Anything else?"

"I think she is very pretty."

"Anything else?"

"I think she is very insulting." (She was looking at me then with a look of supreme aversion.)

"Anything else?"

"I think I should like to go home."

"And never see her again, though she is so pretty?"

"I am not sure that I shouldn't like to see her again, but I should like to go home now."

"You shall go soon," said Miss Havisham, aloud. "Play the game out."

Saving for the one weird smile at first, I should have felt almost sure that Miss Havisham's face could not smile. It had dropped into a watchful and brooding expression,—most likely when all the things about her had become transfixed,—and it looked as if nothing could ever lift it up again. Her chest had dropped, so that she stooped; and her voice had dropped, so that she spoke low, and with a dead lull upon her; altogether, she had the appearance of having dropped body and soul, within and without, under the weight of a crushing blow.

I played the game to an end with Estella, and she beggared me. She threw the cards down on the table when she had won them all, as if she despised them for having been won of me.

"When shall I have you here again?" said Miss Havisham. "Let me think."

I was beginning to remind her that to-day was Wednesday, when she checked me with her former impatient movement of the fingers of her right hand.

"There, there! I know nothing of days of the week; I know nothing of weeks of the year. Come again after six days. You hear?"

"Yes, ma'am."

"Estella, take him down. Let him have something to eat, and let him roam and look about him while he eats. Go, Pip."

I followed the candle down, as I had followed the candle up, and she stood it in the place where we had found it. Until she opened the side entrance, I had fancied, without thinking about it, that it must necessarily be night-time. The rush of the daylight quite confounded me, and made me feel as if I had been in the candlelight of the strange room many hours.

"You are to wait here, you boy," said Estella; and disappeared and closed the door.

I took the opportunity of being alone in the courtyard to look at my coarse hands and my common boots. My opinion of those accessories was not favorable. They had never troubled me before, but they troubled me now, as vulgar appendages. I determined to ask Joe why he had ever taught me to call those picture-cards Jacks, which ought to be called knaves. I wished Joe had been rather more genteelly brought up, and then I should have been so too.

She came back, with some bread and meat and a little mug of beer. She put the mug down on the stones of the yard, and gave me the bread and meat without looking at me, as insolently as if I were a dog in disgrace. I was so humiliated, hurt, spurned, offended, angry, sorry,—I cannot hit upon the right name for the smart—God knows what its name was,—that tears started to my eyes. The moment they sprang there, the girl looked at me with a quick delight in having been the cause of them. This gave me power to keep them back and to look at her: so, she gave a contemptuous toss—but with a sense, I thought, of having made too sure that I was so wounded—and left me.

But when she was gone, I looked about me for a place to hide my face in, and got behind one of the gates in the brewery-lane, and leaned my sleeve against the wall there, and leaned my forehead on it and cried. As I cried, I kicked the wall, and took a hard twist at my hair; so bitter were my feelings, and so sharp was the smart without a name, that needed counteraction.

My sister's bringing up had made me sensitive. In the little world in which children have their existence whosoever brings them up, there is nothing so finely perceived and so finely felt as injustice. It may be only small injustice that the child can be exposed to; but the child is small, and its world is small, and its rocking-horse stands as many hands high, according to scale, as a big-boned Irish hunter. Within myself, I had sustained, from my babyhood, a perpetual conflict with injustice. I had known, from the time when I could speak, that my sister, in her capricious and violent coercion, was unjust to me. I had cherished a profound conviction that her bringing me up by hand gave her no right to bring me up by jerks. Through all my punishments, disgraces, fasts, and vigils, and other penitential performances, I had nursed this assurance; and to my communing so much with it, in a solitary and unprotected way, I in great part refer the fact that I was morally timid and very sensitive.

I got rid of my injured feelings for the time by kicking them into the brewery wall, and twisting them out of my hair, and then I smoothed my face with my sleeve, and came from behind the gate. The bread and meat were acceptable, and the beer was warming and tingling, and I was soon in spirits to look about me.

To be sure, it was a deserted place, down to the pigeon-house in the brewery-yard, which had been blown crooked on its pole by some high wind, and would have made the pigeons think themselves at sea, if there had been any pigeons there to be rocked by it. But there were no pigeons in the dove-cot, no horses in the stable, no pigs in the sty, no malt in the storehouse, no smells of grains and beer in the copper or the vat. All the uses and scents of the brewery might have evaporated with its last reek of smoke. In a by-yard, there was a wilderness of empty casks, which had a certain sour remembrance of better days lingering about them; but it was too sour to be accepted as a sample of the beer that was gone,—and in this respect I remember those recluses as being like most others.

Behind the furthest end of the brewery, was a rank garden with an old wall; not so high but that I could struggle up and hold on long enough to look over it, and see that the rank garden was the garden of the house, and that it was overgrown with tangled weeds, but that there was a track upon the green and yellow paths, as if some one sometimes walked there, and that Estella was walking away from me even then. But she seemed to be everywhere. For when I yielded to the temptation presented by the casks, and began to walk on them, I saw her walking on them at the end of the yard of casks. She had her back towards me, and held her pretty brown hair spread out in her two hands, and never looked round, and passed out of my view directly. So, in the brewery itself,—by which I mean the large paved lofty place in which they used to make the beer, and where the brewing utensils still were. When I first went into it, and, rather oppressed by its gloom, stood near the door looking about me, I saw her pass among the extinguished fires, and ascend some light iron stairs, and go out by a gallery high overhead, as if she were going out into the sky.

It was in this place, and at this moment, that a strange thing happened to my fancy. I thought it a strange thing then, and I thought it a stranger thing long afterwards. I turned my eyes—a little dimmed by looking up at the frosty light—towards a great wooden beam in a low nook of the building near me on my right hand, and I saw a figure hanging there by the neck. A figure all in yellow white, with but one shoe to the feet; and it hung so, that I could see that the faded trimmings of the dress were like earthy paper, and that the face was Miss Havisham's, with a movement going over the whole countenance as if she were trying to call to me. In the terror of seeing the figure, and in the terror of being certain that it had not been there a moment before, I at first ran from it, and then ran towards it. And my terror was greatest of all when I found no figure there.

Nothing less than the frosty light of the cheerful sky, the sight of people passing beyond the bars of the court-yard gate, and the reviving influence of the rest of the bread and meat and beer, would have brought me round. Even with those aids, I might not have come to myself as soon as I did, but that I saw Estella approaching with the keys, to let me out. She would have some fair reason for looking down upon me, I thought, if she saw me frightened; and she would have no fair reason.

She gave me a triumphant glance in passing me, as if she rejoiced that my hands were so coarse and my boots were so thick, and she opened the gate, and stood holding it. I was passing out without looking at her, when she touched me with a taunting hand.

"Why don't you cry?"

"Because I don't want to."

"You do," said she. "You have been crying till you are half blind, and you are near crying again now."

She laughed contemptuously, pushed me out, and locked the gate upon me. I went straight to Mr. Pumblechook's, and was immensely relieved to find him not at home. So, leaving word with the shopman on what day I was wanted at Miss Havisham's again, I set off on the four-mile walk to our forge; pondering, as I went along, on all I had seen, and deeply revolving that I was a common laboring-boy; that my hands were coarse; that my boots were thick; that I had fallen into a despicable habit of calling knaves Jacks; that I was much more ignorant than I had considered myself last night, and generally that I was in a low-lived bad way.

Chapter IX

When I reached home, my sister was very curious to know all about Miss Havisham's, and asked a number of questions. And I soon found myself getting heavily bumped from behind in the nape of the neck and the small of the back, and having my face ignominiously shoved against the kitchen wall, because I did not answer those questions at sufficient length.

If a dread of not being understood be hidden in the breasts of other young people to anything like the extent to which it used to be hidden in mine,—which I consider probable, as I have no particular reason to suspect myself of having been a monstrosity,—it is the key to many reservations. I felt convinced that if I described Miss Havisham's as my eyes had seen it, I should not be understood. Not only that, but I felt convinced that Miss Havisham too would not be understood; and although she was perfectly incomprehensible to me, I entertained an impression that there would be something coarse and treacherous in my dragging her as she really was (to say nothing of Miss Estella) before the contemplation of Mrs. Joe. Consequently, I said as little as I could, and had my face shoved against the kitchen wall.

The worst of it was that that bullying old Pumblechook, preyed upon by a devouring curiosity to be informed of all I had seen and heard, came gaping over in his chaise-cart at tea-time, to have the details divulged to him. And the mere sight of the torment, with his fishy eyes and mouth open, his sandy hair inquisitively on end, and his waistcoat heaving with windy arithmetic, made me vicious in my reticence.

"Well, boy," Uncle Pumblechook began, as soon as he was seated in the chair of honor by the fire. "How did you get on up town?"

I answered, "Pretty well, sir," and my sister shook her fist at me.

"Pretty well?" Mr. Pumblechook repeated. "Pretty well is no answer. Tell us what you mean by pretty well, boy?"

Whitewash on the forehead hardens the brain into a state of obstinacy perhaps. Anyhow, with whitewash from the wall on my forehead, my obstinacy was adamantine. I reflected for some time, and then answered as if I had discovered a new idea, "I mean pretty well."

My sister with an exclamation of impatience was going to fly at me,—I had no shadow of defence, for Joe was busy in the forge,—when Mr. Pumblechook interposed with "No! Don't lose your temper. Leave this lad to me, ma'am; leave this lad to me." Mr. Pumblechook then turned me towards him, as if he were going to cut my hair, and said,—

"First (to get our thoughts in order): Forty-three pence?"

I calculated the consequences of replying "Four Hundred Pound," and finding them against me, went as near the answer as I could—which was somewhere about eightpence off. Mr. Pumblechook then put me through my pence-table from "twelve pence make one shilling," up to "forty pence make three and fourpence," and then triumphantly demanded, as if he had done for me, "Now! How much is forty-three pence?" To which I replied, after a long interval of reflection, "I don't know." And I was so aggravated that I almost doubt if I did know.

Mr. Pumblechook worked his head like a screw to screw it out of me, and said, "Is forty-three pence seven and sixpence three fardens, for instance?"

"Yes!" said I. And although my sister instantly boxed my ears, it was highly gratifying to me to see that the answer spoilt his joke, and brought him to a dead stop.

"Boy! What like is Miss Havisham?" Mr. Pumblechook began again when he had recovered; folding his arms tight on his chest and applying the screw.

"Very tall and dark," I told him.

"Is she, uncle?" asked my sister.

Mr. Pumblechook winked assent; from which I at once inferred that he had never seen Miss Havisham, for she was nothing of the kind.

"Good!" said Mr. Pumblechook conceitedly. ("This is the way to have him! We are beginning to hold our own, I think, Mum?")

"I am sure, uncle," returned Mrs. Joe, "I wish you had him always; you know so well how to deal with him."

"Now, boy! What was she a doing of, when you went in today?" asked Mr. Pumblechook.

"She was sitting," I answered, "in a black velvet coach."

Mr. Pumblechook and Mrs. Joe stared at one another—as they well might—and both repeated, "In a black velvet coach?"

"Yes," said I. "And Miss Estella—that's her niece, I think—handed her in cake and wine at the coach-window, on a gold plate. And we all had cake and wine on gold plates. And I got up behind the coach to eat mine, because she told me to."

"Was anybody else there?" asked Mr. Pumblechook.

"Four dogs," said I.

"Large or small?"

"Immense," said I. "And they fought for veal-cutlets out of a silver basket."

Mr. Pumblechook and Mrs. Joe stared at one another again, in utter amazement. I was perfectly frantic,—a reckless witness under the torture,—and would have told them anything.

"Where was this coach, in the name of gracious?" asked my sister.

"In Miss Havisham's room." They stared again. "But there weren't any horses to it." I added this saving clause, in the moment of rejecting four richly caparisoned coursers which I had had wild thoughts of harnessing.

"Can this be possible, uncle?" asked Mrs. Joe. "What can the boy mean?"

"I'll tell you, Mum," said Mr. Pumblechook. "My opinion is, it's a sedan-chair. She's flighty, you know,—very flighty,—quite flighty enough to pass her days in a sedan-chair."

"Did you ever see her in it, uncle?" asked Mrs. Joe.

"How could I," he returned, forced to the admission, "when I never see her in my life? Never clapped eyes upon her!"

"Goodness, uncle! And yet you have spoken to her?"

"Why, don't you know," said Mr. Pumblechook, testily, "that when I have been there, I have been took up to the outside of her door, and the door has stood ajar, and she has spoke to me that way. Don't say you don't know that, Mum. Howsever, the boy went there to play. What did you play at, boy?"

"We played with flags," I said. (I beg to observe that I think of myself with amazement, when I recall the lies I told on this occasion.)

"Flags!" echoed my sister.

"Yes," said I. "Estella waved a blue flag, and I waved a red one, and Miss Havisham waved one sprinkled all over with little gold stars, out at the coach-window. And then we all waved our swords and hurrahed."

"Swords!" repeated my sister. "Where did you get swords from?"

"Out of a cupboard," said I. "And I saw pistols in it,—and jam,—and pills. And there was no daylight in the room, but it was all lighted up with candles."

"That's true, Mum," said Mr. Pumblechook, with a grave nod. "That's the state of the case, for that much I've seen myself." And then they both stared at me, and I, with an obtrusive show of artlessness on my countenance, stared at them, and plaited the right leg of my trousers with my right hand.

If they had asked me any more questions, I should undoubtedly have betrayed myself, for I was even then on the point of mentioning that there was a balloon in the yard, and should have hazarded the statement but for my invention being divided between that phenomenon and a bear in the brewery. They were so much occupied, however, in discussing the marvels I had already presented for their consideration, that I escaped. The subject still held them when Joe came in from his work to have a cup of tea. To whom my sister, more for the relief of her own mind than for the gratification of his, related my pretended experiences.

Now, when I saw Joe open his blue eyes and roll them all round the kitchen in helpless amazement, I was overtaken by penitence; but only as regarded him,—not in the least as regarded the other two. Towards Joe, and Joe only, I considered myself a young monster, while they sat debating what results would come to me from Miss Havisham's acquaintance and favor. They had no doubt that Miss Havisham would "do something" for me; their doubts related to the form that something would take. My sister stood out for "property." Mr. Pumblechook was in favor of a handsome premium for binding me apprentice to some genteel trade,—say, the corn and seed trade, for instance. Joe fell into the deepest disgrace with both, for offering the bright suggestion that I might only be presented with one of the dogs who had fought for the veal-cutlets. "If a fool's head can't express better opinions than that," said my sister, "and you have got any work to do, you had better go and do it." So he went.

After Mr. Pumblechook had driven off, and when my sister was washing up, I stole into the forge to Joe, and remained by him until he had done for the night. Then I said, "Before the fire goes out, Joe, I should like to tell you something."

"Should you, Pip?" said Joe, drawing his shoeing-stool near the forge. "Then tell us. What is it, Pip?"

"Joe," said I, taking hold of his rolled-up shirt sleeve, and twisting it between my finger and thumb, "you remember all that about Miss Havisham's?"

"Remember?" said Joe. "I believe you! Wonderful!"

"It's a terrible thing, Joe; it ain't true."

"What are you telling of, Pip?" cried Joe, falling back in the greatest amazement. "You don't mean to say it's—"

"Yes I do; it's lies, Joe."

"But not all of it? Why sure you don't mean to say, Pip, that there was no black welwet co—eh?" For, I stood shaking my head. "But at least there was dogs, Pip? Come, Pip," said Joe, persuasively, "if there warn't no weal-cutlets, at least there was dogs?"

"No, Joe."

"A dog?" said Joe. "A puppy? Come?"

"No, Joe, there was nothing at all of the kind."

As I fixed my eyes hopelessly on Joe, Joe contemplated me in dismay. "Pip, old chap! This won't do, old fellow! I say! Where do you expect to go to?"

"It's terrible, Joe; ain't it?"

"Terrible?" cried Joe. "Awful! What possessed you?"

"I don't know what possessed me, Joe," I replied, letting his shirt sleeve go, and sitting down in the ashes at his feet, hanging my head; "but I wish you hadn't taught me to call Knaves at cards Jacks; and I wish my boots weren't so thick nor my hands so coarse."

And then I told Joe that I felt very miserable, and that I hadn't been able to explain myself to Mrs. Joe and Pumblechook, who were so rude to me, and that there had been a beautiful young lady at Miss Havisham's who was dreadfully proud, and that she had said I was common, and that I knew I was common, and that I wished I was not common, and that the lies had come of it somehow, though I didn't know how.

This was a case of metaphysics, at least as difficult for Joe to deal with as for me. But Joe took the case altogether out of the region of metaphysics, and by that means vanquished it.

"There's one thing you may be sure of, Pip," said Joe, after some rumination, "namely, that lies is lies. Howsever they come, they didn't ought to come, and they come from the father of lies, and work round to the same. Don't you tell no more of 'em, Pip. That ain't the way to get out of being common, old chap. And as to being common, I don't make it out at all clear. You are oncommon in some things. You're oncommon small. Likewise you're a oncommon scholar."

"No, I am ignorant and backward, Joe."

"Why, see what a letter you wrote last night! Wrote in print even! I've seen letters—Ah! and from gentlefolks!—that I'll swear weren't wrote in print," said Joe.

"I have learnt next to nothing, Joe. You think much of me. It's only that."

"Well, Pip," said Joe, "be it so or be it son't, you must be a common scholar afore you can be a oncommon one, I should hope! The king upon his throne, with his crown upon his ed, can't sit and write his acts of Parliament in print, without having begun, when he were a unpromoted Prince, with the alphabet.—Ah!" added Joe, with a shake of the head that was full of meaning, "and begun at A too, and worked his way to Z. And I know what that is to do, though I can't say I've exactly done it."

There was some hope in this piece of wisdom, and it rather encouraged me.

"Whether common ones as to callings and earnings," pursued Joe, reflectively, "mightn't be the better of continuing for to keep company with common ones, instead of going out to play with oncommon ones,—which reminds me to hope that there were a flag, perhaps?"

"No, Joe."

"(I'm sorry there weren't a flag, Pip). Whether that might be or mightn't be, is a thing as can't be looked into now, without putting your sister on the Rampage; and that's a thing not to be thought of as being done intentional. Lookee here, Pip, at what is said to you by a true friend. Which this to you the true friend say. If you can't get to be oncommon through going straight, you'll never get to do it through going crooked. So don't tell no more on 'em, Pip, and live well and die happy."

"You are not angry with me, Joe?"

"No, old chap. But bearing in mind that them were which I meantersay of a stunning and outdacious sort,—alluding to them which bordered on weal-cutlets and dog-fighting,—a sincere well-wisher would adwise, Pip, their being dropped into your meditations, when you go upstairs to bed. That's all, old chap, and don't never do it no more."

When I got up to my little room and said my prayers, I did not forget Joe's recommendation, and yet my young mind was in that disturbed and unthankful state, that I thought long after I laid me down, how common Estella would consider Joe, a mere blacksmith; how thick his boots, and how coarse his hands. I thought how Joe and my sister were then sitting in the kitchen, and how I had come up to bed from the kitchen, and how Miss Havisham and Estella never sat in a kitchen, but were far above the level of such common doings. I fell asleep recalling what I "used to do" when I was at Miss Havisham's; as though I had been there weeks or months, instead of hours; and as though it were quite an old subject of remembrance, instead of one that had arisen only that day.

That was a memorable day to me, for it made great changes in me. But it is the same with any life. Imagine one selected day struck out of it, and think how different its course would have been. Pause you who read this, and think for a moment of the long chain of iron or gold, of thorns or flowers, that would never have bound you, but for the formation of the first link on one memorable day.

Chapter X

The felicitous idea occurred to me a morning or two later when I woke, that the best step I could take towards making myself uncommon was to get out of Biddy everything she knew. In pursuance of this luminous conception I mentioned to Biddy when I went to Mr. Wopsle's great-aunt's at night, that I had a particular reason for wishing to get on in life, and that I should feel very much obliged to her if she would impart all her learning to me. Biddy, who was the most obliging of girls, immediately said she would, and indeed began to carry out her promise within five minutes.

The Educational scheme or Course established by Mr. Wopsle's great-aunt may be resolved into the following synopsis. The pupils ate apples and put straws down one another's backs, until Mr. Wopsle's great-aunt collected her energies, and made an indiscriminate totter at them with a birch-rod. After receiving the charge with every mark of derision, the pupils formed in line and buzzingly passed a ragged book from hand to hand. The book had an alphabet in it, some figures and tables, and a little spelling,—that is to say, it had had once. As soon as this volume began to circulate, Mr. Wopsle's great-aunt fell into a state of coma, arising either from sleep or a rheumatic paroxysm. The pupils then entered among themselves upon a competitive examination on the subject of Boots, with the view of ascertaining who could tread the hardest upon whose toes. This mental exercise lasted until Biddy made a rush at them and distributed three defaced Bibles (shaped as if they had been unskilfully cut off the chump end of something), more illegibly printed at the best than any curiosities of literature I have since met with, speckled all over with ironmould, and having various specimens of the insect world smashed between their leaves. This part of the Course was usually lightened by several single combats between Biddy and refractory students. When the fights were over, Biddy gave out the number of a page, and then we all read aloud what we could,—or what we couldn't—in a frightful chorus; Biddy leading with a high, shrill, monotonous voice, and none of us having the least notion of, or reverence for, what we were reading about. When this horrible din had lasted a certain time, it mechanically awoke Mr. Wopsle's great-aunt, who staggered at a boy fortuitously, and pulled his ears. This was understood to terminate the Course for the evening, and we emerged into the air with shrieks of intellectual victory. It is fair to remark that there was no prohibition against any pupil's entertaining himself with a slate or even with the ink (when there was any), but that it was not easy to pursue that branch of study in the winter season, on account of the little general shop in which the classes were holden—and which was also Mr. Wopsle's great-aunt's sitting-room and bedchamber—being but faintly illuminated through the agency of one low-spirited dip-candle and no snuffers.

It appeared to me that it would take time to become uncommon, under these circumstances: nevertheless, I resolved to try it, and that very evening Biddy entered on our special agreement, by imparting some information from her little catalogue of Prices, under the head of moist sugar, and lending me, to copy at home, a large old English D which she had imitated from the heading of some newspaper, and which I supposed, until she told me what it was, to be a design for a buckle.

Of course there was a public-house in the village, and of course Joe liked sometimes to smoke his pipe there. I had received strict orders from my sister to call for him at the Three Jolly Bargemen, that evening, on my way from school, and bring him home at my peril. To the Three Jolly Bargemen, therefore, I directed my steps.

There was a bar at the Jolly Bargemen, with some alarmingly long chalk scores in it on the wall at the side of the door, which seemed to me to be never paid off. They had been there ever since I could remember, and had grown more than I had. But there was a quantity of chalk about our country, and perhaps the people neglected no opportunity of turning it to account.

It being Saturday night, I found the landlord looking rather grimly at these records; but as my business was with Joe and not with him, I merely wished him good evening, and passed into the common room at the end of the passage, where there was a bright large kitchen fire, and where Joe was smoking his pipe in company with Mr. Wopsle and a stranger. Joe greeted me as usual with "Halloa, Pip, old chap!" and the moment he said that, the stranger turned his head and looked at me.

He was a secret-looking man whom I had never seen before. His head was all on one side, and one of his eyes was half shut up, as if he were taking aim at something with an invisible gun. He had a pipe in his mouth, and he took it out, and, after slowly blowing all his smoke away and looking hard at me all the time, nodded. So, I nodded, and then he nodded again, and made room on the settle beside him that I might sit down there.

But as I was used to sit beside Joe whenever I entered that place of resort, I said "No, thank you, sir," and fell into the space Joe made for me on the opposite settle. The strange man, after glancing at Joe, and seeing that his attention was otherwise engaged, nodded to me again when I had taken my seat, and then rubbed his leg—in a very odd way, as it struck me.

"You was saying," said the strange man, turning to Joe, "that you was a blacksmith."

"Yes. I said it, you know," said Joe.

"What'll you drink, Mr.—? You didn't mention your name, by the bye."

Joe mentioned it now, and the strange man called him by it. "What'll you drink, Mr. Gargery? At my expense? To top up with?"

"Well," said Joe, "to tell you the truth, I ain't much in the habit of drinking at anybody's expense but my own."

"Habit? No," returned the stranger, "but once and away, and on a Saturday night too. Come! Put a name to it, Mr. Gargery."

"I wouldn't wish to be stiff company," said Joe. "Rum."

"Rum," repeated the stranger. "And will the other gentleman originate a sentiment."

"Rum," said Mr. Wopsle.

"Three Rums!" cried the stranger, calling to the landlord. "Glasses round!"

"This other gentleman," observed Joe, by way of introducing Mr. Wopsle, "is a gentleman that you would like to hear give it out. Our clerk at church."

"Aha!" said the stranger, quickly, and cocking his eye at me. "The lonely church, right out on the marshes, with graves round it!"

"That's it," said Joe.

The stranger, with a comfortable kind of grunt over his pipe, put his legs up on the settle that he had to himself. He wore a flapping broad-brimmed traveller's hat, and under it a handkerchief tied over his head in the manner of a cap: so that he showed no hair. As he looked at the fire, I thought I saw a cunning expression, followed by a half-laugh, come into his face.

"I am not acquainted with this country, gentlemen, but it seems a solitary country towards the river."

"Most marshes is solitary," said Joe.

"No doubt, no doubt. Do you find any gypsies, now, or tramps, or vagrants of any sort, out there?"

"No," said Joe; "none but a runaway convict now and then. And we don't find them, easy. Eh, Mr. Wopsle?"

Mr. Wopsle, with a majestic remembrance of old discomfiture, assented; but not warmly.

"Seems you have been out after such?" asked the stranger.

"Once," returned Joe. "Not that we wanted to take them, you understand; we went out as lookers on; me, and Mr. Wopsle, and Pip. Didn't us, Pip?"

"Yes, Joe."

The stranger looked at me again,—still cocking his eye, as if he were expressly taking aim at me with his invisible gun,—and said, "He's a likely young parcel of bones that. What is it you call him?"

"Pip," said Joe.

"Christened Pip?"

"No, not christened Pip."

"Surname Pip?"

"No," said Joe, "it's a kind of family name what he gave himself when a infant, and is called by."

"Son of yours?"

"Well," said Joe, meditatively, not, of course, that it could be in anywise necessary to consider about it, but because it was the way at the Jolly Bargemen to seem to consider deeply about everything that was discussed over pipes,—"well—no. No, he ain't."

"Nevvy?" said the strange man.

"Well," said Joe, with the same appearance of profound cogitation, "he is not—no, not to deceive you, he is not—my nevvy."

"What the Blue Blazes is he?" asked the stranger. Which appeared to me to be an inquiry of unnecessary strength.

Mr. Wopsle struck in upon that; as one who knew all about relationships, having professional occasion to bear in mind what female relations a man might not marry; and expounded the ties between me and Joe. Having his hand in, Mr. Wopsle finished off with a most terrifically snarling passage from Richard the Third, and seemed to think he had done quite enough to account for it when he added, "—as the poet says."

And here I may remark that when Mr. Wopsle referred to me, he considered it a necessary part of such reference to rumple my hair and poke it into my eyes. I cannot conceive why everybody of his standing who visited at our house should always have put me through the same inflammatory process under similar circumstances. Yet I do not call to mind that I was ever in my earlier youth the subject of remark in our social family circle, but some large-handed person took some such ophthalmic steps to patronize me.

All this while, the strange man looked at nobody but me, and looked at me as if he were determined to have a shot at me at last, and bring me down. But he said nothing after offering his Blue Blazes observation, until the glasses of rum and water were brought; and then he made his shot, and a most extraordinary shot it was.

It was not a verbal remark, but a proceeding in dumb-show, and was pointedly addressed to me. He stirred his rum and water pointedly at me, and he tasted his rum and water pointedly at me. And he stirred it and he tasted it; not with a spoon that was brought to him, but with a file.

He did this so that nobody but I saw the file; and when he had done it he wiped the file and put it in a breast-pocket. I knew it to be Joe's file, and I knew that he knew my convict, the moment I saw the instrument. I sat gazing at him, spell-bound. But he now reclined on his settle, taking very little notice of me, and talking principally about turnips.

There was a delicious sense of cleaning-up and making a quiet pause before going on in life afresh, in our village on Saturday nights, which stimulated Joe to dare to stay out half an hour longer on Saturdays than at other times. The half-hour and the rum and water running out together, Joe got up to go, and took me by the hand.

"Stop half a moment, Mr. Gargery," said the strange man. "I think I've got a bright new shilling somewhere in my pocket, and if I have, the boy shall have it."

He looked it out from a handful of small change, folded it in some crumpled paper, and gave it to me. "Yours!" said he. "Mind! Your own."

I thanked him, staring at him far beyond the bounds of good manners, and holding tight to Joe. He gave Joe good-night, and he gave Mr. Wopsle good-night (who went out with us), and he gave me only a look with his aiming eye,—no, not a look, for he shut it up, but wonders may be done with an eye by hiding it.

On the way home, if I had been in a humor for talking, the talk must have been all on my side, for Mr. Wopsle parted from us at the door of the Jolly Bargemen, and Joe went all the way home with his mouth wide open, to rinse the rum out with as much air as possible. But I was in a manner stupefied by this turning up of my old misdeed and old acquaintance, and could think of nothing else.

My sister was not in a very bad temper when we presented ourselves in the kitchen, and Joe was encouraged by that unusual circumstance to tell her about the bright shilling. "A bad un, I'll be bound," said Mrs. Joe triumphantly, "or he wouldn't have given it to the boy! Let's look at it."

I took it out of the paper, and it proved to be a good one. "But what's this?" said Mrs. Joe, throwing down the shilling and catching up the paper. "Two One-Pound notes?"

Nothing less than two fat sweltering one-pound notes that seemed to have been on terms of the warmest intimacy with all the cattle-markets in the county. Joe caught up his hat again, and ran with them to the Jolly Bargemen to restore them to their owner. While he was gone, I sat down on my usual stool and looked vacantly at my sister, feeling pretty sure that the man would not be there.

Presently, Joe came back, saying that the man was gone, but that he, Joe, had left word at the Three Jolly Bargemen concerning the notes. Then my sister sealed them up in a piece of paper, and put them under some dried rose-leaves in an ornamental teapot on the top of a press in the state parlor. There they remained, a nightmare to me, many and many a night and day.

I had sadly broken sleep when I got to bed, through thinking of the strange man taking aim at me with his invisible gun, and of the guiltily coarse and common thing it was, to be on secret terms of conspiracy with convicts,—a feature in my low career that I had previously forgotten. I was haunted by the file too. A dread possessed me that when I least expected it, the file would reappear. I coaxed myself to sleep by thinking of Miss Havisham's, next Wednesday; and in my sleep I saw the file coming at me out of a door, without seeing who held it, and I screamed myself awake.

Chapter XI

At the appointed time I returned to Miss Havisham's, and my hesitating ring at the gate brought out Estella. She locked it after admitting me, as she had done before, and again preceded me into the dark passage where her candle stood. She took no notice of me until she had the candle in her hand, when she looked over her shoulder, superciliously saying, "You are to come this way to-day," and took me to quite another part of the house.

The passage was a long one, and seemed to pervade the whole square basement of the Manor House. We traversed but one side of the square, however, and at the end of it she stopped, and put her candle down and opened a door. Here, the daylight reappeared, and I found myself in a small paved courtyard, the opposite side of which was formed by a detached dwelling-house, that looked as if it had once belonged to the manager or head clerk of the extinct brewery. There was a clock in the outer wall of this house. Like the clock in Miss Havisham's room, and like Miss Havisham's watch, it had stopped at twenty minutes to nine.

We went in at the door, which stood open, and into a gloomy room with a low ceiling, on the ground-floor at the back. There was some company in the room, and Estella said to me as she joined it, "You are to go and stand there boy, till you are wanted." "There", being the window, I crossed to it, and stood "there," in a very uncomfortable state of mind, looking out.

It opened to the ground, and looked into a most miserable corner of the neglected garden, upon a rank ruin of cabbage-stalks, and one box-tree that had been clipped round long ago, like a pudding, and had a new growth at the top of it, out of shape and of a different color, as if that part of the pudding had stuck to the saucepan and got burnt. This was my homely thought, as I contemplated the box-tree. There had been some light snow, overnight, and it lay nowhere else to my knowledge; but, it had not quite melted from the cold shadow of this bit of garden, and the wind caught it up in little eddies and threw it at the window, as if it pelted me for coming there.

I divined that my coming had stopped conversation in the room, and that its other occupants were looking at me. I could see nothing of the room except the shining of the fire in the window-glass, but I stiffened in all my joints with the consciousness that I was under close inspection.

There were three ladies in the room and one gentleman. Before I had been standing at the window five minutes, they somehow conveyed to me that they were all toadies and humbugs, but that each of them pretended not to know that the others were toadies and humbugs: because the admission that he or she did know it, would have made him or her out to be a

426

toady and humbug.

They all had a listless and dreary air of waiting somebody's pleasure, and the most talkative of the ladies had to speak quite rigidly to repress a yawn. This lady, whose name was Camilla, very much reminded me of my sister, with the difference that she was older, and (as I found when I caught sight of her) of a blunter cast of features. Indeed, when I knew her better I began to think it was a Mercy she had any features at all, so very blank and high was the dead wall of her face.

"Poor dear soul!" said this lady, with an abruptness of manner quite my sister's. "Nobody's enemy but his own!"

"It would be much more commendable to be somebody else's enemy," said the gentleman; "far more natural."

"Cousin Raymond," observed another lady, "we are to love our neighbor."

"Sarah Pocket," returned Cousin Raymond, "if a man is not his own neighbor, who is?"

Miss Pocket laughed, and Camilla laughed and said (checking a yawn), "The idea!" But I thought they seemed to think it rather a good idea too. The other lady, who had not spoken yet, said gravely and emphatically, "Very true!"

"Poor soul!" Camilla presently went on (I knew they had all been looking at me in the mean time), "he is so very strange! Would anyone believe that when Tom's wife died, he actually could not be induced to see the importance of the children's having the deepest of trimmings to their mourning? 'Good Lord!' says he, 'Camilla, what can it signify so long as the poor bereaved little things are in black?' So like Matthew! The idea!"

"Good points in him, good points in him," said Cousin Raymond; "Heaven forbid I should deny good points in him; but he never had, and he never will have, any sense of the proprieties."

"You know I was obliged," said Camilla,—"I was obliged to be firm. I said, 'It WILL NOT DO, for the credit of the family.' I told him that, without deep trimmings, the family was disgraced. I cried about it from breakfast till dinner. I injured my digestion. And at last he flung out in his violent way, and said, with a D, 'Then do as you like.' Thank Goodness it will always be a consolation to me to know that I instantly went out in a pouring rain and bought the things."

"He paid for them, did he not?" asked Estella.

"It's not the question, my dear child, who paid for them," returned Camilla. "I bought them. And I shall often think of that with peace, when I wake up in the night."

The ringing of a distant bell, combined with the echoing of some cry or call along the passage by which I had come, interrupted the conversation and caused Estella to say to me, "Now, boy!" On my turning round, they all looked at me with the utmost contempt, and, as I went out, I heard Sarah Pocket say, "Well I am sure! What next!" and Camilla add, with indignation, "Was there ever such a fancy! The i-de-a!"

As we were going with our candle along the dark passage, Estella stopped all of a sudden, and, facing round, said in her taunting manner, with her face quite close to mine,—

"Well?"

"Well, miss?" I answered, almost falling over her and checking myself.

She stood looking at me, and, of course, I stood looking at her.

"Am I pretty?"

"Yes; I think you are very pretty."

"Am I insulting?"

"Not so much so as you were last time," said I.

"Not so much so?"

"No."

She fired when she asked the last question, and she slapped my face with such force as she had, when I answered it.

"Now?" said she. "You little coarse monster, what do you think of me now?"

"I shall not tell you."

"Because you are going to tell upstairs. Is that it?"

"No," said I, "that's not it."

"Why don't you cry again, you little wretch?"

"Because I'll never cry for you again," said I. Which was, I suppose, as false a declaration as ever was made; for I was inwardly crying for her then, and I know what I know of the pain she cost me afterwards.

We went on our way upstairs after this episode; and, as we were going up, we met a gentleman groping his way down.

"Whom have we here?" asked the gentleman, stopping and looking at me.

"A boy," said Estella.

He was a burly man of an exceedingly dark complexion, with an exceedingly large head, and a corresponding large hand. He took my chin in his large hand and turned up my face to have a look at me by the light of the candle. He was prematurely bald on the top of his head, and had bushy black eyebrows that wouldn't lie down but stood up bristling. His eyes were set very deep in his head, and were disagreeably sharp and suspicious. He had a large watch-chain, and strong black dots where his beard and whiskers would have been if he had let them. He was nothing to me, and I could have had no foresight then, that he ever would be anything to me, but it happened that I had this opportunity of observing him well.

"Boy of the neighborhood? Hey?" said he.

"Yes, sir," said I.

"How do you come here?"

"Miss Havisham sent for me, sir," I explained.

"Well! Behave yourself. I have a pretty large experience of boys, and you're a bad set of fellows. Now mind!" said he, biting the side of his great forefinger as he frowned at me, "you behave yourself!"

With those words, he released me—which I was glad of, for his hand smelt of scented soap—and went his way downstairs. I wondered whether he could be a doctor; but no, I thought; he couldn't be a doctor, or he would have a quieter and more persuasive manner. There was not much time to consider the subject, for we were soon in Miss Havisham's room, where she and everything else were just as I had left them. Estella left me standing near the door, and I stood there until Miss Havisham cast her eyes upon me from the dressing-table.

"So!" she said, without being startled or surprised: "the days have worn away, have they?"

"Yes, ma'am. To-day is—"

"There, there, there!" with the impatient movement of her fingers. "I don't want to know. Are you ready to play?"

I was obliged to answer in some confusion, "I don't think I am, ma'am."

"Not at cards again?" she demanded, with a searching look.

"Yes, ma'am; I could do that, if I was wanted."

"Since this house strikes you old and grave, boy," said Miss Havisham, impatiently, "and you are unwilling to play, are you willing to work?"

I could answer this inquiry with a better heart than I had been able to find for the other question, and I said I was quite willing.

"Then go into that opposite room," said she, pointing at the door behind me with her withered hand, "and wait there till I come."

I crossed the staircase landing, and entered the room she indicated. From that room, too, the daylight was completely excluded, and it had an airless smell that was oppressive. A fire had been lately kindled in the damp old-fashioned grate, and it was more disposed to go out than to burn up, and the reluctant smoke which hung in the room seemed colder than the clearer air,—like our own marsh mist. Certain wintry branches of candles on the high chimney-piece faintly lighted the chamber; or it would be more expressive to say, faintly troubled its darkness. It was spacious, and I dare say had once been handsome, but every discernible thing in it was covered with dust and mould, and dropping to pieces. The most prominent object was a long table with a tablecloth spread on it, as if a feast had been in preparation when the house and the clocks all stopped together. An epergne or centre-piece of some kind was in the middle of this cloth; it was so heavily overhung with cobwebs that its form was quite undistinguishable; and, as I looked along the yellow expanse out of which I remember its seeming to grow, like a black fungus, I saw speckle-legged spiders with blotchy bodies running home to it, and running out from it, as if some circumstances of the greatest public importance had just transpired in the spider community.

I heard the mice too, rattling behind the panels, as if the same occurrence were important to their interests. But the black beetles took no notice of the agitation, and groped about the hearth in a ponderous elderly way, as if they were short-sighted and hard of hearing, and not on terms with one another.

These crawling things had fascinated my attention, and I was watching them from a distance, when Miss Havisham laid a hand upon my shoulder. In her other hand she had a crutch-headed stick on which she leaned, and she looked like the Witch of the place.

"This," said she, pointing to the long table with her stick, "is where I will be laid when I am dead. They shall come and look at me here."

With some vague misgiving that she might get upon the table then and there and die at once, the complete realization of the ghastly waxwork at the Fair, I shrank under her touch.

"What do you think that is?" she asked me, again pointing with her stick; "that, where those cobwebs are?"

"I can't guess what it is, ma'am."

"It's a great cake. A bride-cake. Mine!"

She looked all round the room in a glaring manner, and then said, leaning on me while her hand twitched my shoulder, "Come, come, come! Walk me, walk me!"

I made out from this, that the work I had to do, was to walk Miss Havisham round and round the room. Accordingly, I started at once, and she leaned upon my shoulder, and we went away at a pace that might have been an imitation (founded on my first impulse under that roof) of Mr. Pumblechook's chaise-cart.

She was not physically strong, and after a little time said, "Slower!" Still, we went at an impatient fitful speed, and as we went, she twitched the hand upon my shoulder, and worked her mouth, and led me to believe that we were going fast because her thoughts went fast. After a while she said, "Call Estella!" so I went out on the landing and roared that name as I had done on the previous occasion. When her light appeared, I returned to Miss Havisham, and we started away again round and round the room.

If only Estella had come to be a spectator of our proceedings, I should have felt sufficiently discontented; but as she brought with her the three ladies and the gentleman whom I had seen below, I didn't know what to do. In my politeness, I would have stopped; but Miss Havisham twitched my shoulder, and we posted on,—with a shame-faced consciousness on my part that they would think it was all my doing.

"Dear Miss Havisham," said Miss Sarah Pocket. "How well you look!"

"I do not," returned Miss Havisham. "I am yellow skin and bone."

Camilla brightened when Miss Pocket met with this rebuff; and she murmured, as she plaintively contemplated Miss Havisham, "Poor dear soul! Certainly not to be expected to look well, poor thing. The idea!"

"And how are you?" said Miss Havisham to Camilla. As we were close to Camilla then, I would have stopped as a matter of course, only Miss Havisham wouldn't stop. We swept on, and I felt that I was highly obnoxious to Camilla.

"Thank you, Miss Havisham," she returned, "I am as well as can be expected."

"Why, what's the matter with you?" asked Miss Havisham, with exceeding sharpness.

"Nothing worth mentioning," replied Camilla. "I don't wish to make a display of my feelings, but I have habitually thought of you more in the night than I am quite equal to."

"Then don't think of me," retorted Miss Havisham.

"Very easily said!" remarked Camilla, amiably repressing a sob, while a hitch came into her upper lip, and her tears overflowed. "Raymond is a witness what ginger and sal volatile I am obliged to take in the night. Raymond is a witness what nervous jerkings I have in my legs.

Chokings and nervous jerkings, however, are nothing new to me when I think with anxiety of those I love. If I could be less affectionate and sensitive, I should have a better digestion and an iron set of nerves. I am sure I wish it could be so. But as to not thinking of you in the night—The idea!" Here, a burst of tears.

The Raymond referred to, I understood to be the gentleman present, and him I understood to be Mr. Camilla. He came to the rescue at this point, and said in a consolatory and complimentary voice, "Camilla, my dear, it is well known that your family feelings are gradually undermining you to the extent of making one of your legs shorter than the other."

"I am not aware," observed the grave lady whose voice I had heard but once, "that to think of any person is to make a great claim upon that person, my dear."

Miss Sarah Pocket, whom I now saw to be a little dry, brown, corrugated old woman, with a small face that might have been made of walnut-shells, and a large mouth like a cat's without the whiskers, supported this position by saying, "No, indeed, my dear. Hem!"

"Thinking is easy enough," said the grave lady.

"What is easier, you know?" assented Miss Sarah Pocket.

"Oh, yes, yes!" cried Camilla, whose fermenting feelings appeared to rise from her legs to her bosom. "It's all very true! It's a weakness to be so affectionate, but I can't help it. No doubt my health would be much better if it was otherwise, still I wouldn't change my disposition if I could. It's the cause of much suffering, but it's a consolation to know I posses it, when I wake up in the night." Here another burst of feeling.

Miss Havisham and I had never stopped all this time, but kept going round and round the room; now brushing against the skirts of the visitors, now giving them the whole length of the dismal chamber.

"There's Matthew!" said Camilla. "Never mixing with any natural ties, never coming here to see how Miss Havisham is! I have taken to the sofa with my staylace cut, and have lain there hours insensible, with my head over the side, and my hair all down, and my feet I don't know where—"

("Much higher than your head, my love," said Mr. Camilla.)

"I have gone off into that state, hours and hours, on account of Matthew's strange and inexplicable conduct, and nobody has thanked me."

"Really I must say I should think not!" interposed the grave lady.

"You see, my dear," added Miss Sarah Pocket (a blandly vicious personage), "the question to put to yourself is, who did you expect to thank you, my love?"

"Without expecting any thanks, or anything of the sort," resumed Camilla, "I have remained in that state, hours and hours, and Raymond is a witness of the extent to which I have choked, and what the total inefficacy of ginger has been, and I have been heard at the piano-forte tuner's across the street, where the poor mistaken children have even supposed it to be pigeons cooing at a distance,—and now to be told—" Here Camilla put her hand to her throat, and began to be quite chemical as to the formation of new combinations there.

When this same Matthew was mentioned, Miss Havisham stopped me and herself, and stood looking at the speaker. This change had a great influence in bringing Camilla's chemistry to a sudden end.

"Matthew will come and see me at last," said Miss Havisham, sternly, "when I am laid on that table. That will be his place,—there," striking the table with her stick, "at my head! And yours will be there! And your husband's there! And Sarah Pocket's there! And Georgiana's there! Now you all know where to take your stations when you come to feast upon me. And now go!"

At the mention of each name, she had struck the table with her stick in a new place. She now said, "Walk me, walk me!" and we went on again.

"I suppose there's nothing to be done," exclaimed Camilla, "but comply and depart. It's something to have seen the object of one's love and duty for even so short a time. I shall think of it with a melancholy satisfaction when I wake up in the night. I wish Matthew could have that comfort, but he sets it at defiance. I am determined not to make a display of my feelings, but it's very hard to be told one wants to feast on one's relations,—as if one was a Giant,—and to be told to go. The bare idea!"

Mr. Camilla interposing, as Mrs. Camilla laid her hand upon her heaving bosom, that lady assumed an unnatural fortitude of manner which I supposed to be expressive of an intention to drop and choke when out of view, and kissing her hand to Miss Havisham, was escorted forth. Sarah Pocket and Georgiana contended who should remain last; but Sarah was too knowing to be outdone, and ambled round Georgiana with that artful slipperiness that the latter was obliged to take precedence. Sarah Pocket then made her separate effect of departing with, "Bless you, Miss Havisham dear!" and with a smile of forgiving pity on her walnut-shell countenance for the weaknesses of the rest.

While Estella was away lighting them down, Miss Havisham still walked with her hand on my shoulder, but more and more slowly. At last she stopped before the fire, and said, after muttering and looking at it some seconds,—

"This is my birthday, Pip."

I was going to wish her many happy returns, when she lifted her stick.

"I don't suffer it to be spoken of. I don't suffer those who were here just now, or any one to speak of it. They come here on the day, but they dare not refer to it."

Of course I made no further effort to refer to it.

"On this day of the year, long before you were born, this heap of decay," stabbing with her crutched stick at the pile of cobwebs on the table, but not touching it, "was brought here. It and I have worn away together. The mice have gnawed at it, and sharper teeth than teeth of mice have gnawed at me."

She held the head of her stick against her heart as she stood looking at the table; she in her once white dress, all yellow and withered; the once white cloth all yellow and withered; everything around in a state to crumble under a touch.

"When the ruin is complete," said she, with a ghastly look, "and when they lay me dead, in my bride's dress on the bride's table,—which shall be done, and which will be the finished curse upon him,—so much the better if it is done on this day!"

She stood looking at the table as if she stood looking at her own figure lying there. I remained quiet. Estella returned, and she too remained quiet. It seemed to me that we continued thus for a long time. In the heavy air of the room, and the heavy darkness that brooded in its remoter corners, I even had an alarming fancy that Estella and I might presently begin to decay.

At length, not coming out of her distraught state by degrees, but in an instant, Miss Havisham said, "Let me see you two play cards; why have you not begun?" With that, we returned to her room, and sat down as before; I was beggared, as before; and again, as before, Miss Havisham watched us all the time, directed my attention to Estella's beauty, and made me notice it the more by trying her jewels on Estella's breast and hair.

Estella, for her part, likewise treated me as before, except that she did not condescend to speak. When we had played some half-dozen games, a day was appointed for my return, and I was taken down into the yard to be fed in the former dog-like manner. There, too, I was again left to wander about as I liked.

It is not much to the purpose whether a gate in that garden wall which I had scrambled up to peep over on the last occasion was, on that last occasion, open or shut. Enough that I saw no gate then, and that I saw one now. As it stood open, and as I knew that Estella had let the visitors out,—for she had returned with the keys in her hand,—I strolled into the garden, and strolled all over it. It was quite a wilderness, and there were old melon-frames and cucumber-frames in it, which seemed in their decline to have produced a spontaneous growth of weak attempts at pieces of old hats and boots, with now and then a weedy offshoot into the likeness of a battered saucepan.

When I had exhausted the garden and a greenhouse with nothing in it but a fallen-down grape-vine and some bottles, I found myself in the dismal corner upon which I had looked out of the window. Never questioning for a moment that the house was now empty, I looked in at another window, and found myself, to my great surprise, exchanging a broad stare with a pale young gentleman with red eyelids and light hair.

This pale young gentleman quickly disappeared, and reappeared beside me. He had been at his books when I had found myself staring at him, and I now saw that he was inky.

"Halloa!" said he, "young fellow!"

Halloa being a general observation which I had usually observed to be best answered by itself, I said, "Halloa!" politely omitting young fellow.

"Who let you in?" said he.

"Miss Estella."

"Who gave you leave to prowl about?"

"Miss Estella."

"Come and fight," said the pale young gentleman.

What could I do but follow him? I have often asked myself the question since; but what else could I do? His manner was so final, and I was so astonished, that I followed where he led, as if I had been under a spell.

"Stop a minute, though," he said, wheeling round before we had gone many paces. "I ought to give you a reason for fighting, too. There it is!" In a most irritating manner he instantly slapped his hands against one another, daintily flung one of his legs up behind him, pulled my hair, slapped his hands again, dipped his head, and butted it into my stomach.

The bull-like proceeding last mentioned, besides that it was unquestionably to be regarded in the light of a liberty, was particularly disagreeable just after bread and meat. I therefore hit out at him and was going to hit out again, when he said, "Aha! Would you?" and began dancing backwards and forwards in a manner quite unparalleled within my limited experience.

"Laws of the game!" said he. Here, he skipped from his left leg on to his right. "Regular rules!" Here, he skipped from his right leg on to his left. "Come to the ground, and go through the preliminaries!" Here, he dodged backwards and forwards, and did all sorts of things while I looked helplessly at him.

I was secretly afraid of him when I saw him so dexterous; but I felt morally and physically convinced that his light head of hair could have had no business in the pit of my stomach, and that I had a right to consider it irrelevant when so obtruded on my attention. Therefore, I followed him without a word, to a retired nook of the garden, formed by the junction of two walls and screened by some rubbish. On his asking me if I was satisfied with the ground, and on my replying Yes, he begged my leave to absent himself for a moment, and quickly returned with a bottle of water and a sponge dipped in vinegar. "Available for both," he said, placing these against the wall. And then fell to pulling off, not only his jacket and waistcoat, but his shirt too, in a manner at once light-hearted, business-like, and bloodthirsty.

Although he did not look very healthy,—having pimples on his face, and a breaking out at his mouth,—these dreadful preparations quite appalled me. I judged him to be about my own age, but he was much taller, and he had a way of spinning himself about that was full of appearance. For the rest, he was a young gentleman in a gray suit (when not denuded for battle), with his elbows, knees, wrists, and heels considerably in advance of the rest of him as to development.

My heart failed me when I saw him squaring at me with every demonstration of mechanical nicety, and eyeing my anatomy as if he were minutely choosing his bone. I never have been so surprised in my life, as I was when I let out the first blow, and saw him lying on his back, looking up at me with a bloody nose and his face exceedingly fore-shortened.

But, he was on his feet directly, and after sponging himself with a great show of dexterity began squaring again. The second greatest surprise I have ever had in my life was seeing him on his back again, looking up at me out of a black eye.

His spirit inspired me with great respect. He seemed to have no strength, and he never once hit me hard, and he was always knocked down; but he would be up again in a moment, sponging himself or drinking out of the water-bottle, with the greatest satisfaction in seconding himself according to form, and then came at me with an air and a show that made me believe he really was going to do for me at last. He got heavily bruised, for I am sorry to record that the more I hit him, the harder I hit him; but he came up again and again and again, until at last he got a bad fall with the back of his head against the wall. Even after that crisis in our affairs, he got up and turned round and round confusedly a few times, not knowing where I was; but finally went on his knees to his sponge and threw it up: at the same time panting out, "That means you have won."

He seemed so brave and innocent, that although I had not proposed the contest, I felt but a gloomy satisfaction in my victory. Indeed, I go so far as to hope that I regarded myself while dressing as a species of savage young wolf or other wild beast. However, I got dressed, darkly wiping my sanguinary face at intervals, and I said, "Can I help you?" and he said "No thankee," and I said "Good afternoon," and he said "Same to you."

When I got into the courtyard, I found Estella waiting with the keys. But she neither asked me where I had been, nor why I had kept her waiting; and there was a bright flush upon her face, as though something had happened to delight her. Instead of going straight to the gate, too, she stepped back into the passage, and beckoned me.

"Come here! You may kiss me, if you like."

I kissed her cheek as she turned it to me. I think I would have gone through a great deal to kiss her cheek. But I felt that the kiss was given to the coarse common boy as a piece of money might have been, and that it was worth nothing.

What with the birthday visitors, and what with the cards, and what with the fight, my stay had lasted so long, that when I neared home the light on the spit of sand off the point on the marshes was gleaming against a black night-sky, and Joe's furnace was flinging a path of fire across the road.

Chapter XII

My mind grew very uneasy on the subject of the pale young gentleman. The more I thought of the fight, and recalled the pale young gentleman on his back in various stages of puffy and incrimsoned countenance, the more certain it appeared that something would be done to me. I felt that the pale young gentleman's blood was on my head, and that the Law would avenge it. Without having any definite idea of the penalties I had incurred, it was clear to me that village boys could not go stalking about the country, ravaging the houses of gentlefolks and pitching into the studious youth of England, without laying themselves open to severe punishment. For some days, I even kept close at home, and looked out at the kitchen door with the greatest caution and trepidation before going on an errand, lest the officers of the County Jail should pounce upon me. The pale young gentleman's nose had stained my trousers, and I tried to wash out that evidence of my guilt in the dead of night. I had cut my knuckles against the pale young gentleman's teeth, and I twisted my imagination into a thousand tangles, as I devised incredible ways of accounting for that damnatory circumstance when I should be haled before the Judges.

When the day came round for my return to the scene of the deed of violence, my terrors reached their height. Whether myrmidons of Justice, specially sent down from London, would be lying in ambush behind the gate;—whether Miss Havisham, preferring to take personal vengeance for an outrage done to her house, might rise in those grave-clothes of hers, draw a pistol, and shoot me dead:—whether suborned boys—a numerous band of mercenaries—might be engaged to fall upon me in the brewery, and cuff me until I was no more;—it was high testimony to my confidence in the spirit of the pale young gentleman, that I never imagined him accessory to these retaliations; they always came into my mind as the acts of injudicious relatives of his, goaded on by the state of his visage and an indignant sympathy with the family features.

However, go to Miss Havisham's I must, and go I did. And behold! nothing came of the late struggle. It was not alluded to in any way, and no pale young gentleman was to be discovered on the premises. I found the same gate open, and I explored the garden, and even looked in at the windows of the detached house; but my view was suddenly stopped by the closed shutters within, and all was lifeless. Only in the corner where the combat had taken place could I detect any evidence of the young gentleman's existence. There were traces of his gore in that spot, and I covered them with garden-mould from the eye of man.

On the broad landing between Miss Havisham's own room and that other room in which the long table was laid out, I saw a garden-chair,—a light chair on wheels, that you pushed from behind. It had been placed there since my last visit, and I entered, that same day, on a regular occupation of pushing Miss Havisham in this chair (when she was tired of walking with her hand upon my shoulder) round her own room, and across the landing, and round the other room. Over and over and over again, we would make these journeys, and sometimes they would last as long as three hours at a stretch. I insensibly fall into a general mention of these journeys as numerous, because it was at once settled that I should return every alternate day at noon for these purposes, and because I am now going to sum up a period of at least eight or ten months.

As we began to be more used to one another, Miss Havisham talked more to me, and asked me such questions as what had I learnt and what was I going to be? I told her I was going to be apprenticed to Joe, I believed; and I enlarged upon my knowing nothing and wanting to know everything, in the hope that she might offer some help towards that desirable end. But she did not; on the contrary, she seemed to prefer my being ignorant. Neither did she ever give me any money,—or anything but my daily dinner,—nor ever stipulate that I should be paid for my services.

Estella was always about, and always let me in and out, but never told me I might kiss her again. Sometimes, she would coldly tolerate me; sometimes, she would condescend to me; sometimes, she would be quite familiar with me; sometimes, she would tell me energetically that she hated me. Miss Havisham would often ask me in a whisper, or when we were alone, "Does she grow prettier and prettier, Pip?" And when I said yes (for indeed she did), would seem to enjoy it greedily. Also, when we played at cards Miss Havisham would look on, with a miserly relish of Estella's moods, whatever they were. And sometimes, when her moods were so many and so contradictory of one another that I was puzzled what to say or do, Miss Havisham would embrace her with lavish fondness, murmuring something in her ear that sounded like "Break their hearts my pride and hope, break their hearts and have no mercy!"

There was a song Joe used to hum fragments of at the forge, of which the burden was Old Clem. This was not a very ceremonious way of rendering homage to a patron saint, but I believe Old Clem stood in that relation towards smiths. It was a song that imitated the measure of beating upon iron, and was a mere lyrical excuse for the introduction of Old Clem's respected name. Thus, you were to hammer boys round—Old Clem! With a thump and a sound—Old Clem! Beat it out, beat it out—Old Clem! With a clink for the stout—Old Clem! Blow the fire, blow the fire—Old Clem! Roaring dryer, soaring higher—Old Clem! One day soon after the appearance of the chair, Miss Havisham suddenly saying to me, with the impatient movement of her fingers, "There, there, there! Sing!" I was surprised into crooning this ditty as I pushed her over the floor. It happened so to catch her fancy that she took it up in a low brooding voice as if she were singing in her sleep. After that, it became customary with

436

us to have it as we moved about, and Estella would often join in; though the whole strain was so subdued, even when there were three of us, that it made less noise in the grim old house than the lightest breath of wind.

What could I become with these surroundings? How could my character fail to be influenced by them? Is it to be wondered at if my thoughts were dazed, as my eyes were, when I came out into the natural light from the misty yellow rooms?

Perhaps I might have told Joe about the pale young gentleman, if I had not previously been betrayed into those enormous inventions to which I had confessed. Under the circumstances, I felt that Joe could hardly fail to discern in the pale young gentleman, an appropriate passenger to be put into the black velvet coach; therefore, I said nothing of him. Besides, that shrinking from having Miss Havisham and Estella discussed, which had come upon me in the beginning, grew much more potent as time went on. I reposed complete confidence in no one but Biddy; but I told poor Biddy everything. Why it came natural to me to do so, and why Biddy had a deep concern in everything I told her, I did not know then, though I think I know now.

Meanwhile, councils went on in the kitchen at home, fraught with almost insupportable aggravation to my exasperated spirit. That ass, Pumblechook, used often to come over of a night for the purpose of discussing my prospects with my sister; and I really do believe (to this hour with less penitence than I ought to feel), that if these hands could have taken a linchpin out of his chaise-cart, they would have done it. The miserable man was a man of that confined stolidity of mind, that he could not discuss my prospects without having me before him,—as it were, to operate upon,—and he would drag me up from my stool (usually by the collar) where I was quiet in a corner, and, putting me before the fire as if I were going to be cooked, would begin by saying, "Now, Mum, here is this boy! Here is this boy which you brought up by hand. Hold up your head, boy, and be forever grateful unto them which so did do. Now, Mum, with respections to this boy!" And then he would rumple my hair the wrong way,—which from my earliest remembrance, as already hinted, I have in my soul denied the right of any fellow-creature to do,—and would hold me before him by the sleeve,—a spectacle of imbecility only to be equalled by himself.

Then, he and my sister would pair off in such nonsensical speculations about Miss Havisham, and about what she would do with me and for me, that I used to want—quite painfully—to burst into spiteful tears, fly at Pumblechook, and pummel him all over. In these dialogues, my sister spoke to me as if she were morally wrenching one of my teeth out at every reference; while Pumblechook himself, self-constituted my patron, would sit supervising me with a depreciatory eye, like the architect of my fortunes who thought himself engaged on a very unremunerative job.

In these discussions, Joe bore no part. But he was often talked at, while they were in progress, by reason of Mrs. Joe's perceiving that he was not favorable to my being taken from the forge. I was fully old enough now to be apprenticed to Joe; and when Joe sat with the poker on his knees thoughtfully raking out the ashes between the lower bars, my sister would so distinctly construe that innocent action into opposition on his part, that she would dive at him, take the poker out of his hands, shake him, and put it away. There was a most irritating end to every one of these debates. All in a moment, with nothing to lead up to it, my sister would stop herself in a yawn, and catching sight of me as it were incidentally, would swoop upon me with, "Come! there's enough of you! You get along to bed; you've given trouble enough for one night, I hope!" As if I had besought them as a favor to bother my life out.

We went on in this way for a long time, and it seemed likely that we should continue to go on in this way for a long time, when one day Miss Havisham stopped short as she and I were walking, she leaning on my shoulder; and said with some displeasure,—

"You are growing tall, Pip!"

I thought it best to hint, through the medium of a meditative look, that this might be occasioned by circumstances over which I had no control.

She said no more at the time; but she presently stopped and looked at me again; and presently again; and after that, looked frowning and moody. On the next day of my attendance, when our usual exercise was over, and I had landed her at her dressing-table, she stayed me with a movement of her impatient fingers:—

"Tell me the name again of that blacksmith of yours."

"Joe Gargery, ma'am."

"Meaning the master you were to be apprenticed to?"

"Yes, Miss Havisham."

"You had better be apprenticed at once. Would Gargery come here with you, and bring your indentures, do you think?"

I signified that I had no doubt he would take it as an honor to be asked.

"Then let him come."

"At any particular time, Miss Havisham?"

"There, there! I know nothing about times. Let him come soon, and come along with you."

When I got home at night, and delivered this message for Joe, my sister "went on the Rampage," in a more alarming degree than at any previous period. She asked me and Joe whether we supposed she was door-mats under our feet, and how we dared to use her so, and what company we graciously thought she was fit for? When she had exhausted a torrent of such inquiries, she threw a candlestick at Joe, burst into a loud sobbing, got out the dustpan,— which was always a very bad sign,—put on her coarse apron, and began cleaning up to a terrible extent. Not satisfied with a dry cleaning, she took to a pail and scrubbing-brush, and cleaned us out of house and home, so that we stood shivering in the back-yard. It was ten o'clock at night before we ventured to creep in again, and then she asked Joe why he hadn't married a Negress Slave at once? Joe offered no answer, poor fellow, but stood feeling his whisker and looking dejectedly at me, as if he thought it really might have been a better speculation.

Chapter XIII

It was a trial to my feelings, on the next day but one, to see Joe arraying himself in his Sunday clothes to accompany me to Miss Havisham's. However, as he thought his court-suit necessary to the occasion, it was not for me to tell him that he looked far better in his working-dress; the rather, because I knew he made himself so dreadfully uncomfortable, entirely on my account, and that it was for me he pulled up his shirt-collar so very high behind, that it made the hair on the crown of his head stand up like a tuft of feathers.

At breakfast-time my sister declared her intention of going to town with us, and being left at Uncle Pumblechook's and called for "when we had done with our fine ladies"—a way of putting the case, from which Joe appeared inclined to augur the worst. The forge was shut up for the day, and Joe inscribed in chalk upon the door (as it was his custom to do on the very rare occasions when he was not at work) the monosyllable HOUT, accompanied by a sketch of an arrow supposed to be flying in the direction he had taken.

We walked to town, my sister leading the way in a very large beaver bonnet, and carrying a basket like the Great Seal of England in plaited Straw, a pair of pattens, a spare shawl, and an umbrella, though it was a fine bright day. I am not quite clear whether these articles were carried penitentially or ostentatiously; but I rather think they were displayed as articles of property,—much as Cleopatra or any other sovereign lady on the Rampage might exhibit her wealth in a pageant or procession.

When we came to Pumblechook's, my sister bounced in and left us. As it was almost noon, Joe and I held straight on to Miss Havisham's house. Estella opened the gate as usual, and, the moment she appeared, Joe took his hat off and stood weighing it by the brim in both his hands; as if he had some urgent reason in his mind for being particular to half a quarter of an ounce.

Estella took no notice of either of us, but led us the way that I knew so well. I followed next to her, and Joe came last. When I looked back at Joe in the long passage, he was still weighing his hat with the greatest care, and was coming after us in long strides on the tips of his toes.

Estella told me we were both to go in, so I took Joe by the coat-cuff and conducted him into Miss Havisham's presence. She was seated at her dressing-table, and looked round at us immediately.

"Oh!" said she to Joe. "You are the husband of the sister of this boy?"

I could hardly have imagined dear old Joe looking so unlike himself or so like some extraordinary bird; standing as he did speechless, with his tuft of feathers ruffled, and his mouth open as if he wanted a worm.

"You are the husband," repeated Miss Havisham, "of the sister of this boy?"

It was very aggravating; but, throughout the interview, Joe persisted in addressing Me instead of Miss Havisham.

"Which I meantersay, Pip," Joe now observed in a manner that was at once expressive of forcible argumentation, strict confidence, and great politeness, "as I hup and married your sister, and I were at the time what you might call (if you was anyways inclined) a single man."

"Well!" said Miss Havisham. "And you have reared the boy, with the intention of taking him for your apprentice; is that so, Mr. Gargery?"

"You know, Pip," replied Joe, "as you and me were ever friends, and it were looked for'ard to betwixt us, as being calc'lated to lead to larks. Not but what, Pip, if you had ever made objections to the business,—such as its being open to black and sut, or such-like,—not but what they would have been attended to, don't you see?"

"Has the boy," said Miss Havisham, "ever made any objection? Does he like the trade?"

"Which it is well beknown to yourself, Pip," returned Joe, strengthening his former mixture of argumentation, confidence, and politeness, "that it were the wish of your own hart." (I saw the idea suddenly break upon him that he would adapt his epitaph to the occasion, before he went on to say) "And there weren't no objection on your part, and Pip it were the great wish of your hart!"

It was quite in vain for me to endeavor to make him sensible that he ought to speak to Miss Havisham. The more I made faces and gestures to him to do it, the more confidential, argumentative, and polite, he persisted in being to Me.

"Have you brought his indentures with you?" asked Miss Havisham.

"Well, Pip, you know," replied Joe, as if that were a little unreasonable, "you yourself see me put 'em in my 'at, and therefore you know as they are here." With which he took them out, and gave them, not to Miss Havisham, but to me. I am afraid I was ashamed of the dear good fellow,—I know I was ashamed of him,—when I saw that Estella stood at the back of Miss Havisham's chair, and that her eyes laughed mischievously. I took the indentures out of his hand and gave them to Miss Havisham.

"You expected," said Miss Havisham, as she looked them over, "no premium with the boy?"

"Joe!" I remonstrated, for he made no reply at all. "Why don't you answer—"

"Pip," returned Joe, cutting me short as if he were hurt, "which I meantersay that were not a question requiring a answer betwixt yourself and me, and which you know the answer to be full well No. You know it to be No, Pip, and wherefore should I say it?"

Miss Havisham glanced at him as if she understood what he really was better than I had thought possible, seeing what he was there; and took up a little bag from the table beside her.

"Pip has earned a premium here," she said, "and here it is. There are five-and-twenty guineas in this bag. Give it to your master, Pip."

As if he were absolutely out of his mind with the wonder awakened in him by her strange figure and the strange room, Joe, even at this pass, persisted in addressing me.

"This is wery liberal on your part, Pip," said Joe, "and it is as such received and grateful welcome, though never looked for, far nor near, nor nowheres. And now, old chap," said Joe, conveying to me a sensation, first of burning and then of freezing, for I felt as if that familiar expression were applied to Miss Havisham,—"and now, old chap, may we do our duty! May you and me do our duty, both on us, by one and another, and by them which your liberal present—have-conweyed—to be—for the satisfaction of mind-of—them as never—" here Joe showed that he felt he had fallen into frightful difficulties, until he triumphantly rescued himself with the words, "and from myself far be it!" These words had such a round and convincing sound for him that he said them twice.

"Good-bye, Pip!" said Miss Havisham. "Let them out, Estella."

"Am I to come again, Miss Havisham?" I asked.

"No. Gargery is your master now. Gargery! One word!"

Thus calling him back as I went out of the door, I heard her say to Joe in a distinct emphatic voice, "The boy has been a good boy here, and that is his reward. Of course, as an honest man, you will expect no other and no more."

How Joe got out of the room, I have never been able to determine; but I know that when he did get out he was steadily proceeding upstairs instead of coming down, and was deaf to all remonstrances until I went after him and laid hold of him. In another minute we were outside the gate, and it was locked, and Estella was gone. When we stood in the daylight alone again, Joe backed up against a wall, and said to me, "Astonishing!" And there he remained so long saying, "Astonishing" at intervals, so often, that I began to think his senses were never coming back. At length he prolonged his remark into "Pip, I do assure you this is as-TON-ishing!" and so, by degrees, became conversational and able to walk away.

I have reason to think that Joe's intellects were brightened by the encounter they had passed through, and that on our way to Pumblechook's he invented a subtle and deep design. My reason is to be found in what took place in Mr. Pumblechook's parlor: where, on our presenting ourselves, my sister sat in conference with that detested seedsman.

"Well?" cried my sister, addressing us both at once. "And what's happened to you? I wonder you condescend to come back to such poor society as this, I am sure I do!"

"Miss Havisham," said Joe, with a fixed look at me, like an effort of remembrance, "made it wery partick'ler that we should give her—were it compliments or respects, Pip?"

"Compliments," I said.

"Which that were my own belief," answered Joe; "her compliments to Mrs. J. Gargery—"

"Much good they'll do me!" observed my sister; but rather gratified too.

"And wishing," pursued Joe, with another fixed look at me, like another effort of remembrance, "that the state of Miss Havisham's elth were sitch as would have—allowed, were it, Pip?"

"Of her having the pleasure," I added.

"Of ladies' company," said Joe. And drew a long breath.

"Well!" cried my sister, with a mollified glance at Mr. Pumblechook. "She might have had the politeness to send that message at first, but it's better late than never. And what did she give young Rantipole here?"

"She giv' him," said Joe, "nothing."

Mrs. Joe was going to break out, but Joe went on.

"What she giv'," said Joe, "she giv' to his friends. 'And by his friends,' were her explanation, 'I mean into the hands of his sister Mrs. J. Gargery.' Them were her words; 'Mrs. J. Gargery.' She mayn't have know'd," added Joe, with an appearance of reflection, "whether it were Joe, or Jorge."

My sister looked at Pumblechook: who smoothed the elbows of his wooden arm-chair, and nodded at her and at the fire, as if he had known all about it beforehand.

"And how much have you got?" asked my sister, laughing. Positively laughing!

"What would present company say to ten pound?" demanded Joe.

"They'd say," returned my sister, curtly, "pretty well. Not too much, but pretty well."

"It's more than that, then," said Joe.

That fearful Impostor, Pumblechook, immediately nodded, and said, as he rubbed the arms of his chair, "It's more than that, Mum."

"Why, you don't mean to say—" began my sister.

"Yes I do, Mum," said Pumblechook; "but wait a bit. Go on, Joseph. Good in you! Go on!"

"What would present company say," proceeded Joe, "to twenty pound?"

"Handsome would be the word," returned my sister.

"Well, then," said Joe, "It's more than twenty pound."

That abject hypocrite, Pumblechook, nodded again, and said, with a patronizing laugh, "It's more than that, Mum. Good again! Follow her up, Joseph!"

"Then to make an end of it," said Joe, delightedly handing the bag to my sister; "it's five-and-twenty pound."

"It's five-and-twenty pound, Mum," echoed that basest of swindlers, Pumblechook, rising to shake hands with her; "and it's no more than your merits (as I said when my opinion was asked), and I wish you joy of the money!"

If the villain had stopped here, his case would have been sufficiently awful, but he blackened his guilt by proceeding to take me into custody, with a right of patronage that left all his former criminality far behind.

"Now you see, Joseph and wife," said Pumblechook, as he took me by the arm above the elbow, "I am one of them that always go right through with what they've begun. This boy must be bound, out of hand. That's my way. Bound out of hand."

"Goodness knows, Uncle Pumblechook," said my sister (grasping the money), "we're deeply beholden to you."

"Never mind me, Mum," returned that diabolical cornchandler. "A pleasure's a pleasure all the world over. But this boy, you know; we must have him bound. I said I'd see to it—to tell you the truth."

The Justices were sitting in the Town Hall near at hand, and we at once went over to have me bound apprentice to Joe in the Magisterial presence. I say we went over, but I was pushed over by Pumblechook, exactly as if I had that moment picked a pocket or fired a rick; indeed, it was the general impression in Court that I had been taken red-handed; for, as Pumblechook shoved me before him through the crowd, I heard some people say, "What's he done?" and others, "He's a young 'un, too, but looks bad, don't he?" One person of mild and benevolent aspect even gave me a tract ornamented with a woodcut of a malevolent young man fitted up with a perfect sausage-shop of fetters, and entitled TO BE READ IN MY CELL.

The Hall was a queer place, I thought, with higher pews in it than a church,—and with people hanging over the pews looking on,—and with mighty Justices (one with a powdered head) leaning back in chairs, with folded arms, or taking snuff, or going to sleep, or writing, or reading the newspapers,—and with some shining black portraits on the walls, which my unartistic eye regarded as a composition of hardbake and sticking-plaster. Here, in a corner my indentures were duly signed and attested, and I was "bound"; Mr. Pumblechook holding me all the while as if we had looked in on our way to the scaffold, to have those little preliminaries disposed of.

When we had come out again, and had got rid of the boys who had been put into great spirits by the expectation of seeing me publicly tortured, and who were much disappointed to find that my friends were merely rallying round me, we went back to Pumblechook's. And there my sister became so excited by the twenty-five guineas, that nothing would serve her but we must have a dinner out of that windfall at the Blue Boar, and that Pumblechook must go over in his chaise-cart, and bring the Hubbles and Mr. Wopsle.

It was agreed to be done; and a most melancholy day I passed. For, it inscrutably appeared to stand to reason, in the minds of the whole company, that I was an excrescence on the entertainment. And to make it worse, they all asked me from time to time,—in short, whenever they had nothing else to do,—why I didn't enjoy myself? And what could I possibly do then, but say I was enjoying myself,—when I wasn't!

However, they were grown up and had their own way, and they made the most of it. That swindling Pumblechook, exalted into the beneficent contriver of the whole occasion, actually took the top of the table; and, when he addressed them on the subject of my being bound, and had fiendishly congratulated them on my being liable to imprisonment if I played at cards, drank strong liquors, kept late hours or bad company, or indulged in other vagaries which the form of my indentures appeared to contemplate as next to inevitable, he placed me standing on a chair beside him to illustrate his remarks.

My only other remembrances of the great festival are, That they wouldn't let me go to sleep, but whenever they saw me dropping off, woke me up and told me to enjoy myself. That, rather late in the evening Mr. Wopsle gave us Collins's ode, and threw his bloodstained sword in thunder down, with such effect, that a waiter came in and said, "The Commercials underneath sent up their compliments, and it wasn't the Tumblers' Arms." That, they were all in excellent spirits on the road home, and sang, O Lady Fair! Mr. Wopsle taking the bass, and asserting with a tremendously strong voice (in reply to the inquisitive bore who leads that piece of music in a most impertinent manner, by wanting to know all about everybody's private affairs) that he was the man with his white locks flowing, and that he was upon the whole the weakest pilgrim going.

Finally, I remember that when I got into my little bedroom, I was truly wretched, and had a strong conviction on me that I should never like Joe's trade. I had liked it once, but once was not now.

Chapter XIV

It is a most miserable thing to feel ashamed of home. There may be black ingratitude in the thing, and the punishment may be retributive and well deserved; but that it is a miserable thing, I can testify.

Home had never been a very pleasant place to me, because of my sister's temper. But, Joe had sanctified it, and I had believed in it. I had believed in the best parlor as a most elegant saloon; I had believed in the front door, as a mysterious portal of the Temple of State whose solemn opening was attended with a sacrifice of roast fowls; I had believed in the kitchen as a chaste though not magnificent apartment; I had believed in the forge as the glowing road to manhood and independence. Within a single year all this was changed. Now it was all coarse and common, and I would not have had Miss Havisham and Estella see it on any account.

How much of my ungracious condition of mind may have been my own fault, how much Miss Havisham's, how much my sister's, is now of no moment to me or to any one. The change was made in me; the thing was done. Well or ill done, excusably or inexcusably, it was done.

Once, it had seemed to me that when I should at last roll up my shirt-sleeves and go into the forge, Joe's 'prentice, I should be distinguished and happy. Now the reality was in my hold, I only felt that I was dusty with the dust of small-coal, and that I had a weight upon my daily remembrance to which the anvil was a feather. There have been occasions in my later life (I suppose as in most lives) when I have felt for a time as if a thick curtain had fallen on all its interest and romance, to shut me out from anything save dull endurance any more. Never has that curtain dropped so heavy and blank, as when my way in life lay stretched out straight before me through the newly entered road of apprenticeship to Joe.

I remember that at a later period of my "time," I used to stand about the churchyard on Sunday evenings when night was falling, comparing my own perspective with the windy marsh view, and making out some likeness between them by thinking how flat and low both were, and how on both there came an unknown way and a dark mist and then the sea. I was quite as dejected on the first working-day of my apprenticeship as in that after-time; but I am glad to know that I never breathed a murmur to Joe while my indentures lasted. It is about the only thing I am glad to know of myself in that connection.

For, though it includes what I proceed to add, all the merit of what I proceed to add was Joe's. It was not because I was faithful, but because Joe was faithful, that I never ran away and went for a soldier or a sailor. It was not because I had a strong sense of the virtue of industry, but because Joe had a strong sense of the virtue of industry, that I worked with tolerable zeal against the grain. It is not possible to know how far the influence of any amiable honest-hearted duty-doing man flies out into the world; but it is very possible to know how it has touched one's self in going by, and I know right well that any good that intermixed itself with my apprenticeship came of plain contented Joe, and not of restlessly aspiring discontented me.

What I wanted, who can say? How can I say, when I never knew? What I dreaded was, that in some unlucky hour I, being at my grimiest and commonest, should lift up my eyes and see Estella looking in at one of the wooden windows of the forge. I was haunted by the fear that she would, sooner or later, find me out, with a black face and hands, doing the coarsest part of my work, and would exult over me and despise me. Often after dark, when I was pulling the bellows for Joe, and we were singing Old Clem, and when the thought how we used to sing it at Miss Havisham's would seem to show me Estella's face in the fire, with her pretty hair fluttering in the wind and her eyes scorning me,—often at such a time I would look towards those panels of black night in the wall which the wooden windows then were, and would fancy that I saw her just drawing her face away, and would believe that she had come at last.

After that, when we went in to supper, the place and the meal would have a more homely look than ever, and I would feel more ashamed of home than ever, in my own ungracious breast.

Chapter XV

As I was getting too big for Mr. Wopsle's great-aunt's room, my education under that preposterous female terminated. Not, however, until Biddy had imparted to me everything she knew, from the little catalogue of prices, to a comic song she had once bought for a half-penny. Although the only coherent part of the latter piece of literature were the opening lines,

When I went to Lunnon town sirs,

Too rul loo rul

Too rul loo rul

Wasn't I done very brown sirs?

Too rul loo rul

Too rul loo rul

—still, in my desire to be wiser, I got this composition by heart with the utmost gravity; nor do I recollect that I questioned its merit, except that I thought (as I still do) the amount of Too rul somewhat in excess of the poetry. In my hunger for information, I made proposals to Mr. Wopsle to bestow some intellectual crumbs upon me, with which he kindly complied. As it turned out, however, that he only wanted me for a dramatic lay-figure, to be contradicted and embraced and wept over and bullied and clutched and stabbed and knocked about in a variety of ways, I soon declined that course of instruction; though not until Mr. Wopsle in his poetic fury had severely mauled me.

Whatever I acquired, I tried to impart to Joe. This statement sounds so well, that I cannot in my conscience let it pass unexplained. I wanted to make Joe less ignorant and common, that he might be worthier of my society and less open to Estella's reproach.

The old Battery out on the marshes was our place of study, and a broken slate and a short piece of slate-pencil were our educational implements: to which Joe always added a pipe of tobacco. I never knew Joe to remember anything from one Sunday to another, or to acquire, under my tuition, any piece of information whatever. Yet he would smoke his pipe at the Battery with a far more sagacious air than anywhere else,—even with a learned air,—as if he considered himself to be advancing immensely. Dear fellow, I hope he did.

It was pleasant and quiet, out there with the sails on the river passing beyond the earthwork, and sometimes, when the tide was low, looking as if they belonged to sunken ships that were still sailing on at the bottom of the water. Whenever I watched the vessels standing out to sea with their white sails spread, I somehow thought of Miss Havisham and Estella; and whenever the light struck aslant, afar off, upon a cloud or sail or green hillside or water-line, it was just the same.—Miss Havisham and Estella and the strange house and the strange life appeared to have something to do with everything that was picturesque.

One Sunday when Joe, greatly enjoying his pipe, had so plumed himself on being "most awful dull," that I had given him up for the day, I lay on the earthwork for some time with my chin on my hand, descrying traces of Miss Havisham and Estella all over the prospect, in the sky and in the water, until at last I resolved to mention a thought concerning them that had been much in my head.

"Joe," said I; "don't you think I ought to make Miss Havisham a visit?"

"Well, Pip," returned Joe, slowly considering. "What for?"

"What for, Joe? What is any visit made for?"

"There is some wisits p'r'aps," said Joe, "as for ever remains open to the question, Pip.

But in regard to wisiting Miss Havisham. She might think you wanted something,—expected something of her."

"Don't you think I might say that I did not, Joe?"

"You might, old chap," said Joe. "And she might credit it. Similarly she mightn't."

Joe felt, as I did, that he had made a point there, and he pulled hard at his pipe to keep himself from weakening it by repetition.

"You see, Pip," Joe pursued, as soon as he was past that danger, "Miss Havisham done the handsome thing by you. When Miss Havisham done the handsome thing by you, she called me back to say to me as that were all."

"Yes, Joe. I heard her."

"ALL," Joe repeated, very emphatically.

"Yes, Joe. I tell you, I heard her."

"Which I meantersay, Pip, it might be that her meaning were,—Make a end on it!—As you was!—Me to the North, and you to the South!—Keep in sunders!"

I had thought of that too, and it was very far from comforting to me to find that he had thought of it; for it seemed to render it more probable.

"But, Joe."

"Yes, old chap."

"Here am I, getting on in the first year of my time, and, since the day of my being bound, I have never thanked Miss Havisham, or asked after her, or shown that I remember her."

"That's true, Pip; and unless you was to turn her out a set of shoes all four round,—and which I meantersay as even a set of shoes all four round might not be acceptable as a present, in a total wacancy of hoofs—"

"I don't mean that sort of remembrance, Joe; I don't mean a present."

But Joe had got the idea of a present in his head and must harp upon it. "Or even," said he, "if you was helped to knocking her up a new chain for the front door,—or say a gross or two of shark-headed screws for general use,—or some light fancy article, such as a toasting-fork when she took her muffins,—or a gridiron when she took a sprat or such like—"

"I don't mean any present at all, Joe," I interposed.

"Well," said Joe, still harping on it as though I had particularly pressed it, "if I was yourself, Pip, I wouldn't. No, I would not. For what's a door-chain when she's got one always up? And shark-headers is open to misrepresentations. And if it was a toasting-fork, you'd go into brass and do yourself no credit. And the oncommonest workman can't show himself oncommon in a gridiron,—for a gridiron IS a gridiron," said Joe, steadfastly impressing it upon me, as if he were endeavouring to rouse me from a fixed delusion, "and you may haim at what you like, but a gridiron it will come out, either by your leave or again your leave, and you can't help yourself—"

"My dear Joe," I cried, in desperation, taking hold of his coat, "don't go on in that way. I never thought of making Miss Havisham any present."

"No, Pip," Joe assented, as if he had been contending for that, all along; "and what I say to you is, you are right, Pip."

"Yes, Joe; but what I wanted to say, was, that as we are rather slack just now, if you would give me a half-holiday to-morrow, I think I would go uptown and make a call on Miss Est—Havisham."

"Which her name," said Joe, gravely, "ain't Estavisham, Pip, unless she have been rechris'ened."

"I know, Joe, I know. It was a slip of mine. What do you think of it, Joe?"

In brief, Joe thought that if I thought well of it, he thought well of it. But, he was particular in stipulating that if I were not received with cordiality, or if I were not encouraged to repeat my visit as a visit which had no ulterior object but was simply one of gratitude for a favor received, then this experimental trip should have no successor. By these conditions I promised to abide.

Now, Joe kept a journeyman at weekly wages whose name was Orlick. He pretended that his Christian name was Dolge,—a clear Impossibility,—but he was a fellow of that obstinate disposition that I believe him to have been the prey of no delusion in this particular, but wilfully to have imposed that name upon the village as an affront to its understanding. He was a broadshouldered loose-limbed swarthy fellow of great strength, never in a hurry, and always slouching. He never even seemed to come to his work on purpose, but would slouch in as if by mere accident; and when he went to the Jolly Bargemen to eat his dinner, or went away at night, he would slouch out, like Cain or the Wandering Jew, as if he had no idea where he was going and no intention of ever coming back. He lodged at a sluice-keeper's out on the marshes, and on working-days would come slouching from his hermitage, with his hands in his pockets and his dinner loosely tied in a bundle round his neck and dangling on his back. On Sundays he mostly lay all day on the sluice-gates, or stood against ricks and barns. He always slouched, locomotively, with his eyes on the ground; and, when accosted or otherwise required to raise them, he looked up in a half-resentful, half-puzzled way, as though the only thought he ever had was, that it was rather an odd and injurious fact that he should never be thinking.

This morose journeyman had no liking for me. When I was very small and timid, he gave me to understand that the Devil lived in a black corner of the forge, and that he knew the fiend very well: also that it was necessary to make up the fire, once in seven years, with a live boy, and that I might consider myself fuel. When I became Joe's 'prentice, Orlick was perhaps confirmed in some suspicion that I should displace him; howbeit, he liked me still less. Not that he ever said anything, or did anything, openly importing hostility; I only noticed that he always beat his sparks in my direction, and that whenever I sang Old Clem, he came in out of time.

Dolge Orlick was at work and present, next day, when I reminded Joe of my half-holiday. He said nothing at the moment, for he and Joe had just got a piece of hot iron between them, and I was at the bellows; but by and by he said, leaning on his hammer,—

"Now, master! Sure you're not a going to favor only one of us. If Young Pip has a half-holiday, do as much for Old Orlick." I suppose he was about five-and-twenty, but he usually spoke of himself as an ancient person.

"Why, what'll you do with a half-holiday, if you get it?" said Joe.

"What'll I do with it! What'll he do with it? I'll do as much with it as him," said Orlick.

"As to Pip, he's going up town," said Joe.

"Well then, as to Old Orlick, he's a going up town," retorted that worthy. "Two can go up town. Tain't only one wot can go up town."

"Don't lose your temper," said Joe.

"Shall if I like," growled Orlick. "Some and their uptowning! Now, master! Come. No favoring in this shop. Be a man!"

The master refusing to entertain the subject until the journeyman was in a better temper, Orlick plunged at the furnace, drew out a red-hot bar, made at me with it as if he were going to run it through my body, whisked it round my head, laid it on the anvil, hammered it out,—as if it were I, I thought, and the sparks were my spirting blood,—and finally said, when he had hammered himself hot and the iron cold, and he again leaned on his hammer,—

"Now, master!"

"Are you all right now?" demanded Joe.

"Ah! I am all right," said gruff Old Orlick.

"Then, as in general you stick to your work as well as most men," said Joe, "let it be a half-holiday for all."

My sister had been standing silent in the yard, within hearing,—she was a most unscrupulous spy and listener,—and she instantly looked in at one of the windows.

"Like you, you fool!" said she to Joe, "giving holidays to great idle hulkers like that. You are a rich man, upon my life, to waste wages in that way. I wish I was his master!"

"You'd be everybody's master, if you durst," retorted Orlick, with an ill-favored grin.

("Let her alone," said Joe.)

"I'd be a match for all noodles and all rogues," returned my sister, beginning to work herself into a mighty rage. "And I couldn't be a match for the noodles, without being a match for your master, who's the dunder-headed king of the noodles. And I couldn't be a match for the rogues, without being a match for you, who are the blackest-looking and the worst rogue between this and France. Now!"

"You're a foul shrew, Mother Gargery," growled the journeyman. "If that makes a judge of rogues, you ought to be a good'un."

("Let her alone, will you?" said Joe.)

"What did you say?" cried my sister, beginning to scream. "What did you say? What did that fellow Orlick say to me, Pip? What did he call me, with my husband standing by? Oh! oh! oh!" Each of these exclamations was a shriek; and I must remark of my sister, what is equally true of all the violent women I have ever seen, that passion was no excuse for her, because it is undeniable that instead of lapsing into passion, she consciously and deliberately took extraordinary pains to force herself into it, and became blindly furious by regular stages; "what was the name he gave me before the base man who swore to defend me? Oh! Hold me! Oh!"

"Ah-h-h!" growled the journeyman, between his teeth, "I'd hold you, if you was my wife. I'd hold you under the pump, and choke it out of you."

("I tell you, let her alone," said Joe.)

"Oh! To hear him!" cried my sister, with a clap of her hands and a scream together,—which was her next stage. "To hear the names he's giving me! That Orlick! In my own house! Me, a married woman! With my husband standing by! Oh! Oh!" Here my sister, after a fit of clappings and screamings, beat her hands upon her bosom and upon her knees, and threw her cap off, and pulled her hair down,—which were the last stages on her road to frenzy. Being by this time a perfect Fury and a complete success, she made a dash at the door which I had fortunately locked.

What could the wretched Joe do now, after his disregarded parenthetical interruptions, but stand up to his journeyman, and ask him what he meant by interfering betwixt himself and Mrs. Joe; and further whether he was man enough to come on? Old Orlick felt that the situation admitted of nothing less than coming on, and was on his defence straightway; so, without so much as pulling off their singed and burnt aprons, they went at one another, like two giants. But, if any man in that neighborhood could stand uplong against Joe, I never saw the man. Orlick, as if he had been of no more account than the pale young gentleman, was very soon among the coal-dust, and in no hurry to come out of it. Then Joe unlocked the door and picked up my sister, who had dropped insensible at the window (but who had seen the fight first, I think), and who was carried into the house and laid down, and who was recommended to revive, and would do nothing but struggle and clench her hands in Joe's hair. Then, came that singular calm and silence which succeed all uproars; and then, with the vague sensation which I have always connected with such a lull,—namely, that it was Sunday, and somebody was dead,—I went upstairs to dress myself.

When I came down again, I found Joe and Orlick sweeping up, without any other traces of discomposure than a slit in one of Orlick's nostrils, which was neither expressive nor ornamental. A pot of beer had appeared from the Jolly Bargemen, and they were sharing it by turns in a peaceable manner. The lull had a sedative and philosophical influence on Joe, who followed me out into the road to say, as a parting observation that might do me good, "On the Rampage, Pip, and off the Rampage, Pip:—such is Life!"

With what absurd emotions (for we think the feelings that are very serious in a man quite comical in a boy) I found myself again going to Miss Havisham's, matters little here. Nor, how I passed and repassed the gate many times before I could make up my mind to ring. Nor, how I debated whether I should go away without ringing; nor, how I should undoubtedly have gone, if my time had been my own, to come back.

Miss Sarah Pocket came to the gate. No Estella.

"How, then? You here again?" said Miss Pocket. "What do you want?"

When I said that I only came to see how Miss Havisham was, Sarah evidently deliberated whether or no she should send me about my business. But unwilling to hazard the responsibility, she let me in, and presently brought the sharp message that I was to "come up."

Everything was unchanged, and Miss Havisham was alone.

"Well?" said she, fixing her eyes upon me. "I hope you want nothing? You'll get nothing."

"No indeed, Miss Havisham. I only wanted you to know that I am doing very well in my apprenticeship, and am always much obliged to you."

"There, there!" with the old restless fingers. "Come now and then; come on your birthday.—Ay!" she cried suddenly, turning herself and her chair towards me, "You are looking round for Estella? Hey?"

I had been looking round,—in fact, for Estella,—and I stammered that I hoped she was well.

"Abroad," said Miss Havisham; "educating for a lady; far out of reach; prettier than ever; admired by all who see her. Do you feel that you have lost her?"

There was such a malignant enjoyment in her utterance of the last words, and she broke into such a disagreeable laugh, that I was at a loss what to say. She spared me the trouble of considering, by dismissing me. When the gate was closed upon me by Sarah of the walnut-shell countenance, I felt more than ever dissatisfied with my home and with my trade and with everything; and that was all I took by that motion.

As I was loitering along the High Street, looking in disconsolately at the shop windows, and thinking what I would buy if I were a gentleman, who should come out of the bookshop but Mr. Wopsle. Mr. Wopsle had in his hand the affecting tragedy of George Barnwell, in which he had that moment invested sixpence, with the view of heaping every word of it on the head of Pumblechook, with whom he was going to drink tea. No sooner did he see me, than he appeared to consider that a special Providence had put a 'prentice in his way to be read at; and he laid hold of me, and insisted on my accompanying him to the Pumblechookian parlor. As I knew it would be miserable at home, and as the nights were dark and the way was dreary, and almost any companionship on the road was better than none, I made no great resistance; consequently, we turned into Pumblechook's just as the street and the shops were lighting up.

As I never assisted at any other representation of George Barnwell, I don't know how long it may usually take; but I know very well that it took until half-past nine o' clock that night, and that when Mr. Wopsle got into Newgate, I thought he never would go to the scaffold, he became so much slower than at any former period of his disgraceful career. I thought it a little too much that he should complain of being cut short in his flower after all, as if he had not been running to seed, leaf after leaf, ever since his course began. This, however, was a mere question of length and wearisomeness. What stung me, was the identification of the whole affair with my unoffending self. When Barnwell began to go wrong, I declare that I felt positively apologetic, Pumblechook's indignant stare so taxed me with it. Wopsle, too, took pains to present me in the worst light. At once ferocious and maudlin, I was made to murder my uncle with no extenuating circumstances whatever; Millwood put me down in argument, on every occasion; it became sheer monomania in my master's daughter to care a button for me; and all I can say for my gasping and procrastinating conduct on the fatal morning, is, that it was worthy of the general feebleness of my character. Even after I was happily hanged and Wopsle had closed the book, Pumblechook sat staring at me, and shaking his head, and saying, "Take warning, boy, take warning!" as if it were a well-known fact that I contemplated murdering a near relation, provided I could only induce one to have the weakness to become my benefactor.

It was a very dark night when it was all over, and when I set out with Mr. Wopsle on the walk home. Beyond town, we found a heavy mist out, and it fell wet and thick. The turnpike lamp was a blur, quite out of the lamp's usual place apparently, and its rays looked solid substance on the fog. We were noticing this, and saying how that the mist rose with a change of wind from a certain quarter of our marshes, when we came upon a man, slouching under the lee of the turnpike house.

"Halloa!" we said, stopping. "Orlick there?"

"Ah!" he answered, slouching out. "I was standing by a minute, on the chance of company."

"You are late," I remarked.

Orlick not unnaturally answered, "Well? And you're late."

"We have been," said Mr. Wopsle, exalted with his late performance,—"we have been indulging, Mr. Orlick, in an intellectual evening."

Old Orlick growled, as if he had nothing to say about that, and we all went on together. I asked him presently whether he had been spending his half-holiday up and down town?

"Yes," said he, "all of it. I come in behind yourself. I didn't see you, but I must have been pretty close behind you. By the by, the guns is going again."

"At the Hulks?" said I.

"Ay! There's some of the birds flown from the cages. The guns have been going since dark, about. You'll hear one presently."

In effect, we had not walked many yards further, when the well-remembered boom came towards us, deadened by the mist, and heavily rolled away along the low grounds by the river, as if it were pursuing and threatening the fugitives.

"A good night for cutting off in," said Orlick. "We'd be puzzled how to bring down a jail-bird on the wing, to-night."

The subject was a suggestive one to me, and I thought about it in silence. Mr. Wopsle, as the ill-requited uncle of the evening's tragedy, fell to meditating aloud in his garden at Camberwell. Orlick, with his hands in his pockets, slouched heavily at my side. It was very dark, very wet, very muddy, and so we splashed along. Now and then, the sound of the signal cannon broke upon us again, and again rolled sulkily along the course of the river. I kept myself to myself and my thoughts. Mr. Wopsle died amiably at Camberwell, and exceedingly game on Bosworth Field, and in the greatest agonies at Glastonbury. Orlick sometimes growled, "Beat it out, beat it out,—Old Clem! With a clink for the stout,—Old Clem!" I thought he had been drinking, but he was not drunk.

Thus, we came to the village. The way by which we approached it took us past the Three Jolly Bargemen, which we were surprised to find—it being eleven o'clock—in a state of commotion, with the door wide open, and unwonted lights that had been hastily caught up and put down scattered about. Mr. Wopsle dropped in to ask what was the matter (surmising that a convict had been taken), but came running out in a great hurry.

"There's something wrong," said he, without stopping, "up at your place, Pip. Run all!"

"What is it?" I asked, keeping up with him. So did Orlick, at my side.

"I can't quite understand. The house seems to have been violently entered when Joe Gargery was out. Supposed by convicts. Somebody has been attacked and hurt."

We were running too fast to admit of more being said, and we made no stop until we got into our kitchen. It was full of people; the whole village was there, or in the yard; and there was a surgeon, and there was Joe, and there were a group of women, all on the floor in the midst of the kitchen. The unemployed bystanders drew back when they saw me, and so I became aware of my sister,—lying without sense or movement on the bare boards where she had been knocked down by a tremendous blow on the back of the head, dealt by some unknown hand when her face was turned towards the fire,—destined never to be on the Rampage again, while she was the wife of Joe.

Chapter XVI

With my head full of George Barnwell, I was at first disposed to believe that I must have had some hand in the attack upon my sister, or at all events that as her near relation, popularly known to be under obligations to her, I was a more legitimate object of suspicion than any one else. But when, in the clearer light of next morning, I began to reconsider the matter and to hear it discussed around me on all sides, I took another view of the case, which was more reasonable.

Joe had been at the Three Jolly Bargemen, smoking his pipe, from a quarter after eight o'clock to a quarter before ten. While he was there, my sister had been seen standing at the kitchen door, and had exchanged Good Night with a farm-laborer going home. The man could not be more particular as to the time at which he saw her (he got into dense confusion when he tried to be), than that it must have been before nine. When Joe went home at five minutes before ten, he found her struck down on the floor, and promptly called in assistance. The fire had not then burnt unusually low, nor was the snuff of the candle very long; the candle, however, had been blown out.

Nothing had been taken away from any part of the house. Neither, beyond the blowing out of the candle,—which stood on a table between the door and my sister, and was behind her when she stood facing the fire and was struck,—was there any disarrangement of the kitchen, excepting such as she herself had made, in falling and bleeding. But, there was one remarkable piece of evidence on the spot. She had been struck with something blunt and heavy, on the head and spine; after the blows were dealt, something heavy had been thrown down at her with considerable violence, as she lay on her face. And on the ground beside her, when Joe picked her up, was a convict's leg-iron which had been filed asunder.

Now, Joe, examining this iron with a smith's eye, declared it to have been filed asunder some time ago. The hue and cry going off to the Hulks, and people coming thence to examine the iron, Joe's opinion was corroborated. They did not undertake to say when it had left the prison-ships to which it undoubtedly had once belonged; but they claimed to know for certain that that particular manacle had not been worn by either of the two convicts who had escaped last night. Further, one of those two was already retaken, and had not freed himself of his iron.

Knowing what I knew, I set up an inference of my own here. I believed the iron to be my convict's iron,—the iron I had seen and heard him filing at, on the marshes,—but my mind did not accuse him of having put it to its latest use. For I believed one of two other persons to have become possessed of it, and to have turned it to this cruel account. Either Orlick, or the strange man who had shown me the file.

Now, as to Orlick; he had gone to town exactly as he told us when we picked him up at the turnpike, he had been seen about town all the evening, he had been in divers companies in several public-houses, and he had come back with myself and Mr. Wopsle. There was nothing against him, save the quarrel; and my sister had quarrelled with him, and with everybody else about her, ten thousand times. As to the strange man; if he had come back for his two bank-notes there could have been no dispute about them, because my sister was fully prepared to restore them. Besides, there had been no altercation; the assailant had come in so silently and suddenly, that she had been felled before she could look round.

It was horrible to think that I had provided the weapon, however undesignedly, but I could hardly think otherwise. I suffered unspeakable trouble while I considered and reconsidered whether I should at last dissolve that spell of my childhood and tell Joe all the story. For months afterwards, I every day settled the question finally in the negative, and reopened and reargued it next morning. The contention came, after all, to this;—the secret was such an old one now, had so grown into me and become a part of myself, that I could not tear it away. In addition to the dread that, having led up to so much mischief, it would be now more likely than ever to alienate Joe from me if he believed it, I had a further restraining dread that he would not believe it, but would assort it with the fabulous dogs and veal-cutlets as a monstrous invention. However, I temporized with myself, of course—for, was I not wavering between right and wrong, when the thing is always done?—and resolved to make a full disclosure if I should see any such new occasion as a new chance of helping in the discovery of the assailant.

The Constables and the Bow Street men from London—for, this happened in the days of the extinct red-waistcoated police—were about the house for a week or two, and did pretty much what I have heard and read of like authorities doing in other such cases. They took up several obviously wrong people, and they ran their heads very hard against wrong ideas, and persisted in trying to fit the circumstances to the ideas, instead of trying to extract ideas from the circumstances. Also, they stood about the door of the Jolly Bargemen, with knowing and reserved looks that filled the whole neighborhood with admiration; and they had a mysterious manner of taking their drink, that was almost as good as taking the culprit. But not quite, for they never did it.

Long after these constitutional powers had dispersed, my sister lay very ill in bed. Her sight was disturbed, so that she saw objects multiplied, and grasped at visionary teacups and wineglasses instead of the realities; her hearing was greatly impaired; her memory also; and her speech was unintelligible. When, at last, she came round so far as to be helped downstairs, it was still necessary to keep my slate always by her, that she might indicate in writing what she could not indicate in speech. As she was (very bad handwriting apart) a more than indifferent speller, and as Joe was a more than indifferent reader, extraordinary complications arose between them which I was always called in to solve. The administration of mutton instead of medicine, the substitution of Tea for Joe, and the baker for bacon, were among the mildest of my own mistakes.

However, her temper was greatly improved, and she was patient. A tremulous uncertainty of the action of all her limbs soon became a part of her regular state, and afterwards, at intervals of two or three months, she would often put her hands to her head, and would then remain for about a week at a time in some gloomy aberration of mind. We were at a loss to find a suitable attendant for her, until a circumstance happened conveniently to relieve us. Mr. Wopsle's great-aunt conquered a confirmed habit of living into which she had fallen, and Biddy became a part of our establishment.

It may have been about a month after my sister's reappearance in the kitchen, when Biddy came to us with a small speckled box containing the whole of her worldly effects, and became a blessing to the household. Above all, she was a blessing to Joe, for the dear old fellow was sadly cut up by the constant contemplation of the wreck of his wife, and had been accustomed, while attending on her of an evening, to turn to me every now and then and say, with his blue eyes moistened, "Such a fine figure of a woman as she once were, Pip!" Biddy instantly taking the cleverest charge of her as though she had studied her from infancy; Joe became able in some sort to appreciate the greater quiet of his life, and to get down to the Jolly Bargemen now and then for a change that did him good. It was characteristic of the police people that they had all more or less suspected poor Joe (though he never knew it), and that they had to a man concurred in regarding him as one of the deepest spirits they had ever encountered.

Biddy's first triumph in her new office, was to solve a difficulty that had completely vanquished me. I had tried hard at it, but had made nothing of it. Thus it was:—

Again and again and again, my sister had traced upon the slate, a character that looked like a curious T, and then with the utmost eagerness had called our attention to it as something she particularly wanted. I had in vain tried everything producible that began with a T, from tar to toast and tub. At length it had come into my head that the sign looked like a hammer, and on my lustily calling that word in my sister's ear, she had begun to hammer on the table and had expressed a qualified assent. Thereupon, I had brought in all our hammers, one after another, but without avail. Then I bethought me of a crutch, the shape being much the same, and I borrowed one in the village, and displayed it to my sister with considerable confidence. But she shook her head to that extent when she was shown it, that we were terrified lest in her weak and shattered state she should dislocate her neck.

When my sister found that Biddy was very quick to understand her, this mysterious sign reappeared on the slate. Biddy looked thoughtfully at it, heard my explanation, looked thoughtfully at my sister, looked thoughtfully at Joe (who was always represented on the slate by his initial letter), and ran into the forge, followed by Joe and me.

"Why, of course!" cried Biddy, with an exultant face. "Don't you see? It's him!"

Orlick, without a doubt! She had lost his name, and could only signify him by his hammer. We told him why we wanted him to come into the kitchen, and he slowly laid down his hammer, wiped his brow with his arm, took another wipe at it with his apron, and came slouching out, with a curious loose vagabond bend in the knees that strongly distinguished him.

I confess that I expected to see my sister denounce him, and that I was disappointed by the different result. She manifested the greatest anxiety to be on good terms with him, was evidently much pleased by his being at length produced, and motioned that she would have him given something to drink. She watched his countenance as if she were particularly wishful to be assured that he took kindly to his reception, she showed every possible desire to conciliate him, and there was an air of humble propitiation in all she did, such as I have seen pervade the bearing of a child towards a hard master. After that day, a day rarely passed without her drawing the hammer on her slate, and without Orlick's slouching in and standing doggedly before her, as if he knew no more than I did what to make of it.

Chapter XVII

I now fell into a regular routine of apprenticeship life, which was varied beyond the limits of the village and the marshes, by no more remarkable circumstance than the arrival of my birthday and my paying another visit to Miss Havisham. I found Miss Sarah Pocket still on duty at the gate; I found Miss Havisham just as I had left her, and she spoke of Estella in the very same way, if not in the very same words. The interview lasted but a few minutes, and she gave me a guinea when I was going, and told me to come again on my next birthday. I may mention at once that this became an annual custom. I tried to decline taking the guinea on the first occasion, but with no better effect than causing her to ask me very angrily, if I expected more? Then, and after that, I took it.

So unchanging was the dull old house, the yellow light in the darkened room, the faded spectre in the chair by the dressing-table glass, that I felt as if the stopping of the clocks had stopped Time in that mysterious place, and, while I and everything else outside it grew older, it stood still. Daylight never entered the house as to my thoughts and remembrances of it, any more than as to the actual fact. It bewildered me, and under its influence I continued at heart to hate my trade and to be ashamed of home.

Imperceptibly I became conscious of a change in Biddy, however. Her shoes came up at the heel, her hair grew bright and neat, her hands were always clean. She was not beautiful,—she was common, and could not be like Estella,—but she was pleasant and wholesome and sweet-tempered. She had not been with us more than a year (I remember her being newly out of mourning at the time it struck me), when I observed to myself one evening that she had curiously thoughtful and attentive eyes; eyes that were very pretty and very good.

It came of my lifting up my own eyes from a task I was poring at—writing some passages from a book, to improve myself in two ways at once by a sort of stratagem—and seeing Biddy observant of what I was about. I laid down my pen, and Biddy stopped in her needlework without laying it down.

"Biddy," said I, "how do you manage it? Either I am very stupid, or you are very clever."

"What is it that I manage? I don't know," returned Biddy, smiling.

She managed our whole domestic life, and wonderfully too; but I did not mean that, though that made what I did mean more surprising.

"How do you manage, Biddy," said I, "to learn everything that I learn, and always to keep up with me?" I was beginning to be rather vain of my knowledge, for I spent my birthday guineas on it, and set aside the greater part of my pocket-money for similar investment; though I have no doubt, now, that the little I knew was extremely dear at the price.

"I might as well ask you," said Biddy, "how you manage?"

"No; because when I come in from the forge of a night, any one can see me turning to at it. But you never turn to at it, Biddy."

"I suppose I must catch it like a cough," said Biddy, quietly; and went on with her sewing.

Pursuing my idea as I leaned back in my wooden chair, and looked at Biddy sewing away with her head on one side, I began to think her rather an extraordinary girl. For I called to mind now, that she was equally accomplished in the terms of our trade, and the names of our different sorts of work, and our various tools. In short, whatever I knew, Biddy knew. Theoretically, she was already as good a blacksmith as I, or better.

"You are one of those, Biddy," said I, "who make the most of every chance. You never had a chance before you came here, and see how improved you are!"

Biddy looked at me for an instant, and went on with her sewing. "I was your first teacher though; wasn't I?" said she, as she sewed.

"Biddy!" I exclaimed, in amazement. "Why, you are crying!"

"No I am not," said Biddy, looking up and laughing. "What put that in your head?"

What could have put it in my head but the glistening of a tear as it dropped on her work? I sat silent, recalling what a drudge she had been until Mr. Wopsle's great-aunt successfully overcame that bad habit of living, so highly desirable to be got rid of by some people. I recalled the hopeless circumstances by which she had been surrounded in the miserable little shop and the miserable little noisy evening school, with that miserable old bundle of incompetence always to be dragged and shouldered. I reflected that even in those untoward times there must have been latent in Biddy what was now developing, for, in my first uneasiness and discontent I had turned to her for help, as a matter of course. Biddy sat quietly sewing, shedding no more tears, and while I looked at her and thought about it all, it occurred to me that perhaps I had not been sufficiently grateful to Biddy. I might have been too reserved, and should have patronized her more (though I did not use that precise word in my meditations) with my confidence.

"Yes, Biddy," I observed, when I had done turning it over, "you were my first teacher, and that at a time when we little thought of ever being together like this, in this kitchen."

"Ah, poor thing!" replied Biddy. It was like her self-forgetfulness to transfer the remark to my sister, and to get up and be busy about her, making her more comfortable; "that's sadly true!"

"Well!" said I, "we must talk together a little more, as we used to do. And I must consult you a little more, as I used to do. Let us have a quiet walk on the marshes next Sunday, Biddy, and a long chat."

My sister was never left alone now; but Joe more than readily undertook the care of her on that Sunday afternoon, and Biddy and I went out together. It was summer-time, and lovely weather. When we had passed the village and the church and the churchyard, and were out on the marshes and began to see the sails of the ships as they sailed on, I began to combine Miss Havisham and Estella with the prospect, in my usual way. When we came to the river-side and sat down on the bank, with the water rippling at our feet, making it all more quiet than it would have been without that sound, I resolved that it was a good time and place for the admission of Biddy into my inner confidence.

"Biddy," said I, after binding her to secrecy, "I want to be a gentleman."

"O, I wouldn't, if I was you!" she returned. "I don't think it would answer."

"Biddy," said I, with some severity, "I have particular reasons for wanting to be a gentleman."

"You know best, Pip; but don't you think you are happier as you are?"

"Biddy," I exclaimed, impatiently, "I am not at all happy as I am. I am disgusted with my calling and with my life. I have never taken to either, since I was bound. Don't be absurd."

"Was I absurd?" said Biddy, quietly raising her eyebrows; "I am sorry for that; I didn't mean to be. I only want you to do well, and to be comfortable."

"Well, then, understand once for all that I never shall or can be comfortable—or anything but miserable—there, Biddy!—unless I can lead a very different sort of life from the life I lead now."

"That's a pity!" said Biddy, shaking her head with a sorrowful air.

Now, I too had so often thought it a pity, that, in the singular kind of quarrel with myself which I was always carrying on, I was half inclined to shed tears of vexation and distress when Biddy gave utterance to her sentiment and my own. I told her she was right, and I knew it was much to be regretted, but still it was not to be helped.

"If I could have settled down," I said to Biddy, plucking up the short grass within reach, much as I had once upon a time pulled my feelings out of my hair and kicked them into the brewery wall,—"if I could have settled down and been but half as fond of the forge as I was when I was little, I know it would have been much better for me. You and I and Joe would have wanted nothing then, and Joe and I would perhaps have gone partners when I was out of my time, and I might even have grown up to keep company with you, and we might have sat on this very bank on a fine Sunday, quite different people. I should have been good enough for you; shouldn't I, Biddy?"

Biddy sighed as she looked at the ships sailing on, and returned for answer, "Yes; I am not over-particular." It scarcely sounded flattering, but I knew she meant well.

"Instead of that," said I, plucking up more grass and chewing a blade or two, "see how I am going on. Dissatisfied, and uncomfortable, and—what would it signify to me, being coarse and common, if nobody had told me so!"

Biddy turned her face suddenly towards mine, and looked far more attentively at me than she had looked at the sailing ships.

"It was neither a very true nor a very polite thing to say," she remarked, directing her eyes to the ships again. "Who said it?"

I was disconcerted, for I had broken away without quite seeing where I was going to. It was not to be shuffled off now, however, and I answered, "The beautiful young lady at Miss Havisham's, and she's more beautiful than anybody ever was, and I admire her dreadfully, and I want to be a gentleman on her account." Having made this lunatic confession, I began to throw my torn-up grass into the river, as if I had some thoughts of following it.

"Do you want to be a gentleman, to spite her or to gain her over?" Biddy quietly asked me, after a pause.

"I don't know," I moodily answered.

"Because, if it is to spite her," Biddy pursued, "I should think—but you know best—that might be better and more independently done by caring nothing for her words. And if it is to gain her over, I should think—but you know best—she was not worth gaining over."

Exactly what I myself had thought, many times. Exactly what was perfectly manifest to me at the moment. But how could I, a poor dazed village lad, avoid that wonderful inconsistency into which the best and wisest of men fall every day?

"It may be all quite true," said I to Biddy, "but I admire her dreadfully."

In short, I turned over on my face when I came to that, and got a good grasp on the hair on each side of my head, and wrenched it well. All the while knowing the madness of my heart to be so very mad and misplaced, that I was quite conscious it would have served my face right, if I had lifted it up by my hair, and knocked it against the pebbles as a punishment for belonging to such an idiot.

Biddy was the wisest of girls, and she tried to reason no more with me. She put her hand, which was a comfortable hand though roughened by work, upon my hands, one after another, and gently took them out of my hair. Then she softly patted my shoulder in a soothing way, while with my face upon my sleeve I cried a little,—exactly as I had done in the brewery yard,—and felt vaguely convinced that I was very much ill-used by somebody, or by everybody; I can't say which.

"I am glad of one thing," said Biddy, "and that is, that you have felt you could give me your confidence, Pip. And I am glad of another thing, and that is, that of course you know you may depend upon my keeping it and always so far deserving it. If your first teacher (dear! such a poor one, and so much in need of being taught herself!) had been your teacher at the present time, she thinks she knows what lesson she would set. But it would be a hard one to learn, and you have got beyond her, and it's of no use now." So, with a quiet sigh for me, Biddy rose from the bank, and said, with a fresh and pleasant change of voice, "Shall we walk a little farther, or go home?"

"Biddy," I cried, getting up, putting my arm round her neck, and giving her a kiss, "I shall always tell you everything."

"Till you're a gentleman," said Biddy.

"You know I never shall be, so that's always. Not that I have any occasion to tell you anything, for you know everything I know,—as I told you at home the other night."

"Ah!" said Biddy, quite in a whisper, as she looked away at the ships. And then repeated, with her former pleasant change, "shall we walk a little farther, or go home?"

I said to Biddy we would walk a little farther, and we did so, and the summer afternoon toned down into the summer evening, and it was very beautiful. I began to consider whether I was not more naturally and wholesomely situated, after all, in these circumstances, than playing beggar my neighbor by candle-light in the room with the stopped clocks, and being despised by Estella. I thought it would be very good for me if I could get her out of my head, with all the rest of those remembrances and fancies, and could go to work determined to relish what I had to do, and stick to it, and make the best of it. I asked myself the question whether I did not surely know that if Estella were beside me at that moment instead of Biddy, she would make me miserable? I was obliged to admit that I did know it for a certainty, and I said to myself, "Pip, what a fool you are!"

We talked a good deal as we walked, and all that Biddy said seemed right. Biddy was never insulting, or capricious, or Biddy to-day and somebody else to-morrow; she would have derived only pain, and no pleasure, from giving me pain; she would far rather have wounded her own breast than mine. How could it be, then, that I did not like her much the better of the two?

"Biddy," said I, when we were walking homeward, "I wish you could put me right."

"I wish I could!" said Biddy.

"If I could only get myself to fall in love with you,—you don't mind my speaking so openly to such an old acquaintance?"

"Oh dear, not at all!" said Biddy. "Don't mind me."

"If I could only get myself to do it, that would be the thing for me."

"But you never will, you see," said Biddy.

It did not appear quite so unlikely to me that evening, as it would have done if we had discussed it a few hours before. I therefore observed I was not quite sure of that. But Biddy said she was, and she said it decisively. In my heart I believed her to be right; and yet I took it rather ill, too, that she should be so positive on the point.

When we came near the churchyard, we had to cross an embankment, and get over a stile near a sluice-gate. There started up, from the gate, or from the rushes, or from the ooze (which was quite in his stagnant way), Old Orlick.

"Halloa!" he growled, "where are you two going?"

"Where should we be going, but home?"

"Well, then," said he, "I'm jiggered if I don't see you home!"

This penalty of being jiggered was a favorite supposititious case of his. He attached no definite meaning to the word that I am aware of, but used it, like his own pretended Christian name, to affront mankind, and convey an idea of something savagely damaging. When I was younger, I had had a general belief that if he had jiggered me personally, he would have done it with a sharp and twisted hook.

Biddy was much against his going with us, and said to me in a whisper, "Don't let him come; I don't like him." As I did not like him either, I took the liberty of saying that we thanked him, but we didn't want seeing home. He received that piece of information with a yell of laughter, and dropped back, but came slouching after us at a little distance.

Curious to know whether Biddy suspected him of having had a hand in that murderous attack of which my sister had never been able to give any account, I asked her why she did not like him.

"Oh!" she replied, glancing over her shoulder as he slouched after us, "because I—I am afraid he likes me."

"Did he ever tell you he liked you?" I asked indignantly.

"No," said Biddy, glancing over her shoulder again, "he never told me so; but he dances at me, whenever he can catch my eye."

However novel and peculiar this testimony of attachment, I did not doubt the accuracy of the interpretation. I was very hot indeed upon Old Orlick's daring to admire her; as hot as if it were an outrage on myself.

"But it makes no difference to you, you know," said Biddy, calmly.

"No, Biddy, it makes no difference to me; only I don't like it; I don't approve of it."

"Nor I neither," said Biddy. "Though that makes no difference to you."

"Exactly," said I; "but I must tell you I should have no opinion of you, Biddy, if he danced at you with your own consent."

I kept an eye on Orlick after that night, and, whenever circumstances were favorable to his dancing at Biddy, got before him to obscure that demonstration. He had struck root in Joe's establishment, by reason of my sister's sudden fancy for him, or I should have tried to get him dismissed. He quite understood and reciprocated my good intentions, as I had reason to know thereafter.

And now, because my mind was not confused enough before, I complicated its confusion fifty thousand-fold, by having states and seasons when I was clear that Biddy was immeasurably better than Estella, and that the plain honest working life to which I was born had nothing in it to be ashamed of, but offered me sufficient means of self-respect and happiness. At those times, I would decide conclusively that my disaffection to dear old Joe and the forge was gone, and that I was growing up in a fair way to be partners with Joe and to keep company with Biddy,—when all in a moment some confounding remembrance of the Havisham days would fall upon me like a destructive missile, and scatter my wits again. Scattered wits take a long time picking up; and often before I had got them well together, they would be dispersed in all directions by one stray thought, that perhaps after all Miss Havisham was going to make my fortune when my time was out.

If my time had run out, it would have left me still at the height of my perplexities, I dare say. It never did run out, however, but was brought to a premature end, as I proceed to relate.

Chapter XVIII

It was in the fourth year of my apprenticeship to Joe, and it was a Saturday night. There was a group assembled round the fire at the Three Jolly Bargemen, attentive to Mr. Wopsle as he read the newspaper aloud. Of that group I was one.

A highly popular murder had been committed, and Mr. Wopsle was imbrued in blood to the eyebrows. He gloated over every abhorrent adjective in the description, and identified himself with every witness at the Inquest. He faintly moaned, "I am done for," as the victim, and he barbarously bellowed, "I'll serve you out," as the murderer. He gave the medical testimony, in pointed imitation of our local practitioner; and he piped and shook, as the aged turnpike-keeper who had heard blows, to an extent so very paralytic as to suggest a doubt regarding the mental competency of that witness. The coroner, in Mr. Wopsle's hands, became Timon of Athens; the beadle, Coriolanus. He enjoyed himself thoroughly, and we all enjoyed ourselves, and were delightfully comfortable. In this cosey state of mind we came to the verdict Wilful Murder.

Then, and not sooner, I became aware of a strange gentleman leaning over the back of the settle opposite me, looking on. There was an expression of contempt on his face, and he bit the side of a great forefinger as he watched the group of faces.

"Well!" said the stranger to Mr. Wopsle, when the reading was done, "you have settled it all to your own satisfaction, I have no doubt?"

Everybody started and looked up, as if it were the murderer. He looked at everybody coldly and sarcastically.

"Guilty, of course?" said he. "Out with it. Come!"

"Sir," returned Mr. Wopsle, "without having the honor of your acquaintance, I do say Guilty." Upon this we all took courage to unite in a confirmatory murmur.

"I know you do," said the stranger; "I knew you would. I told you so. But now I'll ask you a question. Do you know, or do you not know, that the law of England supposes every man to be innocent, until he is proved—proved—to be guilty?"

"Sir," Mr. Wopsle began to reply, "as an Englishman myself, I—"

"Come!" said the stranger, biting his forefinger at him. "Don't evade the question. Either you know it, or you don't know it. Which is it to be?"

He stood with his head on one side and himself on one side, in a bullying, interrogative manner, and he threw his forefinger at Mr. Wopsle,—as it were to mark him out—before biting it again.

"Now!" said he. "Do you know it, or don't you know it?"

"Certainly I know it," replied Mr. Wopsle.

"Certainly you know it. Then why didn't you say so at first? Now, I'll ask you another question,"—taking possession of Mr. Wopsle, as if he had a right to him,—"do you know that none of these witnesses have yet been cross-examined?"

Mr. Wopsle was beginning, "I can only say—" when the stranger stopped him.

"What? You won't answer the question, yes or no? Now, I'll try you again." Throwing his finger at him again. "Attend to me. Are you aware, or are you not aware, that none of these witnesses have yet been cross-examined? Come, I only want one word from you. Yes, or no?"

Mr. Wopsle hesitated, and we all began to conceive rather a poor opinion of him.

"Come!" said the stranger, "I'll help you. You don't deserve help, but I'll help you. Look at that paper you hold in your hand. What is it?"

"What is it?" repeated Mr. Wopsle, eyeing it, much at a loss.

"Is it," pursued the stranger in his most sarcastic and suspicious manner, "the printed paper you have just been reading from?"

"Undoubtedly."

"Undoubtedly. Now, turn to that paper, and tell me whether it distinctly states that the prisoner expressly said that his legal advisers instructed him altogether to reserve his defence?"

"I read that just now," Mr. Wopsle pleaded.

"Never mind what you read just now, sir; I don't ask you what you read just now. You may read the Lord's Prayer backwards, if you like,—and, perhaps, have done it before to-day. Turn to the paper. No, no, no my friend; not to the top of the column; you know better than that; to the bottom, to the bottom." (We all began to think Mr. Wopsle full of subterfuge.) "Well? Have you found it?"

"Here it is," said Mr. Wopsle.

"Now, follow that passage with your eye, and tell me whether it distinctly states that the prisoner expressly said that he was instructed by his legal advisers wholly to reserve his defence? Come! Do you make that of it?"

Mr. Wopsle answered, "Those are not the exact words."

"Not the exact words!" repeated the gentleman bitterly. "Is that the exact substance?"

"Yes," said Mr. Wopsle.

"Yes," repeated the stranger, looking round at the rest of the company with his right hand extended towards the witness, Wopsle. "And now I ask you what you say to the conscience of that man who, with that passage before his eyes, can lay his head upon his pillow after having pronounced a fellow-creature guilty, unheard?"

We all began to suspect that Mr. Wopsle was not the man we had thought him, and that he was beginning to be found out.

"And that same man, remember," pursued the gentleman, throwing his finger at Mr. Wopsle heavily,—"that same man might be summoned as a juryman upon this very trial, and, having thus deeply committed himself, might return to the bosom of his family and lay his head upon his pillow, after deliberately swearing that he would well and truly try the issue joined between Our Sovereign Lord the King and the prisoner at the bar, and would a true verdict give according to the evidence, so help him God!"

We were all deeply persuaded that the unfortunate Wopsle had gone too far, and had better stop in his reckless career while there was yet time.

The strange gentleman, with an air of authority not to be disputed, and with a manner expressive of knowing something secret about every one of us that would effectually do for each individual if he chose to disclose it, left the back of the settle, and came into the space between the two settles, in front of the fire, where he remained standing, his left hand in his pocket, and he biting the forefinger of his right.

"From information I have received," said he, looking round at us as we all quailed before him, "I have reason to believe there is a blacksmith among you, by name Joseph—or Joe—Gargery. Which is the man?"

"Here is the man," said Joe.

The strange gentleman beckoned him out of his place, and Joe went.

"You have an apprentice," pursued the stranger, "commonly known as Pip? Is he here?"

"I am here!" I cried.

The stranger did not recognize me, but I recognized him as the gentleman I had met on the stairs, on the occasion of my second visit to Miss Havisham. I had known him the moment I saw him looking over the settle, and now that I stood confronting him with his hand upon my shoulder, I checked off again in detail his large head, his dark complexion, his deep-set eyes, his bushy black eyebrows, his large watch-chain, his strong black dots of beard and whisker, and even the smell of scented soap on his great hand.

"I wish to have a private conference with you two," said he, when he had surveyed me at his leisure. "It will take a little time. Perhaps we had better go to your place of residence. I prefer not to anticipate my communication here; you will impart as much or as little of it as you please to your friends afterwards; I have nothing to do with that."

Amidst a wondering silence, we three walked out of the Jolly Bargemen, and in a wondering silence walked home. While going along, the strange gentleman occasionally looked at me, and occasionally bit the side of his finger. As we neared home, Joe vaguely acknowledging the occasion as an impressive and ceremonious one, went on ahead to open the front door. Our conference was held in the state parlor, which was feebly lighted by one candle.

It began with the strange gentleman's sitting down at the table, drawing the candle to him, and looking over some entries in his pocket-book. He then put up the pocket-book and set the candle a little aside, after peering round it into the darkness at Joe and me, to ascertain which was which.

"My name," he said, "is Jaggers, and I am a lawyer in London. I am pretty well known. I have unusual business to transact with you, and I commence by explaining that it is not of my originating. If my advice had been asked, I should not have been here. It was not asked, and you see me here. What I have to do as the confidential agent of another, I do. No less, no more."

Finding that he could not see us very well from where he sat, he got up, and threw one leg over the back of a chair and leaned upon it; thus having one foot on the seat of the chair, and one foot on the ground.

"Now, Joseph Gargery, I am the bearer of an offer to relieve you of this young fellow your apprentice. You would not object to cancel his indentures at his request and for his good? You would want nothing for so doing?"

"Lord forbid that I should want anything for not standing in Pip's way," said Joe, staring.

"Lord forbidding is pious, but not to the purpose," returned Mr. Jaggers. "The question is, Would you want anything? Do you want anything?"

"The answer is," returned Joe, sternly, "No."

I thought Mr. Jaggers glanced at Joe, as if he considered him a fool for his disinterestedness. But I was too much bewildered between breathless curiosity and surprise, to be sure of it.

"Very well," said Mr. Jaggers. "Recollect the admission you have made, and don't try to go from it presently."

"Who's a going to try?" retorted Joe.

"I don't say anybody is. Do you keep a dog?"

"Yes, I do keep a dog."

"Bear in mind then, that Brag is a good dog, but Holdfast is a better. Bear that in mind, will you?" repeated Mr. Jaggers, shutting his eyes and nodding his head at Joe, as if he were forgiving him something. "Now, I return to this young fellow. And the communication I have got to make is, that he has great expectations."

Joe and I gasped, and looked at one another.

"I am instructed to communicate to him," said Mr. Jaggers, throwing his finger at me sideways, "that he will come into a handsome property. Further, that it is the desire of the present possessor of that property, that he be immediately removed from his present sphere of life and from this place, and be brought up as a gentleman,—in a word, as a young fellow of great expectations."

My dream was out; my wild fancy was surpassed by sober reality; Miss Havisham was going to make my fortune on a grand scale.

"Now, Mr. Pip," pursued the lawyer, "I address the rest of what I have to say, to you. You are to understand, first, that it is the request of the person from whom I take my instructions that you always bear the name of Pip. You will have no objection, I dare say, to your great expectations being encumbered with that easy condition. But if you have any objection, this is the time to mention it."

My heart was beating so fast, and there was such a singing in my ears, that I could scarcely stammer I had no objection.

"I should think not! Now you are to understand, secondly, Mr. Pip, that the name of the person who is your liberal benefactor remains a profound secret, until the person chooses to reveal it. I am empowered to mention that it is the intention of the person to reveal it at first hand by word of mouth to yourself. When or where that intention may be carried out, I cannot say; no one can say. It may be years hence. Now, you are distinctly to understand that you are most positively prohibited from making any inquiry on this head, or any allusion or reference, however distant, to any individual whomsoever as the individual, in all the communications you may have with me. If you have a suspicion in your own breast, keep that suspicion in your own breast. It is not the least to the purpose what the reasons of this prohibition are; they may be the strongest and gravest reasons, or they may be mere whim. This is not for you to inquire into. The condition is laid down. Your acceptance of it, and your observance of it as binding, is the only remaining condition that I am charged with, by the person from whom I take my instructions, and for whom I am not otherwise responsible. That person is the person from whom you derive your expectations, and the secret is solely held by that person and by me. Again, not a very difficult condition with which to encumber such a rise in fortune; but if you have any objection to it, this is the time to mention it. Speak out."

Once more, I stammered with difficulty that I had no objection.

"I should think not! Now, Mr. Pip, I have done with stipulations." Though he called me Mr. Pip, and began rather to make up to me, he still could not get rid of a certain air of bullying suspicion; and even now he occasionally shut his eyes and threw his finger at me while he spoke, as much as to express that he knew all kinds of things to my disparagement, if he only chose to mention them. "We come next, to mere details of arrangement. You must know that, although I have used the term 'expectations' more than once, you are not endowed with expectations only. There is already lodged in my hands a sum of money amply sufficient for your suitable education and maintenance. You will please consider me your guardian. Oh!" for I was going to thank him, "I tell you at once, I am paid for my services, or I shouldn't render them. It is considered that you must be better educated, in accordance with your altered position, and that you will be alive to the importance and necessity of at once entering on that advantage."

I said I had always longed for it.

"Never mind what you have always longed for, Mr. Pip," he retorted; "keep to the record. If you long for it now, that's enough. Am I answered that you are ready to be placed at once under some proper tutor? Is that it?"

I stammered yes, that was it.

"Good. Now, your inclinations are to be consulted. I don't think that wise, mind, but it's my trust. Have you ever heard of any tutor whom you would prefer to another?"

I had never heard of any tutor but Biddy and Mr. Wopsle's great-aunt; so, I replied in the negative.

"There is a certain tutor, of whom I have some knowledge, who I think might suit the purpose," said Mr. Jaggers. "I don't recommend him, observe; because I never recommend anybody. The gentleman I speak of is one Mr. Matthew Pocket."

Ah! I caught at the name directly. Miss Havisham's relation. The Matthew whom Mr. and Mrs. Camilla had spoken of. The Matthew whose place was to be at Miss Havisham's head, when she lay dead, in her bride's dress on the bride's table.

"You know the name?" said Mr. Jaggers, looking shrewdly at me, and then shutting up his eyes while he waited for my answer.

My answer was, that I had heard of the name.

"Oh!" said he. "You have heard of the name. But the question is, what do you say of it?"

I said, or tried to say, that I was much obliged to him for his recommendation—

"No, my young friend!" he interrupted, shaking his great head very slowly. "Recollect yourself!"

Not recollecting myself, I began again that I was much obliged to him for his recommendation—

"No, my young friend," he interrupted, shaking his head and frowning and smiling both at once,—"no, no, no; it's very well done, but it won't do; you are too young to fix me with it. Recommendation is not the word, Mr. Pip. Try another."

Correcting myself, I said that I was much obliged to him for his mention of Mr. Matthew Pocket—

"That's more like it!" cried Mr. Jaggers.—And (I added), I would gladly try that gentleman.

"Good. You had better try him in his own house. The way shall be prepared for you, and you can see his son first, who is in London. When will you come to London?"

I said (glancing at Joe, who stood looking on, motionless), that I supposed I could come directly.

"First," said Mr. Jaggers, "you should have some new clothes to come in, and they should not be working-clothes. Say this day week. You'll want some money. Shall I leave you twenty guineas?"

He produced a long purse, with the greatest coolness, and counted them out on the table and pushed them over to me. This was the first time he had taken his leg from the chair. He sat astride of the chair when he had pushed the money over, and sat swinging his purse and eyeing Joe.

"Well, Joseph Gargery? You look dumbfoundered?"

"I am!" said Joe, in a very decided manner.

"It was understood that you wanted nothing for yourself, remember?"

"It were understood," said Joe. "And it are understood. And it ever will be similar according."

"But what," said Mr. Jaggers, swinging his purse,—"what if it was in my instructions to make you a present, as compensation?"

"As compensation what for?" Joe demanded.

"For the loss of his services."

Joe laid his hand upon my shoulder with the touch of a woman. I have often thought him since, like the steam-hammer that can crush a man or pat an egg-shell, in his combination of strength with gentleness. "Pip is that hearty welcome," said Joe, "to go free with his services, to honor and fortun', as no words can tell him. But if you think as Money can make compensation to me for the loss of the little child—what come to the forge—and ever the best of friends!—"

O dear good Joe, whom I was so ready to leave and so unthankful to, I see you again, with your muscular blacksmith's arm before your eyes, and your broad chest heaving, and your voice dying away. O dear good faithful tender Joe, I feel the loving tremble of your hand upon my arm, as solemnly this day as if it had been the rustle of an angel's wing!

But I encouraged Joe at the time. I was lost in the mazes of my future fortunes, and could not retrace the by-paths we had trodden together. I begged Joe to be comforted, for (as he said) we had ever been the best of friends, and (as I said) we ever would be so. Joe scooped his eyes with his disengaged wrist, as if he were bent on gouging himself, but said not another word.

Mr. Jaggers had looked on at this, as one who recognized in Joe the village idiot, and in me his keeper. When it was over, he said, weighing in his hand the purse he had ceased to swing:—

"Now, Joseph Gargery, I warn you this is your last chance. No half measures with me. If you mean to take a present that I have it in charge to make you, speak out, and you shall have it. If on the contrary you mean to say—" Here, to his great amazement, he was stopped by Joe's suddenly working round him with every demonstration of a fell pugilistic purpose.

"Which I meantersay," cried Joe, "that if you come into my place bull-baiting and badgering me, come out! Which I meantersay as sech if you're a man, come on! Which I meantersay that what I say, I meantersay and stand or fall by!"

I drew Joe away, and he immediately became placable; merely stating to me, in an obliging manner and as a polite expostulatory notice to any one whom it might happen to concern, that he were not a going to be bull-baited and badgered in his own place. Mr. Jaggers had risen when Joe demonstrated, and had backed near the door. Without evincing any inclination to come in again, he there delivered his valedictory remarks. They were these.

"Well, Mr. Pip, I think the sooner you leave here—as you are to be a gentleman—the better. Let it stand for this day week, and you shall receive my printed address in the meantime. You can take a hackney-coach at the stage-coach office in London, and come straight to me. Understand, that I express no opinion, one way or other, on the trust I undertake. I am paid for undertaking it, and I do so. Now, understand that, finally. Understand that!"

He was throwing his finger at both of us, and I think would have gone on, but for his seeming to think Joe dangerous, and going off.

Something came into my head which induced me to run after him, as he was going down to the Jolly Bargemen, where he had left a hired carriage.

"I beg your pardon, Mr. Jaggers."

"Halloa!" said he, facing round, "what's the matter?"

"I wish to be quite right, Mr. Jaggers, and to keep to your directions; so I thought I had better ask. Would there be any objection to my taking leave of any one I know, about here, before I go away?"

"No," said he, looking as if he hardly understood me.

"I don't mean in the village only, but up town?"

"No," said he. "No objection."

I thanked him and ran home again, and there I found that Joe had already locked the front door and vacated the state parlor, and was seated by the kitchen fire with a hand on each knee, gazing intently at the burning coals. I too sat down before the fire and gazed at the coals, and nothing was said for a long time.

My sister was in her cushioned chair in her corner, and Biddy sat at her needle-work before the fire, and Joe sat next Biddy, and I sat next Joe in the corner opposite my sister. The more I looked into the glowing coals, the more incapable I became of looking at Joe; the longer the silence lasted, the more unable I felt to speak.

At length I got out, "Joe, have you told Biddy?"

"No, Pip," returned Joe, still looking at the fire, and holding his knees tight, as if he had private information that they intended to make off somewhere, "which I left it to yourself, Pip."

"I would rather you told, Joe."

"Pip's a gentleman of fortun' then," said Joe, "and God bless him in it!"

Biddy dropped her work, and looked at me. Joe held his knees and looked at me. I looked at both of them. After a pause, they both heartily congratulated me; but there was a certain touch of sadness in their congratulations that I rather resented.

I took it upon myself to impress Biddy (and through Biddy, Joe) with the grave obligation I considered my friends under, to know nothing and say nothing about the maker of my fortune. It would all come out in good time, I observed, and in the meanwhile nothing was to be said, save that I had come into great expectations from a mysterious patron. Biddy nodded her head thoughtfully at the fire as she took up her work again, and said she would be very particular; and Joe, still detaining his knees, said, "Ay, ay, I'll be ekervally partickler, Pip;" and then they congratulated me again, and went on to express so much wonder at the notion of my being a gentleman that I didn't half like it.

Infinite pains were then taken by Biddy to convey to my sister some idea of what had happened. To the best of my belief, those efforts entirely failed. She laughed and nodded her head a great many times, and even repeated after Biddy, the words "Pip" and "Property." But

I doubt if they had more meaning in them than an election cry, and I cannot suggest a darker picture of her state of mind.

I never could have believed it without experience, but as Joe and Biddy became more at their cheerful ease again, I became quite gloomy. Dissatisfied with my fortune, of course I could not be; but it is possible that I may have been, without quite knowing it, dissatisfied with myself.

Any how, I sat with my elbow on my knee and my face upon my hand, looking into the fire, as those two talked about my going away, and about what they should do without me, and all that. And whenever I caught one of them looking at me, though never so pleasantly (and they often looked at me,—particularly Biddy), I felt offended: as if they were expressing some mistrust of me. Though Heaven knows they never did by word or sign.

At those times I would get up and look out at the door; for our kitchen door opened at once upon the night, and stood open on summer evenings to air the room. The very stars to which I then raised my eyes, I am afraid I took to be but poor and humble stars for glittering on the rustic objects among which I had passed my life.

"Saturday night," said I, when we sat at our supper of bread and cheese and beer. "Five more days, and then the day before the day! They'll soon go."

"Yes, Pip," observed Joe, whose voice sounded hollow in his beer-mug. "They'll soon go."

"Soon, soon go," said Biddy.

"I have been thinking, Joe, that when I go down town on Monday, and order my new clothes, I shall tell the tailor that I'll come and put them on there, or that I'll have them sent to Mr. Pumblechook's. It would be very disagreeable to be stared at by all the people here."

"Mr. and Mrs. Hubble might like to see you in your new gen-teel figure too, Pip," said Joe, industriously cutting his bread, with his cheese on it, in the palm of his left hand, and glancing at my untasted supper as if he thought of the time when we used to compare slices. "So might Wopsle. And the Jolly Bargemen might take it as a compliment."

"That's just what I don't want, Joe. They would make such a business of it,—such a coarse and common business,—that I couldn't bear myself."

"Ah, that indeed, Pip!" said Joe. "If you couldn't abear yourself—"

Biddy asked me here, as she sat holding my sister's plate, "Have you thought about when you'll show yourself to Mr. Gargery, and your sister and me? You will show yourself to us; won't you?"

"Biddy," I returned with some resentment, "you are so exceedingly quick that it's difficult to keep up with you."

("She always were quick," observed Joe.)

"If you had waited another moment, Biddy, you would have heard me say that I shall bring my clothes here in a bundle one evening,—most likely on the evening before I go away."

Biddy said no more. Handsomely forgiving her, I soon exchanged an affectionate good night with her and Joe, and went up to bed. When I got into my little room, I sat down and took a long look at it, as a mean little room that I should soon be parted from and raised above, for ever. It was furnished with fresh young remembrances too, and even at the same moment

I fell into much the same confused division of mind between it and the better rooms to which I was going, as I had been in so often between the forge and Miss Havisham's, and Biddy and Estella.

The sun had been shining brightly all day on the roof of my attic, and the room was warm. As I put the window open and stood looking out, I saw Joe come slowly forth at the dark door, below, and take a turn or two in the air; and then I saw Biddy come, and bring him a pipe and light it for him. He never smoked so late, and it seemed to hint to me that he wanted comforting, for some reason or other.

He presently stood at the door immediately beneath me, smoking his pipe, and Biddy stood there too, quietly talking to him, and I knew that they talked of me, for I heard my name mentioned in an endearing tone by both of them more than once. I would not have listened for more, if I could have heard more; so I drew away from the window, and sat down in my one chair by the bedside, feeling it very sorrowful and strange that this first night of my bright fortunes should be the loneliest I had ever known.

Looking towards the open window, I saw light wreaths from Joe's pipe floating there, and I fancied it was like a blessing from Joe,—not obtruded on me or paraded before me, but pervading the air we shared together. I put my light out, and crept into bed; and it was an uneasy bed now, and I never slept the old sound sleep in it any more.

Chapter XIX

Morning made a considerable difference in my general prospect of Life, and brightened it so much that it scarcely seemed the same. What lay heaviest on my mind was, the consideration that six days intervened between me and the day of departure; for I could not divest myself of a misgiving that something might happen to London in the meanwhile, and that, when I got there, it would be either greatly deteriorated or clean gone.

Joe and Biddy were very sympathetic and pleasant when I spoke of our approaching separation; but they only referred to it when I did. After breakfast, Joe brought out my indentures from the press in the best parlor, and we put them in the fire, and I felt that I was free. With all the novelty of my emancipation on me, I went to church with Joe, and thought perhaps the clergyman wouldn't have read that about the rich man and the kingdom of Heaven, if he had known all.

After our early dinner, I strolled out alone, purposing to finish off the marshes at once, and get them done with. As I passed the church, I felt (as I had felt during service in the morning) a sublime compassion for the poor creatures who were destined to go there, Sunday after Sunday, all their lives through, and to lie obscurely at last among the low green mounds. I promised myself that I would do something for them one of these days, and formed a plan in outline for bestowing a dinner of roast-beef and plum-pudding, a pint of ale, and a gallon of condescension, upon everybody in the village.

If I had often thought before, with something allied to shame, of my companionship with the fugitive whom I had once seen limping among those graves, what were my thoughts on this Sunday, when the place recalled the wretch, ragged and shivering, with his felon iron and badge! My comfort was, that it happened a long time ago, and that he had doubtless been transported a long way off, and that he was dead to me, and might be veritably dead into the bargain.

No more low, wet grounds, no more dikes and sluices, no more of these grazing cattle,—though they seemed, in their dull manner, to wear a more respectful air now, and to face round, in order that they might stare as long as possible at the possessor of such great expectations,—farewell, monotonous acquaintances of my childhood, henceforth I was for London and greatness; not for smith's work in general, and for you! I made my exultant way to the old Battery, and, lying down there to consider the question whether Miss Havisham intended me for Estella, fell asleep.

When I awoke, I was much surprised to find Joe sitting beside me, smoking his pipe. He greeted me with a cheerful smile on my opening my eyes, and said,—

"As being the last time, Pip, I thought I'd foller."

"And Joe, I am very glad you did so."

"Thankee, Pip."

"You may be sure, dear Joe," I went on, after we had shaken hands, "that I shall never forget you."

"No, no, Pip!" said Joe, in a comfortable tone, "I'm sure of that. Ay, ay, old chap! Bless you, it were only necessary to get it well round in a man's mind, to be certain on it. But it took a bit of time to get it well round, the change come so oncommon plump; didn't it?"

Somehow, I was not best pleased with Joe's being so mightily secure of me. I should have liked him to have betrayed emotion, or to have said, "It does you credit, Pip," or something of that sort. Therefore, I made no remark on Joe's first head; merely saying as to his second, that the tidings had indeed come suddenly, but that I had always wanted to be a gentleman, and had often and often speculated on what I would do, if I were one.

"Have you though?" said Joe. "Astonishing!"

"It's a pity now, Joe," said I, "that you did not get on a little more, when we had our lessons here; isn't it?"

"Well, I don't know," returned Joe. "I'm so awful dull. I'm only master of my own trade. It were always a pity as I was so awful dull; but it's no more of a pity now, than it was—this day twelvemonth—don't you see?"

What I had meant was, that when I came into my property and was able to do something for Joe, it would have been much more agreeable if he had been better qualified for a rise in station. He was so perfectly innocent of my meaning, however, that I thought I would mention it to Biddy in preference.

So, when we had walked home and had had tea, I took Biddy into our little garden by the side of the lane, and, after throwing out in a general way for the elevation of her spirits, that I should never forget her, said I had a favor to ask of her.

"And it is, Biddy," said I, "that you will not omit any opportunity of helping Joe on, a little."

"How helping him on?" asked Biddy, with a steady sort of glance.

"Well! Joe is a dear good fellow,—in fact, I think he is the dearest fellow that ever lived,—

but he is rather backward in some things. For instance, Biddy, in his learning and his manners."

Although I was looking at Biddy as I spoke, and although she opened her eyes very wide when I had spoken, she did not look at me.

"O, his manners! won't his manners do then?" asked Biddy, plucking a black-currant leaf.

"My dear Biddy, they do very well here—"

"O! they do very well here?" interrupted Biddy, looking closely at the leaf in her hand.

"Hear me out,—but if I were to remove Joe into a higher sphere, as I shall hope to remove him when I fully come into my property, they would hardly do him justice."

"And don't you think he knows that?" asked Biddy.

It was such a very provoking question (for it had never in the most distant manner occurred to me), that I said, snappishly,—

"Biddy, what do you mean?"

Biddy, having rubbed the leaf to pieces between her hands,—and the smell of a black-currant bush has ever since recalled to me that evening in the little garden by the side of the lane,—said, "Have you never considered that he may be proud?"

"Proud?" I repeated, with disdainful emphasis.

"O! there are many kinds of pride," said Biddy, looking full at me and shaking her head; "pride is not all of one kind—"

"Well? What are you stopping for?" said I.

"Not all of one kind," resumed Biddy. "He may be too proud to let any one take him out of a place that he is competent to fill, and fills well and with respect. To tell you the truth, I think he is; though it sounds bold in me to say so, for you must know him far better than I do."

"Now, Biddy," said I, "I am very sorry to see this in you. I did not expect to see this in you. You are envious, Biddy, and grudging. You are dissatisfied on account of my rise in fortune, and you can't help showing it."

"If you have the heart to think so," returned Biddy, "say so. Say so over and over again, if you have the heart to think so."

"If you have the heart to be so, you mean, Biddy," said I, in a virtuous and superior tone; "don't put it off upon me. I am very sorry to see it, and it's a—it's a bad side of human nature. I did intend to ask you to use any little opportunities you might have after I was gone, of improving dear Joe. But after this I ask you nothing. I am extremely sorry to see this in you, Biddy," I repeated. "It's a—it's a bad side of human nature."

"Whether you scold me or approve of me," returned poor Biddy, "you may equally depend upon my trying to do all that lies in my power, here, at all times. And whatever opinion you take away of me, shall make no difference in my remembrance of you. Yet a gentleman should not be unjust neither," said Biddy, turning away her head.

I again warmly repeated that it was a bad side of human nature (in which sentiment, waiving its application, I have since seen reason to think I was right), and I walked down the little path away from Biddy, and Biddy went into the house, and I went out at the garden gate and took a dejected stroll until supper-time; again feeling it very sorrowful and strange that this, the second night of my bright fortunes, should be as lonely and unsatisfactory as the first.

But, morning once more brightened my view, and I extended my clemency to Biddy, and we dropped the subject. Putting on the best clothes I had, I went into town as early as I could hope to find the shops open, and presented myself before Mr. Trabb, the tailor, who was having his breakfast in the parlor behind his shop, and who did not think it worth his while to come out to me, but called me in to him.

"Well!" said Mr. Trabb, in a hail-fellow-well-met kind of way. "How are you, and what can I do for you?"

Mr. Trabb had sliced his hot roll into three feather-beds, and was slipping butter in between the blankets, and covering it up. He was a prosperous old bachelor, and his open window looked into a prosperous little garden and orchard, and there was a prosperous iron safe let into the wall at the side of his fireplace, and I did not doubt that heaps of his prosperity were put away in it in bags.

"Mr. Trabb," said I, "it's an unpleasant thing to have to mention, because it looks like boasting; but I have come into a handsome property."

A change passed over Mr. Trabb. He forgot the butter in bed, got up from the bedside, and wiped his fingers on the tablecloth, exclaiming, "Lord bless my soul!"

"I am going up to my guardian in London," said I, casually drawing some guineas out of my pocket and looking at them; "and I want a fashionable suit of clothes to go in. I wish to pay for them," I added—otherwise I thought he might only pretend to make them, "with ready money."

"My dear sir," said Mr. Trabb, as he respectfully bent his body, opened his arms, and took the liberty of touching me on the outside of each elbow, "don't hurt me by mentioning that. May I venture to congratulate you? Would you do me the favor of stepping into the shop?"

Mr. Trabb's boy was the most audacious boy in all that country-side. When I had entered he was sweeping the shop, and he had sweetened his labors by sweeping over me. He was still sweeping when I came out into the shop with Mr. Trabb, and he knocked the broom against all possible corners and obstacles, to express (as I understood it) equality with any blacksmith, alive or dead.

"Hold that noise," said Mr. Trabb, with the greatest sternness, "or I'll knock your head off!—Do me the favor to be seated, sir. Now, this," said Mr. Trabb, taking down a roll of cloth, and tiding it out in a flowing manner over the counter, preparatory to getting his hand under it to show the gloss, "is a very sweet article. I can recommend it for your purpose, sir, because it really is extra super. But you shall see some others. Give me Number Four, you!" (To the boy, and with a dreadfully severe stare; foreseeing the danger of that miscreant's brushing me with it, or making some other sign of familiarity.)

Mr. Trabb never removed his stern eye from the boy until he had deposited number four on the counter and was at a safe distance again. Then he commanded him to bring number five, and number eight. "And let me have none of your tricks here," said Mr. Trabb, "or you shall repent it, you young scoundrel, the longest day you have to live."

Mr. Trabb then bent over number four, and in a sort of deferential confidence recommended it to me as a light article for summer wear, an article much in vogue among the nobility and gentry, an article that it would ever be an honor to him to reflect upon a distinguished fellow-townsman's (if he might claim me for a fellow-townsman) having worn. "Are you bringing numbers five and eight, you vagabond," said Mr. Trabb to the boy after that, "or shall I kick you out of the shop and bring them myself?"

I selected the materials for a suit, with the assistance of Mr. Trabb's judgment, and re-entered the parlor to be measured. For although Mr. Trabb had my measure already, and had previously been quite contented with it, he said apologetically that it "wouldn't do under existing circumstances, sir,—wouldn't do at all." So, Mr. Trabb measured and calculated me in the parlor, as if I were an estate and he the finest species of surveyor, and gave himself such a world of trouble that I felt that no suit of clothes could possibly remunerate him for his pains. When he had at last done and had appointed to send the articles to Mr. Pumblechook's on the Thursday evening, he said, with his hand upon the parlor lock, "I know, sir, that London gentlemen cannot be expected to patronize local work, as a rule; but if you would give me a turn now and then in the quality of a townsman, I should greatly esteem it. Good morning, sir, much obliged.—Door!"

The last word was flung at the boy, who had not the least notion what it meant. But I saw him collapse as his master rubbed me out with his hands, and my first decided experience of the stupendous power of money was, that it had morally laid upon his back Trabb's boy.

After this memorable event, I went to the hatter's, and the bootmaker's, and the hosier's, and felt rather like Mother Hubbard's dog whose outfit required the services of so many trades. I also went to the coach-office and took my place for seven o'clock on Saturday morning. It was not necessary to explain everywhere that I had come into a handsome property; but whenever I said anything to that effect, it followed that the officiating tradesman ceased to have his attention diverted through the window by the High Street, and concentrated his mind upon me. When I had ordered everything I wanted, I directed my steps towards Pumblechook's, and, as I approached that gentleman's place of business, I saw him standing at his door.

He was waiting for me with great impatience. He had been out early with the chaise-cart, and had called at the forge and heard the news. He had prepared a collation for me in the Barnwell parlor, and he too ordered his shopman to "come out of the gangway" as my sacred person passed.

"My dear friend," said Mr. Pumblechook, taking me by both hands, when he and I and the collation were alone, "I give you joy of your good fortune. Well deserved, well deserved!"

This was coming to the point, and I thought it a sensible way of expressing himself.

"To think," said Mr. Pumblechook, after snorting admiration at me for some moments, "that I should have been the humble instrument of leading up to this, is a proud reward."

I begged Mr. Pumblechook to remember that nothing was to be ever said or hinted, on that point.

"My dear young friend," said Mr. Pumblechook; "if you will allow me to call you so—"

I murmured "Certainly," and Mr. Pumblechook took me by both hands again, and communicated a movement to his waistcoat, which had an emotional appearance, though it was rather low down, "My dear young friend, rely upon my doing my little all in your absence, by keeping the fact before the mind of Joseph.—Joseph!" said Mr. Pumblechook, in the way of a compassionate adjuration. "Joseph!! Joseph!!!" Thereupon he shook his head and tapped it, expressing his sense of deficiency in Joseph.

"But my dear young friend," said Mr. Pumblechook, "you must be hungry, you must be exhausted. Be seated. Here is a chicken had round from the Boar, here is a tongue had round from the Boar, here's one or two little things had round from the Boar, that I hope you may not despise. But do I," said Mr. Pumblechook, getting up again the moment after he had sat down, "see afore me, him as I ever sported with in his times of happy infancy? And may I—may I—?"

This May I, meant might he shake hands? I consented, and he was fervent, and then sat down again.

"Here is wine," said Mr. Pumblechook. "Let us drink, Thanks to Fortune, and may she ever pick out her favorites with equal judgment! And yet I cannot," said Mr. Pumblechook, getting up again, "see afore me One—and likewise drink to One—without again expressing— May I—may I—?"

I said he might, and he shook hands with me again, and emptied his glass and turned it upside down. I did the same; and if I had turned myself upside down before drinking, the wine could not have gone more direct to my head.

Mr. Pumblechook helped me to the liver wing, and to the best slice of tongue (none of those out-of-the-way No Thoroughfares of Pork now), and took, comparatively speaking, no care of himself at all. "Ah! poultry, poultry! You little thought," said Mr. Pumblechook, apostrophizing the fowl in the dish, "when you was a young fledgling, what was in store for you. You little thought you was to be refreshment beneath this humble roof for one as—Call it a weakness, if you will," said Mr. Pumblechook, getting up again, "but may I? may I—?"

It began to be unnecessary to repeat the form of saying he might, so he did it at once. How he ever did it so often without wounding himself with my knife, I don't know.

"And your sister," he resumed, after a little steady eating, "which had the honor of bringing you up by hand! It's a sad picter, to reflect that she's no longer equal to fully understanding the honor. May—"

I saw he was about to come at me again, and I stopped him.

"We'll drink her health," said I.

"Ah!" cried Mr. Pumblechook, leaning back in his chair, quite flaccid with admiration, "that's the way you know 'em, sir!" (I don't know who Sir was, but he certainly was not I, and there was no third person present); "that's the way you know the noble-minded, sir! Ever forgiving and ever affable. It might," said the servile Pumblechook, putting down his untasted glass in a hurry and getting up again, "to a common person, have the appearance of repeating—but may I—?"

When he had done it, he resumed his seat and drank to my sister. "Let us never be blind," said Mr. Pumblechook, "to her faults of temper, but it is to be hoped she meant well."

At about this time, I began to observe that he was getting flushed in the face; as to myself, I felt all face, steeped in wine and smarting.

I mentioned to Mr. Pumblechook that I wished to have my new clothes sent to his house, and he was ecstatic on my so distinguishing him. I mentioned my reason for desiring to avoid observation in the village, and he lauded it to the skies. There was nobody but himself, he intimated, worthy of my confidence, and—in short, might he? Then he asked me tenderly if I remembered our boyish games at sums, and how we had gone together to have me bound apprentice, and, in effect, how he had ever been my favorite fancy and my chosen friend? If I had taken ten times as many glasses of wine as I had, I should have known that he never had stood in that relation towards me, and should in my heart of hearts have repudiated the idea. Yet for all that, I remember feeling convinced that I had been much mistaken in him, and that he was a sensible, practical, good-hearted prime fellow.

By degrees he fell to reposing such great confidence in me, as to ask my advice in reference to his own affairs. He mentioned that there was an opportunity for a great amalgamation and monopoly of the corn and seed trade on those premises, if enlarged, such as had never occurred before in that or any other neighborhood. What alone was wanting to the realization of a vast fortune, he considered to be More Capital. Those were the two little words, more capital. Now it appeared to him (Pumblechook) that if that capital were got into the business, through a sleeping partner, sir,—which sleeping partner would have nothing to do but walk in, by self or deputy, whenever he pleased, and examine the books,—and walk in twice a year and take his profits away in his pocket, to the tune of fifty per cent,—it appeared to him that that might be an opening for a young gentleman of spirit combined with property, which would be worthy of his attention. But what did I think? He had great confidence in my opinion, and what did I think? I gave it as my opinion. "Wait a bit!" The united vastness and distinctness of this view so struck him, that he no longer asked if he might shake hands with me, but said he really must,—and did.

We drank all the wine, and Mr. Pumblechook pledged himself over and over again to keep Joseph up to the mark (I don't know what mark), and to render me efficient and constant service (I don't know what service). He also made known to me for the first time in my life, and certainly after having kept his secret wonderfully well, that he had always said of me, "That boy is no common boy, and mark me, his fortun' will be no common fortun'." He said with a tearful smile that it was a singular thing to think of now, and I said so too. Finally, I went out into the air, with a dim perception that there was something unwonted in the conduct of the sunshine, and found that I had slumberously got to the turnpike without having taken any account of the road.

There, I was roused by Mr. Pumblechook's hailing me. He was a long way down the sunny street, and was making expressive gestures for me to stop. I stopped, and he came up breathless.

"No, my dear friend," said he, when he had recovered wind for speech. "Not if I can help it. This occasion shall not entirely pass without that affability on your part.—May I, as an old friend and well-wisher? May I?"

We shook hands for the hundredth time at least, and he ordered a young carter out of my way with the greatest indignation. Then, he blessed me and stood waving his hand to me until I had passed the crook in the road; and then I turned into a field and had a long nap under a hedge before I pursued my way home.

I had scant luggage to take with me to London, for little of the little I possessed was adapted to my new station. But I began packing that same afternoon, and wildly packed up things that I knew I should want next morning, in a fiction that there was not a moment to be lost.

So, Tuesday, Wednesday, and Thursday, passed; and on Friday morning I went to Mr. Pumblechook's, to put on my new clothes and pay my visit to Miss Havisham. Mr. Pumblechook's own room was given up to me to dress in, and was decorated with clean towels expressly for the event. My clothes were rather a disappointment, of course. Probably every new and eagerly expected garment ever put on since clothes came in, fell a trifle short of the wearer's expectation. But after I had had my new suit on some half an hour, and had gone through an immensity of posturing with Mr. Pumblechook's very limited dressing-glass, in the futile endeavor to see my legs, it seemed to fit me better. It being market morning at a neighboring town some ten miles off, Mr. Pumblechook was not at home. I had not told him exactly when I meant to leave, and was not likely to shake hands with him again before departing. This was all as it should be, and I went out in my new array, fearfully ashamed of having to pass the shopman, and suspicious after all that I was at a personal disadvantage, something like Joe's in his Sunday suit.

I went circuitously to Miss Havisham's by all the back ways, and rang at the bell constrainedly, on account of the stiff long fingers of my gloves. Sarah Pocket came to the gate, and positively reeled back when she saw me so changed; her walnut-shell countenance likewise turned from brown to green and yellow.

"You?" said she. "You? Good gracious! What do you want?"

"I am going to London, Miss Pocket," said I, "and want to say good-bye to Miss Havisham."

I was not expected, for she left me locked in the yard, while she went to ask if I were to be admitted. After a very short delay, she returned and took me up, staring at me all the way.

Miss Havisham was taking exercise in the room with the long spread table, leaning on her crutch stick. The room was lighted as of yore, and at the sound of our entrance, she stopped and turned. She was then just abreast of the rotted bride-cake.

"Don't go, Sarah," she said. "Well, Pip?"

"I start for London, Miss Havisham, to-morrow," I was exceedingly careful what I said, "and I thought you would kindly not mind my taking leave of you."

"This is a gay figure, Pip," said she, making her crutch stick play round me, as if she, the fairy godmother who had changed me, were bestowing the finishing gift.

"I have come into such good fortune since I saw you last, Miss Havisham," I murmured. "And I am so grateful for it, Miss Havisham!"

"Ay, ay!" said she, looking at the discomfited and envious Sarah, with delight. "I have seen Mr. Jaggers. I have heard about it, Pip. So you go to-morrow?"

"Yes, Miss Havisham."

"And you are adopted by a rich person?"

"Yes, Miss Havisham."

"Not named?"

"No, Miss Havisham."

"And Mr. Jaggers is made your guardian?"

"Yes, Miss Havisham."

She quite gloated on these questions and answers, so keen was her enjoyment of Sarah Pocket's jealous dismay. "Well!" she went on; "you have a promising career before you. Be good—deserve it—and abide by Mr. Jaggers's instructions." She looked at me, and looked at Sarah, and Sarah's countenance wrung out of her watchful face a cruel smile. "Good-bye, Pip!—you will always keep the name of Pip, you know."

"Yes, Miss Havisham."

"Good-bye, Pip!"

She stretched out her hand, and I went down on my knee and put it to my lips. I had not considered how I should take leave of her; it came naturally to me at the moment to do this. She looked at Sarah Pocket with triumph in her weird eyes, and so I left my fairy godmother, with both her hands on her crutch stick, standing in the midst of the dimly lighted room beside the rotten bride-cake that was hidden in cobwebs.

Sarah Pocket conducted me down, as if I were a ghost who must be seen out. She could not get over my appearance, and was in the last degree confounded. I said "Good-bye, Miss Pocket;" but she merely stared, and did not seem collected enough to know that I had spoken. Clear of the house, I made the best of my way back to Pumblechook's, took off my new clothes, made them into a bundle, and went back home in my older dress, carrying it—to speak the truth—much more at my ease too, though I had the bundle to carry.

And now, those six days which were to have run out so slowly, had run out fast and were gone, and to-morrow looked me in the face more steadily than I could look at it. As the six evenings had dwindled away, to five, to four, to three, to two, I had become more and more appreciative of the society of Joe and Biddy. On this last evening, I dressed my self out in my new clothes for their delight, and sat in my splendor until bedtime. We had a hot supper on the occasion, graced by the inevitable roast fowl, and we had some flip to finish with. We were all very low, and none the higher for pretending to be in spirits.

I was to leave our village at five in the morning, carrying my little hand-portmanteau, and I had told Joe that I wished to walk away all alone. I am afraid—sore afraid—that this purpose originated in my sense of the contrast there would be between me and Joe, if we went to the coach together. I had pretended with myself that there was nothing of this taint in the arrangement; but when I went up to my little room on this last night, I felt compelled to admit that it might be so, and had an impulse upon me to go down again and entreat Joe to walk with me in the morning. I did not.

All night there were coaches in my broken sleep, going to wrong places instead of to London, and having in the traces, now dogs, now cats, now pigs, now men,—never horses. Fantastic failures of journeys occupied me until the day dawned and the birds were singing. Then, I got up and partly dressed, and sat at the window to take a last look out, and in taking it fell asleep.

Biddy was astir so early to get my breakfast, that, although I did not sleep at the window an hour, I smelt the smoke of the kitchen fire when I started up with a terrible idea that it must be late in the afternoon. But long after that, and long after I had heard the clinking of the teacups and was quite ready, I wanted the resolution to go downstairs. After all, I remained up there, repeatedly unlocking and unstrapping my small portmanteau and locking and strapping it up again, until Biddy called to me that I was late.

It was a hurried breakfast with no taste in it. I got up from the meal, saying with a sort of briskness, as if it had only just occurred to me, "Well! I suppose I must be off!" and then I kissed my sister who was laughing and nodding and shaking in her usual chair, and kissed Biddy, and threw my arms around Joe's neck. Then I took up my little portmanteau and walked out. The last I saw of them was, when I presently heard a scuffle behind me, and looking back, saw Joe throwing an old shoe after me and Biddy throwing another old shoe. I stopped then, to wave my hat, and dear old Joe waved his strong right arm above his head, crying huskily "Hooroar!" and Biddy put her apron to her face.

I walked away at a good pace, thinking it was easier to go than I had supposed it would be, and reflecting that it would never have done to have had an old shoe thrown after the coach, in sight of all the High Street. I whistled and made nothing of going. But the village was very peaceful and quiet, and the light mists were solemnly rising, as if to show me the world, and I had been so innocent and little there, and all beyond was so unknown and great, that in a moment with a strong heave and sob I broke into tears. It was by the finger-post at the end of the village, and I laid my hand upon it, and said, "Good-bye, O my dear, dear friend!"

Heaven knows we need never be ashamed of our tears, for they are rain upon the blinding dust of earth, overlying our hard hearts. I was better after I had cried than before,—more sorry, more aware of my own ingratitude, more gentle. If I had cried before, I should have had Joe with me then.

So subdued I was by those tears, and by their breaking out again in the course of the quiet walk, that when I was on the coach, and it was clear of the town, I deliberated with an aching heart whether I would not get down when we changed horses and walk back, and have another evening at home, and a better parting. We changed, and I had not made up my mind, and still reflected for my comfort that it would be quite practicable to get down and walk back, when we changed again. And while I was occupied with these deliberations, I would fancy an exact resemblance to Joe in some man coming along the road towards us, and my heart would beat high.—As if he could possibly be there!

We changed again, and yet again, and it was now too late and too far to go back, and I went on. And the mists had all solemnly risen now, and the world lay spread before me.

This is the end of the first stage of Pip's expectations.

Chapter XX

The journey from our town to the metropolis was a journey of about five hours. It was a little past midday when the four-horse stage-coach by which I was a passenger, got into the ravel of traffic frayed out about the Cross Keys, Wood Street, Cheapside, London.

We Britons had at that time particularly settled that it was treasonable to doubt our having and our being the best of everything: otherwise, while I was scared by the immensity of London, I think I might have had some faint doubts whether it was not rather ugly, crooked, narrow, and dirty.

Mr. Jaggers had duly sent me his address; it was, Little Britain, and he had written after it on his card, "just out of Smithfield, and close by the coach-office." Nevertheless, a hackney-coachman, who seemed to have as many capes to his greasy great-coat as he was years old, packed me up in his coach and hemmed me in with a folding and jingling barrier of steps, as if he were going to take me fifty miles. His getting on his box, which I remember to have been decorated with an old weather-stained pea-green hammercloth moth-eaten into rags, was quite a work of time. It was a wonderful equipage, with six great coronets outside, and ragged things behind for I don't know how many footmen to hold on by, and a harrow below them, to prevent amateur footmen from yielding to the temptation.

I had scarcely had time to enjoy the coach and to think how like a straw-yard it was, and yet how like a rag-shop, and to wonder why the horses' nose-bags were kept inside, when I observed the coachman beginning to get down, as if we were going to stop presently. And stop we presently did, in a gloomy street, at certain offices with an open door, whereon was painted MR. JAGGERS.

"How much?" I asked the coachman.

The coachman answered, "A shilling—unless you wish to make it more."

I naturally said I had no wish to make it more.

"Then it must be a shilling," observed the coachman. "I don't want to get into trouble. I know him!" He darkly closed an eye at Mr. Jaggers's name, and shook his head.

When he had got his shilling, and had in course of time completed the ascent to his box, and had got away (which appeared to relieve his mind), I went into the front office with my little portmanteau in my hand and asked, Was Mr. Jaggers at home?

"He is not," returned the clerk. "He is in Court at present. Am I addressing Mr. Pip?"

I signified that he was addressing Mr. Pip.

"Mr. Jaggers left word, would you wait in his room. He couldn't say how long he might be, having a case on. But it stands to reason, his time being valuable, that he won't be longer than he can help."

With those words, the clerk opened a door, and ushered me into an inner chamber at the back. Here, we found a gentleman with one eye, in a velveteen suit and knee-breeches, who wiped his nose with his sleeve on being interrupted in the perusal of the newspaper.

"Go and wait outside, Mike," said the clerk.

I began to say that I hoped I was not interrupting, when the clerk shoved this gentleman out with as little ceremony as I ever saw used, and tossing his fur cap out after him, left me alone.

Mr. Jaggers's room was lighted by a skylight only, and was a most dismal place; the skylight, eccentrically pitched like a broken head, and the distorted adjoining houses looking as if they had twisted themselves to peep down at me through it. There were not so many papers about, as I should have expected to see; and there were some odd objects about, that I should not have expected to see,—such as an old rusty pistol, a sword in a scabbard, several strange-looking boxes and packages, and two dreadful casts on a shelf, of faces peculiarly swollen, and twitchy about the nose. Mr. Jaggers's own high-backed chair was of deadly black horsehair, with rows of brass nails round it, like a coffin; and I fancied I could see how he leaned back in it, and bit his forefinger at the clients. The room was but small, and the clients seemed to have had a habit of backing up against the wall; the wall, especially opposite to Mr. Jaggers's chair, being greasy with shoulders. I recalled, too, that the one-eyed gentleman had shuffled forth against the wall when I was the innocent cause of his being turned out.

I sat down in the cliental chair placed over against Mr. Jaggers's chair, and became fascinated by the dismal atmosphere of the place. I called to mind that the clerk had the same air of knowing something to everybody else's disadvantage, as his master had. I wondered how many other clerks there were upstairs, and whether they all claimed to have the same detrimental mastery of their fellow-creatures. I wondered what was the history of all the odd litter about the room, and how it came there. I wondered whether the two swollen faces were of Mr. Jaggers's family, and, if he were so unfortunate as to have had a pair of such ill-looking relations, why he stuck them on that dusty perch for the blacks and flies to settle on, instead of giving them a place at home. Of course I had no experience of a London summer day, and my spirits may have been oppressed by the hot exhausted air, and by the dust and grit that lay thick on everything. But I sat wondering and waiting in Mr. Jaggers's close room, until I really could not bear the two casts on the shelf above Mr. Jaggers's chair, and got up and went out.

When I told the clerk that I would take a turn in the air while I waited, he advised me to go round the corner and I should come into Smithfield. So I came into Smithfield; and the shameful place, being all asmear with filth and fat and blood and foam, seemed to stick to me. So, I rubbed it off with all possible speed by turning into a street where I saw the great black dome of Saint Paul's bulging at me from behind a grim stone building which a bystander said was Newgate Prison. Following the wall of the jail, I found the roadway covered with straw to deaden the noise of passing vehicles; and from this, and from the quantity of people standing about smelling strongly of spirits and beer, I inferred that the trials were on.

While I looked about me here, an exceedingly dirty and partially drunk minister of justice asked me if I would like to step in and hear a trial or so: informing me that he could give me a front place for half a crown, whence I should command a full view of the Lord Chief Justice in his wig and robes,—mentioning that awful personage like waxwork, and presently offering him at the reduced price of eighteen-pence. As I declined the proposal on the plea of an appointment, he was so good as to take me into a yard and show me where the gallows was kept, and also where people were publicly whipped, and then he showed me the Debtors' Door, out of which culprits came to be hanged; heightening the interest of that dreadful portal by giving me to understand that "four on 'em" would come out at that door the day after to-morrow at eight in the morning, to be killed in a row. This was horrible, and gave me a sickening idea of London; the more so as the Lord Chief Justice's proprietor wore (from his hat down to his boots and up again to his pocket-handkerchief inclusive) mildewed clothes which had evidently not belonged to him originally, and which I took it into my head he had bought cheap of the executioner. Under these circumstances I thought myself well rid of him for a shilling.

I dropped into the office to ask if Mr. Jaggers had come in yet, and I found he had not, and I strolled out again. This time, I made the tour of Little Britain, and turned into Bartholomew Close; and now I became aware that other people were waiting about for Mr. Jaggers, as well as I. There were two men of secret appearance lounging in Bartholomew Close, and thoughtfully fitting their feet into the cracks of the pavement as they talked together, one of whom said to the other when they first passed me, that "Jaggers would do it if it was to be done." There was a knot of three men and two women standing at a corner, and one of the women was crying on her dirty shawl, and the other comforted her by saying, as she pulled her own shawl over her shoulders, "Jaggers is for him, 'Melia, and what more could you have?" There was a red-eyed little Jew who came into the Close while I was loitering there, in company with a second little Jew whom he sent upon an errand; and while the messenger was gone, I remarked this Jew, who was of a highly excitable temperament, performing a jig of anxiety under a lamp-post and accompanying himself, in a kind of frenzy, with the words, "O Jaggerth, Jaggerth, Jaggerth! all otherth ith Cag-Maggerth, give me Jaggerth!" These testimonies to the popularity of my guardian made a deep impression on me, and I admired and wondered more than ever.

At length, as I was looking out at the iron gate of Bartholomew Close into Little Britain, I saw Mr. Jaggers coming across the road towards me. All the others who were waiting saw him at the same time, and there was quite a rush at him. Mr. Jaggers, putting a hand on my shoulder and walking me on at his side without saying anything to me, addressed himself to his followers.

First, he took the two secret men.

"Now, I have nothing to say to you," said Mr. Jaggers, throwing his finger at them. "I want to know no more than I know. As to the result, it's a toss-up. I told you from the first it was a toss-up. Have you paid Wemmick?"

"We made the money up this morning, sir," said one of the men, submissively, while the other perused Mr. Jaggers's face.

"I don't ask you when you made it up, or where, or whether you made it up at all. Has Wemmick got it?"

"Yes, sir," said both the men together.

"Very well; then you may go. Now, I won't have it!" said Mr Jaggers, waving his hand at them to put them behind him. "If you say a word to me, I'll throw up the case."

"We thought, Mr. Jaggers—" one of the men began, pulling off his hat.

"That's what I told you not to do," said Mr. Jaggers. "You thought! I think for you; that's enough for you. If I want you, I know where to find you; I don't want you to find me. Now I won't have it. I won't hear a word."

The two men looked at one another as Mr. Jaggers waved them behind again, and humbly fell back and were heard no more.

"And now you!" said Mr. Jaggers, suddenly stopping, and turning on the two women with the shawls, from whom the three men had meekly separated,—"Oh! Amelia, is it?"

"Yes, Mr. Jaggers."

"And do you remember," retorted Mr. Jaggers, "that but for me you wouldn't be here and couldn't be here?"

"O yes, sir!" exclaimed both women together. "Lord bless you, sir, well we knows that!"

"Then why," said Mr. Jaggers, "do you come here?"

"My Bill, sir!" the crying woman pleaded.

"Now, I tell you what!" said Mr. Jaggers. "Once for all. If you don't know that your Bill's in good hands, I know it. And if you come here bothering about your Bill, I'll make an example of both your Bill and you, and let him slip through my fingers. Have you paid Wemmick?"

"O yes, sir! Every farden."

"Very well. Then you have done all you have got to do. Say another word—one single word—and Wemmick shall give you your money back."

This terrible threat caused the two women to fall off immediately. No one remained now but the excitable Jew, who had already raised the skirts of Mr. Jaggers's coat to his lips several times.

"I don't know this man!" said Mr. Jaggers, in the same devastating strain: "What does this fellow want?"

"Ma thear Mithter Jaggerth. Hown brother to Habraham Latharuth?"

"Who's he?" said Mr. Jaggers. "Let go of my coat."

The suitor, kissing the hem of the garment again before relinquishing it, replied, "Habraham Latharuth, on thuthpithion of plate."

"You're too late," said Mr. Jaggers. "I am over the way."

"Holy father, Mithter Jaggerth!" cried my excitable acquaintance, turning white, "don't thay you're again Habraham Latharuth!"

"I am," said Mr. Jaggers, "and there's an end of it. Get out of the way."

"Mithter Jaggerth! Half a moment! My hown cuthen'th gone to Mithter Wemmick at thith prethent minute, to hoffer him hany termth. Mithter Jaggerth! Half a quarter of a moment! If you'd have the condethenthun to be bought off from the t'other thide—at hany thuperior prithe!—money no object!—Mithter Jaggerth—Mithter—!"

My guardian threw his supplicant off with supreme indifference, and left him dancing on the pavement as if it were red hot. Without further interruption, we reached the front office, where we found the clerk and the man in velveteen with the fur cap.

"Here's Mike," said the clerk, getting down from his stool, and approaching Mr. Jaggers confidentially.

"Oh!" said Mr. Jaggers, turning to the man, who was pulling a lock of hair in the middle of his forehead, like the Bull in Cock Robin pulling at the bell-rope; "your man comes on this afternoon. Well?"

"Well, Mas'r Jaggers," returned Mike, in the voice of a sufferer from a constitutional cold; "arter a deal o' trouble, I've found one, sir, as might do."

"What is he prepared to swear?"

"Well, Mas'r Jaggers," said Mike, wiping his nose on his fur cap this time; "in a general way, anythink."

Mr. Jaggers suddenly became most irate. "Now, I warned you before," said he, throwing his forefinger at the terrified client, "that if you ever presumed to talk in that way here, I'd make an example of you. You infernal scoundrel, how dare you tell ME that?"

The client looked scared, but bewildered too, as if he were unconscious what he had done.

"Spooney!" said the clerk, in a low voice, giving him a stir with his elbow. "Soft Head! Need you say it face to face?"

"Now, I ask you, you blundering booby," said my guardian, very sternly, "once more and for the last time, what the man you have brought here is prepared to swear?"

Mike looked hard at my guardian, as if he were trying to learn a lesson from his face, and slowly replied, "Ayther to character, or to having been in his company and never left him all the night in question."

"Now, be careful. In what station of life is this man?"

Mike looked at his cap, and looked at the floor, and looked at the ceiling, and looked at the clerk, and even looked at me, before beginning to reply in a nervous manner, "We've dressed him up like—" when my guardian blustered out,—

"What? You WILL, will you?"

("Spooney!" added the clerk again, with another stir.)

After some helpless casting about, Mike brightened and began again:—

"He is dressed like a 'spectable pieman. A sort of a pastry-cook."

"Is he here?" asked my guardian.

"I left him," said Mike, "a setting on some doorsteps round the corner."

"Take him past that window, and let me see him."

The window indicated was the office window. We all three went to it, behind the wire blind, and presently saw the client go by in an accidental manner, with a murderous-looking tall individual, in a short suit of white linen and a paper cap. This guileless confectioner was not by any means sober, and had a black eye in the green stage of recovery, which was painted over.

"Tell him to take his witness away directly," said my guardian to the clerk, in extreme disgust, "and ask him what he means by bringing such a fellow as that."

My guardian then took me into his own room, and while he lunched, standing, from a sandwich-box and a pocket-flask of sherry (he seemed to bully his very sandwich as he ate it), informed me what arrangements he had made for me. I was to go to "Barnard's Inn," to young Mr. Pocket's rooms, where a bed had been sent in for my accommodation; I was to remain with young Mr. Pocket until Monday; on Monday I was to go with him to his father's house on a visit, that I might try how I liked it. Also, I was told what my allowance was to be,—it was a very liberal one,—and had handed to me from one of my guardian's drawers, the cards of certain tradesmen with whom I was to deal for all kinds of clothes, and such other things as I could in reason want. "You will find your credit good, Mr. Pip," said my guardian, whose flask of sherry smelt like a whole caskful, as he hastily refreshed himself, "but I shall by this means be able to check your bills, and to pull you up if I find you outrunning the constable. Of course you'll go wrong somehow, but that's no fault of mine."

After I had pondered a little over this encouraging sentiment, I asked Mr. Jaggers if I could send for a coach? He said it was not worth while, I was so near my destination;

Wemmick should walk round with me, if I pleased.

I then found that Wemmick was the clerk in the next room. Another clerk was rung down from upstairs to take his place while he was out, and I accompanied him into the street, after shaking hands with my guardian. We found a new set of people lingering outside, but Wemmick made a way among them by saying coolly yet decisively, "I tell you it's no use; he won't have a word to say to one of you;" and we soon got clear of them, and went on side by side.

Chapter XXI

Casting my eyes on Mr. Wemmick as we went along, to see what he was like in the light of day, I found him to be a dry man, rather short in stature, with a square wooden face, whose expression seemed to have been imperfectly chipped out with a dull-edged chisel. There were some marks in it that might have been dimples, if the material had been softer and the instrument finer, but which, as it was, were only dints. The chisel had made three or four of these attempts at embellishment over his nose, but had given them up without an effort to smooth them off. I judged him to be a bachelor from the frayed condition of his linen, and he appeared to have sustained a good many bereavements; for he wore at least four mourning rings, besides a brooch representing a lady and a weeping willow at a tomb with an urn on it. I noticed, too, that several rings and seals hung at his watch-chain, as if he were quite laden with remembrances of departed friends. He had glittering eyes,—small, keen, and black,—and thin wide mottled lips. He had had them, to the best of my belief, from forty to fifty years.

"So you were never in London before?" said Mr. Wemmick to me.

"No," said I.

"I was new here once," said Mr. Wemmick. "Rum to think of now!"

"You are well acquainted with it now?"

"Why, yes," said Mr. Wemmick. "I know the moves of it."

"Is it a very wicked place?" I asked, more for the sake of saying something than for information.

"You may get cheated, robbed, and murdered in London. But there are plenty of people anywhere, who'll do that for you."

"If there is bad blood between you and them," said I, to soften it off a little.

"O! I don't know about bad blood," returned Mr. Wemmick; "there's not much bad blood about. They'll do it, if there's anything to be got by it."

"That makes it worse."

"You think so?" returned Mr. Wemmick. "Much about the same, I should say."

He wore his hat on the back of his head, and looked straight before him: walking in a self-contained way as if there were nothing in the streets to claim his attention. His mouth was such a post-office of a mouth that he had a mechanical appearance of smiling. We had got to the top of Holborn Hill before I knew that it was merely a mechanical appearance, and that he was not smiling at all.

"Do you know where Mr. Matthew Pocket lives?" I asked Mr. Wemmick.

"Yes," said he, nodding in the direction. "At Hammersmith, west of London."

"Is that far?"

"Well! Say five miles."

"Do you know him?"

"Why, you're a regular cross-examiner!" said Mr. Wemmick, looking at me with an approving air. "Yes, I know him. I know him!"

There was an air of toleration or depreciation about his utterance of these words that rather depressed me; and I was still looking sideways at his block of a face in search of any encouraging note to the text, when he said here we were at Barnard's Inn. My depression was not alleviated by the announcement, for, I had supposed that establishment to be an hotel kept by Mr. Barnard, to which the Blue Boar in our town was a mere public-house. Whereas I now found Barnard to be a disembodied spirit, or a fiction, and his inn the dingiest collection of shabby buildings ever squeezed together in a rank corner as a club for Tom-cats.

We entered this haven through a wicket-gate, and were disgorged by an introductory passage into a melancholy little square that looked to me like a flat burying-ground. I thought it had the most dismal trees in it, and the most dismal sparrows, and the most dismal cats, and the most dismal houses (in number half a dozen or so), that I had ever seen. I thought the windows of the sets of chambers into which those houses were divided were in every stage of dilapidated blind and curtain, crippled flower-pot, cracked glass, dusty decay, and miserable makeshift; while To Let, To Let, To Let, glared at me from empty rooms, as if no new wretches ever came there, and the vengeance of the soul of Barnard were being slowly appeased by the gradual suicide of the present occupants and their unholy interment under the gravel. A frowzy mourning of soot and smoke attired this forlorn creation of Barnard, and it had strewn ashes on its head, and was undergoing penance and humiliation as a mere dust-hole. Thus far my sense of sight; while dry rot and wet rot and all the silent rots that rot in neglected roof and cellar,—rot of rat and mouse and bug and coaching-stables near at hand besides—addressed themselves faintly to my sense of smell, and moaned, "Try Barnard's Mixture."

So imperfect was this realization of the first of my great expectations, that I looked in dismay at Mr. Wemmick. "Ah!" said he, mistaking me; "the retirement reminds you of the country. So it does me."

He led me into a corner and conducted me up a flight of stairs,—which appeared to me to be slowly collapsing into sawdust, so that one of those days the upper lodgers would look out at their doors and find themselves without the means of coming down,—to a set of chambers on the top floor. MR. POCKET, JUN., was painted on the door, and there was a label on the letter-box, "Return shortly."

"He hardly thought you'd come so soon," Mr. Wemmick explained. "You don't want me any more?"

"No, thank you," said I.

"As I keep the cash," Mr. Wemmick observed, "we shall most likely meet pretty often. Good day."

"Good day."

I put out my hand, and Mr. Wemmick at first looked at it as if he thought I wanted something. Then he looked at me, and said, correcting himself,—

"To be sure! Yes. You're in the habit of shaking hands?"

I was rather confused, thinking it must be out of the London fashion, but said yes.

"I have got so out of it!" said Mr. Wemmick,—"except at last. Very glad, I'm sure, to make your acquaintance. Good day!"

When we had shaken hands and he was gone, I opened the staircase window and had nearly beheaded myself, for, the lines had rotted away, and it came down like the guillotine. Happily it was so quick that I had not put my head out. After this escape, I was content to take a foggy view of the Inn through the window's encrusting dirt, and to stand dolefully looking out, saying to myself that London was decidedly overrated.

Mr. Pocket, Junior's, idea of Shortly was not mine, for I had nearly maddened myself with looking out for half an hour, and had written my name with my finger several times in the dirt of every pane in the window, before I heard footsteps on the stairs. Gradually there arose before me the hat, head, neckcloth, waistcoat, trousers, boots, of a member of society of about my own standing. He had a paper-bag under each arm and a pottle of strawberries in one hand, and was out of breath.

"Mr. Pip?" said he.

"Mr. Pocket?" said I.

"Dear me!" he exclaimed. "I am extremely sorry; but I knew there was a coach from your part of the country at midday, and I thought you would come by that one. The fact is, I have been out on your account,—not that that is any excuse,—for I thought, coming from the country, you might like a little fruit after dinner, and I went to Covent Garden Market to get it good."

For a reason that I had, I felt as if my eyes would start out of my head. I acknowledged his attention incoherently, and began to think this was a dream.

"Dear me!" said Mr. Pocket, Junior. "This door sticks so!"

As he was fast making jam of his fruit by wrestling with the door while the paper-bags were under his arms, I begged him to allow me to hold them. He relinquished them with an agreeable smile, and combated with the door as if it were a wild beast. It yielded so suddenly at last, that he staggered back upon me, and I staggered back upon the opposite door, and we both laughed. But still I felt as if my eyes must start out of my head, and as if this must be a dream.

"Pray come in," said Mr. Pocket, Junior. "Allow me to lead the way. I am rather bare here, but I hope you'll be able to make out tolerably well till Monday. My father thought you would get on more agreeably through to-morrow with me than with him, and might like to take a walk about London. I am sure I shall be very happy to show London to you. As to our table, you won't find that bad, I hope, for it will be supplied from our coffee-house here, and (it is only right I should add) at your expense, such being Mr. Jaggers's directions. As to our lodging, it's not by any means splendid, because I have my own bread to earn, and my father hasn't anything to give me, and I shouldn't be willing to take it, if he had. This is our sitting-room,—

just such chairs and tables and carpet and so forth, you see, as they could spare from home. You mustn't give me credit for the tablecloth and spoons and castors, because they come for you from the coffee-house. This is my little bedroom; rather musty, but Barnard's is musty. This is your bedroom; the furniture's hired for the occasion, but I trust it will answer the purpose; if you should want anything, I'll go and fetch it. The chambers are retired, and we shall be alone together, but we shan't fight, I dare say. But dear me, I beg your pardon, you're holding the fruit all this time. Pray let me take these bags from you. I am quite ashamed."

As I stood opposite to Mr. Pocket, Junior, delivering him the bags, One, Two, I saw the starting appearance come into his own eyes that I knew to be in mine, and he said, falling back,—

"Lord bless me, you're the prowling boy!"

"And you," said I, "are the pale young gentleman!"

Chapter XXII

The pale young gentleman and I stood contemplating one another in Barnard's Inn, until we both burst out laughing. "The idea of its being you!" said he. "The idea of its being you!" said I. And then we contemplated one another afresh, and laughed again. "Well!" said the pale young gentleman, reaching out his hand good-humoredly, "it's all over now, I hope, and it will be magnanimous in you if you'll forgive me for having knocked you about so."

I derived from this speech that Mr. Herbert Pocket (for Herbert was the pale young gentleman's name) still rather confounded his intention with his execution. But I made a modest reply, and we shook hands warmly.

"You hadn't come into your good fortune at that time?" said Herbert Pocket.

"No," said I.

"No," he acquiesced: "I heard it had happened very lately. I was rather on the lookout for good fortune then."

"Indeed?"

"Yes. Miss Havisham had sent for me, to see if she could take a fancy to me. But she couldn't,—at all events, she didn't."

I thought it polite to remark that I was surprised to hear that.

"Bad taste," said Herbert, laughing, "but a fact. Yes, she had sent for me on a trial visit, and if I had come out of it successfully, I suppose I should have been provided for; perhaps I should have been what-you-may-called it to Estella."

"What's that?" I asked, with sudden gravity.

He was arranging his fruit in plates while we talked, which divided his attention, and was the cause of his having made this lapse of a word. "Affianced," he explained, still busy with the fruit. "Betrothed. Engaged. What's-his-named. Any word of that sort."

"How did you bear your disappointment?" I asked.

"Pooh!" said he, "I didn't care much for it. She's a Tartar."

"Miss Havisham?"

"I don't say no to that, but I meant Estella. That girl's hard and haughty and capricious to the last degree, and has been brought up by Miss Havisham to wreak revenge on all the male sex."

"What relation is she to Miss Havisham?"

"None," said he. "Only adopted."

"Why should she wreak revenge on all the male sex? What revenge?"

"Lord, Mr. Pip!" said he. "Don't you know?"

"No," said I.

"Dear me! It's quite a story, and shall be saved till dinner-time. And now let me take the liberty of asking you a question. How did you come there, that day?"

I told him, and he was attentive until I had finished, and then burst out laughing again, and asked me if I was sore afterwards? I didn't ask him if he was, for my conviction on that point was perfectly established.

"Mr. Jaggers is your guardian, I understand?" he went on.

"Yes."

"You know he is Miss Havisham's man of business and solicitor, and has her confidence when nobody else has?"

This was bringing me (I felt) towards dangerous ground. I answered with a constraint I made no attempt to disguise, that I had seen Mr. Jaggers in Miss Havisham's house on the very day of our combat, but never at any other time, and that I believed he had no recollection of having ever seen me there.

"He was so obliging as to suggest my father for your tutor, and he called on my father to propose it. Of course he knew about my father from his connection with Miss Havisham. My father is Miss Havisham's cousin; not that that implies familiar intercourse between them, for he is a bad courtier and will not propitiate her."

Herbert Pocket had a frank and easy way with him that was very taking. I had never seen any one then, and I have never seen any one since, who more strongly expressed to me, in every look and tone, a natural incapacity to do anything secret and mean. There was something wonderfully hopeful about his general air, and something that at the same time whispered to me he would never be very successful or rich. I don't know how this was. I became imbued with the notion on that first occasion before we sat down to dinner, but I cannot define by what means.

He was still a pale young gentleman, and had a certain conquered languor about him in the midst of his spirits and briskness, that did not seem indicative of natural strength. He had not a handsome face, but it was better than handsome: being extremely amiable and cheerful. His figure was a little ungainly, as in the days when my knuckles had taken such liberties with it, but it looked as if it would always be light and young. Whether Mr. Trabb's local work would have sat more gracefully on him than on me, may be a question; but I am conscious that he carried off his rather old clothes much better than I carried off my new suit.

As he was so communicative, I felt that reserve on my part would be a bad return unsuited to our years. I therefore told him my small story, and laid stress on my being forbidden to inquire who my benefactor was. I further mentioned that as I had been brought up a blacksmith in a country place, and knew very little of the ways of politeness, I would take it as a great kindness in him if he would give me a hint whenever he saw me at a loss or going wrong.

"With pleasure," said he, "though I venture to prophesy that you'll want very few hints. I dare say we shall be often together, and I should like to banish any needless restraint between us. Will you do me the favour to begin at once to call me by my Christian name, Herbert?"

I thanked him and said I would. I informed him in exchange that my Christian name was Philip.

"I don't take to Philip," said he, smiling, "for it sounds like a moral boy out of the spelling-book, who was so lazy that he fell into a pond, or so fat that he couldn't see out of his eyes, or so avaricious that he locked up his cake till the mice ate it, or so determined to go a bird's-nesting that he got himself eaten by bears who lived handy in the neighborhood. I tell you what I should like. We are so harmonious, and you have been a blacksmith,—-would you mind it?"

"I shouldn't mind anything that you propose," I answered, "but I don't understand you."

"Would you mind Handel for a familiar name? There's a charming piece of music by Handel, called the Harmonious Blacksmith."

"I should like it very much."

"Then, my dear Handel," said he, turning round as the door opened, "here is the dinner, and I must beg of you to take the top of the table, because the dinner is of your providing."

This I would not hear of, so he took the top, and I faced him. It was a nice little dinner,— seemed to me then a very Lord Mayor's Feast,—and it acquired additional relish from being eaten under those independent circumstances, with no old people by, and with London all around us. This again was heightened by a certain gypsy character that set the banquet off; for while the table was, as Mr. Pumblechook might have said, the lap of luxury,—being entirely furnished forth from the coffee-house,—the circumjacent region of sitting-room was of a comparatively pastureless and shifty character; imposing on the waiter the wandering habits of putting the covers on the floor (where he fell over them), the melted butter in the arm-chair, the bread on the bookshelves, the cheese in the coal-scuttle, and the boiled fowl into my bed in the next room,—where I found much of its parsley and butter in a state of congelation when I retired for the night. All this made the feast delightful, and when the waiter was not there to watch me, my pleasure was without alloy.

We had made some progress in the dinner, when I reminded Herbert of his promise to tell me about Miss Havisham.

"True," he replied. "I'll redeem it at once. Let me introduce the topic, Handel, by mentioning that in London it is not the custom to put the knife in the mouth,—for fear of accidents,—and that while the fork is reserved for that use, it is not put further in than necessary. It is scarcely worth mentioning, only it's as well to do as other people do. Also, the spoon is not generally used over-hand, but under. This has two advantages. You get at your mouth better (which after all is the object), and you save a good deal of the attitude of opening oysters, on the part of the right elbow."

He offered these friendly suggestions in such a lively way, that we both laughed and I scarcely blushed.

"Now," he pursued, "concerning Miss Havisham. Miss Havisham, you must know, was a spoilt child. Her mother died when she was a baby, and her father denied her nothing. Her father was a country gentleman down in your part of the world, and was a brewer. I don't know why it should be a crack thing to be a brewer; but it is indisputable that while you cannot possibly be genteel and bake, you may be as genteel as never was and brew. You see it every day."

"Yet a gentleman may not keep a public-house; may he?" said I.

"Not on any account," returned Herbert; "but a public-house may keep a gentleman. Well! Mr. Havisham was very rich and very proud. So was his daughter."

"Miss Havisham was an only child?" I hazarded.

"Stop a moment, I am coming to that. No, she was not an only child; she had a half-brother. Her father privately married again—his cook, I rather think."

"I thought he was proud," said I.

"My good Handel, so he was. He married his second wife privately, because he was proud, and in course of time she died. When she was dead, I apprehend he first told his daughter what he had done, and then the son became a part of the family, residing in the house you are acquainted with. As the son grew a young man, he turned out riotous, extravagant, undutiful,—altogether bad. At last his father disinherited him; but he softened when he was dying, and left him well off, though not nearly so well off as Miss Havisham.—Take another glass of wine, and excuse my mentioning that society as a body does not expect one to be so strictly conscientious in emptying one's glass, as to turn it bottom upwards with the rim on one's nose."

I had been doing this, in an excess of attention to his recital. I thanked him, and apologized. He said, "Not at all," and resumed.

"Miss Havisham was now an heiress, and you may suppose was looked after as a great match. Her half-brother had now ample means again, but what with debts and what with new madness wasted them most fearfully again. There were stronger differences between him and her than there had been between him and his father, and it is suspected that he cherished a deep and mortal grudge against her as having influenced the father's anger. Now, I come to the cruel part of the story,—merely breaking off, my dear Handel, to remark that a dinner-napkin will not go into a tumbler."

Why I was trying to pack mine into my tumbler, I am wholly unable to say. I only know that I found myself, with a perseverance worthy of a much better cause, making the most strenuous exertions to compress it within those limits. Again I thanked him and apologized, and again he said in the cheerfullest manner, "Not at all, I am sure!" and resumed.

"There appeared upon the scene—say at the races, or the public balls, or anywhere else you like—a certain man, who made love to Miss Havisham. I never saw him (for this happened five-and-twenty years ago, before you and I were, Handel), but I have heard my father mention that he was a showy man, and the kind of man for the purpose. But that he was not to be, without ignorance or prejudice, mistaken for a gentleman, my father most strongly asseverates; because it is a principle of his that no man who was not a true gentleman at heart ever was, since the world began, a true gentleman in manner. He says, no varnish can hide the grain of the wood; and that the more varnish you put on, the more the grain will express itself. Well! This man pursued Miss Havisham closely, and professed to be devoted to her. I believe she had not shown much susceptibility up to that time; but all the susceptibility she possessed certainly came out then, and she passionately loved him. There is no doubt that she perfectly idolized him. He practised on her affection in that systematic way, that he got great sums of money from her, and he induced her to buy her brother out of a share in the brewery (which had been weakly left him by his father) at an immense price, on the plea that when he was her husband he must hold and manage it all. Your guardian was not at that time in Miss Havisham's counsels, and she was too haughty and too much in love to be advised by any one. Her relations were poor and scheming, with the exception of my father; he was poor enough, but not time-serving or jealous. The only independent one among them, he warned her that she was doing too much for this man, and was placing herself too unreservedly in his power. She took the first opportunity of angrily ordering my father out of the house, in his presence, and my father has never seen her since."

I thought of her having said, "Matthew will come and see me at last when I am laid dead upon that table;" and I asked Herbert whether his father was so inveterate against her?

"It's not that," said he, "but she charged him, in the presence of her intended husband, with being disappointed in the hope of fawning upon her for his own advancement, and, if he were to go to her now, it would look true—even to him—and even to her. To return to the man and make an end of him. The marriage day was fixed, the wedding dresses were bought, the wedding tour was planned out, the wedding guests were invited. The day came, but not the bridegroom. He wrote her a letter—"

"Which she received," I struck in, "when she was dressing for her marriage? At twenty minutes to nine?"

"At the hour and minute," said Herbert, nodding, "at which she afterwards stopped all the clocks. What was in it, further than that it most heartlessly broke the marriage off, I can't tell you, because I don't know. When she recovered from a bad illness that she had, she laid the whole place waste, as you have seen it, and she has never since looked upon the light of day."

"Is that all the story?" I asked, after considering it.

"All I know of it; and indeed I only know so much, through piecing it out for myself; for my father always avoids it, and, even when Miss Havisham invited me to go there, told me no more of it than it was absolutely requisite I should understand. But I have forgotten one thing. It has been supposed that the man to whom she gave her misplaced confidence acted throughout in concert with her half-brother; that it was a conspiracy between them; and that they shared the profits."

"I wonder he didn't marry her and get all the property," said I.

"He may have been married already, and her cruel mortification may have been a part of her half-brother's scheme," said Herbert. "Mind! I don't know that."

"What became of the two men?" I asked, after again considering the subject.

"They fell into deeper shame and degradation—if there can be deeper—and ruin."

"Are they alive now?"

"I don't know."

"You said just now that Estella was not related to Miss Havisham, but adopted. When adopted?"

Herbert shrugged his shoulders. "There has always been an Estella, since I have heard of a Miss Havisham. I know no more. And now, Handel," said he, finally throwing off the story as it were, "there is a perfectly open understanding between us. All that I know about Miss Havisham, you know."

"And all that I know," I retorted, "you know."

"I fully believe it. So there can be no competition or perplexity between you and me. And as to the condition on which you hold your advancement in life,—namely, that you are not to inquire or discuss to whom you owe it,—you may be very sure that it will never be encroached upon, or even approached, by me, or by any one belonging to me."

In truth, he said this with so much delicacy, that I felt the subject done with, even though I should be under his father's roof for years and years to come. Yet he said it with so much meaning, too, that I felt he as perfectly understood Miss Havisham to be my benefactress, as I understood the fact myself.

It had not occurred to me before, that he had led up to the theme for the purpose of clearing it out of our way; but we were so much the lighter and easier for having broached it, that I now perceived this to be the case. We were very gay and sociable, and I asked him, in the course of conversation, what he was? He replied, "A capitalist,—an Insurer of Ships." I suppose he saw me glancing about the room in search of some tokens of Shipping, or capital, for he added, "In the City."

I had grand ideas of the wealth and importance of Insurers of Ships in the City, and I began to think with awe of having laid a young Insurer on his back, blackened his enterprising eye, and cut his responsible head open. But again there came upon me, for my relief, that odd impression that Herbert Pocket would never be very successful or rich.

"I shall not rest satisfied with merely employing my capital in insuring ships. I shall buy up some good Life Assurance shares, and cut into the Direction. I shall also do a little in the mining way. None of these things will interfere with my chartering a few thousand tons on my own account. I think I shall trade," said he, leaning back in his chair, "to the East Indies, for silks, shawls, spices, dyes, drugs, and precious woods. It's an interesting trade."

"And the profits are large?" said I.

"Tremendous!" said he.

I wavered again, and began to think here were greater expectations than my own.

"I think I shall trade, also," said he, putting his thumbs in his waist-coat pockets, "to the West Indies, for sugar, tobacco, and rum. Also to Ceylon, specially for elephants' tusks."

"You will want a good many ships," said I.

"A perfect fleet," said he.

Quite overpowered by the magnificence of these transactions, I asked him where the ships he insured mostly traded to at present?

"I haven't begun insuring yet," he replied. "I am looking about me."

Somehow, that pursuit seemed more in keeping with Barnard's Inn. I said (in a tone of conviction), "Ah-h!"

"Yes. I am in a counting-house, and looking about me."

"Is a counting-house profitable?" I asked.

"To—do you mean to the young fellow who's in it?" he asked, in reply.

"Yes; to you."

"Why, n-no; not to me." He said this with the air of one carefully reckoning up and striking a balance. "Not directly profitable. That is, it doesn't pay me anything, and I have to—keep myself."

This certainly had not a profitable appearance, and I shook my head as if I would imply that it would be difficult to lay by much accumulative capital from such a source of income.

"But the thing is," said Herbert Pocket, "that you look about you. That's the grand thing. You are in a counting-house, you know, and you look about you."

It struck me as a singular implication that you couldn't be out of a counting-house, you know, and look about you; but I silently deferred to his experience.

"Then the time comes," said Herbert, "when you see your opening. And you go in, and you swoop upon it and you make your capital, and then there you are! When you have once made your capital, you have nothing to do but employ it."

This was very like his way of conducting that encounter in the garden; very like. His manner of bearing his poverty, too, exactly corresponded to his manner of bearing that defeat. It seemed to me that he took all blows and buffets now with just the same air as he had taken mine then. It was evident that he had nothing around him but the simplest necessaries, for everything that I remarked upon turned out to have been sent in on my account from the coffee-house or somewhere else.

Yet, having already made his fortune in his own mind, he was so unassuming with it that I felt quite grateful to him for not being puffed up. It was a pleasant addition to his naturally pleasant ways, and we got on famously. In the evening we went out for a walk in the streets, and went half-price to the Theatre; and next day we went to church at Westminster Abbey, and in the afternoon we walked in the Parks; and I wondered who shod all the horses there, and wished Joe did.

On a moderate computation, it was many months, that Sunday, since I had left Joe and Biddy. The space interposed between myself and them partook of that expansion, and our marshes were any distance off. That I could have been at our old church in my old church-going clothes, on the very last Sunday that ever was, seemed a combination of impossibilities, geographical and social, solar and lunar. Yet in the London streets so crowded with people and so brilliantly lighted in the dusk of evening, there were depressing hints of reproaches for that I had put the poor old kitchen at home so far away; and in the dead of night, the footsteps of some incapable impostor of a porter mooning about Barnard's Inn, under pretence of watching it, fell hollow on my heart.

On the Monday morning at a quarter before nine, Herbert went to the counting-house to report himself,—to look about him, too, I suppose,—and I bore him company. He was to come away in an hour or two to attend me to Hammersmith, and I was to wait about for him. It appeared to me that the eggs from which young Insurers were hatched were incubated in dust and heat, like the eggs of ostriches, judging from the places to which those incipient giants repaired on a Monday morning. Nor did the counting-house where Herbert assisted, show in my eyes as at all a good Observatory; being a back second floor up a yard, of a grimy presence in all particulars, and with a look into another back second floor, rather than a look out.

I waited about until it was noon, and I went upon 'Change, and I saw fluey men sitting there under the bills about shipping, whom I took to be great merchants, though I couldn't understand why they should all be out of spirits. When Herbert came, we went and had lunch at a celebrated house which I then quite venerated, but now believe to have been the most abject superstition in Europe, and where I could not help noticing, even then, that there was much more gravy on the tablecloths and knives and waiters' clothes, than in the steaks. This collation disposed of at a moderate price (considering the grease, which was not charged for), we went back to Barnard's Inn and got my little portmanteau, and then took coach for Hammersmith. We arrived there at two or three o'clock in the afternoon, and had very little way to walk to Mr. Pocket's house. Lifting the latch of a gate, we passed direct into a little garden overlooking the river, where Mr. Pocket's children were playing about. And unless I deceive myself on a point where my interests or prepossessions are certainly not concerned, I saw that Mr. and Mrs. Pocket's children were not growing up or being brought up, but were tumbling up.

Mrs. Pocket was sitting on a garden chair under a tree, reading, with her legs upon another garden chair; and Mrs. Pocket's two nurse-maids were looking about them while the children played. "Mamma," said Herbert, "this is young Mr. Pip." Upon which Mrs. Pocket received me with an appearance of amiable dignity.

"Master Alick and Miss Jane," cried one of the nurses to two of the children, "if you go a bouncing up against them bushes you'll fall over into the river and be drownded, and what'll your pa say then?"

At the same time this nurse picked up Mrs. Pocket's handkerchief, and said, "If that don't make six times you've dropped it, Mum!" Upon which Mrs. Pocket laughed and said, "Thank you, Flopson," and settling herself in one chair only, resumed her book. Her countenance immediately assumed a knitted and intent expression as if she had been reading for a week, but before she could have read half a dozen lines, she fixed her eyes upon me, and said, "I hope your mamma is quite well?" This unexpected inquiry put me into such a difficulty that I began saying in the absurdest way that if there had been any such person I had no doubt she would have been quite well and would have been very much obliged and would have sent her compliments, when the nurse came to my rescue.

"Well!" she cried, picking up the pocket-handkerchief, "if that don't make seven times! What ARE you a doing of this afternoon, Mum!" Mrs. Pocket received her property, at first with a look of unutterable surprise as if she had never seen it before, and then with a laugh of recognition, and said, "Thank you, Flopson," and forgot me, and went on reading.

I found, now I had leisure to count them, that there were no fewer than six little Pockets present, in various stages of tumbling up. I had scarcely arrived at the total when a seventh was heard, as in the region of air, wailing dolefully.

"If there ain't Baby!" said Flopson, appearing to think it most surprising. "Make haste up, Millers."

Millers, who was the other nurse, retired into the house, and by degrees the child's wailing was hushed and stopped, as if it were a young ventriloquist with something in its mouth. Mrs. Pocket read all the time, and I was curious to know what the book could be.

We were waiting, I supposed, for Mr. Pocket to come out to us; at any rate we waited there, and so I had an opportunity of observing the remarkable family phenomenon that whenever any of the children strayed near Mrs. Pocket in their play, they always tripped themselves up and tumbled over her,—always very much to her momentary astonishment, and their own more enduring lamentation. I was at a loss to account for this surprising circumstance, and could not help giving my mind to speculations about it, until by and by Millers came down with the baby, which baby was handed to Flopson, which Flopson was handing it to Mrs. Pocket, when she too went fairly head foremost over Mrs. Pocket, baby and all, and was caught by Herbert and myself.

"Gracious me, Flopson!" said Mrs. Pocket, looking off her book for a moment, "everybody's tumbling!"

"Gracious you, indeed, Mum!" returned Flopson, very red in the face; "what have you got there?"

"I got here, Flopson?" asked Mrs. Pocket.

"Why, if it ain't your footstool!" cried Flopson. "And if you keep it under your skirts like that, who's to help tumbling? Here! Take the baby, Mum, and give me your book."

Mrs. Pocket acted on the advice, and inexpertly danced the infant a little in her lap, while the other children played about it. This had lasted but a very short time, when Mrs. Pocket issued summary orders that they were all to be taken into the house for a nap. Thus I made the second discovery on that first occasion, that the nurture of the little Pockets consisted of alternately tumbling up and lying down.

Under these circumstances, when Flopson and Millers had got the children into the house, like a little flock of sheep, and Mr. Pocket came out of it to make my acquaintance, I was not much surprised to find that Mr. Pocket was a gentleman with a rather perplexed expression of face, and with his very gray hair disordered on his head, as if he didn't quite see his way to putting anything straight.

Chapter XXIII

Mr. Pocket said he was glad to see me, and he hoped I was not sorry to see him. "For, I really am not," he added, with his son's smile, "an alarming personage." He was a young-looking man, in spite of his perplexities and his very gray hair, and his manner seemed quite natural. I use the word natural, in the sense of its being unaffected; there was something comic in his distraught way, as though it would have been downright ludicrous but for his own perception that it was very near being so. When he had talked with me a little, he said to Mrs. Pocket, with a rather anxious contraction of his eyebrows, which were black and handsome, "Belinda, I hope you have welcomed Mr. Pip?" And she looked up from her book, and said, "Yes." She then smiled upon me in an absent state of mind, and asked me if I liked the taste of orange-flower water? As the question had no bearing, near or remote, on any foregone or subsequent transaction, I consider it to have been thrown out, like her previous approaches, in general conversational condescension.

I found out within a few hours, and may mention at once, that Mrs. Pocket was the only daughter of a certain quite accidental deceased Knight, who had invented for himself a conviction that his deceased father would have been made a Baronet but for somebody's determined opposition arising out of entirely personal motives,—I forget whose, if I ever knew,—the Sovereign's, the Prime Minister's, the Lord Chancellor's, the Archbishop of Canterbury's, anybody's,—and had tacked himself on to the nobles of the earth in right of this quite supposititious fact. I believe he had been knighted himself for storming the English grammar at the point of the pen, in a desperate address engrossed on vellum, on the occasion of the laying of the first stone of some building or other, and for handing some Royal Personage either the trowel or the mortar. Be that as it may, he had directed Mrs. Pocket to be brought up from her cradle as one who in the nature of things must marry a title, and who was to be guarded from the acquisition of plebeian domestic knowledge.

So successful a watch and ward had been established over the young lady by this judicious parent, that she had grown up highly ornamental, but perfectly helpless and useless. With her character thus happily formed, in the first bloom of her youth she had encountered Mr. Pocket: who was also in the first bloom of youth, and not quite decided whether to mount to the Woolsack, or to roof himself in with a mitre. As his doing the one or the other was a mere question of time, he and Mrs. Pocket had taken Time by the forelock (when, to judge from its length, it would seem to have wanted cutting), and had married without the knowledge of the judicious parent. The judicious parent, having nothing to bestow or withhold but his blessing, had handsomely settled that dower upon them after a short struggle, and had informed Mr. Pocket that his wife was "a treasure for a Prince." Mr. Pocket had invested the Prince's treasure in the ways of the world ever since, and it was supposed to have brought him in but indifferent interest. Still, Mrs. Pocket was in general the object of a queer sort of respectful pity, because she had not married a title; while Mr. Pocket was the object of a queer sort of forgiving reproach, because he had never got one.

Mr. Pocket took me into the house and showed me my room: which was a pleasant one, and so furnished as that I could use it with comfort for my own private sitting-room. He then knocked at the doors of two other similar rooms, and introduced me to their occupants, by name Drummle and Startop. Drummle, an old-looking young man of a heavy order of architecture, was whistling. Startop, younger in years and appearance, was reading and holding his head, as if he thought himself in danger of exploding it with too strong a charge of knowledge.

Both Mr. and Mrs. Pocket had such a noticeable air of being in somebody else's hands, that I wondered who really was in possession of the house and let them live there, until I found this unknown power to be the servants. It was a smooth way of going on, perhaps, in respect of saving trouble; but it had the appearance of being expensive, for the servants felt it a duty they owed to themselves to be nice in their eating and drinking, and to keep a deal of company downstairs. They allowed a very liberal table to Mr. and Mrs. Pocket, yet it always appeared to me that by far the best part of the house to have boarded in would have been the kitchen,—always supposing the boarder capable of self-defence, for, before I had been there a week, a neighboring lady with whom the family were personally unacquainted, wrote in to say that she had seen Millers slapping the baby. This greatly distressed Mrs. Pocket, who burst into tears on receiving the note, and said that it was an extraordinary thing that the neighbors couldn't mind their own business.

By degrees I learnt, and chiefly from Herbert, that Mr. Pocket had been educated at Harrow and at Cambridge, where he had distinguished himself; but that when he had had the happiness of marrying Mrs. Pocket very early in life, he had impaired his prospects and taken up the calling of a Grinder. After grinding a number of dull blades,—of whom it was remarkable that their fathers, when influential, were always going to help him to preferment, but always forgot to do it when the blades had left the Grindstone,—he had wearied of that poor work and had come to London. Here, after gradually failing in loftier hopes, he had "read" with divers who had lacked opportunities or neglected them, and had refurbished divers others for special occasions, and had turned his acquirements to the account of literary compilation and correction, and on such means, added to some very moderate private resources, still maintained the house I saw.

Mr. and Mrs. Pocket had a toady neighbor; a widow lady of that highly sympathetic nature that she agreed with everybody, blessed everybody, and shed smiles and tears on everybody, according to circumstances. This lady's name was Mrs. Coiler, and I had the honor of taking her down to dinner on the day of my installation. She gave me to understand on the stairs, that it was a blow to dear Mrs. Pocket that dear Mr. Pocket should be under the necessity of receiving gentlemen to read with him. That did not extend to me, she told me in a gush of love and confidence (at that time, I had known her something less than five minutes); if they were all like Me, it would be quite another thing.

"But dear Mrs. Pocket," said Mrs. Coiler, "after her early disappointment (not that dear Mr. Pocket was to blame in that), requires so much luxury and elegance—"

"Yes, ma'am," I said, to stop her, for I was afraid she was going to cry.

"And she is of so aristocratic a disposition—"

"Yes, ma'am," I said again, with the same object as before.

"—That it is hard," said Mrs. Coiler, "to have dear Mr. Pocket's time and attention diverted from dear Mrs. Pocket."

I could not help thinking that it might be harder if the butcher's time and attention were diverted from dear Mrs. Pocket; but I said nothing, and indeed had enough to do in keeping a bashful watch upon my company manners.

It came to my knowledge, through what passed between Mrs. Pocket and Drummle while I was attentive to my knife and fork, spoon, glasses, and other instruments of self-destruction, that Drummle, whose Christian name was Bentley, was actually the next heir but one to a baronetcy. It further appeared that the book I had seen Mrs. Pocket reading in the garden was all about titles, and that she knew the exact date at which her grandpapa would have come into the book, if he ever had come at all. Drummle didn't say much, but in his limited way (he struck me as a sulky kind of fellow) he spoke as one of the elect, and recognized Mrs. Pocket as a woman and a sister. No one but themselves and Mrs. Coiler the toady neighbor showed any interest in this part of the conversation, and it appeared to me that it was painful to Herbert; but it promised to last a long time, when the page came in with the announcement of a domestic affliction. It was, in effect, that the cook had mislaid the beef. To my unutterable amazement, I now, for the first time, saw Mr. Pocket relieve his mind by going through a performance that struck me as very extraordinary, but which made no impression on anybody else, and with which I soon became as familiar as the rest. He laid down the carving-knife and fork,—being engaged in carving, at the moment,—put his two hands into his disturbed hair, and appeared to make an extraordinary effort to lift himself up by it. When he had done this, and had not lifted himself up at all, he quietly went on with what he was about.

Mrs. Coiler then changed the subject and began to flatter me. I liked it for a few moments, but she flattered me so very grossly that the pleasure was soon over. She had a serpentine way of coming close at me when she pretended to be vitally interested in the friends and localities I had left, which was altogether snaky and fork-tongued; and when she made an occasional bounce upon Startop (who said very little to her), or upon Drummle (who said less), I rather envied them for being on the opposite side of the table.

After dinner the children were introduced, and Mrs. Coiler made admiring comments on their eyes, noses, and legs,—a sagacious way of improving their minds. There were four little girls, and two little boys, besides the baby who might have been either, and the baby's next successor who was as yet neither. They were brought in by Flopson and Millers, much as though those two non-commissioned officers had been recruiting somewhere for children and had enlisted these, while Mrs. Pocket looked at the young Nobles that ought to have been as if she rather thought she had had the pleasure of inspecting them before, but didn't quite know what to make of them.

"Here! Give me your fork, Mum, and take the baby," said Flopson. "Don't take it that way, or you'll get its head under the table."

Thus advised, Mrs. Pocket took it the other way, and got its head upon the table; which was announced to all present by a prodigious concussion.

"Dear, dear! Give it me back, Mum," said Flopson; "and Miss Jane, come and dance to baby, do!"

One of the little girls, a mere mite who seemed to have prematurely taken upon herself some charge of the others, stepped out of her place by me, and danced to and from the baby until it left off crying, and laughed. Then, all the children laughed, and Mr. Pocket (who in the meantime had twice endeavored to lift himself up by the hair) laughed, and we all laughed and were glad.

Flopson, by dint of doubling the baby at the joints like a Dutch doll, then got it safely into Mrs. Pocket's lap, and gave it the nut-crackers to play with; at the same time recommending Mrs. Pocket to take notice that the handles of that instrument were not likely to agree with its eyes, and sharply charging Miss Jane to look after the same. Then, the two nurses left the room, and had a lively scuffle on the staircase with a dissipated page who had waited at dinner, and who had clearly lost half his buttons at the gaming-table.

I was made very uneasy in my mind by Mrs. Pocket's falling into a discussion with Drummle respecting two baronetcies, while she ate a sliced orange steeped in sugar and wine, and, forgetting all about the baby on her lap, who did most appalling things with the nut-crackers. At length little Jane, perceiving its young brains to be imperilled, softly left her place, and with many small artifices coaxed the dangerous weapon away. Mrs. Pocket finishing her orange at about the same time, and not approving of this, said to Jane,—

"You naughty child, how dare you? Go and sit down this instant!"

"Mamma dear," lisped the little girl, "baby ood have put hith eyeth out."

"How dare you tell me so?" retorted Mrs. Pocket. "Go and sit down in your chair this moment!"

Mrs. Pocket's dignity was so crushing, that I felt quite abashed, as if I myself had done something to rouse it.

"Belinda," remonstrated Mr. Pocket, from the other end of the table, "how can you be so unreasonable? Jane only interfered for the protection of baby."

"I will not allow anybody to interfere," said Mrs. Pocket. "I am surprised, Matthew, that you should expose me to the affront of interference."

"Good God!" cried Mr. Pocket, in an outbreak of desolate desperation. "Are infants to be nut-crackered into their tombs, and is nobody to save them?"

"I will not be interfered with by Jane," said Mrs. Pocket, with a majestic glance at that innocent little offender. "I hope I know my poor grandpapa's position. Jane, indeed!"

Mr. Pocket got his hands in his hair again, and this time really did lift himself some inches out of his chair. "Hear this!" he helplessly exclaimed to the elements. "Babies are to be nut-crackered dead, for people's poor grandpapa's positions!" Then he let himself down again, and became silent.

We all looked awkwardly at the tablecloth while this was going on. A pause succeeded, during which the honest and irrepressible baby made a series of leaps and crows at little Jane, who appeared to me to be the only member of the family (irrespective of servants) with whom it had any decided acquaintance.

"Mr. Drummle," said Mrs. Pocket, "will you ring for Flopson? Jane, you undutiful little thing, go and lie down. Now, baby darling, come with ma!"

The baby was the soul of honor, and protested with all its might. It doubled itself up the wrong way over Mrs. Pocket's arm, exhibited a pair of knitted shoes and dimpled ankles to the company in lieu of its soft face, and was carried out in the highest state of mutiny. And it gained its point after all, for I saw it through the window within a few minutes, being nursed by little Jane.

It happened that the other five children were left behind at the dinner-table, through Flopson's having some private engagement, and their not being anybody else's business. I thus became aware of the mutual relations between them and Mr. Pocket, which were exemplified in the following manner. Mr. Pocket, with the normal perplexity of his face heightened and his hair rumpled, looked at them for some minutes, as if he couldn't make out how they came to be boarding and lodging in that establishment, and why they hadn't been billeted by Nature on somebody else. Then, in a distant Missionary way he asked them certain questions,—as why little Joe had that hole in his frill, who said, Pa, Flopson was going to mend it when she had time,—and how little Fanny came by that whitlow, who said, Pa, Millers was going to poultice it when she didn't forget. Then, he melted into parental tenderness, and gave them a shilling apiece and told them to go and play; and then as they went out, with one very strong effort to lift himself up by the hair he dismissed the hopeless subject.

In the evening there was rowing on the river. As Drummle and Startop had each a boat, I resolved to set up mine, and to cut them both out. I was pretty good at most exercises in which country boys are adepts, but as I was conscious of wanting elegance of style for the Thames,— not to say for other waters,—I at once engaged to place myself under the tuition of the winner of a prize-wherry who plied at our stairs, and to whom I was introduced by my new allies. This practical authority confused me very much by saying I had the arm of a blacksmith. If he could have known how nearly the compliment lost him his pupil, I doubt if he would have paid it.

There was a supper-tray after we got home at night, and I think we should all have enjoyed ourselves, but for a rather disagreeable domestic occurrence. Mr. Pocket was in good spirits, when a housemaid came in, and said, "If you please, sir, I should wish to speak to you."

"Speak to your master?" said Mrs. Pocket, whose dignity was roused again. "How can you think of such a thing? Go and speak to Flopson. Or speak to me—at some other time."

"Begging your pardon, ma'am," returned the housemaid, "I should wish to speak at once, and to speak to master."

Hereupon, Mr. Pocket went out of the room, and we made the best of ourselves until he came back.

"This is a pretty thing, Belinda!" said Mr. Pocket, returning with a countenance expressive of grief and despair. "Here's the cook lying insensibly drunk on the kitchen floor, with a large bundle of fresh butter made up in the cupboard ready to sell for grease!"

Mrs. Pocket instantly showed much amiable emotion, and said, "This is that odious Sophia's doing!"

"What do you mean, Belinda?" demanded Mr. Pocket.

"Sophia has told you," said Mrs. Pocket. "Did I not see her with my own eyes and hear her with my own ears, come into the room just now and ask to speak to you?"

"But has she not taken me downstairs, Belinda," returned Mr. Pocket, "and shown me the woman, and the bundle too?"

"And do you defend her, Matthew," said Mrs. Pocket, "for making mischief?"

Mr. Pocket uttered a dismal groan.

"Am I, grandpapa's granddaughter, to be nothing in the house?" said Mrs. Pocket. "Besides, the cook has always been a very nice respectful woman, and said in the most natural manner when she came to look after the situation, that she felt I was born to be a Duchess."

There was a sofa where Mr. Pocket stood, and he dropped upon it in the attitude of the Dying Gladiator. Still in that attitude he said, with a hollow voice, "Good night, Mr. Pip," when I deemed it advisable to go to bed and leave him.

Chapter XXIV

After two or three days, when I had established myself in my room and had gone backwards and forwards to London several times, and had ordered all I wanted of my tradesmen, Mr. Pocket and I had a long talk together. He knew more of my intended career than I knew myself, for he referred to his having been told by Mr. Jaggers that I was not designed for any profession, and that I should be well enough educated for my destiny if I could "hold my own" with the average of young men in prosperous circumstances. I acquiesced, of course, knowing nothing to the contrary.

He advised my attending certain places in London, for the acquisition of such mere rudiments as I wanted, and my investing him with the functions of explainer and director of all my studies. He hoped that with intelligent assistance I should meet with little to discourage me, and should soon be able to dispense with any aid but his. Through his way of saying this, and much more to similar purpose, he placed himself on confidential terms with me in an admirable manner; and I may state at once that he was always so zealous and honorable in fulfilling his compact with me, that he made me zealous and honorable in fulfilling mine with him. If he had shown indifference as a master, I have no doubt I should have returned the compliment as a pupil; he gave me no such excuse, and each of us did the other justice. Nor did I ever regard him as having anything ludicrous about him—or anything but what was serious, honest, and good—in his tutor communication with me.

When these points were settled, and so far carried out as that I had begun to work in earnest, it occurred to me that if I could retain my bedroom in Barnard's Inn, my life would be agreeably varied, while my manners would be none the worse for Herbert's society. Mr. Pocket did not object to this arrangement, but urged that before any step could possibly be taken in it, it must be submitted to my guardian. I felt that this delicacy arose out of the consideration that the plan would save Herbert some expense, so I went off to Little Britain and imparted my wish to Mr. Jaggers.

"If I could buy the furniture now hired for me," said I, "and one or two other little things, I should be quite at home there."

"Go it!" said Mr. Jaggers, with a short laugh. "I told you you'd get on. Well! How much do you want?"

I said I didn't know how much.

"Come!" retorted Mr. Jaggers. "How much? Fifty pounds?"

"O, not nearly so much."

"Five pounds?" said Mr. Jaggers.

This was such a great fall, that I said in discomfiture, "O, more than that."

"More than that, eh!" retorted Mr. Jaggers, lying in wait for me, with his hands in his pockets, his head on one side, and his eyes on the wall behind me; "how much more?"

"It is so difficult to fix a sum," said I, hesitating.

"Come!" said Mr. Jaggers. "Let's get at it. Twice five; will that do? Three times five; will that do? Four times five; will that do?"

I said I thought that would do handsomely.

"Four times five will do handsomely, will it?" said Mr. Jaggers, knitting his brows. "Now, what do you make of four times five?"

"What do I make of it?"

"Ah!" said Mr. Jaggers; "how much?"

"I suppose you make it twenty pounds," said I, smiling.

"Never mind what I make it, my friend," observed Mr. Jaggers, with a knowing and contradictory toss of his head. "I want to know what you make it."

"Twenty pounds, of course."

"Wemmick!" said Mr. Jaggers, opening his office door. "Take Mr. Pip's written order, and pay him twenty pounds."

This strongly marked way of doing business made a strongly marked impression on me, and that not of an agreeable kind. Mr. Jaggers never laughed; but he wore great bright creaking boots, and, in poising himself on these boots, with his large head bent down and his eyebrows joined together, awaiting an answer, he sometimes caused the boots to creak, as if they laughed in a dry and suspicious way. As he happened to go out now, and as Wemmick was brisk and talkative, I said to Wemmick that I hardly knew what to make of Mr. Jaggers's manner.

"Tell him that, and he'll take it as a compliment," answered Wemmick; "he don't mean that you should know what to make of it.—Oh!" for I looked surprised, "it's not personal; it's professional: only professional."

Wemmick was at his desk, lunching—and crunching—on a dry hard biscuit; pieces of which he threw from time to time into his slit of a mouth, as if he were posting them.

"Always seems to me," said Wemmick, "as if he had set a man-trap and was watching it. Suddenly-click—you're caught!"

Without remarking that man-traps were not among the amenities of life, I said I supposed he was very skilful?

"Deep," said Wemmick, "as Australia." Pointing with his pen at the office floor, to express that Australia was understood, for the purposes of the figure, to be symmetrically on the opposite spot of the globe. "If there was anything deeper," added Wemmick, bringing his pen to paper, "he'd be it."

Then, I said I supposed he had a fine business, and Wemmick said, "Ca-pi-tal!" Then I asked if there were many clerks? to which he replied,—

"We don't run much into clerks, because there's only one Jaggers, and people won't have him at second hand. There are only four of us. Would you like to see 'em? You are one of us, as I may say."

I accepted the offer. When Mr. Wemmick had put all the biscuit into the post, and had paid me my money from a cash-box in a safe, the key of which safe he kept somewhere down his back and produced from his coat-collar like an iron-pigtail, we went upstairs. The house was dark and shabby, and the greasy shoulders that had left their mark in Mr. Jaggers's room seemed to have been shuffling up and down the staircase for years. In the front first floor, a clerk who looked something between a publican and a rat-catcher—a large pale, puffed, swollen man—was attentively engaged with three or four people of shabby appearance, whom he treated as unceremoniously as everybody seemed to be treated who contributed to Mr. Jaggers's coffers. "Getting evidence together," said Mr. Wemmick, as we came out, "for the Bailey." In the room over that, a little flabby terrier of a clerk with dangling hair (his cropping seemed to have been forgotten when he was a puppy) was similarly engaged with a man with weak eyes, whom Mr. Wemmick presented to me as a smelter who kept his pot always boiling, and who would melt me anything I pleased,—and who was in an excessive white-perspiration, as if he had been trying his art on himself. In a back room, a high-shouldered man with a face-ache tied up in dirty flannel, who was dressed in old black clothes that bore the appearance of having been waxed, was stooping over his work of making fair copies of the notes of the other two gentlemen, for Mr. Jaggers's own use.

This was all the establishment. When we went downstairs again, Wemmick led me into my guardian's room, and said, "This you've seen already."

"Pray," said I, as the two odious casts with the twitchy leer upon them caught my sight again, "whose likenesses are those?"

"These?" said Wemmick, getting upon a chair, and blowing the dust off the horrible heads before bringing them down. "These are two celebrated ones. Famous clients of ours that got us a world of credit. This chap (why you must have come down in the night and been peeping into the inkstand, to get this blot upon your eyebrow, you old rascal!) murdered his master, and, considering that he wasn't brought up to evidence, didn't plan it badly."

"Is it like him?" I asked, recoiling from the brute, as Wemmick spat upon his eyebrow and gave it a rub with his sleeve.

"Like him? It's himself, you know. The cast was made in Newgate, directly after he was taken down. You had a particular fancy for me, hadn't you, Old Artful?" said Wemmick. He then explained this affectionate apostrophe, by touching his brooch representing the lady and the weeping willow at the tomb with the urn upon it, and saying, "Had it made for me, express!"

"Is the lady anybody?" said I.

"No," returned Wemmick. "Only his game. (You liked your bit of game, didn't you?) No; deuce a bit of a lady in the case, Mr. Pip, except one,—and she wasn't of this slender lady-like sort, and you wouldn't have caught her looking after this urn, unless there was something to drink in it." Wemmick's attention being thus directed to his brooch, he put down the cast, and polished the brooch with his pocket-handkerchief.

"Did that other creature come to the same end?" I asked. "He has the same look."

"You're right," said Wemmick; "it's the genuine look. Much as if one nostril was caught up with a horse-hair and a little fish-hook. Yes, he came to the same end; quite the natural end here, I assure you. He forged wills, this blade did, if he didn't also put the supposed testators to sleep too. You were a gentlemanly Cove, though" (Mr. Wemmick was again apostrophizing), "and you said you could write Greek. Yah, Bounceable! What a liar you were! I never met such a liar as you!" Before putting his late friend on his shelf again, Wemmick touched the largest of his mourning rings and said, "Sent out to buy it for me, only the day before."

While he was putting up the other cast and coming down from the chair, the thought crossed my mind that all his personal jewelry was derived from like sources. As he had shown no diffidence on the subject, I ventured on the liberty of asking him the question, when he stood before me, dusting his hands.

"O yes," he returned, "these are all gifts of that kind. One brings another, you see; that's the way of it. I always take 'em. They're curiosities. And they're property. They may not be worth much, but, after all, they're property and portable. It don't signify to you with your brilliant lookout, but as to myself, my guiding-star always is, 'Get hold of portable property'."

When I had rendered homage to this light, he went on to say, in a friendly manner:—

"If at any odd time when you have nothing better to do, you wouldn't mind coming over to see me at Walworth, I could offer you a bed, and I should consider it an honor. I have not much to show you; but such two or three curiosities as I have got you might like to look over; and I am fond of a bit of garden and a summer-house."

I said I should be delighted to accept his hospitality.

"Thankee," said he; "then we'll consider that it's to come off, when convenient to you. Have you dined with Mr. Jaggers yet?"

"Not yet."

"Well," said Wemmick, "he'll give you wine, and good wine. I'll give you punch, and not bad punch. And now I'll tell you something. When you go to dine with Mr. Jaggers, look at his housekeeper."

"Shall I see something very uncommon?"

"Well," said Wemmick, "you'll see a wild beast tamed. Not so very uncommon, you'll tell me. I reply, that depends on the original wildness of the beast, and the amount of taming. It won't lower your opinion of Mr. Jaggers's powers. Keep your eye on it."

I told him I would do so, with all the interest and curiosity that his preparation awakened. As I was taking my departure, he asked me if I would like to devote five minutes to seeing Mr. Jaggers "at it?"

For several reasons, and not least because I didn't clearly know what Mr. Jaggers would be found to be "at," I replied in the affirmative. We dived into the City, and came up in a crowded police-court, where a blood-relation (in the murderous sense) of the deceased, with the fanciful taste in brooches, was standing at the bar, uncomfortably chewing something; while my guardian had a woman under examination or cross-examination,—I don't know which,—and was striking her, and the bench, and everybody present, with awe. If anybody, of whatsoever degree, said a word that he didn't approve of, he instantly required to have it "taken down." If anybody wouldn't make an admission, he said, "I'll have it out of you!" and if anybody made an admission, he said, "Now I have got you!" The magistrates shivered under a single bite of his finger. Thieves and thief-takers hung in dread rapture on his words, and shrank when a hair of his eyebrows turned in their direction. Which side he was on I couldn't make out, for he seemed to me to be grinding the whole place in a mill; I only know that when I stole out on tiptoe, he was not on the side of the bench; for, he was making the legs of the old gentleman who presided, quite convulsive under the table, by his denunciations of his conduct as the representative of British law and justice in that chair that day.

Chapter XXV

Bentley Drummle, who was so sulky a fellow that he even took up a book as if its writer had done him an injury, did not take up an acquaintance in a more agreeable spirit. Heavy in figure, movement, and comprehension,—in the sluggish complexion of his face, and in the large, awkward tongue that seemed to loll about in his mouth as he himself lolled about in a room,—he was idle, proud, niggardly, reserved, and suspicious. He came of rich people down in Somersetshire, who had nursed this combination of qualities until they made the discovery that it was just of age and a blockhead. Thus, Bentley Drummle had come to Mr. Pocket when he was a head taller than that gentleman, and half a dozen heads thicker than most gentlemen.

Startop had been spoilt by a weak mother and kept at home when he ought to have been at school, but he was devotedly attached to her, and admired her beyond measure. He had a woman's delicacy of feature, and was—"as you may see, though you never saw her," said Herbert to me—"exactly like his mother." It was but natural that I should take to him much more kindly than to Drummle, and that, even in the earliest evenings of our boating, he and I should pull homeward abreast of one another, conversing from boat to boat, while Bentley Drummle came up in our wake alone, under the overhanging banks and among the rushes. He would always creep in-shore like some uncomfortable amphibious creature, even when the tide would have sent him fast upon his way; and I always think of him as coming after us in the dark or by the back-water, when our own two boats were breaking the sunset or the moonlight in mid-stream.

Herbert was my intimate companion and friend. I presented him with a half-share in my boat, which was the occasion of his often coming down to Hammersmith; and my possession of a half-share in his chambers often took me up to London. We used to walk between the two places at all hours. I have an affection for the road yet (though it is not so pleasant a road as it was then), formed in the impressibility of untried youth and hope.

When I had been in Mr. Pocket's family a month or two, Mr. and Mrs. Camilla turned up. Camilla was Mr. Pocket's sister. Georgiana, whom I had seen at Miss Havisham's on the same occasion, also turned up. She was a cousin,—an indigestive single woman, who called her rigidity religion, and her liver love. These people hated me with the hatred of cupidity and disappointment. As a matter of course, they fawned upon me in my prosperity with the basest meanness. Towards Mr. Pocket, as a grown-up infant with no notion of his own interests, they showed the complacent forbearance I had heard them express. Mrs. Pocket they held in contempt; but they allowed the poor soul to have been heavily disappointed in life, because that shed a feeble reflected light upon themselves.

These were the surroundings among which I settled down, and applied myself to my education. I soon contracted expensive habits, and began to spend an amount of money that within a few short months I should have thought almost fabulous; but through good and evil I stuck to my books. There was no other merit in this, than my having sense enough to feel my deficiencies. Between Mr. Pocket and Herbert I got on fast; and, with one or the other always at my elbow to give me the start I wanted, and clear obstructions out of my road, I must have been as great a dolt as Drummle if I had done less.

I had not seen Mr. Wemmick for some weeks, when I thought I would write him a note and propose to go home with him on a certain evening. He replied that it would give him much pleasure, and that he would expect me at the office at six o'clock. Thither I went, and there I found him, putting the key of his safe down his back as the clock struck.

"Did you think of walking down to Walworth?" said he.

"Certainly," said I, "if you approve."

"Very much," was Wemmick's reply, "for I have had my legs under the desk all day, and shall be glad to stretch them. Now, I'll tell you what I have got for supper, Mr. Pip. I have got a stewed steak,—which is of home preparation,—and a cold roast fowl,—which is from the cook's-shop. I think it's tender, because the master of the shop was a Juryman in some cases of ours the other day, and we let him down easy. I reminded him of it when I bought the fowl, and I said, "Pick us out a good one, old Briton, because if we had chosen to keep you in the box another day or two, we could easily have done it." He said to that, "Let me make you a present of the best fowl in the shop." I let him, of course. As far as it goes, it's property and portable. You don't object to an aged parent, I hope?"

I really thought he was still speaking of the fowl, until he added, "Because I have got an aged parent at my place." I then said what politeness required.

"So, you haven't dined with Mr. Jaggers yet?" he pursued, as we walked along.

"Not yet."

"He told me so this afternoon when he heard you were coming. I expect you'll have an invitation to-morrow. He's going to ask your pals, too. Three of 'em; ain't there?"

Although I was not in the habit of counting Drummle as one of my intimate associates, I answered, "Yes."

"Well, he's going to ask the whole gang,"—I hardly felt complimented by the word,—"and whatever he gives you, he'll give you good. Don't look forward to variety, but you'll have excellence. And there's another rum thing in his house," proceeded Wemmick, after a moment's pause, as if the remark followed on the housekeeper understood; "he never lets a door or window be fastened at night."

"Is he never robbed?"

"That's it!" returned Wemmick. "He says, and gives it out publicly, "I want to see the man who'll rob me." Lord bless you, I have heard him, a hundred times, if I have heard him once, say to regular cracksmen in our front office, "You know where I live; now, no bolt is ever drawn there; why don't you do a stroke of business with me? Come; can't I tempt you?" Not a man of them, sir, would be bold enough to try it on, for love or money."

"They dread him so much?" said I.

"Dread him," said Wemmick. "I believe you they dread him. Not but what he's artful, even in his defiance of them. No silver, sir. Britannia metal, every spoon."

"So they wouldn't have much," I observed, "even if they—"

"Ah! But he would have much," said Wemmick, cutting me short, "and they know it. He'd have their lives, and the lives of scores of 'em. He'd have all he could get. And it's impossible to say what he couldn't get, if he gave his mind to it."

I was falling into meditation on my guardian's greatness, when Wemmick remarked:—

"As to the absence of plate, that's only his natural depth, you know. A river's its natural depth, and he's his natural depth. Look at his watch-chain. That's real enough."

"It's very massive," said I.

"Massive?" repeated Wemmick. "I think so. And his watch is a gold repeater, and worth a hundred pound if it's worth a penny. Mr. Pip, there are about seven hundred thieves in this town who know all about that watch; there's not a man, a woman, or a child, among them, who wouldn't identify the smallest link in that chain, and drop it as if it was red hot, if inveigled into touching it."

At first with such discourse, and afterwards with conversation of a more general nature, did Mr. Wemmick and I beguile the time and the road, until he gave me to understand that we had arrived in the district of Walworth.

It appeared to be a collection of back lanes, ditches, and little gardens, and to present the aspect of a rather dull retirement. Wemmick's house was a little wooden cottage in the midst of plots of garden, and the top of it was cut out and painted like a battery mounted with guns.

"My own doing," said Wemmick. "Looks pretty; don't it?"

I highly commended it, I think it was the smallest house I ever saw; with the queerest gothic windows (by far the greater part of them sham), and a gothic door almost too small to get in at.

"That's a real flagstaff, you see," said Wemmick, "and on Sundays I run up a real flag. Then look here. After I have crossed this bridge, I hoist it up—so—and cut off the communication."

The bridge was a plank, and it crossed a chasm about four feet wide and two deep. But it was very pleasant to see the pride with which he hoisted it up and made it fast; smiling as he did so, with a relish and not merely mechanically.

"At nine o'clock every night, Greenwich time," said Wemmick, "the gun fires. There he is, you see! And when you hear him go, I think you'll say he's a Stinger."

The piece of ordnance referred to, was mounted in a separate fortress, constructed of lattice-work. It was protected from the weather by an ingenious little tarpaulin contrivance in the nature of an umbrella.

"Then, at the back," said Wemmick, "out of sight, so as not to impede the idea of fortifications,—for it's a principle with me, if you have an idea, carry it out and keep it up,—I don't know whether that's your opinion—"

I said, decidedly.

"—At the back, there's a pig, and there are fowls and rabbits; then, I knock together my own little frame, you see, and grow cucumbers; and you'll judge at supper what sort of a salad I can raise. So, sir," said Wemmick, smiling again, but seriously too, as he shook his head, "if you can suppose the little place besieged, it would hold out a devil of a time in point of provisions."

Then, he conducted me to a bower about a dozen yards off, but which was approached by such ingenious twists of path that it took quite a long time to get at; and in this retreat our glasses were already set forth. Our punch was cooling in an ornamental lake, on whose margin the bower was raised. This piece of water (with an island in the middle which might have been the salad for supper) was of a circular form, and he had constructed a fountain in it, which, when you set a little mill going and took a cork out of a pipe, played to that powerful extent that it made the back of your hand quite wet.

"I am my own engineer, and my own carpenter, and my own plumber, and my own gardener, and my own Jack of all Trades," said Wemmick, in acknowledging my compliments.

"Well; it's a good thing, you know. It brushes the Newgate cobwebs away, and pleases the Aged. You wouldn't mind being at once introduced to the Aged, would you? It wouldn't put you out?"

I expressed the readiness I felt, and we went into the castle. There we found, sitting by a fire, a very old man in a flannel coat: clean, cheerful, comfortable, and well cared for, but intensely deaf.

"Well aged parent," said Wemmick, shaking hands with him in a cordial and jocose way, "how am you?"

"All right, John; all right!" replied the old man.

"Here's Mr. Pip, aged parent," said Wemmick, "and I wish you could hear his name. Nod away at him, Mr. Pip; that's what he likes. Nod away at him, if you please, like winking!"

"This is a fine place of my son's, sir," cried the old man, while I nodded as hard as I possibly could. "This is a pretty pleasure-ground, sir. This spot and these beautiful works upon it ought to be kept together by the Nation, after my son's time, for the people's enjoyment."

"You're as proud of it as Punch; ain't you, Aged?" said Wemmick, contemplating the old man, with his hard face really softened; "there's a nod for you;" giving him a tremendous one; "there's another for you;" giving him a still more tremendous one; "you like that, don't you? If you're not tired, Mr. Pip—though I know it's tiring to strangers—will you tip him one more? You can't think how it pleases him."

I tipped him several more, and he was in great spirits. We left him bestirring himself to feed the fowls, and we sat down to our punch in the arbor; where Wemmick told me, as he smoked a pipe, that it had taken him a good many years to bring the property up to its present pitch of perfection.

"Is it your own, Mr. Wemmick?"

"O yes," said Wemmick, "I have got hold of it, a bit at a time. It's a freehold, by George!"

"Is it indeed? I hope Mr. Jaggers admires it?"

"Never seen it," said Wemmick. "Never heard of it. Never seen the Aged. Never heard of him. No; the office is one thing, and private life is another. When I go into the office, I leave the Castle behind me, and when I come into the Castle, I leave the office behind me. If it's not in any way disagreeable to you, you'll oblige me by doing the same. I don't wish it professionally spoken about."

Of course I felt my good faith involved in the observance of his request. The punch being very nice, we sat there drinking it and talking, until it was almost nine o'clock. "Getting near gun-fire," said Wemmick then, as he laid down his pipe; "it's the Aged's treat."

Proceeding into the Castle again, we found the Aged heating the poker, with expectant eyes, as a preliminary to the performance of this great nightly ceremony. Wemmick stood with his watch in his hand until the moment was come for him to take the red-hot poker from the Aged, and repair to the battery. He took it, and went out, and presently the Stinger went off with a Bang that shook the crazy little box of a cottage as if it must fall to pieces, and made every glass and teacup in it ring. Upon this, the Aged—who I believe would have been blown out of his arm-chair but for holding on by the elbows—cried out exultingly, "He's fired! I heerd him!" and I nodded at the old gentleman until it is no figure of speech to declare that I absolutely could not see him.

The interval between that time and supper Wemmick devoted to showing me his collection of curiosities. They were mostly of a felonious character; comprising the pen with which a celebrated forgery had been committed, a distinguished razor or two, some locks of hair, and several manuscript confessions written under condemnation,—upon which Mr. Wemmick set particular value as being, to use his own words, "every one of 'em Lies, sir." These were agreeably dispersed among small specimens of china and glass, various neat trifles made by the proprietor of the museum, and some tobacco-stoppers carved by the Aged. They were all displayed in that chamber of the Castle into which I had been first inducted, and which served, not only as the general sitting-room but as the kitchen too, if I might judge from a saucepan on the hob, and a brazen bijou over the fireplace designed for the suspension of a roasting-jack.

There was a neat little girl in attendance, who looked after the Aged in the day. When she had laid the supper-cloth, the bridge was lowered to give her means of egress, and she withdrew for the night. The supper was excellent; and though the Castle was rather subject to dry-rot insomuch that it tasted like a bad nut, and though the pig might have been farther off, I was heartily pleased with my whole entertainment. Nor was there any drawback on my little turret bedroom, beyond there being such a very thin ceiling between me and the flagstaff, that when I lay down on my back in bed, it seemed as if I had to balance that pole on my forehead all night.

Wemmick was up early in the morning, and I am afraid I heard him cleaning my boots. After that, he fell to gardening, and I saw him from my gothic window pretending to employ the Aged, and nodding at him in a most devoted manner. Our breakfast was as good as the supper, and at half-past eight precisely we started for Little Britain. By degrees, Wemmick got dryer and harder as we went along, and his mouth tightened into a post-office again. At last, when we got to his place of business and he pulled out his key from his coat-collar, he looked as unconscious of his Walworth property as if the Castle and the drawbridge and the arbor and the lake and the fountain and the Aged, had all been blown into space together by the last discharge of the Stinger.

Chapter XXVI

It fell out as Wemmick had told me it would, that I had an early opportunity of comparing my guardian's establishment with that of his cashier and clerk. My guardian was in his room, washing his hands with his scented soap, when I went into the office from Walworth; and he called me to him, and gave me the invitation for myself and friends which Wemmick had prepared me to receive. "No ceremony," he stipulated, "and no dinner dress, and say to-morrow." I asked him where we should come to (for I had no idea where he lived), and I believe it was in his general objection to make anything like an admission, that he replied, "Come here, and I'll take you home with me." I embrace this opportunity of remarking that he washed his clients off, as if he were a surgeon or a dentist. He had a closet in his room, fitted up for the purpose, which smelt of the scented soap like a perfumer's shop. It had an unusually large jack-towel on a roller inside the door, and he would wash his hands, and wipe them and dry them all over this towel, whenever he came in from a police court or dismissed a client from his room. When I and my friends repaired to him at six o'clock next day, he seemed to have been engaged on a case of a darker complexion than usual, for we found him with his head butted into this closet, not only washing his hands, but laving his face and gargling his throat. And even when he had done all that, and had gone all round the jack-towel, he took out his penknife and scraped the case out of his nails before he put his coat on.

There were some people slinking about as usual when we passed out into the street, who were evidently anxious to speak with him; but there was something so conclusive in the halo of scented soap which encircled his presence, that they gave it up for that day. As we walked along westward, he was recognized ever and again by some face in the crowd of the streets, and whenever that happened he talked louder to me; but he never otherwise recognized anybody, or took notice that anybody recognized him.

He conducted us to Gerrard Street, Soho, to a house on the south side of that street. Rather a stately house of its kind, but dolefully in want of painting, and with dirty windows. He took out his key and opened the door, and we all went into a stone hall, bare, gloomy, and little used. So, up a dark brown staircase into a series of three dark brown rooms on the first floor. There were carved garlands on the panelled walls, and as he stood among them giving us welcome, I know what kind of loops I thought they looked like.

Dinner was laid in the best of these rooms; the second was his dressing-room; the third, his bedroom. He told us that he held the whole house, but rarely used more of it than we saw. The table was comfortably laid—no silver in the service, of course—and at the side of his chair was a capacious dumb-waiter, with a variety of bottles and decanters on it, and four dishes of fruit for dessert. I noticed throughout, that he kept everything under his own hand, and distributed everything himself.

There was a bookcase in the room; I saw from the backs of the books, that they were about evidence, criminal law, criminal biography, trials, acts of Parliament, and such things. The furniture was all very solid and good, like his watch-chain. It had an official look, however, and there was nothing merely ornamental to be seen. In a corner was a little table of papers with a shaded lamp: so that he seemed to bring the office home with him in that respect too, and to wheel it out of an evening and fall to work.

As he had scarcely seen my three companions until now,—for he and I had walked together,—he stood on the hearth-rug, after ringing the bell, and took a searching look at them. To my surprise, he seemed at once to be principally if not solely interested in Drummle.

"Pip," said he, putting his large hand on my shoulder and moving me to the window, "I don't know one from the other. Who's the Spider?"

"The spider?" said I.

"The blotchy, sprawly, sulky fellow."

"That's Bentley Drummle," I replied; "the one with the delicate face is Startop."

Not making the least account of "the one with the delicate face," he returned, "Bentley Drummle is his name, is it? I like the look of that fellow."

He immediately began to talk to Drummle: not at all deterred by his replying in his heavy reticent way, but apparently led on by it to screw discourse out of him. I was looking at the two, when there came between me and them the housekeeper, with the first dish for the table.

She was a woman of about forty, I supposed,—but I may have thought her younger than she was. Rather tall, of a lithe nimble figure, extremely pale, with large faded eyes, and a quantity of streaming hair. I cannot say whether any diseased affection of the heart caused her lips to be parted as if she were panting, and her face to bear a curious expression of suddenness and flutter; but I know that I had been to see Macbeth at the theatre, a night or two before, and that her face looked to me as if it were all disturbed by fiery air, like the faces I had seen rise out of the Witches' caldron.

She set the dish on, touched my guardian quietly on the arm with a finger to notify that dinner was ready, and vanished. We took our seats at the round table, and my guardian kept Drummle on one side of him, while Startop sat on the other. It was a noble dish of fish that the housekeeper had put on table, and we had a joint of equally choice mutton afterwards, and then an equally choice bird. Sauces, wines, all the accessories we wanted, and all of the best, were given out by our host from his dumb-waiter; and when they had made the circuit of the table, he always put them back again. Similarly, he dealt us clean plates and knives and forks, for each course, and dropped those just disused into two baskets on the ground by his chair. No other attendant than the housekeeper appeared. She set on every dish; and I always saw in her face, a face rising out of the caldron. Years afterwards, I made a dreadful likeness of that woman, by causing a face that had no other natural resemblance to it than it derived from flowing hair to pass behind a bowl of flaming spirits in a dark room.

Induced to take particular notice of the housekeeper, both by her own striking appearance and by Wemmick's preparation, I observed that whenever she was in the room she kept her eyes attentively on my guardian, and that she would remove her hands from any dish she put before him, hesitatingly, as if she dreaded his calling her back, and wanted him to speak when she was nigh, if he had anything to say. I fancied that I could detect in his manner a consciousness of this, and a purpose of always holding her in suspense.

Dinner went off gayly, and although my guardian seemed to follow rather than originate subjects, I knew that he wrenched the weakest part of our dispositions out of us. For myself, I found that I was expressing my tendency to lavish expenditure, and to patronize Herbert, and to boast of my great prospects, before I quite knew that I had opened my lips. It was so with all of us, but with no one more than Drummle: the development of whose inclination to gird in a grudging and suspicious way at the rest, was screwed out of him before the fish was taken off.

It was not then, but when we had got to the cheese, that our conversation turned upon our rowing feats, and that Drummle was rallied for coming up behind of a night in that slow amphibious way of his. Drummle upon this, informed our host that he much preferred our room to our company, and that as to skill he was more than our master, and that as to strength he could scatter us like chaff. By some invisible agency, my guardian wound him up to a pitch little short of ferocity about this trifle; and he fell to baring and spanning his arm to show how muscular it was, and we all fell to baring and spanning our arms in a ridiculous manner.

Now the housekeeper was at that time clearing the table; my guardian, taking no heed of her, but with the side of his face turned from her, was leaning back in his chair biting the side of his forefinger and showing an interest in Drummle, that, to me, was quite inexplicable. Suddenly, he clapped his large hand on the housekeeper's, like a trap, as she stretched it across the table. So suddenly and smartly did he do this, that we all stopped in our foolish contention.

"If you talk of strength," said Mr. Jaggers, "I'll show you a wrist. Molly, let them see your wrist."

Her entrapped hand was on the table, but she had already put her other hand behind her waist. "Master," she said, in a low voice, with her eyes attentively and entreatingly fixed upon him. "Don't."

"I'll show you a wrist," repeated Mr. Jaggers, with an immovable determination to show it. "Molly, let them see your wrist."

"Master," she again murmured. "Please!"

"Molly," said Mr. Jaggers, not looking at her, but obstinately looking at the opposite side of the room, "let them see both your wrists. Show them. Come!"

He took his hand from hers, and turned that wrist up on the table. She brought her other hand from behind her, and held the two out side by side. The last wrist was much disfigured,— deeply scarred and scarred across and across. When she held her hands out she took her eyes from Mr. Jaggers, and turned them watchfully on every one of the rest of us in succession.

"There's power here," said Mr. Jaggers, coolly tracing out the sinews with his forefinger. "Very few men have the power of wrist that this woman has. It's remarkable what mere force of grip there is in these hands. I have had occasion to notice many hands; but I never saw stronger in that respect, man's or woman's, than these."

While he said these words in a leisurely, critical style, she continued to look at every one of us in regular succession as we sat. The moment he ceased, she looked at him again. "That'll do, Molly," said Mr. Jaggers, giving her a slight nod; "you have been admired, and can go." She withdrew her hands and went out of the room, and Mr. Jaggers, putting the decanters on from his dumb-waiter, filled his glass and passed round the wine.

"At half-past nine, gentlemen," said he, "we must break up. Pray make the best use of your time. I am glad to see you all. Mr. Drummle, I drink to you."

If his object in singling out Drummle were to bring him out still more, it perfectly succeeded. In a sulky triumph, Drummle showed his morose depreciation of the rest of us, in a more and more offensive degree, until he became downright intolerable. Through all his stages, Mr. Jaggers followed him with the same strange interest. He actually seemed to serve as a zest to Mr. Jaggers's wine.

In our boyish want of discretion I dare say we took too much to drink, and I know we talked too much. We became particularly hot upon some boorish sneer of Drummle's, to the effect that we were too free with our money. It led to my remarking, with more zeal than discretion, that it came with a bad grace from him, to whom Startop had lent money in my presence but a week or so before.

"Well," retorted Drummle; "he'll be paid."

"I don't mean to imply that he won't," said I, "but it might make you hold your tongue about us and our money, I should think."

"You should think!" retorted Drummle. "Oh Lord!"

"I dare say," I went on, meaning to be very severe, "that you wouldn't lend money to any of us if we wanted it."

"You are right," said Drummle. "I wouldn't lend one of you a sixpence. I wouldn't lend anybody a sixpence."

"Rather mean to borrow under those circumstances, I should say."

"You should say," repeated Drummle. "Oh Lord!"

This was so very aggravating—the more especially as I found myself making no way against his surly obtuseness—that I said, disregarding Herbert's efforts to check me,—

"Come, Mr. Drummle, since we are on the subject, I'll tell you what passed between Herbert here and me, when you borrowed that money."

"I don't want to know what passed between Herbert there and you," growled Drummle. And I think he added in a lower growl, that we might both go to the devil and shake ourselves.

"I'll tell you, however," said I, "whether you want to know or not. We said that as you put it in your pocket very glad to get it, you seemed to be immensely amused at his being so weak as to lend it."

Drummle laughed outright, and sat laughing in our faces, with his hands in his pockets and his round shoulders raised; plainly signifying that it was quite true, and that he despised us as asses all.

Hereupon Startop took him in hand, though with a much better grace than I had shown, and exhorted him to be a little more agreeable. Startop, being a lively, bright young fellow, and Drummle being the exact opposite, the latter was always disposed to resent him as a direct personal affront. He now retorted in a coarse, lumpish way, and Startop tried to turn the discussion aside with some small pleasantry that made us all laugh. Resenting this little success more than anything, Drummle, without any threat or warning, pulled his hands out of his pockets, dropped his round shoulders, swore, took up a large glass, and would have flung it at his adversary's head, but for our entertainer's dexterously seizing it at the instant when it was raised for that purpose.

"Gentlemen," said Mr. Jaggers, deliberately putting down the glass, and hauling out his gold repeater by its massive chain, "I am exceedingly sorry to announce that it's half past nine."

On this hint we all rose to depart. Before we got to the street door, Startop was cheerily calling Drummle "old boy," as if nothing had happened. But the old boy was so far from responding, that he would not even walk to Hammersmith on the same side of the way; so Herbert and I, who remained in town, saw them going down the street on opposite sides; Startop leading, and Drummle lagging behind in the shadow of the houses, much as he was wont to follow in his boat.

As the door was not yet shut, I thought I would leave Herbert there for a moment, and run upstairs again to say a word to my guardian. I found him in his dressing-room surrounded by his stock of boots, already hard at it, washing his hands of us.

I told him I had come up again to say how sorry I was that anything disagreeable should have occurred, and that I hoped he would not blame me much.

"Pooh!" said he, sluicing his face, and speaking through the water-drops; "it's nothing, Pip. I like that Spider though."

He had turned towards me now, and was shaking his head, and blowing, and towelling himself.

"I am glad you like him, sir," said I—"but I don't."

"No, no," my guardian assented; "don't have too much to do with him. Keep as clear of him as you can. But I like the fellow, Pip; he is one of the true sort. Why, if I was a fortune-teller—"

Looking out of the towel, he caught my eye.

"But I am not a fortune-teller," he said, letting his head drop into a festoon of towel, and towelling away at his two ears. "You know what I am, don't you? Good night, Pip."

"Good night, sir."

In about a month after that, the Spider's time with Mr. Pocket was up for good, and, to the great relief of all the house but Mrs. Pocket, he went home to the family hole.

Chapter XXVII

"MY DEAR MR PIP:—

"I write this by request of Mr. Gargery, for to let you know that he is going to London in company with Mr. Wopsle and would be glad if agreeable to be allowed to see you. He would call at Barnard's Hotel Tuesday morning at nine o'clock, when if not agreeable please leave word. Your poor sister is much the same as when you left. We talk of you in the kitchen every night, and wonder what you are saying and doing. If now considered in the light of a liberty, excuse it for the love of poor old days. No more, dear Mr. Pip, from your ever obliged, and affectionate servant,

"BIDDY."

"P.S. He wishes me most particular to write what larks. He says you will understand. I hope and do not doubt it will be agreeable to see him, even though a gentleman, for you had ever a good heart, and he is a worthy, worthy man. I have read him all, excepting only the last little sentence, and he wishes me most particular to write again what larks."

I received this letter by the post on Monday morning, and therefore its appointment was for next day. Let me confess exactly with what feelings I looked forward to Joe's coming.

Not with pleasure, though I was bound to him by so many ties; no; with considerable disturbance, some mortification, and a keen sense of incongruity. If I could have kept him away by paying money, I certainly would have paid money. My greatest reassurance was that he was coming to Barnard's Inn, not to Hammersmith, and consequently would not fall in Bentley Drummle's way. I had little objection to his being seen by Herbert or his father, for both of whom I had a respect; but I had the sharpest sensitiveness as to his being seen by Drummle, whom I held in contempt. So, throughout life, our worst weaknesses and meannesses are usually committed for the sake of the people whom we most despise.

I had begun to be always decorating the chambers in some quite unnecessary and inappropriate way or other, and very expensive those wrestles with Barnard proved to be. By this time, the rooms were vastly different from what I had found them, and I enjoyed the honor of occupying a few prominent pages in the books of a neighboring upholsterer. I had got on so fast of late, that I had even started a boy in boots,—top boots,—in bondage and slavery to whom I might have been said to pass my days. For, after I had made the monster (out of the refuse of my washerwoman's family), and had clothed him with a blue coat, canary waistcoat, white cravat, creamy breeches, and the boots already mentioned, I had to find him a little to do and a great deal to eat; and with both of those horrible requirements he haunted my existence.

This avenging phantom was ordered to be on duty at eight on Tuesday morning in the hall, (it was two feet square, as charged for floorcloth,) and Herbert suggested certain things for breakfast that he thought Joe would like. While I felt sincerely obliged to him for being so interested and considerate, I had an odd half-provoked sense of suspicion upon me, that if Joe had been coming to see him, he wouldn't have been quite so brisk about it.

However, I came into town on the Monday night to be ready for Joe, and I got up early in the morning, and caused the sitting-room and breakfast-table to assume their most splendid appearance. Unfortunately the morning was drizzly, and an angel could not have concealed the fact that Barnard was shedding sooty tears outside the window, like some weak giant of a Sweep.

As the time approached I should have liked to run away, but the Avenger pursuant to orders was in the hall, and presently I heard Joe on the staircase. I knew it was Joe, by his clumsy manner of coming upstairs,—his state boots being always too big for him,—and by the time it took him to read the names on the other floors in the course of his ascent. When at last he stopped outside our door, I could hear his finger tracing over the painted letters of my name, and I afterwards distinctly heard him breathing in at the keyhole. Finally he gave a faint single rap, and Pepper—such was the compromising name of the avenging boy—announced "Mr. Gargery!" I thought he never would have done wiping his feet, and that I must have gone out to lift him off the mat, but at last he came in.

"Joe, how are you, Joe?"

"Pip, how AIR you, Pip?"

With his good honest face all glowing and shining, and his hat put down on the floor between us, he caught both my hands and worked them straight up and down, as if I had been the last-patented Pump.

"I am glad to see you, Joe. Give me your hat."

But Joe, taking it up carefully with both hands, like a bird's-nest with eggs in it, wouldn't hear of parting with that piece of property, and persisted in standing talking over it in a most uncomfortable way.

"Which you have that growed," said Joe, "and that swelled, and that gentle-folked;" Joe considered a little before he discovered this word; "as to be sure you are a honor to your king and country."

"And you, Joe, look wonderfully well."

"Thank God," said Joe, "I'm ekerval to most. And your sister, she's no worse than she were. And Biddy, she's ever right and ready. And all friends is no backerder, if not no forarder. 'Ceptin Wopsle; he's had a drop."

All this time (still with both hands taking great care of the bird's-nest), Joe was rolling his eyes round and round the room, and round and round the flowered pattern of my dressing-gown.

"Had a drop, Joe?"

"Why yes," said Joe, lowering his voice, "he's left the Church and went into the playacting. Which the playacting have likeways brought him to London along with me. And his wish were," said Joe, getting the bird's-nest under his left arm for the moment, and groping in it for an egg with his right; "if no offence, as I would 'and you that."

I took what Joe gave me, and found it to be the crumpled play-bill of a small metropolitan theatre, announcing the first appearance, in that very week, of "the celebrated Provincial Amateur of Roscian renown, whose unique performance in the highest tragic walk of our National Bard has lately occasioned so great a sensation in local dramatic circles."

"Were you at his performance, Joe?" I inquired.

"I were," said Joe, with emphasis and solemnity.

"Was there a great sensation?"

"Why," said Joe, "yes, there certainly were a peck of orange-peel. Partickler when he see the ghost. Though I put it to yourself, sir, whether it were calc'lated to keep a man up to his work with a good hart, to be continiwally cutting in betwixt him and the Ghost with 'Amen!' A man may have had a misfortun' and been in the Church," said Joe, lowering his voice to an argumentative and feeling tone, "but that is no reason why you should put him out at such a time. Which I meantersay, if the ghost of a man's own father cannot be allowed to claim his attention, what can, Sir? Still more, when his mourning 'at is unfortunately made so small as that the weight of the black feathers brings it off, try to keep it on how you may."

A ghost-seeing effect in Joe's own countenance informed me that Herbert had entered the room. So, I presented Joe to Herbert, who held out his hand; but Joe backed from it, and held on by the bird's-nest.

"Your servant, Sir," said Joe, "which I hope as you and Pip"—here his eye fell on the Avenger, who was putting some toast on table, and so plainly denoted an intention to make that young gentleman one of the family, that I frowned it down and confused him more—"I meantersay, you two gentlemen,—which I hope as you get your elths in this close spot? For the present may be a werry good inn, according to London opinions," said Joe, confidentially, "and I believe its character do stand it; but I wouldn't keep a pig in it myself,—not in the case that I wished him to fatten wholesome and to eat with a meller flavor on him."

Having borne this flattering testimony to the merits of our dwelling-place, and having incidentally shown this tendency to call me "sir," Joe, being invited to sit down to table, looked all round the room for a suitable spot on which to deposit his hat,—as if it were only on some very few rare substances in nature that it could find a resting place,—and ultimately stood it on an extreme corner of the chimney-piece, from which it ever afterwards fell off at intervals.

"Do you take tea, or coffee, Mr. Gargery?" asked Herbert, who always presided of a morning.

"Thankee, Sir," said Joe, stiff from head to foot, "I'll take whichever is most agreeable to yourself."

"What do you say to coffee?"

"Thankee, Sir," returned Joe, evidently dispirited by the proposal, "since you are so kind as make chice of coffee, I will not run contrairy to your own opinions. But don't you never find it a little 'eating?"

"Say tea then," said Herbert, pouring it out.

Here Joe's hat tumbled off the mantel-piece, and he started out of his chair and picked it up, and fitted it to the same exact spot. As if it were an absolute point of good breeding that it should tumble off again soon.

"When did you come to town, Mr. Gargery?"

"Were it yesterday afternoon?" said Joe, after coughing behind his hand, as if he had had time to catch the whooping-cough since he came. "No it were not. Yes it were. Yes. It were yesterday afternoon" (with an appearance of mingled wisdom, relief, and strict impartiality).

"Have you seen anything of London yet?"

"Why, yes, Sir," said Joe, "me and Wopsle went off straight to look at the Blacking Ware'us. But we didn't find that it come up to its likeness in the red bills at the shop doors; which I meantersay," added Joe, in an explanatory manner, "as it is there drawd too architectooralooral."

I really believe Joe would have prolonged this word (mightily expressive to my mind of some architecture that I know) into a perfect Chorus, but for his attention being providentially attracted by his hat, which was toppling. Indeed, it demanded from him a constant attention, and a quickness of eye and hand, very like that exacted by wicket-keeping. He made extraordinary play with it, and showed the greatest skill; now, rushing at it and catching it neatly as it dropped; now, merely stopping it midway, beating it up, and humoring it in various parts of the room and against a good deal of the pattern of the paper on the wall, before he felt it safe to close with it; finally splashing it into the slop-basin, where I took the liberty of laying hands upon it.

As to his shirt-collar, and his coat-collar, they were perplexing to reflect upon,—insoluble mysteries both. Why should a man scrape himself to that extent, before he could consider himself full dressed? Why should he suppose it necessary to be purified by suffering for his holiday clothes? Then he fell into such unaccountable fits of meditation, with his fork midway between his plate and his mouth; had his eyes attracted in such strange directions; was afflicted with such remarkable coughs; sat so far from the table, and dropped so much more than he ate, and pretended that he hadn't dropped it; that I was heartily glad when Herbert left us for the City.

I had neither the good sense nor the good feeling to know that this was all my fault, and that if I had been easier with Joe, Joe would have been easier with me. I felt impatient of him and out of temper with him; in which condition he heaped coals of fire on my head.

"Us two being now alone, sir,"—began Joe.

"Joe," I interrupted, pettishly, "how can you call me, sir?"

Joe looked at me for a single instant with something faintly like reproach. Utterly preposterous as his cravat was, and as his collars were, I was conscious of a sort of dignity in the look.

"Us two being now alone," resumed Joe, "and me having the intentions and abilities to stay not many minutes more, I will now conclude—leastways begin—to mention what have led to my having had the present honor. For was it not," said Joe, with his old air of lucid exposition, "that my only wish were to be useful to you, I should not have had the honor of breaking wittles in the company and abode of gentlemen."

I was so unwilling to see the look again, that I made no remonstrance against this tone.

"Well, sir," pursued Joe, "this is how it were. I were at the Bargemen t'other night, Pip;"—whenever he subsided into affection, he called me Pip, and whenever he relapsed into politeness he called me sir; "when there come up in his shay-cart, Pumblechook. Which that same identical," said Joe, going down a new track, "do comb my 'air the wrong way sometimes, awful, by giving out up and down town as it were him which ever had your infant companionation and were looked upon as a playfellow by yourself."

"Nonsense. It was you, Joe."

"Which I fully believed it were, Pip," said Joe, slightly tossing his head, "though it signify little now, sir. Well, Pip; this same identical, which his manners is given to blusterous, come to me at the Bargemen (wot a pipe and a pint of beer do give refreshment to the workingman, sir, and do not over stimilate), and his word were, 'Joseph, Miss Havisham she wish to speak to you.'"

"Miss Havisham, Joe?"

"'She wish,' were Pumblechook's word, 'to speak to you.'" Joe sat and rolled his eyes at the ceiling.

"Yes, Joe? Go on, please."

"Next day, sir," said Joe, looking at me as if I were a long way off, "having cleaned myself, I go and I see Miss A."

"Miss A., Joe? Miss Havisham?"

"Which I say, sir," replied Joe, with an air of legal formality, as if he were making his will, "Miss A., or otherways Havisham. Her expression air then as follering: 'Mr. Gargery. You air in correspondence with Mr. Pip?' Having had a letter from you, I were able to say 'I am.' (When I married your sister, sir, I said 'I will;' and when I answered your friend, Pip, I said 'I am.') 'Would you tell him, then,' said she, 'that which Estella has come home and would be glad to see him.'"

I felt my face fire up as I looked at Joe. I hope one remote cause of its firing may have been my consciousness that if I had known his errand, I should have given him more encouragement.

"Biddy," pursued Joe, "when I got home and asked her fur to write the message to you, a little hung back. Biddy says, 'I know he will be very glad to have it by word of mouth, it is holiday time, you want to see him, go!' I have now concluded, sir," said Joe, rising from his chair, "and, Pip, I wish you ever well and ever prospering to a greater and a greater height."

"But you are not going now, Joe?"

"Yes I am," said Joe.

"But you are coming back to dinner, Joe?"

"No I am not," said Joe.

Our eyes met, and all the "Sir" melted out of that manly heart as he gave me his hand.

"Pip, dear old chap, life is made of ever so many partings welded together, as I may say, and one man's a blacksmith, and one's a whitesmith, and one's a goldsmith, and one's a coppersmith. Diwisions among such must come, and must be met as they come. If there's been any fault at all to-day, it's mine. You and me is not two figures to be together in London; nor yet anywheres else but what is private, and beknown, and understood among friends. It ain't that I am proud, but that I want to be right, as you shall never see me no more in these clothes. I'm wrong in these clothes. I'm wrong out of the forge, the kitchen, or off th' meshes. You won't find half so much fault in me if you think of me in my forge dress, with my hammer in my hand, or even my pipe. You won't find half so much fault in me if, supposing as you should ever wish to see me, you come and put your head in at the forge window and see Joe the blacksmith, there, at the old anvil, in the old burnt apron, sticking to the old work. I'm awful dull, but I hope I've beat out something nigh the rights of this at last. And so GOD bless you, dear old Pip, old chap, GOD bless you!"

I had not been mistaken in my fancy that there was a simple dignity in him. The fashion of his dress could no more come in its way when he spoke these words than it could come in its way in Heaven. He touched me gently on the forehead, and went out. As soon as I could recover myself sufficiently, I hurried out after him and looked for him in the neighboring streets; but he was gone.

Chapter XXVIII

It was clear that I must repair to our town next day, and in the first flow of my repentance, it was equally clear that I must stay at Joe's. But, when I had secured my box-place by to-morrow's coach, and had been down to Mr. Pocket's and back, I was not by any means convinced on the last point, and began to invent reasons and make excuses for putting up at the Blue Boar. I should be an inconvenience at Joe's; I was not expected, and my bed would not be ready; I should be too far from Miss Havisham's, and she was exacting and mightn't like it. All other swindlers upon earth are nothing to the self-swindlers, and with such pretences did I cheat myself. Surely a curious thing. That I should innocently take a bad half-crown of somebody else's manufacture is reasonable enough; but that I should knowingly reckon the spurious coin of my own make as good money! An obliging stranger, under pretence of compactly folding up my bank-notes for security's sake, abstracts the notes and gives me nutshells; but what is his sleight of hand to mine, when I fold up my own nutshells and pass them on myself as notes!

Having settled that I must go to the Blue Boar, my mind was much disturbed by indecision whether or not to take the Avenger. It was tempting to think of that expensive Mercenary publicly airing his boots in the archway of the Blue Boar's posting-yard; it was almost solemn to imagine him casually produced in the tailor's shop, and confounding the disrespectful senses of Trabb's boy. On the other hand, Trabb's boy might worm himself into his intimacy and tell him things; or, reckless and desperate wretch as I knew he could be, might hoot him in the High Street. My patroness, too, might hear of him, and not approve. On the whole, I resolved to leave the Avenger behind.

It was the afternoon coach by which I had taken my place, and, as winter had now come round, I should not arrive at my destination until two or three hours after dark. Our time of starting from the Cross Keys was two o'clock. I arrived on the ground with a quarter of an hour to spare, attended by the Avenger,—if I may connect that expression with one who never attended on me if he could possibly help it.

At that time it was customary to carry Convicts down to the dock-yards by stage-coach. As I had often heard of them in the capacity of outside passengers, and had more than once seen them on the high road dangling their ironed legs over the coach roof, I had no cause to be surprised when Herbert, meeting me in the yard, came up and told me there were two convicts going down with me. But I had a reason that was an old reason now for constitutionally faltering whenever I heard the word "convict."

"You don't mind them, Handel?" said Herbert.

"O no!"

"I thought you seemed as if you didn't like them?"

"I can't pretend that I do like them, and I suppose you don't particularly. But I don't mind them."

"See! There they are," said Herbert, "coming out of the Tap. What a degraded and vile sight it is!"

They had been treating their guard, I suppose, for they had a gaoler with them, and all three came out wiping their mouths on their hands. The two convicts were handcuffed together, and had irons on their legs,—irons of a pattern that I knew well. They wore the dress that I likewise knew well. Their keeper had a brace of pistols, and carried a thick-knobbed bludgeon under his arm; but he was on terms of good understanding with them, and stood with them beside him, looking on at the putting-to of the horses, rather with an air as if the convicts were an interesting Exhibition not formally open at the moment, and he the Curator. One was a taller and stouter man than the other, and appeared as a matter of course, according to the mysterious ways of the world, both convict and free, to have had allotted to him the smaller suit of clothes. His arms and legs were like great pincushions of those shapes, and his attire disguised him absurdly; but I knew his half-closed eye at one glance. There stood the man whom I had seen on the settle at the Three Jolly Bargemen on a Saturday night, and who had brought me down with his invisible gun!

It was easy to make sure that as yet he knew me no more than if he had never seen me in his life. He looked across at me, and his eye appraised my watch-chain, and then he incidentally spat and said something to the other convict, and they laughed and slued themselves round with a clink of their coupling manacle, and looked at something else. The great numbers on their backs, as if they were street doors; their coarse mangy ungainly outer surface, as if they were lower animals; their ironed legs, apologetically garlanded with pocket-handkerchiefs; and the way in which all present looked at them and kept from them; made them (as Herbert had said) a most disagreeable and degraded spectacle.

But this was not the worst of it. It came out that the whole of the back of the coach had been taken by a family removing from London, and that there were no places for the two prisoners but on the seat in front behind the coachman. Hereupon, a choleric gentleman, who had taken the fourth place on that seat, flew into a most violent passion, and said that it was a breach of contract to mix him up with such villainous company, and that it was poisonous, and pernicious, and infamous, and shameful, and I don't know what else. At this time the coach was ready and the coachman impatient, and we were all preparing to get up, and the prisoners had come over with their keeper,—bringing with them that curious flavor of bread-poultice, baize, rope-yarn, and hearthstone, which attends the convict presence.

"Don't take it so much amiss, sir," pleaded the keeper to the angry passenger; "I'll sit next you myself. I'll put 'em on the outside of the row. They won't interfere with you, sir. You needn't know they're there."

"And don't blame me," growled the convict I had recognized. "I don't want to go. I am quite ready to stay behind. As fur as I am concerned any one's welcome to my place."

"Or mine," said the other, gruffly. "I wouldn't have incommoded none of you, if I'd had my way." Then they both laughed, and began cracking nuts, and spitting the shells about.—As I really think I should have liked to do myself, if I had been in their place and so despised.

At length, it was voted that there was no help for the angry gentleman, and that he must either go in his chance company or remain behind. So he got into his place, still making complaints, and the keeper got into the place next him, and the convicts hauled themselves up as well as they could, and the convict I had recognized sat behind me with his breath on the hair of my head.

"Good-bye, Handel!" Herbert called out as we started. I thought what a blessed fortune it was, that he had found another name for me than Pip.

It is impossible to express with what acuteness I felt the convict's breathing, not only on the back of my head, but all along my spine. The sensation was like being touched in the marrow with some pungent and searching acid, it set my very teeth on edge. He seemed to have more breathing business to do than another man, and to make more noise in doing it; and I was conscious of growing high-shouldered on one side, in my shrinking endeavors to fend him off.

The weather was miserably raw, and the two cursed the cold. It made us all lethargic before we had gone far, and when we had left the Half-way House behind, we habitually dozed and shivered and were silent. I dozed off, myself, in considering the question whether I ought to restore a couple of pounds sterling to this creature before losing sight of him, and how it could best be done. In the act of dipping forward as if I were going to bathe among the horses, I woke in a fright and took the question up again.

But I must have lost it longer than I had thought, since, although I could recognize nothing in the darkness and the fitful lights and shadows of our lamps, I traced marsh country in the cold damp wind that blew at us. Cowering forward for warmth and to make me a screen against the wind, the convicts were closer to me than before. The very first words I heard them interchange as I became conscious, were the words of my own thought, "Two One Pound notes."

"How did he get 'em?" said the convict I had never seen.

"How should I know?" returned the other. "He had 'em stowed away somehows. Giv him by friends, I expect."

"I wish," said the other, with a bitter curse upon the cold, "that I had 'em here."

"Two one pound notes, or friends?"

"Two one pound notes. I'd sell all the friends I ever had for one, and think it a blessed good bargain. Well? So he says—?"

"So he says," resumed the convict I had recognized,—"it was all said and done in half a minute, behind a pile of timber in the Dock-yard,—'You're a going to be discharged?' Yes, I was. Would I find out that boy that had fed him and kep his secret, and give him them two one pound notes? Yes, I would. And I did."

"More fool you," growled the other. "I'd have spent 'em on a Man, in wittles and drink. He must have been a green one. Mean to say he knowed nothing of you?"

"Not a ha'porth. Different gangs and different ships. He was tried again for prison breaking, and got made a Lifer."

"And was that—Honor!—the only time you worked out, in this part of the country?"

"The only time."

"What might have been your opinion of the place?"

"A most beastly place. Mudbank, mist, swamp, and work; work, swamp, mist, and mudbank."

They both execrated the place in very strong language, and gradually growled themselves out, and had nothing left to say.

After overhearing this dialogue, I should assuredly have got down and been left in the solitude and darkness of the highway, but for feeling certain that the man had no suspicion of my identity. Indeed, I was not only so changed in the course of nature, but so differently dressed and so differently circumstanced, that it was not at all likely he could have known me without accidental help. Still, the coincidence of our being together on the coach, was sufficiently strange to fill me with a dread that some other coincidence might at any moment connect me, in his hearing, with my name. For this reason, I resolved to alight as soon as we touched the town, and put myself out of his hearing. This device I executed successfully. My little portmanteau was in the boot under my feet; I had but to turn a hinge to get it out; I threw it down before me, got down after it, and was left at the first lamp on the first stones of the town pavement. As to the convicts, they went their way with the coach, and I knew at what point they would be spirited off to the river. In my fancy, I saw the boat with its convict crew waiting for them at the slime-washed stairs,—again heard the gruff "Give way, you!" like and order to dogs,—again saw the wicked Noah's Ark lying out on the black water.

I could not have said what I was afraid of, for my fear was altogether undefined and vague, but there was great fear upon me. As I walked on to the hotel, I felt that a dread, much exceeding the mere apprehension of a painful or disagreeable recognition, made me tremble. I am confident that it took no distinctness of shape, and that it was the revival for a few minutes of the terror of childhood.

The coffee-room at the Blue Boar was empty, and I had not only ordered my dinner there, but had sat down to it, before the waiter knew me. As soon as he had apologized for the remissness of his memory, he asked me if he should send Boots for Mr. Pumblechook?

"No," said I, "certainly not."

The waiter (it was he who had brought up the Great Remonstrance from the Commercials, on the day when I was bound) appeared surprised, and took the earliest opportunity of putting a dirty old copy of a local newspaper so directly in my way, that I took it up and read this paragraph:—

Our readers will learn, not altogether without interest, in reference to the recent romantic rise in fortune of a young artificer in iron of this neighborhood (what a theme, by the way, for the magic pen of our as yet not universally acknowledged townsman TOOBY, the poet of our columns!) that the youth's earliest patron, companion, and friend, was a highly respected individual not entirely unconnected with the corn and seed trade, and whose eminently convenient and commodious business premises are situate within a hundred miles of the High Street. It is not wholly irrespective of our personal feelings that we record HIM as the Mentor of our young Telemachus, for it is good to know that our town produced the founder of the latter's fortunes. Does the thought-contracted brow of the local Sage or the lustrous eye of local Beauty inquire whose fortunes? We believe that Quintin Matsys was the BLACKSMITH of Antwerp. VERB. SAP.

I entertain a conviction, based upon large experience, that if in the days of my prosperity I had gone to the North Pole, I should have met somebody there, wandering Esquimaux or civilized man, who would have told me that Pumblechook was my earliest patron and the founder of my fortunes.

Chapter XXIX

Betimes in the morning I was up and out. It was too early yet to go to Miss Havisham's, so I loitered into the country on Miss Havisham's side of town,—which was not Joe's side; I could go there to-morrow,—thinking about my patroness, and painting brilliant pictures of her plans for me.

She had adopted Estella, she had as good as adopted me, and it could not fail to be her intention to bring us together. She reserved it for me to restore the desolate house, admit the sunshine into the dark rooms, set the clocks a-going and the cold hearths a-blazing, tear down the cobwebs, destroy the vermin,—in short, do all the shining deeds of the young Knight of romance, and marry the Princess. I had stopped to look at the house as I passed; and its seared red brick walls, blocked windows, and strong green ivy clasping even the stacks of chimneys with its twigs and tendons, as if with sinewy old arms, had made up a rich attractive mystery, of which I was the hero. Estella was the inspiration of it, and the heart of it, of course. But, though she had taken such strong possession of me, though my fancy and my hope were so set upon her, though her influence on my boyish life and character had been all-powerful, I did not, even that romantic morning, invest her with any attributes save those she possessed. I mention this in this place, of a fixed purpose, because it is the clew by which I am to be followed into my poor labyrinth. According to my experience, the conventional notion of a lover cannot be always true. The unqualified truth is, that when I loved Estella with the love of a man, I loved her simply because I found her irresistible. Once for all; I knew to my sorrow, often and often, if not always, that I loved her against reason, against promise, against peace, against hope, against happiness, against all discouragement that could be. Once for all; I loved her none the less because I knew it, and it had no more influence in restraining me than if I had devoutly believed her to be human perfection.

I so shaped out my walk as to arrive at the gate at my old time. When I had rung at the bell with an unsteady hand, I turned my back upon the gate, while I tried to get my breath and keep the beating of my heart moderately quiet. I heard the side-door open, and steps come across the courtyard; but I pretended not to hear, even when the gate swung on its rusty hinges.

Being at last touched on the shoulder, I started and turned. I started much more naturally then, to find myself confronted by a man in a sober gray dress. The last man I should have expected to see in that place of porter at Miss Havisham's door.

"Orlick!"

"Ah, young master, there's more changes than yours. But come in, come in. It's opposed to my orders to hold the gate open."

I entered and he swung it, and locked it, and took the key out. "Yes!" said he, facing round, after doggedly preceding me a few steps towards the house. "Here I am!"

"How did you come here?"

"I come her," he retorted, "on my legs. I had my box brought alongside me in a barrow."

"Are you here for good?"

"I ain't here for harm, young master, I suppose?"

I was not so sure of that. I had leisure to entertain the retort in my mind, while he slowly lifted his heavy glance from the pavement, up my legs and arms, to my face.

"Then you have left the forge?" I said.

"Do this look like a forge?" replied Orlick, sending his glance all round him with an air of injury. "Now, do it look like it?"

I asked him how long he had left Gargery's forge?

"One day is so like another here," he replied, "that I don't know without casting it up. However, I come here some time since you left."

"I could have told you that, Orlick."

"Ah!" said he, dryly. "But then you've got to be a scholar."

By this time we had come to the house, where I found his room to be one just within the side-door, with a little window in it looking on the courtyard. In its small proportions, it was not unlike the kind of place usually assigned to a gate-porter in Paris. Certain keys were hanging on the wall, to which he now added the gate key; and his patchwork-covered bed was in a little inner division or recess. The whole had a slovenly, confined, and sleepy look, like a cage for a human dormouse; while he, looming dark and heavy in the shadow of a corner by the window, looked like the human dormouse for whom it was fitted up,—as indeed he was.

"I never saw this room before," I remarked; "but there used to be no Porter here."

"No," said he; "not till it got about that there was no protection on the premises, and it come to be considered dangerous, with convicts and Tag and Rag and Bobtail going up and down. And then I was recommended to the place as a man who could give another man as good as he brought, and I took it. It's easier than bellowsing and hammering.—That's loaded, that is."

My eye had been caught by a gun with a brass-bound stock over the chimney-piece, and his eye had followed mine.

"Well," said I, not desirous of more conversation, "shall I go up to Miss Havisham?"

"Burn me, if I know!" he retorted, first stretching himself and then shaking himself; "my orders ends here, young master. I give this here bell a rap with this here hammer, and you go on along the passage till you meet somebody."

"I am expected, I believe?"

"Burn me twice over, if I can say!" said he.

Upon that, I turned down the long passage which I had first trodden in my thick boots, and he made his bell sound. At the end of the passage, while the bell was still reverberating, I found Sarah Pocket, who appeared to have now become constitutionally green and yellow by reason of me.

"Oh!" said she. "You, is it, Mr. Pip?"

"It is, Miss Pocket. I am glad to tell you that Mr. Pocket and family are all well."

"Are they any wiser?" said Sarah, with a dismal shake of the head; "they had better be wiser, than well. Ah, Matthew, Matthew! You know your way, sir?"

Tolerably, for I had gone up the staircase in the dark, many a time. I ascended it now, in lighter boots than of yore, and tapped in my old way at the door of Miss Havisham's room. "Pip's rap," I heard her say, immediately; "come in, Pip."

She was in her chair near the old table, in the old dress, with her two hands crossed on her stick, her chin resting on them, and her eyes on the fire. Sitting near her, with the white shoe, that had never been worn, in her hand, and her head bent as she looked at it, was an elegant lady whom I had never seen.

"Come in, Pip," Miss Havisham continued to mutter, without looking round or up; "come in, Pip, how do you do, Pip? so you kiss my hand as if I were a queen, eh?—Well?"

She looked up at me suddenly, only moving her eyes, and repeated in a grimly playful manner,—

"Well?"

"I heard, Miss Havisham," said I, rather at a loss, "that you were so kind as to wish me to come and see you, and I came directly."

"Well?"

The lady whom I had never seen before, lifted up her eyes and looked archly at me, and then I saw that the eyes were Estella's eyes. But she was so much changed, was so much more beautiful, so much more womanly, in all things winning admiration, had made such wonderful advance, that I seemed to have made none. I fancied, as I looked at her, that I slipped hopelessly back into the coarse and common boy again. O the sense of distance and disparity that came upon me, and the inaccessibility that came about her!

She gave me her hand. I stammered something about the pleasure I felt in seeing her again, and about my having looked forward to it, for a long, long time.

"Do you find her much changed, Pip?" asked Miss Havisham, with her greedy look, and striking her stick upon a chair that stood between them, as a sign to me to sit down there.

"When I came in, Miss Havisham, I thought there was nothing of Estella in the face or figure; but now it all settles down so curiously into the old—"

"What? You are not going to say into the old Estella?" Miss Havisham interrupted. "She was proud and insulting, and you wanted to go away from her. Don't you remember?"

I said confusedly that that was long ago, and that I knew no better then, and the like. Estella smiled with perfect composure, and said she had no doubt of my having been quite right, and of her having been very disagreeable.

"Is he changed?" Miss Havisham asked her.

"Very much," said Estella, looking at me.

"Less coarse and common?" said Miss Havisham, playing with Estella's hair.

Estella laughed, and looked at the shoe in her hand, and laughed again, and looked at me, and put the shoe down. She treated me as a boy still, but she lured me on.

We sat in the dreamy room among the old strange influences which had so wrought upon me, and I learnt that she had but just come home from France, and that she was going to London. Proud and wilful as of old, she had brought those qualities into such subjection to her beauty that it was impossible and out of nature—or I thought so—to separate them from her beauty. Truly it was impossible to dissociate her presence from all those wretched hankerings after money and gentility that had disturbed my boyhood,—from all those ill-regulated aspirations that had first made me ashamed of home and Joe,—from all those visions that had raised her face in the glowing fire, struck it out of the iron on the anvil, extracted it from the darkness of night to look in at the wooden window of the forge, and flit away. In a word, it was impossible for me to separate her, in the past or in the present, from the innermost life of my life.

It was settled that I should stay there all the rest of the day, and return to the hotel at night, and to London to-morrow. When we had conversed for a while, Miss Havisham sent us two out to walk in the neglected garden: on our coming in by and by, she said, I should wheel her about a little, as in times of yore.

So, Estella and I went out into the garden by the gate through which I had strayed to my encounter with the pale young gentleman, now Herbert; I, trembling in spirit and worshipping the very hem of her dress; she, quite composed and most decidedly not worshipping the hem of mine. As we drew near to the place of encounter, she stopped and said,—

"I must have been a singular little creature to hide and see that fight that day; but I did, and I enjoyed it very much."

"You rewarded me very much."

"Did I?" she replied, in an incidental and forgetful way. "I remember I entertained a great objection to your adversary, because I took it ill that he should be brought here to pester me with his company."

"He and I are great friends now."

"Are you? I think I recollect though, that you read with his father?"

"Yes."

I made the admission with reluctance, for it seemed to have a boyish look, and she already treated me more than enough like a boy.

"Since your change of fortune and prospects, you have changed your companions," said Estella.

"Naturally," said I.

"And necessarily," she added, in a haughty tone; "what was fit company for you once, would be quite unfit company for you now."

In my conscience, I doubt very much whether I had any lingering intention left of going to see Joe; but if I had, this observation put it to flight.

"You had no idea of your impending good fortune, in those times?" said Estella, with a slight wave of her hand, signifying in the fighting times.

"Not the least."

The air of completeness and superiority with which she walked at my side, and the air of youthfulness and submission with which I walked at hers, made a contrast that I strongly felt. It would have rankled in me more than it did, if I had not regarded myself as eliciting it by being so set apart for her and assigned to her.

The garden was too overgrown and rank for walking in with ease, and after we had made the round of it twice or thrice, we came out again into the brewery yard. I showed her to a nicety where I had seen her walking on the casks, that first old day, and she said, with a cold and careless look in that direction, "Did I?" I reminded her where she had come out of the house and given me my meat and drink, and she said, "I don't remember." "Not remember that you made me cry?" said I. "No," said she, and shook her head and looked about her. I verily believe that her not remembering and not minding in the least, made me cry again, inwardly,—and that is the sharpest crying of all.

"You must know," said Estella, condescending to me as a brilliant and beautiful woman might, "that I have no heart,—if that has anything to do with my memory."

I got through some jargon to the effect that I took the liberty of doubting that. That I knew better. That there could be no such beauty without it.

"Oh! I have a heart to be stabbed in or shot in, I have no doubt," said Estella, "and of course if it ceased to beat I should cease to be. But you know what I mean. I have no softness there, no—sympathy—sentiment—nonsense."

What was it that was borne in upon my mind when she stood still and looked attentively at me? Anything that I had seen in Miss Havisham? No. In some of her looks and gestures there was that tinge of resemblance to Miss Havisham which may often be noticed to have been acquired by children, from grown person with whom they have been much associated and secluded, and which, when childhood is passed, will produce a remarkable occasional likeness of expression between faces that are otherwise quite different. And yet I could not trace this to Miss Havisham. I looked again, and though she was still looking at me, the suggestion was gone.

What was it?

"I am serious," said Estella, not so much with a frown (for her brow was smooth) as with a darkening of her face; "if we are to be thrown much together, you had better believe it at once. No!" imperiously stopping me as I opened my lips. "I have not bestowed my tenderness anywhere. I have never had any such thing."

In another moment we were in the brewery, so long disused, and she pointed to the high gallery where I had seen her going out on that same first day, and told me she remembered to have been up there, and to have seen me standing scared below. As my eyes followed her white hand, again the same dim suggestion that I could not possibly grasp crossed me. My involuntary start occasioned her to lay her hand upon my arm. Instantly the ghost passed once more and was gone.

What was it?

"What is the matter?" asked Estella. "Are you scared again?"

"I should be, if I believed what you said just now," I replied, to turn it off.

"Then you don't? Very well. It is said, at any rate. Miss Havisham will soon be expecting you at your old post, though I think that might be laid aside now, with other old belongings. Let us make one more round of the garden, and then go in. Come! You shall not shed tears for my cruelty to-day; you shall be my Page, and give me your shoulder."

Her handsome dress had trailed upon the ground. She held it in one hand now, and with the other lightly touched my shoulder as we walked. We walked round the ruined garden twice or thrice more, and it was all in bloom for me. If the green and yellow growth of weed in the chinks of the old wall had been the most precious flowers that ever blew, it could not have been more cherished in my remembrance.

There was no discrepancy of years between us to remove her far from me; we were of nearly the same age, though of course the age told for more in her case than in mine; but the air of inaccessibility which her beauty and her manner gave her, tormented me in the midst of my delight, and at the height of the assurance I felt that our patroness had chosen us for one another. Wretched boy!

At last we went back into the house, and there I heard, with surprise, that my guardian had come down to see Miss Havisham on business, and would come back to dinner. The old wintry branches of chandeliers in the room where the mouldering table was spread had been lighted while we were out, and Miss Havisham was in her chair and waiting for me.

It was like pushing the chair itself back into the past, when we began the old slow circuit round about the ashes of the bridal feast. But, in the funereal room, with that figure of the grave fallen back in the chair fixing its eyes upon her, Estella looked more bright and beautiful than before, and I was under stronger enchantment.

The time so melted away, that our early dinner-hour drew close at hand, and Estella left us to prepare herself. We had stopped near the centre of the long table, and Miss Havisham, with one of her withered arms stretched out of the chair, rested that clenched hand upon the yellow cloth. As Estella looked back over her shoulder before going out at the door, Miss Havisham kissed that hand to her, with a ravenous intensity that was of its kind quite dreadful.

Then, Estella being gone and we two left alone, she turned to me, and said in a whisper,—

"Is she beautiful, graceful, well-grown? Do you admire her?"

"Everybody must who sees her, Miss Havisham."

She drew an arm round my neck, and drew my head close down to hers as she sat in the chair. "Love her, love her, love her! How does she use you?"

Before I could answer (if I could have answered so difficult a question at all) she repeated, "Love her, love her, love her! If she favors you, love her. If she wounds you, love her. If she tears your heart to pieces,—and as it gets older and stronger it will tear deeper,—love her, love her, love her!"

Never had I seen such passionate eagerness as was joined to her utterance of these words. I could feel the muscles of the thin arm round my neck swell with the vehemence that possessed her.

"Hear me, Pip! I adopted her, to be loved. I bred her and educated her, to be loved. I developed her into what she is, that she might be loved. Love her!"

She said the word often enough, and there could be no doubt that she meant to say it; but if the often repeated word had been hate instead of love—despair—revenge—dire death—it could not have sounded from her lips more like a curse.

"I'll tell you," said she, in the same hurried passionate whisper, "what real love is. It is blind devotion, unquestioning self-humiliation, utter submission, trust and belief against yourself and against the whole world, giving up your whole heart and soul to the smiter—as I did!"

When she came to that, and to a wild cry that followed that, I caught her round the waist. For she rose up in the chair, in her shroud of a dress, and struck at the air as if she would as soon have struck herself against the wall and fallen dead.

All this passed in a few seconds. As I drew her down into her chair, I was conscious of a scent that I knew, and turning, saw my guardian in the room.

He always carried (I have not yet mentioned it, I think) a pocket-handkerchief of rich silk and of imposing proportions, which was of great value to him in his profession. I have seen him so terrify a client or a witness by ceremoniously unfolding this pocket-handkerchief as if he were immediately going to blow his nose, and then pausing, as if he knew he should not have time to do it before such client or witness committed himself, that the self-committal has followed directly, quite as a matter of course. When I saw him in the room he had this expressive pocket-handkerchief in both hands, and was looking at us. On meeting my eye, he said plainly, by a momentary and silent pause in that attitude, "Indeed? Singular!" and then put the handkerchief to its right use with wonderful effect.

Miss Havisham had seen him as soon as I, and was (like everybody else) afraid of him. She made a strong attempt to compose herself, and stammered that he was as punctual as ever.

"As punctual as ever," he repeated, coming up to us. "(How do you do, Pip? Shall I give you a ride, Miss Havisham? Once round?) And so you are here, Pip?"

I told him when I had arrived, and how Miss Havisham had wished me to come and see Estella. To which he replied, "Ah! Very fine young lady!" Then he pushed Miss Havisham in her chair before him, with one of his large hands, and put the other in his trousers-pocket as if the pocket were full of secrets.

"Well, Pip! How often have you seen Miss Estella before?" said he, when he came to a stop.

"How often?"

"Ah! How many times? Ten thousand times?"

"Oh! Certainly not so many."

"Twice?"

"Jaggers," interposed Miss Havisham, much to my relief, "leave my Pip alone, and go with him to your dinner."

He complied, and we groped our way down the dark stairs together. While we were still on our way to those detached apartments across the paved yard at the back, he asked me how often I had seen Miss Havisham eat and drink; offering me a breadth of choice, as usual, between a hundred times and once.

I considered, and said, "Never."

"And never will, Pip," he retorted, with a frowning smile. "She has never allowed herself to be seen doing either, since she lived this present life of hers. She wanders about in the night, and then lays hands on such food as she takes."

"Pray, sir," said I, "may I ask you a question?"

"You may," said he, "and I may decline to answer it. Put your question."

"Estella's name. Is it Havisham or—?" I had nothing to add.

"Or what?" said he.

"Is it Havisham?"

"It is Havisham."

This brought us to the dinner-table, where she and Sarah Pocket awaited us. Mr. Jaggers presided, Estella sat opposite to him, I faced my green and yellow friend. We dined very well, and were waited on by a maid-servant whom I had never seen in all my comings and goings, but who, for anything I know, had been in that mysterious house the whole time. After dinner a bottle of choice old port was placed before my guardian (he was evidently well acquainted with the vintage), and the two ladies left us.

Anything to equal the determined reticence of Mr. Jaggers under that roof I never saw elsewhere, even in him. He kept his very looks to himself, and scarcely directed his eyes to Estella's face once during dinner. When she spoke to him, he listened, and in due course answered, but never looked at her, that I could see. On the other hand, she often looked at him, with interest and curiosity, if not distrust, but his face never showed the least consciousness. Throughout dinner he took a dry delight in making Sarah Pocket greener and yellower, by often referring in conversation with me to my expectations; but here, again, he showed no consciousness, and even made it appear that he extorted—and even did extort, though I don't know how—those references out of my innocent self.

And when he and I were left alone together, he sat with an air upon him of general lying by in consequence of information he possessed, that really was too much for me. He cross-examined his very wine when he had nothing else in hand. He held it between himself and the candle, tasted the port, rolled it in his mouth, swallowed it, looked at his glass again, smelt the port, tried it, drank it, filled again, and cross-examined the glass again, until I was as nervous as if I had known the wine to be telling him something to my disadvantage. Three or four times I feebly thought I would start conversation; but whenever he saw me going to ask him anything, he looked at me with his glass in his hand, and rolling his wine about in his mouth, as if requesting me to take notice that it was of no use, for he couldn't answer.

I think Miss Pocket was conscious that the sight of me involved her in the danger of being goaded to madness, and perhaps tearing off her cap,—which was a very hideous one, in the nature of a muslin mop,—and strewing the ground with her hair,—which assuredly had never grown on her head. She did not appear when we afterwards went up to Miss Havisham's room, and we four played at whist. In the interval, Miss Havisham, in a fantastic way, had put some of the most beautiful jewels from her dressing-table into Estella's hair, and about her bosom and arms; and I saw even my guardian look at her from under his thick eyebrows, and raise them a little, when her loveliness was before him, with those rich flushes of glitter and color in it.

Of the manner and extent to which he took our trumps into custody, and came out with mean little cards at the ends of hands, before which the glory of our Kings and Queens was utterly abased, I say nothing; nor, of the feeling that I had, respecting his looking upon us personally in the light of three very obvious and poor riddles that he had found out long ago. What I suffered from, was the incompatibility between his cold presence and my feelings towards Estella. It was not that I knew I could never bear to speak to him about her, that I knew I could never bear to hear him creak his boots at her, that I knew I could never bear to see him wash his hands of her; it was, that my admiration should be within a foot or two of him,—it was, that my feelings should be in the same place with him,—that, was the agonizing circumstance.

We played until nine o'clock, and then it was arranged that when Estella came to London I should be forewarned of her coming and should meet her at the coach; and then I took leave of her, and touched her and left her.

My guardian lay at the Boar in the next room to mine. Far into the night, Miss Havisham's words, "Love her, love her, love her!" sounded in my ears. I adapted them for my own repetition, and said to my pillow, "I love her, I love her, I love her!" hundreds of times. Then, a burst of gratitude came upon me, that she should be destined for me, once the blacksmith's boy. Then I thought if she were, as I feared, by no means rapturously grateful for that destiny yet, when would she begin to be interested in me? When should I awaken the heart within her that was mute and sleeping now?

Ah me! I thought those were high and great emotions. But I never thought there was anything low and small in my keeping away from Joe, because I knew she would be contemptuous of him. It was but a day gone, and Joe had brought the tears into my eyes; they had soon dried, God forgive me! soon dried.

Chapter XXX

After well considering the matter while I was dressing at the Blue Boar in the morning, I resolved to tell my guardian that I doubted Orlick's being the right sort of man to fill a post of trust at Miss Havisham's. "Why of course he is not the right sort of man, Pip," said my guardian, comfortably satisfied beforehand on the general head, "because the man who fills the post of trust never is the right sort of man." It seemed quite to put him into spirits to find that this particular post was not exceptionally held by the right sort of man, and he listened in a satisfied manner while I told him what knowledge I had of Orlick. "Very good, Pip," he observed, when I had concluded, "I'll go round presently, and pay our friend off." Rather alarmed by this summary action, I was for a little delay, and even hinted that our friend himself might be difficult to deal with. "Oh no he won't," said my guardian, making his pocket-handkerchief-point, with perfect confidence; "I should like to see him argue the question with me."

As we were going back together to London by the midday coach, and as I breakfasted under such terrors of Pumblechook that I could scarcely hold my cup, this gave me an opportunity of saying that I wanted a walk, and that I would go on along the London road while Mr. Jaggers was occupied, if he would let the coachman know that I would get into my place when overtaken. I was thus enabled to fly from the Blue Boar immediately after breakfast. By then making a loop of about a couple of miles into the open country at the back of Pumblechook's premises, I got round into the High Street again, a little beyond that pitfall, and felt myself in comparative security.

It was interesting to be in the quiet old town once more, and it was not disagreeable to be here and there suddenly recognized and stared after. One or two of the tradespeople even darted out of their shops and went a little way down the street before me, that they might turn, as if they had forgotten something, and pass me face to face,—on which occasions I don't know whether they or I made the worse pretence; they of not doing it, or I of not seeing it. Still my position was a distinguished one, and I was not at all dissatisfied with it, until Fate threw me in the way of that unlimited miscreant, Trabb's boy.

Casting my eyes along the street at a certain point of my progress, I beheld Trabb's boy approaching, lashing himself with an empty blue bag. Deeming that a serene and unconscious contemplation of him would best beseem me, and would be most likely to quell his evil mind, I advanced with that expression of countenance, and was rather congratulating myself on my success, when suddenly the knees of Trabb's boy smote together, his hair uprose, his cap fell off, he trembled violently in every limb, staggered out into the road, and crying to the populace, "Hold me! I'm so frightened!" feigned to be in a paroxysm of terror and contrition, occasioned by the dignity of my appearance. As I passed him, his teeth loudly chattered in his head, and with every mark of extreme humiliation, he prostrated himself in the dust.

This was a hard thing to bear, but this was nothing. I had not advanced another two hundred yards when, to my inexpressible terror, amazement, and indignation, I again beheld Trabb's boy approaching. He was coming round a narrow corner. His blue bag was slung over his shoulder, honest industry beamed in his eyes, a determination to proceed to Trabb's with cheerful briskness was indicated in his gait. With a shock he became aware of me, and was severely visited as before; but this time his motion was rotatory, and he staggered round and round me with knees more afflicted, and with uplifted hands as if beseeching for mercy. His sufferings were hailed with the greatest joy by a knot of spectators, and I felt utterly confounded.

I had not got as much further down the street as the post-office, when I again beheld Trabb's boy shooting round by a back way. This time, he was entirely changed. He wore the blue bag in the manner of my great-coat, and was strutting along the pavement towards me on the opposite side of the street, attended by a company of delighted young friends to whom he from time to time exclaimed, with a wave of his hand, "Don't know yah!" Words cannot state the amount of aggravation and injury wreaked upon me by Trabb's boy, when passing abreast of me, he pulled up his shirt-collar, twined his side-hair, stuck an arm akimbo, and smirked extravagantly by, wriggling his elbows and body, and drawling to his attendants, "Don't know yah, don't know yah, 'pon my soul don't know yah!" The disgrace attendant on his immediately afterwards taking to crowing and pursuing me across the bridge with crows, as from an exceedingly dejected fowl who had known me when I was a blacksmith, culminated the disgrace with which I left the town, and was, so to speak, ejected by it into the open country.

But unless I had taken the life of Trabb's boy on that occasion, I really do not even now see what I could have done save endure. To have struggled with him in the street, or to have exacted any lower recompense from him than his heart's best blood, would have been futile and degrading. Moreover, he was a boy whom no man could hurt; an invulnerable and dodging serpent who, when chased into a corner, flew out again between his captor's legs, scornfully yelping. I wrote, however, to Mr. Trabb by next day's post, to say that Mr. Pip must decline to deal further with one who could so far forget what he owed to the best interests of society, as to employ a boy who excited Loathing in every respectable mind.

The coach, with Mr. Jaggers inside, came up in due time, and I took my box-seat again, and arrived in London safe,—but not sound, for my heart was gone. As soon as I arrived, I sent a penitential codfish and barrel of oysters to Joe (as reparation for not having gone myself), and then went on to Barnard's Inn.

I found Herbert dining on cold meat, and delighted to welcome me back. Having despatched The Avenger to the coffee-house for an addition to the dinner, I felt that I must open my breast that very evening to my friend and chum. As confidence was out of the question with The Avenger in the hall, which could merely be regarded in the light of an antechamber to the keyhole, I sent him to the Play. A better proof of the severity of my bondage to that taskmaster could scarcely be afforded, than the degrading shifts to which I was constantly driven to find him employment. So mean is extremity, that I sometimes sent him to Hyde Park corner to see what o'clock it was.

Dinner done and we sitting with our feet upon the fender, I said to Herbert, "My dear Herbert, I have something very particular to tell you."

"My dear Handel," he returned, "I shall esteem and respect your confidence."

"It concerns myself, Herbert," said I, "and one other person."

Herbert crossed his feet, looked at the fire with his head on one side, and having looked at it in vain for some time, looked at me because I didn't go on.

"Herbert," said I, laying my hand upon his knee, "I love—I adore—Estella."

Instead of being transfixed, Herbert replied in an easy matter-of-course way, "Exactly. Well?"

"Well, Herbert? Is that all you say? Well?"

"What next, I mean?" said Herbert. "Of course I know that."

"How do you know it?" said I.

"How do I know it, Handel? Why, from you."

"I never told you."

"Told me! You have never told me when you have got your hair cut, but I have had senses to perceive it. You have always adored her, ever since I have known you. You brought your adoration and your portmanteau here together. Told me! Why, you have always told me all day long. When you told me your own story, you told me plainly that you began adoring her the first time you saw her, when you were very young indeed."

"Very well, then," said I, to whom this was a new and not unwelcome light, "I have never left off adoring her. And she has come back, a most beautiful and most elegant creature. And I saw her yesterday. And if I adored her before, I now doubly adore her."

"Lucky for you then, Handel," said Herbert, "that you are picked out for her and allotted to her. Without encroaching on forbidden ground, we may venture to say that there can be no doubt between ourselves of that fact. Have you any idea yet, of Estella's views on the adoration question?"

I shook my head gloomily. "Oh! She is thousands of miles away, from me," said I.

"Patience, my dear Handel: time enough, time enough. But you have something more to say?"

"I am ashamed to say it," I returned, "and yet it's no worse to say it than to think it. You call me a lucky fellow. Of course, I am. I was a blacksmith's boy but yesterday; I am—what shall I say I am—to-day?"

"Say a good fellow, if you want a phrase," returned Herbert, smiling, and clapping his hand on the back of mine—"a good fellow, with impetuosity and hesitation, boldness and diffidence, action and dreaming, curiously mixed in him."

I stopped for a moment to consider whether there really was this mixture in my character. On the whole, I by no means recognized the analysis, but thought it not worth disputing.

"When I ask what I am to call myself to-day, Herbert," I went on, "I suggest what I have in my thoughts. You say I am lucky. I know I have done nothing to raise myself in life, and that Fortune alone has raised me; that is being very lucky. And yet, when I think of Estella—"

("And when don't you, you know?" Herbert threw in, with his eyes on the fire; which I thought kind and sympathetic of him.)

"—Then, my dear Herbert, I cannot tell you how dependent and uncertain I feel, and how exposed to hundreds of chances. Avoiding forbidden ground, as you did just now, I may still say that on the constancy of one person (naming no person) all my expectations depend. And at the best, how indefinite and unsatisfactory, only to know so vaguely what they are!" In saying this, I relieved my mind of what had always been there, more or less, though no doubt most since yesterday.

"Now, Handel," Herbert replied, in his gay, hopeful way, "it seems to me that in the despondency of the tender passion, we are looking into our gift-horse's mouth with a magnifying-glass. Likewise, it seems to me that, concentrating our attention on the examination, we altogether overlook one of the best points of the animal. Didn't you tell me that your guardian,

Mr. Jaggers, told you in the beginning, that you were not endowed with expectations only? And even if he had not told you so,—though that is a very large If, I grant,—could you believe that of all men in London, Mr. Jaggers is the man to hold his present relations towards you unless he were sure of his ground?"

I said I could not deny that this was a strong point. I said it (people often do so, in such cases) like a rather reluctant concession to truth and justice;—as if I wanted to deny it!

"I should think it was a strong point," said Herbert, "and I should think you would be puzzled to imagine a stronger; as to the rest, you must bide your guardian's time, and he must bide his client's time. You'll be one-and-twenty before you know where you are, and then perhaps you'll get some further enlightenment. At all events, you'll be nearer getting it, for it must come at last."

"What a hopeful disposition you have!" said I, gratefully admiring his cheery ways.

"I ought to have," said Herbert, "for I have not much else. I must acknowledge, by the by, that the good sense of what I have just said is not my own, but my father's. The only remark I ever heard him make on your story, was the final one, "The thing is settled and done, or Mr. Jaggers would not be in it." And now before I say anything more about my father, or my father's son, and repay confidence with confidence, I want to make myself seriously disagreeable to you for a moment,—positively repulsive."

"You won't succeed," said I.

"O yes I shall!" said he. "One, two, three, and now I am in for it. Handel, my good fellow;"—though he spoke in this light tone, he was very much in earnest,—"I have been thinking since we have been talking with our feet on this fender, that Estella surely cannot be a condition of your inheritance, if she was never referred to by your guardian. Am I right in so understanding what you have told me, as that he never referred to her, directly or indirectly, in any way? Never even hinted, for instance, that your patron might have views as to your marriage ultimately?"

"Never."

"Now, Handel, I am quite free from the flavor of sour grapes, upon my soul and honor! Not being bound to her, can you not detach yourself from her?—I told you I should be disagreeable."

I turned my head aside, for, with a rush and a sweep, like the old marsh winds coming up from the sea, a feeling like that which had subdued me on the morning when I left the forge, when the mists were solemnly rising, and when I laid my hand upon the village finger-post, smote upon my heart again. There was silence between us for a little while.

"Yes; but my dear Handel," Herbert went on, as if we had been talking, instead of silent, "its having been so strongly rooted in the breast of a boy whom nature and circumstances made so romantic, renders it very serious. Think of her bringing-up, and think of Miss Havisham. Think of what she is herself (now I am repulsive and you abominate me). This may lead to miserable things."

"I know it, Herbert," said I, with my head still turned away, "but I can't help it."

"You can't detach yourself?"

"No. Impossible!"

"You can't try, Handel?"

"No. Impossible!"

"Well!" said Herbert, getting up with a lively shake as if he had been asleep, and stirring the fire, "now I'll endeavor to make myself agreeable again!"

So he went round the room and shook the curtains out, put the chairs in their places, tidied the books and so forth that were lying about, looked into the hall, peeped into the letter-box, shut the door, and came back to his chair by the fire: where he sat down, nursing his left leg in both arms.

"I was going to say a word or two, Handel, concerning my father and my father's son. I am afraid it is scarcely necessary for my father's son to remark that my father's establishment is not particularly brilliant in its housekeeping."

"There is always plenty, Herbert," said I, to say something encouraging.

"O yes! and so the dustman says, I believe, with the strongest approval, and so does the marine-store shop in the back street. Gravely, Handel, for the subject is grave enough, you know how it is as well as I do. I suppose there was a time once when my father had not given matters up; but if ever there was, the time is gone. May I ask you if you have ever had an opportunity of remarking, down in your part of the country, that the children of not exactly suitable marriages are always most particularly anxious to be married?"

This was such a singular question, that I asked him in return, "Is it so?"

"I don't know," said Herbert, "that's what I want to know. Because it is decidedly the case with us. My poor sister Charlotte, who was next me and died before she was fourteen, was a striking example. Little Jane is the same. In her desire to be matrimonially established, you might suppose her to have passed her short existence in the perpetual contemplation of domestic bliss. Little Alick in a frock has already made arrangements for his union with a suitable young person at Kew. And indeed, I think we are all engaged, except the baby."

"Then you are?" said I.

"I am," said Herbert; "but it's a secret."

I assured him of my keeping the secret, and begged to be favored with further particulars. He had spoken so sensibly and feelingly of my weakness that I wanted to know something about his strength.

"May I ask the name?" I said.

"Name of Clara," said Herbert.

"Live in London?"

"Yes, perhaps I ought to mention," said Herbert, who had become curiously crestfallen and meek, since we entered on the interesting theme, "that she is rather below my mother's nonsensical family notions. Her father had to do with the victualling of passenger-ships. I think he was a species of purser."

"What is he now?" said I.

"He's an invalid now," replied Herbert.

"Living on——?"

"On the first floor," said Herbert. Which was not at all what I meant, for I had intended my question to apply to his means. "I have never seen him, for he has always kept his room overhead, since I have known Clara. But I have heard him constantly. He makes tremendous rows,—roars, and pegs at the floor with some frightful instrument." In looking at me and then laughing heartily, Herbert for the time recovered his usual lively manner.

"Don't you expect to see him?" said I.

"O yes, I constantly expect to see him," returned Herbert, "because I never hear him, without expecting him to come tumbling through the ceiling. But I don't know how long the rafters may hold."

When he had once more laughed heartily, he became meek again, and told me that the moment he began to realize Capital, it was his intention to marry this young lady. He added as a self-evident proposition, engendering low spirits, "But you can't marry, you know, while you're looking about you."

As we contemplated the fire, and as I thought what a difficult vision to realize this same Capital sometimes was, I put my hands in my pockets. A folded piece of paper in one of them attracting my attention, I opened it and found it to be the play-bill I had received from Joe, relative to the celebrated provincial amateur of Roscian renown. "And bless my heart," I involuntarily added aloud, "it's to-night!"

This changed the subject in an instant, and made us hurriedly resolve to go to the play. So, when I had pledged myself to comfort and abet Herbert in the affair of his heart by all practicable and impracticable means, and when Herbert had told me that his affianced already knew me by reputation and that I should be presented to her, and when we had warmly shaken hands upon our mutual confidence, we blew out our candles, made up our fire, locked our door, and issued forth in quest of Mr. Wopsle and Denmark.

Chapter XXXI

On our arrival in Denmark, we found the king and queen of that country elevated in two arm-chairs on a kitchen-table, holding a Court. The whole of the Danish nobility were in attendance; consisting of a noble boy in the wash-leather boots of a gigantic ancestor, a venerable Peer with a dirty face who seemed to have risen from the people late in life, and the Danish chivalry with a comb in its hair and a pair of white silk legs, and presenting on the whole a feminine appearance. My gifted townsman stood gloomily apart, with folded arms, and I could have wished that his curls and forehead had been more probable.

Several curious little circumstances transpired as the action proceeded. The late king of the country not only appeared to have been troubled with a cough at the time of his decease, but to have taken it with him to the tomb, and to have brought it back. The royal phantom also carried a ghostly manuscript round its truncheon, to which it had the appearance of occasionally referring, and that too, with an air of anxiety and a tendency to lose the place of reference which were suggestive of a state of mortality. It was this, I conceive, which led to the Shade's being advised by the gallery to "turn over!"—a recommendation which it took extremely ill. It was likewise to be noted of this majestic spirit, that whereas it always appeared with an air of having been out a long time and walked an immense distance, it perceptibly came from a closely contiguous wall. This occasioned its terrors to be received derisively. The Queen of Denmark, a very buxom lady, though no doubt historically brazen, was considered by the public to have too much brass about her; her chin being attached to her diadem by a broad band of that metal (as if she had a gorgeous toothache), her waist being encircled by another, and each of her arms by another, so that she was openly mentioned as "the kettle-drum." The noble boy in the ancestral boots was inconsistent, representing himself, as it were in one breath, as an able seaman, a strolling actor, a grave-digger, a clergyman, and a person of the utmost importance at a Court fencing-match, on the authority of whose practised eye and nice discrimination the finest strokes were judged. This gradually led to a want of toleration for him, and even—on his being detected in holy orders, and declining to perform the funeral service—to the general indignation taking the form of nuts. Lastly, Ophelia was a prey to such slow musical madness, that when, in course of time, she had taken off her white muslin scarf, folded it up, and buried it, a sulky man who had been long cooling his impatient nose against an iron bar in the front row of the gallery, growled, "Now the baby's put to bed let's have supper!" Which, to say the least of it, was out of keeping.

Upon my unfortunate townsman all these incidents accumulated with playful effect. Whenever that undecided Prince had to ask a question or state a doubt, the public helped him out with it. As for example; on the question whether 'twas nobler in the mind to suffer, some roared yes, and some no, and some inclining to both opinions said "Toss up for it;" and quite a Debating Society arose. When he asked what should such fellows as he do crawling between earth and heaven, he was encouraged with loud cries of "Hear, hear!" When he appeared with his stocking disordered (its disorder expressed, according to usage, by one very neat fold in the top, which I suppose to be always got up with a flat iron), a conversation took place in the gallery respecting the paleness of his leg, and whether it was occasioned by the turn the ghost had given him. On his taking the recorders,—very like a little black flute that had just been played in the orchestra and handed out at the door,—he was called upon unanimously for Rule Britannia. When he recommended the player not to saw the air thus, the sulky man said, "And don't you do it, neither; you're a deal worse than him!" And I grieve to add that peals of laughter greeted Mr. Wopsle on every one of these occasions.

But his greatest trials were in the churchyard, which had the appearance of a primeval forest, with a kind of small ecclesiastical wash-house on one side, and a turnpike gate on the other. Mr. Wopsle in a comprehensive black cloak, being descried entering at the turnpike, the gravedigger was admonished in a friendly way, "Look out! Here's the undertaker a coming, to see how you're a getting on with your work!" I believe it is well known in a constitutional country that Mr. Wopsle could not possibly have returned the skull, after moralizing over it, without dusting his fingers on a white napkin taken from his breast; but even that innocent and indispensable action did not pass without the comment, "Wai-ter!" The arrival of the body for interment (in an empty black box with the lid tumbling open), was the signal for a general joy, which was much enhanced by the discovery, among the bearers, of an individual obnoxious to identification. The joy attended Mr. Wopsle through his struggle with Laertes on the brink of the orchestra and the grave, and slackened no more until he had tumbled the king off the kitchen-table, and had died by inches from the ankles upward.

We had made some pale efforts in the beginning to applaud Mr. Wopsle; but they were too hopeless to be persisted in. Therefore we had sat, feeling keenly for him, but laughing, nevertheless, from ear to ear. I laughed in spite of myself all the time, the whole thing was so droll; and yet I had a latent impression that there was something decidedly fine in Mr. Wopsle's elocution,—not for old associations' sake, I am afraid, but because it was very slow, very dreary, very uphill and downhill, and very unlike any way in which any man in any natural circumstances of life or death ever expressed himself about anything. When the tragedy was over, and he had been called for and hooted, I said to Herbert, "Let us go at once, or perhaps we shall meet him."

We made all the haste we could downstairs, but we were not quick enough either. Standing at the door was a Jewish man with an unnatural heavy smear of eyebrow, who caught my eyes as we advanced, and said, when we came up with him,—

"Mr. Pip and friend?"

Identity of Mr. Pip and friend confessed.

"Mr. Waldengarver," said the man, "would be glad to have the honor."

"Waldengarver?" I repeated—when Herbert murmured in my ear, "Probably Wopsle."

"Oh!" said I. "Yes. Shall we follow you?"

"A few steps, please." When we were in a side alley, he turned and asked, "How did you think he looked?—I dressed him."

I don't know what he had looked like, except a funeral; with the addition of a large Danish sun or star hanging round his neck by a blue ribbon, that had given him the appearance of being insured in some extraordinary Fire Office. But I said he had looked very nice.

"When he come to the grave," said our conductor, "he showed his cloak beautiful. But, judging from the wing, it looked to me that when he see the ghost in the queen's apartment, he might have made more of his stockings."

I modestly assented, and we all fell through a little dirty swing door, into a sort of hot packing-case immediately behind it. Here Mr. Wopsle was divesting himself of his Danish garments, and here there was just room for us to look at him over one another's shoulders, by keeping the packing-case door, or lid, wide open.

"Gentlemen," said Mr. Wopsle, "I am proud to see you. I hope, Mr. Pip, you will excuse my sending round. I had the happiness to know you in former times, and the Drama has ever had a claim which has ever been acknowledged, on the noble and the affluent."

Meanwhile, Mr. Waldengarver, in a frightful perspiration, was trying to get himself out of his princely sables.

"Skin the stockings off Mr. Waldengarver," said the owner of that property, "or you'll bust 'em. Bust 'em, and you'll bust five-and-thirty shillings. Shakspeare never was complimented with a finer pair. Keep quiet in your chair now, and leave 'em to me."

With that, he went upon his knees, and began to flay his victim; who, on the first stocking coming off, would certainly have fallen over backward with his chair, but for there being no room to fall anyhow.

I had been afraid until then to say a word about the play. But then, Mr. Waldengarver looked up at us complacently, and said,—

"Gentlemen, how did it seem to you, to go, in front?"

Herbert said from behind (at the same time poking me), "Capitally." So I said "Capitally."

"How did you like my reading of the character, gentlemen?" said Mr. Waldengarver, almost, if not quite, with patronage.

Herbert said from behind (again poking me), "Massive and concrete." So I said boldly, as if I had originated it, and must beg to insist upon it, "Massive and concrete."

"I am glad to have your approbation, gentlemen," said Mr. Waldengarver, with an air of dignity, in spite of his being ground against the wall at the time, and holding on by the seat of the chair.

"But I'll tell you one thing, Mr. Waldengarver," said the man who was on his knees, "in which you're out in your reading. Now mind! I don't care who says contrary; I tell you so. You're out in your reading of Hamlet when you get your legs in profile. The last Hamlet as I dressed, made the same mistakes in his reading at rehearsal, till I got him to put a large red wafer on each of his shins, and then at that rehearsal (which was the last) I went in front, sir, to the back of the pit, and whenever his reading brought him into profile, I called out "I don't see no wafers!" And at night his reading was lovely."

Mr. Waldengarver smiled at me, as much as to say "a faithful Dependent—I overlook his folly;" and then said aloud, "My view is a little classic and thoughtful for them here; but they will improve, they will improve."

Herbert and I said together, O, no doubt they would improve.

"Did you observe, gentlemen," said Mr. Waldengarver, "that there was a man in the gallery who endeavored to cast derision on the service,—I mean, the representation?"

We basely replied that we rather thought we had noticed such a man. I added, "He was drunk, no doubt."

"O dear no, sir," said Mr. Wopsle, "not drunk. His employer would see to that, sir. His employer would not allow him to be drunk."

"You know his employer?" said I.

Mr. Wopsle shut his eyes, and opened them again; performing both ceremonies very slowly. "You must have observed, gentlemen," said he, "an ignorant and a blatant ass, with a rasping throat and a countenance expressive of low malignity, who went through—I will not say sustained—the rôle (if I may use a French expression) of Claudius, King of Denmark. That is his employer, gentlemen. Such is the profession!"

Without distinctly knowing whether I should have been more sorry for Mr. Wopsle if he had been in despair, I was so sorry for him as it was, that I took the opportunity of his turning round to have his braces put on,—which jostled us out at the doorway,—to ask Herbert what he thought of having him home to supper? Herbert said he thought it would be kind to do so; therefore I invited him, and he went to Barnard's with us, wrapped up to the eyes, and we did our best for him, and he sat until two o'clock in the morning, reviewing his success and developing his plans. I forget in detail what they were, but I have a general recollection that he was to begin with reviving the Drama, and to end with crushing it; inasmuch as his decease would leave it utterly bereft and without a chance or hope.

Miserably I went to bed after all, and miserably thought of Estella, and miserably dreamed that my expectations were all cancelled, and that I had to give my hand in marriage to Herbert's Clara, or play Hamlet to Miss Havisham's Ghost, before twenty thousand people, without knowing twenty words of it.

Chapter XXXII

One day when I was busy with my books and Mr. Pocket, I received a note by the post, the mere outside of which threw me into a great flutter; for, though I had never seen the handwriting in which it was addressed, I divined whose hand it was. It had no set beginning, as Dear Mr. Pip, or Dear Pip, or Dear Sir, or Dear Anything, but ran thus:—

"I am to come to London the day after to-morrow by the midday coach. I believe it was settled you should meet me? At all events Miss Havisham has that impression, and I write in obedience to it. She sends you her regard.

"Yours, ESTELLA."

If there had been time, I should probably have ordered several suits of clothes for this occasion; but as there was not, I was fain to be content with those I had. My appetite vanished instantly, and I knew no peace or rest until the day arrived. Not that its arrival brought me either; for, then I was worse than ever, and began haunting the coach-office in Wood Street, Cheapside, before the coach had left the Blue Boar in our town. For all that I knew this perfectly well, I still felt as if it were not safe to let the coach-office be out of my sight longer than five minutes at a time; and in this condition of unreason I had performed the first half-hour of a watch of four or five hours, when Wemmick ran against me.

"Halloa, Mr. Pip," said he; "how do you do? I should hardly have thought this was your beat."

I explained that I was waiting to meet somebody who was coming up by coach, and I inquired after the Castle and the Aged.

"Both flourishing thankye," said Wemmick, "and particularly the Aged. He's in wonderful feather. He'll be eighty-two next birthday. I have a notion of firing eighty-two times, if the neighborhood shouldn't complain, and that cannon of mine should prove equal to the pressure. However, this is not London talk. Where do you think I am going to?"

"To the office?" said I, for he was tending in that direction.

"Next thing to it," returned Wemmick, "I am going to Newgate. We are in a banker's-parcel case just at present, and I have been down the road taking a squint at the scene of action, and thereupon must have a word or two with our client."

"Did your client commit the robbery?" I asked.

"Bless your soul and body, no," answered Wemmick, very drily. "But he is accused of it. So might you or I be. Either of us might be accused of it, you know."

"Only neither of us is," I remarked.

"Yah!" said Wemmick, touching me on the breast with his forefinger; "you're a deep one, Mr. Pip! Would you like to have a look at Newgate? Have you time to spare?"

I had so much time to spare, that the proposal came as a relief, notwithstanding its irreconcilability with my latent desire to keep my eye on the coach-office. Muttering that I would make the inquiry whether I had time to walk with him, I went into the office, and ascertained from the clerk with the nicest precision and much to the trying of his temper, the earliest moment at which the coach could be expected,—which I knew beforehand, quite as well as he. I then rejoined Mr. Wemmick, and affecting to consult my watch, and to be surprised by the information I had received, accepted his offer.

We were at Newgate in a few minutes, and we passed through the lodge where some fetters were hanging up on the bare walls among the prison rules, into the interior of the jail. At that time jails were much neglected, and the period of exaggerated reaction consequent on all public wrongdoing—and which is always its heaviest and longest punishment—was still far off. So, felons were not lodged and fed better than soldiers (to say nothing of paupers), and seldom set fire to their prisons with the excusable object of improving the flavor of their soup. It was visiting time when Wemmick took me in, and a potman was going his rounds with beer; and the prisoners, behind bars in yards, were buying beer, and talking to friends; and a frowzy, ugly, disorderly, depressing scene it was.

It struck me that Wemmick walked among the prisoners much as a gardener might walk among his plants. This was first put into my head by his seeing a shoot that had come up in the night, and saying, "What, Captain Tom? Are you there? Ah, indeed!" and also, "Is that Black Bill behind the cistern? Why I didn't look for you these two months; how do you find yourself?" Equally in his stopping at the bars and attending to anxious whisperers,—always singly,—Wemmick with his post-office in an immovable state, looked at them while in conference, as if he were taking particular notice of the advance they had made, since last observed, towards coming out in full blow at their trial.

He was highly popular, and I found that he took the familiar department of Mr. Jaggers's business; though something of the state of Mr. Jaggers hung about him too, forbidding approach beyond certain limits. His personal recognition of each successive client was comprised in a nod, and in his settling his hat a little easier on his head with both hands, and then tightening the post-office, and putting his hands in his pockets. In one or two instances there was a difficulty respecting the raising of fees, and then Mr. Wemmick, backing as far as possible from the insufficient money produced, said, "it's no use, my boy. I'm only a subordinate. I can't take it. Don't go on in that way with a subordinate. If you are unable to make up your quantum, my boy, you had better address yourself to a principal; there are plenty of principals in the profession, you know, and what is not worth the while of one, may be worth the while of another; that's my recommendation to you, speaking as a subordinate. Don't try on useless measures. Why should you? Now, who's next?"

Thus, we walked through Wemmick's greenhouse, until he turned to me and said, "Notice the man I shall shake hands with." I should have done so, without the preparation, as he had shaken hands with no one yet.

Almost as soon as he had spoken, a portly upright man (whom I can see now, as I write) in a well-worn olive-colored frock-coat, with a peculiar pallor overspreading the red in his complexion, and eyes that went wandering about when he tried to fix them, came up to a corner of the bars, and put his hand to his hat—which had a greasy and fatty surface like cold broth—with a half-serious and half-jocose military salute.

"Colonel, to you!" said Wemmick; "how are you, Colonel?"

"All right, Mr. Wemmick."

"Everything was done that could be done, but the evidence was too strong for us, Colonel."

"Yes, it was too strong, sir,—but I don't care."

"No, no," said Wemmick, coolly, "you don't care." Then, turning to me, "Served His Majesty this man. Was a soldier in the line and bought his discharge."

I said, "Indeed?" and the man's eyes looked at me, and then looked over my head, and then looked all round me, and then he drew his hand across his lips and laughed.

"I think I shall be out of this on Monday, sir," he said to Wemmick.

"Perhaps," returned my friend, "but there's no knowing."

"I am glad to have the chance of bidding you good-bye, Mr. Wemmick," said the man, stretching out his hand between two bars.

"Thankye," said Wemmick, shaking hands with him. "Same to you, Colonel."

"If what I had upon me when taken had been real, Mr. Wemmick," said the man, unwilling to let his hand go, "I should have asked the favor of your wearing another ring—in acknowledgment of your attentions."

"I'll accept the will for the deed," said Wemmick. "By the by; you were quite a pigeon-fancier." The man looked up at the sky. "I am told you had a remarkable breed of tumblers. Could you commission any friend of yours to bring me a pair, if you've no further use for 'em?"

"It shall be done, sir."

"All right," said Wemmick, "they shall be taken care of. Good afternoon, Colonel. Good-bye!" They shook hands again, and as we walked away Wemmick said to me, "A Coiner, a very good workman. The Recorder's report is made to-day, and he is sure to be executed on Monday. Still you see, as far as it goes, a pair of pigeons are portable property all the same." With that, he looked back, and nodded at this dead plant, and then cast his eyes about him in walking out of the yard, as if he were considering what other pot would go best in its place.

As we came out of the prison through the lodge, I found that the great importance of my guardian was appreciated by the turnkeys, no less than by those whom they held in charge. "Well, Mr. Wemmick," said the turnkey, who kept us between the two studded and spiked lodge gates, and who carefully locked one before he unlocked the other, "what's Mr. Jaggers going to do with that water-side murder? Is he going to make it manslaughter, or what's he going to make of it?"

"Why don't you ask him?" returned Wemmick.

"O yes, I dare say!" said the turnkey.

"Now, that's the way with them here, Mr. Pip," remarked Wemmick, turning to me with his post-office elongated. "They don't mind what they ask of me, the subordinate; but you'll never catch 'em asking any questions of my principal."

"Is this young gentleman one of the 'prentices or articled ones of your office?" asked the turnkey, with a grin at Mr. Wemmick's humor.

"There he goes again, you see!" cried Wemmick, "I told you so! Asks another question of the subordinate before his first is dry! Well, supposing Mr. Pip is one of them?"

"Why then," said the turnkey, grinning again, "he knows what Mr. Jaggers is."

"Yah!" cried Wemmick, suddenly hitting out at the turnkey in a facetious way, "you're dumb as one of your own keys when you have to do with my principal, you know you are. Let us out, you old fox, or I'll get him to bring an action against you for false imprisonment."

The turnkey laughed, and gave us good day, and stood laughing at us over the spikes of the wicket when we descended the steps into the street.

"Mind you, Mr. Pip," said Wemmick, gravely in my ear, as he took my arm to be more confidential; "I don't know that Mr. Jaggers does a better thing than the way in which he keeps himself so high. He's always so high. His constant height is of a piece with his immense abilities. That Colonel durst no more take leave of him, than that turnkey durst ask him his intentions respecting a case. Then, between his height and them, he slips in his subordinate,— don't you see?—and so he has 'em, soul and body."

I was very much impressed, and not for the first time, by my guardian's subtlety. To confess the truth, I very heartily wished, and not for the first time, that I had had some other guardian of minor abilities.

Mr. Wemmick and I parted at the office in Little Britain, where suppliants for Mr. Jaggers's notice were lingering about as usual, and I returned to my watch in the street of the coach-office, with some three hours on hand. I consumed the whole time in thinking how strange it was that I should be encompassed by all this taint of prison and crime; that, in my childhood out on our lonely marshes on a winter evening, I should have first encountered it; that, it should have reappeared on two occasions, starting out like a stain that was faded but not gone; that, it should in this new way pervade my fortune and advancement. While my mind was thus engaged, I thought of the beautiful young Estella, proud and refined, coming towards me, and I thought with absolute abhorrence of the contrast between the jail and her. I wished that Wemmick had not met me, or that I had not yielded to him and gone with him, so that, of all days in the year on this day, I might not have had Newgate in my breath and on my clothes. I beat the prison dust off my feet as I sauntered to and fro, and I shook it out of my dress, and I exhaled its air from my lungs. So contaminated did I feel, remembering who was coming, that the coach came quickly after all, and I was not yet free from the soiling consciousness of Mr. Wemmick's conservatory, when I saw her face at the coach window and her hand waving to me.

What was the nameless shadow which again in that one instant had passed?

Chapter XXXIII

In her furred travelling-dress, Estella seemed more delicately beautiful than she had ever seemed yet, even in my eyes. Her manner was more winning than she had cared to let it be to me before, and I thought I saw Miss Havisham's influence in the change.

We stood in the Inn Yard while she pointed out her luggage to me, and when it was all collected I remembered—having forgotten everything but herself in the meanwhile—that I knew nothing of her destination.

"I am going to Richmond," she told me. "Our lesson is, that there are two Richmonds, one in Surrey and one in Yorkshire, and that mine is the Surrey Richmond. The distance is ten miles. I am to have a carriage, and you are to take me. This is my purse, and you are to pay my charges out of it. O, you must take the purse! We have no choice, you and I, but to obey our instructions. We are not free to follow our own devices, you and I."

As she looked at me in giving me the purse, I hoped there was an inner meaning in her words. She said them slightingly, but not with displeasure.

"A carriage will have to be sent for, Estella. Will you rest here a little?"

"Yes, I am to rest here a little, and I am to drink some tea, and you are to take care of me the while."

She drew her arm through mine, as if it must be done, and I requested a waiter who had been staring at the coach like a man who had never seen such a thing in his life, to show us a private sitting-room. Upon that, he pulled out a napkin, as if it were a magic clew without which he couldn't find the way upstairs, and led us to the black hole of the establishment, fitted up with a diminishing mirror (quite a superfluous article, considering the hole's proportions), an anchovy sauce-cruet, and somebody's pattens. On my objecting to this retreat, he took us into another room with a dinner-table for thirty, and in the grate a scorched leaf of a copy-book under a bushel of coal-dust. Having looked at this extinct conflagration and shaken his head, he took my order; which, proving to be merely, "Some tea for the lady," sent him out of the room in a very low state of mind.

I was, and I am, sensible that the air of this chamber, in its strong combination of stable with soup-stock, might have led one to infer that the coaching department was not doing well, and that the enterprising proprietor was boiling down the horses for the refreshment department. Yet the room was all in all to me, Estella being in it. I thought that with her I could have been happy there for life. (I was not at all happy there at the time, observe, and I knew it well.)

"Where are you going to, at Richmond?" I asked Estella.

"I am going to live," said she, "at a great expense, with a lady there, who has the power— or says she has—of taking me about, and introducing me, and showing people to me and showing me to people."

"I suppose you will be glad of variety and admiration?"

"Yes, I suppose so."

She answered so carelessly, that I said, "You speak of yourself as if you were some one else."

"Where did you learn how I speak of others? Come, come," said Estella, smiling delightfully, "you must not expect me to go to school to you; I must talk in my own way. How do you thrive with Mr. Pocket?"

"I live quite pleasantly there; at least—" It appeared to me that I was losing a chance.

"At least?" repeated Estella.

"As pleasantly as I could anywhere, away from you."

"You silly boy," said Estella, quite composedly, "how can you talk such nonsense? Your friend Mr. Matthew, I believe, is superior to the rest of his family?"

"Very superior indeed. He is nobody's enemy—"

"Don't add but his own," interposed Estella, "for I hate that class of man. But he really is disinterested, and above small jealousy and spite, I have heard?"

"I am sure I have every reason to say so."

"You have not every reason to say so of the rest of his people," said Estella, nodding at me with an expression of face that was at once grave and rallying, "for they beset Miss Havisham with reports and insinuations to your disadvantage. They watch you, misrepresent you, write letters about you (anonymous sometimes), and you are the torment and the occupation of their lives. You can scarcely realize to yourself the hatred those people feel for you."

"They do me no harm, I hope?"

Instead of answering, Estella burst out laughing. This was very singular to me, and I looked at her in considerable perplexity. When she left off—and she had not laughed languidly, but with real enjoyment—I said, in my diffident way with her,—

"I hope I may suppose that you would not be amused if they did me any harm."

"No, no you may be sure of that," said Estella. "You may be certain that I laugh because they fail. O, those people with Miss Havisham, and the tortures they undergo!" She laughed again, and even now when she had told me why, her laughter was very singular to me, for I could not doubt its being genuine, and yet it seemed too much for the occasion. I thought there must really be something more here than I knew; she saw the thought in my mind, and answered it.

"It is not easy for even you." said Estella, "to know what satisfaction it gives me to see those people thwarted, or what an enjoyable sense of the ridiculous I have when they are made ridiculous. For you were not brought up in that strange house from a mere baby. I was. You had not your little wits sharpened by their intriguing against you, suppressed and defenceless, under the mask of sympathy and pity and what not that is soft and soothing. I had. You did not gradually open your round childish eyes wider and wider to the discovery of that impostor of a woman who calculates her stores of peace of mind for when she wakes up in the night. I did."

It was no laughing matter with Estella now, nor was she summoning these remembrances from any shallow place. I would not have been the cause of that look of hers for all my expectations in a heap.

"Two things I can tell you," said Estella. "First, notwithstanding the proverb that constant dropping will wear away a stone, you may set your mind at rest that these people never will—never would, in hundred years—impair your ground with Miss Havisham, in any particular, great or small. Second, I am beholden to you as the cause of their being so busy and so mean in vain, and there is my hand upon it."

As she gave it to me playfully,—for her darker mood had been but Momentary,—I held it and put it to my lips. "You ridiculous boy," said Estella, "will you never take warning? Or do you kiss my hand in the same spirit in which I once let you kiss my cheek?"

"What spirit was that?" said I.

"I must think a moment. A spirit of contempt for the fawners and plotters."

"If I say yes, may I kiss the cheek again?"

"You should have asked before you touched the hand. But, yes, if you like."

I leaned down, and her calm face was like a statue's. "Now," said Estella, gliding away the instant I touched her cheek, "you are to take care that I have some tea, and you are to take me to Richmond."

Her reverting to this tone as if our association were forced upon us, and we were mere puppets, gave me pain; but everything in our intercourse did give me pain. Whatever her tone with me happened to be, I could put no trust in it, and build no hope on it; and yet I went on against trust and against hope. Why repeat it a thousand times? So it always was.

I rang for the tea, and the waiter, reappearing with his magic clew, brought in by degrees some fifty adjuncts to that refreshment, but of tea not a glimpse. A teaboard, cups and saucers, plates, knives and forks (including carvers), spoons (various), saltcellars, a meek little muffin confined with the utmost precaution under a strong iron cover, Moses in the bulrushes typified by a soft bit of butter in a quantity of parsley, a pale loaf with a powdered head, two proof impressions of the bars of the kitchen fireplace on triangular bits of bread, and ultimately a fat family urn; which the waiter staggered in with, expressing in his countenance burden and suffering. After a prolonged absence at this stage of the entertainment, he at length came back with a casket of precious appearance containing twigs. These I steeped in hot water, and so from the whole of these appliances extracted one cup of I don't know what for Estella.

The bill paid, and the waiter remembered, and the ostler not forgotten, and the chambermaid taken into consideration,—in a word, the whole house bribed into a state of contempt and animosity, and Estella's purse much lightened,—we got into our post-coach and drove away. Turning into Cheapside and rattling up Newgate Street, we were soon under the walls of which I was so ashamed.

"What place is that?" Estella asked me.

I made a foolish pretence of not at first recognizing it, and then told her. As she looked at it, and drew in her head again, murmuring, "Wretches!" I would not have confessed to my visit for any consideration.

"Mr. Jaggers," said I, by way of putting it neatly on somebody else, "has the reputation of being more in the secrets of that dismal place than any man in London."

"He is more in the secrets of every place, I think," said Estella, in a low voice.

"You have been accustomed to see him often, I suppose?"

"I have been accustomed to see him at uncertain intervals, ever since I can remember. But I know him no better now, than I did before I could speak plainly. What is your own experience of him? Do you advance with him?"

"Once habituated to his distrustful manner," said I, "I have done very well."

"Are you intimate?"

"I have dined with him at his private house."

"I fancy," said Estella, shrinking "that must be a curious place."

"It is a curious place."

I should have been chary of discussing my guardian too freely even with her; but I should have gone on with the subject so far as to describe the dinner in Gerrard Street, if we had not then come into a sudden glare of gas. It seemed, while it lasted, to be all alight and alive with that inexplicable feeling I had had before; and when we were out of it, I was as much dazed for a few moments as if I had been in lightning.

So we fell into other talk, and it was principally about the way by which we were travelling, and about what parts of London lay on this side of it, and what on that. The great city was almost new to her, she told me, for she had never left Miss Havisham's neighborhood until she had gone to France, and she had merely passed through London then in going and returning. I asked her if my guardian had any charge of her while she remained here? To that she emphatically said "God forbid!" and no more.

It was impossible for me to avoid seeing that she cared to attract me; that she made herself winning, and would have won me even if the task had needed pains. Yet this made me none the happier, for even if she had not taken that tone of our being disposed of by others, I should have felt that she held my heart in her hand because she wilfully chose to do it, and not because it would have wrung any tenderness in her to crush it and throw it away.

When we passed through Hammersmith, I showed her where Mr. Matthew Pocket lived, and said it was no great way from Richmond, and that I hoped I should see her sometimes.

"O yes, you are to see me; you are to come when you think proper; you are to be mentioned to the family; indeed you are already mentioned."

I inquired was it a large household she was going to be a member of?

"No; there are only two; mother and daughter. The mother is a lady of some station, though not averse to increasing her income."

"I wonder Miss Havisham could part with you again so soon."

"It is a part of Miss Havisham's plans for me, Pip," said Estella, with a sigh, as if she were tired; "I am to write to her constantly and see her regularly and report how I go on,—I and the jewels,—for they are nearly all mine now."

It was the first time she had ever called me by my name. Of course she did so purposely, and knew that I should treasure it up.

We came to Richmond all too soon, and our destination there was a house by the green,—a staid old house, where hoops and powder and patches, embroidered coats, rolled stockings, ruffles and swords, had had their court days many a time. Some ancient trees before the house were still cut into fashions as formal and unnatural as the hoops and wigs and stiff skirts; but their own allotted places in the great procession of the dead were not far off, and they would soon drop into them and go the silent way of the rest.

A bell with an old voice—which I dare say in its time had often said to the house, Here is the green farthingale, Here is the diamond-hilted sword, Here are the shoes with red heels and the blue solitaire—sounded gravely in the moonlight, and two cherry-colored maids came fluttering out to receive Estella. The doorway soon absorbed her boxes, and she gave me her hand and a smile, and said good night, and was absorbed likewise. And still I stood looking at the house, thinking how happy I should be if I lived there with her, and knowing that I never was happy with her, but always miserable.

I got into the carriage to be taken back to Hammersmith, and I got in with a bad heart-ache, and I got out with a worse heart-ache. At our own door, I found little Jane Pocket coming home from a little party escorted by her little lover; and I envied her little lover, in spite of his being subject to Flopson.

Mr. Pocket was out lecturing; for, he was a most delightful lecturer on domestic economy, and his treatises on the management of children and servants were considered the very best text-books on those themes. But Mrs. Pocket was at home, and was in a little difficulty, on account of the baby's having been accommodated with a needle-case to keep him quiet during the unaccountable absence (with a relative in the Foot Guards) of Millers. And more needles were missing than it could be regarded as quite wholesome for a patient of such tender years either to apply externally or to take as a tonic.

Mr. Pocket being justly celebrated for giving most excellent practical advice, and for having a clear and sound perception of things and a highly judicious mind, I had some notion in my heart-ache of begging him to accept my confidence. But happening to look up at Mrs. Pocket as she sat reading her book of dignities after prescribing Bed as a sovereign remedy for baby, I thought—Well—No, I wouldn't.

Chapter XXXIV

As I had grown accustomed to my expectations, I had insensibly begun to notice their effect upon myself and those around me. Their influence on my own character I disguised from my recognition as much as possible, but I knew very well that it was not all good. I lived in a state of chronic uneasiness respecting my behavior to Joe. My conscience was not by any means comfortable about Biddy. When I woke up in the night,—like Camilla,—I used to think, with a weariness on my spirits, that I should have been happier and better if I had never seen Miss Havisham's face, and had risen to manhood content to be partners with Joe in the honest old forge. Many a time of an evening, when I sat alone looking at the fire, I thought, after all there was no fire like the forge fire and the kitchen fire at home.

Yet Estella was so inseparable from all my restlessness and disquiet of mind, that I really fell into confusion as to the limits of my own part in its production. That is to say, supposing I had had no expectations, and yet had had Estella to think of, I could not make out to my satisfaction that I should have done much better. Now, concerning the influence of my position on others, I was in no such difficulty, and so I perceived—though dimly enough perhaps—that it was not beneficial to anybody, and, above all, that it was not beneficial to Herbert. My lavish habits led his easy nature into expenses that he could not afford, corrupted the simplicity of his life, and disturbed his peace with anxieties and regrets. I was not at all remorseful for having unwittingly set those other branches of the Pocket family to the poor arts they practised; because such littlenesses were their natural bent, and would have been evoked by anybody else, if I had left them slumbering. But Herbert's was a very different case, and it often caused me a twinge to think that I had done him evil service in crowding his sparely furnished chambers with incongruous upholstery work, and placing the Canary-breasted Avenger at his disposal.

So now, as an infallible way of making little ease great ease, I began to contract a quantity of debt. I could hardly begin but Herbert must begin too, so he soon followed. At Startop's suggestion, we put ourselves down for election into a club called The Finches of the Grove: the object of which institution I have never divined, if it were not that the members should dine expensively once a fortnight, to quarrel among themselves as much as possible after dinner, and to cause six waiters to get drunk on the stairs. I know that these gratifying social ends were so invariably accomplished, that Herbert and I understood nothing else to be referred to in the first standing toast of the society: which ran "Gentlemen, may the present promotion of good feeling ever reign predominant among the Finches of the Grove."

The Finches spent their money foolishly (the Hotel we dined at was in Covent Garden), and the first Finch I saw when I had the honor of joining the Grove was Bentley Drummle, at that time floundering about town in a cab of his own, and doing a great deal of damage to the posts at the street corners. Occasionally, he shot himself out of his equipage headforemost over the apron; and I saw him on one occasion deliver himself at the door of the Grove in this unintentional way—like coals. But here I anticipate a little, for I was not a Finch, and could not be, according to the sacred laws of the society, until I came of age.

In my confidence in my own resources, I would willingly have taken Herbert's expenses on myself; but Herbert was proud, and I could make no such proposal to him. So he got into difficulties in every direction, and continued to look about him. When we gradually fell into keeping late hours and late company, I noticed that he looked about him with a desponding eye at breakfast-time; that he began to look about him more hopefully about mid-day; that he drooped when he came into dinner; that he seemed to descry Capital in the distance, rather clearly, after dinner; that he all but realized Capital towards midnight; and that at about two o'clock in the morning, he became so deeply despondent again as to talk of buying a rifle and going to America, with a general purpose of compelling buffaloes to make his fortune.

I was usually at Hammersmith about half the week, and when I was at Hammersmith I haunted Richmond, whereof separately by and by. Herbert would often come to Hammersmith when I was there, and I think at those seasons his father would occasionally have some passing perception that the opening he was looking for, had not appeared yet. But in the general tumbling up of the family, his tumbling out in life somewhere, was a thing to transact itself somehow. In the meantime Mr. Pocket grew grayer, and tried oftener to lift himself out of his perplexities by the hair. While Mrs. Pocket tripped up the family with her footstool, read her book of dignities, lost her pocket-handkerchief, told us about her grandpapa, and taught the young idea how to shoot, by shooting it into bed whenever it attracted her notice.

As I am now generalizing a period of my life with the object of clearing my way before me, I can scarcely do so better than by at once completing the description of our usual manners and customs at Barnard's Inn.

We spent as much money as we could, and got as little for it as people could make up their minds to give us. We were always more or less miserable, and most of our acquaintance were in the same condition. There was a gay fiction among us that we were constantly enjoying ourselves, and a skeleton truth that we never did. To the best of my belief, our case was in the last aspect a rather common one.

Every morning, with an air ever new, Herbert went into the City to look about him. I often paid him a visit in the dark back-room in which he consorted with an ink-jar, a hat-peg, a coal-box, a string-box, an almanac, a desk and stool, and a ruler; and I do not remember that I ever saw him do anything else but look about him. If we all did what we undertake to do, as faithfully as Herbert did, we might live in a Republic of the Virtues. He had nothing else to do, poor fellow, except at a certain hour of every afternoon to "go to Lloyd's"—in observance of a ceremony of seeing his principal, I think. He never did anything else in connection with Lloyd's that I could find out, except come back again. When he felt his case unusually serious, and that he positively must find an opening, he would go on 'Change at a busy time, and walk in and out, in a kind of gloomy country dance figure, among the assembled magnates. "For," says Herbert to me, coming home to dinner on one of those special occasions, "I find the truth to be, Handel, that an opening won't come to one, but one must go to it,—so I have been."

If we had been less attached to one another, I think we must have hated one another regularly every morning. I detested the chambers beyond expression at that period of repentance, and could not endure the sight of the Avenger's livery; which had a more expensive and a less remunerative appearance then than at any other time in the four-and-twenty hours. As we got more and more into debt, breakfast became a hollower and hollower form, and, being on one occasion at breakfast-time threatened (by letter) with legal proceedings, "not unwholly unconnected," as my local paper might put it, "with jewelery," I went so far as to seize the Avenger by his blue collar and shake him off his feet,—so that he was actually in the air, like a booted Cupid,—for presuming to suppose that we wanted a roll.

At certain times—meaning at uncertain times, for they depended on our humor—I would say to Herbert, as if it were a remarkable discovery,—

"My dear Herbert, we are getting on badly."

"My dear Handel," Herbert would say to me, in all sincerity, "if you will believe me, those very words were on my lips, by a strange coincidence."

"Then, Herbert," I would respond, "let us look into our affairs."

We always derived profound satisfaction from making an appointment for this purpose. I always thought this was business, this was the way to confront the thing, this was the way to take the foe by the throat. And I know Herbert thought so too.

We ordered something rather special for dinner, with a bottle of something similarly out of the common way, in order that our minds might be fortified for the occasion, and we might come well up to the mark. Dinner over, we produced a bundle of pens, a copious supply of ink, and a goodly show of writing and blotting paper. For there was something very comfortable in having plenty of stationery.

I would then take a sheet of paper, and write across the top of it, in a neat hand, the heading, "Memorandum of Pip's debts"; with Barnard's Inn and the date very carefully added. Herbert would also take a sheet of paper, and write across it with similar formalities, "Memorandum of Herbert's debts."

Each of us would then refer to a confused heap of papers at his side, which had been thrown into drawers, worn into holes in pockets, half burnt in lighting candles, stuck for weeks into the looking-glass, and otherwise damaged. The sound of our pens going refreshed us exceedingly, insomuch that I sometimes found it difficult to distinguish between this edifying business proceeding and actually paying the money. In point of meritorious character, the two things seemed about equal.

When we had written a little while, I would ask Herbert how he got on? Herbert probably would have been scratching his head in a most rueful manner at the sight of his accumulating figures.

"They are mounting up, Handel," Herbert would say; "upon my life, they are mounting up."

"Be firm, Herbert," I would retort, plying my own pen with great assiduity. "Look the thing in the face. Look into your affairs. Stare them out of countenance."

"So I would, Handel, only they are staring me out of countenance."

However, my determined manner would have its effect, and Herbert would fall to work again. After a time he would give up once more, on the plea that he had not got Cobbs's bill, or Lobbs's, or Nobbs's, as the case might be.

"Then, Herbert, estimate; estimate it in round numbers, and put it down."

"What a fellow of resource you are!" my friend would reply, with admiration. "Really your business powers are very remarkable."

I thought so too. I established with myself, on these occasions, the reputation of a first-rate man of business,—prompt, decisive, energetic, clear, cool-headed. When I had got all my responsibilities down upon my list, I compared each with the bill, and ticked it off. My self-approval when I ticked an entry was quite a luxurious sensation. When I had no more ticks to make, I folded all my bills up uniformly, docketed each on the back, and tied the whole into a symmetrical bundle. Then I did the same for Herbert (who modestly said he had not my administrative genius), and felt that I had brought his affairs into a focus for him.

My business habits had one other bright feature, which I called "leaving a Margin." For example; supposing Herbert's debts to be one hundred and sixty-four pounds four-and-twopence, I would say, "Leave a margin, and put them down at two hundred." Or, supposing my own to be four times as much, I would leave a margin, and put them down at seven hundred. I had the highest opinion of the wisdom of this same Margin, but I am bound to acknowledge that on looking back, I deem it to have been an expensive device. For, we always ran into new debt immediately, to the full extent of the margin, and sometimes, in the sense of freedom and solvency it imparted, got pretty far on into another margin.

But there was a calm, a rest, a virtuous hush, consequent on these examinations of our affairs that gave me, for the time, an admirable opinion of myself. Soothed by my exertions, my method, and Herbert's compliments, I would sit with his symmetrical bundle and my own on the table before me among the stationary, and feel like a Bank of some sort, rather than a private individual.

We shut our outer door on these solemn occasions, in order that we might not be interrupted. I had fallen into my serene state one evening, when we heard a letter dropped through the slit in the said door, and fall on the ground. "It's for you, Handel," said Herbert, going out and coming back with it, "and I hope there is nothing the matter." This was in allusion to its heavy black seal and border.

The letter was signed Trabb & Co., and its contents were simply, that I was an honored sir, and that they begged to inform me that Mrs. J. Gargery had departed this life on Monday last at twenty minutes past six in the evening, and that my attendance was requested at the interment on Monday next at three o'clock in the afternoon.

Chapter XXXV

It was the first time that a grave had opened in my road of life, and the gap it made in the smooth ground was wonderful. The figure of my sister in her chair by the kitchen fire, haunted me night and day. That the place could possibly be, without her, was something my mind seemed unable to compass; and whereas she had seldom or never been in my thoughts of late, I had now the strangest ideas that she was coming towards me in the street, or that she would presently knock at the door. In my rooms too, with which she had never been at all associated, there was at once the blankness of death and a perpetual suggestion of the sound of her voice or the turn of her face or figure, as if she were still alive and had been often there.

Whatever my fortunes might have been, I could scarcely have recalled my sister with much tenderness. But I suppose there is a shock of regret which may exist without much tenderness. Under its influence (and perhaps to make up for the want of the softer feeling) I was seized with a violent indignation against the assailant from whom she had suffered so much; and I felt that on sufficient proof I could have revengefully pursued Orlick, or any one else, to the last extremity.

Having written to Joe, to offer him consolation, and to assure him that I would come to the funeral, I passed the intermediate days in the curious state of mind I have glanced at. I went down early in the morning, and alighted at the Blue Boar in good time to walk over to the forge.

It was fine summer weather again, and, as I walked along, the times when I was a little helpless creature, and my sister did not spare me, vividly returned. But they returned with a gentle tone upon them that softened even the edge of Tickler. For now, the very breath of the beans and clover whispered to my heart that the day must come when it would be well for my memory that others walking in the sunshine should be softened as they thought of me.

At last I came within sight of the house, and saw that Trabb and Co. had put in a funereal execution and taken possession. Two dismally absurd persons, each ostentatiously exhibiting a crutch done up in a black bandage,—as if that instrument could possibly communicate any comfort to anybody,—were posted at the front door; and in one of them I recognized a postboy discharged from the Boar for turning a young couple into a sawpit on their bridal morning, in consequence of intoxication rendering it necessary for him to ride his horse clasped round the neck with both arms. All the children of the village, and most of the women, were admiring these sable warders and the closed windows of the house and forge; and as I came up, one of the two warders (the postboy) knocked at the door,—implying that I was far too much exhausted by grief to have strength remaining to knock for myself.

Another sable warder (a carpenter, who had once eaten two geese for a wager) opened the door, and showed me into the best parlor. Here, Mr. Trabb had taken unto himself the best table, and had got all the leaves up, and was holding a kind of black Bazaar, with the aid of a quantity of black pins. At the moment of my arrival, he had just finished putting somebody's hat into black long-clothes, like an African baby; so he held out his hand for mine. But I, misled by the action, and confused by the occasion, shook hands with him with every testimony of warm affection.

Poor dear Joe, entangled in a little black cloak tied in a large bow under his chin, was seated apart at the upper end of the room; where, as chief mourner, he had evidently been stationed by Trabb. When I bent down and said to him, "Dear Joe, how are you?" he said, "Pip, old chap, you knowed her when she were a fine figure of a—" and clasped my hand and said no more.

Biddy, looking very neat and modest in her black dress, went quietly here and there, and was very helpful. When I had spoken to Biddy, as I thought it not a time for talking I went and sat down near Joe, and there began to wonder in what part of the house it—she—my sister—was. The air of the parlor being faint with the smell of sweet-cake, I looked about for the table of refreshments; it was scarcely visible until one had got accustomed to the gloom, but there was a cut-up plum cake upon it, and there were cut-up oranges, and sandwiches, and biscuits, and two decanters that I knew very well as ornaments, but had never seen used in all my life; one full of port, and one of sherry. Standing at this table, I became conscious of the servile Pumblechook in a black cloak and several yards of hatband, who was alternately stuffing himself, and making obsequious movements to catch my attention. The moment he succeeded, he came over to me (breathing sherry and crumbs), and said in a subdued voice, "May I, dear sir?" and did. I then descried Mr. and Mrs. Hubble; the last-named in a decent speechless paroxysm in a corner. We were all going to "follow," and were all in course of being tied up separately (by Trabb) into ridiculous bundles.

"Which I meantersay, Pip," Joe whispered me, as we were being what Mr. Trabb called "formed" in the parlor, two and two,—and it was dreadfully like a preparation for some grim kind of dance; "which I meantersay, sir, as I would in preference have carried her to the church myself, along with three or four friendly ones wot come to it with willing harts and arms, but it were considered wot the neighbors would look down on such and would be of opinions as it were wanting in respect."

"Pocket-handkerchiefs out, all!" cried Mr. Trabb at this point, in a depressed business-like voice. "Pocket-handkerchiefs out! We are ready!"

So we all put our pocket-handkerchiefs to our faces, as if our noses were bleeding, and filed out two and two; Joe and I; Biddy and Pumblechook; Mr. and Mrs. Hubble. The remains of my poor sister had been brought round by the kitchen door, and, it being a point of Undertaking ceremony that the six bearers must be stifled and blinded under a horrible black velvet housing with a white border, the whole looked like a blind monster with twelve human legs, shuffling and blundering along, under the guidance of two keepers,—the postboy and his comrade.

The neighborhood, however, highly approved of these arrangements, and we were much admired as we went through the village; the more youthful and vigorous part of the community making dashes now and then to cut us off, and lying in wait to intercept us at points of vantage. At such times the more exuberant among them called out in an excited manner on our emergence round some corner of expectancy, "Here they come!" "Here they are!" and we were all but cheered. In this progress I was much annoyed by the abject Pumblechook, who, being behind me, persisted all the way as a delicate attention in arranging my streaming hatband, and smoothing my cloak. My thoughts were further distracted by the excessive pride of Mr. and Mrs. Hubble, who were surpassingly conceited and vainglorious in being members of so distinguished a procession.

And now the range of marshes lay clear before us, with the sails of the ships on the river growing out of it; and we went into the churchyard, close to the graves of my unknown parents, Philip Pirrip, late of this parish, and Also Georgiana, Wife of the Above. And there, my sister was laid quietly in the earth, while the larks sang high above it, and the light wind strewed it with beautiful shadows of clouds and trees.

Of the conduct of the worldly minded Pumblechook while this was doing, I desire to say no more than it was all addressed to me; and that even when those noble passages were read which remind humanity how it brought nothing into the world and can take nothing out, and how it fleeth like a shadow and never continueth long in one stay, I heard him cough a reservation of the case of a young gentleman who came unexpectedly into large property. When we got back, he had the hardihood to tell me that he wished my sister could have known I had done her so much honor, and to hint that she would have considered it reasonably purchased at the price of her death. After that, he drank all the rest of the sherry, and Mr. Hubble drank the port, and the two talked (which I have since observed to be customary in such cases) as if they were of quite another race from the deceased, and were notoriously immortal. Finally, he went away with Mr. and Mrs. Hubble,—to make an evening of it, I felt sure, and to tell the Jolly Bargemen that he was the founder of my fortunes and my earliest benefactor.

When they were all gone, and when Trabb and his men—but not his Boy; I looked for him—had crammed their mummery into bags, and were gone too, the house felt wholesomer. Soon afterwards, Biddy, Joe, and I, had a cold dinner together; but we dined in the best parlor, not in the old kitchen, and Joe was so exceedingly particular what he did with his knife and fork and the saltcellar and what not, that there was great restraint upon us. But after dinner, when I made him take his pipe, and when I had loitered with him about the forge, and when we sat down together on the great block of stone outside it, we got on better. I noticed that after the funeral Joe changed his clothes so far, as to make a compromise between his Sunday dress and working dress; in which the dear fellow looked natural, and like the Man he was.

He was very much pleased by my asking if I might sleep in my own little room, and I was pleased too; for I felt that I had done rather a great thing in making the request. When the shadows of evening were closing in, I took an opportunity of getting into the garden with Biddy for a little talk.

"Biddy," said I, "I think you might have written to me about these sad matters."

"Do you, Mr. Pip?" said Biddy. "I should have written if I had thought that."

"Don't suppose that I mean to be unkind, Biddy, when I say I consider that you ought to have thought that."

"Do you, Mr. Pip?"

She was so quiet, and had such an orderly, good, and pretty way with her, that I did not like the thought of making her cry again. After looking a little at her downcast eyes as she walked beside me, I gave up that point.

"I suppose it will be difficult for you to remain here now, Biddy dear?"

"Oh! I can't do so, Mr. Pip," said Biddy, in a tone of regret but still of quiet conviction. "I have been speaking to Mrs. Hubble, and I am going to her to-morrow. I hope we shall be able to take some care of Mr. Gargery, together, until he settles down."

"How are you going to live, Biddy? If you want any mo—"

"How am I going to live?" repeated Biddy, striking in, with a momentary flush upon her face. "I'll tell you, Mr. Pip. I am going to try to get the place of mistress in the new school nearly finished here. I can be well recommended by all the neighbors, and I hope I can be industrious and patient, and teach myself while I teach others. You know, Mr. Pip," pursued Biddy, with a smile, as she raised her eyes to my face, "the new schools are not like the old, but I learnt a good deal from you after that time, and have had time since then to improve."

"I think you would always improve, Biddy, under any circumstances."

"Ah! Except in my bad side of human nature," murmured Biddy.

It was not so much a reproach as an irresistible thinking aloud. Well! I thought I would give up that point too. So, I walked a little further with Biddy, looking silently at her downcast eyes.

"I have not heard the particulars of my sister's death, Biddy."

"They are very slight, poor thing. She had been in one of her bad states—though they had got better of late, rather than worse—for four days, when she came out of it in the evening, just at tea-time, and said quite plainly, 'Joe.' As she had never said any word for a long while, I ran and fetched in Mr. Gargery from the forge. She made signs to me that she wanted him to sit down close to her, and wanted me to put her arms round his neck. So I put them round his neck, and she laid her head down on his shoulder quite content and satisfied. And so she presently said 'Joe' again, and once 'Pardon,' and once 'Pip.' And so she never lifted her head up any more, and it was just an hour later when we laid it down on her own bed, because we found she was gone."

Biddy cried; the darkening garden, and the lane, and the stars that were coming out, were blurred in my own sight.

"Nothing was ever discovered, Biddy?"

"Nothing."

"Do you know what is become of Orlick?"

"I should think from the color of his clothes that he is working in the quarries."

"Of course you have seen him then?—Why are you looking at that dark tree in the lane?"

"I saw him there, on the night she died."

"That was not the last time either, Biddy?"

"No; I have seen him there, since we have been walking here.—It is of no use," said Biddy, laying her hand upon my arm, as I was for running out, "you know I would not deceive you; he was not there a minute, and he is gone."

It revived my utmost indignation to find that she was still pursued by this fellow, and I felt inveterate against him. I told her so, and told her that I would spend any money or take any pains to drive him out of that country. By degrees she led me into more temperate talk, and she told me how Joe loved me, and how Joe never complained of anything,—she didn't say, of me; she had no need; I knew what she meant,—but ever did his duty in his way of life, with a strong hand, a quiet tongue, and a gentle heart.

"Indeed, it would be hard to say too much for him," said I; "and Biddy, we must often speak of these things, for of course I shall be often down here now. I am not going to leave poor Joe alone."

Biddy said never a single word.

"Biddy, don't you hear me?"

"Yes, Mr. Pip."

"Not to mention your calling me Mr. Pip,—which appears to me to be in bad taste, Biddy,—what do you mean?"

"What do I mean?" asked Biddy, timidly.

"Biddy," said I, in a virtuously self-asserting manner, "I must request to know what you mean by this?"

"By this?" said Biddy.

"Now, don't echo," I retorted. "You used not to echo, Biddy."

"Used not!" said Biddy. "O Mr. Pip! Used!"

Well! I rather thought I would give up that point too. After another silent turn in the garden, I fell back on the main position.

"Biddy," said I, "I made a remark respecting my coming down here often, to see Joe, which you received with a marked silence. Have the goodness, Biddy, to tell me why."

"Are you quite sure, then, that you WILL come to see him often?" asked Biddy, stopping in the narrow garden walk, and looking at me under the stars with a clear and honest eye.

"O dear me!" said I, as if I found myself compelled to give up Biddy in despair. "This really is a very bad side of human nature! Don't say any more, if you please, Biddy. This shocks me very much."

For which cogent reason I kept Biddy at a distance during supper, and when I went up to my own old little room, took as stately a leave of her as I could, in my murmuring soul, deem reconcilable with the churchyard and the event of the day. As often as I was restless in the night, and that was every quarter of an hour, I reflected what an unkindness, what an injury, what an injustice, Biddy had done me.

Early in the morning I was to go. Early in the morning I was out, and looking in, unseen, at one of the wooden windows of the forge. There I stood, for minutes, looking at Joe, already at work with a glow of health and strength upon his face that made it show as if the bright sun of the life in store for him were shining on it.

"Good-bye, dear Joe!—No, don't wipe it off—for God's sake, give me your blackened hand!—I shall be down soon and often."

"Never too soon, sir," said Joe, "and never too often, Pip!"

Biddy was waiting for me at the kitchen door, with a mug of new milk and a crust of bread. "Biddy," said I, when I gave her my hand at parting, "I am not angry, but I am hurt."

"No, don't be hurt," she pleaded quite pathetically; "let only me be hurt, if I have been ungenerous."

Once more, the mists were rising as I walked away. If they disclosed to me, as I suspect they did, that I should not come back, and that Biddy was quite right, all I can say is,—they were quite right too.

Chapter XXXVI

Herbert and I went on from bad to worse, in the way of increasing our debts, looking into our affairs, leaving Margins, and the like exemplary transactions; and Time went on, whether or no, as he has a way of doing; and I came of age,—in fulfilment of Herbert's prediction, that I should do so before I knew where I was.

Herbert himself had come of age eight months before me. As he had nothing else than his majority to come into, the event did not make a profound sensation in Barnard's Inn. But we had looked forward to my one-and-twentieth birthday, with a crowd of speculations and anticipations, for we had both considered that my guardian could hardly help saying something definite on that occasion.

I had taken care to have it well understood in Little Britain when my birthday was. On the day before it, I received an official note from Wemmick, informing me that Mr. Jaggers would be glad if I would call upon him at five in the afternoon of the auspicious day. This convinced us that something great was to happen, and threw me into an unusual flutter when I repaired to my guardian's office, a model of punctuality.

In the outer office Wemmick offered me his congratulations, and incidentally rubbed the side of his nose with a folded piece of tissue-paper that I liked the look of. But he said nothing respecting it, and motioned me with a nod into my guardian's room. It was November, and my guardian was standing before his fire leaning his back against the chimney-piece, with his hands under his coattails.

"Well, Pip," said he, "I must call you Mr. Pip to-day. Congratulations, Mr. Pip."

We shook hands,—he was always a remarkably short shaker,—and I thanked him.

"Take a chair, Mr. Pip," said my guardian.

As I sat down, and he preserved his attitude and bent his brows at his boots, I felt at a disadvantage, which reminded me of that old time when I had been put upon a tombstone. The two ghastly casts on the shelf were not far from him, and their expression was as if they were making a stupid apoplectic attempt to attend to the conversation.

"Now my young friend," my guardian began, as if I were a witness in the box, "I am going to have a word or two with you."

"If you please, sir."

"What do you suppose," said Mr. Jaggers, bending forward to look at the ground, and then throwing his head back to look at the ceiling,—"what do you suppose you are living at the rate of?"

"At the rate of, sir?"

"At," repeated Mr. Jaggers, still looking at the ceiling, "the—rate—of?" And then looked all round the room, and paused with his pocket-handkerchief in his hand, half-way to his nose.

I had looked into my affairs so often, that I had thoroughly destroyed any slight notion

I might ever have had of their bearings. Reluctantly, I confessed myself quite unable to answer the question. This reply seemed agreeable to Mr. Jaggers, who said, "I thought so!" and blew his nose with an air of satisfaction.

"Now, I have asked you a question, my friend," said Mr. Jaggers. "Have you anything to ask me?"

"Of course it would be a great relief to me to ask you several questions, sir; but I remember your prohibition."

"Ask one," said Mr. Jaggers.

"Is my benefactor to be made known to me to-day?"

"No. Ask another."

"Is that confidence to be imparted to me soon?"

"Waive that, a moment," said Mr. Jaggers, "and ask another."

I looked about me, but there appeared to be now no possible escape from the inquiry, "Have-I—anything to receive, sir?" On that, Mr. Jaggers said, triumphantly, "I thought we should come to it!" and called to Wemmick to give him that piece of paper. Wemmick appeared, handed it in, and disappeared.

"Now, Mr. Pip," said Mr. Jaggers, "attend, if you please. You have been drawing pretty freely here; your name occurs pretty often in Wemmick's cash-book; but you are in debt, of course?"

"I am afraid I must say yes, sir."

"You know you must say yes; don't you?" said Mr. Jaggers.

"Yes, sir."

"I don't ask you what you owe, because you don't know; and if you did know, you wouldn't tell me; you would say less. Yes, yes, my friend," cried Mr. Jaggers, waving his forefinger to stop me as I made a show of protesting: "it's likely enough that you think you wouldn't, but you would. You'll excuse me, but I know better than you. Now, take this piece of paper in your hand. You have got it? Very good. Now, unfold it and tell me what it is."

"This is a bank-note," said I, "for five hundred pounds."

"That is a bank-note," repeated Mr. Jaggers, "for five hundred pounds. And a very handsome sum of money too, I think. You consider it so?"

"How could I do otherwise!"

"Ah! But answer the question," said Mr. Jaggers.

"Undoubtedly."

"You consider it, undoubtedly, a handsome sum of money. Now, that handsome sum of money, Pip, is your own. It is a present to you on this day, in earnest of your expectations. And at the rate of that handsome sum of money per annum, and at no higher rate, you are to live until the donor of the whole appears. That is to say, you will now take your money affairs entirely into your own hands, and you will draw from Wemmick one hundred and twenty-five pounds per quarter, until you are in communication with the fountain-head, and no longer with the mere agent. As I have told you before, I am the mere agent. I execute my instructions, and I am paid for doing so. I think them injudicious, but I am not paid for giving any opinion on their merits."

I was beginning to express my gratitude to my benefactor for the great liberality with which I was treated, when Mr. Jaggers stopped me. "I am not paid, Pip," said he, coolly, "to carry your words to any one;" and then gathered up his coat-tails, as he had gathered up the subject, and stood frowning at his boots as if he suspected them of designs against him.

After a pause, I hinted,—

"There was a question just now, Mr. Jaggers, which you desired me to waive for a moment. I hope I am doing nothing wrong in asking it again?"

"What is it?" said he.

I might have known that he would never help me out; but it took me aback to have to shape the question afresh, as if it were quite new. "Is it likely," I said, after hesitating, "that my patron, the fountain-head you have spoken of, Mr. Jaggers, will soon—" there I delicately stopped.

"Will soon what?" asked Mr. Jaggers. "That's no question as it stands, you know."

"Will soon come to London," said I, after casting about for a precise form of words, "or summon me anywhere else?"

"Now, here," replied Mr. Jaggers, fixing me for the first time with his dark deep-set eyes, "we must revert to the evening when we first encountered one another in your village. What did I tell you then, Pip?"

"You told me, Mr. Jaggers, that it might be years hence when that person appeared."

"Just so," said Mr. Jaggers, "that's my answer."

As we looked full at one another, I felt my breath come quicker in my strong desire to get something out of him. And as I felt that it came quicker, and as I felt that he saw that it came quicker, I felt that I had less chance than ever of getting anything out of him.

"Do you suppose it will still be years hence, Mr. Jaggers?"

Mr. Jaggers shook his head,—not in negativing the question, but in altogether negativing the notion that he could anyhow be got to answer it,—and the two horrible casts of the twitched faces looked, when my eyes strayed up to them, as if they had come to a crisis in their suspended attention, and were going to sneeze.

"Come!" said Mr. Jaggers, warming the backs of his legs with the backs of his warmed hands, "I'll be plain with you, my friend Pip. That's a question I must not be asked. You'll understand that better, when I tell you it's a question that might compromise me. Come! I'll go a little further with you; I'll say something more."

He bent down so low to frown at his boots, that he was able to rub the calves of his legs in the pause he made.

"When that person discloses," said Mr. Jaggers, straightening himself, "you and that person will settle your own affairs. When that person discloses, my part in this business will cease and determine. When that person discloses, it will not be necessary for me to know anything about it. And that's all I have got to say."

We looked at one another until I withdrew my eyes, and looked thoughtfully at the floor. From this last speech I derived the notion that Miss Havisham, for some reason or no reason, had not taken him into her confidence as to her designing me for Estella; that he resented this, and felt a jealousy about it; or that he really did object to that scheme, and would have nothing to do with it. When I raised my eyes again, I found that he had been shrewdly looking at me all the time, and was doing so still.

"If that is all you have to say, sir," I remarked, "there can be nothing left for me to say."

He nodded assent, and pulled out his thief-dreaded watch, and asked me where I was going to dine? I replied at my own chambers, with Herbert. As a necessary sequence, I asked him if he would favor us with his company, and he promptly accepted the invitation. But he insisted on walking home with me, in order that I might make no extra preparation for him, and first he had a letter or two to write, and (of course) had his hands to wash. So I said I would go into the outer office and talk to Wemmick.

The fact was, that when the five hundred pounds had come into my pocket, a thought had come into my head which had been often there before; and it appeared to me that Wemmick was a good person to advise with concerning such thought.

He had already locked up his safe, and made preparations for going home. He had left his desk, brought out his two greasy office candlesticks and stood them in line with the snuffers on a slab near the door, ready to be extinguished; he had raked his fire low, put his hat and great-coat ready, and was beating himself all over the chest with his safe-key, as an athletic exercise after business.

"Mr. Wemmick," said I, "I want to ask your opinion. I am very desirous to serve a friend."

Wemmick tightened his post-office and shook his head, as if his opinion were dead against any fatal weakness of that sort.

"This friend," I pursued, "is trying to get on in commercial life, but has no money, and finds it difficult and disheartening to make a beginning. Now I want somehow to help him to a beginning."

"With money down?" said Wemmick, in a tone drier than any sawdust.

"With some money down," I replied, for an uneasy remembrance shot across me of that symmetrical bundle of papers at home—"with some money down, and perhaps some anticipation of my expectations."

"Mr. Pip," said Wemmick, "I should like just to run over with you on my fingers, if you please, the names of the various bridges up as high as Chelsea Reach. Let's see; there's London, one; Southwark, two; Blackfriars, three; Waterloo, four; Westminster, five; Vauxhall, six." He had checked off each bridge in its turn, with the handle of his safe-key on the palm of his hand. "There's as many as six, you see, to choose from."

"I don't understand you," said I.

"Choose your bridge, Mr. Pip," returned Wemmick, "and take a walk upon your bridge, and pitch your money into the Thames over the centre arch of your bridge, and you know the end of it. Serve a friend with it, and you may know the end of it too,—but it's a less pleasant and profitable end."

I could have posted a newspaper in his mouth, he made it so wide after saying this.

"This is very discouraging," said I.

"Meant to be so," said Wemmick.

"Then is it your opinion," I inquired, with some little indignation, "that a man should never—"

"—Invest portable property in a friend?" said Wemmick. "Certainly he should not. Unless he wants to get rid of the friend,—and then it becomes a question how much portable property it may be worth to get rid of him."

"And that," said I, "is your deliberate opinion, Mr. Wemmick?"

"That," he returned, "is my deliberate opinion in this office."

"Ah!" said I, pressing him, for I thought I saw him near a loophole here; "but would that be your opinion at Walworth?"

"Mr. Pip," he replied, with gravity, "Walworth is one place, and this office is another. Much as the Aged is one person, and Mr. Jaggers is another. They must not be confounded together. My Walworth sentiments must be taken at Walworth; none but my official sentiments can be taken in this office."

"Very well," said I, much relieved, "then I shall look you up at Walworth, you may depend upon it."

"Mr. Pip," he returned, "you will be welcome there, in a private and personal capacity."

We had held this conversation in a low voice, well knowing my guardian's ears to be the sharpest of the sharp. As he now appeared in his doorway, towelling his hands, Wemmick got on his great-coat and stood by to snuff out the candles. We all three went into the street together, and from the door-step Wemmick turned his way, and Mr. Jaggers and I turned ours.

I could not help wishing more than once that evening, that Mr. Jaggers had had an Aged in Gerrard Street, or a Stinger, or a Something, or a Somebody, to unbend his brows a little. It was an uncomfortable consideration on a twenty-first birthday, that coming of age at all seemed hardly worth while in such a guarded and suspicious world as he made of it. He was a thousand times better informed and cleverer than Wemmick, and yet I would a thousand times rather have had Wemmick to dinner. And Mr. Jaggers made not me alone intensely melancholy, because, after he was gone, Herbert said of himself, with his eyes fixed on the fire, that he thought he must have committed a felony and forgotten the details of it, he felt so dejected and guilty.

Chapter XXXVII

Deeming Sunday the best day for taking Mr. Wemmick's Walworth sentiments, I devoted the next ensuing Sunday afternoon to a pilgrimage to the Castle. On arriving before the battlements, I found the Union Jack flying and the drawbridge up; but undeterred by this show of defiance and resistance, I rang at the gate, and was admitted in a most pacific manner by the Aged.

"My son, sir," said the old man, after securing the drawbridge, "rather had it in his mind that you might happen to drop in, and he left word that he would soon be home from his afternoon's walk. He is very regular in his walks, is my son. Very regular in everything, is my son."

I nodded at the old gentleman as Wemmick himself might have nodded, and we went in and sat down by the fireside.

"You made acquaintance with my son, sir," said the old man, in his chirping way, while he warmed his hands at the blaze, "at his office, I expect?" I nodded. "Hah! I have heerd that my son is a wonderful hand at his business, sir?" I nodded hard. "Yes; so they tell me. His business is the Law?" I nodded harder. "Which makes it more surprising in my son," said the old man, "for he was not brought up to the Law, but to the Wine-Coopering."

Curious to know how the old gentleman stood informed concerning the reputation of Mr. Jaggers, I roared that name at him. He threw me into the greatest confusion by laughing heartily and replying in a very sprightly manner, "No, to be sure; you're right." And to this hour I have not the faintest notion what he meant, or what joke he thought I had made.

As I could not sit there nodding at him perpetually, without making some other attempt to interest him, I shouted at inquiry whether his own calling in life had been "the Wine-Coopering." By dint of straining that term out of myself several times and tapping the old gentleman on the chest to associate it with him, I at last succeeded in making my meaning understood.

"No," said the old gentleman; "the warehousing, the warehousing. First, over yonder;" he appeared to mean up the chimney, but I believe he intended to refer me to Liverpool; "and then in the City of London here. However, having an infirmity—for I am hard of hearing, sir—"

I expressed in pantomime the greatest astonishment.

"—Yes, hard of hearing; having that infirmity coming upon me, my son he went into the Law, and he took charge of me, and he by little and little made out this elegant and beautiful property. But returning to what you said, you know," pursued the old man, again laughing heartily, "what I say is, No to be sure; you're right."

I was modestly wondering whether my utmost ingenuity would have enabled me to say anything that would have amused him half as much as this imaginary pleasantry, when I was startled by a sudden click in the wall on one side of the chimney, and the ghostly tumbling open of a little wooden flap with "JOHN" upon it. The old man, following my eyes, cried with great triumph, "My son's come home!" and we both went out to the drawbridge.

It was worth any money to see Wemmick waving a salute to me from the other side of the moat, when we might have shaken hands across it with the greatest ease. The Aged was so delighted to work the drawbridge, that I made no offer to assist him, but stood quiet until Wemmick had come across, and had presented me to Miss Skiffins; a lady by whom he was accompanied.

Miss Skiffins was of a wooden appearance, and was, like her escort, in the post-office branch of the service. She might have been some two or three years younger than Wemmick, and I judged her to stand possessed of portable property. The cut of her dress from the waist upward, both before and behind, made her figure very like a boy's kite; and I might have pronounced her gown a little too decidedly orange, and her gloves a little too intensely green. But she seemed to be a good sort of fellow, and showed a high regard for the Aged. I was not long in discovering that she was a frequent visitor at the Castle; for, on our going in, and my complimenting Wemmick on his ingenious contrivance for announcing himself to the Aged, he begged me to give my attention for a moment to the other side of the chimney, and disappeared. Presently another click came, and another little door tumbled open with "Miss Skiffins" on it; then Miss Skiffins shut up and John tumbled open; then Miss Skiffins and John both tumbled open together, and finally shut up together. On Wemmick's return from working these mechanical appliances, I expressed the great admiration with which I regarded them, and he said, "Well, you know, they're both pleasant and useful to the Aged. And by George, sir, it's a thing worth mentioning, that of all the people who come to this gate, the secret of those pulls is only known to the Aged, Miss Skiffins, and me!"

"And Mr. Wemmick made them," added Miss Skiffins, "with his own hands out of his own head."

While Miss Skiffins was taking off her bonnet (she retained her green gloves during the evening as an outward and visible sign that there was company), Wemmick invited me to take a walk with him round the property, and see how the island looked in wintertime. Thinking that he did this to give me an opportunity of taking his Walworth sentiments, I seized the opportunity as soon as we were out of the Castle.

Having thought of the matter with care, I approached my subject as if I had never hinted at it before. I informed Wemmick that I was anxious in behalf of Herbert Pocket, and I told him how we had first met, and how we had fought. I glanced at Herbert's home, and at his character, and at his having no means but such as he was dependent on his father for; those, uncertain and unpunctual. I alluded to the advantages I had derived in my first rawness and ignorance from his society, and I confessed that I feared I had but ill repaid them, and that he might have done better without me and my expectations. Keeping Miss Havisham in the background at a great distance, I still hinted at the possibility of my having competed with him in his prospects, and at the certainty of his possessing a generous soul, and being far above any mean distrusts, retaliations, or designs. For all these reasons (I told Wemmick), and because he was my young companion and friend, and I had a great affection for him, I wished my own good fortune to reflect some rays upon him, and therefore I sought advice from Wemmick's experience and knowledge of men and affairs, how I could best try with my resources to help Herbert to some present income,—say of a hundred a year, to keep him in good hope and heart,—and gradually to buy him on to some small partnership. I begged Wemmick, in conclusion, to understand that my help must always be rendered without Herbert's knowledge or suspicion, and that there was no one else in the world with whom I could advise. I wound up by laying my hand upon his shoulder, and saying, "I can't help confiding in you, though I know it must be troublesome to you; but that is your fault, in having ever brought me here."

Wemmick was silent for a little while, and then said with a kind of start, "Well you know, Mr. Pip, I must tell you one thing. This is devilish good of you."

"Say you'll help me to be good then," said I.

"Ecod," replied Wemmick, shaking his head, "that's not my trade."

"Nor is this your trading-place," said I.

564

"You are right," he returned. "You hit the nail on the head. Mr. Pip, I'll put on my considering-cap, and I think all you want to do may be done by degrees. Skiffins (that's her brother) is an accountant and agent. I'll look him up and go to work for you."

"I thank you ten thousand times."

"On the contrary," said he, "I thank you, for though we are strictly in our private and personal capacity, still it may be mentioned that there are Newgate cobwebs about, and it brushes them away."

After a little further conversation to the same effect, we returned into the Castle where we found Miss Skiffins preparing tea. The responsible duty of making the toast was delegated to the Aged, and that excellent old gentleman was so intent upon it that he seemed to me in some danger of melting his eyes. It was no nominal meal that we were going to make, but a vigorous reality. The Aged prepared such a hay-stack of buttered toast, that I could scarcely see him over it as it simmered on an iron stand hooked on to the top-bar; while Miss Skiffins brewed such a jorum of tea, that the pig in the back premises became strongly excited, and repeatedly expressed his desire to participate in the entertainment.

The flag had been struck, and the gun had been fired, at the right moment of time, and I felt as snugly cut off from the rest of Walworth as if the moat were thirty feet wide by as many deep. Nothing disturbed the tranquillity of the Castle, but the occasional tumbling open of John and Miss Skiffins: which little doors were a prey to some spasmodic infirmity that made me sympathetically uncomfortable until I got used to it. I inferred from the methodical nature of Miss Skiffins's arrangements that she made tea there every Sunday night; and I rather suspected that a classic brooch she wore, representing the profile of an undesirable female with a very straight nose and a very new moon, was a piece of portable property that had been given her by Wemmick.

We ate the whole of the toast, and drank tea in proportion, and it was delightful to see how warm and greasy we all got after it. The Aged especially, might have passed for some clean old chief of a savage tribe, just oiled. After a short pause of repose, Miss Skiffins—in the absence of the little servant who, it seemed, retired to the bosom of her family on Sunday afternoons—washed up the tea-things, in a trifling lady-like amateur manner that compromised none of us. Then, she put on her gloves again, and we drew round the fire, and Wemmick said, "Now, Aged Parent, tip us the paper."

Wemmick explained to me while the Aged got his spectacles out, that this was according to custom, and that it gave the old gentleman infinite satisfaction to read the news aloud. "I won't offer an apology," said Wemmick, "for he isn't capable of many pleasures—are you, Aged P.?"

"All right, John, all right," returned the old man, seeing himself spoken to.

"Only tip him a nod every now and then when he looks off his paper," said Wemmick, "and he'll be as happy as a king. We are all attention, Aged One."

"All right, John, all right!" returned the cheerful old man, so busy and so pleased, that it really was quite charming.

The Aged's reading reminded me of the classes at Mr. Wopsle's great-aunt's, with the pleasanter peculiarity that it seemed to come through a keyhole. As he wanted the candles close to him, and as he was always on the verge of putting either his head or the newspaper into them, he required as much watching as a powder-mill. But Wemmick was equally untiring and gentle in his vigilance, and the Aged read on, quite unconscious of his many rescues. Whenever he looked at us, we all expressed the greatest interest and amazement, and nodded until he resumed again.

As Wemmick and Miss Skiffins sat side by side, and as I sat in a shadowy corner, I observed a slow and gradual elongation of Mr. Wemmick's mouth, powerfully suggestive of his slowly and gradually stealing his arm round Miss Skiffins's waist. In course of time I saw his hand appear on the other side of Miss Skiffins; but at that moment Miss Skiffins neatly stopped him with the green glove, unwound his arm again as if it were an article of dress, and with the greatest deliberation laid it on the table before her. Miss Skiffins's composure while she did this was one of the most remarkable sights I have ever seen, and if I could have thought the act consistent with abstraction of mind, I should have deemed that Miss Skiffins performed it mechanically.

By and by, I noticed Wemmick's arm beginning to disappear again, and gradually fading out of view. Shortly afterwards, his mouth began to widen again. After an interval of suspense on my part that was quite enthralling and almost painful, I saw his hand appear on the other side of Miss Skiffins. Instantly, Miss Skiffins stopped it with the neatness of a placid boxer, took off that girdle or cestus as before, and laid it on the table. Taking the table to represent the path of virtue, I am justified in stating that during the whole time of the Aged's reading, Wemmick's arm was straying from the path of virtue and being recalled to it by Miss Skiffins.

At last, the Aged read himself into a light slumber. This was the time for Wemmick to produce a little kettle, a tray of glasses, and a black bottle with a porcelain-topped cork, representing some clerical dignitary of a rubicund and social aspect. With the aid of these appliances we all had something warm to drink, including the Aged, who was soon awake again. Miss Skiffins mixed, and I observed that she and Wemmick drank out of one glass. Of course I knew better than to offer to see Miss Skiffins home, and under the circumstances I thought I had best go first; which I did, taking a cordial leave of the Aged, and having passed a pleasant evening.

Before a week was out, I received a note from Wemmick, dated Walworth, stating that he hoped he had made some advance in that matter appertaining to our private and personal capacities, and that he would be glad if I could come and see him again upon it. So, I went out to Walworth again, and yet again, and yet again, and I saw him by appointment in the City several times, but never held any communication with him on the subject in or near Little Britain. The upshot was, that we found a worthy young merchant or shipping-broker, not long established in business, who wanted intelligent help, and who wanted capital, and who in due course of time and receipt would want a partner. Between him and me, secret articles were signed of which Herbert was the subject, and I paid him half of my five hundred pounds down, and engaged for sundry other payments: some, to fall due at certain dates out of my income: some, contingent on my coming into my property. Miss Skiffins's brother conducted the negotiation. Wemmick pervaded it throughout, but never appeared in it.

The whole business was so cleverly managed, that Herbert had not the least suspicion of my hand being in it. I never shall forget the radiant face with which he came home one afternoon, and told me, as a mighty piece of news, of his having fallen in with one Clarriker (the young merchant's name), and of Clarriker's having shown an extraordinary inclination towards him, and of his belief that the opening had come at last. Day by day as his hopes grew stronger and his face brighter, he must have thought me a more and more affectionate friend, for I had the greatest difficulty in restraining my tears of triumph when I saw him so happy. At length, the thing being done, and he having that day entered Clarriker's House, and he having talked to me for a whole evening in a flush of pleasure and success, I did really cry in good earnest when I went to bed, to think that my expectations had done some good to somebody.

A great event in my life, the turning point of my life, now opens on my view. But, before I proceed to narrate it, and before I pass on to all the changes it involved, I must give one chapter to Estella. It is not much to give to the theme that so long filled my heart.

Chapter XXXVIII

If that staid old house near the Green at Richmond should ever come to be haunted when I am dead, it will be haunted, surely, by my ghost. O the many, many nights and days through which the unquiet spirit within me haunted that house when Estella lived there! Let my body be where it would, my spirit was always wandering, wandering, wandering, about that house.

The lady with whom Estella was placed, Mrs. Brandley by name, was a widow, with one daughter several years older than Estella. The mother looked young, and the daughter looked old; the mother's complexion was pink, and the daughter's was yellow; the mother set up for frivolity, and the daughter for theology. They were in what is called a good position, and visited, and were visited by, numbers of people. Little, if any, community of feeling subsisted between them and Estella, but the understanding was established that they were necessary to her, and that she was necessary to them. Mrs. Brandley had been a friend of Miss Havisham's before the time of her seclusion.

In Mrs. Brandley's house and out of Mrs. Brandley's house, I suffered every kind and degree of torture that Estella could cause me. The nature of my relations with her, which placed me on terms of familiarity without placing me on terms of favor, conduced to my distraction. She made use of me to tease other admirers, and she turned the very familiarity between herself and me to the account of putting a constant slight on my devotion to her. If I had been her secretary, steward, half-brother, poor relation,—if I had been a younger brother of her appointed husband,—I could not have seemed to myself further from my hopes when I was nearest to her. The privilege of calling her by her name and hearing her call me by mine became, under the circumstances an aggravation of my trials; and while I think it likely that it almost maddened her other lovers, I know too certainly that it almost maddened me.

She had admirers without end. No doubt my jealousy made an admirer of every one who went near her; but there were more than enough of them without that.

I saw her often at Richmond, I heard of her often in town, and I used often to take her and the Brandleys on the water; there were picnics, fête days, plays, operas, concerts, parties, all sorts of pleasures, through which I pursued her,—and they were all miseries to me. I never had one hour's happiness in her society, and yet my mind all round the four-and-twenty hours was harping on the happiness of having her with me unto death.

Throughout this part of our intercourse,—and it lasted, as will presently be seen, for what I then thought a long time,—she habitually reverted to that tone which expressed that our association was forced upon us. There were other times when she would come to a sudden check in this tone and in all her many tones, and would seem to pity me.

"Pip, Pip," she said one evening, coming to such a check, when we sat apart at a darkening window of the house in Richmond; "will you never take warning?"

"Of what?"

"Of me."

"Warning not to be attracted by you, do you mean, Estella?"

"Do I mean! If you don't know what I mean, you are blind."

I should have replied that Love was commonly reputed blind, but for the reason that I always was restrained—and this was not the least of my miseries—by a feeling that it was ungenerous to press myself upon her, when she knew that she could not choose but obey Miss Havisham. My dread always was, that this knowledge on her part laid me under a heavy disadvantage with her pride, and made me the subject of a rebellious struggle in her bosom.

"At any rate," said I, "I have no warning given me just now, for you wrote to me to come to you, this time."

"That's true," said Estella, with a cold careless smile that always chilled me.

After looking at the twilight without, for a little while, she went on to say:—

"The time has come round when Miss Havisham wishes to have me for a day at Satis. You are to take me there, and bring me back, if you will. She would rather I did not travel alone, and objects to receiving my maid, for she has a sensitive horror of being talked of by such people. Can you take me?"

"Can I take you, Estella!"

"You can then? The day after to-morrow, if you please. You are to pay all charges out of my purse, You hear the condition of your going?"

"And must obey," said I.

This was all the preparation I received for that visit, or for others like it; Miss Havisham never wrote to me, nor had I ever so much as seen her handwriting. We went down on the next day but one, and we found her in the room where I had first beheld her, and it is needless to add that there was no change in Satis House.

She was even more dreadfully fond of Estella than she had been when I last saw them together; I repeat the word advisedly, for there was something positively dreadful in the energy of her looks and embraces. She hung upon Estella's beauty, hung upon her words, hung upon her gestures, and sat mumbling her own trembling fingers while she looked at her, as though she were devouring the beautiful creature she had reared.

From Estella she looked at me, with a searching glance that seemed to pry into my heart and probe its wounds. "How does she use you, Pip; how does she use you?" she asked me again, with her witch-like eagerness, even in Estella's hearing. But, when we sat by her flickering fire at night, she was most weird; for then, keeping Estella's hand drawn through her arm and clutched in her own hand, she extorted from her, by dint of referring back to what Estella had told her in her regular letters, the names and conditions of the men whom she had fascinated; and as Miss Havisham dwelt upon this roll, with the intensity of a mind mortally hurt and diseased, she sat with her other hand on her crutch stick, and her chin on that, and her wan bright eyes glaring at me, a very spectre.

I saw in this, wretched though it made me, and bitter the sense of dependence and even of degradation that it awakened,—I saw in this that Estella was set to wreak Miss Havisham's revenge on men, and that she was not to be given to me until she had gratified it for a term. I saw in this, a reason for her being beforehand assigned to me. Sending her out to attract and torment and do mischief, Miss Havisham sent her with the malicious assurance that she was beyond the reach of all admirers, and that all who staked upon that cast were secured to lose. I saw in this that I, too, was tormented by a perversion of ingenuity, even while the prize was reserved for me. I saw in this the reason for my being staved off so long and the reason for my late guardian's declining to commit himself to the formal knowledge of such a scheme. In a word, I saw in this Miss Havisham as I had her then and there before my eyes, and always had had her before my eyes; and I saw in this, the distinct shadow of the darkened and unhealthy house in which her life was hidden from the sun.

The candles that lighted that room of hers were placed in sconces on the wall. They were high from the ground, and they burnt with the steady dulness of artificial light in air that is seldom renewed. As I looked round at them, and at the pale gloom they made, and at the stopped clock, and at the withered articles of bridal dress upon the table and the ground, and at her own awful figure with its ghostly reflection thrown large by the fire upon the ceiling and the wall, I saw in everything the construction that my mind had come to, repeated and thrown back to me. My thoughts passed into the great room across the landing where the table was spread, and I saw it written, as it were, in the falls of the cobwebs from the centre-piece, in the crawlings of the spiders on the cloth, in the tracks of the mice as they betook their little quickened hearts behind the panels, and in the gropings and pausings of the beetles on the floor.

It happened on the occasion of this visit that some sharp words arose between Estella and Miss Havisham. It was the first time I had ever seen them opposed.

We were seated by the fire, as just now described, and Miss Havisham still had Estella's arm drawn through her own, and still clutched Estella's hand in hers, when Estella gradually began to detach herself. She had shown a proud impatience more than once before, and had rather endured that fierce affection than accepted or returned it.

"What!" said Miss Havisham, flashing her eyes upon her, "are you tired of me?"

"Only a little tired of myself," replied Estella, disengaging her arm, and moving to the great chimney-piece, where she stood looking down at the fire.

"Speak the truth, you ingrate!" cried Miss Havisham, passionately striking her stick upon the floor; "you are tired of me."

Estella looked at her with perfect composure, and again looked down at the fire. Her graceful figure and her beautiful face expressed a self-possessed indifference to the wild heat of the other, that was almost cruel.

"You stock and stone!" exclaimed Miss Havisham. "You cold, cold heart!"

"What?" said Estella, preserving her attitude of indifference as she leaned against the great chimney-piece and only moving her eyes; "do you reproach me for being cold? You?"

"Are you not?" was the fierce retort.

"You should know," said Estella. "I am what you have made me. Take all the praise, take all the blame; take all the success, take all the failure; in short, take me."

"O, look at her, look at her!" cried Miss Havisham, bitterly; "Look at her so hard and thankless, on the hearth where she was reared! Where I took her into this wretched breast when it was first bleeding from its stabs, and where I have lavished years of tenderness upon her!"

"At least I was no party to the compact," said Estella, "for if I could walk and speak, when it was made, it was as much as I could do. But what would you have? You have been very good to me, and I owe everything to you. What would you have?"

"Love," replied the other.

"You have it."

"I have not," said Miss Havisham.

"Mother by adoption," retorted Estella, never departing from the easy grace of her attitude, never raising her voice as the other did, never yielding either to anger or tenderness,—"mother by adoption, I have said that I owe everything to you. All I possess is freely yours. All that you have given me, is at your command to have again. Beyond that, I have nothing. And if you ask me to give you, what you never gave me, my gratitude and duty cannot do impossibilities."

"Did I never give her love!" cried Miss Havisham, turning wildly to me. "Did I never give her a burning love, inseparable from jealousy at all times, and from sharp pain, while she speaks thus to me! Let her call me mad, let her call me mad!"

"Why should I call you mad," returned Estella, "I, of all people? Does any one live, who knows what set purposes you have, half as well as I do? Does any one live, who knows what a steady memory you have, half as well as I do? I who have sat on this same hearth on the little stool that is even now beside you there, learning your lessons and looking up into your face, when your face was strange and frightened me!"

"Soon forgotten!" moaned Miss Havisham. "Times soon forgotten!"

"No, not forgotten," retorted Estella,—"not forgotten, but treasured up in my memory. When have you found me false to your teaching? When have you found me unmindful of your lessons? When have you found me giving admission here," she touched her bosom with her hand, "to anything that you excluded? Be just to me."

"So proud, so proud!" moaned Miss Havisham, pushing away her gray hair with both her hands.

"Who taught me to be proud?" returned Estella. "Who praised me when I learnt my lesson?"

"So hard, so hard!" moaned Miss Havisham, with her former action.

"Who taught me to be hard?" returned Estella. "Who praised me when I learnt my lesson?"

"But to be proud and hard to me!" Miss Havisham quite shrieked, as she stretched out her arms. "Estella, Estella, Estella, to be proud and hard to me!"

Estella looked at her for a moment with a kind of calm wonder, but was not otherwise disturbed; when the moment was past, she looked down at the fire again.

"I cannot think," said Estella, raising her eyes after a silence "why you should be so unreasonable when I come to see you after a separation. I have never forgotten your wrongs and their causes. I have never been unfaithful to you or your schooling. I have never shown any weakness that I can charge myself with."

"Would it be weakness to return my love?" exclaimed Miss Havisham. "But yes, yes, she would call it so!"

"I begin to think," said Estella, in a musing way, after another moment of calm wonder, "that I almost understand how this comes about. If you had brought up your adopted daughter wholly in the dark confinement of these rooms, and had never let her know that there was such a thing as the daylight by which she had never once seen your face,—if you had done that, and then, for a purpose had wanted her to understand the daylight and know all about it, you would have been disappointed and angry?"

Miss Havisham, with her head in her hands, sat making a low moaning, and swaying herself on her chair, but gave no answer.

"Or," said Estella,—"which is a nearer case,—if you had taught her, from the dawn of her intelligence, with your utmost energy and might, that there was such a thing as daylight, but that it was made to be her enemy and destroyer, and she must always turn against it, for it had blighted you and would else blight her;—if you had done this, and then, for a purpose, had wanted her to take naturally to the daylight and she could not do it, you would have been disappointed and angry?"

Miss Havisham sat listening (or it seemed so, for I could not see her face), but still made no answer.

"So," said Estella, "I must be taken as I have been made. The success is not mine, the failure is not mine, but the two together make me."

Miss Havisham had settled down, I hardly knew how, upon the floor, among the faded bridal relics with which it was strewn. I took advantage of the moment—I had sought one from the first—to leave the room, after beseeching Estella's attention to her, with a movement of my hand. When I left, Estella was yet standing by the great chimney-piece, just as she had stood throughout. Miss Havisham's gray hair was all adrift upon the ground, among the other bridal wrecks, and was a miserable sight to see.

It was with a depressed heart that I walked in the starlight for an hour and more, about the courtyard, and about the brewery, and about the ruined garden. When I at last took courage to return to the room, I found Estella sitting at Miss Havisham's knee, taking up some stitches in one of those old articles of dress that were dropping to pieces, and of which I have often been reminded since by the faded tatters of old banners that I have seen hanging up in cathedrals. Afterwards, Estella and I played at cards, as of yore,—only we were skilful now, and played French games,—and so the evening wore away, and I went to bed.

I lay in that separate building across the courtyard. It was the first time I had ever lain down to rest in Satis House, and sleep refused to come near me. A thousand Miss Havishams haunted me. She was on this side of my pillow, on that, at the head of the bed, at the foot, behind the half-opened door of the dressing-room, in the dressing-room, in the room overhead, in the room beneath,—everywhere. At last, when the night was slow to creep on towards two o'clock, I felt that I absolutely could no longer bear the place as a place to lie down in, and that I must get up. I therefore got up and put on my clothes, and went out across the yard into the long stone passage, designing to gain the outer courtyard and walk there for the relief of my mind. But I was no sooner in the passage than I extinguished my candle; for I saw Miss Havisham going along it in a ghostly manner, making a low cry. I followed her at a distance, and saw her go up the staircase. She carried a bare candle in her hand, which she had probably taken from one of the sconces in her own room, and was a most unearthly object by its light. Standing at the bottom of the staircase, I felt the mildewed air of the feast-chamber, without seeing her open the door, and I heard her walking there, and so across into her own room, and so across again into that, never ceasing the low cry. After a time, I tried in the dark both to get out, and to go back, but I could do neither until some streaks of day strayed in and showed me where to lay my hands. During the whole interval, whenever I went to the bottom of the staircase, I heard her footstep, saw her light pass above, and heard her ceaseless low cry.

Before we left next day, there was no revival of the difference between her and Estella, nor was it ever revived on any similar occasion; and there were four similar occasions, to the best of my remembrance. Nor, did Miss Havisham's manner towards Estella in anywise change, except that I believed it to have something like fear infused among its former characteristics.

It is impossible to turn this leaf of my life, without putting Bentley Drummle's name upon it; or I would, very gladly.

On a certain occasion when the Finches were assembled in force, and when good feeling was being promoted in the usual manner by nobody's agreeing with anybody else, the presiding Finch called the Grove to order, forasmuch as Mr. Drummle had not yet toasted a lady; which, according to the solemn constitution of the society, it was the brute's turn to do that day. I thought I saw him leer in an ugly way at me while the decanters were going round, but as there was no love lost between us, that might easily be. What was my indignant surprise when he called upon the company to pledge him to "Estella!"

"Estella who?" said I.

"Never you mind," retorted Drummle.

"Estella of where?" said I. "You are bound to say of where." Which he was, as a Finch.

"Of Richmond, gentlemen," said Drummle, putting me out of the question, "and a peerless beauty."

Much he knew about peerless beauties, a mean, miserable idiot! I whispered Herbert.

"I know that lady," said Herbert, across the table, when the toast had been honored.

"Do you?" said Drummle.

"And so do I," I added, with a scarlet face.

"Do you?" said Drummle. "O, Lord!"

This was the only retort—except glass or crockery—that the heavy creature was capable of making; but, I became as highly incensed by it as if it had been barbed with wit, and I immediately rose in my place and said that I could not but regard it as being like the honorable Finch's impudence to come down to that Grove,—we always talked about coming down to that Grove, as a neat Parliamentary turn of expression,—down to that Grove, proposing a lady of whom he knew nothing. Mr. Drummle, upon this, starting up, demanded what I meant by that? Whereupon I made him the extreme reply that I believed he knew where I was to be found.

Whether it was possible in a Christian country to get on without blood, after this, was a question on which the Finches were divided. The debate upon it grew so lively, indeed, that at least six more honorable members told six more, during the discussion, that they believed they knew where they were to be found. However, it was decided at last (the Grove being a Court of Honor) that if Mr. Drummle would bring never so slight a certificate from the lady, importing that he had the honor of her acquaintance, Mr. Pip must express his regret, as a gentleman and a Finch, for "having been betrayed into a warmth which." Next day was appointed for the production (lest our honor should take cold from delay), and next day Drummle appeared with a polite little avowal in Estella's hand, that she had had the honor of dancing with him several times. This left me no course but to regret that I had been "betrayed into a warmth which," and on the whole to repudiate, as untenable, the idea that I was to be found anywhere. Drummle and I then sat snorting at one another for an hour, while the Grove engaged in indiscriminate contradiction, and finally the promotion of good feeling was declared to have gone ahead at an amazing rate.

I tell this lightly, but it was no light thing to me. For, I cannot adequately express what pain it gave me to think that Estella should show any favor to a contemptible, clumsy, sulky booby, so very far below the average. To the present moment, I believe it to have been referable to some pure fire of generosity and disinterestedness in my love for her, that I could not endure the thought of her stooping to that hound. No doubt I should have been miserable whomsoever she had favored; but a worthier object would have caused me a different kind and degree of distress.

It was easy for me to find out, and I did soon find out, that Drummle had begun to follow her closely, and that she allowed him to do it. A little while, and he was always in pursuit of her, and he and I crossed one another every day. He held on, in a dull persistent way, and Estella held him on; now with encouragement, now with discouragement, now almost flattering him, now openly despising him, now knowing him very well, now scarcely remembering who he was.

The Spider, as Mr. Jaggers had called him, was used to lying in wait, however, and had the patience of his tribe. Added to that, he had a blockhead confidence in his money and in his family greatness, which sometimes did him good service,—almost taking the place of concentration and determined purpose. So, the Spider, doggedly watching Estella, outwatched many brighter insects, and would often uncoil himself and drop at the right nick of time.

At a certain Assembly Ball at Richmond (there used to be Assembly Balls at most places then), where Estella had outshone all other beauties, this blundering Drummle so hung about her, and with so much toleration on her part, that I resolved to speak to her concerning him. I took the next opportunity; which was when she was waiting for Mrs. Blandley to take her home, and was sitting apart among some flowers, ready to go. I was with her, for I almost always accompanied them to and from such places.

"Are you tired, Estella?"

"Rather, Pip."

"You should be."

"Say rather, I should not be; for I have my letter to Satis House to write, before I go to sleep."

"Recounting to-night's triumph?" said I. "Surely a very poor one, Estella."

"What do you mean? I didn't know there had been any."

"Estella," said I, "do look at that fellow in the corner yonder, who is looking over here at us."

"Why should I look at him?" returned Estella, with her eyes on me instead. "What is there in that fellow in the corner yonder,—to use your words,—that I need look at?"

"Indeed, that is the very question I want to ask you," said I. "For he has been hovering about you all night."

"Moths, and all sorts of ugly creatures," replied Estella, with a glance towards him, "hover about a lighted candle. Can the candle help it?"

"No," I returned; "but cannot the Estella help it?"

"Well!" said she, laughing, after a moment, "perhaps. Yes. Anything you like."

"But, Estella, do hear me speak. It makes me wretched that you should encourage a man so generally despised as Drummle. You know he is despised."

"Well?" said she.

"You know he is as ungainly within as without. A deficient, ill-tempered, lowering, stupid fellow."

"Well?" said she.

"You know he has nothing to recommend him but money and a ridiculous roll of addle-headed predecessors; now, don't you?"

"Well?" said she again; and each time she said it, she opened her lovely eyes the wider.

To overcome the difficulty of getting past that monosyllable, I took it from her, and said, repeating it with emphasis, "Well! Then, that is why it makes me wretched."

Now, if I could have believed that she favored Drummle with any idea of making me—me—wretched, I should have been in better heart about it; but in that habitual way of hers, she put me so entirely out of the question, that I could believe nothing of the kind.

"Pip," said Estella, casting her glance over the room, "don't be foolish about its effect on you. It may have its effect on others, and may be meant to have. It's not worth discussing."

"Yes it is," said I, "because I cannot bear that people should say, 'she throws away her graces and attractions on a mere boor, the lowest in the crowd.'"

"I can bear it," said Estella.

"Oh! don't be so proud, Estella, and so inflexible."

574

"Calls me proud and inflexible in this breath!" said Estella, opening her hands. "And in his last breath reproached me for stooping to a boor!"

"There is no doubt you do," said I, something hurriedly, "for I have seen you give him looks and smiles this very night, such as you never give to—me."

"Do you want me then," said Estella, turning suddenly with a fixed and serious, if not angry, look, "to deceive and entrap you?"

"Do you deceive and entrap him, Estella?"

"Yes, and many others,—all of them but you. Here is Mrs. Brandley. I'll say no more."

And now that I have given the one chapter to the theme that so filled my heart, and so often made it ache and ache again, I pass on unhindered, to the event that had impended over me longer yet; the event that had begun to be prepared for, before I knew that the world held Estella, and in the days when her baby intelligence was receiving its first distortions from Miss Havisham's wasting hands.

In the Eastern story, the heavy slab that was to fall on the bed of state in the flush of conquest was slowly wrought out of the quarry, the tunnel for the rope to hold it in its place was slowly carried through the leagues of rock, the slab was slowly raised and fitted in the roof, the rope was rove to it and slowly taken through the miles of hollow to the great iron ring. All being made ready with much labor, and the hour come, the sultan was aroused in the dead of the night, and the sharpened axe that was to sever the rope from the great iron ring was put into his hand, and he struck with it, and the rope parted and rushed away, and the ceiling fell. So, in my case; all the work, near and afar, that tended to the end, had been accomplished; and in an instant the blow was struck, and the roof of my stronghold dropped upon me.

Chapter XXXIX

I was three-and-twenty years of age. Not another word had I heard to enlighten me on the subject of my expectations, and my twenty-third birthday was a week gone. We had left Barnard's Inn more than a year, and lived in the Temple. Our chambers were in Garden-court, down by the river.

Mr. Pocket and I had for some time parted company as to our original relations, though we continued on the best terms. Notwithstanding my inability to settle to anything,—which I hope arose out of the restless and incomplete tenure on which I held my means,—I had a taste for reading, and read regularly so many hours a day. That matter of Herbert's was still progressing, and everything with me was as I have brought it down to the close of the last preceding chapter.

Business had taken Herbert on a journey to Marseilles. I was alone, and had a dull sense of being alone. Dispirited and anxious, long hoping that to-morrow or next week would clear my way, and long disappointed, I sadly missed the cheerful face and ready response of my friend.

It was wretched weather; stormy and wet, stormy and wet; and mud, mud, mud, deep in all the streets. Day after day, a vast heavy veil had been driving over London from the East, and it drove still, as if in the East there were an Eternity of cloud and wind. So furious had been the gusts, that high buildings in town had had the lead stripped off their roofs; and in the country, trees had been torn up, and sails of windmills carried away; and gloomy accounts had come in from the coast, of shipwreck and death. Violent blasts of rain had accompanied these rages of wind, and the day just closed as I sat down to read had been the worst of all.

Alterations have been made in that part of the Temple since that time, and it has not now so lonely a character as it had then, nor is it so exposed to the river. We lived at the top of the last house, and the wind rushing up the river shook the house that night, like discharges of cannon, or breakings of a sea. When the rain came with it and dashed against the windows, I thought, raising my eyes to them as they rocked, that I might have fancied myself in a storm-beaten lighthouse. Occasionally, the smoke came rolling down the chimney as though it could not bear to go out into such a night; and when I set the doors open and looked down the staircase, the staircase lamps were blown out; and when I shaded my face with my hands and looked through the black windows (opening them ever so little was out of the question in the teeth of such wind and rain), I saw that the lamps in the court were blown out, and that the lamps on the bridges and the shore were shuddering, and that the coal-fires in barges on the river were being carried away before the wind like red-hot splashes in the rain.

I read with my watch upon the table, purposing to close my book at eleven o'clock. As I shut it, Saint Paul's, and all the many church-clocks in the City—some leading, some accompanying, some following—struck that hour. The sound was curiously flawed by the wind; and I was listening, and thinking how the wind assailed and tore it, when I heard a footstep on the stair.

What nervous folly made me start, and awfully connect it with the footstep of my dead sister, matters not. It was past in a moment, and I listened again, and heard the footstep stumble in coming on. Remembering then, that the staircase-lights were blown out, I took up my reading-lamp and went out to the stair-head. Whoever was below had stopped on seeing my lamp, for all was quiet.

"There is some one down there, is there not?" I called out, looking down.

"Yes," said a voice from the darkness beneath.

"What floor do you want?"

"The top. Mr. Pip."

"That is my name.—There is nothing the matter?"

"Nothing the matter," returned the voice. And the man came on.

I stood with my lamp held out over the stair-rail, and he came slowly within its light. It was a shaded lamp, to shine upon a book, and its circle of light was very contracted; so that he was in it for a mere instant, and then out of it. In the instant, I had seen a face that was strange to me, looking up with an incomprehensible air of being touched and pleased by the sight of me.

Moving the lamp as the man moved, I made out that he was substantially dressed, but roughly, like a voyager by sea. That he had long iron-gray hair. That his age was about sixty. That he was a muscular man, strong on his legs, and that he was browned and hardened by exposure to weather. As he ascended the last stair or two, and the light of my lamp included us both, I saw, with a stupid kind of amazement, that he was holding out both his hands to me.

"Pray what is your business?" I asked him.

"My business?" he repeated, pausing. "Ah! Yes. I will explain my business, by your leave."

"Do you wish to come in?"

"Yes," he replied; "I wish to come in, master."

I had asked him the question inhospitably enough, for I resented the sort of bright and gratified recognition that still shone in his face. I resented it, because it seemed to imply that he expected me to respond to it. But I took him into the room I had just left, and, having set the lamp on the table, asked him as civilly as I could to explain himself.

He looked about him with the strangest air,—an air of wondering pleasure, as if he had some part in the things he admired,—and he pulled off a rough outer coat, and his hat. Then, I saw that his head was furrowed and bald, and that the long iron-gray hair grew only on its sides. But, I saw nothing that in the least explained him. On the contrary, I saw him next moment, once more holding out both his hands to me.

"What do you mean?" said I, half suspecting him to be mad.

He stopped in his looking at me, and slowly rubbed his right hand over his head. "It's disapinting to a man," he said, in a coarse broken voice, "arter having looked for'ard so distant, and come so fur; but you're not to blame for that,—neither on us is to blame for that. I'll speak in half a minute. Give me half a minute, please."

He sat down on a chair that stood before the fire, and covered his forehead with his large brown veinous hands. I looked at him attentively then, and recoiled a little from him; but I did not know him.

"There's no one nigh," said he, looking over his shoulder; "is there?"

"Why do you, a stranger coming into my rooms at this time of the night, ask that question?" said I.

"You're a game one," he returned, shaking his head at me with a deliberate affection, at once most unintelligible and most exasperating; "I'm glad you've grow'd up, a game one! But don't catch hold of me. You'd be sorry arterwards to have done it."

I relinquished the intention he had detected, for I knew him! Even yet I could not recall a single feature, but I knew him! If the wind and the rain had driven away the intervening years, had scattered all the intervening objects, had swept us to the churchyard where we first stood face to face on such different levels, I could not have known my convict more distinctly than I knew him now as he sat in the chair before the fire. No need to take a file from his pocket and show it to me; no need to take the handkerchief from his neck and twist it round his head; no need to hug himself with both his arms, and take a shivering turn across the room, looking back at me for recognition. I knew him before he gave me one of those aids, though, a moment before, I had not been conscious of remotely suspecting his identity.

He came back to where I stood, and again held out both his hands. Not knowing what to do,—for, in my astonishment I had lost my self-possession,—I reluctantly gave him my hands. He grasped them heartily, raised them to his lips, kissed them, and still held them.

"You acted noble, my boy," said he. "Noble, Pip! And I have never forgot it!"

At a change in his manner as if he were even going to embrace me, I laid a hand upon his breast and put him away.

"Stay!" said I. "Keep off! If you are grateful to me for what I did when I was a little child, I hope you have shown your gratitude by mending your way of life. If you have come here to thank me, it was not necessary. Still, however you have found me out, there must be something good in the feeling that has brought you here, and I will not repulse you; but surely you must understand that—I—"

My attention was so attracted by the singularity of his fixed look at me, that the words died away on my tongue.

"You was a saying," he observed, when we had confronted one another in silence, "that surely I must understand. What, surely must I understand?"

"That I cannot wish to renew that chance intercourse with you of long ago, under these different circumstances. I am glad to believe you have repented and recovered yourself. I am glad to tell you so. I am glad that, thinking I deserve to be thanked, you have come to thank me. But our ways are different ways, none the less. You are wet, and you look weary. Will you drink something before you go?"

He had replaced his neckerchief loosely, and had stood, keenly observant of me, biting a long end of it. "I think," he answered, still with the end at his mouth and still observant of me, "that I will drink (I thank you) afore I go."

There was a tray ready on a side-table. I brought it to the table near the fire, and asked him what he would have? He touched one of the bottles without looking at it or speaking, and I made him some hot rum and water. I tried to keep my hand steady while I did so, but his look at me as he leaned back in his chair with the long draggled end of his neckerchief between his teeth—evidently forgotten—made my hand very difficult to master. When at last I put the glass to him, I saw with amazement that his eyes were full of tears.

Up to this time I had remained standing, not to disguise that I wished him gone. But I was softened by the softened aspect of the man, and felt a touch of reproach. "I hope," said I, hurriedly putting something into a glass for myself, and drawing a chair to the table, "that you will not think I spoke harshly to you just now. I had no intention of doing it, and I am sorry for it if I did. I wish you well and happy!"

As I put my glass to my lips, he glanced with surprise at the end of his neckerchief, dropping from his mouth when he opened it, and stretched out his hand. I gave him mine, and then he drank, and drew his sleeve across his eyes and forehead.

"How are you living?" I asked him.

"I've been a sheep-farmer, stock-breeder, other trades besides, away in the new world," said he; "many a thousand mile of stormy water off from this."

"I hope you have done well?"

"I've done wonderfully well. There's others went out alonger me as has done well too, but no man has done nigh as well as me. I'm famous for it."

"I am glad to hear it."

"I hope to hear you say so, my dear boy."

Without stopping to try to understand those words or the tone in which they were spoken, I turned off to a point that had just come into my mind.

"Have you ever seen a messenger you once sent to me," I inquired, "since he undertook that trust?"

"Never set eyes upon him. I warn't likely to it."

"He came faithfully, and he brought me the two one-pound notes. I was a poor boy then, as you know, and to a poor boy they were a little fortune. But, like you, I have done well since, and you must let me pay them back. You can put them to some other poor boy's use." I took out my purse.

He watched me as I laid my purse upon the table and opened it, and he watched me as I separated two one-pound notes from its contents. They were clean and new, and I spread them out and handed them over to him. Still watching me, he laid them one upon the other, folded them long-wise, gave them a twist, set fire to them at the lamp, and dropped the ashes into the tray.

"May I make so bold," he said then, with a smile that was like a frown, and with a frown that was like a smile, "as ask you how you have done well, since you and me was out on them lone shivering marshes?"

"How?"

"Ah!"

He emptied his glass, got up, and stood at the side of the fire, with his heavy brown hand on the mantel-shelf. He put a foot up to the bars, to dry and warm it, and the wet boot began to steam; but, he neither looked at it, nor at the fire, but steadily looked at me. It was only now that I began to tremble.

When my lips had parted, and had shaped some words that were without sound, I forced myself to tell him (though I could not do it distinctly), that I had been chosen to succeed to some property.

"Might a mere warmint ask what property?" said he.

I faltered, "I don't know."

"Might a mere warmint ask whose property?" said he.

I faltered again, "I don't know."

"Could I make a guess, I wonder," said the Convict, "at your income since you come of age! As to the first figure now. Five?"

With my heart beating like a heavy hammer of disordered action, I rose out of my chair, and stood with my hand upon the back of it, looking wildly at him.

"Concerning a guardian," he went on. "There ought to have been some guardian, or such-like, whiles you was a minor. Some lawyer, maybe. As to the first letter of that lawyer's name now. Would it be J?"

All the truth of my position came flashing on me; and its disappointments, dangers, disgraces, consequences of all kinds, rushed in in such a multitude that I was borne down by them and had to struggle for every breath I drew.

"Put it," he resumed, "as the employer of that lawyer whose name begun with a J, and might be Jaggers,—put it as he had come over sea to Portsmouth, and had landed there, and had wanted to come on to you. 'However, you have found me out,' you says just now. Well! However, did I find you out? Why, I wrote from Portsmouth to a person in London, for particulars of your address. That person's name? Why, Wemmick."

I could not have spoken one word, though it had been to save my life. I stood, with a hand on the chair-back and a hand on my breast, where I seemed to be suffocating,—I stood so, looking wildly at him, until I grasped at the chair, when the room began to surge and turn. He caught me, drew me to the sofa, put me up against the cushions, and bent on one knee before me, bringing the face that I now well remembered, and that I shuddered at, very near to mine.

"Yes, Pip, dear boy, I've made a gentleman on you! It's me wot has done it! I swore that time, sure as ever I earned a guinea, that guinea should go to you. I swore arterwards, sure as ever I spec'lated and got rich, you should get rich. I lived rough, that you should live smooth; I worked hard, that you should be above work. What odds, dear boy? Do I tell it, fur you to feel a obligation? Not a bit. I tell it, fur you to know as that there hunted dunghill dog wot you kep life in, got his head so high that he could make a gentleman,—and, Pip, you're him!"

The abhorrence in which I held the man, the dread I had of him, the repugnance with which I shrank from him, could not have been exceeded if he had been some terrible beast.

"Look'ee here, Pip. I'm your second father. You're my son,—more to me nor any son. I've put away money, only for you to spend. When I was a hired-out shepherd in a solitary hut, not seeing no faces but faces of sheep till I half forgot wot men's and women's faces wos like, I see yourn. I drops my knife many a time in that hut when I was a-eating my dinner or my supper, and I says, 'Here's the boy again, a looking at me whiles I eats and drinks!' I see you there a many times, as plain as ever I see you on them misty marshes. 'Lord strike me dead!' I says each time,—and I goes out in the air to say it under the open heavens,—'but wot, if I gets liberty and money, I'll make that boy a gentleman!' And I done it. Why, look at you, dear boy! Look at these here lodgings o'yourn, fit for a lord! A lord? Ah! You shall show money with lords for wagers, and beat 'em!"

In his heat and triumph, and in his knowledge that I had been nearly fainting, he did not remark on my reception of all this. It was the one grain of relief I had.

"Look'ee here!" he went on, taking my watch out of my pocket, and turning towards him a ring on my finger, while I recoiled from his touch as if he had been a snake, "a gold 'un and a beauty: that's a gentleman's, I hope! A diamond all set round with rubies; that's a gentleman's, I hope! Look at your linen; fine and beautiful! Look at your clothes; better ain't to be got! And your books too," turning his eyes round the room, "mounting up, on their shelves, by hundreds! And you read 'em; don't you? I see you'd been a reading of 'em when I come in. Ha, ha, ha! You shall read 'em to me, dear boy! And if they're in foreign languages wot I don't understand, I shall be just as proud as if I did."

Again he took both my hands and put them to his lips, while my blood ran cold within me.

"Don't you mind talking, Pip," said he, after again drawing his sleeve over his eyes and forehead, as the click came in his throat which I well remembered,—and he was all the more horrible to me that he was so much in earnest; "you can't do better nor keep quiet, dear boy. You ain't looked slowly forward to this as I have; you wosn't prepared for this as I wos. But didn't you never think it might be me?"

"O no, no, no," I returned, "Never, never!"

"Well, you see it wos me, and single-handed. Never a soul in it but my own self and Mr. Jaggers."

"Was there no one else?" I asked.

"No," said he, with a glance of surprise: "who else should there be? And, dear boy, how good looking you have growed! There's bright eyes somewheres—eh? Isn't there bright eyes somewheres, wot you love the thoughts on?"

O Estella, Estella!

"They shall be yourn, dear boy, if money can buy 'em. Not that a gentleman like you, so well set up as you, can't win 'em off of his own game; but money shall back you! Let me finish wot I was a telling you, dear boy. From that there hut and that there hiring-out, I got money left me by my master (which died, and had been the same as me), and got my liberty and went for myself. In every single thing I went for, I went for you. 'Lord strike a blight upon it,' I says, wotever it was I went for, 'if it ain't for him!' It all prospered wonderful. As I giv' you to understand just now, I'm famous for it. It was the money left me, and the gains of the first few year wot I sent home to Mr. Jaggers—all for you—when he first come arter you, agreeable to my letter."

O that he had never come! That he had left me at the forge,—far from contented, yet, by comparison happy!

"And then, dear boy, it was a recompense to me, look'ee here, to know in secret that I was making a gentleman. The blood horses of them colonists might fling up the dust over me as I was walking; what do I say? I says to myself, 'I'm making a better gentleman nor ever you'll be!' When one of 'em says to another, 'He was a convict, a few year ago, and is a ignorant common fellow now, for all he's lucky,' what do I say? I says to myself, 'If I ain't a gentleman, nor yet ain't got no learning, I'm the owner of such. All on you owns stock and land; which on you owns a brought-up London gentleman?' This way I kep myself a going. And this way I held steady afore my mind that I would for certain come one day and see my boy, and make myself known to him, on his own ground."

He laid his hand on my shoulder. I shuddered at the thought that for anything I knew, his hand might be stained with blood.

"It warn't easy, Pip, for me to leave them parts, nor yet it warn't safe. But I held to it, and the harder it was, the stronger I held, for I was determined, and my mind firm made up. At last I done it. Dear boy, I done it!"

I tried to collect my thoughts, but I was stunned. Throughout, I had seemed to myself to attend more to the wind and the rain than to him; even now, I could not separate his voice from those voices, though those were loud and his was silent.

"Where will you put me?" he asked, presently. "I must be put somewhere, dear boy."

"To sleep?" said I.

"Yes. And to sleep long and sound," he answered; "for I've been sea-tossed and sea-washed, months and months."

"My friend and companion," said I, rising from the sofa, "is absent; you must have his room."

"He won't come back to-morrow; will he?"

"No," said I, answering almost mechanically, in spite of my utmost efforts; "not to-morrow."

"Because, look'ee here, dear boy," he said, dropping his voice, and laying a long finger on my breast in an impressive manner, "caution is necessary."

"How do you mean? Caution?"

"By G——, it's Death!"

"What's death?"

"I was sent for life. It's death to come back. There's been overmuch coming back of late years, and I should of a certainty be hanged if took."

Nothing was needed but this; the wretched man, after loading wretched me with his gold and silver chains for years, had risked his life to come to me, and I held it there in my keeping! If I had loved him instead of abhorring him; if I had been attracted to him by the strongest admiration and affection, instead of shrinking from him with the strongest repugnance; it could have been no worse. On the contrary, it would have been better, for his preservation would then have naturally and tenderly addressed my heart.

My first care was to close the shutters, so that no light might be seen from without, and then to close and make fast the doors. While I did so, he stood at the table drinking rum and eating biscuit; and when I saw him thus engaged, I saw my convict on the marshes at his meal again. It almost seemed to me as if he must stoop down presently, to file at his leg.

When I had gone into Herbert's room, and had shut off any other communication between it and the staircase than through the room in which our conversation had been held, I asked him if he would go to bed? He said yes, but asked me for some of my "gentleman's linen" to put on in the morning. I brought it out, and laid it ready for him, and my blood again ran cold when he again took me by both hands to give me good night.

I got away from him, without knowing how I did it, and mended the fire in the room where we had been together, and sat down by it, afraid to go to bed. For an hour or more, I remained too stunned to think; and it was not until I began to think, that I began fully to know how wrecked I was, and how the ship in which I had sailed was gone to pieces.

Miss Havisham's intentions towards me, all a mere dream; Estella not designed for me; I only suffered in Satis House as a convenience, a sting for the greedy relations, a model with a mechanical heart to practise on when no other practice was at hand; those were the first smarts I had. But, sharpest and deepest pain of all,—it was for the convict, guilty of I knew not what crimes, and liable to be taken out of those rooms where I sat thinking, and hanged at the Old Bailey door, that I had deserted Joe.

I would not have gone back to Joe now, I would not have gone back to Biddy now, for any consideration; simply, I suppose, because my sense of my own worthless conduct to them was greater than every consideration. No wisdom on earth could have given me the comfort that I should have derived from their simplicity and fidelity; but I could never, never, undo what I had done.

In every rage of wind and rush of rain, I heard pursuers. Twice, I could have sworn there was a knocking and whispering at the outer door. With these fears upon me, I began either to imagine or recall that I had had mysterious warnings of this man's approach. That, for weeks gone by, I had passed faces in the streets which I had thought like his. That these likenesses had grown more numerous, as he, coming over the sea, had drawn nearer. That his wicked spirit had somehow sent these messengers to mine, and that now on this stormy night he was as good as his word, and with me.

Crowding up with these reflections came the reflection that I had seen him with my childish eyes to be a desperately violent man; that I had heard that other convict reiterate that he had tried to murder him; that I had seen him down in the ditch tearing and fighting like a wild beast. Out of such remembrances I brought into the light of the fire a half-formed terror that it might not be safe to be shut up there with him in the dead of the wild solitary night. This dilated until it filled the room, and impelled me to take a candle and go in and look at my dreadful burden.

He had rolled a handkerchief round his head, and his face was set and lowering in his sleep. But he was asleep, and quietly too, though he had a pistol lying on the pillow. Assured of this, I softly removed the key to the outside of his door, and turned it on him before I again sat down by the fire. Gradually I slipped from the chair and lay on the floor. When I awoke without having parted in my sleep with the perception of my wretchedness, the clocks of the Eastward churches were striking five, the candles were wasted out, the fire was dead, and the wind and rain intensified the thick black darkness.

THIS IS THE END OF THE SECOND STAGE OF PIP'S EXPECTATIONS.

Chapter XL

It was fortunate for me that I had to take precautions to ensure (so far as I could) the safety of my dreaded visitor; for, this thought pressing on me when I awoke, held other thoughts in a confused concourse at a distance.

The impossibility of keeping him concealed in the chambers was self-evident. It could not be done, and the attempt to do it would inevitably engender suspicion. True, I had no Avenger in my service now, but I was looked after by an inflammatory old female, assisted by an animated rag-bag whom she called her niece, and to keep a room secret from them would be to invite curiosity and exaggeration. They both had weak eyes, which I had long attributed to their chronically looking in at keyholes, and they were always at hand when not wanted; indeed that was their only reliable quality besides larceny. Not to get up a mystery with these people, I resolved to announce in the morning that my uncle had unexpectedly come from the country.

This course I decided on while I was yet groping about in the darkness for the means of getting a light. Not stumbling on the means after all, I was fain to go out to the adjacent Lodge and get the watchman there to come with his lantern. Now, in groping my way down the black staircase I fell over something, and that something was a man crouching in a corner.

As the man made no answer when I asked him what he did there, but eluded my touch in silence, I ran to the Lodge and urged the watchman to come quickly; telling him of the incident on the way back. The wind being as fierce as ever, we did not care to endanger the light in the lantern by rekindling the extinguished lamps on the staircase, but we examined the staircase from the bottom to the top and found no one there. It then occurred to me as possible that the man might have slipped into my rooms; so, lighting my candle at the watchman's, and leaving him standing at the door, I examined them carefully, including the room in which my dreaded guest lay asleep. All was quiet, and assuredly no other man was in those chambers.

It troubled me that there should have been a lurker on the stairs, on that night of all nights in the year, and I asked the watchman, on the chance of eliciting some hopeful explanation as I handed him a dram at the door, whether he had admitted at his gate any gentleman who had perceptibly been dining out? Yes, he said; at different times of the night, three. One lived in Fountain Court, and the other two lived in the Lane, and he had seen them all go home. Again, the only other man who dwelt in the house of which my chambers formed a part had been in the country for some weeks, and he certainly had not returned in the night, because we had seen his door with his seal on it as we came upstairs.

"The night being so bad, sir," said the watchman, as he gave me back my glass, "uncommon few have come in at my gate. Besides them three gentlemen that I have named, I don't call to mind another since about eleven o'clock, when a stranger asked for you."

"My uncle," I muttered. "Yes."

"You saw him, sir?"

"Yes. Oh yes."

"Likewise the person with him?"

"Person with him!" I repeated.

"I judged the person to be with him," returned the watchman. "The person stopped, when he stopped to make inquiry of me, and the person took this way when he took this way."

"What sort of person?"

The watchman had not particularly noticed; he should say a working person; to the best of his belief, he had a dust-colored kind of clothes on, under a dark coat. The watchman made more light of the matter than I did, and naturally; not having my reason for attaching weight to it.

When I had got rid of him, which I thought it well to do without prolonging explanations, my mind was much troubled by these two circumstances taken together. Whereas they were easy of innocent solution apart,—as, for instance, some diner out or diner at home, who had not gone near this watchman's gate, might have strayed to my staircase and dropped asleep there,—and my nameless visitor might have brought some one with him to show him the way,—still, joined, they had an ugly look to one as prone to distrust and fear as the changes of a few hours had made me.

I lighted my fire, which burnt with a raw pale flare at that time of the morning, and fell into a doze before it. I seemed to have been dozing a whole night when the clocks struck six. As there was full an hour and a half between me and daylight, I dozed again; now, waking up uneasily, with prolix conversations about nothing, in my ears; now, making thunder of the wind in the chimney; at length, falling off into a profound sleep from which the daylight woke me with a start.

All this time I had never been able to consider my own situation, nor could I do so yet. I had not the power to attend to it. I was greatly dejected and distressed, but in an incoherent wholesale sort of way. As to forming any plan for the future, I could as soon have formed an elephant. When I opened the shutters and looked out at the wet wild morning, all of a leaden hue; when I walked from room to room; when I sat down again shivering, before the fire, waiting for my laundress to appear; I thought how miserable I was, but hardly knew why, or how long I had been so, or on what day of the week I made the reflection, or even who I was that made it.

At last, the old woman and the niece came in,—the latter with a head not easily distinguishable from her dusty broom,—and testified surprise at sight of me and the fire. To whom I imparted how my uncle had come in the night and was then asleep, and how the breakfast preparations were to be modified accordingly. Then I washed and dressed while they knocked the furniture about and made a dust; and so, in a sort of dream or sleep-waking, I found myself sitting by the fire again, waiting for—Him—to come to breakfast.

By and by, his door opened and he came out. I could not bring myself to bear the sight of him, and I thought he had a worse look by daylight.

"I do not even know," said I, speaking low as he took his seat at the table, "by what name to call you. I have given out that you are my uncle."

"That's it, dear boy! Call me uncle."

"You assumed some name, I suppose, on board ship?"

"Yes, dear boy. I took the name of Provis."

"Do you mean to keep that name?"

"Why, yes, dear boy, it's as good as another,—unless you'd like another."

"What is your real name?" I asked him in a whisper.

"Magwitch," he answered, in the same tone; "chrisen'd Abel."

"What were you brought up to be?"

"A warmint, dear boy."

He answered quite seriously, and used the word as if it denoted some profession.

"When you came into the Temple last night—" said I, pausing to wonder whether that could really have been last night, which seemed so long ago.

"Yes, dear boy?"

"When you came in at the gate and asked the watchman the way here, had you any one with you?"

"With me? No, dear boy."

"But there was some one there?"

"I didn't take particular notice," he said, dubiously, "not knowing the ways of the place. But I think there was a person, too, come in alonger me."

"Are you known in London?"

"I hope not!" said he, giving his neck a jerk with his forefinger that made me turn hot and sick.

"Were you known in London, once?"

"Not over and above, dear boy. I was in the provinces mostly."

"Were you—tried—in London?"

"Which time?" said he, with a sharp look.

"The last time."

He nodded. "First knowed Mr. Jaggers that way. Jaggers was for me."

It was on my lips to ask him what he was tried for, but he took up a knife, gave it a flourish, and with the words, "And what I done is worked out and paid for!" fell to at his breakfast.

He ate in a ravenous way that was very disagreeable, and all his actions were uncouth, noisy, and greedy. Some of his teeth had failed him since I saw him eat on the marshes, and as he turned his food in his mouth, and turned his head sideways to bring his strongest fangs to bear upon it, he looked terribly like a hungry old dog. If I had begun with any appetite, he would have taken it away, and I should have sat much as I did,—repelled from him by an insurmountable aversion, and gloomily looking at the cloth.

"I'm a heavy grubber, dear boy," he said, as a polite kind of apology when he made an end of his meal, "but I always was. If it had been in my constitution to be a lighter grubber, I might ha' got into lighter trouble. Similarly, I must have my smoke. When I was first hired out as shepherd t'other side the world, it's my belief I should ha' turned into a molloncolly-mad sheep myself, if I hadn't a had my smoke."

As he said so, he got up from table, and putting his hand into the breast of the pea-coat he wore, brought out a short black pipe, and a handful of loose tobacco of the kind that is called Negro-head. Having filled his pipe, he put the surplus tobacco back again, as if his pocket were a drawer. Then, he took a live coal from the fire with the tongs, and lighted his pipe at it, and then turned round on the hearth-rug with his back to the fire, and went through his favorite action of holding out both his hands for mine.

"And this," said he, dandling my hands up and down in his, as he puffed at his pipe,— "and this is the gentleman what I made! The real genuine One! It does me good fur to look at you, Pip. All I stip'late, is, to stand by and look at you, dear boy!"

I released my hands as soon as I could, and found that I was beginning slowly to settle down to the contemplation of my condition. What I was chained to, and how heavily, became intelligible to me, as I heard his hoarse voice, and sat looking up at his furrowed bald head with its iron gray hair at the sides.

"I mustn't see my gentleman a footing it in the mire of the streets; there mustn't be no mud on his boots. My gentleman must have horses, Pip! Horses to ride, and horses to drive, and horses for his servant to ride and drive as well. Shall colonists have their horses (and blood 'uns, if you please, good Lord!) and not my London gentleman? No, no. We'll show 'em another pair of shoes than that, Pip; won't us?"

He took out of his pocket a great thick pocket-book, bursting with papers, and tossed it on the table.

"There's something worth spending in that there book, dear boy. It's yourn. All I've got ain't mine; it's yourn. Don't you be afeerd on it. There's more where that come from. I've come to the old country fur to see my gentleman spend his money like a gentleman. That'll be my pleasure. My pleasure 'ull be fur to see him do it. And blast you all!" he wound up, looking round the room and snapping his fingers once with a loud snap, "blast you every one, from the judge in his wig, to the colonist a stirring up the dust, I'll show a better gentleman than the whole kit on you put together!"

"Stop!" said I, almost in a frenzy of fear and dislike, "I want to speak to you. I want to know what is to be done. I want to know how you are to be kept out of danger, how long you are going to stay, what projects you have."

"Look'ee here, Pip," said he, laying his hand on my arm in a suddenly altered and subdued manner; "first of all, look'ee here. I forgot myself half a minute ago. What I said was low; that's what it was; low. Look'ee here, Pip. Look over it. I ain't a going to be low."

"First," I resumed, half groaning, "what precautions can be taken against your being recognized and seized?"

"No, dear boy," he said, in the same tone as before, "that don't go first. Lowness goes first. I ain't took so many years to make a gentleman, not without knowing what's due to him. Look'ee here, Pip. I was low; that's what I was; low. Look over it, dear boy."

Some sense of the grimly-ludicrous moved me to a fretful laugh, as I replied, "I have looked over it. In Heaven's name, don't harp upon it!"

"Yes, but look'ee here," he persisted. "Dear boy, I ain't come so fur, not fur to be low. Now, go on, dear boy. You was a saying—"

"How are you to be guarded from the danger you have incurred?"

"Well, dear boy, the danger ain't so great. Without I was informed agen, the danger ain't so much to signify. There's Jaggers, and there's Wemmick, and there's you. Who else is there to inform?"

"Is there no chance person who might identify you in the street?" said I.

"Well," he returned, "there ain't many. Nor yet I don't intend to advertise myself in the newspapers by the name of A.M. come back from Botany Bay; and years have rolled away, and who's to gain by it? Still, look'ee here, Pip. If the danger had been fifty times as great, I should ha' come to see you, mind you, just the same."

"And how long do you remain?"

"How long?" said he, taking his black pipe from his mouth, and dropping his jaw as he stared at me. "I'm not a going back. I've come for good."

"Where are you to live?" said I. "What is to be done with you? Where will you be safe?"

"Dear boy," he returned, "there's disguising wigs can be bought for money, and there's hair powder, and spectacles, and black clothes,—shorts and what not. Others has done it safe afore, and what others has done afore, others can do agen. As to the where and how of living, dear boy, give me your own opinions on it."

"You take it smoothly now," said I, "but you were very serious last night, when you swore it was Death."

"And so I swear it is Death," said he, putting his pipe back in his mouth, "and Death by the rope, in the open street not fur from this, and it's serious that you should fully understand it to be so. What then, when that's once done? Here I am. To go back now 'ud be as bad as to stand ground—worse. Besides, Pip, I'm here, because I've meant it by you, years and years. As to what I dare, I'm a old bird now, as has dared all manner of traps since first he was fledged, and I'm not afeerd to perch upon a scarecrow. If there's Death hid inside of it, there is, and let him come out, and I'll face him, and then I'll believe in him and not afore. And now let me have a look at my gentleman agen."

Once more, he took me by both hands and surveyed me with an air of admiring proprietorship: smoking with great complacency all the while.

It appeared to me that I could do no better than secure him some quiet lodging hard by, of which he might take possession when Herbert returned: whom I expected in two or three days. That the secret must be confided to Herbert as a matter of unavoidable necessity, even if I could have put the immense relief I should derive from sharing it with him out of the question, was plain to me. But it was by no means so plain to Mr. Provis (I resolved to call him by that name), who reserved his consent to Herbert's participation until he should have seen him and formed a favorable judgment of his physiognomy. "And even then, dear boy," said he, pulling a greasy little clasped black Testament out of his pocket, "we'll have him on his oath."

To state that my terrible patron carried this little black book about the world solely to swear people on in cases of emergency, would be to state what I never quite established; but this I can say, that I never knew him put it to any other use. The book itself had the appearance of having been stolen from some court of justice, and perhaps his knowledge of its antecedents, combined with his own experience in that wise, gave him a reliance on its powers as a sort of legal spell or charm. On this first occasion of his producing it, I recalled how he had made me swear fidelity in the churchyard long ago, and how he had described himself last night as always swearing to his resolutions in his solitude.

As he was at present dressed in a seafaring slop suit, in which he looked as if he had some parrots and cigars to dispose of, I next discussed with him what dress he should wear. He cherished an extraordinary belief in the virtues of "shorts" as a disguise, and had in his own mind sketched a dress for himself that would have made him something between a dean and a dentist. It was with considerable difficulty that I won him over to the assumption of a dress more like a prosperous farmer's; and we arranged that he should cut his hair close, and wear a little powder. Lastly, as he had not yet been seen by the laundress or her niece, he was to keep himself out of their view until his change of dress was made.

It would seem a simple matter to decide on these precautions; but in my dazed, not to say distracted, state, it took so long, that I did not get out to further them until two or three in the afternoon. He was to remain shut up in the chambers while I was gone, and was on no account to open the door.

There being to my knowledge a respectable lodging-house in Essex Street, the back of which looked into the Temple, and was almost within hail of my windows, I first of all repaired to that house, and was so fortunate as to secure the second floor for my uncle, Mr. Provis. I then went from shop to shop, making such purchases as were necessary to the change in his appearance. This business transacted, I turned my face, on my own account, to Little Britain. Mr. Jaggers was at his desk, but, seeing me enter, got up immediately and stood before his fire.

"Now, Pip," said he, "be careful."

"I will, sir," I returned. For, coming along I had thought well of what I was going to say.

"Don't commit yourself," said Mr. Jaggers, "and don't commit any one. You understand—any one. Don't tell me anything: I don't want to know anything; I am not curious."

Of course I saw that he knew the man was come.

"I merely want, Mr. Jaggers," said I, "to assure myself that what I have been told is true. I have no hope of its being untrue, but at least I may verify it."

Mr. Jaggers nodded. "But did you say 'told' or 'informed'?" he asked me, with his head on one side, and not looking at me, but looking in a listening way at the floor. "Told would seem to imply verbal communication. You can't have verbal communication with a man in New South Wales, you know."

"I will say, informed, Mr. Jaggers."

"Good."

"I have been informed by a person named Abel Magwitch, that he is the benefactor so long unknown to me."

"That is the man," said Mr. Jaggers, "in New South Wales."

"And only he?" said I.

"And only he," said Mr. Jaggers.

"I am not so unreasonable, sir, as to think you at all responsible for my mistakes and wrong conclusions; but I always supposed it was Miss Havisham."

"As you say, Pip," returned Mr. Jaggers, turning his eyes upon me coolly, and taking a bite at his forefinger, "I am not at all responsible for that."

"And yet it looked so like it, sir," I pleaded with a downcast heart.

"Not a particle of evidence, Pip," said Mr. Jaggers, shaking his head and gathering up his skirts. "Take nothing on its looks; take everything on evidence. There's no better rule."

"I have no more to say," said I, with a sigh, after standing silent for a little while. "I have verified my information, and there's an end."

"And Magwitch—in New South Wales—having at last disclosed himself," said Mr. Jaggers, "you will comprehend, Pip, how rigidly throughout my communication with you, I have always adhered to the strict line of fact. There has never been the least departure from the strict line of fact. You are quite aware of that?"

"Quite, sir."

"I communicated to Magwitch—in New South Wales—when he first wrote to me—from New South Wales—the caution that he must not expect me ever to deviate from the strict line of fact. I also communicated to him another caution. He appeared to me to have obscurely hinted in his letter at some distant idea he had of seeing you in England here. I cautioned him that I must hear no more of that; that he was not at all likely to obtain a pardon; that he was expatriated for the term of his natural life; and that his presenting himself in this country would be an act of felony, rendering him liable to the extreme penalty of the law. I gave Magwitch that caution," said Mr. Jaggers, looking hard at me; "I wrote it to New South Wales. He guided himself by it, no doubt."

"No doubt," said I.

"I have been informed by Wemmick," pursued Mr. Jaggers, still looking hard at me, "that he has received a letter, under date Portsmouth, from a colonist of the name of Purvis, or—"

"Or Provis," I suggested.

"Or Provis—thank you, Pip. Perhaps it is Provis? Perhaps you know it's Provis?"

"Yes," said I.

"You know it's Provis. A letter, under date Portsmouth, from a colonist of the name of Provis, asking for the particulars of your address, on behalf of Magwitch. Wemmick sent him the particulars, I understand, by return of post. Probably it is through Provis that you have received the explanation of Magwitch—in New South Wales?"

"It came through Provis," I replied.

"Good day, Pip," said Mr. Jaggers, offering his hand; "glad to have seen you. In writing by post to Magwitch—in New South Wales—or in communicating with him through Provis, have the goodness to mention that the particulars and vouchers of our long account shall be sent to you, together with the balance; for there is still a balance remaining. Good day, Pip!"

We shook hands, and he looked hard at me as long as he could see me. I turned at the door, and he was still looking hard at me, while the two vile casts on the shelf seemed to be trying to get their eyelids open, and to force out of their swollen throats, "O, what a man he is!"

Wemmick was out, and though he had been at his desk he could have done nothing for me. I went straight back to the Temple, where I found the terrible Provis drinking rum and water and smoking negro-head, in safety.

Next day the clothes I had ordered all came home, and he put them on. Whatever he put on, became him less (it dismally seemed to me) than what he had worn before. To my thinking, there was something in him that made it hopeless to attempt to disguise him. The more I dressed him and the better I dressed him, the more he looked like the slouching fugitive on the marshes. This effect on my anxious fancy was partly referable, no doubt, to his old face and manner growing more familiar to me; but I believe too that he dragged one of his legs as if there were still a weight of iron on it, and that from head to foot there was Convict in the very grain of the man.

The influences of his solitary hut-life were upon him besides, and gave him a savage air that no dress could tame; added to these were the influences of his subsequent branded life among men, and, crowning all, his consciousness that he was dodging and hiding now. In all his ways of sitting and standing, and eating and drinking,—of brooding about in a high-shouldered reluctant style,—of taking out his great horn-handled jackknife and wiping it on his legs and cutting his food,—of lifting light glasses and cups to his lips, as if they were clumsy pannikins,—of chopping a wedge off his bread, and soaking up with it the last fragments of gravy round and round his plate, as if to make the most of an allowance, and then drying his finger-ends on it, and then swallowing it,—in these ways and a thousand other small nameless instances arising every minute in the day, there was Prisoner, Felon, Bondsman, plain as plain could be.

It had been his own idea to wear that touch of powder, and I had conceded the powder after overcoming the shorts. But I can compare the effect of it, when on, to nothing but the probable effect of rouge upon the dead; so awful was the manner in which everything in him that it was most desirable to repress, started through that thin layer of pretence, and seemed to come blazing out at the crown of his head. It was abandoned as soon as tried, and he wore his grizzled hair cut short.

Words cannot tell what a sense I had, at the same time, of the dreadful mystery that he was to me. When he fell asleep of an evening, with his knotted hands clenching the sides of the easy-chair, and his bald head tattooed with deep wrinkles falling forward on his breast, I would sit and look at him, wondering what he had done, and loading him with all the crimes in the Calendar, until the impulse was powerful on me to start up and fly from him. Every hour so increased my abhorrence of him, that I even think I might have yielded to this impulse in the first agonies of being so haunted, notwithstanding all he had done for me and the risk he ran, but for the knowledge that Herbert must soon come back. Once, I actually did start out of bed in the night, and begin to dress myself in my worst clothes, hurriedly intending to leave him there with everything else I possessed, and enlist for India as a private soldier.

I doubt if a ghost could have been more terrible to me, up in those lonely rooms in the long evenings and long nights, with the wind and the rain always rushing by. A ghost could not have been taken and hanged on my account, and the consideration that he could be, and the dread that he would be, were no small addition to my horrors. When he was not asleep, or playing a complicated kind of Patience with a ragged pack of cards of his own,—a game that I never saw before or since, and in which he recorded his winnings by sticking his jackknife into the table,—when he was not engaged in either of these pursuits, he would ask me to read to him,—"Foreign language, dear boy!" While I complied, he, not comprehending a single word, would stand before the fire surveying me with the air of an Exhibitor, and I would see him, between the fingers of the hand with which I shaded my face, appealing in dumb show to the furniture to take notice of my proficiency. The imaginary student pursued by the misshapen creature he had impiously made, was not more wretched than I, pursued by the creature who had made me, and recoiling from him with a stronger repulsion, the more he admired me and the fonder he was of me.

This is written of, I am sensible, as if it had lasted a year. It lasted about five days. Expecting Herbert all the time, I dared not go out, except when I took Provis for an airing after dark. At length, one evening when dinner was over and I had dropped into a slumber quite worn out,—for my nights had been agitated and my rest broken by fearful dreams,—I was roused by the welcome footstep on the staircase. Provis, who had been asleep too, staggered up at the noise I made, and in an instant I saw his jackknife shining in his hand.

"Quiet! It's Herbert!" I said; and Herbert came bursting in, with the airy freshness of six hundred miles of France upon him.

"Handel, my dear fellow, how are you, and again how are you, and again how are you? I seem to have been gone a twelvemonth! Why, so I must have been, for you have grown quite thin and pale! Handel, my—Halloa! I beg your pardon."

He was stopped in his running on and in his shaking hands with me, by seeing Provis. Provis, regarding him with a fixed attention, was slowly putting up his jackknife, and groping in another pocket for something else.

"Herbert, my dear friend," said I, shutting the double doors, while Herbert stood staring and wondering, "something very strange has happened. This is—a visitor of mine."

"It's all right, dear boy!" said Provis coming forward, with his little clasped black book, and then addressing himself to Herbert. "Take it in your right hand. Lord strike you dead on the spot, if ever you split in any way sumever! Kiss it!"

"Do so, as he wishes it," I said to Herbert. So, Herbert, looking at me with a friendly uneasiness and amazement, complied, and Provis immediately shaking hands with him, said, "Now you're on your oath, you know. And never believe me on mine, if Pip shan't make a gentleman on you!"

Chapter XLI

In vain should I attempt to describe the astonishment and disquiet of Herbert, when he and I and Provis sat down before the fire, and I recounted the whole of the secret. Enough, that I saw my own feelings reflected in Herbert's face, and not least among them, my repugnance towards the man who had done so much for me.

What would alone have set a division between that man and us, if there had been no other dividing circumstance, was his triumph in my story. Saving his troublesome sense of having been "low" on one occasion since his return,—on which point he began to hold forth to Herbert, the moment my revelation was finished,—he had no perception of the possibility of my finding any fault with my good fortune. His boast that he had made me a gentleman, and that he had come to see me support the character on his ample resources, was made for me quite as much as for himself. And that it was a highly agreeable boast to both of us, and that we must both be very proud of it, was a conclusion quite established in his own mind.

"Though, look'ee here, Pip's comrade," he said to Herbert, after having discoursed for some time, "I know very well that once since I come back—for half a minute—I've been low. I said to Pip, I knowed as I had been low. But don't you fret yourself on that score. I ain't made Pip a gentleman, and Pip ain't a going to make you a gentleman, not fur me not to know what's due to ye both. Dear boy, and Pip's comrade, you two may count upon me always having a gen-teel muzzle on. Muzzled I have been since that half a minute when I was betrayed into lowness, muzzled I am at the present time, muzzled I ever will be."

Herbert said, "Certainly," but looked as if there were no specific consolation in this, and remained perplexed and dismayed. We were anxious for the time when he would go to his lodging and leave us together, but he was evidently jealous of leaving us together, and sat late. It was midnight before I took him round to Essex Street, and saw him safely in at his own dark door. When it closed upon him, I experienced the first moment of relief I had known since the night of his arrival.

Never quite free from an uneasy remembrance of the man on the stairs, I had always looked about me in taking my guest out after dark, and in bringing him back; and I looked about me now. Difficult as it is in a large city to avoid the suspicion of being watched, when the mind is conscious of danger in that regard, I could not persuade myself that any of the people within sight cared about my movements. The few who were passing passed on their several ways, and the street was empty when I turned back into the Temple. Nobody had come out at the gate with us, nobody went in at the gate with me. As I crossed by the fountain, I saw his lighted back windows looking bright and quiet, and, when I stood for a few moments in the doorway of the building where I lived, before going up the stairs, Garden Court was as still and lifeless as the staircase was when I ascended it.

Herbert received me with open arms, and I had never felt before so blessedly what it is to have a friend. When he had spoken some sound words of sympathy and encouragement, we sat down to consider the question, What was to be done?

The chair that Provis had occupied still remaining where it had stood,—for he had a barrack way with him of hanging about one spot, in one unsettled manner, and going through one round of observances with his pipe and his negro-head and his jackknife and his pack of cards, and what not, as if it were all put down for him on a slate,—I say his chair remaining where it had stood, Herbert unconsciously took it, but next moment started out of it, pushed it away, and took another. He had no occasion to say after that that he had conceived an aversion for my patron, neither had I occasion to confess my own. We interchanged that confidence without shaping a syllable.

"What," said I to Herbert, when he was safe in another chair,—"what is to be done?"

"My poor dear Handel," he replied, holding his head, "I am too stunned to think."

"So was I, Herbert, when the blow first fell. Still, something must be done. He is intent upon various new expenses,—horses, and carriages, and lavish appearances of all kinds. He must be stopped somehow."

"You mean that you can't accept—"

"How can I?" I interposed, as Herbert paused. "Think of him! Look at him!"

An involuntary shudder passed over both of us.

"Yet I am afraid the dreadful truth is, Herbert, that he is attached to me, strongly attached to me. Was there ever such a fate!"

"My poor dear Handel," Herbert repeated.

"Then," said I, "after all, stopping short here, never taking another penny from him, think what I owe him already! Then again: I am heavily in debt,—very heavily for me, who have now no expectations,—and I have been bred to no calling, and I am fit for nothing."

"Well, well, well!" Herbert remonstrated. "Don't say fit for nothing."

"What am I fit for? I know only one thing that I am fit for, and that is, to go for a soldier. And I might have gone, my dear Herbert, but for the prospect of taking counsel with your friendship and affection."

Of course I broke down there: and of course Herbert, beyond seizing a warm grip of my hand, pretended not to know it.

"Anyhow, my dear Handel," said he presently, "soldiering won't do. If you were to renounce this patronage and these favors, I suppose you would do so with some faint hope of one day repaying what you have already had. Not very strong, that hope, if you went soldiering! Besides, it's absurd. You would be infinitely better in Clarriker's house, small as it is. I am working up towards a partnership, you know."

Poor fellow! He little suspected with whose money.

"But there is another question," said Herbert. "This is an ignorant, determined man, who has long had one fixed idea. More than that, he seems to me (I may misjudge him) to be a man of a desperate and fierce character."

"I know he is," I returned. "Let me tell you what evidence I have seen of it." And I told him what I had not mentioned in my narrative, of that encounter with the other convict.

"See, then," said Herbert; "think of this! He comes here at the peril of his life, for the realization of his fixed idea. In the moment of realization, after all his toil and waiting, you cut the ground from under his feet, destroy his idea, and make his gains worthless to him. Do you see nothing that he might do, under the disappointment?"

"I have seen it, Herbert, and dreamed of it, ever since the fatal night of his arrival. Nothing has been in my thoughts so distinctly as his putting himself in the way of being taken."

"Then you may rely upon it," said Herbert, "that there would be great danger of his doing it. That is his power over you as long as he remains in England, and that would be his reckless course if you forsook him."

I was so struck by the horror of this idea, which had weighed upon me from the first, and the working out of which would make me regard myself, in some sort, as his murderer, that I could not rest in my chair, but began pacing to and fro. I said to Herbert, meanwhile, that even if Provis were recognized and taken, in spite of himself, I should be wretched as the cause, however innocently. Yes; even though I was so wretched in having him at large and near me, and even though I would far rather have worked at the forge all the days of my life than I would ever have come to this!

But there was no staving off the question, What was to be done?

"The first and the main thing to be done," said Herbert, "is to get him out of England. You will have to go with him, and then he may be induced to go."

"But get him where I will, could I prevent his coming back?"

"My good Handel, is it not obvious that with Newgate in the next street, there must be far greater hazard in your breaking your mind to him and making him reckless, here, than elsewhere? If a pretext to get him away could be made out of that other convict, or out of anything else in his life, now."

"There, again!" said I, stopping before Herbert, with my open hands held out, as if they contained the desperation of the case. "I know nothing of his life. It has almost made me mad to sit here of a night and see him before me, so bound up with my fortunes and misfortunes, and yet so unknown to me, except as the miserable wretch who terrified me two days in my childhood!"

Herbert got up, and linked his arm in mine, and we slowly walked to and fro together, studying the carpet.

"Handel," said Herbert, stopping, "you feel convinced that you can take no further benefits from him; do you?"

"Fully. Surely you would, too, if you were in my place?"

"And you feel convinced that you must break with him?"

"Herbert, can you ask me?"

"And you have, and are bound to have, that tenderness for the life he has risked on your account, that you must save him, if possible, from throwing it away. Then you must get him out of England before you stir a finger to extricate yourself. That done, extricate yourself, in Heaven's name, and we'll see it out together, dear old boy."

It was a comfort to shake hands upon it, and walk up and down again, with only that done.

"Now, Herbert," said I, "with reference to gaining some knowledge of his history. There is but one way that I know of. I must ask him point blank."

"Yes. Ask him," said Herbert, "when we sit at breakfast in the morning." For he had said, on taking leave of Herbert, that he would come to breakfast with us.

With this project formed, we went to bed. I had the wildest dreams concerning him, and woke unrefreshed; I woke, too, to recover the fear which I had lost in the night, of his being found out as a returned transport. Waking, I never lost that fear.

He came round at the appointed time, took out his jackknife, and sat down to his meal. He was full of plans "for his gentleman's coming out strong, and like a gentleman," and urged me to begin speedily upon the pocket-book which he had left in my possession. He considered the chambers and his own lodging as temporary residences, and advised me to look out at once for a "fashionable crib" near Hyde Park, in which he could have "a shake-down." When he had made an end of his breakfast, and was wiping his knife on his leg, I said to him, without a word of preface,—

"After you were gone last night, I told my friend of the struggle that the soldiers found you engaged in on the marshes, when we came up. You remember?"

"Remember!" said he. "I think so!"

"We want to know something about that man—and about you. It is strange to know no more about either, and particularly you, than I was able to tell last night. Is not this as good a time as another for our knowing more?"

"Well!" he said, after consideration. "You're on your oath, you know, Pip's comrade?"

"Assuredly," replied Herbert.

"As to anything I say, you know," he insisted. "The oath applies to all."

"I understand it to do so."

"And look'ee here! Wotever I done is worked out and paid for," he insisted again.

"So be it."

He took out his black pipe and was going to fill it with negro-head, when, looking at the tangle of tobacco in his hand, he seemed to think it might perplex the thread of his narrative. He put it back again, stuck his pipe in a button-hole of his coat, spread a hand on each knee, and after turning an angry eye on the fire for a few silent moments, looked round at us and said what follows.

Chapter XLII

"Dear boy and Pip's comrade. I am not a going fur to tell you my life like a song, or a story-book. But to give it you short and handy, I'll put it at once into a mouthful of English. In jail and out of jail, in jail and out of jail, in jail and out of jail. There, you've got it. That's my life pretty much, down to such times as I got shipped off, arter Pip stood my friend.

"I've been done everything to, pretty well—except hanged. I've been locked up as much as a silver tea-kittle. I've been carted here and carted there, and put out of this town, and put out of that town, and stuck in the stocks, and whipped and worried and drove. I've no more notion where I was born than you have—if so much. I first become aware of myself down in Essex, a thieving turnips for my living. Summun had run away from me—a man—a tinker—and he'd took the fire with him, and left me wery cold.

"I know'd my name to be Magwitch, chrisen'd Abel. How did I know it? Much as I know'd the birds' names in the hedges to be chaffinch, sparrer, thrush. I might have thought it was all lies together, only as the birds' names come out true, I supposed mine did.

"So fur as I could find, there warn't a soul that see young Abel Magwitch, with us little on him as in him, but wot caught fright at him, and either drove him off, or took him up. I was took up, took up, took up, to that extent that I reg'larly grow'd up took up.

"This is the way it was, that when I was a ragged little creetur as much to be pitied as ever I see (not that I looked in the glass, for there warn't many insides of furnished houses known to me), I got the name of being hardened. 'This is a terrible hardened one,' they says to prison wisitors, picking out me. 'May be said to live in jails, this boy.' Then they looked at me, and I looked at them, and they measured my head, some on 'em,—they had better a measured my stomach,—and others on 'em giv me tracts what I couldn't read, and made me speeches what I couldn't understand. They always went on agen me about the Devil. But what the Devil was I to do? I must put something into my stomach, mustn't I?—Howsomever, I'm a getting low, and I know what's due. Dear boy and Pip's comrade, don't you be afeerd of me being low.

"Tramping, begging, thieving, working sometimes when I could,—though that warn't as often as you may think, till you put the question whether you would ha' been over-ready to give me work yourselves,—a bit of a poacher, a bit of a laborer, a bit of a wagoner, a bit of a haymaker, a bit of a hawker, a bit of most things that don't pay and lead to trouble, I got to be a man. A deserting soldier in a Traveller's Rest, what lay hid up to the chin under a lot of taturs, learnt me to read; and a travelling Giant what signed his name at a penny a time learnt me to write. I warn't locked up as often now as formerly, but I wore out my good share of key-metal still.

"At Epsom races, a matter of over twenty years ago, I got acquainted wi' a man whose skull I'd crack wi' this poker, like the claw of a lobster, if I'd got it on this hob. His right name was Compeyson; and that's the man, dear boy, what you see me a pounding in the ditch, according to what you truly told your comrade arter I was gone last night.

"He set up fur a gentleman, this Compeyson, and he'd been to a public boarding-school and had learning. He was a smooth one to talk, and was a dab at the ways of gentlefolks. He was good-looking too. It was the night afore the great race, when I found him on the heath, in a booth that I know'd on. Him and some more was a sitting among the tables when I went in, and the landlord (which had a knowledge of me, and was a sporting one) called him out, and said, 'I think this is a man that might suit you,'—meaning I was.

"Compeyson, he looks at me very noticing, and I look at him. He has a watch and a chain and a ring and a breast-pin and a handsome suit of clothes.

"'To judge from appearances, you're out of luck,' says Compeyson to me.

"'Yes, master, and I've never been in it much.' (I had come out of Kingston Jail last on a vagrancy committal. Not but what it might have been for something else; but it warn't.)

"'Luck changes,' says Compeyson; 'perhaps yours is going to change.'

"I says, 'I hope it may be so. There's room.'

"'What can you do?' says Compeyson.

"'Eat and drink,' I says; 'if you'll find the materials.'

"Compeyson laughed, looked at me again very noticing, giv me five shillings, and appointed me for next night. Same place.

"I went to Compeyson next night, same place, and Compeyson took me on to be his man and pardner. And what was Compeyson's business in which we was to go pardners? Compeyson's business was the swindling, handwriting forging, stolen bank-note passing, and such-like. All sorts of traps as Compeyson could set with his head, and keep his own legs out of and get the profits from and let another man in for, was Compeyson's business. He'd no more heart than a iron file, he was as cold as death, and he had the head of the Devil afore mentioned.

"There was another in with Compeyson, as was called Arthur,—not as being so chrisen'd, but as a surname. He was in a Decline, and was a shadow to look at. Him and Compeyson had been in a bad thing with a rich lady some years afore, and they'd made a pot of money by it; but Compeyson betted and gamed, and he'd have run through the king's taxes. So, Arthur was a dying, and a dying poor and with the horrors on him, and Compeyson's wife (which Compeyson kicked mostly) was a having pity on him when she could, and Compeyson was a having pity on nothing and nobody.

"I might a took warning by Arthur, but I didn't; and I won't pretend I was partick'ler— for where 'ud be the good on it, dear boy and comrade? So I begun wi' Compeyson, and a poor tool I was in his hands. Arthur lived at the top of Compeyson's house (over nigh Brentford it was), and Compeyson kept a careful account agen him for board and lodging, in case he should ever get better to work it out. But Arthur soon settled the account. The second or third time as ever I see him, he come a tearing down into Compeyson's parlor late at night, in only a flannel gown, with his hair all in a sweat, and he says to Compeyson's wife, 'Sally, she really is upstairs alonger me, now, and I can't get rid of her. She's all in white,' he says, 'wi' white flowers in her hair, and she's awful mad, and she's got a shroud hanging over her arm, and she says she'll put it on me at five in the morning.'

"Says Compeyson: 'Why, you fool, don't you know she's got a living body? And how should she be up there, without coming through the door, or in at the window, and up the stairs?'

"'I don't know how she's there,' says Arthur, shivering dreadful with the horrors, 'but she's standing in the corner at the foot of the bed, awful mad. And over where her heart's broke—you broke it!—there's drops of blood.'

"Compeyson spoke hardy, but he was always a coward. 'Go up alonger this drivelling sick man,' he says to his wife, 'and Magwitch, lend her a hand, will you?' But he never come nigh himself.

"Compeyson's wife and me took him up to bed agen, and he raved most dreadful. 'Why look at her!' he cries out. 'She's a shaking the shroud at me! Don't you see her? Look at her eyes! Ain't it awful to see her so mad?' Next he cries, 'She'll put it on me, and then I'm done for! Take it away from her, take it away!' And then he catched hold of us, and kep on a talking to her, and answering of her, till I half believed I see her myself.

"Compeyson's wife, being used to him, giv him some liquor to get the horrors off, and by and by he quieted. 'O, she's gone! Has her keeper been for her?' he says. 'Yes,' says Compeyson's wife. 'Did you tell him to lock her and bar her in?' 'Yes.' 'And to take that ugly thing away from her?' 'Yes, yes, all right.' 'You're a good creetur,' he says, 'don't leave me, whatever you do, and thank you!'

"He rested pretty quiet till it might want a few minutes of five, and then he starts up with a scream, and screams out, 'Here she is! She's got the shroud again. She's unfolding it. She's coming out of the corner. She's coming to the bed. Hold me, both on you—one of each side—don't let her touch me with it. Hah! she missed me that time. Don't let her throw it over my shoulders. Don't let her lift me up to get it round me. She's lifting me up. Keep me down!' Then he lifted himself up hard, and was dead.

"Compeyson took it easy as a good riddance for both sides. Him and me was soon busy, and first he swore me (being ever artful) on my own book,—this here little black book, dear boy, what I swore your comrade on.

"Not to go into the things that Compeyson planned, and I done—which 'ud take a week—I'll simply say to you, dear boy, and Pip's comrade, that that man got me into such nets as made me his black slave. I was always in debt to him, always under his thumb, always a working, always a getting into danger. He was younger than me, but he'd got craft, and he'd got learning, and he overmatched me five hundred times told and no mercy. My Missis as I had the hard time wi'—Stop though! I ain't brought her in—"

He looked about him in a confused way, as if he had lost his place in the book of his remembrance; and he turned his face to the fire, and spread his hands broader on his knees, and lifted them off and put them on again.

"There ain't no need to go into it," he said, looking round once more. "The time wi' Compeyson was a'most as hard a time as ever I had; that said, all's said. Did I tell you as I was tried, alone, for misdemeanor, while with Compeyson?"

I answered, No.

"Well!" he said, "I was, and got convicted. As to took up on suspicion, that was twice or three times in the four or five year that it lasted; but evidence was wanting. At last, me and Compeyson was both committed for felony,—on a charge of putting stolen notes in circulation,—and there was other charges behind. Compeyson says to me, 'Separate defences, no communication,' and that was all. And I was so miserable poor, that I sold all the clothes I had, except what hung on my back, afore I could get Jaggers.

"When we was put in the dock, I noticed first of all what a gentleman Compeyson looked, wi' his curly hair and his black clothes and his white pocket-handkercher, and what a common sort of a wretch I looked. When the prosecution opened and the evidence was put short, aforehand, I noticed how heavy it all bore on me, and how light on him. When the evidence was giv in the box, I noticed how it was always me that had come for'ard, and could be swore to, how it was always me that the money had been paid to, how it was always me that had seemed to work the thing and get the profit. But when the defence come on, then I see the plan plainer; for, says the counsellor for Compeyson, 'My lord and gentlemen, here you has afore you, side by side, two persons as your eyes can separate wide; one, the younger, well brought up, who will be spoke to as such; one, the elder, ill brought up, who will be spoke to as such; one, the younger, seldom if ever seen in these here transactions, and only suspected; t'other, the elder, always seen in 'em and always wi' his guilt brought home. Can you doubt, if there is but one in it, which is the one, and, if there is two in it, which is much the worst one?' And such-like. And when it come to character, warn't it Compeyson as had been to the school, and warn't it his schoolfellows as was in this position and in that, and warn't it him as had been know'd by witnesses in such clubs and societies, and nowt to his disadvantage? And warn't it me as had been tried afore, and as had been know'd up hill and down dale in Bridewells and Lock-Ups! And when it come to speech-making, warn't it Compeyson as could speak to 'em wi' his face dropping every now and then into his white pocket-handkercher,— ah! and wi' verses in his speech, too,—and warn't it me as could only say, 'Gentlemen, this man at my side is a most precious rascal'? And when the verdict come, warn't it Compeyson as was recommended to mercy on account of good character and bad company, and giving up all the information he could agen me, and warn't it me as got never a word but Guilty? And when I says to Compeyson, 'Once out of this court, I'll smash that face of yourn!' ain't it Compeyson as prays the Judge to be protected, and gets two turnkeys stood betwixt us? And when we're sentenced, ain't it him as gets seven year, and me fourteen, and ain't it him as the Judge is sorry for, because he might a done so well, and ain't it me as the Judge perceives to be a old offender of wiolent passion, likely to come to worse?"

He had worked himself into a state of great excitement, but he checked it, took two or three short breaths, swallowed as often, and stretching out his hand towards me said, in a reassuring manner, "I ain't a going to be low, dear boy!"

He had so heated himself that he took out his handkerchief and wiped his face and head and neck and hands, before he could go on.

"I had said to Compeyson that I'd smash that face of his, and I swore Lord smash mine! to do it. We was in the same prison-ship, but I couldn't get at him for long, though I tried. At last I come behind him and hit him on the cheek to turn him round and get a smashing one at him, when I was seen and seized. The black-hole of that ship warn't a strong one, to a judge of black-holes that could swim and dive. I escaped to the shore, and I was a hiding among the graves there, envying them as was in 'em and all over, when I first see my boy!"

He regarded me with a look of affection that made him almost abhorrent to me again, though I had felt great pity for him.

"By my boy, I was giv to understand as Compeyson was out on them marshes too. Upon my soul, I half believe he escaped in his terror, to get quit of me, not knowing it was me as had got ashore. I hunted him down. I smashed his face. 'And now,' says I 'as the worst thing I can do, caring nothing for myself, I'll drag you back.' And I'd have swum off, towing him by the hair, if it had come to that, and I'd a got him aboard without the soldiers.

"Of course he'd much the best of it to the last,—his character was so good. He had escaped when he was made half wild by me and my murderous intentions; and his punishment was light. I was put in irons, brought to trial again, and sent for life. I didn't stop for life, dear boy and Pip's comrade, being here."

He wiped himself again, as he had done before, and then slowly took his tangle of tobacco from his pocket, and plucked his pipe from his button-hole, and slowly filled it, and began to smoke.

"Is he dead?" I asked, after a silence.

"Is who dead, dear boy?"

"Compeyson."

"He hopes I am, if he's alive, you may be sure," with a fierce look. "I never heerd no more of him."

Herbert had been writing with his pencil in the cover of a book. He softly pushed the book over to me, as Provis stood smoking with his eyes on the fire, and I read in it:—

"Young Havisham's name was Arthur. Compeyson is the man who professed to be Miss Havisham's lover."

I shut the book and nodded slightly to Herbert, and put the book by; but we neither of us said anything, and both looked at Provis as he stood smoking by the fire.

Chapter XLIII

Why should I pause to ask how much of my shrinking from Provis might be traced to Estella? Why should I loiter on my road, to compare the state of mind in which I had tried to rid myself of the stain of the prison before meeting her at the coach-office, with the state of mind in which I now reflected on the abyss between Estella in her pride and beauty, and the returned transport whom I harbored? The road would be none the smoother for it, the end would be none the better for it, he would not be helped, nor I extenuated.

A new fear had been engendered in my mind by his narrative; or rather, his narrative had given form and purpose to the fear that was already there. If Compeyson were alive and should discover his return, I could hardly doubt the consequence. That Compeyson stood in mortal fear of him, neither of the two could know much better than I; and that any such man as that man had been described to be would hesitate to release himself for good from a dreaded enemy by the safe means of becoming an informer was scarcely to be imagined.

Never had I breathed, and never would I breathe—or so I resolved—a word of Estella to Provis. But, I said to Herbert that, before I could go abroad, I must see both Estella and Miss Havisham. This was when we were left alone on the night of the day when Provis told us his story. I resolved to go out to Richmond next day, and I went.

On my presenting myself at Mrs. Brandley's, Estella's maid was called to tell that Estella had gone into the country. Where? To Satis House, as usual. Not as usual, I said, for she had never yet gone there without me; when was she coming back? There was an air of reservation in the answer which increased my perplexity, and the answer was, that her maid believed she was only coming back at all for a little while. I could make nothing of this, except that it was meant that I should make nothing of it, and I went home again in complete discomfiture.

Another night consultation with Herbert after Provis was gone home (I always took him home, and always looked well about me), led us to the conclusion that nothing should be said about going abroad until I came back from Miss Havisham's. In the mean time, Herbert and I were to consider separately what it would be best to say; whether we should devise any pretence of being afraid that he was under suspicious observation; or whether I, who had never yet been abroad, should propose an expedition. We both knew that I had but to propose anything, and he would consent. We agreed that his remaining many days in his present hazard was not to be thought of.

Next day I had the meanness to feign that I was under a binding promise to go down to Joe; but I was capable of almost any meanness towards Joe or his name. Provis was to be strictly careful while I was gone, and Herbert was to take the charge of him that I had taken. I was to be absent only one night, and, on my return, the gratification of his impatience for my starting as a gentleman on a greater scale was to be begun. It occurred to me then, and as I afterwards found to Herbert also, that he might be best got away across the water, on that pretence,—as, to make purchases, or the like.

Having thus cleared the way for my expedition to Miss Havisham's, I set off by the early morning coach before it was yet light, and was out on the open country road when the day came creeping on, halting and whimpering and shivering, and wrapped in patches of cloud and rags of mist, like a beggar. When we drove up to the Blue Boar after a drizzly ride, whom should I see come out under the gateway, toothpick in hand, to look at the coach, but Bentley Drummle!

As he pretended not to see me, I pretended not to see him. It was a very lame pretence on both sides; the lamer, because we both went into the coffee-room, where he had just finished his breakfast, and where I ordered mine. It was poisonous to me to see him in the town, for I very well knew why he had come there.

Pretending to read a smeary newspaper long out of date, which had nothing half so legible in its local news, as the foreign matter of coffee, pickles, fish sauces, gravy, melted butter, and wine with which it was sprinkled all over, as if it had taken the measles in a highly irregular form, I sat at my table while he stood before the fire. By degrees it became an enormous injury to me that he stood before the fire. And I got up, determined to have my share of it. I had to put my hand behind his legs for the poker when I went up to the fireplace to stir the fire, but still pretended not to know him.

"Is this a cut?" said Mr. Drummle.

"Oh!" said I, poker in hand; "it's you, is it? How do you do? I was wondering who it was, who kept the fire off."

With that, I poked tremendously, and having done so, planted myself side by side with

Mr. Drummle, my shoulders squared and my back to the fire.

"You have just come down?" said Mr. Drummle, edging me a little away with his shoulder.

"Yes," said I, edging him a little away with my shoulder.

"Beastly place," said Drummle. "Your part of the country, I think?"

"Yes," I assented. "I am told it's very like your Shropshire."

"Not in the least like it," said Drummle.

Here Mr. Drummle looked at his boots and I looked at mine, and then Mr. Drummle looked at my boots, and I looked at his.

"Have you been here long?" I asked, determined not to yield an inch of the fire.

"Long enough to be tired of it," returned Drummle, pretending to yawn, but equally determined.

"Do you stay here long?"

"Can't say," answered Mr. Drummle. "Do you?"

"Can't say," said I.

I felt here, through a tingling in my blood, that if Mr. Drummle's shoulder had claimed another hair's breadth of room, I should have jerked him into the window; equally, that if my own shoulder had urged a similar claim, Mr. Drummle would have jerked me into the nearest box. He whistled a little. So did I.

"Large tract of marshes about here, I believe?" said Drummle.

"Yes. What of that?" said I.

Mr. Drummle looked at me, and then at my boots, and then said, "Oh!" and laughed.

"Are you amused, Mr. Drummle?"

"No," said he, "not particularly. I am going out for a ride in the saddle. I mean to explore those marshes for amusement. Out-of-the-way villages there, they tell me. Curious little public-houses—and smithies—and that. Waiter!"

"Yes, sir."

"Is that horse of mine ready?"

"Brought round to the door, sir."

"I say. Look here, you sir. The lady won't ride to-day; the weather won't do."

"Very good, sir."

"And I don't dine, because I'm going to dine at the lady's."

"Very good, sir."

Then, Drummle glanced at me, with an insolent triumph on his great-jowled face that cut me to the heart, dull as he was, and so exasperated me, that I felt inclined to take him in my arms (as the robber in the story-book is said to have taken the old lady) and seat him on the fire.

One thing was manifest to both of us, and that was, that until relief came, neither of us could relinquish the fire. There we stood, well squared up before it, shoulder to shoulder and foot to foot, with our hands behind us, not budging an inch. The horse was visible outside in the drizzle at the door, my breakfast was put on the table, Drummle's was cleared away, the waiter invited me to begin, I nodded, we both stood our ground.

"Have you been to the Grove since?" said Drummle.

"No," said I, "I had quite enough of the Finches the last time I was there."

"Was that when we had a difference of opinion?"

"Yes," I replied, very shortly.

"Come, come! They let you off easily enough," sneered Drummle. "You shouldn't have lost your temper."

"Mr. Drummle," said I, "you are not competent to give advice on that subject. When I lose my temper (not that I admit having done so on that occasion), I don't throw glasses."

"I do," said Drummle.

After glancing at him once or twice, in an increased state of smouldering ferocity, I said,—

"Mr. Drummle, I did not seek this conversation, and I don't think it an agreeable one."

"I am sure it's not," said he, superciliously over his shoulder; "I don't think anything about it."

"And therefore," I went on, "with your leave, I will suggest that we hold no kind of communication in future."

"Quite my opinion," said Drummle, "and what I should have suggested myself, or done—more likely—without suggesting. But don't lose your temper. Haven't you lost enough without that?"

"What do you mean, sir?"

"Waiter!" said Drummle, by way of answering me.

The waiter reappeared.

"Look here, you sir. You quite understand that the young lady don't ride to-day, and that I dine at the young lady's?"

"Quite so, sir!"

When the waiter had felt my fast-cooling teapot with the palm of his hand, and had looked imploringly at me, and had gone out, Drummle, careful not to move the shoulder next me, took a cigar from his pocket and bit the end off, but showed no sign of stirring. Choking and boiling as I was, I felt that we could not go a word further, without introducing Estella's name, which I could not endure to hear him utter; and therefore I looked stonily at the opposite wall, as if there were no one present, and forced myself to silence. How long we might have remained in this ridiculous position it is impossible to say, but for the incursion of three thriving farmers—laid on by the waiter, I think—who came into the coffee-room unbuttoning their great-coats and rubbing their hands, and before whom, as they charged at the fire, we were obliged to give way.

I saw him through the window, seizing his horse's mane, and mounting in his blundering brutal manner, and sidling and backing away. I thought he was gone, when he came back, calling for a light for the cigar in his mouth, which he had forgotten. A man in a dust-colored dress appeared with what was wanted,—I could not have said from where: whether from the inn yard, or the street, or where not,—and as Drummle leaned down from the saddle and lighted his cigar and laughed, with a jerk of his head towards the coffee-room windows, the slouching shoulders and ragged hair of this man whose back was towards me reminded me of Orlick.

Too heavily out of sorts to care much at the time whether it were he or no, or after all to touch the breakfast, I washed the weather and the journey from my face and hands, and went out to the memorable old house that it would have been so much the better for me never to have entered, never to have seen.

Chapter XLIV

In the room where the dressing-table stood, and where the wax-candles burnt on the wall, I found Miss Havisham and Estella; Miss Havisham seated on a settee near the fire, and Estella on a cushion at her feet. Estella was knitting, and Miss Havisham was looking on. They both raised their eyes as I went in, and both saw an alteration in me. I derived that, from the look they interchanged.

"And what wind," said Miss Havisham, "blows you here, Pip?"

Though she looked steadily at me, I saw that she was rather confused. Estella, pausing a moment in her knitting with her eyes upon me, and then going on, I fancied that I read in the action of her fingers, as plainly as if she had told me in the dumb alphabet, that she perceived I had discovered my real benefactor.

"Miss Havisham," said I, "I went to Richmond yesterday, to speak to Estella; and finding that some wind had blown her here, I followed."

Miss Havisham motioning to me for the third or fourth time to sit down, I took the chair by the dressing-table, which I had often seen her occupy. With all that ruin at my feet and about me, it seemed a natural place for me, that day.

"What I had to say to Estella, Miss Havisham, I will say before you, presently—in a few moments. It will not surprise you, it will not displease you. I am as unhappy as you can ever have meant me to be."

Miss Havisham continued to look steadily at me. I could see in the action of Estella's fingers as they worked that she attended to what I said; but she did not look up.

"I have found out who my patron is. It is not a fortunate discovery, and is not likely ever to enrich me in reputation, station, fortune, anything. There are reasons why I must say no more of that. It is not my secret, but another's."

As I was silent for a while, looking at Estella and considering how to go on, Miss Havisham repeated, "It is not your secret, but another's. Well?"

"When you first caused me to be brought here, Miss Havisham, when I belonged to the village over yonder, that I wish I had never left, I suppose I did really come here, as any other chance boy might have come,—as a kind of servant, to gratify a want or a whim, and to be paid for it?"

"Ay, Pip," replied Miss Havisham, steadily nodding her head; "you did."

"And that Mr. Jaggers—"

"Mr. Jaggers," said Miss Havisham, taking me up in a firm tone, "had nothing to do with it, and knew nothing of it. His being my lawyer, and his being the lawyer of your patron is a coincidence. He holds the same relation towards numbers of people, and it might easily arise. Be that as it may, it did arise, and was not brought about by any one."

Any one might have seen in her haggard face that there was no suppression or evasion so far.

"But when I fell into the mistake I have so long remained in, at least you led me on?" said I.

"Yes," she returned, again nodding steadily, "I let you go on."

"Was that kind?"

"Who am I," cried Miss Havisham, striking her stick upon the floor and flashing into wrath so suddenly that Estella glanced up at her in surprise,—"who am I, for God's sake, that I should be kind?"

It was a weak complaint to have made, and I had not meant to make it. I told her so, as she sat brooding after this outburst.

"Well, well, well!" she said. "What else?"

"I was liberally paid for my old attendance here," I said, to soothe her, "in being apprenticed, and I have asked these questions only for my own information. What follows has another (and I hope more disinterested) purpose. In humoring my mistake, Miss Havisham, you punished—practised on—perhaps you will supply whatever term expresses your intention, without offence—your self-seeking relations?"

"I did. Why, they would have it so! So would you. What has been my history, that I should be at the pains of entreating either them or you not to have it so! You made your own snares. I never made them."

Waiting until she was quiet again,—for this, too, flashed out of her in a wild and sudden way,—I went on.

"I have been thrown among one family of your relations, Miss Havisham, and have been constantly among them since I went to London. I know them to have been as honestly under my delusion as I myself. And I should be false and base if I did not tell you, whether it is acceptable to you or no, and whether you are inclined to give credence to it or no, that you deeply wrong both Mr. Matthew Pocket and his son Herbert, if you suppose them to be otherwise than generous, upright, open, and incapable of anything designing or mean."

"They are your friends," said Miss Havisham.

"They made themselves my friends," said I, "when they supposed me to have superseded them; and when Sarah Pocket, Miss Georgiana, and Mistress Camilla were not my friends, I think."

This contrasting of them with the rest seemed, I was glad to see, to do them good with her. She looked at me keenly for a little while, and then said quietly,—

"What do you want for them?"

"Only," said I, "that you would not confound them with the others. They may be of the same blood, but, believe me, they are not of the same nature."

Still looking at me keenly, Miss Havisham repeated,—

"What do you want for them?"

"I am not so cunning, you see," I said, in answer, conscious that I reddened a little, "as that I could hide from you, even if I desired, that I do want something. Miss Havisham, if you would spare the money to do my friend Herbert a lasting service in life, but which from the nature of the case must be done without his knowledge, I could show you how."

"Why must it be done without his knowledge?" she asked, settling her hands upon her stick, that she might regard me the more attentively.

"Because," said I, "I began the service myself, more than two years ago, without his knowledge, and I don't want to be betrayed. Why I fail in my ability to finish it, I cannot explain. It is a part of the secret which is another person's and not mine."

She gradually withdrew her eyes from me, and turned them on the fire. After watching it for what appeared in the silence and by the light of the slowly wasting candles to be a long time, she was roused by the collapse of some of the red coals, and looked towards me again—at first, vacantly—then, with a gradually concentrating attention. All this time Estella knitted on. When Miss Havisham had fixed her attention on me, she said, speaking as if there had been no lapse in our dialogue,—

"What else?"

"Estella," said I, turning to her now, and trying to command my trembling voice, "you know I love you. You know that I have loved you long and dearly."

She raised her eyes to my face, on being thus addressed, and her fingers plied their work, and she looked at me with an unmoved countenance. I saw that Miss Havisham glanced from me to her, and from her to me.

"I should have said this sooner, but for my long mistake. It induced me to hope that Miss Havisham meant us for one another. While I thought you could not help yourself, as it were, I refrained from saying it. But I must say it now."

Preserving her unmoved countenance, and with her fingers still going, Estella shook her head.

"I know," said I, in answer to that action,—"I know. I have no hope that I shall ever call you mine, Estella. I am ignorant what may become of me very soon, how poor I may be, or where I may go. Still, I love you. I have loved you ever since I first saw you in this house."

Looking at me perfectly unmoved and with her fingers busy, she shook her head again.

"It would have been cruel in Miss Havisham, horribly cruel, to practise on the susceptibility of a poor boy, and to torture me through all these years with a vain hope and an idle pursuit, if she had reflected on the gravity of what she did. But I think she did not. I think that, in the endurance of her own trial, she forgot mine, Estella."

I saw Miss Havisham put her hand to her heart and hold it there, as she sat looking by turns at Estella and at me.

"It seems," said Estella, very calmly, "that there are sentiments, fancies,—I don't know how to call them,—which I am not able to comprehend. When you say you love me, I know what you mean, as a form of words; but nothing more. You address nothing in my breast, you touch nothing there. I don't care for what you say at all. I have tried to warn you of this; now, have I not?"

I said in a miserable manner, "Yes."

"Yes. But you would not be warned, for you thought I did not mean it. Now, did you not think so?"

"I thought and hoped you could not mean it. You, so young, untried, and beautiful, Estella! Surely it is not in Nature."

"It is in my nature," she returned. And then she added, with a stress upon the words, "It is in the nature formed within me. I make a great difference between you and all other people when I say so much. I can do no more."

"Is it not true," said I, "that Bentley Drummle is in town here, and pursuing you?"

"It is quite true," she replied, referring to him with the indifference of utter contempt.

"That you encourage him, and ride out with him, and that he dines with you this very day?"

She seemed a little surprised that I should know it, but again replied, "Quite true."

"You cannot love him, Estella!"

Her fingers stopped for the first time, as she retorted rather angrily, "What have I told you? Do you still think, in spite of it, that I do not mean what I say?"

"You would never marry him, Estella?"

She looked towards Miss Havisham, and considered for a moment with her work in her hands. Then she said, "Why not tell you the truth? I am going to be married to him."

I dropped my face into my hands, but was able to control myself better than I could have expected, considering what agony it gave me to hear her say those words. When I raised my face again, there was such a ghastly look upon Miss Havisham's, that it impressed me, even in my passionate hurry and grief.

"Estella, dearest Estella, do not let Miss Havisham lead you into this fatal step. Put me aside for ever,—you have done so, I well know,—but bestow yourself on some worthier person than Drummle. Miss Havisham gives you to him, as the greatest slight and injury that could be done to the many far better men who admire you, and to the few who truly love you. Among those few there may be one who loves you even as dearly, though he has not loved you as long, as I. Take him, and I can bear it better, for your sake!"

My earnestness awoke a wonder in her that seemed as if it would have been touched with compassion, if she could have rendered me at all intelligible to her own mind.

"I am going," she said again, in a gentler voice, "to be married to him. The preparations for my marriage are making, and I shall be married soon. Why do you injuriously introduce the name of my mother by adoption? It is my own act."

"Your own act, Estella, to fling yourself away upon a brute?"

"On whom should I fling myself away?" she retorted, with a smile. "Should I fling myself away upon the man who would the soonest feel (if people do feel such things) that I took nothing to him? There! It is done. I shall do well enough, and so will my husband. As to leading me into what you call this fatal step, Miss Havisham would have had me wait, and not marry yet; but I am tired of the life I have led, which has very few charms for me, and I am willing enough to change it. Say no more. We shall never understand each other."

"Such a mean brute, such a stupid brute!" I urged, in despair.

"Don't be afraid of my being a blessing to him," said Estella; "I shall not be that. Come! Here is my hand. Do we part on this, you visionary boy—or man?"

"O Estella!" I answered, as my bitter tears fell fast on her hand, do what I would to restrain them; "even if I remained in England and could hold my head up with the rest, how could I see you Drummle's wife?"

"Nonsense," she returned,—"nonsense. This will pass in no time."

"Never, Estella!"

"You will get me out of your thoughts in a week."

"Out of my thoughts! You are part of my existence, part of myself. You have been in every line I have ever read since I first came here, the rough common boy whose poor heart you wounded even then. You have been in every prospect I have ever seen since,—on the river, on the sails of the ships, on the marshes, in the clouds, in the light, in the darkness, in the wind, in the woods, in the sea, in the streets. You have been the embodiment of every graceful fancy that my mind has ever become acquainted with. The stones of which the strongest London buildings are made are not more real, or more impossible to be displaced by your hands, than your presence and influence have been to me, there and everywhere, and will be. Estella, to the last hour of my life, you cannot choose but remain part of my character, part of the little good in me, part of the evil. But, in this separation, I associate you only with the good; and I will faithfully hold you to that always, for you must have done me far more good than harm, let me feel now what sharp distress I may. O God bless you, God forgive you!"

In what ecstasy of unhappiness I got these broken words out of myself, I don't know. The rhapsody welled up within me, like blood from an inward wound, and gushed out. I held her hand to my lips some lingering moments, and so I left her. But ever afterwards, I remembered,—and soon afterwards with stronger reason,—that while Estella looked at me merely with incredulous wonder, the spectral figure of Miss Havisham, her hand still covering her heart, seemed all resolved into a ghastly stare of pity and remorse.

All done, all gone! So much was done and gone, that when I went out at the gate, the light of the day seemed of a darker color than when I went in. For a while, I hid myself among some lanes and by-paths, and then struck off to walk all the way to London. For, I had by that time come to myself so far as to consider that I could not go back to the inn and see Drummle there; that I could not bear to sit upon the coach and be spoken to; that I could do nothing half so good for myself as tire myself out.

It was past midnight when I crossed London Bridge. Pursuing the narrow intricacies of the streets which at that time tended westward near the Middlesex shore of the river, my readiest access to the Temple was close by the river-side, through Whitefriars. I was not expected till to-morrow; but I had my keys, and, if Herbert were gone to bed, could get to bed myself without disturbing him.

As it seldom happened that I came in at that Whitefriars gate after the Temple was closed, and as I was very muddy and weary, I did not take it ill that the night-porter examined me with much attention as he held the gate a little way open for me to pass in. To help his memory I mentioned my name.

"I was not quite sure, sir, but I thought so. Here's a note, sir. The messenger that brought it, said would you be so good as read it by my lantern?"

Much surprised by the request, I took the note. It was directed to Philip Pip, Esquire, and on the top of the superscription were the words, "PLEASE READ THIS, HERE." I opened it, the watchman holding up his light, and read inside, in Wemmick's writing,—

"DON'T GO HOME."

Chapter XLV

Turning from the Temple gate as soon as I had read the warning, I made the best of my way to Fleet Street, and there got a late hackney chariot and drove to the Hummums in Covent Garden. In those times a bed was always to be got there at any hour of the night, and the chamberlain, letting me in at his ready wicket, lighted the candle next in order on his shelf, and showed me straight into the bedroom next in order on his list. It was a sort of vault on the ground floor at the back, with a despotic monster of a four-post bedstead in it, straddling over the whole place, putting one of his arbitrary legs into the fireplace and another into the doorway, and squeezing the wretched little washing-stand in quite a Divinely Righteous manner.

As I had asked for a night-light, the chamberlain had brought me in, before he left me, the good old constitutional rushlight of those virtuous days—an object like the ghost of a walking-cane, which instantly broke its back if it were touched, which nothing could ever be lighted at, and which was placed in solitary confinement at the bottom of a high tin tower, perforated with round holes that made a staringly wide-awake pattern on the walls. When I had got into bed, and lay there footsore, weary, and wretched, I found that I could no more close my own eyes than I could close the eyes of this foolish Argus. And thus, in the gloom and death of the night, we stared at one another.

What a doleful night! How anxious, how dismal, how long! There was an inhospitable smell in the room, of cold soot and hot dust; and, as I looked up into the corners of the tester over my head, I thought what a number of blue-bottle flies from the butchers', and earwigs from the market, and grubs from the country, must be holding on up there, lying by for next summer. This led me to speculate whether any of them ever tumbled down, and then I fancied that I felt light falls on my face,—a disagreeable turn of thought, suggesting other and more objectionable approaches up my back. When I had lain awake a little while, those extraordinary voices with which silence teems began to make themselves audible. The closet whispered, the fireplace sighed, the little washing-stand ticked, and one guitar-string played occasionally in the chest of drawers. At about the same time, the eyes on the wall acquired a new expression, and in every one of those staring rounds I saw written, DON'T GO HOME.

Whatever night-fancies and night-noises crowded on me, they never warded off this DON'T GO HOME. It plaited itself into whatever I thought of, as a bodily pain would have done. Not long before, I had read in the newspapers, how a gentleman unknown had come to the Hummums in the night, and had gone to bed, and had destroyed himself, and had been found in the morning weltering in blood. It came into my head that he must have occupied this very vault of mine, and I got out of bed to assure myself that there were no red marks about; then opened the door to look out into the passages, and cheer myself with the companionship of a distant light, near which I knew the chamberlain to be dozing. But all this time, why I was not to go home, and what had happened at home, and when I should go home, and whether Provis was safe at home, were questions occupying my mind so busily, that one might have supposed there could be no more room in it for any other theme. Even when I thought of Estella, and how we had parted that day forever, and when I recalled all the circumstances of our parting, and all her looks and tones, and the action of her fingers while she knitted,—even then I was pursuing, here and there and everywhere, the caution, Don't go home. When at last I dozed, in sheer exhaustion of mind and body, it became a vast shadowy verb which I had to conjugate. Imperative mood, present tense: Do not thou go home, let him not go home, let us not go home, do not ye or you go home, let not them go home. Then potentially: I may not and I cannot go home; and I might not, could not, would not, and should not go home; until I felt that I was going distracted, and rolled over on the pillow, and looked at the staring rounds upon the wall again.

I had left directions that I was to be called at seven; for it was plain that I must see Wemmick before seeing any one else, and equally plain that this was a case in which his Walworth sentiments only could be taken. It was a relief to get out of the room where the night had been so miserable, and I needed no second knocking at the door to startle me from my uneasy bed.

The Castle battlements arose upon my view at eight o'clock. The little servant happening to be entering the fortress with two hot rolls, I passed through the postern and crossed the drawbridge in her company, and so came without announcement into the presence of Wemmick as he was making tea for himself and the Aged. An open door afforded a perspective view of the Aged in bed.

"Halloa, Mr. Pip!" said Wemmick. "You did come home, then?"

"Yes," I returned; "but I didn't go home."

"That's all right," said he, rubbing his hands. "I left a note for you at each of the Temple gates, on the chance. Which gate did you come to?"

I told him.

"I'll go round to the others in the course of the day and destroy the notes," said Wemmick; "it's a good rule never to leave documentary evidence if you can help it, because you don't know when it may be put in. I'm going to take a liberty with you. Would you mind toasting this sausage for the Aged P.?"

I said I should be delighted to do it.

"Then you can go about your work, Mary Anne," said Wemmick to the little servant; "which leaves us to ourselves, don't you see, Mr. Pip?" he added, winking, as she disappeared.

I thanked him for his friendship and caution, and our discourse proceeded in a low tone, while I toasted the Aged's sausage and he buttered the crumb of the Aged's roll.

"Now, Mr. Pip, you know," said Wemmick, "you and I understand one another. We are in our private and personal capacities, and we have been engaged in a confidential transaction before to-day. Official sentiments are one thing. We are extra official."

I cordially assented. I was so very nervous, that I had already lighted the Aged's sausage like a torch, and been obliged to blow it out.

"I accidentally heard, yesterday morning," said Wemmick, "being in a certain place where I once took you,—even between you and me, it's as well not to mention names when avoidable—"

"Much better not," said I. "I understand you."

"I heard there by chance, yesterday morning," said Wemmick, "that a certain person not altogether of uncolonial pursuits, and not unpossessed of portable property,—I don't know who it may really be,—we won't name this person—"

"Not necessary," said I.

"—Had made some little stir in a certain part of the world where a good many people go, not always in gratification of their own inclinations, and not quite irrespective of the government expense—"

In watching his face, I made quite a firework of the Aged's sausage, and greatly discomposed both my own attention and Wemmick's; for which I apologized.

"—By disappearing from such place, and being no more heard of thereabouts. From which," said Wemmick, "conjectures had been raised and theories formed. I also heard that you at your chambers in Garden Court, Temple, had been watched, and might be watched again."

"By whom?" said I.

"I wouldn't go into that," said Wemmick, evasively, "it might clash with official responsibilities. I heard it, as I have in my time heard other curious things in the same place. I don't tell it you on information received. I heard it."

He took the toasting-fork and sausage from me as he spoke, and set forth the Aged's breakfast neatly on a little tray. Previous to placing it before him, he went into the Aged's room with a clean white cloth, and tied the same under the old gentleman's chin, and propped him up, and put his nightcap on one side, and gave him quite a rakish air. Then he placed his breakfast before him with great care, and said, "All right, ain't you, Aged P.?" To which the cheerful Aged replied, "All right, John, my boy, all right!" As there seemed to be a tacit understanding that the Aged was not in a presentable state, and was therefore to be considered invisible, I made a pretence of being in complete ignorance of these proceedings.

"This watching of me at my chambers (which I have once had reason to suspect)," I said to Wemmick when he came back, "is inseparable from the person to whom you have adverted; is it?"

Wemmick looked very serious. "I couldn't undertake to say that, of my own knowledge. I mean, I couldn't undertake to say it was at first. But it either is, or it will be, or it's in great danger of being."

As I saw that he was restrained by fealty to Little Britain from saying as much as he could, and as I knew with thankfulness to him how far out of his way he went to say what he did, I could not press him. But I told him, after a little meditation over the fire, that I would like to ask him a question, subject to his answering or not answering, as he deemed right, and sure that his course would be right. He paused in his breakfast, and crossing his arms, and pinching his shirt-sleeves (his notion of in-door comfort was to sit without any coat), he nodded to me once, to put my question.

"You have heard of a man of bad character, whose true name is Compeyson?"

He answered with one other nod.

"Is he living?"

One other nod.

"Is he in London?"

He gave me one other nod, compressed the post-office exceedingly, gave me one last nod, and went on with his breakfast.

"Now," said Wemmick, "questioning being over," which he emphasized and repeated for my guidance, "I come to what I did, after hearing what I heard. I went to Garden Court to find you; not finding you, I went to Clarriker's to find Mr. Herbert."

"And him you found?" said I, with great anxiety.

"And him I found. Without mentioning any names or going into any details, I gave him to understand that if he was aware of anybody—Tom, Jack, or Richard—being about the chambers, or about the immediate neighborhood, he had better get Tom, Jack, or Richard out of the way while you were out of the way."

"He would be greatly puzzled what to do?"

"He was puzzled what to do; not the less, because I gave him my opinion that it was not safe to try to get Tom, Jack, or Richard too far out of the way at present. Mr. Pip, I'll tell you something. Under existing circumstances, there is no place like a great city when you are once in it. Don't break cover too soon. Lie close. Wait till things slacken, before you try the open, even for foreign air."

I thanked him for his valuable advice, and asked him what Herbert had done?

"Mr. Herbert," said Wemmick, "after being all of a heap for half an hour, struck out a plan. He mentioned to me as a secret, that he is courting a young lady who has, as no doubt you are aware, a bedridden Pa. Which Pa, having been in the Purser line of life, lies a-bed in a bow-window where he can see the ships sail up and down the river. You are acquainted with the young lady, most probably?"

"Not personally," said I.

The truth was, that she had objected to me as an expensive companion who did Herbert no good, and that, when Herbert had first proposed to present me to her, she had received the proposal with such very moderate warmth, that Herbert had felt himself obliged to confide the state of the case to me, with a view to the lapse of a little time before I made her acquaintance.

When I had begun to advance Herbert's prospects by stealth, I had been able to bear this with cheerful philosophy: he and his affianced, for their part, had naturally not been very anxious to introduce a third person into their interviews; and thus, although I was assured that I had risen in Clara's esteem, and although the young lady and I had long regularly interchanged messages and remembrances by Herbert, I had never seen her. However, I did not trouble Wemmick with these particulars.

"The house with the bow-window," said Wemmick, "being by the river-side, down the Pool there between Limehouse and Greenwich, and being kept, it seems, by a very respectable widow who has a furnished upper floor to let, Mr. Herbert put it to me, what did I think of that as a temporary tenement for Tom, Jack, or Richard? Now, I thought very well of it, for three reasons I'll give you. That is to say: Firstly. It's altogether out of all your beats, and is well away from the usual heap of streets great and small. Secondly. Without going near it yourself, you could always hear of the safety of Tom, Jack, or Richard, through Mr. Herbert. Thirdly. After a while and when it might be prudent, if you should want to slip Tom, Jack, or Richard on board a foreign packet-boat, there he is—ready."

Much comforted by these considerations, I thanked Wemmick again and again, and begged him to proceed.

"Well, sir! Mr. Herbert threw himself into the business with a will, and by nine o'clock last night he housed Tom, Jack, or Richard,—whichever it may be,—you and I don't want to know,—quite successfully. At the old lodgings it was understood that he was summoned to Dover, and, in fact, he was taken down the Dover road and cornered out of it. Now, another great advantage of all this is, that it was done without you, and when, if any one was concerning himself about your movements, you must be known to be ever so many miles off and quite otherwise engaged. This diverts suspicion and confuses it; and for the same reason I recommended that, even if you came back last night, you should not go home. It brings in more confusion, and you want confusion."

Wemmick, having finished his breakfast, here looked at his watch, and began to get his coat on.

"And now, Mr. Pip," said he, with his hands still in the sleeves, "I have probably done the most I can do; but if I can ever do more,—from a Walworth point of view, and in a strictly private and personal capacity,—I shall be glad to do it. Here's the address. There can be no harm in your going here to-night, and seeing for yourself that all is well with Tom, Jack, or Richard, before you go home,—which is another reason for your not going home last night. But, after you have gone home, don't go back here. You are very welcome, I am sure, Mr. Pip"; his hands were now out of his sleeves, and I was shaking them; "and let me finally impress one important point upon you." He laid his hands upon my shoulders, and added in a solemn whisper: "Avail yourself of this evening to lay hold of his portable property. You don't know what may happen to him. Don't let anything happen to the portable property."

Quite despairing of making my mind clear to Wemmick on this point, I forbore to try.

"Time's up," said Wemmick, "and I must be off. If you had nothing more pressing to do than to keep here till dark, that's what I should advise. You look very much worried, and it would do you good to have a perfectly quiet day with the Aged,—he'll be up presently,—and a little bit of—you remember the pig?"

"Of course," said I.

"Well; and a little bit of him. That sausage you toasted was his, and he was in all respects a first-rater. Do try him, if it is only for old acquaintance sake. Good-bye, Aged Parent!" in a cheery shout.

"All right, John; all right, my boy!" piped the old man from within.

I soon fell asleep before Wemmick's fire, and the Aged and I enjoyed one another's society by falling asleep before it more or less all day. We had loin of pork for dinner, and greens grown on the estate; and I nodded at the Aged with a good intention whenever I failed to do it drowsily. When it was quite dark, I left the Aged preparing the fire for toast; and I inferred from the number of teacups, as well as from his glances at the two little doors in the wall, that Miss Skiffins was expected.

Chapter XLVI

Eight o'clock had struck before I got into the air, that was scented, not disagreeably, by the chips and shavings of the long-shore boat-builders, and mast, oar, and block makers. All that water-side region of the upper and lower Pool below Bridge was unknown ground to me; and when I struck down by the river, I found that the spot I wanted was not where I had supposed it to be, and was anything but easy to find. It was called Mill Pond Bank, Chinks's Basin; and I had no other guide to Chinks's Basin than the Old Green Copper Rope-walk.

It matters not what stranded ships repairing in dry docks I lost myself among, what old hulls of ships in course of being knocked to pieces, what ooze and slime and other dregs of tide, what yards of ship-builders and ship-breakers, what rusty anchors blindly biting into the ground, though for years off duty, what mountainous country of accumulated casks and timber, how many rope-walks that were not the Old Green Copper. After several times falling short of my destination and as often overshooting it, I came unexpectedly round a corner, upon Mill Pond Bank. It was a fresh kind of place, all circumstances considered, where the wind from the river had room to turn itself round; and there were two or three trees in it, and there was the stump of a ruined windmill, and there was the Old Green Copper Rope-walk,— whose long and narrow vista I could trace in the moonlight, along a series of wooden frames set in the ground, that looked like superannuated haymaking-rakes which had grown old and lost most of their teeth.

Selecting from the few queer houses upon Mill Pond Bank a house with a wooden front and three stories of bow-window (not bay-window, which is another thing), I looked at the plate upon the door, and read there, Mrs. Whimple. That being the name I wanted, I knocked, and an elderly woman of a pleasant and thriving appearance responded. She was immediately deposed, however, by Herbert, who silently led me into the parlor and shut the door. It was an odd sensation to see his very familiar face established quite at home in that very unfamiliar room and region; and I found myself looking at him, much as I looked at the corner-cupboard with the glass and china, the shells upon the chimney-piece, and the colored engravings on the wall, representing the death of Captain Cook, a ship-launch, and his Majesty King George the Third in a state coachman's wig, leather-breeches, and top-boots, on the terrace at Windsor.

"All is well, Handel," said Herbert, "and he is quite satisfied, though eager to see you. My dear girl is with her father; and if you'll wait till she comes down, I'll make you known to her, and then we'll go upstairs. That's her father."

I had become aware of an alarming growling overhead, and had probably expressed the fact in my countenance.

"I am afraid he is a sad old rascal," said Herbert, smiling, "but I have never seen him. Don't you smell rum? He is always at it."

"At rum?" said I.

"Yes," returned Herbert, "and you may suppose how mild it makes his gout. He persists, too, in keeping all the provisions upstairs in his room, and serving them out. He keeps them on shelves over his head, and will weigh them all. His room must be like a chandler's shop."

While he thus spoke, the growling noise became a prolonged roar, and then died away.

"What else can be the consequence," said Herbert, in explanation, "if he will cut the cheese? A man with the gout in his right hand—and everywhere else—can't expect to get through a Double Gloucester without hurting himself."

He seemed to have hurt himself very much, for he gave another furious roar.

"To have Provis for an upper lodger is quite a godsend to Mrs. Whimple," said Herbert, "for of course people in general won't stand that noise. A curious place, Handel; isn't it?"

It was a curious place, indeed; but remarkably well kept and clean.

"Mrs. Whimple," said Herbert, when I told him so, "is the best of housewives, and I really do not know what my Clara would do without her motherly help. For, Clara has no mother of her own, Handel, and no relation in the world but old Gruffandgrim."

"Surely that's not his name, Herbert?"

"No, no," said Herbert, "that's my name for him. His name is Mr. Barley. But what a blessing it is for the son of my father and mother to love a girl who has no relations, and who can never bother herself or anybody else about her family!"

Herbert had told me on former occasions, and now reminded me, that he first knew Miss Clara Barley when she was completing her education at an establishment at Hammersmith, and that on her being recalled home to nurse her father, he and she had confided their affection to the motherly Mrs. Whimple, by whom it had been fostered and regulated with equal kindness and discretion, ever since. It was understood that nothing of a tender nature could possibly be confided to old Barley, by reason of his being totally unequal to the consideration of any subject more psychological than Gout, Rum, and Purser's stores.

As we were thus conversing in a low tone while Old Barley's sustained growl vibrated in the beam that crossed the ceiling, the room door opened, and a very pretty, slight, dark-eyed girl of twenty or so came in with a basket in her hand: whom Herbert tenderly relieved of the basket, and presented, blushing, as "Clara." She really was a most charming girl, and might have passed for a captive fairy, whom that truculent Ogre, Old Barley, had pressed into his service.

"Look here," said Herbert, showing me the basket, with a compassionate and tender smile, after we had talked a little; "here's poor Clara's supper, served out every night. Here's her allowance of bread, and here's her slice of cheese, and here's her rum,—which I drink. This is Mr. Barley's breakfast for to-morrow, served out to be cooked. Two mutton-chops, three potatoes, some split peas, a little flour, two ounces of butter, a pinch of salt, and all this black pepper. It's stewed up together, and taken hot, and it's a nice thing for the gout, I should think!"

There was something so natural and winning in Clara's resigned way of looking at these stores in detail, as Herbert pointed them out; and something so confiding, loving, and innocent in her modest manner of yielding herself to Herbert's embracing arm; and something so gentle in her, so much needing protection on Mill Pond Bank, by Chinks's Basin, and the Old Green Copper Rope-walk, with Old Barley growling in the beam,—that I would not have undone the engagement between her and Herbert for all the money in the pocket-book I had never opened.

I was looking at her with pleasure and admiration, when suddenly the growl swelled into a roar again, and a frightful bumping noise was heard above, as if a giant with a wooden leg were trying to bore it through the ceiling to come at us. Upon this Clara said to Herbert, "Papa wants me, darling!" and ran away.

"There is an unconscionable old shark for you!" said Herbert. "What do you suppose he wants now, Handel?"

"I don't know," said I. "Something to drink?"

"That's it!" cried Herbert, as if I had made a guess of extraordinary merit. "He keeps his grog ready mixed in a little tub on the table. Wait a moment, and you'll hear Clara lift him up to take some. There he goes!" Another roar, with a prolonged shake at the end. "Now," said Herbert, as it was succeeded by silence, "he's drinking. Now," said Herbert, as the growl resounded in the beam once more, "he's down again on his back!"

Clara returned soon afterwards, and Herbert accompanied me upstairs to see our charge. As we passed Mr. Barley's door, he was heard hoarsely muttering within, in a strain that rose and fell like wind, the following Refrain, in which I substitute good wishes for something quite the reverse:—

"Ahoy! Bless your eyes, here's old Bill Barley. Here's old Bill Barley, bless your eyes. Here's old Bill Barley on the flat of his back, by the Lord. Lying on the flat of his back like a drifting old dead flounder, here's your old Bill Barley, bless your eyes. Ahoy! Bless you."

In this strain of consolation, Herbert informed me the invisible Barley would commune with himself by the day and night together; Often, while it was light, having, at the same time, one eye at a telescope which was fitted on his bed for the convenience of sweeping the river.

In his two cabin rooms at the top of the house, which were fresh and airy, and in which Mr. Barley was less audible than below, I found Provis comfortably settled. He expressed no alarm, and seemed to feel none that was worth mentioning; but it struck me that he was softened,—indefinably, for I could not have said how, and could never afterwards recall how when I tried, but certainly.

The opportunity that the day's rest had given me for reflection had resulted in my fully determining to say nothing to him respecting Compeyson. For anything I knew, his animosity towards the man might otherwise lead to his seeking him out and rushing on his own destruction. Therefore, when Herbert and I sat down with him by his fire, I asked him first of all whether he relied on Wemmick's judgment and sources of information?

"Ay, ay, dear boy!" he answered, with a grave nod, "Jaggers knows."

"Then, I have talked with Wemmick," said I, "and have come to tell you what caution he gave me and what advice."

This I did accurately, with the reservation just mentioned; and I told him how Wemmick had heard, in Newgate prison (whether from officers or prisoners I could not say), that he was under some suspicion, and that my chambers had been watched; how Wemmick had recommended his keeping close for a time, and my keeping away from him; and what Wemmick had said about getting him abroad. I added, that of course, when the time came, I should go with him, or should follow close upon him, as might be safest in Wemmick's judgment. What was to follow that I did not touch upon; neither, indeed, was I at all clear or comfortable about it in my own mind, now that I saw him in that softer condition, and in declared peril for my sake. As to altering my way of living by enlarging my expenses, I put it to him whether in our present unsettled and difficult circumstances, it would not be simply ridiculous, if it were no worse?

He could not deny this, and indeed was very reasonable throughout. His coming back was a venture, he said, and he had always known it to be a venture. He would do nothing to make it a desperate venture, and he had very little fear of his safety with such good help.

Herbert, who had been looking at the fire and pondering, here said that something had come into his thoughts arising out of Wemmick's suggestion, which it might be worth while to pursue. "We are both good watermen, Handel, and could take him down the river ourselves when the right time comes. No boat would then be hired for the purpose, and no boatmen; that would save at least a chance of suspicion, and any chance is worth saving. Never mind the season; don't you think it might be a good thing if you began at once to keep a boat at the Temple stairs, and were in the habit of rowing up and down the river? You fall into that habit, and then who notices or minds? Do it twenty or fifty times, and there is nothing special in your doing it the twenty-first or fifty-first."

I liked this scheme, and Provis was quite elated by it. We agreed that it should be carried into execution, and that Provis should never recognize us if we came below Bridge, and rowed past Mill Pond Bank. But we further agreed that he should pull down the blind in that part of his window which gave upon the east, whenever he saw us and all was right.

Our conference being now ended, and everything arranged, I rose to go; remarking to Herbert that he and I had better not go home together, and that I would take half an hour's start of him. "I don't like to leave you here," I said to Provis, "though I cannot doubt your being safer here than near me. Good-bye!"

"Dear boy," he answered, clasping my hands, "I don't know when we may meet again, and I don't like good-bye. Say good night!"

"Good night! Herbert will go regularly between us, and when the time comes you may be certain I shall be ready. Good night, good night!"

We thought it best that he should stay in his own rooms; and we left him on the landing outside his door, holding a light over the stair-rail to light us downstairs. Looking back at him, I thought of the first night of his return, when our positions were reversed, and when I little supposed my heart could ever be as heavy and anxious at parting from him as it was now.

Old Barley was growling and swearing when we repassed his door, with no appearance of having ceased or of meaning to cease. When we got to the foot of the stairs, I asked Herbert whether he had preserved the name of Provis. He replied, certainly not, and that the lodger was Mr. Campbell. He also explained that the utmost known of Mr. Campbell there was, that he (Herbert) had Mr. Campbell consigned to him, and felt a strong personal interest in his being well cared for, and living a secluded life. So, when we went into the parlor where Mrs. Whimple and Clara were seated at work, I said nothing of my own interest in Mr. Campbell, but kept it to myself.

When I had taken leave of the pretty, gentle, dark-eyed girl, and of the motherly woman who had not outlived her honest sympathy with a little affair of true love, I felt as if the Old Green Copper Rope-walk had grown quite a different place. Old Barley might be as old as the hills, and might swear like a whole field of troopers, but there were redeeming youth and trust and hope enough in Chinks's Basin to fill it to overflowing. And then I thought of Estella, and of our parting, and went home very sadly.

All things were as quiet in the Temple as ever I had seen them. The windows of the rooms on that side, lately occupied by Provis, were dark and still, and there was no lounger in Garden Court. I walked past the fountain twice or thrice before I descended the steps that were between me and my rooms, but I was quite alone. Herbert, coming to my bedside when he came in,—for I went straight to bed, dispirited and fatigued,—made the same report. Opening one of the windows after that, he looked out into the moonlight, and told me that the pavement was as solemnly empty as the pavement of any cathedral at that same hour.

Next day I set myself to get the boat. It was soon done, and the boat was brought round to the Temple stairs, and lay where I could reach her within a minute or two. Then, I began to go out as for training and practice: sometimes alone, sometimes with Herbert. I was often out in cold, rain, and sleet, but nobody took much note of me after I had been out a few times. At first, I kept above Blackfriars Bridge; but as the hours of the tide changed, I took towards London Bridge. It was Old London Bridge in those days, and at certain states of the tide there was a race and fall of water there which gave it a bad reputation. But I knew well enough how to 'shoot' the bridge after seeing it done, and so began to row about among the shipping in the Pool, and down to Erith. The first time I passed Mill Pond Bank, Herbert and I were pulling a pair of oars; and, both in going and returning, we saw the blind towards the east come down. Herbert was rarely there less frequently than three times in a week, and he never brought me a single word of intelligence that was at all alarming. Still, I knew that there was cause for alarm, and I could not get rid of the notion of being watched. Once received, it is a haunting idea; how many undesigning persons I suspected of watching me, it would be hard to calculate.

In short, I was always full of fears for the rash man who was in hiding. Herbert had sometimes said to me that he found it pleasant to stand at one of our windows after dark, when the tide was running down, and to think that it was flowing, with everything it bore, towards Clara. But I thought with dread that it was flowing towards Magwitch, and that any black mark on its surface might be his pursuers, going swiftly, silently, and surely, to take him.

Chapter XLVII

Some weeks passed without bringing any change. We waited for Wemmick, and he made no sign. If I had never known him out of Little Britain, and had never enjoyed the privilege of being on a familiar footing at the Castle, I might have doubted him; not so for a moment, knowing him as I did.

My worldly affairs began to wear a gloomy appearance, and I was pressed for money by more than one creditor. Even I myself began to know the want of money (I mean of ready money in my own pocket), and to relieve it by converting some easily spared articles of jewelery into cash. But I had quite determined that it would be a heartless fraud to take more money from my patron in the existing state of my uncertain thoughts and plans. Therefore, I had sent him the unopened pocket-book by Herbert, to hold in his own keeping, and I felt a kind of satisfaction—whether it was a false kind or a true, I hardly know—in not having profited by his generosity since his revelation of himself.

As the time wore on, an impression settled heavily upon me that Estella was married. Fearful of having it confirmed, though it was all but a conviction, I avoided the newspapers, and begged Herbert (to whom I had confided the circumstances of our last interview) never to speak of her to me. Why I hoarded up this last wretched little rag of the robe of hope that was rent and given to the winds, how do I know? Why did you who read this, commit that not dissimilar inconsistency of your own last year, last month, last week?

It was an unhappy life that I lived; and its one dominant anxiety, towering over all its other anxieties, like a high mountain above a range of mountains, never disappeared from my view. Still, no new cause for fear arose. Let me start from my bed as I would, with the terror fresh upon me that he was discovered; let me sit listening, as I would with dread, for Herbert's returning step at night, lest it should be fleeter than ordinary, and winged with evil news,—for all that, and much more to like purpose, the round of things went on. Condemned to inaction and a state of constant restlessness and suspense, I rowed about in my boat, and waited, waited, waited, as I best could.

There were states of the tide when, having been down the river, I could not get back through the eddy-chafed arches and starlings of old London Bridge; then, I left my boat at a wharf near the Custom House, to be brought up afterwards to the Temple stairs. I was not averse to doing this, as it served to make me and my boat a commoner incident among the water-side people there. From this slight occasion sprang two meetings that I have now to tell of.

One afternoon, late in the month of February, I came ashore at the wharf at dusk. I had pulled down as far as Greenwich with the ebb tide, and had turned with the tide. It had been a fine bright day, but had become foggy as the sun dropped, and I had had to feel my way back among the shipping, pretty carefully. Both in going and returning, I had seen the signal in his window, All well.

As it was a raw evening, and I was cold, I thought I would comfort myself with dinner at once; and as I had hours of dejection and solitude before me if I went home to the Temple, I thought I would afterwards go to the play. The theatre where Mr. Wopsle had achieved his questionable triumph was in that water-side neighborhood (it is nowhere now), and to that theatre I resolved to go. I was aware that Mr. Wopsle had not succeeded in reviving the Drama, but, on the contrary, had rather partaken of its decline. He had been ominously heard of, through the play-bills, as a faithful Black, in connection with a little girl of noble birth, and a monkey. And Herbert had seen him as a predatory Tartar of comic propensities, with a face like a red brick, and an outrageous hat all over bells.

I dined at what Herbert and I used to call a geographical chop-house, where there were maps of the world in porter-pot rims on every half-yard of the tablecloths, and charts of gravy on every one of the knives,—to this day there is scarcely a single chop-house within the Lord Mayor's dominions which is not geographical,—and wore out the time in dozing over crumbs, staring at gas, and baking in a hot blast of dinners. By and by, I roused myself, and went to the play.

There, I found a virtuous boatswain in His Majesty's service,—a most excellent man, though I could have wished his trousers not quite so tight in some places, and not quite so loose in others,—who knocked all the little men's hats over their eyes, though he was very generous and brave, and who wouldn't hear of anybody's paying taxes, though he was very patriotic. He had a bag of money in his pocket, like a pudding in the cloth, and on that property married a young person in bed-furniture, with great rejoicings; the whole population of Portsmouth (nine in number at the last census) turning out on the beach to rub their own hands and shake everybody else's, and sing "Fill, fill!" A certain dark-complexioned Swab, however, who wouldn't fill, or do anything else that was proposed to him, and whose heart was openly stated (by the boatswain) to be as black as his figure-head, proposed to two other Swabs to get all mankind into difficulties; which was so effectually done (the Swab family having considerable political influence) that it took half the evening to set things right, and then it was only brought about through an honest little grocer with a white hat, black gaiters, and red nose, getting into a clock, with a gridiron, and listening, and coming out, and knocking everybody down from behind with the gridiron whom he couldn't confute with what he had overheard. This led to Mr. Wopsle's (who had never been heard of before) coming in with a star and garter on, as a plenipotentiary of great power direct from the Admiralty, to say that the Swabs were all to go to prison on the spot, and that he had brought the boatswain down the Union Jack, as a slight acknowledgment of his public services. The boatswain, unmanned for the first time, respectfully dried his eyes on the Jack, and then cheering up, and addressing Mr. Wopsle as Your Honor, solicited permission to take him by the fin. Mr. Wopsle, conceding his fin with a gracious dignity, was immediately shoved into a dusty corner, while everybody danced a hornpipe; and from that corner, surveying the public with a discontented eye, became aware of me.

The second piece was the last new grand comic Christmas pantomime, in the first scene of which, it pained me to suspect that I detected Mr. Wopsle with red worsted legs under a highly magnified phosphoric countenance and a shock of red curtain-fringe for his hair, engaged in the manufacture of thunderbolts in a mine, and displaying great cowardice when his gigantic master came home (very hoarse) to dinner. But he presently presented himself under worthier circumstances; for, the Genius of Youthful Love being in want of assistance,—on account of the parental brutality of an ignorant farmer who opposed the choice of his daughter's heart, by purposely falling upon the object, in a flour-sack, out of the first-floor window,—summoned a sententious Enchanter; and he, coming up from the antipodes rather unsteadily, after an apparently violent journey, proved to be Mr. Wopsle in a high-crowned hat, with a necromantic work in one volume under his arm. The business of this enchanter on earth being principally to be talked at, sung at, butted at, danced at, and flashed at with fires of various colors, he had a good deal of time on his hands. And I observed, with great surprise, that he devoted it to staring in my direction as if he were lost in amazement.

There was something so remarkable in the increasing glare of Mr. Wopsle's eye, and he seemed to be turning so many things over in his mind and to grow so confused, that I could not make it out. I sat thinking of it long after he had ascended to the clouds in a large watch-case, and still I could not make it out. I was still thinking of it when I came out of the theatre an hour afterwards, and found him waiting for me near the door.

"How do you do?" said I, shaking hands with him as we turned down the street together. "I saw that you saw me."

"Saw you, Mr. Pip!" he returned. "Yes, of course I saw you. But who else was there?"

"Who else?"

"It is the strangest thing," said Mr. Wopsle, drifting into his lost look again; "and yet I could swear to him."

Becoming alarmed, I entreated Mr. Wopsle to explain his meaning.

"Whether I should have noticed him at first but for your being there," said Mr. Wopsle, going on in the same lost way, "I can't be positive; yet I think I should."

Involuntarily I looked round me, as I was accustomed to look round me when I went home; for these mysterious words gave me a chill.

"Oh! He can't be in sight," said Mr. Wopsle. "He went out before I went off. I saw him go."

Having the reason that I had for being suspicious, I even suspected this poor actor. I mistrusted a design to entrap me into some admission. Therefore I glanced at him as we walked on together, but said nothing.

"I had a ridiculous fancy that he must be with you, Mr. Pip, till I saw that you were quite unconscious of him, sitting behind you there like a ghost."

My former chill crept over me again, but I was resolved not to speak yet, for it was quite consistent with his words that he might be set on to induce me to connect these references with Provis. Of course, I was perfectly sure and safe that Provis had not been there.

"I dare say you wonder at me, Mr. Pip; indeed, I see you do. But it is so very strange! You'll hardly believe what I am going to tell you. I could hardly believe it myself, if you told me."

"Indeed?" said I.

"No, indeed. Mr. Pip, you remember in old times a certain Christmas Day, when you were quite a child, and I dined at Gargery's, and some soldiers came to the door to get a pair of handcuffs mended?"

"I remember it very well."

"And you remember that there was a chase after two convicts, and that we joined in it, and that Gargery took you on his back, and that I took the lead, and you kept up with me as well as you could?"

"I remember it all very well." Better than he thought,—except the last clause.

"And you remember that we came up with the two in a ditch, and that there was a scuffle between them, and that one of them had been severely handled and much mauled about the face by the other?"

"I see it all before me."

"And that the soldiers lighted torches, and put the two in the centre, and that we went on to see the last of them, over the black marshes, with the torchlight shining on their faces,—I am particular about that,—with the torchlight shining on their faces, when there was an outer ring of dark night all about us?"

"Yes," said I. "I remember all that."

"Then, Mr. Pip, one of those two prisoners sat behind you tonight. I saw him over your shoulder."

"Steady!" I thought. I asked him then, "Which of the two do you suppose you saw?"

"The one who had been mauled," he answered readily, "and I'll swear I saw him! The more I think of him, the more certain I am of him."

"This is very curious!" said I, with the best assumption I could put on of its being nothing more to me. "Very curious indeed!"

I cannot exaggerate the enhanced disquiet into which this conversation threw me, or the special and peculiar terror I felt at Compeyson's having been behind me "like a ghost." For if he had ever been out of my thoughts for a few moments together since the hiding had begun, it was in those very moments when he was closest to me; and to think that I should be so unconscious and off my guard after all my care was as if I had shut an avenue of a hundred doors to keep him out, and then had found him at my elbow. I could not doubt, either, that he was there, because I was there, and that, however slight an appearance of danger there might be about us, danger was always near and active.

I put such questions to Mr. Wopsle as, When did the man come in? He could not tell me that; he saw me, and over my shoulder he saw the man. It was not until he had seen him for some time that he began to identify him; but he had from the first vaguely associated him with me, and known him as somehow belonging to me in the old village time. How was he dressed? Prosperously, but not noticeably otherwise; he thought, in black. Was his face at all disfigured? No, he believed not. I believed not too, for, although in my brooding state I had taken no especial notice of the people behind me, I thought it likely that a face at all disfigured would have attracted my attention.

When Mr. Wopsle had imparted to me all that he could recall or I extract, and when I had treated him to a little appropriate refreshment, after the fatigues of the evening, we parted. It was between twelve and one o'clock when I reached the Temple, and the gates were shut. No one was near me when I went in and went home.

Herbert had come in, and we held a very serious council by the fire. But there was nothing to be done, saving to communicate to Wemmick what I had that night found out, and to remind him that we waited for his hint. As I thought that I might compromise him if I went too often to the Castle, I made this communication by letter. I wrote it before I went to bed, and went out and posted it; and again no one was near me. Herbert and I agreed that we could do nothing else but be very cautious. And we were very cautious indeed,—more cautious than before, if that were possible,—and I for my part never went near Chinks's Basin, except when I rowed by, and then I only looked at Mill Pond Bank as I looked at anything else.

Chapter XLVIII

The second of the two meetings referred to in the last chapter occurred about a week after the first. I had again left my boat at the wharf below Bridge; the time was an hour earlier in the afternoon; and, undecided where to dine, I had strolled up into Cheapside, and was strolling along it, surely the most unsettled person in all the busy concourse, when a large hand was laid upon my shoulder by some one overtaking me. It was Mr. Jaggers's hand, and he passed it through my arm.

"As we are going in the same direction, Pip, we may walk together. Where are you bound for?"

"For the Temple, I think," said I.

"Don't you know?" said Mr. Jaggers.

"Well," I returned, glad for once to get the better of him in cross-examination, "I do not know, for I have not made up my mind."

"You are going to dine?" said Mr. Jaggers. "You don't mind admitting that, I suppose?"

"No," I returned, "I don't mind admitting that."

"And are not engaged?"

"I don't mind admitting also that I am not engaged."

"Then," said Mr. Jaggers, "come and dine with me."

I was going to excuse myself, when he added, "Wemmick's coming." So I changed my excuse into an acceptance,—the few words I had uttered, serving for the beginning of either,— and we went along Cheapside and slanted off to Little Britain, while the lights were springing up brilliantly in the shop windows, and the street lamp-lighters, scarcely finding ground enough to plant their ladders on in the midst of the afternoon's bustle, were skipping up and down and running in and out, opening more red eyes in the gathering fog than my rushlight tower at the Hummums had opened white eyes in the ghostly wall.

At the office in Little Britain there was the usual letter-writing, hand-washing, candle-snuffing, and safe-locking, that closed the business of the day. As I stood idle by Mr. Jaggers's fire, its rising and falling flame made the two casts on the shelf look as if they were playing a diabolical game at bo-peep with me; while the pair of coarse, fat office candles that dimly lighted Mr. Jaggers as he wrote in a corner were decorated with dirty winding-sheets, as if in remembrance of a host of hanged clients.

We went to Gerrard Street, all three together, in a hackney-coach: And, as soon as we got there, dinner was served. Although I should not have thought of making, in that place, the most distant reference by so much as a look to Wemmick's Walworth sentiments, yet I should have had no objection to catching his eye now and then in a friendly way. But it was not to be done. He turned his eyes on Mr. Jaggers whenever he raised them from the table, and was as dry and distant to me as if there were twin Wemmicks, and this was the wrong one.

"Did you send that note of Miss Havisham's to Mr. Pip, Wemmick?" Mr. Jaggers asked, soon after we began dinner.

"No, sir," returned Wemmick; "it was going by post, when you brought Mr. Pip into the office. Here it is." He handed it to his principal instead of to me.

"It's a note of two lines, Pip," said Mr. Jaggers, handing it on, "sent up to me by Miss Havisham on account of her not being sure of your address. She tells me that she wants to see you on a little matter of business you mentioned to her. You'll go down?"

"Yes," said I, casting my eyes over the note, which was exactly in those terms.

"When do you think of going down?"

"I have an impending engagement," said I, glancing at Wemmick, who was putting fish into the post-office, "that renders me rather uncertain of my time. At once, I think."

"If Mr. Pip has the intention of going at once," said Wemmick to Mr. Jaggers, "he needn't write an answer, you know."

Receiving this as an intimation that it was best not to delay, I settled that I would go to-morrow, and said so. Wemmick drank a glass of wine, and looked with a grimly satisfied air at Mr. Jaggers, but not at me.

"So, Pip! Our friend the Spider," said Mr. Jaggers, "has played his cards. He has won the pool."

It was as much as I could do to assent.

"Hah! He is a promising fellow—in his way—but he may not have it all his own way. The stronger will win in the end, but the stronger has to be found out first. If he should turn to, and beat her—"

"Surely," I interrupted, with a burning face and heart, "you do not seriously think that he is scoundrel enough for that, Mr. Jaggers?"

"I didn't say so, Pip. I am putting a case. If he should turn to and beat her, he may possibly get the strength on his side; if it should be a question of intellect, he certainly will not. It would be chance work to give an opinion how a fellow of that sort will turn out in such circumstances, because it's a toss-up between two results."

"May I ask what they are?"

"A fellow like our friend the Spider," answered Mr. Jaggers, "either beats or cringes. He may cringe and growl, or cringe and not growl; but he either beats or cringes. Ask Wemmick his opinion."

"Either beats or cringes," said Wemmick, not at all addressing himself to me.

"So here's to Mrs. Bentley Drummle," said Mr. Jaggers, taking a decanter of choicer wine from his dumb-waiter, and filling for each of us and for himself, "and may the question of supremacy be settled to the lady's satisfaction! To the satisfaction of the lady and the gentleman, it never will be. Now, Molly, Molly, Molly, Molly, how slow you are to-day!"

She was at his elbow when he addressed her, putting a dish upon the table. As she withdrew her hands from it, she fell back a step or two, nervously muttering some excuse. And a certain action of her fingers, as she spoke, arrested my attention.

"What's the matter?" said Mr. Jaggers.

"Nothing. Only the subject we were speaking of," said I, "was rather painful to me."

The action of her fingers was like the action of knitting. She stood looking at her master, not understanding whether she was free to go, or whether he had more to say to her and would call her back if she did go. Her look was very intent. Surely, I had seen exactly such eyes and such hands on a memorable occasion very lately!

He dismissed her, and she glided out of the room. But she remained before me as plainly as if she were still there. I looked at those hands, I looked at those eyes, I looked at that flowing hair; and I compared them with other hands, other eyes, other hair, that I knew of, and with what those might be after twenty years of a brutal husband and a stormy life. I looked again at those hands and eyes of the housekeeper, and thought of the inexplicable feeling that had come over me when I last walked—not alone—in the ruined garden, and through the deserted brewery. I thought how the same feeling had come back when I saw a face looking at me, and a hand waving to me from a stage-coach window; and how it had come back again and had flashed about me like lightning, when I had passed in a carriage—not alone—through a sudden glare of light in a dark street. I thought how one link of association had helped that identification in the theatre, and how such a link, wanting before, had been riveted for me now, when I had passed by a chance swift from Estella's name to the fingers with their knitting action, and the attentive eyes. And I felt absolutely certain that this woman was Estella's mother.

Mr. Jaggers had seen me with Estella, and was not likely to have missed the sentiments I had been at no pains to conceal. He nodded when I said the subject was painful to me, clapped me on the back, put round the wine again, and went on with his dinner.

Only twice more did the housekeeper reappear, and then her stay in the room was very short, and Mr. Jaggers was sharp with her. But her hands were Estella's hands, and her eyes were Estella's eyes, and if she had reappeared a hundred times I could have been neither more sure nor less sure that my conviction was the truth.

It was a dull evening, for Wemmick drew his wine, when it came round, quite as a matter of business,—just as he might have drawn his salary when that came round,—and with his eyes on his chief, sat in a state of perpetual readiness for cross-examination. As to the quantity of wine, his post-office was as indifferent and ready as any other post-office for its quantity of letters. From my point of view, he was the wrong twin all the time, and only externally like the Wemmick of Walworth.

We took our leave early, and left together. Even when we were groping among Mr. Jaggers's stock of boots for our hats, I felt that the right twin was on his way back; and we had not gone half a dozen yards down Gerrard Street in the Walworth direction, before I found that I was walking arm in arm with the right twin, and that the wrong twin had evaporated into the evening air.

"Well!" said Wemmick, "that's over! He's a wonderful man, without his living likeness; but I feel that I have to screw myself up when I dine with him,—and I dine more comfortably unscrewed."

I felt that this was a good statement of the case, and told him so.

"Wouldn't say it to anybody but yourself," he answered. "I know that what is said between you and me goes no further."

I asked him if he had ever seen Miss Havisham's adopted daughter, Mrs. Bentley Drummle. He said no. To avoid being too abrupt, I then spoke of the Aged and of Miss

Skiffins. He looked rather sly when I mentioned Miss Skiffins, and stopped in the street to blow his nose, with a roll of the head, and a flourish not quite free from latent boastfulness.

"Wemmick," said I, "do you remember telling me, before I first went to Mr. Jaggers's private house, to notice that housekeeper?"

"Did I?" he replied. "Ah, I dare say I did. Deuce take me," he added, suddenly, "I know I did. I find I am not quite unscrewed yet."

"A wild beast tamed, you called her."

"And what do you call her?"

"The same. How did Mr. Jaggers tame her, Wemmick?"

"That's his secret. She has been with him many a long year."

"I wish you would tell me her story. I feel a particular interest in being acquainted with it. You know that what is said between you and me goes no further."

"Well!" Wemmick replied, "I don't know her story,—that is, I don't know all of it. But what I do know I'll tell you. We are in our private and personal capacities, of course."

"Of course."

"A score or so of years ago, that woman was tried at the Old Bailey for murder, and was acquitted. She was a very handsome young woman, and I believe had some gypsy blood in her. Anyhow, it was hot enough when it was up, as you may suppose."

"But she was acquitted."

"Mr. Jaggers was for her," pursued Wemmick, with a look full of meaning, "and worked the case in a way quite astonishing. It was a desperate case, and it was comparatively early days with him then, and he worked it to general admiration; in fact, it may almost be said to have made him. He worked it himself at the police-office, day after day for many days, contending against even a committal; and at the trial where he couldn't work it himself, sat under counsel, and—every one knew—put in all the salt and pepper. The murdered person was a woman,—a woman a good ten years older, very much larger, and very much stronger. It was a case of jealousy. They both led tramping lives, and this woman in Gerrard Street here had been married very young, over the broomstick (as we say), to a tramping man, and was a perfect fury in point of jealousy. The murdered woman,—more a match for the man, certainly, in point of years—was found dead in a barn near Hounslow Heath. There had been a violent struggle, perhaps a fight. She was bruised and scratched and torn, and had been held by the throat, at last, and choked. Now, there was no reasonable evidence to implicate any person but this woman, and on the improbabilities of her having been able to do it Mr. Jaggers principally rested his case. You may be sure," said Wemmick, touching me on the sleeve, "that he never dwelt upon the strength of her hands then, though he sometimes does now."

I had told Wemmick of his showing us her wrists, that day of the dinner party.

"Well, sir!" Wemmick went on; "it happened—happened, don't you see?—that this woman was so very artfully dressed from the time of her apprehension, that she looked much slighter than she really was; in particular, her sleeves are always remembered to have been so skilfully contrived that her arms had quite a delicate look. She had only a bruise or two about her,—nothing for a tramp,—but the backs of her hands were lacerated, and the question was,

Was it with finger-nails? Now, Mr. Jaggers showed that she had struggled through a great lot of brambles which were not as high as her face; but which she could not have got through and kept her hands out of; and bits of those brambles were actually found in her skin and put in evidence, as well as the fact that the brambles in question were found on examination to have been broken through, and to have little shreds of her dress and little spots of blood upon them here and there. But the boldest point he made was this: it was attempted to be set up, in proof of her jealousy, that she was under strong suspicion of having, at about the time of the murder, frantically destroyed her child by this man—some three years old—to revenge herself upon him. Mr. Jaggers worked that in this way: "We say these are not marks of finger-nails, but marks of brambles, and we show you the brambles. You say they are marks of finger-nails, and you set up the hypothesis that she destroyed her child. You must accept all consequences of that hypothesis. For anything we know, she may have destroyed her child, and the child in clinging to her may have scratched her hands. What then? You are not trying her for the murder of her child; why don't you? As to this case, if you will have scratches, we say that, for anything we know, you may have accounted for them, assuming for the sake of argument that you have not invented them?" "To sum up, sir," said Wemmick, "Mr. Jaggers was altogether too many for the jury, and they gave in."

"Has she been in his service ever since?"

"Yes; but not only that," said Wemmick, "she went into his service immediately after her acquittal, tamed as she is now. She has since been taught one thing and another in the way of her duties, but she was tamed from the beginning."

"Do you remember the sex of the child?"

"Said to have been a girl."

"You have nothing more to say to me to-night?"

"Nothing. I got your letter and destroyed it. Nothing."

We exchanged a cordial good-night, and I went home, with new matter for my thoughts, though with no relief from the old.

Chapter XLIX

Putting Miss Havisham's note in my pocket, that it might serve as my credentials for so soon reappearing at Satis House, in case her waywardness should lead her to express any surprise at seeing me, I went down again by the coach next day. But I alighted at the Halfway House, and breakfasted there, and walked the rest of the distance; for I sought to get into the town quietly by the unfrequented ways, and to leave it in the same manner.

The best light of the day was gone when I passed along the quiet echoing courts behind the High Street. The nooks of ruin where the old monks had once had their refectories and gardens, and where the strong walls were now pressed into the service of humble sheds and stables, were almost as silent as the old monks in their graves. The cathedral chimes had at once a sadder and a more remote sound to me, as I hurried on avoiding observation, than they had ever had before; so, the swell of the old organ was borne to my ears like funeral music; and the rooks, as they hovered about the gray tower and swung in the bare high trees of the priory garden, seemed to call to me that the place was changed, and that Estella was gone out of it for ever.

An elderly woman, whom I had seen before as one of the servants who lived in the supplementary house across the back courtyard, opened the gate. The lighted candle stood in the dark passage within, as of old, and I took it up and ascended the staircase alone. Miss Havisham was not in her own room, but was in the larger room across the landing. Looking in at the door, after knocking in vain, I saw her sitting on the hearth in a ragged chair, close before, and lost in the contemplation of, the ashy fire.

Doing as I had often done, I went in, and stood touching the old chimney-piece, where she could see me when she raised her eyes. There was an air of utter loneliness upon her, that would have moved me to pity though she had wilfully done me a deeper injury than I could charge her with. As I stood compassionating her, and thinking how, in the progress of time, I too had come to be a part of the wrecked fortunes of that house, her eyes rested on me. She stared, and said in a low voice, "Is it real?"

"It is I, Pip. Mr. Jaggers gave me your note yesterday, and I have lost no time."

"Thank you. Thank you."

As I brought another of the ragged chairs to the hearth and sat down, I remarked a new expression on her face, as if she were afraid of me.

"I want," she said, "to pursue that subject you mentioned to me when you were last here, and to show you that I am not all stone. But perhaps you can never believe, now, that there is anything human in my heart?"

When I said some reassuring words, she stretched out her tremulous right hand, as though she was going to touch me; but she recalled it again before I understood the action, or knew how to receive it.

"You said, speaking for your friend, that you could tell me how to do something useful and good. Something that you would like done, is it not?"

"Something that I would like done very much."

"What is it?"

I began explaining to her that secret history of the partnership. I had not got far into it, when I judged from her looks that she was thinking in a discursive way of me, rather than of what I said. It seemed to be so; for, when I stopped speaking, many moments passed before she showed that she was conscious of the fact.

"Do you break off," she asked then, with her former air of being afraid of me, "because you hate me too much to bear to speak to me?"

"No, no," I answered, "how can you think so, Miss Havisham! I stopped because I thought you were not following what I said."

"Perhaps I was not," she answered, putting a hand to her head. "Begin again, and let me look at something else. Stay! Now tell me."

She set her hand upon her stick in the resolute way that sometimes was habitual to her, and looked at the fire with a strong expression of forcing herself to attend. I went on with my explanation, and told her how I had hoped to complete the transaction out of my means, but how in this I was disappointed. That part of the subject (I reminded her) involved matters which could form no part of my explanation, for they were the weighty secrets of another.

"So!" said she, assenting with her head, but not looking at me. "And how much money is wanting to complete the purchase?"

I was rather afraid of stating it, for it sounded a large sum. "Nine hundred pounds."

"If I give you the money for this purpose, will you keep my secret as you have kept your own?"

"Quite as faithfully."

"And your mind will be more at rest?"

"Much more at rest."

"Are you very unhappy now?"

She asked this question, still without looking at me, but in an unwonted tone of sympathy. I could not reply at the moment, for my voice failed me. She put her left arm across the head of her stick, and softly laid her forehead on it.

"I am far from happy, Miss Havisham; but I have other causes of disquiet than any you know of. They are the secrets I have mentioned."

After a little while, she raised her head, and looked at the fire again.

"It is noble in you to tell me that you have other causes of unhappiness. Is it true?"

"Too true."

"Can I only serve you, Pip, by serving your friend? Regarding that as done, is there nothing I can do for you yourself?"

"Nothing. I thank you for the question. I thank you even more for the tone of the question. But there is nothing."

She presently rose from her seat, and looked about the blighted room for the means of writing. There were none there, and she took from her pocket a yellow set of ivory tablets, mounted in tarnished gold, and wrote upon them with a pencil in a case of tarnished gold that hung from her neck.

"You are still on friendly terms with Mr. Jaggers?"

"Quite. I dined with him yesterday."

"This is an authority to him to pay you that money, to lay out at your irresponsible discretion for your friend. I keep no money here; but if you would rather Mr. Jaggers knew nothing of the matter, I will send it to you."

"Thank you, Miss Havisham; I have not the least objection to receiving it from him."

She read me what she had written; and it was direct and clear, and evidently intended to absolve me from any suspicion of profiting by the receipt of the money. I took the tablets from her hand, and it trembled again, and it trembled more as she took off the chain to which the pencil was attached, and put it in mine. All this she did without looking at me.

"My name is on the first leaf. If you can ever write under my name, "I forgive her," though ever so long after my broken heart is dust pray do it!"

"O Miss Havisham," said I, "I can do it now. There have been sore mistakes; and my life has been a blind and thankless one; and I want forgiveness and direction far too much, to be bitter with you."

She turned her face to me for the first time since she had averted it, and, to my amazement, I may even add to my terror, dropped on her knees at my feet; with her folded hands raised to me in the manner in which, when her poor heart was young and fresh and whole, they must often have been raised to heaven from her mother's side.

To see her with her white hair and her worn face kneeling at my feet gave me a shock through all my frame. I entreated her to rise, and got my arms about her to help her up; but she only pressed that hand of mine which was nearest to her grasp, and hung her head over it and wept. I had never seen her shed a tear before, and, in the hope that the relief might do her good, I bent over her without speaking. She was not kneeling now, but was down upon the ground.

"O!" she cried, despairingly. "What have I done! What have I done!"

"If you mean, Miss Havisham, what have you done to injure me, let me answer. Very little. I should have loved her under any circumstances. Is she married?"

"Yes."

It was a needless question, for a new desolation in the desolate house had told me so.

"What have I done! What have I done!" She wrung her hands, and crushed her white hair, and returned to this cry over and over again. "What have I done!"

I knew not how to answer, or how to comfort her. That she had done a grievous thing in taking an impressionable child to mould into the form that her wild resentment, spurned affection, and wounded pride found vengeance in, I knew full well. But that, in shutting out the light of day, she had shut out infinitely more; that, in seclusion, she had secluded herself from a thousand natural and healing influences; that, her mind, brooding solitary, had grown diseased, as all minds do and must and will that reverse the appointed order of their Maker, I knew equally well. And could I look upon her without compassion, seeing her punishment in the ruin she was, in her profound unfitness for this earth on which she was placed, in the vanity of sorrow which had become a master mania, like the vanity of penitence, the vanity of remorse, the vanity of unworthiness, and other monstrous vanities that have been curses in this world?

"Until you spoke to her the other day, and until I saw in you a looking-glass that showed me what I once felt myself, I did not know what I had done. What have I done! What have I done!" And so again, twenty, fifty times over, What had she done!

"Miss Havisham," I said, when her cry had died away, "you may dismiss me from your mind and conscience. But Estella is a different case, and if you can ever undo any scrap of what you have done amiss in keeping a part of her right nature away from her, it will be better to do that than to bemoan the past through a hundred years."

"Yes, yes, I know it. But, Pip—my dear!" There was an earnest womanly compassion for me in her new affection. "My dear! Believe this: when she first came to me, I meant to save her from misery like my own. At first, I meant no more."

"Well, well!" said I. "I hope so."

"But as she grew, and promised to be very beautiful, I gradually did worse, and with my praises, and with my jewels, and with my teachings, and with this figure of myself always before her, a warning to back and point my lessons, I stole her heart away, and put ice in its place."

"Better," I could not help saying, "to have left her a natural heart, even to be bruised or broken."

With that, Miss Havisham looked distractedly at me for a while, and then burst out again, What had she done!

"If you knew all my story," she pleaded, "you would have some compassion for me and a better understanding of me."

"Miss Havisham," I answered, as delicately as I could, "I believe I may say that I do know your story, and have known it ever since I first left this neighborhood. It has inspired me with great commiseration, and I hope I understand it and its influences. Does what has passed between us give me any excuse for asking you a question relative to Estella? Not as she is, but as she was when she first came here?"

She was seated on the ground, with her arms on the ragged chair, and her head leaning on them. She looked full at me when I said this, and replied, "Go on."

"Whose child was Estella?"

She shook her head.

"You don't know?"

She shook her head again.

"But Mr. Jaggers brought her here, or sent her here?"

"Brought her here."

"Will you tell me how that came about?"

She answered in a low whisper and with caution: "I had been shut up in these rooms a long time (I don't know how long; you know what time the clocks keep here), when I told him that I wanted a little girl to rear and love, and save from my fate. I had first seen him when I sent for him to lay this place waste for me; having read of him in the newspapers, before I and the world parted. He told me that he would look about him for such an orphan child. One night he brought her here asleep, and I called her Estella."

"Might I ask her age then?"

"Two or three. She herself knows nothing, but that she was left an orphan and I adopted her."

So convinced I was of that woman's being her mother, that I wanted no evidence to establish the fact in my own mind. But, to any mind, I thought, the connection here was clear and straight.

What more could I hope to do by prolonging the interview? I had succeeded on behalf of Herbert, Miss Havisham had told me all she knew of Estella, I had said and done what I could to ease her mind. No matter with what other words we parted; we parted.

Twilight was closing in when I went downstairs into the natural air. I called to the woman who had opened the gate when I entered, that I would not trouble her just yet, but would walk round the place before leaving. For I had a presentiment that I should never be there again, and I felt that the dying light was suited to my last view of it.

By the wilderness of casks that I had walked on long ago, and on which the rain of years had fallen since, rotting them in many places, and leaving miniature swamps and pools of water upon those that stood on end, I made my way to the ruined garden. I went all round it; round by the corner where Herbert and I had fought our battle; round by the paths where Estella and I had walked. So cold, so lonely, so dreary all!

Taking the brewery on my way back, I raised the rusty latch of a little door at the garden end of it, and walked through. I was going out at the opposite door,—not easy to open now, for the damp wood had started and swelled, and the hinges were yielding, and the threshold was encumbered with a growth of fungus,—when I turned my head to look back. A childish association revived with wonderful force in the moment of the slight action, and I fancied that I saw Miss Havisham hanging to the beam. So strong was the impression, that I stood under the beam shuddering from head to foot before I knew it was a fancy,—though to be sure I was there in an instant.

The mournfulness of the place and time, and the great terror of this illusion, though it was but momentary, caused me to feel an indescribable awe as I came out between the open wooden gates where I had once wrung my hair after Estella had wrung my heart. Passing on into the front courtyard, I hesitated whether to call the woman to let me out at the locked gate of which she had the key, or first to go upstairs and assure myself that Miss Havisham was as safe and well as I had left her. I took the latter course and went up.

I looked into the room where I had left her, and I saw her seated in the ragged chair upon the hearth close to the fire, with her back towards me. In the moment when I was withdrawing my head to go quietly away, I saw a great flaming light spring up. In the same moment I saw her running at me, shrieking, with a whirl of fire blazing all about her, and soaring at least as many feet above her head as she was high.

I had a double-caped great-coat on, and over my arm another thick coat. That I got them off, closed with her, threw her down, and got them over her; that I dragged the great cloth from the table for the same purpose, and with it dragged down the heap of rottenness in the midst, and all the ugly things that sheltered there; that we were on the ground struggling like desperate enemies, and that the closer I covered her, the more wildly she shrieked and tried to free herself,—that this occurred I knew through the result, but not through anything I felt, or thought, or knew I did. I knew nothing until I knew that we were on the floor by the great table, and that patches of tinder yet alight were floating in the smoky air, which, a moment ago, had been her faded bridal dress.

Then, I looked round and saw the disturbed beetles and spiders running away over the floor, and the servants coming in with breathless cries at the door. I still held her forcibly down with all my strength, like a prisoner who might escape; and I doubt if I even knew who she was, or why we had struggled, or that she had been in flames, or that the flames were out, until I saw the patches of tinder that had been her garments no longer alight but falling in a black shower around us.

She was insensible, and I was afraid to have her moved, or even touched. Assistance was sent for, and I held her until it came, as if I unreasonably fancied (I think I did) that, if I let her go, the fire would break out again and consume her. When I got up, on the surgeon's coming to her with other aid, I was astonished to see that both my hands were burnt; for, I had no knowledge of it through the sense of feeling.

On examination it was pronounced that she had received serious hurts, but that they of themselves were far from hopeless; the danger lay mainly in the nervous shock. By the surgeon's directions, her bed was carried into that room and laid upon the great table, which happened to be well suited to the dressing of her injuries. When I saw her again, an hour afterwards, she lay, indeed, where I had seen her strike her stick, and had heard her say that she would lie one day.

Though every vestige of her dress was burnt, as they told me, she still had something of her old ghastly bridal appearance; for, they had covered her to the throat with white cotton-wool, and as she lay with a white sheet loosely overlying that, the phantom air of something that had been and was changed was still upon her.

I found, on questioning the servants, that Estella was in Paris, and I got a promise from the surgeon that he would write to her by the next post. Miss Havisham's family I took upon myself; intending to communicate with Mr. Matthew Pocket only, and leave him to do as he liked about informing the rest. This I did next day, through Herbert, as soon as I returned to town.

There was a stage, that evening, when she spoke collectedly of what had happened, though with a certain terrible vivacity. Towards midnight she began to wander in her speech; and after that it gradually set in that she said innumerable times in a low solemn voice, "What have I done!" And then, "When she first came, I meant to save her from misery like mine." And then, "Take the pencil and write under my name, 'I forgive her!'" She never changed the order of these three sentences, but she sometimes left out a word in one or other of them; never putting in another word, but always leaving a blank and going on to the next word.

As I could do no service there, and as I had, nearer home, that pressing reason for anxiety and fear which even her wanderings could not drive out of my mind, I decided, in the course of the night that I would return by the early morning coach, walking on a mile or so, and being taken up clear of the town. At about six o'clock of the morning, therefore, I leaned over her and touched her lips with mine, just as they said, not stopping for being touched, "Take the pencil and write under my name, 'I forgive her.'"

Chapter L

My hands had been dressed twice or thrice in the night, and again in the morning. My left arm was a good deal burned to the elbow, and, less severely, as high as the shoulder; it was very painful, but the flames had set in that direction, and I felt thankful it was no worse. My right hand was not so badly burnt but that I could move the fingers. It was bandaged, of course, but much less inconveniently than my left hand and arm; those I carried in a sling; and I could only wear my coat like a cloak, loose over my shoulders and fastened at the neck. My hair had been caught by the fire, but not my head or face.

When Herbert had been down to Hammersmith and seen his father, he came back to me at our chambers, and devoted the day to attending on me. He was the kindest of nurses, and at stated times took off the bandages, and steeped them in the cooling liquid that was kept ready, and put them on again, with a patient tenderness that I was deeply grateful for.

At first, as I lay quiet on the sofa, I found it painfully difficult, I might say impossible, to get rid of the impression of the glare of the flames, their hurry and noise, and the fierce burning smell. If I dozed for a minute, I was awakened by Miss Havisham's cries, and by her running at me with all that height of fire above her head. This pain of the mind was much harder to strive against than any bodily pain I suffered; and Herbert, seeing that, did his utmost to hold my attention engaged.

Neither of us spoke of the boat, but we both thought of it. That was made apparent by our avoidance of the subject, and by our agreeing—without agreement—to make my recovery of the use of my hands a question of so many hours, not of so many weeks.

My first question when I saw Herbert had been of course, whether all was well down the river? As he replied in the affirmative, with perfect confidence and cheerfulness, we did not resume the subject until the day was wearing away. But then, as Herbert changed the bandages, more by the light of the fire than by the outer light, he went back to it spontaneously.

"I sat with Provis last night, Handel, two good hours."

"Where was Clara?"

"Dear little thing!" said Herbert. "She was up and down with Gruffandgrim all the evening. He was perpetually pegging at the floor the moment she left his sight. I doubt if he can hold out long, though. What with rum and pepper,—and pepper and rum,—I should think his pegging must be nearly over."

"And then you will be married, Herbert?"

"How can I take care of the dear child otherwise?—Lay your arm out upon the back of the sofa, my dear boy, and I'll sit down here, and get the bandage off so gradually that you shall not know when it comes. I was speaking of Provis. Do you know, Handel, he improves?"

"I said to you I thought he was softened when I last saw him."

"So you did. And so he is. He was very communicative last night, and told me more of his life. You remember his breaking off here about some woman that he had had great trouble with.—Did I hurt you?"

I had started, but not under his touch. His words had given me a start.

"I had forgotten that, Herbert, but I remember it now you speak of it."

"Well! He went into that part of his life, and a dark wild part it is. Shall I tell you? Or would it worry you just now?"

"Tell me by all means. Every word."

Herbert bent forward to look at me more nearly, as if my reply had been rather more hurried or more eager than he could quite account for. "Your head is cool?" he said, touching it.

"Quite," said I. "Tell me what Provis said, my dear Herbert."

"It seems," said Herbert, "—there's a bandage off most charmingly, and now comes the cool one,—makes you shrink at first, my poor dear fellow, don't it? but it will be comfortable presently,—it seems that the woman was a young woman, and a jealous woman, and a revengeful woman; revengeful, Handel, to the last degree."

"To what last degree?"

"Murder.—Does it strike too cold on that sensitive place?"

"I don't feel it. How did she murder? Whom did she murder?"

"Why, the deed may not have merited quite so terrible a name," said Herbert, "but, she was tried for it, and Mr. Jaggers defended her, and the reputation of that defence first made his name known to Provis. It was another and a stronger woman who was the victim, and there had been a struggle—in a barn. Who began it, or how fair it was, or how unfair, may be doubtful; but how it ended is certainly not doubtful, for the victim was found throttled."

"Was the woman brought in guilty?"

"No; she was acquitted.—My poor Handel, I hurt you!"

"It is impossible to be gentler, Herbert. Yes? What else?"

"This acquitted young woman and Provis had a little child; a little child of whom Provis was exceedingly fond. On the evening of the very night when the object of her jealousy was strangled as I tell you, the young woman presented herself before Provis for one moment, and swore that she would destroy the child (which was in her possession), and he should never see it again; then she vanished.—There's the worst arm comfortably in the sling once more, and now there remains but the right hand, which is a far easier job. I can do it better by this light than by a stronger, for my hand is steadiest when I don't see the poor blistered patches too distinctly.— You don't think your breathing is affected, my dear boy? You seem to breathe quickly."

"Perhaps I do, Herbert. Did the woman keep her oath?"

"There comes the darkest part of Provis's life. She did."

"That is, he says she did."

"Why, of course, my dear boy," returned Herbert, in a tone of surprise, and again bending forward to get a nearer look at me. "He says it all. I have no other information."

"No, to be sure."

"Now, whether," pursued Herbert, "he had used the child's mother ill, or whether he had used the child's mother well, Provis doesn't say; but she had shared some four or five years of the wretched life he described to us at this fireside, and he seems to have felt pity for her, and forbearance towards her. Therefore, fearing he should be called upon to depose about this destroyed child, and so be the cause of her death, he hid himself (much as he grieved for the child), kept himself dark, as he says, out of the way and out of the trial, and was only vaguely talked of as a certain man called Abel, out of whom the jealousy arose. After the acquittal she disappeared, and thus he lost the child and the child's mother."

"I want to ask—"

"A moment, my dear boy, and I have done. That evil genius, Compeyson, the worst of scoundrels among many scoundrels, knowing of his keeping out of the way at that time and of his reasons for doing so, of course afterwards held the knowledge over his head as a means of keeping him poorer and working him harder. It was clear last night that this barbed the point of Provis's animosity."

"I want to know," said I, "and particularly, Herbert, whether he told you when this happened?"

"Particularly? Let me remember, then, what he said as to that. His expression was, 'a round score o' year ago, and a'most directly after I took up wi' Compeyson.' How old were you when you came upon him in the little churchyard?"

"I think in my seventh year."

"Ay. It had happened some three or four years then, he said, and you brought into his mind the little girl so tragically lost, who would have been about your age."

"Herbert," said I, after a short silence, in a hurried way, "can you see me best by the light of the window, or the light of the fire?"

"By the firelight," answered Herbert, coming close again.

"Look at me."

"I do look at you, my dear boy."

"Touch me."

"I do touch you, my dear boy."

"You are not afraid that I am in any fever, or that my head is much disordered by the accident of last night?"

"N-no, my dear boy," said Herbert, after taking time to examine me. "You are rather excited, but you are quite yourself."

"I know I am quite myself. And the man we have in hiding down the river, is Estella's Father."

Chapter LI

What purpose I had in view when I was hot on tracing out and proving Estella's parentage, I cannot say. It will presently be seen that the question was not before me in a distinct shape until it was put before me by a wiser head than my own.

But when Herbert and I had held our momentous conversation, I was seized with a feverish conviction that I ought to hunt the matter down,—that I ought not to let it rest, but that I ought to see Mr. Jaggers, and come at the bare truth. I really do not know whether I felt that I did this for Estella's sake, or whether I was glad to transfer to the man in whose preservation I was so much concerned some rays of the romantic interest that had so long surrounded me. Perhaps the latter possibility may be the nearer to the truth.

Any way, I could scarcely be withheld from going out to Gerrard Street that night. Herbert's representations that, if I did, I should probably be laid up and stricken useless, when our fugitive's safety would depend upon me, alone restrained my impatience. On the understanding, again and again reiterated, that, come what would, I was to go to Mr. Jaggers to-morrow, I at length submitted to keep quiet, and to have my hurts looked after, and to stay at home. Early next morning we went out together, and at the corner of Giltspur Street by Smithfield, I left Herbert to go his way into the City, and took my way to Little Britain.

There were periodical occasions when Mr. Jaggers and Wemmick went over the office accounts, and checked off the vouchers, and put all things straight. On these occasions, Wemmick took his books and papers into Mr. Jaggers's room, and one of the upstairs clerks came down into the outer office. Finding such clerk on Wemmick's post that morning, I knew what was going on; but I was not sorry to have Mr. Jaggers and Wemmick together, as Wemmick would then hear for himself that I said nothing to compromise him.

My appearance, with my arm bandaged and my coat loose over my shoulders, favored my object. Although I had sent Mr. Jaggers a brief account of the accident as soon as I had arrived in town, yet I had to give him all the details now; and the speciality of the occasion caused our talk to be less dry and hard, and less strictly regulated by the rules of evidence, than it had been before. While I described the disaster, Mr. Jaggers stood, according to his wont, before the fire. Wemmick leaned back in his chair, staring at me, with his hands in the pockets of his trousers, and his pen put horizontally into the post. The two brutal casts, always inseparable in my mind from the official proceedings, seemed to be congestively considering whether they didn't smell fire at the present moment.

My narrative finished, and their questions exhausted, I then produced Miss Havisham's authority to receive the nine hundred pounds for Herbert. Mr. Jaggers's eyes retired a little deeper into his head when I handed him the tablets, but he presently handed them over to Wemmick, with instructions to draw the check for his signature. While that was in course of being done, I looked on at Wemmick as he wrote, and Mr. Jaggers, poising and swaying himself on his well-polished boots, looked on at me. "I am sorry, Pip," said he, as I put the check in my pocket, when he had signed it, "that we do nothing for you."

"Miss Havisham was good enough to ask me," I returned, "whether she could do nothing for me, and I told her No."

"Everybody should know his own business," said Mr. Jaggers. And I saw Wemmick's lips form the words "portable property."

"I should not have told her No, if I had been you," said Mr Jaggers; "but every man ought to know his own business best."

"Every man's business," said Wemmick, rather reproachfully towards me, "is portable property."

As I thought the time was now come for pursuing the theme I had at heart, I said, turning on Mr. Jaggers:—

"I did ask something of Miss Havisham, however, sir. I asked her to give me some information relative to her adopted daughter, and she gave me all she possessed."

"Did she?" said Mr. Jaggers, bending forward to look at his boots and then straightening himself. "Hah! I don't think I should have done so, if I had been Miss Havisham. But she ought to know her own business best."

"I know more of the history of Miss Havisham's adopted child than Miss Havisham herself does, sir. I know her mother."

Mr. Jaggers looked at me inquiringly, and repeated "Mother?"

"I have seen her mother within these three days."

"Yes?" said Mr. Jaggers.

"And so have you, sir. And you have seen her still more recently."

"Yes?" said Mr. Jaggers.

"Perhaps I know more of Estella's history than even you do," said I. "I know her father too."

A certain stop that Mr. Jaggers came to in his manner—he was too self-possessed to change his manner, but he could not help its being brought to an indefinably attentive stop—assured me that he did not know who her father was. This I had strongly suspected from Provis's account (as Herbert had repeated it) of his having kept himself dark; which I pieced on to the fact that he himself was not Mr. Jaggers's client until some four years later, and when he could have no reason for claiming his identity. But, I could not be sure of this unconsciousness on Mr. Jaggers's part before, though I was quite sure of it now.

"So! You know the young lady's father, Pip?" said Mr. Jaggers.

"Yes," I replied, "and his name is Provis—from New South Wales."

Even Mr. Jaggers started when I said those words. It was the slightest start that could escape a man, the most carefully repressed and the sooner checked, but he did start, though he made it a part of the action of taking out his pocket-handkerchief. How Wemmick received the announcement I am unable to say; for I was afraid to look at him just then, lest Mr. Jaggers's sharpness should detect that there had been some communication unknown to him between us.

"And on what evidence, Pip," asked Mr. Jaggers, very coolly, as he paused with his handkerchief half way to his nose, "does Provis make this claim?"

"He does not make it," said I, "and has never made it, and has no knowledge or belief that his daughter is in existence."

For once, the powerful pocket-handkerchief failed. My reply was so unexpected, that Mr. Jaggers put the handkerchief back into his pocket without completing the usual performance, folded his arms, and looked with stern attention at me, though with an immovable face.

Then I told him all I knew, and how I knew it; with the one reservation that I left him to infer that I knew from Miss Havisham what I in fact knew from Wemmick. I was very careful indeed as to that. Nor did I look towards Wemmick until I had finished all I had to tell, and had been for some time silently meeting Mr. Jaggers's look. When I did at last turn my eyes in Wemmick's direction, I found that he had unposted his pen, and was intent upon the table before him.

"Hah!" said Mr. Jaggers at last, as he moved towards the papers on the table. "What item was it you were at, Wemmick, when Mr. Pip came in?"

But I could not submit to be thrown off in that way, and I made a passionate, almost an indignant appeal, to him to be more frank and manly with me. I reminded him of the false hopes into which I had lapsed, the length of time they had lasted, and the discovery I had made: and I hinted at the danger that weighed upon my spirits. I represented myself as being surely worthy of some little confidence from him, in return for the confidence I had just now imparted. I said that I did not blame him, or suspect him, or mistrust him, but I wanted assurance of the truth from him. And if he asked me why I wanted it, and why I thought I had any right to it, I would tell him, little as he cared for such poor dreams, that I had loved Estella dearly and long, and that although I had lost her, and must live a bereaved life, whatever concerned her was still nearer and dearer to me than anything else in the world. And seeing that Mr. Jaggers stood quite still and silent, and apparently quite obdurate, under this appeal, I turned to Wemmick, and said, "Wemmick, I know you to be a man with a gentle heart. I have seen your pleasant home, and your old father, and all the innocent, cheerful playful ways with which you refresh your business life. And I entreat you to say a word for me to Mr. Jaggers, and to represent to him that, all circumstances considered, he ought to be more open with me!"

I have never seen two men look more oddly at one another than Mr. Jaggers and Wemmick did after this apostrophe. At first, a misgiving crossed me that Wemmick would be instantly dismissed from his employment; but it melted as I saw Mr. Jaggers relax into something like a smile, and Wemmick become bolder.

"What's all this?" said Mr. Jaggers. "You with an old father, and you with pleasant and playful ways?"

"Well!" returned Wemmick. "If I don't bring 'em here, what does it matter?"

"Pip," said Mr. Jaggers, laying his hand upon my arm, and smiling openly, "this man must be the most cunning impostor in all London."

"Not a bit of it," returned Wemmick, growing bolder and bolder. "I think you're another."

Again they exchanged their former odd looks, each apparently still distrustful that the other was taking him in.

"You with a pleasant home?" said Mr. Jaggers.

"Since it don't interfere with business," returned Wemmick, "let it be so. Now, I look at you, sir, I shouldn't wonder if you might be planning and contriving to have a pleasant home of your own one of these days, when you're tired of all this work."

Mr. Jaggers nodded his head retrospectively two or three times, and actually drew a sigh. "Pip," said he, "we won't talk about 'poor dreams;' you know more about such things than I, having much fresher experience of that kind. But now about this other matter. I'll put a case to you. Mind! I admit nothing."

He waited for me to declare that I quite understood that he expressly said that he admitted nothing.

"Now, Pip," said Mr. Jaggers, "put this case. Put the case that a woman, under such circumstances as you have mentioned, held her child concealed, and was obliged to communicate the fact to her legal adviser, on his representing to her that he must know, with an eye to the latitude of his defence, how the fact stood about that child. Put the case that, at the same time he held a trust to find a child for an eccentric rich lady to adopt and bring up."

"I follow you, sir."

"Put the case that he lived in an atmosphere of evil, and that all he saw of children was their being generated in great numbers for certain destruction. Put the case that he often saw children solemnly tried at a criminal bar, where they were held up to be seen; put the case that he habitually knew of their being imprisoned, whipped, transported, neglected, cast out, qualified in all ways for the hangman, and growing up to be hanged. Put the case that pretty nigh all the children he saw in his daily business life he had reason to look upon as so much spawn, to develop into the fish that were to come to his net,—to be prosecuted, defended, forsworn, made orphans, bedevilled somehow."

"I follow you, sir."

"Put the case, Pip, that here was one pretty little child out of the heap who could be saved; whom the father believed dead, and dared make no stir about; as to whom, over the mother, the legal adviser had this power: "I know what you did, and how you did it. You came so and so, you did such and such things to divert suspicion. I have tracked you through it all, and I tell it you all. Part with the child, unless it should be necessary to produce it to clear you, and then it shall be produced. Give the child into my hands, and I will do my best to bring you off. If you are saved, your child is saved too; if you are lost, your child is still saved." Put the case that this was done, and that the woman was cleared."

"I understand you perfectly."

"But that I make no admissions?"

"That you make no admissions." And Wemmick repeated, "No admissions."

"Put the case, Pip, that passion and the terror of death had a little shaken the woman's intellects, and that when she was set at liberty, she was scared out of the ways of the world, and went to him to be sheltered. Put the case that he took her in, and that he kept down the old, wild, violent nature whenever he saw an inkling of its breaking out, by asserting his power over her in the old way. Do you comprehend the imaginary case?"

"Quite."

"Put the case that the child grew up, and was married for money. That the mother was still living. That the father was still living. That the mother and father, unknown to one another, were dwelling within so many miles, furlongs, yards if you like, of one another. That the secret was still a secret, except that you had got wind of it. Put that last case to yourself very carefully."

"I do."

"I ask Wemmick to put it to himself very carefully."

And Wemmick said, "I do."

"For whose sake would you reveal the secret? For the father's? I think he would not be much the better for the mother. For the mother's? I think if she had done such a deed she would be safer where she was. For the daughter's? I think it would hardly serve her to establish her parentage for the information of her husband, and to drag her back to disgrace, after an escape of twenty years, pretty secure to last for life. But add the case that you had loved her, Pip, and had made her the subject of those 'poor dreams' which have, at one time or another, been in the heads of more men than you think likely, then I tell you that you had better—and would much sooner when you had thought well of it—chop off that bandaged left hand of yours with your bandaged right hand, and then pass the chopper on to Wemmick there, to cut that off too."

I looked at Wemmick, whose face was very grave. He gravely touched his lips with his forefinger. I did the same. Mr. Jaggers did the same. "Now, Wemmick," said the latter then, resuming his usual manner, "what item was it you were at when Mr. Pip came in?"

Standing by for a little, while they were at work, I observed that the odd looks they had cast at one another were repeated several times: with this difference now, that each of them seemed suspicious, not to say conscious, of having shown himself in a weak and unprofessional light to the other. For this reason, I suppose, they were now inflexible with one another; Mr. Jaggers being highly dictatorial, and Wemmick obstinately justifying himself whenever there was the smallest point in abeyance for a moment. I had never seen them on such ill terms; for generally they got on very well indeed together.

But they were both happily relieved by the opportune appearance of Mike, the client with the fur cap and the habit of wiping his nose on his sleeve, whom I had seen on the very first day of my appearance within those walls. This individual, who, either in his own person or in that of some member of his family, seemed to be always in trouble (which in that place meant Newgate), called to announce that his eldest daughter was taken up on suspicion of shoplifting. As he imparted this melancholy circumstance to Wemmick, Mr. Jaggers standing magisterially before the fire and taking no share in the proceedings, Mike's eye happened to twinkle with a tear.

"What are you about?" demanded Wemmick, with the utmost indignation. "What do you come snivelling here for?"

"I didn't go to do it, Mr. Wemmick."

"You did," said Wemmick. "How dare you? You're not in a fit state to come here, if you can't come here without spluttering like a bad pen. What do you mean by it?"

"A man can't help his feelings, Mr. Wemmick," pleaded Mike.

"His what?" demanded Wemmick, quite savagely. "Say that again!"

"Now look here my man," said Mr. Jaggers, advancing a step, and pointing to the door. "Get out of this office. I'll have no feelings here. Get out."

"It serves you right," said Wemmick, "Get out."

So, the unfortunate Mike very humbly withdrew, and Mr. Jaggers and Wemmick appeared to have re-established their good understanding, and went to work again with an air of refreshment upon them as if they had just had lunch.

Chapter LII

From Little Britain I went, with my check in my pocket, to Miss Skiffins's brother, the accountant; and Miss Skiffins's brother, the accountant, going straight to Clarriker's and bringing Clarriker to me, I had the great satisfaction of concluding that arrangement. It was the only good thing I had done, and the only completed thing I had done, since I was first apprised of my great expectations.

Clarriker informing me on that occasion that the affairs of the House were steadily progressing, that he would now be able to establish a small branch-house in the East which was much wanted for the extension of the business, and that Herbert in his new partnership capacity would go out and take charge of it, I found that I must have prepared for a separation from my friend, even though my own affairs had been more settled. And now, indeed, I felt as if my last anchor were loosening its hold, and I should soon be driving with the winds and waves.

But there was recompense in the joy with which Herbert would come home of a night and tell me of these changes, little imagining that he told me no news, and would sketch airy pictures of himself conducting Clara Barley to the land of the Arabian Nights, and of me going out to join them (with a caravan of camels, I believe), and of our all going up the Nile and seeing wonders. Without being sanguine as to my own part in those bright plans, I felt that Herbert's way was clearing fast, and that old Bill Barley had but to stick to his pepper and rum, and his daughter would soon be happily provided for.

We had now got into the month of March. My left arm, though it presented no bad symptoms, took, in the natural course, so long to heal that I was still unable to get a coat on. My right arm was tolerably restored; disfigured, but fairly serviceable.

On a Monday morning, when Herbert and I were at breakfast, I received the following letter from Wemmick by the post.

"Walworth. Burn this as soon as read. Early in the week, or say Wednesday, you might do what you know of, if you felt disposed to try it. Now burn."

When I had shown this to Herbert and had put it in the fire—but not before we had both got it by heart—we considered what to do. For, of course my being disabled could now be no longer kept out of view.

"I have thought it over again and again," said Herbert, "and I think I know a better course than taking a Thames waterman. Take Startop. A good fellow, a skilled hand, fond of us, and enthusiastic and honorable."

I had thought of him more than once.

"But how much would you tell him, Herbert?"

"It is necessary to tell him very little. Let him suppose it a mere freak, but a secret one, until the morning comes: then let him know that there is urgent reason for your getting Provis aboard and away. You go with him?"

"No doubt."

"Where?"

It had seemed to me, in the many anxious considerations I had given the point, almost indifferent what port we made for,—Hamburg, Rotterdam, Antwerp,—the place signified little, so that he was out of England. Any foreign steamer that fell in our way and would take us up would do. I had always proposed to myself to get him well down the river in the boat; certainly well beyond Gravesend, which was a critical place for search or inquiry if suspicion were afoot. As foreign steamers would leave London at about the time of high-water, our plan would be to get down the river by a previous ebb-tide, and lie by in some quiet spot until we could pull off to one. The time when one would be due where we lay, wherever that might be, could be calculated pretty nearly, if we made inquiries beforehand.

Herbert assented to all this, and we went out immediately after breakfast to pursue our investigations. We found that a steamer for Hamburg was likely to suit our purpose best, and we directed our thoughts chiefly to that vessel. But we noted down what other foreign steamers would leave London with the same tide, and we satisfied ourselves that we knew the build and color of each. We then separated for a few hours: I, to get at once such passports as were necessary; Herbert, to see Startop at his lodgings. We both did what we had to do without any hindrance, and when we met again at one o'clock reported it done. I, for my part, was prepared with passports; Herbert had seen Startop, and he was more than ready to join.

Those two should pull a pair of oars, we settled, and I would steer; our charge would be sitter, and keep quiet; as speed was not our object, we should make way enough. We arranged that Herbert should not come home to dinner before going to Mill Pond Bank that evening; that he should not go there at all to-morrow evening, Tuesday; that he should prepare Provis to come down to some stairs hard by the house, on Wednesday, when he saw us approach, and not sooner; that all the arrangements with him should be concluded that Monday night; and that he should be communicated with no more in any way, until we took him on board.

These precautions well understood by both of us, I went home.

On opening the outer door of our chambers with my key, I found a letter in the box, directed to me; a very dirty letter, though not ill-written. It had been delivered by hand (of course, since I left home), and its contents were these:—

"If you are not afraid to come to the old marshes to-night or to-morrow night at nine, and to come to the little sluice-house by the limekiln, you had better come. If you want information regarding your uncle Provis, you had much better come and tell no one, and lose no time. You must come alone. Bring this with you."

I had had load enough upon my mind before the receipt of this strange letter. What to do now, I could not tell. And the worst was, that I must decide quickly, or I should miss the afternoon coach, which would take me down in time for to-night. To-morrow night I could not think of going, for it would be too close upon the time of the flight. And again, for anything I knew, the proffered information might have some important bearing on the flight itself.

If I had had ample time for consideration, I believe I should still have gone. Having hardly any time for consideration,—my watch showing me that the coach started within half an hour,—I resolved to go. I should certainly not have gone, but for the reference to my Uncle Provis. That, coming on Wemmick's letter and the morning's busy preparation, turned the scale.

It is so difficult to become clearly possessed of the contents of almost any letter, in a violent hurry, that I had to read this mysterious epistle again twice, before its injunction to me to be secret got mechanically into my mind. Yielding to it in the same mechanical kind of way, I left a note in pencil for Herbert, telling him that as I should be so soon going away, I knew not for how long, I had decided to hurry down and back, to ascertain for myself how Miss Havisham was faring. I had then barely time to get my great-coat, lock up the chambers, and make for the coach-office by the short by-ways. If I had taken a hackney-chariot and gone by the streets, I should have missed my aim; going as I did, I caught the coach just as it came out of the yard. I was the only inside passenger, jolting away knee-deep in straw, when I came to myself.

For I really had not been myself since the receipt of the letter; it had so bewildered me, ensuing on the hurry of the morning. The morning hurry and flutter had been great; for, long and anxiously as I had waited for Wemmick, his hint had come like a surprise at last. And now I began to wonder at myself for being in the coach, and to doubt whether I had sufficient reason for being there, and to consider whether I should get out presently and go back, and to argue against ever heeding an anonymous communication, and, in short, to pass through all those phases of contradiction and indecision to which I suppose very few hurried people are strangers. Still, the reference to Provis by name mastered everything. I reasoned as I had reasoned already without knowing it,—if that be reasoning,—in case any harm should befall him through my not going, how could I ever forgive myself!

It was dark before we got down, and the journey seemed long and dreary to me, who could see little of it inside, and who could not go outside in my disabled state. Avoiding the Blue Boar, I put up at an inn of minor reputation down the town, and ordered some dinner. While it was preparing, I went to Satis House and inquired for Miss Havisham; she was still very ill, though considered something better.

My inn had once been a part of an ancient ecclesiastical house, and I dined in a little octagonal common-room, like a font. As I was not able to cut my dinner, the old landlord with a shining bald head did it for me. This bringing us into conversation, he was so good as to entertain me with my own story,—of course with the popular feature that Pumblechook was my earliest benefactor and the founder of my fortunes.

"Do you know the young man?" said I.

"Know him!" repeated the landlord. "Ever since he was—no height at all."

"Does he ever come back to this neighborhood?"

"Ay, he comes back," said the landlord, "to his great friends, now and again, and gives the cold shoulder to the man that made him."

"What man is that?"

"Him that I speak of," said the landlord. "Mr. Pumblechook."

"Is he ungrateful to no one else?"

"No doubt he would be, if he could," returned the landlord, "but he can't. And why? Because Pumblechook done everything for him."

"Does Pumblechook say so?"

"Say so!" replied the landlord. "He han't no call to say so."

"But does he say so?"

"It would turn a man's blood to white wine winegar to hear him tell of it, sir," said the landlord.

I thought, "Yet Joe, dear Joe, you never tell of it. Long-suffering and loving Joe, you never complain. Nor you, sweet-tempered Biddy!"

"Your appetite's been touched like by your accident," said the landlord, glancing at the bandaged arm under my coat. "Try a tenderer bit."

"No, thank you," I replied, turning from the table to brood over the fire. "I can eat no more. Please take it away."

I had never been struck at so keenly, for my thanklessness to Joe, as through the brazen impostor Pumblechook. The falser he, the truer Joe; the meaner he, the nobler Joe.

My heart was deeply and most deservedly humbled as I mused over the fire for an hour or more. The striking of the clock aroused me, but not from my dejection or remorse, and I got up and had my coat fastened round my neck, and went out. I had previously sought in my pockets for the letter, that I might refer to it again; but I could not find it, and was uneasy to think that it must have been dropped in the straw of the coach. I knew very well, however, that the appointed place was the little sluice-house by the limekiln on the marshes, and the hour nine. Towards the marshes I now went straight, having no time to spare.

Chapter LIII

It was a dark night, though the full moon rose as I left the enclosed lands, and passed out upon the marshes. Beyond their dark line there was a ribbon of clear sky, hardly broad enough to hold the red large moon. In a few minutes she had ascended out of that clear field, in among the piled mountains of cloud.

There was a melancholy wind, and the marshes were very dismal. A stranger would have found them insupportable, and even to me they were so oppressive that I hesitated, half inclined to go back. But I knew them well, and could have found my way on a far darker night, and had no excuse for returning, being there. So, having come there against my inclination, I went on against it.

The direction that I took was not that in which my old home lay, nor that in which we had pursued the convicts. My back was turned towards the distant Hulks as I walked on, and, though I could see the old lights away on the spits of sand, I saw them over my shoulder. I knew the limekiln as well as I knew the old Battery, but they were miles apart; so that, if a light had been burning at each point that night, there would have been a long strip of the blank horizon between the two bright specks.

At first, I had to shut some gates after me, and now and then to stand still while the cattle that were lying in the banked-up pathway arose and blundered down among the grass and reeds. But after a little while I seemed to have the whole flats to myself.

It was another half-hour before I drew near to the kiln. The lime was burning with a sluggish stifling smell, but the fires were made up and left, and no workmen were visible. Hard by was a small stone-quarry. It lay directly in my way, and had been worked that day, as I saw by the tools and barrows that were lying about.

Coming up again to the marsh level out of this excavation,—for the rude path lay through it,—I saw a light in the old sluice-house. I quickened my pace, and knocked at the door with my hand. Waiting for some reply, I looked about me, noticing how the sluice was abandoned and broken, and how the house—of wood with a tiled roof—would not be proof against the weather much longer, if it were so even now, and how the mud and ooze were coated with lime, and how the choking vapor of the kiln crept in a ghostly way towards me. Still there was no answer, and I knocked again. No answer still, and I tried the latch.

It rose under my hand, and the door yielded. Looking in, I saw a lighted candle on a table, a bench, and a mattress on a truckle bedstead. As there was a loft above, I called, "Is there any one here?" but no voice answered. Then I looked at my watch, and, finding that it was past nine, called again, "Is there any one here?" There being still no answer, I went out at the door, irresolute what to do.

It was beginning to rain fast. Seeing nothing save what I had seen already, I turned back into the house, and stood just within the shelter of the doorway, looking out into the night. While I was considering that some one must have been there lately and must soon be coming back, or the candle would not be burning, it came into my head to look if the wick were long. I turned round to do so, and had taken up the candle in my hand, when it was extinguished by some violent shock; and the next thing I comprehended was, that I had been caught in a strong running noose, thrown over my head from behind.

"Now," said a suppressed voice with an oath, "I've got you!"

"What is this?" I cried, struggling. "Who is it? Help, help, help!"

Not only were my arms pulled close to my sides, but the pressure on my bad arm caused me exquisite pain. Sometimes, a strong man's hand, sometimes a strong man's breast, was set against my mouth to deaden my cries, and with a hot breath always close to me, I struggled ineffectually in the dark, while I was fastened tight to the wall. "And now," said the suppressed voice with another oath, "call out again, and I'll make short work of you!"

Faint and sick with the pain of my injured arm, bewildered by the surprise, and yet conscious how easily this threat could be put in execution, I desisted, and tried to ease my arm were it ever so little. But, it was bound too tight for that. I felt as if, having been burnt before, it were now being boiled.

The sudden exclusion of the night, and the substitution of black darkness in its place, warned me that the man had closed a shutter. After groping about for a little, he found the flint and steel he wanted, and began to strike a light. I strained my sight upon the sparks that fell among the tinder, and upon which he breathed and breathed, match in hand, but I could only see his lips, and the blue point of the match; even those but fitfully. The tinder was damp,—no wonder there,—and one after another the sparks died out.

The man was in no hurry, and struck again with the flint and steel. As the sparks fell thick and bright about him, I could see his hands, and touches of his face, and could make out that he was seated and bending over the table; but nothing more. Presently I saw his blue lips again, breathing on the tinder, and then a flare of light flashed up, and showed me Orlick.

Whom I had looked for, I don't know. I had not looked for him. Seeing him, I felt that I was in a dangerous strait indeed, and I kept my eyes upon him.

He lighted the candle from the flaring match with great deliberation, and dropped the match, and trod it out. Then he put the candle away from him on the table, so that he could see me, and sat with his arms folded on the table and looked at me. I made out that I was fastened to a stout perpendicular ladder a few inches from the wall,—a fixture there,—the means of ascent to the loft above.

"Now," said he, when we had surveyed one another for some time, "I've got you."

"Unbind me. Let me go!"

"Ah!" he returned, "I'll let you go. I'll let you go to the moon, I'll let you go to the stars. All in good time."

"Why have you lured me here?"

"Don't you know?" said he, with a deadly look.

"Why have you set upon me in the dark?"

"Because I mean to do it all myself. One keeps a secret better than two. O you enemy, you enemy!"

His enjoyment of the spectacle I furnished, as he sat with his arms folded on the table, shaking his head at me and hugging himself, had a malignity in it that made me tremble. As I watched him in silence, he put his hand into the corner at his side, and took up a gun with a brass-bound stock.

"Do you know this?" said he, making as if he would take aim at me. "Do you know where you saw it afore? Speak, wolf!"

"Yes," I answered.

"You cost me that place. You did. Speak!"

"What else could I do?"

"You did that, and that would be enough, without more. How dared you to come betwixt me and a young woman I liked?"

"When did I?"

"When didn't you? It was you as always give Old Orlick a bad name to her."

"You gave it to yourself; you gained it for yourself. I could have done you no harm, if you had done yourself none."

"You're a liar. And you'll take any pains, and spend any money, to drive me out of this country, will you?" said he, repeating my words to Biddy in the last interview I had with her. "Now, I'll tell you a piece of information. It was never so well worth your while to get me out of this country as it is to-night. Ah! If it was all your money twenty times told, to the last brass farden!" As he shook his heavy hand at me, with his mouth snarling like a tiger's, I felt that it was true.

"What are you going to do to me?"

"I'm a going," said he, bringing his fist down upon the table with a heavy blow, and rising as the blow fell to give it greater force,—"I'm a going to have your life!"

He leaned forward staring at me, slowly unclenched his hand and drew it across his mouth as if his mouth watered for me, and sat down again.

"You was always in Old Orlick's way since ever you was a child. You goes out of his way this present night. He'll have no more on you. You're dead."

I felt that I had come to the brink of my grave. For a moment I looked wildly round my trap for any chance of escape; but there was none.

"More than that," said he, folding his arms on the table again, "I won't have a rag of you, I won't have a bone of you, left on earth. I'll put your body in the kiln,—I'd carry two such to it, on my Shoulders,—and, let people suppose what they may of you, they shall never know nothing."

My mind, with inconceivable rapidity followed out all the consequences of such a death. Estella's father would believe I had deserted him, would be taken, would die accusing me; even Herbert would doubt me, when he compared the letter I had left for him with the fact that I had called at Miss Havisham's gate for only a moment; Joe and Biddy would never know how sorry I had been that night, none would ever know what I had suffered, how true I had meant to be, what an agony I had passed through. The death close before me was terrible, but far more terrible than death was the dread of being misremembered after death. And so quick were my thoughts, that I saw myself despised by unborn generations,—Estella's children, and their children,—while the wretch's words were yet on his lips.

"Now, wolf," said he, "afore I kill you like any other beast,—which is wot I mean to do and wot I have tied you up for,—I'll have a good look at you and a good goad at you. O you enemy!"

It had passed through my thoughts to cry out for help again; though few could know better than I, the solitary nature of the spot, and the hopelessness of aid. But as he sat gloating over me, I was supported by a scornful detestation of him that sealed my lips. Above all things, I resolved that I would not entreat him, and that I would die making some last poor resistance to him. Softened as my thoughts of all the rest of men were in that dire extremity; humbly beseeching pardon, as I did, of Heaven; melted at heart, as I was, by the thought that I had taken no farewell, and never now could take farewell of those who were dear to me, or could explain myself to them, or ask for their compassion on my miserable errors,—still, if I could have killed him, even in dying, I would have done it.

He had been drinking, and his eyes were red and bloodshot. Around his neck was slung a tin bottle, as I had often seen his meat and drink slung about him in other days. He brought the bottle to his lips, and took a fiery drink from it; and I smelt the strong spirits that I saw flash into his face.

"Wolf!" said he, folding his arms again, "Old Orlick's a going to tell you somethink. It was you as did for your shrew sister."

Again my mind, with its former inconceivable rapidity, had exhausted the whole subject of the attack upon my sister, her illness, and her death, before his slow and hesitating speech had formed these words.

"It was you, villain," said I.

"I tell you it was your doing,—I tell you it was done through you," he retorted, catching up the gun, and making a blow with the stock at the vacant air between us. "I come upon her from behind, as I come upon you to-night. I giv' it her! I left her for dead, and if there had been a limekiln as nigh her as there is now nigh you, she shouldn't have come to life again. But it warn't Old Orlick as did it; it was you. You was favored, and he was bullied and beat. Old Orlick bullied and beat, eh? Now you pays for it. You done it; now you pays for it."

He drank again, and became more ferocious. I saw by his tilting of the bottle that there was no great quantity left in it. I distinctly understood that he was working himself up with its contents to make an end of me. I knew that every drop it held was a drop of my life. I knew that when I was changed into a part of the vapor that had crept towards me but a little while before, like my own warning ghost, he would do as he had done in my sister's case,—make all haste to the town, and be seen slouching about there drinking at the alehouses. My rapid mind pursued him to the town, made a picture of the street with him in it, and contrasted its lights and life with the lonely marsh and the white vapor creeping over it, into which I should have dissolved.

It was not only that I could have summed up years and years and years while he said a dozen words, but that what he did say presented pictures to me, and not mere words. In the excited and exalted state of my brain, I could not think of a place without seeing it, or of persons without seeing them. It is impossible to overstate the vividness of these images, and yet I was so intent, all the time, upon him himself,—who would not be intent on the tiger crouching to spring!—that I knew of the slightest action of his fingers.

When he had drunk this second time, he rose from the bench on which he sat, and pushed the table aside. Then, he took up the candle, and, shading it with his murderous hand so as to throw its light on me, stood before me, looking at me and enjoying the sight.

"Wolf, I'll tell you something more. It was Old Orlick as you tumbled over on your stairs that night."

I saw the staircase with its extinguished lamps. I saw the shadows of the heavy stair-rails, thrown by the watchman's lantern on the wall. I saw the rooms that I was never to see again; here, a door half open; there, a door closed; all the articles of furniture around.

"And why was Old Orlick there? I'll tell you something more, wolf. You and her have pretty well hunted me out of this country, so far as getting a easy living in it goes, and I've took up with new companions, and new masters. Some of 'em writes my letters when I wants 'em wrote,—do you mind?—writes my letters, wolf! They writes fifty hands; they're not like sneaking you, as writes but one. I've had a firm mind and a firm will to have your life, since you was down here at your sister's burying. I han't seen a way to get you safe, and I've looked arter you to know your ins and outs. For, says Old Orlick to himself, 'Somehow or another I'll have him!' What! When I looks for you, I finds your uncle Provis, eh?"

Mill Pond Bank, and Chinks's Basin, and the Old Green Copper Rope-walk, all so clear and plain! Provis in his rooms, the signal whose use was over, pretty Clara, the good motherly woman, old Bill Barley on his back, all drifting by, as on the swift stream of my life fast running out to sea!

"You with a uncle too! Why, I know'd you at Gargery's when you was so small a wolf that I could have took your weazen betwixt this finger and thumb and chucked you away dead (as I'd thoughts o' doing, odd times, when I see you loitering amongst the pollards on a Sunday), and you hadn't found no uncles then. No, not you! But when Old Orlick come for to hear that your uncle Provis had most like wore the leg-iron wot Old Orlick had picked up, filed asunder, on these meshes ever so many year ago, and wot he kep by him till he dropped your sister with it, like a bullock, as he means to drop you—hey?—when he come for to hear that—hey?"

In his savage taunting, he flared the candle so close at me that I turned my face aside to save it from the flame.

"Ah!" he cried, laughing, after doing it again, "the burnt child dreads the fire! Old Orlick knowed you was burnt, Old Orlick knowed you was smuggling your uncle Provis away, Old Orlick's a match for you and know'd you'd come to-night! Now I'll tell you something more, wolf, and this ends it. There's them that's as good a match for your uncle Provis as Old Orlick has been for you. Let him 'ware them, when he's lost his nevvy! Let him 'ware them, when no man can't find a rag of his dear relation's clothes, nor yet a bone of his body. There's them that can't and that won't have Magwitch,—yes, I know the name!—alive in the same land with them, and that's had such sure information of him when he was alive in another land, as that he couldn't and shouldn't leave it unbeknown and put them in danger. P'raps it's them that writes fifty hands, and that's not like sneaking you as writes but one. 'Ware Compeyson, Magwitch, and the gallows!"

He flared the candle at me again, smoking my face and hair, and for an instant blinding me, and turned his powerful back as he replaced the light on the table. I had thought a prayer, and had been with Joe and Biddy and Herbert, before he turned towards me again.

There was a clear space of a few feet between the table and the opposite wall. Within this space, he now slouched backwards and forwards. His great strength seemed to sit stronger upon him than ever before, as he did this with his hands hanging loose and heavy at his sides, and with his eyes scowling at me. I had no grain of hope left. Wild as my inward hurry was, and wonderful the force of the pictures that rushed by me instead of thoughts, I could yet clearly understand that, unless he had resolved that I was within a few moments of surely perishing out of all human knowledge, he would never have told me what he had told.

Of a sudden, he stopped, took the cork out of his bottle, and tossed it away. Light as it was, I heard it fall like a plummet. He swallowed slowly, tilting up the bottle by little and little, and now he looked at me no more. The last few drops of liquor he poured into the palm of his hand, and licked up. Then, with a sudden hurry of violence and swearing horribly, he threw the bottle from him, and stooped; and I saw in his hand a stone-hammer with a long heavy handle.

The resolution I had made did not desert me, for, without uttering one vain word of appeal to him, I shouted out with all my might, and struggled with all my might. It was only my head and my legs that I could move, but to that extent I struggled with all the force, until then unknown, that was within me. In the same instant I heard responsive shouts, saw figures and a gleam of light dash in at the door, heard voices and tumult, and saw Orlick emerge from a struggle of men, as if it were tumbling water, clear the table at a leap, and fly out into the night.

After a blank, I found that I was lying unbound, on the floor, in the same place, with my head on some one's knee. My eyes were fixed on the ladder against the wall, when I came to myself,—had opened on it before my mind saw it,—and thus as I recovered consciousness, I knew that I was in the place where I had lost it.

Too indifferent at first, even to look round and ascertain who supported me, I was lying looking at the ladder, when there came between me and it a face. The face of Trabb's boy!

"I think he's all right!" said Trabb's boy, in a sober voice; "but ain't he just pale though!"

At these words, the face of him who supported me looked over into mine, and I saw my supporter to be—

"Herbert! Great Heaven!"

"Softly," said Herbert. "Gently, Handel. Don't be too eager."

"And our old comrade, Startop!" I cried, as he too bent over me.

"Remember what he is going to assist us in," said Herbert, "and be calm."

The allusion made me spring up; though I dropped again from the pain in my arm. "The time has not gone by, Herbert, has it? What night is to-night? How long have I been here?" For, I had a strange and strong misgiving that I had been lying there a long time—a day and a night,—two days and nights,—more.

"The time has not gone by. It is still Monday night."

"Thank God!"

"And you have all to-morrow, Tuesday, to rest in," said Herbert. "But you can't help groaning, my dear Handel. What hurt have you got? Can you stand?"

"Yes, yes," said I, "I can walk. I have no hurt but in this throbbing arm."

They laid it bare, and did what they could. It was violently swollen and inflamed, and I could scarcely endure to have it touched. But, they tore up their handkerchiefs to make fresh bandages, and carefully replaced it in the sling, until we could get to the town and obtain some cooling lotion to put upon it. In a little while we had shut the door of the dark and empty sluice-house, and were passing through the quarry on our way back. Trabb's boy—Trabb's overgrown young man now—went before us with a lantern, which was the light I had seen come in at the door. But, the moon was a good two hours higher than when I had last seen the sky, and the night, though rainy, was much lighter. The white vapor of the kiln was passing from us as we went by, and as I had thought a prayer before, I thought a thanksgiving now.

Entreating Herbert to tell me how he had come to my rescue,—which at first he had flatly refused to do, but had insisted on my remaining quiet,—I learnt that I had in my hurry dropped the letter, open, in our chambers, where he, coming home to bring with him Startop whom he had met in the street on his way to me, found it, very soon after I was gone. Its tone made him uneasy, and the more so because of the inconsistency between it and the hasty letter I had left for him. His uneasiness increasing instead of subsiding, after a quarter of an hour's consideration, he set off for the coach-office with Startop, who volunteered his company, to make inquiry when the next coach went down. Finding that the afternoon coach was gone, and finding that his uneasiness grew into positive alarm, as obstacles came in his way, he resolved to follow in a post-chaise. So he and Startop arrived at the Blue Boar, fully expecting there to find me, or tidings of me; but, finding neither, went on to Miss Havisham's, where they lost me. Hereupon they went back to the hotel (doubtless at about the time when I was hearing the popular local version of my own story) to refresh themselves and to get some one to guide them out upon the marshes. Among the loungers under the Boar's archway happened to be Trabb's Boy,—true to his ancient habit of happening to be everywhere where he had no business,—and Trabb's boy had seen me passing from Miss Havisham's in the direction of my dining-place. Thus Trabb's boy became their guide, and with him they went out to the sluice-house, though by the town way to the marshes, which I had avoided. Now, as they went along, Herbert reflected, that I might, after all, have been brought there on some genuine and serviceable errand tending to Provis's safety, and, bethinking himself that in that case interruption must be mischievous, left his guide and Startop on the edge of the quarry, and went on by himself, and stole round the house two or three times, endeavouring to ascertain whether all was right within. As he could hear nothing but indistinct sounds of one deep rough voice (this was while my mind was so busy), he even at last began to doubt whether I was there, when suddenly I cried out loudly, and he answered the cries, and rushed in, closely followed by the other two.

When I told Herbert what had passed within the house, he was for our immediately going before a magistrate in the town, late at night as it was, and getting out a warrant. But,

I had already considered that such a course, by detaining us there, or binding us to come back, might be fatal to Provis. There was no gainsaying this difficulty, and we relinquished all thoughts of pursuing Orlick at that time. For the present, under the circumstances, we deemed it prudent to make rather light of the matter to Trabb's boy; who, I am convinced, would have been much affected by disappointment, if he had known that his intervention saved me from the limekiln. Not that Trabb's boy was of a malignant nature, but that he had too much spare vivacity, and that it was in his constitution to want variety and excitement at anybody's expense. When we parted, I presented him with two guineas (which seemed to meet his views), and told him that I was sorry ever to have had an ill opinion of him (which made no impression on him at all).

Wednesday being so close upon us, we determined to go back to London that night, three in the post-chaise; the rather, as we should then be clear away before the night's adventure began to be talked of. Herbert got a large bottle of stuff for my arm; and by dint of having this stuff dropped over it all the night through, I was just able to bear its pain on the journey. It was daylight when we reached the Temple, and I went at once to bed, and lay in bed all day.

My terror, as I lay there, of falling ill, and being unfitted for to-morrow, was so besetting, that I wonder it did not disable me of itself. It would have done so, pretty surely, in conjunction with the mental wear and tear I had suffered, but for the unnatural strain upon me that to-morrow was. So anxiously looked forward to, charged with such consequences, its results so impenetrably hidden, though so near.

No precaution could have been more obvious than our refraining from communication with him that day; yet this again increased my restlessness. I started at every footstep and every sound, believing that he was discovered and taken, and this was the messenger to tell me so. I persuaded myself that I knew he was taken; that there was something more upon my mind than a fear or a presentiment; that the fact had occurred, and I had a mysterious knowledge of it. As the days wore on, and no ill news came, as the day closed in and darkness fell, my overshadowing dread of being disabled by illness before to-morrow morning altogether mastered me. My burning arm throbbed, and my burning head throbbed, and I fancied I was beginning to wander. I counted up to high numbers, to make sure of myself, and repeated passages that I knew in prose and verse. It happened sometimes that in the mere escape of a fatigued mind, I dozed for some moments or forgot; then I would say to myself with a start, "Now it has come, and I am turning delirious!"

They kept me very quiet all day, and kept my arm constantly dressed, and gave me cooling drinks. Whenever I fell asleep, I awoke with the notion I had had in the sluice-house, that a long time had elapsed and the opportunity to save him was gone. About midnight I got out of bed and went to Herbert, with the conviction that I had been asleep for four-and-twenty hours, and that Wednesday was past. It was the last self-exhausting effort of my fretfulness, for after that I slept soundly.

Wednesday morning was dawning when I looked out of window. The winking lights upon the bridges were already pale, the coming sun was like a marsh of fire on the horizon. The river, still dark and mysterious, was spanned by bridges that were turning coldly gray, with here and there at top a warm touch from the burning in the sky. As I looked along the clustered roofs, with church-towers and spires shooting into the unusually clear air, the sun rose up, and a veil seemed to be drawn from the river, and millions of sparkles burst out upon its waters.

From me too, a veil seemed to be drawn, and I felt strong and well.

Herbert lay asleep in his bed, and our old fellow-student lay asleep on the sofa. I could not dress myself without help; but I made up the fire, which was still burning, and got some coffee ready for them. In good time they too started up strong and well, and we admitted the sharp morning air at the windows, and looked at the tide that was still flowing towards us.

"When it turns at nine o'clock," said Herbert, cheerfully, "look out for us, and stand ready, you over there at Mill Pond Bank!"

Chapter LIV

It was one of those March days when the sun shines hot and the wind blows cold: when it is summer in the light, and winter in the shade. We had our pea-coats with us, and I took a bag. Of all my worldly possessions I took no more than the few necessaries that filled the bag. Where I might go, what I might do, or when I might return, were questions utterly unknown to me; nor did I vex my mind with them, for it was wholly set on Provis's safety. I only wondered for the passing moment, as I stopped at the door and looked back, under what altered circumstances I should next see those rooms, if ever.

We loitered down to the Temple stairs, and stood loitering there, as if we were not quite decided to go upon the water at all. Of course, I had taken care that the boat should be ready and everything in order. After a little show of indecision, which there were none to see but the two or three amphibious creatures belonging to our Temple stairs, we went on board and cast off; Herbert in the bow, I steering. It was then about high-water,—half-past eight.

Our plan was this. The tide, beginning to run down at nine, and being with us until three, we intended still to creep on after it had turned, and row against it until dark. We should then be well in those long reaches below Gravesend, between Kent and Essex, where the river is broad and solitary, where the water-side inhabitants are very few, and where lone public-houses are scattered here and there, of which we could choose one for a resting-place. There, we meant to lie by all night. The steamer for Hamburg and the steamer for Rotterdam would start from London at about nine on Thursday morning. We should know at what time to expect them, according to where we were, and would hail the first; so that, if by any accident we were not taken abroad, we should have another chance. We knew the distinguishing marks of each vessel.

The relief of being at last engaged in the execution of the purpose was so great to me that I felt it difficult to realize the condition in which I had been a few hours before. The crisp air, the sunlight, the movement on the river, and the moving river itself,—the road that ran with us, seeming to sympathize with us, animate us, and encourage us on,—freshened me with new hope. I felt mortified to be of so little use in the boat; but, there were few better oarsmen than my two friends, and they rowed with a steady stroke that was to last all day.

At that time, the steam-traffic on the Thames was far below its present extent, and watermen's boats were far more numerous. Of barges, sailing colliers, and coasting-traders, there were perhaps, as many as now; but of steam-ships, great and small, not a tithe or a twentieth part so many. Early as it was, there were plenty of scullers going here and there that morning, and plenty of barges dropping down with the tide; the navigation of the river between bridges, in an open boat, was a much easier and commoner matter in those days than it is in these; and we went ahead among many skiffs and wherries briskly.

Old London Bridge was soon passed, and old Billingsgate Market with its oyster-boats and Dutchmen, and the White Tower and Traitor's Gate, and we were in among the tiers of shipping. Here were the Leith, Aberdeen, and Glasgow steamers, loading and unloading goods, and looking immensely high out of the water as we passed alongside; here, were colliers by the score and score, with the coal-whippers plunging off stages on deck, as counterweights to measures of coal swinging up, which were then rattled over the side into barges; here, at her moorings was to-morrow's steamer for Rotterdam, of which we took good notice; and here to-morrow's for Hamburg, under whose bowsprit we crossed. And now I, sitting in the stern, could see, with a faster beating heart, Mill Pond Bank and Mill Pond stairs.

"Is he there?" said Herbert.

"Not yet."

"Right! He was not to come down till he saw us. Can you see his signal?"

"Not well from here; but I think I see it.—Now I see him! Pull both. Easy, Herbert. Oars!"

We touched the stairs lightly for a single moment, and he was on board, and we were off again. He had a boat-cloak with him, and a black canvas bag; and he looked as like a river-pilot as my heart could have wished.

"Dear boy!" he said, putting his arm on my shoulder, as he took his seat. "Faithful dear boy, well done. Thankye, thankye!"

Again among the tiers of shipping, in and out, avoiding rusty chain-cables frayed hempen hawsers and bobbing buoys, sinking for the moment floating broken baskets, scattering floating chips of wood and shaving, cleaving floating scum of coal, in and out, under the figure-head of the John of Sunderland making a speech to the winds (as is done by many Johns), and the Betsy of Yarmouth with a firm formality of bosom and her knobby eyes starting two inches out of her head; in and out, hammers going in ship-builders' yards, saws going at timber, clashing engines going at things unknown, pumps going in leaky ships, capstans going, ships going out to sea, and unintelligible sea-creatures roaring curses over the bulwarks at respondent lightermen, in and out,—out at last upon the clearer river, where the ships' boys might take their fenders in, no longer fishing in troubled waters with them over the side, and where the festooned sails might fly out to the wind.

At the stairs where we had taken him abroad, and ever since, I had looked warily for any token of our being suspected. I had seen none. We certainly had not been, and at that time as certainly we were not either attended or followed by any boat. If we had been waited on by any boat, I should have run in to shore, and have obliged her to go on, or to make her purpose evident. But we held our own without any appearance of molestation.

He had his boat-cloak on him, and looked, as I have said, a natural part of the scene. It was remarkable (but perhaps the wretched life he had led accounted for it) that he was the least anxious of any of us. He was not indifferent, for he told me that he hoped to live to see his gentleman one of the best of gentlemen in a foreign country; he was not disposed to be passive or resigned, as I understood it; but he had no notion of meeting danger half way. When it came upon him, he confronted it, but it must come before he troubled himself.

"If you knowed, dear boy," he said to me, "what it is to sit here alonger my dear boy and have my smoke, arter having been day by day betwixt four walls, you'd envy me. But you don't know what it is."

"I think I know the delights of freedom," I answered.

"Ah," said he, shaking his head gravely. "But you don't know it equal to me. You must have been under lock and key, dear boy, to know it equal to me,—but I ain't a going to be low."

It occurred to me as inconsistent, that, for any mastering idea, he should have endangered his freedom, and even his life. But I reflected that perhaps freedom without danger was too much apart from all the habit of his existence to be to him what it would be to another man. I was not far out, since he said, after smoking a little:—

"You see, dear boy, when I was over yonder, t'other side the world, I was always a looking to this side; and it come flat to be there, for all I was a growing rich. Everybody knowed Magwitch, and Magwitch could come, and Magwitch could go, and nobody's head would be troubled about him. They ain't so easy concerning me here, dear boy,—wouldn't be, leastwise, if they knowed where I was."

"If all goes well," said I, "you will be perfectly free and safe again within a few hours."

"Well," he returned, drawing a long breath, "I hope so."

"And think so?"

He dipped his hand in the water over the boat's gunwale, and said, smiling with that softened air upon him which was not new to me:—

"Ay, I s'pose I think so, dear boy. We'd be puzzled to be more quiet and easy-going than we are at present. But—it's a flowing so soft and pleasant through the water, p'raps, as makes me think it—I was a thinking through my smoke just then, that we can no more see to the bottom of the next few hours than we can see to the bottom of this river what I catches hold of. Nor yet we can't no more hold their tide than I can hold this. And it's run through my fingers and gone, you see!" holding up his dripping hand.

"But for your face I should think you were a little despondent," said I.

"Not a bit on it, dear boy! It comes of flowing on so quiet, and of that there rippling at the boat's head making a sort of a Sunday tune. Maybe I'm a growing a trifle old besides."

He put his pipe back in his mouth with an undisturbed expression of face, and sat as composed and contented as if we were already out of England. Yet he was as submissive to a word of advice as if he had been in constant terror; for, when we ran ashore to get some bottles of beer into the boat, and he was stepping out, I hinted that I thought he would be safest where he was, and he said. "Do you, dear boy?" and quietly sat down again.

The air felt cold upon the river, but it was a bright day, and the sunshine was very cheering. The tide ran strong, I took care to lose none of it, and our steady stroke carried us on thoroughly well. By imperceptible degrees, as the tide ran out, we lost more and more of the nearer woods and hills, and dropped lower and lower between the muddy banks, but the tide was yet with us when we were off Gravesend. As our charge was wrapped in his cloak, I purposely passed within a boat or two's length of the floating Custom House, and so out to catch the stream, alongside of two emigrant ships, and under the bows of a large transport with troops on the forecastle looking down at us. And soon the tide began to slacken, and the craft lying at anchor to swing, and presently they had all swung round, and the ships that were taking advantage of the new tide to get up to the Pool began to crowd upon us in a fleet, and we kept under the shore, as much out of the strength of the tide now as we could, standing carefully off from low shallows and mudbanks.

Our oarsmen were so fresh, by dint of having occasionally let her drive with the tide for a minute or two, that a quarter of an hour's rest proved full as much as they wanted. We got ashore among some slippery stones while we ate and drank what we had with us, and looked about. It was like my own marsh country, flat and monotonous, and with a dim horizon; while the winding river turned and turned, and the great floating buoys upon it turned and turned, and everything else seemed stranded and still. For now the last of the fleet of ships was round the last low point we had headed; and the last green barge, straw-laden, with a brown sail, had followed; and some ballast-lighters, shaped like a child's first rude imitation of a boat, lay low in the mud; and a little squat shoal-lighthouse on open piles stood crippled in the mud on stilts and crutches; and slimy stakes stuck out of the mud, and slimy stones stuck out of the mud, and red landmarks and tidemarks stuck out of the mud, and an old landing-stage and an old roofless building slipped into the mud, and all about us was stagnation and mud.

We pushed off again, and made what way we could. It was much harder work now, but Herbert and Startop persevered, and rowed and rowed and rowed until the sun went down. By that time the river had lifted us a little, so that we could see above the bank. There was the red sun, on the low level of the shore, in a purple haze, fast deepening into black; and there was the solitary flat marsh; and far away there were the rising grounds, between which and us there seemed to be no life, save here and there in the foreground a melancholy gull.

As the night was fast falling, and as the moon, being past the full, would not rise early, we held a little council; a short one, for clearly our course was to lie by at the first lonely tavern we could find. So, they plied their oars once more, and I looked out for anything like a house. Thus we held on, speaking little, for four or five dull miles. It was very cold, and, a collier coming by us, with her galley-fire smoking and flaring, looked like a comfortable home. The night was as dark by this time as it would be until morning; and what light we had, seemed to come more from the river than the sky, as the oars in their dipping struck at a few reflected stars.

At this dismal time we were evidently all possessed by the idea that we were followed. As the tide made, it flapped heavily at irregular intervals against the shore; and whenever such a sound came, one or other of us was sure to start, and look in that direction. Here and there, the set of the current had worn down the bank into a little creek, and we were all suspicious of such places, and eyed them nervously. Sometimes, "What was that ripple?" one of us would say in a low voice. Or another, "Is that a boat yonder?" And afterwards we would fall into a dead silence, and I would sit impatiently thinking with what an unusual amount of noise the oars worked in the thowels.

At length we descried a light and a roof, and presently afterwards ran alongside a little causeway made of stones that had been picked up hard by. Leaving the rest in the boat, I stepped ashore, and found the light to be in a window of a public-house. It was a dirty place enough, and I dare say not unknown to smuggling adventurers; but there was a good fire in the kitchen, and there were eggs and bacon to eat, and various liquors to drink. Also, there were two double-bedded rooms,—"such as they were," the landlord said. No other company was in the house than the landlord, his wife, and a grizzled male creature, the "Jack" of the little causeway, who was as slimy and smeary as if he had been low-water mark too.

With this assistant, I went down to the boat again, and we all came ashore, and brought out the oars, and rudder and boat-hook, and all else, and hauled her up for the night. We made a very good meal by the kitchen fire, and then apportioned the bedrooms: Herbert and Startop were to occupy one; I and our charge the other. We found the air as carefully excluded from both, as if air were fatal to life; and there were more dirty clothes and bandboxes under the beds than I should have thought the family possessed. But we considered ourselves well off, notwithstanding, for a more solitary place we could not have found.

While we were comforting ourselves by the fire after our meal, the Jack—who was sitting in a corner, and who had a bloated pair of shoes on, which he had exhibited while we were eating our eggs and bacon, as interesting relics that he had taken a few days ago from the feet of a drowned seaman washed ashore—asked me if we had seen a four-oared galley going up with the tide? When I told him No, he said she must have gone down then, and yet she "took up too," when she left there.

"They must ha' thought better on't for some reason or another," said the Jack, "and gone down."

"A four-oared galley, did you say?" said I.

"A four," said the Jack, "and two sitters."

"Did they come ashore here?"

"They put in with a stone two-gallon jar for some beer. I'd ha' been glad to pison the beer myself," said the Jack, "or put some rattling physic in it."

"Why?"

"I know why," said the Jack. He spoke in a slushy voice, as if much mud had washed into his throat.

"He thinks," said the landlord, a weakly meditative man with a pale eye, who seemed to rely greatly on his Jack,—"he thinks they was, what they wasn't."

"I knows what I thinks," observed the Jack.

"You thinks Custum 'Us, Jack?" said the landlord.

"I do," said the Jack.

"Then you're wrong, Jack."

"AM I!"

In the infinite meaning of his reply and his boundless confidence in his views, the Jack took one of his bloated shoes off, looked into it, knocked a few stones out of it on the kitchen floor, and put it on again. He did this with the air of a Jack who was so right that he could afford to do anything.

"Why, what do you make out that they done with their buttons then, Jack?" asked the landlord, vacillating weakly.

"Done with their buttons?" returned the Jack. "Chucked 'em overboard. Swallered 'em.

657

Sowed 'em, to come up small salad. Done with their buttons!"

"Don't be cheeky, Jack," remonstrated the landlord, in a melancholy and pathetic way.

"A Custum 'Us officer knows what to do with his Buttons," said the Jack, repeating the obnoxious word with the greatest contempt, "when they comes betwixt him and his own light. A four and two sitters don't go hanging and hovering, up with one tide and down with another, and both with and against another, without there being Custum 'Us at the bottom of it." Saying which he went out in disdain; and the landlord, having no one to reply upon, found it impracticable to pursue the subject.

This dialogue made us all uneasy, and me very uneasy. The dismal wind was muttering round the house, the tide was flapping at the shore, and I had a feeling that we were caged and threatened. A four-oared galley hovering about in so unusual a way as to attract this notice was an ugly circumstance that I could not get rid of. When I had induced Provis to go up to bed, I went outside with my two companions (Startop by this time knew the state of the case), and held another council. Whether we should remain at the house until near the steamer's time, which would be about one in the afternoon, or whether we should put off early in the morning, was the question we discussed. On the whole we deemed it the better course to lie where we were, until within an hour or so of the steamer's time, and then to get out in her track, and drift easily with the tide. Having settled to do this, we returned into the house and went to bed.

I lay down with the greater part of my clothes on, and slept well for a few hours. When I awoke, the wind had risen, and the sign of the house (the Ship) was creaking and banging about, with noises that startled me. Rising softly, for my charge lay fast asleep, I looked out of the window. It commanded the causeway where we had hauled up our boat, and, as my eyes adapted themselves to the light of the clouded moon, I saw two men looking into her. They passed by under the window, looking at nothing else, and they did not go down to the landing-place which I could discern to be empty, but struck across the marsh in the direction of the Nore.

My first impulse was to call up Herbert, and show him the two men going away. But reflecting, before I got into his room, which was at the back of the house and adjoined mine, that he and Startop had had a harder day than I, and were fatigued, I forbore. Going back to my window, I could see the two men moving over the marsh. In that light, however, I soon lost them, and, feeling very cold, lay down to think of the matter, and fell asleep again.

We were up early. As we walked to and fro, all four together, before breakfast, I deemed it right to recount what I had seen. Again our charge was the least anxious of the party. It was very likely that the men belonged to the Custom House, he said quietly, and that they had no thought of us. I tried to persuade myself that it was so,—as, indeed, it might easily be. However, I proposed that he and I should walk away together to a distant point we could see, and that the boat should take us aboard there, or as near there as might prove feasible, at about noon. This being considered a good precaution, soon after breakfast he and I set forth, without saying anything at the tavern.

He smoked his pipe as we went along, and sometimes stopped to clap me on the shoulder. One would have supposed that it was I who was in danger, not he, and that he was reassuring me. We spoke very little. As we approached the point, I begged him to remain in a sheltered place, while I went on to reconnoitre; for it was towards it that the men had passed in the night. He complied, and I went on alone. There was no boat off the point, nor any boat drawn up anywhere near it, nor were there any signs of the men having embarked there. But, to be sure, the tide was high, and there might have been some footpints under water.

When he looked out from his shelter in the distance, and saw that I waved my hat to him to come up, he rejoined me, and there we waited; sometimes lying on the bank, wrapped in our coats, and sometimes moving about to warm ourselves, until we saw our boat coming round. We got aboard easily, and rowed out into the track of the steamer. By that time it wanted but ten minutes of one o'clock, and we began to look out for her smoke.

But, it was half-past one before we saw her smoke, and soon afterwards we saw behind it the smoke of another steamer. As they were coming on at full speed, we got the two bags ready, and took that opportunity of saying good-bye to Herbert and Startop. We had all shaken hands cordially, and neither Herbert's eyes nor mine were quite dry, when I saw a four-oared galley shoot out from under the bank but a little way ahead of us, and row out into the same track.

A stretch of shore had been as yet between us and the steamer's smoke, by reason of the bend and wind of the river; but now she was visible, coming head on. I called to Herbert and Startop to keep before the tide, that she might see us lying by for her, and I adjured Provis to sit quite still, wrapped in his cloak. He answered cheerily, "Trust to me, dear boy," and sat like a statue. Meantime the galley, which was very skilfully handled, had crossed us, let us come up with her, and fallen alongside. Leaving just room enough for the play of the oars, she kept alongside, drifting when we drifted, and pulling a stroke or two when we pulled. Of the two sitters one held the rudder-lines, and looked at us attentively,—as did all the rowers; the other sitter was wrapped up, much as Provis was, and seemed to shrink, and whisper some instruction to the steerer as he looked at us. Not a word was spoken in either boat.

Startop could make out, after a few minutes, which steamer was first, and gave me the word "Hamburg," in a low voice, as we sat face to face. She was nearing us very fast, and the beating of her peddles grew louder and louder. I felt as if her shadow were absolutely upon us, when the galley hailed us. I answered.

"You have a returned Transport there," said the man who held the lines. "That's the man, wrapped in the cloak. His name is Abel Magwitch, otherwise Provis. I apprehend that man, and call upon him to surrender, and you to assist."

At the same moment, without giving any audible direction to his crew, he ran the galley abroad of us. They had pulled one sudden stroke ahead, had got their oars in, had run athwart us, and were holding on to our gunwale, before we knew what they were doing. This caused great confusion on board the steamer, and I heard them calling to us, and heard the order given to stop the paddles, and heard them stop, but felt her driving down upon us irresistibly. In the same moment, I saw the steersman of the galley lay his hand on his prisoner's shoulder, and saw that both boats were swinging round with the force of the tide, and saw that all hands on board the steamer were running forward quite frantically. Still, in the same moment, I saw the prisoner start up, lean across his captor, and pull the cloak from the neck of the shrinking sitter in the galley. Still in the same moment, I saw that the face disclosed, was the face of the other convict of long ago. Still, in the same moment, I saw the face tilt backward with a white terror on it that I shall never forget, and heard a great cry on board the steamer, and a loud splash in the water, and felt the boat sink from under me.

It was but for an instant that I seemed to struggle with a thousand mill-weirs and a thousand flashes of light; that instant past, I was taken on board the galley. Herbert was there, and Startop was there; but our boat was gone, and the two convicts were gone.

What with the cries aboard the steamer, and the furious blowing off of her steam, and her driving on, and our driving on, I could not at first distinguish sky from water or shore from shore; but the crew of the galley righted her with great speed, and, pulling certain swift strong strokes ahead, lay upon their oars, every man looking silently and eagerly at the water astern. Presently a dark object was seen in it, bearing towards us on the tide. No man spoke, but the steersman held up his hand, and all softly backed water, and kept the boat straight and true before it. As it came nearer, I saw it to be Magwitch, swimming, but not swimming freely. He was taken on board, and instantly manacled at the wrists and ankles.

The galley was kept steady, and the silent, eager look-out at the water was resumed. But, the Rotterdam steamer now came up, and apparently not understanding what had happened, came on at speed. By the time she had been hailed and stopped, both steamers were drifting away from us, and we were rising and falling in a troubled wake of water. The look-out was kept, long after all was still again and the two steamers were gone; but everybody knew that it was hopeless now.

At length we gave it up, and pulled under the shore towards the tavern we had lately left, where we were received with no little surprise. Here I was able to get some comforts for Magwitch,—Provis no longer,—who had received some very severe injury in the Chest, and a deep cut in the head.

He told me that he believed himself to have gone under the keel of the steamer, and to have been struck on the head in rising. The injury to his chest (which rendered his breathing extremely painful) he thought he had received against the side of the galley. He added that he did not pretend to say what he might or might not have done to Compeyson, but that, in the moment of his laying his hand on his cloak to identify him, that villain had staggered up and staggered back, and they had both gone overboard together, when the sudden wrenching of him (Magwitch) out of our boat, and the endeavor of his captor to keep him in it, had capsized us. He told me in a whisper that they had gone down fiercely locked in each other's arms, and that there had been a struggle under water, and that he had disengaged himself, struck out, and swum away.

I never had any reason to doubt the exact truth of what he thus told me. The officer who steered the galley gave the same account of their going overboard.

When I asked this officer's permission to change the prisoner's wet clothes by purchasing any spare garments I could get at the public-house, he gave it readily: merely observing that he must take charge of everything his prisoner had about him. So the pocket-book which had once been in my hands passed into the officer's. He further gave me leave to accompany the prisoner to London; but declined to accord that grace to my two friends.

The Jack at the Ship was instructed where the drowned man had gone down, and undertook to search for the body in the places where it was likeliest to come ashore. His interest in its recovery seemed to me to be much heightened when he heard that it had stockings on. Probably, it took about a dozen drowned men to fit him out completely; and that may have been the reason why the different articles of his dress were in various stages of decay.

We remained at the public-house until the tide turned, and then Magwitch was carried down to the galley and put on board. Herbert and Startop were to get to London by land, as soon as they could. We had a doleful parting, and when I took my place by Magwitch's side, I felt that that was my place henceforth while he lived.

For now, my repugnance to him had all melted away; and in the hunted, wounded, shackled creature who held my hand in his, I only saw a man who had meant to be my benefactor, and who had felt affectionately, gratefully, and generously, towards me with great constancy through a series of years. I only saw in him a much better man than I had been to Joe.

His breathing became more difficult and painful as the night drew on, and often he could not repress a groan. I tried to rest him on the arm I could use, in any easy position; but it was dreadful to think that I could not be sorry at heart for his being badly hurt, since it was unquestionably best that he should die. That there were, still living, people enough who were able and willing to identify him, I could not doubt. That he would be leniently treated, I could not hope. He who had been presented in the worst light at his trial, who had since broken prison and had been tried again, who had returned from transportation under a life sentence, and who had occasioned the death of the man who was the cause of his arrest.

As we returned towards the setting sun we had yesterday left behind us, and as the stream of our hopes seemed all running back, I told him how grieved I was to think that he had come home for my sake.

"Dear boy," he answered, "I'm quite content to take my chance. I've seen my boy, and he can be a gentleman without me."

No. I had thought about that, while we had been there side by side. No. Apart from any inclinations of my own, I understood Wemmick's hint now. I foresaw that, being convicted, his possessions would be forfeited to the Crown.

"Lookee here, dear boy," said he "It's best as a gentleman should not be knowed to belong to me now. Only come to see me as if you come by chance alonger Wemmick. Sit where I can see you when I am swore to, for the last o' many times, and I don't ask no more."

"I will never stir from your side," said I, "when I am suffered to be near you. Please God, I will be as true to you as you have been to me!"

I felt his hand tremble as it held mine, and he turned his face away as he lay in the bottom of the boat, and I heard that old sound in his throat,—softened now, like all the rest of him. It was a good thing that he had touched this point, for it put into my mind what I might not otherwise have thought of until too late,—that he need never know how his hopes of enriching me had perished.

Chapter LV

He was taken to the Police Court next day, and would have been immediately committed for trial, but that it was necessary to send down for an old officer of the prison-ship from which he had once escaped, to speak to his identity. Nobody doubted it; but Compeyson, who had meant to depose to it, was tumbling on the tides, dead, and it happened that there was not at that time any prison officer in London who could give the required evidence. I had gone direct to Mr. Jaggers at his private house, on my arrival over night, to retain his assistance, and Mr. Jaggers on the prisoner's behalf would admit nothing. It was the sole resource; for he told me that the case must be over in five minutes when the witness was there, and that no power on earth could prevent its going against us.

I imparted to Mr. Jaggers my design of keeping him in ignorance of the fate of his wealth. Mr. Jaggers was querulous and angry with me for having "let it slip through my fingers," and said we must memorialize by and by, and try at all events for some of it. But he did not conceal from me that, although there might be many cases in which the forfeiture would not be exacted, there were no circumstances in this case to make it one of them. I understood that very well. I was not related to the outlaw, or connected with him by any recognizable tie; he had put his hand to no writing or settlement in my favor before his apprehension, and to do so now would be idle. I had no claim, and I finally resolved, and ever afterwards abided by the resolution, that my heart should never be sickened with the hopeless task of attempting to establish one.

There appeared to be reason for supposing that the drowned informer had hoped for a reward out of this forfeiture, and had obtained some accurate knowledge of Magwitch's affairs. When his body was found, many miles from the scene of his death, and so horribly disfigured that he was only recognizable by the contents of his pockets, notes were still legible, folded in a case he carried. Among these were the name of a banking-house in New South Wales, where a sum of money was, and the designation of certain lands of considerable value. Both these heads of information were in a list that Magwitch, while in prison, gave to Mr. Jaggers, of the possessions he supposed I should inherit. His ignorance, poor fellow, at last served him; he never mistrusted but that my inheritance was quite safe, with Mr. Jaggers's aid.

After three days' delay, during which the crown prosecution stood over for the production of the witness from the prison-ship, the witness came, and completed the easy case. He was committed to take his trial at the next Sessions, which would come on in a month.

It was at this dark time of my life that Herbert returned home one evening, a good deal cast down, and said,—

"My dear Handel, I fear I shall soon have to leave you."

His partner having prepared me for that, I was less surprised than he thought.

"We shall lose a fine opportunity if I put off going to Cairo, and I am very much afraid I must go, Handel, when you most need me."

"Herbert, I shall always need you, because I shall always love you; but my need is no greater now than at another time."

"You will be so lonely."

"I have not leisure to think of that," said I. "You know that I am always with him to the full extent of the time allowed, and that I should be with him all day long, if I could. And when I come away from him, you know that my thoughts are with him."

The dreadful condition to which he was brought, was so appalling to both of us, that we could not refer to it in plainer words.

"My dear fellow," said Herbert, "let the near prospect of our separation—for, it is very near—be my justification for troubling you about yourself. Have you thought of your future?"

"No, for I have been afraid to think of any future."

"But yours cannot be dismissed; indeed, my dear dear Handel, it must not be dismissed. I wish you would enter on it now, as far as a few friendly words go, with me."

"I will," said I.

"In this branch house of ours, Handel, we must have a—"

I saw that his delicacy was avoiding the right word, so I said, "A clerk."

"A clerk. And I hope it is not at all unlikely that he may expand (as a clerk of your acquaintance has expanded) into a partner. Now, Handel,—in short, my dear boy, will you come to me?"

There was something charmingly cordial and engaging in the manner in which after saying "Now, Handel," as if it were the grave beginning of a portentous business exordium, he had suddenly given up that tone, stretched out his honest hand, and spoken like a schoolboy.

"Clara and I have talked about it again and again," Herbert pursued, "and the dear little thing begged me only this evening, with tears in her eyes, to say to you that, if you will live with us when we come together, she will do her best to make you happy, and to convince her husband's friend that he is her friend too. We should get on so well, Handel!"

I thanked her heartily, and I thanked him heartily, but said I could not yet make sure of joining him as he so kindly offered. Firstly, my mind was too preoccupied to be able to take in the subject clearly. Secondly,—Yes! Secondly, there was a vague something lingering in my thoughts that will come out very near the end of this slight narrative.

"But if you thought, Herbert, that you could, without doing any injury to your business, leave the question open for a little while—"

"For any while," cried Herbert. "Six months, a year!"

"Not so long as that," said I. "Two or three months at most."

Herbert was highly delighted when we shook hands on this arrangement, and said he could now take courage to tell me that he believed he must go away at the end of the week.

"And Clara?" said I.

"The dear little thing," returned Herbert, "holds dutifully to her father as long as he lasts; but he won't last long. Mrs. Whimple confides to me that he is certainly going."

"Not to say an unfeeling thing," said I, "he cannot do better than go."

"I am afraid that must be admitted," said Herbert; "and then I shall come back for the dear little thing, and the dear little thing and I will walk quietly into the nearest church. Remember! The blessed darling comes of no family, my dear Handel, and never looked into the red book, and hasn't a notion about her grandpapa. What a fortune for the son of my mother!"

On the Saturday in that same week, I took my leave of Herbert,—full of bright hope, but sad and sorry to leave me,—as he sat on one of the seaport mail coaches. I went into a coffee-house to write a little note to Clara, telling her he had gone off, sending his love to her over and over again, and then went to my lonely home,—if it deserved the name; for it was now no home to me, and I had no home anywhere.

On the stairs I encountered Wemmick, who was coming down, after an unsuccessful application of his knuckles to my door. I had not seen him alone since the disastrous issue of the attempted flight; and he had come, in his private and personal capacity, to say a few words of explanation in reference to that failure.

"The late Compeyson," said Wemmick, "had by little and little got at the bottom of half of the regular business now transacted; and it was from the talk of some of his people in trouble (some of his people being always in trouble) that I heard what I did. I kept my ears open, seeming to have them shut, until I heard that he was absent, and I thought that would be the best time for making the attempt. I can only suppose now, that it was a part of his policy, as a very clever man, habitually to deceive his own instruments. You don't blame me, I hope, Mr. Pip? I am sure I tried to serve you, with all my heart."

"I am as sure of that, Wemmick, as you can be, and I thank you most earnestly for all your interest and friendship."

"Thank you, thank you very much. It's a bad job," said Wemmick, scratching his head, "and I assure you I haven't been so cut up for a long time. What I look at is the sacrifice of so much portable property. Dear me!"

"What I think of, Wemmick, is the poor owner of the property."

"Yes, to be sure," said Wemmick. "Of course, there can be no objection to your being sorry for him, and I'd put down a five-pound note myself to get him out of it. But what I look at is this. The late Compeyson having been beforehand with him in intelligence of his return, and being so determined to bring him to book, I do not think he could have been saved. Whereas, the portable property certainly could have been saved. That's the difference between the property and the owner, don't you see?"

I invited Wemmick to come upstairs, and refresh himself with a glass of grog before walking to Walworth. He accepted the invitation. While he was drinking his moderate allowance, he said, with nothing to lead up to it, and after having appeared rather fidgety,—

"What do you think of my meaning to take a holiday on Monday, Mr. Pip?"

"Why, I suppose you have not done such a thing these twelve months."

"These twelve years, more likely," said Wemmick. "Yes. I'm going to take a holiday. More than that; I'm going to take a walk. More than that; I'm going to ask you to take a walk with me."

I was about to excuse myself, as being but a bad companion just then, when Wemmick anticipated me.

"I know your engagements," said he, "and I know you are out of sorts, Mr. Pip. But if you could oblige me, I should take it as a kindness. It ain't a long walk, and it's an early one. Say it might occupy you (including breakfast on the walk) from eight to twelve. Couldn't you stretch a point and manage it?"

He had done so much for me at various times, that this was very little to do for him. I said I could manage it,—would manage it,—and he was so very much pleased by my acquiescence, that I was pleased too. At his particular request, I appointed to call for him at the Castle at half past eight on Monday morning, and so we parted for the time.

Punctual to my appointment, I rang at the Castle gate on the Monday morning, and was received by Wemmick himself, who struck me as looking tighter than usual, and having a sleeker hat on. Within, there were two glasses of rum and milk prepared, and two biscuits. The Aged must have been stirring with the lark, for, glancing into the perspective of his bedroom, I observed that his bed was empty.

When we had fortified ourselves with the rum and milk and biscuits, and were going out for the walk with that training preparation on us, I was considerably surprised to see Wemmick take up a fishing-rod, and put it over his shoulder. "Why, we are not going fishing!" said I. "No," returned Wemmick, "but I like to walk with one."

I thought this odd; however, I said nothing, and we set off. We went towards Camberwell Green, and when we were thereabouts, Wemmick said suddenly,—

"Halloa! Here's a church!"

There was nothing very surprising in that; but again, I was rather surprised, when he said, as if he were animated by a brilliant idea,—

"Let's go in!"

We went in, Wemmick leaving his fishing-rod in the porch, and looked all round. In the mean time, Wemmick was diving into his coat-pockets, and getting something out of paper there.

"Halloa!" said he. "Here's a couple of pair of gloves! Let's put 'em on!"

As the gloves were white kid gloves, and as the post-office was widened to its utmost extent, I now began to have my strong suspicions. They were strengthened into certainty when I beheld the Aged enter at a side door, escorting a lady.

"Halloa!" said Wemmick. "Here's Miss Skiffins! Let's have a wedding."

That discreet damsel was attired as usual, except that she was now engaged in substituting for her green kid gloves a pair of white. The Aged was likewise occupied in preparing a similar sacrifice for the altar of Hymen. The old gentleman, however, experienced so much difficulty in getting his gloves on, that Wemmick found it necessary to put him with his back against a pillar, and then to get behind the pillar himself and pull away at them, while I for my part held the old gentleman round the waist, that he might present an equal and safe resistance. By dint of this ingenious scheme, his gloves were got on to perfection.

The clerk and clergyman then appearing, we were ranged in order at those fatal rails. True to his notion of seeming to do it all without preparation, I heard Wemmick say to himself, as he took something out of his waistcoat-pocket before the service began, "Halloa! Here's a ring!"

I acted in the capacity of backer, or best-man, to the bridegroom; while a little limp pew-opener in a soft bonnet like a baby's, made a feint of being the bosom friend of Miss Skiffins. The responsibility of giving the lady away devolved upon the Aged, which led to the clergyman's being unintentionally scandalized, and it happened thus. When he said, "Who giveth this woman to be married to this man?" the old gentleman, not in the least knowing what point of the ceremony we had arrived at, stood most amiably beaming at the ten commandments. Upon which, the clergyman said again, "WHO giveth this woman to be married to this man?" The old gentleman being still in a state of most estimable unconsciousness, the bridegroom cried out in his accustomed voice, "Now Aged P. you know; who giveth?" To which the Aged replied with great briskness, before saying that he gave, "All right, John, all right, my boy!" And the clergyman came to so gloomy a pause upon it, that I had doubts for the moment whether we should get completely married that day.

It was completely done, however, and when we were going out of church Wemmick took the cover off the font, and put his white gloves in it, and put the cover on again. Mrs. Wemmick, more heedful of the future, put her white gloves in her pocket and assumed her green. "Now, Mr. Pip," said Wemmick, triumphantly shouldering the fishing-rod as we came out, "let me ask you whether anybody would suppose this to be a wedding-party!"

Breakfast had been ordered at a pleasant little tavern, a mile or so away upon the rising ground beyond the green; and there was a bagatelle board in the room, in case we should desire to unbend our minds after the solemnity. It was pleasant to observe that Mrs. Wemmick no longer unwound Wemmick's arm when it adapted itself to her figure, but sat in a high-backed chair against the wall, like a violoncello in its case, and submitted to be embraced as that melodious instrument might have done.

We had an excellent breakfast, and when any one declined anything on table, Wemmick said, "Provided by contract, you know; don't be afraid of it!" I drank to the new couple, drank to the Aged, drank to the Castle, saluted the bride at parting, and made myself as agreeable as I could.

Wemmick came down to the door with me, and I again shook hands with him, and wished him joy.

"Thankee!" said Wemmick, rubbing his hands. "She's such a manager of fowls, you have no idea. You shall have some eggs, and judge for yourself. I say, Mr. Pip!" calling me back, and speaking low. "This is altogether a Walworth sentiment, please."

"I understand. Not to be mentioned in Little Britain," said I.

Wemmick nodded. "After what you let out the other day, Mr. Jaggers may as well not know of it. He might think my brain was softening, or something of the kind."

Chapter LVI

He lay in prison very ill, during the whole interval between his committal for trial and the coming round of the Sessions. He had broken two ribs, they had wounded one of his lungs, and he breathed with great pain and difficulty, which increased daily. It was a consequence of his hurt that he spoke so low as to be scarcely audible; therefore he spoke very little. But he was ever ready to listen to me; and it became the first duty of my life to say to him, and read to him, what I knew he ought to hear.

Being far too ill to remain in the common prison, he was removed, after the first day or so, into the infirmary. This gave me opportunities of being with him that I could not otherwise have had. And but for his illness he would have been put in irons, for he was regarded as a determined prison-breaker, and I know not what else.

Although I saw him every day, it was for only a short time; hence, the regularly recurring spaces of our separation were long enough to record on his face any slight changes that occurred in his physical state. I do not recollect that I once saw any change in it for the better; he wasted, and became slowly weaker and worse, day by day, from the day when the prison door closed upon him.

The kind of submission or resignation that he showed was that of a man who was tired out. I sometimes derived an impression, from his manner or from a whispered word or two which escaped him, that he pondered over the question whether he might have been a better man under better circumstances. But he never justified himself by a hint tending that way, or tried to bend the past out of its eternal shape.

It happened on two or three occasions in my presence, that his desperate reputation was alluded to by one or other of the people in attendance on him. A smile crossed his face then, and he turned his eyes on me with a trustful look, as if he were confident that I had seen some small redeeming touch in him, even so long ago as when I was a little child. As to all the rest, he was humble and contrite, and I never knew him complain.

When the Sessions came round, Mr. Jaggers caused an application to be made for the postponement of his trial until the following Sessions. It was obviously made with the assurance that he could not live so long, and was refused. The trial came on at once, and, when he was put to the bar, he was seated in a chair. No objection was made to my getting close to the dock, on the outside of it, and holding the hand that he stretched forth to me.

The trial was very short and very clear. Such things as could be said for him were said,— how he had taken to industrious habits, and had thriven lawfully and reputably. But nothing could unsay the fact that he had returned, and was there in presence of the Judge and Jury. It was impossible to try him for that, and do otherwise than find him guilty.

At that time, it was the custom (as I learnt from my terrible experience of that Sessions) to devote a concluding day to the passing of Sentences, and to make a finishing effect with the Sentence of Death. But for the indelible picture that my remembrance now holds before me, I could scarcely believe, even as I write these words, that I saw two-and-thirty men and women put before the Judge to receive that sentence together. Foremost among the two-and-thirty was he; seated, that he might get breath enough to keep life in him.

The whole scene starts out again in the vivid colors of the moment, down to the drops of April rain on the windows of the court, glittering in the rays of April sun. Penned in the dock, as I again stood outside it at the corner with his hand in mine, were the two-and-thirty men and women; some defiant, some stricken with terror, some sobbing and weeping, some covering their faces, some staring gloomily about. There had been shrieks from among the women convicts; but they had been stilled, and a hush had succeeded. The sheriffs with their great chains and nosegays, other civic gewgaws and monsters, criers, ushers, a great gallery full of people,—a large theatrical audience,—looked on, as the two-and-thirty and the Judge were solemnly confronted. Then the Judge addressed them. Among the wretched creatures before him whom he must single out for special address was one who almost from his infancy had been an offender against the laws; who, after repeated imprisonments and punishments, had been at length sentenced to exile for a term of years; and who, under circumstances of great violence and daring, had made his escape and been re-sentenced to exile for life. That miserable man would seem for a time to have become convinced of his errors, when far removed from the scenes of his old offences, and to have lived a peaceable and honest life. But in a fatal moment, yielding to those propensities and passions, the indulgence of which had so long rendered him a scourge to society, he had quitted his haven of rest and repentance, and had come back to the country where he was proscribed. Being here presently denounced, he had for a time succeeded in evading the officers of Justice, but being at length seized while in the act of flight, he had resisted them, and had—he best knew whether by express design, or in the blindness of his hardihood—caused the death of his denouncer, to whom his whole career was known. The appointed punishment for his return to the land that had cast him out, being Death, and his case being this aggravated case, he must prepare himself to Die.

The sun was striking in at the great windows of the court, through the glittering drops of rain upon the glass, and it made a broad shaft of light between the two-and-thirty and the Judge, linking both together, and perhaps reminding some among the audience how both were passing on, with absolute equality, to the greater Judgment that knoweth all things, and cannot err. Rising for a moment, a distinct speck of face in this way of light, the prisoner said, "My Lord, I have received my sentence of Death from the Almighty, but I bow to yours," and sat down again. There was some hushing, and the Judge went on with what he had to say to the rest. Then they were all formally doomed, and some of them were supported out, and some of them sauntered out with a haggard look of bravery, and a few nodded to the gallery, and two or three shook hands, and others went out chewing the fragments of herb they had taken from the sweet herbs lying about. He went last of all, because of having to be helped from his chair, and to go very slowly; and he held my hand while all the others were removed, and while the audience got up (putting their dresses right, as they might at church or elsewhere), and pointed down at this criminal or at that, and most of all at him and me.

I earnestly hoped and prayed that he might die before the Recorder's Report was made; but, in the dread of his lingering on, I began that night to write out a petition to the Home Secretary of State, setting forth my knowledge of him, and how it was that he had come back for my sake. I wrote it as fervently and pathetically as I could; and when I had finished it and sent it in, I wrote out other petitions to such men in authority as I hoped were the most merciful, and drew up one to the Crown itself. For several days and nights after he was sentenced I took no rest except when I fell asleep in my chair, but was wholly absorbed in these appeals. And after I had sent them in, I could not keep away from the places where they were, but felt as if they were more hopeful and less desperate when I was near them. In this unreasonable restlessness and pain of mind I would roam the streets of an evening, wandering by those offices and houses where I had left the petitions. To the present hour, the weary western streets of London on a cold, dusty spring night, with their ranges of stern, shut-up mansions, and their long rows of lamps, are melancholy to me from this association.

The daily visits I could make him were shortened now, and he was more strictly kept. Seeing, or fancying, that I was suspected of an intention of carrying poison to him, I asked to be searched before I sat down at his bedside, and told the officer who was always there, that I was willing to do anything that would assure him of the singleness of my designs. Nobody was hard with him or with me. There was duty to be done, and it was done, but not harshly. The officer always gave me the assurance that he was worse, and some other sick prisoners in the room, and some other prisoners who attended on them as sick nurses, (malefactors, but not incapable of kindness, God be thanked!) always joined in the same report.

As the days went on, I noticed more and more that he would lie placidly looking at the white ceiling, with an absence of light in his face until some word of mine brightened it for an instant, and then it would subside again. Sometimes he was almost or quite unable to speak, then he would answer me with slight pressures on my hand, and I grew to understand his meaning very well.

The number of the days had risen to ten, when I saw a greater change in him than I had seen yet. His eyes were turned towards the door, and lighted up as I entered.

"Dear boy," he said, as I sat down by his bed: "I thought you was late. But I knowed you couldn't be that."

"It is just the time," said I. "I waited for it at the gate."

"You always waits at the gate; don't you, dear boy?"

"Yes. Not to lose a moment of the time."

"Thank'ee dear boy, thank'ee. God bless you! You've never deserted me, dear boy."

I pressed his hand in silence, for I could not forget that I had once meant to desert him.

"And what's the best of all," he said, "you've been more comfortable alonger me, since I was under a dark cloud, than when the sun shone. That's best of all."

He lay on his back, breathing with great difficulty. Do what he would, and love me though he did, the light left his face ever and again, and a film came over the placid look at the white ceiling.

"Are you in much pain to-day?"

"I don't complain of none, dear boy."

"You never do complain."

He had spoken his last words. He smiled, and I understood his touch to mean that he wished to lift my hand, and lay it on his breast. I laid it there, and he smiled again, and put both his hands upon it.

The allotted time ran out, while we were thus; but, looking round, I found the governor of the prison standing near me, and he whispered, "You needn't go yet." I thanked him gratefully, and asked, "Might I speak to him, if he can hear me?"

The governor stepped aside, and beckoned the officer away. The change, though it was made without noise, drew back the film from the placid look at the white ceiling, and he looked most affectionately at me.

"Dear Magwitch, I must tell you now, at last. You understand what I say?"

A gentle pressure on my hand.

"You had a child once, whom you loved and lost."

A stronger pressure on my hand.

"She lived, and found powerful friends. She is living now. She is a lady and very beautiful. And I love her!"

With a last faint effort, which would have been powerless but for my yielding to it and assisting it, he raised my hand to his lips. Then, he gently let it sink upon his breast again, with his own hands lying on it. The placid look at the white ceiling came back, and passed away, and his head dropped quietly on his breast.

Mindful, then, of what we had read together, I thought of the two men who went up into the Temple to pray, and I knew there were no better words that I could say beside his bed, than "O Lord, be merciful to him a sinner!"

Chapter LVII

Now that I was left wholly to myself, I gave notice of my intention to quit the chambers in the Temple as soon as my tenancy could legally determine, and in the meanwhile to underlet them. At once I put bills up in the windows; for, I was in debt, and had scarcely any money, and began to be seriously alarmed by the state of my affairs. I ought rather to write that I should have been alarmed if I had had energy and concentration enough to help me to the clear perception of any truth beyond the fact that I was falling very ill. The late stress upon me had enabled me to put off illness, but not to put it away; I knew that it was coming on me now, and I knew very little else, and was even careless as to that.

For a day or two, I lay on the sofa, or on the floor,—anywhere, according as I happened to sink down,—with a heavy head and aching limbs, and no purpose, and no power. Then there came, one night which appeared of great duration, and which teemed with anxiety and horror; and when in the morning I tried to sit up in my bed and think of it, I found I could not do so.

Whether I really had been down in Garden Court in the dead of the night, groping about for the boat that I supposed to be there; whether I had two or three times come to myself on the staircase with great terror, not knowing how I had got out of bed; whether I had found myself lighting the lamp, possessed by the idea that he was coming up the stairs, and that the lights were blown out; whether I had been inexpressibly harassed by the distracted talking, laughing, and groaning of some one, and had half suspected those sounds to be of my own making; whether there had been a closed iron furnace in a dark corner of the room, and a voice had called out, over and over again, that Miss Havisham was consuming within it,—these were things that I tried to settle with myself and get into some order, as I lay that morning on my bed. But the vapor of a limekiln would come between me and them, disordering them all, and it was through the vapor at last that I saw two men looking at me.

"What do you want?" I asked, starting; "I don't know you."

"Well, sir," returned one of them, bending down and touching me on the shoulder, "this is a matter that you'll soon arrange, I dare say, but you're arrested."

"What is the debt?"

"Hundred and twenty-three pound, fifteen, six. Jeweller's account, I think."

"What is to be done?"

"You had better come to my house," said the man. "I keep a very nice house."

I made some attempt to get up and dress myself. When I next attended to them, they were standing a little off from the bed, looking at me. I still lay there.

"You see my state," said I. "I would come with you if I could; but indeed I am quite unable. If you take me from here, I think I shall die by the way."

Perhaps they replied, or argued the point, or tried to encourage me to believe that I was better than I thought. Forasmuch as they hang in my memory by only this one slender thread, I don't know what they did, except that they forbore to remove me.

That I had a fever and was avoided, that I suffered greatly, that I often lost my reason, that the time seemed interminable, that I confounded impossible existences with my own identity; that I was a brick in the house-wall, and yet entreating to be released from the giddy place where the builders had set me; that I was a steel beam of a vast engine, clashing and whirling over a gulf, and yet that I implored in my own person to have the engine stopped, and my part in it hammered off; that I passed through these phases of disease, I know of my own remembrance, and did in some sort know at the time. That I sometimes struggled with real people, in the belief that they were murderers, and that I would all at once comprehend that they meant to do me good, and would then sink exhausted in their arms, and suffer them to lay me down, I also knew at the time. But, above all, I knew that there was a constant tendency in all these people,—who, when I was very ill, would present all kinds of extraordinary transformations of the human face, and would be much dilated in size,—above all, I say, I knew that there was an extraordinary tendency in all these people, sooner or later, to settle down into the likeness of Joe.

After I had turned the worst point of my illness, I began to notice that while all its other features changed, this one consistent feature did not change. Whoever came about me, still settled down into Joe. I opened my eyes in the night, and I saw, in the great chair at the bedside, Joe. I opened my eyes in the day, and, sitting on the window-seat, smoking his pipe in the shaded open window, still I saw Joe. I asked for cooling drink, and the dear hand that gave it me was Joe's. I sank back on my pillow after drinking, and the face that looked so hopefully and tenderly upon me was the face of Joe.

At last, one day, I took courage, and said, "Is it Joe?"

And the dear old home-voice answered, "Which it air, old chap."

"O Joe, you break my heart! Look angry at me, Joe. Strike me, Joe. Tell me of my ingratitude. Don't be so good to me!"

For Joe had actually laid his head down on the pillow at my side, and put his arm round my neck, in his joy that I knew him.

"Which dear old Pip, old chap," said Joe, "you and me was ever friends. And when you're well enough to go out for a ride—what larks!"

After which, Joe withdrew to the window, and stood with his back towards me, wiping his eyes. And as my extreme weakness prevented me from getting up and going to him, I lay there, penitently whispering, "O God bless him! O God bless this gentle Christian man!"

Joe's eyes were red when I next found him beside me; but I was holding his hand, and we both felt happy.

"How long, dear Joe?"

"Which you meantersay, Pip, how long have your illness lasted, dear old chap?"

"Yes, Joe."

"It's the end of May, Pip. To-morrow is the first of June."

"And have you been here all that time, dear Joe?"

"Pretty nigh, old chap. For, as I says to Biddy when the news of your being ill were brought by letter, which it were brought by the post, and being formerly single he is now married though underpaid for a deal of walking and shoe-leather, but wealth were not a object on his part, and marriage were the great wish of his hart—"

"It is so delightful to hear you, Joe! But I interrupt you in what you said to Biddy."

"Which it were," said Joe, "that how you might be amongst strangers, and that how you and me having been ever friends, a wisit at such a moment might not prove unacceptabobble. And Biddy, her word were, 'Go to him, without loss of time.' That," said Joe, summing up with his judicial air, "were the word of Biddy. 'Go to him,' Biddy say, 'without loss of time.' In short, I shouldn't greatly deceive you," Joe added, after a little grave reflection, "if I represented to you that the word of that young woman were, 'without a minute's loss of time.'"

There Joe cut himself short, and informed me that I was to be talked to in great moderation, and that I was to take a little nourishment at stated frequent times, whether I felt inclined for it or not, and that I was to submit myself to all his orders. So I kissed his hand, and lay quiet, while he proceeded to indite a note to Biddy, with my love in it.

Evidently Biddy had taught Joe to write. As I lay in bed looking at him, it made me, in my weak state, cry again with pleasure to see the pride with which he set about his letter. My bedstead, divested of its curtains, had been removed, with me upon it, into the sitting-room, as the airiest and largest, and the carpet had been taken away, and the room kept always fresh and wholesome night and day. At my own writing-table, pushed into a corner and cumbered with little bottles, Joe now sat down to his great work, first choosing a pen from the pen-tray as if it were a chest of large tools, and tucking up his sleeves as if he were going to wield a crow-bar or sledgehammer. It was necessary for Joe to hold on heavily to the table with his left elbow, and to get his right leg well out behind him, before he could begin; and when he did begin he made every downstroke so slowly that it might have been six feet long, while at every upstroke I could hear his pen spluttering extensively. He had a curious idea that the inkstand was on the side of him where it was not, and constantly dipped his pen into space, and seemed quite satisfied with the result. Occasionally, he was tripped up by some orthographical stumbling-block; but on the whole he got on very well indeed; and when he had signed his name, and had removed a finishing blot from the paper to the crown of his head with his two forefingers, he got up and hovered about the table, trying the effect of his performance from various points of view, as it lay there, with unbounded satisfaction.

Not to make Joe uneasy by talking too much, even if I had been able to talk much, I deferred asking him about Miss Havisham until next day. He shook his head when I then asked him if she had recovered.

"Is she dead, Joe?"

"Why you see, old chap," said Joe, in a tone of remonstrance, and by way of getting at it by degrees, "I wouldn't go so far as to say that, for that's a deal to say; but she ain't—"

"Living, Joe?"

"That's nigher where it is," said Joe; "she ain't living."

"Did she linger long, Joe?"

"Arter you was took ill, pretty much about what you might call (if you was put to it) a week," said Joe; still determined, on my account, to come at everything by degrees.

"Dear Joe, have you heard what becomes of her property?"

"Well, old chap," said Joe, "it do appear that she had settled the most of it, which I meantersay tied it up, on Miss Estella. But she had wrote out a little coddleshell in her own hand a day or two afore the accident, leaving a cool four thousand to Mr. Matthew Pocket. And why, do you suppose, above all things, Pip, she left that cool four thousand unto him? 'Because of Pip's account of him, the said Matthew.' I am told by Biddy, that air the writing," said Joe, repeating the legal turn as if it did him infinite good, "'account of him the said Matthew.' And a cool four thousand, Pip!"

I never discovered from whom Joe derived the conventional temperature of the four thousand pounds; but it appeared to make the sum of money more to him, and he had a manifest relish in insisting on its being cool.

This account gave me great joy, as it perfected the only good thing I had done. I asked Joe whether he had heard if any of the other relations had any legacies?

"Miss Sarah," said Joe, "she have twenty-five pound perannium fur to buy pills, on account of being bilious. Miss Georgiana, she have twenty pound down. Mrs.—what's the name of them wild beasts with humps, old chap?"

"Camels?" said I, wondering why he could possibly want to know.

Joe nodded. "Mrs. Camels," by which I presently understood he meant Camilla, "she have five pound fur to buy rushlights to put her in spirits when she wake up in the night."

The accuracy of these recitals was sufficiently obvious to me, to give me great confidence in Joe's information. "And now," said Joe, "you ain't that strong yet, old chap, that you can take in more nor one additional shovelful to-day. Old Orlick he's been a bustin' open a dwelling-ouse."

"Whose?" said I.

"Not, I grant you, but what his manners is given to blusterous," said Joe, apologetically; "still, a Englishman's ouse is his Castle, and castles must not be busted 'cept when done in war time. And wotsume'er the failings on his part, he were a corn and seedsman in his hart."

"Is it Pumblechook's house that has been broken into, then?"

"That's it, Pip," said Joe; "and they took his till, and they took his cash-box, and they drinked his wine, and they partook of his wittles, and they slapped his face, and they pulled his nose, and they tied him up to his bedpust, and they giv' him a dozen, and they stuffed his mouth full of flowering annuals to prewent his crying out. But he knowed Orlick, and Orlick's in the county jail."

By these approaches we arrived at unrestricted conversation. I was slow to gain strength, but I did slowly and surely become less weak, and Joe stayed with me, and I fancied I was little Pip again.

For the tenderness of Joe was so beautifully proportioned to my need, that I was like a child in his hands. He would sit and talk to me in the old confidence, and with the old simplicity, and in the old unassertive protecting way, so that I would half believe that all my life since the days of the old kitchen was one of the mental troubles of the fever that was gone.

He did everything for me except the household work, for which he had engaged a very decent woman, after paying off the laundress on his first arrival. "Which I do assure you, Pip," he would often say, in explanation of that liberty; "I found her a tapping the spare bed, like a cask of beer, and drawing off the feathers in a bucket, for sale. Which she would have tapped yourn next, and draw'd it off with you a laying on it, and was then a carrying away the coals gradually in the soup-tureen and wegetable-dishes, and the wine and spirits in your Wellington boots."

We looked forward to the day when I should go out for a ride, as we had once looked forward to the day of my apprenticeship. And when the day came, and an open carriage was got into the Lane, Joe wrapped me up, took me in his arms, carried me down to it, and put me in, as if I were still the small helpless creature to whom he had so abundantly given of the wealth of his great nature.

And Joe got in beside me, and we drove away together into the country, where the rich summer growth was already on the trees and on the grass, and sweet summer scents filled all the air. The day happened to be Sunday, and when I looked on the loveliness around me, and thought how it had grown and changed, and how the little wild-flowers had been forming, and the voices of the birds had been strengthening, by day and by night, under the sun and under the stars, while poor I lay burning and tossing on my bed, the mere remembrance of having burned and tossed there came like a check upon my peace. But when I heard the Sunday bells, and looked around a little more upon the outspread beauty, I felt that I was not nearly thankful enough,—that I was too weak yet to be even that,—and I laid my head on Joe's shoulder, as I had laid it long ago when he had taken me to the Fair or where not, and it was too much for my young senses.

More composure came to me after a while, and we talked as we used to talk, lying on the grass at the old Battery. There was no change whatever in Joe. Exactly what he had been in my eyes then, he was in my eyes still; just as simply faithful, and as simply right.

When we got back again, and he lifted me out, and carried me—so easily!—across the court and up the stairs, I thought of that eventful Christmas Day when he had carried me over the marshes. We had not yet made any allusion to my change of fortune, nor did I know how much of my late history he was acquainted with. I was so doubtful of myself now, and put so much trust in him, that I could not satisfy myself whether I ought to refer to it when he did not.

"Have you heard, Joe," I asked him that evening, upon further consideration, as he smoked his pipe at the window, "who my patron was?"

"I heerd," returned Joe, "as it were not Miss Havisham, old chap."

"Did you hear who it was, Joe?"

"Well! I heerd as it were a person what sent the person what giv' you the bank-notes at the Jolly Bargemen, Pip."

"So it was."

"Astonishing!" said Joe, in the placidest way.

"Did you hear that he was dead, Joe?" I presently asked, with increasing diffidence.

"Which? Him as sent the bank-notes, Pip?"

"Yes."

"I think," said Joe, after meditating a long time, and looking rather evasively at the window-seat, "as I did hear tell that how he were something or another in a general way in that direction."

"Did you hear anything of his circumstances, Joe?"

"Not partickler, Pip."

"If you would like to hear, Joe—" I was beginning, when Joe got up and came to my sofa.

"Lookee here, old chap," said Joe, bending over me. "Ever the best of friends; ain't us, Pip?"

I was ashamed to answer him.

"Wery good, then," said Joe, as if I had answered; "that's all right; that's agreed upon. Then why go into subjects, old chap, which as betwixt two sech must be for ever onnecessary? There's subjects enough as betwixt two sech, without onnecessary ones. Lord! To think of your poor sister and her Rampages! And don't you remember Tickler?"

"I do indeed, Joe."

"Lookee here, old chap," said Joe. "I done what I could to keep you and Tickler in sunders, but my power were not always fully equal to my inclinations. For when your poor sister had a mind to drop into you, it were not so much," said Joe, in his favorite argumentative way, "that she dropped into me too, if I put myself in opposition to her, but that she dropped into you always heavier for it. I noticed that. It ain't a grab at a man's whisker, not yet a shake or two of a man (to which your sister was quite welcome), that 'ud put a man off from getting a little child out of punishment. But when that little child is dropped into heavier for that grab of whisker or shaking, then that man naterally up and says to himself, 'Where is the good as you are a doing? I grant you I see the 'arm,' says the man, 'but I don't see the good. I call upon you, sir, therefore, to pint out the good.'"

"The man says?" I observed, as Joe waited for me to speak.

"The man says," Joe assented. "Is he right, that man?"

"Dear Joe, he is always right."

"Well, old chap," said Joe, "then abide by your words. If he's always right (which in general he's more likely wrong), he's right when he says this: Supposing ever you kep any little matter to yourself, when you was a little child, you kep it mostly because you know'd as J. Gargery's power to part you and Tickler in sunders were not fully equal to his inclinations. Theerfore, think no more of it as betwixt two sech, and do not let us pass remarks upon onnecessary subjects. Biddy giv' herself a deal o' trouble with me afore I left (for I am almost awful dull), as I should view it in this light, and, viewing it in this light, as I should so put it. Both of which," said Joe, quite charmed with his logical arrangement, "being done, now this to you a true friend, say. Namely. You mustn't go a overdoing on it, but you must have your supper and your wine and water, and you must be put betwixt the sheets."

The delicacy with which Joe dismissed this theme, and the sweet tact and kindness with which Biddy—who with her woman's wit had found me out so soon—had prepared him for it, made a deep impression on my mind. But whether Joe knew how poor I was, and how my great expectations had all dissolved, like our own marsh mists before the sun, I could not understand.

Another thing in Joe that I could not understand when it first began to develop itself, but which I soon arrived at a sorrowful comprehension of, was this: As I became stronger and better, Joe became a little less easy with me. In my weakness and entire dependence on him, the dear fellow had fallen into the old tone, and called me by the old names, the dear "old Pip, old chap," that now were music in my ears. I too had fallen into the old ways, only happy and thankful that he let me. But, imperceptibly, though I held by them fast, Joe's hold upon them began to slacken; and whereas I wondered at this, at first, I soon began to understand that the cause of it was in me, and that the fault of it was all mine.

Ah! Had I given Joe no reason to doubt my constancy, and to think that in prosperity I should grow cold to him and cast him off? Had I given Joe's innocent heart no cause to feel instinctively that as I got stronger, his hold upon me would be weaker, and that he had better loosen it in time and let me go, before I plucked myself away?

It was on the third or fourth occasion of my going out walking in the Temple Gardens leaning on Joe's arm, that I saw this change in him very plainly. We had been sitting in the bright warm sunlight, looking at the river, and I chanced to say as we got up,—

"See, Joe! I can walk quite strongly. Now, you shall see me walk back by myself."

"Which do not overdo it, Pip," said Joe; "but I shall be happy fur to see you able, sir."

The last word grated on me; but how could I remonstrate! I walked no further than the gate of the gardens, and then pretended to be weaker than I was, and asked Joe for his arm. Joe gave it me, but was thoughtful.

I, for my part, was thoughtful too; for, how best to check this growing change in Joe was a great perplexity to my remorseful thoughts. That I was ashamed to tell him exactly how I was placed, and what I had come down to, I do not seek to conceal; but I hope my reluctance was not quite an unworthy one. He would want to help me out of his little savings, I knew, and I knew that he ought not to help me, and that I must not suffer him to do it.

It was a thoughtful evening with both of us. But, before we went to bed, I had resolved that I would wait over to-morrow,—to-morrow being Sunday,—and would begin my new course with the new week. On Monday morning I would speak to Joe about this change, I would lay aside this last vestige of reserve, I would tell him what I had in my thoughts (that Secondly, not yet arrived at), and why I had not decided to go out to Herbert, and then the change would be conquered for ever. As I cleared, Joe cleared, and it seemed as though he had sympathetically arrived at a resolution too.

We had a quiet day on the Sunday, and we rode out into the country, and then walked in the fields.

"I feel thankful that I have been ill, Joe," I said.

"Dear old Pip, old chap, you're a'most come round, sir."

"It has been a memorable time for me, Joe."

"Likeways for myself, sir," Joe returned.

"We have had a time together, Joe, that I can never forget. There were days once, I know, that I did for a while forget; but I never shall forget these."

"Pip," said Joe, appearing a little hurried and troubled, "there has been larks. And, dear sir, what have been betwixt us—have been."

At night, when I had gone to bed, Joe came into my room, as he had done all through my recovery. He asked me if I felt sure that I was as well as in the morning?

"Yes, dear Joe, quite."

"And are always a getting stronger, old chap?"

"Yes, dear Joe, steadily."

Joe patted the coverlet on my shoulder with his great good hand, and said, in what I thought a husky voice, "Good night!"

When I got up in the morning, refreshed and stronger yet, I was full of my resolution to tell Joe all, without delay. I would tell him before breakfast. I would dress at once and go to his room and surprise him; for, it was the first day I had been up early. I went to his room, and he was not there. Not only was he not there, but his box was gone.

I hurried then to the breakfast-table, and on it found a letter. These were its brief contents:—

"Not wishful to intrude I have departed fur you are well again dear Pip and will do better without JO.

"P.S. Ever the best of friends."

Enclosed in the letter was a receipt for the debt and costs on which I had been arrested. Down to that moment, I had vainly supposed that my creditor had withdrawn, or suspended proceedings until I should be quite recovered. I had never dreamed of Joe's having paid the money; but Joe had paid it, and the receipt was in his name.

What remained for me now, but to follow him to the dear old forge, and there to have out my disclosure to him, and my penitent remonstrance with him, and there to relieve my mind and heart of that reserved Secondly, which had begun as a vague something lingering in my thoughts, and had formed into a settled purpose?

The purpose was, that I would go to Biddy, that I would show her how humbled and repentant I came back, that I would tell her how I had lost all I once hoped for, that I would remind her of our old confidences in my first unhappy time. Then I would say to her, "Biddy, I think you once liked me very well, when my errant heart, even while it strayed away from you, was quieter and better with you than it ever has been since. If you can like me only half as well once more, if you can take me with all my faults and disappointments on my head, if you can receive me like a forgiven child (and indeed I am as sorry, Biddy, and have as much need of a hushing voice and a soothing hand), I hope I am a little worthier of you that I was,—not much, but a little. And, Biddy, it shall rest with you to say whether I shall work at the forge with Joe, or whether I shall try for any different occupation down in this country, or whether we shall go away to a distant place where an opportunity awaits me which I set aside, when it was offered, until I knew your answer. And now, dear Biddy, if you can tell me that you will go through the world with me, you will surely make it a better world for me, and me a better man for it, and I will try hard to make it a better world for you."

Such was my purpose. After three days more of recovery, I went down to the old place to put it in execution. And how I sped in it is all I have left to tell.

Chapter LVIII

The tidings of my high fortunes having had a heavy fall had got down to my native place and its neighborhood before I got there. I found the Blue Boar in possession of the intelligence, and I found that it made a great change in the Boar's demeanour. Whereas the Boar had cultivated my good opinion with warm assiduity when I was coming into property, the Boar was exceedingly cool on the subject now that I was going out of property.

It was evening when I arrived, much fatigued by the journey I had so often made so easily. The Boar could not put me into my usual bedroom, which was engaged (probably by some one who had expectations), and could only assign me a very indifferent chamber among the pigeons and post-chaises up the yard. But I had as sound a sleep in that lodging as in the most superior accommodation the Boar could have given me, and the quality of my dreams was about the same as in the best bedroom.

Early in the morning, while my breakfast was getting ready, I strolled round by Satis House. There were printed bills on the gate and on bits of carpet hanging out of the windows, announcing a sale by auction of the Household Furniture and Effects, next week. The House itself was to be sold as old building materials, and pulled down. LOT 1 was marked in whitewashed knock-knee letters on the brew house; LOT 2 on that part of the main building which had been so long shut up. Other lots were marked off on other parts of the structure, and the ivy had been torn down to make room for the inscriptions, and much of it trailed low in the dust and was withered already. Stepping in for a moment at the open gate, and looking around me with the uncomfortable air of a stranger who had no business there, I saw the auctioneer's clerk walking on the casks and telling them off for the information of a catalogue-compiler, pen in hand, who made a temporary desk of the wheeled chair I had so often pushed along to the tune of Old Clem.

When I got back to my breakfast in the Boar's coffee-room, I found Mr. Pumblechook conversing with the landlord. Mr. Pumblechook (not improved in appearance by his late nocturnal adventure) was waiting for me, and addressed me in the following terms:—

"Young man, I am sorry to see you brought low. But what else could be expected! what else could be expected!"

As he extended his hand with a magnificently forgiving air, and as I was broken by illness and unfit to quarrel, I took it.

"William," said Mr. Pumblechook to the waiter, "put a muffin on table. And has it come to this! Has it come to this!"

I frowningly sat down to my breakfast. Mr. Pumblechook stood over me and poured out my tea—before I could touch the teapot—with the air of a benefactor who was resolved to be true to the last.

"William," said Mr. Pumblechook, mournfully, "put the salt on. In happier times," addressing me, "I think you took sugar? And did you take milk? You did. Sugar and milk. William, bring a watercress."

"Thank you," said I, shortly, "but I don't eat watercresses."

"You don't eat 'em," returned Mr. Pumblechook, sighing and nodding his head several times, as if he might have expected that, and as if abstinence from watercresses were consistent with my downfall. "True. The simple fruits of the earth. No. You needn't bring any, William."

I went on with my breakfast, and Mr. Pumblechook continued to stand over me, staring fishily and breathing noisily, as he always did.

"Little more than skin and bone!" mused Mr. Pumblechook, aloud. "And yet when he went from here (I may say with my blessing), and I spread afore him my humble store, like the Bee, he was as plump as a Peach!"

This reminded me of the wonderful difference between the servile manner in which he had offered his hand in my new prosperity, saying, "May I?" and the ostentatious clemency with which he had just now exhibited the same fat five fingers.

"Hah!" he went on, handing me the bread and butter. "And air you a going to Joseph?"

"In heaven's name," said I, firing in spite of myself, "what does it matter to you where I am going? Leave that teapot alone."

It was the worst course I could have taken, because it gave Pumblechook the opportunity he wanted.

"Yes, young man," said he, releasing the handle of the article in question, retiring a step or two from my table, and speaking for the behoof of the landlord and waiter at the door, "I will leave that teapot alone. You are right, young man. For once you are right. I forgit myself when I take such an interest in your breakfast, as to wish your frame, exhausted by the debilitating effects of prodigygality, to be stimilated by the 'olesome nourishment of your forefathers. And yet," said Pumblechook, turning to the landlord and waiter, and pointing me out at arm's length, "this is him as I ever sported with in his days of happy infancy! Tell me not it cannot be; I tell you this is him!"

A low murmur from the two replied. The waiter appeared to be particularly affected.

"This is him," said Pumblechook, "as I have rode in my shay-cart. This is him as I have seen brought up by hand. This is him untoe the sister of which I was uncle by marriage, as her name was Georgiana M'ria from her own mother, let him deny it if he can!"

The waiter seemed convinced that I could not deny it, and that it gave the case a black look.

"Young man," said Pumblechook, screwing his head at me in the old fashion, "you air a going to Joseph. What does it matter to me, you ask me, where you air a going? I say to you, Sir, you air a going to Joseph."

The waiter coughed, as if he modestly invited me to get over that.

"Now," said Pumblechook, and all this with a most exasperating air of saying in the cause of virtue what was perfectly convincing and conclusive, "I will tell you what to say to Joseph. Here is Squires of the Boar present, known and respected in this town, and here is William, which his father's name was Potkins if I do not deceive myself."

"You do not, sir," said William.

"In their presence," pursued Pumblechook, "I will tell you, young man, what to say to Joseph. Says you, "Joseph, I have this day seen my earliest benefactor and the founder of my fortun's. I will name no names, Joseph, but so they are pleased to call him up town, and I have seen that man."

"I swear I don't see him here," said I.

"Say that likewise," retorted Pumblechook. "Say you said that, and even Joseph will probably betray surprise."

"There you quite mistake him," said I. "I know better."

"Says you," Pumblechook went on, "'Joseph, I have seen that man, and that man bears you no malice and bears me no malice. He knows your character, Joseph, and is well acquainted with your pig-headedness and ignorance; and he knows my character, Joseph, and he knows my want of gratitoode. Yes, Joseph,' says you," here Pumblechook shook his head and hand at me, "'he knows my total deficiency of common human gratitoode. He knows it, Joseph, as none can. You do not know it, Joseph, having no call to know it, but that man do.'"

Windy donkey as he was, it really amazed me that he could have the face to talk thus to mine.

"Says you, 'Joseph, he gave me a little message, which I will now repeat. It was that, in my being brought low, he saw the finger of Providence. He knowed that finger when he saw Joseph, and he saw it plain. It pinted out this writing, Joseph. Reward of ingratitoode to his earliest benefactor, and founder of fortun's. But that man said he did not repent of what he had done, Joseph. Not at all. It was right to do it, it was kind to do it, it was benevolent to do it, and he would do it again.'"

"It's pity," said I, scornfully, as I finished my interrupted breakfast, "that the man did not say what he had done and would do again."

"Squires of the Boar!" Pumblechook was now addressing the landlord, "and William! I have no objections to your mentioning, either up town or down town, if such should be your wishes, that it was right to do it, kind to do it, benevolent to do it, and that I would do it again."

With those words the Impostor shook them both by the hand, with an air, and left the house; leaving me much more astonished than delighted by the virtues of that same indefinite "it." I was not long after him in leaving the house too, and when I went down the High Street I saw him holding forth (no doubt to the same effect) at his shop door to a select group, who honored me with very unfavorable glances as I passed on the opposite side of the way.

But, it was only the pleasanter to turn to Biddy and to Joe, whose great forbearance shone more brightly than before, if that could be, contrasted with this brazen pretender. I went towards them slowly, for my limbs were weak, but with a sense of increasing relief as I drew nearer to them, and a sense of leaving arrogance and untruthfulness further and further behind.

The June weather was delicious. The sky was blue, the larks were soaring high over the green corn, I thought all that countryside more beautiful and peaceful by far than I had ever known it to be yet. Many pleasant pictures of the life that I would lead there, and of the change for the better that would come over my character when I had a guiding spirit at my side whose simple faith and clear home wisdom I had proved, beguiled my way. They awakened a tender emotion in me; for my heart was softened by my return, and such a change had come to pass, that I felt like one who was toiling home barefoot from distant travel, and whose wanderings had lasted many years.

The schoolhouse where Biddy was mistress I had never seen; but, the little roundabout lane by which I entered the village, for quietness' sake, took me past it. I was disappointed to find that the day was a holiday; no children were there, and Biddy's house was closed. Some hopeful notion of seeing her, busily engaged in her daily duties, before she saw me, had been in my mind and was defeated.

But the forge was a very short distance off, and I went towards it under the sweet green limes, listening for the clink of Joe's hammer. Long after I ought to have heard it, and long after I had fancied I heard it and found it but a fancy, all was still. The limes were there, and the white thorns were there, and the chestnut-trees were there, and their leaves rustled harmoniously when I stopped to listen; but, the clink of Joe's hammer was not in the midsummer wind.

Almost fearing, without knowing why, to come in view of the forge, I saw it at last, and saw that it was closed. No gleam of fire, no glittering shower of sparks, no roar of bellows; all shut up, and still.

But the house was not deserted, and the best parlor seemed to be in use, for there were white curtains fluttering in its window, and the window was open and gay with flowers. I went softly towards it, meaning to peep over the flowers, when Joe and Biddy stood before me, arm in arm.

At first Biddy gave a cry, as if she thought it was my apparition, but in another moment she was in my embrace. I wept to see her, and she wept to see me; I, because she looked so fresh and pleasant; she, because I looked so worn and white.

"But dear Biddy, how smart you are!"

"Yes, dear Pip."

"And Joe, how smart you are!"

"Yes, dear old Pip, old chap."

I looked at both of them, from one to the other, and then—

"It's my wedding-day!" cried Biddy, in a burst of happiness, "and I am married to Joe!"

They had taken me into the kitchen, and I had laid my head down on the old deal table. Biddy held one of my hands to her lips, and Joe's restoring touch was on my shoulder. "Which he warn't strong enough, my dear, fur to be surprised," said Joe. And Biddy said, "I ought to have thought of it, dear Joe, but I was too happy." They were both so overjoyed to see me, so proud to see me, so touched by my coming to them, so delighted that I should have come by accident to make their day complete!

My first thought was one of great thankfulness that I had never breathed this last baffled hope to Joe. How often, while he was with me in my illness, had it risen to my lips! How irrevocable would have been his knowledge of it, if he had remained with me but another hour!

"Dear Biddy," said I, "you have the best husband in the whole world, and if you could have seen him by my bed you would have—But no, you couldn't love him better than you do."

"No, I couldn't indeed," said Biddy.

"And, dear Joe, you have the best wife in the whole world, and she will make you as happy as even you deserve to be, you dear, good, noble Joe!"

Joe looked at me with a quivering lip, and fairly put his sleeve before his eyes.

"And Joe and Biddy both, as you have been to church to-day, and are in charity and love with all mankind, receive my humble thanks for all you have done for me, and all I have so ill repaid! And when I say that I am going away within the hour, for I am soon going abroad, and that I shall never rest until I have worked for the money with which you have kept me out of prison, and have sent it to you, don't think, dear Joe and Biddy, that if I could repay it a thousand times over, I suppose I could cancel a farthing of the debt I owe you, or that I would do so if I could!"

They were both melted by these words, and both entreated me to say no more.

"But I must say more. Dear Joe, I hope you will have children to love, and that some little fellow will sit in this chimney-corner of a winter night, who may remind you of another little fellow gone out of it for ever. Don't tell him, Joe, that I was thankless; don't tell him, Biddy, that I was ungenerous and unjust; only tell him that I honored you both, because you were both so good and true, and that, as your child, I said it would be natural to him to grow up a much better man than I did."

"I ain't a going," said Joe, from behind his sleeve, "to tell him nothink o' that natur, Pip. Nor Biddy ain't. Nor yet no one ain't."

"And now, though I know you have already done it in your own kind hearts, pray tell me, both, that you forgive me! Pray let me hear you say the words, that I may carry the sound of them away with me, and then I shall be able to believe that you can trust me, and think better of me, in the time to come!"

"O dear old Pip, old chap," said Joe. "God knows as I forgive you, if I have anythink to forgive!"

"Amen! And God knows I do!" echoed Biddy.

"Now let me go up and look at my old little room, and rest there a few minutes by myself. And then, when I have eaten and drunk with you, go with me as far as the finger-post, dear Joe and Biddy, before we say good-bye!"

I sold all I had, and put aside as much as I could, for a composition with my creditors,— who gave me ample time to pay them in full,—and I went out and joined Herbert. Within a month, I had quitted England, and within two months I was clerk to Clarriker and Co., and within four months I assumed my first undivided responsibility. For the beam across the parlor ceiling at Mill Pond Bank had then ceased to tremble under old Bill Barley's growls and was at peace, and Herbert had gone away to marry Clara, and I was left in sole charge of the Eastern Branch until he brought her back.

Many a year went round before I was a partner in the House; but I lived happily with Herbert and his wife, and lived frugally, and paid my debts, and maintained a constant correspondence with Biddy and Joe. It was not until I became third in the Firm, that Clarriker betrayed me to Herbert; but he then declared that the secret of Herbert's partnership had been long enough upon his conscience, and he must tell it. So he told it, and Herbert was as much moved as amazed, and the dear fellow and I were not the worse friends for the long concealment. I must not leave it to be supposed that we were ever a great House, or that we made mints of money. We were not in a grand way of business, but we had a good name, and worked for our profits, and did very well. We owed so much to Herbert's ever cheerful industry and readiness, that I often wondered how I had conceived that old idea of his inaptitude, until I was one day enlightened by the reflection, that perhaps the inaptitude had never been in him at all, but had been in me.

Chapter LIX

For eleven years, I had not seen Joe nor Biddy with my bodily eyes,—though they had both been often before my fancy in the East,—when, upon an evening in December, an hour or two after dark, I laid my hand softly on the latch of the old kitchen door. I touched it so softly that I was not heard, and looked in unseen. There, smoking his pipe in the old place by the kitchen firelight, as hale and as strong as ever, though a little gray, sat Joe; and there, fenced into the corner with Joe's leg, and sitting on my own little stool looking at the fire, was—I again!

"We giv' him the name of Pip for your sake, dear old chap," said Joe, delighted, when I took another stool by the child's side (but I did not rumple his hair), "and we hoped he might grow a little bit like you, and we think he do."

I thought so too, and I took him out for a walk next morning, and we talked immensely, understanding one another to perfection. And I took him down to the churchyard, and set him on a certain tombstone there, and he showed me from that elevation which stone was sacred to the memory of Philip Pirrip, late of this Parish, and Also Georgiana, Wife of the Above.

"Biddy," said I, when I talked with her after dinner, as her little girl lay sleeping in her lap, "you must give Pip to me one of these days; or lend him, at all events."

"No, no," said Biddy, gently. "You must marry."

"So Herbert and Clara say, but I don't think I shall, Biddy. I have so settled down in their home, that it's not at all likely. I am already quite an old bachelor."

Biddy looked down at her child, and put its little hand to her lips, and then put the good matronly hand with which she had touched it into mine. There was something in the action, and in the light pressure of Biddy's wedding-ring, that had a very pretty eloquence in it.

"Dear Pip," said Biddy, "you are sure you don't fret for her?"

"O no,—I think not, Biddy."

"Tell me as an old, old friend. Have you quite forgotten her?

"My dear Biddy, I have forgotten nothing in my life that ever had a foremost place there, and little that ever had any place there. But that poor dream, as I once used to call it, has all gone by, Biddy,—all gone by!"

Nevertheless, I knew, while I said those words, that I secretly intended to revisit the site of the old house that evening, alone, for her sake. Yes, even so. For Estella's sake.

I had heard of her as leading a most unhappy life, and as being separated from her husband, who had used her with great cruelty, and who had become quite renowned as a compound of pride, avarice, brutality, and meanness. And I had heard of the death of her husband, from an accident consequent on his ill-treatment of a horse. This release had befallen her some two years before; for anything I knew, she was married again.

The early dinner hour at Joe's, left me abundance of time, without hurrying my talk with Biddy, to walk over to the old spot before dark. But, what with loitering on the way to look at old objects and to think of old times, the day had quite declined when I came to the place.

There was no house now, no brewery, no building whatever left, but the wall of the old garden. The cleared space had been enclosed with a rough fence, and looking over it, I saw that some of the old ivy had struck root anew, and was growing green on low quiet mounds of ruin. A gate in the fence standing ajar, I pushed it open, and went in.

A cold silvery mist had veiled the afternoon, and the moon was not yet up to scatter it. But, the stars were shining beyond the mist, and the moon was coming, and the evening was not dark. I could trace out where every part of the old house had been, and where the brewery had been, and where the gates, and where the casks. I had done so, and was looking along the desolate garden walk, when I beheld a solitary figure in it.

The figure showed itself aware of me, as I advanced. It had been moving towards me, but it stood still. As I drew nearer, I saw it to be the figure of a woman. As I drew nearer yet, it was about to turn away, when it stopped, and let me come up with it. Then, it faltered, as if much surprised, and uttered my name, and I cried out,—

"Estella!"

"I am greatly changed. I wonder you know me."

The freshness of her beauty was indeed gone, but its indescribable majesty and its indescribable charm remained. Those attractions in it, I had seen before; what I had never seen before, was the saddened, softened light of the once proud eyes; what I had never felt before was the friendly touch of the once insensible hand.

We sat down on a bench that was near, and I said, "After so many years, it is strange that we should thus meet again, Estella, here where our first meeting was! Do you often come back?"

"I have never been here since."

"Nor I."

The moon began to rise, and I thought of the placid look at the white ceiling, which had passed away. The moon began to rise, and I thought of the pressure on my hand when I had spoken the last words he had heard on earth.

Estella was the next to break the silence that ensued between us.

"I have very often hoped and intended to come back, but have been prevented by many circumstances. Poor, poor old place!"

The silvery mist was touched with the first rays of the moonlight, and the same rays touched the tears that dropped from her eyes. Not knowing that I saw them, and setting herself to get the better of them, she said quietly,—

"Were you wondering, as you walked along, how it came to be left in this condition?"

"Yes, Estella."

"The ground belongs to me. It is the only possession I have not relinquished. Everything else has gone from me, little by little, but I have kept this. It was the subject of the only determined resistance I made in all the wretched years."

"Is it to be built on?"

"At last, it is. I came here to take leave of it before its change. And you," she said, in a voice of touching interest to a wanderer,—"you live abroad still?"

"Still."

"And do well, I am sure?"

"I work pretty hard for a sufficient living, and therefore—yes, I do well."

"I have often thought of you," said Estella.

"Have you?"

"Of late, very often. There was a long hard time when I kept far from me the remembrance of what I had thrown away when I was quite ignorant of its worth. But since my duty has not been incompatible with the admission of that remembrance, I have given it a place in my heart."

"You have always held your place in my heart," I answered.

And we were silent again until she spoke.

"I little thought," said Estella, "that I should take leave of you in taking leave of this spot. I am very glad to do so."

"Glad to part again, Estella? To me, parting is a painful thing. To me, the remembrance of our last parting has been ever mournful and painful."

"But you said to me," returned Estella, very earnestly, "'God bless you, God forgive you!' And if you could say that to me then, you will not hesitate to say that to me now,—now, when suffering has been stronger than all other teaching, and has taught me to understand what your heart used to be. I have been bent and broken, but—I hope—into a better shape. Be as considerate and good to me as you were, and tell me we are friends."

"We are friends," said I, rising and bending over her, as she rose from the bench.

"And will continue friends apart," said Estella.

I took her hand in mine, and we went out of the ruined place; and, as the morning mists had risen long ago when I first left the forge, so the evening mists were rising now, and in all the broad expanse of tranquil light they showed to me, I saw no shadow of another parting from her.

About Author

Dickens's literary success began with the 1836 serial publication of The Pickwick Papers. Within a few years he had become an international literary celebrity, famous for his humour, satire, and keen observation of character and society. His novels, most published in monthly or weekly instalments, pioneered the serial publication of narrative fiction, which became the dominant Victorian mode for novel publication. Cliffhanger endings in his serial publications kept readers in suspense. The instalment format allowed Dickens to evaluate his audience's reaction, and he often modified his plot and character development based on such feedback. For example, when his wife's chiropodist expressed distress at the way Miss Mowcher in David Copperfield seemed to reflect her disabilities, Dickens improved the character with positive features. His plots were carefully constructed, and he often wove elements from topical events into his narratives. Masses of the illiterate poor chipped in ha'pennies to have each new monthly episode read to them, opening up and inspiring a new class of readers.

Dickens was regarded as the literary colossus of his age. His 1843 novella, A Christmas Carol, remains popular and continues to inspire adaptations in every artistic genre. Oliver Twist and Great Expectations are also frequently adapted, and, like many of his novels, evoke images of early Victorian London. His 1859 novel, A Tale of Two Cities, set in London and Paris, is his best-known work of historical fiction. Dickens has been praised by fellow writers—from Leo Tolstoy to George Orwell, G. K. Chesterton and Tom Wolfe—for his realism, comedy, prose style, unique characterisations, and social criticism. On the other hand, Oscar Wilde, Henry James, and Virginia Woolf complained of a lack of psychological depth, loose writing, and a vein of sentimentalism. The term Dickensian is used to describe something that is reminiscent of Dickens and his writings, such as poor social conditions or comically repulsive characters.

Early years

Charles John Huffam Dickens was born on 7 February 1812, at 1 Mile End Terrace (now 393 Commercial Road), Landport in Portsea Island (Portsmouth), the second of eight children of Elizabeth Dickens (née Barrow; 1789–1863) and John Dickens (1785–1851). His father was a clerk in the Navy Pay Office and was temporarily stationed in the district. He asked Christopher Huffam, rigger to His Majesty's Navy, gentleman, and head of an established firm, to act as godfather to Charles. Huffam is thought to be the inspiration for Paul Dombey, the owner of a shipping company in Dickens's novel Dombey and Son (1848).

In January 1815, John Dickens was called back to London, and the family moved to Norfolk Street, Fitzrovia. When Charles was four, they relocated to Sheerness, and thence to Chatham, Kent, where he spent his formative years until the age of 11. His early life seems to have been idyllic, though he thought himself a "very small and not-over-particularly-taken-care-of boy".

Charles spent time outdoors, but also read voraciously, including the picaresque novels of Tobias Smollett and Henry Fielding, as well as Robinson Crusoe and Gil Blas. He read and reread The Arabian Nights and the Collected Farces of Elizabeth Inchbald. He retained poignant memories of childhood, helped by an excellent memory of people and events, which he used in his writing. His father's brief work as a clerk in the Navy Pay Office afforded him a few years of private education, first at a dame school, and then at a school run by William Giles, a dissenter, in Chatham.

This period came to an end in June 1822, when John Dickens was recalled to Navy Pay Office headquarters at Somerset House, and the family (except for Charles, who stayed behind to finish his final term of work) moved to Camden Town in London. The family had left Kent amidst rapidly mounting debts, and, living beyond his means, John Dickens was forced by his creditors into the Marshalsea debtors' prison in Southwark, London in 1824. His wife and youngest children joined him there, as was the practice at the time. Charles, then 12 years old, boarded with Elizabeth Roylance, a family friend, at 112 College Place, Camden Town. Roylance was "a reduced [impoverished] old lady, long known to our family", whom Dickens later immortalised, "with a few alterations and embellishments", as "Mrs Pipchin" in Dombey and Son. Later, he lived in a back-attic in the house of an agent for the Insolvent Court, Archibald Russell, "a fat, good-natured, kind old gentleman... with a quiet old wife" and lame son, in Lant Street in Southwark. They provided the inspiration for the Garlands in The Old Curiosity Shop.

On Sundays—with his sister Frances, free from her studies at the Royal Academy of Music—he spent the day at the Marshalsea. Dickens later used the prison as a setting in Little Dorrit. To pay for his board and to help his family, Dickens was forced to leave school and work ten-hour days at Warren's Blacking Warehouse, on Hungerford Stairs, near the present Charing Cross railway station, where he earned six shillings a week pasting labels on pots of boot blacking. The strenuous and often harsh working conditions made a lasting impression on Dickens and later influenced his fiction and essays, becoming the foundation of his interest in the reform of socio-economic and labour conditions, the rigours of which he believed were unfairly borne by the poor. He later wrote that he wondered "how I could have been so easily cast away at such an age". As he recalled to John Forster (from The Life of Charles Dickens):

The blacking-warehouse was the last house on the left-hand side of the way, at old Hungerford Stairs. It was a crazy, tumble-down old house, abutting of course on the river, and literally overrun with rats. Its wainscoted rooms, and its rotten floors and staircase, and the old grey rats swarming down in the cellars, and the sound of their squeaking and scuffling coming up the stairs at all times, and the dirt and decay of the place, rise up visibly before me, as if I were there again. The counting-house was on the first floor, looking over the coal-barges and the river. There was a recess in it, in which I was to sit and work. My work was to cover the pots of paste-blacking; first with a piece of oil-paper, and then with a piece of blue paper; to tie them round with a string; and then to clip the paper close and neat, all round, until it looked as smart as a pot of ointment from an apothecary's shop. When a certain number of grosses of pots had attained this pitch of perfection, I was to paste on each a printed label, and then go on again with more pots. Two or three other boys were kept at similar duty down-stairs on similar wages. One of them came up, in a ragged apron and a paper cap, on the first Monday morning, to show me the trick of using the string and tying the knot. His name was Bob Fagin; and I took the liberty of using his name, long afterwards, in Oliver Twist.

When the warehouse was moved to Chandos Street in the smart, busy district of Covent Garden the boys worked in a room in which the window gave onto the street and little audiences gathered and watched them at work—in Dickens biographer Simon Callow's estimation, the public display was "a new refinement added to his misery".

A few months after his imprisonment, John Dickens's mother, Elizabeth Dickens, died and bequeathed him £450. On the expectation of this legacy, Dickens was released from prison. Under the Insolvent Debtors Act, Dickens arranged for payment of his creditors, and he and his family left Marshalsea, for the home of Mrs Roylance.

Charles's mother, Elizabeth Dickens, did not immediately support his removal from the boot-blacking warehouse. This influenced Dickens's view that a father should rule the family, and a mother find her proper sphere inside the home: "I never afterwards forgot, I never shall forget, I never can forget, that my mother was warm for my being sent back". His mother's failure to request his return was a factor in his dissatisfied attitude towards women.

Righteous indignation stemming from his own situation and the conditions under which working-class people lived became major themes of his works, and it was this unhappy period in his youth to which he alluded in his favourite, and most autobiographical, novel, David Copperfield: "I had no advice, no counsel, no encouragement, no consolation, no assistance, no support, of any kind, from anyone, that I can call to mind, as I hope to go to heaven!"

Dickens was eventually sent to the Wellington House Academy in Camden Town, where he remained until March 1827, having spent about two years there. He did not consider it to be a good school: "Much of the haphazard, desultory teaching, poor discipline punctuated by the headmaster's sadistic brutality, the seedy ushers and general run-down atmosphere, are embodied in Mr Creakle's Establishment in David Copperfield."

Dickens worked at the law office of Ellis and Blackmore, attorneys, of Holborn Court, Gray's Inn, as a junior clerk from May 1827 to November 1828. He was a gifted mimic and impersonated those around him: clients, lawyers, and clerks. He went to theatres obsessively—he claimed that for at least three years he went to the theatre every single day. His favourite actor was Charles Mathews, and Dickens learnt his monopolylogues, (farces in which Mathews played every character), by heart. Then, having learned Gurney's system of shorthand in his spare time, he left to become a freelance reporter. A distant relative, Thomas Charlton, was a freelance reporter at Doctors' Commons, and Dickens was able to share his box there to report the legal proceedings for nearly four years. This education was to inform works such as Nicholas Nickleby, Dombey and Son, and especially Bleak House—whose vivid portrayal of the machinations and bureaucracy of the legal system did much to enlighten the general public and served as a vehicle for dissemination of Dickens's own views regarding, particularly, the heavy burden on the poor who were forced by circumstances to "go to law".

In 1830, Dickens met his first love, Maria Beadnell, thought to have been the model for the character Dora in David Copperfield. Maria's parents disapproved of the courtship and ended the relationship by sending her to school in Paris.

Journalism and early novels

In 1832, at age 20, Dickens was energetic and increasingly self-confident. He enjoyed mimicry and popular entertainment, lacked a clear, specific sense of what he wanted to become, and yet knew he wanted fame. Drawn to the theatre—he became an early member of the Garrick — he landed an acting audition at Covent Garden, where the manager George Bartley and the actor Charles Kemble were to see him. Dickens prepared meticulously and decided to imitate the comedian Charles Mathews, but ultimately he missed the audition because of a cold. Before another opportunity arose, he had set out on his career as a writer.

In 1833, he submitted his first story, "A Dinner at Poplar Walk", to the London periodical Monthly Magazine. William Barrow, a brother of his mother, offered him a job on The Mirror of Parliament and he worked in the House of Commons for the first time early in 1832. He rented rooms at Furnival's Inn and worked as a political journalist, reporting on Parliamentary debates, and he travelled across Britain to cover election campaigns for the Morning Chronicle. His journalism, in the form of sketches in periodicals, formed his first collection of pieces, published in 1836: Sketches by Boz—Boz being a family nickname he employed as a pseudonym for some years. Dickens apparently adopted it from the nickname "Moses", which he had given to his youngest brother Augustus Dickens, after a character in Oliver Goldsmith's The Vicar of Wakefield. When pronounced by anyone with a head cold, "Moses" became "Boses"—later shortened to Boz. Dickens's own name was considered "queer" by a contemporary critic, who wrote in 1849: "Mr Dickens, as if in revenge for his own queer name, does bestow still queerer ones upon his fictitious creations." He contributed to and edited journals throughout his literary career. In January 1835, the Morning Chronicle launched an evening edition, under the editorship of the Chronicle's music critic, George Hogarth. Hogarth invited Dickens to contribute Street Sketches and Dickens became a regular visitor to his Fulham house, excited by Hogarth's friendship with a hero of his, Walter Scott, and enjoying the company of Hogarth's three daughters—Georgina, Mary, and nineteen-year-old Catherine.

Dickens made rapid progress both professionally and socially. He began a friendship with William Harrison Ainsworth, the author of the highwayman novel Rookwood (1834), whose bachelor salon in Harrow Road had become the meeting place for a set that included Daniel Maclise, Benjamin Disraeli, Edward Bulwer-Lytton, and George Cruikshank. All these became his friends and collaborators, with the exception of Disraeli, and he met his first publisher, John Macrone, at the house. The success of Sketches by Boz led to a proposal from publishers Chapman and Hall for Dickens to supply text to match Robert Seymour's engraved illustrations in a monthly letterpress. Seymour committed suicide after the second instalment, and Dickens, who wanted to write a connected series of sketches, hired "Phiz" to provide the engravings (which were reduced from four to two per instalment) for the story. The resulting story became The Pickwick Papers, and though the first few episodes were not successful, the introduction of the Cockney character Sam Weller in the fourth episode (the first to be illustrated by Phiz) marked a sharp climb in its popularity. The final instalment sold 40,000 copies.

In November 1836, Dickens accepted the position of editor of Bentley's Miscellany, a position he held for three years, until he fell out with the owner. In 1836 as he finished the last instalments of The Pickwick Papers, he began writing the beginning instalments of Oliver Twist—writing as many as 90 pages a month—while continuing work on Bentley's and also writing four plays, the production of which he oversaw. Oliver Twist, published in 1838, became one of Dickens's better known stories, and was the first Victorian novel with a child protagonist.

On 2 April 1836, after a one-year engagement, and between episodes two and three of The Pickwick Papers, Dickens married Catherine Thomson Hogarth (1816–1879), the daughter of George Hogarth, editor of the Evening Chronicle. They were married in St. Luke's Church, Chelsea, London. After a brief honeymoon in Chalk in Kent, the couple returned to lodgings at Furnival's Inn. The first of their ten children, Charley, was born in January 1837, and a few months later the family set up home in Bloomsbury at 48 Doughty Street, London, (on which Charles had a three-year lease at £80 a year) from 25 March 1837 until December 1839. Dickens's younger brother Frederick and Catherine's 17-year-old sister Mary, moved in with them. Dickens became very attached to Mary, and she died in his arms after a brief illness in 1837. Unusually for Dickens, as a consequence of his shock, he stopped working, and he and Kate stayed at a little farm on Hampstead Heath for a fortnight. Dickens idealised Mary—the character he fashioned after her, Rose Maylie, he found he could not now kill, as he had planned, in his fiction, and, according to Ackroyd, he drew on memories of her for his later descriptions of Little Nell and Florence Dombey. His grief was so great that he was unable to meet the deadline for the June instalment of Pickwick Papers and had to cancel the Oliver Twist instalment that month as well. The time in Hampstead was the occasion for a growing bond between Dickens and John Forster to develop and Forster soon became his unofficial business manager, and the first to read his work.

His success as a novelist continued. The young Queen Victoria read both Oliver Twist and Pickwick, staying up until midnight to discuss them. Nicholas Nickleby (1838–39), The Old Curiosity Shop (1840–41) and, finally, his first historical novel, Barnaby Rudge: A Tale of the Riots of 'Eighty, as part of the Master Humphrey's Clock series (1840–41), were all published in monthly instalments before being made into books.

In the midst of all his activity during this period, there was discontent with his publishers and John Macrone was bought off, while Richard Bentley signed over all his rights in Oliver Twist. Other signs of a certain restlessness and discontent emerge—in Broadstairs he flirted with Eleanor Picken, the young fiancée of his solicitor's best friend, and one night grabbed her and ran with her down to the sea. He declared they were both to drown there in the "sad sea waves". She finally got free but afterwards kept her distance. In June 1841 he precipitously set out on a two-month tour of Scotland and then, in September 1841, telegraphed Forster that he had decided to go to America. Master Humphrey's Clock was shut down, though Dickens was still keen on the idea of the weekly magazine, a form he liked, a liking that had begun with his childhood reading of the eighteenth-century magazines Tatler and The Spectator.

Dickens was perturbed by the return to power of the Tories, whom Dickens described as "people whom, politically, I despise and abhor." He had been tempted to stand for the Liberals in Reading, but decided against it due to financial straits. He wrote three anti-Tory verse satires ("The Fine Old English Gentleman", "The Quack Doctor's Proclamation", and "Subjects for Painters") which were published in The Examiner.

First visit to the United States

On 22 January 1842, Dickens and his wife arrived in Boston, Massachusetts aboard the RMS Britannia during their first trip to the United States and Canada. At this time Georgina Hogarth, another sister of Catherine, joined the Dickens household, now living at Devonshire Terrace, Marylebone, to care for the young family they had left behind. She remained with them as housekeeper, organiser, adviser, and friend until Dickens's death in 1870. Dickens modeled the character of Agnes Wickfield after Georgina and Mary.

He described his impressions in a travelogue, American Notes for General Circulation. Dickens includes in Notes a powerful condemnation of slavery, which he had attacked as early as

The Pickwick Papers, correlating the emancipation of the poor in England with the abolition of slavery abroad citing newspaper accounts of runaway slaves disfigured by their masters. In spite of the abolitionist sentiments gleaned from his trip to America, some modern commentators have pointed out inconsistencies in Dickens's views on racial inequality, for instance, he has been criticized for his subsequent acquiescence in Governor Eyre's harsh crackdown during the 1860s Morant Bay rebellion in Jamaica and his failure to join other British progressives in condemning it. From Richmond, Virginia, Dickens returned to Washington, D.C., and started a trek westward to St. Louis, Missouri. While there, he expressed a desire to see an American prairie before returning east. A group of 13 men then set out with Dickens to visit Looking Glass Prairie, a trip 30 miles into Illinois.

During his American visit, Dickens spent a month in New York City, giving lectures, raising the question of international copyright laws and the pirating of his work in America. He persuaded a group of twenty-five writers, headed by Washington Irving, to sign a petition for him to take to Congress, but the press were generally hostile to this, saying that he should be grateful for his popularity and that it was mercenary to complain about his work being pirated.

The popularity he gained caused a shift in his self-perception according to critic Kate Flint, who writes that he "found himself a cultural commodity, and its circulation had passed out his control", causing him to become interested in and delve into themes of public and personal personas in the next novels. She writes that he assumed a role of "influential commentator", publicly and in his fiction, evident in his next few books. His trip to the U.S. ended with a trip to Canada: Niagara Falls, Toronto, Kingston and Montreal where he appeared on stage in light comedies.

Soon after his return to England, Dickens began work on the first of his Christmas stories, A Christmas Carol, written in 1843, which was followed by The Chimes in 1844 and The Cricket on the Hearth in 1845. Of these, A Christmas Carol was most popular and, tapping into an old tradition, did much to promote a renewed enthusiasm for the joys of Christmas in Britain and America. The seeds for the story became planted in Dickens's mind during a trip to Manchester to witness the conditions of the manufacturing workers there. This, along with scenes he had recently witnessed at the Field Lane Ragged School, caused Dickens to resolve to "strike a sledge hammer blow" for the poor. As the idea for the story took shape and the writing began in earnest, Dickens became engrossed in the book. He later wrote that as the tale unfolded he "wept and laughed, and wept again" as he "walked about the black streets of London fifteen or twenty miles many a night when all sober folks had gone to bed."

After living briefly in Italy (1844), Dickens travelled to Switzerland (1846), where he began work on Dombey and Son (1846–48). This and David Copperfield (1849–50) mark a significant artistic break in Dickens's career as his novels became more serious in theme and more carefully planned than his early works.

At about this time, he was made aware of a large embezzlement at the firm where his brother, Augustus, worked (John Chapman & Co.). It had been carried out by Thomas Powell, a clerk, who was on friendly terms with Dickens and who had acted as mentor to Augustus when he started work. Powell was also an author and poet and knew many of the famous writers of the day. After further fraudulent activities, Powell fled to New York and published a book called The Living Authors of England with a chapter on Charles Dickens, who was not amused

692

by what Powell had written. One item that seemed to have annoyed him was the assertion that he had based the character of Paul Dombey (Dombey and Son) on Thomas Chapman, one of the principal partners at John Chapman & Co. Dickens immediately sent a letter to Lewis Gaylord Clark, editor of the New York literary magazine The Knickerbocker, saying that Powell was a forger and thief. Clark published the letter in the New-York Tribune, and several other papers picked up on the story. Powell began proceedings to sue these publications, and Clark was arrested. Dickens, realising that he had acted in haste, contacted John Chapman & Co. to seek written confirmation of Powell's guilt. Dickens did receive a reply confirming Powell's embezzlement, but once the directors realised this information might have to be produced in court, they refused to make further disclosures. Owing to the difficulties of providing evidence in America to support his accusations, Dickens eventually made a private settlement with Powell out of court.

Philanthropy

Angela Burdett Coutts, heir to the Coutts banking fortune, approached Dickens in May 1846 about setting up a home for the redemption of fallen women of the working class. Coutts envisioned a home that would replace the punitive regimes of existing institutions with a reformative environment conducive to education and proficiency in domestic household chores. After initially resisting, Dickens eventually founded the home, named "Urania Cottage", in the Lime Grove section of Shepherds Bush, which he managed for ten years, setting the house rules, reviewing the accounts and interviewing prospective residents. Emigration and marriage were central to Dickens's agenda for the women on leaving Urania Cottage, from which it is estimated that about 100 women graduated between 1847 and 1859.

Death

On 8 June 1870, Dickens suffered another stroke at his home after a full day's work on Edwin Drood. He never regained consciousness, and the next day, five years to the day after the Staplehurst rail crash, he died at Gads Hill Place. Biographer Claire Tomalin has suggested Dickens was actually in Peckham when he suffered the stroke, and his mistress Ellen Ternan and her maids had him taken back to Gad's Hill so the public would not know the truth about their relationship. Contrary to his wish to be buried at Rochester Cathedral "in an inexpensive, unostentatious, and strictly private manner", he was laid to rest in the Poets' Corner of Westminster Abbey. A printed epitaph circulated at the time of the funeral reads:

To the Memory of Charles Dickens (England's most popular author) who died at his residence, Higham, near Rochester, Kent, 9 June 1870, aged 58 years. He was a sympathiser with the poor, the suffering, and the oppressed; and by his death, one of England's greatest writers is lost to the world.

His last words were: "On the ground", in response to his sister-in-law Georgina's request that he lie down. On Sunday, 19 June 1870, five days after Dickens was buried in the Abbey, Dean Arthur Penrhyn Stanley delivered a memorial elegy, lauding "the genial and loving humorist whom we now mourn", for showing by his own example "that even in dealing with the darkest scenes and the most degraded characters, genius could still be clean, and mirth could be innocent". Pointing to the fresh flowers that adorned the novelist's grave, Stanley assured those present that "the spot would thenceforth be a sacred one with both the New World and the Old, as that of the representative of literature, not of this island only, but of all who speak our English tongue."

In his will, drafted more than a year before his death, Dickens left the care of his £80,000 estate to his longtime colleague John Forster and his "best and truest friend" Georgina Hogarth who, along with Dickens's two sons, also received a tax-free sum of £8,000 (about £800,000 in present terms). Although Dickens and his wife had been separated for several years at the time of his death, he provided her with an annual income of £600 and made her similar allowances in his will. He also bequeathed £19 19s to each servant in his employment at the time of his death. (Source: Wikipedia)

Lightning Source UK Ltd.
Milton Keynes UK
UKHW012150050320
359866UK00006B/120

9 789353 859695